THE
ANNOTATED LEGENDS

Margaret Weis and Tracy Hickman

Time of the Twins

War of the Twins

Test of the Twins

Edited by Mark Sehestedt
Poetry by Michael Williams
Cover art by Christophe Vacher
Color plates by Larry Elmore, Matt Stawicki, Clyde Caldwell,
and Keith Parkinson
Chapter art by Valerie Valusek

THE ANNOTATED LEGENDS

Cover art by Christophe Vacher
First Printing: September 2003
First Printing of *Time of the Twins*: February 1986
First Printing of *War of the Twins*: May 1986
First Printing of *Test of the Twins*: August 1986
Library of Congress Catalog Card Number: 2003100622

9 8 7 6 5 4 3 2 1

US ISBN: 0-7869-2992-8
UK ISBN: 0-7869-2993-6
620-17978-001-EN

U.S., CANADA,   EUROPEAN HEADQUARTERS
ASIA, PACIFIC, & LATIN AMERICA   Wizards of the Coast, Belgium
Wizards of the Coast, Inc.   T. Hofveld 6D
P.O. Box 707   1702 Groot-Bijgaarden
Renton, WA 98057-0707   Belgium
+1-800-324-6496   +322 457 3350

Visit our web site at **www.wizards.com**

INTRODUCTION
By Tracy Hickman
March 2003

I always begin a story with the end in mind. How we get there and the tortured path we take may be something of a hazy vision with a sketchy map, but I always have a clear idea of where I am going.

This, of course, is not true of real life.

DRAGONLANCE Legends was written while Margaret and I were still employees of TSR, Inc. We were happy enough with our employment at the time, as I recall. I, for one, certainly did not contemplate leaving the company for a writing career. I already had a career as a game designer. The novels were, at the time, a wonderful part of the vision we were creating in the DRAGONLANCE setting as a game. TSR, Inc. even had a retirement planæand, as I recall now, I fully expected to avail myself of its benefits. This was, of course, some time ago, and it all seems pretty naïve of me as I look back on it now.

Some endings blossom into new beginnings. The initial success of Chronicles opened up the opportunity for Margaret and I to write Legends on our own terms. Writing Legends itself differed considerably from Chronicles. We were no longer tied to the game product in terms of story and plot progression. This allowed us the freedom to concentrate on the characters and the stories over the locations and the events. While Legends is as far ranging—and in many ways much more far ranging— than Chronicles, it remains an intimate book. It gives us a close and familiar picture of Raistlin, Caramon, Crysania, and Tasslehoff that would not have been possible in Chronicles.

Sometimes, new beginnings sow the seeds of their own ends. Legends, in many ways, changed life for both Margaret and I. The Legends trilogy's own subsequent success both opened doors of opportunity for us and, in a strange way, led to our leaving TSR. There is nothing so unforgivable as success. Margaret and I leaped from the nest and, I suspect, there were some remaining who were glad for the extra room.

Closing doors on the past and opening doors on a brighter tomorrow is in part what Legends is about—our common footpath toward our story's hoped-for end. Though at times the road will be uncertain, we delight in your company once more on the journey ahead.

AN ALERT TO READERS, FROM MARGARET WEIS:

Since some of the annotations may give away key plot points in the series, we suggest that if you have never before read the DRAGONLANCE Legends series, you might want to start by reading another edition of the books. The Annotated Legends are intended to be useful and interesting to people who have already read the series and who are looking for insight into our work and background information on places, events, and characters. If you are reading this series in this edition and you want to maintain the suspense and the surprise, we recommend you skip over the annotations and come back to them after you've finished the series.

CONCERNING THE POETRY OF MICHAEL WILLIAMS:

As I recall, the poems for DRAGONLANCE Legends came about in a somewhat different way than their predecessors in DRAGONLANCE Chronicles. As Margaret and Tracy wrote the Chronicles, I was in much closer touch with them, a weekly (sometimes daily) audience for the turns in the story, and close by to receive any specific instructions (usually from Margaret) as to the style and subject of the poetry they wanted.

As they worked on the Legends, however, we were in less frequent contact. It was an interesting process for me: one of the dynamic duo would approach me with a general theme or matter, then leave me on my own, more or less. I discovered eventually how liberating this new process could be, but at first, it didn't feel right. I remember telling Tracy I wasn't sure I could do it. His response was a silent, friendly pat on the back, in which I sensed just the hint of a push.

When asked to write commentary on these poems and lyrics, I had initial misgivings because I hadn't looked at them in years and was afraid of what I might find. For the most part, I think I can still stand by them.

—Michael Williams, May 2003

Volume I

Time of the Twins

To Samuel G. and Alta Hickman

My grandpa who tossed me into bed in his own
special way and my grandma nanny who is always
so very wise. Thank you all for the bedtime stories,
life, love, and history. You will live forever.
—Tracy Raye Hickman

This book about the physical and spiritual bonds
binding brothers together could be dedicated
to only one person—my sister.
To Terry Lynn Weis Wilhelm, with love.
—Margaret Weis

ACKNOWLEDGMENTS

We wish to gratefully acknowledge the work of the following:

Michael WIlliams—for splendid poetry and warm friendship.

Steve Sullivan—for his wonderful maps. (Now you know where you are, Steve!)

Patrick Price—for his helpful advice and thoughtful criticism.

Jean Black—our editor, who had faith in us from the beginning.

Ruth Hoyer—for cover and interior design.

Roger Moore—for DRAGON® magazine articles and the story of Tasslehoff and the wolly mammoth.

The DRAGONLANCE® team: Harold Johnson, Laura Hickman, Douglas Niles, Jeff Grubb, Michael Dobson, Michael Breault, Bruce Heard.

The 1987 DRAGONLANCE Calendar artists: Clyde Caldwell, Larry Elmore, Keith Parkinson, and Jeff Easley.

The Meeting

Alone figure trod softly toward the distant light. Walking unheard, his footfalls were sucked into the vast darkness all around him. Bertrem† indulged in a rare flight of fancy as he glanced at the seemingly endless rows of books and scrolls that were part of the *Chronicles of Astinus*† and detailed the history of this world, the history of Krynn.

"It's like being sucked into time," he thought, sighing as he glanced at the still, silent rows. He wished, briefly, that he were being sucked away somewhere, so that he did not have to face the difficult task ahead of him.

"All the knowledge of the world is in these books," he said to himself wistfully. "And I've never found one thing to help make the intrusion upon their author any easier."

Bertrem came to a halt outside the door to summon his courage. His flowing Aesthetic's robes settled themselves about him, falling into correct and orderly folds. His stomach, however, refused to follow the robes' example and lurched about wildly. Bertrem ran his hand across his scalp, a nervous gesture left over from a younger age, before his chosen profession had cost him his hair.

What was bothering him? he wondered bleakly— other than going in to see the Master, of course, something he had not done since . . . since . . . He shuddered. Yes, since the young mage had nearly died upon their doorstep† during the last war.

War . . . change, that was what it was. Like his robes, the world had finally seemed to settle around him, but he felt change coming once again, just as he had felt it two years ago. He wished he could stop it. . . .

Bertrem sighed. "I'm certainly not going to stop anything by standing out here in the darkness," he muttered. He felt uncomfortable anyway, as though surrounded by ghosts. A bright light shone from under the door, beaming out into the hallway. Giving a quick glance backward at the shadows of

As to the origins of the name Bertrem, sometimes I just pluck names out of the air, using them for the way they sound. That's what happened in the case of Bertrem. I discovered later that it is correctly spelled "Bertram," and it is a French name that means "famous raven." The raven represents wisdom, so this would be a suitable name for Bertrem. —MW

I have always been one of those people who asks who is telling the story or who is taking the picture. Stories, if they are passed down to us, must be experienced by someone who either participated or witnessed the events, recorded by someone, told by someone, and passed down until they reach us. I wanted a character who personified the viewpoint of the authors—a literal voice of the text. Astinus makes us believe that there is some way that this story could truly be passed down to us. —TRH

This happened in Dragons of Spring Dawning, Book I, Chapter 5.

the books, peaceful corpses resting in their tombs, the Aesthetic quietly opened the door and entered the study of Astinus† of Palanthas.

Though the man was within, he did not speak, nor even look up.

Walking with gentle, measured tread across the rich rug of lamb's wool that lay upon the marble floor, Bertrem paused before the great, polished wooden desk. For long moments he said nothing, absorbed in watching the hand of the historian guide the quill across the parchment in firm, even strokes.

"Well, Bertrem?" Astinus did not cease his writing.

Bertrem, facing Astinus, read the letters that—even upside down—were crisp and clear and easily decipherable.

This day, as above Darkwatch rising† 29, Bertrem entered my study.

"Crysania† of the House of Tarinius is here to see you, Master. She says she is expected. . . ." Bertrem's voice trailed off in a whisper, it having taken a great deal of the Aesthetic's courage to get that far.

Astinus continued writing.

"Master," Bertrem began faintly, shivering with his daring. "I—we are at a loss. She is, after all, a Revered Daughter of Paladine and I—we found it impossible to refuse her admittance. What sh—"

"Take her to my private chambers," Astinus said without ceasing to write or looking up.

Bertrem's tongue clove to the roof of his mouth, rendering him momentarily speechless. The letters flowed from the quill pen to the white parchment.

This day, as above Afterwatch rising 28, Crysania of Tarinius arrived for her appointment with Raistlin Majere.

"Raistlin Majere!" Bertrem gasped, shock and horror prying his tongue loose. "Are we to admit hi—"

Astinus looked up now, annoyance and irritation creasing his brow. As his pen ceased its eternal scratching on the parchment, a deep unnatural silence settled upon the room. Bertrem paled. The historian's face might have been reckoned handsome in a timeless, ageless fashion. But none who saw his face ever remembered it. They simply remembered the eyes—dark, intent, aware, constantly

I believe that Astinus is, indeed, an Avatar of Gilean—if not the personification of Gilean himself. —TRH

"Darkwatch rising" — This is a reference not to the month or day, but the time of day as measured by the Palanthians. Like many medieval cultures, the Palanthians divide the day not by 24 hours, but by the changing of the city watch.

People often ask us the origin of names in our books. The DRAGONLANCE setting was such a cooperative creation, utilizing the talents of so many people, that it is difficult to remember just who contributed what and when. I do remember, however, that Crysania felt very much like a Christ-archetype, and that may well have influenced her name. After the name had been established in our text, however, the Burger King fast food chain came out with a product called a "Croissandwich," and soon Margaret could not get the idea of a "Crysandwich" out of her mind. I can never read her name now without smiling. —TRH

moving, seeing everything. Those eyes could also communicate vast worlds of impatience, reminding Bertrem that time was passing. Even as the two spoke, whole minutes of history were ticking by, unrecorded.

"Forgive me, Master!" Bertrem bowed in profound reverence, then backed precipitately out of the study, closing the door quietly on his way. Once outside, he mopped his shaved head that was glistening with perspiration, then hurried down the silent, marble corridors of the Great Library of Palanthas.

Astinus paused in the doorway to his private residence, his gaze on the woman who sat within.

Located in the western wing of the Great Library, the residence of the historian was small and, like all other rooms in the library, was filled with books of every type and binding, lining the shelves on the walls and giving the central living area a faint musty odor, like a mausoleum that had been sealed for centuries. The furniture was sparse, pristine. The chairs, wooden and handsomely carved, were hard and uncomfortable to sit upon. A low table, standing by a window, was absolutely free of any ornament or object, reflecting the light from the setting sun upon its smooth black surface. Everything in the room was in the most perfect order. Even the wood for the evening fire—the late spring nights were cool, even this far north†—was stacked in such orderly rows it resembled a funeral pyre.

And yet, cool and pristine and pure as was this private chamber of the historian, the room itself seemed only to mirror the cold, pristine, pure beauty of the woman who sat, her hands folded in her lap, waiting.

Crysania of Tarinius waited patiently. She did not fidget or sigh or glance often at the water-run† timing device in the corner. She did not read— though Astinus was certain Bertrem would have her offered a book. She did not pace the room or examine the few rare ornaments that stood in shadowed nooks within the bookcases. She sat in the straight, uncomfortable, wooden chair, her clear, bright eyes fixed upon the red-stained fringes of the clouds above the mountains as if she were

The decision to put Ansalon on the southern continent was mine. I was deeply aware of the Western European nature of classical, Tolkien-esque fantasy and wanted to make a statement about our world being a very different place. This was from the very beginning of the design, going back to the first maps drawn and the plotting of the climate bands for Ansalon before any book or game was ever produced. —TRH

watching the sun set for possibly the first—or last—time upon Krynn.

So intent was she upon the sight beyond the window that Astinus entered without attracting her attention. He regarded her with intense interest. This was not unusual for the historian, who scrutinized all beings living upon Krynn with the same fathomless, penetrating gaze. What was unusual was that, for a moment, a look of pity and of profound sorrow passed across the historian's face.

Astinus recorded history. He had recorded it since the beginning of time, watching it pass before his eyes and setting it down in his books. He could not foretell the future, that was the province of the gods. But he could sense all the signs of change, those same signs that had so disturbed Bertrem. Standing there, he could hear the drops of water falling in the timing device. By placing his hand beneath them, he could cease the flow of the drops, but time would go on.

Sighing, Astinus turned his attention to the woman, whom he had heard of but never met.

Her hair was black, blue-black, black as the water of a calm sea at night. She wore it combed straight back from a central part, fastened at the back of her head with a plain, unadorned, wooden comb. The severe style was not becoming to her pale, delicate features, emphasizing their pallor. There was no color at all in her face. Her eyes were gray and seemingly much too large. Even her lips were bloodless.†

Some years ago, when she had been young, servants had braided and coiled that thick, black hair into the latest, fashionable styles, tucking in pins of silver and of gold, decorating the somber hues with sparkling jewels. They had tinted her cheeks with the juice of crushed berries and dressed her in sumptuous gowns of palest pinks and powdery blues. Once she had been beautiful. Once her suitors had waited in lines.

The gown she wore now was white, as befitted a cleric of Paladine, and plain though made of fine material. It was unadorned save for the belt of gold that encircled her slim waist. Her only ornament was Paladine's—the medallion of the Platinum Dragon. Her hair was covered by a loose white

hood that enhanced the marble smoothness and coldness of her complexion.

She might have been made of marble, Astinus thought, with one difference—marble could be warmed by the sun.

"Greetings, Revered Daughter of Paladine," Astinus said, entering and shutting the door behind him.

"Greetings, Astinus," Crysania of Tarinius said, rising to her feet.

As she walked across the small room toward him, Astinus was somewhat startled to note the swiftness and almost masculine length of her stride. It seemed oddly incongruous with her delicate features. Her handshake, too, was firm† and strong, not typical of Palanthian women, who rarely shook hands and then did so only by extending their fingertips.

"I must thank you for giving up your valuable time to act as a neutral party in this meeting," Crysania said coolly. "I know how you dislike taking time from your studies."

"As long as it is not wasted time, I do not mind," Astinus replied, holding her hand and regarding her intently. "I must admit, however, that I resent this."

"Why?" Crysania searched the man's ageless face in true perplexity. Then—in sudden understanding— she smiled, a cold smile that brought no more life to her face than the moonlight upon snow. "You don't believe he will come, do you?"

Astinus snorted, dropping the woman's hand as though he had completely lost interest in her very existence. Turning away, he walked to the window and looked out over the city of Palanthas, whose gleaming white buildings glowed in the sun's radiance with a breathtaking beauty, with one exception. One building remained untouched by the sun, even in brightest noontime.

And it was upon this building that Astinus's gaze fixed. Thrusting itself up in the center of the brilliant, beautiful city, its black stone towers† twisted and writhed, its minarets—newly repaired and constructed by the powers of magic—glistened blood-red in the sunset, giving the appearance of rotting, skeletal fingers clawing their way up from some unhallowed burial ground.

good and evil. She sees no shades of gray, no subtle complexities. —MW

Crysania is marked by her handshake as a firm and decisive woman, ready to take action. A woman who imagines that she knows herself. —MW

The contrast of this tower with the surrounding white city reflects the contrast between the central themes of good and evil in the book. I have long been a fan of Bram Stoker's Dracula. *Those darker images are in part the roots of the tower. —TRH*

"Originally there were five Towers of High Sorcery. Built by the ancient wizards as centers for their crafts and learning, they were located in the ancient cities that later came to be called Palanthus, Wayreth, Istar, Daltigoth, and the Ruins.

*"The towers were all alike and yet all different. The general outline of the towers was determined by a central committee of members of all three orders (since all orders use the towers), but the supervision of the construction work was done by wizards who happened to live in the area. This resulted in the same general structure for all towers, but widely varying details and specific layouts." [*DRAGONLANCE *Adventures, by Tracy Hickman and Margaret Weis, TSR, Inc.,1987, p. 29.]*

When working on Chronicles, Tracy and I both realized that Raistlin's story would not end with the Chronicles but would progress from there and that his story and Caramon's needed telling. Thus the foundation for Legends was already being established in Chronicles. —MW

"Two years ago, he entered the Tower of High Sorcery,"† Astinus said in his calm, passionless voice as Crysania joined him at the window. "He entered in the dead of night in darkness, the only moon in the sky was the moon that sheds no light. He walked through the Shoikan Grove—a stand of accursed oak trees that no mortal—not even those of the kender race—dare approach. He made his way to the gates upon which hung still the body of the evil mage who, with his dying breath, cast the curse upon the Tower and leapt from the upper windows, impaling himself upon its gates—a fearsome watchman. But when *he* came there, the watchman bowed before him, the gates opened at his touch, then they shut behind him. And they have not opened again these past two years. He has not left and, if any have been admitted, none have seen them. And you expect *him . . . here?*"

"The master of past and of present," Crysania shrugged. "He came, as was foretold."

Astinus regarded her with some astonishment. "You know his story?"

"Of course," the cleric replied calmly, glancing up at him for an instant, then turning her clear eyes back to look at the Tower, already shrouding itself with the coming night's shadows. "A good general always studies the enemy before engaging in battle. I know Raistlin Majere very well, very well indeed. And I know—he will come this night."

Crysania continued gazing at the dreadful Tower, her chin lifted, her bloodless lips set in a straight, even line, her hands clasped behind her back.

Astinus's face suddenly became grave and thoughtful, his eyes troubled, though his voice was cool as ever. "You seem very sure of yourself, Revered Daughter. How do you know this?"

"Paladine has spoken to me," Crysania replied, never taking her eyes from the Tower. "In a dream, the Platinum Dragon appeared before me and told me that evil—once banished from the world—had returned in the person of this black-robed wizard, Raistlin Majere.† We face dire peril, and it has been given to me to prevent it." As Crysania spoke, her marble face grew smooth, her gray eyes were clear and bright. "It will be the test of my faith I have prayed for!" She glanced at Astinus. "You see, I

have known since childhood that my destiny was to perform some great deed, some great service to the world and its people. This is my chance."

Astinus's face grew graver as he listened, and even more stern.

"Paladine told you this?" he demanded abruptly.

Crysania, sensing, perhaps, this man's disbelief, pursed her lips. A tiny line appearing between her brows was, however, the only sign of her anger, that and an even more studied calmness in her reply.

"I regret having spoken of it, Astinus, forgive me. It was between my god and myself, and such sacred things should not be discussed. I brought it up simply to prove to you that this evil man will come. He cannot help himself. Paladine will bring him."

Astinus's eyebrows rose so that they very nearly disappeared into his graying hair.

"This 'evil man' as you call him, Revered Daughter, serves a goddess as powerful as Paladine— Takhisis, Queen of Darkness! Or perhaps I should not say *serves*," Astinus remarked with a wry smile. "Not of him. . . ."

Crysania's brow cleared, her cool smile returned. "Good redeems its own," she answered gently. "Evil turns in upon itself. Good will triumph again, as it did in the War of the Lance against Takhisis and her evil dragons. With Paladine's help, *I* shall triumph over this evil as the hero, Tanis Half-Elven, triumphed over the Queen of Darkness herself."

"Tanis Half-Elven triumphed with the help of Raistlin Majere," Astinus said imperturbably. "Or is that a part of the legend† you choose to ignore?"

Not a ripple of emotion marred the still, placid surface of Crysania's expression. Her smile remained fixed. Her gaze was on the street.

"Look, Astinus," she said softly. "He comes."

The sun sank behind the distant mountains, the sky, lit by the afterglow, was a gemlike purple. Servants entered quietly, lighting the fire in the small chamber of Astinus. Even it burned quietly, as if the flames themselves had been taught by the historian to maintain the peaceful repose of the Great Library. Crysania sat once more in the uncomfortable chair, her hands folded once more in her lap. Her outward mein was calm and cool as always. Inwardly, her

Why is Astinus, the great historian, speaking of "legend?" History is legend. We in our day believe that history is fact. This is not true nor has it ever been. History—or "His-story" if you will— is the mythology we craft out of the facts at hand that support our viewpoint or the viewpoint of the victor. Indeed, legend is far more compelling than mere "facts." Astinus recognizes this here. (See Appendix A: The Mythic Journey.) —TRH

heart beat with excitement that was visible only by a brightening of her gray eyes.

Born to the noble and wealthy Tarinius family of Palanthas, a family almost as ancient as the city itself, Crysania† had received every comfort and benefit money and rank could bestow. Intelligent, strong-willed, she might easily have grown into a stubborn and willful woman. Her wise and loving parents, however, had carefully nurtured and pruned their daughter's strong spirit so that it had blossomed into a deep and steadfast belief in herself. Crysania had done only one thing in her entire life to grieve her doting parents, but that one thing had cut them deeply. She had turned from an ideal marriage with a fine and noble young man to a life devoted to serving long-forgotten gods.

She first heard the cleric, Elistan, when he came to Palanthas at the end of the War of the Lance. His new religion—or perhaps it should have been called the *old* religion—was spreading like wildfire through Krynn, because new-born legend credited this belief in old gods with having helped defeat the evil dragons and their masters, the Dragon Highlords.

On first going to hear Elistan talk, Crysania had been skeptical. The young woman—she was in her mid-twenties—had been raised on stories of how the gods had inflicted the Cataclysm upon Krynn, hurling down the fiery mountain that rent the lands asunder and plunged the holy city of Istar into the Blood Sea. After this, so people related, the gods turned from men, refusing to have any more to do with them. Crysania was prepared to listen politely to Elistan, but had arguments at hand to refute his claims.

She was favorably impressed on meeting him. Elistan, at that time, was in the fullness of his power. Handsome, strong, even in his middle years, he seemed like one of the clerics of old, who had ridden to battle—so some legends said—with the mighty knight, Huma. Crysania began the evening finding cause to admire him. She ended on her knees at his feet, weeping in humility and joy, her soul at last having found the anchor it had been missing.

The gods had not turned from men,† was the message. It was men who had turned from the gods, demanding in their pride what Huma had sought in

In some ways, I think Crysania was partially modeled on Joan of Arc, which is interesting considering that we utilized a very different approach to Joan of Arc in the War of Souls trilogy.
—TRH

Men are always blaming God for things that are their own doing. God says, "Come to me," but men look for a short cut, wander off, and then wonder where God went. It is a central theme of the question of true faith in Legends. (See Appendix C: Faith and Fantasy.) —TRH

humility. The next day, Crysania left her home, her wealth, her servants, her parents, and her betrothed to move into the small, chill house that was the forerunner of the new Temple Elistan planned to build in Palanthas.

Now, two years later, Crysania† was a Revered Daughter of Paladine, one of a select few who had been found worthy to lead the church through its youthful growing pangs. It was well the church had this strong, young blood. Elistan had given unstintingly of his life and his energy. Now, it seemed, the god he served so faithfully would soon be summoning his cleric to his side. And when that sorrowful event occurred, many believed Crysania would carry on his work.

Certainly Crysania knew that she was prepared to accept the leadership of the church, but was it enough? As she had told Astinus, the young cleric had long felt her destiny was to perform some great service for the world. Guiding the church through its daily routines, now that the war was over, seemed dull and mundane. Daily she had prayed to Paladine to assign her some hard task. She would sacrifice anything, she vowed, even life itself, in the service of her beloved god.

And then had come her answer.

Now, she waited, in an eagerness she could barely restrain. She was not frightened, not even of meeting this man, said to be the most powerful force for evil now living on the face of Krynn. Had her breeding permitted it, her lip would have curled in a disdainful sneer. What evil could withstand the mighty sword of her faith? What evil could penetrate her shining armor?

Like a knight riding to a joust, wreathed with the garlands of his love, knowing that he cannot possibly lose with such tokens fluttering in the wind, Crysania kept her eyes fixed on the door, eagerly awaiting the tourney's first blows. When the door opened, her hands—until now calmly folded—clasped together in excitement.

Bertrem entered. His eyes went to Astinus, who sat immovable as a pillar of stone in a hard, uncomfortable chair near the fire.

"The mage, Raistlin Majere," Bertrem said. His voice cracked on the last syllable. Perhaps he was

"An attractive young woman in her late 20s, Crysania has black hair, white skin, and grey eyes. Her face, in fact, appears colorless and cold to those who first meet her. She is a Revered Daughter of Paladine, a dedicated cleric. Her first and only love is her church."

"The daughter of an ancient, noble family of Palanthus, Crysania is cultured and extremely well-educated. She could have had her choice of husbands, not only because of her manners and attractiveness, but also because of her family's wealth, to which Crysania is the only heir. The young woman wants something more from life, however, than settling down and raising children. She knows that she has been destined for greatness and in her early youth was frustrated and unable to find her calling in life. When she met Elistan, she discovered her destiny. One of the cleric's earliest converts, Crysania left home and wealth and dedicated her life to her faith." [DRAGONLANCE Adventures, by Tracy Hickman and Margaret Weis, TSR, Inc., 1987, p. 112.]

This occurred in Dragons of Spring Dawning, *Book I, Chapter 5*

thinking about the last time he had announced this visitor—the time Raistlin had been dying,† vomiting blood on the steps of the Great Library. Astinus frowned at Bertrem's lack of self-control, and the Aesthetic disappeared back through the door as rapidly as his fluttering robes permitted.

Unconsciously, Crysania held her breath. At first she saw nothing, only a shadow of darkness in the doorway, as if night itself had taken form and shape within the entrance. The darkness paused there.

"Come in, old friend," Astinus said in his deep, passionless voice.

The shadow was lit by a shimmer of warmth—the firelight gleamed on velvety soft, black robes—and then by tiny sparkles, as the light glinted off silver threads, embroidered runes† around a velvet cowl. The shadow became a figure, black robes completely draping the body. For a brief moment, the figure's only human appendage that could be seen was a thin, almost skeletal hand clutching a wooden staff. The staff itself was topped by a crystal ball, held fast in the grip of a carved golden dragon's claw.

Runes were an alphabet developed by the early Germanic peoples. Besides their use as an alphabet, runes were also believed to be powerful magic symbols, which makes them a natural addition to the wizards of Krynn.

As the figure entered the room, Crysania felt the cold chill of disappointment. She had asked Paladine for some difficult task! What great evil was there to fight in this? Now that she could see him clearly, she saw a frail, thin man, shoulders slightly stooped, who leaned upon his staff as he walked, as if too weak to move without its aid. She knew his age, he would be about twenty-eight now. Yet he moved like a human of ninety—his steps slow and deliberate, even faltering.

What test of my faith lies in conquering this wretched creature? Crysania demanded of Paladine bitterly. I have no need to fight him. He is being devoured from within by his own evil!

Facing Astinus, keeping his back to Crysania, Raistlin folded back his black hood.

"Greetings again, Deathless One," he said to Astinus in a soft voice.

"Greetings, Raistlin Majere," Astinus said without rising. His voice had a faint sardonic note, as if sharing some private joke with the mage. Astinus gestured. "May I present Crysania of the House of Tarinius."

Raistlin turned.

Crysania gasped, a terrible ache in her chest caused her throat to close, and for a moment she could not draw a breath. Sharp, tingling pins jabbed her fingertips, a chill convulsed her body. Unconsciously, she shrank back in her chair, her hands clenching, her nails digging into her numb flesh.

All she could see before her were two golden eyes shining from the depths of darkness. The eyes were like a gilt mirror, flat, reflective, revealing nothing of the soul within. The pupils—Crysania stared at the dark pupils in rapt horror. The pupils within the golden eyes were the shape of hourglasses!† And the face—Drawn with suffering, marked with the pain of the tortured existence the young man had led for seven years, ever since the cruel Tests in the Tower of High Sorcery left his body shattered and his skin tinged gold, the mage's face was a metallic mask, impenetrable, unfeeling as the golden dragon's claw upon his staff.

"Revered Daughter of Paladine," he said in a soft voice, a voice filled with respect and—even reverence.

Crysania started, staring at him in astonishment. Certainly that was not what she had expected.

Still, she could not move. His gaze held her, and she wondered in panic if he had cast a spell upon her. Seeming to sense her fear, he walked across the room to stand before her in an attitude that was both patronizing and reassuring. Looking up, she could see the firelight flickering in his golden eyes.

"Revered Daughter of Paladine," Raistlin said again, his soft voice enfolding Crysania like the velvety blackness of his robes. "I hope I find you well?" But now she heard bitter, cynical sarcasm in that voice. This she had expected, this she was prepared for. His earlier tone of respect had taken her by surprise, she admitted to herself angrily, but her first weakness was past. Rising to her feet, bringing her eyes level with his, she unconsciously clasped the medallion of Paladine with her hand. The touch of the cool metal gave her courage.

"I do not believe we need to exchange meaningless social amenities," Crysania stated crisply, her face once more smooth and cold. "We are keeping Astinus from his studies. He will appreciate our completing our business with alacrity."

Raistlin's hour-glass eyes. In a way, they led me to the development of Raistlin as a character. All the characters in Chronicles had been developed by the game group. I was given the task of fleshing out these characters, who had stats and physical descriptions but no background or detail as to their personalities. Larry Elmore had painted a picture of Raistlin, in which he was portrayed as having golden skin and hour-glass eyes. When I asked why he had these features (his twin brother, Caramon, was perfectly normal in appearance) Larry said, "Because it makes him look cool!" I had to come up with a plausible reason for his eyes, and that led me to the notion that this had something to do with Raistlin's magic, which led me to the Test in the Tower, and that led me to the short story called "The Test of the Twins," published first in DRAGON magazine in March, 1984.

On a side note, critics often accuse shared worlds of stifling creativity, but I have found that often they encourage creativity, by encouraging the author to come with creative responses to interesting challenges! I doubt if I would have ever come to know Raistlin if it hadn't been for his eyes. —MW

11

When Raistlin was originally created, his character was given hourglass pupils because someone on the design team thought "it would be cool." It was up to Margaret (in a short story for DRAGON Magazine) to come up with a rational for these pupils—and it helped set the course for the character ever after.
—TRH

"I could not agree more," the black-robed mage said with a slight twist of his thin lip that might have been a smile. "I have come in response to your request. What is it you want of me?"

Crysania sensed he was laughing at her. Accustomed only to the highest respect, this increased her anger. She regarded him with cold gray eyes. "I have come to warn you, Raistlin Majere, that your evil designs are known to Paladine. Beware, or he will destroy you—"

"How?" Raistlin† asked suddenly, and his strange eyes flared with a strange, intense light. "How will he destroy me?" he repeated. "Lightning bolts? Flood and fire? Perhaps another fiery mountain?"

He took another step toward her. Crysania moved coolly away from him, only to back into her chair. Gripping the hard wooden back firmly, she walked around it, then turned to face him.

"It is your own doom you mock," she replied quietly.

Raistlin's lip twisted further still, but he continued talking, as if he had not heard her words. "Elistan?" Raistlin's voice sank to a hissing whisper. "He will send Elistan to destroy me?" The mage shrugged. "But no, surely not. By all reports, the great and holy cleric of Paladine is tired, feeble, dying. . . ."

"No!" Crysania cried, then bit her lip, angry that this man had goaded her into showing her feelings. She paused, drawing a deep breath. "Paladine's ways are not to be questioned or mocked," she said with icelike calm, but she could not help her voice from softening almost imperceptibly. "And Elistan's health is no concern of yours."

"Perhaps I take a greater interest in his health than you realize," Raistlin replied with what was, to Crysania, a sneering smile.

Crysania felt blood pound in her temples. Even as he had spoken, the mage moved around the chair, coming nearer the young woman. He was so close to her now that Crysania could feel a strange, unnatural heat radiate from his body through his black robes. She could smell a faintly cloying but pleasant scent about him. A spiciness—his spell components,† she realized suddenly. The thought sickened and disgusted her. Holding the medallion of Paladine in

Spell components are an integral part of any wizard's supplies in AD&D. Many spells cannot be cast without the proper ingredients.

her hand, feeling its smoothly chiseled edges bite into her flesh, she moved away from him again.

"Paladine came to me in a dream—" she said haughtily.

Raistlin laughed.

Few there were who had ever heard the mage laugh, and those who had heard it remembered it always, resounding through their darkest dreams. It was thin, high-pitched, and sharp as a blade. It denied all goodness, mocked everything right and true, and it pierced Crysania's soul.

"Very well," Crysania said, staring at him with a disdain that hardened her bright, gray eyes to steel blue, "I have done my best to divert you from this course. I have given you fair warning. Your destruction is now in the hands of the gods."

Suddenly, perhaps realizing the fearlessness with which she confronted him, Raistlin's laughter ceased. Regarding her intently, his golden eyes narrowed. Then he smiled, a secret inner smile of such strange joy that Astinus, watching the exchange between the two, rose to his feet. The historian's body blocked the light of the fire. His shadow fell across them both. Raistlin started, almost in alarm. Half-turning, he regarded Astinus with a burning, menacing stare.†

"Beware, old friend," the mage warned, "or would you meddle with history?"

"I do not meddle," Astinus replied, "as you well know. I am an observer, a recorder. In all things, I am neutral. I know your schemes, your plans as I know the schemes and plans of all who draw breath this day. Therefore, hear me, Raistlin Majere, and heed this warning. This one is beloved of the gods†—as her name implies."

"Beloved of the gods? So are we all, are we not, Revered Daughter?" Raistlin asked, turning to face Crysania once more. His voice was soft as the velvet of his robes. "Is that not written in the Disks of Mishakal?† Is that not what the godly Elistan teaches?"

"Yes," Crysania said slowly, regarding him with suspicion, expecting more mockery. But his metallic face was serious, he had the appearance, suddenly, of a scholar—intelligent, wise. "So it is written." She smiled coldly. "I am pleased to find you have read

This scene is filled with symbolism. We have Crysania representing Good, Astinus Neutral, and Raistlin Evil—the forces of the balance that is so central to the cosmology of Krynn. The central conceptual theme of the DRAGONLANCE setting—a triangle moving around a central point— was established before any published word was written. At the grandest conceptual layer, the points of the triangle represented good, evil, and chaos, with the central balance point being Krynn itself. At another layer, you had the three points representing the Whitestone Council, the Dragon Highlords and the neutral nations of Ansalon, with our main group of characters in the middle. On a third level the points represented Laurana, Kitiara, and the world at large with Tanis in the middle. This thematic structure has remained in place through all our works in the DRAGONLANCE setting. —TRH

Astinus's comment here reflects Luke 3:22: "And the Holy Ghost descended in a bodily shape like a dove upon him, and a voice came from heaven, which said, Thou art my beloved Son; in thee I am well pleased." While Crysania is not Christ, her character certainly represents a savior archetype. The reference, while anachronistic, is in my mind a reference to the similar sounds in their names. —TRH

The Disks of Mishakal come from my own theological background. The Book of Mormon, a set of scripture that stands next to the Bible as the foundation of my faith, was translated from ancient writings inscribed on plates of gold. It has always seemed to me also to be a rather enduring method of securing one's records over time; hence the Disks of Mishakal. The ancients apparently agreed, since there are artifacts of writing on metal plates,

the sacred Disks,† though you obviously have not learned from them. Do you not recall what is said in the—"

She was interrupted by Astinus, snorting.

"I have been kept from my studies long enough." The historian crossed the marble floor to the door of the antechamber. "Ring for Bertrem when you are ready to depart. Farewell, Revered Daughter. Farewell . . . old friend."

Astinus opened the door. The peaceful silence of the library flowed into the room, bathing Crysania in refreshing coolness. She felt herself in control and she relaxed. Her hand let loose of the medallion. Formally and gracefully, she bowed her farewell to Astinus, as did Raistlin. And then the door shut behind the historian. The two were alone.

For long moments, neither spoke. Then Crysania, feeling Paladine's power flowing through her, turned to face Raistlin. "I had forgotten that it was you and those with you who recovered the sacred Disks. Of course, you would have read them. I would like to discuss them with you further but, henceforth, in any future dealings we might have, Raistlin Majere," she said in her cool voice, "I will ask you to speak of Elistan more respectfully. He—"

She stopped amazed, watching in alarm as the mage's slender body seemed to crumble before her eyes.

Wracked by spasms of coughing, clutching his chest, Raistlin gasped for breath. He staggered. If it had not been for the staff he leaned upon. he would have fallen to the floor. Forgetting her aversion and her disgust, reacting instinctively, Crysania reached out and, putting her hands upon his shoulders, murmured a healing prayer. Beneath her hands, the black robes were soft and warm. She could feel Raistlin's muscles twisting in spasms, sense his pain and suffering. Pity filled her heart.

Raistlin jerked away from her touch, shoving her to one side. His coughing gradually eased. Able to breathe freely once more, he regarded her with scorn.

"Do not waste your prayers on me, Revered Daughter," he said bitterly. Pulling a soft cloth from his robes, he dabbed his lips and Crysania saw that it came away stained with blood. "There

is no cure for my malady. This is the sacrifice, the price I paid for my magic."

"I don't understand," she murmured. Her hands twitched, as she remembered vividly the velvety soft smoothness of the black robes, and she unconsciously clasped her fingers behind her back.

"Don't you?" Raistlin asked, staring deep into her soul with his strange, golden eyes. "What was the sacrifice you made for *your* power?"†

A faint flush, barely visible in the dying firelight, stained Crysania cheeks with blood, much as the mage's lips were stained. Alarmed at this invasion of her being, she averted her face, her eyes looking once more out the window. Night had fallen over Palanthas. The silver moon, Solinari, was a sliver of light in the dark sky. The red moon that was its twin had not yet risen. The black moon—She caught herself wondering, where is it? Can *he* truly see it?

"I must go," Raistlin said, his breath rasping in his throat. "These spasms weaken me. I need rest."

"Certainly," Crysania felt herself calm once more. All the ends of her emotions tucked back neatly into place, she turned to face him again. "I thank you for coming—"

"But our business is not concluded," Raistlin said softly. "I would like a chance to prove to you that these fears of your god are unfounded. I have a suggestion. Come visit me in the Tower of High Sorcery. There you will see me among my books and understand my studies. When you do, your mind will be at ease. As it teaches in the Disks, we fear only that which is unknown."† He took a step nearer her.

Astounded at his proposal, Crysania's eyes opened wide. She tried to move away from him, but she had inadvertently let herself become trapped by the window. "I cannot go . . . to the Tower," she faltered as his nearness smothered her, stole her breath. She tried to walk around him, but he moved his staff slightly, blocking her path. Coldly, she continued, "The spells laid upon it keep out all—"

"Except those I choose to admit," Raistlin whispered. Folding the blood-stained cloth, he tucked it back into a secret pocket of his robes. Then, reaching out, he took hold of Crysania's hand.

"How brave you are, Revered Daughter," he commented. "You do not tremble at my evil touch."

Raistlin's question is telling. He knows that Crysania has not yet paid the price for her power, and he suspects that she knows it as well. —TRH

In working with magic in a fantasy world, an author has to be careful not to allow the wizard to become too powerful. A reader who knows that the wizard can escape any peril with a wave of his hand is quickly bored with the character and the story. Thus the author must set limits on the magic and on the character who uses it.

In another context, I like to use magic as a metaphor for the creative process. Artists give themselves completely to their art, often sacrificing pleasure, money, sleep, health, etc. in order to create. The artistic endeavor is a very lonely one, sometimes. The reward for the artist lies in the creation, but other people, such as friends and family, often find this difficult to understand and accept. —MW

One of my favorite Twilight Zone *episodes is entitled "Nothing in the Dark"—a wonderful example of this sentiment. —TRH*

"Paladine is with me," Crysania replied disdainfully.

Raistlin smiled, a warm smile, dark and secret—a smile for just the two of them. It fascinated Crysania. He drew her near to him. Then, he dropped her hand. Resting the staff against the chair, he reached out and took hold of her head with his slender hands, placing his fingers over the white hood she wore. Now, Crysania trembled at his touch, but she could not move, she could not speak or do anything more than stare at him in a wild fear she could neither suppress nor understand.

Holding her firmly, Raistlin leaned down and brushed his blood-flecked lips across her forehead. As he did so, he muttered strange words. Then he released her.

Crysania stumbled, nearly falling. She felt weak and dizzy. Her hand went to her forehead where the touch of his lips burned into her skin with a searing pain. "What have you done?" she cried brokenly. "You cannot cast a spell upon me! My faith protects—"

"Of course," Raistlin sighed wearily, and there was an expression of sorrow in his face and voice, the sorrow of one who is constantly suspected, misunderstood. "I have simply given you a charm that will allow you to pass through Shoikan Grove. The way will not be easy"— his sarcasm returned—"but, undoubtedly your *faith* will sustain you!"

Pulling his hood low over his eyes, the mage bowed silently to Crysania, who could only stare at him, then he walked toward the door with slow, faltering steps. Reaching out a skeletal hand, he pulled the bell rope. The door opened and Bertrem entered so swiftly and suddenly that Crysania knew he must have been posted outside. Her lips tightened. She flashed the Aesthetic such a furious, imperious glance that the man paled visibly, though totally unaware of what crime he had committed, and mopped his shining forehead with the sleeve of his robe.

Raistlin started to leave, but Crysania stopped him. "I—I apologize for not trusting you, Raistlin Majere," she said softly. "And, again, I thank you for coming."

Raistlin turned. "And I apologize for my sharp tongue," he said. "Farewell, Revered Daughter. If

you truly do not fear knowledge, then come to the Tower two nights from this night, when Lunitari makes its first appearance in the sky."†

"I will be there," Crysania answered firmly, noting with pleasure Bertrem's look of shocked horror. Nodding in good-bye, she rested her hand lightly on the back of the ornately carved wooden chair.

The mage left the room, Bertrem followed, shutting the door behind him.

Left alone in the warm, silent room, Crysania fell to her knees before the chair. "Oh, thank you, Paladine!" she breathed. "I accept your challenge. I will not fail you! I will not fail!"†

The moons of Krynn always have story significance—and they have a tendency to rise and fall at the whim of the authors. —TRH

Lunitari was the first of the gods to take note of Raistlin's potential. I think that even when he switched to the black robes, he always had a fondness for her and she for him. —MW

And so ends the Prologue of the Legends trilogy. Why was this a prologue and not Chapter 1? What is the difference between a prologue and a first chapter? A Prologue sets the stage for the story proper. This is the Hero's Journey. (See Appendix A: Mythic Journeys.) —TRH

The Oxford English Dictionary *defines the prologue as:* "The preface or introduction to a discourse or performance; a preliminary discourse, poem, preface, preamble; esp. *a discourse or poem spoken as the introduction to a dramatic performance.*" *The goal of this prologue serves to introduce and set up the relationship between two characters around which the rest of the story will revolve.*

One of my creative writing teachers always said that the prologue should not contain any information that is critical to the story, since the author has to assume that not all readers will read the prologue. Thus this prologue does not provide any essential information. It merely introduces Raistlin and Crysania and reveals a bit about each of them—but information that is not critical to the story.

It is important that the book begins with Caramon's story, for he is the central character, and it is his quest for self that drives the story. —MW

BOOK 1

The World of Krynn

The Continent of Ansalon

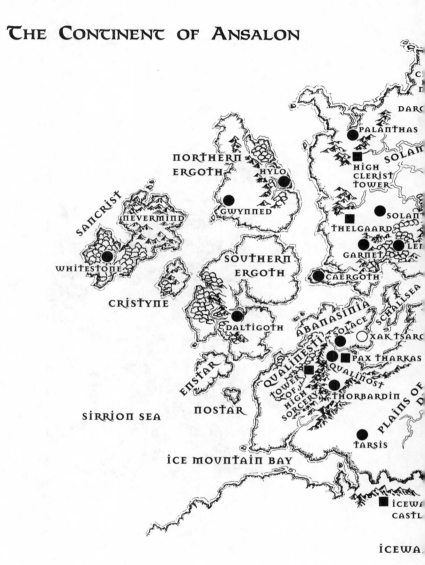

NORTH KEEP

NORDMAAR

VALKINORD

KALAMAN

GARGATH

GODSHOME

KORNEN

NERAKA

SANCTION

KHURI-KHAN

ZAHAKAR

KENDERMORE

BLODEN

TAKAR

SILVANESTI

SHALOST

SILVANOST

TOWERS OF ELI

WINSTON'S
TOWER

KARTHAY

MITHAS

KOTHAS

BLOOD SEA
OF ISTAR

BLOODWATCH

BLOOD
BAY

GOODLUND

THE RUINS

N

CIER

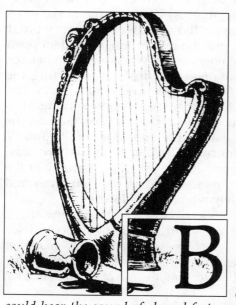

CHAPTER 1[†]

The cycle of the Monomyth (see Appendix A) as defined by Campbell always starts with the hero in a familiar setting like home. Here, we begin our Hero's Journey in the familiar setting of the Inn, tying both Chronicles and Legends together in space as well as giving the reader a reference of how much time has passed. —TRH

Behind her, she could hear the sound of clawed feet, scrapping through the leaves of the forest. Tika tensed, but tried to act as if she didn't hear, luring the creature on. Firmly, she gripped her sword in her hand. Her heart pounded. Closer and closer came the footsteps, she could hear the harsh breathing. The touch of a clawed hand fell upon her shoulder. Whirling about, Tika swung her sword and . . . knocked a tray full of mugs to the floor with a crash.

Dezra[†] shrieked and sprang backward in alarm. Patrons sitting at the bar burst into raucous laughter. Tika knew her face must be as red as her hair. Her heart was pounding, her hands shook.

"Dezra," she said coldly, "you have all the grace and brains of a gully dwarf. Perhaps you and Raf should switch places. *You* carry out the garbage and I'll let *him* wait tables!"

Dezra Phillips is a good friend of Tracy and Laura. Besides, I love the name! —MW

Dezra Despain Phillips is the origin of this name. Dezra was a childhood friend of my wife Laura, and we all went to the same High School together. Years later, Dezra wrote a short story for one of the DRAGONLANCE Tales anthologies. —TRH

Dezra looked up from where she knelt, picking broken pieces of crockery up off the floor, where they floated in a sea of beer. "Perhaps I should!" the waitress cried, tossing the pieces back onto the floor. "Wait tables yourself . . . or is that beneath you now, Tika Majere, Heroine of the Lance?"

Flashing Tika a hurt, reproachful glance, Dezra stood up, kicked the broken crockery out of her way, and flounced out of the Inn.

As the front door banged open, it hit sharply against its frame, making Tika grimace as she envisioned scratches on the woodwork. Sharp words† rose to her lips, but she bit her tongue and stopped their utterance, knowing she would regret them later.

The Hero's Journey of Legends does not start out with the arrival of armies and dark-armored kings. It begins with a domestic disturbance. Our hero must be well grounded in a home before he can be tempted or thrust into the fabled lands of adventure, or else he has nothing to protect behind him and nowhere to which he must return. —TRH

The door remained standing open, letting the bright light of fading afternoon flood the Inn. The ruddy glow of the setting sun gleamed in the bar's freshly polished wood surface and sparkled off the glasses. It even danced on the surface of the puddle on the floor. It touched Tika's flaming red curls teasingly, like the hand of a lover, causing many of the sniggering patrons to choke on their laughter and gaze at the comely woman with longing.

Not that Tika noticed. Now ashamed of her anger, she peered out the window, where she could see Dezra, dabbing at her eyes with an apron. A customer entered the open door, dragging it shut behind him. The light vanished, leaving the Inn once more in cool, half-darkness.

Tika brushed her hand across her own eyes. What kind of monster am I turning into? she asked herself remorsefully. After all, it wasn't Dezra's fault. It's this horrible feeling inside of me! I almost wish there were draconians to fight again. At least then I knew what I feared, at least then I could fight it with my own hands! How can I fight something I can't even name?

Voices broke in on her thoughts, clamoring for ale, for food. Laughter rose, echoing through the Inn of the Last Home.

This is what I came back to find. Tika sniffed and wiped her nose with the bar rag. This is my home. These people are as right and beautiful and warm as the setting sun. I'm surrounded by the sounds of love—laughter, good fellowship, a lapping dog. . . .

Lapping dog! Tika groaned and hurried out from behind the bar.

"Raf!" she exclaimed, staring at the gully dwarf† in despair.

"Beer spill. Me mop up," he said, looking at her and cheerfully wiping his hand across his mouth.

Several of the old-time customers laughed, but there were a few, new to the Inn, who were staring at the gully dwarf in disgust.

"Use this rag to clean it up!" Tika hissed out of the corner of her mouth as she grinned weakly at the customers in apology. She tossed Raf the bar rag and the gully dwarf caught it. But he only held it in his hand, staring at it with a mystified expression.

"What me do with this?"

"Clean up the spill!" Tika scolded, trying unsuccessfully to shield him from the customer's view with her long, flowing skirt.

"Oh! Me not need that," Raf said solemnly. "Me not get nice rag dirty." Handing the cloth back to Tika, the gully dwarf got down on all fours again and began to lick up the spilled beer, now mingled with tracked-in mud.

Her cheeks burning, Tika reached down and jerked Raf up by his collar, shaking him. "Use the rag!" she whispered furiously. "The customers are losing their appetites! And when you're finished with that, I want you to clear off that big table near the fire pit. I'm expecting friends—"† Tika stopped.

Raf was staring at her, wide-eyed, trying to absorb the complicated instructions. He was exceptional, as gully dwarves go. He'd only been there three weeks and Tika had already taught him to count to three (few gully dwarves ever get past two) and had finally gotten rid of his stench. This new-found intellectual prowess combined with cleanliness would have made him a king in a gully dwarf realm, but Raf had no such ambitions. He knew no king lived like he did— "mopping up" spilled beer (if he were quick) and "taking out" the garbage. But there were limits to Raf's talents, and Tika had just reached them.

"I'm expecting friends and—" she started again, then gave up. "Oh, never mind. Just mop this up— *with the rag*," she added severely, "then come to me to find out what to do next."

The most important facets of a gully dwarf's personality are generally agreed to be survival instinct, pride, endurance, and stupidity. Though derided by other intelligent races of Ansalon, gully dwarves continue to thrive under conditions that would have broken many others. Gully dwarves are a proud folk and act with great seriousness. They tend to have inflated ideas of their own places in the grand scheme of things; puncturing their egos is an almost impossible task. DRAGONLANCE Adventures, by Tracy Hickman and Margaret Weis, TSR, Inc., 1987, pp. 67, 68.]

This hearkens back to the beginning of Dragons of Autumn Twlight *when the heroes first gathered at the Inn of the Last Home.*

"Me no drink?" Raf began, then caught Tika's furious glare. "Me do."

Sighing in disappointment, the gully dwarf took the rag back and slopped it around, muttering about "waste good beer." Then he picked up pieces of the broken mugs and, after staring at them a moment, grinned and stuck them in the pockets of his shirt.

Tika† wondered briefly what he planned to do with them, but knew it was wiser not to ask. Returning to the bar, she grabbed some more mugs and filled them, trying not to notice that Raf had cut himself on some of the sharper pieces and was now leaning back on his heels, watching, with intense interest, the blood drip from his hand.

"Have you . . . uh . . . seen Caramon?" Tika asked the gully dwarf casually.

"Nope." Raf wiped his bloody hand in his hair. "But me know where to look." He leaped up eagerly. "Me go find?"

"No!" snapped Tika, frowning. "Caramon's at home."

"Me no think so," Raf said, shaking his head. "Not after sun go down—"

"He's home!" Tika snapped so angrily that the gully dwarf shrank away from her.

"You want to make bet?" Raf muttered, but well under his breath. Tika's temper these days was as fiery as her flaming hair.

Fortunately for Raf, Tika didn't hear him. She finished filling the beer mugs, then carried the tray over to a large party of elves, seated near the door.

I'm expecting friends, she repeated to herself dully. Dear friends. Once she would have been so excited, so eager to see Tanis and Riverwind. Now . . . She sighed, handing out the beer mugs without conscious awareness of what she was doing. Name of the true gods, she prayed, let them come and go quickly! Yes, above all, go quickly! If they stayed . . . If they found out. . . .

Tika's heart sank at the thought. Her lower lip trembled. If they stayed, that would be the end. Plain and simple. Her life would be over. The pain was suddenly more than she could bear. Hurriedly setting the last beer mug down, Tika left the elves, blinking her eyes rapidly. She did not notice the bemused gazes the elves exchanged among themselves as

"Tika is a lovely young woman in her early 20s. A heroine celebrated in legend and song throughout Krynn, Tika could have had her choice of men. She has loved Caramon since she was a girl and her love for him grew deeper during their adventures and perils together. Unfortunately, Tika never fully understood Caramon's relationship with his twin and his dependency on Raistlin. Tika hurried Caramon into marriage following the war, assuming that she could take Raistlin's place in Caramon's heart." [DRAGONLANCE Adventures, *by Tracy Hickman and Margaret Weis, TSR, Inc., 1987, p. 113.*]

they stared at the beer mugs, and she never did remember that they had all ordered wine.

Half blinded by her tears, Tika's only thought was to escape to the kitchen where she could weep unseen. The elves looked about for another waitress, and Raf, sighing in contentment, got back down on his hands and knees, happily lapping up the rest of the beer.

Tanis Half-Elven† stood at the bottom of a small rise, staring up the long, straight, muddy road that stretched ahead of him. The woman he escorted and their mounts waited some distance behind him. The woman had been in need of rest, as had their horses. Though her pride had kept her from saying a word, Tanis saw her face was gray and drawn with fatigue. Once today, in fact, she had nodded off to sleep in the saddle, and would have fallen but for Tanis's strong arm. Therefore, though eager to reach her destination, she had not protested when Tanis stated that he wanted to scout the road ahead alone. He helped her from her horse and saw her settled in a hidden thicket.

He had misgivings about leaving her unattended, but he sensed that the dark creatures pursuing them had fallen far behind. His insistence on speed had paid off, though both he and the woman were aching and exhausted. Tanis hoped to stay ahead of the things until he could turn his companion over to the one person on Krynn who might be able to help her.

They had been riding since dawn, fleeing a horror that had followed them since leaving Palanthas. What it was exactly, Tanis—with all his experience during the wars—could not name. And that made it all the more frightening. Never there when confronted, it was only seen from the corner of the eye that was looking for something else. His companion had sensed it, too, he could tell, though, characteristically, she was too proud to admit to fear.

Walking away from the thicket, Tanis felt guilty. He shouldn't be leaving her alone, he knew. He shouldn't be wasting precious time. All his warrior senses protested. But there was one thing he had to do, and he had to do it alone. To do otherwise would have seemed sacrilege.

And so Tanis stood at the bottom of the hill, summoning his courage to move forward. Anyone looking

The similarities between Tanis's appearance here and at the beginning of Chronicles is intentional. It once more grounds us in the familiar before we fall into the unknown. —TRH

We first see Tanis standing at the bottom of the stairs leading to the Inn of the Last Home because this brings his life full-circle. When we see him on the stairs in Chronicles, his life is in turmoil. He doesn't know who he is or what he wants of life. He has been searching for answers for years and has not been able to find them. Chronicles will bring him knowledge of himself and the answer to his questions. Now he comes back to the Inn as a man complete, secure in his life. —MW

at him might have supposed he was advancing to fight an ogre. But that was not the case. Tanis Half-Elven was returning home. And he both longed for and dreaded his first sight.

The afternoon sun was beginning its downward journey toward night. It would be dark before he reached the Inn, and he dreaded traveling the roads by night. But, once there, this nightmarish journey would be over. He would leave the woman in capable hands and continue on to Qualinesti. But, first, there was this he had to face. With a deep sigh, Tanis Half-Elven drew his green hood up over his head and began the climb.

Topping the rise, his gaze fell upon a large, moss-covered boulder. For a moment, his memories overwhelmed him. He closed his eyes, feeling the sting of swift tears beneath the lids. "Stupid quest," he heard the dwarf's voice echo in his memory. "Silliest thing I ever did!"

Flint! My old friend!

I can't go on, Tanis thought. This is too painful. Why did I ever agree to come back? It holds nothing for me now . . . nothing except the pain of old wounds. My life is good, at last. Finally I am at peace, happy. Why . . . why did I tell them I would come?

Tanis is remembering events from Dragons of Autumn Twlight, *Book I, Chapter 1.*

Drawing a shuddering sigh, he opened his eyes and looked at the boulder. Two years ago†—it would be three this autumn—he had topped this rise and met his long-time friend, the dwarf, Flint Fireforge, sitting on that boulder, carving wood, and complaining—as usual. That meeting had set in motion events that had shaken the world, culminating in the War of the Lance, the battle that cast the Queen of Darkness back into the Abyss, and broke the might of the Dragon Highlords.

These accoutrements mark Tanis's accomplishments from his adventures in the War of the Lance. He has been honored by all of the major races of Ansalon.

Now I am a hero, Tanis thought, glancing down ruefully at the gaudy panoply he wore: breastplate† of a Knight of Solamnia; green silken sash, mark of the Wildrunners of Silvanesti, the elves' most honored legions; the medallion of Kharas, the dwarves' highest honor; plus countless others. No one—human, elf, or half-elf—had been so honored. It was ironic. He who hated armor, who hated ceremony, now forced to wear it as befitting his station. How the old dwarf would have laughed.

"You—a hero!" He could almost hear the dwarf

snort. But Flint was dead†. He had died two years ago this spring in Tanis's arms.

"Why the beard?" He could swear once again that he heard Flint's voice, the first words he had said upon seeing the half-elf in the road. "You were ugly enough. . . ."

Tanis smiled and scratched the beard that no elf on Krynn could grow, the beard that was the outward, visible sign of his half-human heritage. Flint knew well enough why the beard, Tanis thought, gazing fondly at the sun-warmed boulder. He knew me better than I knew myself. He knew of the chaos that raged inside my soul. He knew I had a lesson to learn.

"And I learned it," Tanis whispered to the friend who was with him in spirit only. "I learned it, Flint. But . . . oh, it was bitter!"

The smell of wood smoke came to Tanis. That and the slanting rays of the sun and the chill in the spring air reminded him he still had some distance to travel. Turning, Tanis Half-Elven looked down into the valley where he had spent the bittersweet years of his young manhood. Turning, Tanis Half-Elven looked down upon Solace.

It had been autumn when he last saw the small town. The vallenwood trees† in the valley had been ablaze with the season's colors, the brilliant reds and golds fading into the purple of the peaks of the Kharolis mountains beyond, the deep azure of the sky mirrored in the still waters of Crystalmir Lake.† There had been a haze of smoke over the valley, the smoke of home fires burning in the peaceful town that had once roosted in the vallenwood trees like contented birds. He and Flint had watched the lights flicker on, one by one, in the houses that sheltered among the leaves of the huge trees. Solace—tree city†—one of the beauties and wonders of Krynn.

For a moment, Tanis saw the vision in his mind's eye as clearly as he had seen it two years before. Then the vision faded. Then it had been autumn. Now it was spring. The smoke was there still, the smoke of the home fires. But now it came mostly from houses built on the ground. There was the green of living, growing things, but it only seemed— in Tanis's mind—to emphasize the black scars upon the land; scars† that could never be totally erased,

Flint died in Dragons of Spring Dawning, *Book III, Chapter 3.*

While a missionary in Indonesia, I was so impressed with the banyan trees that I wanted to do something similar in Krynn. More than that, I had a special fondness for tree houses as a child and thought that given the right forest, everyone should live this way. —TRH

The name for Crystalmir Lake comes from "Mirror Lake" and "crystal mirror." —TRH

When I was a child and our family ran out of e-tickets at Disneyland, we would always make our way over to the Swiss Family Robinson tree house. I thought it needed to be bigger. Hence, Solace! —TRH

This is, of course, the aftermath of the Night of Dragons as seen in Dragons of Autumn Twilight, *Book II, Chapter 1.*

though here and there he saw the marks of the plow across them.

Tanis shook his head. Everyone thought that, with the destruction of the Queen's foul temple at Neraka,† the war was over. Everyone was anxious to plow over the black and burned land, scorched by dragonfire, and forget their pain.

See Dragons of Spring Dawning, *Book III, Chapters 12-14.*

His eyes went to a huge circle of black that stood in the center of town. Here, nothing would grow. No plow could turn the soil ravaged by dragonfire and soaked by the blood of innocents, murdered by the troops of the Dragon Highlords.†

Tanis is remembering events from Dragons of Autumn Twilight, *Book II, Chapter 1.*

Tanis smiled grimly. He could imagine how an eyesore like that must irritate those who were working to forget. He was glad it was there. He hoped it would remain, forever.

Softly, he repeated words he had heard Elistan speak, as the cleric dedicated in solemn ceremony the High Clerist's Tower to the memory of those knights who had died there.

"We must remember or we will fall into complacency—as we did before—and the evil will come again."

If it is not already upon us, Tanis thought grimly. And, with that in mind, he turned and walked rapidly back down the hill.

It surprised me during our creation of the DRAGONLANCE *setting how many names we came up with that sounded like real places from history— Abanasinia vs. Abyssinia; Tarsis vs. Tarsus. Whether these were bubbling up from our subconscious or were just accidents of phonetics is impossible to say. —TRH*

The Inn of the Last Home was crowded that evening.

While the war had brought devastation and destruction to the residents of Solace, the end of the war had brought such prosperity that there were already some who were saying it hadn't been "such a bad thing." Solace had long been a crossroads for travelers through the lands of Abanasinia.† But, in the days before the war, the numbers of travelers had been relatively few. The dwarves—except for a few renegades like Flint Fireforge—had shut themselves up in their mountain kingdom of Thorbardin† or barricaded themselves in the hills, refusing to have anything to do with the rest of the world. The elves had done the same, dwelling in the beautiful lands of Qualinesti to the southwest and Silvanesti on the eastern edge of the continent of Ansalon.

I suspect Thor had a great deal of influence on the name Thorbardin. —TRH

The war had changed all that. Elves and dwarves and humans traveled extensively now, their lands and their kingdoms open to all. But it had taken

almost total annihilation to bring about this fragile state of brotherhood.

The Inn of the Last Home—always popular with travelers because of its fine drink and Otik's famous spiced potatoes†—became more popular still. The drink was still fine and the potatoes as good as ever—though Otik had retired—but the real reason for the Inn's increase in popularity was that it had become a place of some renown. The Heroes of the Lance—as they were now called—had been known to frequent this Inn in days gone by.

Otik had, in fact, before his retirement, seriously considered putting up a plaque over the table near the firepit—perhaps something like "Tanis Half-Elven† and Companions Drank Here." But Tika had opposed the scheme so vehemently (the mere thought of what Tanis would say if he caught sight of that made Tika's cheeks burn) that Otik had let it drop. But the rotund barkeep never tired of telling his patrons the story of the night the barbarian woman had sung her strange song and healed Hederick the Theocrat with her blue crystal staff, giving the first proof of the existence of the ancient, true gods.

Tika, who took over management of the Inn upon Otik's retirement and was hoping to save enough money to buy the business, fervently hoped Otik would refrain from telling that story again tonight. But she might have spent her hope on better things.

There were several parties of elves who had traveled all the way from Silvanesti to attend the funeral of Solostaran—Speaker of the Suns† and ruler of the elven lands of Qualinesti. They were not only urging Otik to tell his story, but were telling some of their own, about the Heroes' visit to their land and how they freed it from the evil dragon, Cyan Bloodbane.†

Tika saw Otik glance her direction wistfully at this—Tika had, after all, been one of the members of the group in Silvanesti. But she silenced him with a furious shake of her red curls. *That* was one part of their journey she refused ever to relate or even discuss. In fact, she prayed nightly that she would forget the hideous nightmares of that tortured land.

Otik's spiced potatoes, perhaps the most famous cuisine in all of Ansalon:

1 pound potatoes (any kind)
3 tabelspoons butter
1/2 medium onion, finely chopped
1 to 2 dashes cayenne

Scrub potatoes and remove any eyes. Chop into 1/2-inch cubes with skins. Melt butter in frying pan (traditionally an iron skillet), and heat until sizzling. Add cayenne to butter; stir. Place potatoes in butter and fry until crisp; stir occasionally. Add onion and fry 1 more minute. Serve hot, salted to taste. Serves 2 to 4. [Leaves from the Inn of the Last Home, edited by Margaret Weis and Tracy Hickman, TSR, Inc., 1987, p.253.]

The events Otik so loves to recount are found in Dragons of Autumn Twilight, *Book I, Chapter 3.*

I believe that the intention for the title "Speaker of the Suns" was to equate "suns" with "days." This is opposed to "Speaker of the Stars" equating "stars" with "nights." The reference here is not intended to indicate any special knowledge the elves have regarding the nature of interstellar bodies. —TRH

See Dragons of Winter Night, *Book I, Chapters 10-12.*

31

Tika closed her eyes a moment, wishing the elves would drop the conversation. She had her own nightmares now. She needed no past ones to haunt her. "Just let them come and go quickly," she said softly to herself and to whatever god might be listening.

It was just past sunset. More and more customers entered, demanding food and drink. Tika had apologized to Dezra, the two friends had shed a few tears together, and now were kept busy running from kitchen to bar to table. Tika started every time the door opened, and she scowled irritably when she heard Otik's voice rise above the clatter of mugs and tongues.

". . . beautiful autumn night, as I recall, and I was, of course, busier than a draconian drill sergeant." That always got a laugh. Tika gritted her teeth. Otik had an appreciative audience and was in full swing. There would be no stopping him now. "The Inn was up in the vallenwood trees then, like the rest of our lovely city before the dragons destroyed it.† Ah, how beautiful it was in the old days." He sighed— he always sighed at this point—and wiped away a tear. There was a sympathetic murmur from the crowd. "Where was I?" He blew his nose, another part of the act. "Ah, yes. There I was, behind the bar, when the door opened. . . ."

The door opened. It might have been done on cue, so perfect was the timing. Tika brushed back a strand of red hair from her perspiring forehead and glanced over nervously. Sudden silence filled the room. Tika stiffened, her nails digging into her hands.

A tall man, so tall he had to duck to enter the door, stood in the doorway. His hair was dark, his face grim and stern.

Although cloaked in furs, it was obvious from his walk and stance that his body was strong and muscular. He cast a swift glance around the crowded Inn, sizing up those who were present, wary and watchful of danger.

But it was an instinctive action only, for when his penetrating, somber gaze rested on Tika, his stern face relaxed into a smile and he held his arms open wide.

Tika hesitated, but the sight of her friend suddenly filled her with joy and a strange wave of

The dragons destroyed Solace in Dragons of Autumn Twilight, *Book II, Chapter 1.*

homesickness. Shoving her way through the crowd, she was caught in his embrace.

"Riverwind,† my friend!" she murmured brokenly.

Grasping the young woman in his arms, Riverwind lifted her effortlessly, as though she were a child. The crowd began to cheer, banging their mugs on the table. Most couldn't believe their luck. Here was a Hero of the Lance himself, as if carried on the wings of Otik's story. And he even looked the part! They were enchanted.

For, upon releasing Tika, the tall man had thrown his fur cloak back from his shoulders, and now all could see the Mantle of the Chieftain that the Plainsman wore, its V-shaped sections of alternating furs and tooled leathers each representing one of the Plains tribes over which he ruled. His handsome face, though older and more careworn than when Tika had seen him last, was burned bronze by the sun and weather, and there was an inner joy within the man's eyes which showed that he had found in his life the peace he had been searching for years before.

Tika felt a choking sensation in her throat and turned quickly away, but not quickly enough.

"Tika," he said, his accent thick from living once more among his people, "it is good to see you well and beautiful still. Where's Caramon? I cannot wait to see—Why, Tika, what's wrong?'

"Nothing, nothing," Tika said briskly, shaking her red curls and blinking her eyes. "Come, I have a place saved for you by the fire. You must be exhausted and hungry."

She led him through the crowd, talking nonstop, never giving him a chance to say a word. The crowd inadvertently helped her, keeping Riverwind occupied as they gathered around to touch and marvel over his fur cloak, or tried to shake his hand (a custom Plainsmen consider barbaric) or thrust drinks into his face.

Riverwind accepted it all stoically, as he followed Tika through the excited throng, clasping the beautiful sword of elven make close to his side. His stern face grew a shade darker, and he glanced often out the windows as though already longing to escape the confines of this noisy, hot room and return to the outdoors he loved. But Tika skillfully

Riverwind appeared throughout the Chronicles. His adventures previous to the events in Chronicles are told in Riverwind the Plainsman *by Paul B. Thompson and Tonya C. Cook. He met his death many years later in* Spirit of the Wind *by Chris Pierson.*

shoved the more exuberant patrons aside and soon had her old friend seated by the fire at an isolated table near the kitchen door.

"I'll be back," she said, flashing him a smile and vanishing into the kitchen before he could open his mouth.

The sound of Otik's voice rose once again, accompanied by a loud banging. His story having been interrupted, Otik was using his cane—one of the most feared weapons in Solace—to restore order. The barkeep was crippled in one leg now and he enjoyed telling that story, too—about how he had been injured during the fall of Solace, when, by his own account, he single-handedly fought off the invading armies of draconians.

Grabbing a panful of spiced potatoes and hurrying back to Riverwind, Tika glared at Otik irritably. She knew the true story, how he had hurt his leg being dragged out of his hiding place beneath the floor. But she never told it. Deep within, she loved the old man like a father. He had taken her in and raised her, when her own father disappeared, giving her honest work when she might have turned to thievery. Besides, just reminding him that *she* knew the truth was useful in keeping Otik's tall tales from stretching to new heights.

The crowd was fairly quiet when Tika returned, giving her a chance to talk to her old friend.

Riverwind and Goldmoon's son is named Wanderer. Many years after this, he played a small role in the War of Souls trilogy. See Dragons of a Vanished Moon, *Book I, Chapter 9.*

"How is Goldmoon and your son?"† she asked brightly, seeing Riverwind looking at her, studying her intently.

"She is fine and sends her love," Riverwind answered in his deep, low baritone. "My son"—his eyes glowed with pride—"is but two, yet already stands this tall and sits a horse better than most warriors."

"I was hoping Goldmoon would come with you," Tika said with a sigh she didn't mean Riverwind to hear. The tall Plainsman ate his food for a moment in silence before he answered.

Two daughters: Brightdawn and Moonsong. As adults, both daughters went with their father on his last great adventure in Spirit of the Wind, *by Chris Pierson.*

"The gods have blessed us with two more children,"† he said, staring at Tika with a strange expression in his dark eyes.

"Two?" Tika looked puzzled, then, "oh, twins!" she cried joyfully. "Like Caramon and Rais—" She stopped abruptly, biting her lip.

Riverwind frowned and made the sign that wards off evil. Tika flushed and looked away. There was a roaring in her ears. The heat and the noise made her dizzy. Swallowing the bitter taste in her mouth, she forced herself to ask more about Goldmoon and, after awhile, could even listen to Riverwind's answer.

". . . still too few clerics in our land. There are many converts, but the powers of the gods come slowly. She works hard, too hard to my mind, but she grows more beautiful every day. And the babies, our daughters, both have silver-golden hair—"

Babies. . . . Tika smiled sadly. Seeing her face, Riverwind fell silent, finished eating, and pushed his plate away. "I can think of nothing I would rather do than continue this visit," he said slowly, "but I cannot be gone long from my people. You know the urgency of my mission. Where is Cara—"

"I must go check on your room," Tika said, standing up so quickly she jostled the table, spilling Riverwind's drink. "That gully dwarf is supposed to be making the bed. I'll probably find him sound asleep—"

She hurried away. But she did not go upstairs to the rooms. Standing outside by the kitchen door, feeling the night wind cool her fevered cheeks, she stared out into the darkness. "Let him go away!" she whispered. "Please. . . ."

erhaps most of all, Tanis feared his first sight of the Inn of the Last Home. Here it had all started, three years ago this autumn. Here he and Flint and the irrepressible kender, Tasslehoff Burrfoot, had come that night to meet old friends. Here his world had turned upside down,† never to exactly right itself again.

But, riding toward the Inn, Tanis found his fears eased. It had changed so much it was like coming to some place strange, a place that held no memories. It stood on the ground, instead of in the branches of a great vallenwood.† There were new additions, more rooms had been built to accommodate the influx of travelers, it had a new roof, much more modern in design. All the scars of war had been purged, along with the memories.

Then, just as Tanis was beginning to relax, the front door of the Inn opened. Light streamed out, forming

See Dragons of Autumn Twilight, *Book I, Chapter 2.*

The deciduous vallenwood is the largest species of tree in Ansalon. Some reach heights of almost 300 feet, and the leaves on a mature tree are almost a foot across. The origin of the name "vallenwood" has

a golden path of welcome, the smell of spiced potatoes and the sound of laughter came to him on the
evening breeze. The memories returned in a rush,
and Tanis bowed his head, overcome.

But, perhaps fortunately, he did not have time to
dwell upon the past. As he and his companion
approached the Inn, a stableboy ran out to grab the
horses' reins.

"Food and water," said Tanis, sliding wearily
from the saddle and tossing the boy a coin. He
stretched to ease the cramps in his muscles. "I sent
word ahead that I was to have a fresh horse waiting
for me here. My name is Tanis Half-Elven."

The boy's eyes opened wide; he had already
been staring at the bright armor and rich cloak
Tanis wore. Now his curiosity was replaced by awe
and admiration.

"Y-yes, sir," he stammered, abashed at being
addressed by such a great hero. "T-the horse is
ready, sh-shall I bring him around n-now, sir?"

"No." Tanis smiled. "I will eat first. Bring him in
two hours."

"T-two hours. Yes, sir. Thank you, sir." Bobbing
his head, the boy took the reins Tanis pressed into
his unfeeling hand, then stood there, gaping, completely forgetting his task until the impatient horse
nudged him, nearly knocking him over.

As the boy hurried off, leading Tanis's horse
away, the half-elf turned to assist his companion
down from her saddle.

"You must be made of iron," she said, looking at
Tanis as he helped her to the ground. "Do you really
intend to ride further tonight?"

"To tell the truth, every bone in my body aches,"
Tanis began, then paused, feeling uncomfortable.
He was simply unable to feel at ease around this
woman.

Tanis could see her face reflected in the light
beaming from the Inn. He saw fatigue and pain. Her
eyes were sunken into pale, hollow cheeks. She
staggered as she stepped upon the ground, and
Tanis was quick to give her his arm to lean upon.
This she did, but only for a moment. Then, drawing
herself up she gently but firmly pushed him away
and stood alone, glancing at her surroundings without interest.

been lost. *Natives of Solace
and Abanasinia, when
asked, reply, "They've just
always been called that."
[Adapted from "The
Vallenwoods" by Teri
McLaren (née Williams),*
The History of
Dragonlance, *edited by
Margaret Weis & Tracy
Hickman, TSR 1995, pp.
194-196.]*

SHREDDING
BARK ON
TRUNKS

Every move hurt Tanis, and he could imagine how this woman must feel, unaccustomed as she was to physical exertion or hardship, and he was forced to regard her with grudging admiration. She had not complained once on their long and frightening journey. She had kept up with him, never lagging behind and obeying his instructions without question.

Why, then, he wondered, couldn't he feel anything for her? What was there about her that irritated him and annoyed him? Looking at her face, Tanis had his answer. The only warmth there was the warmth reflected from the Inn's light. Her face itself—even exhausted—was cold, passionless, devoid of—what? Humanity? Thus she had been all this long, dangerous journey. Oh, she had been coolly polite, coolly grateful, coolly distant and remote. She probably would have coolly buried me, Tanis thought grimly. Then, as if to reprimand him for his irreverent thoughts, his gaze was drawn to the medallion she wore around her neck, the Platinum Dragon† of Paladine. He remembered Elistan's parting words, spoken in private just before their journey's beginning.

The dragons were taken straight out of the original Monster Manual—*twelve dragon types, six good and six evil. The* DRAGONLANCE *setting has its roots firmly planted in the* DUNGEONS & DRAGONS *of the 1980s.* —*TRH*

"It is fitting that you escort her, Tanis," said the now-frail cleric. "In many ways, she begins a journey much like your own years ago—seeking self-knowledge. No, you are right, she doesn't know this herself yet." This in answer to Tanis's dubious look. "She walks forward with her gaze fixed upon the heavens," Elistan smiled sadly. "She has not yet learned that, in so doing, one will surely stumble. Unless she learns, her fall may be hard." Shaking his head, he murmured a soft prayer. "But we must put our trust in Paladine."

Tanis had frowned then and he frowned now, thinking about it. Though he had come to a strong belief in the true gods—more through Laurana's love and faith in them than anything else—he felt uncomfortable trusting his life to them, and he grew impatient with those like Elistan who, it seemed, placed too great a burden upon the gods. Let man be responsible for himself for a change, Tanis thought irritably.

"What is it, Tanis?" Crysania asked coldly.

Realizing he had been staring at her all this while, Tanis coughed in embarrassment, cleared his throat,

and looked away. Fortunately, the boy returned for Crysania's horse at this moment, sparing Tanis the need to answer. He gestured at the Inn, and the two walked toward it.

"Actually," Tanis said when the silence grew awkward, "I would like nothing better than to stay here and visit with my friends. But I have to be in Qualinesti the day after tomorrow, and only by hard riding will I arrive in time. My relations with my brother-in-law† are not such that I can afford to offend him by missing Solostaran's funeral." He added with a grim smile, "Both politically and personally, if you take my meaning."

Crysania smiled in turn, but—Tanis saw—it was not a smile of understanding. It was a smile of tolerance, as if this talk of politics and family were beneath her.

They had reached the door to the Inn. "Besides," Tanis added softly, "I miss Laurana.† Funny, isn't it. When she is near and we're busy about our own tasks, we'll sometimes go for days with just a quick smile or a touch and then we disappear into our worlds. But when I'm far away from her, it's like I suddenly awaken to find my right arm cut off. I may not go to bed thinking of my right arm, but when it is gone. . . ."

Tanis stopped abruptly, feeling foolish, afraid he sounded like a lovesick adolescent. But Crysania, he realized, was apparently not paying the least bit of attention to him. Her smooth, marble face had grown, if anything, more cold until the moon's silver light† seemed warm by comparison. Shaking his head, Tanis pushed open the door.

I don't envy Caramon and Riverwind, he thought grimly.

The warm, familiar sounds and smells of the Inn washed over Tanis and, for long moments, everything was a blur. Here was Otik, older and fatter, if possible, leaning upon a cane and pounding him on the back. Here were people he had not seen in years, who had never had much to do with him before, now shaking his hand and claiming his friendship. Here was the old bar, still brightly polished, and somehow he managed to step on a gully dwarf. . . .

And then there was a tall man cloaked in furs, and Tanis was clasped inside his friend's warm embrace.

Tanis has two brothers-in-law: Porthios, the eldest, and Gilthanas—both brothers to Tanis's wife, Laurana. The brother to whom Tanis is referring here is Porthios, who succeeded his father as Speaker of the Suns.

Laurana, wife of Tanis, played a major role in the original DRAGONLANCE Chronicles. Her name was taken from Laura Hickman. [The Annotated Chronicles, by Margaret Weis and Tracy Hickman, Wizards of the Coast, Inc., 1999, p. 315.]

Nothing symbolic in a story is coincidence. The light shines on Crysania with purpose and is part of the deeper structure of the book. —TRH

This "silver light" indicates that Solinari—the moon representing Good—is shining upon her. The other moons—Lunitari, representing Neutral, and Nuitari, representing evil—often come into play with other characters, such as Soth, Raistlin, Dalamar, etc.

"Riverwind," he whispered huskily, holding onto the Plainsman tightly.

"My brother," Riverwind said in Que-shu, the language of his people. The crowd in the Inn was cheering wildly, but Tanis didn't hear them, because a woman with flaming red hair and a smattering of freckles had her hand upon his arm. Reaching out still holding fast to Riverwind, Tanis gathered Tika into their embrace and for long moments the three friends clung to each other—bound together by sorrow and pain and glory.

Riverwind brought them to their senses. Unaccustomed to such public displays of emotion, the tall Plainsman regained his composure with a gruff cough and stood back, blinking his eyes rapidly and frowning at the ceiling until he was master of himself again. Tanis, his reddish beard wet with his own tears, gave Tika another swift hug, then looked around.

"Where's that big lummox of a husband of yours?" he asked cheerfully. "Where's Caramon?"

It was a simple question, and Tanis was totally unprepared for the response. The crowd fell completely silent; it seemed as if someone had shut them all up in a barrel. Tika's face flushed an ugly red, she muttered something unintelligible, and, bending down, dragged a gully dwarf up off the floor and shook him so his teeth rattled in his head.

Startled, Tanis looked at Riverwind, but the Plainsman only shrugged and raised his dark eyebrows. The half-elf turned to ask Tika what was going on, but just then felt a cool touch upon his arm. Crysania! He had completely forgotten her!

His own face flushing, he made his belated introductions.

"May I present Crysania of Tarinius, Revered Daughter of Paladine," Tanis said formally. "Lady Crysania, Riverwind, Chieftain of the Plainsmen, and Tika Waylant Majere."

The name Waylan resonates with mythic significance. Weland was a Germanic god, most often associated with metalworkers, smiths, and swords.

Crysania untied her traveling cloak and drew back her hood. As she did so, the platinum medallion she wore around her neck flashed in the bright candlelight of the Inn. The woman's pure white lamb's wool robes peeped through the folds of her cloak. A murmur—both reverent and respectful—went through the crowd.

"A holy cleric!"

"Did you catch her name? Crysania! Next in line . . ."

"Elistan's successor . . ."†

Crysania inclined her head. Riverwind bowed from the waist, his face solemn, and Tika, her own face still so flushed she appeared feverish, shoved Raf hurriedly behind the bar, then made a deep curtsey.

At the sound of Tika's married name, Majere, Crysania glanced at Tanis questioningly and received his nod in return.

"I am honored," Crysania said in her rich, cool voice, "to meet two whose deeds of courage shine as an example to us all."

Tika flushed in pleased embarrassment. Riverwind's stern face did not change expression, but Tanis saw how much the cleric's praise meant to the deeply religious Plainsman. As for the crowd, they cheered boisterously at this honor to their own and kept on cheering. Otik, with all due ceremony, led his guests to a waiting table, beaming on the heroes as if he had arranged the entire war especially for their benefit.

Sitting down, Tanis at first felt disturbed by the confusion and noise but soon decided it was beneficial. At least he could talk to Riverwind without fear of being overheard. But first, he had to find out—where was Caramon?

Once again, he started to ask, but Tika—after seeing them seated and fussing over Crysania like a mother hen—saw him open his mouth and, turning abruptly, disappeared into the kitchen.

Tanis shook his head, puzzled, but before he could think about it further, Riverwind was asking him questions. The two were soon deeply involved in talk.

"Everyone thinks the war is over," Tanis said, sighing. "And that places us in worse danger than before. Alliances between elves and humans that were strong when times were dark are beginning to melt in the sun. Laurana's in Qualinesti now, attending the funeral of her father† and also trying to arrange an agreement with that stiff-necked brother of hers, Porthios,† and the Knights of Solamnia. The only ray of hope we have is in Porthios's wife, Alhana Starbreeze,"† Tanis smiled. "I never thought I would live to see that elf woman not only tolerant

"Elistan is a prophet of Paladine on Krynn. During the Dragonlance Wars he brought the knowledge of the true gods back to the greater world. Now, however, he is gravely ill. Elistan refuses to allow any to pray to Paladine in an attempt to heal him, saying that the god had granted him life once and his work here is complete. He has brought back knowledge of the true gods and built a beautiful Temple in Palanthus. He now wants only to die in peace.

"Elistan's greatest concern is for the church and for Crysania. He has been given knowledge from Paladine that if Crysania succeeds in her quest, she will be a great leader—a powerful cleric, ruling over the church with wisdom and compassion." [DRAGONLANCE Adventures, *by Tracy Hickman and Margaret Weis, TSR, Inc., 1987, p. 110.]*

Laurana's father is Solostaran, Qualinesti Speaker of the Suns.

Porthios is Solostaran's successor and Tanis's brother-in-law.

Alhana Starbreeze, daughter of the Silvanesti king Lorac Caladon.

of humans and other races, but even warmly supporting them to her intolerant husband."

"A strange marriage," Riverwind commented, and Tanis nodded in agreement. Both men's thoughts were with their friend, the knight, Sturm Brightblade, now lying dead†—hero of the High Clerist's Tower. Both knew Alhana's heart had been buried there in the darkness with Sturm.

Sturm died in Dragons of Winter Night, *Book III, Chapter 13*

The marriage of Alhana and Porthios was a political one, made in hopes of improving relations between the two estranged elven kingdoms.

"Certainly not a marriage of love,"† Tanis shrugged. "But it may be a marriage that will help restore order to the world. Now, what of you, my friend? Your face is dark and drawn with new worries, as well as beaming with new joy. Goldmoon sent Laurana word of the twins."

Riverwind smiled briefly. "You are right. I begrudge every minute I am away," the Plainsman said in his deep voice, "though seeing you again, my brother, lightens my heart's burden. But I left two tribes on the verge of war. So far, I have managed to keep them talking, and there has been no blood shed yet. But malcontents work against me, behind my back. Every minute I am away gives them a chance to stir up old blood feuds."

Tanis clasped his arm. "I am sorry, my friend, and I am grateful you came." Then he sighed again and glanced at Crysania, realizing he had new problems. "I had hoped you would be able to offer this lady your guidance and protection." His voice sank to a murmur. "She travels to the Tower of High Sorcery in Wayreth Forest."†

"The Wayreth Tower's defense is the most unusual [of all the Towers], for one does not seek out the tower, it finds you. The garden about Wayreth Tower has different dimensions at different times and the Tower itself is said to exist without dimension, always existing where it is not. The result is that one could be walking in a forest and suddenly be trespassing within the domains of the wizards of Wayreth." [DRAGONLANCE Adventures, *by Tracy Hickman and Margaret Weis, TSR, Inc., 1987, p. 30.*]

Riverwind's eyes widened in alarm and disapproval. The Plainsman distrusted mages and anything connected with them.

Tanis nodded. "I see you remember Caramon's stories about the time he and Raistlin traveled there. And *they* had been invited. This lady goes without invitation, to seek the mages' advice about—"

Crysania gave him a sharp, imperious glance. Frowning, she shook her head. Tanis, biting his lip, added lamely, "I was hoping you could escort her—"

"I feared as much," said Riverwind, "when I received your message, and that was why I felt I had to come—to offer you some explanation for my refusal. If it were any other time, you know I would gladly help and, in particular, I would be honored to offer my services to a person so revered." He bowed

slightly to Crysania, who accepted his homage with a smile that vanished instantly when she returned her gaze to Tanis. A small, deep line of anger appeared between her brows.

Riverwind continued, "But there is too much at stake. The peace I have established between the tribes, many who have been at war for years, is a fragile one. Our survival as a nation and a people depend upon us uniting and working together to rebuild our land and our lives."

"I understand," Tanis said, touched by Riverwind's obvious unhappiness in having to refuse his request for help. The half-elf caught Lady Crysania's displeased stare, however, and he turned to her with grim politeness. "All will be well, Revered Daughter," he said, speaking with elaborate patience. "Caramon will guide you, and he is worth three of us ordinary mortals, right, Riverwind?"

The Plainsman smiled, old memories returning. "He can eat as much as three ordinary mortals, certainly. And he is as strong as three or more. Do you remember, Tanis, when he used to lift stout Pig-faced William off his feet, when we put on that show in . . . where was it . . . Flotsam?"

"And the time he killed those two draconians by bashing their heads together," Tanis laughed, feeling the darkness of the world suddenly lift in sharing those times with his friend. "And do you remember when we were in the dwarven kingdom and Caramon sneaked up behind Flint and—" Leaning forward, Tanis whispered in Riverwind's ear. The Plainsman's face flushed with laughter. He recounted another tale, and the two men continued, recalling stories of Caramon's strength, his skill with a sword, his courage and honor.

"And his gentleness," Tanis added, after a moment's quiet reflection. "I can see him now, tending to Raistlin so patiently, holding his brother in his arms when those coughing fits nearly tore the mage apart—"

He was interrupted by a smothered cry, a crash, and a thud. Turning in astonishment, Tanis saw Tika staring at him, her face white, her green eyes glimmering with tears.

"Leave now!" she pleaded through pale lips. "Please, Tanis! Don't ask any questions! Just go!"

The plains people of Riverwind and Goldmoon's tribe were always modeled very broadly after Native Americans. —TRH

She grabbed his arm, her nails digging painfully into his flesh.

"Look, what in the name of the Abyss is going on, Tika?" Tanis asked in exasperation, standing up and facing her.

A splintering crash came in answer. The door to the Inn burst open, hit from outside by some tremendous force. Tika jumped back, her face convulsed in such fear and horror as she looked at the door that Tanis turned swiftly, his hand on his sword, and Riverwind rose to his feet.

A large shadow filled the doorway, seeming to spread a pall over the room. The crowd's cheerful noise and laughter ceased abruptly, changing to low, angry mutterings.

Remembering the dark and evil things that had been chasing them, Tanis drew his sword, placing himself between the darkness and Lady Crysania. He sensed, though he did not see, Riverwind's stalwart presence behind him, backing him up.

So, it's caught up with us, Tanis thought, almost welcoming the chance to fight this vague, unknown terror. Grimly he stared at the door, watching as a bloated, grotesque figure entered into the light.

It was a man, Tanis saw, a huge man, but, as he looked more closely, he saw it was a man whose giant girth had run to flab. A bulging belly hung over cinched up leather leggings. A filthy shirt gaped open at the navel, there being too little shirt to cover too much flesh. The man's face—partially obscured by a three-day growth of beard—was unnaturally flushed and splotchy, his hair greasy and unkempt. His clothes, while fine and well-made, were dirty and smelled strongly of vomit and the raw liquor known as dwarf spirits.

Tanis lowered his sword, feeling like a fool. It was just some poor drunken wretch, probably the town bully, using his great size to intimidate the citizenry. He looked at the man with pity and disgust, thinking, even as he did so, that there was something oddly familiar about him. Probably someone he had known when he lived in Solace long ago,† some poor slob who had fallen on hard times.

The half-elf started to turn away, then noticed—to his amazement—that everyone in the Inn was looking at him expectantly.

Tanis spent many happy years in Solace prior to the War of the Lance, though even then he managed an occasional adventure. Some of Tanis's early adventures can be found in The Soulforge *by Margaret Weis,* Tanis: The Shadow Years *by Barbara & Scott Siegel,* Kindred Spirits *by Mark Anthony and Ellen Porath,* Wanderlust *by Mary Kirchoff and Steve Winter,* The Companions *by Tina Daniell, and* Leaves from the Inn of the Last Home *edited by Margaret Weis and Tracy Hickman.*

What do they want me to do, Tanis thought in sudden, swift anger. Attack him? Some hero I'd look—beating up the town drunk!

Then he heard a sob at his elbow. "I told you to leave," Tika moaned, sinking down into a chair. Burying her face in her hands, she began to cry as if her heart would break.

Growing more and more mystified, Tanis glanced at Riverwind, but the Plainsman was obviously as much in the dark as his friend. The drunk, meanwhile, staggered into the room and gazed about in anger.

"Wash ish thish? A party?" he growled. "And nobody in-in-invited their old . . . invited me?"

No one answered. They were fixedly ignoring the slovenly man, their eyes still on Tanis, and now even the drunk's attention turned to the half-elf. Attempting to bring him into focus, the drunk stared at Tanis in a kind of puzzled anger, as though blaming him for being the cause of all his troubles. Then, suddenly, the drunk's eyes widened, his face split into a foolish grin, and he lurched forward, hands outstretched.

"Tanish . . . my fri—"

"Name of the gods," Tanis breathed, recognizing him at last.

The man staggered forward and stumbled over a chair. For a moment he stood swaying unsteadily, like a tree that has been cut and is ready to fall. His eyes rolled back in his head, people scrambled to get out of his way. Then—with a thud that shook the Inn—Caramon Majere,† Hero of the Lance, passed out cold at Tanis's feet.

In Legends, we wanted to make Caramon's character more complex and show him as a true hero. Due to the number of characters in Chronicles, I felt we had short-changed Caramon, making him more of a buffoon than a fleshed-out character. We wanted to remedy that in Legends.

The idea for making him an alcoholic seemed to come naturally, given his co-dependent relationship with his brother. I did quite a bit of study on alcoholism to make certain that I portrayed the disease as accurately as possible, given the fantasy setting. —MW

ame of the gods,"
Tanis repeated in sorrow as he stooped down beside
the comatose warrior. "Caramon . . ."

"Tanis—" Riverwind's voice caused the half-elf to
glance up quickly. The Plainsman held Tika in his
arms, both he and Dezra trying to comfort the distraught young woman. But people were pressing
close, trying to question Riverwind or asking Crysania for a blessing. Others were demanding more ale
or just standing around, gawking.

Tanis rose swiftly to his feet. "The Inn is closed for
the night," he shouted.

There were jeers from the crowd, except for some
scattered applause near the back where several customers thought he was buying a round of drinks.

"No, I mean it," Tanis said firmly, his voice carrying over the noise. The crowd quieted. "Thank you all
for this welcome. I cannot tell you what it means to

me to come back to my homeland. But, my friends and I would like to be alone now. Please, it is late. . . ."

There were murmurs of sympathy and some good-natured clapping. Only a few scowled and muttered comments about the greater the knight the more his own armor glares in his eyes (an old saying from the days when the Solamnic Knights were held in derision).† Riverwind, leaving Dezra to take care of Tika, came forward to prod those few stragglers who assumed Tanis meant everyone except them. The half-elf stood guard over Caramon, who was snoring blissfully on the floor, keeping people from stepping on the big man. He exchanged glances with Riverwind as the Plainsman passed, but neither had time to speak until the Inn was emptied.

Otik Sandeth stood by the door, thanking everyone for coming and assuring each that the Inn would be open again tomorrow night. When everyone else had gone, Tanis stepped up to the retired proprietor, feeling awkward and embarrassed. But Otik stopped him before he could speak.

Gripping Tanis's hand in his, the elderly man whispered, "I'm glad you've come back. Lock up when you're finished." He glanced at Tika, then motioned the half-elf forward conspiratorially. "Tanis," he said in a whisper, "if you happen to see Tika take a little out of the money box, pay it no mind. She'll pay it back someday. I just pretend not to notice." His gaze went to Caramon, and he shook his head sadly. "I know you'll be able to help," he murmured, then he nodded and stumped off into the night, leaning on his cane.

Help! Tanis thought wildly. We came seeking *his* help. Caramon snored particularly loudly, halfwoke himself up, belched up great fumes of dwarf spirits, then settled back down to sleep. Tanis looked bleakly at Riverwind, then shook his head in despair.

Crysania stared down at Caramon in pity mingled with disgust. "Poor man," she said softly. The medallion of Paladine shone in the candlelight. "Perhaps I—"

"There's nothing you can do for him," Tika cried bitterly. "He doesn't need healing. He's drunk, can't you see that? Dead drunk!"

The Knights of Solamnia fell into derision after the Cataclysm.

"Although their land had been spared the worst of the blow, the people of Solamnia still suffered greatly during this time.

"In the end, it was the common people of Solamnia who cast the Knights into disgrace. For centuries, the Knights had kept the peace and safety of the realm. Now, in the hour of their most desperate need, it seemed that the Knights were powerless. Rumors began to spread that the Knights had foreseen the coming of the Cataclysm and had done nothing to stop it. Some Knights, it was said, actually intended to profit by the disaster and increase their land holdings.

"Indeed, there was some truth to these tales, but it was not the Solamnic Order's doing. Lord Soth, Knight of the Rose who ruled in the far northeast reaches of Solamnia at Dargaard Keep had, in fact, been warned by his elven wife of the calamity that was coming."
[DRAGONLANCE Adventures, by Tracy Hickman and Margaret Weis, TSR, Inc., 1987, p. 14, 15.]

The tale of Soth's betrayal of his honor is told in The Cataclysm, DRAGONLANCE Tales II, Volume 2, with contributions by Margaret Weis, Tracy Hickman, Roger E. Moore, Douglas Niles, and more. A more extended version appears in Lord Soth by Edo Van Belkom.

Crysania's gaze turned to Tika in astonishment, but before the cleric could say anything, Tanis hurried back to Caramon. "Help me, Riverwind," he said, bending down. "Let's get him hom—"

"Oh, leave him!" Tika snapped, wiping her eyes with the corner of her apron. "He's spent enough nights on the barroom floor. Another won't matter." She turned to Tanis. "I wanted to tell you. I really did. But I thought . . . I kept hoping . . . He was excited when your letter arrived. He was . . . well, more like himself than I've seen him in a long time. I thought maybe this might do it. He might change. So I let you come." She hung her head. "I'm sorry. . . ."

Tanis stood beside the big warrior, irresolute. "I don't understand. How long—"

"It's why we couldn't come to your wedding, Tanis," Tika said, twisting her apron into knots. "I wanted to, so much! But—" She began to cry again. Dezra put her arms around her.

"Sit down, Tika," Dezra murmured, helping her to a seat in a high-backed, wooden booth.

Tika sank down, her legs suddenly giving out beneath her, then she hid her head in her arms.

"Let's all sit down," Tanis said firmly, "and get our wits about us. You there"—the half-elf beckoned to the gully dwarf, who was peering out at them from beneath the wooden bar. "Bring us a pitcher of ale and some mugs, wine for Lady Crysania, some spiced potatoes—"

Tanis paused. The confused gully dwarf was staring at him, round-eyed, his mouth hanging open in confusion.

"Better let me get it for you, Tanis," Dezra offered, smiling. "You'd probably end up with a pitcher of potatoes if Raf went after it."

"Me help!" Raf protested indignantly.

"You take out the garbage!" Dezra snapped.

"Me big help. . . ." Raf mumbled disconsolately as he shuffled out, kicking at the table legs to relieve his hurt feelings.

"Your rooms are in the new part of the Inn," Tika mumbled. "I'll show you. . . ."

"We'll find them later," Riverwind said sternly, but as he looked at Tika, his eyes were filled with gentle sympathy. "Sit and talk to Tanis. He has to leave soon."

"Damn! My horse!" Tanis said, starting up suddenly. "I asked the boy to bring it around—"

"I will go have them wait," Riverwind offered.

"No, I'll go. It'll just take a moment—"

"My friend," Riverwind said softly as he went past him, "I need to be outdoors! I'll come back to help with—" He nodded his head toward the snoring Caramon.

Tanis sat back down, relieved. The Plainsman left. Crysania sat down beside Tanis on the opposite side of the table, staring at Caramon in perplexity. Tanis kept talking to Tika about small, inconsequential matters until she was able to sit up and even smile a little. By the time Dezra returned with drinks, Tika seemed more relaxed, though her face was still drawn and strained. Crysania, Tanis noticed, barely touched her wine. She simply sat, glancing occasionally at Caramon, the dark line appearing once again between her brows. Tanis knew he should explain to her what was going on, but he wanted someone to explain it to him first.

"When did this—" he began, hesitantly.

"Start?" Tika sighed. "About six months after we got back here." Her gaze went to Caramon. "He was so happy—at first. The town was a mess, Tanis. The winter had been terrible for the survivors. Most of them were starving, the draconians and goblin soldiers took everything. Those whose houses had been destroyed were living in whatever shelter they could find—caves, lean-to hovels. The draconians had abandoned the town by the time we got back, and people were beginning to rebuild. They welcomed Caramon as a hero—the bards had been here already, singing their songs about the defeat of the Queen."

Tika's eyes shimmered with tears and remembered pride.

"He was so happy, Tanis, for a while. People needed him. He worked day and night—cutting trees, hauling timber from the hills, putting up houses. He even took up smithy work, since Theros† was gone. Oh, he wasn't very good at it." Tika smiled sadly. "But he was happy, and no one really minded. He made nails and horseshoes and wagon wheels. That first year was good for us—truly good. We were married, and Caramon seemed to forget about . . . about . . ."

The very first mention of Theros Ironfeld was in Dragons of Autumn Twilight, *Book I, Chapter 3, when he was still the blacksmith in Solace. As the War of the Lance progressed, he would play a vital role in its victory by forging the first new dragonlances. Besides the* Chronicles, *you can find out more about Theros in the novel* Theros Ironfeld, *by Don Perrin.*

Tika swallowed. Tanis patted her hand and, after eating a little and drinking some wine in silence, Tika was able to continue.

"A year ago last spring, though, everything started to change. Something happened to Caramon. I'm not sure what. It had something to do with—" She broke off, shook her head. "The town was prosperous. A blacksmith who had been held captive at Pax Tharkas moved here and took over the smithy trade. Oh, people still needed homes built, but there was no hurry. I took over running the Inn," Tika shrugged. "I guess Caramon just had too much time on his hands."

"No one needed him,"† Tanis said grimly.

Here we see Caramon's desperate need to be needed. —MW

"Not even me. . . ." Tika said, gulping and wiping her eyes. "Maybe it's my fault—"

"No," said Tanis, his thoughts—and his memories—far away. "Not your fault, Tika. I think we know whose fault this is."

"Anyway"—Tika drew a deep breath—"I tried to help, but I was so busy here. I suggested all sorts of things he could do and he tried—he really did. He helped the local constable, tracking down renegade draconians. He was a bodyguard, for a while, hiring out to people traveling to Haven. But no one ever hired him twice." Her voice dropped. "Then one day, last winter, the party he'd been supposed to protect returned, dragging him on a sled. He was dead drunk. *They'd* ended up protecting *him!* Since then, he's spent all his time either sleeping, eating, or hanging out with some ex-mercenaries at the Trough, that filthy place at the other end of town."

Wishing Laurana were here to discuss such matters, Tanis suggested softly, "Maybe a—um—baby?"

"I was pregnant, last summer," Tika said dully, leaning her head on her hand. "But not for long. I miscarried. Caramon never even knew. Since then"—she stared down at the wooden table—"well, we haven't been sleeping in the same room."

Flushing in embarrassment, Tanis could do nothing more than pat her hand and hurriedly change the subject. "You said a moment before 'it had something to do with—' . . . with what?"

Tika shivered, then took another drink of wine. "Rumors started, then, Tanis," she said in a low,

hushed voice. "Dark rumors. You can guess who they were about!"

Tanis nodded.

"Caramon wrote to him, Tanis. I saw the letter. It was—it tore my heart. Not a word of blame or reproach. It was filled with love. He begged his brother to come back and live with us. He pleaded with him to turn his back on the darkness."

"And what happened?" Tanis asked, though he already guessed the answer.

"It came back," Tika whispered. "Unopened. The seal wasn't even broken. And on the outside was written, 'I have no brother. I know no one named Caramon.' And it was signed, *Raistlin!*"

"Raistlin!" Crysania looked at Tika, as if seeing her for the first time. Her gray eyes were wide and startled as they went from the red-haired young woman to Tanis, then to the huge warrior on the floor, who belched comfortably in his drunken sleep. "Caramon . . . This is *Caramon Majere?* This is *his* brother? The twin you were telling me about? The man who could guide me—"

"I'm sorry, Revered Daughter," Tanis said, flushing. "I had no idea he—"

"But Raistlin is so . . . intelligent, powerful. I thought his twin must be the same. Raistlin is sensitive, he exerts such strong control over himself and those who serve him. He is a perfectionist, while this"— Crysania gestured—"this pathetic wretch, while he deserves our pity and our prayers, is—"

"Your 'sensitive and intelligent perfectionist' had a hand in making this man the 'pathetic wretch' you see, Revered Daughter," Tanis said acidly, keeping his anger carefully under control.

"Perhaps it was the other way around," Crysania said, regarding Tanis coldly. "Perhaps it was for lack of love that Raistlin turned from the light to walk in darkness."

Tika looked up at Crysania, an odd expression in her eyes. "Lack of love?" she repeated gently.

Caramon moaned in his sleep and began thrashing about on the floor. Tika rose quickly to her feet.

"We better get him home." She glanced up to see Riverwind's tall figure appear in the doorway, then turned to Tanis. "I'll see you in the morning, won't I? Couldn't you stay . . . just overnight?"

Tanis looked at her pleading eyes and felt like biting off his tongue before he answered. But there was no help for it. "I'm sorry, Tika," he said, taking her hands. "I wish I could, but I must go. It is a long ride to Qualinost from here, and I dare not be late. The fate of two kingdoms, perhaps, depends on my being there."

"I understand," Tika said softly. "This isn't your problem anyway. I'll cope."

Tanis could have torn out his beard with frustration. He longed to stay and help, if he even could help. At least he might talk with Caramon, try to get some sense into that thick skull. But Porthios† would take it as a personal affront if Tanis did not come to the funeral, which would affect not only his personal relationships with Laurana's brother, but would affect the treaty of alliance being negotiated between Qualinesti and Solamnia.

And then, his eyes going to Crysania, Tanis realized he had another problem. He groaned inwardly. He couldn't take her to Qualinost. Porthios had no use for human clerics.

"Look," Tanis said, suddenly getting an idea, "I'll come back, after the funeral." Tika's eyes brightened. He turned to Lady Crysania. "I'll leave you here, Revered Daughter. You'll be safe in this town, in the Inn. Then I can escort you back to Palanthas since your journey has failed—"

"My journey has not failed," Crysania said resolutely. "I will continue as I began. I intend to go to the Tower of High Sorcery at Wayreth, there to council with Par-Salian of the White Robes."

Tanis shook his head. "I cannot take you there," he said. "And Caramon obviously is incapable. Therefore I suggest—"

"Yes," Crysania interrupted complacently. "Caramon is clearly incapacitated. Therefore I will wait for the kender friend of yours to meet me here with the person he was sent to find, then I will continue on my own."

"Absolutely not!" Tanis shouted. Riverwind raised his eyebrows, reminding Tanis who he was addressing. With an effort, the half-elf regained control. "My lady, you have no idea of the danger! Besides those dark things that pursued us—and I think we all know who sent them—I've heard

See note on page 39 concerning Porthios.

Caramon's stories about the Forest of Wayreth. It's darker still! We'll go back to Palanthas, I'll find some Knights—"

For the first time, Tanis saw a pale stain of color touch Crysania's marble cheeks. Her dark brows contracted as she seemed to be thinking. Then her face cleared. Looking up at Tanis, she smiled.

"There is no danger," she said. "I am in Paladine's hands. The dark creatures may have been sent by Raistlin, but they have no power to harm *me!* They have merely strengthened my resolve." Seeing Tanis's face grow even grimmer, she sighed. "I promise this much. I will think about it. Perhaps you are right. Perhaps the journey is too dangerous—"

"And a waste of time!" Tanis muttered, sorrow and exhaustion making him speak bluntly what he had felt all along about this woman's crazy scheme. "If Par-Salian could have destroyed Raistlin, he would have done it long before—"

"Destroy!" Crysania regarded Tanis in shock, her gray eyes cold. "I do not seek his destruction."

Tanis stared at her in amazement.

"I seek to reclaim him," Crysania continued. "I will go to my rooms now, if someone will be so kind as to guide me to them."

Dezra hurried forward. Crysania calmly bade them all good night, then followed Dezra from the room. Tanis gazed after her, totally at a loss for words. He heard Riverwind mutter something in Que-shu. Then Caramon groaned again. Riverwind nudged Tanis. Together they bent over the slumbering Caramon and—with an effort—hauled the big man to his feet.

"Name of the Abyss, he's heavy!" Tanis gasped, staggering under the man's dead weight as Caramon's flacid arms flopped over his shoulders. The putrid smell of the dwarf spirits made him gag.

"How can he drink that stuff?" Tanis said to Riverwind as the two dragged the drunken man to the door, Tika following along anxiously behind.

"I saw a warrior fall victim to that curse once," Riverwind grunted. "He perished leaping over a cliff, being chased by creatures that were there only in his mind."

"I should stay—" Tanis murmured.

"You cannot fight another's battle, my friend,"

Riverwind said firmly. "Especially when it is between a man and his own soul."

It was past midnight when Tanis and Riverwind had Caramon safely at home and dumped—unceremoniously—into his bed. Tanis had never been so tired in his life. His shoulders ached from carrying the dead weight of the giant warrior. He was worn out and felt drained, his memories of the past—once pleasant—were now like old wounds, open and bleeding. And he still had hours to ride before morning.

"I wish I could stay," he repeated again to Tika as they stood together with Riverwind outside her door, gazing out over the sleeping, peaceful town of Solace. "I feel responsible—"

"No, Tanis," Tika said quietly. "Riverwind's right. You can't fight *this* war. You have your own life to live, now. Besides, there's nothing you can do. You might only make things worse."

"I suppose," Tanis frowned. "At any rate, I'll be back in about a week. I'll talk to Caramon then."

"That would be nice," Tika sighed, then, after a pause, changed the subject. "By the way, what did Lady Crysania mean about a kender coming here? Tasslehoff?"

"Yes," Tanis said, scratching his beard. "It has something to do with Raistlin, though I'm not sure what. We ran into Tas in Palanthas. He started in on some of his stories—I warned her that only about half of what he says is true and even that half's nonsense, but he probably convinced her to send him after some person she thinks can help her *reclaim* Raistlin!"

"The woman may be a holy cleric of Paladine," Riverwind said sternly, "and may the gods forgive me if I speak ill of one of their chosen. But I think she's mad." Having made this pronouncement, he slung his bow over his shoulder and prepared to depart.

Tanis shook his head. Putting his arm around Tika, he kissed her. "I'm afraid Riverwind's right," he said to her softly. "Keep an eye on Lady Crysania while she's here. I'll have a talk with Elistan about her when we return. I wonder how much he knew about this wild scheme of hers. Oh, and if Tasslehoff does show up, hang onto him, will you?

I don't want him turning up in Qualinost! I'm going to have enough trouble with Porthios and the elves as it is!"

"Sure, Tanis," Tika said softly. For a moment she nestled close to him, letting herself be comforted by his strength and the compassion she could sense in both his touch and his voice.

Tanis hesitated, holding her, reluctant to let her go. Glancing inside the small house, he could hear Caramon crying out in his sleep.

"Tika—" he began.

But she pushed herself away. "Go along, Tanis," she said firmly. "You've got a long ride ahead of you."

"Tika. I wish—" But there was nothing he could say that would help, and they both knew it.

Turning slowly, he trudged off after Riverwind.

Watching them go, Tika smiled.

"You are very wise, Tanis Half-Elven. But this time you are wrong," she said to herself as she stood alone on her porch. "Lady Crysania *isn't* mad. She's in love."†

*I'm often asked if Crysania loves Raistlin. I do not think she does. She is attracted to him sexually, as he is to her, but that's not the same thing. I think that at this point in their lives, both these people are too selfish to love anyone. They are both using each other to achieve their own goals. Crysania is blind to her flaws throughout much of the book and thus it is only when she is blinded at the end that she sees the truth about Raistlin and the truth about herself.
—MW*

An army of
dwarves was marching around the bedroom, their
steelshod boots going THUD, THUD, THUD. Each
dwarf had a hammer in his hand and, as he marched
past the bed, he banged it against Caramon's head.
Caramon groaned and flapped his hands feebly.

"Get away!" he muttered. "Get away!"

But the dwarves only responded by lifting his bed
up onto their strong shoulders and whirling it around
at a rapid pace, as they continued to march, their boots
striking the wooden floor THUD, THUD, THUD.

Caramon felt his stomach heave. After several desperate tries, he managed to leap out of the revolving
bed and make a clumsy dash for the chamber pot in
the corner. Having vomited, he felt better. His head
cleared. The dwarves disappeared—although he suspected they were hiding beneath the bed, waiting for
him to lie down again.

Instead, he opened a drawer in the tiny bedside table where he kept his small flask of dwarf spirits. Gone! Caramon scowled. So Tika was playing *this* game again, was she? Grinning smugly, Caramon stumbled over to the large clothes chest on the other side of the room. He lifted the lid and rummaged through tunics and pants and shirts that would no longer fit over his flabby body. There it was—tucked into an old boot.

Caramon withdrew the flask lovingly, took a swig of the fiery liquor, belched, and heaved a sigh. There, the hammering in his head was gone. He glanced around the room. Let the dwarves stay under the bed. He didn't care.

There was the clink of crockery in the other room. Tika! Hurriedly, Caramon took another sip, then closed the flask and tucked it back into the boot again. Shutting the lid very, very quietly, he straightened up, ran a hand through his tangled hair, and started to go out into the main living area. Then he caught a glimpse of himself in a mirror as he passed.

"Change my shirt," he muttered thickly.

After much pulling and tugging, he dragged off the filthy shirt he was wearing and tossed it in a corner. Perhaps he should wash? Bah! What was he—a sissy? So he smelled—it was a manly smell. Plenty of women liked it, found it attractive—found *him* attractive! Never complained or nagged, not like Tika. Why couldn't she take him as he was? Struggling into a clean shirt he found at the foot of the bed, Caramon felt very sorry for himself. No one understood him . . . life was hard . . . he was going through a bad time just now . . . but that would change . . . just wait . . . someday—tomorrow maybe. . . .

Lurching out of the bedroom, trying to appear nonchalant, Caramon walked unsteadily across the neat, clean living room and collapsed into a chair at the eating table. The chair creaked beneath his great weight. Tika turned around.

Catching her glance, Caramon sighed. Tika was mad—again. He tried grinning at her, but it was a sickly grin and didn't help. Her red curls bouncing in anger, she whirled around and disappeared through a door into the kitchen. Caramon winced as he heard heavy iron pots bang. The sound brought the dwarves and their hammers back. Within a few

"Twenty-eight years old and 50 pounds overweight . . . Caramon is in terrible physical condition and an alcoholic. He is a sodden wreck of a man, fluctuating between self-pity and self-indulgence. Caramon's testing is the most demanding of all the characters, since it is physical, mental, and spiritual. The trials Caramon undergoes are meant to teach him that he has value as a person and that he must live his own life.

"Following the War of the Lance, Caramon came home a hero. He married Tika and should have lived happily ever after. Unfortunately, once the war had ended and life for people was returning to normal, no one needed Caramon. Even Tika had developed her own life, managing the Inn of the Last Home."
[DRAGONLANCE Adventures, *by Tracy Hickman and Margaret Weis, TSR, Inc., 1987, p. 112.*]

moments, Tika returned, carrying a huge dish of sizzling bacon, fried maize cakes, and eggs. She slammed the plate down in front of him with such force the cakes leaped three inches into the air.

Caramon winced again. He wondered briefly about eating—considering the queasy state of his stomach—then grouchily reminded his stomach who was boss. He was starved, he couldn't remember when he'd eaten last. Tika flounced down in a chair next to him. Glancing up, he saw her green eyes blazing. Her freckles stood out clearly against her skin—a certain sign of fury.

"All right," Caramon growled, shoveling food into his mouth. "What'd I do now?"

"You don't remember." It was a statement.

Caramon cast about hastily in the foggy regions of his mind. Something stirred vaguely. He was supposed to have been somewhere last night. He'd stayed home all day, getting ready. He'd promised Tika . . . but he'd grown thirsty. His flask was empty. He'd just go down to the Trough for a quick nip, then to . . . where . . . why . . .

"I had business to attend to," Caramon said, avoiding Tika's gaze.

"Yes, *we* saw your business," Tika snapped bitterly. "The business that made you pass out right at Tanis's feet!"

"*Tanis!*" Caramon dropped his fork. "Tanis . . . last night . . ." With a heartsick moan, the big man let his aching head sink into his hands.

"You made quite a spectacle of yourself," Tika continued, her voice choked. "In front of the entire town, plus half the elves in Krynn. Not to mention our old friends." She was weeping quietly now. "Our best friends. . . ."

Caramon moaned again. Now he was crying, too. "Why? Why?" he blubbered. "Tanis, of all of them . . ." His self-recriminations were interrupted by a banging on the front door.

"Now what?" Tika muttered, rising and wiping her tears away with the sleeve of her blouse. "Maybe it's Tanis, after all." Caramon lifted his head. "Try at least to *look* like the man you once were." Tika said under her breath as she hurried to the door.

Throwing the bolt, she unlatched it. "Otik?" she said in astonishment. "What are—Whose food?"

The rotund, elderly innkeeper stood in the doorway, a plate of steaming food in his hand. He peered past Tika.

"Isn't she here?" he asked, startled.

"Isn't who here?" Tika replied, confused. "There's no one here."

"Oh, dear," Otik's face grew solemn. Absently, he began to eat the food from the plate. "Then I guess the stableboy was right. She's gone. And after I fixed this nice breakfast."

"Who's gone?" Tika demanded in exasperation, wondering if he meant Dezra.

"Lady Crysania. She's not in her room. Her things aren't there, either. And the stableboy said she came this morning, told him to saddle her horse, and left. I thought—"

"Lady Crysania!" Tika gasped. "She's gone off, by herself. Of course, she would. . . ."

"What?" asked Otik, still munching.

"Nothing," Tika said, her face pale. "Nothing Otik. Uh, you better get back to the Inn. I'll—I may be a little late today."

"Sure, Tika," Otik said kindly, having seen Caramon hunched over the table. "Get there when you can." Then he left, eating as he walked. Tika shut the door behind him.

Seeing Tika return, and knowing he was in for a lecture, Caramon rose clumsily to his feet. "I'm not feeling too good," he said. Lurching across the floor, he staggered into the bedroom, slamming the door shut behind him. Tika could hear the sound of wracking sobs from inside.

She sat down at the table, thinking. Lady Crysania had gone, she was going to find Wayreth Forest by herself. Or rather, she had gone in search of it. No one ever found it, according to legend. *It* found *you!*† Tika shivered, remembering Caramon's stories. The dread Forest was on maps, but—comparing them—no two maps ever agreed on its location. And there was always a symbol of warning beside it. At its center stood the Tower of High Sorcery of Wayreth, where all the power of the mages of Ansalon was now concentrated. Well, almost all—

In sudden resolution, Tika got up and thrust open the bedroom door. Going inside, she found Caramon flat upon the bed, sobbing and blubbering like a

See note concerning the Tower of Wayreth on page 42.

child. Hardening her heart against this pitiful sight, Tika walked with firm steps over to the large chest of clothes. As she threw open the lid and began sorting through the clothes, she found the flask, but simply tossed it into a corner of the room. Then—at the very bottom—she came upon what she had been searching for.

Caramon's armor.

Lifting out a cuisse by its leather strap, Tika stood up and turning around, hurled the polished metal straight at Caramon.

It struck him in the shoulder, bouncing off to fall to the floor with a clatter.

"Ouch!" the big man cried, sitting up. "Name of the Abyss, Tika! Leave me alone for—"

"You're going after her," Tika said firmly, lifting out another piece of armor. "You're going after her, if I have to haul you out of here in a wheelbarrow!"

The term "kender" was originally "kinder," after the German word for "children," but it was quickly pointed out that English readers would read the word as "more kind" rather than with the German pronunciation. Thus the changed spelling kender. —TRH

"Uh, pardon me," said a kender† to a man loitering near the edge of the road on the outskirts of Solace. The man instantly clapped his hand over his purse. "I'm looking for the home of a friend of mine. Well, actually two friends of mine. One's a woman, pretty, with red curls. Her name is Tika Waylan—"

Glaring at the kender, the man jerked a thumb. "Over there yonder."

Tas looked. "There?" he said pointing, impressed. "That truly magnificent house in the new vallenwood?"

"What?" The man gave a brief, sharp laugh. "What'd you call it? Truly magnificent? That's a good one." Still chuckling, he walked off, laughing and hastily counting the coins in his purse at the same time.

How rude! Tas thought, absently slipping the man's pocket knife into one of his pouches. Then, promptly forgetting the incident, the kender headed for Tika's home. His gaze lingered fondly on each detail of the fine house nestled securely in the limbs of the still-growing vallenwood tree.

"I'm so glad for Tika." Tas remarked to what appeared to be a mound of clothes with feet walking beside him. "And for Caramon, too," he added. "But Tika's never really had a true home of her own. How proud she must be!"

As he approached the house, Tas saw it was one of the better homes in the township. It was built in the ages-old tradition of Solace. The delicate turns of the vaulting gables were shaped to appear to be part of the tree itself. Each room extended off from the main body of the house, the wood of the walls carved and polished to resemble the tree trunk. The structure conformed to the shape of the tree, a peaceful harmony existed between man's work and nature's to create a pleasing whole. Tas felt a warm glow in his heart as he thought of his two friends working on and living in such a wonderful dwelling. Then—

"That's funny," said Tas to himself, "I wonder why there's no roof."

As he drew closer, looking at the house more intently, he noticed it was missing quite a few things—a roof among them.

The great vaulting gables actually did nothing more than form a framework for a roof that wasn't there. The walls of the rooms extended only part way around the building. The floor was only a barren platform.

Coming to stand right beneath it, Tas peered upwards, wondering what was going on. He could see hammers and axes and saws lying out in the open, rusting away. From their looks, they hadn't been used in months. The structure itself was showing the effects of long exposure to weather. Tas tugged his topknot thoughtfully. The building had all the makings of the most magnificent structure in all of Solace—if it was ever finished!†

Then Tas brightened. One section of the house *was* finished. All of the glass had been carefully placed into the window frames, the walls were intact, a roof protected the room from the elements. At least Tika has one room of her own, the kender thought. But, as he studied the room more closely, his smile faded. Above the door, he could see clearly, despite some weathering, the carefully crafted mark denoting a wizard's residence.

"I might have known," Tas said, shaking his head. He glanced around. "Well, Tika and Caramon certainly can't be living there. But that man said—Oh."

As he walked around the huge vallenwood tree, he came upon a small house, almost lost amidst

Tika's house is symbolic of Caramon's inability to make anything of his life. He tries to build, to create. He has grandiose ideas, but he can never bring them to fruition. We see in the house that he can't even truly love Tika, for he can't love anyone until he learns to love himself. The only room that is finished is the room Caramon builds for his twin, for at this point, Caramon can find himself only in Raistlin. Tas finds Tika's true house "built in the shadow of a dream."
—MW

61

overgrown weeds, hidden by the shadow of the vallenwood tree. Obviously built only as a temporary measure, it had the look of becoming all too permanent. If ever a building could look unhappy, Tas mused, this one did. Its gables sagged into a frown. Its paint was cracked and peeling. Still, there were flowers in the windowboxes and frilly curtains in the windows. The kender sighed. So this was Tika's house, built in the shadow of a dream.

Approaching the little house, he stood outside the door, listening attentively. There was the most awful commotion going on inside. He could hear thuds and glass breaking and shouts and thumping.

"I think you better wait out here." Tas said to the bundle of clothes.

The bundle grunted and plopped itself comfortably down into the muddy road outside the house. Tas glanced at it uncertainly, then shrugged and walked up to the door. Putting his hand on the doorknob, he turned it and took a step forward, confidently expecting to walk right in. Instead he smashed his nose on the wood. The door was locked.

"That's odd," Tas said, stepping back and looking around. "What is Tika thinking about? Locking doors! How barbaric. And a bolt lock at that. I'm sure I was expected. . . ." He stared at the lock gloomily. The shouts and yells continued inside. He thought he could hear Caramon's deep voice.

"It sure sounds interesting in there." Tas glanced around, and felt cheered immediately. "The window! Of course!"

But, on hurrying over to the window, Tas found it locked, too! "I never would have expected that of Tika, of all people," the kender commented sadly to himself. Studying the lock, he noticed it was a simple one and would open quite easily. From the set of tools in his pouch, Tas removed the lockpicking device that is a kender's birthright. Inserting it, he gave it an expert twist and had the satisfaction of hearing the lock click. Smiling happily, he pushed the paned glass open and crawled inside. He hit the floor without a sound. Peering back out the window, he saw the shapeless bundle napping in the gutter.

Relieved on that point, Tasslehoff paused to look around the house, his sharp eyes taking in everything, his hands touching everything.

"My, isn't this interesting," went Tas's running commentary as he headed for the closed door from beyond which came the crashing sounds. "Tika won't mind if I study it for a moment. I'll put it right back." The object tumbled, of its accord, into his pouch. "And look at this! Uh-oh, there's a crack in it. She'll thank me for telling her about it." That object slipped into another pouch. "And what's the butter dish doing clear over here? I'm sure Tika kept it in the pantry. I better return it to its proper place." The butter dish settled into a third pouch.

By this time, Tas had reached the closed door. Turning the handle— (he was thankful to see Tika hadn't locked it as well!)—he walked inside.

"Hullo," he said merrily. "Remember me? Say, this looks like fun! Can I play? Give me something to throw at him, too, Tika. Gee, Caramon"—Tas entered the bedroom and walked over to where Tika stood, a breastplate in her hand, staring at him in profound astonishment—"what *is* the matter with you—you look *awful*, just *awful!* Say, why are we throwing armor at Caramon, Tika?" Tas asked, picking up a chain mail vest and turning to face the big warrior, who had barricaded himself behind the bed. "Is this something you two do regularly? I've heard married couples do some strange things, but this seems kind of weird—"

"Tasslehoff Burrfoot!" Tika recovered her power of speech. "What in the name of the gods are you doing here?"

"Why, I'm sure Tanis must have told you I was coming," Tas said, hurling the chain mail at Caramon. "Hey—this *is* fun! I found the front door locked." Tas gave her a reproachful glance. "In fact, I had to come in a window, Tika," he said severely. "I think you might have more considera-tion. Anyway, I'm supposed to meet Lady Crysa-nia here and—"

To Tas's amazement, Tika dropped the breast-plate, burst into tears, and collapsed onto the floor. The kender looked over at Caramon, who was rising up from behind the backboard like a spectre rising from the grave. Caramon stood looking at Tika with a lost and wistful expression. Then he picked his way through pieces of armor that lay scattered about on the floor and knelt down beside her.

"Tika," he whispered pathetically, patting her shoulder. "I'm sorry. I didn't mean all those things I said, you know that. I love you! I've always loved you. It's just . . . I don't know what to do!"

"You know what to do!" Tika shouted. Pulling away from him, she sprang to her feet. "I just told you! Lady Crysania's in danger. You've got to go to her!"

"Who is this Lady Crysania?" Caramon yelled back. "Why should I give a damn whether she's in danger or not?"

"Listen to me for once in your life," Tika hissed through clenched teeth, her anger drying her tears. "Lady Crysania is a powerful cleric of Paladine, one of the most powerful in the world, next to Elistan. She was warned in a dream that Raistlin's evil could destroy the world. She is going to the Tower of High Sorcery in Wayreth to talk to Par-Salian to—"

"To get help destroying him, isn't that it?" Caramon snarled.

"And what if they did?" Tika flared. "Does he deserve to live? He'd kill you without a second thought!"

Caramon's eyes flashed dangerously, his face flushed. Tas gulped, seeing the big man's fist clench, but Tika walked right up to stand in front of him. Though her head barely came to his chin, Tas thought the big man cowered at her anger. His hand opened weakly.

"But, no, Caramon," Tika said grimly, "she doesn't want to destroy him. She's just as big a fool as you are. She loves your brother, may the gods help her. She wants to save him, to turn him from evil."

Caramon stared at Tika in wonder. His expression softened.

"Truly?" he said.

"Yes, Caramon," Tika said wearily. "That's why she came here, to see you. She thought you might be able to help. Then, when she saw you last night—"

Caramon's head drooped. His eyes filled with tears. "A woman, a stranger, wants to help Raist. And risks her life to do it." He began to blubber again.

Tika stared at him in exasperation. "Oh, for the love of—Go after her, Caramon!" she cried, stamping her foot on the floor. "She'll never reach the

Tower alone. You know that! You've been through the Forest of Wayreth."

"Yes," Caramon said, sniffing. "I went with Raist. I took him there, so he could find the Tower and take the Test. That evil Test! I guarded him. He needed me . . . then."

"And Crysania needs you now!" Tika said grimly. Caramon was still standing, irresolute, and Tas saw Tika's face settle in firm, hard lines. "You don't have much time to lose, if you're going to catch up with her. Do you remember the way?"

"I do!" shouted Tas in excitement. "That is, I have a map," Tika and Caramon turned around to stare at the kender in astonishment, both having forgotten his existence.

"I dunno," Caramon said, regarding Tas darkly. "I remember your maps.† One of them took us to a seaport that didn't have any sea!"†

"That wasn't my fault!" Tas cried indignantly. "Even Tanis said so. My map was drawn before the Cataclysm struck and took the sea away. But you *have* to take me with you, Caramon! I'm supposed to meet Lady Crysania. She sent me on a quest, a real quest. And I completed it. I found"—sudden movement caught Tas's attention—"oh, here she is."

He waved his hand, and Tika and Caramon turned to see the shapeless bundle of clothes standing in the door to their bedroom. Only now the bundle had grown two black, suspicious eyes.

"Me hungry," said the bundle to Tas accusingly. "When we eat?"

"I went on a quest for Bupu,"† Tasslehoff Burrfoot said proudly.†

"But what in the name of the Abyss does Lady Crysania want with a gully dwarf?" Tika said in absolute mystification. She had taken Bupu to the kitchen, given her some stale bread and half a cheese, then sent her back outside—the gully dwarf's smell doing nothing to enhance the comfort of the small house. Bupu returned happily to the gutter, where she supplemented her meal by drinking water out of a puddle in the street.

"Oh, I promised I wouldn't tell," Tas said importantly. The kender was helping Caramon to strap on his armor—a rather involved task, since the big man was considerably bigger since the last time he'd

See Dragons of Winter Night, *Book I, Chapter 3.*

This "seaport that didn't have any sea" was Tarsis, and for once, Tasslehoff's excuse is valid. Tarsis was indeed a port city until the Cataclysm, when the remaking of the continent of Ansalon left the city in the midst of the Plains of Dust.

I believe I came up with this name—something of a combination of the Indonesian word "Bapak," meaning father, and "Ibu," meaning mother. —TRH

Tas is recalling events from Dragons of Autumn Twilight, *Book I, Chapter 17.*

I believe I also came up with the name Fizban—most probably some subconscious bubble from my childhood. It certainly sounds nearly identical to the fictitious game of "fizbin flush" that James T. Kirk used in "A Piece of the Action." I always liked to think it sounded a lot like "Whizbang" in my own head. —TRH

Tasslehoff's confusion here is understandable. Fizban the Fabulous is an avatar (the physical manifestation of a god on the mortal plane) of Paladine.

"Since he is a god (Paladine), Fizban is interested in people learning about themselves and developing their true potential. When Fizban tries to help characters out of a fix, it often seems as if he is simply making the situation worse instead of better. Fizban always allows others freedom of choice and does not interfere with their decisions. Fizban's purpose is to restore the balance of good and evil to the world, not to make one triumph over the other." [DRAGONLANCE *Adventures, by Tracy Hickman and Margaret Weis, TSR, Inc., 1987, p. 108.]*

Par-Salian is the Head of the Conclave of Wizards. "[He] is not a wizard of action, preferring to spend his time in study. It was primarily because of his vast knowledge of magic that he obtained his high rank. It was he who made the important decision to

worn it. Both Tika and Tas worked until they were sweating, tugging on straps, pushing and prodding rolls of fat beneath the metal.

Caramon groaned and moaned, sounding very much like a man being stretched on the rack. The big man's tongue licked his lips and his longing gaze went more than once to the bedroom and the small flask Tika had so casually tossed into the corner.

"Oh, come now, Tas," Tika wheedled, knowing the kender couldn't keep a secret to save his life. "I'm sure Lady Crysania wouldn't mind—"

Tas's face twisted in agony. "She-she made me promise and swear to Paladine, Tika!" The kender's face grew solemn. "And you know that Fizban†—I mean Paladine†—and I are *personal* friends." The kender paused. "Suck in your gut, Caramon," he ordered irritably. "How did you ever get yourself into this condition, anyway?"

Putting his foot against the big man's thigh, Tas tugged. Caramon yelped in pain.

"I'm in fine shape," the big man mumbled angrily. "It's the armor. It's shrunk or something."

"I didn't know this kind of metal shrinks," Tas said with interest. "I'll bet it has to be heated! How did you do that? Or did it just get real, real hot around here?"

"Oh, shut up!" Caramon snarled.

"I was only being helpful," Tas said, wounded. "Anyway, oh, about Lady Crysania." His face took on a lofty look. "I gave my sacred oath. All I can say is she wanted me to tell her everything I could remember about Raistlin. And I did. And this has to do with that. Lady Crysania's truly a wonderful person, Tika," Tas continued solemnly. "You might not have noticed, but I'm not very religious. Kender aren't as a rule. But you don't have to be religious to know that there is something *truly good* about Lady Crysania. She's smart, too. Maybe even smarter than Tanis."

Tas's eyes were bright with mystery and importance. "I think I can tell you this much," he said in a whisper. "She has a plan! A plan to help save Raistlin! Bupu's part of the plan. She's taking her to Par-Salian!"†

Even Caramon looked dubious at this, and Tika was privately beginning to think maybe Riverwind

and Tanis were right. Maybe Lady Crysania was mad. Still, anything that might help Caramon, might give him some hope—

But Caramon had apparently been working things out in his own mind. "You know. It's all the fault of this Fis-Fistandoodlet or whatever his name was," he said, tugging uncomfortably at the leather straps where they bit into his flabby flesh. "You know, that mage Fizban—er—Paladine told us about. And Par-Salian knows something about that, too!" His face brightened. "We'll fix everything. I'll bring Raistlin back here, like we planned, Tika! He can move into the room we've got fixed up for him. We'll take care of him, you and I. In our new house. It's going to be fine, fine!" Caramon's eyes shone. Tika couldn't look at him. He sounded so much like the old Caramon, the Caramon she had loved. . . .

Keeping her expression stern, she turned abruptly and headed for the bedroom. "I'll go get the rest of your things—"

"Wait!" Caramon stopped her. "No, uh—thanks, Tika. I can manage. How about you—uh—pack us something to eat."

"I'll help," Tas offered, heading eagerly for the kitchen.

"Very well," Tika said. Reaching out, she caught hold of the kender by the topknot of hair that tumbled down his back. "Just one minute, Tasslehoff Burrfoot. You're not going anywhere until you sit down and empty out every one of your pouches!"

Tas wailed in protest. Under cover of the confusion, Caramon hurried into the bedroom and shut the door. Without pausing, he went straight for the corner and retrieved the flask. Shaking it, he found it over half-full. Smiling to himself in satisfaction, he thrust it deep into his pack, then hastily crammed some additional clothes in on top of it.

"Now, I'm all set!" he called out cheerfully to Tika.

"I'm all set," Caramon repeated, standing disconsolately on the porch.

He was a ludicrous sight. The stolen dragon armor he had worn during the last months of the campaign had been completely refurbished by the big warrior when he arrived back in Solace. He had beaten the dents out, cleaned and polished and redesigned it so

allow the young mage, Raistlin Majere, to take the Test at an age earlier than most. Some wizards believed that it was because of this decision that Fistandantilus was able to seal a bargain with the young mage and thus lead him into paths of evil.

"Par-Salian is aware, however, that without Raistlin's skill and power, the War of the Lance would never have been won. He knows that Raistlin chose for himself the path he walks. At this point in his life, Par-Salian would like very much to give up the burden of heading the Conclave, but he cannot while Raistlin's threat to the world exists." [DRAGONLANCE Adventures, by Tracy Hickman and Margaret Weis, TSR, Inc., 1987, p. 110.]

Caramon is trying to say "Fistandantilus" here. Fistandantilus is one of mine as well—much to the dismay of many DRAGONLANCE writers! I always liked the way it rolled off the tongue when I spoke it aloud. This is no doubt part of my fondness for the Indonesian language, which features words with some of the longest strings of syllables you can imagine. —TRH

completely that it no longer resembled the original. He had taken a great deal of care with it, then packed it away lovingly. It was still in excellent condition. Only now, unfortunately, there was a large gap between the shining black chain mail that covered his chest and the big belt that girdled his rotund waist. Neither he nor Tas had been able to strap the metal plates that guarded his legs around his flabby thighs. He had stowed these away in his pack. He groaned when he lifted his shield and looked at it suspiciously, as if certain someone had filled it with lead weights during the last two years. His sword belt would not fit around his sagging gut. Blushing furiously, he strapped the sword in its worn scabbard onto his back.

At this point, Tas was forced to look somewhere else. The kender thought he was going to laugh but was startled to find himself on the verge of tears.

"I look a fool," Caramon muttered, seeing Tas turn away hurriedly. Bupu was staring at him with eyes as wide as tea-cups, her mouth hanging open.

"Him look just like my Highbulp,† Phudge I," Bupu sighed.

Highbulp, Phudge I was a character from Dragons of Autumn Twilight, *Book I, Chapter 19.*

A vivid memory of the fat, slovenly king of the gully dwarf clan in Xak Tsaroth came to Tas's mind. Grabbing the gully dwarf, he stuffed a hunk of bread in her mouth to shut her up. But the damage had been done. Apparently Caramon, too, remembered.

"That does it," he snarled, flushing darkly and hurling his shield to the wooden porch where it banged and clattered loudly. "I'm not going! This was a stupid idea anyway!" He stared accusingly at Tika, then, turning around, he started for the door. But Tika moved to stand in front of him.

"No," she said quietly. "You're not coming back into my house, Caramon, until you come back one whole person."

"Him more like *two* whole person," mumbled Bupu in a muffled voice. Tas stuffed more bread in her mouth.

"You're not making any sense!" Caramon snapped viciously, putting his hand on her shoulder. "Get out of my way, Tika!"

"Listen to me, Caramon," Tika said. Her voice was soft, but penetrating; her eyes caught and held the big man's attention. Putting her hand on his chest, she

looked up at him earnestly. "You offered to follow Raistlin into darkness, once. Do you remember?"

Caramon swallowed, then nodded silently, his face pale.

"He refused." Tika continued gently, "saying it would mean your death. But, don't you see, Caramon—you *have* followed him into darkness! And you're dying by inches! Raistlin himself told you to walk your own path and let him walk his. But you haven't done that! You're trying to walk both paths, Caramon. Half of you is living in darkness and the other half is trying to drink away the pain and the horror you see there."

"It's my fault!" Caramon began to blubber, his voice breaking. "It's my fault he turned to the Black Robes.† I drove him to it! That's what Par-Salian tried to make me see—"

Caramon is remembering events from the latter chapters of Dragons of Winter Night, *Book I, Chapter 9.*

Tika bit her lip. Tas could see her face grow grim and stern with anger, but she kept it inside. "Perhaps," was all she said. Then she drew a deep breath. "But you are not coming back to me as husband or even friend until you come back at peace with yourself."

Caramon stared at her, looking as though he was seeing her for the first time. Tika's face was resolute and firm, her green eyes were clear and cold. Tas suddenly remembered† her fighting draconians in the Temple at Neraka that last horrible night of the War. She had looked just the same.

This occurred in the latter chapters of Dragons of Spring Dawning.

"Maybe that'll be never," Caramon said surlily. "Ever think of that, huh, my fine lady?"

"Yes," Tika said steadily. "I've thought of it. Good-bye,† Caramon."

Turning away from her husband, Tika walked back through the door of her house and shut it. Tas heard the bolt slide home with a click. Caramon heard it, too, and flinched at the sound. He clenched his huge fists, and for a minute Tas feared he might break down the door. Then his hands went limp. Angrily, trying to salvage some of his shattered dignity, Caramon stomped off the porch.

"I'll show her," he muttered, striding off, his armor clanking and clattering. "Come back, three or four days, with that Lady Cryslewhatever. Then we'll talk about this. She can't do this to me! No, by all the gods! Three, four days, she'll be begging

". . . though Tika loves Caramon dearly, the independent, strong-willed young woman can never need Caramon the way Raistlin needed him. Tika is wise enough to know that this type of relationship is poison anyway. Tika blames herself, however, for Caramon's slow descent into the bottle. She is ashamed of him and of herself and tries to hide this worsening condition from their friends. Tika

realizes, finally, that Caramon will die unless he changes and therefore she throws him out, telling him not to return to her as husband or friend until he knows himself." [DRAGONLANCE Adventures, *by Tracy Hickman and Margaret Weis, TSR, Inc., 1987, p. 113.*]

Tasslehoff is another character that we felt we'd like to develop. He's comic relief, of course, but he also represents all those friends and family of alcoholics. Tas represents innocent wisdom. He sees Caramon far more clearly than anyone else, even Raistlin. —MW

me to come back. But maybe I will and maybe I won't. . . ."

Tas stood, irresolute. Behind him, inside the house, his sharp kender ears could hear grief-stricken sobbing. He knew that Caramon, between his own self-pitying ramblings and his clanking armor, could hear nothing. But what could he do?

"I'll take care of him, Tika!" Tas shouted, then, grabbing Bupu, they hurried along after the big man. Tas sighed. Of all the adventures he had been on, this one was certainly starting out all wrong.

CHAPTER 5

Throughout man's history, the concept of a glorious and lost past has been an evocative archetype. From Xanadu to Atlantis, people have told tales of the ancient days that were great and now lost to us. —TRH

alanthas—fabled[†] city of beauty.

A city that has turned its back upon the world and sits gazing, with admiring eyes, into its mirror.

Who had described it thus? Kitiara,[†] seated upon the back of her blue dragon, Skie, pondered idly as she flew within sight of the city walls. The late, unlamented Dragon Highlord Ariakas, perhaps. It sounded pretentious enough, like something he would say. But he had been right about the Palanthians, Kit was forced to admit. So terrified were they of seeing their beloved city laid waste, they had negotiated a separate peace with the Highlords. It wasn't until right before the end of the war—when it was obvious they had nothing to lose—that they had reluctantly joined with others to fight the might of the Dark Queen.

Because of the heroic sacrifice of the Knights of Solamnia, the city of Palanthas was spared the

Kitiara is named after my wife, Kate—and there the similarity between the two ends. Really! [Jeff Grubb, from The Annotated Chronicles, by Margaret Weis and Tracy Hickman, Wizards of the Coast, Inc., 1999, p. 39.]

See Dragons of Spring Dawning, *Book I, Chapter 9.*

destruction† that had laid other cities—such as Solace and Tarsis—to waste. Kit, flying within arrow shot of the walls, sneered. Now, once more, Palanthas had turned her eyes to her mirror, using the new influx of prosperity to enhance her already legendary charm.

Thinking this, Kitiara laughed out loud as she saw the stir upon the Old City walls. It had been two years since a blue dragon had flown above the walls. She could picture the chaos, the panic. Faintly, on the still night air, she could hear the beating of drums and the clear calls of trumpets.†

Kitiara is, by nature, a skeptic and a cynic. She always looks for the flaws in a building, but in so doing she is more often right than not. Here, she sees the cracks in the foundations of Palanthas. —TRH

Skie, too, could hear. His blood stirred at the sounds of war, and he turned a blazing red eye round to Kitiara, begging her to reconsider.

"No, my pet," Kitiara called, reaching down to pat his neck soothingly. "Now is not the time! But soon—if we prove successful! Soon, I promise you!"

Skie was forced to content himself with that. He achieved some satisfaction, however, by breathing a bolt of lightning from his gaping jaws, blackening the stone wall as he soared past, keeping just out of arrow range. The troops scattered like ants at his coming, the dragonfear sweeping over them in waves.

Kitiara flew slowly, leisurely. None dared touch her—a state of peace existed between her armies in Sanction and the Palanthians, though there were some among the Knights who were trying to persuade the free peoples of Ansalon to unite and attack Sanction where Kitiara had retreated following the war. But the Palanthians couldn't be bothered. The war was over, the threat gone.

"And daily I grow in strength and in might," Kit said to them as she flew above the city, taking it all in, storing it in her mind for future reference.

The general layout of Palanthas was influenced by early twentieth-century concepts in planned "communities of tomorrow," as well as their progeny, the Israeli kibbutzim. —TRH

Palanthas† is built like a wheel. All of the important buildings—the palace of the reigning lord, government offices, and the ancient homes of the nobles—stand in the center. The city revolves around this hub. In the next circle are built the homes of the wealthy guildsmen—the "new" rich—and the summer homes of those who live outside the city walls. Here, too, are the educational centers, including the Great Library of Astinus. Finally, near the walls of Old City, is the marketplace and shops of every type and description.

Eight wide avenues lead out from the center of Old City, like spokes on the wheel. Trees line these avenues, lovely trees, whose leaves are like golden lace all year long. The avenues lead to the seaport to the north and to the seven gates of Old City Wall.

Surrounding the wall, Kit saw New City, built just like Old City, in the same circular pattern. There are no walls around New City, since walls "detract from the overall design," as one of the lords put it.

Kitiara smiled. She did not see the beauty of the city. The trees were nothing to her. She could look upon the dazzling marvels of the seven gates without a catch in her throat—well, perhaps, a small one. How easy it would be, she thought with a sigh, to capture!

Two other buildings attracted her interest. One was a new one being built in the center of the city—a Temple, dedicated to Paladine. The other building was her destination. And, on this one, her gaze rested thoughtfully.

Itt stood out in such vivid contrast to the beauty of the city around it that even Kitiara's cold, unfeeling gaze noted it. Thrusting up from the shadows that surrounded it like a bleached fingerbone, it was a thing of darkness and twisted ugliness, all the more horrible because once it must have been the most wonderful building in Palanthas—the ancient Tower of High Sorcery.

Shadow surrounded it by day and by night, for it was guarded by a grove of huge oak trees, the largest trees growing on Krynn, some of the more well-traveled whispered in awe. No one knew for certain because there were none, even of the kender race which fears little on this world, who could walk in the trees' dread darkness.

"The Shoikan Grove," Kitiara murmured to an unseen companion. "No living being of any race dared enter it. Not until *he* came—*the master of past and of present.*" If she said this with a sneer in her voice, it was a sneer that quivered as Skie began to circle nearer and nearer that patch of blackness.

The blue dragon settled down upon the empty, abandoned streets near the Shoikan Grove. Kit had urged Skie with everything from bribes to dire threats to fly her over the Grove to the Tower itself. But Skie, although he would have shed the last

"During the Age of Might, the wizards grew so powerful that many people feared they might take over the world. Among these was the Kingpriest. He turned the people against the wizards.

"It would have been easy for the wizards to have destroyed the people, but they knew that in so doing they would destroy the world. Rather than do this, they chose to sacrifice their own power in the world. They destroyed two of the Towers of High Sorcery—those at Daltigoth and the Ruins. They turned the Tower at Istar over to the Kingpriest and were intending to give him the Tower at Palanthas but for the terrible event that was to befall it. In return, they were allowed to retain the Tower at Wayreth, and it was here that they brought as much of their libraries and as many of their magical artifacts as was possible.

"At the beginning of the ceremony to turn over the Tower of Palanthas to the Kingpriest's representative, an evil wizard—driven insane by the downfall of his art—leaped from an upper window and impaled himself upon the spikes of the tower's gate. As his blood flowed to the ground, he cast a curse upon the tower, saying that no living being would inhabit it until the Master of Past and Present returned with power." [DRAGONLANCE Adventures, by Tracy Hickman and Margaret Weis, TSR, Inc., 1987, p.31, 33.]

Kitiara is foreshadowing for us the special status of Raistlin's journey. —TRH

drop of his blood for his master, refused her this. It was beyond his power. No mortal being, not even a dragon, could enter that accursed ring of guardian oaks.†

Skie stood glaring into the grove with hatred, his red eyes burning, while his claws nervously tore up the paving stones. He would have prevented his master from entering, but he knew Kitiara well. Once her mind was set upon something, nothing could deter her. So Skie folded his great, leathery wings around his body and gazed at this fat, beautiful city while thoughts of flames and smoke and death filled him with longing.

Kitiara dismounted from her dragonsaddle slowly. The silver moon, Solinari, was a pale, severed head in the sky. Its twin, the red moon Lunitari, had just barely risen and now flickered on the horizon like the wick of a dying candle. The faint light of both moons shimmered in Kitiara's dragonscale armor, turning it a ghastly blood-hued color.

Kit studied the grove intently, took a step toward it, then stopped nervously. Behind her, she could hear a rustle—Skie's wings giving unspoken advice— *Let us flee this place of doom, lady! Flee while we still have our lives!*

Kitiara swallowed. Her tongue felt dry and swollen. Her stomach muscles knotted painfully. Vivid memories of her first battle returned to her, the first time she had faced an enemy and known that she must kill this man—or she herself would be dead. Then, she had conquered with the skillful thrust of her sword blade. But this?

"I have walked many dark places upon this world," Kit said to her unseen companion in a deep, low voice, "and I have not known fear. But I cannot enter here."

"Simply hold the jewel he gave you high in your hand," said her companion, materializing out of the night. "The Guardians of the Grove will be powerless to harm you."

Kitiara looked into the dense ring of tall trees. Their vast, spreading branches blotted out the light of moons and stars by night, of the sun by day. Around their roots flowed perpetual night. No soft breeze touched their hoary arms, no storm wind moved the great limbs. It was said that even during

the awful days before the Cataclysm, when storms the like of which had not been known before on Krynn swept the land, the trees of Shoikan Grove alone had not bent to the anger of the gods.

But, more horrible even than their everlasting darkness, was the echo of everlasting life that pulsed from deep within. Everlasting life, everlasting misery and torment . . .

"What you say my head believes," Kitiara answered, shivering, "but my heart does not, Lord Soth."†

"Turn back, then," the death knight answered, shrugging. "Show *him* that the most powerful Dragon Highlord in the world is a coward."

Kitiara stared at Soth from the eye slits of her dragonhelm.

Her brown eyes glinted, her hand closed spasmodically over the hilt of her sword. Soth returned her gaze, the orange flame flickering within his eye sockets burned bright in hideous mockery. And if *his* eyes laughed at her, what would those golden eyes of the mage reveal? Not laughter—triumph!

Compressing her lips tightly, Kitiara reached for the chain around her neck where hung the charm Raistlin had sent her. Grasping hold of the chain, she gave it a quick jerk, snapping it easily. Then she held the jewel in her gloved hand.

Black as dragon's blood, the jewel felt cold to the touch, radiating a chill even through her heavy, leather gloves. Unshining, unlovely, it lay heavy in her palm.

"How can these Guardians see it?" Kitiara demanded, holding it to the moons' light. "Look, it does not gleam or sparkle. It seems I hold nothing more than a lump of coal in my hand."

"The moon that shines upon the night jewel you cannot see, nor can any see save those who worship it," Lord Soth replied. "Those—and the dead who, like me, have been damned to eternal life. *We* can see it! For us, it shines more clearly than any light in the sky. Hold it high, Kitiara, hold it high and walk forward. The Guardians will not stop you. Take off your helm, that they may look upon your face and see the light of the jewel reflected in your eyes."

Kitiara hesitated a moment longer. Then—with thoughts of Raistlin's mocking laughter ringing

Lord Soth sprang to life one afternoon in my cubicle at TSR. I was working on the design of a module entitled Dragons of War *and was pondering the disposition of armed forces that were attacking the tower. Suddenly, there was Lord Soth, full blown in my mind. In that moment, I knew his history and his tragic fate.*

Soth is such a powerful presence that we, as writers, are somewhat in awe of him. Whenever he is allowed into a story, he has a tendency to take it over and start dragging it in the direction he wants it to take. We have to be very careful whenever Lord Soth appears in our stories lest he dominate it! —TRH

in her ears—the Dragon Highlord removed the horned dragonhelm from her head. Still she stood, glancing around. No wind ruffled her dark curls. She felt cold sweat trickle down her temple. With an angry flick of her glove, she wiped it away. Behind her, she could hear the dragon whimper—a strange sound, one she had never heard Skie make before. Her resolution faltered. The hand holding the jewel shook.

"They feed off fear, Kitiara," said Lord Soth softly. "Hold the jewel high, let them see it reflected in your eyes!"

Show him you are a coward! Those words echoed in her mind. Clutching the nightjewel, lifting it high above her head, Kitiara entered Shoikan Grove.

Darkness descended, dropping over her so suddenly Kitiara thought for one horrible, paralyzing moment she had been struck blind. Only the sight of Lord Soth's flaming eyes flickering within his pale, skeletal visage reassured her. She forced herself to stand there calmly, letting that debilitating moment of fear fade. And then she noticed, for the first time, a light gleam from the jewel. It was like no other light she had ever seen. It did not illuminate the darkness so much as allow Kitiara to distinguish all that lived within the darkness from the darkness itself.

By the jewel's power, Kitiara could begin to make out the trunks of the living trees. And now she could see a path forming at her feet. Like a river of night, it flowed onward, into the trees, and she had the eerie sensation that she was flowing along with it.

Fascinated, she watched her feet move, carrying her forward without her volition. The Grove had tried to keep her out, she realized in horror. Now, it was drawing her in!

Desperately she fought to regain control of her own body. Finally, she won—or so she presumed. At least, she quit moving. But now she could do nothing but stand in that flowing darkness and shiver, her body racked by spasms of fear. Branches creaked overhead, cackling at the joke. Leaves brushed her face. Frantically, Kit tried to bat them away, then she stopped. Their touch was chill, but not unpleasant. It was almost a caress, a gesture of respect. She had been recognized, known for one

"Black as an evil dragon's blood, the jewel protects any who enter Shoikan Grove as long as they have the courage and will to use it. The Nightjewel helps to alleviate the fear generated by the Grove, though it does not cancel it completely. The Nightjewel can be used in defense against the undead who stalk the Grove, but the person using it must have the courage to touch the undead with the jewel if the undead attack.

"The Nightjewel is black, unlovely to look at, and cold to the touch. It can be worn about the neck on a silver chain, but must be held in the hand, high in the air, when entering the Grove."
[DRAGONLANCE Adventures, by Tracy Hickman and Margaret Weis, TSR, Inc., 1987, p. 98.]

of their own. Immediately, Kit was in command of herself once more. Lifting her head, she made herself look at the path.

It was not moving. That had been an illusion borne of her own terror. Kit smiled grimly. The trees themselves were moving! Standing aside to let her pass. Kitiara's confidence rose. She walked the path with firm steps and even turned to glance triumphantly at Lord Soth, who walked a few paces behind her. The death knight did not appear to notice her, however.

"Probably communing with his fellow spirits," Kit said to herself with a laugh that was twisted, suddenly, into a shriek of sheer terror.

Something had caught hold of her ankle! A bone-freezing chill was seeping slowly through her body, turning her blood and her nerves to ice. The pain was intense. She screamed in agony. Clutching at her leg, Kitiara saw what had grabbed her—a white hand! Reaching up from the ground, its bony fingers were wrapped tightly around her ankle. It was sucking the life out of her, Kit realized, feeling the warmth leave. And then, horrified, she saw her foot begin to disappear into the oozing soil.

Panic swept her mind. Frantically she kicked at the hand, trying to break its freezing grip. But it held her fast, and yet another hand reached up from the black path and grabbed hold of her other ankle. Screaming in terror, Kitiara lost her balance and plunged to the ground.

"Don't drop the jewel!" came Lord Soth's lifeless voice. "They will drag you under!"

Kitiara kept hold of the jewel, clutching it in her hand even as she fought and twisted, trying to escape the deathly grasp that was slowly drawing her down to share its grave. "Help me!" she cried, her terror-stricken gaze seeking Soth.

"I cannot," the death knight answered grimly. "My magic will not work here. The strength of your own will is all that can save you now, Kitiara. Remember the jewel. . . ."

For a moment, Kitiara lay quite still, shivering at the chilling touch. And then anger coursed through her body. *How dare he do this to me!* she thought, seeing, once more, mocking golden eyes enjoying her torture. Her anger thawed the chill of fear and

burned away the panic. She was calm now. She knew what she must do. Slowly, she pushed herself up out of the dirt. Then, coldly and deliberately, she held the jewel down next to the skeletal hand and, shuddering, touched the jewel to the pallid flesh.

A muffled curse rumbled from the depths of the ground. The hand quivered, then released its grip, sliding back into the rotting leaves beside the trail.

Swiftly, Kitiara touched the jewel to the other hand that grasped her. It, too, vanished. The Dragon Highlord scrambled to her feet and stared around. Then she held the jewel aloft.

"See this, you accursed creatures of living death?" she screamed shrilly. "You will not stop me! I will pass! Do you hear me? I *will* pass!"

There was no answer. The branches creaked no longer, the leaves hung limply. After standing a moment longer in silence, the jewel in her hand, Kitiara started walking down the trail once more, cursing Raistlin beneath her breath. She was aware of Lord Soth near her.

"Not much farther," he said. "Once again, Kitiara, you have earned my admiration."

Kitiara did not answer. Her anger was gone, leaving a hollow place in the pit of her stomach that was rapidly filling up again with fear. She did not trust herself to speak. But she kept walking, her eyes now focused grimly on the path ahead of her. All around her now, she could see the fingers digging through the soil, seeking the living flesh they both craved and hated. Pale, hollow visages glared at her from the trees, black and shapeless things flitted about her, filling the cold, clammy air with a foul scent of death and decay.

But, though the gloved hand that held the jewel shook, it never wavered. The fleshless fingers did not stop her. The faces with their gaping mouths howled in vain for her warm blood. Slowly, the oak trees continued to part before Kitiara, the branches bending back out of the way.

There, standing at the trail's end, was Raistlin.

"I should kill you, you damned bastard!" Kitiara said through numb lips, her hand on the hilt of her sword.

"I am overjoyed to see you, too, my sister," Raistlin replied in his soft voice.

It was the first time brother and sister had met in over two years. Now that she was out from among the darkness of the trees, Kitiara could see her brother, standing in Solinari's pale light. He was dressed in robes of the finest black velvet. Hanging from his slightly stooped, thin shoulders, they fell in soft folds around his slender body. Silver runes were stitched about the hood that covered his head, leaving all but his golden eyes in shadow. The largest rune was in the center—an hourglass. Other silver runes sparkled in the moons' light upon the cuffs of his wide, full sleeves. He leaned upon the Staff of Magius, its crystal, which flamed into light only upon Raistlin's command—dark and cold, clutched in a golden dragon's claw.

"I should kill you!" Kitiara repeated, and, before she was quite aware of what she did, she cast a glance at the death knight, who seemed to form out of the darkness of the grove. It was a glance, not of command, but of invitation—an unspoken challenge.

Raistlin smiled, the rare smile that few ever saw. It was, however, lost in the shadows of his hood.

"Lord Soth," he said, turning to greet the death knight.

Kitiara bit her lip as Raistlin's hourglass eyes studied the undead knight's armor. Here were still the graven symbols of a Knight of Solamnia—the Rose and the Kingfisher and the Sword—but all were blackened as if the armor burned in a fire.

"Knight of the Black Rose," continued Raistlin, "who died in flames in the Cataclysm† before the curse of the elfmaid you wronged dragged you back to bitter life."

"Such is my tale," the death knight said without moving. "And you are Raistlin, master of past and present, the one foretold."†

The two stood, staring at each other, both forgetting Kitiara, who—feeling the silent, deadly contest being waged between the two—forgot her own anger, holding her breath to witness the outcome.

"Your magic is strong," Raistlin commented. A soft wind stirred the branches of the oak trees, caressed the black folds of the mage's robes.

"Yes," said Lord Soth quietly. "I can kill with a single word. I can hurl a ball of fire into the midst of my enemies. I rule a squadron of skeletal warriors,

See also The Cataclysm, DRAGONLANCE *Tales II, Volume 2, with contributions by Margaret Weis, Tracy Hickman, Roger E. Moore, Douglas Niles, and more; and* Lord Soth, *by Edo von Belkom.*

The Prophecy is a part of the monomyth as explained by Campbell. It is part of the Call to Adventure, which the hero hears and which takes him from his familiar surroundings to the realms of the new and magical. Interestingly, this so-called "prophecy" was uttered by Raistlin himself after he had traveled backward in time. Something of a "sure-bet" for a prophecy, wouldn't you say? —TRH

who can destroy by touch alone. I can raise a wall of ice to protect those I serve. The invisible is discernible to my eyes. Ordinary magic spells crumble in my presence."

Raistlin nodded, the folds of his hood moving gently.

Lord Soth stared at the mage without speaking. Walking close to Raistlin, he stopped only inches from the mage's frail body. Kitiara's breath came fast.

Then, with a courtly gesture, the cursed Knight of Solamnia placed his hand over that portion of his anatomy that had once contained his heart.

"But I bow in the presence of a master," Lord Soth said.

Kitiara chewed her lip, checking an exclamation.

Raistlin glanced over at her quickly, amusement flashing in his golden, hourglass eyes.

"Disappointed, my dear sister?"

But Kitiara was well accustomed to the shifting winds of fate. She had scouted out the enemy, discovered what she needed to know. Now she could proceed with the battle. "Of course not, little brother," she answered with the crooked smile that so many had found so charming. "After all, it was you I came to see. It's been too long since we visited. You look well."

"Oh, I am, dear sister," Raistlin said. Coming forward, he put his thin hand upon her arm. She started at his touch, his flesh felt hot, as though he burned with fever. But—seeing his eyes intent upon her, noting every reaction—she did not flinch. He smiled.

"It has been so long since we saw each other last. What, two years?† Two years ago this spring, in fact," he continued, conversationally, holding Kitiara's arm within his hand. His voice was filled with mockery. "It was in the Temple of the Queen of Darkness at Neraka, that fateful night when my queen met her downfall and was banished from the world—"

"Thanks to your treachery," Kitiara snapped, trying, unsuccessfully, to break free of his grip. Raistlin kept his hand upon Kitiara's arm. Though taller and stronger than the frail mage, and seemingly capable of breaking him in two with her bare hands, Kitiara—nevertheless—found herself longing

Raistlin is discussing events from Dragons of Spring Dawning, *Book III, Chapters 11-12.*

Neraka is the Indonesian word for Hell. Some time ago, I got an email from a lovely young woman whose mother had named her Nereka because she liked the way it sounded. This young woman wanted to know the meaning of her name now that she was older. I was obliged to tell her—with my apologies.
—TRH

to pull away from that burning touch, yet not daring to move.

Raistlin laughed and, drawing her with him, led her to the outer gates of the Tower of High Sorcery.

"Shall we talk of treachery, dear sister? Didn't you rejoice when I used my magic to destroy Lord Ariakas's shield of protection, allowing Tanis Half-Elven the chance to plunge his sword into the body of *your* lord and master?† Did not I—by that action—make you the most powerful Dragon Highlord in Krynn?"

"A lot of good it has done me!" Kitiara returned bitterly. "Kept almost a prisoner in Sanction† by the foul Knights of Solamnia, who rule the lands all about! Guarded day and night by golden dragons, my every move watched. My armies scattered, roaming the land. . . ."

"Yet you came here," Raistlin said simply. "Did the gold dragons stop you? Did the Knights know of your leaving?"

Kitiara stopped on the path leading to the tower, staring at her brother in amazement. "Your doing?"

"Of course!" Raistlin shrugged. "But, we will talk of these matters later, dear sister," he said as they walked. "You are cold and hungry. The Shoikan Grove shakes the nerves of the most stalwart. Only one other person has successfully passed through its borders, with my help, of course. I expected you to do well, but I must admit I was a bit surprised at the courage of Lady Crysania—"

"Lady Crysania!" Kitiara repeated, stunned. "A Revered Daughter of Paladine! You allowed her—here?"

"I not only allowed her, I invited her," Raistlin answered imperturbably. "Without that invitation and a charm of warding, of course, she could never have passed."

"And she came?"

"Oh, quite eagerly, I assure you." Now it was Raistlin who paused. They stood outside the entrance to the Tower of High Sorcery. Torchlight from the windows shone upon his face. Kitiara could see it clearly. The lips were twisted in a smile, his flat golden eyes shone cold and brittle as winter sunlight. "Quite eagerly," he repeated softly.

Kitiara began to laugh.

See Dragons of Spring Dawning, *Book III, Chapter 9.*

The city of Sanction is the oldest part of Krynn, at least in terms of its design. This city surrounded by three volcanoes was the central part of my design for a game and story that I designed months before being hired by TSR. I actually called the game Sanction, and it became the foundation of the design I renamed the Dragonlance *setting. —TRH*

Late that night, after the two moons had set, in the still dark hours before the dawn, Kitiara sat in Raistlin's study, a glass of dark-red wine in her hands, her brows creased in a frown.

The study was comfortable, or so it seemed to look upon. Large, plush chairs of the best fabric and finest construction stood upon hand-woven carpets only the wealthiest people in Krynn could afford to own. Decorated with woven pictures of fanciful beasts and colorful flowers, they drew the eye, tempting the viewer to lose himself for long hours in their beauty. Carved wooden tables stood here and there, objects rare and beautiful—or rare and ghastly—ornamented the room.

But its predominant feature were the books. It was lined with deep wooden shelves, holding hundreds and hundreds of books. Many were similar in appearance, all bound with a nightblue binding, decorated with runes of silver. It was a comfortable room, but, despite a roaring fire blazing in a huge, gaping fireplace at one end of the study, there was a bone-chilling cold in the air. Kitiara was not certain, but she had the feeling it came from the books.

Lord Soth stood far from the fire's light, hidden in the shadows. Kit could not see him, but she was aware of his presence—as was Raistlin. The mage sat opposite his half-sister in a large chair behind a gigantic desk of black wood, carved so cunningly that the creatures decorating it seemed to watch Kitiara with their wooden eyes.

This is the first real hint that Ansalon is really only a part of a larger world. When we first started designing the DRAGONLANCE setting, we were struggling to determine what would make an acceptable fantasy world. The only real model we had of any use was Tolkien's Middle-earth, and so much of the DRAGONLANCE setting was modeled on that great, epic work. It is no coincidence that Ansalon is almost identical in geographic size to the known map of Middle-earth—and no surprise that Middle-earth itself is close to Europe in size. —TRH

Squirming uncomfortably, she drank her wine, too fast. Although well accustomed to strong drink, she was beginning to feel giddy, and she hated that feeling. It meant she was losing control. Angrily, she thrust the glass away from her, determined to drink no more.

"This plan of yours is crazy!" she told Raistlin irritably. Not liking the gaze of those golden eyes upon her, Kitiara stood up and began to pace the room. "It's senseless! A waste of time. With your help, we could rule Ansalon, you and I. In fact"— Kitiara turned suddenly, her face alight with eagerness— "with your power we could rule the world!† We don't need Lady Crysania or our hulking brother—"

"Rule the world," Raistlin repeated softly, his eyes burning. "Rule the *world*? You still don't understand,

do you, my dear sister? Let me make this as plain as I know how." Now it was his turn to stand up. Pressing his thin hands upon the desk, he leaned toward her, like a snake.

"I don't give a damn about the world!" he said softly. "I could rule it tomorrow if I wanted it! I don't."

"You don't want the world," Kit shrugged, her voice bitter with sarcasm. "Then that leaves only—"

Kitiara almost bit her tongue. She stared at Raistlin in wonder. In the shadows of the room, Lord Soth's flaming eyes blazed more brightly than the fire.

"*Now* you understand," Raistlin smiled in satisfaction and resumed his seat once more. "Now you see the importance of this Revered Daughter of Paladine! It was fate brought her to me, just when I was nearing the time for my journey."

Kitiara could only stare at him, aghast. Finally, she found her voice. "How—how do you know she will follow you? Surely you didn't tell her!"

"Only enough to plant the seed in her breast," Raistlin† smiled, looking back to that meeting. Leaning back, he put his thin fingers to his lips. "My performance was, frankly, one of my best. Reluctantly I spoke, my words drawn from me by her goodness and purity. They came out, stained with blood, and she was mine . . . lost through her own pity." He came back to the present with a start. "She will come," he said coldly, sitting forward once more. "She and that buffoon of a brother.† He will serve me unwittingly, of course. But then, that's how he does everything."

Kitiara put her hand to her head, feeling her blood pulse. It was not the wine, she was cold sober now. It was fury and frustration. He could help me! she thought angrily. He is truly as powerful as they said. More so! But he's insane. He's lost his mind. . . . Then, unbidden, a voice spoke to her from somewhere deep inside.

What if he isn't insane? What if he really means to go through with this?

Coldly, Kitiara considered his plan, looking at it carefully from all angles. What she saw horrified her. No. He could not win! And, worse, he would probably drag her down with him!

Raistlin begins Legends supremely self-confident. He represents chaos, seeking to overthrow order, represented by the gods. To this end, he has plans and ambitions, and he knows exactly how he's going to achieve them. He has no care for anyone. He is willing to use people, even resort to murder, to achieve his goals. All this might make Raistlin a very unlikable character but for the fact that he has a heart and a soul, neither of which he wants, for he believes love and sympathy for his fellow men to be weaknesses. In the end, love for his brother and empathy for the weak and downtrodden (represented by Bupu) are the strengths that will redeem Raistlin.
—MW

The sibling rivalry between Raistlin and Caramon has been part of the DRAGONLANCE *setting since the very first tale in* Dragons of Autumn Twilight, *but later works developed the early years between the brothers. See* The Soulforge *by* Margaret Weis, Brothers in Arms *by Margaret Weis and Don Perrin, and* The Brothers Majere *by* Kevin Stein.

These thoughts passed through Kit's mind swiftly, and none of them showed on her face. In fact, her smile grew only more charming. Many were the men who had died, that smile their last vision.

Raistlin might have been considering that as he looked at her intently. "You can be on a winning side for a change, my sister."

Kitiara's conviction wavered. If he *could* pull it off, it would be glorious! Glorious! Krynn would be hers.

Kit looked at the mage. Twenty-eight years ago, he had been a newborn baby, sick and weakly, a frail counterpart to his strong, robust twin brother.

"Let 'im die. 'Twill be best in the long run," the midwife had said. Kitiara had been a teenager then. Appalled, she heard her mother weepingly agree.

But Kitiara had refused. Something within her rose to the challenge. The baby would live! She would *make* him live, whether he wanted to or not. "My first fight," she used to tell people proudly, "was with the gods. And I won!"

And now! Kitiara studied him. She saw the man. She saw—in her mind's eye—that whining, puking baby. Abruptly, she turned away.

"I must get back," she said, pulling on her gloves. "You will contact me upon your return?"

"If I am successful, there will be no need to contact you," Raistlin said softly. "You will *know*."

Kitiara almost sneered but caught herself quickly. Glancing at Lord Soth, she prepared to leave the room. "Farewell then, my brother." Controlled as she was, she could not keep an edge of anger from her voice. "I am sorry you do not share my desire for the good things of *this* life! We could have done much together, you and I!"

"Farewell, Kitiara," Raistlin† said, his thin hand summoning the shadowy forms of those who served him to show his guests to the door. "Oh, by the way," he added as Kit stood in the doorway, "I owe you my life, dear sister. At least, so I have been told. I just wanted to let you know that—with the death of Lord Ariakas, who would, undoubtedly, have killed you—I consider my debt paid. I owe you nothing!"

Kitiara stared into the mage's golden eyes, seeking threat, promise, what? But there was nothing

Characters are like real people to me as an author. Some of them become intimate friends, while some are merely acquaintances. Some I like very much; others I can't stand! And some very, very few become as close as family. Raistlin Majere was one of the latter. When I started to study him, to try to understand him, I realized I understood him and empathized with him. I knew him, knew exactly how he would react to certain situations. I knew his ambition, knew his darkest secrets, knew his love-hate relationship with his brother, which would prove to be the relationship that had the most impact on his life. —MW

there. Absolutely nothing. And then, in an instant, Raistlin spoke a word of magic and vanished from her sight.

The way out of Shoikan Grove was not difficult. The guardians had no care for those who left the Tower. Kitiara and Lord Soth walked together, the death knight moving soundlessly through the Grove, his feet leaving no impression on the leaves that lay dead and decaying on the ground. Spring did not come to Shoikan Grove.

Kitiara did not speak until they had passed the outer perimeter of trees and once more stood upon the solid paving stones of the city of Palanthas. The sun was rising, the sky brightening from its deep night blue to a pale gray. Here and there, those Palanthians whose business called for them to rise early were waking. Far down the street, past the abandoned buildings that surrounded the Tower, Kitiara could hear marching feet, the changing of the watch upon the wall. She was among the living once again.

She drew a deep breath, then, "He must be stopped,"† she said to Lord Soth.

The death knight made no comment, one way or the other.

"It will not be easy, I know," Kitiara said, drawing the dragonhelm over her head and walking rapidly toward Skie, who had reared his head in triumph at her approach. Patting her dragon lovingly upon his neck, Kitiara turned to face the death knight.

"But we do not have to confront Raistlin directly. His scheme hinges upon Lady Crysania. Remove her, and we stop him. He need never know I had anything to do with it, in fact. Many have died, trying to enter the Forest of Wayreth. Isn't that so?"

Lord Soth nodded, his flaming eyes flaring slightly.

"You handle it. Make it appear to be . . . fate," Kitiara said. "My little brother believes in that, apparently." She mounted her dragon. "When he was small, I taught him that to refuse to do my bidding meant a whipping. It seems he must learn that lesson again!"

At her command, Skie's powerful hind legs dug into the pavement, cracking and breaking the stones. He leaped into the air, spread his wings, and soared into the morning sky. The people of Palanthas felt a

"Kitiara is a gambler with fate. Having considered the odds, she has decided to put her money on the Dark Queen instead of her half-brother, Raistlin. It is a pretty good bet, since she undoubtedly believes she could worm her way back into Raistlin's favor should he succeed." [DRAGONLANCE Adventures, *by Tracy Hickman and Margaret Weis, TSR, Inc., 1987, p. 108.*]

shadow lift from their hearts, but that was all they knew. Few saw the dragon or its rider leave.

Lord Soth remained standing upon the fringes of Shoikan Grove.

"I, too, believe in fate, Kitiara," the death knight murmured. "The fate a man makes himself."

Glancing up at the windows of the Tower of High Sorcery, Soth saw the light extinguished from the room where they had been. For a brief instant, the Tower was shrouded in the perpetual darkness that seemed to linger around it, a darkness the sun's light could not penetrate. Then one light gleamed forth, from a room at the top of the tower.

The mage's laboratory, the dark and secret room where Raistlin worked his magic.

"Who will learn this lesson, I wonder?" Soth murmured. Shrugging, he disappeared, melting into the waning shadows as daylight approached.

CHAPTER 6

et's stop at this place," Caramon said, heading for a ramshackle building that stood huddled back away from the trail, lurking in the forest like a sulking beast. "Maybe she's been in here."

"I really doubt it," said Tas, dubiously eyeing the sign that hung by one chain over the door. "The 'Cracked Mug't doesn't seem quite the place—"

"Nonsense," growled Caramon, as he had growled more times on this journey already than Tas could count, "she has to eat. Even great, muckety-muck clerics have to eat. Or maybe someone in here will have seen some sign of her on the trail. *We're* not having any luck."

"No," muttered Tasslehoff beneath his breath, "but we might have more luck if we searched the road, not taverns."

They had been on the road three days, and

Taverns are the customary settings for the launching of adventures, a logical choice, for it is in taverns that we find both strangers and friends coming together to relax in company with others. The tavern is often the center of news of the world, for travelers share their tales here. —MW

The monomyth begins at home, a familiar place from whence the hero is called out into the realms of unknown adventure. That many games and stories begin in inns—a traditional gathering place to hear stories—is no coincidence. They share a common mythic ancestry with heroes from Odysseus to Luke Skywalker. (See Appendix A) —TRH

*"Most kender are
encountered during
wanderlust, a particular
phase in a kender's life that
occurs for most kender
during their early 20s.
Apparently the kender's
natural curiosity and
desire for action suddenly
go into overdrive at this
time, and kender are driven
to wander the land as far
as they can go. Wanderlust
may last for many years,
and some kender have a
habit of making maps of
their travels during this
time. Sadly, most kender
are poor mapmakers,
lacking the patience and
skills to chart their travels
accurately. Kender may
collect other maps during
this time to satisfy their
curiosity about other
places. This wanderlust is
responsible for spreading
kender communities across
the continent of Ansalon."*
[DRAGONLANCE
Adventures, *by Tracy
Hickman and Margaret
Weis, TSR, Inc., 1987,
p. 52.]*

Tas's worst misgivings about this adventure had
proved true.

Ordinarily, kender are enthusiastic travelers. All
kender are stricken with wanderlust† somewhere
near their twentieth year. At this time, they gleefully
strike out for parts unknown, intent on finding nothing except adventure and whatever beautiful, horrible, or curious items might by chance fall into their
bulging pouches. Completely immune to the self-
preserving emotion of fear, afflicted by unquench-
able curiosity, the kender population on Krynn
was not a large one, for which most of Krynn was
devoutly grateful.

Tasslehoff Burrfoot, now nearing his thirtieth year
(at least as far as he could remember), was, in most
regards, a typical kender. He had journeyed the
length and breadth of the continent of Ansalon, first
with his parents before they had settled down in
Kenderhome. After coming of age, he wandered by
himself until he met Flint Fireforge, the dwarven
metalsmith and his friend, Tanis Half-Elven. After
Sturm Brightblade, Knight of Solamnia, and the
twins, Caramon and Raistlin, joined them, Tas
became involved in the most wonderful adventure
of his life—the War of the Lance.

But, in some respects, Tasslehoff was *not* a typical
kender, although he would have denied this if it
were mentioned. The loss of two people he loved
dearly—Sturm Brightblade and Flint—touched the
kender deeply. He had come to know the emotion
of fear, not fear for himself, but fear and concern for
those he cared about. His concern for Caramon,
right now, was deep.

And it grew daily.

At first, the trip had been fun. Once Caramon got
over his fit of sulks about Tika's hard-heartedness
and the inability of the world in general to understand him, he had taken a few swigs from his flask
and felt better. After several more swigs, he began to
relate stories about his days helping to track down
draconians. Tas found this amusing and entertaining
and, though he continually had to watch Bupu to
make certain she didn't get run over by a wagon or
wander into a mudhole, he enjoyed his morning.

By afternoon, the flask was empty, and Caramon
was even in such a good humor as to be ready to

listen to some of Tas's stories, which the kender never tired of relating. Unfortunately, right at the best part, when he was escaping with the woolly mammoth and the wizards were shooting lightning bolts at him, Caramon came to a tavern.

"Just fill up the flask," he mumbled and went inside.

Tas started to follow, then saw Bupu staring in openmouthed wonder at the red-hot blacksmith's forge across the road. Realizing she would either set herself or the town or both on fire, and knowing that he couldn't take her into the tavern (most refused to serve gully dwarves), Tas decided to stay out and keep an eye on her. After all, Caramon would probably be only a few minutes. . . .

Two hours later, the big man stumbled out.

"Where in the Abyss have you been?" Tas demanded, pouncing on Caramon like a cat.

"Jusht having a . . . having a little . . ." Caramon swayed unsteadily, "one for the . . . road."

"I'm on a quest!" Tas yelled in exasperation. "My first quest, given to me by an Important Person, who may be in danger. And I've been stuck out here two hours with a gully dwarf!" Tas pointed at Bupu, who was asleep in a ditch. "I've never been so bored in my life, and *you're* in there soaking up dwarf spirits!"

Caramon glared at him, his lips pursed into a pout. "You know something," the big man muttered as he staggered off down the road, "you're st-starting to shound a lot like Tika. . ."

Things went rapidly downhill from there.

That night they came to the crossroads.

"Let's go this way," Tas said, pointing. "Lady Crysania's certain to know people are going to try to stop her. She'll take a route that's not very well traveled to try and throw off pursuit. I think we should follow the same trail we took two years ago,† when we left Solace—"

"Nonsense!" Caramon snorted. "She's a woman and a cleric to boot. She'll take the easiest road. We'll go by way of Haven."†

Tas had been dubious about this decision, and his doubts proved well-founded. They hadn't traveled more than a few miles when they came to another tavern.

Tas is referring to the events told in Dragons of Autumn Twilight, Book I, *Chapter 5.*

Solace and Haven were both named by me and were intended to be evocative of home, the place where all heroic journeys begin. —TRH

Caramon went in to find out if anyone had seen a person matching Lady Crysania's description, leaving Tas—once again—with Bupu. An hour later the big man emerged, his face flushed and cheerful.

"Well, has anyone seen her?" Tas asked irritably.

"Seen who? Oh—her. No. . . ."

And now, two days later,† they were only about halfway to Haven. But the kender could have written a book describing the taverns along the way.

Although Solace and Haven are only a little over twenty miles apart as the crow flies, travelers must go the long way around due to Darken Wood, which separates the two villages.

"In the old days," Tas fumed, "we could have walked to Tarsis and back in this time!"

"I was younger then, and immature. My body's mature now, and I have to build up my strength," Caramon said loftily, "little by little."

"He's building up something little by little," Tas said to himself grimly, "but strength isn't it!"

Caramon could not walk much more than an hour before he was forced to sit down and rest. Often he collapsed completely, moaning in pain, sweat rolling off his body. It would take Tas, Bupu, and the flask of dwarf spirits to get him back on his feet again. He complained bitterly and continually. His armor chafed, he was hungry, the sun was too hot, he was thirsty. At night, he insisted that they stop in some wretched inn. Then Tas had the thrill of watching the big man drink himself senseless. Tas and the bartender would haul him to his room where he would sleep until half the morning was gone.

After the third day of this (and their twentieth tavern) and still no sign of Lady Crysania, Tasslehoff was beginning to think seriously about returning to Kenderhome, buying a nice little house, and retiring from adventuring.

It was about midday when they arrived at the Cracked Mug. Caramon immediately disappeared inside. Heaving a sigh that came from the toes of his new, bright green shoes, Tas stood with Bupu, looking at the outside of the slovenly place in grim silence.

"Me no like this anymore," Bupu announced. She glared at Tas accusingly. "You say we go find pretty man in red robes. All we find is one fat drunk. I go back home, back to Highbulp, Phudge I."

"No, don't leave! Not yet!" Tas cried desperately. "We'll find the—uh—pretty man. Or at least a pretty lady who wants to help the pretty man. Maybe . . . maybe we'll learn something here.

It was obvious Bupu didn't believe him. Tas didn't believe himself.

"Look," he said, "just wait for me here. It won't be much farther. I know—I'll bring you something to eat. Promise you won't leave?"

Bupu smacked her lips, eyeing Tas dubiously. "Me wait," she said, plopping down into the muddy road. "At least till after lunch."

Tas, his pointed chin jutting out firmly, followed Caramon into the tavern. He and Caramon were going to have a little talk—

As it turned out, however, that wasn't necessary.

"Your health, gentlemen," Caramon said, raising a glass to the slovenly crowd gathered in the bar. There weren't many—a couple of traveling dwarves, who sat near the door, and a party of humans, dressed like rangers,† who lifted their mugs in return to Caramon's salute.

Tas sat down next to Caramon, so depressed that he actually returned a purse his hands had (without his knowing it) removed from the belt of one of the dwarves as he passed.

"I think you dropped this," Tas mumbled, handing it back to the dwarf, who stared at him in amazement.

"We're looking for a young woman," Caramon said, settling down for the afternoon. He recited her description as he had recited it in every tavern from Solace on. "Black hair, small, delicate, pale face, white robes. She's a cleric—"

"Yeah, we've seen her," said one of the rangers.

Beer spurted from Caramon's mouth. "You have?" he managed to gasp, choking.

Tas perked up. "Where?" he asked eagerly.

"Wandering about the woods east of here," said the ranger, jerking his thumb.

"Yeah?" Caramon said suspiciously. "What're you doing out in the woods yourselves?"

"Chasing goblins. There's a bounty for them in Haven."

"Three gold pieces for goblin ears," said his friend, with a toothless grin, "if you care to try your luck."

"What about the woman?" Tas pursued.

"She's a crazy one, I guess." The ranger shook his head. "We told her the land out around here was crawling with goblins and she shouldn't be out alone. She just said she was in the hands of Paladine, or some such name, and he would take care of her."

Caramon heaved a sigh and lifted his drink to his lips. "That sounds like her all right—"

Leaping up, Tas snatched the glass from the big man's hand.

"What the—" Caramon glared at him angrily.

"Come on!" Tas said, tugging at him. "We've got to go! Thanks for the help," he panted, dragging Caramon to the door. "Where did you say you saw her?"

"About ten miles east of here. You'll find a trail out back, behind the tavern. Branches off the main road. Follow it and it'll take you through the forest. Used to be a short cut to Gateway, before it got too dangerous to travel."

"Thanks again!" Tas pushed Caramon, still protesting, out the door.

"Confound it, what's the hurry?" Caramon snarled angrily, jerking away from Tas's prodding hands. "We coulda at least had dinner. . . ."

"Caramon!" said Tas urgently, dancing up and down. "Think! Remember! Don't you realize where she is? Ten miles east of here! Look—" Yanking open one of his pouches, Tas pulled out a whole sheaf of maps. Hurriedly, he sorted through them, tossing them onto the ground in his haste. "Look," he repeated finally, unrolling one and thrusting it into Caramon's flushed face.

The big man peered at it, trying to bring it into focus.

"Huh?"

"Oh, for—Look, here's where we are, near as I can figure. And here's Haven, still south of us. Across here is Gateway. Here's the path they were talking about and here—" Tas's finger pointed.

Caramon squinted. "Dark-dar-dar Darken† Wood," he mumbled. "Darken Wood. That seems familiar. . . ."

"Of course it seems familiar! We nearly died there!"† Tas yelled, waving his arms. "It took Raistlin to save us—"

Seeing Caramon scowl, Tas hurried on. "What if she should wander in there alone?" he asked pleadingly.

"Few physical details exist about Darken Wood. It stretched through all the land between Haven and Solace Vale, from the White-rage Cut north to Haven Road. Its trees were interspersed with mountain ridges. In the north (near the Twin Peaks which guarded Haven Road through Shadow Canyon) was Starlight Canyon, home of the pegasi. In the center were the Dryad Forests, and stretching south to Haven were the Centaur Reaches. Just north of the Dryad Forests was Unicorn Grove, home of the Forestmaster." [The Atlas of the DRAGONLANCE World, *by Karen Wynn Fonstad, TSR, Inc., 1987, p. 14.]*

The Companions' adventures in Darken Wood can be found in Dragons of Autumn Twilight, *Book I, Chapters 10-11.*

Caramon looked out into the forest, his bleary eyes peering at the narrow, overgrown trail. His scowl deepened. "I suppose you expect me to stop her," he grumbled.

"Well, naturally we'll have to stop her!" Tas began, then came to a sudden halt. "You never meant to," the kender said softly, staring at Caramon. "All along, you never meant to go after her. You were just going to stumble around here for a few days, have a few drinks, a few laughs, then go back to Tika, tell her you're a miserable failure, figuring she'd take you back, same as usual—"

"So what did you expect me to do?" Caramon growled, turning away from Tas's reproachful gaze. "How can I help this woman find the Tower of High Sorcery, Tas?" He began to whimper. "I don't *want* to find it! I swore I'd never go near that foul place again! They destroyed him there, Tas. When he came out, his skin was that strange gold color. They gave him those cursed eyes so that all he sees is death. They shattered his body. He couldn't take a breath without coughing. And they made him . . . they made him kill me!" Caramon choked and buried his face in his hands, sobbing in pain, trembling in terror.

"He-he didn't kill you,† Caramon," Tas said, feeling completely helpless. "Tanis told me. It was just an image of you. And he was sick and scared and hurting real bad inside. He didn't know what he was doing—"

But Caramon only shook his head. And the tender-hearted kender couldn't blame him. No wonder he doesn't want to go back there, Tas thought remorsefully. Perhaps I should take him home. He certainly isn't much good to anyone in this state. But then Tas remembered Lady Crysania, out there all alone, blundering into Darken Wood. . . .

"I talked to a spirit there once," Tas murmured, "but I'm not certain they'd remember me. And there're goblins out there. And, while I'm not afraid of them, I don't suppose I'd be much good fighting off more than three or four."

Tasslehoff was at a loss. If only Tanis were here! The half-elf always knew what to say, what to do. He'd make Caramon listen to reason. But Tanis isn't here, said a stern voice inside of the kender that

Of all archetypes, the struggle of brother against brother is one of the most powerful. It is a classic theme to have the main and impact character so closely related and yet at such odds in a story. It is reflected down through the centuries from Cain and Able, Jacob and Esau, and in countless tales of the Arabian Nights. —TRH

sounded at times suspiciously like Flint. It's up to you, you doorknob!

I don't want it to be up to me! Tas wailed, then waited for a moment to see if the voice answered. It didn't. He was alone.

"Caramon," Tas said, making his voice as deep as possible and trying very hard to sound like Tanis, "look, just come with us as far as the edges of the Forest of Wayreth. Then you can go home. We'll probably be safe after that—"

But Caramon wasn't listening. Awash in liquor and self-pity he collapsed onto the ground. Leaning back against a tree, he babbled incoherently about nameless horrors, begging Tika to take him back.

Bupu stood up and came to stand in front of the big warrior. "Me go," she said in disgust. "Me want fat, slobbering drunk me find plenty back home." Nodding her head, she started off down the path. Tas ran after her, caught her, and dragged her back.

"No, Bupu! You can't! We're almost there!"

Suddenly Tasslehoff's patience ran out. Tanis wasn't here. No one was here to help. It was just like the time† when he'd broken the dragon orb. Maybe what he was doing wasn't the right thing, but it was the only thing he could think of to do.

Tas's breaking of the dragon orb can be found in Dragons of Winter Night, *Book III, Chapter 6.*

Tas walked up and kicked Caramon in the shins.

"Ouch!" Caramon gulped. Startled, he stared at Tas, a hurt and puzzled look on his face. "What'dya do that for?"

In answer, Tas kicked him again, hard. Groaning, Caramon grabbed his leg.

"Hey, now we have some fun," Bupu said. Running forward gleefully, she kicked Caramon in the other leg. "Me stay now."

The big man roared. Blundering to his feet, he glared at Tas. "Blast it, Burrfoot, if this is one of your games—"

"It's no game, you big ox!" the kender shouted. "I've decided to kick some sense into you, that's all! I've had enough of your whining! All you've done, all these years, is whine! The noble Caramon, sacrificing everything for his ungrateful brother. Loving Caramon, always putting Raistlin first! Well—maybe you did and maybe you didn't. I'm starting to think you always put Caramon first!

And maybe Raistlin knew, deep inside, what I'm just beginning to figure out! You only did it because it made *you* feel good! Raistlin didn't need you—you needed him! You lived his life because you're too scared to live a life of your own!"

Caramon's eyes glowed feverishly, his face paled with anger. Slowly, he stood up, his big fists clenched. "You've gone too far this time, you little bastard—"

"Have I?" Tas was screaming now, jumping up and down. "Well, listen to this, Caramon! You're always blubbering about how no one needs you. Did you ever stop to think that Raistlin needs you now more than he's ever needed you before? And Lady Crysania—she needs you! And there you stand, a big blob of quivering jelly with your brain all soaked and turned to mush!"

Tasslehoff thought for a moment he *had* gone too far. Caramon took an unsteady step forward, his face blotched and mottled and ugly. Bupu gave a yelp and ducked behind Tas. The kender stood his ground—just as he had when the furious elf lords had been about to slice him in two† for breaking the dragon orb. Caramon loomed over him, the big man's liquor-soaked breath nearly making Tas gag. Involuntarily, he closed his eyes. Not from fear, but from the look of terrible anguish and rage on Caramon's face.

This incident can also be found in Dragons of Winter Night, *Book III, Chapter 6.*

He stood, braced, waiting for the blow that would likely smash his nose back through to the other side of his head.

But the blow never fell. There was the sound of tree limbs ripping apart, huge feet stomping through dense brush.

Cautiously, Tas opened his eyes. Caramon was gone, crashing down the trail into the forest. Sighing, Tas stared after him. Bupu crept out from behind his back.

"That fun," she announced. "I stay after all. Maybe we play game again?"

"I don't think so, Bupu," Tas said miserably. "Come on. I guess we better go after him."

"Oh, well," the gully dwarf reflected philosophically. "Some other game come along, just as fun."

"Yeah," Tas agreed absently. Turning around, afraid that perhaps someone in the wretched inn

had overheard and might start trouble, the kender's eyes opened wide.

The Cracked Mug tavern was gone. The dilapidated building, the sign swinging on one chain, the dwarves, the rangers, the bartender, even the glass Caramon had lifted to his lips. All had disappeared into the midafternoon air like an evil dream upon awakening.

Chapter 7

Sing† as the spirits move you,
Sing to your doubling eye,
Plain Jane becomes Lovable Lindas
When six moons shine in the sky.

Sing to a sailor's courage,
Sing while the elbows bend,
A ruby port your harbor,
Hoist three sheets to the wind.

Sing while the heart is cordial,
Sing to the absinthe of cares,
Sing to the one for the weaving road,
And the dog, and each of his hairs.

All of the waitresses love you,
Every dog is your friend,
Whatever you say is just what you mean,
So hoist three sheets to the wind.†

I still have an affection for drinking songs, even though my own intake these days is seldom more than a solitary beer. The kender drinking song in Chronicles (mistakenly called a Trailsong, whatever that is, in **Leaves From the Inn of the Last Home**) is very dear to me, as is "Three Sheets to the Wind." I don't know if the phrase "three sheets to the wind" to describe advanced drunkenness is common nationwide or simply a southernism I picked up along the way, but it fit in here nicely.

My favorite line is "all of the waitresses love you." It describes the third stage of advanced inebriation, right between "to hell with dinner" and mild coma. You can ask Larry Elmore about the waitress with feathers in the Milwaukee bar. The joke will be on me, of course, but he stood back and let me embarrass myself. —Michael Williams

Michael Williams, the poet laureate of the DRAGONLANCE setting, was occasionally known to indulge himself now and then. While I have always had an abiding respect and admiration for Michael's abilities as a poet, this sweet little poem—filled with its dual and occasionally triple meanings—is very much my favorite of his work.
—TRH

By evening, Caramon was roaring drunk.

Tasslehoff and Bupu caught up with the big man as he was standing in the middle of the trail, draining the last of the dwarf spirits from the flask. He leaned his head back, tilting it to get every drop. When he finally lowered the flask, it was to peer inside it in disappointment. Wobbling unsteadily on his feet, he shook it.

"All gone," Tas heard him mumble unhappily.

The kender's heart sank.

"Now I've done it," Tas said to himself in misery. "I can't tell him about the disappearing inn. Not when he's in this condition! I've only made things worse!"

But he hadn't realized quite how much worse until he came up to Caramon and tapped him on the shoulder. The big man whirled around in drunken alarm.

"What ish it? Who'sh there?" He peered around the rapidly darkening forest.

"Me, down here," said Tas in a small voice. "I—I just wanted to say I was sorry, Caramon, and—"

"Uh? Oh . . ." Staggering backwards, Caramon stared at him, then grinned foolishly. "Oh, hullo there, little fellow. A kender"—his gaze wandered to Bupu—"and a gu-gul-gullgullydorf," he finished with a rush. He bowed. "Whashyournames?"

"What?" Tas asked.

"Whashyournames?" Caramon repeated with dignity.

"You know me, Caramon," Tas said, puzzled. "I'm Tasslehoff."

"Me Bupu," answered the gully dwarf, her face lighting up, obviously hoping this was another game. "Who you?"

"You know who he is," Tas began irritably, then nearly swallowed his tongue as Caramon interrupted.

"I'm Raistlin," said the big man solemnly with another, unsteady bow. "A—a great and pow—pow—powerfulmagicuser."

"Oh, come off it, Caramon!" Tas said in disgust. "I said I was sorry, so don't—"

"Caramon?" The big man's eyes opened wide, then narrowed shrewdly. "Caramon's dead. I killed him. Long ago in the Tow—the Twowr—the Twer-HighSorshry."

"By Reorx's beard!" Tas breathed.

"Him not Raistlin!" snorted Bupu. Then she paused, eyeing him dubiously. "Is him?"

"N-no! Of course not," Tasslehoff snapped.

"This not fun game!" Bupu said with firm decision. "Me no like! Him not pretty man so nice to me. Him fat drunk. Me go home." She looked around. "Which way home?"

"Not now, Bupu!" What was going on? Tas wondered bleakly. Clutching at his topknot, he gave his hair a hard yank. His eyes watered with the pain, and the kender sighed in relief. For a moment, he thought he'd fallen asleep without knowing it and was walking around in some weird dream.

But apparently it was all real—too real. Or at least for him. For Caramon, it was quite a different story.

"Watch," Caramon was saying solemnly, weaving back and forth. "I'll casht a magicshpell." Raising his hands, he blurted out a string of gibberish. "Ashanddust and ratsnests! Burrung!" He pointed at a tree. "Poof," he whispered, stumbling backward. "Up in flames! Up! Up! Burning, burning, burning . . . jusht like poor Caramon." He staggered forward, wobbling down the trail.

"All of the waitresshes love you," he sang. "Every dog ish your friend. Whatever you shay is jusht what you m-mean—"

Wringing his hands, Tas hurried after him. Bupu trotted along behind.

"Tree *not* burn," she said to Tas sternly.

"I know!" Tas groaned. "It's just . . . he thinks—"

"Him one bad magician. My turn." Rummaging around in the huge bag that kept tripping her periodically, Bupu gave a triumphant yell and pulled out a very stiff, very dead rat.

"Not now, Bupu—" Tas began, feeling what was left of his own sanity start to slip. Caramon, ahead of them, had quit singing and was shouting something about covering the forest in cobwebs.

"I going to say secret magic word," Bupu stated. "You no listen. Spoil secret."

"I won't listen," Tas said impatiently, trying to catch up with Caramon, who, for all his wobbling, was moving along at a fair rate of speed.

"You listening?" Bupu asked, panting along after him.

"No," Tas said, sighing.

"Why not?"

"You told me not to!" Tas shouted in exasperation.

"But how you know when to no listen if you no listen?" Bupu demanded angrily. "You try to steal secret magic word! Me go home."

The gully dwarf came to a dead stop, turned around, and trotted back down the path. Tas skidded to a halt. He could see Caramon now, clinging to a tree, conjuring up a host of dragons, by the sounds of it. The big man looked like he would stay put for a while at least. Cursing under his breath, the kender turned and ran after the gully dwarf.

"Stop, Bupu!" he cried frantically, catching hold of a handful of filthy rags that he mistook for her shoulder. "I swear, I'd never steal your secret magic word!"

"You stole it!" she shrieked, waving the dead rat at him. "You said it!"

"Said what?" Tasslehoff asked, completely baffled.

"Secret magic word! You say!" Bupu screamed in outrage. "Here! Look!" Holding out the dead rat, she pointed ahead of them, down the trail, and yelled, "I say secret magic word now—*secret magic word*! There. *Now* we see some hot magic."

Tas put his hand to his head. He felt giddy.

"Look! Look!" Bupu shouted in triumph, pointing a grubby finger. "See? I start fire. Secret magic word never fail. Umphf. Some bad magic-user—him."

Glancing down the path, Tas blinked. There *were* flames visible ahead of them on the trail.

"I'm definitely going back to Kenderhome," Tas mused quietly to himself. "I'll get a little house . . . or maybe move in with the folks for a few months until I feel better."

"Who's out there?" called a clear, crystalline voice.

Relief flooded over Tasslehoff. "It's a campfire!" he babbled, nearly hysterical with joy. And the voice! He hurried forward, running through the darkness toward the light. "It's me—Tasslehoff Burrfoot. I've—oof!"

The "oof" was occasioned by Caramon plucking the kender off of his feet, lifting him in his strong arms, and clapping his hand over Tas's mouth.

"Shhhh," whispered Caramon close to Tas's ear. The fumes from his breath made the kender's head swim. "There's shomeone out there!"

"Mpf blsxtchscat!" Tas wriggled frantically, trying to loosen Caramon's hold. The kender was slowly being smothered to death.

"That's who I thought it was," Caramon whispered, nodding to himself solemnly as his hand clamped even more firmly over the kender's mouth.

Tas began to see bright blue stars. He fought desperately, tearing at Caramon's hands with all his strength, but it would have been the end of the kender's brief but exciting life had not Bupu suddenly appeared at Caramon's feet.

"Secret magic word!" she shrieked, thrusting the dead rat into Caramon's face. The distant firelight was reflected in the corpse's black eyes and glittered off the sharp teeth fixed in a perpetual grin.

"Ayiii!" Caramon screamed and dropped the kender. Tas fell heavily to the ground, gasping for breath.

"What is going on out there?" said a cold voice.

"We've come . . . to rescue you. . . ." said Tasslehoff, standing up dizzily.

A white-robed figure cloaked in furs appeared on the path in front of them. Bupu looked up at it in deep suspicion.

"Secret magic word," said the gully dwarf, waving the dead rat at the Revered Daughter of Paladine.

"You'll forgive me if I'm not wildly grateful," said Lady Crysania to Tasslehoff as they sat around the fire later that evening.

"I know. I'm sorry," Tasslehoff said, sitting hunched in misery on the ground. "I made a mess of things. I generally do," he continued woefully. "Ask anyone. I've often been told I drive people crazy—but this is the first time I ever did it for real!"

Snuffling, the kender cast an anxious gaze at Caramon. The big man sat near the fire, huddled in his cape. Still under the influence of the potent dwarf spirits, he was now sometimes Caramon and sometimes Raistlin. As Caramon, he ate voraciously, cramming food into his mouth with gusto. He then regaled them with several bawdy ballads—to the delight of Bupu, who clapped along out of time and came in strong on the choruses. Tas was torn by a strong desire to giggle wildly or crawl beneath a rock and die in shame.

But, the kender decided with a shudder, he would take Caramon—bawdy songs and all—over Caramon/Raistlin. The transformation occurred suddenly, right in the middle of a song, in fact. The big man's frame collapsed, he began to cough, then—looking at them with narrow eyes—he coldly ordered himself to shut up.

"You didn't do this to him," Lady Crysania said to Tas, regarding Caramon with a cool gaze. "It is the drink. He is gross, thick-headed, and obviously lacking in self-control. He has let his appetites rule him. Odd, isn't it, that he and Raistlin are twins? His brother is so much in control, so disciplined, intelligent, and refined."

She shrugged. "Oh, there is no doubt this poor man is to be greatly pitied." Standing up, she walked over to where her horse was tethered and began to unstrap her bedroll from its place behind her saddle. "I shall remember him in my prayers to Paladine."

"I'm sure prayers won't hurt," Tas said dubiously, "but I think some strong tarbean tea might be better just now."

Lady Crysania turned and regarded the kender with a reproving stare. "I am certain you did not mean to blaspheme. Therefore I will take your statement in the sense it was uttered. Do endeavor to look at things with a more serious attitude, however."

"I *was* serious," Tas protested. "All Caramon needs is a few mugs of good, thick tarbean tea—"

Lady Crysania's dark eyebrows rose so sharply that Tas fell silent, though he hadn't the vaguest idea what he had said to upset her. He began to unpack his own blankets, his spirits just about as low as he could ever remember them being. He felt just as he had when he had ridden dragonback† with Flint during the Battle of Estwilde† Plains. The dragon had soared into the clouds, then it dove out, spinning round and round. For a few moments, up had been down, sky had been below, ground above, and then—whoosh! into a cloud, and everything was lost in the haze.

His mind felt just like it did then. Lady Crysania admired Raistlin and pitied Caramon. Tas wasn't certain, but that seemed all backward. Then there

Tas is remembering events found in Dragons of Spring Dawning, *Book I, Chapter 9.*

The origin of the name "Estwilde" is pretty obvious. It's a rather easy twisting of "east wild."
—TRH

was Caramon who was Caramon and then wasn't Caramon. Inns that were there one minute and gone the next. A secret magic word he was supposed to listen for so he'd know when not to listen. Then he'd made a perfectly logical, commonsense suggestion about tarbean tea and been reprimanded for blasphemy!

"After all," he mumbled to himself, jerking at his blankets, "Paladine and I are *close* personal friends. *He'd* know what I meant."

Sighing, the kender pillowed his head upon a rolled-up cloak. Bupu—now quite convinced that Caramon was Raistlin—was sound asleep, curled up with her head resting adoringly on the big man's foot. Caramon himself was sitting quietly now, his eyes closed, humming a song to himself. Occasionally he would cough, and once he demanded in a loud voice that Tas bring him his spellbook so that he could study his magic. But he seemed peaceful enough. Tas hoped he would soon doze and sleep off the effects of the dwarf spirits.

The fire burned low. Lady Crysania spread out her blankets on a bed of pine needles she had gathered to keep out the damp. Tas yawned. She was certainly getting on better than he'd expected. She had chosen a good, sensible location to make camp—near the trail, a stream of clear running water close by. Just as well not to have to wander too far in these dark and spooky woods—

Spooky wood† . . . what did that remind him of? Tas caught himself as he was slipping over the edge of sleep. Something important. Spooky wood. Spooks . . . talk to spooks . . .

"Darken Wood!" he said in alarm, sitting bolt upright.

"What?" asked Lady Crysania, wrapping her cloak around her and preparing to lie down.

"Darken Wood!" Tas repeated in alarm. He was now thoroughly awake. "We're close to Darken Wood. We came to warn you! It's a horrible place. You might have blundered into it. Maybe we're in it already—"

"Darken Wood?" Caramon's eyes flared open. He stared around him vaguely.

"Nonsense," Lady Crysania said comfortably, adjusting beneath her head a small traveling pillow she had brought with her. "We are not in Darken

Darken Wood finds some of its roots in Mirkwood of The Hobbit, *as well as in the mythic traditions of leaving home. The trees themselves, reaching into the ground, seem symbols of the great monomyth, and as such have been used down the ages. —TRH*

Wood, not yet. It is about five miles distant. Tomorrow we will come to a path that will take us there."

"You—you *want* to go there!" Tas gasped.

"Of course," Lady Crysania said coldly. "I go there to seek the Forestmaster's† help. It would take me many long months to travel from here to the Forest of Wayreth, even on horseback. Silver dragons dwell in Darken Wood with the Forestmaster. They will fly me to my destination."

The Companions met the Forestmaster in Dragons of Autumn Twilight, *Book I, Chapter 11.*

"But the spectres, the ancient dead king and his followers—"†

More inhabitants of Darken Wood. See Dragons of Autumn Twilight, *Book I, Chapter 10.*

"—were released from their terrible bondage when they answered the call to fight the Dragon Highlords," Lady Crysania said, somewhat sharply. "You really should study the history of the war, Tasslehoff. Especially since you were involved in it. When the human and elven forces combined to recapture Qualinesti, the spectres of Darken Wood fought with them and thus broke the dark enchantment that held them bound to dreadful life. They left this world and have been seen no more."

"Oh," said Tas stupidly. After glancing about for a moment, he sat back down on his bedroll. "I talked to them," he continued wistfully. "They were very polite—sort of abrupt in their comings and goings, but very polite. It's kind of sad to think—"

"I am quite tired," interrupted Lady Crysania. "And I have a long journey ahead of me tomorrow. I will take the gully dwarf and continue on to Darken Wood. You can take your besotted friend back home where he will—hopefully—find the help he needs. Now go to sleep."

"Shouldn't one of us . . . stay on watch?" Tas asked hesitantly. "Those rangers said—" He stopped suddenly. Those "rangers" had been in the inn that wasn't.

I've never been much on the concept of avatars, per se. Fizban is the mortal guise of Paladine. Paladine is a god but a lesser one, not the High God of the DRAGONLANCE *universe. The pantheon of Krynn masks a central god figure and has from the beginning of the design. —TRH*

"Nonsense. Paladine will guard our rest," said Lady Crysania sharply. Closing her eyes, she began to recite soft words of prayer.

Tas gulped. "I wonder if we know the same Paladine?" he asked, thinking of Fizban† and feeling very lonesome. But he said it under his breath, not wanting to be accused of blasphemy again. Lying down, he squirmed in his blankets but could not get comfortable. Finally, still wide awake, he sat back up and leaned against a tree trunk. The spring

night was cool but not unpleasantly chill. The sky was clear, and there was no wind. The trees rustled with their own conversations, feeling new life running through their limbs, waking after their long winter's sleep. Running his hand over the ground, Tas fingered the new grass poking up beneath the decaying leaves.

The kender sighed. It was a nice night. Why did he feel uneasy? Was that a sound? A twig breaking?† Tas started and looked around, holding his breath to hear better. Nothing. Silence. Glancing up into the heavens, he saw the constellation of Paladine, the Platinum Dragon, revolving around the constellation of Gilean, the Scales of Balance. Across from Paladine—each keeping careful watch† upon the other—was the constellation of the Queen of Darkness—Takhisis, the Five-Headed Dragon.

"You're awfully far away up there," Tas said to the Platinum Dragon. "And you've got a whole world to watch, not just us. I'm sure you won't mind if *I* guard our rest tonight, too. No disrespect intended, of course. It's just that I have the feeling Someone Else up there is watching us tonight, too, if you take my meaning." The kender shivered. "I don't know why I feel so queer all of a sudden. Maybe it's just being so close to Darken Wood and—well, I'm responsible for everyone apparently!"

It was an uncomfortable thought for a kender. Tas was accustomed to being responsible for himself, but when he'd traveled with Tanis and the others, there had always been someone else responsible for the group. There had been strong, skilled warriors—

What was that? He'd definitely heard something *that* time! Jumping up, Tas stood quietly, staring into the darkness. There was silence, then a rustle, then—

A squirrel. Tas heaved a sigh that came from his toes.

"While I'm up, I'll just go put another log on the fire," he said to himself. Hurrying over, he glanced at Caramon and felt a pang. It would have been much easier standing watch in the darkness if he knew he could count on Caramon's strong arm. Instead, the warrior had fallen over on his back, his eyes closed, his mouth open, snoring in drunken contentment. Curled about Caramon's boot, her head on his foot, Bupu's snores mingled with his.

Concerning James Fenimore Cooper's Leatherstocking Tales, Mark Twain wrote: "Another stage-property that he pulled out of his box pretty frequently was his broken twig. He prized his broken twig above all the rest of his effects, and worked it the hardest. It is a restful chapter in any book of his when somebody doesn't step on a dry twig and alarm all the reds and whites for two hundred yards around. Every time a Cooper person is in peril, and absolute silence is worth four dollars a minute, he is sure to step on a dry twig. There may be a hundred handier things to turn out and find a dry twig; and if he can't do it, go and borrow one. In fact the Leather Stocking Series ought to have been called the Broken Twig Series." ["Fenimore Cooper's Literary Offenses," by Mark Twain, The Unabridged Mark Twain, Lawrence Teacher, ed., Running Press, 1976, pp. 1239-1250.]

"Paladine's constellation guards Gilean's constellation (the Book of Knowledge). According to tradition, Paladine's constellation occupies this position because truth and knowledge are essential weapons in combating Evil." [TALES OF THE LANCE Boxed Set, World Book of Ansalon, TSR, Inc., 1992, p. 113.]

Across from them, as far away as possible, Lady Crysania slept peacefully, her smooth cheek resting on her folded hands.

With a trembling sigh, Tas cast the logs on the fire. Watching it blaze up, he settled himself down to watch, staring intently into the night-shrouded trees whose whispering words now had an ominous tone. Then, there it was again.

"Squirrel!" Tas whispered resolutely.

Was that something moving in the shadows? There was a distinct crack—like a twig snapping in two. No squirrel did that! Tas fumbled about in his pouch until his hand closed over a small knife.

The forest was moving! The trees were closing in!

Tas tried to scream a warning, but a thin-limbed branch grabbed hold of his arm. . . .

"Aiiii," Tas shouted, twisting free and stabbing at the branch with his knife.

There was a curse and yelp of pain. The branch let loose its hold, and Tas breathed a sigh. No tree he had ever met yelped in pain. Whatever they were facing was living, breathing. . . .

"Attack!" the kender yelled, stumbling backward. "Caramon! Help! Caramon—"

Two years before, the big warrior would have been on his feet instantly, his hand closing over the hilt of his sword, alert and ready for battle. But Tas, scrambling to get his back to the fire, his small knife the only thing keeping whatever it was at bay, saw Caramon's head loll to one side in drunken contentment.

"Lady Crysania!" Tas screamed wildly, seeing more dark shapes creep from the woods. "Wake up! Please, wake up!"

He could feel the heat of the fire now. Keeping an eye on the menacing shadows, Tas reached down and grabbed a smoldering log by one end—he hoped it was the cool end. Lifting it up, he thrust the firebrand out before him.

There was movement as one of the creatures made a dive for him. Tas swiped out with his knife, driving it back. But in that instant, as it came into the light of his brand, he'd caught a glimpse of it.

"Caramon!" he shrieked. "Draconians!"

Lady Crysania was awake now; Tas saw her sit up, staring around in sleepy confusion.

"The fire!" Tas shouted to her desperately. "Get

near the fire!" Stumbling over Bupu, the kender kicked Caramon. "Draconians!" he yelled again.

One of Caramon's eyes opened, then the other, glaring around muzzily.

"Caramon! Thank the gods!" Tas gasped in relief.

Caramon sat up. Peering around the camp, completely disoriented and confused, he was still warrior enough to be hazily aware of danger. Rising unsteadily to his feet, he gripped the hilt of his sword and belched.

"Washit?" he mumbled, trying to focus his eyes.

"Draconians!" Tasslehoff screeched, hopping around like a small demon, waving his firebrand and his knife with such vigor that he actually succeeded in keeping his enemies at bay.

"Draconians?" Caramon muttered, staring around in disbelief. Then he caught a glimpse of a twisted reptilian face in the light of the dying fire. His eyes opened wide. "Draconians!" he snarled. "Tanis! Sturm! Come to me! Raistlin—your magic! We'll take them."

Yanking his sword from its scabbard, Caramon plunged ahead with a rumbling battle cry—and fell flat on his face.

Bupu clung to his foot.

"Oh, no!" Tas groaned.

Caramon lay on the ground, blinking and shaking his head in wonder, trying to figure out what hit him. Bupu, rudely awakened, began to howl in terror and pain, then bit Caramon on the ankle.

Tas started forward to help the fallen warrior—at least drag Bupu off him—when he heard a cry. Lady Crysania! Damn! He'd forgotten about her! Whirling around, he saw the cleric struggling with one of the dragon men.

Tas hurtled forward and stabbed viciously at the draconian. With a shriek, it let loose of Crysania and fell backward, its body turning to stone† at Tas's feet. Just in time, the kender remembered to retrieve his knife or the stony corpse would have kept it fast.

Tas dragged Crysania back with him toward the fallen Caramon, who was trying to shake the gully dwarf off his leg.

The draconians closed in. Glancing about feverishly, Tas saw they were surrounded by the creatures. But why weren't they attacking full force?

It was my idea to have the draconians die in ways that were perilous to the attacker. I suspect you, too, hear the dice rolling again on this one. I thought it would be interesting in the game to make the actual death of a creature dangerous to the attacker. It was easy to implement in the game—but how to explain it in story? —TRH

What were they waiting for?

"Are you all right?" he managed to ask Crysania.

"Yes," she said. Though very pale, she appeared calm and—if frightened—was keeping her fear under control. Tas saw her lips move—presumably in silent prayer. The kender's own lips tightened.

"Here, lady," he said, shoving the firebrand in her hand. "I guess you're going to have to fight and pray at the same time."

"Elistan did. So can I," Crysania said, her voice shaking only slightly.

Shouted commands rang out from the shadows. The voice wasn't draconian. Tas couldn't make it out. He only knew that just hearing it gave him cold chills. But there wasn't time to wonder about it. The draconians, their tongues flicking out of their mouths, jumped for them.

Crysania lashed out with the smoldering brand clumsily, but it was enough to make the draconians hesitate. Tas was still trying to pry Bupu off Caramon. But it was a draconian who, inadvertently, came to their aid. Shoving Tas backward, the dragon man laid a clawed hand on Bupu.

Gully dwarves are noted throughout Krynn for their extreme cowardice and total unreliability in battle. But—when driven into a corner—they can fight like rabid rats.

"Glupsludge!" Bupu screamed in anger and, turning from gnawing on Caramon's ankle, she sank her teeth into the scaly hide of the draconian's leg.

Bupu didn't have many teeth, but what she did have were sharp and she bit into the draconian's green flesh with a relish occasioned by the fact that she hadn't eaten much dinner.

The draconian gave a hideous yell. Raising its sword, it was about to end Bupu's days upon Krynn when Caramon—bumbling around trying to see what was going on—accidentally sliced off the creature's arm. Bupu sat back, licking her lips, and looked about eagerly for another victim.

"Hurrah! Caramon!" Tas cheered wildly, his small knife stabbing here and there as swiftly as a striking snake. Lady Crysania smashed one draconian with her firebrand, crying out the name of Paladine. The creature pitched over.

There were only two or three draconians still

standing that Tas could see, and the kender began to feel elated. The creatures lurked just outside the firelight, eyeing the big warrior, Caramon, warily as he staggered to his feet. Seen only in the shadows, he still cut the menacing figure he had in the old days. His sword blade gleamed wickedly in the red flames.

"Get 'em, Caramon!" Tas yelled shrilly. "Clunk their heads—"†

The kender's voice died as Caramon turned slowly to face him, a strange look on his face.

"I'm not Caramon," he said softly. "I'm his twin, Raistlin. Caramon's dead.† I killed him." Glancing down at the sword in his hand, the big warrior dropped it as if it stung him. "What am I doing with cold steel in my hands?" he asked harshly. "I can't cast spells with a sword and shield!"

Tasslehoff choked, casting an alarmed glance at the draconians. He could see them exchanging shrewd looks. They began to move forward slowly, though they all kept their gazes fixed upon the big warrior, probably suspecting a trap of some sort.

"You're not Raistlin! You're Caramon!" Tas cried in desperation, but it was no use. The man's brain was still pickled in dwarf spirits. His mind completely unhinged, Caramon closed his eyes, lifted his hands, and began to chant.

"Antsnests silverash bookarah," he murmured, weaving back and forth.

The grinning face of a draconian loomed up before Tas. There was a flash of steel, and the kender's head seemed to explode in pain. . . .

Tas was on the ground. Warm liquid was running down his face, blinding him in one eye, trickling into his mouth. He tasted blood. He was tired . . . very tired. . . .

But the pain was awful. It wouldn't let him sleep. He was afraid to move his head, afraid if he did it might separate into two pieces. And so he lay perfectly still, watching the world from one eye.

He heard the gully dwarf screaming on and on, like a tortured animal, and then the screams suddenly ended. He heard a deep cry of pain, a smothered groan, and a large body crashed to the ground beside him. It was Caramon, blood flowing from his mouth, his eyes wide open and staring.

Caramon has somewhat of a reputation for dispatching his foes by bashing their heads together. See Dragons of Autumn Twilight, *Book I, Chapter 4.*

Here Caramon, in his drunken hallucination, kills himself, so to speak, and takes on the identity of his twin. At this point, Caramon hits bottom and he can either start trying to struggle out of the darkness or let it consume him. —MW

Tas couldn't feel sad. He couldn't feel anything except the terrible pain in his head. A huge draconian stood over him, sword in hand. He knew that the creature was going to finish him off. Tas didn't care. End the pain, he pleaded. End it quickly.

Then there was a flurry of white robes and a clear voice calling upon Paladine. The draconian disappeared abruptly with the sound of clawed feet scrambling through the brush. The white robes knelt beside him, Tas felt the touch of a gentle hand upon his head, and heard the name of Paladine again. The pain vanished. Looking up, he saw the cleric's hand touch Caramon, saw the big man's eyelids flutter and close in peaceful sleep.

It's all right! Tas thought in elation. They've gone! We're going to be all right. Then he felt the hand tremble. Regaining some of his senses as the cleric's healing powers flooded through his body, the kender raised his head, peering ahead with his good eye.

Something was coming. Something had called off the draconians. Something was walking into the light of the fire.

Tas tried to cry out a warning, but his throat closed. His mind tumbled over and over. For a moment, too frightened† and dizzy to think clearly, he thought someone had mixed up adventures on him.

He saw Lady Crysania rise to her feet, her white robes sweeping the dirt near his head. Slowly, she began backing away from the thing that stalked her. Tas heard her call to Paladine, but the words fell from lips stiff with terror.

Tas himself wanted desperately to close his eyes. Fear and curiosity warred in his small body. Curiosity won out. Peering out of his one good eye, Tas watched the horrible figure draw nearer and nearer to the cleric. The figure was dressed in the armor of a Solamnic Knight, but that armor was burned and blackened. As it drew near Crysania, the figure stretched forth an arm that did not end in a hand. It spoke words that did not come from a mouth. Its eyes flared orange, its transparent legs strode right through the smoldering ashes of the fire. The chill of the regions where it was forced to eternally dwell flowed from its body, freezing the very marrow in Tas's bones.

A kender frightened? I suspect he was frightened for Crysania, not himself. Yeah, that's got to be it. —TRH

A problem with writing kender is that they are supposedly fearless. However, if a situation arises where an author wants to create fear in a reader, the author needs to do that through making a character feel fear. Thus, when Tas meets Lord Soth, we needed to make the reader feel how truly fearsome the death knight is. If Tas didn't feel any fear, then the reader wouldn't either. In addition, it makes Tas a very shallow character. Thus we came up with the idea that Tas could feel fear for people he cared for, even if he didn't feel fear himself. This also adds considerable depth to Tas's character and makes him more "human." —MW

Fearfully, Tas raised his head. He saw Lady Crysania backing away. He saw the death knight walk toward her with slow, steady steps.

The knight raised its right hand and pointed at Crysania with a pale, shimmering finger.

Tas felt a sudden, uncontrollable terror seize him. "No!" he moaned, shivering, though he had no idea what awful thing was about to happen.

The knight spoke one word.

"Die."

At that moment, Tas saw Lady Crysania raise her hand and grasp the medallion she wore around her neck. He saw a bright flash of pure white light well from her fingers and then she fell to the ground as though stabbed by the fleshless finger.

"No!" Tasslehoff heard himself cry. He saw the orange flaring eyes turn their attention to him, and a chill, dank darkness, like the darkness of a tomb, sealed shut his eyes and closed his mouth. . . .

*Dalamar was named for a young man I met at Gen Con. I noticed his name when I was signing a book for him, and I just loved it. I asked him if I could use it and he gave me permission. It worked perfectly for the dark elf.
—MW*

alamart approached the door to the mage's laboratory with trepidation, tracing a nervous finger over the runes of protection stitched onto the fabric of his black robes as he hastily rehearsed several spells of warding in his mind. A certain amount of caution would not have been thought unseemly in any young apprentice approaching the inner, secret chambers of a dark and powerful master. But Dalamar's precautions were extraordinary. And with good reason. Dalamar had secrets of his own to hide, and he dreaded and feared nothing more in this world than the gaze of those golden, hourglass eyes.

And yet, deeper than his fear, an undercurrent of excitement pulsed in Dalamar's blood as it always did when he stood before this door. He had seen wonderful things inside this chamber, wonderful . . . fearful. . . .

Raising his right hand,† he made a quick sign in the air before the door and muttered a few words in the language of magic. There was no reaction. The door had no spell cast upon it. Dalamar breathed a bit easier, or perhaps it was a sigh of disappointment. His master was not engaged in any potent, powerful magic, otherwise Raistlin would have cast a spell of holding† upon the door. Glancing down at the floor, the dark elf† saw no flickering, flaring lights beaming from beneath the heavy wooden door. He smelled nothing except the usual smells of spice and decay. Dalamar placed the five fingertips of his left hand upon the door and waited in silence.

Within the space of time it took the dark elf to draw a breath came the softly spoken command, "Enter, Dalamar."

Bracing himself, Dalamar stepped into the chamber as the door swung silently open before him. Raistlin sat at a huge and ancient stone table, so large that one of the tall, broad-shouldered race of minotaurs living upon Mithas might have lain down upon it, stretched out his full height, and still had room to spare. The stone table, in fact the entire laboratory, were part of the original furnishings Raistlin had discovered when he claimed the Tower of High Sorcery in Palanthas as his own.

The great, shadowy chamber seemed much larger than it could possibly have been, yet the dark elf could never determine whether it was the chamber itself that seemed larger or he himself who seemed smaller whenever he entered it. Books lined the walls, here as in the mage's study. Runes and spidery writing glowed through the dust gathered on their spines. Glass bottles and jars of twisted design stood on tables around the sides of the chamber, their bright-colored contents bubbling and boiling with hidden power.

Here, in this laboratory long ago, great and powerful magic had been wrought. Here, the wizards of all three Robes—the White of Good, the Red of Neutrality, and the Black of Evil—joined in alliance to create the Dragon Orbs—one of which was now in Raistlin's possession. Here, the three Robes had come together in a final, desperate battle to save their Towers, the bastions of their strength, from the Kingpriest of Istar and the mobs. Here

In the AD&D game rules as they existed when we were writing Legends, spells required various actions by the caster: verbal (spoken incantations), somatic (hand movements), and material (various spell components, such as bat wings, rose petals, etc.) I hear the dice rolling again. Still, it makes for exciting and visual spell casting!
—TRH

Hold Portal: *This spell magically bars a door, gate, or valve of wood, metal, or stone. The magical closure holds the portal fast, just as if it were securely closed and locked. [2nd Edition* ADVANCED DUNGEONS & DRAGONS *Player's Handbook, by David "Zeb" Cook, TSR, 1997, p. 175.]*

"Dark elves" in the DRAGONLANCE *setting are not to be confused with the dark elves (or drow) of other* DUNGEONS & DRAGONS *settings. The dark elves of Krynn are not a separate race; they are those elves, most often from the Silvanesti or Qualinesti, who have chosen to follow the dark arts and have been exiled by their people, or "cast from the light." Hence, the term "dark elf." Every now and then in early* DRAGONLANCE *books, you'll run across the word "drow." This is because during those early days all of this was still being worked out in the minds of the authors and designers.*

they had failed, believing it was better to live in defeat than fight, knowing that their magic could destroy the world.

The mages had been forced to abandon this Tower, carrying their spellbooks and other paraphernalia to the Tower of High Sorcery, hidden deep within the magical Forest of Wayreth. It was when they abandoned this Tower that the curse had been cast upon it. The Shoikan Grove had grown to guard it from all comers until—as foretold— "the master of past and present shall return with power."

And the master had returned. Now he sat in the ancient laboratory, crouched over the stone table that had been dragged, long ago, from the bottom of the sea. Carved with runes that ward off all enchantments, it was kept free of any outside influences that might affect the mage's work. The table's surface was ground smooth and polished to an almost mirrorlike finish. Dalamar could see the nightblue bindings of the spellbooks that sat upon it reflected in the candlelight.

Scattered about on its surface were other objects, too—objects hideous and curious, horrible and lovely: the mage's spell components. It was on these Raistlin was working now, scanning a spellbook, murmuring soft words as he crushed something between his delicate fingers, letting it trickle into a phial he held.

"*Shalafi*," Dalamar said quietly, using the elven word for "master."

Raistlin looked up.

Dalamar felt the stare of those golden eyes pierce his heart with an indefinable pain. A shiver of fear swept over the dark elf, the words, *He knows!* seethed in his brain. But none of this emotion was outwardly visible. The dark elf's handsome features remained fixed, unchanged, cool. His eyes returned Raistlin's gaze steadily. His hands remained folded within his robes as was proper.

So dangerous was this job that—when *They* had deemed it necessary to plant a spy inside the mage's household—They had asked for volunteers, none of them willing to take responsibility for cold-bloodedly commanding anyone to accept this deadly assignment. Dalamar had stepped forward immediately.

"Dalamar is a young dark elf of 90 years, which figures out to about 25 in human years. Dalamar is a very handsome elf with long, flowing brown hair, brown eyes, and an extremely charming and winning personality. He is in excellent health and condition, well-built and muscular."
[DRAGONLANCE Adventures, *by Tracy Hickman and Margaret Weis, TSR, Inc., 1987, p. 111-112.*]

Magic was Dalamar's only home. Originally† from Silvanesti, he now neither claimed nor was claimed by that noble race of elves. Born to a low caste, he had been taught only the most rudimentary of the magical arts, higher learning being for those of royal blood. But Dalamar had tasted the power, and it became his obsession. Secretly he worked, studying the forbidden, learning wonders reserved for only the high-ranking elven mages. The dark arts impressed him most, and thus, when he was discovered wearing the Black Robes that no true elf could even bear to look upon, Dalamar was cast out of his home and his nation. And he became known as a "dark elf," one who is outside of the light. This suited Dalamar well for, early on, he had learned that there is power in darkness.

And so Dalamar had accepted the assignment.† When asked to give his reasons why he would willingly risk his life performing this task, he had answered coldly, "I would risk my soul for the chance to study with the greatest and most powerful of our order who has *ever* lived!"

"You may well be doing just that," a sad voice had answered him.

The memory of that voice returned to Dalamar at odd moments, generally in the darkness of the night—which was so *very* dark inside the Tower. It returned to him now. Dalamar forced it out of his mind.

"What is it?" Raistlin asked gently.

The mage always spoke gently and softly, sometimes not even raising his voice above a whisper. Dalamar had seen fearful storms rage in this chamber. The blazing lightning and crashing thunder had left him partially deaf for days. He had been present when the mage summoned creatures from the planes above and below to do his bidding; their screams and wails and curses still sounded in his dreams at night. Yet, through it all, he had never heard Raistlin raise his voice. Always that soft, sibilant whisper penetrated the chaos and brought it under control.

"Events are transpiring in the outside world, *Shalafi,* that demand your attention."

"Indeed?" Raistlin looked down again, absorbed in his work.

"Lady Crysania—"

The tale of Dalamar's early years can be found in Dalamar the Dark, *by Nancy Varian Berberick.*

"A skilled young wizard, Dalamar has just complete his Test. His first task as an apprentice is to serve Raistlin, the Master of the Tower of High Sorcery in Palanthus.

"The Conclave of Wizards fears Raistlin more than any other threat in the history of their Orders. In a secret meeting, they asked for a volunteer to serve as Raistlin's apprentice and to spy on him for the Conclave. Dalamar volunteered without hesitation." [DRAGONLANCE Adventures, *by Tracy Hickman and Margaret Weis, TSR, Inc., 1987, p. 112.*]

Raistlin's hooded head lifted quickly. Dalamar, reminded forcibly of a striking snake, involuntarily fell back a step before that intense gaze.

"What? Speak!" Raistlin hissed the word.

"You—you should come, *Shalafi*," Dalamar faltered. "The Live Ones† report. . . ."

The dark elf spoke to empty air. Raistlin had vanished.

Heaving a trembling sigh, the dark elf pronounced the words that would take him instantly to his master's side.

Far below the Tower of High Sorcery, deep beneath the ground, was a small round room magically carved from the rock that supported the Tower. This room had *not* been in the Tower originally. Known as the Chamber of Seeing, it was Raistlin's creation.

Within the center of the small room of cold stone was a perfectly round pool of still, dark water. From the center of the strange, unnatural pond spurted a jet of blue flame. Rising to the ceiling of the chamber, it burned eternally, day and night. And around it, eternally, sat the Live Ones.

Though the most powerful mage living upon Krynn, Raistlin's power was far from complete, and no one realized that more than the mage himself. He was always forcibly reminded of his weaknesses when he came into this room—one reason he avoided it, if possible. For here were the visible, outward symbols of his failures—the Live Ones.

Wretched creatures mistakenly created by magic gone awry, they were held in thrall in this chamber, serving their creator. Here they lived out their tortured lives, writhing in a larva-like, bleeding mass about the flaming pool. Their shining wet bodies made a horrible carpet for the floor, whose stones, made slick with their oozings, could be seen only when they parted to make room for their creator.

Yet, despite their lives of constant, twisted pain, the Live Ones spoke no word of complaint. Far better their lot than those who roamed the Tower, those known as the Dead Ones. . . .

Raistlin materialized within the Chamber of Seeing, a dark shadow emerging out of darkness. The blue flame sparkled off the silver threads that decorated his robes, shimmered within the black cloth. Dalamar appeared beside him, and the two

In the Live Ones, we see Raistlin's ambition to achieve godhood. He attempts to create life. He fails, of course, because he is mortal. —MW

walked over to stand beside the surface of the still, black water.

"Where?" Raistlin asked.

"Here, M-master," blurbled one of the Live Ones, pointing a misshapen appendage.

Raistlin hurried to stand beside it, Dalamar walking by his side, their black robes making a soft, whispering sound upon the slimy stone floor. Staring into the water, Raistlin motioned Dalamar to do the same. The dark elf looked into the still surface, seeing for an instant only the reflection of the jet of blue flame. Then the flame and the water merged, then parted, and he was in a forest. A big human male, clad in ill-fitting armor, stood staring down at the body of a young human female, dressed in white robes. A kender knelt beside the body of the woman, holding her hand in his. Dalamar heard the big man speak as clearly as if he had been standing by his side.

"She's dead. . . ."

"I—I'm not sure, Caramon. I think—"

"I've seen death often enough, believe me. She's dead. And it's all my fault . . . my fault. . . ."

"Caramon, you imbecile!" Raistlin snarled with a curse. "What happened? What went wrong?"

As the mage spoke, Dalamar saw the kender look up quickly.

"Did you say something?" the kender asked the big human, who was working in the soil.

"No. It was just the wind."

"What are you doing?"

"Digging a grave. We've got to bury her."

"Bury her?" Raistlin gave a brief, bitter laugh. "Oh, of course, you bumbling idiot! That's all you can think of to do!" The mage fumed. "Bury her! I must know what happened!" He turned to the Live One. "What did you see?"

"T-they c-camp in t-trees, M-master." Froth dribbled from the creature's mouth, its speech was practically unrecognizable. "D-draco k-kill—"

"Draconians?" Raistlin repeated in astonishment. "Near Solace? Where did they come from?"

"D-dunno! Dunno!" The Live One cowered in terror. "I-I—"

"Shhh," Dalamar warned, drawing his master's attention back to the pond where the kender was arguing.

It is unclear in the text whether funeral pyres are a proper tradition of the people of Solace, of Palanthas, or of the disciples of Paladine. Caramon was well traveled and would have familiarity with all of these cultural traditions. His own nature would make him concerned for giving Crysania a proper farewell. —TRH

"Caramon, you can't bury her! She's—"

"We don't have any choice. I know it's not proper,†
but Paladine will see that her soul journeys in peace. We
don't dare build a funeral pyre, not with those dragon-
men around—"

"But, Caramon, I really think you should come look at
her! There's not a mark on her body!"

"I don't want to look at her! She's dead! It's my fault!
We'll bury her here, then I'll go back to Solace, go back to
digging my own grave—"

"Caramon!"

"Go find some flowers and leave me be!"

Dalamar saw the big man tear up the moist dirt
with his bare hands, hurling it aside while tears
streamed down his face. The kender remained
beside the woman's body, irresolute, his face covered with dried blood, his expression a mixture of
grief and doubt.

"No mark, no wound, draconians coming out of
nowhere . . ." Raistlin frowned thoughtfully. Then,
suddenly, he knelt beside the Live One, who shrank
away from him. "Speak. Tell me everything. I must
know. Why wasn't I summoned earlier?"

"Th-the d-draco k-kill, M-master," the Live One's
voice bubbled in agony. "B-but the b-big m-man
k-kill, too. T-then b-big ddark c-come! E-eyes of f-
fire. I-I s-scared. I-I f-fraid f-fall in wa-water. . . ."

"I found the Live One lying at the edge of the pool,"
Dalamar reported coolly, "when one of the others
told me something strange was going on. I looked
into the water. Knowing of your interest in this
human female, I thought you—"

"Quite right," Raistlin murmured, cutting off Dalamar's explanation impatiently. The mage's golden
eyes narrowed, his thin lips compressed. Feeling his
anger, the poor Live One dragged its body as far from
the mage as possible. Dalamar held his breath. But
Raistlin's anger was not directed at them.

" 'Big dark, eyes of fire'—Lord Soth! So, my sister,
you betray me," Raistlin whispered. "I smell your
fear, Kitiara! You coward! I could have made you
queen of this world. I could have given you wealth
immeasurable, power unlimited. But no. You are,
after all, a weak and petty-minded worm!"

Raistlin stood quietly, pondering, staring into the
still pond. When he spoke next, his voice was soft,

lethal. "I will not forget this, my dear sister. You are fortunate that I have more urgent, pressing matters at hand, or you would be residing with the phantom lord who serves you!" Raistlin's thin fist clenched, then—with an obvious effort—he forced himself to relax. "But, now, what to do about this? I must do something before my brother plants the cleric in a flower bed!"

"Shalafi, what has happened?" Dalamar ventured, greatly daring. "This—woman. What is she to you? I do not understand."

Raistlin glanced at Dalamar irritably and seemed about to rebuke him for his impertinence. Then the mage hesitated. His golden eyes flared once with a flash of inner light that made Dalamar cringe, before returning to their flat, impassive stare.

"Of course, apprentice. You shall know everything. But first—"

Raistlin stopped. Another figure had entered the scene in the forest they watched so intently. It was a gully dwarf, bundled in layers and layers of bright, gaudy clothing, a huge bag dragging behind her as she walked.

"Bupu!" Raistlin whispered, the rare smile touching his lips. "Excellent. Once more you shall serve me, little one."

Reaching out his hand, Raistlin touched the still water. The Live Ones around the pool cried out in horror, for they had seen many of their own kind stumble into that dark water, only to shrivel and wither and become nothing more than a wisp of smoke, rising with a shriek into the air. But Raistlin simply murmured soft words, then withdrew his hand. The fingers were white as marble, a spasm of pain crossed his face. Hurriedly, he slid his hand into a pocket of his robe.

"Watch," he whispered exultantly.

Dalamar stared into the water, watching the gully dwarf approach the still, lifeless form of the woman.

"Me help."

"No, Bupu!"

"You no like my magic! Me go home. But first me help pretty lady."

"What in the name of the Abyss—" Dalamar muttered.

"Watch!" Raistlin commanded.

Dalamar watched as the gully dwarf's small, grubby hand dove into the bag at her side. After fumbling about for several moments, it emerged with a loathsome object—a dead, stiff lizard with a leather thong wrapped around its neck. Bupu approached the woman and—when the kender tried to stop her—thrust her small fist into his face warningly. With a sigh and a sideways glance at Caramon, who was digging furiously, his face a mask of grief and blood, the kender stepped back. Bupu plopped down beside the woman's lifeless form and carefully placed the dead lizard on the unmoving chest.

Dalamar gasped.

The woman's chest moved, the white robes shivered. She began breathing, deeply and peacefully.

The kender let out a shriek.

"Caramon! Bupu's cured her! She's alive! Look!"

"What the—" The big man stopped digging and stumbled over, staring at the gully dwarf in amazement and fear.

Bupu's lizard cure hearkens back to Dragons of Autumn Twilight, *Book I, Chapter 18.*

"Lizard cure,"† Bupu said in triumph. *"Work every time."*

"Yes, my little one," Raistlin said, still smiling. "It works well for coughs, too, as I remember." He waved his hand over the still water. The mage's voice became a lulling chant. "And now, sleep, my brother, before you do anything else stupid. Sleep, kender, sleep, little Bupu. And sleep as well, Lady Crysania, in the realm where Paladine protects you."

Still chanting, Raistlin made a beckoning motion with his hand. "And now come, Forest of Wayreth. Creep up on them as they sleep. Sing them your magical song. Lure them onto your secret paths."

The spell was ended. Rising to his feet, Raistlin turned to Dalamar. "And you come, too, apprentice"— there was the faintest sarcasm in the voice that made the dark elf shudder— "come to my study. It is time for us to talk."

CHAPTER 9

Dalamar sat in the mage's study in the same chair Kitiara had occupied on her visit. The dark elf was far less comfortable, far less secure than Kitiara had been. Yet his fears were well-contained. Outwardly he appeared relaxed, composed. A heightened flush upon his pale elven features could be attributed, perhaps, to his excitement at being taken into his master's confidence.

Dalamar had been in the study† often, though not in the presence of his master. Raistlin spent his evenings here alone, reading, studying the tomes that lined his walls. No one dared disturb him then. Dalamar entered the study only during the daylight hours, and then only when Raistlin was busy elsewhere. At that time the dark elf apprentice was allowed—no, required—to study the spellbooks himself, some of them, that is. He had

Wizards in Ansalon must spend most of their time studying, researching, etc. The wizards, besides being wielders of great magics, are devoted scholars.

been forbidden to open or even touch those with the nightblue binding.

Dalamar had done so once, of course. The binding felt intensely cold, so cold it burned his skin. Ignoring the pain, he managed to open the cover, but after one look, he quickly shut it. The words inside were gibberish, he could make nothing of them. And he had been able to detect the spell of protection cast over them. Anyone looking at them too long without the proper key to translate them would go mad.

Seeing Dalamar's injured hand, Raistlin asked him how it happened. The dark elf replied coolly that he had spilled some acid from a spell component he was mixing. The archmage smiled and said nothing. There was no need. Both understood.

But now he was in the study by Raistlin's invitation, sitting here on a more or less equal basis with his master. Once again, Dalamar felt the old fear laced by intoxicating excitement.

Raistlin sat before him at the carved wooden table, one hand resting upon a thick nightblue-bound spellbook. The archmage's fingers absently caressed the book, running over the silver runes upon the cover. Raistlin's eyes stared fixedly at Dalamar. The dark elf did not stir or shift beneath that intense, penetrating gaze.

"You were very young, to have taken the Test," Raistlin said abruptly in his soft voice.

Dalamar blinked. This was not what he had expected.

"Not so young as you, *Shalafi*," the dark elf replied. "I am in my nineties, which figures to about twenty-five of your human years. You, I believe, were only twenty-one when you took the Test."

"Yes," Raistlin murmured, and a shadow passed across the mage's golden-tinted skin. "I was . . . twenty-one."

Dalamar saw the hand that rested upon the spellbook clench in swift, sudden pain; he saw the golden eyes flare. The young apprentice was not surprised at this show of emotion. The Test is required of any mage seeking to practice the arts of magic at an advanced level. Administered in the Tower of High Sorcery at Wayreth, it is conducted by the leaders of all three Robes. For, long ago, the magic-users of

Krynn realized what had escaped the clerics—if the balance of the world† is to be maintained, the pendulum must swing freely back and forth among all three—Good, Evil, Neutrality. Let one grow too powerful—any one—and the world would begin to tilt toward its destruction.

The Test is brutal. The higher levels of magic, where true power is obtained, are no place for inept bunglers. The Test was designed to get rid of those—permanently; death being the penalty for failure. Dalamar still had nightmares about his own testing, so he could well understand Raistlin's reaction.

"I passed," Raistlin whispered, his eyes staring back to that time. "But when I came out of that terrible place I was as you see me now. My skin had this golden tint, my hair was white, and my eyes . . ." He came back to the present, to look fixedly at Dalamar. "Do you know what I see with these hourglass eyes?"

"No, *Shalafi.*"

"I see time as it affects all things," Raistlin replied. "Human flesh withers before these eyes, flowers wilt and die, the rocks themselves crumble as I watch. It is always winter in my sight. Even you, Dalamar"—Raistlin's eyes caught and held the young apprentice in their horrible gaze—"even elven flesh that ages so slowly the passing of the years are as rain showers in the spring—even upon your young face, Dalamar—I see the mark of death!"

Dalamar shivered, and this time could not hide his emotion. Involuntarily, he shrank back into the cushions of the chair. A shield spell† came quickly to his mind, as did—unbidden—a spell designed to injure, not defend. Fool! he sneered at himself, quickly regaining control, what puny spell of mine could kill *him*?

"True, true," Raistlin murmured, answering Dalamar's thoughts, as he often did. "There live none upon Krynn who has the power to harm me. Certainly not you, apprentice. But you are brave. You have courage. Often you have stood beside me in the laboratory, facing those I have dragged from the planes of their existence. You knew that if I but drew a breath at the wrong time, they would rip the

The concept of balance was part of the original design structure for the world. Imagine three points of a triangle around a central sphere. These points— good, evil and chaos—are constantly pulling against each other for dominance over the central sphere that represents each of us. This concept—that our willful, free choice between these poles brings motion and growth to the universe— is at the heart of all the DRAGONLANCE setting and was from the beginning. At the highest level of the story, the points represent the cosmic forces of good, evil, and chaos pulling on the world of Krynn. At a more intimate level of the story, the points represent the Solamnic Knights (good), the Dragon Highlords (evil), and the different people of Ansalon (chaos) with the Heroes of the Lance in the center. At the most intimate level of the story we have Laurana (good), Kitiara (evil), and the demands of the world (chaos) all pulling on the central figure of Tanis. In many ways, this also reflects my personal belief in the workings of our own cosmos. —TRH

Shield: *When this spell is cast, an invisible barrier comes into being in front of the wizard. [2nd Edition ADVANCED DUNGEONS & DRAGONS Player's Handbook, by David "Zeb" Cook, TSR, 1997, p. 178.]*

living hearts from our bodies and devour them while we writhed before them in torment."

"It was my privilege," Dalamar murmured.

"Yes," Raistlin replied absently, his thoughts abstracted. Then he raised an eyebrow. "And you knew, didn't you, that if such an event occurred, I would save myself but not you?"

"Of course, *Shalafi*," Dalamar answered steadily. "I understand and I take the risk"—the dark elf's eyes glowed. His fears forgotten, he sat forward eagerly in his chair—"no, *Shalafi*, I *invite* the risks! I would sacrifice anything for the sake of—"

"The magic," Raistlin finished.

"Yes! The sake of the magic!" Dalamar cried.

"And the power it confers," Raistlin nodded. "You are ambitious. But—how ambitious, I wonder? Do you, perhaps, seek rulership of your kinsmen? Or possibly a kingdom somewhere, holding a monarch in thrall while you enjoy the wealth of his lands? Or perhaps an alliance with some dark lord, as was done in the days of the dragons not far back. My sister, Kitiara, for example, found you quite attractive. She would enjoy having you about. Particularly if you have any magic arts you practice in the bedroom—"

"*Shalafi*, I would not desecrate—"

Raistlin waved a hand. "I joke, apprentice. But you take my meaning. Does one of those reflect your dreams?"

"Well, certainly, *Shalafi*." Dalamar hesitated, confused. Where was all this leading? To some information he could use and pass on, he hoped, but how much of himself to reveal? "I—"

Raistlin cut him off. "Yes, I see I have come close to the mark. I have discovered the heights of your ambition. Have you never guessed at mine?"

Dalamar felt a thrill of joy surge through his body. *This* is what he had been sent to discover. The young mage answered slowly, "I have often wondered, *Shalafi*. You are so powerful"—Dalamar motioned at the window where the lights of Palanthas could be seen, shining in the night— "this city, this land of Solamnia, this continent of Ansalon could be yours."

"This *world*† could be mine!" Raistlin smiled, his thin lips parting slightly. "We have seen the lands

This appears to be the first recognition of any substantive lands beyond the shores of Ansalon. We already recognized that the world of Krynn was getting smaller with every passing tale. Although Raist alludes to other lands, at the time it was written those shores were only vague outlines in our minds. They had no substance beyond dreams. —TRH

beyond the seas, haven't we, apprentice. When we look into the flaming water, we can see them and those who dwell there. To control them would be simplicity itself—"

Raistlin rose to his feet. Walking to the window, he stared out over the sparkling city spread out before him. Feeling his master's excitement, Dalamar left his chair and followed him.

"I could give you that kingdom,† Dalamar," Raistlin said softly. His hand drew back the curtain, his eyes lingered upon the lights that gleamed more warmly than the stars above. "I could give you not only rulership of your miserable kinsmen, but control of the elves everywhere in Krynn." Raistlin shrugged. "I could give you my sister."

Turning from the window, Raistlin faced Dalamar, who watched him eagerly.

"But I care nothing for that"—Raistlin gestured, letting the curtain fall— "nothing. My ambition goes further."

"But, *Shalafi*, there is not much left if you turn down the world." Dalamar faltered, not understanding. "Unless you have seen worlds beyond this one that are hidden from my eyes. . . ."

"Worlds beyond?" Raistlin pondered. "Interesting thought. Perhaps someday I should consider that possibility. But, no, that is not what I meant." The mage paused and, with a motion of his hand, beckoned Dalamar closer. "You have seen the great door in the very back of the laboratory? The door of steel, with runes of silver and of gold set within? The door without a lock?"

"Yes, *Shalafi*," Dalamar replied, feeling a chill creep over him that not even the strange heat of Raistlin's body so near him could dispel.

"Do you know where that door leads?"

"Yes . . . *Shalafi*." A whisper.

"And you know why it is not opened?"

"You cannot open it, *Shalafi*. Only one of great and powerful magic and one of true holy powers may together open—" Dalamar stopped, his throat closing in fear, choking him.

"Yes," Raistlin murmured, "you understand. 'One of true holy powers.' Now you know why I need *her*! Now you understand the heights—and the depths— of my ambition."

The Tempter is an archetype from nearly all mythology. This temptation is reminiscent of Christ's temptation by Satan. —TRH

"Again, the devil taketh him up into an exceeding high mountain, and sheweth him all the kingdoms of the world, and the glory of them; and saith unto him, All these things will I give thee, if thou wilt fall down and worship me." [Matthew 4:8-9 KJV]

"This is madness!" Dalamar gasped, then lowered his eyes in shame. "Forgive me, *Shalafi*, I meant no disrespect."

"No, and you are right. It *is* madness, with my limited powers." A trace of bitterness tinged the mage's voice. "That is why I am about to undertake a journey."

"Journey?" Dalamar looked up. "Where?"

"Not where—when," Raistlin corrected. "You have heard me speak of Fistandantilus?"

"Many times, *Shalafi*," Dalamar said, his voice almost reverent. "The greatest of our Order. Those are his spellbooks, the ones with the nightblue binding."

"Inadequate," Raistlin muttered, dismissing the entire library with a gesture. "I have read them all, many times in these past years, ever since I obtained the Key to their secrets from the Queen of Darkness herself. But they only frustrate me!" Raistlin clenched his thin hand. "I read these spellbooks and I find great gaps—entire volumes missing! Perhaps they were destroyed in the Cataclysm or, later, in the Dwarfgate Wars† that proved Fistandantilus's undoing. These missing volumes, this knowledge of his that has been lost, will give me the power I need!"

"And so your journey will take you—" Dalamar stopped in disbelief.

"Back in time," Raistlin finished calmly. "Back to the days just prior to the Cataclysm, when Fistandantilus was at the height of his power."

Dalamar felt dizzy, his thoughts swirled in confusion. What would *They* say? Amidst all Their speculation, They had certainly not foreseen this!

"Steady, my apprentice." Raistlin's soft voice seemed to come to Dalamar from far away. "This has unnerved you. Some wine?"

The mage walked over to a table. Lifting a carafe, he poured a small glass of blood-red liquid and handed it to the dark elf. Dalamar took it gratefully, startled to see his hand shaking. Raistlin poured a small glass for himself.

"I do not drink this strong wine often, but tonight it seems we should have a small celebration. A toast to—how did you put it?—one of true holy powers. This, then, to Lady Crysania!"

Raistlin drank his wine in small sips. Dalamar

The Dwarfgate Wars occurred approximately thirty-nine years after the Cataclysm.

gulped his down. The fiery liquid bit into his throat. He coughed.

"*Shalafi,* if the Live One reported correctly, Lord Soth cast a death spell† upon Lady Crysania, yet she still lives. Did you restore her life?"

Raistlin shook his head. "No, I simply gave her visible signs of life so that my dear brother would not bury her. I cannot be certain what happened, but it is not difficult to guess. Seeing the death knight before her and knowing her fate, the Revered Daughter fought the spell with the only weapon she had, and a powerful one it was—the holy medallion of Paladine. The god protected her, transporting her soul to the realms where the gods dwell, leaving her body a shell upon the ground. There are none—not even I—who can bring her soul and body back together again. Only a high cleric of Paladine has that power."

Death Spell: When a death spell is cast, it snuffs out the life forces of creatures in the area of effect instantly and irrevocably. [2nd Edition ADVANCED DUNGEONS & DRAGONS Player's Handbook, by David "Zeb" Cook, TSR, 1997, pp. 222, 223.]

"Elistan?"

"Bah, the man is sick, dying. . . ."

"Then she is lost to you!"

"No," said Raistlin gently. "You fail to understand, apprentice. Through inattention, I lost control. But I have regained it quickly. Not only that, I will make this work to my advantage. Even now, they approach the Tower of High Sorcery. Crysania was going there, seeking the help of the mages. When she arrives, she will find that help, and so will my brother."

"You *want* them to help her?" Dalamar asked in confusion. "She plots to destroy you!"

Raistlin quietly sipped his wine, watching the young apprentice intently. "Think about it, Dalamar," he said softly, "think about it, and you will come to understand. But"—the mage set down his empty glass—"I have kept you long enough."

Dalamar glanced out the window. The red moon, Lunitari, was starting to sink out of sight behind the black jagged edges of the mountains. The night was nearing its midpoint.

"You must make *your* journey and be back before I leave in the morning," Raistlin continued. "There will undoubtedly be some last-minute instructions, besides many things I must leave in your care. You will be in charge here, of course, while I am gone."

Dalamar nodded, then frowned. "You spoke of *my* journey, *Shalafi*? I am not going anywhere—" The dark elf stopped, choking as he remembered that he did, indeed, have somewhere to go, a report to make.

Raistlin stood regarding the young elf in silence, the look of horrified realization dawning on Dalamar's face reflected in the mage's mirrorlike eyes. Then, slowly, Raistlin advanced upon the young apprentice, his black robes rustling gently about his ankles. Stricken with terror, Dalamar could not move. Spells of protection slipped from his grasp. His mind could think of nothing, see nothing, except two flat, emotionless, golden eyes.

Slowly, Raistlin lifted his hand and laid it gently upon Dalamar's chest, touching the young man's black robes with the tips of five fingers.

The pain was excruciating. Dalamar's face turned white, his eyes widened, he gasped in agony. But the dark elf could not withdraw from that terrible touch. Held fast by Raistlin's gaze, Dalamar could not even scream.

"Relate to them accurately both what I have told you," Raistlin whispered, "and what you may have guessed. And give the great Par-Salian my regards . . . apprentice!"

The mage withdrew his hand.

Dalamar collapsed upon the floor, clutching his chest, moaning. Raistlin walked around him without even a glance. The dark elf could hear him leave the room, the soft swish of the black robes, the door opening and closing.

In a frenzy of pain, Dalamar ripped open his robes. Five red, glistening trails of blood streamed down his breast, soaking into the black cloth, welling from five holes that had been burned into his flesh.

CHAPTER
10

Caramon! Get up! Wake up!"

No. I'm in my grave. It's warm here beneath the ground, warm and safe. You can't wake me, you can't reach me. I'm hidden in the clay, you can't find me.

"Caramon, you've got to see this! Wake up!"

A hand shoved aside the darkness, tugged at him.

No, Tika, go away! You brought me back to life once,† back to pain and suffering. You should have left me in the sweet realm of darkness below the Blood Sea of Istar.† But I've found peace now at last. I dug my grave and I buried myself.

"Hey, Caramon, you better wake up and take a look at this!"

Those words! They were familiar. Of course, I said them! I said them to Raistlin long ago, when he and I first came to this forest. So how can I be hearing them? Unless I *am* Raistlin. . . . Ah, that's—

Caramon is recalling events found in Dragons of Spring Dawning, *Book II, Chapter 5.*

"The fifth angel sounded his trumpet, and I saw a star that had fallen from the sky to the earth. The star was given the key to the shaft of the Abyss. When he opened the Abyss, smoke rose from it like the smoke from a gigantic furnace. The sun and sky were darkened by the smoke from the Abyss." [Revelation 9:1-2 NIV]

129

There was a hand on his eyelid! Two fingers were prying it open! At the touch, fear ran prickling through Caramon's bloodstream, starting his heart beating with a jolt.

"Arghhhh!" Caramon roared in alarm, trying to crawl into the dirt as that one, forcibly opened eye saw a gigantic face hovering over him—the face of a gully dwarf!

"Him awake," Bupu reported. "Here," she said to Tasslehoff, "you hold this eye. I open other one."

"No!" Tas cried hastily. Dragging Bupu off the warrior, Tas shoved her behind him. "Uh . . . you go get some water."

"Good idea," Bupu remarked and scuttled off.

"It—it's all right, Caramon," Tas said, kneeling beside the big man and patting him reassuringly. "It was only Bupu. I'm sorry, but I was—uh— looking at the . . . well, you'll see . . . and I forgot to watch her."

Groaning, Caramon covered his face with his hand. With Tas's help, he struggled to sit up. "I dreamed I was dead," he said heavily. "Then I saw that face—I knew it was all over. I was in the Abyss."

"You may wish you were," Tas said somberly.

Caramon looked up at the sound of the kender's unusually serious tone. "Why? What do you mean?" he asked harshly.

Instead of answering, Tas asked, "How do you feel?"

Caramon scowled. "I'm sober, if that's what you want to know," the big man muttered. "And I wish to the gods I wasn't. So there."

Tasslehoff regarded him thoughtfully for a moment, then, slowly, he reached into a pouch and drew forth a small leather-bound bottle. "Here, Caramon," he said quietly, "if you really think you need it."

The big man's eyes flashed. Eagerly, he stretched out a trembling hand and snatched the bottle. Uncorking the top, he sniffed at it, smiled, and raised it to his lips.

"Quit staring at me!" he ordered Tas sullenly.

"I'm s-sorry," Tas flushed. He rose to his feet. "I-I'll just go look after Lady Crysania—"

"Crysania . . ." Caramon lowered the flask, untasted. He rubbed his gummed eyes. "Yeah, I

forgot about her. Good idea, you looking after her. Take her and get out of here, in fact. You and that vermin-ridden gully dwarf of yours! Get out and leave me alone!" Raising the bottle to his lips again, Caramon took a long pull. He coughed once, lowered the bottle, and wiped his mouth with the back of his hand. "Go on," he repeated, staring at Tas dully, "get out of here! All of you! Leave me alone!"

"I'm sorry, Caramon," Tas said quietly. "I really wish we could. But we can't."

"Why?" snarled Caramon.

Tas drew a deep breath. "Because, if I remember the stories Raistlin told me, I think the Forest of Wayreth has found us."

For a moment, Caramon stared at Tas, his blood-shot eyes wide.

"That's impossible," he said after a moment, his words little more than a whisper. "We're miles from there! I—it took me and Raist . . . it took us months to find the Forest! And the Tower is far south of here! It's clear past Qualinesti, according to your map," Caramon regarded Tas balefully. "That isn't the same map that showed Tarsis by the sea, is it?"

"It could be," Tas hedged, hastily rolling up the map and hiding it behind his back. "I have so many. . . ." He hurriedly changed the subject. "But Raistlin said it was a magic forest, so I suppose it could have found us, if it was so inclined."

"It *is* a magic forest," Caramon murmured, his voice deep and trembling. "It's a place of horror." He closed his eyes and shook his head, then—suddenly—he looked up, his face full of cunning. "This is a trick, isn't it? A trick to keep me from drinking! Well, it won't work—"

"It's no trick, Caramon," Tas sighed. Then he pointed. "Look over there. It's just like Raistlin described to me once."

Turning his head, Caramon saw, and he shuddered, both at the sight and at the bitter memories of his brother it brought back.

The glade they were camped in was a small, grassy clearing some distance from the main trail. It was surrounded by maple trees, pines, walnut trees, and even a few aspens. The trees were just

beginning to bud out. Caramon had looked at them while digging Crysania's grave. The branches shimmered in the early morning sunlight with the faint yellow-green glow of spring. Wild flowers bloomed at their roots, the early flowers of spring—crocuses and violets.

As Caramon looked around now, he saw that these same trees surrounded them still—on three sides. But now—on the fourth, the southern side—the trees had changed.

These trees, mostly dead, stood side-by-side, lined up evenly, row after row. Here and there, as one looked deeper into the Forest, a living tree might be seen, watching like an officer over the silent ranks of his troops. No sun shone in this Forest. A thick, noxious mist flowed out of the trees, obscuring the light. The trees themselves were hideous to look upon, twisted and deformed, their limbs like great claws dragging the ground. Their branches did not move, no wind stirred their dead leaves. But—most horrible—things within the Forest moved. As Caramon and Tas watched, they could see shadows flitting among the trunks, skulking among the thorny underbrush.

"Now, look at this," Tas said. Ignoring Caramon's alarmed shout, the kender ran straight for the Forest. As he did so, the trees parted! A path opened wide, leading right into the Forest's dark heart. "Can you beat that?" Tas cried in wonder, coming to a halt right before he set foot upon the path. "And when I back away—"

The kender walked backward, away from the trees, and the trunks slid back together again, closing ranks, presenting a solid barrier.

"You're right," Caramon said hoarsely. "It is the Forest of Wayreth. So it appeared, one morning, to us." He lowered his head. "I didn't want to go in. I tried to stop Raist. But he wasn't afraid! The trees parted for him, and he entered. 'Stay by me, my brother,' he told me, 'and I will keep you from harm.' How often had I said those words to *him?* He wasn't afraid! I was!"

Suddenly, Caramon stood up. "Let's get out of here!" Feverishly grabbing his bedroll with shaking hands, he slopped the contents of the bottle all over the blanket.

"No good," Tas said laconically. "I tried. Watch."

Turning his back on the trees, the kender walked north. The trees did not move. But—inexplicably—Tasslehoff was walking *toward* the Forest once more. Try as he might, turn as he might, he always ended up walking straight into the tree's fog-bound, night-marish ranks.

Sighing, Tas came over to stand beside Caramon. The kender looked solemnly up into the big man's tear-stained, red-rimmed eyes and reached out a small hand, resting it on the warrior's once-strong arm.

"Caramon, you're the only one who's been through here! You're the only one who knows the way. And, there's something else," Tas pointed. Caramon turned his head. "You asked about Lady Crysania. There she is. She's alive, but she's dead at the same time. Her skin is like ice. Her eyes are fixed in a terrible stare. She's breathing, her heart's beating, but it might just as well be pumping through her body that spicy stuff the elves use to preserve their dead!"† The kender drew a deep, quivering breath.

"We've got to get help for her, Caramon. Maybe in there"—Tas pointed to the Forest—"the mages can help her! I can't carry her." He raised his hands help-lessly. "I need you, Caramon. She needs you! I guess you could say you owe it to her."

"Since it's my fault she's hurt?" Caramon mut-tered savagely.

"No, I didn't mean that," Tas said, hanging his head and brushing his hand across his eyes. "It's no one's fault, I guess."

"No, it *is* my fault," Caramon said. Tas glanced up at him, hearing a note in Caramon's voice he hadn't heard in a long, long time. The big man stood, staring at the bottle in his hands. "It's time I faced up to it. I've blamed everyone else—Raistlin, Tika. . . . But all the time I knew—deep inside—it was me. It came to me, in that dream. I was lying at the bottom of a grave, and I realized—this *is* the bottom! I can't go any lower. I either stay here and let them throw dirt on top of me—just like I was going to bury Crysania—or I climb out," Caramon sighed, a long, shuddering sigh. Then, in sudden resolution, he put the cork on the bottle and handed

This is, of course, a marked difference to the pyre that Caramon insists on building for Crysania back in Chapter 8. The intention here is to highlight very real and deep differences in the two cultures. —TRH

133

it back to Tas. "Here," he said softly. "It's going to be long climb, and I'm going to need help, I expect. But not that kind of help."

"Oh, Caramon!" Tas threw his arms around the big man's waist as far as he could reach, hugging him tightly. "I wasn't afraid of that spooky wood, not really. But I *was* wondering how I was going to get through by myself. Not to mention Lady Crysania and—Oh, Caramon! I'm so glad you're back! I—"

"There, there," Caramon muttered, flushing in embarrassment and shoving Tasslehoff gently away from him. "It's all right. I'm not sure how much help I'll be—I was scared to death the first time I went into that place. But, you're right. Maybe they can help Crysania." Caramon's face hardened. "Maybe they can answer a few questions I have about Raist, too. Now, where's that gully dwarf gotten to? And"—he glanced down at his belt—"where's my dagger?"

"What dagger?" Tas asked, skipping around, his gaze on the Forest.

Reaching out, his face grim, Caramon caught hold of the kender. His gaze went to Tas's belt. Tas's followed. His eyes opened wide in astonishment.

"You mean *that* dagger? My goodness, I wonder how it got there? You know," he said thoughtfully, "I'll bet you dropped it, during the fight."

"Yeah," Caramon muttered. Growling, he retrieved his dagger and was just putting it back into its sheath when he heard a noise behind him. Whirling around in alarm, he got a bucketful of icy water, right in the face.

"Him awake now," Bupu announced complacently, dropping the bucket.

While drying his clothes, Caramon sat and studied the trees, his face drawn with the pain of his memories. Finally, heaving a sigh, he dressed, checked his weapons, then stood up. Instantly, Tasslehoff was right next to him.

"Let's go!" he said eagerly.

Caramon stopped. "Into the Forest?" he asked in a hopeless voice.

"Well, of course!" Tas said, startled. "Where else?"

Caramon scowled, then sighed, then shook his head. "No, Tas," he said gruffly. "You stay here with

Lady Crysania. Now, look," he said in answer to the kender's indignant squawk of protest, "I'm just going into the Forest for a little ways—to, er, check it out."

"You think there's something in there, don't you?" Tas accused the big man. "That's why you're making me stay out! You'll go in there and there'll be a big fight. You'll probably kill it, and I'll miss the whole thing!"

"I doubt that," Caramon muttered. Glancing into the fog-ridden Forest apprehensively, he tightened his sword belt.

"At least you might tell me what you think it is," Tas said. "And, say, Caramon, what am I supposed to do if *it* kills *you?* Can I go in then? How long should I wait? Could it kill you in—say—five minutes? Ten? Not that I think it will," he added hastily, seeing Caramon's eyes widen. "But I really should know, I mean, since you're leaving me in charge."

Bupu studied the slovenly warrior speculatively. "Me say—two minutes. It kill him in two minutes. You make bet?" She looked at Tas.

Caramon glared grimly at both of them, then heaved another sigh. Tas was only being logical, after all.

"I'm not sure what to expect," Caramon muttered. "I-I remember last time, we . . . we met this thing . . . a wraith. It—Raist . . ." Caramon fell silent. "I don't know what you should do," he said after a moment. Shoulders slumping, he turned away and began to walk slowly toward the Forest. "The best you can, I guess."

"I got nice snake here, me say he last two minutes," Bupu said to Tas, rummaging around in her bag. "What stakes you put up?"

"Shhhh," Tas said softly, watching Caramon walk away. Then, shaking his head, he scooted over to sit beside Crysania, who lay on the ground, her sightless eyes staring up at the sky. Gently, Tas drew the cleric's white hood over her head, shading her from the sun's rays. He had tried unsuccessfully to shut those staring eyes, but it was as if her flesh had turned to marble.

Raistlin seemed to walk beside Caramon every step of the way into the Forest. The warrior could

almost hear the soft whisper of his brother's red robes—they had been red then! He could hear his brother's voice—always gentle, always soft, but with that faint hiss of sarcasm that grated so on their friends. But it had never bothered Caramon. He had understood—or anyway thought he had.

The trees in the Forest suddenly shifted at Caramon's approach, just as they had shifted at the kender's approach.

Just as they shifted when we approached . . . how many years ago, Caramon thought. Seven? Has it only been seven years? No, he realized sadly. It's been a lifetime, a lifetime for both of us.

As Caramon came to the edge of the wood, the mist flowed out along the ground, chilling his ankles with a cold that seared through flesh and bit into bone. The trees stared at him, their branches writhing in agony. He remembered† the tortured woods of Silvanesti, and that brought more memories of his brother. Caramon stood still a moment, looking into the Forest. He could see the dark and shadowy shapes waiting for him. And there was no Raistlin to keep them at bay. Not this time.

"I was never afraid of anything until I entered the Forest of Wayreth," Caramon said to himself softly. "I only went in last time because you were with me, my brother. Your courage alone kept me going. How can I go in there now without you? It's magic. I don't understand magic! I can't fight it! What hope is there?" Caramon put his hands over his eyes to blot out the hideous sight. "I can't go in there," he said wretchedly. "It's too much to ask of me!"

Pulling his sword from its sheath, he held it out. His hand shook so he nearly dropped the weapon. "Hah!" he said bitterly. "See? I couldn't fight a child. This is too much to ask. No hope. There is no hope. . . ."

"It is easy to have hope in the spring, warrior, when the weather is warm and the vallenwoods are green. It is easy to have hope in the summer when the vallenwoods glitter with gold. It is easy to have hope in the fall when the vallenwoods are as red as living blood. But in the winter, when the air is sharp and bitter and the skies are gray, does the vallenwood die, warrior?"

Caramon is remembering events that occurred in Dragons of Winter Night, Book I, Chapters 9 ff.

"Who spoke?" Caramon cried, staring around wildly, clutching his sword in his trembling hand.

"What does the vallenwood do in the winter, warrior, when all is dark and even the ground is frozen? It digs deep, warrior. It sends its root down, down, into the soil, down to warm heart of the world. There, deep within, the vallenwood finds nourishment to help it survive the darkness and the cold, so that it may bloom again in the spring."

"So?" Caramon asked suspiciously, backing up a step and looking around.

"So you stand in the darkest winter of your life, warrior. And so you must dig deep to find the warmth and the strength that will help you survive the bitter cold and the terrible darkness. No longer do you have the bloom of spring or the vigor of summer. You must find the strength you need in your heart, in your soul. Then, like the vallenwoods, you will grow once more."

"Your words are pretty—" Caramon began, scowling, distrusting this talk of spring and trees. But he could not finish, his breath caught in his throat.

The Forest was changing before his eyes.

The twisting, writhing trees straightened as he watched, lifting their limbs to the skies, growing, growing, growing. He bent his head back so far he nearly lost his balance, but still he couldn't see their tops. They were vallenwood trees! Just like those in Solace before the coming of the dragons. As he watched in awe, he saw dead limbs burst into life—green buds sprouted, burst open, blossomed into green glistening leaves that turned summer gold—seasons changing as he drew a shivering breath.

The noxious fog vanished, replaced by a sweet fragrance drifting from beautiful flowers that twined among the roots of the vallenwoods. The darkness in the forest vanished, the sun shed its bright light upon the swaying trees. And as the sunlight touched the trees' leaves, the calls of birds filled the perfumed air.

Easeful the forest, easeful its mansions per
   fected
Where we grow and decay no longer, our
   trees ever green,

Margaret wanted a "poem about a magically changing forest." Yeah, that's what she gave me. I remember asking, "Good change or bad change?" and receiving a little more description, but I think they were still working on parts of the scene in which it appears—especially upon the immediate reactions of Caramon and Tas.

Margaret nailed it—just flat-out nailed it—in her description of Caramon's response. Because the song is supposed to suggest a kind of perfection and completion that both gives you hope and makes you a little sad, that lets both those sentiments rest together.

The poem was fun metrically, because it is in what is known as dactylic trimeter, very popular in Classical lyrics. I don't read Greek, but my Latin in passable, and I lifted the rhythm straight out of Catullus, my favorite of the Roman lyric poets.
—Michael Williams

Ripe fruit never falling, streams still and
  transparent
As glass, as the heart in repose this lasting day.

Beneath these branches the willing surrender
  of movement,
The business of birdsong, of love, left on the
  borders
With all of the fevers, the failures of memory.
Easeful the forest, easeful its mansions per
  fected.

And light upon light, light as dismissal of
  darkness,
Beneath these branches no shade, for shade is
  forgotten
In the warmth of the light and the cool smell
  of the leaves
Where we grow and decay; no longer, our
  trees ever green.

Here there is quiet, where music turns in
  upon silence,
Here at the world's imagined edge, where
  clarity
Completes the senses, at long last where we
  behold
Ripe fruit never falling, streams still and
  transparent.

Where the tears are dried from our faces. or
  settle,
Still as a stream in accomplished countries of
  peace,
And the traveler opens, permitting the
  voyage of light
As air, as the heart in repose this lasting day.

Easeful the forest, easeful its mansions per
  fected
Where we grow and decay no longer, our
  trees ever green,
Ripe fruit never falling, streams still and
  transparent
As air, as the heart in repose this lasting day.

Caramon's eyes filled with tears. The beauty of the song pierced his heart. There was hope! Inside the Forest, he would find all the answers! He'd find the help he sought.

"Caramon!" Tasslehoff was jumping up and down with excitement. "Caramon, that's wonderful! How did you do it? Hear the birds? Let's go! Quickly."

"Crysania—" Caramon said, starting to turn back. "We'll have to make a litter. You'll have to help—" But before he could finish, he stopped, staring in astonishment at two white-robed figures, who glided out of the golden woods. Their white hoods were pulled low over their heads, he could not see their faces. Both bowed before him solemnly, then walked across the glade to where Crysania lay in her deathlike sleep. Lifting her still body with ease, they bore her gently back to where Caramon stood. Coming to the edge of the Forest, they stopped, turning their hooded heads, looking at him expectantly.

"I think they're waiting for you to go in first, Caramon," Tas said cheerfully. "You go on ahead, I'll get Bupu."

The gully dwarf remained standing in the center of the glade, regarding the Forest with deep suspicion, which Caramon looking at the white-robed figures, suddenly shared.

"Who are you?" he asked.

They did not answer. They simply stood, waiting.

"Who cares who they are!" Tas said, impatiently grabbing hold of Bupu and dragging her along, her sack bumping against her heels.

Caramon scowled. "You go first." He gestured at the white-robed figures. They said nothing, nor did they move.

"Why are you waiting for me to enter that Forest?" Caramon stepped back a pace. "Go ahead"—he gestured—"take her to the Tower. You can help her. You don't need me—"

The figures did not speak, but one raised his hand, pointing.

"C'mon, Caramon," Tas urged. "Look, it's like he was inviting us!"

They will not bother us, brother. . . . We have been invited! Raistlin's words, spoken seven years ago.

"Mages invited us. I don't trust 'em." Caramon softly repeated the answer he had made then.

Suddenly, the air was filled with laughter—strange, eerie, whispering laughter. Bupu threw her arms around Caramon's leg, clinging to him in terror. Even Tasslehoff seemed a bit disconcerted. And then came a voice, as Caramon had heard it seven years before.

Does that include me, dear brother?

CHAPTER
II

T he hideous apparition came closer and closer to her. Crysania was possessed by a fear such as she had never known, a fear she could never have believed† existed. As she shrank back before it, Crysania, for the first time in her life, contemplated death—her own death. It was not the peaceful transition to a blessed realm she had always believed existed. It was savage pain and howling darkness, eternal days and nights spent envying the living.

She tried to cry out for help, but her voice failed. There was no help anyway. The drunken warrior lay in a pool of his own blood. Her healing arts had saved him, but he would sleep long hours. The kender could not help her. Nothing could help her against this. . . .

On and on the dark figure walked, nearer and nearer he came. Run! her mind screamed. Her limbs

Crysania is considering the teachings of her own religion at this point as opposed to the reality that is before her. Each of the different religions in Krynn has its own beliefs regarding the afterlife. Not one of these religions, from the authors' rather omniscient perspective, have a clear and complete understanding of what the afterlife is all about. Each of them have that part of the truth that they need to progress to the next part of their learning journey. That these truths appear to conflict is due to their own mortal understanding, not a discrepancy in the will of the High God. —TRH

would not obey. It was all she could do to creep backward, and then her body seemed to move of its own volition, not through any direction of hers. She could not even look away from him. The orange flickering lights that were his eyes held her fast.

He raised a hand, a spectral hand. She could see through it, see through him, in fact, to the night-shadowed trees behind.

The silver moon was in the sky, but it was not its bright light that gleamed off the antique armor of a long-dead Solamnic Knight. The creature shone with an unwholesome light of his own, glowing with the energy of his foul decay. His hand lifted higher and higher, and Crysania knew that when his hand reached a level even with her heart, she would die.

Through lips numb with fear, Crysania called out a name, "Paladine," she prayed. The fear did not leave her, she still could not wrench her soul away from the terrible gaze of those fiery eyes. But her hand went to her throat. Grasping hold of the medallion, she ripped it from her neck. Feeling her strength draining, her consciousness ebbing, Crysania raised her hand. The platinum medallion caught Solinari's light and flared bluewhite. The hideous apparition spoke— "Die!"

Crysania felt herself falling. Her body hit the ground, but the ground did not catch her. She was falling through it, or away from it. Falling . . . falling . . . closing her eyes . . . sleeping. . . . dreaming. . . .

She was in a grove of oak trees. White hands clutched at her feet, gaping mouths sought to drink her blood. The darkness was endless, the trees mocked her, their creaking branches laughing horribly.

"Crysania," said a soft, whispering voice.

What was that, speaking her name from the shadows of the oaks? She could see it, standing in a clearing, robed in black.

"Crysania," the voice repeated.

"Raistlin!" She sobbed in thankfulness. Stumbling out of the terrifying grove of oak trees, fleeing the bone-white hands that sought to drag her down to join their endless torment, Crysania felt thin arms hold her. She felt the strange burning touch of slender fingers.

"Rest easy, Revered Daughter," the voice said softly. Trembling in his arms, Crysania closed her eyes. "Your trials are over. You have come through the Grove safely. There was nothing to fear, lady. You had my charm."

"Yes," Crysania murmured. Her hand touched her forehead where his lips had pressed against her skin. Then, realizing what she had been through, and realizing, too, that she had allowed him to see her give way to weakness, Crysania pushed the mage's arms away. Standing back from him, she regarded him coldly.

"Why do you surround yourself with such foul things?" she demanded. "Why do you feel the need for such . . . such guardians!" Her voice quavered in spite of herself.

Raistlin looked at her mildly, his golden eyes shining in the light of his staff. "What kind of guardians do you surround yourself with, Revered Daughter?" he asked. "What torment would I endure if I set foot upon the Temple's sacred grounds?"

Crysania opened her mouth for a scathing reply, but the words died on her lips. Indeed, the Temple *was* consecrated ground. Sacred to Paladine, if any who worshipped the Queen of Darkness entered its precincts, they would feel Paladine's wrath. Crysania saw Raistlin smile, his thin lips twitch. She felt her skin flush. How was he capable of doing this to her? Never had any man been able to humiliate her so! Never had any man cast her mind in such turmoil!

Ever since the evening she had met Raistlin at the home of Astinus, Crysania had not been able to banish him from her thoughts. She had looked forward to visiting the Tower this night, looked forward to it and dreaded it at the same time. She had told Elistan all about her talk with Raistlin, all—that is—except the "charm" he had given her. Somehow, she could not bring herself to tell Elistan that Raistlin had touched her, had—No, she wouldn't mention it.

Elistan had been upset enough as it was. He knew Raistlin, he had known the young man of old—the mage having been among the companions who rescued the cleric from Verminaard's prison at Pax Tharkas.† Elistan had never liked or trusted

This occurred in Dragons of Autumn Twilight, *Book II, Chapters 13-14.*

Raistlin, but then no one had, not really. The cleric had not been surprised to hear that the young mage had donned the Black Robes. He was not surprised to hear about Crysania's warning from Paladine. He *was* surprised at Crysania's reaction to meeting Raistlin, however. He was surprised—and alarmed—at hearing Crysania had been invited to visit Raistlin in the Tower—a place where now beat the heart of evil in Krynn. Elistan would have forbidden Crysania to go, but freedom of will† was a teaching of the gods.

He told Crysania his thoughts and she listened respectfully. But she had gone to the Tower, drawn by a lure she could not begin to understand—although she told Elistan it was to "save the world."

"The world is getting on quite well," Elistan replied gravely.

But Crysania did not listen.

"Come inside," Raistlin said. "Some wine will help banish the evil memories of what you have endured." He regarded her intently. "You are very brave, Revered Daughter," he said and she heard no sarcasm in his voice. "Few there are with the strength to survive the terror of the Grove."

He turned away from her then, and Crysania was glad he did. She felt herself blushing at his praise.

"Keep near me," he warned as he walked ahead of her, his black robes rustling softly around his ankles. "Keep within the light of my staff."

Crysania did as she was bidden, noticing as she walked near him how the staff's light made her white robes shine as coldly as the light of the silver moon, a striking contrast to the strange warmth it shed over Raistlin's soft velvety black robes.

He led her through the dread Gates. She stared at them in curiosity, remembering the gruesome story of the evil mage who had cast himself down upon them, cursing them with his dying breath. *Things* whispered and jabbered around her. More than once, she turned at the sound, feeling cold fingers upon her neck or the touch of a chill hand upon hers. More than once, she saw movement out of the corner of her eye, but when she looked, there was never anything there. A foul mist rose up from the ground, rank with the smell of decay, making her bones ache. She began to shake uncontrollably and

when, suddenly, she glanced behind her and saw two disembodied, staring eyes—she took a hurried step forward and slipped her hand around Raistlin's thin arm.

He regarded her with curiosity and a gentle amusement that made her blush again.

"There is no need to be afraid," he said simply. "I am master here. I will not let you come to harm."

"I-I'm not afraid," she said, though she knew he could feel her body quivering. "I . . . was just . . . unsure of my steps, that was all."

"I beg your pardon, Revered Daughter," Raistlin said, and now she could not be certain if she heard sarcasm in his voice or not. He came to a halt. "It was impolite of me to allow you to walk this unfamiliar ground without offering you my assistance. Do you find the walking easier now?"

"Yes, much," she said, flushing deeply beneath that strange gaze.

He said nothing, merely smiled. She lowered her eyes, unable to face him, and they resumed walking. Crysania berated herself for her fear all the way to the Tower, but she did not remove her hand from the mage's arm. Neither of them spoke again until they reached the door to the Tower itself. It was a plain wooden door with runes carved on the outside of its surface. Raistlin said no word, made no motion that Crysania could see, but—at their approach—the door slowly opened. Light streamed out from inside, and Crysania felt so cheered by its bright and welcoming warmth, that—for an instant— she did not see another figure standing silhouetted within it.

When she did, she stopped and drew back in alarm.

Raistlin touched her hand with his thin, burning fingers.

"That is only my apprentice, Revered Daughter," he said. "Dalamar is flesh and blood, he walks among the living—at least for the moment."

Crysania did not understand that last remark, nor did she pay it much attention, hearing the underlying laughter in Raistlin's voice. She was too startled by the fact that live people *lived* here. How silly, she scolded herself. What kind of monster have I pictured this man? He *is* a man, nothing more. He is human, he is flesh and blood. The thought relieved

her, made her relax. Stepping through the doorway, she felt almost herself. She extended her hand to the young apprentice as she would have given it to a new acolyte.

"My apprentice, Dalamar," Raistlin said, gesturing toward him. "Lady Crysania, Revered Daughter of Paladine."

"Lady Crysania," said the apprentice with becoming gravity, accepting her hand and bringing it to his lips, bowing slightly. Then he lifted his head, and the black hood that shadowed his face fell back.

"An elf!" Crysania gasped. Her hand remained in his. "But, that's not possible," she began in confusion. "Not serving evil—"

"I am a dark elf, Revered Daughter," the apprentice said, and she heard a bitterness in his voice. "At least, that is what my people call me."†

Crysania murmured in embarrassment. "I'm sorry. I didn't mean—"

She faltered and fell silent, not knowing where to look. She could almost feel Raistlin laughing at her. Once again, he had caught her off-balance. Angrily, she snatched her hand away from the apprentice's cool grip and withdrew her other hand from Raistlin's arm.

"The Revered Daughter has had a fatiguing journey, Dalamar," Raistlin said. "Please show her to my study and pour her a glass of wine. With your permission, Lady Crysania"—the mage bowed—"there are a few matters that demand my attention. Dalamar, anything the lady requires, you will provide at once."

"Certainly, *Shalafi*," Dalamar answered respectfully.

Crysania said nothing as Raistlin left, suddenly overwhelmed with a sense of relief and a numbing exhaustion. Thus must the warrior feel, battling for his life against a skilled opponent, she observed silently as she followed the apprentice up a narrow, winding staircase.

Raistlin's study was nothing like she had expected.

What *had* I expected, she asked herself. Certainly not this pleasant room filled with strange and fascinating books. The furniture was attractive and comfortable, a fire burned on the hearth, filling the room with warmth that was welcome after the chill of the

"When an elf embraces evil, worships the gods of Darkness, or is considered a threat to his or her people, elven society moves swiftly to punish the guilty. The elven respect for life does not permit them to execute these individuals. Instead, those elves deemed dangerous are cast out and named dark elves.

"To be named a dark elf is to be without a country and a people. Forbidden to interact with all other elves, regardless of nationality, a dark elf is forced to roam the world in exile, always dreaming of the homeland that will never be seen again." [DRAGONLANCE Campaign Setting, Wizards of the Coast, 2003]

walk to the Tower. The wine that Dalamar poured was delicious. The warmth of the fire seemed to seep into her blood as she drank a small sip.

Dalamar brought forward a small, ornately carved table and set it at her right hand. Upon this, he placed a bowl of fruit and a loaf of fragrant, still-warm bread.

"What is this fruit?" Crysania asked, picking up a piece and examining it in wonder. "I've never seen anything like this before."

"Indeed not, Revered Daughter," Dalamar answered, smiling. Unlike Raistlin, Crysania noticed, the young apprentice's smile was reflected in his eyes. "*Shalafi* has it brought to him from the Isle of Mithas."

"Mithas?" Crysania repeated in astonishment. "But that's on the other side of the world! The minotaurs live there. They allow none to enter their kingdom! Who brings it?"

She had a sudden, terrifying vision of the servant who might have been summoned to bring such delicacies to such a master. Hastily, she returned the fruit to the bowl.

"Try it, Lady Crysania," Dalamar said without a trace of amusement in his voice. "You will find it quite delicious. The *Shalafi's* health is delicate. There are so few things he can tolerate. He lives on little else but this fruit, bread, and wine."

Crysania's fear ebbed. "Yes," she murmured, her eyes going to the door involuntarily. "He is dreadfully frail, isn't he? And that terrible cough . . ." Her voice was soft with pity.

"Cough? Oh, yes," Dalamar† said smoothly, "his . . . cough." He did not continue and, if Crysania thought this odd, she soon forgot it in her contemplation of the room.

The apprentice stood a moment, waiting to see if she required anything else. When Crysania did not speak, he bowed. "If you need nothing more, lady, I will retire. I have my own studies to pursue."

"Of course. I will be fine here," Crysania said, coming out of her thoughts with a start. "He is your teacher, then," she said in sudden realization. Now it was her turn to look at Dalamar intently. "Is he a good one? Do you learn from him?"

"He is the most gifted of any in our Order, Lady Crysania," Dalamar said softly. "He is brilliant,

Dalamar proved to be one of my favorite characters. He is important to the story in that, although he is a Black Robe and therefore "evil," he realizes the importance of laws and the need to impose order on chaos in order for the world to continue to progress. He is ambitious, but he has come to learn that ambition must have its limits or it will end in destruction. —MW

skilled, controlled. Only one has lived who was as powerful—the great Fistandantilus. And my *Shalafi* is young, only twenty-eight. If he lives, he may well—"

"If he lives?" Crysania repeated, then felt irritated that she had unintentionally let a note of concern creep into her voice. It is right to feel concern, she told herself. After all, he is one of the gods' creatures. All life is sacred.

"The Art is fraught with danger, my lady," Dalamar was saying. "And now, if you will excuse me. . . ."

"Certainly," Crysania murmured.

Bowing again, Dalamar padded quietly from the room, shutting the door behind him. Toying with her wine glass, Crysania stared into the dancing flames, lost in thought. She did not hear the door open—if indeed it did. She felt fingers touching her hair. Shivering, she looked around, only to see Raistlin sitting in a high-backed wooden chair behind his desk.

"Can I send for anything else? Is everything to your liking?" he asked politely.

"Y-yes," Crysania stammered, setting her wine glass down so that he would not see her hand shake. "Everything is fine. More than fine, actually. Your apprentice—Dalamar? He is quite charming."

"Isn't he?" said Raistlin dryly. He placed the tips of the five fingers of each hand together and rested them upon the table.

"What marvelous hands you have," Crysania said, without thinking. "How slender and supple the fingers are, and so delicate." Suddenly realizing what she had been saying, she flushed and stammered. "B-but I-I suppose that is requisite to your Art—"

"Yes," Raistlin said, smiling, and this time Crysania thought she saw actual pleasure in his smile. He held his hands to the light cast by the flames. "When I was just a child, I could amaze and delight my brother with the tricks these hands could—even then—perform." Taking a golden coin from one of the secret pockets of his robes, Raistlin placed the coin upon the knuckles of his hand. Effortlessly, he made it dance and spin and whirl across his hand. It glistened in and out of his fingers. Flipping into the

air, it vanished, only to reappear in his other hand. Crysania gasped in delight. Raistlin glanced up at her, and she saw the smile of pleasure twist into one of bitter pain.

"Yes," he said, "it was my one skill, my one talent. It kept the other children amused. Sometimes it kept them from hurting me."

"Hurting you?" Crysania asked hesitantly, stung by the pain in his voice.

He did not answer at once, his eyes on the golden coin he still held in his hand. Then he drew a deep breath. "I can picture your childhood," he murmured. "You come from a wealthy family, so they tell me. You must have been beloved, sheltered, protected, given anything you wanted. You were admired, sought after, liked."

Crysania could not reply. She felt suddenly over-whelmed with guilt.

"How different was my childhood." Again, that smile of bitter pain. "My nickname was the Sly One. I was sickly and weak. And too smart. They were such fools! Their ambitions so petty—like my brother, who never thought deeper than his food dish! Or my sister, who saw the only way to attain her goals was with her sword. Yes, I was weak. Yes, they protected me. But some day, I vowed I wouldn't need their protection! I would rise to greatness on my own, using my gift—*my magic*."

His hand clenched, his golden-tinted skin turned pale. Suddenly he began to cough, the wrenching, wracking cough that twisted his frail body. Crysania rose to her feet, her heart aching with pain. But he motioned her to sit down. Drawing a cloth from a pocket, he wiped the blood from his lips.

"And this was the price I paid for my magic,"† he said when he could speak again. His voice was little more than a whisper. "They shattered my body and gave me this accursed vision, so that all I look upon I see dying before my eyes. But it was worth it, worth it all! For I have what I sought—power. I don't need them—any of them—anymore."

"But this power is evil!" Crysania said, leaning forward in her chair and regarding Raistlin earnestly.

"Is it?" asked Raistlin suddenly. His voice was mild. "Is ambition evil? Is the quest for power, for control over others evil?† If so, then I fear, Lady

Sacrifice is a question of balance: the giving up of one thing for another. Here, again, we see a restatement of the theme of balance. —TRH

Here Raistlin calls into question whether there is any difference between a zealot and a tyrant. This is very much a central theme in Legends, particularly when it comes to the Kingpriest. Very clearly, here, a zealot is a tyrant in a different set of robes. —TRH

Crysania, that you may as well exchange those white robes for black."

"How dare you?" Crysania cried, shocked. "I don't—"

"Ah, but you do," Raistlin said with a shrug. "You would not have worked so hard to rise to the position you have in the church without having your share of ambition, of the desire for power."† Now it was his turn to lean forward. "Haven't you always said to yourself—there is something *great* I am destined to do? *My* life will be different from the lives of others. *I* am not content to sit and watch the world pass by. I want to shape it, control it, mold it!"

Held fast by Raistlin's burning gaze, Crysania could not move or utter a word. How could he know? she asked herself, terrified. Can he read the secrets of my heart?

"Is that evil, Lady Crysania?" Raistlin repeated gently, insistently.

Slowly, Crysania shook her head. Slowly, she raised her hand to her throbbing temples. No, it wasn't evil. Not the way he spoke of it, but something wasn't quite right. She couldn't think. She was too confused. All that kept running through her mind was: *How alike we are, he and I!*

He was silent, waiting for her to speak. She had to say something. Hurriedly, she took a gulp of wine to give herself time to collect her scattered thoughts.

"Perhaps I do have those desires," she said, struggling to find the words, "but, if so, my ambition is not for myself. I use my skills and talents for others, to help others. I use it for the church—"

"The church!" Raistlin sneered.

Crysania's confusion vanished, replaced by cold anger. "Yes," she replied, feeling herself on safe and secure ground, surrounded by the bastion of her faith. "It was the power of good, the power of Paladine, that drove away the evil in the world. It is that power I seek. That power that—"

"Drove away the evil?" Raistlin interrupted.

Crysania blinked. Her thoughts had carried her forward.

She hadn't even been totally aware of what she was saying. "Why, yes—"

"But evil and suffering still remain in the world," Raistlin persisted.

"Crysania is devout, but she is also ambitious. She knows that she has within her the strength and the ability to lead the church when Elistan is gone. What she does not yet understand is that she must also have compassion, humility, and tolerance or she will follow in the footsteps of the Kingpriest." [DRAGONLANCE Adventures, *by Tracy Hickman and Margaret Weis, TSR, Inc., 1987, p. 112.*]

"Because of such as you!" Crysania cried passionately.

"Ah, no, Revered Daughter," Raistlin said. "Not through any act of mine. Look—" He motioned her near with one hand, while with the other he reached once again into the secret pockets of his robe.

Suddenly wary and suspicious, Crysania did not move, staring at the object he drew forth. It was a small, round piece of crystal, swirling with color, very like a child's marble. Lifting a silver stand from where it stood on a corner of his desk, Raistlin placed the marble on top of it. The thing appeared ludicrous, much too small for the ornate stand. Then Crysania gasped. The marble was growing! Or perhaps *she* was shrinking! She couldn't be certain. But the glass globe was now the right size and rested comfortably upon the silver stand.

"Look into it," Raistlin said softly.

"No," Crysania drew back, staring fearfully at the globe. "What is that?"

"A dragon orb," Raistlin replied, his gaze holding her fast. "It is the only one left on Krynn. It obeys my commands. I will not allow you to come to harm. Look inside the orb, Lady Crysania—unless you fear the truth."

"How do I know it will show me the truth?" Crysania demanded, her voice shaking. "How do I know it won't show me just what you tell it to show me?"

"If you know the way the dragons orbs were made long ago," Raistlin replied, "you know they were created by all three of the Robes—the White, the Black, and the Red. They are not tools of evil, they are not tools of good. They are everything and nothing. You wear the medallion of Paladine"—the sarcasm had returned— "and you are strong in your faith. Could I force you to see what you did not want to see?"

"What will I see?" Crysania whispered, curiosity and a strange fascination drawing her near the desk.

"Only what your eyes have seen, but refused to look at."

Raistlin placed his thin fingers upon the glass, chanting words of command. Hesitantly, Crysania leaned over the desk and looked into the dragon orb. At first she saw nothing inside the glass globe but a faint swirling green color. Then she drew back. There were hands inside the orb! Hands that were reaching out. . . .

"Do not fear," murmured Raistlin. "The hands come for me."

And, indeed, even as he spoke, Crysania saw the hands inside the orb reach out and touch Raistlin's hands. The image vanished. Wild, vibrant colors whirled madly inside the orb for an instant, making Crysania dizzy with their light and their brilliance. Then they, too, were gone. She saw . . .

"Palanthas," she said, startled. Floating on the mists of morning, she could see the entire city, gleaming like a pearl, spread out before her eyes. And then the city began to rush up at her, or perhaps she was falling down into it. Now she was hovering over New City, now she was over the Wall, now she was inside Old City. The Temple of Paladine rose before her, the beautiful, sacred grounds peaceful and serene in the morning sunlight. And then she was *behind* the Temple, looking over a high wall.

She caught her breath. "What is this?" she asked.

"Have you never seen it?" Raistlin replied. "This alley so near the sacred grounds?"

Crysania shook her head, "N-no," she answered, her voice breaking. "And, yet, I must have. I have lived in Palanthas all my life. I know all of—"

"No, lady," Raistlin said, his fingertips lightly caressing the dragon orb's crystalline surface. "No, you know very little."

Crysania could not answer. He spoke the truth, apparently, for she did not know this part of the city. Littered with refuse, the alley was dark and dismal. Morning's sunlight did not find its way past the buildings that leaned over the street as if they had no more energy to stand upright. Crysania recognized the buildings now. She had seen them from the front. They were used to store everything from grain to casks of wine and ale. But how much different they looked from the front! And who were these people, these wretched people?

"They live there," Raistlin answered her unspoken question.

"Where?" Crysania asked in horror. "There? Why?"

"They live where they can. Burrowing into the heart of the city like maggots, they feed off its decay.

As for why?" Raistlin shrugged. "They have nowhere else to go."

"But this is terrible! I'll tell Elistan. We'll help them, give them money—"

"Elistan knows," Raistlin said softly.

"No, he can't! That's impossible!"

"You knew. If not about this, then you knew of other places in your fair city that are not so fair."

"I didn't—" Crysania began angrily, then stopped. Memories washed over her in waves—her mother averting her face as they rode in their carriage through certain parts of town, her father quickly drawing shut the curtains in the carriage windows or leaning out to tell the driver to take a different road.

The scene shimmered, the colors swirled, it faded and was replaced by another, and then another. Crysania watched in agony as the mage ripped the pearl-white facade from the city, showing her blackness and corruption beneath. Bars, brothels, gambling dens, the wharves, the docks . . . all spewed forth their refuse of misery and suffering before Crysania's shocked vision. No longer could she avert her face, there were no curtains to pull shut. Raistlin dragged her inside, brought her close to the hopeless, the starving, the forlorn, the forgotten.

"No," she pleaded, shaking her head and trying to back away from the desk. "Please show me no more."

But Raistlin was pitiless. Once again the colors swirled, and they left Palanthas. The dragon orb carried them around the world, and everywhere Crysania looked, she saw more horrors. Gully dwarves, a race cast off from their dwarven kin, living in squalor in whatever part of Krynn they could find that no one else wanted. Humans eking out a wretched existence in lands where rain had ceased to fall. The Wilder elves, enslaved by their own people. Clerics, using their power to cheat and amass great wealth at the expense of those who trusted them.†

It was too much. With a wild cry, Crysania covered her face with her hands. The room swayed beneath her feet. Staggering, she nearly fell. And then Raistlin's arms were around her. She felt that strange, burning warmth from his body and the soft touch of the black velvet. There was a smell of spices,

One might be tempted to say that this theme of corrupt clergy was sparked by the televangelist scandals of the 1980s. They may have had an influence, but more carnage and death have been visited on the world in the name of religion than nearly any other single concept. The massacres of the Christian Crusades, the "convert or die" of Islam, the Ku Klux Klan, and "the Troubles" in Northern Ireland are all extensions in parts large or small of myopic zealotry. I do not believe that blood and hate are the province of the true prophets of God.
—TRH

rose petals, and other, more mysterious odors. She could hear his shallow breathing rattle in his lungs.

Gently, Raistlin led Crysania back to her chair. She sat down, quickly drawing away from his touch. His nearness was both repelling and attracting at the same time, adding to her feelings of loss and confusion. She wished desperately that Elistan were here. He would know, he would understand. For there had to be an explanation! Such terrible suffering, such evil should not be allowed. Feeling empty and hollow, she stared into the fire.

"We are not so very different." Raistlin's voice seemed to come from the flames. "I live in my Tower, devoting myself to my studies. You live in your Tower, devoting yourself to your faith. And the world turns around us."

"And that is true evil," Crysania said to the flames. "To sit and do nothing."†

"The only thing necessary for the triumph of evil is for good men to do nothing." —Edmund Burke (1729-1797)

"Now you understand," Raistlin said. "No longer am I content to sit and watch. I have studied long years for one reason, with one aim. And now that is within my grasp. *I* will make a difference, Crysania. *I* will change the world. *That* is my plan."

Crysania looked up swiftly. Her faith had been shaken, but its core was strong. "Your plan! It is the plan Paladine warned me of in my dream. This plan to change the world will cause the world's destruction!" Her hand clenched in her lap. "You must not go through with it! Paladine—"

Raistlin made an impatient gesture with his hand. His golden eyes flashed and, for a moment, Crysania shrank back, catching a glimpse of the smoldering fires within the man.

"Paladine will not stop me," Raistlin said, "for I seek to depose his greatest enemy."

Crysania stared at the mage, not understanding. What enemy could that be? What enemy could Paladine have upon this world? Then Raistlin's meaning became clear. Crysania felt the blood drain from her face, cold fear made her shudder convulsively. Unable to speak, she shook her head. The enormity of his ambition and his desires was too fearful, too impossible to even contemplate.

"Listen," he said, softly. "I will make it clear. . . ."

And he told her his plans. She sat for what seemed like hours before the fire, held by the gaze of his

strange, golden eyes, mesmerized by the sound of his soft, whispering voice, hearing him tell her of the wonders of his magic and of the magic now long lost, the wonders discovered by Fistandantilus.

Raistlin's voice fell silent. Crysania sat for long moments, lost and wandering in a realm far from any she had ever known. The fire burned low in the gray hour before dawn. The room became lighter. Crysania shivered in the suddenly chill chamber.

Raistlin coughed, and Crysania looked up at him, startled. He was pale with exhaustion, his eyes seemed feverish, his hands shook. Crysania rose to her feet.

"I am sorry," she said, her voice low. "I have kept you awake all night, and you are not well. I must go."

Raistlin rose with her. "Do not worry about my health, Revered Daughter," he said with a twisted smile. "The fire that burns within me is fuel enough to warm this shattered body. Dalamar will accompany you back through Shoikan Grove, if you like."

"Yes, thank you," Crysania murmured. She had forgotten that she must go back through that evil place. Taking a deep breath, she held her hand out to Raistlin. "Thank you for meeting with me," she began formally. "I hope—"

Raistlin took her hand in his, the touch of his smooth flesh burned. Crysania looked into his eyes. She saw herself reflected there, a colorless woman dressed in white, her face framed by her dark, black hair.

"You cannot do this," Crysania whispered. "It is wrong, you must be stopped." She held onto his hand very tightly.

"Prove to me that it is wrong," Raistlin answered, drawing her near. "Show me that this is evil. Convince me that the ways of good are the means of saving the world."

"Will you listen?" Crysania asked wistfully. "You are surrounded by darkness. How can I reach you?"

"The darkness parted, didn't it?" Raistlin said. "The darkness parted, and you came in."

"Yes . . ." Crysania was suddenly aware of the touch of his hand, the warmth of his body. Flushing uncomfortably, she stepped back. Removing

her hand from his grasp, she absently rubbed it, as if it hurt.

"Farewell, Raistlin Majere," she said, without meeting his eyes.

"Farewell, Revered Daughter of Paladine," he said.

The door opened and Dalamar stood within it, though Crysania had not heard Raistlin summon the young apprentice. Drawing her white hood up over her hair, Crysania turned from Raistlin and walked through the door. Moving down the gray, stone hallway, she could feel his golden eyes burning through her robes. When she arrived at the narrow winding staircase leading down, his voice reached her.

"Perhaps Paladine did not send you to stop me, Lady Crysania. Perhaps he sent you to help."

Crysania paused and looked back. Raistlin was gone, the gray hall was bleak and empty. Dalamar stood beside her in silence, waiting.

Slowly, gathering the folds of her white robes in her hand so that she did not trip, Crysania descended the stairs.

And kept on descending . . . down . . . down . . . into unending sleep.

CHAPTER
12

The Tower of High Sorcery in Wayreth had been, for centuries, the last outpost of magic upon the continent of Ansalon. Here the mages had been driven, when the Kingpriest† ordered them from the other Towers. Here they had come, leaving the Tower in Istar,† now under the waters of the Blood Sea, leaving the accursed and blackened Tower in Palanthas.†

The Tower in Wayreth was an imposing structure, an unnerving sight. The outer walls formed an equilateral triangle. A small tower stood at each angle of the perfect geometric shape. In the center stood the two main towers, slanted slightly, twisting just a little, enough to make the viewer blink and say to himself—aren't those crooked?

The walls were built of black stone. Polished to a high gloss, it shone brilliantly in the sunlight and, in the night, reflected the light of two moons and mirrored

*The Kingpriest is the personification of myopic zealotry. His mortal mind, incapable of conceiving in any significant part the mind of God, believes that his limited understanding is the only real perspective on existence. He is a blind man at the bottom of a well who believes that the universe is four feet wide.
—TRH*

*I put the name Istar on the original map of Krynn with no conscious knowledge that it meant anything. Ishtar was indeed an ancient Babylonian goddess, but the Istar of the DRAGONLANCE setting is not named after her.
—TRH*

One reads these passages and is reminded of Sodom and Gomorrah but one might as easily be reminded of Atlantis or the Flood in Noah's time. Every now and then, it seems, God decides to clean house. —TRH

the darkness of the third. Runes were carved upon the surface of the stone, runes of power and strength, shielding and warding; runes that bound the stones to each other; runes that bound the stones to the ground. The tops of the walls were smooth. There were no battlements for soldiers to man. There was no need.

Far from any centers of civilization, the Tower at Wayreth was surrounded by its magic wood. None could enter who did not belong, none came to it without invitation. And so the mages protected their last bastion of strength, guarding it well from the outside world.

Yet, the Tower was not lifeless. Ambitious apprentice magic-users came from all over the world to take the rigorous—and sometimes fatal—Test. Wizards of high standing arrived daily, continuing their studies, meeting, discussing, conducting dangerous and delicate experiments. To these, the Tower was open day and night. They could come and go as they chose—Black Robes, Red Robes, White Robes.

Though far apart in philosophies—in their ways of viewing and of living with the world—all the Robes met in peace in the Tower. Arguments were tolerated only as they served to advance the Art. Fighting of any sort was prohibited—the penalty was swift, terrible death.

The Art. It was the one thing that united them all. It was their first loyalty—no matter who they were, whom they served, what color robes they wore. The young magic-users who faced death calmly when they agreed to take the Test understood this. The ancient wizards who came here to breathe their last and be entombed within the familiar walls understood this. The Art—Magic. It was parent, lover, spouse, child. It was soil, fire, air, water. It was life. It was death. It was beyond death.

Par-Salian thought of all this as he stood within his chambers in the northernmost of the two tall towers, watching Caramon and his small retinue advance toward the gates.

As Caramon remembered the past, so, too, did Par-Salian. Some wondered if it was with regret.

No, he said silently, watching Caramon come up the path, his battlesword clanking against his flabby thighs. I do not regret the past. I was given a terrible choice and I made it.

Who questions the gods? They demanded a sword.
I found one. And—like all swords—it was two-edged.

Caramon and his group had arrived at the outer
gate. There were no guards. A tiny silver bell rang in
Par-Salian's quarters.

The old mage raised his hand. The gates swung
open.

It was twilight when they entered the outer gates
of the Tower of High Sorcery. Tas glanced around,
startled. It had been morning only moments ago.†
Or at least it seemed like it had been morning!
Looking up, he could see red rays streaking across
the sky, gleaming eerily off the polished stone walls
of the Tower.

Tas shook his head. "How does anyone tell time
around here?" he asked himself. He stood in a vast
courtyard bounded by the outer walls and the inner
two towers. The courtyard was stark and barren.
Paved with gray flagstone, it looked cold and
unlovely. No flowers grew, no trees broke the unre-
lieved monotony of the gray stone. And it was empty,
Tas noticed in disappointment. There was absolutely
no one around, no one in sight.

Or was there? Tas caught a glimpse of movement
out of the corner of his eye, a flutter of white. Turning quickly, however, he was amazed to see it was
gone! No one was there. And then, he saw, out of the
corner of the other eye, a face and a hand and a red
robed sleeve. He looked at it directly—and it was
gone! Suddenly, Tas had the impression he was
surrounded by people, coming and going, talking,
or just sitting and staring, even sleeping! Yet—the
courtyard was still silent, still empty.

"These must be mages taking the Test!" Tas said
in awe. "Raistlin told me they traveled all over, but
I never imagined anything like this! I wonder if
they can see me? Do you suppose I could touch one,
Caramon, if I—Caramon?"

Tas blinked. Caramon was gone! Bupu was gone!
The white-robed figures and Lady Crysania were
gone. He was alone!

Not for long. There was a flash of yellow light, a
most horrible smell, and a black-robed mage stood
towering before him. The mage extended a hand, a
woman's hand.

Time does seem rather flexible here in our story. Mystic places often have a "timelessness" to them. From Eden to Shangri-la and many tales in between, such strange variations in time have been an archetypal theme. —TRH

"You have been summoned."

Tas gulped. Slowly, he held out his hand. The woman's fingers closed over his wrist. He shivered at their cold touch. "Perhaps I'm going to be magicked!" he said to himself hopefully.

The courtyard, the black stone walls, the red streaks of sunlight, the gray flagstone, all began to dissolve around Tas, running down the edges of his vision like a rain-soaked painting. Thoroughly delighted, the kender felt the woman's black robes wrap around him. She tucked them up around his chin. . . .

When Tasslehoff came to his senses, he was lying on a very hard, very cold, stone floor. Next to him, Bupu snored blissfully. Caramon was sitting up, shaking his head, trying to clear away the cobwebs.

"Ouch." Tas rubbed the back of his neck. "Funny kind of accommodations, Caramon," he grumbled, getting to his feet. "You'd think they could at least magic up beds. And if they want a fellow to take a nap, why don't they just say so instead of sending—oh—"

Hearing Tas's voice break off in a strange sort of gurgle, Caramon glanced up quickly.

They were not alone.

"I know this place," Caramon whispered.

They were in a vast chamber carved of obsidian. It was so wide that its perimeter was lost in shadow, so high that its ceiling was obscured in shadow. No pillars supported it, no lights lit it. Yet light there was, though none could name its source. It was a pale light, white—not yellow. Cold and cheerless, it gave no warmth.

The last time Caramon had been in this chamber, the light shone upon one old man, dressed in white robes, sitting by himself in a great stone chair. This time, the light shone upon the same old man, but he was no longer alone. A half-circle of stone chairs sat around him—twenty-one to be exact. The white-robed old man sat in the center. To his left were three indistinct figures, whether male or female, human or some other race, it was difficult to tell. Their hoods were pulled low over their faces. They were dressed in red robes. To their left sat six figures, clothed all in black. One chair among them was empty. On the old

man's right sat four more red-robed figures, and—to their right, six dressed all in white. Lady Crysania lay on the floor before them, her body on a white pallet, covered with white linen.

Of all the Conclave, only the old man's face was visible.

"Good evening," Tasslehoff said, bowing and backing up and bowing and backing up until he bumped into Caramon. "Who *are* these people?" the kender whispered loudly. "And what are they doing in our bedroom?"

"The old man in the center is Par-Salian," Caramon said softly. "And we're not in a bedroom. This is the central hall, the Hall of Mages or some such thing. You better wake up the gully dwarf."

"Bupu!" Tas kicked the snoring dwarf with his foot.

"Gulphphunger spawn," she snarled, rolling over, her eyes tightly closed. "Go way. Me sleep."

"Bupu!" Tas was desperate; the old man's eyes seemed to go right through him. "Hey, wake up. Dinner."

"Dinner!" Opening her eyes, Bupu jumped to her feet. Glancing around eagerly, she caught sight of the twenty robed figures, sitting silently, their hooded faces invisible.

Bupu let out a scream like a tortured rabbit.† With a convulsive leap, she threw herself at Caramon and wrapped her arms around his ankle in a deathlike grip. Aware of the glittering eyes watching him, Caramon tried to shake her loose, but it was impossible. She clung to him like a leech, shivering, peering at the mages in terror. Finally, Caramon gave up.

The old man's face creased in what might have been a smile. Tas saw Caramon look down self-consciously at his smelly clothes. He saw the big man finger his unshaven jowls and run a hand through his tangled hair. Embarrassed, he flushed uncomfortably. Then his expression hardened. When he spoke, it was with simple dignity.

"Par-Salian," Caramon said, the words booming out too loudly in the vast, shadowy hall, "do you remember me?"

"I remember you, warrior," said the mage. His voice was soft, yet it carried in the chamber. A dying whisper would have carried in that chamber.

The image of the rabbit is used deliberately here as a reference to the twins, stemming from Michael Williams's joke about Caramon. Caramon and Raistlin are standing in front of a monstrous fire dragon, who is about to roast them. When asked what Caramon would do and say in this dire situation, Michael Williams made a shadow puppet with his fingers and replied, "Look, Raist, bunnies!" We all loved that remark, and I was able to use it in a more tender moment in the twins' lives when Caramon tries to alleviate his brother's pain by making shadow puppets. The final reference to the "bunnies" comes at the very end of the series, when Raistlin sacrifices himself and his brother's love redeems him. —MW

161

He said nothing more. None of the other mages spoke. Caramon shifted uncomfortably. Finally he gestured at Lady Crysania. "I have brought her here, hoping you could help her. Can you? Will she be all right?"

"Whether she will be all right or not is not in our hands," Par-Salian answered. "It is beyond our skill to care for her. In order to protect her from the spell the death knight cast upon her—a spell that surely would have meant her death—Paladine heard her last prayer and sent her soul to dwell in his peaceful realms.

Caramon's head bowed. "It's my fault," he said huskily. "I-I failed her. I might have been able—"

"To protect her?" Par-Salian shook his head. "No, warrior, you could not have protected her from the Knight of the Black Rose. You would have lost your own life trying. Is that not true, kender?"

Tas, suddenly finding the gaze of the old man's blue eyes upon him felt tingling sparks shoot through his body. "Y-Yes," he stammered. "I-I saw him—it," Tasslehoff shuddered.

"This from one who knows no fear," Par-Salian said mildly. "No, warrior, do not blame yourself. And do not give up hope for her. Though we ourselves cannot restore her soul to her body, we know of those who can. But, first, tell me why Lady Crysania sought us out. For we know she was searching for the Forest of Wayreth."

"I'm not sure." Caramon mumbled.

"She came because of Raistlin," Tas chimed in helpfully. But his voice sounded shrill and discordant in the hall. The name rang out eerily. Par-Salian frowned, Caramon turned to glare at him. The mages' hooded heads shifted slightly, as if they were glancing at each other, their robes rustled softly. Tas gulped and fell silent.

"Raistlin," the name hissed softly from Par-Salian's lips. He stared at Caramon intently. "What does a cleric of good have to do with your brother? Why did she undertake this perilous journey for his sake?"

Caramon shook his head, unwilling or unable to talk.

"You know of his evil?" Par-Salian pursued sternly.

Caramon stubbornly refused to answer, his gaze was fixed on the stone floor.

"I know—" Tas began, but Par-Salian made a slight movement with his hand and the kender hushed.

"You know that now we believe he intends to conquer the world?" Par-Salian continued, his relentless words hitting Caramon like darts. Tas could see the big man flinch. "Along with your half-sister, Kitiara†—or the Dark Lady, as she is known among her troops—Raistlin has begun to amass armies. He has dragons, flying citadels. And in addition we know—"

A sneering voice rang through the hall. "You know nothing, Great One. You are a fool!"

The words fell like drops of water into a still pond, causing ripples of movement to spread among the mages. Startled, Tas turned, searching for the source of the strange voice, and saw, behind him, a figure emerging from the shadows. Its black robes rustled as it walked past them to face Par-Salian. At that moment, the figure removed its hood.

Tas felt Caramon stiffen. "What is it?" the kender whispered, unable to see.

"A dark elf!" Caramon muttered.

"Really?" Tas said, his eyes brightening. "You know, in all the years I've lived on Krynn, I've never seen a dark elf." The kender started forward only to be caught by the collar of his tunic. Tas squawked in irritation, as Caramon dragged him back, but neither Par-Salian nor the black-robed figure appeared to notice the interruption.

"I think you should explain yourself, Dalamar," Par-Salian said quietly. "Why am I a fool?"

"Conquer the world!" Dalamar sneered. "*He* does not plan to conquer the world! The world means nothing to him. He could have the world tomorrow, tonight, if he wanted it!"

"Then what does he want?" This question came from a red-robed mage seated near Par-Salian.

Tas, peering out around Caramon's arm, saw the delicate, cruel features of the dark elf relax in a smile—a smile that made the kender shiver.

"He wants to become a god,"† Dalamar answered softly. "He will challenge the Queen of Darkness herself. That is his plan."

The mages said nothing, they did not move, but their silence seemed to stir among them like shifting

Kitiara is a wonderful foil for Raistlin, for while she is as power-hungry as he is, Kitiara is much more pragmatic. Raistlin represents the spiritual/mental side of life. He is physically frail, surviving by the power of his mind. Kitiara is physically strong. She believes that all problems can be solved with force. Kitiara believes only in what she can see, touch, taste, and smell. She has no use for the gods, and she views people who are faithful to the gods as being inherently weak. Kitiara has ambitions, but they are practical. She wants things. She wants control over things: money, people, armies, cities. Because she doesn't understand the spiritual side of life, she secretly fears it and therefore refuses to face it—a refusal that will ultimately result in her downfall. —MW

Raistlin's ambition mirrors that of another would-be usurper:
"12 How art thou fallen from heaven, O Lucifer, son of the morning! How art thou cut down to the ground, which didst weaken the nations!
13 For thou hast said in thine heart, I will ascend into heaven, I will exalt my throne above the stars of God....
14 I will ascend above the heights of the clouds; I will be like the most High.
15 Yet thou shalt be brought down to hell, to the sides of the pit."
[Isaiah 14:12-15 KJV]

currents of air as they stared at Dalamar with glittering, unblinking eyes.

Then Par-Salian sighed. "I think you overestimate him."

There was a ripping, rending sound, the sound of cloth being torn apart. Tas saw the dark elf's arms jerk, tearing open the fabric of his robes.

"Is this overestimating him?" Dalamar cried.

The mages leaned forward, a gasp whispered through the vast hall like a chill wind. Tas struggled to see, but Caramon's hand held him fast. Irritably, Tas glanced up at Caramon's face. Wasn't he curious? But Caramon appeared totally unmoved.

"You see the mark of his hand upon me," Dalamar hissed. "Even now, the pain is almost more than I can bear." The young elf paused, then added through clenched teeth. "He said to give you his regards, Par-Salian!"

The great mage's head bent. The hand rising to support it shook as with a palsy. He seemed old, feeble, weary. For a moment, the mage sat with his eyes covered, then he raised his head and looked intently at Dalamar.

"So—our worst fears are realized." Par-Salian's eyes narrowed questioningly. "He knows, then, that *we* sent you—"

"To spy on him?" Dalamar laughed, bitterly. "Yes, he knows!" The dark elf spit the words. "He's known all along. He's been using me—using all of us—to further his own ends."

"I find this all very difficult to believe," stated the red-robed mage in a mild voice. "We all admit that young Raistlin is certainly powerful, but I find this talk of challenging a goddess quite ridiculous . . . quite ridiculous indeed."

There were murmured assents from both halves of the semi-circle.

"Oh, do you?" Dalamar asked, and there was a lethal softness in his voice. "Then, let me tell you fools that you have no idea of the meaning of the word *power*. Not as it relates to him! You cannot begin to fathom the depths of his power or to soar the heights! I can! I have seen"—for a moment Dalamar paused, his voice lost its anger and was filled with wonder—"I have seen such things as none of you have dared imagine! I have walked the

realms of dreams with my eyes open! I have seen beauty to make the heart burst with pain. I have descended into nightmares—I have witnessed horrors"—he shuddered—"horrors so nameless and terrible that I begged to be struck dead rather than look upon them!" Dalamar glanced around the semi-circle, gathering them all together with his flashing, dark-eyed gaze. "And all these wonders *he* summoned, *he* created, *he* brought to life with his magic."†

There was no sound, no one moved.

"You are wise to be afraid, Great One," Dalamar's voice sank to a whisper. "But no matter how great your fear, you do not fear him enough. Oh, yes, he lacks power to cross that dread threshold. But that power he goes to find. Even as we speak, he is preparing himself for the long journey. Upon my return tomorrow, he will leave."

Par-Salian raised his head. "Your return?" he asked, shocked. "But he knows you for what you are—a spy, sent by us, the Conclave, his fellows." The great mage's glance went to the chair that stood empty amidst the Black Robes, then he rose to his feet. "No, young Dalamar. You are very courageous, but I cannot allow you to return to what would undoubtedly be tortured death at his hands."

"You cannot stop me," Dalamar said, and there was no emotion in his voice. "I said before—I would give my soul to study with such as he. And now, though it costs me my life, I will stay with him. He expects me back. He leaves me in charge of the Tower of High Sorcery in his absence."

"He leaves you to guard?" the red-robed mage said dubiously. "You, who have betrayed him?"

"He knows me," Dalamar said bitterly. "He knows he has ensnared me. He has stung my body and sucked my soul dry, yet I will return to the web. Nor will I be the first," Dalamar motioned down at the still, white form lying on the pallet before him. Then, half-turning, the dark elf glanced at Caramon. "Will I, *brother*?" he said with a sneer.

At last, Caramon seemed driven to action. Angrily shaking Bupu loose from his foot, the warrior took a step forward, both the kender and the gully dwarf crowding close behind him.

"Who is this?" Caramon demanded, scowling at

"Dalamar's first love and loyalty is to his magic and to the Conclave. He admires Raistlin, however, and is fascinated by the power of the archmage. Thus he willingly risks his life to study with him and serve as his apprentice. But Dalamar is smart enough to know that man was not meant to challenge the gods and that only destruction can result from such vast ambition."
[DRAGONLANCE Adventures, *by Tracy Hickman and Margaret Weis, TSR, Inc., 1987, p. 112.]

the dark elf. "What's going on? Who are you talking about?"

Before Par-Salian could answer, Dalamar turned to face the big warrior.

"I am called Dalamar," the dark elf said coldly. "And I speak of your twin brother, Raistlin. He is my master. I am his apprentice. I am, in addition, a spy, sent by this august company you see before you to report on the doings of your brother."

Caramon did not answer. He may not have even heard. His eyes—wide with horror—were fixed on the dark elf's chest. Following Caramon's gaze, Tas saw five burned and bloody holes in Dalamar's flesh. The kender swallowed, feeling suddenly queasy.

"Yes, your brother's hand did this," Dalamar remarked, guessing Caramon's thoughts. Smiling grimly, the dark elf gripped the torn edges of his black robes with his hand and pulled them together, hiding the wounds. "It is no matter," he muttered, "it was no more than I deserved."

Caramon turned away, his face so pale Tas slipped his hand in the big man's hand, fearing he might collapse. Dalamar regarded Caramon with scorn.

"What's the matter?" he asked. "Didn't you believe him capable of this?" The dark elf shook his head in disbelief, his eyes swept the assemblage before him. "No, you are like the rest of them. Fools . . . all of you, fools!"

The mages murmured together, some voices angry, some fearful, most questioning. Finally, Par-Salian raised his hand for silence.

"Tell us, Dalamar, what he plans. Unless, of course, he has forbidden you to speak of it." There was a note of irony in the mage's voice that the dark elf did not miss.

"No," Dalamar smiled grimly. "I know his plans. Enough of them, that is. He even asked that I be certain and report them to you accurately."

There were muttered words and snorts of derision at this. But Par-Salian only looked more concerned, if that were possible. "Continue," he said, almost without voice.

Dalamar drew a breath.

"He journeys back in time, to the days just prior to the Cataclysm, when the great Fistandantilus was at the height of his power. It is my *Shalafi's* intention to

meet this great mage, to study with him, and to recover those works of Fistandantilus we know were lost during the Cataclysm. For my *Shalafi* believes, from what he has read in the spellbooks he took from the Great Library at Palanthas, that Fistandantilus learned how to cross the threshold that exists between god and men. Thus, the great wizard was able to prolong his life after the Cataclysm to fight the Dwarven Wars. Thus, he was able to survive the terrible explosion that devastated the lands of Dergoth. Thus, was he able to live until he found a new receptacle for his soul."

"I don't understand any of this! Tell me what's going on!" Caramon demanded, striding forward angrily. "Or I'll tear this place down around your miserable heads! Who is this Fistandantilus? What does he have to do with my brother?"

"Shhh," Tas said, glancing apprehensively at the mages.

"We understand, kenderken," Par-Salian said, smiling at Tas gently. "We understand his anger and his sorrow. And he is right—we owe him an explanation," The old mage sighed. "Perhaps what I did was wrong. And yet—did I have a choice? Where would we be today if I had not made the decision I made?"

Tas saw Par-Salian turn to look at the mages who sat on either side of him, and suddenly the kender realized Par-Salian's answer was for them as much as for Caramon. Many had cast back their hoods and Tas could see their faces now. Anger marked the faces of those wearing the black robes, sadness and fear were reflected in the pale faces of those wearing white. Of the red robes, one man in particular caught Tas's attention, mainly because his face was smooth, impassive, yet the eyes were dark and stirring. It was the mage who had doubted Raistlin's power. It seemed to Tas that it was to this man in particular that Par-Salian directed his words.

"Over seven years ago, Paladine appeared to me," Par-Salian's eyes stared into the shadows. "The great god warned me that a time of terror was going to engulf the world. The Queen of Darkness had awakened the evil dragons and was planning to wage war upon the people in an effort to conquer them. 'One among your Order you will choose to help fight this evil.' Paladine told me. 'Choose well, for

this person shall be as a sword to cleave the darkness. You may tell him nothing of what the future holds, for by his decisions, and the decisions of others, will your world stand or fall forever into eternal night.' "

Par-Salian was interrupted by angry voices, coming particularly from those wearing the black robes. Par-Salian glanced at them, his eyes flashing. Within that moment, Tas saw revealed the power and authority that lay within the feeble old mage.

"Yes, perhaps I should have brought the matter before the Conclave," Par-Salian said, his voice sharp. "But I believed then—as I believe now—that it was my decision alone. I knew well the hours that the Conclave would spend bickering, I knew well none of you would agree! I made my decision. Do any of you challenge my right to do so?"

Tas held his breath, feeling Par-Salian's anger roll around the hall like thunder. The Black Robes sank back into their stone seats, muttering. Par-Salian was silent for a moment, then his eyes went back to Caramon, and their stern glance softened.

"I chose Raistlin," he said.

Caramon scowled. "Why?" he demanded.

"I had my reasons," Par-Salian said gently. "Some of them I cannot explain to you, not even now. But I can tell you this—he was born with the gift. And that is most important. The magic dwells deep within your brother. Did you know that, from the first day Raistlin attended school, his own master held him in fear and awe. How does one teach a pupil who knows more than the teacher? And combined with the gift of magic is intelligence. Raistlin's mind is never at rest. It seeks knowledge, demands answers. And he is courageous—perhaps more courageous than you are, warrior. He fights pain every day of his life. He has faced death more than once and defeated it. He fears nothing—neither the darkness nor the light. And his soul . . ." Par-Salian paused. "His soul burns with ambition, the desire for power, the desire for more knowledge. I knew that nothing, not even the fear of death itself, would stop him from attaining his goals. And I knew that the goals he sought to attain might well benefit the world, even if he, himself, should choose to turn his back upon it."

Par-Salian paused. When he spoke, it was with sorrow. "But first he had to take the Test."

"You should have foreseen the outcome," the red-robed mage said, speaking in the same mild tone. "We all knew *he* was waiting, biding his time. . . ."

"I had no choice!" Par-Salian snapped, his blue eyes flashing. "Our time was running out. The world's time was running out. The young man had to take the Test and assimilate what he had learned. I could delay no longer."

Caramon stared from one to the other. "You knew Raist was in some kind of danger when you brought him here?"

"There is always danger," Par-Salian answered. "The Test is designed to weed out those who might be harmful to themselves, to the Order, to the innocents in the world." He put his hand to his head, rubbing his brows. "Remember, too, that the Test is designed to teach as well. We hoped to teach your brother compassion to temper his selfish ambition, we hoped to teach him mercy, pity. And, it was, perhaps, in my eagerness to teach that I made a mistake. I forgot Fistandantilus."

"Fistandantilus?" Caramon said in confusion. "What do you mean—forgot him? From what you've said, that old mage is dead."

"Dead? No," Par-Salian's face darkened. "The blast that killed thousands in the Dwarven Wars† and laid waste a land that is still devastated and barren did not kill Fistandantilus. His magic was powerful enough to defeat death itself. He moved to another plane of existence,† a plane far from here, yet not far enough. Constantly he watched, biding his time, searching for a body to accept his soul. And he found that body—your brother's."

Caramon listened in tense silence, his face deathly white. Out of the corner of his eye, Tas saw Bupu start edging backward. He grabbed her hand and held onto her tightly, keeping the terrified gully dwarf from turning and fleeing headlong out of the hall.

"Who knows what deal the two made during the Test? None of us, probably," Par-Salian smiled slightly. "I know this. Raistlin did superbly, yet his frail health was failing him. Perhaps he could have survived the final test—the confrontation with the

The Dwarfgate Wars were first alluded to in an AD&D adventure module that I wrote for the DRAGONLANCE setting. That section of the game never made it into the Chronicles, so it was nice to be able to use it here in Legends. —TRH

This is not to be confused with the planes of AD&D. I have personally never believed the DRAGONLANCE setting to be in any so-called plane connected to other AD&D worlds. I always thought it rather cheap to do so. The DRAGONLANCE setting, for me, has always existed on its own and separate from any other settings. —TRH

169

dark elf—if Fistandantilus had not aided him. Perhaps not."

"Aided him? He saved his life?"

Par-Salian shrugged. "We know only this, warrior—it was not any of us who left your brother with that gold-tinted skin. The dark elf cast a fireball† at him, and Raistlin survived. Impossible, of course—"

"Not for Fistandantilus," interrupted the red-robed mage.

"No," Par-Salian agreed sadly, "not for Fistandantilus. I wondered at the time, but I was not able to investigate. Events in the world were rushing to a climax. Your brother was himself when he came out of the Test. More frail, of course, but that was only to be expected. And I was right"—Par-Salian cast a swift, triumphant glance around the semicircle—"*he was strong in his magic!* Who else could have gained power over a dragon orb without years of study?"

"Of course," the red-robed mage said, "he had help from one who'd *had* years of study."

Par-Salian frowned and did not answer.

"Let me get this straight," Caramon said, glowering at the white-robed mage. "This Fistandantilus . . . took over Raistlin's soul? *He's* the one that made Raistlin take the Black Robes."

"Your brother made his own choice," Par-Salian spoke sharply. "As did we all."

"I don't believe it!" Caramon shouted. "Raistlin didn't make this decision. You're lying—all of you! You tortured my brother, and then one of your old wizards claimed what was left of his body!" Caramon's words boomed through the chamber and sent the shadows dancing in alarm.

Tas saw Par-Salian regard the warrior grimly, and the kender cringed, waiting for the spell that would sizzle Caramon like a spitted chicken. It never came. The only sound was Caramon's ragged breathing.

"I'm going to get him back," Caramon said finally, tears gleaming in his eyes. "If he can go back in time to meet this old wizard, so can I. You can send me back. And when I find Fistandantilus, I'll kill him. Then Raist will be . . ." He choked back a sob, fighting for control. "He'll be Raist again. And he'll forget all this nonsense about challenging th-the Queen of Darkness and . . . becoming a god."

A classic AD&D spell:
Fireball: *A fireball is an explosive burst of flame, which detonates with a low roar. [2nd Edition* ADVANCED DUNGEONS & DRAGONS *Player's Handbook, by David "Zeb" Cook, TSR, 1997, pp. 191, 192.]*
The thing Par-Salian isn't telling you here is that the necessary spell components are sulphur and a tiny ball of bat guano.

The semi-circle broke into chaos. Voices raised, clamboring in anger. "Impossible! He'll change history! You've gone too far, Par-Salian—"

The white-robed mage rose to his feet and, turning, stared at every mage in the semi-circle, his eyes going to each individually. Tas could sense the silent communication, swift and searing as lightning.

Caramon wiped his hand across his eyes, staring at the mages defiantly. Slowly, they all sank back into their seats. But Tas saw hands clench, he saw faces that were unconvinced, faces filled with anger. The red-robed mage stared at Par-Salian speculatively, one eyebrow raised. Then he, too, sat back. Par-Salian cast a final, quick glance around the Conclave before he turned to face Caramon.

"We will consider your offer," Par-Salian said. "It might work. Certainly, it is not something he would expect—"

Dalamar began to laugh.

CHAPTER 13

xpects?" Dalamar laughed until he could scarcely breathe. "He *planned* all of this! Do you think this great idiot"—he waved at Caramon—"could have found his way here by himself? When creatures of darkness pursued Tanis Half-Elven and Lady Crysania—pursued but never caught them—who do you think sent them? Even the encounter with the death knight, an encounter plotted by his sister, an encounter that could have wrecked his plans—my *Shalafi* has turned to his own advantage. For, undoubtedly you fools will send this woman, Lady Crysania, back in time to the only ones who can heal her†—the Kingpriest and his followers. You will send her back in time to meet Raistlin! Not only that, you'll even provide her with this man—his brother—as bodyguard. Just what the *Shalafi* wants."

Tas saw Par-Salian's clawlike fingers clench over

the cold stone arms of his chair, the old man's blue eyes gleamed dangerously.

"We have suffered enough of your insults, Dalamar," Par-Salian said. "I begin to think your loyalty to your *Shalafi* is too great. If that is true, your usefulness to this Conclave is ended."

Ignoring the threat, Dalamar smiled bitterly. "My *Shalafi*—" he repeated softly, then sighed. A shudder convulsed his slender body, he gripped the torn robes in his hand and bowed his head. "I am caught in the middle, as he intended," the dark elf whispered. "I don't know who I serve anymore, if anyone." He raised his dark eyes, and their haunted look made Tas's heart ache. "But I know this—if any of you came and tried to enter the Tower while he was gone, I would kill you. That much loyalty I owe him. Yet, I am just as frightened of him as you are. I'll help you, if I can."

Par-Salian's hands relaxed, though he still continued to regard Dalamar sternly. "I fail to understand why Raistlin told you of his plans? Surely he must know we will move to prevent him from succeeding in his terrifying ambitions."

"Because—like me—he has you where he wants you," Dalamar said. Suddenly he staggered, his face pale with pain and exhaustion. Par-Salian made a motion, and a chair materialized out of the shadows. The dark elf slumped into it. "You must go along with his plans. You must send this man back into time"—he gestured at Caramon—"along with the woman. It is the only way he can succeed—"

"And it is the only way we can stop him," Par-Salian said, his voice low. "But why Lady Crysania? What possible interest could he have in one so good, so pure—"

"So powerful," Dalamar said with a grim smile. "From what he has been able to gather from the writings of Fistandantilus that still survive, he will need a cleric to go with him to face the dread Queen. And only a cleric of good has power enough to defy the Queen and open the Dark Door. Oh, Lady Crysania was not the *Shalafi's* first choice. He had vague plans to use the dying Elistan—but I won't relate that. As it turned out, however, Lady Crysania fell into his hands—one might say literally. She is good, strong in her faith, powerful—"

"And drawn to evil as a moth is drawn to the flame," Par-Salian murmured, looking at Crysania with deep pity.

Tas, watching Caramon, wondered if the big man was even absorbing half of this. He had a vague, dull-witted look about him, as if he wasn't quite certain where—or who—he was. Tas shook his head dubiously. They're going to send *him* back in time? the kender thought.

"Raistlin has other reasons for wanting both this woman and his brother back in time with him, of that you may be certain," the red-robed mage said to Par-Salian. "He has not revealed his game, not by any means. He has told us—through our agent— just enough to leave us confused. I say we thwart his plans!"

Par-Salian did not reply. But, lifting his head, he stared at Caramon for long moments and in his eyes was a sadness that pierced Tas's heart. Then, shaking his head, he lowered his gaze, looking fixedly at the hem of his robes. Bupu whimpered, and Tas patted her absently. Why that strange look at Caramon? the kender wondered uneasily. Surely they wouldn't send him off to certain death? Yet, wasn't that what they'd be doing if they sent him back the way he was now—sick, depressed, confused? Tas shifted from one foot to the other, then yawned. No one was paying any attention to him. All this talk was boring. He was hungry, too. If they were going to send Caramon back in time, he wished they'd just *do* it.

Suddenly, he felt one part of his mind (the part that was listening to Par-Salian) tug at the other part. Hurriedly, Tas brought both parts together to listen to what was being said.

Dalamar was talking. "She spent the night in his study. I do not know what was discussed, but I know that when she left in the morning, she appeared distraught and shaken. His last words to her were these, 'Has it occurred to you that Paladine did not send you to stop me but to help me?' "

"And what answer did she make?"

"She did not answer him," Dalamar replied. "She walked back through the Tower and then through the Grove like one who can neither see nor hear."

"What I do not understand is why Lady Crysania was traveling here to seek our help in sending her

back? Surely she must have known we would refuse such a request!" the red-robed mage stated.

"I can answer that!" Tasslehoff said, speaking before he thought.

Now Par-Salian was paying attention to him, now all the mages in the semi-circle were paying attention to him. Every head turned in his direction. Tas had talked to spirits in Darken Wood, he had spoken at the Council of White Stone† but, for a moment, he was awed at this silent, solemn audience. Especially when it occurred to him what he had to say.

"Please, Tasslehoff Burrfoot," Par-Salian spoke with great courtesy, "tell us what you know." The mage smiled. "Then, perhaps, we can bring this meeting to a close and you can have your dinner."

Tas blushed, wondering if Par-Salian could, perhaps, see through his head and read his thoughts printed on his brain like he read words printed on a sheet of parchment.

"Oh! Yes, dinner would be great. But, now, um— about Lady Crysania." Tas paused to collect his thoughts, then launched into his tale. "Well, I'm not certain about this, mind you. I just know from what little I was able to pick up here and there. To begin at the beginning, I met Lady Crysania when I was in Palanthas visiting my friend, Tanis Half-Elven. You know him? And Laurana, the Golden General? I fought with them in the War of the Lance. I helped save Laurana from the Queen of Darkness." The kender spoke with pride. "Have you ever heard that story? I was in the Temple at Neraka—"

Par-Salian's eyebrows raised ever so slightly, and Tas stuttered.

"Uh, w-well, I'll tell that later. Anyway, I met Lady Crysania at Tanis's home and I heard their plans to travel to Solace to see Caramon. As it happened, I-I sort of . . . well, found a letter Lady Crysania had written to Elistan. I think it must have fallen out of her pocket."

The kender paused for breath. Par-Salian's lips twitched, but he refrained from smiling.

"I read it," Tas continued, now enjoying the attention of his audience, "just to see if it was important. After all, she might have thrown it away. In the letter, she said she was more—uh, how did it go— 'firmly convinced than ever, after my talk with

Tas spoke to spirits in Darken Wood in Dragons of Autumn Twilight, *Book I, Chapter 10 and spoke at the Whitestone Council in* Dragons of Winter Night, *Book III, Chapter 6.*

This is, in part, homage to Luke Skywalker in The Return of the Jedi. *Margaret, a big STAR WARS fan and a downright Darth Vader groupie, absolutely hated the end of that film. I wrote a new ending for her where the Darth that was burned on the pyre was actually a clone of the real Darth Vader who was using Luke to off the Emperor and give Vader control of the galaxy. She seemed satisfied with that. Might I ask you to keep that in mind when you get to the end of this book?*
—TRH

Back in Dragons of Autumn Twilight, *Bupu was one of the few characters to whom Raistlin ever showed any kindness or affection.*

Goldmoon killed the black dragon Khisanth in Dragons of Autumn Twilight, *Book I, Chapter 21.*

Tanis, that there was good in Raistlin't and that he could be 'turned from his evil path. I must convince the mages of this—' Anyhow, I saw that the letter was important, so l took it to her. She was *very* grateful to get it back," Tas said solemnly. "She hadn't realized she'd lost it."

Par-Salian put his fingers on his lips to control them.

"I said I could tell her lots of stories about Raistlin, if she wanted to hear them. She said she'd like that a lot, so I told her all the stories I could think of. She was particularly interested in the ones I told her about Bupu—

" 'If only I could find the gully dwarf!'† she said to me one night. 'I'm certain I could convince Par-Salian that there is hope, that he may be reclaimed!' "

At this, one of the Black Robes snorted loudly. Par-Salian glanced sharply in that direction, the wizards hushed. But Tas saw many of them—particularly the Black Robes—fold their arms across their chests in anger. He could see their eyes glittering from the shadows of their hoods.

"Uh, I'm s-sure I didn't mean to offend," Tas stuttered. "I know I always thought Raistlin looked much better in black—with that golden skin of his and all. *I* certainly don't believe everyone has to be good, of course. Fizban—he's really Paladine—we're great *personal* friends, Paladine and I—Anyway, Fizban said that there had to be a balance in the world, that we were fighting to restore the balance. So that means that there has to be Black Robes as well as White, doesn't it?"

"We know what you mean, kenderken," Par-Salian said gently. "Our brethren take no offense at your words. Their anger is directed elsewhere. Not everyone in the world is as wise as the great Fizban the Fabulous."

Tas sighed. "I miss him, sometimes. But, where was I? Oh, yes, Bupu. That's when I had my idea. Maybe, if Bupu told her story, the mages would believe her, I said to Lady Crysania. She agreed and I offered to go and find Bupu. I hadn't been to Xak Tsaroth since Goldmoon killed the black dragon† and it was just a short hop from where we were and Tanis said it would be fine with him. He seemed quite pleased to see me off, actually.

"The Highpulp let me take Bupu, after a—uh—small bit of discussion and some interesting items that I had in my pouch. I took Bupu to Solace, but Tanis had already gone and so had Lady Crysania. Caramon was—" Tas stopped, hearing Caramon clear his throat behind him. "Caramon was—wasn't feeling too good, but Tika—that's Caramon's wife and a great friend of mine—anyway, Tika said we had to go after Lady Crysania, because the Forest of Wayreth was a terrible place and—No offense meant, I'm certain, but did you ever stop to think that your Forest is really nasty? I mean, it is *not* friendly"— Tas glared at the mages sternly—"and I don't know why you let it wander around loose! I think it's irresponsible!"

Par-Salian's shoulders quivered.

"Well, that's all I know," Tas said. "And, there's Bupu, and she can—" Tas stopped, looking around. "Where'd she go?"

"Here," Caramon said grimly, dragging the gully dwarf out from behind his back where she had been cowering in abject terror. Seeing the mages staring at her, the gully dwarf gave a shriek and collapsed onto the floor, a quivering bundle of ragged clothes.

"I think you had better tell us her story," Par-Salian said to Tas. "If you can, that is."

"Yes," Tas replied, suddenly subdued. "I know what it was Lady Crysania wanted me to tell. It happened back during the war, when we were in Xak Tsaroth.† The only ones who knew anything about that city were gully dwarves. But most wouldn't help us. Raistlin cast a charm spell† on one of them— Bupu. Charmed wasn't exactly the word for what it did to her. She fell in love with him," Tas paused, sighing, then continued in a remorseful tone. "Some of us thought it was funny, I guess. But Raistlin didn't. He was really kind to her, and he even saved her life, once, when draconians attacked us. Well, after we left Xak Tsaroth, Bupu came with us. She couldn't bear to leave Raistlin."

Tas's voice dropped. "One night, I woke up. I heard Bupu crying. I started to go to her, but I saw Raistlin had heard her, too. She was homesick. She wanted to go back to her people, but she couldn't leave him. I don't know what he said, but I saw him lay his hand on her head. And it seemed that I

"Perched near a 1,000-foot cliff that plunged to Newsea in the midst of the Cursed Lands were the ruins of the once ancient and beautiful city of Xak Tsaroth. Prior to the Cataclysm, 300 years before the War of the Lance, the city had been inland, a major trading center of such importance that even the far eastern city of Istar purchased products from its huge open-air markets. With the fall of the fiery mountain on Istar . . . the city slid down the face of a cliff into a vast cavern formed by the huge rents in the ground." [The Atlas of the DRAGONLANCE *World, by Karen Wynn Fonstad, TSR, Inc. 1987, p. 20.]*

Another AD&D spell. **Charm Person:** *If the spell recipient fails his saving throw, he regards the caster as a trusted friend and ally to be heeded and protected. The spell does not enable the caster to control the charmed creature as if it were an automaton, but any word or action of the caster is viewed in the most favorable way. [2ⁿᵈ Edition* ADVANCED DUNGEONS & DRAGONS *Player's Handbook, by David "Zeb" Cook, TSR, 1997, p. 171.]*

could see a light shining all around Bupu. And, then, he sent her home. She had to travel through a land filled with terrible creatures but, somehow, I *knew* she would be safe. And she was," Tas finished solemnly.

There was a moment's silence, then it seemed that all the mages began to talk at once. Those of the Black Robes shook their heads. Dalamar sneered.

"The kender was dreaming," he said scornfully.

"Who believes kender anyway?" said one.

Those of the Red Robes and the White Robes appeared thoughtful and perplexed.

"If this is true," said one, "perhaps we have misjudged him. Perhaps we should take this chance, however slim."

Finally Par-Salian raised a hand for silence.

"I admit I find this difficult to believe," he said at last. "I mean no disparagement to you, Tasslehoff Burrfoot," he added gently, smiling at the indignant kender. "But all know your race has a most lamentable tendency to, uh, exaggerate. It is obvious to me that Raistlin simply charmed this—this *creature*"— Par-Salian spoke with disgust—"to use her and—"

"Me no creature!"

Bupu lifted her tear-stained, mud-streaked face from the floor, her hair frizzed up like an angry cat's. Glaring at Par-Salian, she stood up and started forward, tripped over the bag she carried, and sprawled flat on the floor. Undaunted, the gully dwarf picked herself up and faced Par-Salian.

"Me know nothing 'bout big, powerful wizards." Bupu waved a grubby hand. "Me know nothing 'bout no charm spell. Me know magic is in this"— she scrabbled around in the bag, then drew forth the dead rat and waved it in Par-Salian's direction— "and me know that man you talk 'bout here is nice man. Him nice to me." Clutching the dead rat to her chest, Bupu stared tearfully at Par-Salian. "The others—the big man, the kender—they laugh at Bupu. They look at me like me some sort of bug."

Bupu rubbed her eyes. There was a lump in Tas's throat, and he felt lower than a bug himself.

Bupu continued, speaking softly. "Me know how me look." Her filthy hands tried in vain to smooth her dress, leaving streaks of dirt down it. "Me know me not pretty, like lady lying there." The gully dwarf

snuffled, but then she wiped her hand across her nose and—raising her head—looked at Par-Salian defiantly. "But him not call me 'creature!' Him call me 'little one.' Little one," she repeated.

For a moment, she was quiet, remembering. Then she heaved a gusty sigh. "I-I want to stay with him. But him tell me, 'no.' Him say he must walk roads that be dark. Him tell me, he want me to be safe. Him lay his hand on my head"—Bupu bowed her head, as if in memory— "and I feel warm inside. Then him tell me, 'Farewell, Bupu.' Him call me 'little one.'" Looking up, Bupu glanced around at the semi-circle. "Him never laugh at me," she said, choking. "Never!" She began to cry.

The only sounds in the room, for a moment, were the gully dwarf's sobs. Caramon put his hands over his face, overcome. Tas drew a shuddering breath and fished around for a handkerchief. After a few moments, Par-Salian rose from his stone chair and came to stand in front of the gully dwarf, who was regarding him with suspicion and hiccuping at the same time.

The great mage extended his hand. "Forgive me, Bupu," he said gravely, "if I offended you. I must confess that I spoke those cruel words on purpose, hoping to make you angry enough to tell your story. For, only then, could we be certain of the truth." Par-Salian laid his hand on Bupu's head, his face was drawn and tired, but he appeared exultant. "Maybe we did not fail, maybe he did learn some compassion,"† he murmured. Gently he stroked the gully dwarf's rough hair. "No, Raistlin would never laugh at you, little one. He knew, he remembered. There were too many who had laughed at him."

Tas couldn't see through his tears, and he heard Caramon weeping quietly beside him. The kender blew his nose on his handkerchief, then went up to retrieve Bupu, who was blubbering into the hem of Par-Salian's white robe.

"So this is the reason Lady Crysania made this journey?" Par-Salian asked Tas as the kender came near. The mage glanced at the still, white, cold form lying beneath the linen, her eyes staring sightlessly into the shadowy darkness. "She believes that she can rekindle the spark of goodness that we tried to light and failed?"

While Par-Salian is onto something here, he is still misjudging Raistlin. Raistlin did not learn compassion. On the contrary, it is compassion that is at the very heart of Raistlin's ambition. Treated as a "weakling" as a child and constantly overshadowed by his brother, Raistlin developed a great empathy and compassion for the "underdogs" of the world. This is why he was so kind to Bupu but so cruel and dismissive to others. This compassion is also the root of Raistlin's evil. He champions the down-trodden, but this has twisted into a hatred for the strong and powerful. This is why he gave Crysania the vision of the downtrodden back in Chapter 11. Hence his comment to Crysania: "We are not so very different." Raistlin is thus more of a tragic hero rather than a classical hero or villain.

"Yes," Tas answered, suddenly uncomfortable beneath the gaze of the mage's penetrating blue eyes.

"And why does she want to attempt this?" Par-Salian persisted.

Tas dragged Bupu to her feet and handed her his handkerchief, trying to ignore the fact that she stared at it in wonder, obviously having no idea what she was supposed to do with it. She blew her nose on the hem of her dress.

"Uh, well, Tika said—" Tas stopped, flushing.

"What did Tika say?" Par-Salian asked softly.

"Tika said"—Tas swallowed—"Tika said she was doing it . . . because she l-loved him—Raistlin."

Par-Salian nodded. His gaze went to Caramon. "What about you, twin?" he asked suddenly. Caramon's head lifted, he stared at Par-Salian with haunted eyes.

"Do you love him still? You have said you would go back to destroy Fistandantilus. The danger you face will be great. Do you love your brother enough to undertake this perilous journey? To risk your life for him, as this lady has done? Remember, before you answer, you do not go back on a quest to save the world. You go back on a quest to save a soul, nothing more. Nothing less."

Caramon's lips moved, but no sound came from them. His face was lighted by joy, however, a happiness that sprang from deep within him. He could only nod his head.

Par-Salian turned to face the assembled Conclave.

"I have made my decision," he began.

One of the Black Robes rose and cast her hood back. Tas saw that it was the woman who had brought him here. Anger burned in her eyes. She made a swift, slashing motion with her hand.

"We challenge this decision, Par-Salian," she said in a low voice. "And you know that means you cannot cast the spell."

"The Master of the Tower may cast the spell alone, Ladonna,"† Par-Salian replied grimly. "That power is given to all the Masters. Thus did Raistlin discover the secret when he became Master of the Tower in Palanthas. I do not need the help of either Red or Black."

There was a murmur from the Red Robes, as well; many looking at the Black Robes and nodding in agreement with them. Ladonna smiled.

The name Ladonna is evocative of Belladonna, a poisonous Old World plant in the nightshade family— a fitting name for the head of the Black Robes.

"Indeed, Great One," she said, "I know this. You do not need us for the casting of the spell, but you need us nonetheless. You need our cooperation, Par-Salian, our silent cooperation—else the shadows of our magic will rise and blot out the light of the silver moon. And you will fail."†

Par-Salian's face grew cold and gray. "What of the life of this woman?" he demanded, gesturing at Crysania.

"What is the life of a cleric of Paladine to us?" Ladonna sneered. "Our concerns are far greater and not to be discussed among outsiders. Send these away"—she motioned at Caramon—"and we will meet privately."

"I believe that is wise, Par-Salian," said the red-robed mage mildly. "Our guests are tired and hungry, and they would find our family disagreements most boring."

"Very well," Par-Salian said abruptly. But Tas could see the white-robed mage's anger as he turned to face them. "You will be summoned."

"Wait!" Caramon shouted, "I demand to be present! I—"

The big man stopped, nearly strangling himself. The Hall was gone, the mages were gone, the stone chairs were gone. Caramon was yelling at a hat stand.

Dizzily, Tas looked around. He and Caramon and Bupu were in a cozy room that might have come straight from the Inn of the Last Home. A fire burned in the grate, comfortable beds stood at one end. A table laden with food was near the fire, the smells of fresh-baked bread and roasted meat made his mouth water. Tas sighed in delight.

"I think this is the most wonderful place in the whole world," he said.

This reflects again the underlying themes of the story: when one side gets overbalanced, the other two sides unite to work back toward balance, even if those sides are otherwise opposed to each other.
—TRH

CHAPTER 14

The old white-robed mage sat in a study that was much like Raistlin's in the Tower of Palanthas, except that the books which lined Par-Salian's shelves were bound in white leather. The silver runes traced upon their spines and covers glinted in the light of a crackling fire. To anyone entering, the room seemed hot and stuffy. But Par-Salian was feeling the chill of age enter his bones. To him, the room was quite comfortable.

He sat at his desk, his eyes staring into the flames. He started slightly at a soft knock upon his door, then, sighing, he called softly, "Enter."

A young, white-robed mage opened the door, bowing to the black-robed mage who walked past him—as was proper to one of her standing. She accepted the homage without comment. Casting her hood aside, she swept past him into Par-Salian's

chamber and stopped, just inside the doorway. The white-robed mage gently shut the door behind her, leaving the two heads of their Orders alone together.

Ladonna† cast a quick, penetrating glance about the room. Much of it was lost in shadow, the fire casting the only light. Even the drapes had been closed, blotting out the moons' eerie glow. Raising her hand, Ladonna murmured a few, soft words. Several items in the room began to gleam with a weird, reddish light indicating that they had magical properties—a staff leaning up against the wall, a crystal prism on Par-Salian's desk, a branched candelabra, a gigantic hourglass, and several rings on the old man's fingers among others. These did not seem to alarm Ladonna, she simply looked at each and nodded. Then, satisfied, she sat down in a chair near the desk. Par-Salian watched her with a slight smile on his lined face.

"There are no Creatures from Beyond lurking in the corners, Ladonna, I assure you," the old mage said dryly. "Had I wanted to banish you from this plane, I could have done so long ago, my dear."

"When we were young?" Ladonna cast aside her hood. Iron-gray hair, woven into an intricate braid coiled about her head, framed a face whose beauty seemed enhanced by the lines of age that appeared to have been drawn by a masterful artist, so well did they highlight her intelligence and dark wisdom. "That would have been a contest indeed, Great One."

"Drop the title, Ladonna," Par-Salian said. "We have known each other too long for that."

"Known each other long and well, Par-Salian," Ladonna said with a smile. "Quite well," she murmured softly, her eyes going to the fire.

"Would you go back to our youth, Ladonna?" Par-Salian asked.

She did not answer for a moment, then she looked up at him and shrugged. "To trade power and wisdom and skill for what? Hot blood? Not likely, my dear. What about you?"

"I would have answered the same twenty years ago," Par-Salian said, rubbing his temples. "But now . . . I wonder."

"I did not come to relive old times, no matter how pleasant," Ladonna said, clearing her throat,

"An extraordinarily beautiful human female in her 60s, Ladonna is a powerful wizardess who rules over the Black Robes only because Raistlin has never challenged her. Despite her age—which she scorns to hide by means of magical arts—Ladonna is still a woman of striking appearance. She has iron gray hair that she wears woven in the most intricate designs upon her head. Her black robes are rich and luxurious, glittering with runes of protection stitched in silver. She wears many jewels, some of which are magical and others not, for Ladonna has a weakness for fine jewelry. In their youth, Ladonna and Par-Salian were lovers and there is still a kind of affection and understanding between them.." [DRAGONLANCE Adventures, by Tracy Hickman and Margaret Weis, TSR, Inc., 1987, p. 111.]

183

her voice suddenly stern and cold. "I have come to oppose this madness." She leaned forward, her dark eyes flashing. "You are not serious, I hope, Par-Salian? Even you cannot be soft-hearted or soft-headed enough to send that stupid human back in time to try and stop Fistandantilus? Think of the danger! He could change history! We could all cease to exist!"

"Bah! Ladonna, *you* think!" Par-Salian snapped. "Time is a great flowing river, vaster and wider than any river we know. Throw a pebble into the rushing water—does the water suddenly stop? Does it begin to flow backward? Does it turn in its course and flow another direction? Of course not! The pebble creates a few ripples on the surface, perhaps, but then it sinks. The river flows onward, as it has ever done."

"What are you saying?" Ladonna asked, regarding Par-Salian warily.

"That Caramon and Crysania are pebbles, my dear. They will no more affect the flow of time than two rocks thrown into the Thon-Tsalariant would affect its course. They are pebbles—" he repeated.

The prefix Thon *signifies both "river" and "road" since the elves used the rivers primarily as a means of transportation.*

"We underestimate Raistlin, Dalamar says," Ladonna interrupted. "He must be fairly certain of his success, or he would not take this risk. He is no fool, Par-Salian."

"He is certain of acquiring the magic. In that we cannot stop him. But that magic will be meaningless to him without the cleric. He needs Crysania." The white-robed mage sighed. "And that is why we must send her back in time."

"I fail to see—"

"She must die, Ladonna!" Par-Salian snarled. "Must I conjure a vision for you? She must be sent back to a time when *all* clerics passed from this land. Raistlin said that we would have to send her back. We would have no choice. As he himself said—this is the one way we can thwart his plans! It is his greatest hope—and his greatest fear. He needs to take her with him to the Gate, but he needs her to come willingly! Thus he plans to shake her faith, disillusion her enough so that she will work with him." Par-Salian waved his hand irritably. "We are wasting time. He leaves in the morning. We must act at once."

"Then keep her here!" Ladonna said scornfully. "That seems simple enough."

Par-Salian shook his head. "He would simply return for her. And—by then he will have the magic. He will have the power to do what he chooses."

"Kill her."

"That has been tried and failed. Besides, could even you, with your arts, kill her while she is under Paladine's protection?"

"Perhaps the god will prevent her going, then?"

"No. The augury I cast was neutral. Paladine has left the matter in our hands. Crysania is nothing but a vegetable here, nor will ever be anything more, since none alive today have the power to restore her. Perhaps Paladine intends her to die in a place and time where her death will have meaning so that she may fulfill her life's cycle."

"So you will send her to her death," Ladonna murmured, looking at Par-Salian in amazement. "Your white robes will be stained red with blood, my old friend."

Par-Salian slammed his hands upon the table, his face contorted in agony. "I don't enjoy this, damn it! But what can I do? Can't you see the position I'm in? Who sits now as the Head of the Black Robes?"

"I do," Ladonna replied.

"Who sits as the Head if *he* returns victorious?"

Ladonna frowned and did not answer.

"Precisely. My days are numbered, Ladonna. I know that. Oh"—he gestured—"my powers are still great. Perhaps they have never been greater. But every morning when I awake, I feel the fear. Will today be the day it fails? Every time I have trouble recalling† a spell, I shiver. Someday, I know, I will not be able to remember the correct words." He closed his eyes. "I am tired, Ladonna, very tired. I want to do nothing more than stay in this room, near this warm fire, and record in these books the knowledge I have acquired through the years. Yet I dare not step down now, for I know who would take my place."

The old mage sighed. "I will choose my successor, Ladonna," he said softly. "I will not have my position wrested from my hands. My stake in this is greater than any of yours."

"Perhaps not," Ladonna said, staring at the flames. "If he returns victorious, there will no longer be a

This rather nice story element is inspired by AD&D. Concerning the casting of spells, the Player's Handbook states ". . . it is the memorization that is important. To draw on magical energy, the wizard must shape specific mental patterns in his mind. These patterns are very complicated and alien to normal thought, so they don't register in the mind as normal learning. To shape these patterns, the wizard must spend time memorizing the spell, twisting his thoughts and recasting the energy patters each time to account for subtle changes—planetary motions, seasons, times of day, and more. [2ⁿᵈ Edition ADVANCED DUNGEONS & DRAGONS *Player's Handbook, by David "Zeb" Cook, TSR, 1997, p. 107.]*

185

Conclave. We shall all be his servants." Her hand clenched. "I still oppose this, Par-Salian! The danger is too great! Let her remain here, let Raistlin learn what he can from Fistandantilus. We can deal with him when he returns! He is powerful, of course, but it will take him years to master the arts that Fistandantilus knew when he died! We can use that time to arm ourselves against him! We can—"

There was rustling in the shadows of the room. Ladonna started and turned, her hand darting immediately to a hidden pocket in her robe.

"Hold, Ladonna," said a mild voice. "You need not waste your energies on a shield spell. I am no Creature from Beyond, as Par-Salian has already stated." The figure stepped into the light of the fire, its red robes gleaming softly.

The name Justarius is evocative of "just" and "justice," perhaps suggesting that the head of the Red Robes, who stand for Neutrality, must be neutral or impartial in order to be just.

Ladonna settled back with a sigh, but there was a glint of anger in her eyes that would have made an apprentice start back in alarm. "No, Justarius."† she said coolly, "you are no Creature from Beyond. So you managed to hide yourself from me? How clever you have become, Red Robe." Twisting around in her chair, she regarded Par-Salian with scorn. "You *are* getting old, my friend, if you required help to deal with me!"

"Oh, I'm sure Par-Salian is just as surprised to see me here as you are, Ladonna," Justarius stated. Wrapping his red robes around him, he walked slowly forward to sit down in another chair before Par-Salian's desk. He limped as he walked, his left foot dragging the ground. Raistlin was not the only mage ever injured in the Test.

Justarius smiled. "Though the Great One has become quite adept at hiding his feelings," he added.

"I was aware of you," Par-Salian said softly. "You know me better than that, my friend."

Justarius shrugged. "It doesn't really matter. I was interested in hearing what you had to say to Ladonna—"

"I would have said the same to you."

"Probably less, for I would not have argued as she has. I agree with you, I have from the beginning. But that is because we know the truth, you and I."

"What truth?" Ladonna repeated. Her gaze went from Justarius to Par-Salian, her eyes dilating with anger.

"You will have to show her," Justarius† said, still in the same mild voice. "She will not be convinced otherwise. Prove to her how great the danger is."

"You will show me nothing!" Ladonna said, her voice shaking. "I would believe nothing you two devised—"

"Then let her do it herself," Justarius suggested, shrugging.

Par-Salian frowned, then—scowling—he shoved the crystal prism upon the desk toward her. He pointed. "The staff in the corner belonged to Fistandantilus—the greatest, most powerful wizard who has ever lived. Cast a Spell of Seeing, Ladonna. Look at the staff."

Ladonna touched the prism hesitantly, her glance moving suspiciously once more from Par-Salian to Justarius, then back.

"Go ahead!" Par-Salian snapped. "I have not tampered with it." His gray eyebrows came together. "You know I cannot lie to you, Ladonna."

"Though you may lie to others," Justarius said softly.

Par-Salian cast the red-robed mage an angry look but did not reply.

Ladonna picked up the crystal with sudden resolution. Holding it in her hand, she raised it to her eyes, chanting words that sounded harsh and sharp. A rainbow of light beamed from the prism to the plain wooden staff that leaned up against the wall in a dark corner of the study. The rainbow expanded as it welled out from the crystal to encompass the entire staff. Then it wavered and coalesced, forming into the shimmering image of the owner of the staff.

Ladonna stared at the image for long moments, then slowly lowered the prism from her eye. The moment she withdrew her concentration from it, the image vanished, the rainbow light winked out. Her face was pale.

"Well, Ladonna," Par-Salian asked quietly, after a moment. "Do we go ahead?"

"Let me see the Time Travel spell," she said, her voice taut.

Par-Salian made an impatient gesture. "You know that is not possible, Ladonna! Only the Masters of the Tower may know this spell—"

"A human male in his late 40s, Justarius is considered by many to be next in line as Head of the Conclave when Par-Salian retires. A big, robust man with an open, honest face, Justarius walks with a pronounced limp. His left leg was crippled during the magical Test. How or why no one knows, but it is rumored that Justarius was exceptionally proud of his physical prowess when young and that his Test forced him to choose between physical strength or his magic."
[DRAGONLANCE Adventures, by Tracy Hickman and Margaret Weis, TSR, Inc., 1987, p. 110.]

"I am within my rights to see the description, at least," Ladonna returned coldly. "Hide the components and the words from my sight, if you will. But I demand to see the expected results." Her expression hardened. "Forgive me if I do not trust you, old friend, as I might once have done. But your robes seem to be turning as gray as your hair."

Justarius† smiled, as if this amused him.

Par-Salian sat for a moment, irresolute.

"Tomorrow morning, friend," Justarius murmured.

Angrily, Par-Salian rose to his feet. Reaching beneath his robes, he drew forth a silver key that he wore around his neck on a silver chain—the key that only the Master of a Tower of High Sorcery may use. Once there were five, now only two remained. As Par-Salian took the key from around his neck and inserted it into an ornately carved wooden chest standing near his desk, all three mages present were wondering silently if Raistlin was—even now—doing the same thing with the key *he* possessed, perhaps even drawing out the same spellbook, bound in silver. Perhaps even turning slowly and reverently through the same pages, casting his gaze upon the spells known only to the Masters of the Towers.

Par-Salian opened the book, first muttering the prescribed words that only the Masters know. If he had not, the book would have vanished from beneath his hand. Arriving at the correct page, he lifted the prism from where Ladonna had set it, then held it above the page, repeating the same harsh, sharp words Ladonna had used.

The rainbow light streamed down from the prism, brightening the page. At a command from Par-Salian, the light from the prism beamed out to strike a bare wall opposite them.

"Look," Par-Salian said, his anger still apparent in his voice. "There, upon the wall. Read the description of the spell."

Ladonna and Justarius turned to face the wall where they could read the words as the prism presented them. Neither Ladonna nor Justarius could read the components needed or the words required. Those appeared as gibberish, either through Par-Salian's art or the conditions imposed by the spell itself. But the description of the spell was clear.

The ability to travel back in time is available to elves, humans, and ogres, since these were the races created by the gods at the beginning of time and so travel within its flow. The spell may not be used by dwarves, gnomes, or kender, since the creation of these races was an accident, unforeseen by the gods. (Refer to the Gray Stone of Gargarth, see Appendix G.) The introduction of any of these races into a previous time span could have serious repercussions on the present, although what these might be is unknown. (A note in Par-Salian's wavering handwriting had the word 'draconian' inked in among the forbidden races.

There are dangers, however, that the spellcaster needs to be fully aware of before proceeding. If the spellcaster dies while back in time, this will affect nothing in the future, for it will be as if the spellcaster died this day in the present. His other death will affect neither the past nor the present nor the future, except as it would have normally affected those. Therefore, we do not waste power on any type of protection spell.

The spellcaster will not be able to change or affect what has occurred previously in any way.† That is an obvious precaution. Thus this spell is really useful only for study. That was the purpose for which it was designed. (Another note, this time in a handwriting much older than Par-Salian's adds on the margin—*"It is not possible to prevent the Cataclysm. So we have learned to our great sorrow and at a great cost. May his soul rest with Paladine."*)

"So *that's* what happened to him,"† Justarius said with a low whistle of surprise. "That was a well-kept secret."

"They were fools to even try it," Par-Salian said, "but they were desperate."

"As are we," Ladonna added bitterly. "Well, is there more?"

"Yes, the next page," Par-Salian replied.

If the spellcaster is not going himself but is sending back another (please note racial precaution on previous page), he or she should equip the one traveling with a device that can be activated at will and so return the traveler to his own time. Descriptions of such devices and their making will be found following—

"And so forth," Par-Salian said. The rainbow light disappeared, swallowed in the mage's hand as Par-Salian wrapped his fingers around it. "The

This is true of the cosmology of Krynn and to a certain extent forms the basis not only of time travel in this novel but also of events in the War of Souls trilogy. For a more complete explanation of time travel and its proscriptions and oddities in Krynn, please see Appendix B. —TRH

Him who? People want to know the story behind the mysterious time traveler. We'll never tell! —MW

rest is devoted to the technical details of making such a device. I have an ancient one. I will give it to Caramon."

His emphasis on the man's name was unconscious, but everyone in the room noticed it. Ladonna smiled wryly, her hands softly caressing her black robes. Justarius shook his head. Par-Salian himself, realizing the implications, sank down in his chair, his face lined with sorrow.

"So Caramon will use it alone," Justarius said. "I understand why we send Crysania, Par-Salian. She must go back, never to return. But Caramon?"

"Caramon is my redemption," Par-Salian said without looking up. The old mage stared at his hands that lay, trembling, on the open spellbook. "He is going on a journey to save a soul, as I told him. But it will not be his brother's." Par-Salian looked up, his eyes filled with pain. His gaze went first to Justarius, then to Ladonna. Both met that gaze with complete understanding.

"The truth could destroy him," Justarius said.

"There is very little left to destroy, if you ask me," Ladonna remarked coldly. She rose to her feet. Justarius rose with her, staggering a little until he obtained his balance on his crippled leg. "As long as you get rid of the woman, I care little what you do about the man, Par-Salian. If you believe it will wash the blood from your robes, then help him, by all means," She smiled grimly. "In a way, I find this quite funny. Maybe—as we get older—we aren't so different after all, are we, my dear?"

"The differences are there, Ladonna," Par-Salian said, smiling wearily. "It is the crisp, clear outlines that begin to fade and blur in our sight. Does this mean the Black Robes will go along with my decision?"

"It seems we have no choice," Ladonna said without emotion. "If you fail—"

"Enjoy my downfall," Par-Salian said wryly.

"I will," the woman answered softly, "the more so as it will probably be the last thing I enjoy in this life. Farewell, Par-Salian."

"Farewell, Ladonna," he said.

"A wise woman," Justarius remarked as the door shut behind her.

"A rival worthy of you, my friend." Par-Salian

returned to his seat behind the desk. "I will enjoy watching you two do battle for my position."

"I sincerely hope you have the opportunity to do so," Justarius said, his hand on the door. "When will you cast the spell?"

"Early morning," Par-Salian said, speaking heavily. "It takes days of preparation. I have already spent long hours working on it."

"What about assistance?"

"No one, not even an apprentice. I will be exhausted at the end. See to the disbanding of the Conclave, will you, my friend?"

"Certainly. And the kender and the gully dwarf?"

"Return the gully dwarf to her home with whatever small treasures you think she would like. As for the kender"—Par-Salian smiled—"you may send him wherever he would like to go—barring the moons, of course.† As for treasure, I'm certain *he* will have acquired a sufficient amount before he leaves. Do a surreptitious check on his pouches, but, if it's nothing important, let him keep what he finds."

Justarius nodded. "And Dalamar?"

Par-Salian's face grew grim. "The dark elf has undoubtedly left already. He would not want to keep his *Shalafi* waiting." Par-Salian's fingers drummed on the desk, his brow furrowed in frustration. "It is a strange charm Raistlin possesses! You never met him, did you? No. I felt it myself and I cannot understand. . . ."

"Perhaps I can," Justarius said. "We've all been laughed at one time in our lives. We've all been jealous of a sibling. We have felt pain and suffered, just as he has suffered.† And we've all longed—just once—for the power to crush our enemies! We pity him. We hate him. We fear him—all because there is a little of him in each of us, though we admit it to ourselves only in the darkest part of the night."

"If we admit it to ourselves at all. That wretched cleric! Why did she have to get involved?" Par-Salian clasped his head in his shaking hands.

"Farewell, my friend," Justarius said gently. "I will wait for you outside the laboratory should you need help when it is all over."

"Thank you," Par-Salian whispered without raising his head.

This comment may not be as absurd as it seems. In the novel Darkness and Light, *by Paul B. Thompson and Tonya C. Cook, Sturm and Kitiara had an adventure on the moon Lunitari.*

This provides us the key to Raistlin's character and the main reason why so many readers can empathize with him. —MW

This is why Raistlin is so identifiable for all of us—because we, too, have been Raistlin at one point or another in our lives. —TRH

Justarius limped from the study. Shutting the door too hastily, he caught the hem of his red robe and was forced to open it again to free himself. Before he closed the door again, he heard the sound of weeping.

CHAPTER 15

asslehoff Burr-
foot was bored.

And, as everyone knows, there is nothing more
dangerous on Krynn than a bored kender.

Tas and Bupu and Caramon had finished their
meal—a very dull one. Caramon, lost in his thoughts,
never said a word but sat wrapped in bleak silence
while absent-mindedly devouring nearly everything
in sight. Bupu did not even sit. Grabbing a bowl, she
scooped out the contents with her hands, shoveling
it into her mouth with a rapidity learned long ago at
gully dwarf dining tables. Putting that one down, she
started on another and polished off a dish of gravy,
the butter, the sugar and cream, and finally half a dish
of milk potatoes† before Tas realized what she was
doing. He just barely saved a salt cellar.

"Well," said Tas brightly. Pushing back his empty
plate, he tried to ignore the sight of Bupu grabbing it

*Milk potatoes are what we
know as "mashed"
potatoes—that is, potatoes
that are mashed up and
then mixed with milk. Not
as popular in Ansalon as
Otik's famous spiced
potatoes. —MW*

and licking it clean. "I'm feeling much better. How about you, Caramon? Let's go explore!"

"Explore!" Caramon gave him such a horrified look that Tas was momentarily taken aback. "Are you mad? I wouldn't set foot outside that door for all the wealth in Krynn!"

"Really?" Tas asked eagerly. "Why not? Oh, tell me, Caramon! What's out there?"

"I don't know." The big man shuddered. "But it's bound to be awful."

"I didn't see any guards—"

"No, and there's a damn good reason for that," Caramon snarled. "Guards aren't needed around here. I can see that look in your eye, Tasslehoff, and you just forget about it right now! Even if you could get out"—Caramon gave the door to the room a haunted look—"which I doubt, you'd probably walk into the arms of a lich† or worse!"

Tas's eyes opened wide. He managed, however, to squelch an exclamation of delight. Looking down at his shoes, he muttered, "Yeah, I guess you're right, Caramon. I'd forgotten where we were."

"I guess you did," Caramon said severely. Rubbing his aching shoulders, the big man groaned. "I'm dead tired. I've got to get some sleep. You and what's-er-name there turn in, too. All right?"

"Sure, Caramon," Tasslehoff said.

Bupu, belching contently, had already wrapped herself up in a rug before the fire, using the remainder of the bowl of milk potatoes for a pillow.

Caramon eyed the kender suspiciously. Tas assumed the most innocent look a kender could possibly assume, the result of which was that Caramon shook his finger at him sternly.

"Promise me you won't leave this room, Tasslehoff Burrfoot. Promise just like you'd promise . . . say, Tanis, if he were here."

"I promise," Tas said solemnly, "just like I'd promise Tanis—if he were here."

"Good." Caramon sighed and collapsed onto a bed that creaked in protest, the mattress sagging clear to the floor beneath the big man's weight. "I guess someone'll wake us up when they decide what they're going to do."

"Will you really go back in time, Caramon?" Tas asked wistfully, sitting down on his own bed and

Although the word "lich" is literally just an archaic term for "corpse," in the DRAGONLANCE setting it is far more ominous. A lich is a powerful wizard who, in his quest for immortality, has become one of the undead, but one still in possession of all of his arcane powers.

pretending to unlace his boots.

"Yeah, sure. 'S no big thing," Caramon murmured sleepily. "Now get some sleep and . . . thanks, Tas. You've been . . . you've been . . . a big help. . . ." His words trailed off into a snore.

Tas held perfectly still, waiting until Caramon's breathing became even and regular. That didn't take long because the big man was emotionally and physically exhausted. Looking at Caramon's pale, careworn, and tear-streaked face, the kender felt a moment's twinge of conscience. But kender are accustomed to dealing with twinges of conscience— just as humans are accustomed to dealing with mosquito bites.

"He'll never know I've been gone," Tas said to himself as he sneaked across the floor past Caramon's bed. "And I really didn't promise *him* I wouldn't go anywhere. I promised Tanis. And Tanis isn't here, so the promise doesn't count. Besides, I'm certain he would have wanted to explore, if he hadn't been so tired."

By the time Tas crept past Bupu's grubby little body, he had firmly convinced himself that Caramon had ordered him to look around before going to bed. He tried the door handle with misgivings, remembering Caramon's warning. But it opened easily. We *are* guests then, not prisoners. Unless there was a lich standing guard outside. Tas poked his head around the door frame. He looked up the hall, then down the hall. Nothing. Not a lich in sight. Sighing a bit in disappointment, Tas slipped out the door, then shut it softly behind him.

The hallway ran to his left and to his right, vanishing around shadowy corners at either end. It was barren, cold, and empty. Other doors branched off from the hallway, all of them dark, all of them closed. There were no decorations of any kind, no tapestries hung on the walls, no carpets covered the stone floor. There weren't even any lights, no torches, no candles. Apparently the mages were supposed to provide their own if they did any wandering about after dark.

A window at one end did allow the light of Solinari, the silver moon, to filter through its glass panes, but that was all. The rest of the hallway was completely dark. Too late Tas thought of sneaking

back into the room for a candle. No. If Caramon woke up, he might not remember he had told the kender to go exploring.

"I'll just pop into one of these other rooms and borrow a candle," Tas said to himself. "Besides, that's a good way to meet people."

Gliding down the hall quieter than the moonbeams that danced on the floor, Tas reached the next door. "I won't knock, in case they're asleep," he reasoned and carefully turned the doorknob. "Ah, locked!" he said, feeling immensely cheered.

This would give him something to do for a few minutes at least. Pulling out his lock-picking tools, he held them up to the moonlight to select the proper size wire for this particular lock.

"I hope it's not magically locked," he muttered, the sudden thought making him grow cold. Magicians did that sometimes, he knew—a habit kender consider highly unethical. But maybe in the Tower of High Sorcery, surrounded by mages, they wouldn't figure it would be worthwhile. "I mean, anyone could just come along and *blow* the door down," Tas reasoned.

Sure enough, the lock opened easily. His heart beating with excitement, Tas shoved the door open quietly and peered inside. The room was lit only by the faint glow of a dying fire. He listened. He couldn't hear anyone in it, no sounds of snoring or breathing, so he walked in, padding softly. His sharp eyes found the bed. It was empty. No one home.

"Then they won't mind if I borrow their candle," the kender said to himself happily. Finding a candlestick, he lit the wick with a glowing coal. Then he gave himself up to the delights of examining the occupant's belongings, noticing as he did so that whoever resided in this room was *not* a very tidy person.

About two hours and many rooms later, Tas was wearily returning to his own room, his pouches bulging with the most fascinating items—all of which he was fully determined to return to their owners in the morning. He had picked most of them up off the tops of tables where they had obviously been carelessly tossed. He found more than a few on the floor (he was certain the owners had lost them) and had even rescued several from the pockets of

robes that were probably destined to be laundered, in which case these items would certainly have been misplaced.

Looking down the hall, he received a severe shock, however, when he saw light streaming out from under their door!

"Caramon!" He gulped, but at that moment a hundred plausible excuses for being out of the room entered his brain. Or perhaps Caramon might not even have missed him yet. Maybe he was into the dwarf spirits. Considering this possibility, Tas tiptoed up to the closed door of their room and pressed his ear against it, listening.

He heard voices. One he recognized immediately— Bupu's. The other . . . he frowned. It seemed familiar . . . where had he heard it?

"Yes, I am going to send you back to the Highpulp, if that is where you want to go? But first you must tell where the Highpulp is."

The voice sound faintly exasperated. Apparently, this had been going on for some time. Tas put his eye to the keyhole. He could see Bupu, her hair clotted with milk potatoes, glaring suspiciously at a red-robed figure. Now Tas remembered where he'd heard the voice—that was the man at the Conclave, who kept questioning Par-Salian!

"High*bulp*!" Bupu repeated indignantly. "Not Highpulp! And Highbulp is home. You send me home."

"Yes, of course. Now where is home?"

"Where Highbulp is."

"And where is the Highpul-bulp?" the red-robed mage asked in hopeless tones.

"Home," Bupu stated succinctly. "I tell you that before. You got ears under that hood? Maybe you deaf." The gully dwarf disappeared from Tas's sight for a moment, diving into her bag. When she reappeared, she held another dead lizard, a leather thong wrapped around its tail. "Me cure. You stick tail in ear and—"

"Thank you," said the mage hastily, "but my hearing is quite perfect, I assure you. Uh, what do you call your home? What is the name?"

"The Pitt. Two Ts. Some fancy name, huh?" Bupu said proudly. "That Highbulp's idea. Him ate book once. Learned lots. All right here." She patted her stomach.

Tas clapped his hand over his mouth to keep from giggling. The red-robed mage was experiencing similar problems as well. Tas saw the man's shoulders shake beneath his red robes, and it took him a while to respond. When he did, his voice had a faint quiver.

"What . . . what do humans call the name of your—the—uh—Pitt?"

Tas saw Bupu scowl. "Dumb name. Sound like someone spit up. Skroth."

"Skroth," the red-robed mage repeated, mystified. "Skroth," he muttered. Then he snapped his fingers. "I remember. The kender said it in the Conclave. Xak Tsaroth?"

"Me say that once already. You sure you not want lizard cure for ears? You put tail—"

Heaving a sigh of relief, the red-robed mage held his hand out over Bupu's head. Sprinkling what looked like dust down over her (Bupu sneezed violently), Tas heard the mage chant strange words.†

"Me go home now?" Bupu asked hopefully.

The mage did not answer, he kept chanting.

"Him not nice," she muttered to herself, sneezing again as the dust slowly coated her hair and body. "None of them nice. Not like my pretty man." She wiped her nose, snuffling. "Him not laugh . . . him call me 'little one.' "

The dust on the gully dwarf began to glow a faint yellow. Tas gasped softly. The glow grew brighter and brighter, changing color, turning yellow-green, then green, then green-blue, then blue and suddenly—

"Bupu!" Tas whispered.

The gully dwarf was gone!

"And I'm next!" Tas realized in horror. Sure enough, the red-robed mage was limping across the room to the bed where the thoughtful kender had made up a dummy of himself so that Caramon wouldn't be worried in case he woke up.

"Tasslehoff Burrfoot" the red-robed mage called softly. He had passed beyond Tas's sight. The kender stood frozen, waiting for the mage to discover he was missing. Not that he was afraid of getting caught. He was used to getting caught and was fairly certain he could talk his way out of it. But he *was* afraid of being sent home! They didn't really expect Caramon to go anywhere without him, did they?

Notice that the mage is casting the spell just like he would in a game of AD&D: using spell components in conjunction with an incantation.

"Caramon *needs* me!" Tas whispered to himself in agony. "They don't know what bad shape he's in. Why, what would happen if he didn't have me along to drag him out of bars?"

"Tasslehoff," the red-robed mage's voice repeated. He must be nearing the bed.

Hurriedly, Tas's hand dove into his pouch. Pulling out a fistful of junk, he hoped against hope he'd found something useful. Opening his small hand, he held it up to the candlelight. He had come up with a ring, a grape, and a lump of mustache wax. The wax and the grape were obviously out. He tossed them to the floor.

"Caramon!" Tas heard the red-robed mage say sternly. He could hear Caramon grunt and groan and pictured the mage shaking him. "Caramon, wake up. Where's the kender?"

Trying to ignore what was happening in the room, Tas concentrated on examining the ring. It was probably magical. He'd picked it up in the third room to the left. Or was it the fourth? And magical rings *usually* worked just by being worn. Tas was an expert on the subject. He'd accidentally put on a magical ring once that had teleported him right into the heart of an evil wizard's palace.† There was every possibility this might do the same. He had no idea what it did.

Maybe there was some sort of clue on the ring?

Tas turned it over, nearly dropping it in his haste. Thank the gods Caramon was so hard to wake up!

It was a plain ring, carved out of ivory, with two small pink stones. There were some runes traced on the inside. Tas recalled† his magical Glasses of Seeing with a pang, but they were lost in Neraka, unless some draconian was wearing them.

"Wha . . . wha . . ." Caramon was babbling. "Kender? I told him . . . don't go out there . . . liches. . . ."

"Damn!" The red-robed mage was heading for the door.

Please, Fizban! the kender whispered, if you remember me at all, which I don't suppose you do, although you might—I was the one who kept finding your hat. Please, Fizban! Don't let them send Caramon off without me. Make this a Ring of Invisibility. Or at least a Ring of Something that will keep them from catching me!

This is one of Tasslehoff's famous kender tales (which may or may not have actually happened), which he first began telling back in Dragons of Autumn Twilight, *Book I, Chapter 9.*

For more on what Tas is remembering here, see Dragons of Winter Night, *Book I, Chapter 6.*

Closing his eyes tightly so he wouldn't see any-thing Horrible he might accidentally conjure up, Tas thrust the ring over his thumb. (At the last moment he opened his eyes, so that he wouldn't miss seeing anything Horrible he might conjure up.)

At first, nothing happened. He could hear the red-robed mage's halting footsteps coming nearer and nearer the door.

Then—something *was* happening, although not quite what Tas expected. The hall was growing! There was a rushing sound in the kender's ears as the walls swooped past him and the ceiling soared away from him. Open-mouthed, he watched as the door grew larger and larger, until it was an immense size.

What have I done? Tas wondered in alarm. Have I made the Tower grow? Do you suppose anyone'll notice? If they do, will they be *very* upset?

The huge door opened with a gust of wind that nearly flattened the kender. An enormous red-robed figure filled the doorway.

A giant! Tas gasped. I've not only made the Tower grow! I've made the mages grow, too! Oh, dear. I guess they'll notice *that!* At least they will the first time they try to put on their shoes! And I'm sure they'll be upset. I would be if I was twenty feet tall and none of my clothes fit.

But the red-robed mage didn't seem at all per-turbed about suddenly shooting up in height, much to Tas's astonishment. He just peered up and down the hall, yelling, "Tasslehoff Burrfoot!"

He even looked right at where Tas was standing—and didn't see him!

"Oh, thank you, Fizban!" the kender squeaked. Then he coughed. His voice certainly did sound funny. Experimentally, he said, "Fizban?" again. Again, he squeaked.

At that moment, the red-robed mage glanced down.

"Ah, ha! And whose room have you escaped from, my little friend?" the mage said.

As Tasslehoff watched in awe, a giant hand reached down—it was reaching down for him! The fingers got nearer and nearer. Tas was so startled he couldn't run or do anything except wait for that gigantic hand to grab him. Then it would be all

over! They'd send him home instantly, if they didn't inflict a worse punishment on him for enlarging their Tower when he wasn't at all certain that they wanted it enlarged.

The hand hovered over him and then picked him up by his tail.

"My tail!" Tas thought wildly, squirming in midair as the hand lifted him off the floor. "I haven't got a tail! But I must! The hand's got hold of me by something!"

Twisting his head around. Tas saw that indeed, he did have a tail! Not only a tail, but four pink feet! Four! And instead of bright blue leggings, he was wearing white fur!

"Now, then," boomed a stern voice right in one of his ears, "answer me, little rodent! Whose familiar are you?"

"The wizard's familiar is
another staple of the
AD&D wizard. Familiars
are typically small
creatures, such as cats,
frogs, ferrets, crows,
hawks, snakes, owls,
ravens, toads, weasels, or
even mice. A creature
acting as a familiar can
benefit a wizard, conveying
its sensory powers to its
master, conversing with
him, and serving as a
guard/scout/spy as well."
[2nd Edition ADVANCED
DUNGEONS & DRAGONS
Player's Handbook, by
David "Zeb" Cook, TSR,
1997, p. 174.]

amiliar! Tassle-
hoff clutched at the word. Familiar. . . . Talks with
Raistlin came back to his fevered mind.

"Some magi have animals that are bound to do
their bidding,"† Raistlin had told him once. "These
animals, or *familiars* as they are called, can act as an
extension of a mage's own senses. They can go places
he cannot, see things he is unable to see, hear conversations he has not been invited to share."

At the time, Tasslehoff had thought it a wonderful idea, although he recalled Raistlin had not
been impressed. He seemed to consider it a weakness, to be so heavily dependent upon another
living being.

"Well, answer me?" the red-robed mage demanded,
shaking Tasslehoff by the tail. Blood rushed to the
kender's head, making him dizzy, plus being held
by the tail was quite painful, to say nothing of the

indignity! All he could do, for a moment, was to give thanks that Flint couldn't see him.

I suppose, he thought bleakly, that familiars can talk. I hope they speak Common, not something strange—like Mouse, for example.

"I'm—I—uh—belong to"—what was a good name for a mage?—"Fa—Faikus," Tas squeaked, remembering hearing Raistlin use this name in connection with a fellow student long ago.

"Ah," the red-robed mage said with a frown, "I might have known. Were you out upon some errand for your master or simply roaming around loose?"

Fortunately for Tas, the mage changed his hold upon the kender, releasing his tail to grasp him firmly in his hand. The kender's front paws rested quivering on the red-robed mage's thumb, his now beady, bright-red eyes stared into the mage's cool, dark ones.

What shall I answer? Tas wondered frantically. Neither choice sounded very good.

"It—it's my n-night off," Tas said in what he hoped was an indignant tone of squeak.

"Humpf!" The mage sniffed. "You've been around that lazy Faikus too long, that's for certain. I'll have a talk with that young man in the morning. As for you, no, you needn't start squirming! Have you forgotten that Sudora's familiar prowls the halls at night? You could have been Marigold's dessert! Come along with me. After I'm finished with this evening's business, I'll return you to your master."

Tas, who had just been ready to sink his sharp little teeth into the mage's thumb, suddenly thought better of the idea. "Finished with this evening's business!" Of course, that had to be Caramon! This was better than being invisible! He would just go along for the ride!

The kender hung his head in what he imagined was a mousy expression of meekness and contrition. It seemed to satisfy the red-robed mage, for he smiled in a preoccupied manner and began to search the pocket of his robes for something.

"What is it, Justarius?" There was Caramon, looking befuddled and still half asleep, He peered vaguely up and down the hallway. "You find Tas?"

"The kender? No." The mage smiled again, this time rather ruefully. "It may be a while before we find him, I'm afraid—kender being very adept at hiding."

"You won't hurt him?" Caramon asked anxiously, so anxiously Tas felt sorry for the big man and longed to reassure him.

"No, of course not," Justarius replied soothingly, still searching through his robes. "Though," he added as an afterthought, "he might inadvertently hurt himself. There are objects lying around here it wouldn't be advisable to play with. Well, now, are you ready?"

"I really don't want to go until Tas is back and I know he's all right," Caramon said stubbornly.

"I'm afraid you haven't any choice," the mage said, and Tas heard the man's voice grow cool. "Your brother travels in the morning. You must be prepared to go then as well. It takes hours for Par-Salian to memorize and cast this complex spell. Already he has started. I have stayed too long searching for the kender, in fact. We are late. Come along."

"Wait . . . my things. . . ." Caramon said pathetically. "My sword . . ."

"You need not worry about any of that," Justarius answered. Apparently finding what he had been searching for, he drew a silken bag out of the pocket of his robes. "You may not go back in time with any weapon or any device from this time period. Part of the spell will see to it that you are suitably dressed for the period you journey within."

Caramon looked down at his body, bewildered. "Y-you mean, I'll have to change clothes? I won't have a sword? What—"

And you're sending this man back in time *by himself!* Tas thought indignantly. He'll last five minutes. Five minutes, if that long! No, by all the gods, I'm—

Just exactly what the kender was going to do was lost as he suddenly found himself popped headfirst into the silken bag!

Everything went inky black. He tumbled down to the bottom of the bag, feet over tail, landing on his head. From somewhere inside of him came a horrifying fear of being on his back in a vulnerable position. Frantically, he fought to right himself, scrabbling wildly at the slick sides of the bag with his clawed feet. Finally he was right side up, and the terrible feeling subsided.

So *that's* what it's like to be panic-stricken, Tas thought with a sigh. I don't think much of it, that's certain. And I'm very glad kender don't get that way, as a general rule. Now what?

Forcing himself to calm down and his little heart to stop racing, Tas crouched in the bottom of the silken bag and tried to think what to do next. He appeared to have lost track of what was going on in his wild scrambling, for—by listening—he could hear two pairs of footsteps walking down a stone hall; Caramon's heavy, booted feet and the mage's shuffling tread.

He also experienced a slight swaying motion, and he could hear the soft sounds of cloth rubbing against cloth. It suddenly occurred to him that the red-robed mage had undoubtedly suspended the sack he was in from his belt!

"What am I supposed to do back there? How'm I supposed to get back here afterwards—"

That was Caramon's voice, muffled a bit by the cloth bag but still fairly clear.

"All that will be explained to you." The mage's voice sounded overly patient. "I wonder—Are you having doubts, second thoughts perhaps. If so, you should tell us now—"

"No," Caramon's voice sounded firm, firmer than it had in a long time. "No, I'm not having doubts. I'll go. I'll take Lady Crysania back. It's my fault she's hurt, no matter what that old man says. I'll see that she gets the help she needs and I'll take care of this Fistandantilus for you."

"M-m-m-m."

Tas heard that "m-m-m-m," though he doubted Caramon could. The big man was rambling on about what he would do to Fistandantilus when he caught up with him. But Tas felt chilled, as he had when Par-Salian gave Caramon that strange, sad look in the Hall. The kender, forgetting where he was, squeaked in frustration.

"Shhhh," Justarius murmured absently, patting the bag with his hand. "This is only for a short while, then you'll be back in your cage, eating corn."

"Huh?" Caramon said. Tas could almost see the big man's startled look. The kender gnashed his small teeth. The word "cage" called up a dreadful picture in his mind and a truly alarming thought occurred to him—what if I can't get back to being myself?

"Oh, not you!" the mage said hastily. "I was talking to my little furry friend here. He's getting restless. If we weren't late, I'd take him back right now." Tas froze. "There, he seems to have settled down. Now, what were you saying?"

Tas didn't pay any more attention. Miserably, he clung to the bag with his small feet as it swayed back and forth, bumping gently against the mage's thigh as he limped along. Surely the spell could be reversed by simply taking off the ring?

Tas's fingers itched to try it and see The last magic ring he'd put on he hadn't been able to get off! What if this was the same? Was he doomed to a life of white fur and pink feet forever? At the thought, Tas wrapped one foot around the ring that was still stuck to a toe (or whatever) and almost pulled it off, just to make sure.

But the thought of suddenly bursting out of a silk bag, a full-grown kender, and landing at the mage's feet came to his mind. He forced his quivering little paw to stop. No. At least this way he was being taken to wherever Caramon was being taken. If nothing else, maybe he could go back with him in mouse shape. There might be worse things. . . .

How was he going to get out of the bag!

The kender's heart sank to his hind feet. Of course, getting out was easy if he turned back into himself. Only then they'd catch him and send him home! But if he stayed a mouse, he'd end up eating corn with Faikus! The kender groaned and hunkered down, his nose between his paws. This was by far the worst predicament he'd ever been in in his entire life, even counting the time the two wizards caught him running off with their woolly mammoth.† To top it off, he was beginning to feel queasy, what with the swaying motion of the bag, being cooped up, the funny smell inside the bag, and the bumping around and all.

"The whole mistake lay in saying a prayer to Fizban," the kender told himself gloomily. "He may be Paladine in reality, but I bet somewhere that wacky old mage is getting a real chuckle out of this."

Thinking about Fizban and how much he missed the crazy old mage wasn't making Tas feel any better, so he put the thought out of his mind and tried once more to concentrate on his surroundings, hoping to

The first mention of this is particular kender tale was in Dragons of Autumn Twilight, *Book I, Chapter 9. This one, at least, may have actually happened, as we find out in* Kendermore *by Mary Kirchoff.*

figure a way out. He stared into the silky darkness and suddenly—

"You idiot!" he told himself excitedly. "You lame-brained doorknob of a kender, as Flint would say! Or lamebrained mouse, because I'm not a kender anymore! I'm a mouse . . . and I have teeth!"

Hurriedly Tas took an experimental nibble. At first he couldn't get a grip on the slick fabric and he despaired once more.

"Try the seam, fool," he scolded himself severely, and sank his teeth into the thread that held the fabric together. It gave way almost instantly as his sharp little teeth sheared right through. Tas quickly nibbled away several more stitches and soon he could see something red—the mage's red robes! He caught a whiff of fresh air (what *had* that man been keeping in here!) and was so elated he quickly started to chew through some more.

Then he stopped. If he enlarged the hole anymore, he'd fall out. And he wasn't ready to, at least not yet. Not until they got to wherever it was they were going. Apparently that wasn't far off. It occurred to Tas that they had been climbing a series of stairs for some time now. He could hear Caramon wheezing from the unaccustomed exercise and even the red-robed mage appeared a bit winded.

"Why can't you just magic us up to this labora-tory place?" Caramon grumbled, panting.

"No!" Justarius answered softly, his voice tinged with awe. "I can feel the very air tingle and crackle with the power Par-Salian extends to perform this spell. I would have no minor spell of mine disturb the forces that are at work here this night!"

Tas shivered at this beneath his fur, and he thought Caramon might have done the same, for he heard the big man clear his throat nervously and then continue to climb in silence. Suddenly, they came to a halt.

"Are we here?" Caramon asked, trying to keep his voice steady.

"Yes," came the whispered answer. Tas strained to hear. "I will take you up these last few stairs, then—when we come to the door at the top—I will open it very softly and allow you to enter. Speak no word! Say nothing that might disturb Par-Salian in his con-centration. This spell takes days of preparation—"

"You mean he knew days ago he was going to be doing this?" Caramon interrupted harshly.

"Hush!" Justarius ordered, and his voice was tinged with anger. "Of course, he knew this was a possibility. He had to be prepared. It was well he did so, for we had no idea your brother intended to move this fast!" Tas heard the man draw a deep breath. When he spoke again, it was in calmer tones. "Now, I repeat, when we climb these last few stairs—speak no word! Is that understood?"

"Yes," Caramon sounded subdued.

"Do exactly as Par-Salian commands you to do. Ask no questions! Just obey. Can you do that?"

"Yes," Caramon sounded more subdued still. Tas heard a small tremor in the big man's reply.

He's scared, Tas realized. Poor Caramon. Why are they doing this to him? I don't understand. There's more going on here than meets the eye. Well, that makes it final. I don't care if I *do* break Par-Salian's concentration. I'll just have to risk it. Somehow, someway—I'm going to go with Caramon! He needs me. Besides—the kender sighed—to travel back in time! How wonderful. . . .

"Very well." Justarius hesitated, and Tas could feel his body grow tense and rigid. "I will say my farewells here, Caramon. May the gods go with you. What you are doing is dangerous . . . for us all. You cannot begin to comprehend the danger." This last was spoken so softly only Tas heard it, and the kender's ears twitched in alarm. Then the red-robed mage sighed. "I wish I could say I thought your brother was worth it"

"He is," Caramon said firmly. "You will see."

"I pray Gilean you are right. . . . Now, are you ready?"

"Yes."

Tas heard a rustling sound, as if the hooded mage nodded his head. Then they began to move again, climbing the stairs slowly. The kender peered out of the hole in the bottom of the sack, watching the shadowy steps slide by underneath him. He would have seconds only, he knew.

The stairs came to an end. He could see a broad stone landing beneath him. This is it! he told himself with a gulp. He could hear the rustling sound again and feel the mage's body move. A door creaked.

Quickly, Tas's sharp teeth sliced through the remaining threads that held the seam together. He heard Caramon's slow steps, entering the door. He heard the door starting to close. . . .

The seam gave way. Tas fell out of the sack. He had a passing moment to wonder if mice always landed on their feet—like cats. (He had once dropped a cat off the roof of his house to see if that old saying was true. It is.) And then he hit the stone floor running. The door was shut, the red-robed mage had turned away. Without stopping to look around, the kender darted swiftly and silently across the floor. Flattening his small body, he wriggled through the crack between the door and the floor and dove beneath a bookcase that was standing near the wall.

Tas paused to catch his breath and listen.

What if Justarius discovered him missing? Would he come back and look for him?

Stop this, Tas told himself sternly. He won't know where I fell out. And he probably wouldn't come back here, anyway. Might disturb the spell.

After a few moments, the kender's tiny heart slowed down its pace so that he could hear over the blood pounding in his ears. Unfortunately, his ears told him very little. He could hear a soft murmuring, as if someone were rehearsing lines for a street play. He could hear Caramon try to catch his breath from the long climb and still keep his breathing muffled so as not to disturb the mage. The big man's leather boots creaked as he shifted nervously from one foot to the other.

But that was all.

"I have to see!" Tas said to himself. "Otherwise I won't know what's going on."

Creeping out from underneath the bookcase, the kender truly began to experience this tiny, unique world he had tumbled into. It was a world of crumbs, a world of dust balls and thread, of pins and ash, of dried rose petals and damp tea leaves.† The insignificant was suddenly a world in itself. Furniture soared above him, like trees in a forest, and served about the same purpose—it provided cover. A candle flame was the sun, Caramon a monstrous giant.

Tas circled the man's huge feet warily. Catching a glimpse of movement out of one corner of his eye, he

Some of these details are part of the clutter of any old room, but things like dried rose petals, damp tea leaves, and perhaps even ash are meant to be understood as spell components.

saw a slippered foot beneath a white robe. Par-Salian. Swiftly, Tas made a dart for the opposite end of the room, which was, fortunately, lit only by candles.

Then Tas skidded to a stop. He had been in a mage's laboratory once before this, when he'd been wearing that cursed teleporting ring. The strange and wonderful sights he'd seen there remained with him, and now he halted just before he stepped inside a circle drawn on the stone floor with silver powder. Within the center of the circle that glistened in the candlelight lay Lady Crysania, her sightless eyes still staring up at nothing, her face as white as the linen that shrouded her.

This was where the magic would be performed!

The fur rising on the back of his neck, Tas hastily scrambled back, out of the way, cowering beneath an overturned chamber pot.† On the outside of the circle stood Par-Salian, his white robes glowing with an eerie light. In his hands, he held an object encrusted with jewels that sparkled and flashed as he turned it. It looked like a sceptre Tas had seen a Nordmaar† king holding once, yet this device looked far more fascinating. It was faceted and jointed in the most unique fashion. Parts of it moved, Tas saw, while— more amazing still—other parts moved without moving! Even as he watched, Par-Salian deftly manipulated the object, folding and bending and twisting, until it was no bigger than an egg. Muttering strange words over it, the archmage dropped it into the pocket of his robe.

Then, though Tas could have sworn Par-Salian never took a step, he was suddenly standing inside the silver circle, next to Crysania's inert figure. The mage bent over her, and Tas saw him place something in the folds of her robes. Then Par-Salian began to chant the language of magic, moving his gnarled hands above her in ever-widening circles. Glancing quickly at Caramon, Tas saw him standing near the circle, a strange expression on his face. It was the expression of one who is somewhere unfamiliar, yet who feels completely at home.

Of course, Tas thought wistfully, he grew up with magic. Maybe this is just like being back with his brother again.

Par-Salian rose to his feet, and the kender was shocked at the change that had come over the man.

In medieval times, the chamber pot was a large pot kept in the room that served, among other things, as a toilet. The servants would empty them out. If this one is overturned, one can only imagine Tasslehoff's dire surroundings.

Nordmaar is an area of northeastern Ansalon, where the city of Kalaman is located. The Companions spent some time there during the War of the Lance.

His face had aged years, it was gray in color, and he staggered as he stood. He made a beckoning motion to Caramon and the man came forward, walking slowly, stepping carefully over the silver powder. His face fixed in a dreamlike trance, he stood silently beside the still form of Crysania.

Par-Salian removed the device from his pocket and held it out to Caramon. The big man placed his hand on it and, for a moment, the two stood holding it together. Tas saw Caramon's lips move, though he heard no sound. It was as if the warrior were reading to himself, memorizing some magically communicated information. Then Caramon ceased to speak. Par-Salian raised his hands and, with the motion, lifted himself from the floor and floated backward out of the circle into the shadowy darkness of the laboratory.

Tas could no longer see him, but he could hear his voice. The chanting grew louder and louder and suddenly a wall of silver light sprang from the circle traced upon the floor. It was so bright it made Tas's red mouse eyes burn, but the kender could not look away. Par-Salian cried out now with such a loud voice that the very stones of the chamber themselves began to answer in a chorus of voices that rose from the depths of the ground.

Tas's gaze was fixed upon that shimmering curtain of power. Within it, he could see Caramon standing near Crysania, still holding the device in his hand. Then Tas gasped a tiny gasp that made no more sound in the chamber than a mouse's breath. He could still see the laboratory itself through that shimmering curtain, but now it seemed to wink on and off, as if fighting for its own existence. And— when it winked out—the kender caught a glimpse of somewhere else! Forests, cities, lakes, and oceans blurred in his vision, coming and going, people seen for an instant than vanishing, replaced by others.

Caramon's body began to pulse with the same regularity as the strange visions as he stood within the column of light. Crysania, too, was there and then she wasn't.

Tears streaked down past Tas's quivering nose, sliding down his whiskers. "Caramon's going on the greatest adventure of all time!" the kender thought bleakly. "And he's leaving *me* behind!"

For one wild moment, Tas fought with himself. Everything inside of him that was logical and con-scientious and Tanis-like told him—Tasslehoff, don't be a fool. This is Big Magic. You're likely to really Mess Things Up! Tas heard that voice, but it was being drowned out by all the chanting and the stones singing and, soon, it vanished altogether. . . .

Par-Salian never heard the small squeak. Lost in his casting of the spell, he caught only the barest glimpse of movement out of the comer of his eye. Too late, he saw the mouse streak out of its hiding place, heading straight for the silvery wall of light! Horrified, Par-Salian ceased his chant, the voices of the stones rang hollow and died. In the silence he could now hear the tiny voice, "Don't leave me, Caramon! Don't leave me! You know what trouble you'll get into without me!"

The mouse ran through the silver powder, scat-tering a sparkling trail behind it, and burst into the lighted circle. Par-Salian heard a small, tinging sound and saw a ring roll round and round on the stone floor. He saw a third figure materialize in the circle, and he gasped in horror. Then the puls-ing figures were gone. The light of the circle was sucked into a great vortex, the laboratory was plunged into darkness.

Weak and exhausted, Par-Salian collapsed onto the floor. His last thought, before he lost conscious-ness, was a terrible one.

He had sent a kender back in time.†

Of all the ominous, doom-laden sentences ever written in DRAGONLANCE, *this is one of my favorites.*
—MW

Book I concludes with Crysania as the representative of Good, Raistlin as the agent of Evil, Tas as the unwitting agent of Chaos, and Caramon as everyman stuck in the middle. These themes will continue to be played out both in Dragons of Summer Flame *and throughout the War of Souls trilogy.*
—TRH

BOOK 2

North is this way
of course...

Well guarded—
boring!

Solam

Palanthas

Dargaard
Keep

? ?

gnomes

Sancrist

Ergoth

(I wonder if the
silver Dragon is here?)

Solace will
be here

Qualinesti

xak Tsaroth
(before it sank)

Tarsis

Tower of High Sorcery

* it is by
the sea

Ice Wall

Nordmar
(I think)

Karthay

Mithas   minotaurs
Kothas   (rude bunch)

City of Istar
(where we came)

Istar
Temple

Balifor
(kenders!!)

Silvanost

Lorac is King
(I met him)

Map of Ansalon

Circa 962 I.A.

asslehoff Burrfoot (himself)

enubis walked with slow steps through the wide, airy halls of the light-filled Temple of the Gods in Istar. His thoughts were abstracted, his gaze on the marble floor's intricate patterns. One might have supposed, seeing him walk thus aimlessly and preoccupied, the cleric was insensible of the fact that he was walking in the heart of the universe. But Denubis was not insensible of this fact, nor was it one he was likely to forget. Lest he should, the Kingpriest reminded him of it daily in his morning call to prayers.

"We are the heart of the universe,"† the Kingpriest would say in the voice whose music was so beautiful one occasionally forgot to listen to the words. "Istar, city beloved of the gods,† is the center of the universe and we—being at the heart of the city—are therefore the heart of the universe. As the blood flows from the heart, bringing nourishment to even the smallest

The idea behind the Kingpriest was to show the antithesis of the separation of church and state under the United States Constitution. Here was a single man who possessed both aspects of his culture and enforced both views with a law tailored to his own beliefs and viewpoint. —TRH

This description about Istar—a fabled land long held just beyond our vision in Chronicles—now makes the city very real. Good fantasy keeps much of its past shrouded by the intervening mists of time and distance. Istar can only be described well here because there is a great deal more history even further back on which it can rest. —TRH

toe, so our faith and our teachings flow from this great temple to the smallest, most insignificant among us. Remember this as you go about your daily duties, for you who work here are favored of the gods. As one touch upon the tiniest strand of the silken web will send tremors through the entire web, so your least action could spread tremors throughout Krynn."

Denubis shivered. He wished the Kingpriest would not use that particular metaphor. Denubis detested spiders. He hated all insects, in fact; something he never admitted and, indeed, felt guilty about. Was he not commanded to love all creatures, except, of course, those created by the Queen of Darkness? That included ogres, goblins, trolls, and other evil races, but Denubis was not certain about spiders. He kept meaning to ask, but he knew this would entail an hour-long philosophical argument among the Revered Sons, and he simply didn't think it was worth it. Secretly, he would continue to hate spiders.

Denubis slapped himself gently on his balding head. How had his mind wandered to spiders? I'm getting old, he thought with a sigh. I'll soon be like poor Arabacus, doing nothing all day but sitting in the garden and sleeping until someone wakens me for dinner. At this, Denubis sighed again, but it was nearer a sigh of envy than one of pity. Poor Arabacus, indeed! At least he is spared—

"Denubis. . ."

Denubis† paused. Glancing this way and that around the large corridor, he saw no one. The cleric shuddered. Had he heard that soft voice, or just imagined it?

"Denubis," came the voice again.

This scene somewhat mirrors an event early in the life of the prophet Samuel, although with Denubis it is a negative example. See I Samuel 3.

This time the cleric looked more closely into the shadows formed by the huge marble columns supporting the gilded ceiling. A darker shadow, a patch of blackness within the darkness was now discernible. Denubis checked an exclamation of irritation. Suppressing the second shudder that swept over his body, he halted in his course and moved slowly over to the figure that stood in the shadows, knowing that the figure would never move out of the shadows to meet him. It was not that light was harmful to the one who awaited Denubis, as light is

harmful to some of the creatures of darkness. In fact, Denubis wondered if anything on the face of this world could be harmful to this man. No, it was simply that he preferred shadows. Theatrics, Denubis thought sarcastically.

"You called me, Dark One?" Denubis asked in a voice he tried hard to make sound pleasant.

He saw the face in the shadows smile, and Denubis knew at once that all of his thoughts were well-known to this man.

"Damn it!" Denubis cursed (a habit frowned upon by the Kingpriest but one which Denubis, a simple man, had never been able to overcome). "Why does the Kingpriest keep him around the court? Why not send him away, as the others were banished?"

He said this to himself, of course, because— deep within his soul—Denubis knew the answer. This one was too dangerous, too powerful. This one was not like the others. The Kingpriest kept him as a man keeps a ferocious dog to protect his house; he knows the dog will attack when ordered, but he must constantly make certain that the dog's leash is secure. If the leash ever broke, the animal would go for his throat.

"I am sorry to disturb you, Denubis," said the man in his soft voice, "especially when I see you absorbed in such weighty thought. But an event of great importance is happening, even as we speak. Take a squadron of the Temple guards and go to the marketplace. There, at the crossroads, you will find a Revered Daughter of Paladine. She is near death. And there, also, you will find the man who assaulted her."

Denubis's eyes opened wide, then narrowed in sudden suspicion.

"How do you know this?" he demanded.

The figure within the shadows stirred, the dark line formed by the thin lips widened—the figure's approximation of a laugh.

"Denubis," the figure chided, "you have known me many years. Do you ask the wind how it blows? Do you question the stars to find out why they shine? I *know*, Denubis. Let that be enough for you."

"But—" Denubis put his hand to his head in confusion. This would entail explanations, reports to the

proper authorities. One did not simply conjure up a squadron of Temple guards!

"Hurry, Denubis," the man said gently. "She will not live long. . . ."

Denubis swallowed. A Revered Daughter of Paladine, assaulted! Dying—in the marketplace! Probably surrounded by gaping crowds. The scandal! The Kingpriest would be highly displeased—

The cleric opened his mouth, then shut it again. He looked for a moment at the figure in the shadows, then, finding no help there, Denubis whirled about and, in a flurry of robes, ran back down the corridor the way he had come, his leather sandals slapping on the marble floor.

Reaching the central headquarters of the Captain of the Guard, Denubis managed to gasp out his request to the lieutenant on duty. As he had foreseen, this caused all sorts of commotion. Waiting for the Captain himself to appear, Denubis collapsed in a chair and tried to catch his breath.

The identity of the creator of spiders might be open to question, Denubis thought sourly, but there was no doubt in his mind at all about the creator of *that* creature of darkness who, no doubt, was standing back there in the shadows laughing at him.

"Tasslehoff!"

The kender opened his eyes. For a moment, he had no idea where he was or even who he was. He had heard a voice speaking a name that sounded vaguely familiar. Confused, the kender looked around. He was lying on top of a big man, who was flat on his back in the middle of a street. The big man was regarding him with utter astonishment, perhaps because Tas was perched upon his broad stomach.

"Tas?" the big man repeated, and this time his face grew puzzled. "Are you supposed to be here?"

"I-I'm really not sure," the kender said, wondering who "Tas" was. Then it all came back to him— hearing Par-Salian chanting, ripping the ring off his thumb, the blinding light, the singing stones, the mage's horrified shriek. . . .

"Of course, I'm supposed to be here," Tas snapped irritably, blocking out the memory of Par-Salian's

fearful yell. "You don't think they'd let you come back here by yourself, do you?" The kender was practically nose to nose with the big man.

Caramon's puzzled look darkened to a frown. "I'm not sure," he muttered, "but I don't think you—"

"Well, I'm here." Tas rolled off Caramon's rotund body to land on the cobblestones beneath them. "Wherever 'here' is," he muttered beneath his breath. "Let me help you up," he said to Caramon, extending his small hand, hoping this action would take Caramon's mind off him. Tas didn't know whether or not he could be sent back, but he didn't intend to find out.

Caramon struggled to sit up, looking for all the world like an overturned turtle, Tas thought with a giggle. And it was then the kender noticed that Caramon was dressed much differently than he had been when they left the Tower. He had been wearing his own armor (as much of it that fit), a loose-fitting tunic made of fine cloth, sewn together with Tika's loving care.

But, now, he was wearing coarse cloth, slovenly stitched together. A crude leather vest hung from his shoulders. The vest might have had buttons once, but, if so, they were gone now. Buttons weren't needed anyway, Tas thought, for there was no way the vest would have stretched to fit over Caramon's sagging gut. Baggy leather breeches and patched leather boots with a big hole over one toe completed the unsavory picture.

"Whew!" Caramon muttered, sniffing. "What's that horrible smell?"

"You," Tas said, holding his nose and waving his hand as though this might dissipate the odor. Caramon reeked of dwarf spirits! The kender regarded him closely. Caramon had been sober when they'd left, and he certainly looked sober now. His eyes, if confused, were clear and he was standing straight, without weaving.

The big man looked down and, for the first time, saw himself.

"What? How?" he asked, bewildered.

"You'd think," Tas said sternly, regarding Caramon's clothes in disgust, "that the mages could afford something better than this! I mean, I know this spell must be hard on clothes, but surely—"

A sudden thought occurred to him. Fearfully, Tas looked down at his clothes, then breathed a sigh of relief. Nothing had happened to him. Even his pouches were with him, all perfectly intact. A nagging voice inside him mentioned that this was probably because he wasn't supposed to have come along, but the kender conveniently ignored it.

"Well, let's have a look around," Tas said cheerfully, suiting his action to his words. He'd already been able to guess where they were by the odor—in a alley. The kender wrinkled his nose. He'd thought Caramon smelled bad! Filled with garbage and refuse of every kind, the alley was dark, overshadowed by a huge stone building. But it was daylight, Tas could tell, glancing down at the end of the alley where he could see what appeared to a busy street, thronged with people who were coming and going.

"I think that's a market," Tas said with interest, starting to walk nearer the end of the alley to investigate. "What city did you say they sent us to?"

"Istar," he heard Caramon mumble from behind him. Then, "Tas!"

Hearing a frightened tone in Caramon's voice, the kender turned around hurriedly, his hand going immediately to the little knife he carried in his belt. Caramon was kneeling by something lying the alley.

"What is it?" Tas called, running back.

"Lady Crysania," Caramon said, lifting a dark cloak.

"Caramon!" Tas drew a horrified breath. "What did they do to her? Did their magic go wrong?"

"I don't know," Caramon said softly, "but we've got to get help." He carefully covered the woman's bruised and bloody face with the cloak.

"I'll go," Tas offered, "you stay here with her. This doesn't look like a really good part of town, if you take my meaning."

"Yeah," Caramon said, sighing heavily.

"It'll be all right," Tas said, patting the big man on his shoulder reassuringly. Caramon nodded but said nothing. With a final pat, Tas turned and ran back down the alley toward the street. Reaching the end, he darted out onto the sidewalk.

"Hel—" he began, but just then a hand closed

over his arm in a grip of iron, hoisting him clear up off the sidewalk.

"Here, now," said a stern voice, "where are you going?"

Tas twisted around to see a bearded man, his face partially covered by the shining visor of his helm, staring at him with dark, cold eyes.

Townguard, the kender realized quickly, having had a great deal of experience with this type of official personage.

"Why, I was coming to look for you," Tas said,† trying to wriggle free and assume an innocent air at the same time.

"*That's* a likely story from a kender!" The guard snorted, getting an even firmer grasp on Tas. "It'd be a history-making event† in Krynn, if it was true, that's for certain."

"But it *is* true," Tas said, glaring at the man indignantly. "A friend of ours is hurt, down there."

He saw the guard glance over at a man he had not noticed before—a cleric, dressed in white robes. Tas brightened. "Oh? A cleric? How—"

The guard clapped his hand over the kender's mouth.

"What do you think, Denubis? That's Beggar's Alley down there. Probably a knifing, nothing more than thieves falling out."

The cleric was a middle-aged man with thinning hair and a rather melancholy, serious face. Tas saw him look around the marketplace and shake his head. "The Dark One said the crossroads, and this is it—or near enough. We should investigate."

"Very well." The guardsman shrugged. Detailing two of his men, he watched them advance cautiously down the filthy alleyway. He kept his hand over the kender's mouth, and Tas, slowly being smothered, made a pathetic, squeaking sound.

The cleric, gazing anxiously after the guards, glanced around.

"Let him breathe, Captain," he said.

"We'll have to listen to him chatter," the captain grumbled irritably, but he removed his hand from Tas's mouth.

"He'll be quiet, won't you?" the cleric asked, looking at Tas with eyes that were kind in a preoccupied fashion. "He realizes how serious this is, don't you?"

It is interesting to note that Caramon and Tas have traveled backward through the centuries, yet they are still capable of communicating directly with the local inhabitants. Realistically, language is a dynamic thing, changing over time with use and circumstance. Considering the time and distance Caramon and Tas have traveled, they probably should not be quite this conversant. —TRH

The irony is that this truly is a history-making event! —MW

Not quite certain whether the cleric was addressing him or the captain or both, Tas thought it best simply to nod in agreement. Satisfied, the cleric turned back to watch the guards. Tas twisted enough in the captain's grasp so that he, too, was able to see. He saw Caramon stand up, gesturing at the dark, shapeless bundle lying beside him. One of the guards knelt down and drew aside the cloak.

"Captain!" he shouted as the other guard immediately grabbed hold of Caramon. Startled and angry at the rough treatment, the big man jerked out of the guard's grasp. The guard shouted, his companion rose to his feet. There was a flash of steel.

"Damn!"† swore the captain. "Here, watch this little bastard, Denubis!" He thrust Tasslehoff in the cleric's direction.

"Shouldn't I go?" Denubis protested, catching hold of Tas as the kender stumbled into him.

"No!" The captain was already running down the alley, his own shortsword drawn. Tas heard him mutter something about "big brute . . . dangerous."

"Caramon isn't dangerous," Tas protested, looking up at the cleric called Denubis in concern. "They won't hurt him, will they? What's wrong?"

"I'm afraid we'll find out soon enough," Denubis said in a stern voice, but holding Tas in such a gentle grip that the kender could easily have broken free. At first Tas considered escape—there was no better place in the world to hide than in a large city market. But the thought was a reflexive one, just like Caramon's breaking away from the guard. Tas couldn't leave his friend.

"They won't hurt him, if he comes peacefully." Denubis sighed. "Though if he's done—" The cleric shivered and for a moment paused. "Well, if he's done *that*, he might find an easier death here."

"Done what?" Tas was growing more and more confused. Caramon, too, appeared confused, for Tas saw him raise his hands in a protestation of innocence.

But even as he argued, one of the guards came up behind the big man and struck him in the back of his knees with the shaft of his spear. Caramon's legs buckled. As he staggered, the guard in front of him knocked the big man to the ground with an almost nonchalant blow to the chest.

It is true that the curse words of a culture tell us important things about the culture itself. Curse words, however, are only the tip of the linguistic iceberg. It is not realistic to think that people of another time, culture, or world would speak English (such as the story was originally written in) or any other language which we might know. However, if the society and its language are truly different, then we quickly loose connection with the characters and their story. All translation is an adaptation; perhaps we should look at the text in this light. —TRH

Caramon hadn't even hit the pavement before the point of the spear was at his throat. He lifted his hands feebly in a gesture of surrender. Quickly, the guards rolled him over onto his stomach and, grasping his hands, tied them behind his back with rapid expertise.

"Make them stop!" Tas cried, straining forward. "They can't do that—"

The cleric caught him. "No, little friend, it would be best for you to stay with me. Please," Denubis said, gently gripping Tas by the shoulders. "You cannot help him, and trying will only make things worse for you."

The guards dragged Caramon to his feet and began to search him thoroughly, even reaching their hands down into his leather breeches. They found a dagger at his belt—this they handed to their captain—and a flagon of some sort. Opening the top, they sniffed and then tossed it away in disgust.

One of the guards motioned to the dark bundle on the pavement. The captain knelt down and lifted the cloak. Tas saw him shake his head. Then the captain, with the other guard's help, carefully lifted the bundle and turned to walk out of the alley. He said something to Caramon as he passed. Tas heard the filthy word with riveting shock, as did Caramon, apparently, for the big man's face went deathly white.

Glancing up at Denubis, Tas saw the cleric's lips tighten, the fingers on Tas's shoulder trembled.

Then Tas understood.

"No," he whispered softly in agony, "oh, no! They can't think that! Caramon wouldn't harm a mouse! He didn't hurt Lady Crysania! He was only trying to help her! That's why we came here. Well, one reason anyway. Please!" Tas whirled around to face Denubis, clasping his hands together. "Please, you've got to believe me! Caramon's a soldier. He's killed things—sure. But only nasty things like draconians and goblins. Please, please believe me!"

But Denubis only looked at him sternly.

"No! How could you think that? I hate this place! I want to go back home!" Tas cried miserably, seeing Caramon's stricken, confused expression. Bursting into tears, the kender buried his face in his hands and sobbed bitterly.

Then Tas felt a hand touch him, hesitate, then pat him gently.

"There, there, now," Denubis said. "You'll have a chance to tell your story. Your friend will, too. And, if you're innocent, no harm will come to you." But Tas heard the cleric sigh. "Your friend had been drinking, hadn't he?"

"No!" Tas snuffled, looking up at Denubis pleadingly. "Not a drop, I swear. . . ."

The kender's voice died, however, at the sight of Caramon as the guards led him out of the alley into the street where Tas and the cleric stood. Caramon's face was covered with muck and filth from the alley, blood dribbled from a cut on his lip. His eyes were wild and blood-shot, the expression on his face vacant and filled with fear. The legacy of past drinking bouts was marked plainly in his puffy, red cheeks and shaking limbs. A crowd, which had begun to form at the sight of the guards, began to jeer.

Tas hung his head. What was Par-Salian doing? he wondered in confusion. Had something gone wrong? Were they even in Istar? Were they lost somewhere? Or maybe this was some terrible nightmare. . . .

"Who— What happened?" Denubis asked the captain. "Was the Dark One right?"

"Right? Of course, he was right. Have you ever known him to be wrong?" the captain snapped. "As for who—I don't know who she is, but she's a member of your order. Wears the medallion of Paladine around her neck. She's hurt pretty bad, too. I thought she was dead, in fact, but there's a faint lifebeat in her neck."

"Do you think she was . . . she was . . ." Denubis faltered.

"I don't know," the captain said grimly. "But she's been beaten up. She's had some kind of fit, I guess. Her eyes are wide open, but she doesn't seem to see or hear anything."

"We must convey her to the Temple at once," Denubis said briskly, though Tas heard a tremor in the man's voice. The guards were dispersing the crowd, holding their spears in front of them and pushing back the curious.

"Everything's in hand. Move along, move along.

Market's about to close for the day. You best finish
your shopping while there's still time."

"I didn't hurt her!" Caramon said bleakly. He was
shivering in terror. "I didn't hurt her," he repeated,
tears streaking down his face.

"Yeah!" the captain said bitterly. "Take these two
to the prisons," he ordered his guards.

Tas whimpered. One of the guards grabbed him
roughly, but the kender—confused and stunned—
caught hold of Denubis's robes and refused to let go.
The cleric, his hand resting on Lady Crysania's lifeless form, turned around when he felt the kender's
clinging hands.

"Please," Tas begged, "please, he's telling the
truth."

Denubis's stern face softened. "You are a loyal
friend," he said gently. "A rather unusual trait to
find in a kender. I hope your faith in this man is
justified." Absently, the cleric stroked Tas's topknot
of hair, his expression sad. "But, you must realize
that sometimes, when a man has been drinking, the
liquor makes him do things—"

"Come along, you!" the guard snarled, jerking Tas
backward. "Quit your little act. It won't work."

"Don't let this upset you, Revered Son," the captain said. "You know kender!"

"Yes," Denubis replied, his eyes on Tas as the
two guards led the kender and Caramon away
through the rapidly thinning crowd in the marketplace. "I do know kender. And that's a remarkable one." Then, shaking his head, the cleric turned
his attention back to Lady Crysania. "If you will
continue holding her, Captain," he said softly, "I
will ask Paladine to convey us to the Temple with
all speed."

Tas, twisting around in the guard's grip, saw the
cleric and the Captain of the Guard standing alone
in the marketplace. There was a shimmer of white
light, and they were gone.

Tas blinked and, forgetting to look where he was
going stumbled over his feet. He tumbled to the
cobblestone pavement, skinning his knees and his
hands painfully. A firm grip on his collar jerked
him upright, and a firm hand gave him a shove in
the back.

"Come along. None of your tricks."

Tas moved forward, too miserable and upset to even look around at his surroundings. His gaze went to Caramon, and the kender felt his heart ache. Overwhelmed by shame and fear, Caramon plodded down the street blindly, his steps unsteady.

"I didn't hurt her!" Tas heard him mumble. "There must be some sort of mistake. . . ."

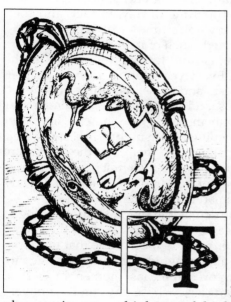

CHAPTER 2

The beautiful elven voices rose higher and higher, their sweet notes spiraling up the octaves as though they would carry their prayers to the heavens simply by ascending the scales. The faces of the elven women, touched by the rays of the setting sun slanting through the tall crystal windows, were tinged a delicate pink, their eyes shone with fervent inspiration.

The listening pilgrims wept for the beauty, causing the choir's white and blue robes—white robes for the Revered Daughters of Paladine, blue robes for the Daughters of Mishakal—to blur in their sight. Many would swear later that they had seen the elven women transported skyward, swathed in fluffy clouds.

When their song reached a crescendo of sweetness, a chorus of deep, male voices joined in, keeping the prayers that had been sweeping upward like

freed birds tied to the ground—clipping the wings, so to speak, Denubis thought sourly. He supposed he was jaded. As a young man, he, too, had cleansed his soul with tears when he first heard the Evening Hymn. Then, years later, it had become routine. He could well remember the shock he had experienced when he first realized his thoughts had wandered to some pressing piece of church business during the singing. Now it was worse than routine. It had become an irritant, cloying and annoying. He had come to dread this time of day, in fact, and took advantage of every opportunity to escape.

Why? He blamed much of it on the elven women. Racial prejudice, he told himself morosely. Yet, he couldn't help it. Every year a party of elven women, Revered Daughters and those in training, journeyed from the glorious lands of Silvanesti to spend a year in Istar, devoting themselves to the church. This meant they sang the Evening Hymn nightly and spent their days reminding all around them that the elves were the favored of the gods—created first of all the races,† granted a lifespan of hundreds of years. Yet nobody but Denubis seemed to take offense at this.

Here we see mythos on top of mythos—a glimpse of the mythology in which the characters themselves believe. —TRH

Tonight, in particular, the singing was irritating to Denubis because he was worried about the young woman he had brought to the Temple that morning. He had, in fact, almost avoided coming this evening but had been captured at the last moment by Gerald, an elderly human cleric whose days on Krynn were numbered and who found his greatest comfort in attending Evening Prayers. Probably, Denubis reflected, because the old man was almost totally deaf. This being the case, it had been completely impossible to explain to Gerald that he—Denubis— had somewhere else to go. Finally Denubis gave up and gave the old cleric his arm in support. Now Gerald stood next to him, his face rapt, picturing in his mind, no doubt, the beautiful plane to which he, someday, would ascend.

Denubis was thinking about this and about the young woman, whom he had not seen or heard anything about since he had brought her to the Temple that morning, when he felt a gentle touch upon his arm. The cleric jumped and glanced about guiltily, wondering if his inattention had been observed and would be reported. At first he couldn't figure out

who had touched him, both of his neighbors apparently lost in their prayers. Then he felt the touch again and realized it came from behind. Glancing in back of him, he saw a hand had slipped unobtrusively through the curtain that separated the balcony on which the Revered Sons stood from the antechambers around the balcony.

The hand beckoned, and Denubis, puzzled, left his place in line and fumbled awkwardly with the curtain, trying to leave without calling undue attention to himself. The hand had withdrawn and Denubis couldn't find the separation in the folds of the heavy velvet curtains. Finally, after he was certain every pilgrim in the place must have his eyes fixed on him in disgust, he found the opening and stumbled through it.

A young acolyte, his face smooth and placid, bowed to the flushed and perspiring cleric as if nothing were amiss.

"My apologies for interrupting your Evening Prayers, Revered Son, but the Kingpriest requests that you honor him with a few moments of your time, if it is convenient." The acolyte spoke the prescribed words with such casual courtesy that it would not have seemed unusual to any observer if Denubis had replied, "No, not now. I have other matters I must attend to directly. Perhaps later?"

Denubis, however, said nothing of the sort. Paling visibly, he mumbled something about "being much honored," his voice dying off at the end. The acolyte was accustomed to this, however, and—nodding acknowledgment—turned and led the way through the vast, airy, winding halls of the Temple to the quarters of the Kingpriest of Istar.

Hurrying behind the youth, Denubis had no need to wonder what this could be about. The young woman, of course. He had not been in the Kingpriest's presence for well over two years, and it could not be coincidence that brought him this summons on the very day he had found a Revered Daughter lying near death in an alley.

Perhaps she has died, Denubis thought sadly. The Kingpriest is going to tell me in person. It would certainly be kind of the man. Out of character, perhaps, in one who had such weighty affairs as the fate of nations on his mind, but certainly kind.

He hoped she hadn't died. Not just for her sake, but for the sake of the human and the kender. Denubis had been thinking a lot about them, too. Particularly the kender. Like others on Krynn, Denubis hadn't much use for kender, who had no respect at all for rules or personal property—either their own or other people's. But this kender seemed different. Most kender Denubis knew (or thought he knew) would have run off at the first sign of trouble. This one had stayed† by his big friend with touching loyalty and had even spoken up in his friend's defense.

Denubis shook his head sadly. If the girl died, they would face—No, he couldn't think about it. Murmuring a sincere prayer to Paladine to protect everyone concerned (if they were worthy),† Denubis wrenched his mind from its depressing thoughts and forced it to admire the splendors of the King-priest's private residence in the Temple.

He had forgotten the beauty—the milky white walls, glowing with a soft light of their own that came—so legend had it—from the very stones themselves. So delicately shaped and carved were they, that they glistened like great white rose petals springing up from the polished white floor. Running through them were faint veins of light blue, softening the harshness of the stark white.

The wonders of the hallway gave way to the beauties of the antechamber. Here the walls flowed upward to support the dome overhead, like a mortal's prayer ascended to the gods. Frescoes of the gods were painted in soft colors. They, too, seemed to glow with their own light—Paladine, the Platinum Dragon, God of Good; Gilean of the Book, God of Neutrality; even the Queen of Darkness was represented here—for the Kingpriest would offend no god overtly. She was portrayed as the five-headed dragon, but such a meek and inoffensive dragon Denubis wondered she didn't roll over and lick Paladine's foot.

He thought that only later, however, upon reflection. Right now, he was much too nervous to even look at the wonderful paintings. His gaze was fixed on the carefully wrought platinum doors that opened into the heart of the Temple itself.

The doors swung open, emitting a glorious light. His time of audience had come.

This passages shows us the growth that Tasslehoff has experienced. All characters grow—whether through change or through the strengthening of their steadfast qualities. Static characters are a waste of typesetting. —TRH

What a wonderful statement—how one tries to put caveats on which of his children their God should bless. Prayer as a bargaining tool! That someone should try to dictate restraints to God's actions seems not only hypocritical but the very definition of hubris. —TRH

Denubis's prayer reflects the dangerous nature of the Kingpriest's religious teachings in that only those who are considered worthy should receive Paladine's protection. —MW

The Hall of Audience first gave those who came here a sense of their own meekness and humility.† This was the heart of goodness. Here was represented the glory and power of the church. The doors opened onto a huge circular room with a floor of polished white granite. The floor continued upward to form the walls into the petals of a gigantic rose, soaring skyward to support a great dome. The dome itself was of frosted crystal that absorbed the glow of the sun and the moons. Their radiance filled every part of the room.

I know this may seem hard to believe, but the description of this room is due, in no small part, to a flower vase I made in my Junior High School pottery class! —TRH

A great arching wave of seafoam blue swept up from the center of the floor into an alcove that stood opposite the door. Here stood a single throne. More brilliant than the light streaming down from the dome was the light and warmth that flowed from this throne.

Denubis entered the room with his head bowed and his hands folded before him as was proper. It was evening and the sun had now set. The Hall Denubis walked into was lit only by candles. Yet, as always, Denubis had the distinct impression he had stepped into an open-air courtyard bathed in sunlight.

Indeed, for a moment his eyes were dazzled by the brilliance. Keeping his gaze lowered, as was proper until he was given leave to raise it, he caught glimpses of the floor and objects and people present in the Hall. He saw the stairs as he ascended them. But the radiance welling from the front of the room was so splendid that he literally noticed nothing else.

"Raise your eyes, Revered Son of Paladine," spoke a voice whose music brought tears to Denubis's eyes when the lovely music of the elven women could move him no longer.

Denubis looked up, and his soul trembled in awe. It had been two years since he had been this near the Kingpriest, and time had dulled his memory. How different it was to observe him every morning from a distance—seeing him as one sees the sun appearing on the horizon, basking in its warmth, feeling cheered at its light. How different to be summoned into the presence of the sun, to stand before it and feel one's soul burned by the purity and clarity of its brilliance.

This time, I'll remember, thought Denubis sternly. But no one, returning from an audience with the

Kingpriest, could ever recall exactly what he looked
like.† It seemed sacrilegious to attempt to do so, in
fact—as though thinking of him in terms of mere
flesh was a desecration. All anyone ever remembered was that they had been in the presence of
someone incredibly beautiful.

The aura of light surrounded Denubis, and he
was immediately rent by the most terrible guilt for
his doubts and misgivings and questionings. In contrast to the Kingpriest, Denubis saw himself as the
most wretched creature on Krynn. He fell to his
knees, begging forgiveness, almost totally unaware
of what he was doing, knowing only that it was the
right thing to do.

And forgiveness was granted. The musical voice
spoke, and Denubis was immediately filled with a
sense of peace and sweet calm. Rising to his feet,
he faced the Kingpriest in reverent humility and
begged to know how he could serve him.

"You brought a young woman, a Revered Daughter of Paladine, to the Temple this morning," said
the voice, "and we understand you have been concerned about her—as is only natural and most
proper. We thought it would give you comfort to
know that she is well and fully recovered from her
terrible ordeal. It may also ease your mind, Denubis, beloved son of Paladine, to know that she was
not physically injured."

Denubis offered his thanks to Paladine for the
young woman's recovery and was just preparing to
stand aside and bask for a few moments in the glorious light when the full import of the Kingpriest's
words struck him.

"She—she was not assaulted?" Denubis managed
to stammer.

"No, my son," answered the voice, sounding a
joyous anthem. "Paladine in his infinite wisdom
had gathered her soul to himself, and I was able,
after many long hours of prayer, to prevail upon him
to return such a treasure to us, since it had been
snatched untimely from its body. The young woman
now finds rest in a life-giving sleep."

. "But the marks on her face?" Denubis protested,
confused. "The blood—"

"There were no marks," the Kingpriest said mildly,
but with a hint of reproof that made Denubis feel

unaccountably miserable. "I told you, she was not physically injured."

"I—I am delighted I was mistaken," Denubis answered sincerely. "All the more so because it means that young man who was arrested is innocent as he claimed and may now go free."

"I am truly thankful, even as you are thankful, Revered Son, to know that a fellow creature in this world did not commit a crime as foul as was first feared. Yet who among us is truly innocent?"†

The musical voice paused and seemed to be awaiting an answer. And answers were forthcoming. The cleric heard murmured voices all around him give the proper response, and Denubis became consciously aware for the first time that there were others present near the throne. Such was the influence of the Kingpriest that he had almost believed himself alone with the man.

The Biblical motif is once again evident in this section of the story: "He who is without sin, let him cast the first stone." (John 8:1-11; Romans 3:10) —TRH

Denubis mumbled the response to this question along with the rest and suddenly knew without being told that he was dismissed from the august presence. The light no longer beat upon him directly, it had turned from him to another. Feeling as if he had stepped from brilliant sun into the shade, he stumbled, half-blind, back down the stairs. Here, on the main floor, he was able to catch his breath, relax, and look around.

The Kingpriest sat at one end, surrounded by light. But, it seemed to Denubis that his eyes were becoming accustomed to the light, so to speak, for he could at last begin to recognize others with him. Here were the heads of the various orders—the Revered Sons and Revered Daughters. Known almost jokingly as "the hands and feet of the sun," it was these who handled the mundane, day-to-day affairs of the church. It was these who ruled Krynn. But there were others here, besides high church officials. Denubis felt his gaze drawn to a corner of the Hall, the only corner, it seemed, that was in shadow.

There sat a figure robed in black, his darkness outshone by the Kingpriest's light. But Denubis, shuddering, had the distinct impression that the darkness was only waiting, biding its time, knowing that— eventually—the sun must set.

The knowledge that the Dark One, as Fistandantilus was known around the court, was allowed within the Kingpriest's Hall of Audience came as a shock to Denubis. The Kingpriest was trying to rid the world of evil, yet it was here—in his court! And then a comforting thought came to Denubis—perhaps, when the world was totally free of evil, when the last of the ogre races had been eliminated, then Fistandantilus himself would fall.

But even as he thought this and smiled at the thought, Denubis saw the cold glitter of the mage's eyes turn their gaze toward him. Denubis shivered and looked away hurriedly. What a contrast there was between that man and the Kingpriest! When basking in the Kingpriest's light, Denubis felt calm and peaceful. Whenever he happened to look into the eyes of Fistandantilus, he was reminded forcefully of the darkness within himself.

And, under the gaze of those eyes, he suddenly found himself wondering what the Kingpriest had meant by the curious statement, "who of us is truly innocent?"

Feeling uncomfortable, Denubis walked into an antechamber where stood a gigantic banquet table.

The smell of the luscious, exotic foods, brought from all over Ansalon by worshipful pilgrims or purchased in the huge open-air markets of cities as far away as Xak Tsaroth, made Denubis remember that he had not eaten since morning. Taking a plate, he browsed among the wonderful food, selecting this and that until his plate was filled and he had only made it halfway down the table that literally groaned under its aromatic burden.

A servant brought round cups of fragrant, elven wine. Taking one of these and juggling the plate and his eating implements in one hand, the wine in the other, Denubis sank into a chair and began to eat heartily. He was just enjoying the heavenly combination of a mouthful of roast pheasant and the lingering taste of the elven wine when a shadow fell across his plate.

Denubis glanced up, choked, and bolted the remainder of the mouthful, dabbing at the wine dribbling down his chin in embarrassment.

"R-revered Son," he stuttered, making a feeble attempt to rise in the gesture of respect that the Head of the Brethren deserved.

Quaratht regarded him with sardonic amusement and waved a hand languidly. "Please, Revered Son, do not let me disturb you. I have no intention of interrupting your dinner. I merely wanted a word with you. Perhaps, when you are finished—"

"Quite . . . quite finished," Denubis said hastily, handing his half-full plate and glass to a passing servant. "I don't seem to be as hungry as I thought." That, at least, was true. He had completely lost his appetite.

Quarath smiled a delicate smile. His thin elven face with its finely sculpted features seemed to be made of fragile porcelain, and he always smiled carefully, as if fearing his face would break.

"Very well, if the desserts do not tempt you?"

"N-no, not in the slightest. Sweets . . . bad for th-the digestion th-this late—"

"Then, come with me, Revered Son. It has been a long time since we talked." Quarath took Denubis's arm with casual familiarity—though it had been months since the cleric had last seen his superior.

First the Kingpriest, now Quarath. Denubis felt a cold lump in the pit of his stomach. As Quarath was leading him out of the Audience Hall, the Kingpriest's musical voice rose. Denubis glanced backward, basking for one more moment in that wondrous light. Then, as he looked away with a sigh, his gaze came to rest upon the black-robed mage. Fistandantilus smiled and nodded. Shuddering, Denubis hurriedly accompanied Quarath out the door.

The two clerics walked through sumptuously decorated corridors until they came to a small chamber, Quarath's own. It, too, was splendidly decorated inside, but Denubis was too nervous to notice any detail.

"Please, sit down, Denubis. I may call you that, since we are comfortably alone."

Denubis didn't know about the comfortably, but they were certainly alone. He sat on the edge of the seat Quarath offered him, accepted a small glass of cordial which he didn't drink, and waited. Quarath talked of inconsequential nothings for a few moments, asking after Denubis's work—he translated passages of the Disks of Mishakal into his native language, Solamnict—and other items in which he obviously wasn't the least bit interested.

Quarath also plays a role in Chris Pierson's Kingpriest Trilogy, *which tells the story of how the last Kingpriest came to power and how his reign led to the Cataclysm. See* Chosen of the Gods, Divine Hammer, *and* Sacred Fire.

Solamnic was loosely based on Latin structure, although true scholars of that great, ancient language would find my inept attempts humorous at best. Although I have written entire song lyrics in this language, its structure and form only loosely exist in my head.
—TRH

Then, after a pause, Quarath said casually, "I couldn't help but hear you questioning the King-priest."

Denubis set his cordial down on a table, his hand shaking so he barely avoided spilling it. "I . . . I was . . . simply concerned . . . about—about the young man . . . they arrested erroneously," he stammered faintly.

Quarath nodded gravely. "Very right, too. Very proper. It is written that we should be concerned about our fellows in this world.† It becomes you, Denubis, and I shall certainly note that in my yearly report."

Yet more allusions to Biblical sources, best summed up in "Love thy neighbor."

"Thank you, Revered Son," Denubis murmured, not certain what else to say.

Quarath said nothing more but sat regarding the cleric opposite with his slanted, elven eyes.

Denubis mopped his face with the sleeve of his robe. It was unbelievably hot in this room. Elves had such thin blood.†

This is another slight nod to the AD&D rules. In the game, each race has unique benefits and drawbacks, and the elves were stuck with a penalty to their Constitution (health, well-being, physical endurance, etc.).

"Was there something else?" Quarath asked mildly.

Denubis drew a deep breath. "My lord," he said earnestly, "about that young man. Will he be released? And the kender?" He was suddenly inspired. "I thought perhaps I could be of some help, guide them back to the paths of good. Since the young man is innocent—"

"Who of us is truly innocent?" Quarath questioned, looking at the ceiling as if the gods themselves might write the answer there for him.

"I'm certain that is a very good question," Denubis said meekly, "and one no doubt worthy of study and discussion, but this young man is, apparently innocent—at least as innocent as he's likely to be of anything—" Denubis stopped, slightly confused.

Quarath smiled sadly. "Ah, there, you see?" he said, spreading his hands and turning his gaze upon the cleric. "The fur of the rabbit covers the tooth of the wolf, as the saying goes."

Leaning back in his chair, Quarath once again regarded the ceiling. "The two are being sold in the slave markets tomorrow."

Denubis half rose from his chair. "What? My lord—"

Quarath's gaze instantly fixed itself upon the cleric, freezing the man where he stood.

"Questioning? Again?"

"But . . . he's innocent!" was all Denubis could think of to say.

Quarath smiled again, this time wearily, indulgently.

"You are a good man, Denubis. A good man, a good cleric. A simple man, perhaps, but a good one. This was not a decision we made lightly. We questioned the man. His accounts of where he came from and what he was doing in Istar are confused, to say the least. If he was innocent of the girl's injuries, he undoubtedly has other crimes that are tearing at his soul. That much is visible upon his face. He has no means of support, there was no money on him. He is a vagrant and likely to turn to thievery if left on his own. We are doing him a favor by providing him with a master who will care for him. In time, he can earn his freedom and, hopefully, his soul will have been cleansed of its burden of guilt. As for the kender—" Quarath waved a negligent hand.

"Does the Kingpriest know?" Denubis summoned up courage to ask.

Quarath sighed, and this time the cleric saw a faint wrinkle of irritation appear on the elf's smooth brow. "The Kingpriest† has many more pressing issues on his mind, Revered Son Denubis," he said coldly. "He is so good that the pain of this one man's suffering would upset him for days. He did not specifically say the man was to be freed, so we simply removed the burden of this decision from his thoughts."

Seeing Denubis's haggard face fill with doubt, Quarath sat forward, regarding his cleric with a frown. "Very well, Denubis, if you must know— there were some very strange circumstances regarding the young woman's discovery. Not the least of which is that it was instituted, we understand, by the Dark One."

Denubis swallowed and sank back into his seat. The room no longer seemed hot. He shivered. "That is true," he said miserably, passing his hand over his face. "He met me—"

"I know!" Quarath snapped. "He told me. The young woman will stay here with us. She is a Revered Daughter. She wears the medallion of Paladine. She, also, is somewhat confused, but that is to be expected. We can keep an eye on her. But I'm certain

The Kingpriest is an immensely complicated character and one that was very difficult to develop, for he had to be so good that he was evil, which is an interesting dichotomy! Here again, the concept of free will comes into play. The Kingpriest decides that in order to force the people to adhere to his concept of good, he has to deprive people of their free will, which is precisely what the gods of evil want to do. He also uses the time-honored method of the "scapegoat" in order to unite people to his cause, targeting certain people and races as evil and ordering their destruction. —MW

239

By "Elder Days," I believe Quarath is referring here to the First Age. —TRH

There is a sick condescension hidden in this statement that very much is the oppressor's justification for owning slaves. "We are more enlightened than that," Quarath says, and you can hear his voice coming down from the high place he has put himself. This same hollow and sickly phrase rings in the concept of the supposed "White Man's Burden" to "civilize" the supposedly "less advanced barbarians" in the world. —TRH

you realize how impossible it is that we allow that young man to simply wander off. In the Elder Days,† they would have tossed him in a dungeon and thought no more of it. We are more enlightened than that. We will provide a decent home for him and be able to watch over him at the same time."†

Quarath makes it sound like a charitable act, selling a man into slavery, Denubis thought in confusion. Perhaps it is. Perhaps I am wrong. As he says, I am a simple man. Dizzily, he rose from his chair. The rich food he had eaten sat in his stomach like a cobblestone. Mumbling an apology to his superior, he started toward the door. Quarath rose, too, a conciliatory smile on his face.

"Come visit with me again, Revered Son," he said, standing by the door. "And do not fear to question us. That is how we learn."

Denubis nodded numbly, then paused. "I—I have one more question, then," he said hesitantly. "You mentioned the Dark One. What do you know of him? I mean, why is he here? He—he frightens me."

Quarath's face was grave, but he did not appear displeased at this question. Perhaps he was relieved that Denubis's mind had turned to another subject. "Who knows anything of the ways of magic-users," he answered, "except that their ways are not our ways, nor yet the ways of the gods. It was for that reason the Kingpriest felt compelled to rid Ansalon of them, as much as was possible. Now they are holed up in their one remaining Tower of High Sorcery in that cast-off Forest of Wayreth. Soon, even that will disappear as their numbers dwindle, since we have closed the schools. You heard about the cursing of the Tower at Palanthas?"

Denubis nodded silently.

"That terrible incident!" Quarath frowned. "It just goes to show you how the gods have cursed these wizards, driving that one poor soul to such madness that he impaled himself upon the gates, bringing down the wrath of the gods and sealing the Tower forever, we suppose. But, what were we discussing?"

"Fistandantilus," Denubis murmured, sorry he had brought it up. Now he wanted only to get back to his room and take his stomach powder.

Quarath raised his feathery eyebrows. "All I know of him is that he was here when I came, some

one hundred years ago. He is old—older even than many of my kindred, for there are few even of the eldest of my race who can remember a time when his name was not whispered. But he is human and therefore must use his magic arts to sustain his life. How, I dare not imagine." Quarath looked at Denubis intently. "You understand now, of course, why the Kingpriest keeps him at court?"

"He fears him?" Denubis asked innocently.

Quarath's porcelain smile became fixed for a moment, then it was the smile of a parent explaining a simple matter to a dull child. "No, Revered Son," he said patiently. "Fistandantilus is of great use to us. Who knows the world† better? He has traveled its width and breadth. He knows the languages, the customs, the lore of every race on Krynn. His knowledge is vast. He is useful to the Kingpriest, and so we allow him to remain here, rather than banish him to Wayreth, as we have banished his fellows."

When he is referring to "the world" here, he is talking strictly about Ansalon and not all of Krynn. It is all the world he really knows or cares about. —TRH

Denubis nodded. "I understand," he said, smiling weakly. "And . . . and now, I must go. Thank you for your hospitality, Revered Son, and for clearing up my doubts. I—I feel much better now."

"I am glad to have been able to help," Quarath said gently. "May the gods grant you restful sleep, my son."

"And you as well," Denubis murmured the reply, then left, hearing, with relief, the door shut behind him.

The cleric walked hurriedly past the Kingpriest's audience chamber. Light welled from the door, the sound of the sweet, musical voice tugged at his heart as he went by, but he feared he might be sick and so resisted the temptation to return.

Longing for the peace of his quiet room, Denubis walked quickly through the Temple. He became lost once, taking a wrong turn in the crisscrossing corridors. But a kindly servant led him back the direction he needed to take to reach the part of the Temple where he lived.

This part was austere, compared to that where the Kingpriest and the court resided, although still filled with every conceivable luxury by Krynnish standards. But as Denubis walked the halls, he thought how homey and comforting the soft candlelight appeared. Other clerics passed him with smiles and

whispered evening greetings. This was where he belonged. It was simple, like himself.

Heaving another sigh of relief, Denubis reached his own small room and opened the door (nothing was ever locked in the Temple—it showed a distrust of one's fellows) and started to enter. Then he stopped. Out of the corner of his eye he had glimpsed movement, a dark shadow within darker shadows. He stared intently down the corridor. There was nothing there. It was empty.

I *am* getting old. My eyes are playing tricks, Denubis told himself, shaking his head wearily. Walking into the room, his white robes whispering around his ankles, he shut the door firmly, then reached for his stomach powder.

key rattled in the lock of the cell door.

Tasslehoff sat bolt upright. Pale light crept into the cell through a tiny, barred window set high in the thick, stone wall. Dawn, he thought sleepily. The key rattled again, as if the jailer was having trouble opening the lock. Tas cast an uneasy glance at Caramon on the opposite side of the cell. The big man lay on the stone slab that was his bed without moving or giving any sign that he heard the racket.

A bad sign, Tas thought anxiously, knowing the well-trained warrior (when he wasn't drunk) would once have awakened at the sound of footsteps outside the room. But Caramon had neither moved nor spoken since the guards brought them here yesterday. He had refused food and water (although Tas had assured him it was a cut above most prison food). He lay on the stone slab and stared up at the

ceiling until nightfall. Then he had moved, a little at least—he had shut his eyes.

The key was rattling louder than ever, and added to its noise was the sound of the jailer swearing. Hurriedly Tas stood up and crossed the stone floor, plucking straw out of his hair and smoothing his clothes as he went. Spotting a battered stool in the corner, the kender dragged it over to the door, stood upon it, and peered through the barred window in the door down at the jailer on the other side.

"Good morning," Tas said cheerfully. "Having some trouble?"

The jailer jumped three feet at the unexpected sound and nearly dropped his keys. He was small man, wizened and gray as the walls. Glaring up at the kender's face through the bars the jailer snarled and, inserting the key in the lock once more poked and shook it vigorously. A man standing behind the jailer scowled. He was a large, well-built man, dressed in fine clothes and wrapped against the morning chill in a bear-skin cape. In his hand, he held a piece of slate, a bit of chalkrock dangling from it by a leather thong.

"Hurry up," the man snarled at the jailer. "The market opens at midday and I've got to get this lot cleaned up and decent-looking by then."

"Must be broken," muttered the jailer.

"Oh, no, it's not broken," Tas said helpfully. "Actually, in fact, I think your key would fit just fine if my lockpick wasn't in the way."

The jailer slowly lowered the keys and raised his eyes to look balefully at the kender.

"It was the oddest accident," Tas continued. "You see, I was rather bored last night—Caramon fell asleep early—and you had taken away all my things, so, when I just happened to discover that you'd missed a lockpick I keep in my sock, I decided to try it on this door, just to keep my hand in, so to speak, and to see what kind of jails you built back here. You do build a very nice jail, by the way," Tas said solemnly. "One of the nicest I've ever been in—er, one of the nicest I've ever seen. By the way, my name is Tasslehoff Burrfoot." The kender squeezed his hand through the bar in case either of them wanted to shake it. They didn't. "And I'm from Solace. So's my friend. We're here on a sort of mission you might

say and— Oh, yes, the lock. Well, you needn't glare at me so, it wasn't *my* fault. In fact, it was your stupid lock that broke my lockpick! One of my best too. My father's," the kender said sadly. "He gave it to me on the day I came of age. I really think," Tas added in a stern voice, "that you could at least apologize."

At this, the jailer made a strange sound, sort of a snort and an explosion. Shaking his ring of keys at the kender, he snapped something incoherent about "rotting in that cell forever" and started walking off, but the man in the bear-skin cape grabbed hold of him.

"Not so fast. I need the one in here."

"I know, I know," the jailer whined in a thin voice, "but you'll have to wait for the locksmith—"

"Impossible. My orders are to put 'im on the block today."

"Well, then you come up with some way to get them outta there." The jailer sneered. "Get the kender a new lockpick. Now, do you want the rest of the lot or not?"

He started to totter off, leaving the bear-skin man staring grimly at the door. "You know where my orders come from," he said in ominous tones.

"My orders come from the same place," the jailer said over his bony shoulder, "and if *they* don't like it they can come *pray* the door open. If that don't work, they can wait for the locksmith, same as everyone else."

"Are you going to let us out?" Tas asked eagerly. "If you are, we might be able to help—" Then a sudden thought crossed his mind. "You're not going to execute us, are you? Because, in that case, I think we'd just as soon wait for the locksmith. . . ."

"Execute!" the bear-skin man growled. "Hasn't been an execution in Istar in ten years. Church forbade it."

"Aye, a quick, clean death was too good for a man," cackled the jailer, who had turned around again. "Now, what do you mean about helping, you little beast?"

"Well," Tas faltered, "if you're not going to execute us, what are you going to do with us, then? I don't suppose you're letting us go? We are innocent, after all. I mean, we didn't—"

"I'm not going to do anything with *you*," the bear-skin man said sarcastically. "It's your friend I want. And, no, they're not letting him go."

"Quick, clean death," the old jailer muttered, grinning toothlessly. "Always a nice crowd gathered to watch, too. Made a man feel his going out meant something, which is just what Harry Snaggle said to me as they was marching him off to be hung. He hoped there would be a good crowd and there was. Brought a tear to his eye. 'All these people,' he says to me, 'giving up their holiday just to come give me a sendoff.' A gentleman to the end."

"He's going on the block!" the bear-skin man said loudly, ignoring the jailer.

"Quick, clean." The jailer shook his head.

"Well," Tas said dubiously, "I'm not sure what that means, but if you're truly letting us out, perhaps Caramon can help."

The kender disappeared from the window, and they heard him yelling, "Caramon, wake up! They're wanting to let us out and they can't get the door open and I'm afraid it's my fault, well, partly—"

"You realize you've got to take them both," the jailer said cunningly.

"What?" The bear-skin man turned to glare at the jailer. "That was never mentioned—"

"They're to be sold together. Those are my orders, and since your orders and my orders come from the same place—"

"Is this in writing?" The man scowled.

"Of course." The jailer was smug.

"I'll lose money! Who'll buy a kender?"

The jailer shrugged. It was none of his concern.

The bear-skin man opened his mouth again, then shut it as another face appeared framed in the cell door. It wasn't the kender's this time. It was the face of a human, a young man, around twenty-eight. The face might once have been handsome, but now the strong jawline was blurred with fat, the brown eyes were lackluster, the curly hair tangled and matted.

"How is Lady Crysania?" Caramon asked.

The bear-skin man blinked in confusion.

"Lady Crysania. They took her to the Temple," Caramon repeated.

The jailer prodded the bear-skin man in the ribs. "You know—the woman he beat up."

"I didn't touch her," Caramon said evenly. "Now, how is she?"

"That's none of your concern," the bear-skin man snapped, suddenly remembering what time it was, "Are you a locksmith? The kender said something about you being able to open the door."

"I'm not a locksmith," Caramon said, "but maybe I can open it." His eyes went to the jailer. "If you don't mind it breaking?"

"Lock's broken now!" the jailer said shrilly. "Can't see as you could hurt it much worse unless you broke the door down."

"That's what I intend to do," Caramon said coolly.

"Break the door down?" the jailer's shrieked. "You're daft! Why—"

"Wait." The bear-skin man had caught a glimpse of Caramon's shoulders and bull-like neck through the bars in the door. "Let's see this. If he does, I'll pay damages."

"You bet you will!" the jailer jabbered. The bear-skin man glanced at him out of the corner of his eye, and the jailer fell silent.

Caramon closed his eyes and drew several deep breaths, letting each out slowly. The bear-skin man and the jailer backed away from the door. Caramon disappeared from sight. They heard a grunt and then the sound of a tremendous blow hitting the solid wooden door. The door shuddered on its hinges, indeed, even the stone walls seemed to shake with the force of the blow. But the door held. The jailer, however, backed up another step, his mouth wide open.

There was another grunt from inside the cell, then another blow. The door exploded with such force that the only remaining, recognizable pieces were the twisted hinges and the lock—still fastened securely to the doorframe. The force of Caramon's momentum sent him flying into the corridor. Muffled sounds of cheering could be heard from surrounding cells where other prisoners had their faces pressed to the bars.

"You'll pay for this!" the jailer squeaked at the bear-skin man.

"It's worth every penny," the man said, helping Caramon to his feet and dusting him off, eyeing him

critically at the same time. "Been eating a bit too well, huh? Enjoy your liquor, too, I'll bet? Probably what got you in here. Well, never mind. That's soon mended. Name's—Caramon?"

The big man nodded morosely.

"And I'm Tasslehoff Burrfoot," said the kender, stepping out through the broken door and extending his hand again. "I go everywhere with him, absolutely everywhere. I promised Tika I would and—"

The bear-skin man was writing something down on his slate and only glanced at the kender absently. "Mmmmm, I see."

"Well, now," the kender continued, putting his hand into his pocket with a sigh, "if you'd take these chains off our feet, it would certainly be easier to walk."

"Wouldn't it?" the bear-skin man murmured, jotting down some figures on the slate. Adding them up, he smiled. "Go ahead," he instructed the jailer. "Get any others you've got for me today."

The old man shuffled off, first casting a vicious glance at Tas and Caramon.

"You two, sit over there by the wall until we're ready to go," the bear-skin man ordered.

Caramon crouched down on the floor, rubbing his shoulder. Tas sat next to him with a happy sigh. The world outside the jail cell looked brighter already. Just like he'd told Caramon— "Once we're out, we'll have a chance! We've got no chance at all, cooped up in here."

"Oh, by the way," Tas called after the retreating figure of the jailer, "would you please see that my lockpick's returned to me? Sentimental value, you know."

"A chance, huh?" Caramon said to Tas as the blacksmith prepared to bolt on the iron collar. It had taken a while to find one big enough, and Caramon was the last of the slaves to have this sign of his bondage fastened around his neck. The big man winced in pain as the smith soldered the bolt with a red-hot iron. There was a smell of burning flesh.

Tas tugged miserably at his collar and winced in sympathy for Caramon's suffering. "I'm sorry," he

said, snuffling. "I didn't know he meant '*on* the block'! I thought he said '*down* the block.' Like, we're going to take a walk 'down the block.' They talk kinda funny back here. Honestly, Caramon . . ."

"That's all right," Caramon said with a sigh. "It's not your fault."

"But it's somebody's fault," Tas said reflectively, watching with interest as the smith slapped grease over Caramon's burn, then inspected his work with a critical eye. More than one blacksmith in Istar had lost his job when a slave-owner turned up, demanding retribution for a runaway slave who had slipped his collar.

"What do you mean?" Caramon muttered dully, his face settling into its resigned, vacant look.

"Well," Tas whispered, with a glance at the smith, "stop and think. Look how you were dressed when we got here. You looked just like a ruffian. Then there was that cleric and those guards turning up, just like they were expecting us. And Lady Crysania, looking like she did."

"You're right," Caramon said, a gleam of life flickering in his dull eyes. The gleam became a flash, igniting a smoldering fire. "Raistlin," he murmured. "He knows I'm going to try and stop him. *He's* done this!"

"I'm not so sure," Tas said after some thought. "I mean, wouldn't he be more likely to just burn you to a crisp or make you into a wall hanging or something like that?"

"No!" Caramon said, and Tas saw excitement in his eyes. "Don't you see? He *wants* me back here . . . to do something. He wouldn't murder us. That . . . that dark elf† who works for him told us, remember?"

He is speaking, of course, of Dalamar, who is Raistlin's apprentice.

Tas looked dubious and started to say something, but just then the blacksmith pushed the warrior to his feet. The bear-skin man, who had been peering in at them impatiently from the doorway of the smith's shop, motioned to two of his own personal slaves. Hurrying inside, they roughly grabbed hold of Caramon and Tas, shoving them into line with the other slaves. Two more slaves came up and began attaching the leg chains of all the slaves together until they were strung out in a line. Then—at a gesture from the bear-skin man—

the wretched living chain of humans, half-elves, and two goblins shuffled forward.

They hadn't taken more than three steps before they were all immediately tangled up by Tasslehoff, who had mistakenly started off in the wrong direction.

After much swearing and a few lashes with a willow stick (first looking to see if any clerics were about), the bear-skin man got the line moving. Tas hopped about trying to get into step. It was only after the kender was twice dragged to his knees, imperiling the entire line again, that Caramon finally wrapped his big arm around his waist, lifted him up—chain and all—and carried him.

"That was kind of fun," Tas commented breathlessly. "Especially where I fell over. Did you see that man's face? I—"

"What did you mean, back there?" Caramon interrupted. "What makes you think Raistlin's not behind this?"

Tas's face grew unusually serious and thoughtful. "Caramon," he said after a moment, putting his arms around Caramon's neck and speaking into his ear to be heard above the rattling of chains and the sounds of the city streets. "Raistlin must have been awfully busy, what with traveling back here and all. Why, it took Par-Salian days to cast that time-traveling spell and he's a really powerful mage. So it must have taken a lot of Raistlin's energy. How could he have possibly done that and done this to us at the same time?"

"Well," Caramon said, frowning. "If he didn't, who did?"

"What about—Fistandantilus?" Tas whispered dramatically.

Caramon sucked in his breath, his face grew dark.

"He—he's a really powerful wizard," Tas reminded him, "and, well, you didn't make any secret of the fact that you've come back here to—uh—well, do him in, so to speak. I mean, you even said that right in the Tower of High Sorcery. And we *know* Fistandantilus can hang around in the Tower. That's where he met Raistlin, wasn't it? What if he was standing there and heard you? I guess he'd be pretty mad."

"Bah! If he's that powerful, he would have just killed me on the spot!" Caramon scowled.

"No, he can't," Tas said firmly. "Look, I've got this all figured out. He can't murder his own pupil's brother. Especially if Raistlin's brought you back here for a reason. Why, for all Fistandantilus knows, Raistlin may love you, deep down inside."

Caramon's face paled, and Tas immediately felt like biting off his tongue. "Anyway," he went on hurriedly, "he can't get rid of you right away. He's got to make it look good."

"So?"

"So—" Tas drew a deep breath. "Well, they don't execute people around here, but they apparently have other ways of dealing with those no one wants hanging around. That cleric and the jailer both talked about executions being 'easy' death compared to what was going on now."

The lash of a whip across Caramon's back ended further conversation. Glaring furiously at the slave who had struck him—an ingratiating, sniveling fellow, who obviously enjoyed his work—Caramon lapsed into gloomy silence, thinking over what Tas had told him. It certainly made sense. He had seen how much power and concentration Par-Salian had exerted casting this difficult spell. Raistlin may be powerful, but not like that! Plus, he was still weak physically.

Caramon suddenly saw everything quite clearly. Tasslehoff's right! We're being set up. Fistandantilus will do away with me somehow and then explain my death to Raistlin as an accident.

Somewhere, in the back of Caramon's mind, he heard a gruff old dwarvish voice say, "I don't know who's the bigger ninny—you or that door-knob of a kender! If either of you make it out of this alive, I'll be surprised!" Caramon smiled sadly at the thought of his old friend. But Flint wasn't here, neither was Tanis or anyone else who could advise him. He and Tas were on their own and, if it hadn't been for the kender's impetuous leap into the spell, he might very well have been back here by himself, without anyone! That thought appalled him. Caramon shivered.

"All this means is that I've got to get to this Fistandantilus before he gets to me," he said to himself softly.

The great spires of the Temple looked down on city streets kept scrupulously clean—all except the back alleys. The streets were thronged with people. Temple guards† roamed about, keeping order, standing out from the crowd in their colorful mantles and plumed helms. Beautiful women cast admiring glances at the guards from the corners of their eyes as they strolled among the bazaars and shops, their fine gowns sweeping the pavement as they moved. There was one place in the city the women didn't go near, however, though many cast curious glances toward it—the part of the square where the slave market stood.

The slave market was crowded, as usual. Auctions were held once a week—one reason the bear-skin man, who was the manager, had been so eager to get his weekly quotient of slaves from the prisons. Though the money from the sales of prisoners went into the public coffers, the manager got his cut, of course. This week looked particularly promising.

As he had told Tas, there were no longer executions in Istar or parts of Krynn that it controlled. Well, few. The Knights of Solamnia still insisted on punishing knights who betrayed their Order in the old barbaric fashion—slitting the knight's throat with his own sword. But the Kingpriest was counseling with the Knights, and there was hope that soon even that heinous practice would be stopped.

Of course, the halting of executions in Istar had created another problem—what to do with the prisoners, who were increasing in number and becoming a drain on the public coffers. The church, therefore, conducted a study.† It was discovered that most prisoners were indigent, homeless, and penniless. The crimes they had committed—thievery, burglary, prostitution, and the like—grew out of this.

"Isn't it logical, therefore," said the Kingpriest to his ministers on the day he made the official pronouncement, "that slavery is not only the answer† to the problem of overcrowding in our prisons but is a most kind and beneficent way of dealing with these poor people, whose only crime is that they have been caught in a web of poverty from which they cannot escape?

The description of the Temple guards is reminiscent of the Vatican's Swiss Guard.

This phrase may have been inspired by my own frustrations with endless corporate meetings that never resulted in any action. —TRH

Once again we see the "White Man's Burden" argument. The condescension in these statements makes my skin crawl. —TRH

"Of course it is. It is our duty, therefore, to help them. As slaves, they will be fed and clothed and housed. They will be given everything they lacked that forced them to turn to a life of crime. We will see to it that they are well-treated, of course, and provide that after a certain period of servitude—if they have done well—they may purchase their own freedom. They will then return to us as productive members of society."

The idea was put into effect at once and had been practiced for about ten years now. There had been problems. But these had never reached the attention of the Kingpriest—they had not been serious enough to demand his concern. Underministers had dealt efficiently with them, and now the system ran quite smoothly. The church had a steady income from the money received for the prison slaves (to keep them separate from slaves sold by private concerns), and slavery even appeared to act as a deterrent from crime.

The problems that had arisen concerned two groups of criminals—kenders and those criminals whose crimes were particularly unsavory. It was discovered that it was impossible to sell a kender to anyone, and it was also difficult to sell a murderer, rapist, the insane, etc. The solutions were simple. Kender were locked up overnight and then escorted to the city gates (this resulted in a small procession every morning). Institutions had been created to handle the more obdurate type of criminal.

It was to the dwarven head of one of these institutions that the bear-skin man stood talking animatedly that morning, pointing at Caramon as he stood with the other prisoners in the filthy, foul-smelling pen behind the block, and making a dramatic motion of knocking a door down with his shoulder.

The head of the institution did not seem impressed. This was not unusual, however. He had learned, long ago, that to seem impressed over a prisoner resulted in the asking price doubling on the spot. Therefore, the dwarf scowled at Caramon, spit on the ground, crossed his arms and, planting his feet firmly on the pavement, glared up at the bear-skin man.

"He's out of shape, too fat. Plus he's a drunk, look at his nose." The dwarf shook his head. "And he

doesn't look mean. What did you say he did? Assaulted a cleric? Humpf!" The dwarf snorted. "The only thing it looks like he could assault'd be a wine jug!"

The bear-skin man was accustomed to this, of course.

"You'd be passing up the chance of a lifetime, Rockbreaker," he said smoothly. "You should have seen him bash that door down. I've never seen such strength in any man. Perhaps he is overweight, but that's easily cured. Fix him up and he'll be a heart-throb. The ladies'll adore him.† Look at those melting brown eyes and that wavy hair." The bear-skin man lowered his voice. "It would be a real shame to lose him to the mines. . . . I tried to keep word of what he had done quiet, but Haarold got wind of it, I'm afraid."

Both the bear-skin man and the dwarf glanced at a human standing some distance away, talking and laughing with several of his burly guards. The dwarf stroked his beard, keeping his face impassive.

The bear-skin man went on, "Haarold's sworn to have him at all costs. Says he'll get the work of two ordinary humans out of him. Now, you being a preferred customer, I'll try to swing things your direction."

"Let Haarold have him," growled the dwarf. "Fat slob."

But the bear-skin man saw the dwarf regarding Caramon with a speculative eye. Knowing from long experience when to talk and when to keep quiet, the bear-skin man bowed to the dwarf and went on his way, rubbing his hands.

Overhearing this conversation, and seeing the dwarf's gaze run over him like a man looks at a prize pig, Caramon felt the sudden, wild desire to break out of his bonds, crash through the pen where he stood caged, and throttle both the bear-skin man and the dwarf. Blood hammered in his brain, he strained against his bonds, the muscles in his arms rippled—a sight that caused the dwarf to open his eyes wide and caused the guards standing around the pen to draw their swords from their scabbards. But Tasslehoff suddenly jabbed him in the ribs with his elbow.

"Caramon, look!" the kender said in excitement.

We were inspired here both by "professional" wrestling and the Roman Circus. Come to think of it, professional wrestling and the Roman Circus have a lot in common. —TRH

For a moment, Caramon couldn't hear over the throbbing in his ears. Tas poked him again.

"Look, Caramon. Over there, at the edge of the crowd, standing by himself. See?"

Caramon drew a shaking breath and forced himself to calm down. He looked over to where the kender was pointing, and suddenly the hot blood in his veins ran cold.

Standing on the fringes of the crowd was a black-robed figure. He stood alone. Indeed, there was even a wide, empty circle around him. None in the crowd came near him. Many made detours, going out of their way to avoid coming close to him. No one spoke to him, but all were aware of his presence. Those near him, who had been talking animatedly, fell into uncomfortable silence, casting nervous glances his direction.

The man's robes were a deep black, without ornamentation. No silver thread glittered on his sleeves, no border surrounded the black hood he wore pulled low over his face. He carried no staff, no familiar walked by his side. Let other mages wear runes of warding and protection, let other mages carry staves of power or have animals do their bidding. This man needed none. His power sprang from within—so great, it had spanned the centuries, spanned even planes of existence. It could be felt, it shimmered around him like the heat from the smith's furnace.

He was tall and well-built, the black robes fell from shoulders that were slender but muscular. His white hands—the only parts of his body that were visible—were strong and delicate and supple. Though so old that few on Krynn could venture even to guess his age, he had the body of one young and strong. Dark rumors told how he used his magic arts to overcome the debilities of age.

And so he stood alone, as if a black sun had been dropped into the courtyard. Not even the glitter of his eyes could be seen within the dark depths of his hood.

"Who's that?" Tas asked a fellow prisoner conversationally, nodding at the black-robed figure.

"Don't you know?" the prisoner said nervously, as if reluctant to reply.

"I'm from out of town," Tas apologized.

"Why, that's the Dark One—Fistandantilus. You've heard of him, I suppose?"

"Yes," Tas said, glancing at Caramon as much as to say *I told you so!* "We've heard of him."

CHAPTER
4

hen Crysania first awakened from the spell Paladine had cast upon her, she was in such a state of bewilderment and confusion that the clerics were greatly concerned, fearing her ordeal had unbalanced her mind.

She spoke of Palanthas, so they assumed she must come from there. But she called continually for the Head of her Order—someone named Elistan. The clerics were familiar with the Heads of all the Orders on Krynn and this Elistan was not known. But she was so insistent that there was, at first, some fear that something might have happened to the current Head in Palanthas. Messengers were hastily dispatched.

Then, too, Crysania spoke of a Temple in Palanthas, where no Temple existed. Finally she talked quite wildly of dragons and the "return of the gods,"† which caused those in the room—Quarath and Elsa,

Speaking of the "return of the gods" is a blasphemous act inasmuch as it would require that at some point the gods had departed— that being a blasphemous thought in the strictly structured world of Istar's Kingpriest. —TRH

257

head of the Revered Daughters—to look at each other in horror and make the signs of protection against blasphemy. Crysania was given an herbal potion, which calmed her, and eventually she fell asleep. The two stayed with her for long moments after she slept, discussing her case in low voices. Then the Kingpriest entered the room, coming to allay their fears.

"I cast an augury," said the musical voice, "and was told that Paladine called her to him to protect her from a spell of evil magic that had been used upon her. I don't believe any of us find that difficult to doubt."

Quarath and Elsa shook their head, exchanging knowing glances. The Kingpriest's hatred of magic-users was well known.

"She has been with Paladine, therefore, living in that wondrous realm which we seek to recreate upon this soil. Undoubtedly, while there, she was given knowledge of the future. She speaks of a beautiful Temple being built in Palanthas. Have we not plans to build such a Temple? She talks of this Elistan, who is probably some cleric destined to rule there."

"But . . . dragons, return of the gods?" murmured Elsa.

"As to the dragons," the Kingpriest said in a voice radiating warmth and amusement, "that is probably some tale† of her childhood that haunted her in her illness, or perhaps had something to do with the spell cast upon her by the magic-user." His voice became stern. "It is said, you know, that the wizards have the power to make people see that which does not exist. As for her talk of the 'return of the gods'. . ."

The Kingpriest† was silent for a moment. When he spoke again, it was with a hushed and breathless quality. "You two, my closest advisors, know of the dream in my heart. You know that someday— and that day is fast approaching—I will go to the gods and demand their help to fight the evil that is still present among us. On that day, Paladine himself will heed my prayers. He will come to stand at my side, and together we will battle the darkness until it is forever vanquished! This is what she has foreseen! This is what she means by the 'return of the gods!' "

During the Third Dragonwar, Huma Dragonbane defeated the Queen of Darkness and her minions. In defeat, Takhisis agreed to depart for the Abyss and take her dragons with her. The good dragons departed as well. It was Takhisis's breaking of this covenant and the return of the dragons to Ansalon that sparked the War of the Lance. But, at this time in history, the War of the Lance is still hundreds of years away. Dragons have been relegated to myths and folktales, which explains why the Kingpriest does not believe in them.

Although his personal name is never given in the Legends trilogy, we learn in Chosen of the Gods *by Chris Pierson that the Kingpriest's name is Beldinas. Throughout the Kingpriest trilogy, Beldinas is referred to as "the Light-bringer," which, translated into Latin, is "Lucifer."*

Light filled the room, Elsa whispered a prayer, and even Quarath lowered his eyes.

"Let her sleep," said the Kingpriest. "She will be better by morning. I will mention her in my prayers to Paladine."

He left the room and it grew darker with his passing. Elsa stood looking after him in silence. Then, as the door shut to Crysania's chamber, the elven woman turned to Quarath.

"Does he have the power?" Elsa asked her male counterpart as he stood staring thoughtfully at Crysania. "Does he truly intend to do . . . what he spoke of doing?"

"What?" Quarath's thoughts had been far away. He glanced after the Kingpriest. "Oh, that? Of course he has the power. You saw how he healed this young woman. And the gods speak to him through the augury, or so he claims. When was the last time you healed someone, Revered Daughter?"

"Then you believe all that about Paladine taking her soul and letting her see the future?" Elsa appeared amazed. "You believe he truly healed her?"

"I believe there is something very strange about this young woman and about those two who came with her," Quarath said gravely. "I will take care of *them*. You keep an eye on her. As for the Kingpriest"—Quarath shrugged—"let him call down the power of the gods. If they come down to fight for him, fine. If not, it doesn't matter to us. We know who does the work of the gods on Krynn."

"I wonder," remarked Elsa, smoothing Crysania's dark hair back from her slumbering face. "There was a young girl in our Order who had the power of true healing. That young girl who was seduced by the Solamnic knight. What was his name?"

"Soth," said Quarath. "Lord Soth, of Dargaard Keep. Oh, I don't doubt it. You occasionally find some, particularly among the very young or the very old, who have the power. Or think they do. Frankly, I am convinced most of it is simply a result of people wanting to believe in something so badly that they convince themselves it is true. Which doesn't hurt any of us. Watch this young woman closely, Elsa. If she continues to talk about such things in the morning, after she is recovered, we may need to take drastic measures. But, for now—"

He fell silent. Elsa nodded. Knowing that the young woman would sleep soundly under the influence of the potion, the two of them left Crysania alone, asleep in a room in the great Temple of Istar.

Crysania woke the next morning feeling as if her head were stuffed with cotton. There was a bitter taste in her mouth and she was terribly thirsty. Dizzily, she sat up, trying to piece together her thoughts. Nothing made any sense. She had a vague, horrifying memory of a ghastly creature from beyond the grave approaching her. Then she had been with Raistlin in the Tower of High Sorcery, and then a dim memory of being surrounded by mages dressed in white, red, and black, an impression of singing stones, and a feeling of having taken a long journey.

Crysania is referencing events that occurred in Dragons of Autumn Twilight, *Book II, Chapters 12-13.*

She also had a memory of awakening and finding herself in the presence of a man whose beauty had been overpowering, whose voice filled her mind and her soul with peace. But he said he was the Kingpriest and that she was in the Temple of the Gods in Istar. That made no sense at all. She remembered calling for Elistan, but no one seemed to have heard of him. She told them about him—how he was healed by Goldmoon,† cleric of Mishakal, how he led the fight against the evil dragons, and how he was telling the people about the return of the gods. But her words only made the clerics regard her with pity and alarm. Finally, they gave her an odd-tasting potion to drink, and she had fallen asleep.

Though she is several hundred years in the past, Crysania's current surroundings are far better than what she—even as a wealthy member of a great city—is used to. It seems that every culture longs for "the good old days" when things were better. The Arabs, it has been said, long for the great days of the Persian Empire and dream of reestablishing that greatness. The Jewish nation longs after the greatness of Herod's Temple. People in the United States have a long tradition of looking back with longing on their own short history. The truth is that the good old days were not nearly so good as we believe them to be; nevertheless it is a common and recurring theme in mythology. —TRH

Now she was still confused but determined to find out where she was and what was happening. Getting out of bed, she forced herself to wash as she did every morning, then she sat down at the strange-looking dressing table and calmly brushed and braided her long, dark hair. The familiar routine made her feel more relaxed.

She even took time to look around the bedroom, and she couldn't help but admire its beauty and splendor. But she did think, however, that it seemed rather out of place in a Temple devoted to the gods, if that was truly where she was. Her bedroom in her parent's home in Palanthas had not been half so splendid,† and it had been furnished with every luxury money could buy.

Her mind went suddenly to what Raistlin had shown her—the poverty and want so near the Temple—and she flushed uncomfortably.

"Perhaps this is a guest room," Crysania said to herself, speaking out loud, finding the familiar sound of her own voice comforting. "After all, the guest rooms in our new Temple are certainly designed to make our guests comfortable. Still"—she frowned, her gaze going to a costly golden statue of a dryad,† holding a candle in her golden hands—"that is extravagant. It would feed a family for months."

How thankful she was he couldn't see this! She would speak to the Head of this Order, whoever he was. (Surely she must have been mistaken, thinking he said he was the Kingpriest!)

Having made up her mind to action, feeling her head clear, Crysania removed the night clothes she had been wearing and put on the white robes she found laid out neatly at the foot of her bed.

What quaint, old-fashioned robes, she noticed, slipping them over her head. Not at all like the plain, austere white robes worn by those of her Order in Palanthas. These were heavily decorated. Golden thread sparkled on the sleeves and hem, crimson and purple ribbon ornamented the front, and a heavy golden belt gathered the folds around her slender waist. More extravagance. Crysania bit her lip in displeasure, but she also took a peep at herself in a gilt-framed mirror. It certainly was becoming, she had to admit, smoothing the folds of the gown.

It was then that she felt the note in her pocket.

Reaching inside, she pulled out a piece of rice paper that had been folded into quarters. Staring at it curiously, wondering idly if the owner of the robes had left it by accident, she was startled to see it addressed to herself. Puzzled, she opened it.

Lady Crysania,

I knew you intended to seek my help in returning to the past in an effort to prevent the young mage, Raistlin, from carrying out the evil he plots. Upon your way to us, however, you were atacked by a death knight. To save you, Paladine took your soul to his heavenly dwelling. There are none among us now, even Elistan himself, who can bring you back.† Only those clerics living at the time of the Kingpriest have this power. So we have

"If any creature can be called a child of nature, it's the dryad. Depending on when you meet one, you could easily mistake her for an elf maiden. Dryads are beautiful, thin, pale, creatures, the very essence of a woman that a human lad might lose his heart to at first sight. However, they have no human blood within them—they're not even mortal." [The Bestiary, by Steven "Stan!" Brown, Wizards of the Coast, Inc., 1998, p. 104.]

On reflection, this seems like a very convenient disease—at least for the authors—doesn't it?
—TRH

sent you back in time to Istar, right before the Cata-
clysm, in the company of Raistlin's brother, Caramon.
We send you to fulfill a twofold purpose. First, to heal
you of your grievous wound and, second, to allow you
to try to succeed in your efforts to save the young mage
from himself.

If, in this, you see the workings of the gods, perhaps
then you may consider your efforts blessed. I would
counsel only this—that the gods work in ways strange
to mortal men, since we see only that part of the picture
being painted around us. I had hoped to discuss this
with you personally, before you left, but that proved
impossible. I can only caution you of one thing—beware
of Raistlin.

You are virtuous, steadfast in your faith, and proud of
both your virtue and your faith. This is a deadly combination, my dear. He will take full advantage of it.

Remember this, too. You and Caramon have gone back
in dangerous times. The days of the Kingpriest are numbered. Caramon is on a mission that could prove dangerous to his life.

But you, Crysania, are in danger of both your life and
your soul. I foresee that you will be forced to choose—to
save one, you must give up the other.† There are many
ways for you to leave this time period, one of which is
through Caramon. May Paladine be with you.

Par-Salian
Order of the White Robes
The Tower of High Sorcery
Wayreth

Another Biblical reference.
—TRH

"24 Then said Jesus unto
his disciples, If any man
will come after me, let him
deny himself, and take up
his cross, and follow me.
25 For whosoever will save
his life shall lose it: and
whosoever will lose his life
for my sake shall find it.
26 For what is a man
profited, if he shall gain the
whole world, and lose his
own soul? or what shall a
man give in exchange for
his soul?"
[Matthew 16: 24-26 KJV]

Crysania sank down on the bed, her knees
giving way beneath her. The hand that held the
letter trembled. Dazedly, she stared at it, reading it
over and over without comprehending the words.
After a few moments, however, she grew calmer
and forced herself to go over each word, reading
one sentence at a time until she was certain she had
grasped the meaning.

This took nearly a half hour of reading and pondering. At last she believed she understood. Or at
least most of it. The memory of why she had been
journeying to the Forest of Wayreft returned. So,
Par-Salian had known. He had been expecting her.
All the better. And he was right—the attack by the
death knight had obviously been an example of

Paladine's intervention, insuring that she come back here to the past. As for that remark about her faith and her virtue—!

Crysania rose to her feet. Her pale face was fixed in firm resolve, there was a faint spot of color in each cheek, and her eyes glittered in anger. She was only sorry she had *not* been able to confront him with that in person! How dare he?

Her lips drawn into a tight, straight line, Crysania refolded the note, drawing her fingers across it swiftly, as though she would like to tear it apart. A small golden box—the kind of box used by ladies of the court to hold their jewelry—stood on the dressing table beside the gilt-edged mirror and the brush. Picking up the box, Crysania withdrew the small key from the lock, thrust the letter inside, and snapped the lid shut. She inserted the key, twisted it, and heard the lock click. Dropping the key into the pocket where she had found the note, Crysania looked once more into the mirror.

She smoothed the black hair back from her face, drew up the hood of her robe, and draped it over her head. Noticing the flush on her cheeks, Crysania forced herself to relax, allow her anger to seep away. The old mage meant well, after all, she reminded herself. And how could one of magic possibly understand one of faith? She could rise above petty anger. She was, after all, hovering on the edge of her moment of greatness. Paladine was with her. She could almost sense his presence. And the man she had met was truly the Kingpriest!

She smiled, remembering the feeling of goodness he had inspired. How could he have been responsible for the Cataclysm? No, her soul refused to believe it. History must have maligned him. True, she had been with him for only a few seconds, but a man so beautiful, so good and holy†—responsible for such death and destruction? It was impossible! Perhaps she would be able to vindicate him. Perhaps that was another reason Paladine had sent her back here—to discover the truth!

Joy filled Crysania's soul. And, at that moment, she heard her joy answered, it seemed, in the pealing of the bells ringing for Morning Prayers. The beauty of the music brought tears to her eyes. Her heart bursting with excitement and happiness, Crysania

Lucifer, too, was said to be the most beautiful of the angels. —TRH

left her room and hurried out into the magnificent corridors, nearly running into Elsa.

"In the name of the gods," exclaimed Elsa in astonishment, "can it be possible? How are you feeling?"

"I am feeling much better, Revered Daughter," Crysania said in some confusion, remembering that what they had heard her say earlier must have seemed to be wild and incoherent ramblings. "As—as though I had awakened from a strange and vivid dream."

"Paladine be praised," murmured Elsa, regarding Crysania with narrowed eyes and a sharp, penetrating gaze.

"I have not neglected to do so, you may be certain," said Crysania sincerely. In her own joy, she did not notice the elf woman's odd look. "Were you going to Morning Prayers? If so, may I accompany you?" She looked around the splendid building in awe. "I fear it will be some time before I learn my way around."

"Of course," Elsa said, recovering herself. "This way." They started back down the corridor.

"I was also concerned about the—the young man who was . . . was found with me," Crysania stammered, suddenly remembering she knew very little about the circumstances regarding her appearance in this time.

Elsa's face grew cold and stern. "He is where he will be well cared for, my dear. Is he a friend of yours?"

"No, of course not," Crysania said quickly, remembering her last encounter with the drunken Caramon. "He—he was my escort. Hired escort," she stammered, realizing suddenly that she was very poor at lying.

"He is at the School of the Games," Elsa replied. "It would be possible to send him a message, if you are concerned."

Crysania had no idea what this school was, and she was afraid to ask too many more questions. Thanking Elsa, therefore, she let the matter drop, her mind at ease. At least now she knew where Caramon was and that he was safe. Feeling reassured, knowing that she had a way back to her own time, she allowed herself to relax completely.

"Ah, look, my dear," Elsa said, "here comes another to inquire after your health."

"Revered Son," Crysania bowed in reverence as Quarath came up to the two women. Thus she missed his swift glance of inquiry at Elsa and the elf-woman's slight nod.

"I am overjoyed to see you up and around," Quarath said, taking Crysania's hand and speaking with such feeling and warmth that the young woman flushed with pleasure. "The Kingpriest spent the night in prayer for your recovery. This proof of his faith and power will be extremely gratifying. We will present you to him formally this evening. But, now"—he interrupted whatever Crysania had been about to say—"I am keeping you from Prayers. Please, do not let me detain you further."

Bowing to them both with exquisite grace, Quarath walked past, heading down the corridor.

"Isn't he attending services?" Crysania asked, her gaze following the cleric.

"No, my dear," Elsa said, smiling at Crysania's naiveté, "he attends the Kingpriest in his own private ceremonies early each morning. Quarath is, after all, second only to the Kingpriest and has matters of great importance to deal with each day. One might say that, if the Kingpriest is the heart and soul of the church, Quarath is the brain."

"My, how odd," murmured Crysania, her thoughts on Elistan.

"Odd, my dear?" Elsa said, with a slightly reproving air. "The Kingpriest's thoughts are with the gods. He cannot be expected to deal with such mundane matters as the day-to-day business of the church, can he?"

"Oh, of course not." Crysania flushed in embarrassment.

How provincial she must seem to these people; how simple and backward. As she followed Elsa down the bright and airy halls, the beautiful music of the bells and the glorious sound of a children's choir filled her very soul with ecstasy. Crysania remembered the simple service Elistan held every morning. And he still did most of the work of the church himself!

That simple service seemed shabby to her now, Elistan's work demeaning. Certainly it had taken a toll on his health. Perhaps, she thought with a pang of regret, he might not have shortened his own life

if he had been surrounded by people like these to help him.

Well, that would change, Crysania resolved suddenly, realizing that this must be another reason why she had been sent back—she had been chosen to restore the glory of the church! Trembling in excitement, her mind already busy with plans for change, Crysania asked Elsa to describe the inner workings of the church hierarchy. Elsa was only too glad to expand upon it as the two continued down the corridor.

Lost in her interest in the conversation, attentive to Elsa's every word, Crysania thought no more of Quarath, who was—at that moment—quietly opening the door to her bedroom and slipping inside.

Chapter 5

uarath found the letter from Par-Salian within a matter of moments. He had noticed, almost immediately on entering, that the golden box that stood on top of the dressing table had been moved. A quick search of the drawers revealed it and, since he had the master key to the locks of every box and drawer and door in the Temple, he opened it easily.

The letter itself, however, was not so easily understood by the cleric. It took him only seconds to absorb its contents. These would remain imprinted on his mind; Quarath's phenomenal ability to memorize instantly anything he saw being one of his greatest gifts. So it was that he had the complete text of the letter locked in his mind within seconds. But, he realized, it would take hours of pondering to make sense of it.

Absently, Quarath folded the parchment and put

it back into the box, then returned the box to its exact position within the drawer. He locked it with the key, glanced through the other drawers without much interest, and—finding nothing—left the young woman's room, lost in thought.

So perplexing and disturbing were the contents of the letter that he canceled his appointments for that morning or shifted them onto the shoulders of underlings. Then he went to his study. Here he sat, recalling each word, each phrase.

At last, he had it figured out—if not to his complete satisfaction, then, at least, enough to allow him to determine a course of action. Three things were apparent. One, the young woman might be a cleric, but she was involved with magic-users and was, therefore, suspect. Two, the Kingpriest was in danger. That was not surprising, the magic-users had good reason to hate and fear the man. Three, the young man who had been found with Crysania was, undoubtedly, an assassin. Crysania, herself might be an accomplice.

Quarath smiled grimly, congratulating himself on having already taken appropriate measures to deal with the threat. He had seen to it that the young man—Caramon was his name apparently—was serving his time in a place where unfortunate accidents occurred from time to time.

As for Crysania, she was safely within the walls of the Temple where she could be watched and subtly interrogated.

Breathing easier, his mind clearing, the cleric rang for the servant to bring his lunch, thankful to know that, for the moment at least, the Kingpriest was safe.

Quarath was an unusual man in many respects, not the least of which was that, though highly ambitious, he knew the limits of his own abilities. He needed the Kingpriest, he had no desire to take his place.† Quarath was content to bask in the light of his master, all the while extending his own control and authority and power over the world—all in the name of the church.

And, as he extended his own authority, so he extended the power of his race. Imbued with a sense of their superiority over all others, as well as with a sense of their own innate goodness, the elves were a moving force behind the church.

It has become very cliché in fantasy fiction that the villain (usually a "Dark Lord") wants to rule the world. It's never explained why, exactly. That's just what dark lords are supposed to do. But Quarath breaks the cliché and is a more realistic character. He wants the power to control others, but he recognizes that it is much safer to do it from the background. Better to let the puppet do the ruling while he pulls the strings.

It was unfortunate, Quarath felt, that the gods had seen fit to create other, weaker races. Races such as humans, who—with their short and frantic lives—were easy targets for the temptations of evil. But the elves were learning to deal with this. If they could not completely wipe out the evil in the world (and they were working on it), then they could at least bring it under control. It was freedom that brought about evil—freedom of choice.† Especially to humans, who continually abused this gift. Give them strict rules to follow, make it clear what was right and what was wrong in no uncertain terms, restrict this wild freedom that they misused. Thus, Quarath believed, the humans would fall in line. They would be content.

This is the fatal flaw at the heart of all the Kingpriest's logic. The freedom of man to think and choose— man's agency of independent thought and choice—is the heart of humanity's relationship to God. The denial of agency and the suppression of alternate ideas and opinions was Satan's plan from the beginning and was rejected by God. The Kingpriest is following Satan's logic here. See Appendix C. —TRH

As for the other races on Krynn, gnomes and dwarves and (sigh) kender, Quarath (and the church) was rapidly forcing them into small, isolated territories where they could cause little trouble and would, in time, probably die out. (This plan was working well with the gnomes and the dwarves, who hadn't much use for the rest of Krynn anyhow. Unfortunately, however, the kender didn't take to it at all and were still happily wandering about the world, causing no end of trouble and enjoying life thoroughly.)

All of this passed through Quarath's mind as he ate his lunch and began to make his plans. He would do nothing in haste about this Lady Crysania. That was not his way, nor the way of the elves, for that matter. Patience in all things. Watch. Wait. He needed only one thing now, and that was more information. To this end, he rang a small golden bell. The young acolyte who had taken Denubis to the Kingpriest appeared so swiftly and quietly at the summons that he might have slipped beneath the door instead of opening it.

"What is your bidding, Revered Son?"

"Two small tasks," Quarath said without looking up, being engaged in writing a note. "Take this to Fistandantilus. It has been some time since he was my guest at dinner, and I desire to talk with him."

"Fistandantilus is not here, my lord," said the acolyte. "In fact, I was on my way to report this to you."

Quarath raised his head in astonishment.

"Not here?"

"No, Revered Son. He left last night, or so we suppose. At least that was the last anyone saw of him. His room is empty, his things gone. It is believed, from certain things he said, that he has gone to the Tower of High Sorcery at Wayreth. Rumor has it that the wizards are holding a Conclave there, though none know for certain."

"A Conclave," Quarath repeated, frowning. He was silent a moment, tapping the paper with the tip of the quill. Wayreth was far away . . . still, perhaps it was not far enough. . . . Cataclysm . . . that odd word that had been used in the letter. Could it be possible that the magic-users were plotting some devastating catastrophe? Quarath felt chilled. Slowly, he crumpled the invitation he had been penning.

"Have his movements been traced?"

"Of course, Revered Son. As much as is possible with him. He has not left the Temple for months, apparently. Then, yesterday, he was seen in the slave market."

"The slave market?" Quarath felt the chill spread throughout his body. "What business did he have there?"

"He bought two slaves, Revered Son."

Quarath said nothing, interrogating the cleric with a look.

"He did not purchase the slaves himself, my lord. The purchase was made through one of his agents."

"Which slaves?" Quarath knew the answer.

"The ones that were accused of assaulting the female cleric, Revered Son."

"I gave orders that those two were to be sold either to the dwarf or the mines."

"Barak did his best and, indeed, the dwarf bid for them, my lord. But the Dark One's agents outbid him. There was nothing Barak could do. Think of the scandal. Besides, his agent sent them to the school anyway—"

"Yes," Quarath muttered. So, it was all falling into place. Fistandantilus had even had the temerity to purchase the young man, the assassin! Then he had vanished. Gone to report, undoubtedly. But why should the mages bother with assassins? Fistandantilus himself could have murdered the

Kingpriest on countless occasions. Quarath had the unpleasant impression that he had inadvertently walked from a clear, well-lighted path into a dark and treacherous forest.

He sat in troubled silence for so long that the young acolyte cleared his throat as a subtle reminder of his presence three times before the cleric noticed him.

"You had another task for me, Revered Son?"

Quarath nodded slowly. "Yes, and this news makes this task even more important. I wish you to undertake it yourself. I must talk to the dwarf."

The acolyte bowed and left. There was no need to ask who Quarath meant—there was only one dwarf in Istar.

Just who Arack Rockbreaker was or where he came from no one knew. He never made reference to his past and generally scowled so ferociously if this subject came up that it was usually immediately dropped. There were several interesting speculations concerning this, the favorite being that he was an outcast from Thorbardin—ancient home of the mountain dwarves, where he had committed some crime resulting in exile. Just what that might have been, no one knew. Nor did anyone take into account the fact that dwarves never punished any crime by exile; execution being considered more humane.

Other rumors insisted he was actually a Dewar†— a race of evil dwarves nearly exterminated by their cousins and now driven to living a wretched, embittered existence in the very bowels of the world. Though Arack didn't particularly look or act like a Dewar, this rumor was popular due to the fact that Arack's favorite (and only) companion was an ogre. Other rumor had it that Arack didn't even come from Ansalon at all, but from somewhere over the sea.†

Certainly, he was the meanest looking of his race anyone could remember seeing. The jagged scars that crossed his face vertically gave him a perpetual scowl. He was not fat, there wasn't a wasted ounce on his frame. He moved with the grace of a feline and, when he stood, planted his feet so firmly that they seemed part of the ground itself.

The Dewar, or "Dark Dwarves," should not be confused with the Daewar, a noble clan of Mountain Dwarves.

"The dark dwarves include two clans of mountain dwarves who prefer to live completely in darkness. Considered mad by other dwarves, dark dwarves are known for evil and murderous acts. They claim loyalty to the High Thane and the dwarven race, but more than once the dark dwarves have betrayed their kin. [DRAGONLANCE Campaign Setting, Wizards of the Coast, 2003, p. 14.]

When the DRAGONLANCE setting was first created, there was a vague notion of there being "other lands" across the oceans, but these were thought of much like the destination of Tolkien's elves when they went "into the West." Originally, there was no further thought to the coastlines of these other lands than appear here in these brief words. —TRH

This later changed, of course, as the DRAGONLANCE setting

grew in popularity. TSR soon began publishing AD&D game products set in other continents of Krynn, the most notable being the DRAGONLANCE Time of the Dragon *Boxed Set, which detailed the continent of Taladas far to the northeast of Ansalon, and the* DRAGONLANCE *accessory* Otherlands, *which dealt with "lost" lands beyond even Taladas.*

Wherever he came from, Arack had made Istar his home for so many years now that the subject of his origin rarely came up. He and the ogre, whose name was Raag, had come for the Games in the old days when the Games had been real. They immediately became great favorites with the crowds. People in Istar still told how Raag and Arack defeated the mighty minotaur, Darmoork, in three rounds. It started when Darmoork hurled the dwarf clear out of the arena. Raag, in a berserk fit of anger, lifted the minotaur off his feet and—ignoring several terrible stab wounds—impaled him upon the huge Freedom Spire in the center of the ring.

Though neither the dwarf (who survived only by the fact that a cleric had been standing in the street when the dwarf sailed over the arena wall and landed practically at his feet) nor the ogre won his freedom that day, there was no doubt who had been winner of the contest. (Indeed, it was many days before anyone reached the Golden Key on the Spire, since it took that long to remove the remains of the minotaur.)

Arack related the gruesome details of this fight to his two new slaves.

"That's how I got this old cracked face of mine," the dwarf said to Caramon as he led the big man and the kender through the streets of Istar. "And that's how me and Raag made our name in the Games."

"What games?" asked Tas, stumbling over his chains and sprawling flat on his face, to the great delight of the crowd in the market place.

Arack scowled in irritation. "Take those durn things off 'im," he ordered the gigantic, yellow-skinned ogre, who was acting as guard. "I guess you won't run off and leave yer friend behind, will you?" The dwarf studied Tas intently. "No, I didn't think so. They said you had a chance to run away once and you didn't. Just mind you don't run away on me!" Arack's natural scowl deepened. "I'd have never bought a kender, but I didn't have much choice. *They* said you two was to be sold together. Just remember that—as far as I'm concerned—yer worthless. Now, what fool question was you asking?"

"How are you going to get the chains off? Don't you need a key? Oh—" Tas watched in delighted

astonishment as the ogre took the chains in either hand and, with a quick jerk, yanked them apart.

"Did you see that, Caramon?" Tas asked as the ogre picked him up and set him on his feet, giving him a push that nearly sent the kender into the dirt again. "He's really strong! I never met an ogre before. What was I saying? Oh, the games. What games?"

"Why, *the Games*," Arack snapped in exasperation.

Tas glanced up at Caramon, but the big man shrugged and shook his head, frowning. This was obviously something everyone knew about here. Asking too many questions would seem suspicious. Tas cast about in his mind, dragging up every memory and every story he had ever heard about the ancient days before the Cataclysm. Suddenly he caught his breath. "The Games!" he said to Caramon, forgetting the dwarf was listening. "The great Games of Istar! Don't you remember?"

Caramon's face grew grim.

"You mean that's where we're going?" Tas turned to the dwarf, his eyes wide. "We're going to be gladiators? And fight in the arena, with the crowd watching and all! Oh, Caramon, think of it! The great Games of Istar! Why I've heard stories—"

"So have I," the big man said slowly, "and you can forget it, dwarf. I've killed men before, I admit—but only when it was my life or theirs. I never enjoyed killing. I can still see their faces, sometimes, at night. I won't murder for sport!"

He said this so sternly that Raag glanced questioningly at the dwarf and raised his club slightly, an eager look on his yellow, warty face. But Arack glared at him and shook his head.

Tas was regarding Caramon with new respect. "I never thought of that," the kender said softly. "I guess you're right, Caramon." He turned to the dwarf again. "I'm really sorry, Arack, but we won't be able to fight for you."

Arack cackled. "You'll fight. Why? Because it's the only way to get that collar off yer neck, that's why."

Caramon shook his head stubbornly. "I won't kill—"

The dwarf snorted. "Where have you two been living? At the bottom of the Sirrion?† Or are they all

The Sirrion Sea lies to the west of Ansalon.

273

We know that Solace became a tree-city after the Cataclysm, when the people took to the treetops for protection. Did Solace exist before that? It might have, as a very small village, which means it is unlikely that Arack would have heard of it. The dwarf's comment here is probably in reference to something Caramon said about being from a town named Solace. —MW

Ancient Roman gladiatorial combat was every bit as contrived in many instances as today's professional wrestling. It seems that people in all ages find the spectacle more important than an honest contest of skills. This, I believe, is because of how we, as a race of beings, perceive the world. See Appendix A. —TRH

The fact that the games are fake further emphasizes the idea that Istar is built on a foundation of sham, trickery, hypocrisy, and illusion. —MW

as dumb as you in Solace?† No one fights to kill in the arena anymore." Arack's eyes grew misty. He rubbed them with a sigh. "Those days are gone for good, more's the pity. It's all fake."†

"Fake?" Tas repeated in astonishment. Caramon glowered at the dwarf and said nothing, obviously not believing a word.

"There hasn't been a real, true fight in the old arena in ten years," Arack avowed. "It all started with the elves"—the dwarf spat on the ground. "Ten years ago, the elven clerics—curse them to the Abyss where they belong—convinced the Kingpriest to put an end to the Games. Called 'em 'barbaric'! Barbaric, hah!" The dwarf's scowl twisted into a snarl, then—once more—he sighed and shook his head.

"All the great gladiators left," Arack said wistfully, his eyes looking back to that glorious time. "Danark the Hobgoblin—as vicious a fighter as you'll ever come across. And Old Josepf One-Eye. Remember him, Raag?" The ogre nodded sadly. "Claimed he was a Knight of Solamnia, old Josepf did. Always fought in full battle armor. They all left, except me and Raag." A gleam appeared deep in the dwarf's cold eyes. "We didn't have nowhere to go, you see, and besides—I had a kind of feeling that the Games weren't over. Not yet."

Arack and Raag stayed in Istar. Keeping their quarters inside the deserted arena, they became, as it were, unofficial caretakers. Passers-by saw them there daily—Raag lumbering among the stands, sweeping the aisles with a crude broom or just sitting, staring down dully into the arena where Arack worked, the dwarf lovingly tending the machines in the Death Pits, keeping them oiled and running. Those who saw the dwarf sometimes noticed a strange smile on his bearded, broken-nosed face.

Arack was right. The Games hadn't been banned many months before the clerics began noticing that their peaceful city wasn't so peaceful anymore. Fights broke out in bars and taverns with alarming frequency, there were brawls in the streets and once, even, a full-scale riot. There were reports that the Games had gone underground (literally) and were now being held in caves outside of town. The

discovery of several mauled and mutilated bodies appeared to bear this out. Finally, in desperation, a group of human and elf lords sent a delegation to the Kingpriest to request that the Games be started again.

"Just as a volcano must erupt to let the steam and poisonous vapors escape from the ground," said one elflord, "so it seems that humans, in particular, use the Games as an outlet for their baser emotions."

While this speech certainly did nothing to endear the elflord to his human counterparts, they were forced to admit there was some justification to it. At first, the Kingpriest wouldn't hear of it. He had always abhorred the brutal contests. Life was a sacred gift of the gods, not something to be taken away just to provide pleasure to a blood-thirsty crowd.

"And then it was me gave 'em their answer," Arack† said smugly. "They weren't going to let me in their fine and fancy Temple." The dwarf grinned. "But no one keeps Raag out of wherever he's a mind to go. So they hadn't much choice.

" 'Start the Games again,' I told 'em, and they looked down at their long noses at me. 'But there needn't be no killing,' I says. 'No real killing, that is. Now, listen me out. You've seen the street actors do Huma, ain't you? You've seen the knight fall to the ground, bleedin' and moanin' and floppin' around. Yet five minutes later he's up and drinking ale at the tavern down the block. I've done a bit of street work in my time, and . . . well . . . watch this. Come here, Raag.'

"Raag came over, a big grin on his ugly, yellow face.

" 'Give me your sword, Raag,' I orders. Then, before they could say a word, I plunges the sword in Raag's gut. You shoulda seen him. Blood all over! Running down my hands, spurting from his mouth. He gave a great bellow and fell to the floor, twitchin' and groanin'.

"You shoulda heard 'em yell," the dwarf said gleefully, shaking his head over the memory. "I thought we was gonna have to pick them elflords up off the floor. So, before they could call the guards to come haul me away, I kicked old Raag, here.

" 'You can get up now, Raag,' I says.

> "Arack's past is unknown. Once a gladiator in the Games when they were real, Arack now runs the fake Games for the vicarious delight of the wealthy of Istar. The dwarf is one of the strongest of his race and extremely ugly. A long scar that runs vertically across his face gives him a perpetual scowl that appears especially sinister when he is smiling."
> [DRAGONLANCE Adventures, by Tracy Hickman and Margaret Weis, TSR, Inc., 1987, p. 90.]

"And he sat up, giving them a big grin. Well, they all started talking at once." The dwarf mimicked high-pitched elven voices.

" 'Remarkable! How is it done? This could be the answer—' "

"How *did* you do it?" Tas asked eagerly.

Arack shrugged. "You'll learn. A lot of chicken blood, a sword with a blade that collapses down into the handle—it's simple. That's what I told 'em. Plus, it's easy to teach gladiators how to act like they're hurt, even a dummy like old Raag† here."

Tas glanced at the ogre apprehensively, but Raag was only grinning fondly at the dwarf. "Most of 'em beefed up their fights anyway, to make it look good for the gulls—audience, I should say. Well, the King-priest, he went for it and"—the dwarf drew himself up proudly— "he even made me Master. And that's my title, now. Master of the Games."

"I don't understand," Caramon said slowly. "You mean people pay to be tricked? Surely they must have figured it out—"

"Oh, sure," Arack sneered. "We've never made no big secret of it. And now it's the most popular sport on Krynn. People travel fer hundreds of miles to see the Games. The elflords come—and even the King-priest himself, sometimes. Well, here we are," Arack said, coming to a halt outside a huge stadium and looking up at it with pride.

It was made of stone and was ages old, but what it might have been built for originally, no one remembered. On Game days, bright flags fluttered from the tops of the stone towers and it would have been thronged with people. But there were no Games today, nor would there be until summer's end. It was gray and colorless, except for the garish paintings on the walls portraying great events in the history of the sport. A few children stood around the outside, hoping for a glimpse of one of their heroes. Snarling at them, Arack motioned to Raag to open the massive, wooden doors.

"You mean no one gets killed," Caramon persisted, staring somberly at the arena with its bloody paintings.

The dwarf looked oddly at Caramon, Tas saw. Arack's expression was suddenly cruel and calculating, his dark, tangled eyebrows creased over his small

"A gigantic and not overly bright ogre, Raag is Arack's devoted bodyguard and the dwarf's only friend. Raag is extremely fond of Arack and would unhesitantly lay down his life for the dwarf. Arack is also fond of Raag—the two have been together a long, long time."
[DRAGONLANCE Adventures, *by Tracy Hickman and Margaret Weis, TSR, Inc., 1987, p. 95.]*

eyes. Caramon didn't notice, he was still inspecting the wall paintings. Tas made a sound, and Caramon suddenly glanced around at the dwarf. But, by that time, Arack's expression had changed.

"No one," the dwarf said with a grin, patting Caramon's big arm. "No one. . . ."

CHAPTER 6

The ogre led Caramon and Tas into a large room. Caramon had the fevered impression of its being filled with people.

"Him new man," grunted Raag, jerking a yellow, filthy thumb in Caramon's direction as the big man stood next to him. It was Caramon's introduction to the "school." Flushing, acutely conscious of the iron collar around his neck that branded him someone's property, Caramon kept his eyes on the straw-covered, wooden floor. Hearing only a muttered response to Raag's statement, Caramon glanced up. He was in a mess hall, he saw now. Twenty or thirty men of various races and nationalities sat about in small groups, eating dinner.

Some of the men were looking at Caramon with interest, most weren't looking at him at all. A few nodded, the majority continued eating. Caramon wasn't certain what to do next, but Raag solved the

problem. Laying a hand on Caramon's shoulder, the ogre shoved him roughly toward a table. Caramon stumbled and nearly fell, managing to catch himself before he smashed into the table. Whirling around, he glared angrily at the ogre. Raag stood grinning at him, his hands twitching.

I'm being baited, Caramon realized, having seen that look too many times in bars where someone was always trying to goad the big man into a fight. And this was one fight he knew he couldn't win. Though Caramon stood almost six and a half feet tall, he didn't even quite come to the ogre's shoulder, while Raag's vast hand could wrap itself around Caramon's thick neck twice. Caramon swallowed, rubbed his bruised leg, and sat down on the long wooden bench.

Casting a sneering glance at the big human, Raag's squinty-eyed gaze took in everyone in the mess hall. With shrugs and low murmurs of disappointment, the men went back to their dinners. From a table in a corner, where sat a group of minotaurs, there was laughter. Grinning back at them, Raag left the room.

Feeling himself blush self-consciously, Caramon hunkered down on the bench and tried to disappear. Someone was sitting across from him, but the big warrior couldn't bear to meet the man's gaze. Tasslehoff had no such inhibitions, however. Clambering up on the bench beside Caramon, the kender regarded their neighbor with interest.

"I'm Tasslehoff Burrfoot," he said, extending his small hand to a large, black-skinned human†—also wearing an iron collar—sitting across them. "I'm new, too," the kender added, feeling wounded that he had not been introduced. The black man looked up from his food, glanced at Tas, ignored the kender's hand, then turned his gaze on Caramon.

"You two partners?"

"Yeah," Caramon answered, thankful the man hadn't referred to Raag in any way. He was suddenly aware of the smell of food and sniffed hungrily, his mouth watering. Looking appreciatively at the man's plate, which was stacked high with roast deer meat, potatoes, and slabs of bread, he sighed. "Looks like they feed us well, at any rate."

Caramon saw the black-skinned man glance at his round belly and then exchange amused looks

Tolkien's original fantasy was written with a British audience in mind. Tolkien himself said that his purpose was to write an "Anglo-Saxon mythology." Even so, he managed to address wide and deep racial issues under the guise of elves and dwarves. His audience, we now know, is global. I have always wished that diverse people of color, representative of that wider world, were a larger part of fantasy. —TRH

with a tall, extraordinarily beautiful woman who took her seat next to him, her plate loaded with food as well. Looking at her, Caramon's eyes widened. Clumsily, he attempted to stand up and bow.

"Your servant, ma'am—" he began.

"Sit down, you great oaf!" the woman snapped angrily, her tan skin darkening. "You'll have them all laughing!"

Indeed, several of the men chuckled. The woman turned and glared at them, her hand darting to a dagger she wore in her belt. At the sight of her flashing green eyes, the men swallowed their laughter and went back to their food. The woman waited until she was certain all had been properly cowed, then she, too, turned her attention back to her meal, jabbing at her meat with swift, irritated thrusts of her fork.

"I—I'm sorry," Caramon stammered, his big face flushed. "I didn't mean—"

"Forget it," the woman said in a throaty voice. Her accent was odd, Caramon couldn't place it. She appeared to be human, except for that strange way of talking—stranger even than the other people around here—and the fact that her hair was a most peculiar color—sort of a dull, leaden green. It was thick and straight, and she wore it in a long braid down her back. "You're new here, I take it. You'll soon understand—you don't treat me any different than the others. Either in or out of the arena. Got that?"

"The arena?" Caramon said in blank astonishment. "You—you're a gladiator?"

"One of the best, too," the black-skinned man across from them said, grinning. "I am Pheragas of Northern Ergoth and this is Kiiri the Sirine—"†

"A Sirine! From below the sea?" Tas asked in excitement. "One of those women who can change shapes and—"

The woman flashed the kender a glance of such fury that Tas blinked and fell silent. Then her gaze went swiftly to Caramon. "Do you find that funny, *slave*?" Kiiri asked, her eyes on Caramon's new collar.

Caramon put his hand over it, flushing again. Kiiri gave a short, bitter laugh, but Pheragas regarded him with pity.

A Krynnish version of the classical siren. —TRH

"You'll get used to it, in time," he said with a shrug.

"I'll never get used to it!" Caramon said, clenching his big fist.

Kiiri glanced at him. "You will, or your heart will break and you will die," she said coolly. So beautiful was she, and so proud her bearing, that her own iron collar might have been a necklace of finest gold, Caramon thought. He started to reply but was interrupted by a fat man in a white, greasy apron who slammed a plate of food down in front of Tasslehoff.

"Thank you," said the kender politely.

"Don't get used to the service," the cook snarled. "After this, you pick up yer own plate, like everyone else. Here"—he tossed a wooden disk down in front of the kender—"there's your meal chit. Show that, or you don't eat. And here's yours," he added, flipping one to Caramon.

"Where's my food?" Caramon asked, pocketing the wooden disk.

Plopping a bowl down in front of the big man, the cook turned to leave.

"What's this?" Caramon growled, staring at the bowl.

Tas leaned over to look. "Chicken broth," he said helpfully.

"I know *what* it is," Caramon said, his voice deep. "I mean, what is this, some kind of joke? Because it's not funny," he added, scowling at Pheragas and Kiiri, who were both grinning at him. Twisting around on the bench, Caramon reached out and grabbed hold of the cook, jerking him backward. "Get rid of this dishwater and bring me something to eat!"

With surprising quickness and dexterity, the cook broke free of Caramon's grip, twisted the big man's arm behind his back and shoved his head face-first into the bowl of soup.

"Eat it and like it," the cook snarled, dragging Caramon's dripping head up out of the soup by the hair. "Because—as far as food goes—that's all you're gonna be seeing for about a month."

Tasslehoff stopped eating, his face lighting up. The kender noticed that everyone else in the room had stopped eating again, too, certain that—this time—there would be a fight.

Caramon's face, dripping with soup, was deathly white. There were red splotches in the cheeks, and his eyes glinted dangerously.

The cook was watching him smugly, his own fists clenched.

Eagerly, Tas waited to see the cook splattered all over the room. Caramon's big fists clenched, the knuckles turned white. One of the big hands lifted and—slowly—Caramon began to wipe the soup from his face.

With a snort of derision, the cook turned and swaggered off.

Tas sighed. That certainly wasn't the old Caramon, he thought sadly, remembering the man who had killed two draconians by bashing their heads together with his bare hands, the Caramon who had once left fifteen ruffians in various stages of hurt when they made the mistake of trying to rob the big man. Glancing at Caramon out of the corner of his eye, Tas swallowed the sharp words that had been on his tongue and went back to his dinner, his heart aching.

Caramon ate slowly, spooning up the soup and gulping it down without seeming to taste it. Tas saw the woman and the black-skinned man exchange glances again and, for a moment, the kender feared they would laugh at Caramon. Kiiri, in fact, started to say something, but—on looking up toward the front of the room—she shut her mouth abruptly and went back to her meal. Tas saw Raag enter the mess hall again, two burly humans trundling along behind him.

Walking over, they came to a halt behind Caramon. Raag poked the big warrior.

Caramon glanced around slowly. "What is it?" he asked in a dull voice that Tas didn't recognize.

"You come now," Raag said.

"I'm eating," Caramon began, but the two humans grabbed the big man by the arms and dragged him off the bench before he could even finish his sentence. Then Tas saw a glimmer of Caramon's old spirit. His face an ugly, dark red, Caramon aimed a clumsy blow at one. But the man, grinning derisively, dodged it easily. His partner kicked Caramon savagely in the gut. Caramon collapsed with a groan, falling to the floor on all fours. The two humans

hauled him to his feet. His head hanging, Caramon allowed himself to be led away.

"Wait! Where—" Tas stood up, but felt a strong hand close over his own.

Kiiri shook her head warningly, and Tas sat back down.

"What are they going to do to him?" he asked.

The woman shrugged. "Finish your meal," she said in a stern voice.

Tas set his fork down. "I'm not very hungry," he mumbled despondently, his mind going back to the dwarf's strange, cruel look at Caramon outside the arena.

The black-skinned man smiled at the kender, who sat across from him. "Come on," he said, standing up and holding out his hand to Tas in a friendly manner, "I'll show you to your room. We all go through it the first day. Your friend will be all right—in time."

"In time," Kiiri snorted, shoving her plate away.

Tas lay all alone in the room he had been told he would share with Caramon. It wasn't much. Located beneath the arena, it looked more like a prison cell than a room. But Kiiri told him that all the gladiators lived in rooms like these.

"They are clean and warm," she said. "There are not many in this world who can say that of where they sleep. Besides, if we lived in luxury, we would grow soft."

Well, there was certainly no danger of that, as far as the kender could see, glancing around at the bare, stone walls, the straw-covered floor, a table with a water pitcher and a bowl, and the two small chests that were supposed to hold their possessions. A single window, high up in the ceiling right at ground level, let in a shaft of sunlight. Lying on the hard bed, Tas watched the sun travel across the room. The kender might have gone exploring, but he had the feeling he wouldn't enjoy himself much until he found out what they had done to Caramon.

The sun's line on the floor grew longer and longer. A door opened and Tas leaped up eagerly, but it was only another slave, tossing a sack in onto the floor, then shutting the door again. Tas inspected the sack and his heart sank. It was Caramon's belongings! Everything he'd had on him—including his clothes!

Tas studied them anxiously, looking for bloodstains. Nothing. They appeared all right. . . . His hand closed over something hard in an inner, secret pocket.

Quickly, Tas pulled it out. The kender caught his breath. The magical device from Par-Salian! How had they missed it, he wondered, marveling at the beautiful jeweled pendant as he turned it over in his hand. Of course, it was magical, he reminded himself. It looked like nothing more than a bauble now, but he had himself seen Par-Salian transform it from a sceptre-like object. Undoubtedly it had the power to avoid discovery if it didn't *want* to be discovered.

Feeling it, holding it, watching the sunlight sparkle on its radiant jewels, Tas sighed with longing. This was the most exquisite, marvelous, fantastic thing he'd ever seen in his life. He wanted it most desperately. Without thinking, his little body rose and was heading for his pouches when he caught himself.

Tasslehoff Burrfoot, said a voice that sounded uncomfortably like Flint's, this is Serious Business you're meddling with. This is the Way Home. Par-Salian himself, the Great Par-Salian gave it to Caramon in a solemn ceremony. It belongs to Caramon. It's his, you have no right to it!

Tas shivered. He had certainly never thought thoughts like these before in his life. Dubiously, he glanced at the device. Perhaps *it* was putting these uncomfortable thoughts in his head!

He decided he didn't want any part of them. Hurriedly, he carried the device over and put it in Caramon's chest. Then, as an extra precaution, he locked the chest and stuffed the key in Caramon's clothes. Even more miserable, he returned to his bed.

The sunlight had just about disappeared and the kender was growing more and more anxious when he heard a noise outside. The door was kicked open violently.

"Caramon!" Tas cried in horror, springing to his feet.

The two burly humans dragged the big man in over the doorstep and flung him down on the bed. Then, grinning, they left, slamming the door shut behind them. There was a low, moaning sound from the bed.

"Caramon!" Tas whispered. Hurriedly grabbing up the water pitcher, he dumped some water in the

bowl and carried it over to the big warrior's bedside. "What did they do?" he asked softly, moistening the man's lips with water.

Caramon moaned again and shook his head weakly. Tas glanced quickly at the big man's body. There were no visible wounds, no blood, no swelling, no purple welts or whip-lash marks. Yet he had been tortured, that much was obvious. The big man was in agony. His body was covered with sweat, his eyes had rolled back in his head. Every now and then, various muscles in his body twitched spasmodically and a groan of pain escaped his lips.

"Was . . . was it the rack?" Tas asked, gulping. "The wheel, maybe? Thumb-screws?" None of those left marks on the body, at least so he had heard.

Caramon mumbled a word.

"What?" Tas bent near him, bathing his face in water. "What did you say? Cali—cali—what? I didn't catch that." The kender's brow furrowed. "I never heard of a torture called calisomething," he muttered. "I wonder what it could be."

Caramon repeated it, moaning again.

"Cali . . . cali . . . calisthenics!" Tas said triumphantly. Then he dropped the water pitcher onto the floor. "Calisthenics? That's not torture!"

Caramon groaned again.

"That's exercises, you big baby!" Tas yelled. "Do you mean I've been waiting here, worried sick, imagining all sorts of horrible things, and you've been out doing exercises!"

Caramon had just strength enough to raise himself off the bed. Reaching out one big hand, he gripped Tas by the collar of his shirt and dragged him over to stare him in the eye.

"I was captured by goblins once," Caramon said in a hoarse whisper, "and they tied me to a tree and spent the night tormenting me. I was wounded by draconians in Xak Tsaroth. Baby dragons chewed on my leg in the dungeons of the Queen of Darkness.† And, I swear to you, that I am in more pain now than I have ever been in my life! Leave me alone, and let me die in peace."

With another groan, Caramon's hand dropped weakly to his side. His eyes closed. Smothering a grin, Tas crept back to his bed.

Lord Toede's goblins captured Caramon in Dragons of Autumn Twilight, *Book II, Chapter 2. He was captured and slightly wounded by draconians in* Dragons of Autumn Twilight, *Book I, Chapter 13. Dragon hatchlings chewed on him while he was crossing an underground stream in the dungeons of the Queen of Darkness in* Dragons of Spring Dawning, *Book III, Chapter 10.*

"He thinks he's in pain now," the kender reflected, "wait until morning!"

Summer in Istar ended. Fall came, one of the most beautiful in anyone's memory. Caramon's training began, and the warrior did not die, though there were times when he thought death might be easier. Tas, too, was strongly tempted on more than one occasion to put the big, spoiled baby out of his misery. One of these time had been during the night, when Tas had been awakened by a heart-breaking sob.

"Caramon?" Tas said sleepily, sitting up in bed.

No answer, just another sob.

"What is it?" Tas asked, suddenly concerned. He got out of bed and trotted across the cold, stone floor. "Did you have a dream?"

He could see Caramon nod in the moonlight.

"Was it about Tika?" asked the tenderhearted kender, feeling tears come to his own eyes at the sight of the big man's grief. "No. Raistlin? No. Yourself? Are you afraid—"

"A muffin!" Caramon sobbed.

"What?" Tas asked blankly.

"A muffin!" Caramon blubbered. "Oh, Tas! I'm so hungry. And I had a dream about this muffin, like Tika used to bake, all covered with sticky honey and those little, crunchy nuts. . . ."

Picking up a shoe, Tas threw it at him and went back to bed in disgust.

But by the end of the second month of rigorous training, Tas looked at Caramon, and the kender had to admit that this was just exactly what the big man had needed. The rolls of fat around the big man's waist were gone, the flabby thighs were once more hard and muscular, muscles rippled in his arms and across his chest and back. His eyes were bright and alert, the dull, vacant stare gone. The dwarf spirits had been sweated and soaked from his body, the red had gone from his nose, and the puffy look was gone from his face. His body was tanned a deep bronze from being out in the sun. The dwarf decreed that Caramon's brown hair be allowed to grow long, as this style was currently popular in Istar, and now it curled around his face and down his back.†

We wanted Caramon to look sexy for the DRAGONLANCE calendar painting! The TSR artists were renowned for their pictures of scantily clad females. Several of the women who worked there thought that turnabout was fair play, so we urged the artists to paint a "beefcake" painting of Caramon as a gladiator. Clyde Caldwell and Larry Elmore both did splendid jobs. —MW

He was a superbly skilled warrior now, too. Although Caramon had been well-trained before, it had been informal training, his weapons technique picked up mostly from his older half-sister, Kitiara. But Arack† imported trainers from all over the world, and now Caramon was learning techniques from the best.

Not only this, but he was forced to hold his own in daily contests between the gladiators themselves. Once proud of his wrestling skill, Caramon had been deeply shamed to find himself flat on his back after only two rounds against the woman, Kiiri. The black man, Pheragas, sent Caramon's sword flying after one pass, then bashed him over the head with his own shield for good measure.

But Caramon was an apt, attentive pupil. His natural ability made him a quick study, and it wasn't long before Arack was watching in glee as the big man flipped Kiiri with ease, then coolly wrapped Pheragas up in his own net, pinning the black man to the arena floor with his own trident.

Caramon, himself, was happier than he had been in a long time. He still detested the iron collar, and rarely a day went by at first without his longing to break it and run. But, these feelings lessened as he became interested in his training. Caramon had always enjoyed military life. He liked having someone tell him what to do and when to do it. The only real problem he was having was with his acting abilities.

Always open and honest, even to a fault, the worst part of his training came when he had to pretend to be losing. He was supposed to cry out loudly in mock pain when Rolf stomped on his back. He had to learn how to collapse as though horribly wounded when the Barbarian lunged at him with the fake, collapsible swords.

"No! No! No! you big dummy!" Arack screamed over and over. Swearing at Caramon one day, the dwarf walked over and punched him hard, right in the face.

"Arrgh!" Caramon cried out in real pain, not daring to fight back with Raag watching in glee.

"There—" Arack said, standing back in triumph, his fists clenched, blood on the knuckles. "Remember that yell. The gulls'll love it."

"Arack has two major interests: money and the Games. He is a born showman and knows exactly what will please an audience. He takes great pride in his Games and works extremely hard to make them a success. He hires the best trainers in all areas of fighting and takes excellent care of his athletes, despite the fact that they are slaves." [DRAGONLANCE Adventures, *by Tracy Hickman and Margaret Weis, TSR, Inc., 1987, p. 90.]*

But, in acting, Caramon appeared hopeless. Even when he did yell, it sounded "more like some wench getting her behind pinched than like anyone dying," Arack told Kiiri in disgust. And then, one day, the dwarf had an idea.

It came to him as he was watching the training sessions that afternoon. There happened to be a small audience at the time. Arack occasionally allowed certain members of the public in, having discovered that this was good for business. At this time, he was entertaining a nobleman, who had traveled here with his family from Solamnia. The nobleman had two very charming young daughters and, from the moment they entered the arena, they had never taken their eyes from Caramon.

"Why didn't we see him fight the other night?" one asked their father.

The nobleman looked inquiringly at the dwarf.

"He's new," Arack said gruffly. "He's still in train-ing. He's just about ready, mind you. In fact, I was thinking of putting him in—when did you say you were coming back to the Games?"

"We weren't," the nobleman began, but his daugh-ters both cried out in dismay. "Well," he amended, "perhaps—if we can get tickets."

The girls both clapped their hands, their eyes going back to Caramon, who was practicing his sword work with Pheragas. The young man's tanned body glistened with sweat, his hair clung in damp curls to his face, he moved with the grace of a well-trained athlete. Seeing the girls' admiring gaze, it suddenly occurred to the dwarf what a remarkably handsome young man Caramon was.

"He must win," said one of the girls, sighing. "I could not bear to see him lose!"

"He will win," said the other. "He was meant to win. He looks like a victor."

"Of course! That solves all my problems!" said the dwarf suddenly, causing the noblemen and his family to stare at him, puzzled. "The Victor! That's how I'll bill 'im. Never defeated! Doesn't know how to lose! Vowed to take his own life, he did, if anyone ever beat him!"

"Oh, no!" both girls cried in dismay. "Don't tell us that."

"It's true," the dwarf said solemnly, rubbing his hands.

"They'll come from miles around," he told Raag that night, "hoping to be there the night he loses. And, of course, he won't lose—not for a good, long while. Meanwhile, he'll be a heartbreaker. I can see that now. And I have just the costume. . . ."

Tasslehoff, meanwhile, was finding his own life in the arena quite interesting. Although at first deeply wounded when told he couldn't be a gladiator (Tas had visions of himself as another Kronin Thistleknot—the hero of Kenderhome), Tas had moped around for a few days in boredom. This ended in his nearly getting killed by an enraged minotaur who discovered the kender happily going through his room.

The minotaurs were furious. Fighting at the arena for the love of the sport only, they considered themselves a superior race, living and eating apart from the others. Their quarters were sacrosanct and inviolate.

Dragging the kender before Arack, the minotaur demanded that he be allowed to slit him open and drink his blood. The dwarf might have agreed—not having overly much use for kenders himself—but Arack remembered the talk he'd had with Quarath shortly after he'd purchased these two slaves. For some reason, the highest church authority in the land was interested in seeing that nothing happened to these two. He had to refuse the minotaur's request, therefore, but mollified him by giving him a boar he could butcher in sport. Then, Arack took Tas aside, cuffed him across the face a few times, and finally gave him permission to leave the arena and explore the town if the kender promised to come back at night.

Tas, who had already been sneaking out of the arena anyway, was thrilled at this, and repaid the dwarf's kindness by bringing him back any little trinket he thought Arack might like. Appreciative of this attention, Arack only beat the kender with a stick when he caught Tas trying to sneak pastry to Caramon, instead of whipping him as he would have otherwise.

Thus, Tas came and went about Istar pretty much as he liked, learning quickly to dodge the town guards, who had a most unreasonable dislike for kender. And so it was that Tasslehoff was able to enter the Temple itself.

Amid his training and dieting and other problems, Caramon had never lost sight of his real goal. He had received a cold, terse message from Lady Crysania, so he knew she was all right. But that was all. Of Raistlin, there was no sign.

At first, Caramon despaired of finding his brother or Fistandantilus, since he was never allowed outside the arena. But he soon realized that Tas could go places and see things much easier than he could, even if he had been free. People had a tendency to treat kender the same way they treated children— as if they weren't there. And Tas was even more expert than most kender at melting into shadows and ducking behind curtains or sneaking quietly through halls.

Plus there was the advantage that the Temple itself was so vast and filled with so many people, coming and going at nearly all hours, that one kender was easily ignored or—at most—told irritably to get out of the way. This was made even easier by the fact that there were several kender slaves working in the kitchens and even a few kender clerics, who came and went freely.

Tas would have dearly loved to make friends of these and to ask questions about his homeland— particularly the kender clerics, since he'd never known these existed. But he didn't dare. Caramon had warned him about talking too much and, for once, Tas took this warning seriously. Finding it nerve-racking to be on constant guard against talking about dragons or the Cataclysm or something that would get everyone all upset, he decided it would be easier to avoid temptation altogether. So he contented himself with nosing around the Temple and gathering information.

"I've seen Crysania," he reported to Caramon one night after they'd returned from dinner and a game of arm wrestling with Pheragas. Tas lay down on the bed while Caramon practiced with a mace and chain in the center of the room, Arack wanting him skilled in weapons other than the sword. Seeing that Caramon still needed a lot of practice, Tas crept to the far end of the bed—well out of the way of some of the big man's wilder swings.

"How is she?" Caramon asked, glancing over at the kender with interest.

Tas shook his head. "I don't know. She *looks* all right, I guess. At least she doesn't look sick. But she doesn't look happy, either. Her face is pale and, when I tried to talk to her, she just ignored me. I don't think she recognized me."

Caramon frowned. "See if you can find out what the matter is," he said. "She was looking for Raistlin, too, remember. Maybe it has something to do with him."

"All right," the kender replied, then ducked as the mace whistled by his head. "Say, be careful! Move back a little." He felt his topknot anxiously to see if all his hair was still there.

"Speaking of Raistlin," Caramon said in a subdued voice. "I don't suppose you found out anything today either?"

Tas shook his head. "I've asked and asked. Fistandantilus has apprentices that come and go sometimes. But no one's seen anyone answering Raistlin's description. And, you know, people with golden skin and hourglass eyes do tend to stand out in a crowd. But"—the kender looked more cheerful—"I may find out something soon. Fistandantilus is back, I heard."

"He is?" Caramon stopped swinging the mace and turned to face Tas.

"Yes. I didn't see him, but some of the clerics were talking about it. I guess he reappeared last night, right in the Kingpriest's Hall of Audience. Just—poof! There he was. Quite dramatic."

"Yeah," Caramon grunted. Swinging the mace thoughtfully, he was quiet for so long that Tas yawned and started to drift off to sleep. Caramon's voice brought him back to consciousness with a start.

"Tas," Caramon said, "this is our chance."

"Our chance to what?" The kender yawned again.

"Our chance to murder Fistandantilus," the warrior said quietly.

CHAPTER 7

aramon's cold statement woke the kender up quickly.

"M-murder! I, uh, think you ought to think about this, Caramon," Tas stammered. "I mean, well, look at it this way. This Fistandantilus is a really, really *good*, I—I mean, *talented* magic-user. Better even than Raistlin and Par-Salian put together, if what they say is true. You just don't sneak up and murder a guy like that. Especially when you've never murdered anybody! Not that I'm saying we should practice, mind you, but—"

"He has to sleep, doesn't he?" Caramon asked.

"Well," Tas faltered, "I suppose so. Everybody has to sleep, I guess, even magic-users—"

"Magic-users most of all," Caramon interrupted coldly. "You remember how weak Raist'd be if he didn't sleep? And that holds true of all wizards, even the most powerful. That's one reason they lost

the great battles—the Lost Battles.† They had to rest. And quit talking about this 'we' stuff. *I'll* do it. You don't even have to come along. Just find out where his room is, what kind of defenses he has, and when he goes to bed. I'll take care of it from there."

"Caramon," Tas began hesitantly, "do you suppose it's right? I mean, I know that's why the mages sent you back here. At least I *think* that's why. It all got sort of muddled there at the end. And I know this Fistandantilus is supposed to be a really *evil* person and he wears the black robes and all that, but is it right to *murder* him? I mean, it seems to me that this just makes us as evil as he is, doesn't it?"

"I don't care," Caramon said without emotion, his eyes on the mace he was slowly swinging back and forth. "It's his life or Raistlin's,† Tas. If I kill Fistandantilus now, back in this time, he won't be able to come forward and grab Raistlin. I could free Raistlin from that shattered body, Tas, and make him whole! Once I wrench this man's evil hold from him—then I know he'd be just like the old Raist. The little brother I loved." Caramon's voice grew wistful and his eyes moist. "He could come and live with us, Tas."

"What about Tika?" Tas asked hesitantly. "How's she going to feel about you murdering somebody?"

Caramon's brown eyes flashed in anger. "I told you before—don't talk about her, Tas!"

"But, Caramon—"

"I mean it, Tas!"

And this time the big man's voice held the tone that Tas knew meant he had gone too far. The kender sat hunched miserably in his bed. Looking over at him, Caramon sighed.

"Look, Tas," he said quietly, "I'll explain it once. I-I haven't been very good to Tika. She was right to throw me out, I see that now, though there was a time I thought I'd never forgive her." The big man was quiet a moment, sorting out his thoughts. Then, with another sigh, he continued. "I told her once that, as long as Raistlin lived, he'd come first in my thoughts. I warned her to find someone who could give her all his love. I thought at first *I* could, when Raistlin went off on his own. But"—he shook his head—"I dunno. It didn't work. Now, I've got to do this, don't you see? And I can't think about Tika! She-she only gets in the way. . . ."

*"19 PC—Siege on Sorcery: Afraid and jealous of a magic he cannot understand, the Kingpriest urges the people of Krynn to lay siege to the Towers of High Sorcery. Two towers are nearly overwhelmed. Rather than lose their towers to ignorant masses, the Wizards of High Sorcery destroy two of the towers (the Towers of Goodlund and Daltigoth), unleashing a terrifying backlash of magical power. Fearful of the rampant magic that might arise if all five towers are destroyed, the Kingpriest grants the mages exile to the Tower of Wayreth (the most isolated of the remaining towers) if they leave the remaining towers intact (the Towers of Palanthas and Istar). The Orders of High Sorcery reluctantly agree. The Kingpriest moves into the Tower of Istar, claiming it as his own. The Tower of Palanthas is cursed by the Black Robe wizard Rannoch to remain closed until opened by the Master of Past and Present." [*DRAGONLANCE Campaign Setting, Wizards of the Coast, 2003, p. 203.]*

Caramon is considering committing an act of evil—the murder of Fistandantilus—in order to save his brother. His rationalization for the act is essentially that "the end justifies the means." It is a short-cut sort of answer to his problem, however, that does not really address the complexity of the problem at hand. It is the fallacy of situational ethics. —TRH

"But Tika loves you so much!" was all Tas could say. And, of course, it was the wrong thing. Caramon scowled and began swinging the mace again.

"All right, Tas," he said, his voice so deep it might have come from beneath the kender's feet, "I guess this means good-bye. Ask the dwarf for a different room. I'm going to do this and, if anything goes wrong, I wouldn't want to get you into trouble—"

"Caramon, you know I didn't mean I wouldn't help," Tas mumbled. "You need me!"

"Yeah, I guess," Caramon muttered, flushing. Then, looking over at Tas, he smiled in apology. "I'm sorry. Just don't talk about Tika anymore, all right?"

"All right," Tas said unhappily. He smiled back at Caramon in return, watching as the big man put his weapons away and prepared for bed. But it was a sickly smile and, when Tas crawled into his own bed, he felt more depressed and unhappy than he had since Flint died.

"He† wouldn't have approved, that's for sure," Tas said to himself, thinking of the gruff, old dwarf. "I can hear him now. 'Stupid, doorknob of a kender!' he'd say. 'Murdering wizards! Why don't you just save everyone trouble and do away with yourself!' And then there's Tanis," Tas thought, even more miserable. "I can just imagine what *he'd* say!" Rolling over, Tas pulled the blankets up around his chin. "I wish he was here! I wish *someone* was here to help us! Caramon's not thinking right, I know he isn't! But what can *I* do? I've got to help him. He's my friend. And he'd likely get into no end of trouble without me!"

The next day was Caramon's first day in the Games. Tas made his visit to the Temple in the early morning and was back in time to see Caramon's fight, which would take place that afternoon. Sitting on the bed, swinging his short legs back and forth, the kender made his report as Caramon paced the floor nervously, waiting for the dwarf and Pheragas to bring him his costume.

"You're right," Tas admitted reluctantly. "Fistandantilus needs lots of sleep, apparently. He goes to bed early every night and sleeps like the dead—I m-mean"—Tas stuttered—"sleeps soundly till morning."

Notice how Tasslehoff's conscience seems to manifest itself through his friend's (supposed) views. It is moments like these that made Tasslehoff one of the DRAGONLANCE setting's most endearing characters.

Caramon looked at him grimly.

"Guards?"

"No," Tas said, shrugging. "He doesn't even lock his door. No one locks doors in the Temple. After all, it is a holy place, and I guess everyone either trusts everyone or they don't have anything to lock up. You know," the kender said on reflection, "I always detested door locks, but now I've decided that life without them would be really boring. I've been in a few rooms in the Temple"—Tas blissfully ignored Caramon's horrified glance—"and, believe me, it's not worth the bother. You'd think a magic-user would be different, but Fistandantilus doesn't keep any of his spell stuff there. I guess he just uses his room to spend the night when he's visiting the court. Besides," the kender pointed out with a sudden brilliant flash of logic, "he's the only evil person in the court, so he wouldn't need to protect himself from anyone other than himself!"

Caramon, who had quit listening long ago, muttered something and kept pacing. Tas frowned uncomfortably. It had suddenly occurred to him that he and Caramon now ranked right up there with evil magic-users. This helped him make up his mind.

"Look, I'm sorry, Caramon," Tas said, after a moment. "But I don't think I can help you, after all. Kender aren't very particular, sometimes, about their own things, or other people's for that matter, but I don't believe a kender ever in his life *murdered* anybody!" He sighed, then continued in a quivering voice. "And, I got to thinking about Flint and . . . and Sturm. You know Sturm wouldn't approve! He was so honorable. It just isn't right, Caramon! It makes us just as bad as Fistandantilus. Or maybe worse."

Caramon opened his mouth and was just about to reply when the door burst open and Arack marched in.

"How're we doing, big guy?" the dwarf said, leering up at Caramon. "Quite a change from when you first came here, ain't it?" He patted the big man's hard muscles admiringly, then—balling up his fist—suddenly slammed it into Caramon's gut. "Hard as steel," he said, grinning and shaking his hand in pain.

Caramon glowered down at the dwarf in disgust, glanced at Tas, then sighed. "Where's my costume?" he grumbled. "It's nearly High Watch."

The dwarf held up a sack. "It's in here. Don't worry, it won't take you long to dress."

Grabbing the sack nervously, Caramon opened it. "Where's the rest of it?" he demanded of Pheragas, who had just entered the room.

"That's it!" Arack cackled. "I told you it wouldn't take long to dress!"

Caramon's face flushed a deep red. "I—I can't wear . . . just this. . . ." he stammered, shutting the sack hastily. "You said there'd be ladies. . . ."

"And they'll love every bronze inch!" Arack hooted. Then the laughter vanished from the dwarf's broken face, replaced by the dark and menacing scowl. "Put it on, you great oaf. What do you think they pay to see? A dancing school? No—they pay to see bodies covered in sweat and blood. The more body, the more sweat, the more blood—real blood— the better!"

"*Real* blood?" Caramon looked up, his brown eyes flaring. "What do you mean? I thought you said—"

"Bah! Get him ready, Pheragas. And while you're at it, explain the facts of life to the spoiled brat. Time to grow up, Caramon, my pretty poppet." With that and a grating laugh, the dwarf stalked out.

Pheragas stood aside to let the dwarf pass, then entered the small room. His face, usually jovial and cheerful, was a blank mask. There was no expression in his eyes, and he avoided looking directly at Caramon.

"What did he mean? Grow up?" Caramon asked. "Real blood?"

"Here," Pheragas said gruffly, ignoring the question. "I'll help with these buckles. It takes a bit of getting used to at first. They're strictly ornamental, made to break easily. The audience loves it if a piece comes loose or falls off."

He lifted an ornate shoulder guard from the bag and began strapping it onto Caramon, working around behind him, keeping his eyes fixed on the buckles.

"This is made out of gold," Caramon said slowly.

Pheragas grunted.

"Butter would stop a knife sooner than this stuff," Caramon continued, feeling it. "And look at all these

fancy do-dads! A sword point'll catch and stick in any of 'em."

"Yeah." Pheragas laughed, but it was forced laughter. "As you can see, it's almost better to be naked than wear this stuff."

"I don't have much to worry about then," Caramon remarked grimly, pulling out the leather loincloth that was the only other object in the sack, besides an ornate helmet. The loincloth, too, was ornamented in gold and barely covered his private parts decently. When he and Pheragas had him dressed, even the kender blushed at the sight of Caramon from the rear.

Pheragas started to go, but Caramon stopped him, his hand on his arm. "You better tell me, my friend. That is, if you still are my friend."

Pheragas looked at Caramon intently, then shrugged. "I thought you'd have figured it out by now. We use edged weapons. Oh, the swords still collapse," he added, seeing Caramon's eyes narrow. "But, if you get hit, you bleed—for real. That's why we harped on your stabbing thrusts."

"You mean people really get hurt? I could hurt someone? Someone like Kiiri, or Rolf, or the Barbarian?" Caramon's voice raised in anger. "What else goes on! What else didn't you tell me—friend!"

Pheragas regarded Caramon coldly. "Where did you think I got these scars? Playing with my nanny? Look, someday you'll understand. There's not time to explain it now. Just trust us, Kiiri and I. Follow our lead. And—keep your eyes on the minotaurs. They fight for themselves, not for any masters or owners. They answer to no one. Oh, they agree to abide by the rules—they have to or the Kingpriest would ship them back to Mithas. But . . . well, they're favorites with the crowd. The people like to see them draw blood. And they can take as good as they give."

"Get out!" Caramon snarled.

Pheragas stood staring at him a moment, then he turned and started out the door. Once there, however, he stopped.

"Listen, friend," he said sternly, "these scars I get in the ring are badges of honor, every bit as good as some knight's spurs he wins in a contest! It's the only kind of honor we can salvage out of this tawdry

show! The arena's got its own code, Caramon, and it doesn't have one damn thing to do with those knights and noblemen who sit out there and watch us slaves bleed for their own amusement. They talk of *their* honor. Well, we've got our own. It's what keeps us alive." He fell silent. It seemed he might say something more, but Caramon's gaze was on the floor, the big man stubbornly refusing to acknowledge his words or presence.

Finally, Pheragas said "You've got five minutes," and left, slamming the door behind him.

Tas longed to say something but, seeing Caramon's face, even the kender knew it was time to keep silent.

Go into a battle with bad blood, and it'll be spilled by nightfall. Caramon couldn't remember what gruff old commander had told him that, but he'd found it a good axiom. Your life often depended on the loyalty of those you fought with. It was a good idea to get any quarrels between you settled. He didn't like holding grudges either. It generally did nothing for him but upset his stomach.

It was an easy thing, therefore, to shake Pheragas's hand when the black man started to turn away from him prior to entering the arena and to make his apologies. Pheragas accepted these warmly, while Kiiri—who obviously had heard all about the episode from Pheragas—indicated her approval with a smile. She indicated her approval of Caramon's costume, too; looking at him with such open admiration in her flashing green eyes that Caramon flushed in embarrassment.

The three stood talking in the corridors that ran below the arena, waiting to make their entrance. With them were the other gladiators who would fight today, Rolf, the Barbarian, and the Red Minotaur. Above them, they could hear occasional roars from the crowd, but the sound was muffled. Craning his neck, Caramon could see out the entryway door. He wished it was time to start. Rarely had he ever felt this nervous, more nervous than going into battle, he realized.

The others felt the tension, too. It was obvious in Kiiri's laughter that was too shrill and loud and the sweat that poured down Pheragas's face. But it was

a good kind of tension, mingled with excitement. And, suddenly, Caramon realized he was looking forward to this.

"Arack's called our names," Kiiri said. She and Pheragas and Caramon walked forward—the dwarf having decided that since they worked well together they should fight as a team. (He also hoped that the two pros would cover up for any of Caramon's mistakes!)

The first thing Caramon noticed as he stepped out into the arena was the noise. It crashed over him in thunderous waves, one after another, coming seemingly from the sun-drenched sky above him. For a moment he felt lost in confusion. The by-now familiar arena—where he had worked and practiced so hard these last few months—was a strange place suddenly. His gaze went to the great circular rows of stands surrounding the arena, and he was overwhelmed at the sight of the thousands of people, all—it seemed—on their feet screaming and stomping and shouting.

The colors swam in his eyes—gaily fluttering banners that announced a Games Day, silk banners of all the noble families of Istar, and the more humble banners of those who sold everything from fruited ice to tarbean tea, depending on the season of the year. And it all seemed to be in motion, making him dizzy, and suddenly nauseous. Then he felt Kiiri's cool hand upon his arm. Turning, he saw her smile at him in reassurance. He saw the familiar arena behind her, he saw Pheragas and his other friends.

Feeling better, he quickly turned his attention back to the action. He had better keep his mind on business, he told himself sternly. If he missed a single rehearsed move, he would not only make himself look foolish, but he might accidentally hurt someone. He remembered how particular Kiiri had been that he timed his swordthrusts just right. Now, he thought grimly, he knew why.

Keeping his eyes on his partners and the arena, ignoring the noise and the crowd, he took his place, waiting to start. The arena looked different, somehow, and for a moment he couldn't figure it out. Then he realized that, just as they were in costume, the dwarf had decorated the arena, too. Here were the same old sawdust-covered platforms

where he fought every day, but now they were tricked out with symbols representing the four corners of the world.

Around these four platforms, the hot coals blazed, the fire roared, the oil boiled and bubbled. Bridges of wood spanned the Death Pits as they were called, connecting the four platforms. These Pits had, at first, alarmed Caramon. But he had learned early in the game that they were for effect only. The audience loved it when a fighter was driven from the arena onto the bridges. They went wild when the Barbarian held Rolf by his heels over the boiling oil. Having seen it all in rehearsal, Caramon could laugh with Kiiri at the terrified expression on Rolf's face and the frantic efforts he made to save himself that resulted—as always—in the Barbarian being hit over the head by a blow from Rolf's powerful arms.

The sun reached its zenith and a flash of gold brought Caramon's eyes to the center of the arena. Here stood the Freedom Spire—a tall structure made of gold, so delicate and ornate that it seemed out of place in such crude surroundings. At the top hung a key—a key that would open a lock on any of the iron collars. Caramon had seen the spire often enough in practice, but he had never seen the key, which was kept locked in Arack's office. Just looking at it made the iron collar around his neck feel unusually heavy. His eyes filled with sudden tears. Freedom. . . . To wake in the morning and be able to walk out a door, to go anywhere in this wide world you wanted. It was such a simple thing. Now, how much he missed it!

Then he heard Arack call out his name, he saw him point at them. Gripping his weapon, Caramon turned to face Kiiri, the sight of the Golden Key still in his mind. At the end of the year, any slave who had done well in the Games could fight for the right to climb that spire and get the key. It was all fake, of course. Arack always selected those guaranteed to draw the biggest audiences. Caramon had never thought about it before—his only concern being his brother and Fistandantilus. But, now, he realized he had a new goal. With a wild yell, he raised his phony sword high in the air in salute.

Soon, Caramon began to relax and have fun. He found himself enjoying the roars and applause of the crowd. Caught up in their excitement, he discovered he was playing up to them—just as Kiiri had told him he would. The few wounds he'd received in the warm-up bouts were nothing, only scratches. He couldn't even feel the pain. He laughed at himself for his worry. Pheragas had been right not to mention such a silly thing. He was sorry he had made such a big deal of it.

"They like you," Kiiri said, grinning at him during one of their rest periods. Once again, her eyes swept admiringly over Caramon's muscular, practically nude body. "I don't blame them. I'm looking forward to our wrestling match."

Kiiri laughed at his blush, but Caramon saw in her eyes that she wasn't kidding and he was suddenly acutely aware of her femaleness—something that had never occurred to him in practice. Perhaps it was her own scanty costume, which seemed designed to reveal everything, yet hid all that was most desirable. Caramon's blood burned, both with passion and the pleasure he always found in battle. Confused memories of Tika came to his mind, and he looked away from Kiiri hurriedly, realizing he had been saying more with his own eyes than he intended.

This ploy was only partly successful, because he found himself staring into the stands—right into the eyes of many admiring and beautiful women, who were obviously trying to capture his attention.

"We're on again," Kiiri nudged him, and Caramon returned thankfully to the ring.

He grinned at the Barbarian as the tall man strode forward. This was their big number, and he and Caramon had practiced it many times. The Barbarian winked at Caramon as they faced each other, their faces twisted into looks of ferocious hatred. Growling and snarling like animals, both men crouched over, stalking each other around the ring a suitable amount of time to build up tension. Caramon caught himself about to grin and had to remind himself that he was supposed to look mean. He liked the Barbarian. A Plainsman, the man reminded him in many ways of Riverwind— tall, dark-haired, though not nearly as serious as the stern ranger.

The Barbarian was a slave as well, but the iron collar around his neck was old and scratched from countless battles. He would be one chosen to go after the golden key this year, that was certain.

Caramon thrust out with the collapsible sword. The Barbarian dodged with ease and, catching Caramon with his heel, neatly tripped him. Caramon went down with a roar. The audience groaned (the women sighed), but there were many cheers for the Barbarian, who was a favorite. The Barbarian lunged at the prone Caramon with a spear. The women screamed in terror. At the last moment, Caramon rolled to one side and, grabbing the Barbarian's foot, jerked him down to the sawdust platform.

Thunderous cheers. The two men grappled on the floor of the arena. Kiiri rushed out to aid her fallen comrade and the Barbarian fought them both off, to the crowd's delight. Then, Caramon, with a gallant gesture, ordered Kiiri back behind the line. It was obvious to the crowd that he would take care of this insolent opponent himself.

Kiiri patted Caramon on his rump (that wasn't in the script and nearly caused Caramon to forget his next move), then she ran off. The Barbarian lunged at Caramon, who pulled his collapsible dagger. This was the show-stopper—as they had planned. Ducking beneath the Barbarian's upraised arm with a skillful maneuver, Caramon thrust the dummy dagger right into the Barbarian's gut where a bladder of chicken blood was cleverly concealed beneath his feathered breastplate.

It worked! The chicken blood splashed out over Caramon, running down his hand and his arm. Caramon looked into the Barbarian's face, ready for another wink of triumph. . . .

Something was wrong.

The man's eyes had widened, as was in the script. But they had widened in true pain and in shock. He staggered forward—that was in the script, too—but not the gasp of agony. As Caramon caught him, he realized in horror that the blood washing over his arm was warm!

Wrenching his dagger free, Caramon stared at it, even as he fought to hold onto the Barbarian, who was collapsing against him. The blade was real!

"Caramon . . ." The man choked. Blood spurted from his mouth.

The audience roared. They hadn't seen special effects like this in months!

"Barbarian! I didn't know!" Caramon cried, staring at dagger in horror. "I swear!"

And then Pheragas and Kiiri were by his side, helping to ease the dying Barbarian down onto the arena floor.

"Keep up the act!" Kiiri snapped harshly.

Caramon nearly struck her in his rage, but Pheragas caught his arm. "Your life, our lives depend on it!" the black man hissed. "*And* the life of your little friend!"

Caramon stared at them in confusion. What did they mean? What were they saying? He had just killed a man—a friend! Groaning, he jerked away from Pheragas and knelt beside the Barbarian. Dimly he could hear the crowd cheering, and he knew—somewhere inside of him—that they were eating this up. The Victor paying tribute to the "dead."

"Forgive me," he said to the Barbarian, who nodded.

"It's not your fault," the man whispered. "Don't blame yoursel—" His eyes fixed in his head, a bubble of blood burst on his lips.

"We've got to get him out of the arena," Pheragas whispered sharply to Caramon, "and make it look good. Like we rehearsed. Do you understand?"

Caramon nodded dully. *Your life . . . the life of your little friend.* I am a warrior. I've killed before. Death is nothing new. *The life of your little friend.* Obey orders. I'm used to that. Obey orders, then I'll figure out the answers. . . .

Repeating that over and over, Caramon was able to subdue the part of his mind that burned with rage and pain. Coolly and calmly, he helped Kiiri and Pheragas lift the Barbarian's "lifeless" corpse to its feet as they had done countless times in rehearsal. He even found the strength to turn and face the crowd and bow. Pheragas, with a skillful motion of his free arm, made it seem as if the "dead" Barbarian were bowing, too. The crowd loved it and cheered wildly. Then the three friends dragged the corpse off the stage, down into the dark aisles below.

Once there, Caramon helped them ease the Barbarian down onto the cold stone. For long moments, he stared at the corpse, dimly aware of the other gladiators, who had been waiting their turn to go up into the arena, looking at the lifeless body, then melting back into the shadows.

Slowly, Caramon stood up. Turning around, he grabbed hold of Pheragas and, with all his strength, hurled the black man up against the wall. Drawing the bloodstained dagger from his belt, Caramon held it up before Pheragas's eyes.

"It was an accident," Pheragas said through clenched teeth.

"Edged weapons!" Caramon cried, shoving Pheragas's head roughly into the stone wall. "Bleed a little! Now, you tell me! What in the name of the Abyss is going on!"

"It was an accident, oaf," came a sneering voice.

Caramon turned. The dwarf stood before him, his squat body a small, twisted shadow in the dark and dank corridor beneath the arena.

"And now I'll tell you about accidents," Arack said, his voice soft and malevolent. Behind him loomed the giant figure of Raag, his club in his huge hand. "Let Pheragas go. He and Kiiri have to get back to the arena and take their bows. You all were the winners today."

Caramon glanced at Pheragas for a moment, then dropped his hand. The dagger slipped from his nerveless fingers onto the floor, he slumped back against the wall. Kiiri regarded him in mute sympathy, laying her hand on his arm. Pheragas sighed, cast the smug dwarf a venomous glance, then both he and Kiiri left the corridor. They walked around the body of the Barbarian, which lay, untouched, on the stone.

"You told me no one got killed!" Caramon said in a voice choked with anger and pain.

The dwarf came over to stand in front of the big man. "It was an accident," Arack repeated. "Accidents happen around here. Particularly to people who aren't careful. They could happen to you, if you're not careful. Or to that little friend of yours. Now, the Barbarian, here, he wasn't careful. Or rather, his master wasn't careful."

Caramon raised his head, staring at the dwarf, his eyes wide with shock and horror.

"Ah, I see you finally got it figured out," Arack nodded.

"This man died because his owner crossed someone," Caramon said softly.

"Yeah." The dwarf grinned and tugged at his beard. "Civilized, ain't it? Not like the old days. And no one's the wiser. Except his master, of course. I saw his face this afternoon. He knew, as soon as you stuck the Barbarian. You might as well have thrust that dagger into him. He got the message all right."

"This was a warning?" Caramon asked in strangled tones.

The dwarf nodded again and shrugged.

"Who? Who was his owner?"

Arack hesitated, regarding Caramon quizzically, his broken face twisted into a leer. Caramon could almost see him calculating, figuring how much he could gain from telling, how much he might gain by keeping silent. Apparently, the money added up quickly in the "telling" column, because he didn't hesitate long. Motioning Caramon to lean down, he whispered a name in his ear.

Caramon looked puzzled.

"High cleric, a Revered Son of Paladine," the dwarf added. "Number two to the Kingpriest himself. But he's made a bad enemy, a bad enemy." Arack shook his head.

A burst of muffled cheering roared from above them. The dwarf glanced up, then back at Caramon. "You'll have to go up, take a bow. It's expected. You're a winner."

"What about him?" Caramon asked, his gaze going to the Barbarian. "He won't be going up. Won't they wonder?"

"Pulled muscle. Happens all the time. Can't make his final bow," the dwarf said casually. "We'll put the word out he retired, was given his freedom."

Given his freedom! Tears filled his eyes. He looked away, down the corridor. There was another cheer. He would have to go. *Your life. Our lives. The life of your little friend.*

"That's why," Caramon said thickly, "that's why you had me kill him! Because now you've got me! You know I won't talk—"

"I knew that anyway," Arack said, grinning wickedly. "Let's say having you kill him was just a

little extra touch. The customers like that, shows I care. You see, it was *your* master who sent this warning! I thought he'd appreciate it, having his own slave carry it out. Course that puts you in a bit of danger. The Barbarian's death'll have to be avenged. But, it'll do wonders for business, once the rumor spreads."

"*My* master!" Caramon gasped. "But, you bought me! The school—"

"Ah, I acted as agent only." The dwarf cackled. "I thought maybe you didn't know!"

"But who is my—" And then Caramon knew the answer. He didn't even hear the words the dwarf said. He couldn't hear them over the sudden roaring sound that echoed in his brain. A blood-red tide surged over him, suffocating him. His lungs ached, his stomach heaved, and his legs gave way beneath him.

The next thing he knew, he was sitting in the corridor, the ogre holding his head down between his knees. The dizziness passed. Caramon gasped and lifted his head, shaking off the ogre's grasp.

"I'm all right," he said through bloodless lips.

Raag glanced at him, then up at the dwarf.

"We can't take him out there in this condition," Arack said, regarding Caramon with disgust. "Not looking like a fish gone belly up. Haul him to his room."

"No," said a small voice from the darkness. "I-I'll take care of him."

Tas crept out of the shadows, his face nearly as pale as Caramon's.

Arack hesitated, then snarled something and turned away. With a gesture to the ogre, he hurried off, clambering up the stairs to make the awards to the victors.

Tasslehoff knelt beside Caramon, his hand on the big man's arm. The kender's gaze went to the body that lay forgotten on the stone floor. Caramon's gaze followed. Seeing the pain and anguish in his eyes, Tas felt a lump come to his throat. He couldn't say a word, he could only pat Caramon's arm.

"How much did you hear?" Caramon asked thickly.

"Enough," Tas murmured. "Fistandantilus."

"He planned this all along," Caramon sighed and leaned his head back, wearily closing his eyes. "This

is how he'll get rid of us. He won't even have to do it himself. Just let this . . . this cleric. . . ."

"Quarath."

"Yeah, he'll let this Quarath kill us." Caramon's fists clenched. "The wizard's hands will be clean! Raistlin will never suspect. And all the time, every fight from now on, I'll wonder. Is that dagger Kiiri holds real?" Opening his eyes, Caramon looked at the kender. "And you, Tas. You're in this, too. The dwarf said so. I can't leave, but you could! You've got to get out of here!"

"Where would I go?" Tas asked helplessly. "He'd find me, Caramon. He's the most powerful magic-user that ever lived. Even kender can't hide from people like him."

For a moment the two sat together in silence, the roar of the crowd echoing above them. Then Tas's eyes caught a gleam of metal across the corridor. Recognizing the object, he rose to his feet and crept over to retrieve it.

"I can get us inside the Temple," he said, taking a deep breath, trying to keep his voice steady. Picking up the bloodstained dagger, he brought it back and handed it to Caramon.

"I can get us in tonight."

"Solinari is the hand of
white magic, the patron
deity of all the White Robe
Wizards of High Sorcery.
Solinari's primary
ambition is to spread
magic throughout the
world, and to bring more
worthy mages to the
Order of the White Robes.
He works closely with his
cousins Lunitari and
Nuitari to protect and
foster magic on Krynn."
[DRAGONLANCE
Campaign Setting,
Wizards of the Coast, Inc.,
2003, p. 125.]

he silver moon,
Solinari,† flickered on the horizon. Rising up over
the central tower of the Temple of the Kingpriest, the
moon looked like a candle flame burning on a tall,
fluted wick. Solinari was full and bright this night,
so bright that the services of the lightwalkers were
not needed and the boys who earned their living
lighting party-goers from one house to another with
their quaint, silver lamps spent the night at home,
cursing the bright moonlight that robbed them of
their livelihood.

Solinari's twin, the blood-red Lunitari, had not
risen, nor would it rise for several more hours,
flooding the streets with its eerie purplish brilliance.
As for the third moon, the black one, its dark round-
ness among the stars was noted by one man, who
gazed at it briefly as he divested himself of his black
robes, heavy with spell components, and put on the

simpler, softer, black sleeping gown. Drawing the black hood up over his head to blot out Solinari's cold, piercing light, he lay down on his bed and drifted into the restful sleep so necessary to him and his Art.

At least that is what Caramon envisioned him doing as he and the kender walked the moonlit, crowded streets. The night was alive with fun. They passed group after group of merrymakers—parties of men laughing boisterously and discussing the games; parties of women, who clung together and shyly glanced at Caramon out of the corners of their eyes. Their filmy dresses floated around them in the soft breeze that was mild for late autumn. One such group recognized Caramon, and the big man almost ran, fearing they would call guards to take him back to the arena.

But Tas—wiser about the ways of the world—made him stay. The group was enchanted with him. They had seen him fight that afternoon and, already, he had won their hearts. They asked inane questions about the Games, then didn't listen to his answers—which was just as well. Caramon was so nervous, he made very little sense. Finally they went on their way, laughing and bidding him good fortune. Caramon glanced at the kender wonderingly at this, but Tas only shook his head.

"Why did you think I made you dress up?" he asked Caramon shortly.

Caramon had, in fact, been wondering about this very thing. Tas had insisted that he wear the golden, silken cape he wore in the ring, plus the helmet he had worn that afternoon. It didn't seem at all suitable for sneaking into Temples—Caramon had visions of crawling through sewers or climbing over rooftops. But when he balked, Tas's eyes had grown cold. Either Caramon did as he was told or he could forget it, he said sharply.

Caramon, sighing, dressed as ordered, putting the cape on over his regular loose shirt and leather breeches. He put the bloodstained dagger in his belt. Out of habit, he had started to clean it, then stopped. No, it would be more suitable this way.

It had been a simple matter for the kender to unlock their door after Raag locked them in that night, and the two had slipped through the sleeping

section of the gladiators' quarters without incident; most of the fighters either being asleep or—in the case of the minotaurs—roaring drunk.

The two walked the streets openly, to Caramon's vast discomfort. But the kender seemed unperturbed. Unusually moody and silent, Tas continually ignored Caramon's repeated questions. They drew nearer and nearer the Temple. It loomed before them in all its pearl and silver radiance, and finally Caramon stopped.

"Wait a minute, Tas," he said softly, pulling the kender into a shadowy corner, "just how do you plan to get us in here?"

"Through the front doors," Tas answered quietly.

"The front doors?" Caramon repeated in blank astonishment. "Are you mad? The guards! They'll stop us—"

"It's a Temple, Caramon," Tas said with a sigh. "A Temple to the gods. Evil things just don't enter."

"Fistandantilus enters," Caramon said gruffly.

"But only because the Kingpriest allows it," Tas said, shrugging. "Otherwise, he *couldn't* get in here. The gods wouldn't permit it. At least that's what one of the clerics told me when I asked."

Caramon frowned. The dagger in his belt seemed heavy, the metal was hot against his skin. Just his imagination, he told himself. After all, he'd worn daggers before. Reaching beneath his cloak, he touched it reassuringly. Then, his lips pressed tightly together, he started walking toward the Temple. After a moment's hesitation, Tas caught up with him.

"Caramon," said the kender in a small voice, "I-I think I know what you were thinking. I've been thinking the same thing. What if the gods won't let *us* in?"

"We're out to destroy evil," Caramon said evenly, his hand on the dagger's hilt. "They'll help us, not hinder us. You'll see."

"But, Caramon—" Now it was Tas's turn to ask questions and Caramon's turn to grimly ignore him. Eventually, they reached the magnificent steps leading up to the Temple.

Caramon stopped, staring at the building. Seven towers rose to the heavens, as if praising the gods for their creation. But one spiraled above them all.

s beautiful cityscape of Istar, Matt Stawicki creates one of the firs
es for the DRAGONLANCE world with his rendition of *Time of the T*

n this memorable cover for the 1987 DRAGONLANCE Calendar

Gleaming in Solinari's light, it seemed not to praise the gods but sought to rival them. The beauty of the Temple, its pearl and rose-colored marble gleaming softly in the moonlight, its still pools of water reflecting the stars, its vast gardens of lovely, fragrant flowers, its ornamentation of silver and of gold, all took Caramon's breath away, piercing his heart. He could not move but was held as though spellbound by the wonder.

And then, in the back of his mind, came a lurking feeling of horror. He had seen this before! Only he had seen it in a nightmare—the towers twisted and misshapen. . . . Confused, he closed his eyes. Where? How? Then, it came to him. The Temple at Neraka, where he'd been imprisoned!† The Temple of the Queen of Darkness! It had been this very Temple, perverted by her evil, corrupted, turned to a thing of horror. Caramon trembled. Overwhelmed by this terrible memory, wondering at its portent, he thought for a moment of turning around and fleeing.

Caramon is remembering events from Dragons of Spring Dawning, *Book III, Chapters 11-12.*

Then he felt Tas tug at his arm. "Keep moving!" the kender ordered. "You look suspicious!"

Caramon shook his head, clearing it of stupid memories that meant nothing, he told himself. The two approached the guards at the door.

"Tas!" Caramon said suddenly, gripping the kender by the shoulder so tightly he squeaked in pain. "Tas, this is a test! If the gods let us in, I'll know we're doing the right thing! We'll have their blessing!"

Tas paused. "Do you think so?" he asked hesitantly.

"Of course!" Caramon's eyes shone in Solinari's bright light. "You'll see. Come on." His confidence restored, the big man strode up the stairs. He was an imposing sight, the golden, silken cape fluttering about him, the golden helmet flashing in the moonlight. The guards stopped talking and turned to watch him. One nudged the other, saying something and making a swift, stabbing motion with his hand. The other guard grinned and shook his head, regarding Caramon with admiration.

Caramon knew immediately what the pantomime represented and he nearly stopped walking, feeling once again the warm blood splash over his hand and hearing the Barbarian's last, choked words. But he had come too far to quit now. And, perhaps this too was a sign, he told himself. The Barbarian's spirit, lingering near, anxious for its revenge.

Tas glanced up at him anxiously. "Better let me do the talking," the kender whispered.

Caramon nodded, swallowing nervously.

"Greetings, gladiator," called one of the guards. "You're new to the Games, are you not? I was telling my companion on watch, here, that he missed a pretty fight today. Not only that, but you won me six silver pieces, as well. What is it you are called?"

"He's the 'Victor,'" Tas said glibly. "And today was just the beginning. He's never been defeated in battle, and he never will be."

"And who are you, little cutpurse? His manager?"

This was met by roars of laughter from the other guard and nervous high-pitched laughter from Caramon. Then he glanced down at Tas and knew immediately they were in trouble. Tas's face was white. Cutpurse! The most dreadful insult, the worst thing in the world one could call a kender! Caramon's big hand clapped over Tas's mouth.

"Sure," said Caramon, keeping a firm grip on the wriggling kender, "and a good one, too."

"Well, keep an eye on him," the other guard added, laughing even harder. "We want to see you slit throats—not pockets!"

Tasslehoff's ears—the only part visible above Caramon's wide hand—flushed scarlet. Incoherent sounds came from behind Caramon's palm. "I-I think we better go on in," the big warrior stammered, wondering how long he could hold Tas. "We're late."

The guards winked at each other knowingly, one of them shook his head in envy. "I saw the women watching you today," he said, his gaze going to Caramon's broad shoulders. "I should have known you'd be invited here for, uh, dinner."

What were they talking about? Caramon's puzzled look caused the guards to break out in renewed laughter.

"Name of the gods!" one sputtered. "Look at him! He *is* new!"

"Go ahead," the other guard waved him on by. "Good appetite!"

More laughter. Flushing red, not knowing what to say and still trying to hold onto Tas, Caramon

entered the Temple. But, as he walked, he heard crude jokes pass between the guards, giving him sudden clear insight into their meaning. Dragging the wriggling kender down a hallway, he darted around the first corner he came to. He hadn't the vaguest idea where he was.

Once the guards were out of sight and hearing, he let Tas go. The kender was pale, his eyes dilated.

"Why, those—those— I'll— They'll regret—"

"Tas!" Caramon shook him. "Stop it. Calm down. Remember why we're here!"

"Cutpurse! As if I were a common thief!" Tas was practically frothing at the mouth. "I—"

Caramon glowered at him, and the kender choked. Getting control of himself, he drew a deep breath and let it out again slowly. "I'm all right, now," he said sullenly. "I said I'm all right," he snapped as Caramon continued to regard him dubiously.

"Well, we got inside, though not quite the way I expected," Caramon muttered. "Did you hear what they were saying?"

"No, not after 'cu-cut' . . . after that word. You had part of your hand over my ears," Tas said accusingly.

"They . . . they sounded like . . . the ladies invited m-men here for-for . . . you know. . . ."

"Look, Caramon," Tas said, exasperated. "You got your sign. They let us in. They were probably just teasing you. You know how gullible you are. You'll believe anything! Tika's always saying so."

A memory of Tika came to Caramon's mind. He could hear her say those very words, laughing. It cut him like a knife. Glaring at Tas, he shoved the memory away immediately.

"Yeah," he said bitterly, flushing, "you're probably right. They're having their joke on me. And I fell for it, too! But"—he lifted his head and, for the first time, looked around at the splendor of the Temple. He began to realize where he was—this holy place, this palace of the gods. Once more he felt the reverence and awe he had experienced as he stood gazing at it, bathed in Solinari's radiant light—"you're right—the gods have given us our sign!"

There was a corridor in the Temple where few came and, of those that did, none went voluntarily. If

forced to come here on some errand, they did their
business quickly and left as swiftly as possible.

There was nothing wrong with the corridor itself.
It was just as splendid as the other halls and corridors of the Temple. Beautiful tapestries done in
muted colors graced its walls, soft carpets covered
its marble floors, graceful statues filled its shadowy
alcoves. Ornately carved wooden doors opened off
of it, leading to rooms as pleasingly decorated as
other rooms in the Temple. But the doors opened no
longer. All were locked. All the rooms were empty—
all except one.

That room was at the very far end of the corridor,
which was dark and silent even in the daytime. It was
as if the occupant of this one room cast a pall over the
very floor he walked, the very air he breathed. Those
who entered this corridor complained of feeling
smothered. They gasped for breath like someone
dying inside a burning house.

This room was the room of Fistandantilus. It had
been his for years, since the Kingpriest came to
power and drove the magic-users from their Tower
in Palanthas—the Tower where Fistandantilus had
reigned as Head of the Conclave.

What bargain had they struck—the leading
powers of good and of evil in the world? What deal
had been made that allowed the Dark One to live
inside the most beautiful, most holy place on Krynn?
None knew, many speculated. Most believed it was
by the grace of the Kingpriest, a noble gesture to a
defeated foe.

But even he—even the Kingpriest himself—did
not walk this corridor. Here, at least, the great mage
reigned in dark and terrifying supremacy.

At the far end of the corridor stood a tall
window. Heavy plush curtains were drawn over
it, blotting out the sunlight in the daytime, the
moons' rays at night. Rarely did light penetrate
the curtains' thick folds. But this night, perhaps
because the servants had been driven by the Head
of Household to clean and dust the corridor, the
curtains were parted the slightest bit, letting Solinari's silver light shine into the bleak, empty corridor. The beams of the moon the dwarves call Night
Candle pierced the darkness like a long, thin blade
of glittering steel.

Or perhaps the thin, white finger of a corpse, Caramon thought, looking down that silent corridor. Stabbing through the glass, the finger of moonlight ran the length of the carpeted floor and, reaching the length of the hall, touched him where he stood at the end.

"That's his door," the kender said in such a soft whisper Caramon could barely hear him over the beating of his own heart. "On the left."

Caramon reached beneath his cloak once more, seeking the dagger's hilt, its reassuring presence. But the handle of the knife was cold. He shuddered as he touched it and quickly withdrew his hand.

It seemed a simple thing, to walk down this corridor. Yet he couldn't move. Perhaps it was the enormity of what he contemplated—to take a man's life, not in battle, but as he slept. To kill a man in his sleep—of all times, the time we are most defenseless, when we place ourselves in the hands of the gods. Was there a more heinous, cowardly crime?

The gods gave me a sign, Caramon reminded himself, and sternly he made himself remember the dying Barbarian. He made himself remember his brother's torment in the Tower. He remembered how powerful this evil mage was when awake. Caramon drew a deep breath and grasped the hilt of the dagger firmly. Holding it tightly, though he did not draw it from his belt, he began to walk down the still corridor, the moonlight seeming now to beckon him on.

He felt a presence behind him, so close that, when he stopped, Tas bumped into him.

"Stay here," Caramon ordered.

"No—" Tas began to protest, but Caramon hushed him.

"You've got to. Someone has to stand on watch at this end of the corridor. If anyone comes, make a noise or something."

"But—"

Caramon glared down at the kender. At the sight of the big man's grim expression and cold, emotionless glare, Tas gulped and nodded. "I-I'll just stand over there, in that shadow." He pointed and crept away.

Caramon waited until he was certain Tas wouldn't "accidentally" follow him. But the kender

hunched miserably in the shadow of huge, potted tree that had died months ago. Caramon turned and continued on.

Standing next to the brittle skeleton whose dry leaves rustled when the kender moved, Tas watched Caramon walk down the hallway. He saw the big man reach the end, stretch out a hand, and wrap it around the door handle. He saw Caramon give it a gentle push. It yielded to his pressure and opened silently. Caramon disappeared inside the room.

Tasslehoff began to shake. A horrible, sick feeling spread from his stomach throughout his body, a whimper escaped his lips. Clasping his hand over his mouth so that he wouldn't yelp, the kender pressed himself up against the wall and thought about dying, alone, in the dark.

Caramon eased his big body around the door, opening it only a crack in case the hinges should squeak. But it was silent. Everything in the room was silent. No noise from anywhere in the Temple came into this chamber, as if all life itself had been swallowed by the choking darkness. Caramon felt his lungs burn, and he remembered vividly the time he had nearly drowned in the Blood Sea of Istar. Firmly, he resisted the urge to gasp for air.

He paused a moment in the doorway, trying to calm his racing heart, and looked around the room. Solinari's light streamed in through a gap in the heavy curtains that covered the window. A thin sliver of silver light slit the darkness, slicing through it in a narrow cut that led straight to the bed at the far end of the room.

The chamber was sparsely furnished. Caramon saw the shapeless bulk of a heavy black robe draped over a wooden chair. Soft leather boots stood next to it. No fire burned in the grate, the night was too warm. Gripping the hilt of the knife, Caramon drew it slowly and crossed the room, guided by the moon's silver light.

A sign from the gods, he thought, his pounding heartbeat nearly choking him. He felt fear, fear such as he had rarely experienced in his life—a raw, gut-wrenching, bowel-twisting fear that made his mus-

cles jerk and dried his throat. Desperately, he forced himself to swallow so that he wouldn't cough and wake the sleeper.

I must do this quickly! he told himself, more than half afraid he might faint or be sick. He crossed the room, the soft carpet muffling his swift footsteps. Now he could see the bed and the figure asleep within it. He could see the figure clearly, the moonlight slicing a neat line across the floor, up the bedstead, over the coverlet, slanting upward to the head lying on the pillow, its hood pulled over the face to blot out the light.

"Thus the gods point my way," Caramon murmured, unaware that he was speaking. Creeping up to the side of the bed, he paused, the dagger in his hand, listening to the quiet breathing of his victim, trying to detect any change in the deep, even rhythm that would tell him he had been discovered.

In and out . . . in and out . . . the breathing was strong, deep, peaceful. The breathing of a healthy young man. Caramon shuddered, recalling how old this wizard was supposed to be, recalling the dark tales he had heard about how Fistandantilus renewed his youth. The man's breathing was steady, even. There was no break, no quickening. The moonlight poured in, cold, unwavering, a sign. . . .

Caramon raised the dagger. One thrust—swift and neat—deep in the chest and it would be over. Moving forward, Caramon hesitated. No, before he struck, he would look upon the face—the face of the man who had tortured his brother.

No! Fool! a voice screamed inside Caramon. Stab now, quickly! Caramon even lifted the knife again, but his hand shook. He *had* to see the face! Reaching out a trembling hand, he gently touched the black hood. The material was soft and yielding. He pushed it aside.

Solinari's silver moonlight touched Caramon's hand, then touched the face of the sleeping mage, bathing it in radiance. Caramon's hand stiffened, growing white and cold as that of a corpse as he stared down at the face on the pillow.

It was not the face of an ancient evil wizard, scarred with countless sins. It was not even the face of some tormented being whose life had been stolen from his body to keep the dying mage alive.

It was the face of a young magic-user, weary from long nights of study at his books, but now relaxed, finding welcome rest. It was the face of one whose tenacious endurance of constant pain was marked in the firm, unyielding lines about the mouth. It was a face as familiar to Caramon as his own, a face he had looked upon in sleep countless times, a face he had soothed with cooling water. . . .

The hand holding the dagger stabbed down, plunging the blade into the mattress. There was a wild, strangled shriek, and Caramon fell to his knees beside the bed, clutching at the coverlet with fingers curled in agony. His big body shook convulsively, wracked with shuddering sobs.

Raistlin opened his eyes and sat up, blinking in Solinari's bright light. He drew his hood over his eyes once more, then, sighing in irritation, reached out and carefully removed the dagger from his brother's nerveless grip.

his was truly
stupid, my brother," said Raistlin, turning the
dagger over in his slender hands, studying it idly.
"I find it hard to believe, even of you."

Kneeling on the floor by the bedside, Caramon
looked up at his twin. His face was haggard, drawn
and deathly pale. He opened his mouth.

" 'I don't understand, Raist,' " Raistlin whined,
mocking him.

Caramon clamped his lips shut, his face hardened into a dark, bitter mask. His eyes glanced at
the dagger his brother still held. "Perhaps it would
have been better if I hadn't drawn aside the hood,"
he muttered.

Raistlin smiled, though his brother did not see
him.

"You had no choice," he replied. Then he sighed
and shook his head. "My brother, did you honestly

think to simply walk into my room and murder me as I slept? You know what a light sleeper I am, have always been."

"No, not you!" Caramon cried brokenly, lifting his gaze. "I thought—" He could not go on.

Raistlin stared at him, puzzled for a moment, then suddenly began to laugh. It was horrible laughter, ugly and taunting, and Tasslehoff—still standing at the end of the hall—clasped his hands over his ears at the sound, even as he began creeping down the corridor toward it to see what was going on.

"You were going to murder Fistandantilus!" Raistlin said, regarding his brother with amusement. He laughed again at the thought. "Dear brother," he said, "I had forgotten how entertaining you could be."

Caramon flushed, and rose unsteadily to his feet.

"I was going to do it . . . for you," he said. Walking over to the window, he pulled aside the curtain and stared moodily out into the courtyard of the Temple that shimmered with pearl and silver in Solinari's light.

"Of course you were," Raistlin snapped, a trace of the old bitterness creeping into his voice. "Why did you ever do anything, except for me?"

Speaking a sharp word of command, Raistlin caused a bright light to fill the room, gleaming from the Staff of Magius that leaned against the wall in a corner. The mage threw back the coverlet and rose from his bed. Walking over to the grate, he spoke another word and flames leaped up from the bare stone. Their orange light beat upon his pale, thin face and was reflected in the clear, brown eyes.

"Well, you are late, my brother," Raistlin continued, holding his hands out to warm them at the blaze, flexing and exercising his supple fingers. "Fistandantilus is dead. By my hands."

Caramon turned around sharply to stare at his brother, caught by the odd tone in Raistlin's voice. But his brother remained standing by the fire, staring into the flames.

"You thought to walk in and stab him as he slept," Raistlin murmured, a grim smile on his thin lips. "The greatest mage who ever lived—up until now."

Caramon saw his brother lean against the mantel-piece, as if suddenly weak.

"He was surprised to see me," said Raistlin softly. "And he mocked me, as he mocked me in the Tower. But he was afraid. I could see it in his eyes.

" 'So, little mage,' " Fistandantilus sneered, 'and how did you get here? Did the great Par-Salian send you?'

" 'I came on my own,' I told him. 'I am the Master of the Tower now.'

"He had not expected that. 'Impossible,' he said, laughing. '*I* am the one whose coming the prophecy foretold. *I* am master of past and present. When I am ready, I will return to my property.'

"But the fear grew in his eyes, even as he spoke, for he read my thoughts. 'Yes,' I answered his unspoken words, 'the prophecy did not work as you hoped. You intended to journey from the past to the present, using the lifeforce you wrenched from me to keep you alive. But you forgot, or perhaps you didn't care, that I could draw upon your *spiritual* force! You had to keep me alive in order to keep sucking out my living juices. And—to that end—you gave me the words and taught me to use the dragon orb. When I lay dying at Astinus's feet,† you breathed air into this wretched body you had tortured. You brought me to the Dark Queen and beseeched her to give me the Key to unlock the mysteries of the ancient magic texts I could not read. And, when you were finally ready, you intended to enter the shattered husk of my body and claim it for your own.' "

Raistlin turned to face his brother, and Caramon stepped back a pace, frightened at the hatred and fury he saw burning within the eyes, brighter than the dancing flames of the fire.

"So he thought to keep me weak and frail. But I fought him! I fought him!" Raistlin repeated softly, intently, his gaze staring far away. "I used him! I used his spirit and I lived with the pain and I overcame it! '*You* are master of the past,' I told him, 'but you lack the strength to get into the present. *I* am master of the present, about to become master of the past!' "

Raistlin sighed, his hand dropped, the light flickered in his eyes and died, leaving them dark and haunted. "I killed him," he murmured, "but it was a bitter battle."

When did Raistlin lay dying at Astinus's feet? See Dragons of Spring Dawning, *Book I, Chapter 5.*

"You killed him? They-they said you came back to learn from him," Caramon stammered, confusion twisting his face.

"I did," Raistlin said softly. "Long months I spent with him, in another guise, revealing myself to him only when I was ready. This time, I sucked *him* dry!"

Caramon shook his head. "That's impossible. You didn't leave until the same time we did, that night. . . . At least that's what the dark elf said—"

Raistlin shook his head irritably. "Time to you, my brother, is a journey from sunrise to sunset. Time to those of us who have mastered its secrets is a journey beyond suns.† Seconds become years, hours—millennia. I have walked these halls as Fistandantilus for months now. These last few weeks I have traveled to all the Towers of High Sorcery—those still standing, that is—to study and to learn. I have been with Lorac, in the elven kingdom, and taught him to use the dragon orb—a deadly gift, for one as weak and vain as he. It will snare him, later on. I have spent long hours with Astinus in the Great Library. And, before that, I studied with the great Fistandantilus. Other places I have visited, seeing horrors and wonders beyond your imagining. But, to Dalamar, for example, I have been gone no more than a day and a night. As have you."

This was beyond Caramon. Desperately, he sought to grab at some fraction of reality.

"Then . . . does this mean that you're . . . all right, now? I mean, in the present? In our time?" He gestured. "Your skin isn't gold anymore, you've lost the hourglass eyes. You look . . . like you did when you were young, and we rode to the Tower, seven years ago. Will you be like that when we go back?"

"No, my brother," Raistlin said, speaking with the patience one uses explaining things to a child. "Surely Par-Salian explained this? Well, perhaps not. Time is a river. I have not changed the course of its flow. I have simply climbed out and jumped in at a point farther upstream. It carries me along its course. I—"

Raistlin stopped suddenly, casting a sharp glance at the door. Then, with a swift motion of his hand, he caused the door to burst open and Tasslehoff Burrfoot tumbled inside, falling down face first.

Raistlin is showing off here, demonstrating his greater knowledge and understanding of the universe. It is interesting to note that this is typical of Raistlin: a man who has great knowledge and power, yet here puts it to no greater use than to belittle his brother. —TRH

"Oh, hullo," Tas said, cheerfully picking himself up off the floor. "I was just going to knock." Dusting himself off, he turned eagerly to Caramon. "*I have it figured out!* You see—it used to be Fistandantilus becoming Raistlin becoming Fistandantilus. Only now it's Fistandantilus becoming Raistlin becoming Fistandantilus, then becoming Raistlin again. See?"

No, Caramon did not. Tas turned around to the mage. "Isn't that right, Raist—"

The mage didn't answer. He was staring at Tasslehoff with such a queer, dangerous expression in his eyes that the kender glanced uneasily at Caramon and took a step or two nearer the warrior—just in case Caramon needed help, of course.

Suddenly Raistlin's hand made a swift, slight, summoning motion. Tasslehoff felt no sensation of movement, but there was a blurring in the room for half a heartbeat, and then he was being held by his collar within inches of Raistlin's thin face.

"Why did Par-Salian send *you*?" Raistlin asked in a soft voice that "shivered" the kender's skin, as Flint used to say.

"Well, he thought Caramon needed help, of course and—" Raistlin's grip tightened, his eyes narrowed. Tas faltered. "Uh, actually, I don't think he, uh, really intended to s-send me." Tas tried to twist his head around to look beseechingly at Caramon, but Raistlin's grip was strong and powerful, nearly choking the kender. "It-it was, more or less, an accident, I guess, at least as far as he was c-concerned. And I could t-talk better if you'd let me breathe . . . every once in awhile."

"Go on!" Raistlin ordered, shaking Tas slightly.

"Raist, stop—" Caramon began, taking a step toward him, his brow furrowed.

"Shut up!" Raistlin commanded furiously, never taking his burning eyes off the kender. "Continue."

"There-there was a ring someone had dropped . . . well, maybe not dropped—" Tas stammered, alarmed enough by the expression in Raistlin's eyes into telling the truth, or as near as was kenderly possible. "I-I guess I was sort of going into someone else's room, and it f-fell in-into my pouch, I suppose, because I don't know how it got there, but when th-the red-robed man sent Bupu home, I knew I was

next. And I couldn't leave Caramon! So I-I said a prayer to F-Fizban—I mean Paladine—and I put the ring on and—poof!"—Tas held up his hands—"I was a mouse!"

The kender paused at this dramatic moment, hoping for an appropriately amazed response from his audience. But Raistlin's eyes only dilated with impatience and his hand twisted the kender's collar just a bit more, so Tas hurried on, finding it increasingly difficult to breathe.

"And so I was able to hide," he squeaked, not unlike the mouse he had been, "and sneaked into Par-Salian's labra-labora-lavaratory—and he was doing the most wonderful things and the rocks were singing and Crysania was lying there all pale and Caramon looked terrified and I *couldn't* let him go alone—so . . . so . . ." Tas shrugged and looked at Raistlin with disarming innocence, "here I am. . . ."

Raistlin continued clutching him for a moment, devouring him with his eyes, as if he would strip the skin from his bones and see inside his very soul. Then, apparently satisfied, the mage let the kender drop to the floor and turned back to stare into the fire, his thoughts abstracted.

"What does this mean?" he murmured. "A kender—by all the laws of magic forbidden! Does this mean the course of time *can* be altered? Is he telling the truth? Or is this how they plot to stop me?"

"What did you say?" Tas asked with interest, looking up from where he sat on the carpet, trying to catch his breath. "The course of time altered? By *me?* Do you mean that I could—"

Raistlin whirled, glaring at the kender so viciously that Tas shut his mouth and began edging his way back to where Caramon stood.

"I was sure surprised to find your brother. Weren't you?" Tas asked Caramon, ignoring the spasm of pain that crossed Caramon's face. "Raistlin was surprised to see me, too, wasn't he? That's odd, because I saw him in the slave market and I assumed he must have seen us—"

"Slave market!" Caramon said suddenly. Enough of this talk about rivers and time. This was something he could understand! "Raist—you said you've been here months! That means *you* are the

one who made them think I attacked Crysania! You're the one who bought me! You're the one who sent me to the Games!"

Raistlin made an impatient gesture, irritated at having his thoughts interrupted.

But Caramon persisted. "Why!" he demanded angrily. "Why that place?"

"Oh, in the name of the gods, Caramon!" Raistlin turned around again, his eyes cold. "What possible use could you be to me in the condition you were in when you came here? I need a strong warrior where we're going next—not a fat drunk.'

"And . . . and you ordered the Barbarian's death?" Caramon asked, his eyes flashing. "You sent the warning to what's-his-name—Quarath?"

"Don't be a dolt, my brother," Raistlin said grimly. "What do I care for these petty court intrigues? Their little, mindless games? If I wanted to do away with an enemy, his life would be snuffed out in a matter of seconds. Quarath flatters himself to think I would take such an interest in him."

"But the dwarf said—"

"The dwarf hears only the sound of money being dropped into his palm. But, believe what you will." Raistlin shrugged. "It matters little to me."

Caramon was silent long moments, pondering. Tas opened his mouth—there were at least a hundred questions he was dying to ask Raistlin—but Caramon glared at him and the kender closed it quickly. Caramon, slowly going over in his mind all that his brother had told him, suddenly raised his gaze.

"What do you mean—'where we go next'?"

"My counsel is mine to keep," Raistlin replied. "You will know when the time comes, so to speak. My work here progresses, but it is not quite finished. There is one other here besides you who must be beaten down and hammered into shape."

"Crysania," Caramon murmured. "This has something to do with challenging the-the Dark Queen, doesn't it? Like they said? You need a cleric—"

"I am very tired, my brother," Raistlin interrupted. At his gesture, the flames in the fireplace vanished. At a word, the light from the Staff winked out. Darkness, chill and bleak, descended on the three who stood there. Even Solinari's light was gone, the moon having sunk behind the buildings. Raistlin crossed the room, heading for his bed. His black robes rustled softly. "Leave me to my rest. You should not remain here long in any event. Undoubtedly, spies have reported your presence, and Quarath can be a deadly enemy. Try to avoid getting yourself killed. It would annoy me greatly to have to train another bodyguard. Farewell, my brother. Be ready. My summons will come soon. Remember the date."

Caramon opened his mouth, but he found himself talking to a door. He and Tas were standing outside in the now-dark corridor.

"That's really incredible!" the kender said, sighing in delight. "I didn't even feel myself moving, did you? One minute we were there, the next we're here. Just a wave of the hand. It must be wonderful being a mage," Tas said wistfully, staring at the closed door. "Zooming through time and space and closed doors."

"Come on," Caramon said abruptly, turning and stalking down the corridor.

The Ansalonian equivalent of the birthday present.

"Say Caramon," Tas said softly, hurrying after him. "What did Raistlin mean—'remember the date'? Is it his Day of Life Gift† coming up or something? Are you supposed to get him a present?"

"No," Caramon growled. "Don't be silly."

*Many cultures throughout the world hold celebrations in the depths of their winter season. This, I believe, is natural to the cycle of seasons and humanity's relationship to them. The Yule celebrations on Krynn reflect that concept. The Christmas of Christianity was placed on December 25th not because there was any real historic precedent for it being the actual day of Christ's birth, but rather so that it would compete with and ultimately usurp many other pagan festivals that took place around this same time. The Yule of Krynn reflects the tradition of all such winter festivals rather than Christmas per se.
—TRH*

"I'm not being silly," Tas protested, offended. "After all, Yuletide† is in a few weeks, and he's probably expecting a present for that. At least, I suppose they celebrate Yuletide back here in Istar the same as we celebrate it in our time. Do you think—"

Caramon came to a sudden halt.

"What is it?" Tas asked, alarmed at the horrified expression on the big man's face. Hurriedly, the kender glanced around, his hand closing over the hilt of a small knife he had tucked into his own belt. "What do you see? I don't—"

"The date!" Caramon cried. "The date, Tas! Yuletide! In Istar!" Whirling around, he grabbed the startled kender. "What year is it? What year?"

"Why . . ." Tas gulped, trying to think. "I believe, yes, someone told me it was—962."

Caramon groaned, his hands dropped Tas and clutched at his head.

'What *is* it?" Tas asked.

"Think, Tas, think!" Caramon muttered. Then, clutching at his head in misery, the big man stumbled blindly down the corridor in the darkness. "What do they want me to do? What *can* I do?"

Tas followed more slowly. "Let's see. This is Yuletide, year 962 I.A. Such a ridiculously high number. For some reason it sounds familiar. Yuletide, 962. . . . Oh, I remember!" he said triumphantly. "That was the last Yuletide right before . . . right before. . . ."

The thought took the kender's breath away.

"Right before the Cataclysm!" he whispered.

CHAPTER
10

enubis set down the quill pen and rubbed his eyes. He sat in the quiet of the copying room, his hand over his eyes, hoping that a brief moment of rest would help him. But it didn't. When he opened his eyes and grasped the quill pen to begin his work again, the words he was trying to translate still swam together in a meaningless jumble.

Sternly, he reprimanded himself and ordered himself to concentrate and—finally—the words began to make sense and sort themselves out. But it was difficult going. His head ached. It had ached, it seemed, for days now, with a dull, throbbing pain that was present even in his dreams.

"It's this strange weather," he told himself repeatedly. "Too hot for the beginning of Yule season."

It was too hot, strangely hot. And the air was thick with moisture, heavy and oppressive. The fresh

breezes had seemingly been swallowed up by the heat. One hundred miles away at Karthay,† so he had heard, the ocean lay flat and calm beneath the fiery sun, so calm that no ships could sail. They sat in the harbor, their captains cursing, their cargo rotting.

Mopping his forehead, Denubis tried to continue working diligently, translating the Disks of Mishakal into Solamnic.† But his mind wandered. The words made him think of a tale he had heard some Solamnic knights discussing last night—a gruesome tale that Denubis kept trying to banish from his mind.

A knight named Soth had seduced a young elven cleric and then married her, bringing her home to his castle at Dargaard Keep as his bride.† But this Soth had already been married, so the knights said, and there was more than one reason to believe that his first wife had met a most foul end.

The knights had sent a delegation to arrest Soth and hold him for trial, but Dargaard Keep, it was said, was now an armed fortress—Soth's own loyal knights defending their lord. What made it particularly haunting was that the elven woman the lord had deceived remained with him, steadfast in her love and loyalty to the man, even though his guilt had been proven.

Denubis shuddered and tried to banish the thought. There! He made an error. This was hopeless! He started to lay the quill down again, then heard the door to the copying room opening. Hastily, he lifted the quill pen and began to write rapidly.

"Denubis," said a soft, hesitant voice.

The cleric looked up. "Crysania, my dear," he said, with a smile.

"Am I disturbing your work? I can come back—"

"No, no," Denubis assured her. "I am glad to see you. Very glad." This was quite true. Crysania had a way of making him feel calm and tranquil. Even his headache seemed to lessen. Leaving his high-backed writing stool, he found a chair for her and one for himself, then sat down near her, wondering why she had come.

As if in answer, Crysania looked around the still, peaceful room and smiled. "I like it here," she said. "It's so quiet and, well, private." Her smile faded. "I sometimes get tired of . . . of so many people," she

"Karthay was the only major Istari city in the north, and it served both as one of the nation's major trade ports and as the main guardian of the entrance to the Bay of Istar. One of Karthay's main landmarks was Winston's Tower, a massive lighthouse and fortress that was equipped with catapults able to fire flaming pitch several miles into the strait it overlooked." ["Istar: Land of the Kingpriests," by Steve Miller, Wizards of the Coast, Inc., 2003]

The text here does not state the language in which the Disks of Mishakal were originally written—only that the Kingpriest is attempting to translate them into Solamnic, a language that was fairly universal at the close of the Third Age. That Denubis is having difficulty with the work is a subtle evidence that his faith has strayed. Latter Day Saints history records that the Golden Plates containing the Book of Mormon could not be read whenever the translator lacked faith. So, too, here with the Kingpriest. —TRH

Lord Soth's story is a great Gothic romance. This entire backstory came to me in a rush all at once. It was an extraordinary experience. —TRH

said, her gaze going to the door that led to the main part of the Temple.

"Yes, it is quiet," Denubis said. "Now, at any rate. It wasn't so, in past years. When I first came, it was filled with scribes, translating the words of the gods into languages so that everyone could read them. But the Kingpriest didn't think that was necessary and—one by one—they all left, finding more important things to do. Except me." He sighed. "I guess I'm too old," he added gently, apologetically. "I tried to think of something important to do, and I couldn't. So I stayed here. No one seemed to mind . . . very much."

He couldn't help frowning slightly, remembering those long talks with Revered Son, Quarath, prodding and poking at him to make something of himself. Eventually, the higher cleric gave up, telling Denubis he was hopeless. So Denubis had returned to his work, sitting day after day in peaceful solitude, translating the scrolls and the books and sending them off to Solamnia where they sat, unread, in some great library.

"But, enough about me," he added, seeing Crysania's wan face. "What is the matter, my dear? Are you not feeling well? Forgive me, but I couldn't help but notice, these past few weeks, how unhappy you've seemed."

Crysania stared down at her hands in silence, then glanced back up at the cleric. "Denubis," she began hesitantly, "do . . . do you think the church is . . . what it should be?"

That wasn't at all what he had expected. She had more the look of a young girl deceived by a lover. "Why, of course, my dear," Denubis said in some confusion.

"Really?" Lifting her gaze, she looked into his eyes with an intent stare that made Denubis pause. "You have been with the church for a long time, before the coming of the Kingpriest and Quar—his ministers. You talk about the old days. You have seen it change. Is it better?"

Denubis opened his mouth to say, certainly, yes, it was better. How could it be otherwise with such a good and holy man as the Kingpriest at its head? But Lady Crysania's gray eyes were staring straight into his soul, he realized suddenly, feeling their

searching, seeking gaze bringing light to all the dark corners where he had been hiding things—he knew—for years. He was reminded, uncomfortably, of Fistandantilus.

"I—well—of course—it's just—" He was babbling and he knew it. Flushing, he fell silent. Crysania nodded gravely, as if she had expected the answer.

"No, it *is* better," he said firmly, not wanting to see her young faith bruised, as his had been. Taking her hand, he leaned forward. "I'm just a middle-aged old man, my dear. And middle-aged old men don't like change. That's all. To us, everything was better in the old days. Why"—he chuckled—"even the water tasted better, it seems. I'm not used to modern ways. It's hard for me to understand. The church is doing a world of good, my dear. It's bringing order to the land and structure to society—"

"Whether society wants it or not," Crysania muttered, but Denubis ignored her.

"It's eradicating evil," he continued, and suddenly the story of that knight—that Lord Soth—floated to the top of his mind, unbidden. He sank it hurriedly, but not before he had lost his place in his lecture. Lamely, he tried to pick it up again, but it was too late.

"Is it?" Lady Crysania was asking him. "Is it eradicating evil? Or are we like children, left alone in the house at night, who light candle after candle to keep away the darkness? We don't see that the darkness has a purpose—though we may not understand it†—and so, in our terror, we end up burning down the house!"

Denubis blinked, not understanding this at all; but Crysania continued, growing more and more restless as she talked. It was obvious, Denubis realized uncomfortably, that she had kept this pent up inside her for weeks.

"We don't try to help those who have lost their way find it again! We turn our backs on them, calling them unworthy, or we get rid of them! Do you know"—she turned on Denubis— "that Quarath has proposed ridding the world of the ogre races?"

"But, my dear, ogres are, after all, a murderous, villainous lot—" Denubis ventured to protest feebly.

"Created by the gods, just as we were," Crysania said. "Do we have the right, in our imperfect

Here Crysania confronts her own flaw in the person of Denubis. She is not so much doubting good as she is coming to question Denubis (and her own) understanding of what really constitutes good and evil. Their own understanding depends solely on their own myopic rites, rituals, and dogma rather than on inspiration and acceptance of a larger perspective of deity. Denubis's problem is that he is leaning on his own understanding. See Appendix C. —TRH

understanding of the great scheme of things, to destroy anything the gods created?"

"Even spiders?" Denubis asked wistfully, without thinking. Seeing her irritated expression, he smiled. "Never mind. The ramblings of an old man."

"I came here, convinced that the church was everything good and true, and now I—I—" She put her head in her hands.

Denubis's heart ached nearly as much as his head. Reaching out a trembling hand, he gently stroked the smooth, blue-black hair, comforting her as he would have comforted the daughter he never had.

"Don't feel ashamed of your questioning, child," he said, trying to forget that he had been feeling ashamed of his. "Go, talk to the Kingpriest. He will answer your doubts. He has more wisdom than I."

Crysania looked up hopefully.

"Do you think—"

"Certainly," Denubis smiled. "See him tonight, my dear. He will be holding audience. Do not be afraid. Such questions do not anger him."

"Very well," Crysania said, her face filled with resolve. "You are right. It's been foolish of me to wrestle with this myself, without help. I'll ask the Kingpriest. Surely, he can make this darkness light."

Denubis smiled and rose to his feet as Crysania rose. Impulsively, she leaned over and kissed him gently on the cheek. "Thank you, my friend," she said softly. "I'll leave you to your work."

Watching her walk from the still, sunlit room, Denubis felt a sudden, inexplicable sorrow and, then, a very great fear. It was as if he stood in a place of bright light, watching her walk into a vast and terrible darkness. The light around him grew brighter and brighter, while the darkness around her grew more horrible, more dense.

Confused, Denubis put his hand to his eyes. The light was real! It was streaming into this room, bathing him in a radiance so brilliant and beautiful that he couldn't look upon it. The light pierced his brain, the pain in his head was excruciating. And still, he thought desperately, I must warn Crysania, I must stop her. . . .

The light engulfed him, filling his soul with its radiant brilliance. And then, suddenly, the bright light was gone. He was once more standing in the

sunlit room. But he wasn't alone. Blinking, trying to accustom his eyes to the darkness, he looked around and saw an elf standing in the room with him, observing him coolly. The elf was elderly, balding, with a long, meticulously groomed, white beard. He was dressed in long, white robes, the medallion of Paladine hung about his neck. The expression on the elf's face was one of sadness, such sadness that Denubis was moved to tears, though he had no idea why.

"I'm sorry," Denubis said huskily. Putting his hand to his head, he suddenly realized it didn't hurt anymore. "I-I didn't see you come in. Can I help you? Are you looking for someone?"

"No, I have found the one I seek," the elf said calmly, but still with the same sad expression, "if you are Denubis."

"I am Denubis," the cleric replied, mystified. "But, forgive me, I can't place you—"

"My name is Loralon," said the elf.

Denubis gasped. The greatest of the elven clerics, Loralon had, years ago, fought Quarath's rise to power. But Quarath was too strong. Powerful forces backed him. Loralon's words of reconciliation and peace were not appreciated. In sorrow, the old cleric had returned to his people, to the wondrous land of Silvanesti that he loved, vowing never to look upon Istar again.

What was he doing here?

"Surely, you seek the Kingpriest," Denubis stammered, "I'll—"

"No, there is only one in this Temple I seek and that is you, Denubis," Loralon said. "Come, now. We have a long journey ahead of us."

"Journey!" Denubis repeated stupidly, wondering if he were going mad. "That's impossible. I've not left Istar since I came here, thirty years—"

"Come along, Denubis," said Loralon gently.

"Where? How? I don't understand—" Denubis cried. He saw Loralon standing in the center of the sunlit, peaceful room, watching him, still with that same expression of deep, unutterable sadness. Reaching up, Loralon touched the medallion he wore around his neck.

And then Denubis knew. Paladine gave his cleric insight. He saw the future. Blanching in horror, he shook his head.

"No," he whispered. "That is too dreadful."

"All is not decided. The scales of balance are tipping, but they have not yet been upset. This journey may be only temporary, or it may last for time beyond reckoning. Come, Denubis, you are needed here no longer."

The great elven cleric stretched out his hand. Denubis felt blessed with a sense of peace and understanding he had never before experienced, even in the presence of the Kingpriest. Bowing his head, he reached out and took Loralon's hand. But, as he did so, he could not help weeping. . . .

Crysania sat in a corner of the Kingpriest's sumptuous Hall of Audience, her hands folded calmly in her lap, her face pale but composed. Looking at her, no one would have guessed the turmoil in her soul. No one, perhaps, except one man, who had entered the room unnoticed by anyone and who now stood in a shadowy alcove, watching Crysania.

Sitting there, listening to the musical voice of the Kingpriest, hearing him discuss important matters of state with his ministers, hearing him go from politics to solving the great mysteries of the universe with other ministers, Crysania actually blushed to think she had even considered approaching him with her petty questions.

Words of Elistan's came to her mind. "Do not go to others for the answers. Look in your own heart, search your own faith. You will either find the answer or come to see that the answer is with the gods themselves, not with man."

And so Crysania sat, preoccupied with her thoughts, searching her heart. Unfortunately, the peace she sought eluded her. Perhaps there were no answers to her questions, she decided abruptly. Then she felt a hand on her arm. Starting, Crysania looked up.

"There *are* answers to your questions, Revered Daughter," said a voice that sent a thrill of shocked recognition through her nerves, "there are answers, but you refuse to listen to them."

She knew the voice, but—looking eagerly into the shadows of the hood, she could not recognize the face. She glanced at the hand on her shoulder, thinking she knew that hand. Black robes fell

around it, and her heart lurched. But there were no silver runes upon the robes, such as *he* wore. Once more, she stared into the face. All she could see was the glitter of hidden eyes, pale skin. . . . Then the hand left her shoulder and, reaching up, turned back the front of the hood.

At first, Crysania felt bitter disappointment. The young man's eyes were not golden, not shaped like the hourglass that had become his symbol. The skin was not tinted gold, the face was not frail and sickly. This man's face was pale, as if from long hours of study, but it was healthy, even handsome, except for its look of perpetual, bitter cynicism. The eyes were brown, clear and cold as glass, reflecting back all they saw, revealing nothing within. The man's body was slender, but well-muscled. The black, unadorned robes he wore revealed the outline of strong shoulders, not the stooped and shattered frame of the mage. And then the man smiled, the thin lips parted slightly.

"It *is* you!" Crysania breathed, starting up from her chair.

The man placed his hand upon her shoulder again, exerting a gentle pressure that forced her back down. "Please, remain seated, Revered Daughter," he said. "I will join you. It is quiet here, and we can talk without interruption." Turning, he motioned with a graceful gesture and a chair that had been across the room suddenly stood next to him. Crysania gasped slightly and glanced around the room. But, if anyone else had noticed, they were all studiously intent upon ignoring the mage. Looking back, Crysania found Raistlin watching her in amusement, and she felt her skin grow warm.

"Raistlin," she said formally, to cover her confusion, "I am pleased to see you."

"And I am pleased to see you, Revered Daughter," he said in that mocking voice that grated on her nerves. "But my name is not Raistlin."

She stared at him, flushing even more now in her embarrassment. "Forgive me," she said, looking intently at his face, "but you reminded me strongly of someone I know—once knew."

"Perhaps this will clear up the mystery," he said softly. "My name, to those around here, is Fistandantilus."

Crysania shivered involuntarily, the lights in the room seemed to darken. "No," she said, shaking her head slowly, "that cannot be! You came back . . . to learn from him!"

"I came back to *become* him," Raistlin replied.

"But . . . I've heard stories. He's evil, foul—" She drew away from Raistlin, her gaze fixed on him in horror.

"The evil is no more," Raistlin replied. "He is dead."

"You?" The word was a whisper.

"He would have killed me, Crysania," Raistlin said simply, "as he has murdered countless others. It was my life or his."

"We have exchanged one evil for another," Crysania answered in a sad, hopeless voice. She turned away.

I am losing her! Raistlin realized instantly. Silently, he regarded her. She had shifted in her chair, turning her face from him. He could see her profile, cold and pure as Solinari's light. Coolly he studied her, much as he studied the small animals that came under his knife when he probed for the secrets of life itself. Just as he stripped away their skins to see the beating hearts beneath, so he mentally stripped away Crysania's outer defenses to see her soul.

She was listening to the beautiful voice of the Kingpriest, and on her face was a look of profound peace. But Raistlin remembered her face as he had seen it on entering. Long accustomed to observing others and reading the emotions they thought they hid, he had seen the slight line appear between her black eyebrows, he had seen her gray eyes grow dark and clouded.

She had kept her hands in her lap, but he had seen the fingers twist the cloth of her gown. He knew of her conversation with Denubis. He knew she doubted, that her faith was wavering, teetering on the edge of the precipice. It would take little to shove her over the edge. And, with a bit of patience on his part, she might even jump over of her own accord.

Raistlin remembered how she had flinched at his touch. Drawing near her, he reached out and took hold of her wrist. She started and almost immediately tried to break free of his hold. But his grip

was firm. Crysania looked up into his eyes and could not move.

"Do you truly believe that of me?" Raistlin asked in the voice of one who has suffered long and then returned to find it was all for nothing. He saw his sorrow pierce her heart. She tried to speak, but Raistlin continued, twisting the knife in her soul.

"Fistandantilus planned to return to our time, destroy me, take my body, and pick up where the Queen of Darkness left off. He plotted to bring the evil dragons under his control. The Dragon Highlords, like my sister, Kitiara, would have flocked to his standard. The world would be plunged into war, once again," Raistlin paused. "That threat is now ended," he said softly.

His eyes held Crysania, just as his hand held her wrist. Looking in them, she saw herself reflected in their mirrorlike surface. And she saw herself, not as the pale, studious, severe cleric she had heard herself called more than once, but as someone beautiful and caring. This man had come to her in trust and she had let him down. The pain in his voice was unendurable, and Crysania tried once again to speak, but Raistlin continued, drawing her ever nearer.

"You know my ambitions," he said. "To you, I opened my heart. Is it my design to renew the war? Is it my desire to conquer the world? My sister, Kitiara, came to me to ask this very thing, to seek my help. I refused, and you, I fear, paid the consequences." Raistlin sighed and lowered his eyes. "I told her about you, Crysania, and of your goodness and your power. She was enraged and sent her death knight to destroy you, thinking to end your influence over me."

"Do I have influence over you then?" Crysania asked softly, no longer trying to break free of Raistlin's hold. Her voice trembled with joy. "Can I dare hope that you have seen the ways of the church and—"

"The ways of *this* church?"† Raistlin asked, his voice once again bitter and mocking. Withdrawing his hand abruptly, he sat back in his chair, gathering his black robes about him and regarding Crysania with a sneering smile.

Embarrassment, anger, and guilt stained Crysania's cheeks a faint pink, her gray eyes darkened to

Raistlin is disgusted with the church, but not necessarily with faith. His reference to "this church" conveys his distrust of a single, exclusionary dogma and the myopic society it represents. It does reflect the thoughts of many people who believe in God but have trouble believing in an organized church. See Appendix C. —TRH

deep blue. The color in her cheeks spread to her lips and suddenly she *was* beautiful, something Raistlin noticed without meaning to. The thought annoyed him beyond all bounds, threatening to disrupt his concentration. Irritably, he pushed it away.

"l know your doubts, Crysania," he continued abruptly. "I know what you have seen. You have found the church to be far more concerned with running the world than teaching the ways of the gods. You have seen its clerics double-dealing, dabbling in politics, spending money for show that might have fed the poor. You thought to vindicate the church, when you came back; to discover that others caused the gods in their righteous anger to hurl the fiery mountain down upon those who forsook them. You sought to blame . . . magic-users, perhaps."

Crysania's flush deepened, she could not look at him and turned her face away, but her pain and humiliation were obvious.

Raistlin continued mercilessly. "The time of the Cataclysm draws near. Already, the true clerics have left the land. . . . Yes, didn't you know? Your friend, Denubis, has gone. You, Crysania, are the only true cleric left in the land."

Crysania stared at Raistlin in shock. "That's . . . impossible," she whispered. Her eyes glanced around the room. And she could hear, for the first time, the conversations of those gathered in knots away from the Kingpriest. She heard talk of the Games, she heard arguments over the distribution of public funds, the routing of armies, the best means to bring a rebellious land under control—all in the name of the church.

And then, as if to drown out the other, harsh voices, the sweet, musical voice of the Kingpriest welled up in her soul, calming her troubled spirit. The Kingpriest was here, still. Turning from the darkness, she looked toward his light and felt her faith, once more strong and pure, rise up to defend her. Coolly, she looked back at Raistlin.

"There is still goodness in the world," she said sternly. Standing she started to leave. "As long as that holy man, who is surely blessed of the gods, rules, I cannot believe that the gods visited their wrath upon the church. Say, rather, it was on the world for ignoring the church," she continued, her

voice low and passionate. Raistlin had risen as well and, watching her intently, moved nearer to her.

She did not seem to notice but kept on. "Or for ignoring the Kingpriest! He must foresee it! Perhaps even now he is trying to prevent it! Begging the gods to have mercy!"

"Look at this man," Raistlin whispered, " 'blessed' of the gods." Reaching out, the mage took hold of Crysania with his strong hands and forced her to face the Kingpriest. Overwhelmed with guilt for having doubted and angry with herself for having carelessly allowed Raistlin to see within her, Crysania angrily tried to free herself of his hold, but he gripped her firmly, his fingers burning into her skin.

"Look!" he repeated. Shaking her slightly, he made her raise her head to look directly into the light and glory that surrounded the Kingpriest.

Raistlin felt the body he held so near his own start to tremble, and he smiled in satisfaction. Moving his black-hooded head near hers, Raistlin whispered in her ear, his breath touching her cheek.

"What do you see, Revered Daughter?"

His only answer was a heartbroken moan.

Raistlin's smile deepened. "Tell me," he persisted.

"A man." Crysania faltered, her shocked gaze on the Kingpriest. "Only a human man. He looks weary and . . . and frightened. His skin sags, he hasn't slept for nights. Pale blue eyes dart here and there in fear—" Suddenly, she realized what she had been saying. Acutely aware of Raistlin's nearness, the warmth and the feel of the strong, muscled body beneath the soft, black robes, Crysania broke free of his grip.

"What spell is this you have cast over me?" she demanded angrily, turning to confront him.

"No spell, Revered Daughter," Raistlin said quietly. "I have broken the spell he weaves around himself in his fear. It is that fear which will prove his undoing and bring down destruction upon the world."

Crysania stared at Raistlin wildly. She wanted him to be lying, she willed him to be lying. But then she realized that, even if he was, it didn't matter. She could no longer lie to herself.

Confused, frightened, and bewildered, Crysania turned around and, half-blinded by her tears, ran out of the Hall of Audience.

Raistlin watched her go, feeling neither elation nor satisfaction at his victory. It was, after all, no more than he had expected. Sitting down again, near the fire, he selected an orange from a bowl of fruit sitting on a table and casually tore off its peel as he stared thoughtfully into the flames.

One other person in the room watched Crysania flee the audience chamber. He watched as Raistlin ate the orange, draining the fruit of its juice first, then devouring the pulp.

His face pale with anger vying with fear, Quarath left the Hall of Audience, returning to his own room, where he paced the floor until dawn.

CHAPTER II

t became known in later history as the Night of Doom, that night the true clerics left Krynn.† Where they went and what their fate may have been, not even Astinus records. Some say they were seen during the bleak, bitter days of the War of the Lance, three hundred years later. There are many elves who will swear on all they hold dear that Loralon, greatest and most devout of the elven clerics, walked the tortured lands of Silvanesti, grieving at its downfall and blessing the efforts of those who gave of themselves to help in its rebuilding.

But, for most on Krynn, the passing of the true clerics went unnoticed. That night, however, proved to be a Night of Doom in many ways for others.

Crysania fled the Hall of Audience of the King-priest in confusion and fear. Her confusion was easily explained. She had seen that greatest of

This is, of course, a direct reference to the concept of the Rapture, as held by many modern evangelical Christians. There are many traditions around the world of a similar concept. In some beliefs the "good" are taken off the earth and the "wicked" are left to be destroyed. In others, the "good" are left behind and the "wicked" are taken away to destruction. Who is which may at that moment be a matter of personal opinion, but apparently we are either going or staying one way or the other! — TRH

beings, the Kingpriest, the man that even clerics in her own day still revered, as a human afraid of his own shadow, a human who hid himself behind spells and who let others rule for him. All of the doubts and misgivings she had developed about the church and its purpose on Krynn† returned.

As for what she feared, that she could not or would not define.

On first leaving the Hall, she stumbled along blindly without any clear idea of where she was going or what she was doing. Then she sought refuge in a corner, dried her tears, and pulled herself together. Ashamed of her momentary loss of control, she knew at once what she had to do.

She must find Denubis. She would prove Raistlin wrong.

Walking through the empty corridors lit by Solinari's waning light, Crysania went to Denubis's chamber. This tale of vanishing clerics could not be true. Crysania had, in fact, never believed in the old legends about the Night of Doom, considering them children's tales. Now, she still refused to believe it. Raistlin was . . . mistaken.

She hurried on without pause, familiar with the way. She had visited Denubis in his chambers several times to discuss theology or history, or to listen to his stories of his homeland. She knocked on the door.

There was no answer.

"He's asleep," Crysania said to herself, irritated at the sudden shiver that shook her body. "Of course, it's past Deep Watch. I'll return in the morning."

But she knocked again and even called out softly, "Denubis."

Still no answer.

"I'll come back. After all, it's only been a few hours since I saw him," she said to herself again, but she found her hand on the doorknob, gently turning it. "Denubis?" she whispered, her heart throbbing in her throat. The room was dark, it faced into an inner courtyard and so the window let in nothing of the moon's light. For a moment Crysania's will failed her. "This is ridiculous!" she reprimanded herself, already envisioning Denubis's embarrassment and her own if the man woke up to find her creeping into his bedchamber in the dead of night.

This climactic period of Krynn's history has been the subject of many short stories. See especially The Reign of Istar *and* The Cataclysm*, both edited by Margaret Weis and Tracy Hickman. —TRH*

Firmly, Crysania threw open the door, letting the light from the torches in the corridor shine into the small room. It was just the way he had left it—neat, orderly . . . and empty.

Well, not quite empty. The man's books, his quill pens, even his clothes were still there, as if he had just stepped out for a few minutes, intending to return directly. But the spirit of the room was gone, leaving it cold and vacant as the still-made bed.

For a moment, the lights in the corridor blurred before Crysania's eyes. Her legs felt weak and she leaned against the door. Then, as before, she forced herself to be calm, to think rationally. Firmly, she shut the door and, even more firmly, made herself walk down the sleeping corridors toward her own room.

Very well, the Night of Doom had come. The true clerics were gone. It was nearly Yule. Thirteen days after Yule, the Cataclysm would strike. That thought brought her to a halt. Feeling weak and sick, she leaned against a window and stared unseeing into a garden bathed in white moonlight. So this was the end of her plans, her dreams, her goals. She would be forced to go back to her own time and report nothing but dismal failure.

The silver garden swam in her sight. She had found the church corrupt, the Kingpriest apparently at fault for the terrible destruction of the world. She had even failed in her original intent, to draw Raistlin from the folds of darkness. He would never listen to her. Right now, probably, he was laughing at her with that terrible, mocking laugh. . . .

"Revered Daughter?" came a voice.

Hastily wiping her eyes, Crysania turned. "Who is there?" she asked, trying to clear her throat. Blinking rapidly, she stared into the darkness, then caught her breath as a dark, robed figure emerged from the shadows. She could not speak, her voice failed.

"I was on my way to my chambers when I saw you standing here," said the voice, and it was not laughing or mocking. It was cool and tinged with cynicism, but there was a strange quality to it, a warmth, that made Crysania tremble.

"I hope you are not ill," Raistlin said, coming over to stand beside her. She could not see his face, hidden by the shadows of the dark hood. But she could see his eyes, glittering, clear and cold in the moonlight.

"No," Crysania murmured in confusion and turned her face away, devoutly hoping that all traces of tears were gone. But it did little good. Weariness, strain, and her own failings overwhelmed her. Though she sought desperately to control them, the tears came again, sliding down her cheeks.

"Go away, please," she said, squeezing her eyes shut, swallowing the tears like bitter medicine.

She felt warmth envelop her and the softness of velvet black robes brush against her bare arm. She smelled the sweet scent of spices and rose petals and a vaguely cloying scent of decay—bat's wings, perhaps, the skull of some animal—those mysterious things magicians used to cast their spells. And then she felt a hand touch her cheek, slender fingers, sensitive and strong and burning with that strange warmth.

Either the fingers brushed the tears away or they dried at their burning touch, Crysania wasn't certain. Then the fingers gently lifted her chin and turned her head away from the moonlight. Crysania couldn't breathe, her heartbeat stifled her. She kept her eyes closed, fearing what she might see. But she could feel Raistlin's slender body, hard beneath the soft robes, press against hers. She could feel that terrible warmth . . .

Crysania suddenly wanted his darkness to enfold her and hide her and comfort her. She wanted that warmth to burn away the cold inside of her. Eagerly, she raised her arms and reached out her hands . . . and he was gone. She could hear the rustle of his robes receding in the stillness of the corridor.

Startled, Crysania opened her eyes. Then, weeping once more, she pressed her cheek against the cold glass. But these were tears of joy.

"Paladine," she whispered, "thank you. My way is clear. I will not fail!"

A dark-robed figure stalked the Temple halls. Any who met it shrank away from it in terror, shrank from the anger that could be felt if not seen on the hooded face. Raistlin at last entered his own deserted corridor, hit the door to his room with a blast that nearly shattered it, and caused flames to leap up in the grate with nothing more than a glance. The fire roared up the chimney and Raistlin paced,

hurling curses at himself until he was too tired to walk. Then he sank into a chair and stared at the fire with a feverish gaze.

"Fool!" he repeated. "I should have foreseen this!" His fist clenched. "I should have known. This body, for all its strength, has the great weakness common to mankind. No matter how intelligent, how disciplined the mind, how controlled the emotions, *that* waits in the shadows like a great beast, ready to leap out and take over." He snarled in rage and dug his nails into his palm until it bled. "I can still see her! I can see her ivory skin, her pale, soft lips. I can smell her hair and feel the curving softness of her body next to mine!"

"No!" This was fairly a shriek. "This must not, will not be allowed to happen! Or perhaps. . . ." A thought. "What if I were to seduce her? Would that not put her even more in my power?" The thought was more than tempting, it brought such a rush of desire to the young man that his entire body shook.

But the cold and calculating, logical part of Raistlin's mind took over. "What do you know of lovemaking?" he asked himself with a sneer. "Of seduction? In this, you are a child, more stupid than your behemoth of a brother."

Memories of his youth† came back to him in a flood. Frail and sickly, noted for his biting sarcasm and his sly ways, Raistlin had certainly never attracted the attention of women, not like his handsome brother. Absorbed, obsessed by his studies of magic, he had not felt the loss—much. Oh, once he had experimented. One of Caramon's girlfriends, bored by easy conquest, thought the big man's twin brother might prove more interesting. Goaded by his brother's gibes and those of his fellows, Raistlin had given way to her coarse overtures. It had been a disappointing experience for both of them. The girl returned gratefully to Caramon's arms. For Raistlin, it had simply proved what he had long suspected—that he found true ecstasy only in his magic.

But this body—younger, stronger, more like his brother's—ached with a passion he had never before experienced. Yet he could not give way to it. "I would end up destroying myself"— he saw with cold clarity—"and, far from furthering my objective, might well harm it. She is virgin, pure in mind and

Accounts of Raistlin's youth can be found in The Soulforge *by Margaret Weis.*

345

Many cultures place great reverence upon virginity, the most obvious being the Virgin Mary. There were also the vestal virgins of antiquity, and even Merlin. In her Author's Note to The Crystal Cave, *Mary Stewart wrote: "There is so strong a connection in legend (and indeed in history) between celibacy, or virginity, and power, that I have thought it reasonable to insist on Merlin's virginity." [The Crystal Cave, by Mary Stewart, Fawcett Crest Edition, 1989, p. 383.]*

body. That purity is her strength.† I need it tarnished, but I need it intact."

Having firmly resolved this and being long experienced in the practice of exerting strict mental control over his emotions, the young mage relaxed and sat back in his chair, letting weariness sweep over him. The fire died low, his eyes closed in the rest that would renew his flagging power.

But, before he drifted off to sleep, still sitting in the chair, he saw once more, with unwanted vividness, a single tear glistening in the moonlight.

The Night of Doom continued. An acolyte was awakened from a sound sleep and told to report to Quarath. He found the elven cleric sitting in his chambers.

"Did you send for me, my lord?" the acolyte asked, attempting to stifle a yawn. He looked sleepy and rumpled. Indeed, his outer robes had been put on backward in his haste to answer the summons that had come so late in the night.

"What is the meaning of this report?" Quarath demanded, tapping at a piece of paper on his desk.

The acolyte bent over to look, rubbing the sleep out of his eyes enough to make the writing coherent.

"Oh, that," he said after a moment. "Just what it says, my lord."

"That Fistandantilus was *not* responsible for the death of my slave? I find that very difficult to believe."

"Nonetheless, my lord, you may question the dwarf yourself. He confessed—after a great deal of monetary persuasion—that he had in reality been hired by the lord named there, who was apparently incensed at the church's takeover of his holdings on the outskirts of the city."

"I know what he's incensed about!" Quarath snapped. "And killing my slave would be just like Onygion—sneaky and underhanded. He doesn't dare face me directly."

Quarath sat, musing. "Then why did that big slave commit the deed?" he asked suddenly, giving the acolyte a shrewd glance.

"The dwarf stated that this was something arranged privately between himself and Fistandantilus. Apparently the first 'job' of this nature that came his way was to be given to the slave, Caramon."

"That wasn't in the report," Quarath said, eyeing the young man sternly.

"No," the acolyte admitted, flushing. "I—I really don't like putting anything about . . . the magic-user . . . down in writing. Anything like that, where he might read it—"

"No, I don't suppose I blame you," Quarath muttered. "Very well, you may go."

The acolyte nodded, bowed, and returned thankfully to his bed.

Quarath did not go to his bed for long hours, however, but sat in his study, going over and over the report. Then, he sighed. "I am becoming as bad as the Kingpriest, jumping at shadows that aren't there. If Fistandantilus wanted to do away with me, he could manage it within seconds. I should have realized—this is not his style." He rose to his feet, finally. "Still, he was with her tonight. I wonder what that means? Perhaps nothing. Perhaps the man is more human than I would have supposed. Certainly the body he has appeared in this time is better than those he usually dredges up."

The elf smiled grimly to himself as he straightened his desk and filed the report away carefully. "Yule is approaching. I will put this from my mind until the holiday season is past. After all, the time is fast coming when the Kingpriest will call upon the gods to eradicate evil from the face of Krynn. That will sweep this Fistandantilus and those who follow him back into the darkness which spawned them."

He yawned, then, and stretched. "But I'll take care of Lord Onygion first."

The Night of Doom was nearly ended. Morning lit the sky as Caramon lay in his cell, staring into the gray light. Tomorrow was another game, his first since the "accident."

Life had not been pleasant for the big warrior these last few days. Nothing had changed outwardly. The other gladiators were old campaigners, most of them, long accustomed to the ways of the Game.

"It is not a bad system," Pheragas said with a shrug when Caramon confronted him the day after his return from the Temple. "Certainly better than a thousand men killing each other on the fields of battle. Here, if one nobleman feels offended by

another, their feud is handled secretly, in private, to the satisfaction of all."

"Except the innocent man who dies for a cause he doesn't care about or understand!" Caramon said angrily.

"Don't be such a baby!" Kiiri snorted, polishing one of her collapsible daggers. "By your own account, you did some mercenary work. Did you understand or care about the cause then? Didn't you fight and kill because you were being well paid?† Would you have fought if you weren't? I don't see the difference."

"The difference is I had a choice!" Caramon responded, scowling. "And I knew the cause I fought for! I never would have fought for anyone I didn't believe was in the right! No matter how much money they paid me! My brother felt the same. He and I—" Caramon abruptly fell silent.

Kiiri looked at him strangely, then shook her head with a grin. "Besides," she added lightly, "it adds spice, an edge of real tension. You'll fight better from now on. You'll see."

Thinking of this conversation as he lay in the darkness, Caramon tried to reason it out in his slow, methodical fashion. Maybe Kiiri and Pheragas were correct, maybe he *was* being a baby, crying because the bright, glittering toy he had enjoyed playing with suddenly cut him. But—looking at it every way possible—he still couldn't believe it was right. A man deserved a choice, to choose his own way to live, his own way to die. No one else had the right to determine that for him.

And then, in the predawn, a crushing weight seemed to fall on Caramon. He sat up, leaning on one elbow, staring unseeing into the gray cell. If that was true, if every man deserved a choice, then what about his brother? Raistlin had made his choice—to walk the ways of night instead of day. Did Caramon have the right to drag his brother from those paths?

His mind went back to those days he had unwittingly recalled when talking to Kiiri and Pheragas—those days right before the Test, those days that had been the happiest in his life—the days of mercenary work with his brother.

The two fought well together,† and they were always welcomed by nobles. Though warriors

Kiiri knows that Caramon had indeed been a mercenary in his younger years, but her knowledge of the specifics is quite lacking. Many of Caramon's early adventures can be found in Brothers in Arms *by Margaret Weis and Don Perrin, and* Brothers Majere *by Kevin Stein.*

One account of the early days is in Brothers in Arms *by Margaret Weis and Don Perrin. Besides detailing the adventures of Caramon and Raistlin, the book features one of the rarest creatures found in Ansalon—a half-kender.*

were common as leaves in the trees, magic-users who could and would join the fighting were another thing altogether. Though many nobles looked somewhat dubious when they saw Raistlin's frail and sickly appearance, they were soon impressed by his courage and his skill. The brothers were paid well and were soon much in demand.

But they always selected the cause they fought for with care.

"That was Raist's doing," Caramon whispered to himself wistfully. "I would have fought for anyone, the cause mattered little to me. But Raistlin insisted that the cause had to be a just one.† We walked away from more than one job because he said it involved a strong man trying to grow stronger by devouring others. . . .

"But that's what Raistlin's doing!" Caramon said softly, staring up at the ceiling. "Or is it? That's what they *say he's* doing, those magic-users. But can I trust them? Par-Salian was the one who got him into this, he admitted that! Raistlin rid the world of this Fistandantilus creature. By all accounts, that's a good thing. And Raist told me he didn't have anything to do with the Barbarian's death. So he hasn't really done anything wrong. Maybe we've misjudged him. . . . Maybe we have *no right* to try to force him to change. . . ."†

Caramon sighed. "What should I do?" Closing his eyes in forlorn weariness, he fell asleep, and soon the smell of warm, freshly baked muffins filled his mind.

The sun lit the sky. The Night of Doom ended. Tasslehoff rose from his bed, eagerly greeted the new day, and decided that he—he personally—would stop the Cataclysm.

One of the great strengths of this book for me is the examination of the nature of good and evil. Caramon never thought of such questions much, but Raistlin—a character that we primarily identify as evil—was deeply concerned with the ethics of his actions. To a very great extent, Raistlin's central flaw is identical to that of the Kingpriest: a single-minded commitment to his own point of view over all others. Yet here we see that it is that same commitment that sets them both above Caramon, who has remained uncommitted all his life to anything except his brother. —TRH

This is the central theme of Legends: that we have no right to force change on anyone. Change—true change—comes only from within. It is motivated, inspired, or invoked in others but never enforced. Faith is not dictated; it must come from within. Goodness and righteousness are not mandated; they must come from within. Every soul must chose for itself. This is the greatest gift of God. This simple lesson, if we could all learn it, would eliminate terrorism and warfare. It would revolutionize the world we know today. It can revolutionize our own personal worlds as well— the world of our acquaintances, friends, and supposed enemies. It can change the world—one soul at a time. —TRH

349

CHAPTER 12

The rose is an important symbol in the books. Down through time, the rose has been associated with love, because the rose is beautiful to look upon, with a sweet fragrance, while its thorns can also pierce the flesh and draw blood. Crysania is portrayed as the white rose, pure and virginal. Lord Soth is the black rose, the personification of death and dishonor. Tas finds joy amidst the red roses of Yule, though the unusually warm weather is a hint of ominous changes coming.
—MW

lter time!" Tasslehoff said eagerly, slipping over the garden wall into the sacred Temple area and dropping down to land in the middle of a flower bed. Some clerics were walking in the garden, talking among themselves about the merriment of the forthcoming Yule season. Rather than interrupt their conversation, Tas did what he considered the polite thing and flattened himself down among the flowers until they left, although it meant getting his blue leggings dirty.

It was rather pleasant, lying among the red Yule roses,† so called because they grew only during the Yule season. The weather was warm, too warm, most people said. Tas grinned. Trust humans. If the weather was cold, Yule-type weather, they'd complain about that, too. He thought the warmth was delightful. A trifle hard to breathe in the heavy air, perhaps, but— after all—you couldn't have everything.

Tas listened to the clerics with interest. The Yule parties must be splendid things, he thought, and briefly considered attending. The first one was tonight—Yule Welcoming. It would end early, since everyone wanted to get lots of sleep in preparation for the big Yule parties themselves, which would begin at dawn tomorrow and run for days—the last celebration before the harsh, dark winter set in.

"Perhaps I'll attend that party tomorrow," Tas thought. He had supposed that a Yule Welcoming party in the Temple would be solemn and grand and, therefore, dull and boring—at least from a kender viewpoint. But the way these clerics talked, it sounded quite lively.

Caramon was fighting tomorrow—the Games being one of the highlights of the Yule season. Tomorrow's fight determined which teams would have the right to face each other in the Final Bout—the last game of the year before winter forced the closing of the arena. The winners of this last game would win their freedom. Of course, it was already predetermined who would win tomorrow—Caramon's team. For some reason, this news had sent Caramon into a gloomy depression.

Tas shook his head. He never would understand that man, he decided. All this sulking about honor. After all, it was only a game. Anyway, it made things easy. It would be simple for Tas to sneak off and enjoy himself.

But then the kender sighed. No, he had serious business to attend to—stopping the Cataclysm was more important than a party, maybe even a couple of parties. He'd sacrifice his own amusement to this great cause.

Feeling very self-righteous and noble (and suddenly quite bored), the kender glared at the clerics irritably, wishing they'd hurry up. Finally, they strolled inside, leaving the garden empty. Heaving a sigh of relief, Tas picked himself up and brushed off the dirt. Plucking a Yule rose, he stuck it in his topknot for decoration in honor of the season, then slipped into the Temple.

It, too, was decorated for the Yule season, and the beauty and splendor took the kender's breath away. He stared around in delight, marveling at the thousands of Yule roses that had been raised in gardens

all over Krynn and brought here to fill the Temple corridors with their sweet fragrance. Wreaths of everbloom added a spicy scent, sunlight glistened off its pointed, polished leaves twined with red velvet and swans' feathers. Baskets of rare and exotic fruits stood on nearly every table—gifts from all over Krynn to be enjoyed by everyone in the Temple. Plates of wonderful cakes and sweetmeats stood beside them. Thinking of Caramon, Tas stuffed his pouches full, happily picturing the big man's delight. He had never known Caramon to stay depressed in the face of a crystal sugared almond puff.

Tas roamed the halls, lost in happiness. He almost forgot why he had come and had to remind himself continually of his Important Mission. No one paid any attention to him. Everyone he passed was intent on the upcoming celebration or on the business of running the government or the church or both. Few even gave Tas a second glance. Occasionally, a guard stared sternly at him, but Tas just smiled cheerily, waved, and went on. It was an old kender proverb— *Don't change color to match the walls. Look like you belong and the walls will change color to match you.*

Finally, after many windings and turnings (and several stops to investigate interesting objects, some of which happened to fall into the kender's pouches), Tas found himself in the one corridor that was *not* decorated, that was *not* filled with merry people making gleeful party arrangements, that was *not* resounding with the sounds of choirs practicing their Yule hymns. In this corridor, the curtains were still drawn, denying the sun admittance. It was chill and dark and forbidding, more so than ever because of the contrast to the rest of the world.

Tas crept down the hall, not walking softly for any particular reason except that the corridor was so grimly silent and gloomy it seemed to expect everyone who entered to be the same and would be highly offended if he weren't. The last thing Tas wanted to do was offend a corridor, he told himself, so he walked quietly. The possibility that he might be able to sneak up on Raistlin without the mage knowing it and catch a glimpse of some wonderful magical experiment certainly never crossed the kender's mind.

Drawing near the door, he heard Raistlin speaking and, from the tone, it sounded like he had a visitor.

"Drat," was Tas's first thought. "Now I'll have to wait to talk to him until this person leaves. And I'm on an Important Mission, too. How inconsiderate. I wonder how long they're going to be."

Putting his ear to the keyhole—to see if he could figure out how much longer the person planned to stay—Tas was startled to hear a woman's voice answer the mage.

"That voice sounds familiar," said the kender to himself, pressing closer to listen. "Of course! Crysania! I wonder what she's doing here."

"You're right, Raistlin." Tas heard her say with a sigh, "this *is* much more restful than those garish corridors. When I first came here, I was frightened. You smile! But I was. I admit it. This corridor seemed so bleak and desolate and cold. But now the hallways of the Temple are filled with an oppressive, stifling warmth. Even the Yule decorations depress me. I see so much waste, money squandered that could be helping those in need."

She stopped speaking, and Tas heard a rustle. Since no one was talking, the kender quit listening and put his eyes to the keyhole. He could see inside the room quite clearly. The heavy curtains were drawn, but the chamber was lit with soft candlelight. Crysania sat in a chair, facing him. The rustling sound he heard was apparently her stirring in impatience or frustration. She rested her head on her hand, and the look on her face was one of confusion and perplexity.

But that was not what made the kender open his eyes wide. Crysania had changed! Gone were the plain, unadorned white robes, the severe hair style. She was dressed as the other female clerics in white robes, but these were decorated with fine embroidery. Her arms were bare, though a slender golden band adorned one, enhancing the pure whiteness of her skin. Her hair fell from a central part to sweep down around her shoulders with feathery softness. There was a flush of color in her cheeks, her eyes were warm and their gaze lingered on the black-robed figure that sat across from her, his back to Tas.

"Humpf," said the kender with interest. "Tika was right."

"I don't know why I come here," Tas heard Crysania say after a moment's pause.

I do, the kender thought gleefully, quickly moving his ear back to the keyhole so he could hear better.

Her voice continued. "I am filled with such hope when I come to visit you, but I always leave depressed and unhappy. I plan to show you the ways of righteousness and truth, to prove to you that only by following those ways can we hope to bring peace to our world. But you always turn my words upside down and inside out."

"Your questions are your own," Tas heard Raistlin say, and there was another rustling sound, as if the mage moved closer to the woman. "I simply open your heart so that you may hear them. Surely Elistan counsels against blind faith. . . ."

Tas heard a sarcastic note in the mage's voice, but apparently Crysania did not detect it, for she answered quickly and sincerely, "Of course. He encourages us to question and often tells us of Goldmoon's example—how her questioning led to the return of the true gods. But questions should lead one to better understanding, and your questions only make me confused and miserable!"

"How well I know that feeling." Raistlin murmured so softly that Tas almost didn't hear him. The kender heard Crysania move in her chair and risked a quick peep. The mage was near her, one hand resting on her arm. As he spoke those words, Crysania moved nearer him, impulsively placing her hand over his. When she spoke, there was such hope and love and joy in her voice that Tas felt warm all over.

"Do you mean that?" Crysania asked the mage. "Are my poor words touching some part of you? No, don't look away! I can see by your expression that you have thought of them and pondered them. We are so alike! I knew that the first time I met you. Ah, you smile again, mocking me. Go ahead. *I* know the truth. You told me the same thing, in the Tower. You said I was as ambitious as you were. I've thought about it, and you're right. Our ambitions take different forms, but perhaps they are not as dissimilar as I once believed. We both live lonely lives, dedicated to our studies. We open our hearts to no one, not even those who would be closest to us. You

surround yourself with darkness, but, Raistlin, I have seen beyond that. The warmth, the light . . ."

Tas quickly put his eye back to the keyhole. He's going to kiss her! he thought, wildly excited. This is wonderful! Wait until I tell Caramon.

"Come on, fool!" he instructed Raistlin impatiently as the mage sat there, his hands on Crysania's arms. "How can he resist?" the kender muttered, looking at the woman's parted lips, her shining eyes.

Suddenly Raistlin let loose of Crysania and turned away from her, abruptly rising out of his chair. "You had better go," he said in a husky voice. Tas sighed and drew away from the door in disgust. Leaning against the wall, he shook his head.

There was the sound of coughing, deep and harsh, and Crysania's voice, gentle and filled with concern.

"It is nothing," Raistlin said as he opened the door. "I have felt unwell for several days. Can you not guess the reason?" he asked, pausing with the door half ajar. Tas pressed back against the wall so they wouldn't see him, not wanting to interrupt (or miss) anything. "Haven't you felt it?"

"I have felt something," Crysania murmured breathlessly. "What do you mean?"

"The anger of the gods," Raistlin answered, and it was obvious to Tas that this wasn't the answer Crysania had hoped for. She seemed to droop. Raistlin did not notice, but continued on. "Their fury beats upon me, as if the sun were drawing nearer and nearer to this wretched planet. Perhaps that is why you are feeling depressed and unhappy."

"Perhaps," murmured Crysania.

"Tomorrow is Yule,"† Raistlin continued softly. "Thirteen days after that, the Kingpriest will make his demand. Already, he and his ministers plan for it. The gods know. They have sent him a warning— the vanishing of the clerics. But he did not heed it. Every day, from Yule on, the warning signs will grow stronger, clearer. Have you ever read Astinus's *Chronicles of the Last Thirteen Days?*† They are not pleasant reading, and they will be less pleasant to live through."

Crysania looked at him, her face brightening. "Come back with us before then," she said eagerly. "Par-Salian gave Caramon a magical device that

*"On the fifth day of Yule,
The Kingpriest forced on
 me
Five Sorcery Towers
Four Solamnic Knights
Three Edicts
Two Gladiators
And a Kender in a
 paradox!"
—TRH*

*These thirteen warnings
are very much after the
Biblical Plagues of Egypt
found in the book of
Exodus. —TRH*

*"The gods sent thirteen
omens to warn the folk of
Ansalon of their coming
doom. How quickly the
people forgot the prophesy
foretold by the elven priest,
Loralon: 'That if ever man,
in pride, should challenge
the gods, woe betide the
world.' These thirteen
signs passed all but
unnoticed among the folk."
[TALES OF THE LANCE
Boxed Set, World Book
of Ansalon, TSR, Inc.,
1992, p. 24.]*

will take us back to our own time. The kender told me—"

"What magical device?" Raistlin demanded suddenly, and the strange tone of his voice sent a thrill through the kender and startled Crysania. "What does it look like? How does it work?" His eyes burned feverishly.

"I-I don't know," Crysania faltered.

"Oh, I'll tell you," Tas offered, stepping out from against the wall. "Gee, I'm sorry. I didn't mean to scare you. It's just that I couldn't help overhearing. Merry Yule to you both, by the way," Tas extended his small hand, which no one took.

Both Raistlin and Crysania were staring at him with the same expressions worn on the faces of those who suddenly see a spider drop into their soup at dinner. Unabashed, Tas continued prattling cheerfully, putting his hand in his pocket. "What were we talking about? Oh, the magical device. Yes, well," Tas continued more hurriedly, seeing Raistlin's eyes narrow in an alarming fashion, "when it's unfolded, it's shaped like a . . . a sceptre and it has a . . . a ball at one end, all glittering with jewels. It's about this big." The kender spread his hands about an arm's length apart. "That's when it's stretched out. Then, Par-Salian did something to it and it—"

"Collapsed in upon itself," Raistlin finished, "until you could carry it in your pocket."

"Why, yes!" Tas said excitedly. "That's right! How did you know?"

"I am familiar with the object," Raistlin replied, and Tas noticed again a strange sound to the mage's voice, a quivering, a tenseness—fear? Or elation? The kender couldn't tell. Crysania noticed it, too.

"What is it?" she asked.

Raistlin didn't answer immediately, his face was suddenly a mask, unreadable, impassive, cold. "I hesitate to say," he told her. "I must study on this matter." Flicking a glance at the kender—"What is it you want? Or are you simply listening at keyholes!"

"Certainly not!" Tas said, insulted. "I came to talk to you, if you and Lady Crysania are finished, that is," he amended hastily, his glance going to Crysania.

She regarded him with quite an unfriendly expression, the kender thought, then turned away from him to Raistlin. "Will I see you tomorrow?" she asked.

"I think not," he said. "I will not, of course, be attending the Yule party."

"Oh, but I don't want to go either—" Crysania began.

"You will be expected," Raistlin said abruptly. "Besides, I have too long neglected my studies in the pleasure of your company."

"I see," Crysania said. Her own voice was cool and distant and, Tasslehoff could tell, hurt and disappointed.

"Farewell, gentlemen," she said after a moment, when it was apparent Raistlin wasn't going to add anything further. Bowing slightly, she turned and walked down the dark hall, her white robes seeming to take the light away as she left.

"I'll tell Caramon you send your regards," Tas called after her helpfully, but Crysania didn't turn around. The kender turned to Raistlin with a sigh. "I'm afraid Caramon didn't make much of an impression on her. But, then, he was all fuddled because of the dwarf spirits—"

Raistlin coughed. "Did you come here to discuss my brother?" he interrupted coldly, "because, if so, you can leave—"

"Oh, no!" Tas said hastily. Then he grinned up at the mage. "I came to stop the Cataclysm!"

For the first time in his life, the kender had the satisfaction of seeing his words absolutely stun Raistlin. It was not a satisfaction he enjoyed long, however. The mage's face went white and stiff, his mirrorlike eyes seemed to shatter, allowing Tas to see inside, into those dark, burning depths the mage kept hidden. Hands as strong as the claws of a predatory bird sank into the kender's shoulders, hurting him. Within seconds, Tas found himself thrown inside Raistlin's room. The door slammed shut with a shattering bang.

"What gave you this idea?" Raistlin demanded.

Tas shrank backward, startled, and glanced around the room uneasily, his kender instincts telling him he better look for someplace to hide.

"Uh—you d-did," Tas stammered. "Well, n-not exactly. But you said something about m-my coming back here and being able to alter time. And, I thought, st-stopping the Cataclysm would be a sort of good thing—"

"How did you plan to do it?" Raistlin asked, and his eyes burned with a hot fire that made Tas sweat just looking into it.

"Well, I planned to discuss it with you first, of course," the kender said, hoping Raistlin was still subject to flattery, "and then I thought—if you said it was all right—that I would just go and talk to the Kingpriest and tell him he was making a really big mistake—one of the All Time Big Mistakes, if you take my meaning. And, I'm sure, once I explained, that he'd listen—"

"I'm sure," Raistlin said, and his voice was cool and controlled. But Tas thought he detected, oddly, a note of vast relief. "So"—the mage turned away—"you intend to talk to the Kingpriest. And what if he refuses to listen? What then?"

Tas paused, his mouth open. "I guess I hadn't considered that," the kender said, after a moment. He sighed, then shrugged. "We'll go home."

"There's another way," Raistlin said softly, sitting down in his chair and regarding the kender with his mirrorlike eyes. "A sure way! A way you could stop the Cataclysm without fail."

"There is?" Tas said eagerly. "What?"

"The magical device," Raistlin answered, spreading his slender hands. "Its powers are great, far beyond what Par-Salian told that idiot brother of mine. Activate it on the Day of the Cataclysm, and its magic will destroy the fiery mountain high above the world, so that it harms no one."

"Really?" Tas gasped. "That's wonderful." Then he frowned. "But, how can I be sure? Suppose it doesn't work—"

"What have you got to lose?" Raistlin asked. "If, for some reason, it fails, and I truly doubt it." The mage smiled at the kender's naiveté. "It was, after all, created by the highest level magic-users—"

"Like dragon orbs?"† Tas interrupted.

"Like dragon orbs," Raistlin snapped, irritated at the interruption. "But if it did fail, you could always use it to escape at the last moment."

"With Caramon and Crysania," Tas added.

Raistlin did not answer, but the kender didn't notice in his excitement. Then he thought of something.

"What if Caramon decides to leave before then?"

"The Orbs of Dragonkind *(also called* Dragon Orbs*) are fragile, etched crystal globes. The orbs* were employed long before the Cataclysm for the purpose of destroying evil dragons—according to legends, at least. These legends are common throughout the civilized lands of Krynn. What is not known . . . is that the orbs' actual purpose is to summon evil dragons. Powerful mages of old would* summon *the dragons with the orbs, and then destroy them with powerful magic."* [DRAGONLANCE Adventures, *by Tracy Hickman and Margaret Weis, TSR, Inc., 1987, p. 95.]*

he asked fearfully.

"He won't," Raistlin answered softly. "Trust me," he added, seeing Tas about to argue.

The kender pondered again, then sighed. "I just thought of something. I don't think Caramon will let me have the device. Par-Salian told him to guard it with his life. He never lets it out of his sight and locks it up in a chest when he has to leave. And I'm sure he wouldn't believe me if I tried to explain why I wanted it."

"Don't tell him. The day of the Cataclysm is the day of the Final Bout," Raistlin said, shrugging. "If it is gone for a short time, he'll never miss it."

"But, that would be stealing!"† Tas said, shocked.

Raistlin's lips twitched. "Let us say—borrowing," the mage amended soothingly. "It's for such a worthy cause! Caramon won't be angry. I know my brother. Think how proud he will be of you!"

"You're right," Tas said, his eyes shining. "I'd be a true hero, greater than Kronin Thistleknot himself! How do I find out how to work it?"

"I'll give you instructions," Raistlin said, rising. He began to cough again. "Come back . . . in three days' time. And now . . . I must rest."

"Sure," Tas said cheerfully, getting to his feet. "I hope you feel better." He started for the door. Once there, however, he hesitated. "Oh, say, I don't have a gift for you. I'm sorry—"

"You have given me a gift," Raistlin said, "a gift of inestimable value. Thank you."

"I have!" Tas said, astonished. "Oh, you must mean stopping the Cataclysm. Well, don't mention it. I—"

Tas suddenly found himself in the middle of the garden, staring at the rosebushes and an extremely surprised cleric who had seen the kender apparently materialize out of nowhere, right in the middle of the path.

"Great Reorx's† beard! I wish I knew how to do that," Tasslehoff said wistfully.

When the characters were first put together for the DRAGONLANCE setting, it was initially with the idea of a balanced party for AD&D games. This, of course, would include the thief character class. Now, while the abilities of a thief in a group of adventurers are essential, I found the entire idea of stealing morally wrong. However, I was reminded of the old joke of a neighbor who is constantly borrowing things and never returning them. This evolved into the concept of "borrowing" for the kender—and gave the race such great depth. Roger Moore then "borrowed" this concept from me when he wrote the first story about Tasslehoff and really breathed life into the character. Margaret and I then "borrowed" Tasslehoff back in this form. People have been "borrowing" this little kender ever since! —TRH

"According to the dwarves and gnomes, Reorx, the god of the forge, is the greatest god of the entire pantheon. Reorx is the supreme god of the dwarves, who consider themselves his chosen people—although gnomes also consider themselves the 'true chosen of Reorx.' In actuality, Reorx loves both races equally." [DRAGONLANCE Campaign Setting, Wizards of the Coast, Inc., 2003, p. 127.]

†n Yule day
came the first of what would be later known as the
Thirteen Calamities, (note that Astinus records them
in the *Chronicles* as the Thirteen Warnings).†

The day dawned hot and breathless. It was the
hottest Yule day anyone—even the elves—could
remember. In the Temple, the Yule roses drooped
and withered, the everbloom wreaths smelled as if
they had been baked in an oven, the snow that
cooled the wine in silver bowls melted so rapidly
that the servants did nothing all day but run back
and forth from the depths of the rock cellars to the
party rooms, carrying buckets of slush.

Raistlin woke on that morning, in the dark hour
before the dawn, so ill he could not rise from his bed.
He lay naked, bathed in sweat, a prey to the fevered
hallucinations that had caused him to rip off his
robes and the bedcovers. The gods were indeed near,

*So what's the difference
between "calamities" and
"warnings?" Thirteen
Calamities sounds like an
accident. Thirteen
Warnings, on the other
hand, as Astinus corrects,
denotes that the events
should have been a sign to
the people that something
terrible was coming. This
difference points again to
the myopia of the people of
Istar at the time and their
inability to accept their
own responsibility for what
is coming. —TRH*

but it was the closeness of one god in particular—his goddess, the Queen of Darkness—that was affecting him. He could feel her anger, as he could sense the anger of all the gods at the Kingpriest's attempt to destroy the balance they sought to achieve in the world.

Thus he had dreamed of his Queen, but she had chosen not to appear to him in her anger as might have been expected. He had not dreamed of the terrible five-headed dragon,† the Dragon of All Colors and of None that would try to enslave the world in the Wars of the Lance. He had not seen her as the Dark Warrior, leading her legions to death and destruction. No, she had appeared to him as the Dark Temptress, the most beautiful of all women, the most seductive, and thus she had spent the night with him, tantalizing him with the weakness, the glory of the flesh.

When the DRAGONLANCE setting was originally proposed, it would have featured one adventure module for each of the twelve different types of dragons in the Monster Manual at the time. Thus, Takhisis was very much modeled after Tiamat from that work. —TRH

Closing his eyes, shivering in the room that was cool despite the heat outdoors, Raistlin pictured to himself once again the fragrant dark hair hanging over him; he felt her touch, her warmth. Reaching up his hands, letting himself sink beneath her spell, he had parted the tangled hair—and seen Crysania's face!

The dream ended, shattered as his mind took control once more. And now he lay awake, exultant in his victory, yet knowing the price it had cost. As if to remind him, a wrenching coughing fit seized him.

"I will not give in," he muttered when he could breathe. "You will not win me over so easily, my Queen." Staggering out of bed, so weak he had to pause more than once to rest, he put on the black robes and made his way to his desk. Cursing the pain in his chest, he opened an ancient text on magical paraphernalia and began his laborious search.

Crysania, too, had slept poorly. Like Raistlin, she felt the nearness of all the gods, but of her god—Paladine—most of all. She felt his anger, but it was tinged with a sorrow so deep and devastating that Crysania could not bear it. Overwhelmed with guilt, she turned away from that gentle face and began to run. She ran and ran, weeping, unable to see where she was going. She stumbled and was falling into nothingness, her soul torn with fear.

Then strong arms caught her. She was enfolded in soft black robes, held near a muscular body. Slender fingers stroked her hair, soothing her. She looked into a face—

Bells. Bells broke the stillness. Startled, Crysania sat up in bed, looking around wildly. Then, remembering the face she had seen, remembering the warmth of his body and the comfort she had found there, she put her aching head in her hands and wept.

Tasslehoff, on waking, at first felt disappointment. Today was Yule, he remembered, and also the day Raistlin said Dire Things would begin to happen. Looking around in the gray light that filtered through their window, the only dire thing Tas saw was Caramon, down on the floor, huffing and puffing his way grimly through morning exercises.

Although Caramon's days were filled with weapons' practice, working out with his team members, developing new parts of their routine, the big man still fought a never-ending battle with his weight. He had been taken off his diet and allowed to eat the same food as the others. But the sharp-eyed dwarf soon noticed that Caramon was eating about five times more than anyone else!

Once, the big man had eaten for pleasure. Now, nervous and unhappy and obsessed by thoughts of his brother, Caramon sought consolation in food as another might seek consolation in drink. (Caramon had, in fact, tried that once, ordering Tas to sneak a bottle of dwarf spirits in to him. But, unused to the strong alcohol, it had made him violently sick—much to the kender's secret relief.)

Arack decreed, therefore, that Caramon could eat only if he performed a series of strenuous exercises each day. Caramon often wondered how the dwarf knew if he missed a day, since he did them early in the morning before anyone else was up. But Arack *did* know, somehow. The one morning Caramon had skipped the exercises, he had been denied access to the mess hall by a grinning, club-wielding Raag.

Growing bored with listening to Caramon grunt and groan and swear, Tas climbed up on a chair, peering out the window to see if there was anything dire happening outside. He felt cheered immediately.

"Caramon! Come look!" he called in excitement. "Have you ever seen a sky that peculiar shade before?"

"Ninety-nine, one hundred," puffed the big man. Then Tas heard a large "ooof." With a thud that shook the room, Caramon flopped down on his now rock-hard belly to rest. Then the big man heaved himself up off the stone floor and came to look out the barred window, mopping the sweat from his body with a towel.

Casting a bored glance outside, expecting nothing but an ordinary sunrise, the big man blinked, then his eyes opened wide.

"No," he murmured, draping the towel around his neck and coming to stand behind Tas, "I never did. And I've seen some strange things in my time, too."

"Oh, Caramon!" Tas cried, "Raistlin was right. He said—"

"Raistlin!"

Tas gulped. He hadn't meant to bring that up.

"Where did you see Raistlin?" Caramon demanded, his voice deep and stern.

"In the Temple, of course," Tas answered as if it were the most common thing in the world. "Didn't I mention I went there yesterday?"

"Yes, but you—"

"Well, why else would I go except to see our friends?"

"You never—"

"I saw Lady Crysania and Raistlin. I'm sure I mentioned that. You never do listen to me, you know," Tas complained, wounded. "You sit there on that bed, every night, brooding and sulking and talking to yourself. 'Caramon,' I could say, 'the roof's caving in,' and you'd say, 'That's nice, Tas.' "

"Look, kender, I know that if I had heard you mention—"

"Lady Crysania, Raistlin, and I had a wonderful little chat," Tas hurried on, "all about Yule—by the way, Caramon, you should see how beautifully they've decorated the Temple! It's filled with roses and everbloom and, say, did I remember to give you that candy? Wait, it's right over there in my pouch. Just a minute"—the kender tried to jump off the chair but Caramon had him cornered—"well, I guess it can wait. Where was I? Oh, yes"—seeing Caramon scowl—"Raistlin and Lady Crysania and I were talking and, oh, Caramon! It's so exciting. Tika was right, she's in love with your brother."

Caramon blinked, having completely lost the thread of the conversation, which Tas, being rather careless with his pronouns, didn't help.

"No, I don't mean Tika's in love with your brother," Tas amended, seeing Caramon's confusion. "I mean Lady Crysania's in love with your brother! It was great fun. I was sort of leaning against Raistlin's closed door, resting, waiting for them to finish their conversation, and I happened to glance in the keyhole and he almost kissed her, Caramon! Your brother! Can you imagine! But he didn't." The kender sighed. "He practically yelled at her to leave. She did, but she didn't want to, I could tell. She was all dressed up and looked really pretty."

Seeing Caramon's face darken and the preoccupied look steal over it, Tas began to breathe a bit easier. "We got to talking about the Cataclysm, and Raistlin mentioned how Dire Things would begin happening today—Yule—as the gods tried to warn the people to change."

"In love with him?" Caramon muttered. Frowning, he turned away, letting Tas slip off the chair.

"Right. Unmistakably," the kender said glibly, hurrying over to his pouch and digging through it until he came to the batch of sweetmeats he had brought back. They were half-melted, sticking together in a gooey mass, and they had also acquired an outer coating of various bits and pieces from the kender's pouch, but Tas was fairly certain Caramon would never notice. He was right. The big man accepted the treat and began to eat without even glancing at it.

"He needs a cleric, they said," Caramon mumbled, his mouth full. "Were they right, after all? Is he going to go through with it? Should I let him? Should I try to stop him? Do I have the right to stop him? If she chooses to go with him, isn't that her choice? Maybe that would be the best thing for him," Caramon said softly, licking his sticky fingers. "Maybe, if she loves him enough. . . ."

Tasslehoff sighed in relief and sank down on his bed to wait for the breakfast call. Caramon hadn't

thought to ask the kender *why* he'd gone to see Raistlin in the first place. And Tas was certain now, that he'd never remember he hadn't. His secret was safe. . . .

The sky was clear that Yule day, so clear it seemed one could look up into the vast dome that covered the world and see realms beyond. But, though everyone glanced up, few cared to fix their gazes upon it long enough to see anything. For the sky was indeed "a peculiar shade," as Tas said—it was green.

A strange, noxious, ugly green that, combined with the stifling heat and the heavy, hard-to-breathe air, effectively sucked the joy and merriment out of Yule. Those forced to go outside to attend parties hurried through the sweltering streets, talking about the odd weather irritably, viewing it as a personal insult. But they spoke in hushed voices, each feeling a tiny sliver of fear prick their holiday spirit.

The party inside the Temple was somewhat more cheerful, being held in the Kingpriest's chambers that were shut away from the outside world. None could see the strange sky, and all those who came within the presence of the Kingpriest felt their irritation and fear melt away. Away from Raistlin, Crysania was once again under the Kingpriest's spell and sat near him a long time. She did not speak, she simply let his shining presence comfort her and banish the dark, nighttime thoughts. But she, too, had seen the green sky. Remembering Raistlin's words, she tried to recall what she had heard of the Thirteen Days.

But it was all children's tales that were muddled together with the dreams she had had last night. Surely, she thought, the Kingpriest will notice! He will heed the warnings. . . . She willed time to change or, if that were not possible, she willed the Kingpriest innocent. Sitting within his light, she banished from her mind the picture she had seen of the frightened mortal with his pale blue, darting eyes. She saw a strong man, denouncing the ministers who had deceived him, an innocent victim of their treachery. . . .

The crowd at the arena that day was sparse, most not caring to sit out beneath the green sky, whose

color deepened and darkened more and more fearfully as the day wore on.

The gladiators themselves were uneasy, nervous, and performed their acts half-heartedly. Those spectators who came were sullen, refusing to cheer, catcalling and hurling gibes at even their favorites.

"Do you often have such skies?" Kiiri asked, glancing up with a shudder as she and Caramon and Pheragas stood in the corridors, awaiting their turn in the arena. "If so, I know why my people choose to live beneath the sea!"

"My father sailed the sea," growled Pheragas, "as did my grandfather before him, as did I, before I tried to knock some sense into the first mate's head with a belaying pin and got sent here for my pains. And I've never seen a sky this color. Or heard of one either. It bodes ill, I'll wager."

"No doubt," Caramon said uncomfortably. It had suddenly begun to sink into the big man that the Cataclysm was thirteen days away! Thirteen days . . . and these two friends, who had grown as dear to him as Sturm and Tanis, these two friends would perish! The rest of the inhabitants of Istar meant little to him. From what he had seen, they were a selfish lot, living mainly for pleasure and money (though he found he could not look upon the children without a pang of sorrow), but these two— He had to warn them, somehow. If they left the city, they might escape.

Lost in his thoughts, he had paid little attention to the fight in the arena. It was between the Red Minotaur, so called because the fur that covered his bestial face had a distinctly reddish-brown cast to it, and a young fighter—a new man, who had arrived only a few weeks before. Caramon had watched the young man's training with patronizing amusement.

But then he felt Pheragas, who was standing next to him, stiffen. Caramon's gaze went immediately to the ring. "What is it?"

"That trident,"† Pheragas said quietly, "have you ever seen one like it in the prop room?"

Caramon stared hard at the Red Minotaur's weapon, squinting against the harsh sun blazing in the green-glazed sky. Slowly, he shook his head, feeling anger stir inside of him. The young man was completely outclassed by the minotaur, who

This trident, oddly enough, may have come from my memory of comic fight between Zero Mostel and a gladiator in A Funny Thing Happened on the Way to the Forum. *—TRH*

had fought in the arena for months and who, in fact, was rivaling Caramon's team for the championship. The only reason the young man had lasted as long as he had was the skilled showmanship of the minotaur, who blundered around in a pretended battle rage that actually won a few laughs from the audience.

"A real trident. Arack intends to blood the young man, no doubt," Caramon muttered. "Look there, I was right," pointing to three bleeding scratches that suddenly appeared on the young man's chest.

Pheragas said nothing, only flicked a glance at Kiiri, who shrugged.

"What is it?" Caramon shouted above the roar of the crowd. The Red Minotaur had just won by neatly tripping up his opponent and pinning him to the mat, thrusting the points of the trident down around his neck.

The young man staggered to his feet, feigning shame, anger, and humiliation as he had been taught. He even shook his fist at his victorious opponent before he stalked from the arena. But, instead of grinning as he passed Caramon and his team, enjoying a shared joke on the audience, the young man appeared strangely preoccupied and never looked at them. His face was pale, Caramon saw, and beads of sweat stood out on his forehead. His face twisted with pain, and he had his hand clasped over the bloody scratches.

"Lord Onygion's man," Pheragas said quietly, laying a hand on Caramon's arm. "Count yourself fortunate, my friend. You can quit worrying."

"What?" Caramon gaped at the two in confusion. Then he heard a shrill scream and a thud from within the underground tunnel. Whirling around, Caramon saw the young man fall into a writhing heap on the floor, clutching his chest and screaming in agony.

"No!" Kiiri commanded, holding onto Caramon. "Our turn next. Look, Red Minotaur comes off."

The minotaur sauntered past them, ignoring them as that race ignores all it considers beneath them. The Red Minotaur also walked past the dying young man without a glance. Arack came scurrying down the tunnel, Raag behind. With a gesture, the dwarf ordered the ogre to remove the now lifeless body.

Caramon hesitated, but Kiiri sank her nails into his arm, dragging him out into the hideous sunlight. "The score for the Barbarian is settled," she hissed out of the corner of her mouth. "Your master had nothing to do with it, apparently. It was Lord Onygion, and now he and Quarath are even."

The crowd began to cheer and the rest of Kiiri's words were lost. The spectators had begun to forget their oppression at the sight of their favorite trio. But Caramon didn't hear them. Raistlin had told him the truth! He hadn't had anything to do with the Barbarian's death. It had been coincidence, or perhaps the dwarf's perverted idea of a joke. Caramon felt a sensation of relief flow over him.

He could go home! At last he understood. Raistlin had tried to tell him. Their paths were different, but his brother had the right to walk his as he chose. Caramon was wrong, the magic-users were wrong, Lady Crysania was wrong. He would go home and explain. Raistlin wasn't harming anyone, he wasn't a threat. He simply wanted to pursue his studies in peace.

Walking out into the arena, Caramon waved back to the cheering crowd in elation.

The big man even enjoyed that day's fighting. The bout was rigged, of course, so that his team would win—setting up the final battle between them and the Red Minotaur on the day of the Cataclysm. But Caramon didn't need to worry about that. He would be long gone, back at home with Tika. He would warn his two friends first, of course, and urge them to leave this doomed city. Then he'd apologize to his brother, tell him he understood, take Lady Crysania and Tasslehoff back to their own time, and begin his life anew. He'd leave tomorrow, or perhaps the day after.

But it was at the moment when Caramon and his team were taking their bows after a well-acted battle that the cyclone struck the Temple of Istar.

The green sky had deepened to the color of dark and stagnant swamp water when the swirling clouds appeared, snaking down out of the vast emptiness to wrap their sinuous coils about one of the seven towers of the Temple and tear it from its foundations. Lifting it into the air, the cyclone broke the marble into fragments fine as hail and sent it rattling down upon the city in a stinging rain.

No one was hurt seriously, though many suffered small cuts from being struck by the sharp pieces of rock. The part of the Temple that was destroyed was used for study and for the work of the church. It had—fortunately—been empty during the holiday. But the inhabitants of the Temple and the city itself were thrown into a panic.

Fearing that cyclones might start descending everywhere, people fled the arena and clogged the streets in panicked efforts to reach their homes. Within the Temple, the Kingpriest's musical voice fell silent, his light wavered. After surveying the wreckage, he and his ministers—the Revered Sons and Daughters of Paladine—descended to an inner sanctuary to discuss the matter. Everyone else hurried about, trying to clean up, the wind having overturned furniture, knocked paintings off the walls, and sent clouds of dust drifting down over everything.

This is the beginning, Crysania thought fearfully, trying to force her numb hands to quit shaking as she picked up fragments of fine china from the dining hall. This is only the beginning . . .

And it will get worse.

CHAPTER 14

t is the forces of evil, working to defeat me," cried the Kingpriest, his musical voice sending a thrill of courage through the souls of those listening. "But I will not give in! Neither must you! We must be strong in the face of this threat. . . ."

"No," Crysania whispered to herself in despair. "No, you have it all wrong! You don't understand! How can you be so blind!"

She was sitting at Morning Prayers,† twelve days after the First of the Thirteen Warnings had been given—but had not been heeded. Since then, reports had poured in from all parts of the continent, telling of other strange events—a new one each day.

"King Lorac reports that, in Silvanesti, the trees wept blood for an entire day," the Kingpriest recounted, his voice swelling with the awe and horror of the events he related. "The city of Palanthas is

As a missionary in Java in 1976, I remember well listening to the call to prayers from the mosques.
—TRH

covered in a dense white fog so thick people wander around lost if they venture out into the streets.

"In Solamnia, no fires will burn. Their hearths lie cold and barren. The forges are shut down, the coals might as well be ice for all the warmth they give. Yet, on the plains of Abanasinia, the prairie grass has caught fire. The flames rage out of control, filling the skies with black smoke and driving the Plainsmen from their tribal lodges.

"Just this morning, the griffonst carried word that the elven city of Qualinost is being invaded by the forest animals, suddenly turned strange and savage—"

Crysania could bear it no longer. Though the women glanced at her in shock as she stood up, she ignored their glowering looks and left the Services, fleeing into the corridors of the Temple.

A jagged flash of lightning blinded her, the vicious crack of thunder immediately following made her cover her face with her hands.

"This must cease or I will go mad!" she murmured brokenly, cowering in a corner.

For twelve days, ever since the cyclone, a thunderstorm raged over Istar, flooding the city with rain and hail. The flash of lightning and peals of thunder were almost continuous, shaking the Temple, destroying sleep, battering the mind. Tense, numb with fatigue and exhaustion and terror, Crysania sank down in a chair, her head in her hands.

A gentle touch on her arm made her start in alarm, jumping up. She faced a tall, handsome young man wrapped in a sopping wet cloak. She could see the outlines of strong, muscular shoulders.

"I'm sorry, Revered Daughter, I didn't mean to scare you," he said in a deep voice that was as vaguely familiar as his face.

"Caramon!" Crysania gasped in relief, clutching at him as something real and solid. There was another bright flash and explosion. Crysania squeezed her eyes shut, gritting her teeth, feeling even Caramon's strong, muscular body tense nervously. He held onto her, steadying her.

"I-I had to go to Morning Prayers," Crysania said when she could be heard. "It must be horrible out there. You're soaked to the skin!"

"I've tried for days to see you—" Caramon began.

"In case you don't know, a griffon is a weird-looking creature with the head, wings, and front claws of a golden eagle, and the body of a lion. They're one of the finest hunters in the skies, and probably on the ground, too.

"I have absolutely no idea who first thought of capturing and training such a deadly beast, but it was either the bravest or stupidest person ever to draw breath [and probably both]. As near as I can tell, though, a Silvanesti elf did it.

"At the very least, the Silvanesti were the first to ride griffons into battle. Kith-Kanan founded the Windriders as an arm of House Protector during the Kinslayer War." [The Bestiary, by Steven "Stan!" Brown, Wizards of the Coast, Inc., 1998, p. 46.]

"I-I know," Crysania faltered. "I'm sorry. It's just that I-I've been busy—"

"Lady Crysania," Caramon interrupted, trying to keep his voice steady. "We're not talking about an invitation to a Yule Party. Tomorrow this city will cease to exist! I—"

"Hush!" Crysania commanded. Nervously, she glanced about. "We cannot talk here!" A flash of lightning and a shattering crash made her cringe, but she regained control almost immediately. "Come with me."

Caramon hesitated then, frowning, followed her as she led the way through the Temple into one of several dark, inner rooms. Here, the lightning at least could not penetrate and the thunder was muffled. Shutting the door carefully, Crysania sat down in a chair and motioned Caramon to do the same.

Caramon stood a moment, then sat down, uncomfortable and on edge, acutely conscious of the circumstances of their last meeting when his drunkenness had nearly gotten them all killed. Crysania might have been thinking of this, too. She regarded him with eyes that were cold and gray as the dawn. Caramon flushed.

"I am glad to see your health has improved," Crysania said, trying to keep the severity out of her voice and failing entirely.

Caramon's flush grew deeper. He looked down at the floor.

"I'm sorry," Crysania said abruptly. "Please forgive me. I-I haven't slept for nights, ever since this started." She put a trembling hand to her forehead. "I can't think," she added hoarsely. "This incessant noise. . . ."

"I understand," Caramon said, glancing up at her. "And you have every right to despise me. I despise myself for what I was. But that really doesn't matter now. We've got to leave, Lady Crysania!"

"Yes, you're right" Crysania drew a deep breath. "We've got to get out of here. We have only hours left to escape. I am well aware of it, believe me." Sighing, she looked down at her hands. "I have failed," she said dully. "I kept hoping, up until this last moment, that somehow things might change. But the Kingpriest is blind! Blind!"

"That's not why you've been avoiding me though,

is it?" Caramon asked, his voice expressionless. "Preventing me from leaving?"

Now it was Crysania who blushed. She looked down at her hands, twisting in her lap. "No," she said so softly Caramon barely heard. "No, I-I didn't want to leave without . . . without . . ."

"Raistlin," Caramon finished. "Lady Crysania, he has magic of his own. It brought him here in the first place. He has made his choice. I've come to realize that. We should leave—"

"Your brother has been terribly ill," Crysania said abruptly.

Caramon looked up quickly, his face drawn with concern.

"I have tried for days to see him, ever since Yule, but he refused admittance to all, even to me. And now, today, he has sent for me," Crysania continued, feeling her face burn under Caramon's penetrating gaze. "I am going to talk to him, to persuade him to come with us. If his health is impaired, he will not have the strength to use his magic."

"Yes," Caramon muttered, thinking about the difficulty involved in casting such a powerful, complex spell. It had taken Par-Salian days, and he was in good health. "What's wrong with Raist?" he asked suddenly.

"The nearness of the gods affects him," Crysania replied, "as it does others, though they refuse to admit it." Her voice died in sorrow, but she pressed her lips together tightly for a moment, then continued. "We must be prepared to move quickly, if he agrees to come with us—"

"If he doesn't?" Caramon interrupted.

Crysania blushed. "I think . . . he will," she said, overcome by confusion, her thoughts going back to the time in his chambers when he had been so near her, the look of longing and desire in his eyes, the admiration. "I've been . . . talking to him . . . about the wrongness of his ways. I've shown him how evil can never build or create, how it can only destroy and turn in upon itself.† He has admitted the validity of my arguments and promised to think about them."

"And he loves you," Caramon said softly.

Crysania could not meet the man's gaze. She could not answer. Her heart beat so she could not, for a moment, hear above the pulsing of her blood.

There are three themes that run throughout all classic DRAGONLANCE:
1.) Good redeems its own.
2.) Evil feeds on itself.
3.) It is the struggle between the two that brings motion to the world. Here we see the first two themes stated.
—TRH

She could sense Caramon's dark eyes regarding her steadily as the thunder rumbled and shook the Temple around them. Crysania gripped her hands together to stop their trembling. Then she was aware of Caramon rising to his feet.

"My lady," he said in a hushed, solemn voice, "if you are right, if your goodness and your love can turn him from those dark paths that he walks and lead him—by his own choice—into the light, I would . . . I would—" Caramon choked and turned his head hurriedly.

Hearing so much love in the big man's voice and seeing the tears he tried to hide, Crysania was overcome with pain and remorse. She began to wonder if she had misjudged him. Standing up, she gently touched the man's huge arm, feeling its great muscles tense as Caramon fought to bring himself under control.

"Must you return? Can't you stay—"

"No" Caramon shook his head. "I've got to get Tas, and the device Par-Salian gave me. It's locked away. And then, I have friends. . . . I've been trying to convince them to leave the city. It may be too late, but I've got to make one more attempt—"

"Certainly," Crysania said. "I understand. Return as quickly as you can. Meet me . . . meet me in Raistlin's rooms."

"I will, my lady," he replied fervently. "And now I must go, before my friends leave for practice." Taking her hand in his, he clasped it firmly, then hurried away. Crysania watched him walk back out into the corridor, whose torchlights shone in the gloomy darkness. He moved swiftly and surely, not even flinching when he passed a window at the end of the corridor and was suddenly illuminated by a brilliant flash of lightning. It was hope† that anchored his storm-tossed spirit, the same hope Crysania felt suddenly welling up inside her.

Caramon vanished into the darkness and Crysania, catching up her white robes in one hand, quickly turned and climbed the stairs to the part of the Temple that housed the black-robed mage.

Her good spirits and her hope failed slightly as she entered that corridor. Here the full fury of the storm seemed to rage unabated. Not even the heaviest curtains could keep out the blinding lightning, the

The struggle for hope in the face of adversity is a theme running throughout the DRAGONLANCE *setting:*

"Still," the kender said softly, "we have to keep trying and hoping. That's what's important, the trying and the hoping. Maybe that's the most important of all." [Dragons of Autumn Twilight, *Book II, "The Wedding."]*

The darkness might conquer, but it could never extinguish hope. And though one candle, or many, might flicker and die, new candles would be lit from the old.

Thus hope's flame always burns, lighting the darkness until the coming of day. [Dragons of Spring Dawning, *Book II, Chapter 9.]*

thickest walls could not muffle the peals of thunder. Perhaps because of some ill-fitting window, even the wind itself seemed to have penetrated the Temple walls. Here no torches would burn, not that they were needed, so incessant was the lighting.

Crysania's black hair blew in her eyes, her robes fluttered around her. As she neared the mage's room at the end of the corridor, she could hear the rain beat against the glass. The air was cold and damp. Shivering, she hastened her steps and had raised her hand to knock upon the door when the corridor suddenly sizzled with a blue-white flash of lightning. The simultaneous explosion of thunder knocked Crysania against the door. It flew open, and she was in Raistlin's arms.

It was like her dream. Almost sobbing in her terror, she nestled close to the velvet softness of the black robes and warmed herself by the heat of his body. At first, that body next to hers was tense, then she felt it relax. His arms tightened around her almost convulsively, a hand reached up to stroke her hair, soothingly, comfortingly.

"There, there," he whispered as one might to a frightened child, "fear not the storm, Revered Daughter. Exult in it! Taste the power of the gods, Crysania! Thus do they frighten the foolish. They cannot harm us—not if you choose otherwise."

Gradually Crysania's sobs lessened. Raistlin's words were not the gentle murmurings of a mother. Their meaning struck home to her. She lifted her head, looking up at him.

"What do you mean?" she faltered, suddenly frightened. A crack had appeared in his mirrorlike eyes, permitting her to see the soul burning within.

Involuntarily, she started to push away from him, but he reached out and, smoothing the tangled black hair from her face with trembling hands, whispered, "Come with me, Crysania! Come with me to a time when you will be the only cleric in the world, to the time when we may enter the portal and challenge the gods, Crysania! Think of it! To rule, to show the world such power as this!"

Raistlin let go his grasp. Raising his arms, the black robes shimmering about him as the lightning flared and the thunder roared, he laughed. And then Crysania saw the feverish gleam in his eyes and

the bright spots of color on his deathly pale cheeks. He was thin, far thinner than when she had seen him last.

"You're ill," she said, backing up, her hands behind her, reaching for the door. "I'll get help. . ."

"No!" Raistlin's shout was louder than the thunder. His eyes regained their mirrored surface, his face was cold and composed. Reaching out, he grasped her wrist with a painful grip and jerked her back into the room. The door slammed shut behind her. "I am ill," he said more quietly, "but there is no help, no cure for my malady but to escape this insanity. My plans are almost completed. Tomorrow, the day of the Cataclysm, the attention of the gods will be turned to the lesson they must inflict upon these poor wretches. The Dark Queen will not be able to stop me as I work my magic and carry myself forward to the one time in history when *she* is vulnerable to the power of a true cleric!"

"Let me go!" Crysania cried, pain and outrage submerging her fear. Angrily, she wrenched her arm free of his grasp. But she still remembered his embrace, the touch of his hands. . . . Hurt and ashamed, Crysania turned away. "You must work your evil without me," she said, her voice choked with her tears. "I will not go with you."

"Then you will die," Raistlin said grimly.

"Do you dare threaten me!" Crysania cried, whirling around to face him, shock and fury drying her eyes.

"Oh, not by my hand," Raistlin said with a strange smile. "You will die by the hands of those who sent you here."

Crysania blinked, stunned. Then she quickly regained her composure. "Another trick?" she asked coldly, backing away from him, the pain in her heart at his deception almost more than she could bear. She wanted only to leave before he saw how much he had been able to hurt her—

"No trick, Revered Daughter," Raistlin said simply. He gestured to a book with red binding that lay open upon his desk. "See for yourself. Long I studied—" He swept his hand about the rows and rows of books that lined the wall. Crysania gasped. These had not been here the last time. Looking at her, he nodded. "Yes, I brought them from far-off

places. I traveled far in search of many of them. This one I finally found in the Tower of High Sorcery at Wayreth, as I suspected all along I might. Come, look at it."

"What is it?" Crysania stared at the volume as if it might have been a coiled, poisonous serpent.

"A book, nothing more." Raistlin smiled wearily. "I assure you it will not change into a dragon and carry you off at my command. I repeat—it is a book, an encyclopedia, if you will. A very ancient one, written during the Age of Dreams."†

"Why do you want me to see this? What does it have to do with me?" Crysania asked suspiciously. But she had ceased edging her way toward the door. Raistlin's calm demeanor reassured her. She had even ceased to notice, for the moment, the lightning and cracking of the storm outside.

"It is an encyclopedia of magical devices produced during the Age of Dreams," Raistlin continued imperturbably, never taking his eyes from Crysania. seeming to draw her nearer with his gaze as he stood beside the desk. "Read—"

"I cannot read the language of magic,"† Crysania said, frowning, then her brow cleared. "Or are you going to 'translate' for me?" she inquired haughtily.

Raistlin's eyes flared in swift anger, but the anger was almost instantly replaced by a look of sadness and exhaustion that went straight to Crysania's heart. "It is not written in the language of magic," he said softly. "I would not have asked you here otherwise." Glancing down at the black robes he wore, he smiled the twisted, bitter smile. "Long ago, I willingly paid the penalty. I do not know why I should have hoped you would trust me."

Biting her lip, feeling deeply ashamed, though she had no idea why, Crysania crossed around to the other side of the desk. She stood there, hesitantly. Sitting down, Raistlin beckoned to her, and she took a step forward to stand beside the open book. The mage spoke a word of command, and the staff that leaned up against the wall near Crysania burst into a flood of yellow light, startling her nearly as much as the lightning.

"Read," Raistlin said, indicating the page.

Trying to compose herself, Crysania glanced down, scanning the page, though she had no idea what she

Before the DRAGONLANCE setting was ever in print, I worked on a background history for the world that went back three thousand years. The Age of Dreams was a part of that history from the very beginning. —TRH

The language of magic follows the grammatical structure of the Indonesian language that I learned as a missionary, although the individual roots, prefixes, and suffixes have usually been changed. —TRH

377

sought. Then, her attention was captured. *Device of Time Journeying* read one of the entries and, beside it, was pictured a device similar to the one the kender had described.

"This is it?" she asked, looking up at Raistlin. "The device Par-Salian gave Caramon to get us back?"

The mage nodded, his eyes reflecting the yellow light of the staff.

"Read," he repeated softly.

Curious, Crysania scanned the text. There was little more than a paragraph, describing the device, the great mage—now long forgotten—who had designed and built it—the requirements for its use. Much of the description was beyond her understanding, dealing with things arcane. She grasped at bits and pieces—

. . . will carry the person already under a time spell forward or backward . . . must be assembled correctly and the facets turned in the prescribed order. . . . will transport one person only, the person to whom it is given at the time the spell is cast . . . device's use is restricted to elves, humans, ogres . . . no spell word required. . . .

Crysania came to the end and glanced up at Raistlin uncertainly. He was watching her with a strange, expectant look. There was something there he was waiting for her to find. And, deep within, she felt a disquiet, a fear, a numbness, as if her heart understood the text more quickly than her brain.

"Again," Raistlin said.

Trying to concentrate, though she was now once more aware of the storm outside that seemed to be growing in intensity, Crysania looked back at the text.

And there it was. The words leaped out at her, reaching for her throat, choking her.

Transport one person only. . . .

Transport one person only!

Crysania's legs gave way. Fortunately, Raistlin moved a chair behind her or she might have fallen to the floor.

For long moments she stared into the room. Though lit by lightning and the magical light of the staff, it had, for her, grown suddenly dark.

"Does he know?" she asked finally, through numb lips.

"Caramon?" Raistlin snorted. "Of course not. If they had told him, he would have broken his fool neck trying to get it to you and would beg you on his knees to use it and give him the privilege of dying in your stead. I can think of little else that would make him happier.

"No, Lady Crysania, he would have used it confidently, with you standing beside him as well as the kender, no doubt. And he would have been devastated when they explained to him why he returned alone. I wonder how Par-Salian would have managed that," Raistlin added with a grim smile. "Caramon is quite capable of tearing that Tower down around their ears. But that is neither here nor there."

His gaze caught hers, though she would have avoided it. He compelled her, by the force of his will, to look into his eyes. And, once again, she saw herself, but this time alone and terribly frightened.

"They sent you back here to die, Crysania," Raistlin said in a voice that was little more than a breath, yet it penetrated to Crysania's very core, echoing louder in her mind than the thunder. "This is the good you tell me about? Bah! They live in fear, as does the Kingpriest! They fear you as they fear me. The only path to good, Crysania, is my path!† Help me defeat the evil. I need you. . . ."

Crysania closed her eyes. She could see once again, vividly, Par-Salian's handwriting on the note she had found—*your life or your soul—gain one and you will lose the other! There are many ways back for you, one of which is through Caramon.* He had purposely misled her! What other way existed, besides Raistlin's? Is this what the mage meant? Who could answer her? Was there anyone, anyone in this bleak and desolate world she could trust?

Her muscles twitching, contracting, Crysania pushed herself up from her chair. She did not look at Raistlin, she stared ahead at nothing. "I must go . . ." she muttered brokenly, "I must think. . . ."

Raistlin did not try to stop her. He did not even stand. He spoke no word—until she reached the door.

"Tomorrow," he whispered. "Tomorrow. . . ."

Here Raistlin tempts Crysania in a scene reminiscent of the temptations of Christ. It is interesting to me, as I read this, that Raistlin's argument is exactly the same as that of the Kingpriest! —TRH

CHAPTER
15

t took all of
Caramon's strength, plus that of two of the Temple
guards, to force the great doors of the Temple open
and let him out into the storm. The wind hit him
full force, driving the big man back against the
stone wall and pinning him there for an instant, as
if he were no bigger than Tas. Struggling, Caramon
fought against it and finally won, the gale force
relenting enough to allow him to continue down
the stairs.

The fury of the storm was somewhat lessened as
he walked among the tall buildings of the city, but it
was still difficult going. Water ran a foot deep in
some places, swirling about his legs, threatening
more than once to sweep him off his feet. The lightning half-blinded him, the thunder was deafening.

Needless to say, he saw few other people. The
inhabitants of Istar cowered indoors, alternately

cursing or calling upon the gods. The occasional traveler he passed, driven out into the storm by who knows what desperate reason, clung to the sides of the buildings or stood huddled miserably in doorways.

But Caramon trudged on, anxious to get back to the arena. His heart was filled with hope, his spirits were high, despite the storm. Or perhaps because of the storm. Surely now Kiiri and Pheragas would listen to him instead of giving him strange, cold looks when he tried to persuade them to flee Istar.

"I can't tell you how I know, I just know!" he pleaded. "There's disaster coming, I can smell it!"

"And miss the final tournament?" Kiiri said coolly.

"They won't hold it in this weather!" Caramon waved his arms.

"No storm this fierce ever lasts long!" Pheragas said. "It will blow itself out, and we'll have a beautiful day. Besides"—his eyes narrowed—"what would you do without us in the arena?"

"Why, fight alone, if need be," Caramon said, somewhat flustered. He planned to be long gone by that time—he and Tas, Crysania and perhaps . . . perhaps. . . .

"If need be . . ." Kiiri had repeated in an odd, harsh tone, exchanging glances with Pheragas. "Thanks for thinking of us, friend," she said with a scathing glance at the iron collar Caramon wore, the collar that matched her own, "but no thanks. Our lives would be forfeit—runaway slaves! How long do you think we'd live out there?"

"It won't matter, not after . . . after . . ." Caramon sighed and shook his head miserably. What could he say? How could he make them understand? But they had not given him the chance. They walked off without another word, leaving him sitting alone in the mess hall.

But, surely, now they would listen! They would see that this was no ordinary storm. Would they have time to get away safely? Caramon frowned and wished, for the first time, he had paid more attention to books. He had no idea how wide an area the devastating effect of the fall of the fiery mountain encompassed. He shook his head. Maybe it was already too late.

Well, he had tried, he told himself, slogging along through the water. Wrenching his mind from the plight of his friends, he forced himself to think more cheerful thoughts. Soon he would be gone from this terrible place. Soon this would all seem like a bad dream.

He would be back home with Tika. Maybe with Raistlin! "I'll finish building the new house," he said, thinking regretfully of all the time he had wasted. A picture came into his mind. He could see himself, sitting by the fire in their new home, Tika's head resting in his lap. He'd tell her all about their adventures. Raistlin would sit with them, in the evenings; reading, studying, dressed in white robes. . . .

"Tika won't believe a word of this," Caramon said to himself. "But it won't matter. She'll have the man she fell in love with home again. And this time, he won't leave her, ever, for anything!" He sighed, feeling her crisp red curls wrap around his fingers, seeing them shine in the firelight.

These thoughts carried Caramon through the storm and to the arena. Pulling out the block in the wall that was used by all the gladiators on their nocturnal rambles. (Arack was aware of its existence but, by tacit arrangement, turned a blind eye to it as long as the privilege wasn't abused.) No one was in the arena, of course. Practice sessions had all been canceled. Everyone was huddled inside, cursing the foul weather and making bets on whether or not they would fight tomorrow.

Arack was in a mood nearly as foul as the elements, counting over and over the pieces of gold that would slip through his fingers if he had to cancel the Final Bout—the sporting event of the year in Istar. He tried to cheer himself up with the thought that *he* had promised him fine weather and *he*, if anyone, should know. Still, the dwarf stared gloomily outside.

From his vantage point, a window high above the grounds in the tower of the arena, he saw Caramon creep through the stone wall. "Raag!" He pointed. Looking down, Raag nodded in understanding and, grabbing the huge club, waited for the dwarf to put away his account† books.

Mark (friendly neighborhood editor) pointed out that in many of our works, accountants are presented as part of the side of evil! (There's Arack here, and Morham Targonne in War of Souls.) I do not think this is intentional. The representation is a preoccupation with the material things of the world. —TRH

Sherlock Holmes maintained that a love of chess was indicative of a devious mind. For me, it's accountants! —MW

Caramon hurried to the cell he shared with the kender, eager to tell him about Crysania and Raistlin. But when he entered, the small room was empty.

"Tas?" he said, glancing around to make certain he hadn't overlooked him in the shadows. But a flash of lightning illuminated the room more brightly than daylight. There was no sign of the kender.

"Tas, come out! This is no time for games!" Caramon ordered sternly. Tasslehoff had nearly frightened him out of six years' growth one day by hiding under the bed, then leaping out when Caramon's back was turned. Lighting a torch, the big man got down, grumbling, on his hands and knees and flashed the light under the bed. No Tas.

"I hope the little fool didn't try to go out in this storm!" Caramon said to himself, his irritation changing to sudden concern. "He'd get blown back to Solace. Or maybe he's in the mess hall, waiting for me. Maybe he's with Kiiri and Pheragas. That's it! I'll just grab the device, then join him—"

Talking to himself, Caramon went over to the small, wooden chest where he kept his armor. Opening it, he took out the fancy, gold costume. Giving it a scornful glance, he tossed the pieces on the floor. "At least I won't have to wear that get-up again," he said thankfully. "Though"—he grinned somewhat shamefacedly—"it'd be fun to see Tika's reaction when I put that on! Wouldn't she laugh? But I'll bet she'd like it, just the same." Whistling cheerfully, Caramon quickly took everything out of the chest and, using the edge of one of the collapsible daggers, carefully prized up the false bottom he had built into it.

The whistle died on his lips.

The chest was empty.

Frantically, Caramon felt all over the inside of the chest, though it was quite obvious that a pendant as large as the magical device wouldn't have been likely to slip through a crack. His heart beating wildly with fear, Caramon scrambled to his feet and began to search the room, flashing the torchlight into every corner, peering once more under the beds. He even ripped up his straw mattress and was starting to work on Tas's when he suddenly noticed something.

Not only was the kender gone, but so were his pouches, all his beloved possessions. And so was his cloak.

And then Caramon knew. Tas had taken the device.

But why? . . . Caramon felt for a moment as if lightning had struck him, the sudden understanding sizzling his way from his brain to his body with a shock that paralyzed him.

Tas had seen Raistlin—he had told Caramon about that. But what had Tas been doing there? *Why* had he gone to see Raistlin? Caramon suddenly realized that the kender had skillfully steered the conversation away from that point.

Caramon groaned. The curious kender had, of course, questioned him about the device, but Tas had always seemed satisfied with Caramon's answers. Certainly, he had never bothered it. Caramon checked, occasionally, to make sure it was still there—one did that as a matter of habit when living with a kender. But, if Tas had been curious enough about it, he would have taken it to Raistlin. . . . He did that often in the old days, when he found something magical.

Or maybe Raistlin tricked Tas into bringing it to him! Once he had the device, Raistlin could force them to go with him. Had he been plotting this all along? Had he tricked Tas and deceived Crysania? Caramon's mind stumbled about his head in confusion. Or maybe—

"Tas!" Caramon cried, suddenly latching onto firm, positive action. "I have to find Tas! I have to stop him!"

Feverishly, the big man grabbed up his soaking wet cloak. He was barreling out the door when a huge dark shadow blocked his path.

"Out of my way, Raag," Caramon growled, completely forgetting, in his anxiety, where he was.

Raag reminded him instantly, his giant hand closing over Caramon's huge shoulder. "Where go, slave?"

Caramon tried to shake off the ogre's grip, but Raag's hand simply tightened its grip. There was a crunching sound, and Caramon gasped in pain.

"Don't hurt him, Raag," came a voice from somewhere around Caramon's kneecaps. "He's got to fight tomorrow. What's more, he's got to win!"

Raag pushed Caramon back into the cell with as little effort as a grown man playfully tosses a child. The big warrior stumbled backward, falling heavily on the stone floor.

"You sure are busy today," Arack said conversationally, entering the cell and plopping down on the bed.

Sitting up, Caramon rubbed his bruised shoulder. He cast a quick glance at Raag, who was still standing, blocking the door. Arack continued.

"You've already been out once in this foul weather, and now you're heading out again?" The dwarf shook his head. "No, no. I can't allow it. You might catch cold. . . ."

"Hey," Caramon said, grinning weakly and licking his dry lips. "I was just going to the mess hall to find Tas—" He cringed involuntarily as a bolt of lightning exploded outside. There was a cracking sound and a sudden odor of burning wood.

"Forget it. The kender left," Arack said, shrugging, "and it looked to me like he left for good—had his stuff all packed."

Caramon swallowed, clearing his throat. "Let me go find him then—" he began.

Arack's grin twisted suddenly into a vicious scowl. "I don't give a damn about the little bastard! I got my money's worth outta him, I figure, in what he stole for me already. But you—I've got quite an investment in you. Your little escape plan's failed, slave."

"Escape?" Caramon laughed hollowly. "I never— You don't understand—"

"So I don't understand?" Arack snarled. "I don't understand that you've been trying to get two of my best fighters to leave? Trying to ruin me, are you?" The dwarf's voice rose to a shrill shriek above the howl of the wind outside. "Who put you up to this?" Arack's expression became suddenly shrewd and cunning. "It wasn't your master, so don't lie. He's been to see me."

"Raist—er—Fist-Fistandantil—" Caramon stammered, his jaw dropping.

The dwarf smiled smugly. "Yeah. And Fistandantilus warned me you might try something like this. Said I should watch you carefully. He even suggested a fitting punishment for you. The final fight

tomorrow will not be between your team and the minotaurs. It will be you against Kiiri and Pheragas and the Red Minotaur!" The dwarf leaned over, leering into Caramon's face. "And their weapons will be real!"†

Caramon stared at Arack uncomprehendingly for a moment. Then, "Why?" he murmured bleakly. "Why does he want to kill me?"

"Kill you?" The dwarf cackled. "He doesn't want to kill you! He thinks you'll win! 'It's a test,' he says to me, 'I don't want a slave who isn't the best! And this will prove it. Caramon showed me what he could do against the Barbarian. That was his first test. Let's make *this* test harder on him,' he says. Oh, he's a rare one, your master!"

The dwarf chuckled, slapping his knees at the thought, and even Raag gave a grunt that might have been indicative of amusement.

"I won't fight," Caramon said, his face hardening into firm, grim lines. "Kill me! I won't fight my friends. And they won't fight me!"

"He said you'd say that!" The dwarf roared. "Didn't he, Raag! The very words. By gar, he knows you! You'd think you two was kin! 'So,' he says to me, 'if he refuses to fight, and he will, I have no doubt, then you tell him that his friends will fight in his stead, only they will fight the Red Minotaur and it will be the minotaur who has the real weapons.' "

Caramon remembered vividly the young man writhing in agony on the stone floor as the poison from the minotaur's trident coursed through his body.

"As for your friends fighting you"—the dwarf sneered— "Fistandantilus took care of that, too. After what he told them, I think they're gonna be real eager to get in the arena!"

Caramon's head sank to his chest. He began to shake. His body convulsed with chills, his stomach wrenched. The enormity of his brother's evil overwhelmed him, his mind filled with darkness and despair.

Raistlin has deceived us all, deceived Crysania, Tas, me! It was Raistlin who made me kill the Barbarian. He lied to me! And he's lied to Crysania, too. He's no more capable of loving her than the dark

moon is capable of lighting the night skies. He's using her! And Tas? Tas! Caramon closed his eyes. He remembered Raistlin's look when he discovered the kender, his words—"kender can alter time. . . . is this how they plan to stop me?" Tas was a danger to him, a threat! He had no doubt, now, where Tas had gone. . . .

The wind outside howled and shrieked, but not as loudly as the pain and anguish in Caramon's soul. Sick and nauseous, wracked by icy spasms of needle-sharp pain, the big warrior completely lost any comprehension of what was going on around him. He didn't see Arack's gesture, nor feel Raag's huge hands grab hold of him. He didn't even feel the bindings on his wrists. . . .

It was only later, when the awful feelings of sickness and horror passed, that he woke to a realization of his surroundings. He was in tiny, windowless cell far underground, probably beneath the arena. Raag was fastening a chain to the iron collar around his neck and was bolting that chain to a ring in the stone wall. Then the ogre shoved him to the floor and checked the leather thongs that bound Caramon's wrists.

"Not too tight," Caramon heard the dwarf's voice warn, "he's got to fight tomorrow. . . ."

There was a distant rumble of thunder, audible even this far beneath the ground. At the sound, Caramon looked up hopefully. We can't fight in this weather—

The dwarf grinned as he followed Raag out the wooden door. He started to slam it shut, then poked his head around the corner, his beard wagging in glee as he saw the look on Caramon's face.

"Oh, by the way. Fistandantilus says it's going to be a beautiful day tomorrow. A day that everyone on Krynn will long remember. . . ."

The door slammed shut and locked.

Caramon sat alone in the dense, damp darkness. His mind was calm, the sickness and shock having wiped it clean as slate of any feeling, any emotion. He was alone. Even Tas was gone. There was no one he could turn to for advice, no one to make his decisions for him anymore. And then, he realized, he didn't need anyone. Not to make this decision.

Now he knew, now he understood. *This* is why the mages had sent him back. They knew the truth. They wanted him to learn it for himself. His twin was lost, never to be reclaimed.

Raistlin must die.

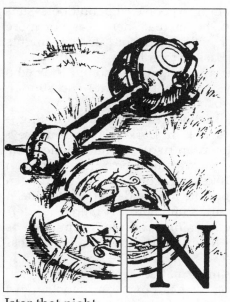

CHAPTER 16

None slept in Istar that night.

The storm increased in fury until it seemed it must destroy everything in its path. The wind's keening was like the deadly wail of the banshee,† piercing even the continuous crashing of the thunder. Splintered lightning danced among the streets, trees exploded at its fiery touch. Hail rattled and bounced among the streets, knocking bricks and stones from houses, shattering the thickest glass, allowing the wind and rain to rush into homes like savage conquerors. Flood waters roared through the streets, carrying away the market stalls, the slave pens, carts and carriages.

Yet, no one was hurt.

It was as if the gods, in this last hour, held their hands cupped protectively over the living; hoping, begging them to heed the warnings.

". . . [B]anshees are a kind of undead creature found only among the elves. These spirits of dead elf women find themselves painfully tied to the world even after their lives have ended." [The Bestiary, by Steven "Stan!" Brown, Wizards of the Coast, Inc., 1998, p. 158.]

Storms are often of great portent in DRAGONLANCE *stories. Besides this one, there's also the Maelstrom over the Blood Sea, and most recently the Great Storm that heralded the rise of Mina and the One God in the War of Souls trilogy.*

Tasslehoff talked to the spooks of Darken Wood back in Dragons of Autumn Twilight, *Book I, Chapter 10.*

One of Tas's famed dragon flights can be found in Dragons of Spring Dawning, *Book I, Chapter 9.*

How close did Tas get? Find out in Dragons of Spring Dawning, *Book I, Chapter 6.*

Tas broke the dragon orb in Dragons of Winter Night, *Book III, Chapter 6.*

The defeat of the Queen of Darkness is the struggle that takes up the entire Chronicles trilogy, but it all came to conclusion in Dragons of Spring Dawning, *Book III, Chapters 8-14.*

At dawn, the storm† ceased. The world was suddenly filled with a profound silence. The gods waited, not even daring to breathe, lest they miss the one small cry that might yet save the world.

The sun rose in a pale blue, watery sky. No bird sang to welcome it, no leaves rustled in the morning breeze, for there was no morning breeze. The air was still and deathly calm. Smoke rose from the smoldering trees in straight lines to the heavens, the flood waters dwindled away rapidly as though whisked down a huge drain. The people crept outdoors, staring around in disbelief that there was not more damage and then, exhausted from sleepless nights preceding, went back to their beds.

But there was, after all, one person in Istar who slept peacefully through the night. The sudden silence, in fact, woke him up.

As Tasslehoff Burrfoot was fond of recounting— he had talked to spooks in Darken Wood,† met several dragons (flown on two)†, come *very* near the accursed Shoikan Grove† (how near improved with each telling), broke a dragon orb,† and had been personally responsible for the defeat of the Queen of Darkness† (with some help). A mere thunderstorm, even the likes of a thunderstorm such as this one, wasn't likely to frighten him, much less disturb his sleep.

It had been a simple matter to retrieve the magical device. Tas shook his head over Caramon's naive pride in the cleverness of his hiding place. Tas had refrained from telling the big man, but that false bottom could have been detected by any kender over the age of three.

Tas lifted the magical device out of the box eagerly, staring at it with wonder and delight. He had forgotten how charming and lovely it was, folded down into an oval pendant. It seemed impossible that his hands would transform it into a device that would perform such a miracle!

Hurriedly, Tas went over Raistlin's instructions in his mind. The mage had given them to him only a few days before and had made him memorize them—figuring that Tas would promptly lose written instructions, as Raistlin had told him caustically.

They were not difficult, and Tas had them in moments.

Thy† time is thy own
Though across it you travel.
Its expanses you see
Whirling through forever,
Obstruct not its flow.
Grasp firmly the end and the beginning,
Turn them back upon themselves, and
All that is loose shall be secure.
Destiny be over your own head.

Tracy wrote this poem
about the time-travel
device. —MW

The device was so beautiful, Tas could have lingered, admiring it, for long moments. But he didn't have long moments, so he hastily thrust it into one of his pouches, grabbed his other pouches (just in case he found anything worth carrying along—or anything found him), put on his cloak and hurried out. On the way, he thought about his last conversation with the mage just a few days previous.

" 'Borrow' the object the night before," Raistlin had counseled him. "The storm will be frightening, and Caramon might take it into his head to leave. Besides, it will be easiest for you to slip into the room known as the Sacred Chamber of the Temple unnoticed while the storm rages. The storm will end in the morning, and then the Kingpriest and his ministers will begin the processional. They will be going to the Sacred Chamber, and it is there that the Kingpriest will make his demands of the gods.

"You must be in the chamber and you must activate the device at the very moment the Kingpriest ceases to speak—"

"How will it stop it?" Tas interrupted eagerly. "Will I see it shoot a ray of light up to heaven or something? Will it knock the Kingpriest flat?"

"No," Raistlin answered, coughing softly, "it will not—um—knock the Kingpriest flat. But you are right about the light."

"I am?" Tas's mouth gaped open. "I just guessed! That's fantastic! I must be getting good at this magic stuff."

"Yes," Raistlin replied dryly, "now, to continue before I was interrupted—"

"Sorry, it won't happen again," Tas apologized, then shut his mouth as Raistlin glared at him.

"You must sneak into the Sacred Chamber during the night. The area behind the altar is lined with curtains. Hide there and you will not be discovered."

"Then I'll stop the Cataclysm, go back to Caramon, and tell him all about it! I'll be a hero—" Tas stopped, a sudden thought crossing his mind. "But, how can I be a hero if I stop something that never started? I mean, how will they know I did anything if I didn't—"

"Oh, they'll know. . . ." said Raistlin softly.

"They will? But I still don't see—Oh, you're busy, I guess. I suppose I should go? All right. Say, well, you're leaving after this is all over," Tas said, being rather firmly propelled toward the door by Raistlin's hand on his shoulder. "Where are you going?"

"Where I choose," said Raistlin.

"Could I come with you?" Tas asked eagerly.

"No, you'll be needed back in your own time," Raistlin answered, staring at the kender very strangely—or so Tas thought at the time. "To look after Caramon. . . ."

"Yes, I guess you're right." The kender sighed. "He does take a lot of looking after." They reached the door. Tas regarded it for a moment, then looked up wistfully at Raistlin. "I don't suppose you could . . . sort of swoosh me somewhere, like you did the last time? It's great fun. . . ."

Checking a sigh, Raistlin obligingly "swooshed" the kender into a duck pond, to Tas's vast amusement. The kender couldn't recall, in fact, when Raistlin had been so nice to him.

It must be because of my ending the Cataclysm, Tas decided. He's probably really grateful, just doesn't know how to express it properly. Or maybe he's not allowed to be grateful since he's evil.

That was an interesting thought and one Tas considered as he waded out of the pond and went, dripping, back to the arena.

Tas recalled it again as he left the arena the night before the Cataclysm that wasn't going to happen, but his thoughts about Raistlin were rudely interrupted. He hadn't realized quite how bad the storm had grown and was somewhat amazed at the ferocity of the wind that literally picked him up and slammed him back against the stone wall of the arena when he first darted outside. After pausing a

moment to recover his breath and check to see if anything was broken, the kender picked himself up and started off toward the Temple again, the magical device firmly in hand.

This time, he had presence of mind enough to hug the buildings, finding that the wind didn't buffet him so there. Walking through the storm proved to be rather an exhilarating experience, in fact. Once lightning struck a tree next to him, smashing it to smithereens. (He had often wondered, what exactly was a smithereen?)† Another time he misjudged the depth of the water running in the street and found himself being washed down the block at a rapid rate. This was amusing and would have been even more fun if he had been able to breathe. Finally, the water dumped him rather abruptly in an alley, where he was able to get back onto his feet and continue his journey.

At last the question can be answered. According to The New Shorter Oxford Dictionary, "smithereens" is from the Irish Gaelic smidirín. According to my Irish Gaelic dictionary, smidirín means "smithereens." The mystery lives on. . . .

Tas was almost sorry to reach the Temple after so many adventures, but—reminding himself of his Important Mission—he crept through the garden and made his way inside. Once there, it was, as Raistlin had predicted, easy to lose himself in the confusion created by the storm. Clerics were running everywhere, trying to mop up water and broken glass from shattered windows, relighting blown out torches, comforting those who could no longer stand the strain.

He had no idea where the Sacred Chamber was, but there was nothing he enjoyed more than wandering around strange places. Two or three hours (and several bulging pouches later), he ran across a room that precisely matched Raistlin's description.

No torches lit the room; it was not being used at present, but flashes of lightning illuminated it brightly enough for the kender to see the altar and the curtains Raistlin had described. By this time, being rather fatigued, Tas was glad to rest. After investigating the room and finding it boringly empty, he made his way past the altar (empty as well) and ducked behind the curtains, rather hoping (even if he was tired) to find some kind of secret cave where the Kingpriest performed holy rites forbidden to the eyes of mortal men.

Looking around, he sighed. Nothing. Just a wall, covered by curtains. Sitting down behind the curtains,

Tas spread out his cloak to dry, wrung the water out of his topknot, and—by the flashes of lightning coming through the stained glass windows—began to sort through the interesting objects that had made their way into his pouches.

After a while, his eyes grew too heavy to keep open and his yawns were beginning to hurt his jaws. Curling up on the floor, he drifted off to sleep, only mildly annoyed by the booming of the thunder. His last thought was to wonder if Caramon had missed him yet and, if so, was he very angry? . . .

The next thing Tas knew, it was quiet. Now, why that should have startled him out of perfectly sound sleep was at first a complete mystery. It was also somewhat of a mystery as to where he was, exactly, but then he remembered.

Oh, yes. He was in the Sacred Chamber of the Temple of the Kingpriest of Istar. Today was the day of the Cataclysm, or it would have been. Perhaps, more accurately, today wasn't the day of the Cataclysm. Or today *had been* the day of the Cataclysm. Finding this all very confusing—altering time was such a bother—Tas decided not to think about it and to try to figure out, instead, why it was so quiet.

Then, it occurred to him. The storm had stopped! Just like Raistlin said it would. Rising to his feet, he peeked out from between the curtains into the Sacred Chamber. Through the windows, he could see bright sunlight. Tas gulped in excitement.

He had no idea what time it was but, from the brilliance of the sunlight, it must be close to mid-morning. The processional would start soon, he remembered, and would take a while to wind through the Temple. The Kingpriest had called upon the gods at High Watch, when the sun reached its zenith in the sky.

Sure enough, just as Tas was thinking about it, bells pealed out, right above him, it seemed, their clanging startling him more than the thunder. For a moment he wondered if he might be doomed to go through life hearing nothing but bonging sounds ring in his ears. Then the bells in the tower above stopped and, after a few moments more, so did the bells in his head. Heaving a sigh of relief, he peeked out between the curtains into the Chamber again and was just wondering if there was a chance

someone might come back here to clean when he saw a shadowy figure slip into the room.

Tas drew back. Keeping the curtains open only a crack, he peered through with one eye. The figure's head was bowed, its steps were slow and uncertain. It paused a moment to lean against one of the stone benches that flanked the altar as if too tired to continue further, then it sank down to its knees. Though it was dressed in white robes like nearly everyone in the Temple, Tas thought this figure looked familiar, so, when he was fairly certain the figure's attention wasn't on him, he risked widening the opening.

"Crysania!" he said to himself with interest. "I wonder why she's here so early?" Then he was seized with a sudden overwhelming disappointment. Suppose she was here to stop the Cataclysm as well! "Drat! Raistlin said I could," Tas muttered.

Then, he realized she was talking—either to herself or praying—Tas wasn't sure which. Crowding as close to the curtain as he dared, he listened to her soft words.

"Paladine, greatest, wisest god of eternal goodness, hear my voice on this most tragic of days. I know I cannot stop what is to come. And, perhaps it is a sign of a lack of faith that I even question what you do. All I ask is this—help me to understand! If it is true that I must die, let me know why. Let me see that my death will serve some purpose. Show me that I have not failed in all I came back here to accomplish.

"Grant that I may stay here, unseen, and listen to what no mortal ever heard and lived to relate—the words of the Kingpriest. He is a good man, too good, perhaps." Crysania's head sank into her hands. "My faith hangs by a thread," she said so softly Tas could barely hear. "Show me some justification for this terrible act. If it is your capricious whim, I will die as I was intended to, perhaps, among those who long ago lost their faith in the true gods—"

"Say not that they lost their faith, Revered Daughter," came a voice from the air that so startled the kender he nearly fell through the curtains. "Say, rather, that their faith in the true gods was replaced by their faith in false ones—money, power, ambition. . . ."†

This concept is very much in line with Latter Day Saints and Protestant perspectives on the Reformation. It also has roots in the televangelist scandals of the 1980s.
—TRH

Crysania raised her head with a gasp that Tas echoed, but it was the sight of her face, not the sight of a shimmering figure of white materializing beside her, that made the kender draw in his breath. Crysania had obviously not slept for nights, her eyes were dark and wide, sunken into her face. Her cheeks were hollow, her lips dry and cracked. She had not bothered to comb her hair—it fell down about her face like black cobwebs as she stared in fear and alarm at the strange, ghostly figure.

"Who—who are you?" she faltered.

This is the same Loralon who gave the prophecy concerning the Thirteen Warnings. See note p. 265.

"My name is Loralon.† And I have come to take you away. You were not intended to die, Crysania. You are the last true cleric now on Krynn and you may join us, who left many days ago.

"Loralon, the great cleric of Silvanesti," Crysania murmured. For long moments, she looked at him, then, bowing her head, she turned away, her eyes looking toward the altar. "I cannot go," she said firmly, her hands clasped nervously before her as she knelt. "Not yet. I must hear the Kingpriest. I must understand. . . ."

"Don't you understand enough already?" Loralon asked sternly. "What have you felt in your soul this night?"

Genesis 3:5 has Satan telling Eve that if she and Adam will partake of the fruit, they shall be "as gods." This very much foreshadows Raistlin's intent and resonated back to the original temptation here in the foundations of the Bible. —TRH

Crysania swallowed, then brushed back her hair with a trembling hand. "Awe, humility," she whispered. "Surely, all must feel that before the power of the gods. . . ."

"Nothing else?" Loralon pursued. "Envy, perhaps? A desire to emulate them? To exist on the same level?"†

"No!" Crysania answered angrily, then flushed, averting her face.

"Come with me now, Crysania," Loralon persisted. "A true faith needs no demonstrations, no justification for believing what it knows in its heart to be right."

Crysania has not yet learned that truth does not lie in the words of others but in her own heart. It is a lesson that she will learn with great pain and sacrifice. —TRH

"The words my heart speaks echo hollow in my mind," Crysania returned. "They are no more than shadows. I must see the truth, shining in the clear light of day!† No, I will not leave with you. I will stay and hear what he says! I will know if the gods are justified!"

Crysania will not see the truth until she is blind. —MW

Loralon regarded her with a look that was more pitying than angry. "You do not look into the

light, you stand in front of it. The shadow you see cast before you is your own. The next time you will see clearly, Crysania, is when you are blinded by darkness . . . darkness unending. Farewell, Revered Daughter."

Tasslehoff blinked and looked around. The old elf was gone! Had he ever really been there? the kender wondered uneasily. But he must have, because Tas could still remember his words. He felt chilled and confused. What had he meant? It all sounded so strange. And what had Crysania meant—being sent here to die?

Then the kender cheered up. Neither of them knew that the Cataclysm wasn't going to happen. No wonder Crysania was feeling gloomy and out of sorts.

"She'll probably perk up quite a bit when she finds out that the world isn't going to be devastated after all," Tas said to himself.

And then the kender heard distant voices raised in song. The processional! It was beginning. Tas almost whooped in excitement. Fearing discovery, he quickly covered his mouth with his hands. Then he took a last, quick peek out at Crysania. She sat forlornly, cringing at the sound of the music. Distorted by distance, it was shrill, harsh, and unlovely. Her face was so ashen Tas was momentarily alarmed, but then he saw her lips press together firmly, her eyes darken. She stared, unseeing, at her folded hands.

"You'll feel better soon," Tas told her silently, then the kender ducked back behind the curtain to remove the wonderful magical device from his pouch. Sitting down, he held the device in his hands, and waited.

The processional lasted forever, at least as far as the kender was concerned. He yawned. Important Missions were certainly dull, he decided irritably, and hoped someone would appreciate what he'd gone through when it was all over. He would have dearly loved to tinker with the magical device, but Raistlin had impressed upon him that he was to *leave it alone* until the time came and then *follow the instructions to the letter*. So intent had been the look in Raistlin's eyes and so cold his voice that it had penetrated even the kender's

careless attitude. Tas sat holding the magical object, almost afraid to move.

Then, just as he was beginning to give up in despair (and his left foot was slowing losing all sensation), he heard a burst of beautiful voices right outside the room! A brilliant light welled through the curtains. The kender fought his curiosity, but finally couldn't resist just one peep. He had, after all, never seen the Kingpriest. Telling himself that he needed to see what was going on, he peeked through the crack in the curtains again.

The light nearly blinded him.

"Great Reorx!" the kender muttered, covering his eyes with his hands. He recalled once looking up at the sun when a child, trying to figure out if it really *was* a giant gold coin and, if so, how he could get it out of the sky. He'd been forced to go to bed for three days with cold rags over his eyes.

"I wonder how he does that?" Tas asked, daring to peep† through his fingers again. He stared into the heart of the light just as he had stared into the sun. And he saw the truth. The sun wasn't a golden coin. The Kingpriest was just a man.

The kender did not experience the terrible shock felt by Crysania when she saw through the illusion to the real man. Perhaps this was because Tas had no preconceived notions of what the Kingpriest *should* look like. Kender hold absolutely no one and nothing in awe (though Tas had to admit he felt a bit queer around the death knight, Lord Soth). He was, therefore, only mildly surprised to see that the most holy Kingpriest was simply a middle-aged human, balding, with pale blue eyes and the terrified look of a deer caught in a thicket. Tas was surprised—and disappointed.

"I've gone to all this trouble for nothing," the kender thought irritably. "There isn't going to be a Cataclysm. I don't think this man could make me angry enough to throw a pie at him, let alone a whole fiery mountain."

But Tas had nothing else to do (and he was really dying to work the magical device), so he decided to stick around and watch and listen. Something might happen after all. He tried to see Crysania, wondering how she felt about this, but

A bit of a nod to The Wizard of Oz *here, as Tas peeks behind the curtain to see that the Kingpriest is a mere mortal. It should be noted that, like Dorothy and her dog (who represent symbolically the Fool and his dog on the Tarot cards), the innocent kender sees and understands the truth about the Kingpriest.* —MW

"Pay no attention to that man behind the curtain!" (A nod to The Wizard of Oz.*) —TRH*

the halo of light surrounding the Kingpriest was so bright he couldn't see anything else in the room.

The Kingpriest walked to the front of the altar, moving slowly, his eyes darting left and right. Tas wondered if the Kingpriest would see Crysania, but apparently he was blinded by his own light as well, for his eyes passed right over her. Arriving at the altar, he did not kneel to pray, as had Crysania. Tas thought he might have started to, but then the Kingpriest angrily shook his head and remained standing.

From his vantage point behind and slightly to the left of the altar, Tas had an excellent look at the man's face. Once again, the kender gripped the magical device in excitement. For, the look of sheer terror in the watery eyes had been hidden by a mask of arrogance.

"Paladine," the Kingpriest trumpeted, and Tas had the distinct impression that the man was conferring with some underling. "Paladine, you see the evil that surrounds me! You have been witness to the calamities that have been the scourge of Krynn these past days. You know that this evil is directed against me, personally, because I am the only one fighting it! Surely you must see now that this doctrine of balance will not work!"

The Kingpriest's voice lost the harsh blare, becoming soft as a flute. "I understand, of course. You had to practice this doctrine in the old days, when you were weak. But you have me now, your right arm, your true representative upon Krynn. With our combined might, I can sweep evil from this world! Destroy the ogre races! Bring the wayward humans into line! Find new homelands far away for the dwarves and kender and gnomes, those races not of your own creation—"

How insulting! Tas thought, incensed. I've half a mind to let them go ahead and drop a mountain on him!

"And I will rule in glory," the Kingpriest's voice rose to a crescendo, "creating an age to rival even the fabled Age of Dreams!" The Kingpriest spread his arms wide. "You gave this and more to Huma,† Paladine, who was nothing but a renegade knight of low birth! I demand that you give me, too, the power to drive away the shadows of evil that darken this land!"

Huma's tale is told in The Legend of Huma *by Richard A. Knaak.*

The Kingpriest fell silent, waiting, his arms upraised.

Tas held his breath, waiting, too, clutching the magical device in his hands.

And then, the kender felt it—the answer. A horror crept over him, a fear he'd never experienced before, not even in the presence of Lord Soth or the Shoikan Grove. Trembling, the kender sank to his knees and bowed his head, whimpering and shaking, pleading with some unseen force for mercy, for forgiveness. Beyond the curtain, he could hear his own incoherent mumblings echoed, and he knew Crysania was there and that she, too, felt the terrible hot anger that rolled over him like the thunder from the storm.

But the Kingpriest did not speak a word. He simply remained, staring up expectantly into the heavens he could not see through the vast walls and ceilings of his Temple . . . the heavens he could not see because of his own light.

CHAPTER
17

H is mind firmly
resolved upon a course of action, Caramon fell into
an exhausted sleep and, for a few hours, was blessed
with oblivion. He awakened with a start to find
Raag bending over him, breaking his chains.

"What about these?" Caramon asked, raising his
bound wrists.

Raag shook his head. Although Arack didn't
really think even Caramon would be foolish enough
to try and overpower the ogre unarmed, the dwarf
had seen enough madness in the man's eyes last
night not to risk taking chances.

Caramon sighed. He had, indeed, considered
that possibility as he had considered many others
last night, but had rejected it. The important thing
was to stay alive—at least until he had made certain Raistlin was dead. After that, it didn't matter
anymore. . . .

Poor Tika. . . . She would wait and wait, until one day she would wake and realize he was never coming home.

"Move!" Raag grunted.

Caramon moved, following the ogre up the damp and twisting stairs leading from the storage rooms beneath the arena. He shook his head, clearing it of thoughts of Tika. Those might weaken his resolve, and he could not afford that. Raistlin must die. It was as if the lightning last night had illuminated a part of Caramon's mind that had lain in darkness for years. At last he saw the true extent of his brother's ambition, his lust for power. At last Caramon quit making excuses for him. It galled him, but he had to admit that even that dark elf, Dalamar, knew Raistlin far better than he, his twin brother.

Love had blinded him, and it had, apparently, blinded Crysania, too. Caramon recalled a saying of Tanis's' "I've never seen anything done out of love come to evil." Caramon snorted. Well, there was a first time for everything—that had been a favorite saying of old Flint's. A first time . . . and a last.

Just how he was going to kill his brother, Caramon didn't know. But he wasn't worried. There was a strange feeling of peace within him. He was thinking with a clarity and a logic that amazed him. He *knew* he could do it. Raistlin wouldn't be able to stop him either, not this time. The magic time travel spell would require the mage's complete concentration. The only thing that could possibly stop Caramon was death itself.

And therefore, Caramon said grimly to himself, I'll have to live.

He stood quietly without moving a muscle or speaking a word as Arack and Raag struggled to get him into his armor.

"I don't like it," the dwarf muttered more than once to the ogre as they dressed Caramon. The big man's calm, emotionless expression made the dwarf more uneasy than if he had been a raging bull. The only time Arack saw a flicker of life on Caramon's stoic face was when he buckled his shortsword onto his belt. Then the big man had glanced down at it, recognizing the useless prop for what it was. Arack saw him smile bitterly.

"Keep your eye on him," Arack instructed, and Raag nodded. "And keep him away from the others until he goes into the arena."

Raag nodded again, then led Caramon, hands bound, into the corridors beneath the arena where the others waited. Kiiri and Pheragas glanced over at Caramon as he entered. Kiiri's lip curled, and she turned coldly away. Caramon met Pheragas's gaze unflinchingly, his eyes neither begging nor pleading. This was not what Pheragas had expected, apparently. At first the black man seemed confused, then—after a few whispered words from Kiiri—he, too, turned away. But Caramon saw the man's shoulders slump and he saw him shake his head.

There was a roar from the crowd then, and Caramon shifted his gaze to what he could see of the stands. It was nearly midday, the Games started promptly at High Watch. The sun shone in the sky, the crowd—having had some sleep—was large and in a particularly good humor. There were some preliminary fights scheduled—to whet the crowd's appetite and to heighten the tension. But the true attraction was the Final Bout—the one that would determine the champion—the slave who wins either his freedom or—in the Red Minotaur's case—wealth enough to last him years.

Arack wisely kept up the pacing of the first few fights, making them light, even comic. He'd imported a few gully dwarves† for the occasion. Giving them real weapons (which, of course, they had no idea how to use), he sent them into the arena. The audience howled its delight, laughing until many were in tears at the sight of the gully dwarves tripping over their own swords, viciously stabbing each other with the hilts of their daggers, or turning and running, shrieking, out of the arena. Of course, the audience didn't enjoy the event nearly as much as the gully dwarves themselves, who finally tossed aside all weapons and launched into a mud fight. They had to be forcibly removed from the ring.

The crowd applauded, but now many began to stomp their feet in good humored, if impatient, demand for the main attraction. Arack allowed this to go on for several moments, knowing—like the showman he was—that it merely heightened

"The following aspects to a gully dwarf's personality sum up the entire race: keen survival instinct, a strong (if baffling) pride in themselves, unflagging endurance, a pitiable aspect, a desperate will to live, and low cunning and lower intelligence. The cornerstone of gully dwarf existence is simple survival. Gully dwarves do whatever it takes to stay alive. When danger threatens, their first thought is to run if possible, and grovel and cry piteously if not. Gully dwarves are not completely helpless, however. If backed into a corner, gully dwarves fight viciously, with the desperate fury of the cornered rat. Gully dwarves resort to any tactics to survive: biting, gnawing, scratching, and pummeling. 'Fighting dirty' is the only way a gully dwarf knows how to fight." [DRAGONLANCE Campaign Setting, Wizards of the Coast, Inc., 2003, p. 14.]

their excitement. He was right. Soon the stands were rocking as the crowd clapped and stomped and chanted.

And thus it was that no one in the crowd felt the first tremor.

Caramon felt it, and his stomach lurched as the ground shuddered beneath his feet. He was chilled with fear—not fear of dying, but fear that he might die without accomplishing his objective. Glancing up anxiously into the sky, he tried to recall every legend he had ever heard about the Cataclysm. It had struck near mid-afternoon, he thought he remembered. But there had been earthquakes, volcanic eruptions, dreadful natural disasters of all kinds throughout Krynn, even before the fiery mountain smashed the city of Istar so far beneath the ground that the seas rushed in to cover it.

This occurred in Dragons of Spring Dawning, *Book I, Chapter 4.*

Vividly, Caramon saw the wreckage of this doomed city as he had seen it† after their ship had been sucked into the whirlpool of what was now known as the Blood Sea† of Istar. The sea elves had rescued them then, but there would be no rescue for these people. Once more, he saw the twisted and shattered buildings. His soul recoiled in horror and he realized, with a start, that he had been keeping that terrible sight from his mind.

I never really believed it would happen, he realized, shivering with fear as the ground shivered in sympathy. I have hours only, maybe not that long. I must get out of here! I must reach Raistlin!

Then, he calmed down. Raistlin was expecting him. Raistlin needed him—or at least he needed a "trained fighter." Raistlin would ensure that he had plenty of time—time to win and get to him. Or time to lose and be replaced.

"The Blood Sea is one of the more spectacular legacies of the Cataclysm. Where the mighty city of Istar once stood, there is now a churning maelstrom almost 250 miles across. A perpetual storm rages above it. The bravest of captains occasionally skirts the maelstrom, as its outer currents allow ships traveling in the right direction to gain more speed. This is a dangerous gambit, however, as many good ships and crews have fallen victim to the swirling currents. Legend has it that the churning water leads to the Abyss, and that all those drawn into it end up in eternal servitude to Takhisis and the other Evil gods." [DRAGONLANCE Classics 15th Anniversary Edition, *by Steve Miller and Stan! Wizards of the Coast, 1999, p. 187.*]

But it was with a feeling of vast relief that Caramon felt the tremor cease. Then he heard Arack's voice coming from the center of the arena, announcing the Final Bout.

"Once they fought as a team, ladies and gentlemen, and as all of you know, they were the best team we've seen here in long years. Many's the time you saw each one risk his or her life to save a teammate. They were like brothers"—Caramon flinched at this—"but now they're bitter enemies, ladies and gentlemen. For when it comes to freedom, to

wealth, to winning this greatest of all the Games—
love has to sit in the back row. They'll give their all,
you may be sure of that, ladies and gentlemen.
This is a fight to the death between Kiiri the Sirine,
Pheragas of Ergoth, Caramon the Victor, and the
Red Minotaur. They won't leave this arena unless
it's feet first!"

The crowd cheered and roared. Even though they
knew it was fake, they loved convincing themselves
it wasn't.† The roaring grew louder as the Red Minotaur entered, his bestial face disdainful as always.
Kiiri and Pheragas glanced at him, then at the trident he held, then at each other. Kiiri's hand closed
tightly around her dagger.

Caramon felt the ground shake again. Then Arack
called his name. It was time for the Game to begin.

*This tells us more about
the people of Istar than
they know about
themselves. They would
rather convince themselves
that a falsehood is true in
order to justify their lives.
—TRH*

Tasslehoff felt the first tremors and for a moment
thought it was just his imagination, a reaction to that
terrible anger rolling around them. Then he saw the
curtains swaying back and forth, and he realized
that this was it. . . .

Activate the device! came a voice into Tasslehoff's
brain. His hands trembling, looking down at the
pendant, Tas repeated the instructions.

"*Thy time is thy own,* let's see, I turn the face
toward me. There. *Though across it you travel.* I shift
this plate from right to left. *Its expanses you see*—back
plate drops to form two disks connected by rods . . .
it works!" Highly excited, Tas continued. "*Whirling
through forever,* twist top facing me counterclockwise
from bottom. *Obstruct not its flow.* Make sure the
pendant chain is clear. There, that's right. Now, *Grasp
firmly the end and the beginning.* Hold the disks at
both ends. *Turn them back upon themselves,* like so,
and *All that is loose shall be secure.* The chain will
wind itself into the body! Isn't this wonderful! It's
doing it! Now, *Destiny be over your own head.* Hold it
over my head and—Wait! Something's not right! I
don't think this is supposed to be happening. . . ."

A tiny jeweled piece fell off the device, hitting Tas
on the nose. Then another, and another, until the distraught kender was standing in a perfect rain of
small, jeweled pieces.

"What?" Tas stared wildly at the device he held
up over his head. Frantically he twisted the ends

again. This time the rain of jeweled pieces became a positive downpour, clattering on the floor with bright, chime-like tones.

Tasslehoff wasn't sure, but he didn't think it was supposed to do this. Still, one never knew, especially about wizard's toys. He watched it, holding his breath, waiting for the light. . . .

The ground suddenly leaped beneath his feet, hurling him through the curtains and sending him sprawling on the floor at the feet of the Kingpriest. But the man never noticed the ashen-faced kender. The Kingpriest was staring about him in magnificent unconcern, watching with detached curiosity the curtains that rippled like waves, the tiny cracks that suddenly branched through the marble altar. Smiling to himself, as if assured that this was the acquiescence of the gods, the Kingpriest turned from the crumbling altar and made his way back down the central aisle, past the shuddering benches, and out into the main part of the Temple.

"No!" Tas moaned, rattling the device. At that moment, the tubes connecting either end of the sceptre separated in his hands. The chain slipped between his fingers. Slowly, trembling nearly as much as the floor on which he lay, Tasslehoff struggled to his feet. In his hand, he held the broken pieces of the magical device.

"What have I done?" Tas wailed. "I followed Raistlin's instructions, I'm sure I did! I—"

And suddenly the kender knew. Tears caused the glimmering, shattered pieces to blur in his gaze. "He was so nice to me," Tas murmured. "He made me repeat the instructions over and over—*to make certain you have them right*, he said." Tas squeezed shut his eyes, willing that when he opened them, this would all be a bad dream.

But when he did, it wasn't.

"I had them right. He *meant* for me to break it!" Tas whimpered, shivering. "Why? To strand us all back here? To leave us all to die? No! He wants Crysania, they said so, the mages in the Tower. That's it!" Tas whirled around. "Crysania!"

But the cleric neither heard nor saw him. Staring straight unhead, unmoved, even though the ground shook beneath her knees as she knelt, Crysania's gray eyes glowed with an eerie, inner light. Her

hands, still folded as if in prayer, clenched each other so tightly that the fingers had turned purplish red, the knuckles white.

Her lips moved. Was she praying?

Scrambling back behind the curtains, Tas quickly picked up every tiny jeweled piece of the device, gathered up the chain that had nearly slipped down a crack in the floor, then stuck everything into one pouch, closing it securely. Giving the floor a final look, he crept out into the Sacred Chamber.

"Crysania," he whispered. He hated to disturb her prayers, but this was too urgent to give up.

"Crysania?" he said, coming over to stand in front of her, since it was obvious she wasn't even aware of his existence.

Watching her lips, he read their unspoken utterings.

"I know," she was saying, "I know his mistake! Perhaps for me, the gods will grant what they denied him!"

Drawing a deep breath, she lowered her head. "Paladine, thank you! Thank you!" Tas heard her intone fervently. Then, swiftly, she rose to her feet. Glancing around in some astonishment at the objects in the room that were moving in a deadly dance, her gaze flicked, unseeing, right over the kender.

"Crysania!" Tas babbled, this time clutching at her white robes. "Crysania, I broke it! Our only way back! I broke a dragon orb once. But that was on purpose! I never meant to break this. Poor Caramon! You've got to help me! Come with me, talk to Raistlin, make him fix it!"

The cleric stared down at Tasslehoff blankly, as if he were a stranger accosting her on the street. "Raistlin!" she murmured, gently but firmly detaching the kender's hands from her robes. "Of course! He tried to tell me, but I wouldn't listen. And now I know, now I know the truth!"

Thrusting Tas away from her, Crysania gathered up her flowing white robes, darted out from among the benches, and ran down the center aisle without a backward glance as the Temple shook on its very foundations.

It wasn't until Caramon started to mount the stairs leading out into the arena that Raag finally removed the bindings from the gladiator's wrists.

Flexing his fingers, grimacing, Caramon followed Kiiri and Pheragas and the Red Minotaur out into the center of the arena. The audience cheered. Caramon, taking his place between Kiiri and Pheragas, looked up at the sky nervously. It was past High Watch, the sun was beginning its slow descent.

Istar would never live to see the sunset.

Thinking of this, and thinking that he, too, would never again see the sun's red rays stream over a battlement, or melt into the sea, or light the tops of the vallenwoods, Caramon felt tears sting his eyes. He wept not so much for himself, but for those two who stood beside him, who must die this day, and for all those innocents who would perish without understanding why.

He wept, too, for the brother he had loved, but his tears for Raistlin were for someone who had died long ago.

"Kiiri, Pheragas," Caramon said in a low voice when the Minotaur strode forward to take his bow alone, "I don't know what the mage told you, but I never betrayed you."

Kiiri refused to even look at him. He saw her lip curl. Pheragas, glancing at him from the corner of his eye, saw the stain of tears upon Caramon's face and hesitated, frowning, before he, too, turned away.

"It doesn't matter, really," Caramon continued, "whether you believe me or not. You can kill each other for the key if you want, because I'm finding my freedom my own way."

Now Kiiri looked at him, her eyes wide in disbelief. The crowd was on its feet, yelling for the Minotaur, who was walking around the arena, waving his trident above his head.

"You're mad!" she whispered as loudly as she dared. Her gaze went meaningfully to Raag. As always, the ogre's huge, yellowish body blocked the only exit.

Caramon's gaze followed imperturbably, his face not changing expression.

"Our weapons are real, my friend," Pheragas said harshly. "Yours are not!"

Caramon nodded, but did not answer.

"Don't do this!" Kiiri edged closer. "We'll help you fake it in the arena today. I-I guess neither of us really believed the black-robed one. You must

admit, it seemed weird—you trying to get us to leave the city! We thought, like he said, that you wanted the prize all to yourself. Look, pretend you're injured real early. Get yourself carried off. We'll help you escape tonight—"

"There will be no tonight," Caramon said softly. "Not for me, not for any of us. I haven't got much time. I can't explain. All I ask is this—just don't try to stop me."

Pheragas took a breath, but the words died on his lips as another tremor, this one more severe, shook the ground.

Now, everyone noticed. The arena swayed on its stilts, the bridges over the Death Pits creaked, the floor rose and fell, nearly knocking the Red Minotaur to his feet. Kiiri grabbed hold of Caramon. Pheragas braced his legs like a sailor on board a heaving vessel.† The crowd in the stands fell suddenly silent as their seats rocked beneath them. Hearing the cracking of the wood, some screamed. Several even rose to their feet. But the tremor stopped as quickly as it had begun.

Little details like this spring from my love of boating. As often as life permits, I love to go boating, especially on Lake Powell on the Utah-Arizona border. —TRH

Everything was quiet, too quiet. Caramon felt the hair rise on his neck and his skin prickle. No birds sang, not a dog barked. The crowd was silent, waiting in fear. *I have to get out of here!* Caramon resolved. His friends didn't matter anymore, nothing mattered. He had just one fixed objective—to stop Raistlin.

And he must act now, before the next shock hit and before people recovered from this one. Glancing quickly around, Caramon saw Raag standing beside the exit, the ogre's yellow, mottled face creased in puzzlement, his slow brain trying to figure out what was going on. Arack† had appeared suddenly beside him, staring around, probably hoping he wouldn't be forced to refund his customers' money. Already the crowd was starting to settle down, though many glanced about uneasily.

". . . Arack is a political realist. He knows that the Games have become a means of settling accounts among the wealthy and he sees no reason why he shouldn't make a profit out of it. Large sums of money are wagered on the athletes and the nobleman who owns a popular fighter generally makes a considerable fortune.

*"The only person Arack is truly loyal to (and will not betray) is his bodyguard, Raag the ogre." [*DRAGONLANCE Adventures, by Tracy Hickman and Margaret Weis, TSR, Inc., 1987, p. 95.]*

Caramon drew a deep breath, then, gripping Kiiri in his arms, he heaved with all his strength, hurling the startled woman right into Pheragas, sending them both tumbling to the ground.

Seeing them fall, Caramon whirled around and propelled his massive body straight at the ogre, driving his shoulder into Raag's gut with all the strength his months of training had given him. It was a blow that would have killed a human, but it only knocked the wind out of the ogre. The force of Caramon's charge sent them both crashing backward into the wall.

Desperately, while Raag was gasping for breath, Caramon grappled for the ogre's stout club. But just as he yanked it out of Raag's grip, the ogre recovered. Howling in anger, Raag brought both massive hands up under Caramon's chin with a blow that sent the big warrior flying back into the arena.

Landing heavily, Caramon could see nothing for a moment except sky and arena whirling around and around him. Groggy from the blow his warrior's instincts took over. Catching a glimpse of movement to his left, Caramon rolled over just as the minotaur's trident came down where his sword arm had been. He could hear the minotaur snarling and growling in bestial fury.

Caramon struggled to regain his feet, shaking his head to clear it, but he knew he could never hope to avoid the minotaur's second strike. And then a black body was between him and the Red Minotaur. There was a flash of steel as Pheragas's sword blocked the trident blow that would have finished Caramon. Staggering, Caramon backed up to catch his breath and felt Kiiri's cool hands helping to support him.

"Are you all right?" she muttered.

"Weapon!" Caramon managed to gasp, his head still ringing from the ogre's blow.

"Take mine," Kiiri said, thrusting her shortsword into Caramon's hands. "Then rest a moment. I'll handle Raag."

The ogre, wild with rage and the excitement of battle, barreled toward them, his slavering jaws wide open.

"No! You need it—" Caramon began to protest, but Kiiri only grinned at him.

"Watch!" she said lightly, then spoke strange words that reminded Caramon vaguely of the language of magic. These, however, had a faint accent, almost elvish.

And, suddenly Kiiri was gone. In her place stood a gigantic she-bear. Caramon gasped, unable—for a moment—to comprehend what had happened. Then

he remembered—Kiiri was a Sirine,† gifted with the power to change her shape!

Rearing up on her hind legs, the she-bear towered over the huge ogre. Raag came to a halt, his eyes wide open in alarm at the sight. Kiiri roared in rage, her sharp teeth gleamed. The sunlight glinted off her claws as one of her giant paws lashed out and caught Raag across his mottled face.

The ogre howled in pain, streams of yellowish blood oozed from the claw marks, one eye disappeared in a mass of bleeding jelly. The bear leaped on the ogre. Watching in awe, Caramon could see nothing but yellow skin and blood and brown fur.

The crowd, too, although they had yelled in delight at the beginning, suddenly became aware that this fight wasn't faked. This was for real. People were going to die. There was a moment of shocked silence, then—here and there—someone cheered. Soon the applause and wild yells were deafening.

Caramon quickly forgot the people in the stands, however. He saw his chance. Only the dwarf stood blocking the exit now, and Arack's face, though twisted in anger, was twisted in fear as well. Caramon could easily get past him. . . .

At that moment, he heard a grunt of pleasure from the minotaur. Turning, Caramon saw Pheragas slump over in pain, catching the butt end of the trident in his solar plexus. The minotaur reversed the stroke, raising the weapon to kill, but Caramon yelled loudly, distracting the minotaur long enough to throw him off stride.

The Red Minotaur turned to face this new challenge, a grin on his red-furred face. Seeing Caramon armed only with a shortsword, the minotaur's grin broadened. Lunging at Caramon, the minotaur sought to end the fight quickly. But Caramon sidestepped deftly. Raising his foot, he kicked, shattering the minotaur's kneecap. It was a painful, crippling blow, and sent the minotaur stumbling to the ground.

Knowing his enemy was out for at least a few moments, Caramon ran over to Pheragas. The black man remained huddled over, grasping his stomach.

"C'mon," Caramon grunted, putting his arm around him. "I've seen you take a hit like that, get up, and eat a five-course meal. What's the matter?"

Concerning Sirines, Caramon Majere would later write, "If you ever see a group of these elusive creatures [or even a lone one], my best advice is to sail on and leave them be." [The Bestiary, by Steven "Stan!" Brown, Wizards of the Coast, Inc., 1998, p. 106.]

But there was no answer. Caramon felt the man's body shiver convulsively, and he saw that the shining black skin was wet with sweat. Then Caramon saw the three bleeding slashes the trident had cut in the man's arm. . . .

Pheragas looked up at his friend. Seeing Caramon's horrified gaze, he realized he understood. Shuddering in pain from the poison that was coursing through his veins, Pheragas sank to his knees. Caramon's big arms closed around him.

"Take . . . take my sword." Pheragas choked. "Quickly, fool!" Hearing from the sounds his enemy was making that the minotaur was back on his feet, Caramon hesitated only a second, then took the large sword from Pheragas's shaking hand.

Pheragas pitched over, writhing in pain.

Gripping the sword, tears blinding his eyes, Caramon rose and whirled, blocking the Red Minotaur's sudden thrust. Even though limping on one leg, the minotaur's strength was such that he easily compensated for the painful injury. Then, too, the minotaur knew that all it took was a scratch to kill his victim, and Caramon would have to come inside the trident's range to use his sword.

Slowly the two stalked each other, circling round and round. Caramon no longer heard the crowd that was stamping and whistling and cheering madly at the sight of real blood. He no longer thought of escape, he had no idea—even—where he was. His warrior's instincts had taken over. He knew one thing. He had to kill.

And so he waited. Minotaurs had one major fault, Pheragas taught him. Believing themselves to be superior to all other races, minotaurs generally underestimate an opponent. They make mistakes, if you wait them out. The Red Minotaur was no exception. The minotaur's thoughts became clear to Caramon—pain and anger, outrage at the insult, an eagerness to end the life of this dull-witted, puny human.

The two edged nearer and nearer the spot where Kiiri was still locked in a vicious battle with Raag, as Caramon could tell by the sounds of growling and shrieking from the ogre. Suddenly, apparently preoccupied with watching Kiiri, Caramon slipped in a pool of yellow, slimy blood. The Red Minotaur,

howling in delight, lunged forward to impale the human's body on the trident.

But the slip had been feigned. Caramon's sword flashed in the sunlight. The minotaur, seeing he had been fooled, tried to recover from this forward lunge. But he had forgotten his crippled knee. It would not bear his weight, and the Red Minotaur fell to the arena floor, Caramon's sword cleaving cleanly through the bestial head.

Jerking his sword free, Caramon heard a horrible snarling behind him and turned just in time to see the great she-bear's jaws clamp over Raag's huge neck. With a shake of her head, Kiiri bit deeply into the jugular vein. The ogre's mouth opened wide in a scream none would ever hear.

Caramon started toward them when he caught sudden movement to his right. Quickly he turned, every sense alert as Arack hurtled past him, the dwarf's face an ugly mask of grief and fury. Caramon saw the dagger flash in the dwarf's hand and he hurled himself forward, but he was too late. He could not stop the blade that buried itself in the bear's chest. Instantly, the dwarf's hand was awash in red, warm blood. The great she-bear roared in pain and anger. One huge paw lashed out. Catching hold of the dwarf, with her last convulsive strength, Kiiri lifted Arack and threw him across the arena. The dwarf's body smashed against the Freedom Spire where hung the golden key, impaling it upon one of the countless ornate protrusions. The dwarf gave a fearsome shriek, then the entire pinnacle collapsed, crashing into the flame-filled pits below.

Kiiri fell, blood pouring from the gash in her breast. The crowd was going wild, screaming and yelling Caramon's name. The big man did not hear. Bending down, he took Kiiri in his arms. The magical spell she had woven unraveled. The bear was gone, and he held Kiiri close to his chest.

"You've won, Kiiri," Caramon whispered. "You're free."

Kiiri looked up at him and smiled. Then her eyes widened, the life left them. Their dying gaze remained fixed upon the sky, almost—it seemed to Caramon—expectantly, as if now she knew what was coming.

Gently laying her body down upon the blood-soaked arena floor, Caramon rose to his feet. He saw Pheragas's body frozen in its last, agonized throes. He saw Kiiri's sightless, staring eyes.

"You will answer for this, my brother," Caramon said softly.

There was a noise behind him, a murmuring like the angry roar of the sea before the storm. Grimly, Caramon gripped his sword and turned, preparing to face whatever new enemy awaited him. But there was no enemy, only the other gladiators. At the sight of Caramon's, tear-streaked and blood-stained face, one by one, they stood aside, making way for him to pass.

Looking at them, Caramon realized that—at last—*he* was free. Free to find his brother, free to put an end to this evil forever. He felt his soul soar, death held little meaning and no fear for him anymore. The smell of blood was in his nostrils, and he was filled with the sweet madness of battle.

Thirsting now with the desire for revenge, Caramon ran to the edge of the arena, preparing to descend the stairs that led down to the tunnels beneath it, when the first of the earthquakes shattered the doomed city of Istar.

CHAPTER 18

C rysania neither
saw nor heard Tasslehoff. Her mind was blinded
by a myriad colors that swirled within its depths,
sparkling like splendid jewels, for suddenly she
understood. *This* was why Paladine had brought
her back here—not to redeem the memory of the
Kingpriest—but to learn from his mistakes. And she
knew, she knew in her soul, that she *had* learned. *She*
could call upon the gods and they would answer—
not with anger—but with power! The cold darkness
within her broke open, and the freed creature sprang
from its shell, bursting into the sunlight.

In a vision, she saw herself—one hand holding
high the medallion of Paladine, its platinum flashing in the sun. With her other hand, she called forth
legions of believers, and they swarmed around her
with adoring, rapt expressions as she led them to
lands of beauty beyond imagining.

She didn't have the Key yet to unlock the door, she knew. And it could not happen here, the wrath of the gods was too great for her to penetrate. But where to find the Key, where to find the door, even? The dancing colors made her dizzy, she could not see or think. And then she heard a voice, a small voice, and felt hands clutching at her robes. "Raistlin. . ." she heard the voice say, the rest of the words were lost. But suddenly her mind cleared. The colors vanished, as did the light, leaving her alone in the darkness that was calm and soothing to her soul.

"Raistlin," she murmured. "He tried to tell me. . . ."

Still the hands clutched at her. Absently, she disengaged them and thrust them aside. Raistlin would take her to the Portal, he would help her find the Key. Evil turns in upon itself, Elistan said. So Raistlin would unwittingly help her. Crysania's soul sang in a joyous anthem to Paladine. *When I return in my glory, with goodness in my hand, when all the evil in the world is vanquished, then Raistlin himself will see my†might, he will come to understand and believe.*

"Crysania!"

The ground shook beneath Crysania's feet, but she did not notice the tremor. She heard a voice call her name, a soft voice, broken by coughing.

"Crysania " It spoke again. "There is not much time. Hurry!"

Raistlin's voice! Looking around wildly, Crysania searched for him, but she saw no one. And then she realized, he was speaking to her mind, guiding her. "Raistlin," she murmured, "I hear you. I am coming"

Turning, she ran down the aisle and out into the Temple. The kender's cry behind her fell on deaf ears.

"Raistlin?" said Tas, puzzled, glancing around. Then he understood. Crysania was going to Raistlin! Somehow, magically, he was calling to her and she was going to find him! Tasslehoff dashed out into the corridor of the Temple after Crysania. Surely, she would make Raistlin fix the device. . . .

Once in the corridor, Tas glanced up and down and spotted Crysania quickly. But his heart nearly

Crysania has not yet learned the lesson of the Kingpriest. In using the words "I" and "my" here she is walking down that same slippery slope as the Kingpriest and Raistlin. —TRH

jumped out on the floor—she was running so swiftly she had nearly reached the end of the hall.

Making certain the broken pieces of the magical device were secure in his pouch, Tas ran grimly after Crysania, keeping her fluttering white robes in his sight for as long as possible.

Unfortunately, that wasn't very long. She immediately vanished around a corner.

The kender ran as he had never run before, not even when the imagined terrors of Shoikan Grove had been chasing him.† His topknot of hair streamed out behind him, his pouches bounced around wildly, spilling their contents, leaving behind a glittering trail of rings and bracelets and baubles.

This occurred in Dragons of Spring Dawning, *Book I, Chapter 6.*

Keeping a firm grip on the pouch with the magical device, Tas reached the end of the hall and skidded around it, slamming up against the opposite wall in his haste. Oh, no! His heart went from jumping around in his chest to land with a thud at his feet. He began to wish irritably that his heart would stay put. Its gyrations were making him nauseous.

The hall was filled with clerics, all dressed in white robes! How was he ever to spot Crysania? Then he saw her, about half-way down the hall, her black hair shining in the torchlight. He saw, too, that clerics swirled about in her wake, shouting or glowering after her as she ran by.

Tas leaped to the pursuit, hope rising again; Crysania had been necessarily slowed in her wild flight by the crowd of people in the Temple. The kender sped past them, ignoring cries of outrage, skipping out of the way of grasping hands.

"Crysania," he yelled desperately.

The crowd of clerics in the hall became thicker, everyone hurrying out to wonder about the strange tremblings of the ground, trying to guess what this portended.

Tas saw Crysania halt more than once, pushing her way through the crowd. She had just freed herself when Quarath came around the corner, calling for the Kingpriest. Not watching where she was going, Crysania ran right into him, and he caught hold of her.

"Stop! My dear," Quarath cried, shaking her, thinking her hysterical. "Calm yourself!"

"Let me go!" Crysania struggled in his grasp.

"She's gone mad with terror! Help me hold her!" Quarath called to several other clerics standing nearby.

It suddenly occurred to Tas that Crysania *did* look mad. He could see her face as he drew near her, now. Her black hair was a tangled mass, her eyes were deep, deep gray, the color of the storm clouds, and her face was flushed with exertion. She seemed to hear nothing, no voices penetrated her consciousness, except, perhaps, one.

Other clerics caught hold of her at Quarath's command. Screaming incoherently, Crysania fought them, too. Desperation gave her strength, she came close to escaping more than once. Her white robes tore in their hands as they tried to hold her, Tas thought he saw blood on more than one cleric's face.

Running up, he was just about to leap on the back of the nearest cleric and bop him over the head when he was blinded by a brilliant light that brought everyone—even Crysania—to a halt.

No one moved. All Tas could hear for a moment were Crysania's gasps for breath and the heavy breathing of those who had tried to stop her. Then a voice spoke.

"The gods come," said the musical voice from out of the center of the light, "at my command—"†

The Kingpriest has gone from serving the gods to insisting that they serve him.

The ground beneath Tasslehoff's feet leaped high in the air, tossing the kender up like a feather. It sank rapidly as Tas was going up, then flew up to meet him as he was coming down. The kender slammed into the floor, the impact knocking the breath from his small body.

The air exploded with dust and glass and splinters, screams and shrieks and crashes. Tas could do nothing except fight to try to breathe. Lying on the marble floor as it jumped and rocked and shook beneath him, he watched in amazement as columns cracked and crumbled, walls split, pillars fell, and people died.

The Temple of Istar was collapsing.

Crawling forward on his hands and knees, Tas tried desperately to keep Crysania in sight. She seemed oblivious to what was happening around her. Those who had been holding her let go in their terror, and Crysania, still hearing only Raistlin's voice, started on her way again. Tas yelled, Quarath

was lunging at her, but, even as the cleric hurtled toward her, a huge marble column next to her toppled and fell.

Tas caught his breath. He couldn't see a thing for an instant then the marble dust settled. Quarath was nothing but a bloody mass on the floor. Crysania, apparently unhurt, stood staring dazedly down at the elf, whose blood had spattered all over her white robes.

"Crysania!" Tasslehoff shouted hoarsely. But she didn't notice him. Turning away, she stumbled through the wreckage, unseeing, hearing nothing but the voice that called to her more urgently now than ever.

Staggering to his feet, his body bruised and aching, Tas ran after her. Nearing the end of the hall, he saw Crysania make a turn to her right and go down a flight of stairs. Before he followed her, Tas risked a quick look behind him, drawn by a terrible curiosity.

The brilliant light still filled the corridor, illuminating the bodies of the dead and dying. Cracks gaped in the Temple walls, the ceiling sagged, dust choked the air. And within that light, Tas could still hear the voice, only now its lovely music had faded. It sounded harsh, shrill, and off-key.

"The gods come. . . ."

Outside the great arena, running through Istar, Caramon fought his way through death-choked streets. Much like Crysania's, his mind, too, heard Raistlin's voice. But it was not calling to him. No, Caramon heard it as he had heard it in their mother's womb, he heard the voice of his twin, the voice of the blood they shared.

And so Caramon paid no heed to the screams of the dying, or the pleas for help from those trapped beneath the wreckage. He paid no heed to what was happening around him. Buildings tumbled down practically on top of him, stones plummeted into the streets, narrowly missing him. His arms and upper body were soon bleeding from small, jagged cuts. His legs were gashed in a hundred places.

But he did not stop. He did not even feel the pain. Climbing over debris, lifting giant beams of wood and hurling them out of his way, Caramon slowly

made his way through the dying streets of Istar to the Temple that gleamed in the sun before him. In his hand, he carried a bloodstained sword.

Tasslehoff followed Crysania down, down, down into the very bowels of the ground—or so it seemed to the kender. He hadn't even known such places in the Temple existed, and he wondered how he had come to miss all these hidden staircases in his many ramblings. He wondered, too, how Crysania came to know of their existence. She passed through secret doors that were not visible even to Tas's kender eyes.

The earthquake ended, the Temple shook a moment longer in horrified memory, then shivered and was still once more. Outside was death and chaos, but inside all was still and silent. It seemed to Tas as if everything in the world was holding its breath, waiting. . . .

Down here—wherever *here* was—Tas saw little damage, perhaps because it was so far beneath the ground. Dust clouded the air, making it hard to breathe or see and occasionally a crack appeared in a wall, or a torch fell to the floor. But most of the torches were still in their sconces on the wall, still burning, casting an eerie glow in the drifting dust.

Crysania never paused or hesitated, but pressed on rapidly, though Tas soon lost all sense of direction or of where he was. He had managed to keep up with her fairly easily, but he was growing more and more tired and hoped that they would get to wherever they were going soon. His ribs hurt dreadfully. Each breath he drew burned like fire, and his legs felt like they must belong to a thick-legged, iron-shod dwarf.

He followed Crysania down another flight of marble stairs, forcing his aching muscles to keep moving. Once at the bottom, Tas looked up wearily and his heart rose for a change. They were in a dark, narrow hallway that ended, thankfully, in a wall, not another staircase!

Here, a single torch burned in a sconce above a darkened doorway.

With a glad cry, Crysania hurried through the doorway, vanishing into the darkness beyond.

"Of course!" Tas realized thankfully. "Raistlin's laboratory! It must be down here."

Hurrying forward, he was very near the door when a great, dark shape bore down on him from him behind, tripping him. Tas tumbled to the floor, the pain in his ribs making him catch his breath.

Looking up, fighting the pain, the kender saw the flash of golden armor and the torchlight glisten upon the blade of a sword. He recognized the man's bronze, muscular body, but the man's face—the face that should have been so familiar—was the face of someone Tas had never seen before.

"Caramon?" he whispered as the man surged past him. But Caramon neither saw him nor heard him. Frantically, Tas tried to stand up.

Then the aftershock hit and the ground rocked out from beneath Tas's feet. Lurching back against a wall, he heard a cracking sound above him and saw the ceiling start to give way.

"Caramon!" he cried, but his voice was lost in the sound of wood tumbling down on top of him, knocking him in the head. Tas struggled to stay conscious, despite the pain. But his brain, as if stubbornly refusing to have anything more to do with this mess, snuffed out the lights. Tas sank into darkness.

CHAPTER 19

Hearing in her mind Raistlin's calm voice drawing her past death and destruction, Crysania ran without hesitation into the room that lay far below the Temple. But, on entering, her eager steps faltered. Hesitantly, she glanced around, her pulse beating achingly in her throat.

She had been blind to the horrors of the stricken Temple. Even now, she glanced at the blood on her dress and could not remember how it got there. But here, in this room, things stood out with vivid clarity, though the laboratory was lit only by light streaming from a crystal atop a magical staff. Staring around, overawed by a sense of evil, she could not make herself walk beyond the door.

Suddenly, she heard a sound and felt a touch on her arm. Whirling in alarm, she saw dark, living, shapeless creatures, trapped and held in cages. Smelling

her warm blood, they stirred in the staff's light, and it was the touch of one of their grasping hands she had felt. Shuddering, Crysania backed out of their way and bumped into something solid.

It was an open casket containing the body of what might have once been a young man. But the skin was stretched like parchment across his bones, his mouth was open in a ghastly, silent scream. The ground lurched beneath her feet, and the body in the casket bounced up wildly, staring at her from empty eye sockets.

Crysania gasped, no sound came from her throat, her body was chilled by cold sweat. Clutching her head in shaking hands, she squeezed her eyes shut to blot out the horrible sight. The world started to slip away, then she heard a soft voice.

"Come, my dear," said the voice that had been in her mind. "Come. You are safe with me, now. The creatures of Fistandantilus's evil cannot harm you while I am here."

Crysania felt life return to her body. Raistlin's voice brought comfort. The sickness passed, the ground quit shaking, the dust settled. The world lapsed into deathly silence.

Thankfully, Crysania opened her eyes. She saw Raistlin standing some distance from her, watching her from the shadows of his hooded head, his eyes glittering in the light of his staff. But, even as Crysania looked at him, she caught a glimpse of the writhing, caged shapes. Shuddering, she kept her gaze on Raistlin's pale face.

"Fistandantilus?" she asked through dry lips. "He built this?"

"Yes, this laboratory is his," Raistlin replied coolly. "It is one he created years and years ago. Unbeknownst to any of the clerics, he used his great magic to burrow beneath the Temple like a worm, eating away solid rock, forming it into stairs and secret doors, casting his spells upon them so that few knew of their existence."

Crysania saw a thin-lipped sardonic smile cross Raistlin's face as he turned to the light.

"He showed it to few, over the years. Only a handful of apprentices were ever allowed to share the secret," Raistlin shrugged. "And none of these lived to tell about it." His voice softened. "But then

Fistandantilus made a mistake. He showed it to one young apprentice. A frail, brilliant, sharp-tongued young man, who observed and memorized every turn and twist of the hidden corridors, who studied every word of every spell that revealed secret doorways, reciting them over and over, committing them to memory, before he slept, night after night. And thus, we stand here, you and I, safe—for the moment— from the anger of the gods."

Making a motion with his hand, he gestured for Crysania to come to the back part of the room where he stood at a large, ornately carved, wooden desk. On it rested a silver-bound spellbook he had been reading. A circle of silver powder was spread around the desk. "That's right. Keep your eyes on me. The darkness is not so terrifying then, is it?"

Crysania could not answer. She realized that, once again, she had allowed him, in her weakness, to read more in her eyes than she had intended him to see. Flushing, she looked quickly away.

"I—I was only startled, that's all," she said. But she could not repress a shudder as she glanced back at the casket. "What is—or was—that?" she whispered in horror.

"One of the Fistandantilus's apprentices, no doubt," Raistlin answered. "The mage sucked the life force from him to extend his own life. It was something he did . . . frequently."

Raistlin coughed, his eyes grew shadowed and dark with some terrible memory, and Crysania saw a spasm of fear and pain pass over his usually impassive face. But before she could ask more, there was the sound of a crash in the doorway. The black-robed mage quickly regained his composure. He looked up, his gaze going past Crysania.

"Ah, enter, my brother. I was just thinking of the Test, which naturally brought you to mind."

Caramon! Faint with relief, Crysania turned to welcome the big man with his solid, reassuring presence, his jovial, good-natured face. But her words of greeting died on her lips, swallowed up by the darkness that only seemed to grow deeper with the warrior's arrival.

"Speaking of tests, I am pleased you survived yours, brother," Raistlin said, his sardonic smile returned. "This lady"—he glanced at Crysania—

"will have need of a bodyguard where we go. I can't tell you how much it means to me to have someone along I know and trust."

Crysania shrank from the terrible sarcasm, and she saw Caramon flinch as though Raistlin's words had been tiny, poisoned barbs, shooting in his flesh. The mage seemed neither to notice nor care, however. He was reading his spellbook, murmuring soft words and tracing symbols in the air with his delicate hands.

"Yes, I survived your test," Caramon said quietly. Entering the room, he came into the light of the staff. Crysania caught her breath in fear.

"Raistlin!" she cried, backing away from Caramon as the big man came slowly forward, the bloody sword in his hand. "Raistlin, look!" Crysania said, stumbling into the desk near where the mage was standing, unknowingly stepping into the circle of silver powder. Grains of it clung to the bottom of her robe, shimmering in the staff's light.

Irritated at the interruption, the mage glanced up.

"I survived your test," Caramon repeated, "as you survived the Test in the Tower. There, they shattered your body. Here, you shattered my heart. In its place is nothing now, just a cold emptiness as black as your robes. And, like this swordblade, it is stained with blood. A poor wretch of a minotaur died upon this blade. A friend gave his life for me, another died in my arms. You've sent the kender to *his* death, haven't you? And how many more have died to further your evil designs?" Caramon's voice dropped to a lethal whisper. "This ends it, my brother. No more will die because of you. Except one—myself. It's fitting, isn't it, Raist? We came into this world together; together, we'll leave it."

He took another step forward. Raistlin seemed about to speak, but Caramon interrupted.

"You cannot use your magic to stop me, not this time. I know about this spell you plan to cast. I know it will take all of your power, all of your concentration. If you use even the smallest bit of magic against me, you will not have the strength to leave this place, and my end will be accomplished all the same. If you do not die at my hands, you will die at the hands of the gods."

Raistlin gazed at his brother without comment, then, shrugging, he turned back to read in his

book. It was only when Caramon took one more step forward, and Raistlin heard the man's golden armor clank, that the mage sighed in exasperation and glanced up at his twin. His eyes, glittering from the depths of his hood, seemed the only points of light in the room.

"You are wrong, my brother," Raistlin said softly. "There is one other who will die." His mirrorlike gaze went to Crysania, who stood alone, her white robes shimmering in the darkness, between the two brothers.

Caramon's eyes were soft with pity as he, too, looked at Crysania, but the resolution on his face did not waver. "The gods will take her to them," he said gently. "She is a true cleric. None of the true clerics died in the Cataclysm. That is why Par-Salian sent her back." Holding out his hand, he pointed. "Look, there stands one, waiting."

Crysania had no need to turn and look, she felt Loralon's presence.

"Go to him, Revered Daughter," Caramon told her. "Your place is in the light, not here in the darkness."

Raistlin said nothing, he made no motion of any kind, just stood quietly at the desk, his slender hand resting upon the spellbook.

Crysania did not move. Caramon's words beat in her mind like the wings of the evil creatures who fluttered about the Tower of High Sorcery. She heard the words, yet they held no meaning for her. All she could see was herself, holding the shining light in her hand, leading the people. The Key . . . the Portal. . . . She saw Raistlin holding the Key in his hand, she saw him beckoning to her. Once more, she felt the touch of Raistlin's lips, burning, upon her forehead.

A light flickered and died. Loralon was gone.

"I cannot," Crysania tried to say, but no voice came. None was needed. Caramon understood. He hesitated, looking at her for one, long moment, then he sighed.

"So be it," Caramon said coolly, as he, too, advanced into the silver circle. "Another death will not matter much to either of us now, will it, my brother?"

Crysania stared, fascinated, at the bloodstained sword shining in the staff's light. Vividly, she pictured

it piercing her body and, looking up into Caramon's eyes, she saw that he pictured the same thing, and that even this would not deter him. She was nothing to him, not even a living, breathing human. She was merely an obstacle in his path, keeping him from his true objective—his brother.

What terrible hatred, Crysania thought, and then, looking deep into the eyes that were so near her own now, she had a sudden flash of insight—what terrible love!

Caramon lunged at her with an outstretched hand, thinking to catch her and hurl her aside. Acting out of panic, Crysania dodged his grasp, stumbling back up against Raistlin, who made no move to touch her. Caramon's hand gripped nothing but a sleeve of her robe, ripping and tearing it. In a fury, he cast the white cloth to the ground, and now Crysania knew she must die. Still, she kept her body between him and his brother.

Caramon's sword flashed.

In desperation, Crysania clutched the medallion of Paladine she wore around her throat.

"Halt!" She cried the word of command even as she shut her eyes in fear. Her body cringed, waiting for the terrible pain as the steel tore through her flesh. Then, she heard a moan and the clatter of a sword falling to the stone. Relief surged through her body, making her weak and faint. Sobbing, she felt herself falling.

But slender hands caught and held her; thin, muscular arms gathered her near, a soft voice spoke her name in triumph. She was enveloped in warm blackness, drowning in warm blackness, sinking down and down. And in her ear, she heard whispered the words of the strange language of magic.

Like spiders or caressing hands, the words crawled over her body. The chanting of the words grew louder and louder, Raistlin's voice stronger and stronger. Silver light flared, then vanished. The grip of Raistlin's arms around Crysania tightened in ecstasy, and she was spinning around and around, caught up in that ecstasy, whirling away with him into the blackness.

She put her arms about him and laid her head on his chest and let herself sink into the darkness. As she fell, the words of magic mingled with the

singing of her blood and the singing of the stones in the Temple. . . .

And through it all, one discordant note—a harsh, heartbroken moan.

Tasslehoff Burrfoot heard the stones singing, and he smiled dreamily. He was a mouse, he remembered, scampering forward through the silver powder while the stones sang. . . .

Tast woke up suddenly. He was lying on a cold stone floor, covered with dust and debris. The ground beneath him was beginning to shiver and shake once more. Tas knew, from the strange and unfamiliar feeling of fear building up inside of him that this time the gods meant business. This time, the earthquake would not end.

"Crysania! Caramon!" Tas shouted, but he heard only the echo of his shrill voice come back, bouncing hollowly off the shivering walls.

Staggering to his feet, ignoring the pain in his head, Tas saw that the torch still shone above that darkened room Crysania had entered, that part of the building seemingly the only part untouched by the convulsive heaving of the ground. *Magic*, Tas thought vaguely, making his way inside and recognizing wizardly things. He looked for signs of life, but all he saw were the horrible caged creatures, hurling themselves upon their cell doors, knowing the end of their tortured existence was near, yet unwilling to give up life, no matter how painful.

Tas stared around wildly. Where had everyone gone? "Caramon?" he said in a small voice. But there was no answer, only a distant rumbling as the shaking of the ground grew worse and worse. Then, in the dim light of the torch outside, Tas caught a glimpse of metal shining on the floor near a desk. Staggering across the floor, Tas managed to reach it.

His hand closed about the golden hilt of a gladiator's sword. Leaning back against the desk for support, he stared at the silver blade, stained black with blood. Then he lifted something else that had been lying on the floor beneath the sword—a remnant of white cloth. He saw golden embroidery portraying the symbol of Paladine shine dully in the torchlight. There was a circle of powder on the floor, powder

That Istar was destroyed by a meteor strike because of the folly of the Kingpriest and his followers was part of the background history from before Chronicles was written. That Tasslehoff happened to be right in the middle of it with a ringside seat allowed us to be there, too, but presented quite a dilemma for Margaret as we soon shall see. —TRH

that once might have been silver but was now burned black.

"They've gone," Tas said softly to the caged, gibbering creatures. "They've gone. . . . I'm all alone."

A sudden heaving of the ground sent the kender to the floor on his hands and knees. There was a snapping and rending sound, so loud it nearly deafened him, causing Tas to raise his head. As he stared up at the ceiling in awe, it split wide open. The rock cracked. The foundation of the Temple parted.

And then the Temple itself shattered. The walls flew asunder. The marble separated. Floor after floor burst open, like the petals of a rose spreading in the morning's light, a rose that would die by nightfall. The kender's gaze followed the dreadful progress until, finally, he saw the very tower of the Temple itself split wide, falling to the ground with a crash that was more devastating than the earthquake.

Unable to move, protected by the powerful dark spells cast by an evil mage long dead, Tas† stood in the laboratory of Fistandantilus, looking up into the heavens.

And he saw the sky begin to rain fire.†

It should be noted that as I was writing this, I had no idea how we were going to rescue Tasslehoff from being destroyed by the fiery mountain. When I finished this scene, I called Tracy to tell him that unless he came up with a solution, we had just killed off one of our most beloved characters! Tracy promised he knew what happened to Tas, and his solution turned out to be brilliant. —MW

12 " 'You were the model of perfection, full of wisdom and perfect in beauty.
15 You were blameless in your ways from the day you were created till wickedness was found in you.
17 Your heart became proud on account of your beauty,
and you corrupted your wisdom because of your splendor.
So I threw you to the earth; I made a spectacle of you before kings.
18 By your many sins and dishonest trade you have desecrated your sanctuaries. So I made a fire come out from you, and it consumed you, and I reduced you to ashes on the ground in the sight of all who were watching.
19 All the nations who knew you are appalled at you; you have come to a horrible end and will be no more.' "
[Ezekiel 28:12, 15, 17-19 NIV]

VOLUME 2

WAR OF THE TWINS

BOOK 1

This book is dedicated to
you who are sharing our journeys through Krynn.
Thank you, reader, for walking this path with us.
—Margaret Weis and Tracy Hickman

The River Flows On . . .

The dark waters of time† swirled about the archmage's black robes, carrying him and those with him forward through the years.

The sky rained fire, the mountain fell upon the city of Istar, plunging it down, down into the depths of the ground. The sea waters, taking mercy on the terrible destruction, rushed in to fill the void. The great Temple, where the Kingpriest was still waiting for the gods to grant him his demands, vanished from the face of the world. Even those sea elves who ventured into the newly-created Blood Sea of Istar looked in wonder at the place where the Temple had stood.† There was nothing there now but a deep black pit.† The sea water within was so dark and chill that even these elves, born and bred and living beneath the water, dared not swim near it.

But there were many on Ansalon who envied the inhabitants of Istar. For them at least, death had come swiftly.

For those who survived the immediate destruction on Ansalon, death came slowly, in hideous aspect—starvation, disease, murder . . .

War.

I have been a fan of time travel stories since first reading H.G. Wells and watching The Time Tunnel *on television. Of all the theories of time travel paradox, I have always liked the image of time as a river that is somewhat self-correcting. It helped fudge out many of the more nasty paradoxes that time travel potentially creates. See Appendix B. —TRH*

Mythology and legend are replete with examples of lost civilizations being brought down to their doom—Atlantis being the most famous in Western cultures. —TRH

The greater the good that is aspired to, the further the fall in failure. Lucifer in the Christian tradition was the greatest of the angels before he fell from grace. —TRH

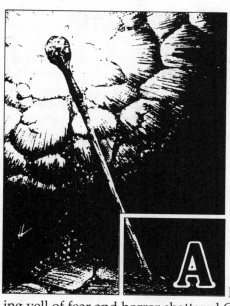

CHAPTER I

A hoarse,[†] bellowing yell of fear and horror shattered Crysania's sleep. So sudden and awful was the yell and so deep her sleep that, for a moment, she could not even think what had wakened her. Terrified and confused, she stared around, trying to understand where she was, trying to discover what had frightened her so that she could scarcely breathe.

She was lying on a damp, hard floor. Her body shook convulsively from the chill that penetrated her bones; her teeth chattered from the cold. Holding her breath, she sought to hear something or see something. But the darkness around was thick and impenetrable, the silence was intense.

She let go her breath and tried to draw another, but the darkness seemed to be stealing it away. Panic gripped her. Desperately she tried to structure the darkness, to people it with shapes and forms. But

Thus begins the second volume in the Legends trilogy. Why a trilogy? Thanks in large part to J.R.R. Tolkien, trilogy has come to mean three bound volumes of a single, epic story. Legends—and Chronicles before it—certainly follows this format. —TRH

none came to her mind. There was only the darkness and it had no dimension. It was eternal. . . .

Then she heard the yell again and recognized it as what had awakened her. And, though she came near gasping in relief at the sound of another human voice, the fear she heard in that yell echoed in her soul.

Desperately, frantically trying to penetrate the darkness, she forced herself to think, to remember. . . .

There had been singing stones, a chanting voice—Raistlin's voice—and his arms around her. Then the sensation of stepping into water† and being carried into a swift, vast darkness.

Once again we see time as a river. See Appendix B. —TRH

Raistlin! Reaching out a trembling hand, Crysania felt nothing near her but damp, chill stone. And then memory returned with horrifying impact. Caramon lunging at his brother with the flashing sword in his hand. . . . Her words as she cast a clerical spell to protect the mage. . . . The sound of a sword clanging on stone.

But that yell—it was Caramon's voice! What if he—

"Raistlin!" Crysania called fearfully, struggling to her feet. Her voice vanished, disappeared, swallowed up by the darkness. It was such a terrible feeling that she dared not speak again. Clasping her arms about her, shivering in the intense cold, Crysania's hand went involuntarily to the medallion of Paladine that hung around her neck. The god's blessing flowed through her.

"Light," she whispered and, holding the medallion fast, she prayed to the god to light the darkness.

Soft light welled from the medallion between her fingers, pushing back the black velvet that smothered her, letting her breathe. Lifting the chain over her head, Crysania held the medallion aloft. Shining it about her surroundings, she tried to remember the direction from which the yell had come.

She had quick impressions of shattered, blackened furniture, cobwebs, books lying scattered about the floor, bookshelves falling off walls. But these were almost as frightening as the darkness itself; it was the darkness that gave them birth. These objects had more right to this place than she.

And then the yell came again.

Her hand shaking, Crysania turned swiftly toward the sound. The light of the god parted the darkness,

bringing two figures into shockingly stark relief. One, dressed in black robes, lay still and silent on the cold floor. Standing above that unmoving figure was a huge man. Dressed in blood-stained golden armor, an iron collar bolted around his neck, he stared into the darkness, his hands outstretched, his mouth open wide, his face white with terror.

The medallion slipped from Crysania's nerveless hand as she recognized the body lying huddled at the feet of the warrior.

"Raistlin!" she whispered.

Only as she felt the platinum chain slither through her fingers, only as the precious light around her wavered, did she think to catch the medallion as it fell.

She ran across the floor, her world reeling with the light that swung crazily from her hand. Dark shapes scurried from beneath her feet, but Crysania never noticed them. Filled with a fear more suffocating than the darkness, she knelt beside the mage.

He lay face down upon the floor, his hood cast over his head. Gently, Crysania lifted him, turning him over. Fearfully she pushed the hood back from his face and held the glowing medallion above him. Fear chilled her heart.

The mage's skin was ashen, his lips blue, his eyes closed and sunken into his hollow cheekbones.

"What have you done?" she cried to Caramon,† looking up from where she knelt beside the mage's seemingly lifeless body. "What have you done?" she demanded, her voice breaking in her grief and her fury.

"Crysania?" Caramon whispered hoarsely.

The light from the medallion cast strange shadows over the form of the towering gladiator. His arms still outstretched, his hands grasping feebly at the air, he bent his head toward the sound of her voice. "Crysania?" he repeated again, with a sob. Taking a step toward her, he fell over his brother's legs and plunged headlong to the floor.†

Almost instantly, he was up again, crouched on his hands and knees, his breath coming in quick gasps, his eyes still wide and staring. He reached out his hand.

"Crysania?" He lunged toward the sound of her voice. "Your light! Bring us your light! Quickly!"

The first person Crysania finds in the darkness is Caramon. This not only builds up our suspense, wondering what has happened to Tasslehoff and Raistlin, but it presages the ending, where Crysania will turn to Caramon to lead her out of darkness. —MW

Caramon began the first book in a drunken stupor. Now he is blind and cannot see. There is a resonance to these two images that tells us he still has much to learn. This motif, however, is inverted in the case of Crysania, as we shall see. —TRH

"I have a light, Caramon! I—Blessed Paladine!" Crysania murmured, staring at him in the medallion's soft glow. "You are blind!"

Reaching out her hand, she took hold of his grasping, twitching fingers. At her touch, Caramon sobbed again in relief. His clinging hand closed over hers with crushing strength, and Crysania bit her lip with the pain. But she held onto him firmly with one hand, the medallion with the other.

Rising to her feet, she helped Caramon to his. The warrior's big body shook, and he clutched at her in desperate terror, his eyes still staring straight ahead, wild, unseeing. Crysania peered into the darkness, searching desperately for a chair, a couch . . . something.

And then she became aware, suddenly, that the darkness was looking back.†

Hurriedly averting her eyes, keeping her gaze carefully within the light of her medallion, she guided Caramon to the only large piece of furniture she saw.

"Here, sit down," she instructed. "Lean up against this."

She settled Caramon on the floor, his back against an ornately carved wooden desk that, she thought, seemed vaguely familiar to her. The sight brought a rush of painful, familiar memories—she had seen it somewhere. But she was too worried and preoccupied to give it much thought.

"Caramon?" she asked shakily. "Is Raistlin d— Did you kill—" Her voice broke.

"Raistlin?" Caramon turned his sightless eyes toward the sound of her voice. The expression on his face grew alarmed. He tried to stand. "Raist! Where—"

"No. Sit back!" Crysania ordered in swift anger and fear. Her hand on his shoulder, she shoved him down.

Caramon's eyes closed, a wry smile twisted his face. For a moment, he looked very like his twin.

"No, I didn't kill him!" he said bitterly. "How could I? The last thing I heard was you cry out to Paladine, then everything went dark. My muscles wouldn't move, the sword fell from my hand. And then—"

But Crysania wasn't listening. Running back to where Raistlin lay a few feet from them, she knelt

Crysania is blind, yet the darkness can see her.
—MW

down beside the mage once again. Holding the medallion near his face, she reached her hand inside the black hood to feel for the lifebeat in his neck. Closing her eyes in relief, she breathed a silent prayer to Paladine.

"He's alive!" she whispered. "But then, what's wrong with him?"

"What *is* wrong with him?" Caramon asked, bitterness and fear still tinging his voice. "I can't see—"

Flushing almost guiltily, Crysania described the mage's condition.

Caramon shrugged. "Exhausted by the spell casting," he said, his voice expressionless. "And, remember, he was weak to begin with, at least so you told me. Sick from the nearness of the gods or some such thing." His voice sank. "I've seen him like that before. The first time he used the dragon orb,† he could scarcely move afterward. I held him in my arms—"

He broke off, staring into the darkness, his face calm now, calm and grim, "There's nothing we can do for him," he said. "He has to rest."

This occurred in Dragons of Winter Night, *Book III, Chapter 3.*

After a short pause, Caramon asked quietly, "Lady Crysania, can you heal me?"

Crysania's skin burned. "I—I'm afraid not," she replied, distraught. "It—it must have been my spell that blinded you." Once more, in her memory, she saw the big warrior, the bloodstained sword in his hand, intent on killing his twin, intent on killing her—if she got in his way.

"I'm sorry," she said softly, feeling so tired and chilled she was almost sick. "But I was desperate and . . . and afraid. Don't worry, though," she added, "the spell is not permanent. It will wear off, in time."

Caramon sighed. "I understand," he said. "Is there a light in this room? You said you had one."

"Yes," she answered. "I have the medallion—"

"Look around. Tell me where we are. Describe it."

"But Raistlin—"

"He'll be all right!" Caramon snapped, his voice harsh and commanding. "Come back here, near me. Do as I say! Our lives—his life—may depend on it! Tell me where we are!"

Looking into the darkness, Crysania felt her fear return. Reluctantly leaving the mage, she came back to sit beside Caramon.

"I—I don't know," she faltered, holding the glowing medallion high again. "I can't see much of anything beyond the medallion's light. But it seems to be some place I've been before, I just can't place it. There's furniture lying around, but it's all broken and charred, as though it had been in a fire. There are lots of books scattered about. There's a big wooden desk—you're leaning against it. It seems to be the only piece of furniture not broken. And it seems familiar to me," she added softly, puzzled. "It's beautiful, carved with all sorts of strange creatures."

Caramon felt beneath him with his hand. "Carpet," he said, "over stone."

"Yes, the floor is covered with carpet—or was. But it's torn now, and it looks like something's eaten it—"

She choked, seeing a dark shape suddenly skitter away from her light.

"What?" Caramon asked sharply.

"What's been eating the carpet apparently," Crysania replied with a nervous little laugh. "Rats." She tried to continue, "There's a fireplace, but it hasn't been used in years. It's all filled with cobwebs. In fact, the place is covered with cobwebs—"

But her voice gave out. Sudden images of spiders dropping from the ceiling and rats running past her feet made her shudder and gather her torn white robes around her. The bare and blackened fireplace reminded her of how cold she was.

Feeling her body tremble, Caramon smiled bleakly and reached out for her hand. Clasping it tightly, he said in a voice that was terrible in its calm, "Lady Crysania, if all we have to face are rats and spiders, we may count ourselves lucky."

She remembered the shout of sheer terror that had awakened her. Yet he hadn't been able to see! Swiftly, she glanced about. "What is it? You must have heard or sensed something, yet—"

"Sensed," Caramon repeated softly. "Yes, I *sensed* it. There are *things* in this place, Crysania. Horrible things. I can feel them watching us! I can feel their hatred. Wherever we are, we have intruded upon them. Can't you feel it, too?"

Crysania stared into the darkness. So it *had* been looking back at her. Now that Caramon spoke of it,

she could sense something out there. Or, as Caramon said, some *things*!

The longer she looked and concentrated upon them, the more real they became. Although she could not see them, she knew they waited, just beyond the circle of light cast by the medallion. Their hatred was strong, as Caramon had said, and, what was worse, she felt their evil flow chillingly around her. It was like . . . like . . .

Crysania caught her breath.

"What?" Caramon cried, starting up.

"Sst," she hissed, gripping his hand tightly. "Nothing. It's just—I know where we are!" she said in hushed tones.

He did not answer but turned his sightless eyes toward her.

"The Tower of High Sorcery at Palanthas!" she whispered.

"Where Raistlin lives?" Caramon looked relieved.

"Yes . . . no," Crysania shrugged helplessly. "It's the same room I was in—his study—but it doesn't look the same. It looks like no one's lived here for maybe a hundred years or more and—Caramon! That's it! He said he was taking me to 'a place and time when there were no clerics!' That must be after the Cataclysm and before the war. Before—"

"Before he returned to claim this Tower as his own,"† Caramon said grimly. "And that means the curse is still upon the Tower, Lady Crysania. That means we are in the one place in Krynn where evil reigns supreme. The one place more feared than any other upon the face of the world. The one place where no mortal dare tread, guarded by the Shoikan Grove and the gods know what else! He has brought us here! We have materialized within its heart!"

Raistlin claimed the Tower in the very last chapter, "The Homecoming," in Dragons of Spring Dawning.

Crysania suddenly saw pale faces appear outside the circle of light, as if summoned by Caramon's voice. Disembodied heads, staring at her with eyes long ago closed in dark and dismal death, they floated in the cold air, their mouths opening wide in anticipation of warm, living blood.

"Caramon, I can see them!" Crysania choked, shrinking close to the big man. "I can see their faces!"

"I felt their hands on me," Caramon said. Shivering convulsively, feeling her shivering as well, he put his arm about her, drawing her close to him.

"They attacked me. Their touch froze my skin. That was when you heard me yell."

"But why didn't I see them before? What keeps them from attacking now?"

"You, Lady Crysania," Caramon said softly. "You are a cleric of Paladine. These are creatures spawned of evil, created by the curse. They do not have the power to harm you."

Crysania looked at the medallion in her hands. The light welled forth still, but—even as she stared at it—it seemed to dim. Guiltily, she remembered the elven cleric, Loralon. She remembered her refusal to accompany him. His words rang in her mind: *You will see only when you are blinded by the darkness. . . .*

"I am a cleric, true," she said softly, trying to keep the despair from her voice, "but my faith is . . . imperfect. These things sense my doubts, my weakness. Perhaps a cleric as strong as Elistan would have the power to fight them.† I don't think I do." The glow dimmed further. "My light is failing, Caramon," she said, after a moment. Looking up, she could see the pallid faces eagerly drift nearer, and she shrank closer to him. "What can we do?"

"What *can* we do! I have no weapon! I can't see!" Caramon cried out in agony, clenching his fist.

"Hush!" Crysania ordered, grasping his arm, her eyes on the shimmering figures. "They seem to grow stronger when you talk like that! Perhaps they feed off fear. Those in the Shoikan Grove do, so Dalamar told me."

Caramon drew a deep breath. His body glistened with sweat, and he began to shake violently.

"We've got to try to wake up Raistlin," Crysania said.

"No good!" Caramon whispered through chattering teeth. "I know—"

"We have to try!" Crysania said firmly, though she shuddered at the thought of walking even a few feet under that terrible scrutiny.

"Be careful, move slowly," Caramon advised, letting her go.

Holding the medallion high, her eyes on the eyes of the darkness, Crysania crept over to Raistlin. She placed one hand on the mage's thin, black-robed shoulder. "Raistlin!" she said as loudly as she dared, shaking him. "Raistlin!"

I believe that faith is a power in this world. Crysania sees evidence of this now in her own story. —TRH

There was no response. She might as well have tried to rouse a corpse. Thinking of that, she glanced out at the waiting figures. Would they kill *him*? she wondered. After all, he didn't exist in this time. The "master of past and present" had not yet returned to claim his property—this Tower.

Or had he?

Crysania called to the mage again and, as she did so, she kept her eyes on the undead, who were moving nearer as her light grew weaker.

"Fistandantilus!" she said to Raistlin.

"Yes!" Caramon cried, hearing her and understanding. "They recognize *that* name. What's happening? I feel a change. . . ."

"They've stopped!" Crysania said breathlessly. "They're looking at him now."

"Get back!"† Caramon ordered, rising to a half-crouch. "Keep away from him. Get that light away from him! Let them see him as he exists in *their* darkness!"†

"No!" Crysania retorted angrily. "You're mad! Once the light's gone, they'll devour him—"

"It's our only chance!"

Lunging for Crysania blindly, Caramon caught her off guard. He grabbed her in his strong arms and yanked her away from Raistlin, hurling her to the floor. Then he fell across her smashing the breath from her body.

"Caramon!" She gasped for air. "They'll kill him! No—" Frantically, Crysania struggled against the big warrior, but he held her pinned beneath him.

The medallion was still clutched in her fingers. Its light glowed weaker and weaker. Twisting her body, she saw Raistlin, lying in darkness now, outside the circle of her light.

"Raistlin!" she screamed. "No! Let me up, Caramon! They're going to him. . . ."

But Caramon held her all the more firmly, pressing her down against the cold floor. His face was anguished, yet grim and determined, his sightless eyes staring down at her. His flesh was cold against her own, his muscles tense and knotted.

She would cast another spell on him! The words were on her lips when a shrill cry of pain pierced the darkness.

"Paladine, help me!" Crysania prayed. . . .

Note that here we see Caramon's knowledge and wisdom coming to the fore.
—MW

The creatures here perceive the world in their own way. This darkness is not just an absence of light but the condition of their souls.
—TRH

Nothing happened.

Weakly, she tried one more time to escape Caramon, but it was hopeless and she knew it. And now, apparently, even her god had abandoned her. Crying out in frustration, cursing Caramon, she could only watch.

The pale, shimmering figures surrounded Raistlin now. She could see him only by the light of the horrid aura their decaying bodies cast. Her throat ached and a low moan escaped her lips as one of the ghastly creatures raised its cold hands and laid them upon his body.

Raistlin screamed. Beneath the black robes, his body jerked in spasms of agony.

Caramon, too, heard his brother's cry. Crysania could see it reflected in his deathly, pale face. "Let me up!" she pleaded. But, though cold sweat beaded his forehead, he shook his head resolutely, holding her hands tightly.

Raistlin screamed again. Caramon shuddered, and Crysania felt his muscles grow flaccid. Dropping the medallion, she freed her arms to strike at him with her clenched fists. But as she did so, the medallion's light vanished, plunging them both into complete darkness. Caramon's body was suddenly wrenched off hers. His hoarse, agonized scream mingled with the screams of his brother.

Dizzily, her heart racing in terror, Crysania struggled to sit up, her hand pawing the floor frantically for the medallion.

A face came near hers. She glanced up quickly from her search, thinking it was Caramon. . . .

It wasn't. A disembodied head floated near her.

"No!" she whispered, unable to move, feeling life drain from her hands, her body, her very heart. Fleshless hands grasped her arms, drawing her near; bloodless lips gaped, eager for warmth.

"Paladi—" Crysania tried to pray, but she felt her soul being sucked from her body by the creature's deadly touch.

Then she heard, dimly and far away, a weak voice chanting words of magic. Light exploded around her. The head so near her own vanished with a shriek the fleshless hands loosed their grasp. There was an acrid smell of sulfur.

"*Shirak.*" The explosive light was gone. A soft glow lit the room.

Crysania sat up. "Raistlin!" she whispered thankfully. Staggering to her hands and knees, she crawled forward across the blackened, blasted floor to reach the mage, who lay on his back, breathing heavily. One hand rested on the Staff of Magius. Light radiated from the crystal ball clutched in the golden dragon's claw atop the staff.

"Raistlin! Are you all right?"

Kneeling beside him, she looked into his thin, pale face as he opened his eyes. Wearily, he nodded. Then, reaching up, he drew her down to him. Embracing her, he stroked her soft, black hair. She could feel his heart beat. The strange warmth of his body drove away the chill.

"Don't be afraid!" he whispered soothingly, feeling her tremble. "They will not harm us. They have seen me and recognized me. They didn't hurt you?"

She could not speak but only shook her head. He sighed again. Crysania, her eyes closed, lay in his embrace, lost in comfort.

Then, as his hand went to her hair once more, she felt his body tense. Almost angrily, he grasped her shoulders and pushed her away from him.

"Tell me what happened," he ordered in a weak voice.

"I woke up here—" Crysania faltered. The horror of her experience and the memory of Raistlin's warm touch confused and unnerved her. Seeing his eyes grow cold and impatient, however, she made herself continue, keeping her voice steady. "I heard Caramon shout—"

Raistlin's eyes opened wide. "My brother?" he said, startled. "So the spell brought him, too. I'm amazed I am still alive. Where is he?" Lifting his head weakly, he saw his brother, lying unconscious on the floor. "What's the matter with him?"

"I—I cast a spell. He's blind," Crysania said, flushing. "I didn't mean to, it was when he was trying to ki-kill you—in Istar, right before the Cataclysm—"

"You blinded him! Paladine . . . blinded *him*!" Raistlin laughed. The sound reverberated off the cold stones, and Crysania cringed, feeling a chill of horror. But the laughter caught in Raistlin's throat. The mage began to choke and gag, gasping for breath.

Crysania watched, helpless, until the spasm passed and Raistlin lay quietly once more. "Go on," he whispered irritably.

"I heard him yell, but I couldn't see in the darkness. The medallion gave me light, though, and I found him and I—I knew he was blind. I found you, too. You were unconscious. We couldn't wake you. Caramon told me to describe where we were and then I saw"—she shuddered—"I saw those . . . those horrible—"

"Continue," Raistlin said.

Crysania drew a deep breath, "Then the light from the medallion began to fail—"

Raistlin nodded.

"—and those . . . things came toward us. I called out to you, using the name Fistandantilus. That made them pause. Then"—Crysania's voice lost its fear and was edged with anger—"your brother grabbed me and threw me down on the floor, shouting something about 'let them see him as he exists in their own darkness!' When Paladine's light no longer touched you, those creature—" She shuddered and covered her face with her hands, still hearing Raistlin's terrible scream echoing in her mind.

"My brother said that?" Raistlin asked softly after a moment.

Crysania moved her hands to look at him, puzzled at his tone of mingled admiration and astonishment. "Yes," she said coldly after a moment. "Why?"

"He saved our lives," Raistlin remarked, his voice once more caustic. "The great dolt actually had a good idea. Perhaps you should leave him blind—it aids his thinking."

Raistlin tried to laugh, but it turned to a cough that nearly choked him instead. Crysania started toward him to help him, but he halted her with a fierce look, even as his body twisted in pain. Rolling to his side, he retched.

He fell back weakly, his lips stained with blood, his hands twitching. His breathing was shallow and too fast. Occasionally a coughing spasm wrenched his body.

Crysania stared at him helplessly.

"You told me once that the gods could not heal this malady. But you're dying, Raistlin! Isn't there

something I can do?" she asked softly, not daring to touch him.

He nodded, but for a minute could neither speak nor move. Finally, with an obvious effort, he lifted a trembling hand from the chill floor and motioned Crysania near. She bent over him. Reaching up, he touched her cheek, drawing her face close to his. His breath was warm against her skin.

"Water!" He gasped inaudibly. She could understand him only by reading the movements of his blood-caked lips. "A potion . . . will help. . . ." Feebly, his hand moved to a pocket in his robes. "And . . . and warmth, fire! I . . . have not . . . the strength. . . ."

Crysania nodded, to show she understood.

"Caramon?" His lips formed the words.

"Those—those things attacked him," she said, glancing over at the big warrior's motionless body. "I'm not sure if he's still alive. . . ."

"We need him! You . . . must . . . heal him!" He could not continue but lay panting for air, his eyes closed.

Crysania swallowed, shivering. "Are—are you sure?" she asked hesitantly. "He tried to murder you—"

Raistlin smiled, then shook his head. The black hood rustled gently at the motion. Opening his eyes, he looked up at Crysania and she could see deep within their brown depths. The flame within the mage burned low, giving the eyes a soft warmth much different from the raging fire she had seen before.

"Crysania . . ." he breathed, "I . . . am going . . . to lose consciousness. . . . You . . . will . . . be alone . . . in this place of darkness. . . . My brother . . . can help. . . . Warmth . . ." His eyes closed, but his grasp on Crysania's hand tightened, as though endeavoring to use her lifeforce to cling to reality. With a violent struggle, he opened his eyes again to look directly into hers. "Don't leave this room!" he mouthed. His eyes rolled back in his head.

You will be alone! Crysania glanced around fearfully, feeling suffocated with terror. Water! Warmth! How could she manage? She couldn't! Not in this chamber of evil!

"Raistlin!" she begged, grasping his frail hand in both her hands and resting her cheek against it.

"Raistlin, please don't leave me!" she whispered, cringing at the touch of his cold flesh. "I can't do what you ask! I haven't the power! I can't create water out of dust—"

Raistlin's eyes opened. They were nearly as dark as the room in which he lay. Moving his hand, the hand she held, he traced a line from her eyes down her cheek. Then the hand went limp, his head lolled to one side.

Crysania raised her own hand to her skin in confusion, wondering what he meant by such a strange gesture? It had not been a caress. He was trying to tell her something, that much had been apparent by his insistent gaze. But what? Her skin burned at his touch . . . bringing back memories. . . .

And then she knew.

I can't create water out of dust. . . .

"My tears!" she murmured.

Many writers in many different fields of writing find the Second Act to be the most difficult to write. In trilogies, the second book often feels the weakest of the three. My experience, however, has been different. I have often liked our second books best of the three. —TRH

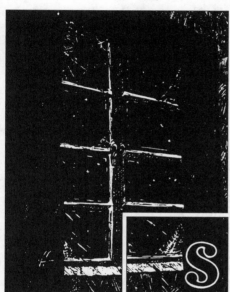

CHAPTER
2

itting alone in
the chill chamber, kneeling beside Raistlin's still
body, seeing Caramon lying nearby, pale and lifeless, Crysania suddenly envied both of them
fiercely. How easy it would be, she thought, to slip
into unconsciousness and let the darkness take me!
The evil of the place—which had seemingly fled at
the sound of Raistlin's voice—was returning. She
could feel it on her neck like a cold draft. Eyes stared
at her from the shadows, eyes that were kept back,
apparently, only by the light of the Staff of Magius,†
which still gleamed. Even unconscious, Raistlin's
hand rested on it.

Crysania lay the archmage's other hand, the hand
she held, gently across his chest. Then she sat back, her
lips pressed tightly together, swallowing her tears.

"He's depending on me," she said to herself, talking to dispel the sounds of whispering she heard

*"Magius was a wizard of
legend who aided Huma in
his quests. His staff was
one of the most revered
artifacts, not for its
powers, but in honor of the
mage who used it. Indeed,
compared to other devices,
it seems to be of little use.
But many have suspected
that there was more magic
to the staff than met the
eye. In later years, the staff
was given to Raistlin
Majere at the completion
of his tests."*
[DRAGONLANCE
Adventures, *by Tracy
Hickman and Margaret
Weis, TSR, Inc., 1987,
p. 97.]*

451

around her. "In his weakness, he is relying on my strength. All my life," she continued, wiping tears from her eyes and watching the water gleam on her fingers in the staff's light, "I have prided myself on my strength. Yet, until now, I never knew what true strength was." Her eyes went to Raistlin. "Now, I see it in him! I will not let him down!

"Warmth," she said, shivering so much that she could barely stand. "He needs warmth. We all do." She sighed helplessly. "Yet how am I to do that! If we were in Ice Wall Castle, my prayers alone would be enough to keep us warm. Paladine would aid us. But this chill is not the chill of ice or snow.

"It is deeper than that—freezing the spirit more than the blood. Here, in this place of evil, my faith might sustain me, but it will never warm us!"

Thinking of this and glancing around the room dimly seen by the light of the staff, Crysania saw the shadowy forms of tattered curtains hanging from the windows. Made of heavy velvet, they were large enough to cover all of them. Her spirits rose, but sank almost instantly as she realized they were far across the room. Barely visible within the writhing darkness, the windows were outside of the staff's circle of bright light.

"I'll have to walk over there," she said to herself, "in the shadows!" Her heart almost failed her, her strength ebbed. "I will ask Paladine's help." But, as she spoke, her gaze went to the medallion lying cold and dark on the floor.

Bending down to pick it up, she hesitated, fearing for a moment to touch it, remembering in sorrow how its light had died at the coming of the evil.

Once again, she thought of Loralon, the great elven cleric who had come to take her away before the Cataclysm. She had refused, choosing instead to risk her life, to hear the words of the Kingpriest—the words that called down the wrath of the gods. Was Paladine angry? Had he abandoned *her* in his anger, as many believed he had abandoned all of Krynn following the terrible destruction of Istar? Or was his divine guidance simply unable to penetrate the chill layers of evil that shrouded the accursed Tower of High Sorcery?

Confused and frightened, Crysania lifted the medallion. It did not glow. It did nothing. The metal

felt cold in her hand. Standing in the center of the room, holding the medallion, her teeth chattering, she willed herself to walk to a window.

"If I don't," she muttered through stiff lips, "I'll die of the cold.† We'll all die," she added, her gaze going back to the brothers. Raistlin wore his black velvet robes, but she remembered the icy feel of his hand in hers. Caramon was still dressed as he had been for the gladiator games in little more than golden armor and a loincloth.

Lifting her chin, Crysania cast a defiant glance at the unseen, whispering things that lurked around her, then she walked steadfastly out of the circle of magical light shed by Raistlin's staff.

Almost instantly, the darkness came alive!† The whispers grew louder and, in horror, she realized she could understand the words!

> How† loud your heart is calling, love,
> How close the darkness at your breast,
> How hectic are the rivers, love,
> Drawn through your dying wrist.
>
> And love, what heat your frail skin hides,
> As pure as salt, as sweet as death,
> And in the dark the red moon rides
> The foxfire of your breath.

There was a touch of chill fingers on her skin. Crysania started in terror and shrank back, only to see nothing there! Nearly sick with fear and the horror of the gruesome love song of the dead, she could not move for a long moment.

"No!" she said angrily. "I *will* go on! These creatures of evil shall not stop me! I am a cleric of Paladine! Even if my god has abandoned me, I will not abandon my faith!"†

Raising her head, Crysania thrust out her hand as though she would actually part the darkness like a curtain. Then she continued to walk to the window. The hiss of whispers sounded around her, she heard eerie laughter, but nothing harmed her, nothing touched her. Finally, after a journey that seemed miles long, she reached the windows.

Clinging to the curtains, shaking, her legs weak, she drew them aside and looked out, hoping to see

The chill that Crysania is feeling is not a condition of actual temperature but rather the chill of the grave and the dead. It is a cold that goes directly to our bones. —TRH

The ghostly visages are reminiscent of the river of the dead in War of Souls. These images resonate as knowledge beyond mortality is confronted by all-too-mortal beings. —TRH

This song was supposed to be vampiric, and I think it is—or at least blood-obsessed in an erotic, creepy kind of way. Man, I must have been reading a lot of Yeats at the time— the ballad form, the slant rhyme of "breast" and "wrist." Also, the line "Drawn through your dying wrist" is an attempt to do the kind of thing Yeats does so well, reversing the first metrical foot so that the accent hits your ear at the beginning of the line, brings you up short, and makes your eye and your thoughts stagger a little.

I know I'm not Yeats. Not even in the same league. But then again, neither are any of you. —Michael Williams

Crysania's comment on faith here indicates that her faith is, in reality, based on

(contiued from last page)

her own arrogance. She believes in her heart that she is better than even Paladine, who has abandoned his people, yet even though he has hurt her, she will not abandon him. Thus she, like Raistlin and the Kingpriest, sees herself as superior to the gods. —MW

A central theme in the DRAGONLANCE saga has been that the perceived "abandonment" of the world by the gods is really just a matter of perspective, that it was actually man who abandoned the gods. Crysania here says that Paladine has abandoned her, but it is she who is wandering from her god, having not followed the admonition of his clerics to leave with them before the Cataclysm. Crysania here is trying to convince herself that she must hold on to her beliefs even if she feels the reason for those beliefs is no longer watching over her. —TRH

the lights of the city of Palanthas to comfort her. There are other living beings out there, she said to herself, pressing her face against the glass. I'll see the lights—

But the prophecy had not yet been fulfilled. Raistlin—as master of the past and the present—had not yet returned with power to claim the Tower as would happen in the future. And so the Tower remained cloaked in impenetrable darkness, as though a perpetual black fog hung about it. If the lights of the beautiful city of Palanthas glowed, she could not see them.

With a bleak sigh, Crysania grasped hold of the cloth and yanked. The rotting fabric gave way almost instantly, nearly burying her in a shroud of velvet brocade as the curtains tumbled down around her. Thankfully, she wrapped the heavy material around her shoulders like a cloak, huddling gratefully in its warmth.

Clumsily tearing down another curtain, she dragged it back across the dark room, hearing it scrape against the floor as it collected broken pieces of furniture on its way.

The staff's magical light gleamed, guiding her through the darkness. Reaching it finally, she collapsed upon the floor, shaking with exhaustion and the reaction to her terror.

She hadn't realized until now how tired she was. She had not slept in nights, ever since the storm began in Istar. Now that she was warmer, the thought of wrapping up in the curtain and slipping into oblivion was irresistibly tempting.

"Stop it!" she ordered herself. Forcing herself to stand up, she dragged the curtain over to Caramon and knelt beside him. She covered him with the heavy fabric, pulling it up over his broad shoulders. His chest was still, he was barely breathing. Placing her cold hand on his neck, she felt for the lifebeat. It was slow and irregular. And then she saw marks upon his neck, dead white marks—as of fleshless lips.

The disembodied head floated in Crysania's memory. Shuddering, she banished it from her thoughts and, wrapped in the curtain, placed her hands upon Caramon's forehead.

"Paladine," she prayed softly, "if you have not turned from† your cleric in anger, if you will only try

to understand that what she does she does to honor *you*, if you can part this terrible darkness long enough to grant this one prayer—heal this man! If his destiny has *not* been fulfilled, if there is still something more he must do, grant him health. If not, then gather his soul gently to your arms, Paladine, that he may dwell eternally—"

Crysania could not go on. Her strength gave out. Weary, drained by terror and her own internal struggles, lost and alone in the vast darkness, she let her head sink into her hands and began to cry the bitter sobs of one who sees no hope.

And then she felt a hand touch hers. She started in terror, but this hand was strong and warm. "There now, Tika," said a deep, sleepy sounding voice. "It'll be all right. Don't cry."

Lifting her tear-stained face, Crysania saw Caramon's chest rise and fall with deep breaths. His face lost its deathly pallor, the white marks on his neck faded. Patting her hand soothingly, he smiled.

"It's jus' a bad dream, Tika," he mumbled. "Be all gone . . . by morning. . . ."

Gathering the curtain up around his neck, snuggling in its warmth, Caramon gave a great, gaping yawn and rolled over onto his side to drift into a deep, peaceful sleep.

Too tired and numb even to offer thanks, Crysania could only sit and watch the big man sleep for a moment. Then a sound caught her ear—the sound of water dripping! Turning, she saw—for the first time—a glass beaker resting on the edge of the desk. The beaker's long neck was broken and it lay upon its side, its mouth hanging over the edge. It had been empty a long time apparently, its contents spilled one hundred years before. But now it shone with a clear liquid† that dripped upon the floor, gently, one drop at a time, each drop sparkling in the light of the staff.

Reaching out her hand, Crysania caught some of the drops in her palm, then lifted her hand hesitantly to her lips.

"Water!" she breathed.

The taste was faintly bitter, almost salty, but it seemed to her the most delicious water she had ever drunk. Forcing her aching body to move, she poured more water into her hand, gulping thirstily. Standing

A miracle—just enough of a miracle for Crysania to go on and no more. The greatest miracles in our lives, I believe, are those that may seem the smallest to others. —TRH

the beaker upright on the desk, she saw the water level rise again, replacing what she had taken.

Now she could thank Paladine with words that rose from the very depths of her being, so deep that she could not speak them. Her fear of the darkness and the creatures in it vanished. Her god had not abandoned her—he was with her still, even though—perhaps—she had disappointed him.

Her fears at ease, she took a final look at Caramon. Seeing him sleeping peacefully, the lines of pain smoothed from his face, she turned from him and walked over to where his brother lay huddled in his robes, his lips blue with cold.

Lying down beside the mage, knowing that the heat of their bodies would warm them both, Crysaniat wrapped the curtain over them and, resting her head on Raistlin's shoulder, she closed her eyes and let the darkness enfold her.

Crysania was a very interesting character to write. In order to have a foil for Raistlin, we wanted to give him someone who would be his equal in ambition and with a hunger for power. Crysania is first portrayed as Raistlin's mirror image, but in her own way, her ambition for power is as overweening and as selfish as his. He knows her flaws and he very cleverly uses them against her from the beginning. —MW

Chapter 3

"She called him 'Raistlin!'"

"But then—'Fistandantilus!'"

"How can we be certain? This is not right!† He came
not through the Grove, as was foretold. He came not with
power! And these others? He was supposed to come alone!"

"Yet sense his magic! I dare not defy him. . . ."

"Not even for such rich reward?"

"The blood smell has driven you mad! If it is he, and he
discovers you have feasted on his chosen, he will send you
back to the everlasting darkness where you will dream
always of warm blood and never taste it!"

"And if it is not, and we fail in our duties to guard this
place, then She will come in her wrath and make that fate
seem pleasant!"

Silence. Then,

"There is a way we can make certain. . . ."

"It is dangerous. He is weak, we might kill him."

*Here is the first indication
to us that the flow of time
has been diverted from its
previous course. —TRH*

457

"We must know! Better for him to die than for us to fail in our duty to Her Dark Majesty."

"Yes. . . . His death could be explained. His life . . . maybe not."

Cold, searing pain penetrated the layers of unconsciousness like slivers of ice piercing his brain. Raistlin struggled in their grasp, fighting through the fog of sickness and exhaustion to return for one brief moment to conscious awareness. Opening his eyes, fear nearly suffocated him as he saw two pallid heads floating above him, staring at him with eyes of vast darkness. Their hands were on his chest—it was the touch of those icy fingers that tore through his soul.

Looking into those eyes, the mage knew what they sought and sudden terror seized him. "No," he spoke without breath, "I will not live that again!"

"You will. We must know!" was all they said.

Anger at this outrage gripped Raistlin. Snarling a bitter curse, he tried to raise his arms from the floor to wrest the ghostly hands from their deadly grip. But it was useless. His muscles refused to respond, a finger twitched, nothing more.

Fury and pain and bitter frustration made him shriek, but it was a sound no one heard—not even himself. The hands tightened their grasp, the pain stabbed him, and he sank—not into darkness—but into remembrance.

There were no windows in the Learning Room where the seven apprentice magic-users worked that morning. No sunlight was admitted, nor was the light of the two moons—silver and red. As for the third moon, the black moon,† its presence could be felt here as elsewhere on Krynn without being seen.

The room was lit by thick beeswax candles that stood in silver candleholders on the table. The candles could thus be easily picked up and carried about to suit the convenience of the apprentices as they went about their studies.

This was the only room in the great castle of Fistandantilus lit by candles. In all others, glass globes with continual light spells cast upon them hovered in the air, shedding magical radiance to lighten the gloom that was perpetual in this dark fortress. The globes were not used in the Learning Room,

Why put three moons in Krynn's skies? Perhaps it was the influence of AD&D on us, but Margaret and I have always tried to take fantasy literature in new directions. Krynn is a world wholly distinct from Earth, unlike Tolkien's Middle-earth. Time travel itself was a science-fiction notion we applied to fantasy. We have even written fantasies taking place in the far future (The Deathgate Cycle)! —TRH

however, for one very good reason—if brought into this room, their light would instantly fail—a Dispel Magic† spell was in constant effect here. Thus the need for candles and the need to keep out any influence that might be gleaned from the sun or the two light-shedding moons.

Six of the apprentices sat near each other at one table, some talking together, a few studying in silence. The seventh sat apart, at a table far across the room. Occasionally one of the six would raise his head and cast an uneasy glance at the one who sat apart, then lower his head quickly, for, no matter who looked or at what time, the seventh always seemed to be staring back at them.

The seventh found this amusing, and he indulged in a bitter smile. Raistlin had not found much to smile about during these months he had been living in the castle of Fistandantilus. It had not been an easy time for him. Oh, it had been simple enough to maintain the deception, keeping Fistandantilus from guessing his true identity, concealing his true powers, making it seem as if he were simply one of this group of fools working to gain the favor of the great wizard and thus become his apprentice.

Deception was life's blood to Raistlin. He even enjoyed his little games of oneupsmanship with the apprentices, always doing things just a little bit better, always keeping them nervous, offguard. He enjoyed his game with Fistandantilus, too. He could sense the archmage watching him. He knew what the great wizard was thinking—who *is* this apprentice? Where does he get the power that the archmage could feel burn within the young man but could not define.

Sometimes Raistlin thought he could detect Fistandantilus studying his face, as though thinking it looked familiar. . . .

No, Raistlin enjoyed the game. But it was totally unexpected that he come upon something he had *not* enjoyed. And that was to be forcibly reminded of the most unhappy time of his life—his old school days.

The Sly One†—that had been his nickname among the apprentices at his old Master's school. Never liked,† never trusted, feared even by his own Master, Raistlin spent a lonely, embittered youth. The only person who ever cared for him had been his twin

Dispel Magic: *When a wizard casts this spell, it has a chance to neutralize or negate magic it comes in contact with. [2nd Edition* ADVANCED DUNGEONS & DRAGONS *Player's Handbook, by David "Zeb" Cook, TSR, 1997, p. 191.]*

See The Soulforge, *Book II, Chapter 1, by Margaret Weis.*

So many of us identify with Raistlin for this very reason: we were all on the outside of the group to which we longed to belong. —TRH

459

brother, Caramon, and *his* love was so patronizing and smothering that Raistlin often found the hatred of his classmates easier to accept.

And now, even though he despised these idiots seeking to please a Master who would—in the end—only murder the one chosen, even though he enjoyed fooling them and taunting them, Raistlin still felt a pang sometimes, in the loneliness of the night, when he heard them together, laughing. . . .

Angrily, he reminded himself that this was all beneath his concern. He had a greater goal to achieve. He had to concentrate, conserve his strength. For today was the day, the day Fistandantilus would choose his apprentice.

You six will leave, Raistlin thought to himself. You will leave hating and despising me, and none of you will ever know that one of you owes me his life!

The door to the Learning Room opened with a creak, sending a jolt of alarm through the six black-robed figures sitting at the table. Raistlin, watching them with a twisted smile, saw the same sneering smile reflected on the wizened, gray face of the man who stood in the doorway.

The wizard's glittering gaze went to each of the six in turn, causing each to pale and lower his hooded head while hands toyed with spell components or clenched in nervousness.

Finally, Fistandantilus turned his black eyes to the seventh apprentice, who sat apart. Raistlin met his gaze without flinching, his twisted smile twisted further—into mockery. Fistandantilus's brows contracted. In swift anger, he slammed the door shut. The six apprentices started at the booming sound that shattered the silence.

The bloodstone is my birthstone (March), and it has always fascinated me, mainly because it is the ugliest of all the birthstones, in my opinion. I studied it to find out why it was so revered and discovered that it was popularly believed to be able to staunch bleeding and that it could draw out impurities from the blood. I own just such a bloodstone pendant as is described.
—MW

The wizard walked to the front of the Learning Room, his steps slow and faltering. He leaned upon a staff and his old bones creaked as he lowered himself into a chair. The wizard's gaze went once more to the six apprentices seated before him and, as he looked at them—at their youthful, healthy bodies—one of Fistandantilus's withered hands raised to caress a pendant he wore on a long, heavy chain around his neck. It was an odd-looking pendant—a single, oval bloodstone† set in plain silver.

Often the apprentices discussed this pendant among themselves, wondering what it did. It was

the only ornamentation Fistandantilus ever wore, and all knew it must be highly valuable. Even the lowest level apprentice could sense the powerful spells of protection and warding laid upon it, guarding it from every form of magic. What did it do? they whispered, and their speculations ranged from drawing beings from the celestial† planes to communicating with Her Dark Majesty herself.

One of their number, of course, could have told them. Raistlin knew what it did. But he kept his knowledge to himself.

Fistandantilus's gnarled and trembling hand closed over the bloodstone eagerly, as his hungry gaze went from one apprentice to the other. Raistlin could have sworn the wizard licked his lips, and the young mage felt a moment of sudden fear.

What if I fail? he asked himself, shuddering. He is powerful! The most powerful wizard who ever lived! Am I strong enough? What if—

"Begin the test," Fistandantilus said in a cracked voice, his gaze going to the first of the six.

Firmly, Raistlin banished his fears. This was what he had worked a lifetime to attain. If he failed, he would die. He had faced death before. In fact, it would be like meeting an old friend. . . .

One by one, the young mages rose from their places, opened their spellbooks, and recited their spells. If the Dispel Magic had not been laid upon the Learning Room, it would have been filled with wonderful sights. Fireballs would have exploded within its walls, incinerating all who were within range; phantom dragons would have breathed illusory fire; dread beings would have been dragged shrieking from other planes of existence. But, as it was, the room remained in candlelit calm, silent except for the chantings of the spellcasters and the rustling of the leaves of the spellbooks.

One by one, each mage completed his test, then resumed his seat. All performed remarkably well. This was not unexpected. Fistandantilus permitted only seven of the most skilled of the young male magic-users who had already passed the grueling Test at the Tower of High Sorcery to study further with him. Out of that number, he would choose one to be his assistant.

So they supposed.

The concept of the planes came, no doubt, from our AD&D roots. However, I have never much cared for the concept of "shared universes" or that all worlds published by TSR were somehow linked into some great cosmic reality. I have always viewed the universe of DRAGONLANCE as unique and separate. I have always considered "migration" from one world to another—from Krynn to Ravenloft, for example—to be the equivalent of one of those "special" television episodes where the crew from STAR TREK appears on GUNSMOKE. It may be sound like a good idea but ends up being unsettling at best. I prefer to keep my universes separate—but that is strictly my personal opinion. —TRH

The archmage's hand touched the bloodstone. His gaze went to Raistlin. "Your turn, mage," he said. There was a flicker in the old eyes. The wrinkles on the wizard's forehead deepened slightly, as though trying to recall the young man's face.

Slowly, Raistlin rose to his feet, still smiling the bitter, cynical smile, as if this were all beneath him. Then, with a nonchalant shrug, he slammed shut his spellbook. The other six apprentices exchanged grim glances at this. Fistandantilus frowned, but there was a spark in his dark eyes.

Glibly, sneeringly, Raistlin began to recite the complicated spell from memory. The other apprentices stirred at this show of skill, glaring at him with hatred and undisguised envy. Fistandantilus watched, his frown changing to a look of hunger so malevolent that it nearly broke Raistlin's concentration.

Forcing himself to keep his mind firmly on his work, the young mage completed the spell, and—suddenly—the Learning Room was lit by a brilliant flare of multicolored light, its silence shattered by the sound of an explosion!

Fistandantilus started, the grin wiped off his face. The other apprentices gasped.

"How did you break the Dispel Magic spell?" Fistandantilus demanded angrily. "What strange power is this?"

In answer, Raistlin opened his hands. In his palms he held a ball of blue and green flame, blazing with such radiance that no one could look at it directly. Then, with that same, sneering smile, he clapped his hands. The flame vanished.

The Learning Room was silent once more, only now it was the silence of fear as Fistandantilus rose to his feet. His rage shimmering around him like a halo of flame, he advanced upon the seventh apprentice.

Raistlin did not shrink from that anger. He remained standing calmly, coolly watching the wizard's approach.

"How did you—" Fistandantilus's voice grated. Then his gaze fell upon the young mage's slender hands. With a vicious snarl, the wizard reached out and grasped Raistlin's wrist.

Raistlin gasped in pain, the archmage's touch was cold as the grave. But he made himself smile still, though he knew his grin must look like a death's head.

"Flash powder!" Fistandantilus jerked Raistlin forward, holding his hand under the candlelight so that all could see. "A common sleight-of-hand trick, fit only for street illusionists!"†

"Thus I earned my living," Raistlin said through teeth clenched against the pain. "I thought it suitable for use in such a collection of amateurs as you have gathered together, Great One."

Fistandantilus tightened his grip. Raistlin choked in agony, but he did not struggle or try to withdraw. Nor did he lower his gaze from that of his Master. Though his grip was painful, the wizard's face was interested, intrigued.

"So you consider yourself better than these?" Fistandantilus asked Raistlin in a soft, almost kindly voice, ignoring the angry mutterings of the apprentices.

Raistlin had to pause to gather the strength to speak through the haze of pain. "You know I am!"

Fistandantilus stared at him, his hand still grasping him by the wrist. Raistlin saw a sudden fear in the old man's eyes, a fear that was quickly quenched by that look of insatiable hunger. Fistandantilus loosed his hold on Raistlin's arm. The young mage could not repress a sigh of intense relief as he sank into his chair, rubbing his wrist. The mark of the archmage's hand could be seen upon it plainly—it had turned his skin icy white.

"Get out!" Fistandantilus snapped. The six mages rose, their black robes rustling about them. Raistlin rose, too. "You stay," the archmage said coldly.

Raistlin sat back down, still rubbing his injured wrist. Warmth and life were returning to it. As the other young mages filed out, Fistandantilus followed them to the door. Turning back, he faced his new apprentice.

"These others will soon be gone and we shall have the castle to ourselves. Meet me in the secret chambers far below when it is Darkwatch. I am conducting an experiment that will require your . . . assistance."

Raistlin watched in a kind of horrible fascination as the old wizard's hand went to the bloodstone, stroking it lovingly. For a moment, Raistlin could not answer. Then, he smiled sneeringly—only this time it was at himself, for his own fear.

"I will be there, Master," he said.

I always liked stage magic. It occurred to me that this would be a wonderful way for Raistlin to transition from early years in sleight-of-hand to real wizardry later in life—and to show his contempt here for the petty practices of his peers.
—TRH

Raistlin lay upon the stone slab in the laboratory located far beneath the archmage's castle. Not even his thick black velvet robes could keep out the chill, and Raistlin shivered uncontrollably. But whether it was from the cold, fear, or excitement, he could not tell.

He could not see Fistandantilus, but he could hear him—the whisper of his robes, the soft thud of the staff upon the floor, the turning of a page in the spellbook. Lying upon the slab, feigning to be helpless under the wizard's influence, Raistlin tensed. The moment fast approached.

As if in answer, Fistandantilus appeared in his line of vision, leaning over the young mage with that look of eager hunger, the bloodstone pendant swinging from the chain around his neck.

"Yes," said the wizard, "you are skilled. More skilled and more powerful than any young apprentice I have met in these many, many years."

"What will you do to me?" Raistlin asked hoarsely. The note of desperation in his voice was not entirely forced. He *must* know how the pendant worked.

"How can that matter?" Fistandantilus questioned coolly, laying his hand upon the young mage's chest.

"My . . . object in coming to you was to learn," Raistlin said, gritting his teeth and trying not to writhe at the loathsome touch. "I would learn, even to the last!"

"Commendable," Fistandantilus nodded, his eyes gazing into the darkness, his thoughts abstracted. Probably going over the spell in his mind, Raistlin thought to himself. "I am going to enjoy inhabiting a body and a mind so thirsty† for knowledge, as well as one that is innately skilled in the Art. Very well, I will explain. My last lesson, apprentice. Learn it well.

"You cannot know, young man, the horrors of growing old. How well I remember my first life and how well I remember the terrible feeling of anger and frustration I felt when I realized that I—the most powerful magic-user who had ever lived—was destined to be trapped in a weak and wretched body that was being consumed by age! My mind—my mind was sound! Indeed, I was stronger mentally

This scene shows us Raistlin's strength of will and his keen desire to learn as much as he can about his art, even when facing what might be a terrible death. He is not simply trying to trick Fistandantilus into revealing his plans, but he is truly intent on learning, as witnessed by his question about the words to the spell. —MW

than I had ever been in my life! But all this power, all this vast knowledge would be wasted—turned to dust! Devoured by worms!†

"I wore the Red Robes then—

"You start. Are you surprised? Taking the Red Robes was a conscious, cold-blooded decision, made after seeing how best I could gain. In neutrality,† one learns better, being able to draw from both ends of the spectrum and being beholden to neither. I went to Gilean, God of Neutrality, with my plea to be allowed to remain upon this plane and extend my knowledge. But, in this, the God of the Book could not help me. Humans were his creation, and it was because of my impatient human nature and the knowledge of the shortness of my life that I had pressed on with my studies. I was counseled to accept my fate."

Fistandantilus shrugged. "I see comprehension in your eyes, apprentice. In a way, I am sorry to destroy you. I think we could have developed a rare understanding. But, to make a long story short, I walked out into the darkness. Cursing the red moon, I asked that I be allowed to look upon the black. The Queen of Darkness heard my prayer and granted my request. Donning the Black Robes, I dedicated myself to her service and, in return, I was taken to her plane of existence. I have seen the future, I have lived the past. She gave me this pendant, so that I am able to choose a new body during my stay in this time. And, when I choose to cross the boundaries of time and enter the future, there is a body prepared and ready to accept my soul."

Raistlin could not repress a shudder at this. His lip curled in hatred. *His* was the body the wizard spoke of! Ready and waiting. . . .

But Fistandantilus did not notice. The wizard raised the bloodstone pendant, preparing to cast the spell.

Looking at the pendant as it glistened in the pale light cast by a globe in the center of the laboratory, Raistlin felt his heartbeat quicken. His hands clenched.

With an effort, his voice trembling with excitement that he hoped would be mistaken for terror, he whispered, "Tell me how it works! Tell me what will happen to me!"

"And the LORD God said, Behold, the man is become as one of us, to know good and evil: and now, lest he put forth his hand, and take also of the tree of life, and eat, and live for ever . . . "
[Genesis 3:22 KJV]

This is Fistandantilus's rationalization for the red robes. However, I believe he shows us in his actions that his choice was a false one and his reasoning flawed. There is no true neutrality. —TRH

Fistandantilus smiled, his hand slowly revolving the bloodstone above Raistlin's chest. "I will place this upon your breast, right over your heart. And, slowly, you will feel your lifeforce start to ebb from your body. The pain is, I believe, quite excruciating. But it will not last long, apprentice, if you do not struggle against it. Give in and you will quickly lose consciousness. From what I have observed, fighting only prolongs the agony."

"Are there no words to be spoken?" Raistlin asked, shivering.

"Of course," Fistandantilus replied coolly, his body bending down near Raistlin's, his eyes nearly on a level with the young mage's. Carefully, he placed the bloodstone on Raistlin's chest. "You are about to hear them. . . . They will be the last sounds you ever hear. . . ."

Raistlin felt his flesh crawl at the touch and for a moment could barely restrain himself from breaking away and fleeing. No, he told himself coldly, clenching his hands, digging his nails into the flesh so that the pain would distract his thoughts from fear, *I must hear the words!*

Quivering, he forced himself to lie there, but he could not refrain from closing his eyes, blotting out the sight of the evil, wizened face so near his own that he could smell the decaying breath. . . .

"That's right," said a soft voice, "relax. . . ." Fistandantilus began to chant.

Concentrating on the complex spell, the wizard closed his own eyes, swaying back and forth as he pressed the bloodstone pendant into Raistlin's flesh. Fistandantilus did not notice, therefore, that his words were being repeated, murmured feverishly by the intended victim. By the time he realized something was wrong, he had ended the reciting of the spell and was standing, waiting, for the first infusion of new life to warm his ancient bones.

There was nothing.

Alarmed, Fistandantilus opened his eyes. He stared in astonishment at the black-robed young mage lying on the cold stone slab, and then the wizard made a strange, inarticulate sound and staggered backward in a sudden fear he could not hide.

"I see you recognize me at last," said Raistlin, sitting up. One hand rested upon the stone slab,

but the other was in one of the secret pockets of his robes. "So much for the body waiting for you in the future."

Fistandantilus did not answer. His gaze darted to Raistlin's pocket, as though he would pierce through the fabric with his black eyes.

Quickly he regained his composure. "Did the great Par-Salian send you back here, little mage?" he asked derisively. But his gaze remained on the mage's pocket.

Raistlin shook his head as he slid off the stone slab. Keeping one hand in the pocket of his robes, he moved the other to draw back the black hood, allowing Fistandantilus to see his true face, not the illusion he had maintained for these past long months. "I came myself. I am Master of the Tower now."

"That's impossible," the wizard snarled.

Raistlin smiled, but there was no answering smile in his cold eyes, which kept Fistandantilus always in their mirrorlike gaze. "So you thought. But you made a mistake. You underestimated me. You wrenched part of my lifeforce from me during the Test, in return for protecting me from the drow.† You forced me to live a life of constant pain in a shattered body, doomed me to dependence on my brother. You taught me to use the dragon orb and kept me alive when I would have died at the Great Library† of Palanthas. During the War of the Lance, you helped me drive the Queen of Darkness back to the Abyss where she was no longer a threat to the world—or to you. Then, when you had gained enough strength in this time, you intended to return to the future and claim *my* body! *You* would have become *me*."

Raistlin saw Fistandantilus's eyes narrow, and the young mage tensed, his hand closing over the object he carried in his robes. But the wizard only said mildly, "That is all correct. What do you intend to do about it? Murder me?"

"No," said Raistlin softly, "*I* intend to become *you*!"

"Fool!" Fistandantilus laughed shrilly. Raising a withered hand, he held up the bloodstone pendant. "The only way you could do that is to use this on me! And it is protected against all forms of magic by charms the power of which you have no conception, little mage—"

The word "drow" does pop up occasionally in early DRAGONLANCE novels and game product, which is a continual source of confusion to new readers. In the DRAGONLANCE setting, the word "drow" is meant to refer elves who have been cast out from their societies. They are the "dark elf" exiles of the DRAGONLANCE setting, not the entirely separate race of drow that are found in the FORGOTTEN REALMS and GREYHAWK settings.

See Dragons of Spring Dawning, Book I, Chapter 5.

467

His voice died away to a whisper, strangled in sudden fear and shock as Raistlin removed his hand from his robe. In his palm lay the bloodstone pendant.

"Protected from all forms of magic," said the young mage, his grin like that of a skull's, "but not protected† against sleight-of-hand. Not protected against the skills of a common street illusionist. . . ."

Raistlin saw the wizard turn deathly pale. Fistandantilus's eyes went feverishly to the chain on his neck. Now that the illusion was revealed, he realized he held nothing in his hand.

A rending, cracking sound shattered the silence. The stone floor beneath Raistlin's feet heaved, sending the young mage stumbling to his knees. Rock blew apart as the foundation of the laboratory broke in half. Above the chaos rose Fistandantilus's voice, chanting a powerful spell of summoning.†

Recognizing it, Raistlin responded, clutching the bloodstone in his hand as he cast a spell of shielding† around his body to give himself time to work his magic. Crouched on the floor, he twisted around to see a figure burst through the foundation, its hideous shape and visage something seen only in insane dreams.

"Seize him, hold him!" Fistandantilus shrieked, pointing at Raistlin. The apparition surged across the crumbling floor toward the young mage and reached for him with its writhing coils.

Fear overwhelmed Raistlin as the creature from beyond† worked its own horrible magic on him. The shielding spell crumbled beneath the onslaught. The apparition would devour his soul and feast upon his flesh.

Control! Long hours of study, long-practiced strength and rigorous self-discipline brought the words of the spell Raistlin needed to his mind. Within moments, it was complete. As the young mage began to chant the words of banishment, he felt the ecstasy of his magic flow through his body, delivering him from the fear.

The apparition hesitated.

Fistandantilus, furious, ordered it on.

Raistlin ordered it to halt.

The apparition glared at each, its coils twisting, its very appearance shifting and shimmering in the

---

It is the unexpected, the unlooked-for, that always brings about our downfall. Fistandantilus looks here for the great magic he should counter and thus being misdirected fails to notice the simple switch.
—TRH

"Conjuration/ summoning *spells bring something to the caster from elsewhere. Conjuration normally produces matter or items from some other place. Summoning enables the caster to compel living creatures and powers to appear in his presence or to channel extraplanar energies through himself."* [2nd Edition ADVANCED DUNGEONS & DRAGONS Player's Handbook, *by David "Zeb" Cook, TSR, 1997, p. 107.]*

Shield: *When this spell is cast, an invisible barrier comes into being in front of the wizard. [2nd Edition* ADVANCED DUNGEONS & DRAGONS Player's Handbook, *by David "Zeb" Cook, TSR, 1997, p. 178.]*

Of course, this had to be a "creature from beyond" since we couldn't write the word "demon" under TSR guidelines. For that matter, we were not all that sure

what kind of creature was summoned in the first place! —TRH

gusty winds of its creation. Both mages held it in check, watching the other intently, waiting for the eye blink, the lip twitch, the spasmodic jerk of a finger that would prove fatal.

Neither moved, neither seemed likely to move. Raistlin's endurance was greater, but Fistandantilus's magic came from ancient sources; he could call upon unseen powers to support him.

Finally, it was the apparition itself who could no longer endure. Caught between two equal, conflicting powers, tugged and pulled in opposite directions, its magical being could be held together no longer. With a brilliant flash, it exploded.

The force hurled both mages backward, slamming them into the walls. A horrible smell filled the chamber, and broken glass fell like rain. The walls of the laboratory were blackened and charred. Here and there, small fires burned with bright, multicolored flames, casting a lurid glow over the site of the destruction.

Raistlin staggered swiftly to his feet, wiping blood from a cut on his forehead. His enemy was no less quick, both knowing weakness meant death. The two mages faced each other in the flickering light.

"So, it comes to this!" Fistandantilus said in his cracked and ancient voice. "You could have gone on, living a life of ease. I would have spared you the debilities, the indignities of old age. Why rush to your own destruction!"

"You know," Raistlin said softly, breathing heavily, his strength nearly spent.

Fistandantilus nodded slowly, his eyes on Raistlin. "As I said," he murmured softly, "it is a pity this must happen. We could have done much together, you and I. Now—"

"Life for one. Death for the other," Raistlin said. Reaching out his hand, he carefully laid the bloodstone pendant upon the cold slab. Then he heard the words of chanting and raised his voice in an answering chant himself.

The battle lasted long. The two guardians of the Tower who watched the sight they had conjured up from the memories of the black-robed mage lying within their grasp, were lost in confusion. They had,

up to this point, seen everything through Raistlin's vision. But so close now were the two magic-users that the Tower's guardians saw the battle through the eyes of *both* opponents.

Lightning crackled from fingertips, black-robed bodies twisted in pain, screams of agony and fury echoed amidst the crash of rock and timber.

Magical walls of fire thawed walls of ice, hot winds blew with the force of hurricanes. Storms of flame swept the hallways, apparitions sprang from the Abyss at the behest of their masters, elementals shook the very foundations of the castle. The great dark fortress of Fistandantilus began to crack, stones tumbling from the battlements.

And then, with a fearful shriek of rage and pain, one of the black-robed mages collapsed, blood flowing from his mouth.

Which was which? Who had fallen? The guardians sought frantically to tell, but it was impossible.

The other mage, nearly spent, rested a moment, then managed to drag himself across the floor. His trembling hand reached up to the top of the stone slab, groped about, then found and grasped the bloodstone pendant. With his last strength, the black-robed mage gripped the pendant and crawled back to kneel beside the still-living body of his victim.†

I am always asked which mage won this battle, Raistlin or Fistandantilus. The truth is that I don't know, and Raistlin would never know either. This, to me, is perhaps one of the most horrifying scenes in the entire series, because Raistlin can never know which person he is. In committing this murder, he has lost himself in the truest sense of the word.
—MW

The mage on the floor could not speak, but his eyes, as they gazed into the eyes of his murderer, cast a curse of such hideous aspect that the two guardians of the Tower felt even the chill of their tormented existence grow warm by comparison.

The black-robed mage holding the bloodstone hesitated. He was so close to his victim's mind that he could read the unspoken message of those eyes, and his soul shrank from what it saw. But then his lips tightened. Shaking his hooded head and giving a grim smile of triumph, he carefully and deliberately pressed the pendant down on the black-robed chest of his victim.

The body on the floor writhed in tormented agony, a shrill scream bubbled from his blood-frothed lips. Then, suddenly, the screams ceased. The mage's skin wrinkled and cracked like dry parchment, his eyes stared sightlessly into the darkness. He slowly withered away.

With a shuddering sigh, the other mage collapsed on top of the body of his victim, he himself weak, wounded, near death. But clutched in his hand was the bloodstone and flowing through his veins was new blood, giving him life that would—in time—fully restore him to health. In his mind was knowledge, memories of hundreds of years of power, spells, visions of wonders and terrors that spanned generations. But there, too, were memories of a twin brother, memories of a shattered body, of a prolonged, painful existence.

As two lives mingled within him, as hundreds of strange, conflicting memories surged through him, the mage reeled at the impact. Crouching beside the corpse of his rival, the black-robed mage who had been the victor stared at the bloodstone in his hand. Then he whispered in horror.

"Who am I?"†

The question that has been asked since the book was published is: So, who won? Astute readers will realize that it is a question Raistlin himself asks at the end of this chapter when he says, "Who am I?" Raistlin himself does not really know the answer to this question. However, I believe, in light of the War of Souls, that the answer is clear. For better or worse, Raistlin triumphed.
—TRH

CHAPTER 4

T he guardians slid away from Raistlin, staring at him with hollow eyes. Too weak to move, the mage stared back, his own eyes reflecting the darkness.

"I tell you this"—he spoke to them without a voice and was understood—"touch me again, and I will turn you to dust—as I did *him*."

"Yes, Master," the voices whispered as their pale visages faded back into the shadows.

"What—" murmured Crysania sleepily. "Did you say something?" Realizing she had been sleeping with her head upon his shoulder, she flushed in confusion and embarrassment and hurriedly sat up. "Can-can I get you anything?" she asked.

"Hot water"—Raistlin lay back limply—"for . . . my potion."

Crysania glanced around, brushing her dark hair out of her eyes. Gray light seeped through the

windows. Thin and wispy as a ghost, it brought no comfort. The Staff of Magius cast its light still, keeping away the dark things of the night. But it shed no warmth. Crysania rubbed her aching neck. She was stiff and sore and she knew she must have been asleep for hours. The room was still freezing cold. Bleakly, she looked over at the cold and blackened firegrate.

"There's wood," she faltered, her gaze going to the broken furniture lying about, "but I-I have no tinder or flint. I can't—"

"Wake my brother!" snarled Raistlin, and immediately began to gasp for breath. He tried to say something further, but could do no more than gesture feebly. His eyes glittered with such anger and his face was twisted with such rage that Crysania stared at him in alarm, feeling a chill that was colder than the air around her.

Raistlin closed his eyes wearily and his hand went to his chest.† "Please," he whispered in agony, "the pain . . ."

"Of course," Crysania said gently, overwhelmed with shame. What would it be like to live with such pain, day after day? Leaning forward, she drew the curtain from her own shoulders and tucked it carefully around Raistlin. The mage nodded thankfully but could not speak. Then, shivering, Crysania crossed the room to where Caramon lay.

Putting her hand out to touch his shoulder, she hesitated. What if he's still blind? she thought, or what if he can see and decides . . . decides to kill Raistlin?

But her hesitation lasted only a moment. Resolutely, she put her hand on his shoulder and shook him. If he does, she said to herself grimly, I will stop him. I did it once, I can do it again.

Even as she touched him, she was aware of the pale guardians, lurking in the darkness, watching her every move.

"Caramon," she called softly, "Caramon, wake up. Please! We need—"

"What?" Caramon sat up quickly, his hand going reflexively to his sword hilt—that wasn't there. His eyes focused on Crysania, and she saw with relief tinged with fear that he could see her. He stared at

The effects of Raistlin's chronic illness appear to be similar to a form of tuberculosis. However, the question has always remained just how affected Raistlin actually was by his illness.

When we were first playing the first adventure module for the first DRAGONLANCE game, my friend Terry Phillips took the part of Raistlin. When he spoke in character during the game, he affected the hoarse, rasping voice. Each time he did, the room went silent as everyone strained to hear what he had to say. Margaret, also playing in the game, picked up on that. She realized that this was something Raistlin would do even if his voice were well, just so as to command attention.

We may never know the extent of Raistlin's chronic illness, due in part to the fact that Raistlin himself used this illness to manipulate people and may well have exaggerated it from time to time for his own ends. —TRH

her blankly, however, without recognition, then looked quickly around his surroundings.

Then Crysania saw remembrance in the darkening of his eyes, saw them fill with a haunted pain. She saw remembrance in the clenching of his jaw muscles and the cold gaze he turned upon her. She was about to say something—apologize, explain, rebuke—when his eyes grew suddenly tender as his face softened with concern.

"Lady Crysania," he said, sitting up and dragging the curtain from his body, "you're freezing! Here, put this around you."

Before she could say a word in protest, Caramon wrapped the curtain around her snugly. She noticed as he did so that he looked once at his twin. But his gaze passed quickly over Raistlin, as if he did not exist.

Crysania caught hold of his arm. "Caramon," she said, "he saved our lives. He cast a spell. Those things out there in the darkness leave us alone because he told them to!"

"Because they recognize one of their own!" Caramon said harshly, lowering his gaze and trying to withdraw his arm from her grasp. But Crysania held him fast, more with her eyes than her cold hand.

"You can kill him now," she said angrily. "Look, he's helpless, weak. Of course, if you do, we'll all die. But you were prepared to do that anyway, weren't you!"

"I can't kill him," Caramon said. His brown eyes were clear and cold, and Crysania—once again—saw a startling resemblance between the twins. "Let's face it, Revered Daughter, if I tried, you'd only blind me again."

Caramon brushed her hand from his arm.

"One of us, at least, should see clearly," he said.

See Time of the Twins, Book II, Chapter 19.

Crysania felt herself flush in shame and anger, hearing Loralon's words† echo in the warrior's sarcasm. Turning away from her, Caramon stood up quickly.

"I'll build a fire," he said in a cold, hard voice, "if those"—he waved a hand—"friends of my brother's out there will let me."

"I believe they will," Crysania said, speaking with equal coolness as she, too, rose to her feet.

"They did not hinder me when . . . when I tore down the curtains." She could not help a quiver creeping into her voice at the memory of being trapped by those shadows of death.

Caramon glanced around at her and, for the first time, it occurred to Crysania what she must look like. Wrapped in a rotting black velvet curtain, her white robes torn and stained with blood, black with dust and ash from the floor. Involuntarily, her hand went to her hair—once so smooth, carefully braided and coiled. Now it hung about her face in straggling wisps. She could feel the dried tears upon her cheeks, the dirt, the blood. . . .

Self-consciously, she wiped her hand across her face and tried to pat back her hair. Then, realizing how futile and even stupid she must look, and angered still further by Caramon's pitying expression, she drew herself up with shabby dignity.

"So, I am no longer the marble maiden you first met," she said haughtily, "just as you are no longer the sodden drunk. It seems we have both learned a thing or two on our journey."

"I know *I* have," Caramon said gravely.

"Have you?" Crysania retorted. "I wonder! Did you learn—as I did—that the mages sent *me* back in time, knowing that I would not return?"

Caramon stared at her. She smiled grimly.

"No. You were unaware of that small fact, or so your brother said. The time device could be used by only one person—the person to whom it was given—you! The mages sent me back in time to die—because they feared me!"

Caramon frowned. He opened his mouth, closed it, then shook his head. "You could have left Istar with that elf who came for you"

"Would *you* have gone?" Crysania demanded. "Would you have given up your life in our time if you could help it? No! Am I so different?"

Caramon's frown deepened and he started to reply, but at that moment, Raistlin coughed. Glancing at the mage, Crysania sighed and said, "You better build the fire, or we'll all perish anyway." Turning her back on Caramon, who still stood regarding her silently, she walked over to his brother.

Looking at the frail mage, Crysania wondered

if he had heard. She wondered if he were even still conscious.

He was conscious, but if Raistlin was at all aware of what had passed between the other two, he appeared to be too weak to take any interest in it. Pouring some of the water into a cracked bowl, Crysania knelt down beside him. Tearing a piece from the cleanest portion of her robe, she wiped his face; it burned with fever even in the chill room.

Behind her, she heard Caramon gathering up bits of the broken wooden furniture and stacking it in the grate.

"I need something for tinder," the big man muttered to himself. "Ah, these books—"

At that, Raistlin's eyes flared open, his head moved and he tried feebly to rise.

"Don't, Caramon!" Crysania cried, alarmed. Caramon stopped, a book in his hand.

"Dangerous, my brother!" Raistlin gasped weakly. "Spellbooks! Don't touch them. . . ."

His voice failed, but the gaze of his glittering eyes was fixed on Caramon with a look of such apparent concern that even Caramon seemed taken aback. Mumbling something unintelligible, the big man dropped the book and began to search about the desk. Crysania saw Raistlin's eyes close in relief.†

While one might read this moment as Raist being concerned for his books, I like to think he was relieved that his brother was not hurt. —TRH

"Here's— Looks like . . . letters," Caramon said after a moment of shuffling through paper on the floor. "Would—would these be all right?" he asked gruffly.

Raistlin nodded wordlessly, and, within moments, Crysania heard the crackling of flame. Lacquer-finished, the wood of the broken furniture caught quickly, and soon the fire burned with a bright, cheering light. Glancing into the shadows, Crysania saw the pallid faces withdraw—but they did not leave.

"We must move Raistlin near the fire," she said, standing up, "and he said something about a potion—"

"Yes," Caramon answered tonelessly. Coming to stand beside Crysania, he stared down at his brother. Then he shrugged. "Let him magic himself over there if that's what he wants."

Crysania's eyes flashed in anger. She turned to Caramon, scathing words on her lips, but, at a

weak gesture from Raistlin, she bit her lower lip and kept silent.

"You pick an inopportune time to grow up, my brother," the mage whispered.

"Maybe," said Caramon slowly, his face filled with unutterable sorrow. Shaking his head, he walked back over to stand by the fire. "Maybe it doesn't matter anymore."

Crysania, watching Raistlin's gaze follow his brother, was startled to see him smile a swift, secret smile and nod in satisfaction. Then, as he looked up at her, the smile vanished quickly. Lifting one arm, he motioned her to come near him.

"I can stand," he breathed, "with your help."

"Here, you'll need your staff," she said, extending her hand for it.

"Don't touch it!" Raistlin ordered, catching hold of her hand in his. "No," he repeated more gently, coughing until he could scarcely breathe. "Other hands . . . touch it . . . light fails. . . ."

Shivering involuntarily, Crysania cast a swift glance around the room. Raistlin, seeing her, and seeing the shimmering shapes hovering just outside the light of the staff,† shook his head. "No, I do not believe they would attack us," he said softly as Crysania put her arms around him and helped him to rise. "They know who I am." His lip curled in a sneer at this, and he choked. "They know who I am," he repeated more firmly, "and they dare not cross me. But—" he coughed again, and leaned heavily upon Crysania, one arm around her shoulder, the other hand clutching his staff—"it will be safer to keep the light of the staff burning."

This staff-light was a common AD&D technique of casting a Light spell on a staff in order to make one's way through the darkness. The concept most likely originated with Gandalf's lit staff in Moria. —TRH

The mage staggered as he spoke and nearly fell. Crysania paused to let him catch his breath. Her own breath was coming more rapidly than normal, revealing the confused tangle of her emotions. Hearing the harsh rattle of Raistlin's labored breathing, she was consumed with pity for his weakness. Yet, she could feel the burning heat of the body pressed so near hers. There was the intoxicating scent of his spell components—rose petals, spice—and his black robes were soft to the touch, softer than the curtain around her shoulders. His gaze met hers as they stood there; for a moment, the mirrorlike surface of his eyes cracked and she saw warmth and passion. His arm around her tightened reflexively, drawing her closer without seeming to mean to do so.

Crysania flushed, wanting desperately to both run away and stay forever in that warm embrace. Quickly, she lowered her gaze, but it was too late. She felt Raistlin stiffen. Angrily, he withdrew his arm. Pushing her aside, he gripped his staff for support.

But he was still too weak. He staggered and started to fall. Crysania moved to help him, but suddenly a huge body interposed itself between her and the mage. Strong arms caught Raistlin up as if he were no more than a child. Caramon carried his brother to a frayed and blackened, heavily cushioned chair he had dragged near the fire.

For a few moments, Crysania could not move from where she stood, leaning against the desk. It was only when she realized that she was alone in the darkness, outside the light of both fire and staff, that she walked hurriedly over near the fire herself.

"Sit down, Lady Crysania," said Caramon, drawing up another chair and beating the dust and ash off with his hands as best he could.

"Thank you," she murmured, trying, for some reason, to avoid the big man's gaze. Sinking down into the chair, she huddled near the blaze, staring fixedly into the flames until she felt she had regained some of her composure.

When she was able to look around, she saw Raistlin lying back in his chair, his eyes closed, his breathing ragged. Caramon was heating water in a battered iron pot that he had dragged, from the looks of it, out of the ashes of the fireplace.

He stood before it, staring intently into the water. The firelight glistened on his golden armor, glowed on his smooth, tan skin. His muscles rippled as he flexed his great arms to keep warm.

He is truly a magnificently built man, Crysania thought, then shuddered. Once again, she could see him entering that room beneath the doomed Temple, the bloody sword in his hand, death in his eyes. . . .

"The water's ready," Caramon announced, and Crysania returned to the Tower with a start.

"Let me fix the potion," she said quickly, thankful for something to do.

Raistlin opened his eyes as she came near him. Looking into them, she saw only a reflection of herself, pale, wan, disheveled. Wordlessly, he held out a small, velvet pouch. As she took it, he gestured to his brother, then sank back, exhausted.†

Raistlin is one of the most powerful people in Ansalon, yet he is also one of the most helpless at times.

Taking the pouch, Crysania turned to find Caramon watching her, a look of mingled perplexity and sadness giving his face an unaccustomed gravity. But all he said was, "Put a few of the leaves in this cup, then fill it with the hot water."

"What is it?" Crysania asked curiously. Opening the pouch, her nose wrinkled at the strange, bitter scent of the herbs. Caramon poured the water into the cup she held.

"I don't know," he said, shrugging. "Raist always gathered the herbs and mixed them himself. Par-Salian gave the recipe to him after . . . after the Test, when he was so sick. I know"—he smiled at her—"it smells awful and must taste worse." His glance went almost fondly to his brother. "But it will help him." His voice grated harshly. Abruptly, he turned away.

Crysania carried the steaming potion to Raistlin, who clutched at it with trembling hands and eagerly brought the cup to his lips. Sipping at it, he breathed a sigh of relief and, once more, sank back among the cushions of the chair.

An awkward silence fell. Caramon was staring down at the fire once more. Raistlin, too, looked into the flames and drank his potion without comment. Crysania returned to her own chair to do what each of the others must be doing, she realized—trying to sort out thoughts, trying to make some sense of what had happened.

Hours ago, she had been standing in a doomed city, a city destined to die by the wrath of the gods. She had been on the verge of complete mental and physical collapse. She could admit this now, though she could not have then. How fondly she had imagined her soul to be girded round by the steel walls of her faith. Not steel, she saw now, with shame and regret. Not steel, but ice. The ice had melted in the harsh light of truth, leaving her exposed and vulnerable. If it had not been for Raistlin, she would have perished back there in Istar.

Raistlin . . . Her face flushed. This was something else she had never thought to contend with—love,

passion. She had been betrothed to a young man, years ago, and she had been quite fond of him. But she had not loved him. She had, in fact, never really believed in love—the kind of love that existed in tales told to children. To be that wrapped up in another person seemed a handicap, a weakness to be avoided. She remembered something Tanis Half-Elven had said about his wife, Laurana—what was it? "When she is gone, it is like I'm missing my right arm. . . ."

What romantic twaddle, she had thought at the time. But now she asked herself, did she feel that way about Raistlin? Her thoughts went to the last day in Istar, the terrible storm, the flashing of the lightning, and how she had suddenly found herself in Raistlin's arms. Her heart contracted with the swift ache of desire as she felt, once again, his strong embrace. But there was also a sharp fear, a strange revulsion. Unwillingly, she remembered the feverish gleam in his eyes, his exultation in the storm—as if he himself had called it down.

It was like the strange smell of the spell components that clung to him—the pleasant smell of roses and spice, but—mingled with it—the cloying odor of decaying creatures, the acrid smell of sulfur. Even as her body longed for his touch,† something in her soul shrank away in horror. . . .

Caramon's stomach rumbled loudly. The sound, in the deathly still chamber, was startling.

Looking up, her thoughts shattered, Crysania saw the big man blush deeply in embarrassment. Suddenly reminded of her own hunger—she couldn't remember the last time she had been able to choke down a mouthful of food—Crysania began to laugh.

Caramon looked at her dubiously, perhaps thinking her hysterical. At the puzzled look on the big man's face, Crysania only laughed harder. It felt good to laugh, in fact. The darkness in the room seemed pushed back, the shadows lifted from her soul. She laughed merrily and, finally, caught by the infectious nature of her mirth, Caramon began to laugh, too, though he still shook his head, his face red.

"Thus do the gods remind us we're human," Crysania said when she could speak, wiping the

Crysania's behavior is terribly codependent. Love and hate are both strong and overwhelming emotions when they are not held in check. Unable to master either of them, Crysania often has trouble differentiating between the two and finds herself overwhelmed and confused by their power. It is a self-destructive behavior. —TRH

tears from her eyes. "Here we are, in the most horrible place imaginable, surrounded by creatures waiting eagerly to devour us whole, and all I can think of right now is how desperately hungry I am!"

"We need food," said Caramon soberly, suddenly serious. "And decent clothing, if we're going to be here long." He looked at his brother. "How long *are* we going to be here?"

"Not long," Raistlin replied. He had finished the potion, and his voice was already stronger. Some color had returned to his pale face. "I need time to rest, to recover my strength, and to complete my studies. This lady"—his glittering gaze went to Crysania, and she shivered at the sudden impersonal tone in his voice—"needs to commune with her god and renew her faith. Then, we will be ready to enter the Portal. At which time, my brother, you may go where you will."

Crysania felt Caramon's questioning glance, but she kept her face smooth and expressionless, though Raistlin's cool, casual mention of entering the dread Portal, of going into the Abyss and facing the Queen of Darkness froze her heart. She refused to meet Caramon's eyes, therefore, and stared into the fire.

The big man sighed, then he cleared his throat. "Will you send me home?" he asked his twin.

"If that is where you wish to go."

"Yes," Caramon said, his voice deep and stern. "I want to go back to Tika and to . . . talk to Tanis." His voice broke. "I'll have to . . . to explain, somehow, about Tas dying . . . back there in Istar. . . ."

"In the name of the gods, Caramon," Raistlin snapped, making an irritated motion with his slender hand, "I thought we had seen some glimmer of an adult lurking in that hulking body of yours! You will undoubtedly return to find Tasslehoff sitting in your kitchen, regaling Tika with one stupid story after another, having robbed you blind in the meantime!"

"What?" Caramon's face grew pale, his eyes widened.

"Listen to me, my brother!" Raistlin hissed, pointing a finger at Caramon. "The kender doomed himself when he disrupted Par-Salian's spell. There is a very good reason for the prohibition against those of

his race† and the races of dwarves and gnomes traveling back in time. Since they were created by accident, through a quirk of fate and the god, Reorx's, carelessness, these races are not within the flow of time, as are humans, elves, and ogres—those races first created by the gods.

"Thus, the kender† could have altered time, as he was quick to realize when I inadvertently let slip that fact. I could not allow that to happen! Had he stopped the Cataclysm, as he intended, who knows what might have occurred? Perhaps we might have returned to our own time† to find the Queen of Darkness reigning supreme and unchallenged, since the Cataclysm was sent, in part, to prepare the world to face her coming and give it the strength† to defy her—"

"So you murdered him!" Caramon interrupted hoarsely.

"I told him to get the device"—Raistlin bit the words—"I taught him how to use it, and I sent him home!"

Caramon blinked. "You did?" he asked suspiciously.

Raistlin sighed and laid his head back into the cushions of the chair. "I did, but I don't expect you to believe me,† my brother." His hands plucked feebly at the black robes he wore. "Why should you, after all?"

"You know," said Crysania softly, "I seem to remember, in those last horrible moments before the earthquake struck, seeing Tasslehoff. He . . . he was with me . . . in the Sacred Chamber. . . ."

She saw Raistlin open his eyes a slit. His glittering gaze pierced her heart and startled her, distracting her thoughts for a moment.

"Go on," Caramon urged.

"I—I remember . . . he had the magical device. At least I think he did. He said something about it." Crysania put her hand to her forehead. "But I can't think what it was. It-it's all so dreadful and confused. But—I'm certain he said he had the device!"

Raistlin smiled slightly. "Surely, you will believe Lady Crysania, my brother?" He shrugged. "A cleric of Paladine will not lie."†

"So Tasslehoff's home? Right now?" Caramon said, trying to assimilate this startling information. "And, when I go back, I'll find him—"

"—safe and sound and loaded down with most of your personal possessions," Raistlin finished wryly. "But, now, we must turn our attention to more pressing matters. You are right, my brother. We need food and warm clothing, and we are not likely to find either here. The time we have come forward to is about one hundred years after the Cataclysm. This Tower"—he waved his hand—"has been deserted all those years. It is now guarded by the creatures of darkness called forth by the curse of the magic-user whose body is still impaled upon the spikes of the gates below us. The Shoikan Grove has grown up around it, and there are none on Krynn who dare enter.

"None except myself, of course. No, no one can get inside. But the guardians will not prevent one of us—you, my brother, for example—from leaving. You will go into Palanthas and buy food and clothing. I could produce it with my magic, but I dare not expend any unnecessary energy between now and when I—that is Crysania and I—enter the Portal."

Caramon's eyes widened. His gaze went to the soot-blackened window, his thoughts to the horrifying stories of the Shoikan Grove beyond.

"I will give you a charm to guard you, my brother," Raistlin added in exasperation, seeing the frightened look on Caramon's face. "A charm will be necessary, in fact, but not to aid your way through the Grove. It is far more dangerous in here. The guardians obey me, but they hunger for your blood. Do not set foot outside this room without me. Remember that. You, too, Lady Crysania."

"Where is this . . . this Portal?" Caramon asked abruptly.

"In the laboratory, above us, at the top of the Tower," Raistlin replied. "The Portals were kept in the most secure place the wizards could devise because, as you can imagine, they are extremely dangerous!"

"It's like wizards to go tampering with what they should best leave alone," Caramon growled. "Why in the name of the gods did they create a gateway to the Abyss?"

Placing the tips of his fingers together, Raistlin stared into the fire, speaking to the flames as if they were the only ones with the power to understand him.

seems to triumph in the moment, it ultimately sews the seeds both of its own destruction and lays a foundation for future good. —TRH

The irony here is that Raistlin is, in fact, lying. Raistlin thought he had arranged for Tas to die so that he would not endanger his plans by disrupting time. —MW

Raistlin goes from self-pity to sarcasm. This is the nature of how Raistlin sees his relationships, as being based entirely on manipulation. Caramon has, of course, fed this over the years in their codependent relationship by being an enabler. In many ways, Caramon's basic compassion and desire to care for his brother has crippled them both. —TRH

"In the hunger for knowledge, many things are created. Some are good, that benefit us all. A sword in your hands, Caramon, champions the cause of righteousness and truth and protects the innocent. But a sword in the hands of, say, our beloved sister, Kitiara, would split the heads of the innocent wide open if it suited her. Is this the fault of the sword's creator?"

"N—" Caramon began, but his twin ignored him.

"Long ago, during the Age of Dreams, when magic-users were respected and magic flourished upon Krynn, the five Towers of High Sorcery stood as beacons of light in the dark sea of ignorance that was this world. Here, great magics were worked, benefiting all. There were plans for greater still. Who knows but that now we might have been riding on the winds, soaring the skies like dragons. Maybe even leaving this wretched world and inhabiting other worlds, far away . . . far away. . . ."

His voice grew soft and quiet. Caramon and Crysania held very still, spellbound by his tone, caught up in the vision of his magic.

He sighed. "But that was not to be. In their desire to hasten their great works, the wizards decided they needed to communicate directly with each other, from one Tower to another, without the need for cumbersome teleportation spells. And so, the Portals were constructed."

"They succeeded?" Crysania's eyes shone with wonder.

"They succeeded!" Raistlin snorted. "Beyond their wildest dreams"†—his voice dropped—"their worst nightmares. For the Portals could not only provide movement in one step between any of the far-flung Towers and fortresses of magic—but also into the realms of the gods, as an inept wizard of my own order discovered to his misfortune."

Raistlin shivered, suddenly, and drew his black robes more tightly around him, huddling close to the fire.

"Tempted by the Queen of Darkness, as only she can tempt mortal man when she chooses"—Raistlin's face grew pale—"he used the Portal to enter her realm and gain the prize she offered him nightly, in his dreams," Raistlin laughed, bitter, mocking laughter. "Fool! What happened to him, no one

The theme of science outstripping our wisdom is a classic theme of science fiction. Knowledge of magical power in this world is directly analogous to scientific knowledge. Ian Malcolm's comment in the Jurassic Park *film— "They were so busy figuring out if they could, they never stopped to ask if they should"—has resonance with this theme and with Raistlin's comment here. —TRH*

knows. But he never returned through the Portal. The Queen, however, did. And with her, came legions of dragons—"

"The first Dragon Wars!"† Crysania gasped.

"Yes, brought upon us by one of my own kind with no discipline, no self-control. One who allowed himself to be seduced—" Breaking off, Raistlin stared broodingly into the fire.

"But, I never heard that!" Caramon protested. "According to the legends, the dragons came together—"

"Your history is limited to bedtime tales, my brother!" Raistlin said impatiently. "And just proves how little you know of dragons. They are independent creatures, proud, self-centered, and completely incapable of coming together to cook dinner, much less coordinate any sort of war effort. No, the Queen entered the world completely that time, not just the shadow she was during our war with her. She waged war upon the world, and it was only through Huma's great sacrifice that she was driven back."†

Raistlin paused, hands to his lips, musing. "Some say that Huma did *not* use the Dragonlance to physically destroy her, as the legend goes. But, rather, the lance had some magical property allowing him to drive her back into the Portal and seal it shut. The fact that he *did* drive her back proves that—in this world—she is vulnerable." Raistlin stared fixedly into the flames. "Had there been someone—someone of *true* power at the Portal when she entered, someone capable of destroying her utterly instead of simply driving her back—then history might well have been rewritten."

No one spoke. Crysania stared into the flames, seeing, perhaps, the same glorious vision as the archmage. Caramon stared at his twin's face.

Raistlin's gaze suddenly left the flames, flashing into focus with a clear, cold intensity. "When I am stronger, tomorrow, I will ascend to the laboratory alone"—his stern glance swept over both Caramon and Crysania—"and begin my preparations. You, lady, had best start communing with your god."

Crysania swallowed nervously. Shivering, she drew her chair nearer the fire. But suddenly Caramon was on his feet, standing before her. Reaching

The First Dragon War was the first major conflict in Krynn.

The gods of Krynn, in many ways, more closely resemble the gods of Olympus—flawed and fallible. When I first began designing the world of Krynn, I was faced with the question of a theology for the world. I wanted a multi-theistic, diverse theology, but this also rankled against my own personal monotheistic beliefs. So I created a layer of gods—the gods of Krynn, who were more like a layer of "middle management" between Krynn and the High God. I also placed this High God—at least in my mind—in a place so removed from Krynn that few, if any, of the mortals walking its surface were even aware of the High God's existence. This concept of a High God later found its way into Dragons of Summer Flame—albeit as something of an impostor. The High God again became an important concept in the War of Souls. At the time of this writing, however, the High God was still a mystery to the people of Krynn, who were forging ahead with the all-too-fallible gods they knew. —TRH

down, his strong hands gripped her arms, forcing her to look up into his eyes.

"This is madness, lady," he said, his voice soft and compassionate. "Let me take you from this dark place! You're frightened—you have reason to be afraid! Maybe not everything Par-Salian said about Raistlin was true. Maybe everything I thought about him wasn't true, either. Perhaps I've misjudged him. But I see this clearly, lady. You're frightened and I don't blame you! Let Raistlin do this thing alone! Let *him* challenge the gods—if that's what he wants! But you don't have to go with him! Come home! Let me take you back to our time, away from here."

Raistlin did not speak, but his thoughts echoed in Crysania's mind as clearly as if he had. *You heard the Kingpriest! You said yourself that you know his mistake! Paladine favors you. Even in this dark place, he grants your prayers. You are his chosen! You will succeed where the Kingpriest failed! Come with me, Crysania. This is our destiny!*

"I am frightened," Crysania said, gently disengaging Caramon's hands from her arms. "And I am truly touched by your concern. But this fear of mine is a weakness in me that I must combat. With Paladine's help, I will overcome it—before I enter the Portal with your brother."

"So be it," Caramon said heavily, turning away.

Raistlin smiled, a dark, secret smile that was not reflected in either his eyes or his voice.

"And now, Caramon," he said caustically, "if you are quite through meddling in matters you are completely incapable of comprehending, you had best prepare for your journey. It is midmorning, now. The markets—such as they are in these bleak times—are just opening." Reaching into a pocket in his black robes, Raistlin withdrew several coins† and tossed them at his brother. "That should be sufficient for our needs."

I'm not entirely certain when Raistlin had time to go to the coin exchange and trade for this currency. I can only hope the people in the marketplace didn't check the dates on those coins too carefully. —TRH

Caramon caught the coins without thinking. Then he hesitated, staring at his brother with the same look Crysania had seen him wear in the Temple at Istar, and she remembered thinking, *what terrible hate . . . what terrible love!*

Finally, Caramon lowered his gaze, stuffing the money into his belt.

"Come here to me, Caramon," Raistlin said softly.

"Why?" he muttered, suddenly suspicious.

"Well, there is the matter of that iron collar around your neck. Would you walk the streets with the mark of slavery still? And then there is the charm." Raistlin spoke with infinite patience. Seeing Caramon hesitate still, he added, "I would not advise you leave this room without it. Still, that is your decision—"

Glancing over at the pallid faces, who were still watching intently from the shadows, Caramon came to stand before his brother, his arms crossed before his chest. "Now what?" he growled.

"Kneel down before me."

Caramon's eyes flashed with anger. A bitter oath burned on his lips, but, his eyes going furtively to Crysania, he choked back and swallowed his words.

Raistlin's pale face appeared saddened. He sighed. "I am exhausted, Caramon. I do not have the strength to rise. Please—"

His jaw clenched, Caramon slowly lowered himself, bending knee to floor so that he was level with his frail, black-robed twin.

Raistlin spoke a soft word. The iron collar split apart and fell from Caramon's neck, landing with a clatter on the floor.

"Come nearer," Raistlin said.

Swallowing, rubbing his neck, Caramon did as he was told. though he stared at his brother bitterly. "I'm doing this for Crysania," he said, his voice taut. "If it were just you and me, I'd let you rot in this foul place!"

Reaching out his hands, Raistlin placed them on either side of his twin's head with a gesture that was tender, almost caressing. "Would you, my brother?" the mage asked so softly it was no more than a breath. "Would you leave me? Back there, in Istar— would you truly have killed me?"

Caramon only stared at him, unable to answer. Then, Raistlin bent forward and kissed his brother on the forehead. Caramon flinched, as though he had been touched with a red-hot iron.

Raistlin released his grip.

Caramon stared at him in anguish. "I don't know!" he murmured brokenly. "The gods help me—I don't know!"

With a shuddering sob, he covered his face with his hands. His head sank into his brother's lap.

Raistlin stroked his brother's brown, curling hair. "There, now, Caramon," he said gently. "I have given you the charm. The things of darkness cannot harm you, not so long as I am here."

aramon stood in the doorway to the study, peering out into the darkness of the corridor beyond—a darkness that was alive with whispers and eyes. Beside him was Raistlin, one hand on his twin's arm, the Staff of Magius in his other.

"All will be well, my brother," Raistlin said softly. "Trust me."

Caramon glanced at his twin out of the corner of his eye. Seeing his look, Raistlin smiled sardonically. "I will send one of these with you," the mage continued, motioning with his slender hand.

"I'd rather not!"† Caramon muttered, scowling as the pair of disembodied eyes nearest him drew nearer still.

"Attend him," Raistlin commanded the eyes. "He is under my protection. You see me? You know who I am?"

I'm paying homage here to one of my favorite authors, *Charles Dickens. In* A Christmas Carol, *Jacob Marley offers Scrooge the chance to save himself by a visit from the three ghosts. Scrooge's reply, "I think I'd rather not." —MW*

The eyes lowered their gaze in reverence, then fixed their cold and ghastly stare upon Caramon. The big warrior shuddered and cast one final glance at Raistlin, only to see his brother's face turn grim and stern.

"The guardians will guide you safely through the Grove. You may have more to fear, however, once you leave it. Be wary, my brother. This city is not the beautiful, serene place it will become in two hundred years Now, refugees pack it, living in the gutters, the streets, wherever they can. Carts rumble over the cobblestones every morning, removing the bodies of those who died during the night.† There are men out there who will murder you for your boots. Buy a sword, first thing, and carry it openly in your hand."

"I'll worry about the town," Caramon snapped. Turning abruptly, he walked off down the corridor, trying without much success to ignore the pale, glowing eyes that floated near his shoulder.

Raistlin watched until his brother and the guardian had passed beyond the staff's radius of magical light and were swallowed up by the noisome darkness. Waiting until even the echoes of his brother's heavy footfalls had faded, Raistlin turned and reentered the study.

Lady Crysania sat in her chair, trying without much success to comb her fingers through her tangled hair. Padding softly across the floor to stand near her, unseen, Raistlin reached into one of the pockets of his black robes and drew forth a handful of fine white sand. Coming up behind her, the mage raised his hand and let the sand drift down over the woman's dark hair.

"*Ast tasark simiralan krynawi,*"† Raistlin whispered, and almost immediately Crysania's head drooped, her eyes closed, and she drifted into a deep, magical sleep. Moving to stand before her, Raistlin stared at her for long moments.

Though she had washed the stain of tears and blood from her face, the marks of her journey through darkness were still visible in the blue shadows beneath her long lashes, a cut upon her lip, and the pallor of her complexion. Reaching out his hand, Raistlin gently brushed back the hair that fell in dark tendrils across her eyes.

"Bring out your dead! Bring out your dead!"
"I'm not dead yet!"
"He says he's not dead!"
"He will be in a minute."
"I don't want to go on the cart!"
"Oh, don't be such a baby!"
—*TRH (quoting* Monty Python and the Holy Grail)

This phrase, while it does utilize Indonesian language forms, is essentially meaningless. Still, it looks good on the page! —*TRH*

Crysania had cast aside the velvet curtain she had been using as a blanket as the room was warmed by the fire. Her white robes, torn and stained with blood, had come loose around her neck. Raistlin could see the soft curves of her breasts beneath the white cloth rising and falling with her deep, even breathing.

"Were I as other men, she would be mine," he said softly.

His hand lingered near her face, her dark, crisp hair curling around his fingers.

"But I am not as other men," Raistlin murmured. Letting her hair fall, he pulled the velvet curtain up around her shoulders and across her slumbering form. Crysania smiled from some sweet dream, perhaps, and nestled more snugly into the chair, resting her cheek upon her hand as she laid her head on the armrest.

Raistlin's hand brushed against the smooth skin of her face, recalling vivid memories. He began to tremble. He had but to reverse the sleep spell, take her in his arms, hold her as he held her when he cast the magic spell that brought them to this place. They would have an hour alone together before Caramon returned. . . .

"I am *not* as other men!" Raistlin snarled.

Abruptly walking away, his dour gaze encountered the staring, watchful eyes of the guardians.

"Watch over her while I am gone," he said to several half-seen, hovering spectres lurking in the dark shadows in the corner of the study. "You two," he ordered the two who been with him when he awakened, "accompany me."

"Yes, Master," the two murmured. As the staff's light fell upon them, the faint outlines of black robes could be seen.

Stepping out into the corridor, Raistlin carefully closed the door to the study behind him. He gripped the staff, spoke a soft word of command, and was instantly taken† to the laboratory at the top of the Tower of High Sorcery.

He had not even drawn a breath when, materializing out of the darkness, he was attacked.

Shrieks and howls of outrage screamed around him. Dark shapes darted out of the air, daring the light of the staff as bone-white fingers clutched for

Teleport: When this spell is used, the wizard instantly transports himself . . . to a well-known destination. [2nd Edition ADVANCED DUNGEONS & DRAGONS Player's Handbook, by David "Zeb" Cook, TSR, 1997, p. 219.]

his throat and grasped his robes, rending the cloth. So swift and sudden was the attack and so awful the sense of hatred that Raistlin very nearly lost control.

But he was in command of himself quickly. Swinging the staff in a wide arc, shouting hoarse words of magic, he drove back the spectres.

"Talk to them!" he commanded the two guardians with him. "Tell them who I am!"

"Fistandantilus," he heard them say through a roaring in his ears, ". . . though his time has not yet come as was foretold . . . some magical experiment. . . ."

Weakened and dizzy, Raistlin staggered to a chair and slumped down into it. Bitterly cursing himself for not being prepared for such an onslaught and cursing the frail body that was, once again, failing him, he wiped blood from a jagged cut upon his face and fought to remain conscious.

This is *your* doing, my Queen. His thoughts came grimly through a haze of pain. You dare not fight me openly. I am too strong for you on this—my plane—of existence! You have your foothold in this world. Even now, the Temple has appeared in its perverted form in Neraka. You have wakened the evil dragons. They are stealing the eggs of the good dragons.† But the door remains closed, the Foundation Stone has been blocked by self-sacrificing love. And that was your mistake. For now, by your entry into *our* plane, you have made it possible for us to enter *yours*! I cannot reach you yet . . . you cannot reach me. . . . But the time will come . . . the time will come. . . .

These events, of course, set up the great conflict found in the DRAGONLANCE *Chronicles.*

"Are you unwell, Master?" came a frightened voice near him. "I am sorry we could not prevent them from harming you, but you moved too swiftly! Please, forgive us. Let us help—"

"There is nothing you can do!" Raistlin snarled, coughing. He felt the pain in his chest ease. "Leave me a moment. . . . Let me rest. Drive these others out of here."

"Yes, Master."

Closing his eyes, waiting for the horrible dizziness and pain to pass, Raistlin sat for an hour in the darkness, going over his plans in his mind. He needed two weeks of unbroken rest and study to prepare himself. That time he would find here easily enough. Crysania was his—she would follow him willingly, eagerly in fact, calling down the power of

Paladine to assist him in opening the Portal and fighting the dread Guardians beyond.

He had the knowledge of Fistandantilus, knowledge accumulated by the mage over the ages. He had his own knowledge, too, plus the strength of his younger body. By the time he was ready to enter, he would be at the height of his powers—the greatest archmage ever to have lived upon Krynn!

The thought comforted him and gave him renewed energy. The dizziness subsided finally, the pain eased. Rising to his feet, he cast a quick glance about the laboratory. He recognized it, of course. It looked exactly the same as when he had entered it in a past that was now two hundred years in the future. *Then* he had come with power—as foretold. The gates had opened, the evil guardians had greeted him reverently—not attacked him.

As he walked through the laboratory, the Staff of Magius shining to light his way, Raistlin glanced about curiously. He noticed odd, puzzling changes. Everything should have been *exactly* as it was when he would arrive two hundred years from now. But a beaker now standing intact had been broken when he found it. A spellbook now resting on the large stone table, he had discovered on the floor.

"Do the guardians disturb things?" he asked the two who remained with him. His robes rustled about his ankles as he made his way to the very back of the huge laboratory, back to the Door That Was Never Opened.

"Oh, no, Master," said one, shocked. "We are not permitted to touch anything."

Raistlin shrugged. Lots of things could happen in two hundred years to account for such occurrences. "Perhaps an earthquake," he said to himself, losing interest in the matter as he approached the shadows where the great Portal stood.

Raising the Staff of Magius, he shone its magical light ahead of him. The shadows fled the far corner of the laboratory, the corner where stood the Portal with its platinum carvings of the five dragon heads and its huge silver-steel door that no key upon Krynn could unlock.

Raistlin held the staff high . . . and gasped.

For long moments he could do nothing but stare, the breath wheezing in his lungs, his thoughts

seething and burning. Then, his shrill scream of anger and rage and fury pierced the living fabric of the Tower's darkness.

So dreadful was the cry, echoing through the dark corridors of the Tower, that the evil guardians cowered back into their shadows, wondering if perhaps their dread Queen had burst in upon them.

Caramon heard the cry as he entered the door at the bottom of the Tower. Shivering with sudden terror, he dropped the packages he carried and, with trembling hands, lit the torch he had brought. Then, the naked blade of his new sword in his hand, the big warrior raced up the stairs two at a time.

Bursting into the study, he saw Lady Crysania looking around in sleepy fearfulness.

"I heard a scream—" she said, rubbing her eyes and rising to her feet.

"Are you all right?" Caramon gasped, trying to catch his breath.

"Why, yes," she said, looking startled, as she realized what he was thinking. "It wasn't me. I must have fallen asleep. It woke me—"

"Where's Raist?" Caramon demanded.

"Raistlin!" she repeated, alarmed, and started to push her way past Caramon when he caught hold of her.

"This is why you slept," he said grimly, brushing fine white sand from her hair. "Sleep spell."

Crysania blinked. "But why—"

"We'll find out."

"Warrior," said a cold voice almost in his ear.

Whirling, Caramon thrust Crysania behind him, raising his sword as a black-robed, spectral figure materialized out of the darkness. "You seek the wizard? He is above, in the laboratory. He is in need of assistance, and we have been commanded not to touch him."

"I'll go," Caramon said, "alone."

"I'm coming with you," Crysania said. "*I will* come with you," she repeated firmly, in response to Caramon's frown.

Caramon started to argue, then, remembering that she *was* a cleric of Paladine and had once before exerted her powers over these creatures of darkness,† shrugged and gave in, though with little grace.

It is a common theme in legend and folklore that priests or holy men are feared by the forces of darkness. This later found its way into Advanced Dungeons & Dragons *with clerics beings especially useful in combating the undead and other forces of darkness.*

"What happened to him, if you were commanded not to touch him?" Caramon asked the spectre gruffly as he and Crysania followed it from the study out into the dark corridor. "Keep close to me," he muttered to Crysania, but the command was not necessary.

If the darkness had seemed alive before, it throbbed and pulsed and jittered and jabbered with life now as the guardians, upset by the scream, thronged the corridors. Though he was now warmly dressed, having purchased clothes at the marketplace, Caramon shivered convulsively with the chill that flowed from their undead bodies. Beside him, Crysania shook so she could barely walk.

"Let me hold the torch," she said through clenched teeth. Caramon handed her the torch, then encircled her with his right arm, drawing her near. She clasped her arm about him, both of them finding comfort in the touch of living flesh as they climbed the stairs after the spectre.

"What happened?" he asked again, but the spectre did not answer. It simply pointed up the spiral stairs.

Holding his sword in his left hand, his sword hand, Caramon and Crysania followed the spectre as it flowed up the stairs, the torchlight dancing and wavering.

After what seemed an endless climb, the two reached the top of the Tower of High Sorcery, both of them aching and frightened and chilled to the very heart.

"We must rest," Caramon said through lips so numb he was practically inaudible. Crysania leaned against him, her eyes closed, her breath coming in labored gasps. Caramon himself did not think he could have climbed another stair, and he was in superb physical condition.

"Where is Raist—Fistandantilus?" Crysania stammered after her breathing had returned somewhat to normal.

"Within." The spectre pointed again, this time to a closed door and, as it pointed, the door swung silently open.

Cold air flowed from the room in a dark wave, ruffling Caramon's hair and blowing aside Crysania's cloak. For a moment Caramon could not move. The sense of evil coming from within that chamber was overwhelming. But Crysania, her hand firmly clasped over the medallion of Paladine, began to walk forward.

Reaching out, Caramon drew her back. "Let me go first."

Crysania smiled at him wearily. "In any other case but this, warrior," she said, "I would grant you that privilege. But, here, the medallion I hold is as formidable a weapon as your sword."

"You have no need for any weapon," the spectre stated coldly. "The Master commanded us to see that you come to no harm. We will obey his request."

"What if he's dead?" Caramon asked harshly, feeling Crysania stiffen in fear beside him.

"If he had died," the spectre replied, its eyes gleaming, "your warm blood would already be upon our lips. Now enter."

Hesitantly, Crysania pressed close beside him, Caramon entered the laboratory. Crysania lifted the torch, holding it high, as both paused, looking around.

"There," Caramon whispered, the innate closeness that existed between the twins leading him to find the dark mass, barely visible on the floor at the back of the laboratory.

Her fears forgotten, Crysania hurried forward, Caramon following more slowly, his eyes warily scanning the darkness.

Raistlin lay on his side, his hood drawn over his face. The Staff of Magius lay some distance from him, its light gone out, as though Raistlin—in bitter anger—had hurled it from him. In its flight, it had, apparently, broken a beaker and knocked a spellbook to the floor.

Handing Caramon the torch, Crysania knelt beside the mage and felt for the lifebeat in his neck. It was weak and irregular, but he lived. She sighed in relief, then shook her head. "He's all right. But I don't understand. What happened to him?"

"He is not hurt physically," the spectre said, hovering near them. "He came to this part of the laboratory as though looking for something. And then he walked over here, muttering about a portal. Holding his staff high, he stood where he lies now, staring straight ahead. Then he screamed, hurled the staff from him, and fell to the floor, cursing in fury until he lost consciousness."

Puzzled, Caramon held the torch up. "I wonder what could have happened?" he murmured. "Why, there's nothing here! Nothing but a bare, blank wall!"

CHAPTER
6

How has he been?" Crysania asked softly as she entered the room. Drawing back the white hood from her head, she untied her cloak to allow Caramon to remove it from around her shoulders.

"Restless," the warrior replied with a glance toward a shadowed corner. "He has been impatient for your return."

Crysania sighed and bit her lip. "I wish I had better news," she murmured.

"I'm glad you don't," Caramon said grimly, folding Crysania's cloak over a chair. "Maybe he'll give up this insane idea and come home."

"I can't—" began Crysania, but she was interrupted.

"If you two are *quite* finished with whatever it is you are doing there in the darkness, perhaps you will come tell me what you discovered, lady."

Crysania flushed deeply. Casting an irritated glance at Caramon, she hurried across the room to where Raistlin lay on a pallet near the fire.

The mage's rage had been costly. Caramon had carried him from the laboratory where they'd found him lying before the empty stone wall to the study. Crysania had made up a bed on the floor, then watched, helplessly, as Caramon ministered to his brother as gently as a mother to a sick child. But there was little even the big man could do for his frail twin. Raistlin lay unconscious for over a day, muttering strange words in his sleep. Once he wakened and cried out in terror, but he immediately sank back into whatever darkness he wandered.

Bereft of the light of the staff that even Caramon dared not touch and was forced to leave in the laboratory, he and Crysania sat huddled near Raistlin. They kept the fire burning brightly, but both were always conscious of the presence of the shadows of the guardians of the Tower, waiting, watching.

Finally, Raistlin awoke. With his first breath, he ordered Caramon to prepare his potion and, after drinking this, was able to send one of the guardians to fetch the staff. Then he beckoned to Crysania. "You must go to Astinus," he whispered.

"Astinus!" Crysania repeated in blank astonishment. "The historian?† But why—I don't understand—"

Raistlin's eyes glittered, a spot of color burned into his pale cheek with feverish brilliance. "The Portal *is not here!*" he snarled, grinding his teeth in impotent fury. His hands clenched and almost immediately he began to cough. He glared at Crysania.

"Don't waste my time with fool questions! Just go!" he commanded in such terrible anger that she shrank away, startled. Raistlin fell back, gasping for breath.

Caramon glanced up at Crysania in concern. She walked to the desk, staring down unseeing at some of the tattered and blackened spellbooks that lay upon it.

"Now wait just a minute, lady," Caramon said softly, rising and coming to her. "You're not really considering going? Who is this Astinus anyway? And how do you plan to get through the Grove without a charm?"

Is Astinus actually Gilean? Many people hold divergent thoughts on this subject. I, personally, believe that he is. —TRH

"I have a charm," Crysania murmured, "given to me by your brother when—when we first met. As for Astinus, he is the keeper of the Great Library of Palanthas, the Chronicler of the History of Krynn."

"He may be that in our time, but he won't be there now!" Caramon said in exasperation. "Think, lady!"

"I am thinking," Crysania snapped, glancing at him in anger. "Astinus is known as the Ageless One. He was first to set foot upon Krynn, so the legends say, and he will be the last to leave it."

Caramon regarded her skeptically.

"He records all history as it passes. He knows everything that has happened in the past and is happening in the present. But"—Crysania glanced at Raistlin with a worried look—"he cannot see into the future. So I'm not certain what help he can be to us."

Caramon, still dubious and obviously not believing half of this wild tale, had argued long against her going. But Crysania only grew more determined, until, finally, even Caramon realized they had no choice. Raistlin grew worse instead of better. His skin burned with fever, he lapsed into periods of incoherence and, when he was himself, angrily demanded to know why Crysania hadn't been to see Astinus yet.

So† she had braved the terrors of the Grove and the equally appalling terrors of the streets of Palanthas. Now she knelt beside the mage's bed, her heart aching as she watched him struggle to sit up—with his brother's help—his glittering gaze fixed eagerly upon her.

"Tell me everything!" he ordered hoarsely. "Exactly as it occurred. Leave out nothing."

Nodding wordlessly, still shaken by the terrifying walk through the Tower, Crysania tried to force herself to calm down and sort out her thoughts.

"I went to the Great Library and—and asked to see Astinus," she began, nervously smoothing the folds of the plain, white robe Caramon had brought her to replace the blood-stained gown she had worn. "The Aesthetics refused to admit me, but then I showed them the medallion of Paladine. That threw them into confusion, as you might well imagine." She smiled. "It has been a hundred years since any sign of the old gods has come, so, finally, one hurried off to report to Astinus.

It is important to pay attention to the pace. All stories have a meter to them, a pacing to the events as the story is told. This tempo and the varying of the tempo are very important to the flow of the story as it unfolds, and they give an important dynamic to the text. While it might have been interesting to see every detail of Crysania's journey here, it would have needlessly slowed down the story and ruined the pacing. One of my favorite devices in the great Arabian classic A Thousand Nights and a Night *is: "And he rehearsed to her from first to last all that had happened to him." This quick phrase covers a lot of story that we already know and communicates it to another character in the story. —TRH*

"After waiting for some time, I was taken to his chamber where he sits all day long and many times far into the night, recording the history of the world." Crysania paused, suddenly frightened at the intensity of Raistlin's gaze. It seemed he would snatch the words from her heart, if he could.

Looking away for a moment to compose herself, she continued, her own gaze now on the fire. "I entered the room, and he—he just sat there, writing, ignoring me. Then the Aesthetic who was with me announced my name, 'Crysania of the House of Tarinius,' as you told me to tell him. And then—"

She stopped, frowning slightly.

Raistlin stirred. "What?"

"Astinus looked up *then*," Crysania said in a puzzled tone, turning to face Raistlin. "He actually ceased writing and laid his pen down. And he said, '*You!*' in such a thundering voice that I was startled and the Aesthetic with me nearly fainted. But before I could say anything or ask what he meant or even how he knew me, he picked up his pen and—going to the words he had just written—crossed them out!"

"Crossed them out," Raistlin repeated thoughtfully, his eyes dark and abstracted. "Crossed them out," he murmured, sinking back down onto his pallet.

Seeing Raistlin absorbed in his thoughts, Crysania kept quiet until he looked up at her again.

"What did he do then?" the mage asked weakly.

"He wrote something down over the place where he had made the error, if that's what it was. Then he raised his gaze to mine again and I thought he was going to be angry. So did the Aesthetic, for I could feel him shaking. But Astinus was quite calm. He dismissed the Aesthetic and bade me sit down. Then he asked why I had come.

"I told him we were seeking the Portal. I added, as you instructed, that we had received information that led us to believe it was located in the Tower of High Sorcery at Palanthas, but that, upon investigation, we had discovered our information was wrong. The Portal was not there.

"He nodded, as if this did not surprise him. 'The Portal was moved when the Kingpriest attempted to take over the Tower. For safety's sake, of course. In time, it may return to the Tower of High Sorcery at Palanthas, but it is not there now.'

" 'Where is it, then?' I asked.

"For long moments, he did not answer me. And then—" Here Crysania faltered and glanced over at Caramon fearfully, as if warning him to brace himself.

Seeing her look, Raistlin pushed himself up on the pallet. "Tell me!" he demanded harshly.

Crysania drew a deep breath. She would have looked away, but Raistlin caught hold of her wrist and, despite his weakness, held her so firmly, she found she could not break free of his deathlike grip.

"He—he said such information would cost you. Every man has his price, even he."

"Cost me!" Raistlin repeated inaudibly, his eyes burning.

Crysania tried unsuccessfully to free herself as his grasp tightened painfully.

"What *is* the cost?" Raistlin demanded.

"He said you would know!" Crysania gasped. "He said you had promised it to him, long ago."

Raistlin loosed her wrist. Crysania sank back away from him, rubbing her arm, avoiding Caramon's pitying gaze. Abruptly, the big man rose to his feet and stalked away. Ignoring him, ignoring Crysania, Raistlin sank back onto his frayed pillows, his face pale and drawn, his eyes suddenly dark and shadowed.

Crysania stood up and went to pour herself a glass of water. But her hand shook so she slopped most of it on the desk and was forced to set the pitcher down. Coming up behind her, Caramon poured the water and handed her the glass, a grave expression on his face.

Raising the glass to her lips, Crysania was suddenly aware of Caramon's gaze going to her wrist. Looking down, she saw the marks of Raistlin's hand upon her flesh. Setting the glass back down upon the desk, Crysania quickly drew her robe over her injured arm.

"He's doesn't mean to hurt me,"† she said softly in answer to Caramon's stern, unspoken glare. "His pain makes him impatient. What is our suffering, compared to his? Surely you of all people must understand that? He is so caught up in his greater vision that he doesn't know when he hurts others."

Turning away, she walked back to where Raistlin lay, staring unseeing into the fire.

Crysania is very quick to conjure up her own excuses and explanations for Raistlin's terrible treatment of her. This is evidence, purposely put in the text, of Crysania's codependent and abusive relationship with the mage. It is a tragedy to which all too many women fall prey—and all too many men prey upon. Crysania tells herself that she can fix Raistlin with her love and goodness, but Raistlin simply abuses her. The more he abuses her the more she tries to "love him" into change, and the downward spiral has no reason to be broken. Many women who have written to Margaret and I express this same desire: their attraction to Raistlin in order to redeem him. I am concerned that they may fall into this same trap in their own lives. —TRH

"Oh, he knows all right," Caramon muttered to himself. "I'm just beginning to realize—he's known all along!"

Astinus of Palanthas, historian of Krynn, sat in his chamber, writing. The hour was late, very late, past Darkwatch, in fact. The Aesthetics had long ago closed and barred the doors to the Great Library. Few were admitted during the day, none at night. But bars and locks were nothing to the man who entered the Library and who now stood, a figure of darkness, before Astinus.

The historian did not glance up. "I was beginning to wonder where you were," he said, continuing to write.

"I have been unwell," the figure replied, its black robes rustling. As if reminded, the figure coughed softly.

"I trust you are feeling better?" Astinus still did not raise his head.

"I am returning to health slowly," the figure replied. "Many things tax my strength."

"Be seated, then," Astinus remarked, gesturing with the end of his quill pen to a chair, his gaze still upon his work.

The figure, a twisted smile on its face, padded over to the chair and sat down. There was silence within the chamber for many minutes, broken only by the scratching of Astinus's pen and the occasional cough of the black-robed intruder.

Finally, Astinus laid the pen down and lifted his gaze to meet that of his visitor. His visitor drew back the black hood from his face. Regarding him silently for long moments, Astinus nodded to himself.

"I do not know this face, Fistandantilus, but I know your eyes. There is something strange in them, however. I see the future in their depths. So you have become master of time, yet you do not return with power, as was foretold."

"My name is not Fistandantilus, Deathless One. It is Raistlin, and that is sufficient explanation for what has happened." Raistlin's smile vanished, his eyes narrowed. "But surely you knew that?" He gestured. "Surely the final battle between us is recorded—"

"I recorded the name as I recorded the battle,"

Astinus said coolly. "Would you care to see the entry
. . . Fistandantilus?"

Raistlin frowned, his eyes glittered dangerously.
But Astinus remained unperturbed. Leaning back in
his chair, he studied the archmage calmly.

"Have you brought what I asked for?"

"I have," Raistlin replied bitterly. "Its making cost
me days of pain and sapped my strength, else I
would have come sooner."

And now, for the first time, a hint of emotion shone
on Astinus's cold and ageless face. Eagerly, he leaned
forward, his eyes shining as Raistlin slowly drew
aside the folds of his black robes, revealing what
seemed an empty, crystal globe hovering within his
hollow chest cavity like a clear, crystalline heart.

Even Astinus could not repress a start at this
sight, but it was apparently nothing more than an
illusion, for, with a gesture, Raistlin sent the globe
floating forward. With his other hand, he drew the
black fabric back across his thin chest.

As the globe drifted near him, Astinus placed his
hands upon it, caressing it lovingly. At his touch, the
globe was filled with moonlight—silver, red, even
the strange aura of the black moon was visible.
Beneath the moons whirled vision after vision.

"You see time passing, even as we sit here,"
Raistlin said, his voice tinged with an unconscious
pride. "And thus, Astinus, no longer will you have
to rely on your unseen messengers from the planes
beyond for your knowledge of what happens in the
world around you.† Your own eyes will be your
messengers from this point forward."

This tells us that although Astinus may indeed be a god—or at the very least possess many godlike powers—he is not all-knowing. His knowledge is limited.

"Yes! Yes!" Astinus breathed, the eyes that looked
into the globe glimmering with tears, the hands that
rested upon it shaking.

"And now my payment," Raistlin continued
coldly. "Where is the Portal?"

Astinus looked up from the globe. "Can you not
guess, Man of the Future and the Past? You have
read the histories. . . ."

Raistlin stared at Astinus without speaking, his
face growing pale and chill until it might have been
a deathmask.

Zhaman is, indeed, an Indonesian word meaning "days, age, era" or "epoch." —TRH

"You are right. I *have* read the histories. So that is
why Fistandantilus went to Zhaman,"† the archmage said finally.

Astinus nodded wordlessly.

"Zhaman, the magical fortress, located in the Plains of Dergoth . . . near Thorbardin—home of the mountain dwarves. And Zhaman is in land controlled by the mountain dwarves," Raistlin went on, his voice expressionless as though reading from a textbook. "And where, even now, their cousins, the hill dwarves, go—driven by the evil that has consumed the world since the Cataclysm to demand shelter within the ancient mountain home."

"The Portal is located—"

"—deep within the dungeons of Zhaman," Raistlin said bitterly. "Here, Fistandantilus fought the Great Dwarven War—"

"*Will* fight . . ." Astinus corrected.

"*Will* fight," Raistlin murmured, "the war that will encompass his own doom!"

The mage fell silent. Then, abruptly, he rose to his feet and moved to Astinus's desk. Placing his hands upon the book, he turned it around to face him. Astinus observed him with cool, detached interest.

"You are right," Raistlin said, scanning the still-wet writing on the parchment. "I *am* from the future. I have read the *Chronicles*, as you penned them.† Parts of them, at any rate. I remember reading this entry—one you *will* write there." He pointed to a blank space, then recited from memory. " 'As of this date, After Darkwatch falling 30, Fistandantilus brought me the Globe of Present Time Passing.' "

Astinus did not reply. Raistlin's hand began to shake. "You *will* write that?" he persisted, anger grating in his voice.

Astinus paused, then acquiesced with a slight shrug of his shoulders.

Raistlin sighed. "So I am doing nothing that *has not been done before!*" His hand clenched suddenly and, when he spoke again, his voice was tight with the effort it was taking to control himself.

"Lady Crysania came to you, several days ago. She said you were writing as she entered and that, after seeing her, you crossed something out. Show me what that was."

Astinus frowned.

"Show me!" Raistlin's voice cracked, it was almost a shriek.

Margaret and I have often said, while creating these books, that we felt more as though we were writing down events that had happened than that we were making up stories. In the back of our minds, we pictured both Chronicles and Legends as somehow being originally penned by Astinus. —TRH

Placing the globe to one side of the table, where it hovered near him, Astinus reluctantly removed his hands from its crystal surface. The light blinked out, the globe grew dark and empty. Reaching around behind him, the historian pulled out a great, leather-bound volume and, without hesitation, found the page requested.

He turned the book so that Raistlin could see.

The archmage read what had been written, then read the correction. When he stood up, his black robes whispering about him as he folded his hands within his sleeves, his face was deathly pale but calm.

"This alters time."

"This alters nothing," Astinus said coolly. "She came in his stead, that is all. An even exchange. Time flows on, undisturbed."†

"And carries me with it?"

"Unless you have the power to change the course of rivers by tossing in a pebble,"† Astinus remarked wryly.

Raistlin looked at him and smiled, swiftly, briefly. Then he pointed at the globe. "Watch, Astinus," he whispered, "watch for the pebble! Farewell, Deathless One."

The room was empty, suddenly, except for Astinus. The historian sat silently, pondering. Then, turning the book back, he read once more what he had been writing when Crysania had entered.

On this date, Afterwatch rising 15, Denubis, a cleric of Paladine, arrived here, having been sent by the great archmage, Fistandantilus, to discover the whereabouts of the Portal. In return for my help, Fistandantilus will make what he has long promised me—the Globe of Present Time Passing. . . .

Denubis's name had been crossed out, Crysania's written in.

The River of Time was a concept that I brought to Legends as part of the underlying structure. See Appendix B. —TRH

See Appendix B. —TRH

CHAPTER 7

*We deliberately build up
the suspense, letting the
reader wonder if Tasslehoff
is dead through six
chapters, then introduce
him in Chapter Seven
with the phrase, "I'm
dead," which he says
aloud, indicating that, of
course, he's very much
alive. —MW*

"I'm dead,"† said Tasslehoff Burrfoot.

He waited expectantly a moment.

"I'm dead," he said again. "My, my. This must be the Afterlife."

Another moment passed.

"Well," said Tas, "one thing I can say for it—it certainly is *dark*."

Still nothing happened. Tas found his interest in being dead beginning to wane. He was, he discovered, lying on his back on something extremely hard and uncomfortable, cold and stony-feeling.

"Perhaps I'm laid out on a marble slab, like Huma's," he said, trying to drum up some enthusiasm. "Or a hero's crypt, like where we buried Sturm."

That thought entertained him a while, then, "Ouch!" He pressed his hand to his side, feeling a stabbing pain in his ribs and, at the same time, he

*I was sitting in my
home office one day when
I got a call from Margaret.
She had just finished the
first book of Legends and
was working on the
manuscript for the second
book.*

*"What are we going to
do?" she said. "I think I
just killed Tasslehoff!"*

*"What do you mean?" I
asked.*

*"Well, he was standing
right under the fiery
mountain falling out of
the sky at the end of the
last book."*

"Uh-huh."

*"He was in the middle
of Istar at the moment of
the Cataclysm!"*

"Uh-huh."

*"But we need him for
later in the books!"*

*"Uh-huh. No problem. I
know what happens."*

"What?"

"He dies."

"What?"

*"Yes, he dies," I said.
"But let me tell you what
happens after he dies."
—TRH*

noticed another pain in his head. He also came to realize that he was shivering, a sharp rock was poking him in the back, and he had a stiff neck.

"Well, I certainly didn't expect this," he snapped irritably. "I mean, by all accounts when you're dead, you're not supposed to feel anything." He said this quite loudly, in case someone was listening. "I said you're not supposed to feel anything!" he repeated pointedly when the pain did not go away.

"Drat!"† muttered Tas. "Maybe it's some sort of mix-up. Maybe I'm dead and the word just hasn't gotten around my body yet. I certainly haven't gone all stiff, and I'm *sure* that's supposed to happen. So I'll just wait."

Squirming to get comfortable (first removing the rock from beneath his back), Tas folded his hands across his chest and stared up into the thick, impenetrable darkness. After a few minutes of this, he frowned.

"If this is being dead, it sure isn't all it's cracked up to be," he remarked sternly. "Now I'm not only dead, I'm bored, too. Well," he said after a few more moments of staring into the darkness, "I guess I can't do much about being dead, but I can do something about being bored. There's obviously been a mix-up. I'll just have to go talk to someone about this."

Sitting up, he started to swing his legs around to jump off the marble slab, only to discover that he was—apparently—lying on a stone floor. "How rude!" he commented indignantly. "Why not just dump me in someone's root cellar?"

Stumbling to his feet, he took a step forward and bumped into something hard and solid. "A rock," he said gloomily, running his hands over it. "Humpf! Flint dies† and *he* gets a tree! *I* die and I get a rock. It's obvious someone's done something all wrong.

"Hey!—" he cried, groping around in the darkness. "Is anyone—Well, what do you know? I've still got my pouches! They let me bring everything with me, even the magical device. At least that was considerate. Still"—Tas's lips tightened with firm resolve—"someone better do something about this pain. I simply won't put up with it."

Investigating with his hands, since he couldn't see a thing, Tas ran his fingers curiously over the big

---

I imagine that most kender talk to themselves, due to a love of talking and the notion that they travel so much that they often have only themselves to talk to. That and the fact that even when they do talk to other people, they tend not to listen, so it's almost like talking to themselves anyway. —MW

Flint died in Dragons of Spring Dawning, *Book III, Chapter 3.*

rock. It seemed to be covered with carved images—runes, maybe? And *that* struck him as familiar. The shape of the huge rock, too, was odd.

"It isn't a rock after all! It's a table, seemingly," he said, puzzled. "A rock table carved with runes—" Then his memory returned. "I know!" he shouted triumphantly. "It's that big stone desk in the laboratory where I went to hunt for Raistlin and Caramon and Crysania, and found that they'd all gone and left me behind. I was standing there when the fiery mountain came down on top of me! In fact, that's the place where I died!"†

See Time of the Twins, Book II, Chapter 19.

He felt his neck. Yes, the iron collar was still there—the collar they had put on him when he was sold as a slave. Continuing to grope around in the darkness, Tas tripped over something. Reaching down, he cut himself on a something sharp.

"Caramon's sword!" he said, feeling the hilt. "I remember. I found it on the floor. And that means," said Tas with growing outrage, "that they didn't even *bury* me! They just left my body where it was! I'm in the basement of a ruined Temple." Brooding, he sucked his bleeding finger. A sudden thought occurred to him. "And I suppose they intend for me to *walk* to wherever it is I'm going in the Afterlife. They don't even provide transportation! This is really the last straw!"

He raised his voice to a shout. "Look!" he said, shaking his small fist. "I want to talk to whoever's in charge!"

But there was no sound.

"No light," Tas grumbled, falling over something else. "Stuck down in the bottom of a ruined temple—dead! Probably at the bottom of the Blood Sea of Istar. . . . Say," he said, pausing to think, "maybe I'll meet some sea elves, like Tanis told me about.† But, no, I forgot"—he sighed—"I'm dead, and you can't, as far as I'm able to understand, meet people after you're dead. Unless you're an undead, like Lord Soth." The kender cheered up considerably. "I wonder how you get that job? I'll ask. Being a death knight must be *quite* exciting. But, first, I've got to find out where I'm supposed to be and why I'm not there!"

Tanis encountered the sea elves in Dragons of Spring Dawning, *Book II, Chapter 6.*

Picking himself up again, Tas managed to make his way to what he figured was probably the front

of the room beneath the Temple. He was thinking
about the Blood Sea of Istar and wondering why
there wasn't more water about when something else
suddenly occurred to him.

"Oh, dear!" he muttered. "The Temple *didn't* go into
the Blood Sea! It went to Neraka! I was in the Temple,
in fact, when I defeated the Queen of Darkness."

Tas came to a doorway—he could tell by feeling
the frame—and peered out into the darkness that
was *so very* dark.

"Neraka, huh," he said, wondering if that was
better or worse than being at the bottom of an ocean.

Cautiously, he took a step forward and felt something beneath his foot. Reaching down, his small
hand closed over—"A torch! It must have been the
one over the doorway. Now, somewhere in here,
I've got a tinderbox—" Rummaging through several
pouches, he came up with it at last.

"Strange," he said, glancing about the corridor
as the torch flared to light. "It looks just like it did
when I left it—all broken and crumbled after the
earthquake. You'd think the Queen would have
tidied up a bit by now. I don't remember it being in
such a mess when I was in it in Neraka. I wonder
which is the way out."

He looked back toward the stairs he had come
down in his search for Crysania and Raistlin. Vivid
memories of the walls cracking and columns falling
came to his mind. "That's no good, that's for sure,"
he muttered, shaking his head. "Ouch, that hurts."
He put his hand to his forehead. "But that was the
only way out, I seem to recall." He sighed, feeling a
bit low for a moment. But his kender cheerfulness
soon surfaced. "There sure are a lot of cracks in the
walls, though. Perhaps something's opened up."

Walking slowly, mindful of the pain in his head
and his ribs, Tas stepped out into the corridor. He
carefully checked out each wall without seeing anything promising until he reached the very end of
the hall. Here he discovered a very large crack in the
marble that, unlike the others, made an opening
deeper than Tas's torchlight could illuminate.

No one but a kender could have squeezed into
that crack, and, even for Tas, it was a tight fit, forcing him to rearrange all his pouches and slide
through sideways.

"All I can say is—being dead is certainly a lot of bother!" he muttered, squeezing through the crack and ripping a hole in his blue leggings.

Matters didn't improve. One of his pouches got hung up on a rock, and he had to stop and tug at it until it was finally freed. Then the crack got so very narrow he wasn't at all certain he would make it. Taking off all his pouches, he held them and the torch over his head and, after holding his breath and tearing his shirt, he gave a final wiggle and managed to pop through. By this time, however, he was aching, hot, sweaty, and in a bad mood.

"I always wondered why people objected to dying," he said, wiping his face. "Now I know!"†

Pausing to catch his breath and rearrange his pouches, the kender was immensely cheered to see light at the far end of the crack. Flashing his torch around, he discovered that the crack was getting wider, so—after a moment—he went on his way and soon reached the end—the source of the light.

Reaching the opening, Tas peered out, drew a deep breath and said, "Now *this* is more what I had in mind!"

The landscape was certainly like nothing he had ever seen before in his life. It was flat and barren, stretching on and on into a vast, empty sky that was lit with a strange glow, as if the sun had just set or a fire burned in the distance. But the whole sky was that strange color, even above him. And yet, for all the brightness, things around him were very dark. The land seemed to have been cut out of black paper and pasted down over the eerie-looking sky. And the sky itself was empty—no sun, no moons, no stars. Nothing.

Tas took a cautious step or two forward. The ground felt no different from any other ground, even though—as he walked on it—he noticed that it took on the same color as the sky. Looking up, he saw that, in the distance, it turned black again. After a few more steps, he stopped to look behind him at the ruins of the great Temple.

"Great Reorx's beard!" Tas gasped, nearly dropping his torch.

There was nothing behind him! Wherever it was he had come from was gone! The kender turned around in a complete circle. Nothing ahead

I remember watching a TV show—Amazing Stories, I think it was—in which a man finds himself in hell. It turns out to be a granny-decorated living room with a middle-aged couple showing an eternal and endless progression of bad slides from their vacation. The man complained to Satan who explained that for that man's soul this was hell. "The funny thing is," Satan says as he is leaving, "there is another room just like this one in heaven."

The idea intrigued me that everyman's heaven—or hell—is unique. Face it. Tasslehoff would probably find fire and brimstone to be a pretty amazing thing, so we tried to picture what real hell would be like for a kender. We believed it would be essentially one eternal "time out!" —TRH

of him, nothing behind him, nothing in any direction he looked.

Tasslehoff Burrfoot's heart sank right down to the bottom of his green shoes and stayed there, refusing to be comforted. This was, without a doubt, the most *boring* place he'd ever seen in his entire existence!

"This can't be the Afterlife," the kender said miserably. "This *can't* be right! There *must* be some mistake. Hey, wait a minute! I'm supposed to meet Flint here! Fizban said so† and Fizban may have been a bit muddled about other things, but he didn't sound muddled about *that*!

Tas is absolutely right. See Dragons of Spring Dawning, *Book III, Chapter 14.*

"Let's see—how did that go? There was a big tree, a beautiful tree, and beneath it sat a grumbling, old dwarf, carving wood and—Hey! There's the tree! Now, where did that come from?"

The kender blinked in astonishment. Right ahead of him, where nothing had been just a moment before, he now saw a large tree.

"Not exactly my idea of a beautiful tree," Tas muttered, walking toward it, noticing—as he did so—that the ground had developed a curious habit of trying to slide out from under his feet. "But then, Fizban had odd taste and so, come to think of it, did Flint."

He drew nearer the tree, which was black—like everything else—and twisted and hunched over like a witch he'd seen once. It had no leaves on it. "That thing's been dead at least a hundred years!" Tas sniffed. "If Flint thinks *I'm* going to spend my Afterlife sitting under a dead tree with him, he's got another think coming. I—Hey, Flint!" The kender cried out, coming up to the tree and peering around. "Flint? Where are you? I—Oh, there you are," he said, seeing a short, bearded figure sitting on the ground on the other side of the tree. "Fizban told me I'd find you here. I'll bet you're surprised to see me! I—"

The kender came round the tree, then stopped short. "Say," he cried angrily, "you're not Flint! Who—Arack!"

Tas staggered backward as the dwarf who had been the Master of the Games in Istar suddenly turned his head and looked at him with such an evil grin on his twisted face that the kender felt his

blood run cold—an unusual sensation; he couldn't remember ever experiencing it before. But before he had time to enjoy it, the dwarf leaped to his feet and, with a vicious snarl, rushed at the kender.

With a startled yelp, Tas swung his torch to keep Arack back, while with his other hand he fumbled for the small knife he wore in his belt. But, just as he pulled his knife out, Arack vanished. The tree vanished. Once again, Tas found himself standing smack in the center of nothing† beneath that fire-lit sky.

"All right now," Tas said, a small quiver creeping into his voice, though he tried his best to hide it, "I don't think this is at all fun. It's miserable and horrible and, while Fizban didn't exactly promise the Afterlife would be one endless party, I'm *certain* he didn't have anything like this in mind!" The kender slowly turned around, keeping his knife drawn and his torch held out in front of him.

"I know I haven't been very religious," Tas added with a snuffle, looking out into the bleak landscape and trying to keep his feet on the weird ground, "but *I* thought I led a pretty good life. And I *did* defeat the Queen of Darkness. Of course, I had some help," he added, thinking that this might be a good time for honesty, "and I *am* a *personal* friend of Paladine and—"

"In the name of Her Dark Majesty," said a soft voice behind him, "what are *you* doing here?"

Tasslehoff sprang three feet into the air in alarm—a sure sign that the kender was completely unnerved—and whirled around. There—where there hadn't been anyone standing a moment before— stood a figure that reminded him very much of the cleric of Paladine, Elistan, only *this* figure wore black clerical robes instead of white and around its neck— instead of the medallion of Paladine—hung the medallion of the Five-Headed Dragon.†

"Uh, pardon me, sir," stammered Tas, "but I'm not at all sure *what* I'm doing here. I'm not at all sure where *here* is, to be perfectly truthful, and—oh, by the way, my name's Tasslehoff Burrfoot." He extended his small hand politely. "What's yours?"

But the figure, ignoring the kender's hand, threw back its black cowl and took a step nearer. Tas was considerably startled to see long, iron-gray hair flow out from beneath the cowl, hair so long, in

I had a difficult time coming up with a description of hell that would fit a kender. Dante's vision of hell, for example, would have been as exciting as a carnival to kender, sent them flocking to it in droves. So for Tasslehoff, I went with the vision of hell written by T.S. Eliot in The Cocktail Party:

> *Hell is oneself,*
> *Hell is alone, the other figures in it*
> *Merely projections.*
> *There is nothing to escape from*
> *And nothing to escape to. One is always alone.*
> —MW

The symbol of Takhisis.

fact, that it would easily have touched the ground if it had not floated around the figure in a weird sort of way, as did the long, gray beard that suddenly seemed to sprout out of the skull-like face.

"S-say, that's quite . . . remarkable," Tas stuttered, his mouth dropping open. "How did you do that? And, I don't suppose you could tell me, but where did you say I was? You s-see—" The figure took another step nearer and, while Tas certainly wasn't afraid of him, or it, or whatever it was, the kender found that he didn't want it or him coming any closer for some reason. "I-I'm dead," Tas continued, trying to back up only to find that, for some unaccountable reason, something was blocking him, "and—by the way"—indignation got the better of fear—"are you in charge around here? Because I don't think this death business is being handled at all well! I hurt!" Tas said, glaring at the figure accusingly. "My head hurts and my ribs. And then I had to walk all this way, coming up out of the basement of the Temple—"

"The basement of the Temple!" The figure stopped now, only inches from Tasslehoff. Its gray hair floated as if stirred by a hot wind. Its eyes, Tas could see now, were the same red color as the sky, its face gray as ash.

"Yes!" Tas gulped. Besides everything else, the figure had a most horrible smell. "I—I was following Lady Crysania and she was following Raistlin and—"

"Raistlin!" The figure spoke the name in a voice that made Tas's hair literally stand up on his head. "Come with me!"

The figure's hand—a most peculiar-looking hand—closed over Tasslehoff's wrist. "Ow!" squeaked Tas, as pain shot through his arm. "You're hurting—"

But the figure paid no attention. Closing its eyes, as though lost in deep concentration, it gripped the kender tightly, and the ground around Tas suddenly began to shift and heave. The kender gasped in wonder as the landscape itself took on a rapid, fluid motion.

We're not moving, Tas realized in awe, the ground is!

"Uh," said Tas in a small voice, "where did you say I was?"

"You are in the Abyss," said the figure in a sepulchral tone.

"Oh, dear," Tas said sorrowfully, "I didn't think I was *that* bad." A tear trickled down his nose. "So this is the Abyss. I hope you don't mind me telling you that I'm frightfully disappointed in it. I always supposed the Abyss would be a fascinating place. But so far it isn't. Not in the least. It—it's awful boring and . . . ugly . . . and, I really don't mean to be rude, but there is a most peculiar smell." Sniffling, he wiped his nose on his sleeve, too unhappy even to reach for a pocket handkerchief. "Where did you say we were going?"

"You asked to see the person in charge," the figure said, and its skeletal hand closed over the medallion it wore around its neck.

The landscape changed. It was every city Tas had ever been in, it seemed, and yet none. It was familiar, yet he didn't recognize a thing. It was black, flat, and lifeless, yet teeming with life. He couldn't see or hear anything, yet all around him was sound and motion.

Tasslehoff stared at the figure beside him, at the shifting planes beyond and above and below him, and the kender was stricken dumb. For only the second time in his life (the first had been when he found Fizban alive when the old man was supposed to have been decently dead),† Tas couldn't speak a word.

This happened in Dragons of Winter Night, *Book II, Chapter 9.*

If every kender on the face of Krynn had been asked to name Places I'd Most Like To Visit, the plane of existence where the Queen of Darkness dwelled would have come in at least third on many lists.

But now, here was Tasslehoff Burrfoot, standing in the waiting† room of the great and terrible Queen, standing in one of the most interesting places known to man or kender, and he had never felt unhappier in his life.

First, the room the gray-haired, black-robed cleric told him to stay in was completely empty. There weren't any tables with interesting little objects on them, there weren't any chairs (which was why he was standing). There weren't even any *walls*! In fact, the only way he knew he was in a room at all was

Another aspect of Tasslehoff's personalized hell—having to wait for anything! I'm sure that anyone who has had to sit in any waiting room can sympathize with Tasslehoff's misery and agree that it is deserving of some aspect of hell. —TRH

that when the cleric told him to "stay in the waiting room," Tas suddenly *felt* he was in a room.

But, as far as he could see, he was standing in the middle of nothing. He wasn't even certain, at this point, which way was up or which way was down. Both looked alike—an eerie glowing, flame-like color.

He tried to comfort himself by telling himself over and over that he was going to meet the Dark Queen. He recalled stories Tanis told about meeting the Queen in the Temple at Neraka.

"I was surrounded by a great darkness," Tanis had said, and, even though it was months after the experience, his voice still trembled, "but it seemed more a darkness of my own mind than any actual physical presence. I couldn't breathe. Then the darkness lifted, and she spoke to me, though she said no word. I heard her in my mind. And I saw her in all her forms—the Five-Headed Dragon, the Dark Warrior, the Dark Temptress—for she was not completely in the world yet. She had not yet gained control."

Tas remembered Tanis shaking his head. "Still, her majesty and might were very great. She is, after all, a goddess—one of the creators of the world. Her dark eyes stared into my soul, and I couldn't help myself—I sank to my knees and worshipped her. . . ."

And now he, Tasslehoff Burrfoot; was going to meet the Queen as she was in her own plane of existence—strong and powerful. "Perhaps she'll appear as the Five-Headed Dragon." Tas said to cheer himself up. But even *that* wonderful prospect didn't help, though he had never seen a five-headed anything before, much less a dragon. It was as if all the spirit of adventure and curiosity were oozing out of the kender like blood dripping from a wound.

"I'll sing a bit," he said to himself, just to hear the sound of his own voice. "That generally raises my spirits."

He began to hum the first song that came into his head—a Hymn to the Dawn that Goldmoon had taught him.

Even the night must fail
For light sleeps in the eyes

And dark becomes dark on dark
Until the darkness dies.

Soon the eye resolves
Complexities of night
Into stillness, where the heart
Falls into fabled light.

Tas was just starting in on the second verse when he became aware, to his horror, that his song was echoing back to him—only the words were now twisted and terrible. . . .

Even the night must fail
When light sleeps in the eyes,
When dark becomes dark on dark
And into darkness dies.

Soon the eye dissolves,
Perplexed by the teasing night,
Into a stillness of the heart
A fable of fallen light.†

"Stop it," cried Tas frantically into the eerie, burning silence that resounded with his song. "I didn't mean to say that! I—"

With startling suddenness, the black-robed cleric materialized in front of Tasslehoff, seeming to coalesce out of the bleak surroundings.

"Her Dark Majesty will see you now," the cleric said, and, before Tasslehoff could blink, he found himself in another place.

He knew it was another place, not because he had moved a step or even because this place was different from the last place, but that he *felt* he was someplace else. There was still the same weird glow, the same emptiness, except now he had the impression he wasn't alone.

The moment he realized this, he saw a black, smooth wooden chair appear—its back to him. Seated in it was a figure dressed in black, a hood pulled up over its head.

Thinking perhaps some mistake had been made and that the cleric had taken him to the wrong place, Tasslehoff—gripping his pouches nervously in his hand—walked cautiously around the chair to

What was immeasurably fun about these two songs—which are kind of "companion songs," I suppose—was finding ways to vary the lines, either to retain the words and twist them in the second, more denying poem, or to construct a line from the second poem as an echo of the sounds of its original ("Perplexed" and "tease" in line 6, for example, are supposed to pun on "complexities" in the first poem). Some of the lines (especially the very one I have quoted) strain that connection a little, I think. But strained connections are part of the fun as well. How far can you vary the words or echo the sounds before the resemblance breaks down?

Perhaps all this sounds technical and nerdy. If it does, I don't particularly care. Technical challenges, after all, are part of the playfulness and joy of writing lyrics, and when it is no longer fun . . . why, go out and see a good movie. —Michael Williams

see the figure's face. Or perhaps the chair turned to around to see *his* face. The kender wasn't certain.

But, as the chair moved, the figure's face came into view.

Tasslehoff knew no mistake had been made.

It was not a Five-Headed Dragon he saw. It was not a huge warrior in black, burning armor. It was not even the Dark Temptress, who so haunted Raistlin's dreams. It was a woman dressed all in black, a tight-fitting hood pulled up over her hair, framing her face in a black oval. Her skin was white and smooth and ageless, her eyes large and dark. Her arms, encased in tight black cloth, rested on the arms of her chair, her white hands curved calmly around the ends of the armrests.

The expression on her face was not horrifying, nor terrifying, nor threatening, nor awe-inspiring; it was, in fact, not even an expression at all.† Yet Tas was aware that she was scrutinizing him intensely, delving into his soul, studying parts of him that he wasn't even aware existed.

Her aspect is a particularly frightening one tailored to shake kender—no expression at all. —TRH

"I-I'm Tasslehoff Burrfoot, M-majesty," said the kender, reflexively stretching out his small hand. Too late, he realized his offense and started to withdraw his hand and bow, but then he felt the touch of five fingers in his palm. It was a brief touch, but Tas might have grabbed a handful of nettles. Five sting-ing branches of pain shot through his arm and bored into his heart, making him gasp.

But, as swiftly as they touched him, they were gone. He found himself standing very dose to the lovely, pale woman, and so mild was the expression in her eyes that Tas might well have doubted she was the cause of the pain, except that—looking down at his palm—he saw a mark there, like a five-pointed star.

Tell me your story.

Tas started. The woman's lips had not moved, but he heard her speak. He realized, also, in sudden fright, that she probably knew more of his story than he did.

Sweating, clutching his pouches nervously, Tassle-hoff Burrfoot made history that day—at least as far as kender storytelling was concerned. He told the entire story of his trip to Istar in under five seconds. And every word was true.

"Par-Salian accidentally sent me back in time with my friend Caramon. We were going to kill Fistandantilus only we discovered it was Raistlin so we didn't. I was going to stop the Cataclysm with a magical device, but Raistlin made me break it. I followed a cleric named Lady Crysania down to a laboratory beneath the Temple of Istar to find Raistlin and make him fix the device. The roof caved in and knocked me out. When I woke up, they had all left me and the Cataclysm struck and now I'm dead and I've been sent to the Abyss."

Tasslehoff drew a deep, quivering breath and mopped his face with the end of his long topknot of hair. Then, realizing his last comment had been less than complimentary, he hastened to add, "Not that I'm complaining, Your Majesty. I'm certain whoever did this must have had quite a good reason. After all, I did break a dragon orb,† and I seem to recall once someone said I took something that didn't belong to me, and . . . and I wasn't as respectful of Flint as I should have been, I guess, and once, for a joke, I hid Caramon's clothes while he was taking a bath and he had to walk into Solace stark naked. But"—Tas could not help a snuffle—"I always helped Fizban find his hat!"

You are not dead, said the voice, *nor have you been sent here. You are not, in fact, supposed to be here at all.*

At this startling revelation, Tasslehoff looked up directly into the Queen's dark and shadowy eyes. "I'm not?" he squeaked, feeling his voice go all queer. "Not dead?" Involuntarily, he put his hand to his head—which still ached. "So that explains it! I just thought someone had botched things up—"

Kender are not allowed† here, continued the voice.

"That doesn't surprise me," Tas said sadly, feeling much more himself since he wasn't dead. "There are quite a number of places on Krynn kender aren't allowed."

The voice might not have even heard him. *When you entered the laboratory of Fistandantilus, you were protected by the magical enchantment he had laid on the place. The rest of Istar was plunged far below the ground at the time the Cataclysm struck. But I was able to save the Temple of the Kingpriest. When I am ready, it will return to the world, as will I, myself.*

"But you won't win," said Tas before he thought.

See Dragons of Winter Night, *Book III, Chapter 6.*

Some consider this ban on kender to be Takhisis's method of preventing hell from becoming truly hellish. However, what she means is that due to their innocence and their perpetually cheerful outlook on life, kender are not really welcome in hell. —MW

Kender are innocent before the gods. They do not steal. They only "borrow indefinitely." They are without guile or malice. They therefore are not accountable to the gods for such acts (no matter what the Solamnic Knights may think) and therefore, having not chosen evil, do not qualify for hell. I believe the same applies to the innocents of our own world. —TRH

"I—I k-know," he stuttered as the dark-eyed gaze shot right through him. "I was th-there."

No, you were not there, for that has not happened yet. You see, kender, by disrupting Par-Salian's spell, you have made it possible to alter time. Fistandantilus—or Raistlin, as you know him—told you this. That was why he sent you to your death—or so he supposed. He did not want time altered: The Cataclysm was necessary to him so that he could bring this cleric of Paladine forward to a time when he will have the only true cleric in the land.

It seemed to Tasslehoff that he saw, for the first time, a flicker of dark amusement in the woman's shadowy eyes, and he shivered without understanding why.

How soon you will come to regret that decision, Fistandantilus, my ambitious friend. But it is too late. Poor, puny mortal. You have made a mistake—a costly mistake. You are locked in your own time loop. You rush forward to your own doom.

"I don't understand," cried Tas.

Yes, you do, said the voice calmly. *Your coming has shown me the future. You have given me the chance to change it. And, by destroying you, Fistandantilus has destroyed his only chance of breaking free. His body will perish again, as he perished long ago. Only this time, when his soul seeks another body to house it, I will stop him. Thus, the young mage, Raistlin, in the future, will take the Test in the Tower of High Sorcery, and he will die there. He will not live to thwart my plans. One by one, the others will die. For without Raistlin's help, Goldmoon will not find the blue crystal staff. Thus—the beginning of the end for the world.*

"No!" Tas whimpered, horror-stricken. "This—this can't be! I-I didn't mean to do this. I-I just wanted to-to go with Caramon on-on this adventure! He-he couldn't have made it alone. He *needed* me!"

The kender stared around frantically, seeking some escape. But, though there seemed everywhere to run, there was nowhere to hide. Dropping to his knees before the black-clothed woman, Tas stared up at her. "What have I done? What have I done?" he cried frantically.

You have done such that even Paladine might be tempted to turn his back upon you, kender.

"What will you do to me?" Tas sobbed wretchedly. "Where will I go?" He lifted a tear-streaked face. "I

don't suppose you c-could send me back to Caramon? Or back to my own time?"

Your time no longer exists. As for sending you to Caramon, that is quite impossible, as you surely must understand. No, you will remain here, with me, so I may insure that nothing goes wrong.

"Here?"† Tas gasped. "How long?"

The woman began to fade before his eyes, shimmering and finally vanishing into the nothingness around him. *Not long, I should imagine, kender. Not long at all. Or perhaps always. . . .*

"What do you—what does she mean?" Tas turned to face the gray-haired cleric, who had sprung up to fill the void left by Her Dark Majesty. "Not long or always?"

"Though not dead, you are—even now—dying. Your lifeforce is ebbing from you, as it must for any of the living who mistakenly venture down here and who have not the power to fight the evil that devours them from within. When you are dead, the gods will determine your fate."

"I see," said Tas, choking back a lump in his throat. He hung his head. "I deserve it, I suppose. Oh, Tanis, I'm sorry! I truly didn't mean to do it. . . ."

The cleric gripped his arm painfully. The surroundings changed, the ground shifted away beneath his feet. But Tasslehoff never noticed. His eyes filling with tears, he gave himself up to dark despair and hoped death would come quickly.

The hero braving the land of the dead is a long-standing theme of mythology—from Odysseus and Aeneas to the many Celtic heroes being drawn into the Otherworld. This chapter fits into a long-standing theme in mythology.

CHAPTER 8

"Here you are,"
said the dark cleric.

"Where?" Tas asked listlessly, more out of force of habit than because he cared.

The cleric paused, then shrugged. "I suppose if there were a prison in the Abyss, you would be in it now."

Tas looked around. As usual, there was nothing there—simply a vast barren stretch of eerie emptiness. There were no walls, no cells, no barred windows, no doors, no locks, no jailer. And he knew, with deep certainty, that—this time—there was no escape.

"Am I supposed to just stand here until I drop?" Tas asked in a small voice. "I mean, couldn't I at least have a bed and a-a stool—oh!"

As he spoke, a bed materialized before his eyes, as did a three-legged, wooden stool. But even these familiar objects appeared so horrifying, sitting in the

middle of nothing, that Tas could not bear to look at them long.

"Th-thank you," he stammered, walking over to sit down upon the stool with a sigh. "What about food and water?"

He waited a moment, to see if these, too, would appear. But they didn't. The cleric shook his head, his gray hair forming a swirling cloud around him.

"No, the needs of your mortal body will be cared for while you are here. You will feel no hunger or thirst. I have even healed your wounds."

Tas suddenly noticed that his ribs had stopped hurting and the pain in his head was gone. The iron collar had vanished from around his neck.

"There is no need for your thanks," the cleric continued, seeing Tas open his mouth. "We do this so that you will not interrupt us in our work. And, so, farewell—"

The dark cleric raised his hands, obviously preparing to depart.

"Wait!" Tas cried, leaping up from his stool and clutching at the dark, flowing robes. "Won't I see you again? Don't leave me alone!" But he might as well have tried to grab smoke. The flowing robes slipped through his fingers, and the dark cleric disappeared.

"When you are dead, we will return your body to lands above and see that your soul speeds on its way . . . or stays here, as you may be judged. Until that time, we have no more need of contact with you."

"I'm alone!" Tas said, glancing around his bleak surroundings in despair. "Truly alone . . . alone until I die. . . . Which won't be long," he added sadly. Walking over, he sat down upon his stool. "I might as well die as fast as possible and get it over with. At least I'll probably go someplace different—I hope." He looked up into the empty vastness.

"Fizban," Tas said softly, "you probably can't hear me from clear down here. And I don't suppose there's anything you could do for me anyway, but I *did* want to tell you, before I die, that I didn't *mean* to cause all this trouble, disrupting Par-Salian's spell and going back in time when I wasn't supposed to got and all that."

Heaving a sigh, Tas pressed his small hands together, his lower lip quivering. "Maybe that doesn't

A similar incident sets off the War of Souls. The roots for our later works all find their origins in the seeds of our earlier works. This scene resonates down through our works. —TRH

count for much . . . and I suppose that—if I must be honest—part of me went along with Caramon just because"—he swallowed the tears that were beginning to trickle down his nose—"just because it sounded like so much fun! But, truly, part of me went with him because he had no business going back into the past alone! He was fuddled because of the dwarf spirits, you see. And I promised Tika I'd look after him. Oh, Fizban! If there were just some way out of this mess, I'd try my best to straighten everything out. Honestly—"

"Hullothere."

"What?" Tas nearly fell off his stool. Whirling around, half thinking he might see Fizban, he saw, instead, only a short figure—shorter even than himself—dressed in brown britches, a gray tunic, and a brown leather apron.

"Isaidhullothere," repeated the voice, rather irritably.

"Oh, he-hello," Tas stammered, staring at the figure. It certainly didn't *look* like a dark cleric, at least Tas had never heard of any that wore brown leather aprons. But, he supposed, there could always be exceptions especially considering the fact that brown leather aprons are such useful things. Still, this person bore a strong resemblance to someone he knew, if only he could remember. . . .

"Gnosh!" Tas exclaimed suddenly, snapping his fingers. "You're a gnome! Uh, pardon me for asking such a personal question"—the kender flushed in embarrassment—"but are you—uh—dead?"

"Areyou?" the gnome asked, eyeing the kender suspiciously.

"No," said Tas, rather indignantly.

"WellI'mnoteither!" snapped the gnome.

"Uh, could you slow down a bit?" Tas suggested. "I know your people talk rapidly, but it makes it hard for us to understand, sometimes—"

"I said I'm not either!" the gnome shouted loudly.

"Thank you," Tas said politely. "And I'm not hard of hearing. You can talk in a normal tone of voice—er, talk *slowly* in a normal tone of voice," the kender hurried to add, seeing the gnome draw in a breath.

"What's . . . your . . . name?" the gnome asked, speaking at a snail's pace.

"Tasslehoff . . . Burrfoot." The kender extended a small hand, which the gnome took and shook heartily. "What's . . . yours? I mean—what's yours? Oh, no! I didn't mean—"

But it was too late. The gnome was off.

"Gnimshmarigongalesefrahootsputhturandot-samanella—"†

"The short form!" Tas cried when the gnome stopped for breath.

"Oh." The gnome appeared downcast. "Gnimsh."

"Thank you. Nice meeting you—uh—Gnimsh," Tas said, sighing in relief. He had completely forgotten that every gnome's name provides the unwary listener with a complete account of the gnome's family's life history,† beginning with his earliest known (or imagined) ancestor.

"Nice meeting you, Burrfoot," the gnome said, and they shook hands again.

"Will you be seated?" Tas said, sitting down on the bed and gesturing politely toward the stool. But Gnimsh gave the stool a scathing glance and sat down in a chair that materialized right beneath him. Tas gasped at the sight. It was truly a remarkable chair†—it had a footrest that went up and down and rockers on the bottom that let the chair rock back and forth and it even tilted completely backward, letting the person sitting in it lie down if so inclined.

Unfortunately, as Gnimsh sat down, the chair tilted too far backward†, flipping the gnome out on his head. Grumbling, he climbed back in it and pressed a lever. This time, the footrest flew up, striking him in the nose. At the same time, the back came forward and, before long, Tas had to help rescue Gnimsh from the chair, which appeared to be eating him.

"Drat," said the gnome and, with a wave of his hand, he sent the chair back to wherever it had come from, and sat down, disconsolately, on Tasslehoff's stool.

Having visited gnomes and seen their inventions before, Tasslehoff mumbled what was proper. "Quite interesting . . . truly an advanced design in chairs. . . ."

"No, it isn't," Gnimsh snapped, much to Tas's amazement. "It's a rotten design. Belonged to my

I no longer remember who came up with the gnomish naming conventions, but Jeff Grubb may be highly suspect. —TRH

My own religious background may have influenced this interest in the "instant" genealogy of the gnomes. —TRH

I have had a few mishaps in my time in a recliner. —TRH

This is in homage to Tracy. When I first moved to Wisconsin, I had a very cheap car (all I could afford), and parts of it were always falling apart. One day, when I went to pick up Tracy at his house, he sat down in the passenger's seat. As he started to comfortably lean into the cushion, the seat collapsed, leaving him lying flat on his back, staring at the roof. I laughed so hard I couldn't drive, and we were nearly late for our meeting. I couldn't resist putting it into the book. —MW

wife's first cousin. I should have known better than to think of it. But"—he sighed—"sometimes I get homesick."

"I know," Tas said, swallowing a sudden lump in his throat. "If-if you don't mind my asking, what are you doing here, if you're—uh—not dead?"

"Will you tell me what *you're* doing here?" Gnimsh countered.

"Of course," said Tas, then he had a sudden thought. Glancing around warily, he leaned forward. "No one *minds*, do they?" he asked in a whisper. "That we're talking, I mean? Maybe we're not supposed to—"

"Oh, *they* don't care," Gnimsh said scornfully. "As long as we leave them alone, we're free to go around anywhere. Of course," he added, "anywhere looks about the same as here, so there's not much point."

"I see," Tas said with interest. "How do you travel?"

"With your mind. Haven't you figured that out yet? No, probably not." The gnome snorted. "Kender were never noted for their brains."

"Gnomes and kender *are* related," Tas pointed out in miffed tones.

"So I've heard," Gnimsh replied skeptically, obviously not believing any of it.

Tasslehoff decided, in the interests of maintaining peace, to change the subject. "So, if I want to go somewhere, I just think of that place and I'm there?"

"Within limits, of course," Gnimsh said. "You can't, for example, enter any of the holy precincts where the dark clerics go—"

"Oh." Tas sighed, that having been right up at the top of his list of tourist attractions. Then he cheered up again. "You made that chair come out of nothing and, come to think of it, *I* made this bed and this stool. If I think of something, will it just appear?"

"Try it," Gnimsh suggested.

Tas thought of something.

Gnimsh snorted as a hatrack appeared at the end of the bed. "Now *that's* handy."

"I was just practicing," Tas said in hurt tones.

"You better watch it," the gnome said, seeing Tas's face light up. "Sometimes things appear, but not quite the way you expected."

"Yeah." Tas suddenly remembered the tree and the dwarf. He shivered. "I guess you're right. Well, at least we have each other. Someone to talk to. You can't imagine how *boring* it was." The kender settled back on the bed, first imagining—with caution—a pillow. "Well, go ahead. Tell me your story."

"You start." Gnimsh glanced at Tas out of the corner of his eye.

"No, you're my guest."

"I insist."

"*I* insist."

"You. After all, I've been here longer."

"How do you know?"

"I just do. . . . Go on."

"But—" Tas suddenly saw this was getting nowhere, and though they apparently had all eternity, he didn't plan on spending it arguing with a gnome. Besides, there was no real reason why he *shouldn't* tell his story. He enjoyed telling stories, anyway. So, leaning back comfortably, he told his tale. Gnimsh listened with interest, though he did rather irritate Tas by constantly interrupting and telling him to "get on with it," just at the most exciting parts.

Finally, Tas came to his conclusion. "And so here I am. Now yours," he said, glad to pause for breath.

"Well," Gnimsh said hesitantly, looking around darkly as though afraid someone might be listening, "it all began years and years ago with my family's Life Quest. You do know"—he glared at Tas—"what a Life Quest is?"†

"Sure," said Tas glibly. "My friend Gnosh had a Life Quest. Only his was dragon orbs. Each gnome has assigned to him a particular project that he must complete successfully or never get into the Afterlife." Tas had a sudden thought. "That's not why you're here, is it?"

"No." The gnome shook his wispy-haired head. "My family's Life Quest was developing an invention that could take us from one dimensional plane of existence to another. And"—Gnimsh heaved a sigh—"mine worked."

"It worked?" Tas said, sitting up in astonishment.

"Perfectly," Gnimsh answered with increasing despondency.

Tasslehoff was stunned. He'd never before heard

"Science is a gnome's life, so much so that every gnome chooses a special Life Quest upon reaching adulthood. More important than family ties, the Life Quest defines the gnome. The Life Quest is always related to furthering knowledge or developing technology.

*"The goal is specific and usually out of reach. It is not uncommon for Life Quests to be handed down from one generation to the next multiple times before it is achieved. Successful completion of a Life Quest ensures the gnome, and any forebear working on the same quest, a place in the afterlife with Reorx. [*DRAGONLANCE *Campaign Setting, Wizards of the Coast, Inc., 2003, p. 25.]*

of such a thing—a gnomish invention that worked
. . . and perfectly, too!

Gnimsh glanced at him. "Oh, I know what you're
thinking," he said. "I'm a failure. You don't know
the half of it. You see—*all* of my inventions work.
Every one."

Gnimsh put his head in his hands.

"How—how does that make you a failure?" Tas
asked, confused.

Gnimsh raised his head, staring at him. "Well,
what good is inventing something if it works?†
Where's the challenge? The need for creativity? For
forward thinking? What would become of progress?
You know," he said with deepening gloom, "that if I
hadn't come here, they were getting ready to exile
me. They said I was a distinct threat to society. I set
scientific exploration back a hundred years."

Gnimsh's head drooped. "That's why I don't mind
being here. Like you, I deserve it. It's where I'm
likely to wind up anyway."

"Where is your device?" Tas asked in sudden
excitement.

"Oh, *they* took it away, of course," Gnimsh
answered, waving his hand.

"Well!"—the kender thought—"can't you imagine one? You imagined up that chair?"

"And you saw what *it* did!" Gnimsh replied.
"Likely I'd end up with my father's invention. It
took him to another plane of existence, all right.
The Committee† on Exploding Devices is studying
it now, in fact, or at least they were when I got stuck
here. What are you trying to do? Find a way out of
the Abyss?"

"I have to," Tas said resolutely. "The Queen of
Darkness will win the war, otherwise, and it will all
be my fault. Plus, I've got some friends who are in
terrible danger. Well, one of them isn't exactly a
friend, but he *is* an interesting person and, while he
did try to kill me by making me break the magical
device, I'm certain it was nothing personal. He had
a good reason. . . ."

Tas stopped.

"That's it!" he said, springing up off the bed.
"That's it!" he cried in such excitement that a whole
forest of hatracks appeared around the bed, much to
the gnome's alarm.

*Jeff Grubb is responsible
for all things gnomish.
—MW*

*This preoccupation with
departments may have
been a reflection of our
corporate life at TSR.
—TRH*

Gnimsh slid off his stool, eyeing Tas warily. "What's it?" he demanded, bumping into a hatrack.

"Look!" Tas said, fumbling with his pouches. He opened one, then another. "Here it is!" he said, holding a pouch open to show Gnimsh. But, just as the gnome was peering into it, Tas suddenly slammed it shut. "Wait!"

"What?" Gnimsh asked, startled.

"Are *they* watching?" Tas asked breathlessly. "Will they know?"

"Know what?"

"Just—will they know?"

"No, I don't suppose so," Gnimsh answered hesitantly. "I can't say for sure, since I don't know what it is they're not supposed to know. But I do know that they're all pretty busy,† right now, from what I can tell. Waking up evil dragons and that sort of thing. Takes a lot of work."

Again, we see the known gods of Krynn mirroring the qualities of the gods of Olympus. —TRH

"Good," Tas said grimly, sitting on the bed. "Now, look at this." He opened his pouch and dumped out the contents. "What does that remind you of?"

"The year my mother invented the device designed to wash dishes," the gnome said. "The kitchen was knee-deep in broken crockery. We had to—"

"No!" Tas snapped irritably. "Look, hold this piece next to this one and—"

"My dimensional traveling device!" Gnimsh gasped. "You're right! It *did* look something like this. Mine didn't have all these gewgaw jewels, but. . . . No, look. You've got it all wrong. I think that goes here, not there. Yes. See? And then this chain hooks on here and wraps around like so. No, that's not quite the way. It must go . . . Wait, I see. This has to fit in there first." Sitting down on the bed, Gnimsh picked up one of the jewels and stuck it into place. "Now, I need another one of these red gizmos." He began sorting through the jewels. "What did you do to this thing, anyway?" he muttered. "Put it into a meat grinder?"

But the gnome, absorbed in his task, completely ignored Tas's answer. The kender, meanwhile, took advantage of the opportunity to tell his story again. Perching on the stool, Tas talked blissfully and without interruption while, totally forgetting the kender's existence, Gnimsh began to arrange the myriad jewels and little gold and silver things and chains, stacking them into neat piles.

All the while Tas was talking, though, he was watching Gnimsh, hope filling his heart. Of course, he thought with a pang, he *had* prayed to Fizban, and there was every possibility that, if Gnimsh got this device working, it might whisk them onto a moon† or turn them both into chickens or something. But, Tas decided, he'd just have to take that chance. After all, he'd promised he'd try to straighten things out, and though finding a failed gnome wasn't quite what he'd had in mind, it was better than sitting around, waiting to die.

Gnimsh, meanwhile, had imagined up a piece of slate and a bit of chalk and was sketching diagrams, muttering, "Slide jewel A into golden gizmo B—"†

This may not be as impossible as it sounds. See Darkness and Light *by Paul B. Thompson and Tonya C. Cook.*

Tracy devised the time travel device and wrote the poem that goes with it. He is also the only one who ever understood the Raistlin/Fistandantilus time loop and—honest to God—he had to explain it to me by drawing a diagram on a chalkboard at TSR. The diagram covered two chalkboards, as I recall. In honor of this, we see Gnimsh at the end of the chapter working with a chalkboard. —MW

CHAPTER
9

Awretched place, my brother," Raistlin remarked softly as he slowly and stiffly dismounted from his horse.

"We've stayed in worse," Caramon commented, helping Lady Crysania from her mount. "It's warm and dry inside, which makes it one hundred times better than out here. Besides," he added gruffly, glancing at his brother, who had collapsed against the side of his horse, coughing and shivering, "we none of us can ride farther without rest. I'll see to the horses. You two go on in."

Crysania, huddled in her sodden cloak, stood in the foot-deep mud and stared dully at the inn. It was, as Raistlin said, a wretched place.

What the name might have been, no one knew, for no sign hung above the door. The only thing, in fact, that marked it as an inn at all was a crudely lettered slate stuck in the broken front window that read,

"WayFarrers WelCum". The stone building itself was old and sturdily constructed. But the roof was falling in, though attempts had been made, here and there, to patch it with thatch. One window was broken. An old felt hat covered it, supposedly to keep out the rain. The yard was nothing but mud and a few bedraggled weeds.

Raistlin had gone ahead. Now he stood in the open doorway, looking back at Crysania. Light glowed from inside, and the smell of wood smoke promised a fire. As Raistlin's face hardened into an expression of impatience, a gust of wind blew back the hood of Crysania's cloak, driving the slashing rain into her face. With a sigh, she slogged through the mud to reach the front door.

"Welcome, master. Welcome, missus."

Crysania started at the voice that came from beside her—she had not seen anyone when she entered. Turning, she saw an ill-favored man huddling in the shadows behind the door, just as it slammed shut.

"A raw day, master," the man said, rubbing his hands together in a servile manner. That, a grease-stained apron, and a torn rag thrown over his arm marked him as the innkeeper. Glancing around the filthy, shabby inn, Crysania thought it appropriate enough. The man drew nearer to them, still rubbing his hands, until he was so close to Crysania that she could smell the foul odor of his beery breath. Covering her face with her cloak, she drew away from him. He seemed to grin at this, a drunken grin that might have appeared foolish had it not been for the cunning expression in his squinty eyes.

Looking at him, Crysania felt for a moment that she would almost prefer to go back out into the storm. But Raistlin, with only a sharp, penetrating glance at the innkeeper, said coldly, "A table near the fire."

"Aye, master, aye. A table near the fire, aye. Good on such a wicked day as this be. Come, master, missus, this way." Bobbing and bowing in a fawning manner that was, once again, belied by the look in his eyes, the man shuffled sideways across the floor, never taking his gaze from them, herding them toward a dirty table.

"A wizard be ye, master?" asked the innkeeper, reaching out a hand to touch Raistlin's black robes but

withdrawing it immediately at the mage's piercing glance. "One of the Black 'unst too. It's been a long while since we've seen the like, that it has," he continued. Raistlin did not answer. Overcome by another fit of coughing, he leaned heavily upon his staff. Crysania helped him to a chair near the fire. Sinking down into it, he huddled gratefully toward the warmth.

"Hot water," ordered Crysania, untying her wet cloak.

"What be the matter with 'im?" the innkeeper asked suspiciously, drawing back. "Not the burning fever, is it? Cause if it is, ye can go back out—"

"No," Crysania snapped, throwing off her cloak. "His illness is his own, of no harm to others." Leaning down near the mage, she glanced back up at the innkeeper. "I asked for hot water," she said peremptorily.

"Aye." His lip curled. He no longer rubbed his hands but shoved them beneath the greasy apron before he shuffled off.

Her disgust lost in her concern for Raistlin, Crysania forgot the innkeeper as she tried to make the mage more comfortable. She unfastened his traveling cloak and helped him remove it then spread it to dry before the fire. Searching the inn's common room, she discovered several shabby chair cushions and, trying to ignore the dirt that covered them, brought them back to arrange around Raistlin so that he could lean back and breathe more easily.

Kneeling beside him to help remove his wet boots, she felt a hand touch her hair.

"Thank you," Raistlin whispered, as she looked up.

Crysania flushed with pleasure. His brown eyes seemed warmer than the fire, and his hand brushed back the wet hair from her face with a gentle touch. She could not speak or move but remained, kneeling at his side, held fast by his gaze.

"Be you his woman?"

The innkeeper's harsh voice, coming from behind her, made Crysania start. She had neither seen him approach nor heard his shuffling step. Rising to her feet, unable to look at Raistlin, she turned abruptly to face the fire, saying nothing.

"She is a lady of one of the royal houses of Palanthas," said a deep voice from the doorway. "And I'll thank you to speak of her with respect, innkeep."

All text has a voice, even the narrative. Characters all have their own voice, a distinctive way of speaking. It is important for a writer to be aware of the voice of every character and to reflect that in the text. —TRH

"Aye, master, aye," muttered the innkeeper, seemingly daunted by Caramon's massive girth as the big man came inside, bringing in a gust of wind and rain with him. "I'm sure I intended no disrespect and I hopes none was taken."

Crysania did not answer. Half-turning, she said in a muffled voice, "Here, bring that water to the table."

As Caramon shut the door and came over to join them, Raistlin drew forth the pouch that contained the herbal concoction for his potion. Tossing it onto the table, he directed Crysania, with a gesture, to prepare his drink. Then he sank back among the cushions, his breath wheezing, gazing into the flames. Conscious of Caramon's troubled gaze upon her, Crysania kept her gaze on the potion she was preparing.

"The horses are fed and watered. We've ridden them easy enough, so they'll be able to go on after an hour's rest. I want to reach Solanthus before nightfall," Caramon said after a moment's uncomfortable silence. He spread his cloak before the fire. The steam rose from it in clouds. "Have you ordered food?" he asked Crysania abruptly.

"No, just the—the hot water," she murmured, handing Raistlin his drink.

"Innkeep, wine for the lady and the mage, water for me, and whatever you have to eat," Caramon said, sitting down near the fire on the opposite side of the table from his brother. After weeks of traveling this barren land toward the Plains of Dergoth, they had all learned that one ate what was on hand at these roadside inns, if—indeed—there was anything at all.

"This is only the beginning of the fall storms," Caramon said quietly to his brother as the innkeeper slouched out of the room again. "They will get worse the farther south we travel. Are you resolved on this course of action? It could be the death of you."

"What do you mean by that?" Raistlin's voice cracked. Starting up, he sloshed some of the hot potion from the cup.

"Nothing, Raistlin," Caramon said, taken aback by his brother's piercing stare. "Just—just . . . your cough. It's always worse in the damp."

Staring sharply at his twin, and seeing that, apparently, Caramon meant no more than he had said, Raistlin leaned back into the cushions once more. "Yes, I am resolved upon this course of action. So should you be too, my brother. For it is the only way you will ever see your precious home again."

"A lot of good it will do me if you die on the way," Caramon growled.

Crysania looked at Caramon in shock, but Raistlin only smiled bitterly. "Your concern touches me, brother. But do not fear for my health. My strength will be sufficient to get there and cast the final spell, if I do not tax myself overly in the meantime."

"It seems you have someone who will take care you do not do that," Caramon replied gravely, his gaze on Crysania.

She flushed again and would have made some remark, but the innkeeper returned. Standing beside them, a kettle of some steaming substance in one hand and a cracked pitcher in the other, he regarded them warily.

"Pardon my asking, masters," he whined, "but I'll see the color of yer money first. Times being what they are—"

"Here," said Caramon, taking a coin from his purse and tossing it upon the table. "Will that suit?"

"Aye, masters, aye." The innkeeper's eyes shone nearly as brightly as the silver piece. Setting down the kettle and pitcher, slopping stew onto the table, he grabbed the coin greedily, watching the mage all the while as though fearful he might make it disappear.

Thrusting the coin into his pocket, the innkeeper shuffled behind the slovenly bar and returned with three bowls, three horn spoons, and three mugs. These he also slapped down on the table, then stood back, his hands once more rubbing together. Crysania picked up the bowls and, staring at them in disgust, immediately began to wash them in the remaining hot water.

"Will there be anything else, masters, missus?" the innkeeper asked in such fawning tones that Caramon grimaced.

"Do you have bread and cheese?"

"Yes, master."

"Wrap some up then, in a basket."

"Ye'll be . . . traveling on, will ye?" the innkeeper asked.

Placing the bowls back upon the table, Crysania looked up, aware of a subtle change in the man's voice. She glanced at Caramon to see if he noticed, but the big man was stirring the stew, sniffing at it hungrily. Raistlin, seeming not to have heard, stared fixedly into the fire, his hands clasping the empty mug limply.

"We're certainly not spending the night here," Caramon said, ladling stew into the bowls.

"Ye'll find no better lodgings in—Where did you say you was headed?" the innkeeper asked.

"It's no concern of yours," Crysania replied coldly. Taking a full bowl of stew, she brought it to Raistlin. But the mage, after one look at the thick, grease-covered substance, waved it away. Hungry as she was, Crysania could only choke down a few mouthfuls of the mixture. Shoving the bowl aside, she wrapped herself in her still-damp cloak and curled up in her chair, closing her eyes and trying not to think that in an hour she'd be back on her horse, riding through the bleak, storm-ridden land once again.

Raistlin had already fallen asleep. The only sounds made were by Caramon, eating the stew with the appetite of an old campaigner, and by the innkeeper, returning to the kitchen to fix the basket as ordered.

Within an hour, Caramon brought the horses round from the stable—three riding horses and one pack horse, heavily laden, its burden covered with a blanket and secured with strong ropes. Helping his brother and Lady Crysania to mount, and seeing them both settled wearily into their saddles, Caramon mounted his own gigantic steed. The innkeeper stood out in the rain, bareheaded, holding the basket. He handed it up to Caramon, grinning and bobbing as the rain soaked through his clothes.

With curt thanks, and tossing another coin that landed in the mud at the innkeeper's feet, Caramon grabbed the reins of the pack horse and started off. Crysania and Raistlin followed, heavily muffled in their cloaks against the downpour.

The innkeeper, apparently oblivious to the rain, picked up the coin and stood watching them ride

away. Two figures emerged from the confines of the stables, joining him.

Tossing the coin in the air, the innkeeper glanced at them. "Tell 'im—they travel the Solanthus road."

They fell easy victims to the ambush.

Riding in the failing light of the dismal day, beneath thick trees whose branches dripped water monotonously and whose fallen leaves obscured even the sound of their own horses' footfalls, each was lost in his or her own gloomy thoughts. None heard the galloping of hooves or the ring of bright steel until it was too late.

Before they knew what was happening, dark shapes dropped out of the trees like huge, terrifying birds, smothering them with their black-cloaked wings. It was all done quietly, skillfully.

One clambered up behind Raistlin, knocking the mage unconscious before he could turn. Another dropped from a branch beside Crysania, clasping his hand over her mouth and holding the point of his dagger to her throat. But it took three of them to drag Caramon from his horse and wrestle the big man to the ground, and, when the struggle was finally over, one of the robbers† did not get to his feet. Nor would he, ever again, it seemed. He lay quite still in the mud, his head facing the wrong direction.

After the Cataclysm, most of Ansalon fell into chaos. This happened in our own history—the fall of the Roman Empire led to the Dark Ages, the Civil War gave rise to the "lawlessness" of the West.

"Neck's broke," reported one of the robbers to a figure who came up—after all was over—to survey the handiwork.

"Neat job of it, too," the robber commented coolly, eyeing Caramon, who was being held in the grip of four men, his big arms bound with bowstrings. A deep cut on his head bled freely, the rainwater washing the blood down his face. Shaking his head, trying to clear it, Caramon continued to struggle.

The leader, noticing the bulging muscles that strained the strong, wet bowstrings until several of his guards looked at them apprehensively, shook his head in admiration.

Caramon, finally clearing the fuzziness from his head and shaking the blood and rainwater from his eyes, glanced around. At least twenty or thirty heavily armed men stood around them. Looking up at their leader, Caramon breathed a muttered oath.

"Half-ogres are usually born out of violence and slavery. They are considered weak and soft by ogre standards, and bestial and ugly by human standards." — [DRAGONLANCE Campaign Setting, Wizards of the Coast, Inc., 2003, p.41.]

This man was easily the biggest human Caramon had ever seen!

His thoughts went instantly back to Raag and the gladiator arena in Istar. "Part ogre,"† he said to himself, spitting out a tooth that had been knocked loose in the fight. Remembering vividly the huge ogre who had helped Arack train the gladiators for the Games, Caramon saw that, though obviously human, this man had a yellow, ogre-ish cast to his skin and the same, flat-nosed face. He was larger than most humans, too—towering head and shoulders over the tall Caramon—with arms like tree trunks. But he walked with an odd gait, Caramon noticed, and he wore a long cloak that dragged the ground, hiding his feet.

Having been taught in the arena to size up an enemy and search out every weakness, Caramon watched the man closely. When the wind blew aside the thick fur cloak that covered him, Caramon saw in astonishment that the man had only one leg. The other was a steel pegleg.

Noticing Caramon's glance at his pegleg, the half-ogre grinned broadly and took a step nearer the big man. Reaching out a huge hand, the robber patted Caramon tenderly on the cheek.

"I admire a man who puts up a good fight," he said in a soft voice. Then, with startling swiftness, he doubled his hand into a fist, drew back his arm, and slugged Caramon in the jaw. The force of the blow knocked the big warrior backward, nearly causing those who held him to fall over, too. "But you'll pay for the death of my man."

Gathering his long, fur cloak around him, the half-ogre stumped over to where Crysania stood, held securely in the arms of one of the robbers. Her captor still had his hand over her mouth, and, though her face was pale, her eyes were dark and filled with anger.

"Isn't this nice," the half-ogre said softly. "A present, and it's not even Yule." His laughter boomed through the trees. Reaching out, he caught hold of her cloak and ripped it from her neck. His gaze flicked rapidly over her curving figure, well revealed as the rain soaked instantly through her white robes. His smile widened and his eyes glinted. He reached out a huge hand.

Crysania shrank away from him, but the half-ogre grabbed hold of her easily, laughing.

"Why, what's this bauble you wear, sweet one?" he asked, his gaze going to the medallion of Paladine she wore around her slender neck. "I find it . . . unbecoming. Pure platinum, it is!" He whistled. "Best let me keep it for you, dear. I fear that, in the pleasures of our passion, it might get lost—"

Caramon had recovered enough by now to see the half-ogre grasp the medallion in his hand. There was a glint of grim amusement in Crysania's eyes, though she shuddered visibly at the man's touch. A flash of pure, white light crackled through the driving rain. The half-ogre clutched at his hand. Drawing it back with a snarl of pain, he released Crysania.

There was a muttering among the men standing watching. The man holding Crysania suddenly loosened his grip and she jerked free, glaring at him angrily and pulling her cloak back around her.

The half-ogre raised his hand, his face twisted in rage. Caramon feared he would strike Crysania, when, at that moment, one of the man yelled out.

"The wizard, he's comin' to!"

The half-ogre's eyes were still on Crysania, but he lowered his hand. Then, he smiled. "Well, witch, you have won the first round, it seems." He glanced back at Caramon. "I enjoy contests—both in fighting and in love. This promises to be a night of amusement, all around."

Giving a gesture, he ordered the man who had been holding Crysania to take her in hand again, and the man did, though Caramon noticed it was with extreme reluctance. The half-ogre walked over to where Raistlin lay upon the ground, groaning in pain.

"Of all of them, the wizard's the most dangerous. Bind his hands behind his back and gag him," ordered the robber in a grating voice. "If he so much as croaks, cut out his tongue. That'll end his spellcasting days for good."†

"Why don't we just kill him now?" one of the men growled.

"Go ahead, Brack," said the half-ogre pleasantly, turning swiftly to regard the man who had spoken. "Take your knife and slit his throat."

"Not with *my* hands," the man muttered, backing up a step.

He is correct. Spellcasting requires incantation, hand motions, the mixing of spell components, or some combination of them all, depending upon the spell.

"No? You'd rather *I* was the one cursed for murdering a Black Robe?" the leader continued, still in the same, pleasant tone. "You'd enjoy seeing *my* sword hand wither and drop off?"

"I—I didn't mean that, of course, Steeltoe. I—I wasn't thinking, that's all."

"Then start thinking. He can't harm us now. Look at him," Steeltoe gestured to Raistlin. The mage lay on his back, his hands bound in front of him. His jaws had been forced open and a gag tied around his mouth. However, his eyes gleamed from the shadows of his hood in a baleful rage, and his hands clenched in such impotent fury that more than one of the strong men standing about wondered uneasily if such measures were adequate.

Perhaps feeling something of this himself, Steeltoe† limped over to where Raistlin lay staring up at him with bitter hatred. As he stopped near the mage, a smile creased the half-ogre's yellowish face, and he suddenly slammed the steel toe of his pegleg against the side of Raistlin's head. The mage went limp. Crysania cried out in alarm, but her captor held her fast. Even Caramon was amazed to feel swift, sharp pain contract his heart as he saw his brother's form lying huddled in the mud.

"That should keep him quiet for a while. When we reach camp, we'll blindfold him and take him for a walk up on the Rock. If he slips and falls over the cliff, well, that's the way of things, isn't it, men? His blood won't be on our hands."

There was some scattered laughter, but Caramon saw more than a few glance uneasily at each other, shaking their heads.

Steeltoe turned away from Raistlin to examine with gleaming eyes the heavily laden pack horse. "We've made a rich haul this day, men," he said in satisfaction. Stumping back around, he came to where Crysania stood, pinned in the arms of her somewhat nervous captor.

"A rich haul, indeed," he murmured. One huge hand grasped Crysania's chin roughly. Bending down, he pressed his lips against hers in a brutal kiss. Trapped in the arms of her captor, Crysania could do nothing. She did not struggle; perhaps some inner sense told her this was precisely what the man wanted. She stood straight, her body rigid.

"The half-ogre is about seven feet tall, powerfully built, with a steel peg leg in place of his missing lower left leg (lost in a battle with a griffon). Attached at the knee, the peg leg has a round toe and is a formidable weapon.

*"The half-ogre is skilled in wrestling techniques and swordsmanship. He is a brutish-looking man with a yellowish cast to his complexion and a large, flat nose. He appears human in all other aspects." [*Dragonlance Adventures, *by Tracy Hickman and Margaret Weis, TSR, Inc., 1987, p. 90.]*

But Caramon saw her hands clench and, when Steeltoe released her, she could not help but avert her face, her dark hair falling across her cheek.

"You know my policy, men," Steeltoe said, fondling her hair coarsely, "share the spoils among us—after I've taken my cut, of course."

There was more laughter at this and, here and there, some scattered cheering. Caramon had no doubt of the man's meaning and he guessed, from the few comments he heard, that this wouldn't be the first time "spoils" had been "shared."

But there were some young faces who frowned, glancing at each other in disquiet, shaking their heads. And there were even a few muttered comments, such as, "I'll have nought to do with a witch!" and "I'd sooner bed the wizard!"

Witch! There was that term again. Vague memories stirred in Caramon's mind—memories of the days† when he and Raistlin had traveled with Flint, the dwarven metalsmith; days before the return of the true gods. Caramon shivered, suddenly remembering with vivid clarity the time they had come into a town that was going to burn an old woman at the stake for witchcraft. He recalled how his brother and Sturm, the ever noble knight, had risked their lives to save the old crone, who turned out to be nothing more than a second-rate illusionist.

But Caramon had forgotten, until now, how the people of this time viewed any type of magical powers, and Crysania's clerical powers—in these days when there were no true clerics—would be even more suspect. He shuddered, then forced himself to think with cold logic. Burning was a harsh death, but it was a far quicker one than—

"Bring the witch to me." Steeltoe limped across the trail to where one of his men held his horse. Mounting, he gestured. "Then follow with the others."

Crysania's captor dragged her forward. Reaching down, Steeltoe grabbed her under the arms and lifted her onto the horse, seating her in front of him. Grasping the reins in his hands, his thick arms wrapped around her, completely engulfing her. Crysania sat staring straight ahead, her face cold and impassive.

Does she know? Caramon wondered, watching helplessly as Steeltoe rode past him, the man's

We included stories like this in order to give depth to the characters, to provide them with interesting backgrounds, and to tantalize the readers by allowing them to imagine how this encounter might have come about, what might have happened, what the characters might have done and said. It is important to us that these backstories never be told but should be left to the reader's imagination. —MW

yellowish face twisted into a leer. She's always been sheltered, protected from things like this. Perhaps she doesn't realize what dreadful acts these men are capable of committing.

And then Crysania glanced back at Caramon. Her face was calm and pale, but there was a look of such horror in her eyes, horror and pleading, that he hung his head, his heart aching.

She knows. . . . The gods help her. She knows. . . .

Someone shoved Caramon from behind. Several men grabbed him and flung him, headfirst, over the saddle of his horse. Hanging upside down, his strong arms bound with the bowstrings that were cutting into his flesh, Caramon saw the men lift his brother's limp body and throw it over his own horse's saddle. Then the bandits mounted up and led their captives deeper into the forest.

The rain streamed down on Caramon's bare head as the horse plodded through the mud, jouncing him roughly. The pommel of the saddle jabbed him in the side; the blood rushing to his head made him dizzy. But all he could see in his mind as they rode were those dark, terror-filled eyes, pleading with him for help.

And Caramon knew, with sick certainty, that no help would come.

CHAPTER 10

Raistlin walked across a burning desert. A line of footsteps† stretched before him in the sand, and he was walking in these footsteps. On and on the footsteps led him, up and down dunes of brilliant white, blazing in the sun. He was hot and tired and terribly thirsty. His head hurt, his chest ached, and he wanted to lie down and rest. In the distance was a water hole, cooled by shady trees. But, try as he might, he could not reach it. The footsteps did not go that way, and he could not move his feet any other direction.

On and on he plodded, his black robes hanging heavily about him. And then, nearly spent, he looked up and gasped in terror. The footsteps led to a scaffold! A black-hooded figure knelt with its head upon the block. And, though he could not see the face, he knew with terrible certainty that it was he himself who knelt there, about to die. The executioner stood above him, a bloody axe in his hand. The executioner, too, wore a black hood that covered his face. He

Raistlin's nightmare of the footsteps in the desert reflects his inner agony at being constrained to follow in the path of Fistandantilus. Raistlin has realized that he is a prisoner of the time loop that he himself created and that it will lead to his destruction. —MW

*raised the axe and held it poised above Raistlin's neck.
And as the axe fell, Raistlin saw in his last moments a
glimpse of his executioner's face. . . .*

"Raist!" whispered a voice.

The mage shook his aching head. With the voice
came the comforting realization that he had been
dreaming. He struggled to wake up, fighting off
the nightmare.

"Raist!" hissed the voice, more urgently.

A sense of real danger, not dreamed danger, roused
the mage further. Waking fully, he lay still for a
moment, keeping his eyes closed until he was more
completely aware of what was going on.

He lay on wet ground, his hands bound in front of
him, his mouth gagged. There was throbbing pain in
his head and Caramon's voice in his ears.

Around him, he could hear sounds of voices and
laughter, he could smell the smoke of cooking
fires. But none of the voices seemed very near,
except his brother's. And then everything came
back to him. He remembered the attack, he remembered a man with a steel leg. . . . Cautiously, Raistlin
opened his eyes.

Caramon lay near him in the mud, stretched out
on his stomach, his arms bound tightly with bowstrings. There was a familiar glint in his twin's brown
eyes, a glint that brought back a rush of memories of
old days, times long past—fighting together, com-
bining steel and magic.

And, despite the pain and the darkness around
them, Raistlin felt a sense of exhilaration he had not
experienced in a long time.

Brought together† by danger, the bond between
the two was strong now, letting them communicate
with both word and thought. Seeing his brother fully
cognizant of their plight, Caramon wriggled as close
as he dared, his voice barely a breath.

"Is there any way you can free your hands? Do
you still carry the silver dagger?"

Raistlin nodded once, briefly. At the beginning
of time, magic-users were prohibited by the gods
from carrying any type of weapon or wearing any
sort of armor. The reason being, ostensibly, that they
needed to devote time to study that could not be
spent achieving proficiency in the art of weaponry.
But, after the magic-users had helped Huma defeat

*Caramon and Raistlin do
work together well when
confronting a common foe.
—TRH*

the Queen of Darkness by creating the magical dragon orbs, the gods granted them the right to carry daggers upon their persons—in memory of Huma's lance.

Bound to his wrist by a cunning leather thong that would allow the weapon to slip down into his hand when needed, the silver dagger was Raistlin's last means of defense, to be used only when all his spells were cast . . . or at a time like this.

"Are you strong enough to use your magic?" Caramon whispered.

Raistlin closed his eyes wearily for a moment. Yes, he was strong enough. But—this meant a further weakening, this meant more time would be needed to regain strength to face the Guardians of the Portal. Still, if he didn't live that long . . .

Of course, he *must* live! he thought bitterly. Fistandantilus had lived! He was doing nothing more than following footsteps through the sand.

Angrily, Raistlin banished the thought. Opening his eyes, he nodded. *I am strong enough,* he told his brother mentally, and Caramon sighed in relief.

"Raist," the big man whispered, his face suddenly grave and serious, "you . . . you can guess what . . . what they plan for Crysania."

Raistlin had a sudden vision of that hulking, ogre-ish human's rough hands upon Crysania, and he felt a startling sensation—rage and anger such as he had rarely experienced gripped him. His heart contracted painfully and, for a moment, he was blinded by a blood-dimmed haze.

Seeing Caramon regarding him with astonishment, Raistlin realized that his emotions must be apparent on his face. He scowled, and Caramon continued hurriedly. "I have a plan."

Raistlin nodded irritably, already aware of what his brother had in mind.

Caramon whispered, "If I fail—"

—*I'll kill her first, then myself,* Raistlin finished. But, of course, there would be no need. He was safe . . . protected. . . .

Then, hearing men approaching, the mage closed his eyes, thankfully feigning unconsciousness again. It gave him time to sort his tangled emotions and force himself to regain control. The silver dagger was cold against his arm. He flexed the muscles that would release the thong. And, all the while, he pondered that strange reaction he'd felt about a woman he cared nothing for . . . except her usefulness to him as a cleric, of course.

Two men jerked Caramon to his feet and shoved him forward. Caramon was thankful to notice that, beyond a quick glance to make certain the mage was still unconscious, neither man paid any attention to his twin. Stumbling along over the uneven ground, gritting his teeth against the pain from cramped, chilled leg muscles, Caramon found himself thinking about that odd expression on his brother's face when he mentioned Lady Crysania. Caramon would have called it the outraged expression of a lover, if seen on the face of any other man. But his brother? Was Raistlin capable of such an emotion? Caramon had decided in Istar that Raistlin wasn't, that he had been completely consumed by evil.

But now, his twin seemed different, much more like the old Raistlin, the brother he had fought side by side with so many times before, their lives in each other's keeping. What Raistlin had told Caramon about Tas made sense. So he hadn't killed the kender after all. And, though sometimes irritable, Raistlin was always unfailingly gentle with Crysania. Perhaps—

One of the guards jabbed him painfully in the ribs, recalling Caramon to the desperateness of their situation. Perhaps! He snorted. Perhaps it would all end here and now. Perhaps the only thing he would buy with his life would be swift death for the other two.

Walking through the camp, thinking over all he had seen and heard since the ambush, Caramon mentally reviewed his plan.

The bandit's camp was more like a small town than a thieves' hideout. They lived in crudely built log huts, keeping their animals sheltered in a large cave. They had obviously been here some time, and apparently feared no law—giving mute testimony to the strength and leadership capabilities of the half-ogre, Steeltoe.†

But Caramon, having had more than a few runins with thieves in his day, saw that many of these men were not loutish ruffians. He had seen several

"The product of a loathsome alliance between an ogre and a wretched human woman, Steeltoe was abandoned by his mother at birth. A nobleman of Solamnia found the child, took pity on him, and gave him a home. The half-ogre proved unusually intelligent. The nobleman provided for his education and made Steeltoe master of his estates when the half-ogre reached maturity. Steeltoe repaid his master's kindness by murdering the nobleman and stealing his money.

"Crimes of this sort were not unusual in the bitter days following the Cataclysm. The half-ogre escaped easily into the wilderness of Solamnia, gathering around him other men living outside the law. Because of his education, Steeltoe found it easy to attract many disillusioned young men, particularly reviled Knights of Solamnia, who otherwise would have had nothing to do with bandits. Steeltoe is a clever speech maker, continually reminding his men that the world owes them a living and it is their right to take what they want."
[DRAGONLANCE Adventures, by Tracy Hickman and Margaret Weis, TSR, Inc., 1987, p. 90.]

glance at Crysania and shake their heads in obvious distaste for what was to come. Though dressed in little more than rags, several carried fine weapons— steel swords of the kind passed down from father to son, and they handled them with the care given a family heirloom, not booty. And, though he could not be certain in the failing light of the stormy day, Caramon thought he had noted on many of the swords the Rose and the Kingfisher—the ancient symbol of the Solamnic Knights.

The men were clean-shaven, without the long mustaches that marked such knights, but Caramon could detect in their stern, young faces traces of his friend, the knight, Sturm Brightblade. And, reminded of Sturm, Caramon was reminded, too, of what he knew of the history† of the knighthood following the Cataclysm.

Blamed by most of their neighbors for bringing about the dreadful calamity, the knights had been driven from their homes by angry mobs. Many had been murdered, their families killed before their eyes. Those who survived went into hiding, roaming the land on their own or joining outlaw bands—like this one.

Glancing at the men as they stood about the camp cleaning their weapons and talking in low voices, Caramon saw the mark of evil deeds upon many faces, but he also saw looks of resignation and hopelessness. He had known hard times himself. He knew what it could drive a man to do.

All this gave him hope that his plan might succeed.

A bonfire blazed in the center of the encampment, not far from where he and Raistlin had been dumped on the ground. Glancing behind, he saw his brother still feigning unconsciousness. But he also saw, knowing what to look for, that the mage had managed to twist his body around into a position where he could both see and hear clearly.

As Caramon stepped forward into the fire's light, most of the men stopped what they were doing and followed, forming a half-circle around him. Sitting in a large wooden chair near the blaze was Steeltoe, a flagon in his hand. Standing near him, laughing and joking, were several men Caramon recognized at once as typical toadies, fawning over their leader. And he was not surprised to see,

The concept of a great society breaking down and collapsing into anarchy is an old and established theme. From the tales of Atlantis to our own rosy reflections on more recent history, it seems that everyone looks back on "the good old days" and feels that society has fallen apart. Socrates felt the same way in his time. The background history for the DRAGONLANCE setting that I originally created prominently featured this theme in the Cataclysm. In some ways, Legends is not only a sequel but a kind of prequel, showing us events that happened before Chronicles. —TRH

at the edge of the crowd, the grinning, ill-favored face of their innkeeper.

Sitting in a chair beside Steeltoe was Crysania. Her cloak had been taken from her. Her dress was ripped open at the bodice—he could imagine by whose hands. And, Caramon saw with growing anger, there was a purplish blotch on her cheek. One corner of her mouth was swollen.

But she held herself with rigid dignity, staring straight ahead and trying to ignore the crude jokes and frightful tales being bandied back and forth. Caramon smiled grimly in admiration. Remembering the panic-stricken state of near madness to which she had been reduced during the last days of Istar, and thinking of her previous soft and sheltered life, he was pleased, if amazed, to see her reacting to this dangerous situation with a coolness Tika might have envied.

Tika. . . . Caramon scowled. He had not meant to think of Tika—especially not in connection with Lady Crysania! Forcing his thoughts to the present, he coldly averted his eyes from the woman to his enemy, concentrating on him.

Seeing Caramon, Steeltoe turned from his conversation and gestured broadly for the warrior to approach.

"Time to die, warrior," Steeltoe said to him, still in the same pleasant tone of voice. He glanced over lazily at Crysania. "I'm certain, lady, you won't mind if our tryst is postponed a few moments while I take care of this matter. Just think of this as a little before-bed entertainment, my dear." He stroked Crysania's cheek with his hand. When she moved away from him, her dark eyes flashing in anger, he changed his caress to a slap, hitting her across the face.

Crysania did not cry out. Raising her head, she stared back at her tormentor with grim pride.

Knowing that he could not let himself be distracted by concern for her, Caramon kept his gaze on the leader, studying him calmly. This man rules by fear and brute force, he thought to himself. Of those who follow, many do so reluctantly. They're all afraid of him; he's probably the only law in this godforsaken land. But he's obviously kept them well fed and alive when they would otherwise have

perished. So they're loyal, but just how far will their loyalty go?

Keeping his voice evenly modulated, Caramon drew himself up, regarding the half-ogre with a look of disdain. "Is this how you show your bravery? Beating up women?" Caramon sneered. "Untie me and give me my sword, and we'll see what kind of man you really are!"

Steeltoe regarded him with interest and, Caramon saw uneasily, a look of intelligence on his brutish face.

"I had thought to have something more original out of you, warrior," Steeltoe said with a sigh that was part show and part not as he rose to his feet. "Perhaps you will not be such a challenge to me as I first thought. Still, I have nothing better to do this evening. *Early* in the evening, that is," he amended, with a leer and a rakish bow to Crysania, who ignored him.

The half-ogre threw aside the great fur cloak he wore and, turning, commanded one of his men to bring him his sword. The toadies scattered to do his bidding, while the other men moved to surround a cleared space to one side of the bonfire—obviously this was a sport that had been enjoyed before. During the confusion, Caramon managed to catch Crysania's eye.

Inclining his head, he glanced meaningfully toward where Raistlin lay. Crysania understood his meaning at once. Looking over at the mage, she smiled sadly and nodded. Her hand closed about the medallion of Paladine and her swollen lips moved.

Caramon's guards shoved him into the circle, and he lost sight of her. "It'll take more than prayers to Paladine to get us out of this one, lady," he muttered, wondering with a certain amount of amusement, if his brother was, at that moment, praying to the Queen of Darkness for help as well.

Well, he had no one to pray to, nothing to help him but his own muscle and bone and sinew.

They cut the bindings on his arms. Caramon flinched at the pain of blood returning to his limbs, but he flexed his stiff muscles, rubbing them to help the circulation and to warm himself. Then he stripped off his soaking-wet shirt and his breeches to fight naked. Clothes gave the enemy a chance for

a hand-hold, so his old instructor, Arack the dwarf, had taught him in the Games Arena in Istar.

At the sight of Caramon's magnificent physique, there was a murmur of admiration from the men standing around the circle. The rain streamed down over his tan, well-muscled body, the fire gleamed on his strong chest and shoulders, glinting off his numerous battle scars. Someone handed Caramon a sword, and the warrior swung it with practiced ease and obvious skill. Even Steeltoe, entering the ring of men, seemed a bit disconcerted at the sight of the former gladiator.

But if Steeltoe was—momentarily—startled at the appearance of his opponent, Caramon was no less taken aback at the appearance of Steeltoe. Half-ogre and half-human, the man had inherited the best traits of both races. He had the girth and muscle of the ogres, but he was quick on his feet and agile, while, in his eyes, was the dangerous intelligence of a human. He, too, fought almost naked, wearing nothing but a leather loincloth. But what made Caramon's breath whistle between his teeth was the weapon the half-ogre carried—easily the most wonderful sword the warrior had ever seen in his life.

A gigantic blade, it was designed for use as a two-handed weapon. Indeed, Caramon thought, eyeing it expertly, there were few men he knew who could even have lifted it, much less wielded it. But, not only did Steeltoe heft it with ease, he used it with one hand! And he used it well, that much Caramon could tell from the half-ogre's practiced, well-timed swings. The steel blade caught the fire's light as he slashed the air. It hummed as it sliced through the darkness, leaving a blazing trail of light behind it.

As his opponent limped into the ring, his steel pegleg gleaming, Caramon saw with despair that he faced not the brutish, stupid opponent he had expected, but a skilled swordsman, an intelligent man, who had overcome his handicap to fight with a mastery two-legged men might well envy.

Not only had Steeltoe overcome his handicap, Caramon discovered after their first pass, but the half-ogre made use of it in a most deadly fashion.

The two stalked each other, feinting, each watching for any weakness in the opponent's defense.

Then, suddenly, balancing himself easily on his good leg, Steeltoe used his steel leg as another weapon. Whirling around, he struck Caramon with the steel leg with such force that it sent the big man crashing to the ground. His sword flew from his hands.

Quickly regaining his balance, Steeltoe advanced with his huge sword, obviously intending to end the battle and get on to other amusements. But, though caught off guard, Caramon had seen this type of move in the arena. Lying on the ground, gasping for breath, feigning having had the wind knocked out of him, Caramon waited until his enemy closed on him. Then, reaching out, he grabbed hold of Steeltoe's good leg and jerked it out from beneath him.

The men standing around cheered and applauded. As the sound brought back vivid memories of the arena at Istar, Caramon felt his blood race. Worries about black-robed brothers and white-robed clerics vanished. So did thoughts of home. His self-doubts disappeared. The thrill of fighting, the intoxicating drug of danger, coursed through his veins, filling him with an ecstasy much like his twin felt using his magic.

Scrambling to his feet, seeing his enemy do the same, Caramon made a sudden, desperate lunge for his sword, which lay several feet from him. But Steeltoe was quicker. Reaching Caramon's sword first, he kicked it, sending it flying.

Even as he kept an eye on his opponent, Caramon glanced about for another weapon and saw the bonfire, blazing at the far end of the ring.

But Steeltoe saw Caramon's glance. Instantly guessing his objective, the half-ogre moved to block him.

Caramon made a run for it. The half-ogre's slashing blade sliced through the skin on his abdomen, leaving a glistening trail of blood behind. With a leaping dive, Caramon rolled near the logs, grabbed one by the end, and was on his feet as Steeltoe drove his blade into the ground where the big man's head had been only seconds before.

The sword arced through the air again. Caramon heard it humming and barely was able to parry the blow with the log in time. Chips and sparks flew as the sword bit into the wood, Caramon having grabbed a log that was burning at one end. The force of Steeltoe's blow was tremendous, making Caramon's hands

ring and the sharp edges of the log dig painfully into his flesh. But he held fast, using his great strength to drive the half-ogre backward as Steeltoe fought to recover his balance.

The half-ogre held firm, finally shoving his pegleg into the ground and pushing Caramon back. The two men slowly took up their positions again, circling each other. Then the air was filled with the flashing light of steel and flaming cinders.

How long they fought, Caramon had no idea. Time drowned in a haze of stinging pain and fear and exhaustion. His breath came in ragged gasps. His lungs burned like the end of the log, his hands were raw and bleeding. But still he gained no advantage. He had never in his life faced such an opponent. Steeltoe, too, who had entered the fight with a sneer of confidence, now faced his enemy with grim determination. Around them, the men stood silently now, enthralled by the deadly contest.

The only sounds at all, in fact, were the crackling of the fire, the heavy breathing of the opponents, or perhaps the splash of a body as one went down into the mud, or the grunt of pain when a blow told.

The circle of men and the firelight began to blur in Caramon's eyes. To his aching arms, the log felt heavier than a whole tree, now. Breathing was agony. His opponent was as exhausted as he, Caramon knew, from the fact that Steeltoe had neglected to follow up an advantageous blow, being forced to simply stand and catch his breath. The half-ogre had an ugly purple welt running along his side where Caramon's log had caught him. Everyone in the circle had heard the snapping of his ribs and seen the yellowish face contort in pain.

But he came back with a swipe of his sword that sent Caramon staggering backward, flailing away with the log in a frantic attempt to parry the stroke. Now the two stalked each other, neither hearing nor caring about anything else but the enemy across from him. Both knew that the next mistake would be fatal.

And then Steeltoe slipped in the mud. It was just a small slip, sending him down on his good knee, balancing on his pegleg. At the beginning of the battle, he would have been up in seconds. But his strength was giving out and it took a moment longer to struggle up again.

That second was what Caramon had been waiting for. Lurching forward, using the last bit of strength in his own body, Caramon lifted the log and drove it down as hard as he could on the knee to which the pegleg was attached. As a hammer strikes a nail, Caramon's blow drove the pegleg deep into the sodden ground.

Snarling in fury and pain, the half-ogre turned and twisted, trying desperately to drag his leg free, all the while attempting to keep Caramon back with slashing blows of his sword. Such was his tremendous strength that he almost succeeded. Even now, seeing his opponent trapped, Caramon had to fight the temptation to let his hurting body rest, to let his opponent go.

But there could be only one end to this contest. Both men had known that from the beginning. Staggering forward, grimly swinging his log, Caramon caught the half-ogre's blade and sent it flying from his hands. Seeing death in Caramon's eyes, Steeltoe still fought defiantly to free himself. Even at the last moment, as the log in the big man's hands whistled through the air, the half-ogre's huge hands made a clutching grasp for Caramon's arms—

The log smashed into the half-ogre's head with a wet, sodden thud and the crunch of bone, flinging the half-ogre backward. The body twitched, then was still. Steeltoe lay in the mud, his steel pegleg still pinning him to the ground, the rain washing away the blood and brains that oozed from the cracks in his skull.

Stumbling in weariness and pain, Caramon sank to his knees, leaning on the blood- and rain-soaked log, trying to catch his breath. There was a roaring in his ears—the angry shouts of men surging forward to kill him. He didn't care. It didn't matter. Let them come. . . .

But no one attacked.

Confused by this, Caramon raised his blurred gaze to a black-robed figure kneeling down beside him. He felt his brother's slender arm encircle him protectively, and he saw flickering darts of lightning flash warmingly from the mage's fingers. Closing his eyes, Caramon leaned his head against his brother's frail chest and drew a deep, shuddering breath.

Then he felt cool hands touch his skin and he heard a soft voice murmur a prayer to Paladine.

Caramon's eyes flared open. He shoved the startled Crysania away, but it was too late. Her healing influence spread through his body. He could hear the men gathered around him gasp as the bleeding wounds vanished, the bruises disappeared, and the color returned to his deathly pale face. Even the archmage's pyrotechnics had not created the outburst of alarm and shocked cries the healing did.

"Witchcraft! She healed him! Burn the witch!"

"Burn them both, witch and wizard!"

"They hold the warrior in thrall. We'll take them and free his soul!"

Glancing at his brother, he saw—from the grim expression on Raistlin's face—that the mage, too, was reliving old memories and understood the danger.

"Wait!" Caramon gasped, rising to his feet as the crowd of muttering men drew near. Only the fear of Raistlin's magic kept the men from rushing them, he knew, and—hearing his brother's sudden racking cough—Caramon feared Raistlin's strength might soon give out.

Catching hold of the confused Crysania, Caramon thrust her protectively behind him as he confronted the crowd of frightened, angry men.

"Touch this woman, and you will die as your leader died," he shouted, his voice loud and clear above the driving rain.

"Why should we let a witch live?" snarled one, and there were mutters of agreement.

"Because she's *my* witch!" Caramon said sternly, casting a defiant gaze around. Behind him, he heard Crysania draw in a sharp breath, but Raistlin gave her a warning glance and, if she had been going to speak, she sensibly kept quiet. "She does not hold me in thrall but obeys my commands and those of the wizard. She will do you no harm, I swear."

There were murmurs among the men, but their eyes, as they looked at Caramon, were no longer threatening. Admiration there had been—now he could see grudging respect and a willingness to listen.

"Let us be on our way," Raistlin began in his soft voice, "and we—"

"Wait!" rasped Caramon. Gripping his brother's arm, he drew him near and whispered. "I've got an idea. Watch over Crysania!"

Nodding, Raistlin moved to stand near Crysania, who stood quietly, her eyes on the now silent group of bandits. Caramon walked over to where the body of the half-ogre lay in the reddening mud. Leaning down, he wrested the great sword from Steeltoe's deathgrip and raised it high over his head. The big warrior was a magnificent sight, the firelight reflecting off his bronze skin, the muscles rippling in his arms as he stood in triumph above the body of his slain enemy.

"I have destroyed your leader. Now I claim the right to take his place!" Caramon shouted, his voice echoing among the trees. "I ask only one thing—that you leave this life of butchery and rape and robbery. We travel south—"

That got an unexpected reaction. "South! They travel south!" several voices cried and there was scattered cheering. Caramon stared at them, taken aback, not understanding. Raistlin, coming forward, clutched at him.

"What are you doing?" the mage demanded, his face pale.

Caramon shrugged, looking about in puzzled amazement at the enthusiasm he had created. "It just seemed a good idea to have an armed escort, Raistlin," he said. "The lands south of here are, by all accounts, wilder than those we have ridden through. I figured we could take a few of these men with us, that's all. I don't understand—"

A young man of noble bearing, who more than any of the others, recalled Sturm to Caramon's mind, stepped forward. Motioning the others to quiet down, he asked, "You're going south? Do you, perchance, seek the fabled wealth of the dwarves in Thorbardin?"

Raistlin scowled. "*Now* do you understand?" he snarled. Choking, he was shaken by a fit of coughing that left him weak and gasping. Had it not been for Crysania hurrying to support him, he might have fallen.

"I understand you need rest," Caramon replied grimly. "We all do. And unless we come up with some sort of armed escort, we'll never have a peaceful night's sleep. What do the dwarves in Thorbardin have to do with anything? What's going on?"

In this book, we see Caramon really coming to the forefront, becoming a true hero, who will prevail in the end, and also proving to the reader and to his brother that he is not the dullard many have taken him for. Caramon also starts to realize this, as well, and starts to gain in self-respect and self-esteem. —MW

Raistlin stared at the ground, his face hidden by the shadows of his hood. Finally, sighing, he said coldly, "Tell them yes, we go south. We're going to attack the dwarves."

Caramon's eyes opened wide. "Attack Thorbardin?"

"I'll explain later," Raistlin snarled softly. "Do as I tell you."

Caramon hesitated.

Shrugging his thin shoulders, Raistlin smiled unpleasantly. "It is your only way home, my brother! And maybe our only way out of here alive."

Caramon glanced around. The men had begun to mutter again during this brief exchange, obviously suspicious of their intentions. Realizing he had to make a decision quickly or lose them for good—and maybe even face another attack—he turned back, vying for time to try to think things through further.

"We go south," he said, "it is true. But for our own reasons. What is this you say of wealth in Thorbardin?"

"It is said that the dwarves have stored great wealth in the kingdom beneath the mountain," the young man answered readily. Others around him nodded.

"Wealth they stole from humans," added one.

"Aye! Not just money," cried out a third, "but grain and cattle and sheep. They'll eat like kings this winter, while our bellies go empty!"

"We have talked before of going south to take our share," the young man continued, "but Steeltoe said things were well enough here. There are some, though, who were having second thoughts."

Caramon pondered, wishing he knew more of history. He had heard of the Great Dwarfgate Wars,† of course. His old dwarf friend, Flint, talked of little else. Flint was a hill dwarf. He had filled Caramon's head with tales of the cruelty of the mountain dwarves of Thorbardin, saying much the same things these men said. But to hear Flint tell it, the wealth the mountain dwarves stole had been taken from their cousins, the hill dwarves.

If this were true, then Caramon might well be justified in making this decision. He could, of course, do as his brother commanded. But something inside Caramon had snapped in Istar. Even though he was

The Dwarfgate War: Humans and hill dwarves demand entry into Thorbardin and access to its food stores.
*[*DRAGONLANCE *Campaign Setting, Wizards of the Coast, Inc., 2003, p. 204.]*

beginning to think he had misjudged his brother, he knew him well enough to continue to distrust him. Never again would he obey Raistlin blindly.

But then he sensed Raistlin's glittering eyes upon him, and he heard his brother's voice echo in his mind.

Your only way back home!

Caramon clenched his fist in swift anger, but Raistlin had him, he knew. "We go south to Thorbardin," he said harshly, his troubled gaze on the sword in his hand. Then he raised his head to look at the men around him. "Will you come with us?"

There was a moment's hesitation. Several of the men came forward to talk to the young nobleman, who was now apparently their spokesman. He listened, nodded, then faced Caramon once more.

"We would follow *you* without hesitation, great warrior," said the young man, "but what have you to do with this black-robed wizard? Who is *he*, that we should follow him?"

"My name is Raistlin," the mage replied. "This man is my bodyguard."

There was no response, only dubious frowns and doubtful looks.

"I am his bodyguard, that is true," Caramon said quietly, "but the mage's real name is Fistandantilus."

At this, there were sharp intakes of breath among the men. The frowns changed to looks of respect, even fear and awe.

"My name is Garic," the young man said, bowing to the archmage with the old-fashioned courtesy of the Knights of Solamnia. "We have heard of you, Great One. And though your deeds are dark as your robes, we live in a time of dark deeds, it seems. We will follow you and the great warrior you bring with you."

Stepping forward, Garic laid his sword at Caramon's feet.† Others followed suit, some eagerly, others more warily. A few slunk off into the shadows. Knowing them for the cowardly ruffians they were, Caramon let them go.

He was left with about thirty men; a few of the same noble bearing as Garic, but most of them were ragged, dirty thieves and scoundrels.

"My army," Caramon said to himself with a grim smile that night as he spread his blanket in

An ancient sign of submission. The Gallic leader Vercingetorix, when surrendering to the Romans, instead drove his sword into the ground between Julius Caesar's feet. After parading Vercingetorix through Rome, Caesar had him executed.

557

Steeltoe's hut the half-ogre had built for his own personal use. Outside the door, he could hear Garic talking to the other man Caramon had decided looked trustworthy enough to stand watch.

Bone-weary, Caramon had assumed he'd fall asleep quickly. But he found himself lying awake in the darkness, thinking, making plans.

Like most young soldiers, Caramon had often dreamed of becoming an officer. Now, unexpectedly, here was his chance. It wasn't much of a command, maybe, but it was a start. For the first time since they'd arrived in this god-forsaken time, he felt a glimmer of pleasure.

Plans tumbled over and over in his mind. Training, the best routes south, provisioning, supplies . . . These were new and different problems for the former mercenary soldier. Even in the War of the Lance, he had generally followed Tanis's lead. His brother knew nothing of these matters; Raistlin had informed Caramon coldly that he was on his own in this. Caramon found this challenging and— oddly—refreshing. These were flesh-and-blood problems, driving the dark and shadowy problems with his brother from his mind.

Thinking of his twin, Caramon glanced over to where Raistlin lay huddled near a fire that blazed in a huge stone fireplace. Despite the heat, he was wrapped in his cloak and as many blankets as Crysania had been able to find. Caramon could hear his brother's breath rattle in his lungs, occasionally he coughed in his sleep.

Crysania slept on the other side of the fire. Although exhausted, her sleep was troubled and broken. More than once she cried out and sat up suddenly, pale and trembling. Caramon sighed. He would have liked to comfort her—to take her in his arms and soothe her to sleep. For the first time, in fact, he realized how *much* he would like to do this. Perhaps it had been telling the men she was his. Perhaps it was seeing the half-ogre's hands on her, feeling the same sense of outrage he had seen reflected on his brother's face.

Whatever the reason, Caramon caught himself watching her that night in a much different way than he had watched her before, thinking thoughts that, even now, made his skin burn and his pulse quicken.

Closing his eyes, he willed images of Tika, his wife, to come to his mind. But he had banished these memories for so long that they were unsatisfying. Tika was a hazy, misty picture and she was far away. Crysania was flesh and blood and she was here! He was very much aware of her soft, even breathing. . . .

Damn! Women! Irritably, Caramon flopped over on his stomach, determined to sweep all thoughts of females beneath the rug of his other problems. It worked. Weariness finally stole over him.

As he drifted into sleep, one thing remained to trouble him, hovering in the back of his mind. It was not logistics, or red-haired warrior women, or even lovely, white-robed clerics.

It was nothing more than a look—the strange look he had seen Raistlin give him when Caramon had said the name "Fistandantilus."

It had not been a look of anger or irritation, as Caramon might have expected. The last thing Caramon saw before sleep erased the memory was Raistlin's look of stark, abject terror.

BOOK 2

I have always considered the book divisions within these books as theatrical acts. This, perhaps, is why my own books tend to be divided into three sections when I write them. —TRH

The Army Of Fistandantilus

As the band of men under Caramon's command traveled south toward the great dwarven kingdom of Thorbardin, their fame grew—and so did their numbers. The fabled "wealth beneath the mountain" had long been legend among the wretched, half-starved people of Solamnia. That summer, they had seen most of their crops wither and die in the fields. Dread diseases stalked the land, more feared and deadly than even the savage bands of goblins and ogres who had been driven from their ancient lands by hunger.

Though it was autumn still, the chill of coming winter was in the night air. Faced with nothing but the bleak prospect of watching their children perish through starvation or cold or the illnesses that the clerics of these new gods could not cure, the men and women of Solamnia believed they had nothing to lose. Abandoning their homes, they packed up their families and their meager possessions to join the army and travel south.

From having to worry about feeding thirty men, Caramon suddenly found himself responsible for several hundred, plus women and children as well. And more came to the camp daily. Some were knights, trained with sword and spear; their nobility apparent even through their rags. Others were farmers, who held the swords Caramon put in their hands as they might have held their hoes. But there was a kind of grim nobility about them, too. After years of helplessly facing Famine and Want, it was an exhilarating thought to be preparing to face an enemy that could be killed and conquered.

Without quite realizing how it happened, Caramon found himself general of what was now being called the "Army of Fistandantilus."

At first, he had all he could manage to do in acquiring food for the vast numbers of men and their families. But memories of the lean days of mercenary life returned to him. Discovering those who were skilled hunters, he sent them ranging far afield in search of game. The women smoked

the meat or dried it, so that what was not immediately used could be stored.

Many of those who came brought what grain and fruit they had managed to harvest. This Caramon pooled, ordering the grain pounded into flour or maize, baking it into the rock-hard but life-sustaining trail bread a traveling army could live on for months. Even the children had their tasks—snaring or shooting small game, fishing, hauling water, chopping wood.

Then he had to undertake the training of his raw recruits—drilling them in the use of spear and bow, of sword and shield.

Finally, he had to find those spears and bows, swords and shields.

And, as the army moved relentlessly south, word of their coming spread. . . .†

The extensive background for the DRAGONLANCE *setting was initially meant to remain just that . . . background. With the success of Chronicles, however, we were given the opportunity to write a story in this same world. We decided to do a time travel story that would allow us and our readers to experience just a little of the foundations that were laid for Chronicles. That this evolved into our characters taking the parts of their own legends was a wonderful discovery for us as writers. —TRH*

CHAPTER I

ax Tharkas—a monument to peace.† Now it had become a symbol of war.

Pax is the Latin word for "peace."

The history of the great stone fortress of Pax Tharkas has its roots in an unlikely legend—the story of a lost race of dwarves known as the Kal-thax.

As humans cherish steel—the forging of bright weapons, the glitter of bright coin; as elves cherish their woodlands—the bringing forth and nurturing of life; so the dwarves cherish stone—the shaping of the bones of the world.

Before the Age of Dreams was the Age of Twilight when the history of the world is shrouded in the mists of its dawning. There dwelt in the great halls of Thorbardin a race of dwarves whose stonework was so perfect and so remarkable that the god Reorx, Forger of the World, looked upon it and marveled. Knowing in his wisdom that once such perfection

had been attained by mortals there was nothing left in life to strive for, Reorx took up the entire Kal-thax race and brought them to live with him near heaven's forge.

Few examples remain of the ancient craftwork of the Kal-thax. These are kept within the dwarven kingdom of Thorbardin and are valued above all other things. After the time of the Kal-thax, it was the lifelong ambition of each dwarf to gain such perfection in his stonework that he, too, might be taken up to live with Reorx.

As time went by, however, this worthy goal became perverted and twisted into an obsession. Thinking and dreaming of nothing but stone, the lives of the dwarves became as inflexible and unchanging as the medium of their craft. They burrowed deep into their ancient halls beneath the mountain, shunning the outside world. And the outside world shunned them.

Time passed and brought the tragic wars between elves and men. This ended with the signing of the Swordsheath Scroll and the voluntary exile of Kith-Kanan and his followers from the ancient elven homeland of Silvanesti. By the terms of the Swordsheath Scroll, the Qualinesti elves (meaning "freed nation")† were given the lands west of Thorbardin for the establishment of their new homeland.

This was agreeable to both humans and elves. Unfortunately, no one bothered to consult the dwarves. Seeing this influx of elves as a threat to their way of life beneath the mountain, the dwarves† attacked. Kith-Kanan found, to his sorrow, that he had walked away from one war only to find himself embroiled in another.

After many long years, the wise elven king managed to convince the stubborn dwarves that the elves had no interest in their stone. They wanted only the living beauty of their wilderness. Though this love for something changeable and wild was totally incomprehensible to the dwarves, they at last came to accept the idea. The elves were no longer seen as a threat. The races could, at last, become friends.

To honor this agreement, Pax Tharkas was built. Guarding the mountain pass between Qualinesti and

I was the primary person who put together the various language conventions for the DRAGONLANCE setting. I still on rare occasions get a call from the book department asking if I could give them an Elvish or Dwarvish word or name for a new place or a magic phrase. —TRH

The conflict between dwarves, elves, and humans is part of the conventional vision of fantasy, but it also has a deeper meaning. Their conflicts reflect the centuries-old racial conflicts with which we as humanity still struggle, both as societies and as individuals. My hope is that we can learn from the dwarves and elves that we should set aside our prejudices. —TRH

Thorbardin, the fortress was dedicated as a monument to differences—a symbol of unity and diversity.

In those times, before the Cataclysm, elves and dwarves had together manned the battlements of this mighty fortress. But now, dwarves alone kept watch from its two tall towers. For the evil time brought division once again to the races.

Retreating into their forested homeland of Qualinesti, nursing the wounds that drove them to seek solitude, the elves left Pax Tharkas. Safe inside their woodlands, they closed their borders to all. Trespassers—whether human or goblin, dwarf or ogre—were killed instantly and without question.

Duncan,† King of Thorbardin, thought of this as he watched the sun drop down behind the mountains, falling from the sky into Qualinesti. He had a sudden, playful vision of the elves attacking the sun itself for daring to enter their land, and he snorted derisively. Well, they have good reason to be paranoid, he said to himself. They have good reason to shut out the world. What did the world do for them?

Entered their lands, raped their women, murdered their children, burned their homes, stole their food. And was it goblins or ogres, spawn of evil? No! Duncan growled savagely into his beard. It was those they had trusted, those they had welcomed as friends—humans.

And now it's our turn, Duncan thought, pacing the battlements, an eye on the sunset that had bathed the sky in blood. It's our turn to shut our doors and tell the world good riddance! Go to the Abyss in your own way and let us go to it in ours!

Lost in his thoughts, Duncan only gradually became aware that another person had joined him in his pacing; iron-shod steps keeping time with his. The new dwarf was head and shoulders taller than his king and, with his long legs, could have taken two steps for his king's one. But he had, out of respect, slowed his pace to match his monarch's.

Duncan frowned uncomfortably. At any other time, he would have welcomed this person's company. Now it came to him as a sign of ill omen. It threw a shadow over his thoughts, as the sinking sun caused the chill shadow of the mountain peaks to lengthen and stretch out their fingers toward Pax Tharkas.

Why are the dwarves so often portrayed as quasi-Scotsmen? A large part of my ancestry is traced to Scotland, though I lay no claim to any knowledge of their ancient traditions. I hope they do not mind that our dwarven fellows here have taken on their voices and adopted some of their society. —TRH

"They'll guard our western border well," Duncan said by way of opening the conversation, his gaze on the borders of Qualinesti.

"Aye, Thane," the other dwarf answered, and Duncan cast a sharp glance at him from beneath his thick, gray eyebrows. Though the taller dwarf had spoken in agreement with his king, there was a reserve, a coolness in the dwarf's voice indicative of his disapproval.

Snorting in irritation, Duncan whirled abruptly in his pacing, heading the other direction, and had the amused satisfaction of having caught his fellow dwarf off guard. But the taller dwarf, instead of stumbling to turn around and catch up with his king, simply stopped and stood staring sadly out over the battlements of Pax Tharkas into the now shadowy elven lands beyond.

Irritably, Duncan first considered simply continuing on without his companion, then he came to a halt, giving the tall dwarf time to catch up. The tall dwarf made no move, however, so finally with an exasperated expression, Duncan turned and stomped back.

"By Reorx's† beard, Kharas," he growled, "what is it?"

"I think you should meet with Fireforge," Kharas said slowly, his eyes on the sky that was now deepening to purple. Far above, a single, bright star sparkled in the darkness.

"I have nothing to say to him," Duncan said shortly.

"The Thane is wise," Kharas spoke the ritual words with a bow, but he accompanied it with a heavy sigh, clasping his hands behind his back.

Duncan exploded. "What you mean to say is 'The Thane's a stupid ass!'" The king poked Kharas in the arm. "Isn't that nearer the mark?"

Kharas turned his head, smiling, stroking the silken tresses of his long, curling beard that shone in the light of the torches being lit upon the walls. He started to reply, but the air was suddenly filled with noise—the ringing of boots, the stamping of feet and calling of voices, the clash of axes against steel: the changing of the watch. Captains shouted commands, men left their positions, others took them over. Kharas, observing this in silence, used it

Doug Niles was my model for the dwarves. Every Gen Con for many years, Tracy and I put on a "traveling road show"—a reader's theater that portrayed scenes from the novels. Doug was always cast as Flint in these productions and he was Flint. To this day, I hear Doug's voice when I write dwarf characters. —MW

as a meaningful backing for his statement when he finally did speak.

"I think you should listen to what he has to say to you, Thane Duncan," Kharas said simply. "There is talk that you are goading our cousins into war—"

"Me!" Duncan roared in a rage. "Me goading them into war! *They're* the ones who're on the march, swarming down out of their hills like rats! It was they who left the mountain. *We* never asked them to abandon their ancestral home! But no, in their stiff-necked pride they—" He sputtered on, relating a long history of wrongs, both justified and imagined. Kharas allowed him to talk, waiting patiently until Duncan had blown off most of his anger.

Then the tall dwarf said patiently, "It will cost you nothing to listen, Thane, and might buy us great gains in the long run. Other eyes than those of our cousins are watching, you may be certain."

Duncan growled, but he kept silent, thinking. Contrary to what he had accused Kharas of thinking, King Duncan was *not* a stupid dwarf. Nor did Kharas consider him such: Quite the contrary. One of seven thanes ruling the seven clans of the dwarven kingdom, Duncan had managed to ally the other thanedoms under his leadership, giving the dwarves of Thorbardin a king for the first time in centuries. Even the Dewar acknowledged Duncan their leader, albeit reluctantly.

The Dewar, or so-called dark dwarves, dwelt far beneath the ground, in dimly lit, foul-smelling caves that even the mountain dwarves of Thorbardin, who lived most of their lives below ground, hesitated to enter. Long ago, a trace of insanity had shown up in this particular clan, causing them to be shunned by the others. Now, after centuries of inbreeding forced upon them by isolation, the insanity was more pronounced, while those judged sane were an embittered, dour lot.

But they had their uses as well. Quick to anger, ferocious killers who took pleasure in killing, they were a valued part of the Thane's army. Duncan treated them well for that reason and because, at heart, he was a kind and just dwarf. But he was smart enough not to turn his back on them.

Likewise, Duncan was smart enough to consider the wisdom of Kharas's words. "Other eyes will be

watching." That was true enough. He cast a glance back to the west, this time a wary one. The elves wanted no trouble, of that he felt certain. Nevertheless, if they thought the dwarves likely to provoke war, they would act swiftly to protect their homeland. Turning, he looked to the north. Rumor had it that the warlike Plainsmen of Abanasinia were considering an alliance with the hill dwarves, whom they had allowed to camp upon their lands. In fact, for all Duncan knew, this alliance could have already been made. At least if he talked to this hill dwarf, Fireforge, he might find out.

Then, too, there were darker rumors still . . . rumors of an army marching from the shattered lands of Solamnia, an army led by a powerful, black-robed wizard. . . .

"Very well!" King Duncan snarled with no good grace. "You have won again, Kharas. Tell the hill dwarf I will meet him in the Hall of Thanes at the next watch. See if you can dredge up representatives from the other thanes. We'll do this above board, since that's what you recommend."

Smiling, Kharas† bowed, his long beard nearly sweeping the tops of his boots. With a surly nod, Duncan turned and stomped below, his boots ringing out the measure of his displeasure. The other dwarves along the battlements bowed as their king passed but almost immediately turned back to their watch. Dwarves are an independent lot, loyal to their clans first and anyone else second. Though all respected Duncan, he was not revered and he knew it. Maintaining his position was a daily struggle.

Conversation, briefly interrupted by the passage of the king, renewed almost immediately. These dwarves knew war was coming, were eager for it, in fact. Hearing their deep voices, listening to their talk of battles and fighting, Kharas gave another sigh.

Turning in the opposite direction, he started off in search of the delegation of hill dwarves, his heart nearly as heavy as the gigantic war hammer he carried—a hammer few other dwarves could even lift. Kharas, too, saw war coming. He felt as he had felt once when, as a young child, he had traveled to the city of Tarsis† and stood on the beach, watching in wonder as the waves crashed upon the shore. That war was coming seemed as

"Kharas" is the Solamnic word for "knight." [Dragonlance Adventures *by Tracy Hickman and Margaret Weis, TSR, Inc., 1987, p.109.]*

I put this name on the original map of Krynn with no conscious knowledge that any place remotely sounding like it ever existed. Now that I have displayed my complete lack of education regarding ancient geography. —TRH

(Editor's note: The Apostle Paul was from the city of Tarsus.)

inevitable and unstoppable as the waves themselves. But he was determined to do what he could to try to prevent it.

Kharas made no secret of his hatred of war, he was strong in his arguments for peace. Many among the dwarves found this odd, for Kharas was the acknowledged hero of his race. As a young dwarf in the days before the Cataclysm, he had been among those who fought the legions of goblins and ogres in the Great Goblin Wars fomented by the Kingpriest of Istar.

That was a time when there was still trust among races. Allies of the Knights, the dwarves had gone to their aid when the goblins invaded Solamnia. The dwarves and knights fought side by side, and young Kharas had been deeply impressed by the knightly Code and the Measure. The Knights, in turn, had been impressed by the young dwarf's fighting skill.

Taller and stronger than any others of his race, Kharas wielded a huge hammer that he had made himself—legend said it was with the god, Reorx's, help—and there were countless times he held the field alone until his men could rally behind him to drive off the invaders.

For his valor, the Knights awarded him the name "Kharas," which means "knight" in their language. There was no higher honor they could bestow upon an outsider.

When Kharas returned home, he found his fame had spread.

He could have been the military leader of the dwarves; indeed, he might have been king himself, but he had no such ambitions. He had been one of Duncan's strongest supporters, and many believed Duncan owed his rise to power in his clan to Kharas. But, if so, that fact had not poisoned their relationship. The older dwarf and the younger hero became close friends—Duncan's rock-hard practicality keeping Kharas's idealism well-grounded.

And then came the Cataclysm. In those first, terrible years following the shattering of the land, Kharas's courage shone as an example to his beleaguered people. His had been the speech that led the thanes to join together and name Duncan king. The Dewar trusted Kharas, when they trusted no

other. Because of this unification, the dwarves had survived and even managed to thrive.

Now, Kharas was in his prime. He had been married once, but his beloved wife perished during the Cataclysm, and dwarves, when they wed, wed for life. There would be no sons bearing his name, for which Kharas, contemplating the bleak future he foresaw ahead for the world, was almost thankful.

"Reghar Fireforge, of the hill dwarves, and party."

The herald pronounced the name, stamping the butt end of his ceremonial spear upon the hard, granite floor. The hill dwarves entered, walking proudly up to the throne where Duncan sat in what was now called the Hall of Thanes in the fortress of Pax Tharkas. Behind him, in shorter chairs that had been hastily dragged in for the occasion, sat the six representatives of the other clans to act as witnesses for their thanes. They were witnesses only, there to report back to their thanes what had been said and done. Since it was war time, all authority rested with Duncan. (At least as much of it as he could claim.)

The witnesses were, in fact, nothing more than captains of their respective divisions. Though supposedly a single unit made up collectively of all the dwarves from each clan, the army was, nonetheless, merely a collection of clans gathered together. Each clan provided its own units with its own leaders; each clan lived separate and apart from the others. Fights among the clans were not uncommon—there were blood feuds that went back for generations. Duncan had tried his best to keep a tight lid on these boiling cauldrons, but—every now and then—the pressure built too high and the lid blew off.

Now, however, facing a common foe, the clans were united. Even the Dewar representative, a dirty-faced, ragged captain named Argat who wore his beard braided in knots in a barbaric fashion and who amused himself during the proceedings by skillfully tossing a knife into the air and catching it as it descended, listened to the proceedings with less than his usual air of sneering contempt.

There was, in addition, the captain of a squadron of gully dwarves. Known as the Highgug, he was there by Duncan's courtesy only. The word "gug" meaning "private" in gully dwarf language, this dwarf was

therefore nothing more than a "high private," a rank considered laughable in the rest of the army. It was an outstanding honor among gully dwarves, however, and the Highgug was held in awe by most of his troops. Duncan, always politic, was unfailingly polite to the Highgug and had, therefore, won his undying loyalty. Although there were many who thought this might have been more of a hindrance than a help, Duncan replied that you never knew when such things could come in handy.

And so the Highgug† was here as well, though few saw him. He had been given a chair in an obscure corner and told to sit still and keep quiet, instructions he followed to the letter. In fact, they had to return to remove him two days later.

"Dwarves is dwarves," was an old saying common to the populace of the rest of Krynn when referring to the differences between the hill dwarves and the mountain dwarves.

But there *were* differences—vast differences, to the dwarvish mind, though these might not have been readily apparent to any outside observer. Oddly enough, and neither the elves nor the dwarves would admit it, the hill dwarves had left the ancient kingdom of Thorbardin for many of the same reasons that the Qualinesti elves left the traditional homeland of Silvanesti.

The dwarves of Thorbardin lived rigid, highly structured lives. Everyone knew his or her place within his or her own clan. Marriage between clans was unheard of; loyalty to the clan being the binding force of every dwarf's life. Contact with the outside world was shunned—the very worst punishment that could be inflicted upon a dwarf was exile; even execution was considered more merciful. The dwarf's idea of an idyllic life was to be born, grow up, and die without ever sticking one's nose outside the gates of Thorbardin.

Unfortunately, this was—or at least had been in the past—a dream only. Constantly called to war to defend their holdings, the dwarves were forced to mix with the outside world. And—if there were no wars—there were always those who sought the dwarven skill in building and who were willing to pay vast sums to acquire it. The beautiful city of Palanthas had been lovingly constructed by a veritable army of dwarves,

Gully dwarves are a lot of fun to write, and I always enjoyed working with them. Gully dwarves are not bright, and one often wonders how they survive. They do so by a combination of strong survival instincts and "street smarts." The inability to do higher mathematics probably helps, as well. —MW

as had many of the other cities in Krynn. Thus a race of well-traveled, free-spirited, independent dwarves came about. They talked of intermarriage between the clans, they spoke matter-of-factly about trade with humans and elves. They actually expressed a desire to live in the open air. And—most heinous of all—they expressed the belief that other things in life might hold more importance than the crafting of stone.

This, of course, was seen by the more rigid dwarves as a direct threat to dwarvish society itself, so, inevitably, the split occurred. The independent dwarves left their home beneath the mountain in Thorbardin. The parting did not occur peacefully. There were harsh words on both sides. Blood feuds started then that would last for hundreds of years. Those who left took to the hills where, if life wasn't all they had hoped for, at least it was free—they could marry whom they chose, come and go as they chose, earn their own money. The dwarves left behind simply closed ranks and became even more rigid, if that were possible.

The two dwarves facing each other now were thinking of this, as they sized each other up. They were also thinking, perhaps, that this was a historic moment—the first time both sides had met in centuries.

Reghar Fireforge was the elder of the two, a top-ranking member of the strongest clan of hill dwarves. Though nearing his two-hundredth Day of Life Gift, the old dwarf was hale and hearty still. He came of a long-lived clan. The same could not be said of his sons, however. Their mother had died of a weak heart and the same malady seemed to run in the family. Reghar had lived to bury his eldest son and, already, he could see some of the same symptoms of an early death in his next oldest—a young man of seventy-five, just recently married.†

We always delight in finding ideas that resonate with other ideas in our books. This origin of Flint's heart condition adds such resonating structure to Chronicles and, therefore, greater depth to the overall storyline. —TRH

Dressed in furs and animal skins, looking as barbaric (if cleaner) than the Dewar, Reghar stood with his feet wide apart, staring at Duncan, his rock-hard eyes glittering from beneath brows so thick many wondered how the old dwarf could see at all. His hair was iron gray, so was his beard, and he wore it plaited and combed and tucked into his belt in hill-dwarf fashion. Flanked by an escort of hill

dwarves—all dressed much the same—the old dwarf was an impressive sight.

King Duncan returned Reghar's gaze without faltering—this staring-down contest was an ancient dwarvish practice and, if the parties were particularly stubborn, had been known to result in both dwarves keeling over from exhaustion unless interrupted by some neutral third party. Duncan, as he regarded Reghar grimly, began to stroke his own curled and silky beard that flowed freely over his broad stomach. It was a sign of contempt, and Reghar, noticing it without admitting that he noticed it, flushed in anger.

The six clan members sat stoically in their chairs, prepared for a long sitting. Reghar's escort spread their feet and fixed their eyes on nothing. The Dewar continued to toss his knife in the air—much to everyone's annoyance. The Highgug sat in his corner, forgotten except for the redolent odor of gully dwarf that pervaded the chill room. It seemed likely, from the look of things, that Pax Tharkas would crumble with age around their heads before anyone spoke. Finally, with a sigh, Kharas stepped in between Reghar and Duncan. Their line of vision broken, each party could drop his gaze without losing dignity.

Bowing to his king, Kharas turned and bowed to Reghar with profound respect. Then he retreated. Both sides were now free to talk on an equal basis, though each side privately had its own ideas about how equal that might be.

"I have granted you audience," Duncan stated, starting matters off with formal politeness that, among dwarves, never lasted long, "Reghar Fireforge, in order to hear what brings our kinsmen on a journey to a realm they chose to leave long ago."

"A good day it was for us when we shook the dust of the moldy old tomb from our feet," Reghar growled, "to live in the open like honest men instead of skulking beneath the rock like lizards."

Reghar patted his plaited beard, Duncan stroked his. Both stared at each other. Reghar's escort wagged their heads, thinking their chieftain had come off better in the first verbal contest.

"Then why is it that the honest men have returned to the moldy old tomb, except that they come as

grave robbers?" Duncan snapped, leaning back with an air of self-satisfaction.

There was a murmur of appreciation from the six mountain dwarves, who clearly thought their thane had scored a point.

Reghar flushed. "Is the man who takes back what was stolen from him first a thief?" he demanded.

"I fail to understand the point of that question," Duncan said smoothly, "since you have nothing of value anyone would want to steal. It is said even the kender avoid your land."

There was appreciative laughter from the mountain dwarves, while the hill dwarves literally shook with rage—that being a mortal insult. Kharas sighed.

"I'll tell you about stealing!" Reghar snarled, his beard quivering with anger. "Contracts—that's what you've stolen! Underbidding us, working at a loss to take the bread from our mouths! And there've been raids into our lands—stealing our grain and cattle! We've heard the stories of the wealth you've amassed and we've come to claim what is rightfully ours! No more, no less!"

"Lies!" roared Duncan, leaping to his feet in a fury. "All lies! What wealth lies below the mountain we've worked for, with honest sweat! And here you come back, like spendthrift children, whining that your bellies are empty after wasting the days carousing when you should have been working!" He made an insulting gesture. "You even look like beggars!"

"Beggars, is it?" Reghar roared in his turn, his face turning a deep shade of purple. "No, by Reorx's beard! If I was starving and you handed me a crust of bread, I'd spit on your shoes! Deny that you're fortifying this place, practically on our borders! Deny that you've roused the elves against us, causing them to cut off their trade! Beggars! No! By Reorx's beard and his forge and his hammer, we'll come back, but it'll be as conquerors! We'll have what is rightfully ours and teach you a lesson to boot!"

"You'll come, you sniveling cowards"—Duncan sneered—"hiding behind the skirts of a black-robed wizard and the bright shields of human warriors, greedy for spoils! They'll stab you in the back and then rob your corpses!"

"Who should know better about robbing corpses!" Reghar shouted. "You've been robbing ours for years!"

The six clan members sprang out of their chairs, and Reghar's escort jumped forward. The Dewar's high-pitched laughter rose above the thundering shouts and threats. The Highgug crouched in his corner, his mouth wide open.

The war might have started then and there had not Kharas run between the two sides, his tall figure towering over everyone. Pushing and shoving, he forced both sides to back off. Still, even after the two were separated, there was the shout of derision, the occasional insult hurled. But—at a stern glance from Kharas—these soon ceased and all fell into a sullen, surly silence.

Kharas spoke, his deep voice gruff and filled with sadness. "Long ago, I prayed the god to grant me the strength to fight injustice and evil in the world. Reorx answered my prayer by granting me leave to use his forge, and there, on the forge of the god himself, I made this hammer.† It has shone in battle since fighting the evil things of this world and protecting my homeland, the homeland of my people. Now, you, my king, would ask of me that I go to war against my kinsmen? And you, my kinsmen, would threaten to bring war to our land? Is this where your words are leading you—that I should use this hammer against my own blood?"

The famed Hammer of Kharas, which will play a major role in the War of the Lance.

Neither side spoke. Both glowered at each other from beneath tangled brows, both seemed almost half-ashamed. Kharas's heartfelt speech touched many. Only two heard it unmoved. Both were old men, both had long ago lost any illusions about the world, both knew this rift had grown too wide to be bridged by words. But the gesture had to be made.

"Here is my offer, Duncan, King of Thorbardin," Reghar said, breathing heavily. "Withdraw your men from this fortress. Give Pax Tharkas and the lands that surround it to us and our human allies. Give us one-half of the treasure beneath the mountain—the half that is rightfully ours—and allow those of us who might choose to do so to return to the safety of the mountain if the evil grows in this land. Persuade the elves to lift their trade barriers, and split all contracts for masonry work fifty-fifty.

"In return, we will farm the land around Thorbardin and trade our crops to you for less than it's costing you to grow them underground. We'll help protect your borders and the mountain itself, if need arises."

Kharas gave his lord a pleading look, begging him to consider—or at least negotiate. But Duncan was beyond reasoning, it seemed.

"Get out!" he snarled. "Return to your blackrobed wizard! Return to your human friends! Let us see if your wizard is powerful enough to blow down the walls of this fortress, or uproot the stones of our mountain. Let us see how long your human friends remain friends when the winter winds swirl about the campfires and their blood drips on the snow!"

Reghar gave Duncan a final look, filled with such enmity and hatred it might well have been a blow. Then, turning on his heel, he motioned to his followers. They stalked out of the Hall of Thanes and out of Pax Tharkas.

Word spread quickly. By the time the hill dwarves were ready to leave, the battlements were lined with mountain dwarves, shouting and hooting derisively. Reghar and his party rode off, their faces stern and grim, never once looking back.

Kharas, meanwhile, stood in the Hall of Thanes, alone with his king (and the forgotten Highgug). The six witnesses had all returned to their clans, spreading the news. Kegs of ale and the potent drink known as dwarf spirits were broached that night in celebration. Already, the sounds of singing and raucous laughter could be heard echoing through the great stone monument to peace.

"What would it have hurt to negotiate, Thane?" Kharas asked, his voice heavy with sorrow.

Duncan, his sudden anger apparently vanished, looked at the taller dwarf and shook his head, his graying beard brushing against his robes of state. He was well within his rights to refuse to answer such an impertinent question. Indeed, no one but Kharas would have had the courage to question Duncan's decision at all.

"Kharas," Duncan said, putting his hand on his friend's arm affectionately, "tell me—is there treasure beneath the mountain? Have we robbed our

kinsmen? Do we raid their lands, or the lands of the humans, for that matter? Are their accusations just?"

"No," Kharas answered, his eyes meeting those of his sovereign steadily.

Duncan sighed. "You have seen the harvest. You know that what little money remains in the treasury we will spend to lay in what we can for this winter."

"Tell them this!" Kharas said earnestly. "Tell them the truth! They are not monsters! They are our kinsmen, they will understand—"

Duncan smiled sadly, wearily. "No, they are not monsters. But, what is worse, they have become like children." He shrugged. "Oh, we could tell them the truth—show them even. But they would not believe us. They would not believe their own eyes. Why? Because they *want* to believe otherwise!"

Kharas frowned, but Duncan continued patiently. "They want to believe, my friend. More than that, they *have* to believe. It is their only hope for survival. They have nothing, nothing except that hope. And so they are willing to fight for it. I understand them." The old king's eyes dimmed for a moment, and Kharas—staring at him in amazement—realized then that his anger had been all feigned, all show.

"Now they can return to their wives and their hungry children and they can say, 'We will fight the usurpers! When we win, you will have full bellies again.' And that will help them forget their hunger, for a while."

Kharas's face twisted in anguish. "But to go this far! Surely, we can share what little—"

"My friend," Duncan said softly, "by Reorx's Hammer, I swear this—if I agree to their terms, we would all perish. Our race would cease to exist."

Kharas stared at him. "As bad as that?" he asked.

Duncan nodded. "Aye, as bad as that. Few only know this—the leaders of the clans, and now you. And I swear you to secrecy. The harvest was disastrous. Our coffers are nearly empty, and now we must hoard what we can to pay for this war. Even for our own people, we will be forced to ration food this winter. With what we have, we calculate that we can make it—barely. Add hundreds of more mouths—" He shook his head.

Kharas stood pondering, then he lifted his head, his dark eyes flashing. "If that is true, then so be it!"

he said sternly. "Better we all starve to death, than die fighting each other!"

"Noble words, my friend," Duncan answered. The beating of drums thrummed through the room and deep voices raised in stirring war chants, older than the rocks of Pax Tharkas, older—perhaps—than the bones of the world itself. "You can't eat noble words, though, Kharas. You can't drink them or wrap them around your feet or burn them in your firepit or give them to children crying in hunger."

"What about the children who will cry when their father leaves, never to return?" Kharas asked sternly.

Duncan raised an eyebrow. "They will cry for a month," he said simply, "then they will eat his share of the food. And wouldn't he want it that way?"

With that, he turned and left the Hall of Thanes, heading for the battlements once more.

As Duncan counseled Kharas in the Hall of Thanes, Reghar Fireforge and his party were guiding their short-statured, shaggy hill ponies out of the fortress of Pax Tharkas, the hoots and laughter of their kinsmen ringing in their ears.

Reghar did not speak a word for long hours, until they were well out of sight of the huge double towers of the fortress. Then, when they came to a crossing in the road, the old dwarf reined in his horse.

Turning to the youngest member of the party, he said in a grim, emotionless voice, "Continue north, Darren Ironfist." The old dwarf drew forth a battered, leather pouch. Reaching inside, he pulled out his last gold piece. For a long moment he stood staring at it, then he pressed it into the hands of the dwarf. "Here. Buy passage across the New Sea. Find this Fistandantilus and tell him . . . tell him—"

Reghar paused, realizing the enormity of his action. But, he had no choice. This had been decided before he left. Scowling, he snarled, "Tell him that, when he gets here, he'll have an army waiting to fight for him."

CHAPTER
2

The night was cold and dark over the lands of Solamnia. The stars above gleamed with a sparkling, brittle light. The constellations of the Platinum Dragon, Paladine, and Takhisis, Queen of Darkness, circled each other endlessly around Gilean's Scales of Balance. It would be two hundred years or more before these same constellations vanished from the skies, as the gods and men waged war over Krynn.

For now, each was content with watching the other.

If either god had happened to glance down, he or she would, perhaps, have been amused to see what appeared to be mankind's feeble attempts to imitate their celestial glory. On the plains of Solamnia, outside the mountain fortress city of Garnet, campfires dotted the flat grasslands, lighting the night below as the stars lit the night above.

The Army of Fistandantilus.

The flames of the campfires were reflected in shield and breastplate, danced off sword blades and flashed on spear tip. The fires shone on faces bright with hope and new-found pride, they burned in the dark eyes of the camp followers and leaped up to light the merry play of the children.

Around the campfires stood or sat groups of men, talking and laughing, eating and drinking, working over their equipment. The night air was filled with jests and oaths and tall tales. Here and there were groans of pain, as men rubbed shoulders and arms that ached from unaccustomed exercise. Hands calloused from swinging hoes were blistered from wielding spears. But these were accepted with good-natured shrugs. They could watch their children play around the campfires and know that they had eaten, if not well, at least adequately that night. They could face their wives with pride. For the first time in years, these men had a goal, a purpose in their lives.

There were some who knew this goal might well be death, but those who knew this recognized and understood it and made the choice to remain anyway.

"After all," said Garic to himself as his replacement came to relieve him of his guard duty, "death comes to all. Better a man meet it in the blazing sunlight, his sword flashing in his hand, than to have it come creeping up on him in the night unawares, or clutch at him with foul, diseased hands."

The young man, now that he was off duty, returned to his campfire and retrieved a thick cloak from his bedroll. Hastily gulping down a bowl of rabbit stew, he then walked among the campfires.

Headed for the outskirts of the camp, he walked with purpose, ignoring many invitations to join friends around their fires. These he waved off genially and continued on his way. Few thought anything of this. A great many fled the lights of the fires at night. The shadows were warm with soft sighs and murmurs and sweet laughter.

Garic *did* have an appointment in the shadows, but it was not with a lover, though several young women in camp would have been more than happy to share the night with the handsome young nobleman. Coming to a large boulder, far from camp and

far from other company, Garic wrapped his cloak about him, sat down, and waited.

He did not wait long.

"Garic?" said a hesitant voice.

"Michael!" Garic cried warmly, rising to his feet. The two men clasped hands and then, overcome, embraced each other warmly.

"I couldn't believe my eyes when I saw you ride into camp today, cousin," Garic continued, gripping the other young man's hand as though afraid to let him go, afraid he might disappear into the darkness.

"Nor I you," said Michael, holding fast to his kinsmen and trying to rid his throat of a huskiness it seemed to have developed. Coughing, he sat down on the boulder and Garic joined him. Both remained silent for a few moments as they cleared their throats and pretended to be stern and soldierly.

"I thought it was a ghost," Michael said with a hollow attempt at a laugh. "We heard you were dead. . . ." His voice died and he coughed again. "Confounded damp weather," he muttered, "gets in a man's windpipes."

"I escaped," Garic said quietly. "But my father, my mother, and my sister were not so lucky."

"Anne?" Michael† murmured, pain in his voice.

"She died quickly," Garic said quietly, "as did my mother. My father saw to that, before the mob butchered him. It made them mad. They mutilated his body—"

Garic choked. Michael gripped his arm in sympathy. "A noble man, your father. He died as a true Knight, defending his home. A better death than some face," he added grimly, causing Garic to look at him with a sharp, penetrating glance. "But, what is your story? How did you get away from the mob? Where have you been this last year?"

"I did not get away from them," Garic said bitterly. "I arrived when it was all over. Where I had been did not matter"—the young man flushed—"but I should have been with them, to die with them!"

"No, your father would not have wanted that." Michael shook his head. "You live. You will carry on the name."

Garic frowned, his eyes glinted darkly. "Perhaps. Though I have not lain with a woman since—" He

A few common names help ground the text when we read it. It gives this strange world a more familiar feeling. Besides, you certainly wouldn't want everyone to have a name as terrible to type as Fistandantilus, would you? —TRH

shook his head. "At any rate, I could only do for them what I could. I set fire to the castle—"

Michael gasped, but Garic continued, unhearing.

"—so that the mobs should not take it over. My family's ashes remain there, among the blackened stones of the hall my great-great-grandfather built. Then I rode aimlessly, for a time, not much caring what happened to me. Finally, I met up with a group of other men, many like myself—driven from their homes for various reasons.

"They asked no questions. They cared nothing about me except that I could wield a sword with skill. I joined them and we lived off our wits."

"Bandits?" Michael asked, trying to keep a startled tone from his voice and failing, apparently, for Garic cast him a dark glance.

"Yes, bandits," the young man answered coldly. "Does that shock you? That a Knight of Solamnia should so forget the Code and the Measure that he joins with bandits? I'll ask you this, Michael—where were the Code and the Measure when they murdered my father, your uncle? Where are they anywhere in this wretched land?"

"Nowhere, perhaps," Michael returned steadily, "except in our hearts."

Garic was silent. Then he began to weep, harsh sobs that tore at his body. His cousin put his arms around him, holding him close. Garic gave a shuddering sigh, wiping his eyes with the back of his hand.

"I have not cried once since I found them," he said in a muffled voice. "And you are right, cousin. Living with robbers, I had sunk into a pit from which I might not have escaped, but for the general—"

"This Caramon?"

Garic nodded. "We ambushed him and his party one night. And that opened my eyes. Before, I had always robbed people without much thought or, sometimes, I even enjoyed it—telling myself it was dogs like these who had murdered my father. But in this party there was a woman and the magic-user. The wizard was ill. I hit him, and he crumpled at my touch like a broken doll. And the woman—I knew what they would do to her and the thought sickened me. But, I was afraid of the leader—Steeltoe, they called him. He was a beast! Half-ogre.

"But the general challenged him. I saw true nobility that night—a man willing to give his life to protect those weaker than himself. And he won." Garic grew calmer. As he talked, his eyes shone with admiration. "I saw, then, what my life had become. When Caramon asked if we would come with him, I agreed, as did most of the others. But it wouldn't have mattered about them—I would have gone with him anywhere."

"And now you're part of his personal guard?" Michael said, smiling.

Garic nodded, flushing with pleasure. "I—I told him I was no better than the others—a bandit, a thief. But he just looked at me, as though he could see inside my soul, and smiled and said every man had to walk through a dark, starless night and, when he faced the morning, he'd be better for it."

"Strange," Michael said. "I wonder what he meant?"

"I think I understand," Garic said. His glance went to the far edge of the camp where Caramon's huge tent stood, smoke from the fires curling around the fluttering, silken flag that was a black streak against the stars. "Sometimes, I wonder if he isn't walking through his own 'dark night.' I've seen a look on his face, sometimes—" Garic shook his head. "You know," he said abruptly, "he and the wizard are twin brothers."

Michael's eyes opened wide. Garic confirmed it with a nod. "It is a strange relationship. There's no love lost between them."

"One of the Black Robes?" Michael said, snorting. "I should think not! I wonder the mage even travels with us. From what I have heard, these wizards can ride the night winds and summon forces from the graves to do their battles."

"This one could do that, I've no doubt,"† Garic replied, giving a smaller tent next to the general's a dark glance. "Though I have seen him do his magic only once—back at the bandit camp—I know he is powerful. One look from his eyes, and my stomach shrivels inside of me, my blood turns to water. But, as I said, he was not well when we first met up with them. Night after night, when he still slept in his brother's tent, I heard him cough until I did not think he could draw breath again. How can a man live with such pain, I asked myself more than once."

Not only did we want to portray how "every man" viewed the twins at this juncture, we wanted to show that Caramon has gained the respect and admiration of his followers, as opposed to the way he was often viewed by others in Chronicles. —MW

"But he seemed fine when I saw him today."

"His health has improved greatly. He does nothing to tax it, however. Just spends all day in his tent, studying the spellbooks he carries with him in those great, huge chests. But he's walking his 'dark night,' too," Garic added. "A gloom hangs about him, and it's been growing the farther south we travel. He is haunted by terrible dreams. I've heard him cry out in his sleep. Horrible cries— they'd wake the dead."

Michael shuddered, then, sighing, looked over at Caramon's tent. "I had grave misgivings about joining an army led, they say, by one of the Black Robes. And of all the wizards who have ever lived, this Fistandantilus is rumored to be the most powerful. I had not fully committed myself to join when I rode in today. I thought I would look things over, find out if it's true they go south to help the oppressed people of Abanasinia in their fight against mountain dwaves."

Sighing again, he made a gesture as if to stroke long mustaches, but his hand stopped. He was cleanshaven, having removed the ages-old symbol of the Knights—the symbol that led, these days, to death.

"Though my father still lives, Garic," Michael continued, "I think he might well trade his life for your father's death. We were given a choice by the lord of Vingaard† Keep—we could stay in the city and die or leave and live. Father would have died. I, too, if we'd had only ourselves to think of. But we could not afford the luxury of honor. A bitter day it was when we packed what we could on a mean cart and left the Hall. I saw them settled in a wretched cottage in Throtyl. They'll be all right, for the winter at least. Mother is strong and does the work of a man. My little brothers are good hunters. . . ."

"Your father?" Garic asked gently when Michael stopped talking.

"His heart broke that day," Michael said simply. "He sits staring out the window, his sword on his lap. He has not spoken one word to anyone since the day we left the family hall."

Michael suddenly clenched his fist. "Why am I lying to you, Garic? I don't give a damn about oppressed people in Abanasinia! I came to find the treasure! The treasure beneath the mountain! And

Most of the early map placenames were of my design. Very early on, I had created a map of Ansalon and spent quite some time placing sites and their names on that map.
—TRH

glory! Glory to bring back the light in his eyes! If we win, the Knights can lift their heads once more!"

He, too, gazed at the small tent next to the large one—the small tent that had the sign of a wizard's residence hung upon it, the small tent that everyone in the camp avoided, if possible. "But, to find this glory, led by the man called the Dark One. The Knights of old would not have done so. Paladine—"

"Paladine has forgotten us," Garic said bitterly. "We are left on our own. I know nothing of black-robed wizards, I care little about that one. I stay here and I follow because of one man—the general. If he leads me to my fortune, well and good. If not"—Garic sighed deeply—"then he has at least led me to find peace within myself. I could wish the same for him," he said, beneath his breath. Then, rising, he shook off his gloomy thoughts.

Michael rose, too.

"I must return to camp and get some sleep. It is early waking tomorrow," Garic said. "We're preparing to march within the week, so I hear. Well, cousin, will you stay?"

Michael looked at Garic. He looked at Caramon's tent, its bright-colored flag with the nine-pointed star fluttering in the chill air. He looked at the wizard's tent. Then, he nodded. Garic grinned widely. The two clasped hands and walked back to the campfires, arms around each other's shoulders.

"Tell me this, though," Michael said in a hushed voice as they walked, "is it true this Caramon keeps a witch?"

I'm sure that we had some reason for giving Caramon a nine-pointed star, but for the life of me, I can't remember what it was supposed to symbolize. Tracy, can you? —MW

Why a nine-pointed star? One point is a dot. Two points is a line. Three points is a triangle. Four points is a square. Five points . . . well, that is a star, but it is also a pentagram, and TSR at the time certainly would not have allowed that even if I would. Six is a Star of David, and that would be another set of connotations and problems altogether. Seven felt like it had been used already. Eight was just too symmetrical for my tastes, which leads us to—you guessed it—the nine-pointed star. —TRH

Where are you
going?" Caramon demanded harshly. Stepping into
his tent, his eyes blinked rapidly to try to get accustomed to the shadowy darkness after the chill glare
of the autumn sun.

"I'm moving out," Crysania said, carefully folding her white clerical robes and placing them in the
chest that had been stored beneath her cot. Now it
sat open on the floor beside her.

"We've been through this," Caramon growled
in a low voice. Glancing behind him at the guards
outside the tent entrance, he carefully lowered the
tent flap.

Caramon's tent was his pride and joy. Having
originally belonged to a wealthy Knight of Solamnia, it had been brought to Caramon as a gift by two
young, stern-faced men, who—though they claimed
to have "found" it—handled it with such skilled

hands and loving care that it was obvious they had no more "found" it than they had found their own arms or legs.

Made of some fabric none in this day and age could identify, it was so cunningly woven that not a breath of wind penetrated even the seams. Rainwater rolled right off it; Raistlin said it had been treated with some sort of oil. It was large enough for Caramon's cot, several large chests containing maps, the money, and jewels they brought from the Tower of High Sorcery, clothes and armor, plus a cot for Crysania, as well as a chest for her clothing. Still, it did not seem crowded when Caramon received visitors.

Raistlin slept and studied in a smaller tent made of the same fabric and construction that was pitched near his brother's. Though Caramon had offered to share the larger tent, the mage had insisted upon privacy. Knowing his twin's need for solitude and quiet, and not particularly enjoying being around his brother anyway, Caramon had not argued. Crysania, however, had openly rebelled when told she must remain in Caramon's tent.

In vain, Caramon argued that it was safer for her there. Stories about her "witchcraft," the strange medallion of a reviled god she wore, and her healing of the big warrior had spread quickly through the camp and were eagerly whispered to all newcomers. The cleric never left her tent but that dark glances followed her. Women grabbed their babies to their breasts when she came near. Small children ran from her in fear that was half mocking and half real.

"I am well aware of your arguments," Crysania remarked, continuing to fold her clothes and pack them away without looking up at the big man. "And I don't concede them. Oh"—she stopped him as he drew a breath to speak—"I've heard your stories of witch-burning. More than once! I do not doubt their validity, but that was in a day and age far removed from this one."

"Whose tent are you moving to, then?" Caramon asked, his face flushing. "My brother's?"

Crysania ceased folding the clothes, holding them for long moments over her arm, staring straight ahead. Her face did not change color. It grew, if

possible, a shade more pale. Her lips pressed tightly together. When she answered, her voice was cold and calm as a winter's day. "There is another small tent, similar to his. I will live in that one. You may post a guard, if you think it necessary."

"Crysania, I'm sorry," Caramon said, moving toward her. She still did not look at him. Reaching out his hands, he took hold of her arms, gently, and turned her around, forcing her to face him. "I . . . I didn't mean that. Please forgive me. And, yes, I think it *is* necessary to post a guard! But there is no one I trust, Crysania, unless it is myself. And, even then—" His breathing quickened, the hands on her arms tightened almost imperceptibly.

Perhaps Caramon makes a habit of taking women from Raistlin (the first instance we know of was way back in Chapter 4, Book IV, of The Soulforge) *because he subconsciously feels that it is the only area in which he can compete with Raistlin and win. —TRH*

"I love you,† Crysania," he said softly. "You're not like any other woman I've ever known! I didn't mean to. I don't know how it happened. I—I didn't even really much *like* you when I first met you. I thought you were cold and uncaring, wrapped up in that religion of yours. But when I saw you in the clutches of that half-ogre, I saw your courage, and when I thought about what—what they might do to you—"

He felt her shudder involuntarily; she still had dreams about that night. She tried to speak, but Caramon took advantage of her reaction to hurry on.

"I've seen you with my brother. It reminds me of the way I was, in the old days"—his voice grew wistful—"you care for him so tenderly, so patiently."

Crysania did not break free of his grasp. She simply stood there, looking up at him with clear, gray eyes, holding the folded white robe close against her chest. "This, too, is a reason, Caramon," she said sadly. "I have sensed your growing"—now she flushed, slightly—"affection for me and, while I know you too well to believe you would ever force attentions on me that I would consider unwelcome, I do not feel comfortable sleeping in the same tent alone with you."

"Crysania!" Caramon began, his face anguished, his hands trembling as they held her.

"What you feel for me isn't love, Caramon," Crysania said softly. "You are lonely, you miss your wife. It is *her* you love. I know, I've seen the tenderness in your eyes when you talk about Tika."

His face darkened at the sound of Tika's name.

"What would you know of love?" Caramon asked abruptly, releasing his grasp and looking away. "I love Tika, sure. I've loved lots of women. Tika's loved her share of men, too, I'll wager." He drew in an angry breath. That wasn't true, and he knew it. But it eased his own guilt, guilt he'd been wrestling with for months. "Tika's human!" he continued surlily. "*She's* flesh and blood—not some pillar of ice!"

"What do *I* know of love?" Crysania repeated, her calm slipping, her gray eyes darkening in anger. "I'll tell you what I know of love. I—"

"Don't say it!" Caramon cried in a low voice, completely losing control of himself and grabbing her in his arms. "Don't say you love Raistlin! He doesn't deserve your love! He's using you, just like he used me! And he'll throw you away when he's finished!"

"Let go of me!" Crysania demanded, her cheeks stained pink, her eyes a deep gray.

"Can't you see!" Caramon cried, almost shaking her in his frustration. "Are you blind?"†

"Pardon me," said a soft voice, "if I am interrupting. But there is urgent news."

At the sound of that soft voice, Crysania's face went white, then scarlet. Caramon, too, started at the sound, his hands loosening their hold. Crysania drew back from him and, in her haste, stumbled over the chest and fell to her knees. Her face well hidden by her long, black, flowing hair, she remained kneeling beside the chest, pretending to rearrange her things with hands that shook.

Scowling, his own face flushed an ugly red, Caramon turned to face his twin.

Raistlin coolly regarded his brother with his mirrorlike eyes. There was no expression on his face, as there had been no expression in his voice when he spoke upon first entering. But Caramon had seen, for a split second, the eyes crack. The glimpse of the dark and burning jealousy inside appalled him, hitting him an almost physical blow. But the look was gone instantly, leaving Caramon to doubt if he had truly seen it. Only the tight, knotted feeling in the pit of his stomach and the sudden bitter taste in his mouth made him believe it had been there.

This comment was deliberately put here—a foreshadowing. —TRH

"What news?" he growled, clearing his throat.

"Messengers have arrived from the south," Raistlin said.

"Yes?" Caramon prompted, as his brother paused.

Casting off his hood, Raistlin stepped forward, his gaze holding his brother's gaze, binding them together, making the resemblance between them strong. For an instant, the mage's mask dropped.

"The dwarves of Thorbardin are preparing for war!" Raistlin hissed, his slender hand clenching into a fist. He spoke with such intense passion that Caramon blinked at him in astonishment and Crysania raised her head to regard him with concern.

Confused and uncomfortable, Caramon broke free of his brother's feverish stare and turned away, pretending to shuffle some maps on the map table. The warrior shrugged. "I don't know what else you expected," he said coolly. "It was your idea, after all. Talking of hidden wealth. We've made no secret of the fact that's where we're headed. In fact, it's practically become our recruiting slogan! 'Join up with Fistandantilus and raid the mountain!'"

Caramon tossed this off thoughtlessly, but its effect was startling. Raistlin went livid. He seemed to try to speak, but no intelligible sounds came from his lips, only a blood-stained froth. His sunken eyes flared, as the moon on an ice-bound lake. His fist still clenched, he took a step toward his brother.

Crysania sprang to her feet. Caramon—truly alarmed—took a step backward, his hand closing over the hilt of his sword. But, slowly and with a visible effort, Raistlin regained control. With a vicious snarl, he turned and walked from the tent, his intense anger still so apparent, however, that the guards shivered as he passed them.

Caramon remained standing, lost in confusion and fear, unable to comprehend why his brother had reacted as he did. Crysania, too, stared after Raistlin in perplexity until the sound of shouting voices outside the tent roused both of them from their thoughts. Shaking his head, Caramon walked over to the entrance. Once there, he half-turned but did not look at Crysania as he spoke.

"If we are truly preparing for war," he said coldly, "I can't take time to worry about you. As I have

stated before, you won't be safe in a tent by your-self. So you'll continue to sleep here. I'll leave you alone, you may be certain of that. You have my word of honor."

With this, he stepped outside the tent and began conferring with his guards.

Flushing in shame, yet so angry she could not speak, Crysania remained in the tent for a moment to regain her composure. Then she, too, walked from the tent. One glance at the guards' faces and she realized at once that, despite the fact that she and Caramon had kept their voices low, part of their conversation had been overheard.

Ignoring the curious, amused glances, she looked around quickly and saw the flutter of black robes disappearing into the forest. Returning to the tent, she caught up her cloak and, tossing it hur-riedly around her shoulders, headed off in the same direction.

Caramon saw Crysania enter the woods near the edge of camp. Though he had not seen Raistlin, he had a pretty good idea of why Crysania was headed in that direction. He started to call to her. Though he did not know of any real danger lurking in the scraggly forest of pine trees that stood at the base of the Garnet Mountains, in these unsettled times, it was best not to take chances.

As her name was on his lips, however, he saw two of his men exchange knowing looks. Caramon had a sudden vivid picture of himself calling after the cleric like some love-sick youth, and his mouth snapped shut. Besides, here was Garic coming up, followed by a weary-looking dwarf and a tall, dark-skinned young man decked out in the furs and feathers of a barbarian.

The messengers, Caramon realized. He would have to meet with them. But— His gaze went once more to the forest. Crysania had vanished. A premo-nition of danger seized Caramon. It was so strong that he almost crashed through the trees after her, then and there. Every warrior's instinct called to him. He could put no name to his fear, but it was there, it was real.

Yet, he could not rush off, leaving these emis-saries, while he went chasing after a girl. His men would never respect him again. He could send a guard, but that would make him look almost as foolish. There was no help for it. Let Paladine look after her, if that was what she wanted. Gritting his teeth, Caramon turned to greet the messengers and lead them into his tent.

Once there, once he had made them comfortable and had exchanged formal and meaningless pleasantries, once food had been brought and drinks poured, he excused himself and slipped out the back. . . .

Footsteps in the sand, leading me on. . . .

Looking up, I see the scaffold, the hooded figure with its head on the block, the hooded figure of the executioner, the sharp blade of the axe glinting in the burning sun.

The axe falls, the victim's severed head rolls on the wooden platform, the hood comes off—

"My head!"† Raistlin whispered feverishly, twisting his thin hands together in anguish.

The executioner, laughing, removes his hood, revealing—

"My face!" Raistlin murmured, his fear spreading through his body like a malign growth, making him sweat and chill by turns. Clutching at his head, he tried to banish the evil visions that haunted his dreams continually, night after night, and lingered to disturb his waking hours as well, turning all he ate or drank to ashes in his mouth.

But they would not depart. "Master of Past and Present!" Raistlin laughed hollowly—bitter, mocking laughter. "I am Master of nothing! All this power, and I am trapped! Trapped! Following in *his* footsteps, knowing that every second that passes has *passed before*! I see people I've never seen, yet I know them! I hear the echo of my own words before I speak them! This face!" His hands pressed against his cheeks. "This face! *His* face! Not mine! Not mine! Who am I? I am my own executioner!"

His voice rose to a shriek. In a frenzy, not realizing what he was doing, Raistlin began to claw at his skin with his nails as though his face were a mask, and he could tear it from his bones.

"Stop! Raistlin, what are you doing? Stop, please!"

He could barely hear the voice. Firm but gentle hands grasped his wrists, and he fought them, struggling. But then the madness passed. The dark and frightful waters in which he had been drowning

Inspired, of course, by the scene in STAR WARS: The Empire Strikes Back *when Luke defeats Vader in the tree on Dagobah. Vader's head rolls to the ground—and inside Luke sees his own face. Margaret was such a great* STAR WARS *fan.* —TRH

This scene was not only a homage to STAR WARS: The Empire Strikes Back, *it also once more portrays Raistlin's agony over not knowing whether he is victim or executioner. Of course, he is both.* —MW

receded, leaving him calm and drained. Once more, he could see and feel and hear. His face stung. Looking down, he saw blood on his nails.

"Raistlin!" It was Crysania's voice. Lifting his gaze, he saw her standing before him, holding his hands away from his face, her eyes wide and filled with concern.

"I'm all right," Raistlin said coldly. "Leave me alone!" But, even as he spoke, he sighed and lowered his head again, shuddering as the horror of the dream washed over him. Pulling a clean cloth from a pocket, he began to dab at the wounds on his face.

"No, you're not," Crysania murmured, taking the cloth from his shaking hand and gently touching the bleeding gouges. "Please, let me do this," she said, as he snarled something unintelligible. "I know you won't let me heal you, but there is a clear stream near. Come, drink some water, rest and let me wash these "

Sharp, bitter words were on Raistlin's lips. He raised a hand to thrust her away. But then he realized that he didn't want her to leave. The darkness of the dream receded when she was with him. The touch of warm, human flesh was comforting after the cold fingers of death.

And so, he nodded with a weary sigh.

Her face pale with anguish and concern, Crysania put her arm around him to support his faltering steps, and Raistlin allowed himself to be led through the forest, acutely conscious of the warmth and the motion of her body next to his.

Reaching the bank of the stream, the archmage sat down upon a large, flat rock, warmed by the autumn sun. Crysania dipped her cloth in the water and, kneeling next to him, cleaned the wounds on his face. Dying leaves fell around them, muffling sound, falling into the stream to be whisked away by the water.

Raistlin did not speak. His gaze followed the path of the leaves, watching as each clung to the branch with its last, feeble strength, watching as the ruthless wind tore it from its hold, watching as it swirled in the air to fall into the water, watching as it was carried off into oblivion by the swift-running stream. Looking past the leaves into the

water, he saw the reflection of his face wavering there. He saw two long, bloody marks down each cheek, he saw his eyes—no longer mirrorlike, but dark and haunted. He saw fear, and he sneered at himself derisively.

"Tell me," said Crysania hesitantly, pausing in her ministrations and placing her hand over his, "tell me what's wrong. I don't understand. You've been brooding ever since we left the Tower. Has it something to do with the Portal being gone? With what Astinus told you back in Palanthas?"

Raistlin did not answer. He did not even look at her. The sun was warm on his black robes, her touch was warmer than the sun. But, somewhere, some part of his mind was coldly balancing, calculating— tell her? What will I gain? More than if I kept silent?

Yes . . . draw her nearer, enfold her, wrap her up, accustom her to the darkness. . . .

"I know," he said finally, speaking as if reluctantly, yet—for some reason—still not looking at her as he spoke, but staring into the water, "that the Portal is in a place near Thorbardin, in the magical fortress called Zhaman. This I discovered from Astinus.

"Legend tells us that Fistandantilus undertook what some call the Dwarfgate Wars so that he could claim the mountain kingdom of Thorbardin for his own. Astinus relates much the same thing in his *Chronicles*"—Raistlin's voice grew bitter— "*much* the same thing! But, read between the lines, read closely, as I *should* have read but, in my arrogance, did not, and you will read the truth!"

His hands clenched. Crysania sat before him, the damp, blood-stained cloth held fast, forgotten as she listened, enthralled.

"Fistandantilus came here to do *the very same thing I came here to do*!" Raistlin's words hissed with a strange, foreboding passion. "He cared nothing for Thorbardin! It was all a sham, a ruse! He wanted one thing—and that was to reach the Portal! The dwarves stood in his way, as they stand in mine. They controlled the fortress then, they controlled the land for miles around it. The only way he could reach it was to start a war so that he could get close enough to gain access to it! And, so, history repeats itself.

"For I must do what he did. . . . I *am* doing what he did!"

His expression bitter, he stared silently into the water.

"From what I have read of Astinus's *Chronicles*," Crysania began, speaking hesitantly, "the war was bound to come anyway. There has long been bad blood between the hill dwarves and their cousins. You can't blame yourself—"

Raistlin snarled impatiently. "I don't give a damn about the dwarves! They can sink into the Sirrion, for all I care." Now he looked at her, coldly, steadily. "You say you have read Astinus's works on this. If so, think! What caused the end of the Dwarfgate Wars?"

Crysania's eyes grew unfocused as she sought back in her mind, trying to recall. Then her face paled. "The explosion," she said softly. "The explosion that destroyed the Plains of Dergoth. Thousands died and so did—"

"*So did Fistandantilus!*" Raistlin said with grim emphasis.

For long moments, Crysania could only stare at him. Then the full realization of what he meant sank in. "Oh, but surely not!" she cried, dropping the blood-stained cloth and clutching Raistlin's hands with her own. "You're not the same person! The circumstances are different. They must be! You've made a mistake!"

Raistlin shook his head, smiling cynically. Gently disengaging his hand from hers, he reached out and touched her chin, raising her head so that she looked directly into his eyes. "No, the circumstances are *not* different. I have *not* made a mistake. I am caught in time, rushing forward to my own doom."

"How do you know? How can you be certain?"

"I know because—one other perished with Fistandantilus that day."

"Who?" Crysania asked, but even before he told her she felt a dark mantle of fear settle upon her shoulders, falling around her with a rustle as soft as the dying leaves.

"An old friend of yours," Raistlin's smile twisted. "Denubis!"

"Denubis!" she repeated soundlessly.

"Yes," Raistlin replied, unconsciously letting his fingers trace along her firm jaw, cup her chin in his hand. "That much I learned from Astinus. If you will recall, your cleric friend was already drawn to Fistandantilus, even though he refused to admit it to himself. He had his doubts about the church, much the same as yours. I can only assume that during those final, horrifying days in Istar, Fistandantilus persuaded him to come—"

"You didn't persuade *me*," Crysania interrupted firmly. "I chose to come! It was my decision!"

"Of course," Raistlin said smoothly, letting go of her. He hadn't realized what he was doing, caressing her soft skin. Now, unbidden, he felt his blood stir. He found his gaze going to her curving lips, her white neck. He had a sudden vivid image of her in his brother's arms. He remembered the wild surge of jealousy he had felt.

This must not happen! he reprimanded himself. It will interfere with my plans. . . . He started to rise, but Crysania caught hold of his hand with both of hers and rested her cheek in his palm.

"No," she said softly, her gray eyes looking up at him, shining in the bright sunlight that filtered through the leaves, holding him with her steadfast gaze, "we will alter time, you and I! You are more powerful than Fistandantilus. I am stronger in my faith than Denubis! I heard the Kingpriest's demands of the gods. I know his mistake! Paladine will answer my prayers as he has in the past. Together, we will change the ending . . . you and I. . . ."

Caught up in the passion of her words, Crysania's eyes deepened to blue, her skin, cool on Raistlin's hand, flushed a delicate pink. Beneath his fingers, he could feel the lifeblood pulse in her neck. He felt her tenderness, her softness, her smoothness . . . and suddenly he was down on his knees beside her. She was in his arms. His mouth sought her lips, his lips touched her eyes, her neck. His fingers tangled in her hair. Her fragrance filled his nostrils, and the sweet ache of desire filled his body.

She yielded to his fire, as she had yielded to his magic, kissing him eagerly. Raistlin sank down into the soft carpet of dying leaves. Lying back, he drew Crysania down with him, holding her in his arms.

Larry Elmore gives us this touching scene from *War of the Twins*.

Caramon and Tasslehoff prepare for a battle against time in
Matt Stawicki's 2000 update of *War of the Twins*.

Keith Parkinson perfectly defines the moment in Raistlin's
quest for power when he confronts Fistandantilus in the past.

The sunlight in the blue autumn sky was brilliant, blinding him. The sun itself beat upon his black robes with a unbearable heat, almost as unbearable as the pain inside his body.

Crysania's skin was cool to his feverish touch, her lips like sweet water to a man dying of thirst. He gave himself up to the light, shutting his eyes againstt it. And then, the shadow of a face appeared in his mind: a goddess—dark-haired, dark-eyed, exultant, victorious, laughing. . . .

"No!" Raistlin cried. "No!" he shrieked in half-strangled tones as he hurled Crysania from him. Trembling and dizzy, he staggered to his feet.

His eyes burned in the sunlight. The heat upon his robes was stifling, and he felt himself gasping for air. Drawing his black hood over his head, he stood, shaking, trying to regain his composure, his control.

"Raistlin!" Crysania cried, clinging to his hand. Her voice was warm with passion. Her touch worsened the pain, even as it promised to ease it. His resolve began to crumble, the pain tore at him. . . .

Furiously, Raistlin snatched his hand free. Then, his face grim, he reached out and grasped the fragile white cloth of her robes. With a jerk, he ripped it from her shoulders, while, with the other hand, he shoved her half-naked body down into the leaves.

"Is this what you want?" he asked, his voice taut with anger. "If so, wait here for my brother. He's bound to be along soon!" He paused, struggling for breath.

Lying on the leaves, seeing her nakedness reflected starkly in those mirrorlike eyes, Crysania clutched the torn cloth to her breast and stared at him wordlessly.

"Is *this* what we have come here to attain?" Raistlin continued relentlessly. "I thought your aim was higher, Revered Daughter! You boast of Paladine, you boast of your powers. Did you think that this might be the answer to your prayers? That I would fall victim to your charms?"

That shot told! He saw her flinch, her gaze waver. Closing her eyes, she rolled over, sobbing in agony, clasping her torn robe to her body. Her black hair fell across her bare shoulders, the skin of her back was white and soft and smooth. . . .

Many cultures, both modern and ancient, hold virginity sacred. Mary Stewart used this motif in her Arthurian series—Merlin was very powerful until a woman seduced him. Greece had the vestal virgins. Many cultures once required priests and servants to be eunuchs. Although Crysania is good, she is also Raistlin's ultimate temptation. She promises to be the downfall of both of them. Raistlin must resist sexual passion in order to preserve his power.

Turning abruptly, Raistlin walked away. He walked rapidly and, as he walked, he felt calm return to him. The ache of passion subsided, leaving him once more able to think clearly.

His eyes caught a glimpse of movement, a flash of armor. His smile curled into a sneer. As he had predicted, there went Caramon, setting out in search of her. Well, they were welcome to each other. What did it matter to him?

Reaching his tent, Raistlin entered its cool, dark confines. The sneer still curled his lips but, recalling his weakness, recalling how close he'd come to failure, recalling—against his will—her soft, warm lips, it faded. Shaking, he collapsed into a chair and let his head sink into his hands.

But the smile was back, half an hour later, when Caramon burst into his tent. The big man's face was flushed, his eyes dilated, his hand on the hilt of his sword.

"I should kill you, you damned bastard!" he said in a choked voice.

"What for this time, my brother?" Raistlin asked in irritation, continuing to read the spellbook he was studying. "Have I murdered another of your pet kender?"

"You know damn well what for!" Caramon snarled with an oath. Lurching forward, he grabbed the spellbook and slammed it shut. His fingers burned as he touched its nightblue binding, but he didn't even feel the pain. "I found Lady Crysania in the woods, her clothes ripped off, crying her heart out! Those marks on your face—"

"Were made by my hands. Did she tell you what happened?" Raistlin interrupted.

"Yes, but—"

"Did she tell you that *she* offered herself to *me*?"

"I don't believe—"

"And that *I* turned her down," Raistlin continued coldly, his eyes meeting his brother's unwaveringly.

"You arrogant son of a—"

"And even now, she probably sits weeping in her tent, thanking the gods that I love her enough to cherish her virtue." Raistlin gave a bitter, mocking laugh that pierced Caramon like a poisoned dagger.

"I don't believe you!" Caramon said softly. Grabbing hold of his brother's robes, he yanked Raistlin from his chair. "I don't believe her! She'd say anything to protect your miserable—"

"Remove your hands, brother!" Raistlin said in a flat, soft whisper.

"I'll see you in the Abyss!"

"I said remove your hands!" There was a flash of blue light, a crackle and sizzling sound, and Caramon screamed in pain, loosening his hold as a jarring, paralyzing shock surged through his body.

"I warned you," Raistlin straightened his robes and resumed his seat.

"By the gods, I *will* kill you this time!" Caramon said through clenched teeth, drawing his sword with a trembling hand.

"Then do so," Raistlin snapped, looking up from the spellbook he had reopened, "and get it over with. This constant threatening becomes boring!"

There was an odd gleam in the mage's eyes, an almost eager gleam—a gleam of invitation.

"Try it!" he whispered, staring at his brother. "Try to kill me! You will *never* get home again. . . ."

"That doesn't matter!" Lost in blood-lust, overwhelmed by jealousy and hatred, Caramon took a step toward his brother, who sat, waiting, that strange, eager look upon his thin face.

"Try it!" Raistlin ordered again.

Caramon raised his sword.

"General Caramon!" Alarmed voices shouted outside; there was the sound of running footsteps. With an oath, Caramon checked his swing and hesitated, half-blinded by tears of rage, staring grimly at his brother.

"General! Where are you?" The voices sounded closer, and there were the answering voices of his guard, directing them to Raistlin's tent.

"Here!" Caramon finally shouted. Turning from his brother, he thrust the sword back into its scabbard and yanked open the tent flap. "What is it?"

"General, I—Sir, your hands! They're burned. How—?"

"Never mind. What's the matter?"

"The witch, sir. She's gone!"

"Gone?" Caramon repeated in alarm. Casting his brother a vicious glance, the big man hurried out of

the tent. Raistlin heard his booming voice demanding explanations, the men giving them.

Raistlin did not listen. He closed his eyes with a sigh. Caramon had not been allowed to kill him.

Ahead of him, stretched out before him in a straight, narrow line, the footsteps led inexorably on.

CHAPTER
4

Caramon had once complimented her on her riding skill. Until leaving Palanthas with Tanis Half-Elven to ride south to seek the magical Forest of Wayreft, Crysania had never been nearer a horse than seated inside one of her father's elegant carriages. Women of Palanthas did not ride, not even for pleasure, as did the other Solamnic women.

But that had been in her other life.

Her other life. Crysania smiled grimly to herself as she leaned over her mount's neck and dug her heels into its flanks, urging it forward at a trot. How far away it seemed; long ago and distant.

She checked a sigh, ducking her head to avoid some low-hanging branches. She did not look behind her. Pursuit would not be very swift in coming, she hoped. There were the messengers—Caramon would have to deal with them first—and

he dared not send any of his guards out without him. Not after the witch!

Suddenly, Crysania laughed. If anyone ever looked like a witch, I do! She had not bothered to change her torn robes. When Caramon had found her in the woods, he had fastened them together with clasps from his cloak. The robes had ceased, long ago, to be snowy white; from travel and wear and being washed in streams, they had dulled to a dove-colored gray. Now, torn and mud-spattered, they fluttered around her like bedraggled feathers. Her cloak whipped out behind her as she rode. Her black hair was a tangled mass. She could scarcely see through it.

She rode out of the woods. Ahead of her stretched the grasslands, and she reined in the horse for a moment to study the land lying ahead of her. The animal, used to plodding along with the ranks of the slow-moving army, was excited by this unaccustomed exercise. It shook its head and danced sideways a few steps, looking longingly at the smooth expanse of grass, begging for a run. Crysania patted its neck.

"Come on, boy," she urged, giving it free rein.

Nostrils flaring, the horse laid back its ears and sprang forward, galloping across the open grasslands, thrilling in its newfound freedom. Clinging to the creature's neck, Crysania gave herself up to the pleasure of *her* newfound freedom. The warm afternoon sun was a pleasant contrast to the sharp, biting wind in her face. The rhythm of the animal's gallop, the excitement of the ride, and the faint edge of fear she always felt on horseback numbed her mind, easing the ache in her heart.

As she rode, her plans crystallized in her mind, becoming clearer and sharper. Ahead of her, the land darkened with the shadows of a pine forest; above her, to her right, the snowcapped peaks of the Garnet Mountains† glistened in the bright sunshine. Giving the reins a sharp jerk to remind the animal that she was in control, Crysania slowed the horse's mad gallop and guided it toward the distant woods.†

Crysania had been gone from camp almost an hour before Caramon managed to get matters organized enough to set off in pursuit. As Crysania had

The Garnet Mountains are a small mountain chain in southern Solamnia.

Who designed the original geography of Krynn? That would be me. I sat down and created the original map, primarily on hexagon paper, which is why the early coastlines all look the odd way that they do.

It may be interesting to note that I designed the Ansalonian continent to the same size as Tolkien's Middle-earth. In those days, we really weren't all that sure of what we were doing, and there was no other model on which to base any world design. So we simply took the size of Tolkien's stage and duplicated it in scale, hoping it would be just the right size for a campaign.

As to which came first— the story or the setting—I must say the setting came first. —TRH

foreseen, he had to explain the emergency to the messengers and make certain they were not offended before he could leave. This involved some time, because the Plainsman spoke very little Common and no dwarven, and, while the dwarf spoke Common fairly well (one reason he had been chosen as messenger), he couldn't understand Caramon's strange accent and was constantly forcing the big man to repeat himself.

Caramon had begun trying to explain who Crysania was and what her relationship was to him, but that proved impossible for either the dwarf or the Plainsman to comprehend. Finally, Caramon gave up and told them, bluntly, what they were bound to hear in camp anyway—that she was his woman and she had run off.

The Plainsman nodded in understanding. The women of his tribe, being notably wild, occasionally took it into their heads to do the same thing.† He suggested that when Caramon caught her, he have all her hair cut off—the sign of a disobedient wife. The dwarf was somewhat astonished—a dwarven woman would as soon think of running away from home and husband as she would of shaving her chin whiskers. But, he reminded himself dourly, he was among humans and what could you expect?

A slight nod to Goldmoon, whose flight from her people helped to set in motion the events of Dragonlance *Chronicles.*

Both bid Caramon a quick and successful journey and settled down to enjoy the camp's stock of ale. Heaving a sigh of relief, Caramon hurried out of his tent to find that Garic had saddled a horse and was holding it ready for him.

"We picked up her trail, General," the young man said, pointing. "She rode north, following a small animal trail into the woods. She's on a fast horse—" Garic shook his head a moment in admiration. "She stole one of the best, I'll say that for her, sir. But, I wouldn't think she'd get far."

Caramon mounted. "Thank you, Garic," he began, then stopped as he saw another horse being led up. "What's this?" he growled. "I said I was going alone—"

"I am coming, too, my brother," spoke a voice from the shadows.

Caramon looked around. The archmage came out of his tent, dressed in his black traveling cloak and boots. Caramon scowled, but Garic was already respectfully helping Raistlin to mount the thin,

nervous black horse the archmage favored. Caramon dared not say anything in front of the men—and his brother knew it. He saw the amused glint in Raistlin's eyes as he raised his head, the sunlight hitting their mirrored surface.

"Let's be off, then," Caramon muttered, trying to conceal his anger. "Garic, you're in command while I'm gone. I don't expect it will be long. Make certain that our guests are fed and get those farmers back out there on the field. I want to see them spearing those straw dummies when I return, not each other!"

"Yes, sir," Garic said gravely, giving Caramon the Knight's salute.

A vivid memory of Sturm Brightblade came to Caramon's mind, and with it days of his youth; days when he and his brother had traveled with their friends—Tanis, Flint the dwarven metalsmith, Sturm. . . . Shaking his head, he tried to banish the memories as he guided his horse out of camp.

But they returned to him more forcefully when he reached the trail into the woods and caught a glimpse of his brother riding next to him, the mage keeping his horse just a little behind the warrior's, as usual. Though he did not particularly like riding, Raistlin rode well, as he did all things well if he set his mind to it. He did not speak nor even look at his brother, keeping his hood cast over his head, lost in his own thoughts. This was not unusual—the twins had sometimes traveled for days with little verbal communication.

But there was a bond between them, nonetheless, a bond of blood and bone and soul. Caramon felt himself slipping into the old, easy comradeship. His anger began to melt away—it had been partly at himself, anyhow.

Half-turning, he spoke over his shoulder.

"I—I'm sorry . . . about . . . back there, Raist," he said gruffly as they rode deeper into the forest, following Crysania's clearly marked trail. "What you said was true—she did tell me that . . . that she—" Caramon floundered, blushing. He twisted around in the saddle. "That she—Damn it, Raist! Why did you have to be so rough with her?"

Raistlin lifted his hooded head, his face now visible to his brother. "I had to be rough," he said in

his soft voice. "I had to make her see the chasm yawning at her feet, a chasm that, if we fell into it, would destroy us all!"

Caramon stared at his twin in wonder. "You're not human!"

To his astonishment, Raistlin sighed. The mage's harsh, glittering eyes softened a moment. "I am more human than you realize, my brother," he said in a wistful tone that went straight to Caramon's heart.

"Then love her, man!" Caramon said, dropping back to ride beside his brother. "Forget this nonsense about chasms and pits or whatever! You may be a powerful wizard and she may be a holy cleric, but, underneath those robes, you're both flesh and blood! Take her in your arms and . . . and. . . ."

Caramon was so carried away that he checked his horse, stopping in the middle of the trail, his face lit with his passion and enthusiasm. Raistlin brought his horse to a stop, too. Leaning forward, he laid his hand on his brother's arm, his burning fingers searing Caramon's skin. His expression was hard, his eyes once again brittle and cold as glass.

"Listen to me, Caramon, and try to understand," Raistlin said in an expressionless tone that made his twin shudder. "I am incapable of love. Haven't you realized that, yet? Oh, yes, you are right—beneath these robes I am flesh and blood, more's the pity. Like any other man, I am capable of lust. That's all it is . . . lust."

He shrugged. "It would probably matter little to me if I gave in to it, perhaps weaken me some temporarily, nothing more. It would certainly not affect my magic. But"—his gaze went through Caramon like a sliver of ice—"it would destroy Crysania when she found out. And she *would* find out!"

"You black-hearted bastard!" Caramon said through clenched teeth.

Raistlin raised an eyebrow. "Am I?" he asked simply. "If I were, wouldn't I just take my pleasure as I found it? I am capable of understanding and controlling myself—unlike others."

Caramon blinked. Spurring his horse, he proceeded down the trail again, lost in confusion. Somehow, his brother had managed, once again, to turn everything upside down. Suddenly he, Caramon, felt consumed with guilt—a prey to animal instincts he wasn't man enough to control, while his brother—by admitting he was incapable of love— appeared noble and self-sacrificing. Caramon shook his head.

The two followed Crysania's trail deeper into the woods. It was easy going, she had kept to the path, never veering, never bothering, even, to cover her tracks.

"Women!" Caramon muttered after a time. "If she was going to have a sulking fit, why didn't she just do it the easy way and walk! Why did she have to take a blasted horseback ride halfway into the countryside?"

"You do not understand her, my brother," Raistlin said, his gaze on the trail. "Such is not her intent. She has a purpose in this ride, believe me."

"Bah!" Caramon snorted. "This from the expert on women! I've been married! I know! She's ridden off in a huff, knowing we'll come after her. We'll find her somewhere along here, her horse ridden into the ground, probably lame. She'll be cold and haughty. We'll apologize and . . . and I'll let her have her damn tent if she wants it and—see there! What'd I tell you?" Bringing his horse to a halt, he gestured across the flat grasslands. "There's a trail a blind gully dwarf could follow! Come on."

Raistlin did not answer, but there was a thoughtful look on his thin face as he galloped after his brother. The two followed Crysania's trail across the grasslands. They found where she entered the woods again, came to a stream and crossed it. But there, on the bank of the stream Caramon brought his horse to a halt.

"What the—" He looked left and right, guiding his animal around in a circle. Raistlin stopped, sighing, and leaned over the pommel of his saddle.

"I told you," he said grimly. "She has a purpose. She is clever, my brother. Clever enough to know your mind and how it works . . . when it *does* work!"

Caramon glowered at his twin but said nothing.

Crysania's trail had disappeared.

As Raistlin said, Crysania had a purpose. She was clever and intelligent, she guessed what Caramon would think and she purposefully misled him. Though certainly not skilled in woodslore herself,

for months now, she had been with those who were. Often lonely—few spoke to the "witch"—and often left to her own devices by Caramon, who had problems of command to deal with, and Raistlin, who was wrapped up in his studies, Crysania had little to do but ride by herself, listening to the stories of those about her and learning from them.

Thus it had been a simple thing to double back on her own trail, riding her horse down the center of the stream, leaving no tracks to follow. Coming to a rocky part of the shore where, again, her horse would leave no tracks, she left the stream. Entering the woods, she avoided the main trail, searching instead for one of the many, smaller animal trails that led to the stream. Once on it, she covered her tracks as best she could. Although she did it crudely, she was fairly certain Caramon would not give her credit enough even for that, so she had no fear he would follow her.

If Crysania had known Raistlin rode with his brother, she might have had misgivings, for the mage seemed to know her mind better than she did herself. But she didn't, so she continued ahead at a leisurely pace—to rest the horse and to give herself time to go over her plans.

In her saddlebags, she carried a map, stolen from Caramon's tent. On the map was marked a small village nestled in the mountains. It was so small it didn't even have a name—at least not one marked on the map. But this village was her destination. Here she planned to accomplish a two-fold purpose: she would alter time and she would prove—to Caramon and his brother and herself—that she was more than a piece of useless, even dangerous, baggage. She would prove her own worth.

Here, in this village, Crysania intended to bring back the worship of the ancient gods.

This was not a new thought for her. It was something she had often considered attempting but had not for a variety of reasons. The first was that both Caramon and Raistlin had absolutely forbidden her to use any clerical powers while in camp. Both feared for her life, having seen witch-burnings themselves in their younger days.† (Raistlin had, in fact, nearly been a victim himself, until rescued by Sturm and Caramon.)

These events (and others) are told in The Soulforge *by Margaret Weis.*

Crysania herself had enough common sense to know that none of the men or their families traveling with the army would listen to her, all of them firmly believing that she *was* a witch. The thought had crossed her mind that if she could get to people who knew nothing of her, tell them her story, give them the message that the gods had *not* abandoned man, but that man had abandoned the gods, then they would follow her as they would follow Goldmoon two hundred years later.

But it was not until she had been stung by Raistlin's harsh words that she had gathered the courage to act. Even now, leading the horse at a walk through the quiet forest in the twilight, she could still hear his voice and see his flashing eyes as he reprimanded her.

I deserved it, she admitted to herself. I had abandoned my faith. I was using my "charms" to try to bring him to me, instead of my example to bring him to Paladine. Sighing, she absently brushed her fingers through her tangled hair. If it had not been for *his* strength of will, I would have fallen.

Her admiration for the young archmage, already strong, deepened—as Raistlin had foreseen. She determined to restore his faith in her and prove herself worthy, once more, of his trust and regard. For, she feared, blushing, he must have a very low opinion of her now. By returning to camp with a corps of followers, of true believers, she planned not only to show him that he was wrong—that time could be altered by bringing clerics into a world where, before, there were none—but also she hoped to extend her teachings throughout the army itself.

Thinking of this, making her plans, Crysania felt more at peace with herself than she had in the months since they'd come to this time period. For once she was doing something on her own. She wasn't trailing along behind Raistlin or being ordered about by Caramon. Her spirits rose. By her calculations, she should reach the village just before dark.

The trail she was on had been steadily climbing up the side of the mountain. Now it topped a rise and then dipped down, descending into a small valley. Crysania halted the horse. There, nestled in the valley, she could at last see the village that was her destination.

Something struck her as odd about the village, but she was not yet a seasoned enough traveler to have learned to trust her instincts about such things. Knowing only that she wanted to reach the village before darkness fell, and eager to put her plan into immediate action, Crysania mounted her horse once more and rode down the trail, her hand closing over the medallion of Paladine she wore around her neck.

"Well, what do we do now?" Caramon asked, sitting astride his horse and looking both up and down the stream.

"*You're* the expert on women," Raistlin retorted.

"All right, I made a mistake," Caramon grumbled. "That doesn't help us. It'll be dark soon, and then we'll never find her trail. I haven't heard you come up with any helpful suggestions," he grumbled, glancing at his brother balefully. "Can't you magic up something?"

"I would have 'magicked up' brains for you long ago, if I could have," Raistlin snapped peevishly. "What would you like me to do—make her appear out thin air or look for her in my crystal ball? No, I won't waste my strength. Besides it's not necessary. Have you a map, or did you manage to think that far ahead?"

"I have a map," Caramon said grimly, drawing it out of his belt and handing it to his brother.

"You might as well water the horses and let them rest," Raistlin said, sliding off his. Caramon dismounted as well and led the horses to the stream while Raistlin studied the map.

By the time Caramon had tethered the horses to a bush and returned to his brother, the sun was setting. Raistlin held the map nearly up to his nose trying to read it in the dusk. Caramon heard him cough and saw him hunch down into his traveling cloak.

"You shouldn't be out in the night air," Caramon said gruffly.

Coughing again, Raistlin gave him a bitter glance. "I'll be all right."

Shrugging, Caramon peered over his brother's shoulder at the map. Raistlin pointed a slender finger at a small spot, halfway up the mountainside.

"There," he said.

"Why? What would she go to some out-of-the-way place like that for?" Caramon asked, frowning, puzzled. "That doesn't make any sense."

"Because you have still not seen her purpose!" Raistlin returned. Thoughtfully, he rolled up the map, his eyes staring into the fading light. A dark line appeared between his brows.

"Well?" Caramon prompted skeptically. "What is this great purpose you keep mentioning? What's the matter?"

"She has placed herself in grave danger," Raistlin said suddenly, his cool voice tinged with anger. Caramon stared at him in alarm.

"What? How do you know? Do you see—"

"Of course I can't see, you great idiot!" Raistlin snarled over his shoulder as he walked rapidly to his horse. "I think! I use my brain! She is going to this village to establish the old religion. She is going there to tell them of the true gods!"

"Name of the Abyss!" Caramon swore, his eyes wide. "You're right, Raist," he said, after a moment's thought. "I've heard her talk about trying that, now I think of it. I never believed she was serious, though."

Then, seeing his brother untying his horse and preparing to mount, he hurried forward and laid his hand on his brother's bridle. "Just a minute, Raist! There's nothing we can do now. We'll have to wait until morning." He gestured into the mountains. "You know as well as I do that we don't dare ride those wretched trails after dark. We'd be taking a chance on the horses stumbling into a hole and breaking a leg. To say nothing of what *lives* in these god-forsaken woods."

"I have my staff for light," Raistlin said, motioning to the Staff of Magius, snug in its leather carrier on the side of saddle. He started to pull himself up, but a fit of coughing forced him to pause, clinging to the saddle, gasping for breath.

Caramon waited until the spasm eased. "Look, Raist," he said in milder tones, "I'm just as worried about her as you are—but I think you're overreacting. Let's be sensible. It's not as if she were riding into a den of goblins! That magical light'll draw to us whatever's lurking out there in the night like moths to a candleflame. The horses are winded. You're in no shape to go on, much less fight if we have to.

We'll make camp here for the night. You get some rest, and we'll start fresh in the morning."

Raistlin paused, his hands on his saddle, staring at his brother. It seemed as if he might argue, then a coughing fit seized him. His hands slipped to his side, he laid his forehead against the horse's flank as if too exhausted to move.

"You are right, my brother," he said, when he could speak.

Startled at this unusual display of weakness, Caramon almost went to help his twin, but checked himself in time—a show of concern would only bring a bitter rebuke. Acting as if nothing were at all amiss, he began untying his brother's bedroll, chatting along, not really thinking about what he was saying.

"I'll spread this out, and you rest. We can probably risk a small fire, and you can heat up that potion of yours to help your cough. I've got some meat here and a few vegetables Garic threw together for me." Caramon prattled on, not even realizing what he was saying. "I'll fix up a stew. It'll be just like the old days.

"By the gods!" He paused a moment, grinning. "Even though we never knew where our next steel piece was coming from, we still ate well in those days! Do you remember? There was a spice you had. You'd toss it in the pot. What was it?" He gazed off into the distance, as though he could part the mists of time with his eyes. "Do you remember the one I'm talking about? You use it in your spell-casting. But it made damn good stews, too! The name . . . it was like ours—marjere, marjorie? Hah!"—Caramon laughed—"I'll never forget the time that old master of yours† caught us cooking with his spell components! I thought he'd turn himself inside out!"

That would be Master Theobold, one of Raistlin's early teachers. See The Soulforge *by Margaret Weis.*

Sighing, Caramon went back to work, tugging at the knots. "You know, Raist," he said softly, after a moment, "I've eaten wondrous food in wondrous places since then—palaces and elf woods and all. But nothing could quite match that. I'd like to try it again, to see if it was like I remember it. It'd be like old times—"

There was a soft rustle of cloth. Caramon stopped, aware that his brother had turned his black hooded

head and was regarding him intently. Swallowing, Caramon kept his eyes fixedly on the knots he was trying to untie. He hadn't meant to make himself vulnerable and now he waited grimly for Raistlin's rebuke, the sarcastic gibe.

There was another soft rustle of cloth, and then Caramon felt something soft pressed into his hand— a tiny bag.

Marjoram is named for the god Majere. See The Soulforge *by Margaret Weis, Book II, Chapter 1.*

"Marjoram,"† Raistlin said in a soft whisper. "The name of the spice is marjoram. . . ."

CHAPTER
5

It wasn't until
Crysania rode into the outskirts of the village itself
that she realized something was wrong.

Caramon, of course, would have noticed it when
he first looked down at the village from the top of the
hill. He would have detected the absence of smoke
from the cooking fires. He would have noted the
unnatural silence—no sounds of mothers calling for
children or the plodding thuds of cattle coming in
from the fields or neighbors exchanging cheerful
greetings after a long day's work. He would have
seen that no smoke rose from the smithy's forge,
wondered uneasily at the absence of candlelight
glowing from the windows. Glancing up, he would
have seen with alarm the large number of carrion
birds in the sky, circling. . . .

All this Caramon or Tanis Half-Elven or Raistlin
or any of them would have noted and, if forced to go

on, he would have approached the village with hand on sword or a defensive magic spell on the lips.

But it was only after Crysania cantered into the village and, staring around, wondered where everyone was, that she experienced her first glimmerings of uneasiness. She became aware of the birds, then, as their harsh cries and calls of irritation at her presence intruded on her thoughts. Slowly, they flapped away, in the gathering darkness, or perched sullenly on trees, melting into the shadows.

Dismounting in front of a building whose swinging sign proclaimed it an inn, Crysania tied the horse to a post and approached the front door. If it was an inn, it was a small one, but well-built and neat with ruffled curtains in the windows and a general air of cheery welcome about it that seemed, somehow, sinister in the eerie silence. No light came from the window. Darkness was rapidly swallowing the little town. Crysania, pushing open the door, could barely see inside.

"Hello?" she called hesitantly. At the sound of her voice, the birds outside squawked raucously, making her shiver. "Is anyone here? I'd like a room—"

But her voice died. She knew, without doubt that this place was empty, deserted. Perhaps everyone had left to join the army? She had known of entire villages to do so. But, looking around, she realized that that wasn't true in this case. There would have been nothing left here except furniture; the people would have taken their possessions with them.

Here, the table was set for dinner. . . .

Stepping farther inside as her eyes adjusted to the dimness, she could see glasses still filled with wine, the bottles sitting open in the center of the table. There was no food. Some of the dishes had been knocked off and lay broken on the floor, next to some gnawed-on bones. Two dogs and a cat skulking about, looking half-starved, gave her an idea of how that had happened.

A staircase ran up to the second floor. Crysania thought about going up it, but her courage failed her. She would look around the town first. Surely someone was here, someone who could tell her what was going on.

Picking up a lamp, she lit it from the tinder box† in her pack, then went back out into the street, now

The tinder box was a staple of any self-respecting adventurer's AD&D game.

616

almost totally dark. What had happened? Where was everyone? It did not look as if the town had been attacked. There were no signs of fighting—no broken furniture, no blood, no weapons lying about. No bodies.

Her uneasiness grew as she walked outside the door of the inn. Her horse whinnied at the sight of her. Crysania suppressed a wild desire to leap up on it and ride away as fast as she could. The animal was tired; it could go no farther without rest. It needed food. Thinking of that, Crysania untied it and led it around to the stable behind the inn. It was empty. Not unusual—horses were a luxury these days. But it was filled with straw and there was water, so at least the inn was prepared to receive travelers. Placing her lamp on a stand, Crysania unsaddled her exhausted animal and rubbed it down, crudely and clumsily she knew, having never done it before.

But the horse seemed satisfied enough and, when she left, was munching oats it found in a trough.

Taking her lamp, Crysania returned to the empty, silent streets. She peered into dark houses, looked into darkened shop windows. Nothing. No one. Then, walking along, she heard a noise. Her heart stopped beating for an instant, the lamplight wavered in her shaking hand. She stopped, listening, telling herself it was a bird or an animal.

No, there it was again. And again. It was an odd sound, a kind of swishing, then a plop. Then a swish again, followed by a plop. Certainly there was nothing sinister or threatening about it. But still Crysania stood there, in the center of the street, unwilling to move toward the noise to investigate.

"What nonsense!" she told herself sternly. Angry at herself, disappointed at the failure—apparently—of her plans, and determined to discover what was going on, Crysania boldly walked forward. But her hand, she noted nervously, seemed of its own accord to reach for the medallion of her god.

The sound grew louder. The row of houses and small shops came to an end. Turning a corner, walking softly, she suddenly realized she should have doused her lamplight. But the thought came too late. At the sight of the light, the figure that had been making the odd sound turned abruptly, flung up his arm to shield his eyes, and stared at her.

"Who are you?" the man's voice called. "What do you want?" He did not sound frightened, only desperately tired, as if her presence were an additional, great burden.

But instead of answering, Crysania walked closer. For now she had figured out what the sound was. He had been shoveling! He held the shovel in his hand. He had no light. He had obviously been working so hard he was not even aware that night had fallen.

Raising her lamp to let the light shine on both of them, Crysania studied the man curiously. He was young, younger than she†—probably about twenty or twenty-one. He was human, with a pale, serious face, and he was dressed in robes that, save for some strange, unrecognizable symbol upon them, she would have taken for clerical garb. As she drew nearer, Crysania saw the young man stagger. If his shovel had not been in the ground, he would have fallen. Instead, he leaned upon it, as if exhausted past all endurance.

Her own fears forgotten, Crysania hurried forward to help him. But, to her amazement, he stopped her with a motion of his hand.

"Keep away!" he shouted.

"What?" Crysania asked, startled.

"Keep away!" he repeated more urgently. But the shovel would support him no longer. He fell to his knees, clutching his stomach as if in pain.

"I'll do no such thing," Crysania said firmly, recognizing that the young man was ill or injured. Hurrying forward, she started to put her arm around him to help him up when her gaze fell upon what he had been doing.

She halted, staring in horror.

He had been filling in a grave—a mass grave.

Looking down into a huge pit, she saw bodies— men, women, children. There was not a mark upon them, no sign of blood. Yet they were all dead; the entire town, she realized numbly.

And then, turning, she saw the young man's face, she saw sweat pouring from it, she saw the glazed, feverish eyes. And then she knew.

"I tried to warn you," he said wearily, choking. "The burning fever."

"Come along," said Crysania, her voice trembling with grief. Turning her back firmly on the ghastly

I hesitate to say exactly how old Crysania is, but I recall envisioning her as being in her mid-thirties. —TRH

sight behind her, she put her arms around the young man. He struggled weakly.

"No! Don't!" he begged. "You'll catch it! Die . . . within hours. . . ."

"You are sick. You need rest," she said. Ignoring his protests, she led him away.

"But the grave," he whispered, his horrified gaze going to the dark sky where the carrion birds circled. "We can't leave the bodies—"

"Their souls are with Paladine," Crysania said, fighting back her own nausea at the thought of the gruesome feasting that would soon commence. Already she could hear the cackles of triumph. "Only their shells still lie there. They understand that the living come first."

Sighing, too weak to argue, the young man bowed his head and put his arm around Crysania's neck. He was, she noted, unbelievably thin—she scarcely felt his weight at all as he leaned against her. She wondered how long it had been since he'd eaten a good meal.

Walking slowly, they left the gravesite. "My house, there," he said, gesturing feebly to a small cabin on the edge of the village.

Crysania nodded. "Tell me what happened," she said, to keep his thoughts and her own from the sound of flapping birds' wings behind them.

"There's not much to tell," he said, shivering with chills. "It strikes quickly, without warning. Yesterday, the children were playing in the yards. Last night, they were dying in their mothers' arms. Tables were laid for dinner that no one was able to eat. This morning, those who were still able to move dug that grave, their own grave, as we all knew then. . . ."

His voice failed, a shudder of pain gripping him.

"It will be all right now," Crysania said. "We'll get you in bed. Cool water and sleep. I'll pray. . . ."

"Prayers!" The young man laughed bitterly. "I am their cleric!" He waved a hand back at the grave. "You see what good prayers have done!"

"Hush, save your strength," Crysania said as they arrived at the small house. Helping him lie down upon the bed, she shut the door and, seeing a fire laid, lit it with the flame from her lamp. Soon it was blazing. She lit candles and then returned to her

patient. His feverish eyes had been following her every move.

Drawing a chair up next to the bed, she poured water into a bowl, dipped a cloth into it, then sat down beside him, to lay the cool cloth across his burning forehead.

"I am a cleric, too," she told him, lightly touching the medallion she wore around her neck, "and I am going to pray to my god to heal you."

Setting the bowl of water on a small table beside the bed, Crysania reached out to the young man and placed her hands upon his shoulders. Then she began to pray. "Paladine—"

"What?" he interrupted, clutching at her with a hot hand. "What are you doing?"

"I am going to heal you," Crysania said, smiling at him with gentle patience. "I am a cleric of Paladine."

"Paladine!" The young man grimaced in pain, then—catching his breath—looked up at her in disbelief. "That's who I thought you said. How can you be one of *his* clerics? They vanished, so it's told, right before the Cataclysm."

"It's a long story," Crysania replied, drawing the sheets over the young man's shivering body, "and one I will tell you later. But, for now, believe that I am truly a cleric of this great god and that he will heal you!"

"No!" the young man cried, his hand wrapping around hers so tightly it hurt. "I am a cleric, too, a cleric of the Seeker† gods. I tried to heal my people"— his voice cracked—"but there . . . there was nothing I could do. They died!" His eyes closed in agony. "I prayed! The gods . . . didn't answer."

"That's because these gods you pray to are false gods," Crysania said earnestly, reaching out to smooth back the young man's sweat-soaked hair. Opening his eyes, he regarded her intently. He was handsome, Crysania saw, in a serious, scholarly fashion. His eyes were blue, his hair golden.

"Water," he murmured through parched lips. She helped him sit up. Thirstily, he drank from the bowl, then she eased him back down on the bed. Staring at her still, he shook his head, then shut his eyes wearily.

"You know of Paladine, of the ancient gods?" Crysania asked softly.

The Seekers were primarily an invention of mine. They were not so much identifiable with a particular sect or creed in our own world as they were with a general attitude toward God and how man relates to Him through religion and faith.
—TRH

The young man's eyes opened, there was a gleam of light in them. "Yes," he said bitterly. "I know of them. I know they smashed the land. I know they brought storms and pestilence upon us. I know evil things have been unleashed in this land. And then they left. In our hour of need, they abandoned us!"

Now it was Crysania's turn to stare. She had expected denial, disbelief, or even total ignorance of the gods. She knew she could handle that. But this bitter anger?† This was not the confrontation she had been prepared to face. Expecting superstitious mobs, she had found instead a mass grave and a dying young cleric.

"The gods did *not* abandon us," she said, her voice quivering in her earnestness. "They are here, waiting only for the sound of a prayer. The evil that came to Krynn man brought upon himself, through his own pride and willful ignorance."

The story of Goldmoon healing the dying Elistan and thereby converting him to the ancient faith came vividly to Crysania filling her with exultation.† She would heal this young cleric, convert him. . . .

"I am going to help you," she said. "Then there will be time to talk, time for you to understand."

Kneeling down beside the bed once more, she clasped the medallion she wore around her neck and again began, "Paladine—"

A hand grabbed her roughly, hurting her, breaking her hold on the medallion. Startled, she looked up. It was the young cleric. Half-sitting up, weak, shivering with fever, he still stared at her with a gaze that was intense but calm.

"No," he said steadily, "*you* must understand. You don't need to convince me. I believe you!" He looked up into the shadows above him with a grim and bitter smile. "Yes, Paladine is with you. I can sense his great presence. Perhaps my eyes have been opened the nearer I approach death."

"This is wonderful!" Crysania cried ecstatically. "I can—"

"Wait!" The cleric gasped for breath, still holding her hand. "Listen! *Because* I believe I refuse . . . to let you heal me."

"What?" Crysania stared at him, uncomprehending. Then, "You're sick, delirious," she said firmly. "You don't know what you're saying."

Everyone after the Cataclysm seems to blame the gods for what happened. It is rather like a child blaming their parent for being punished and disconnecting their own responsibility for the justice of the punishment. I am reminded of small babies who, unable to adequately control their motor skills, often will hit themselves in the face. Their first reaction is to look at their parent with outraged expression as if it were the parent that hit them. I think we, too, as humanity, look to blame God for the choices we have made in life—better to blame anyone than face our own mistakes. —TRH

See Dragons of Autumn Twilight, Book II, Chapters 12-13.

"I do," he replied. "Look at me. Am I rational? Yes?"

Crysania, studying him, had to nod her head.

"Yes, you must admit it. I am . . . not delirious. I am fully conscious, comprehending."

"Then, why—?"

"Because," he said softly, each breath coming from him with obvious pain, "if Paladine is here—and I believe he is, now—then why is he . . . letting this happen! Why did he let my people die? Why does he permit this suffering? Why did he cause it?† Answer me!" He clutched at her angrily. "Answer me!"

Her own questions! Raistlin's questions! Crysania felt her mind stumbling in confused darkness. How could she answer him, when she was searching so desperately for these answers herself?

Through numb lips, she repeated Elistan's words: "We must have faith. The ways of the gods cannot be known to us, we cannot see—"

Lying back down, the young man shook his head wearily and Crysania herself fell silent, feeling helpless in the face of such violent, intense anger. I'll heal him anyway, she determined. He is sick and weak in mind and body. He cannot be expected to understand. . . .

Then she sighed. No. In other circumstances, Paladine might have allowed it. The god will not grant my prayers, Crysania knew in despair. In his divine wisdom, he will gather the young man to himself and then all will be made clear.

But it could not be so now.

Suddenly, Crysania realized bleakly that time could not be altered, at least not this way, not by her. Goldmoon would restore man's faith in the ancient gods in a time when terrible anger such as this had died, when man would be ready to listen and to accept and believe. Not before.

Her failure overwhelmed her. Still kneeling by the bed, she bowed her head in her hands and asked to be forgiven for not being willing to accept or understand.†

Feeling a hand touch her hair, she looked up. The young man was smiling wanly at her.

"I'm sorry," he said gently, his fever-parched lips twitching. "Sorry . . . to disappoint you."

"I understand," Crysania said quietly, "and I will respect your wishes."

These questions have plagued mankind since the dawn of thought. I have found my own answer in the concept of perspectives— the narrow limits of my own and the unfathomable, eternal grandness of God's. We are so willing to lay our faith in our own limited, myopic few.

In my game seminars and in various novels— including this one—I have tried to express this view: that the point is not whether we will die or not, for we all will die, but rather the point is what we do with the life that we have. See Appendix C.

It is a lesson that Crysania still struggles with at this point in the story. —TRH

Crysania is finally beginning to learn humility. She isn't all the way there yet, but she's well on her way.

"Thank you," he replied. He was silent. For long moments, the only sound that could be heard was his labored breathing. Crysania started to stand up, but she felt his hot hand close over hers. "Do one thing for me," he whispered.

"Anything," she said, forcing herself to smile, though she could barely see him through her tears.

"Stay with me tonight . . . while I die. . . ."

CHAPTER 6

limbing the stairs leading up to the scaffold. Head bowed. Hands tied behind my back. I struggle to free myself, even as I mount the stairs, though I know it is useless—I have spent days, weeks, struggling to free myself, to no avail.

The black robes trip me. I stumble. Someone catches me, keeps me from falling, but drags me forward, nonetheless. I have reached the top. The block, stained dark with blood, is before me. Frantically now I seek to free my hands! If only I can loosen them! I can use my magic! Escape! Escape!

"There is no escape!" laughs my executioner, and I know it is myself speaking! My laughter! My voice! "Kneel, pathetic wizard! Place your head upon the cold and bloody pillow!"

No! I shriek with terror and rage and fight desperately, but hands grab me from behind. Viciously, they force me to my knees. My shrinking flesh touches the chill and

slimy block! Still I wrench and twist and scream and still they force me down.

A black hood is drawn over my head . . . but I can hear the executioner coming closer, I can hear his black robes rustling around his ankles, I can hear the blade being lifted . . . lifted. . . .

"Raist! Raistlin! Wake up!"

Raistlin's eyes opened. Staring upward, dazed and wild with terror, he had no idea for a moment where he was or who had wakened him.

"Raistlin, what is it?" the voice repeated.

Strong hands held him firmly, a familiar voice, warm with concern, blotting out the whistling scream of the executioner's falling axe blade. . . .

"Caramon!" Raistlin cried, clutching at his brother. "Help me! Stop them! Don't let them murder me! Stop them! Stop them!"†

"Shhhh, I won't let them do anything to you, Raist," Caramon murmured, holding his brother close, stroking the soft brown hair. "Shhh, you're all right. I'm here . . . I'm here."

Laying his head on Caramon's chest, hearing his twin's steady, slow heartbeat, Raistlin gave a deep, shuddering sigh. Then he closed his eyes against the darkness and sobbed like a child.

Even though Raistlin is one of the most powerful mortals in Ansalon, he has moments like this of extreme vulnerability. He isn't Superman.

"Ironic, isn't it?" Raistlin muttered bitterly some time later, as his brother stirred up the fire and set an iron pot filled with water on it to boil. "The most powerful mage who has ever lived, and I am reduced to a squalling babe by a dream!"

"So you're human," Caramon grunted, bending over the pot, watching it closely with the rapt attention all pay to the business of forcing water to boil more quickly. He shrugged. "You said it yourself."

"Yes . . . human!" Raistlin repeated savagely, huddled, shivering, in his black robes and traveling cloak.

Caramon glanced at him uneasily at this, remembering what Par-Salian and the other mages had told him at the Conclave held in the Tower of High Sorcery. *Your brother intends to challenge the gods! He seeks to become a god himself!*

But even as Caramon looked at his brother, Raistlin drew his knees up close to his body, rested his hands upon his knees, and laid his head down upon them

wearily. Feeling a strange choking sensation in his throat, vividly remembering the warm and wonderful feeling he had experienced when his brother had reached out to him for comfort, Caramon turned his attention back to the water.

Raistlin's head snapped up, suddenly.

"What was that?" he asked at the same time Caramon, hearing the sound as well, rose to his feet.

"I dunno," Caramon said softly, listening. Padding soft-footed, the big man moved with surprising swiftness to his bedroll, grasped his sword, and drew it from its scabbard.

Acting in the same moment, Raistlin's hand closed over the Staff of Magius that lay beside him. Twisting to his feet like a cat, he doused the fire, upending the kettle over it. Darkness descended on them with a soft, hissing sound as the coals sputtered and died.

Giving their eyes time to become accustomed to the sudden change, both the brothers stood still, concentrating on their hearing.

The stream near which they were camped burbled and lapped among the rocks, branches creaked and leaves rattled as a sharp breeze sprang up, slicing through the autumn night. But what they had heard was neither wind in the trees nor water.

"There it is," said Raistlin in a whisper as his brother came to stand beside him. "In the woods, across the stream."

It was a scrabbling sound, like someone trying unsuccessfully to creep through unfamiliar territory. It lasted a few moments, then stopped, then began again. Either some *one* unfamiliar with the territory or some *thing*—clumsy, heavy-booted.

"Goblins!" hissed Caramon.

Gripping his sword, he and his brother exchanged glances. The years of darkness, of estrangement between them, the jealousy, hatred—everything vanished within that instant. Reacting to the shared danger, they were one, as they had been in their mother's womb.

Moving cautiously, Caramon set foot in the stream. The red moon, Lunitari, glimmered through the trees. But it was new tonight. Looking like the wick of a pinched-out candle, it gave little light. Fearing to turn his foot upon a stone, Caramon tested each step

carefully before he put his weight upon it. Raistlin followed, holding his darkened staff in one hand, resting his other lightly upon his brother's shoulder for balance.

They crossed the stream as silently as the wind whispering across the water and reached the opposite bank. They could still hear the noise. It was made by something living, though, there was no doubt. Even when the wind died, they could hear the rustling sound.

"Rear guard. Raiding party!" Caramon mouthed, half-turning so that his brother could hear.

Raistlin nodded. Goblin raiding parties customarily sent scouts to keep watch upon the trail when they rode in to loot a village. Since it was a boring job and meant that the goblins elected had no share in the killing or the spoils, it generally fell to those lowest in rank—the least skilled, most expendable members of the party.

Raistlin's hand closed suddenly over Caramon's arm, halting him momentarily.

"Crysania!" the mage whispered. "The village! We must know where the raiding party is!"

Caramon scowled. "I'll take it alive!" He indicated this with a gesture of his huge hand wrapping itself around an imaginary goblin neck.

Raistlin smiled grimly in understanding. "And I will question it," he hissed, making a gesture of his own.

Together, the twins crept up the trail, taking care to keep in the shadows so that even the faintest glimmer of moonlight should not be reflected from buckle or sword. They could still hear the sound. Though it ceased sometimes, it always started again. It remained in the same location. Whoever or whatever it was appeared to have no idea of their approach. They drew toward it, keeping to the edges of the trail until they were—as well as they could judge—practically opposite it.

The sound, they could tell now, was in the woods, about twenty feet off the trail. Glancing swiftly around, Raistlin's sharp eyes spotted a thin trail. Barely visible in the pale light of moon and stars, it branched off from the main one—an animal trail, probably leading down to the stream. A good place for scouts to lie hidden, giving them quick access to

the main trail if they decided to attack, an easy escape route if the opposition proved too formidable.

"Wait here!" Caramon signed.

A rustle of his black hood was Raistlin's response. Reaching out to hold aside a low, overhanging branch, Caramon entered the forest, moving slowly and stealthily about two feet away from the faint animal trail that led into it.

Raistlin stood beside a tree, his slender fingers reaching into one of his many, secret pockets, hastily rolling a pinch of sulfur up in a tiny ball of bat guano.† The words to the spell were in his mind. He repeated them to himself. Even as he did this, however, he was acutely conscious of the sound of his brother's movements.

Both necessary components to cast a fireball in AD&D rules.

Though Caramon was trying to be quiet, Raistlin could hear the creak of the big man's leather armor, the metal buckles' jingle, the crack of a twig beneath his feet as he moved away from his waiting twin. Fortunately, their quarry was continuing to make so much noise that the warrior would probably proceed unheard. . . .

A horrible shriek rang through the night, followed by a frightful yelling and thrashing sound, as if a hundred men were crashing through the wilderness.

Raistlin started.

Then a voice shouted, "Raist! Help! Aiiihh!"

More thrashing, the sound of tree limbs snapping, a thumping sound. . . .

Gathering his robes around him, Raistlin ran swiftly onto the animal trail, the time for concealment and secrecy past. He could hear his brother yelling, still. The sound was muffled, but clear, not choked or as if he were in pain.

Racing through the woods, the archmage ignored the branches that slapped his face and the brambles that caught at his robes. Breaking suddenly and unexpectedly into a clearing; he stopped, crouching, beside a tree. Ahead of him, he could see movement—a gigantic black shadow that seemed to be hovering in the air, floating above the ground. Grappling with the shadowy creature, yelling and cursing horribly, was—by the sound—Caramon!

Another magical phrase of mine. There are a few more Indonesian elements in this, and it does follow the grammatical form, but it is, nevertheless, nonsense.
—TRH

"*Ast kiranann Soth-aran/Suh kali Jalaran.*"† Raistlin chanted the words and tossed the small ball of sulfur high above him, into the leaves of the trees. An

instantaneous burst of light in the branches was accompanied by a low, booming explosion. The tree-tops burst into flame, illuminating the scene below.

Raistlin darted forward, the words of a spell on his lips, magical fire crackling from his fingertips.

He stopped, staring in astonishment.

Before him, hanging upside down by one leg from a rope suspended over a tree branch, was Caramon. Suspended next to him, scrabbling frantically in fear of the flames, was a rabbit.

Raistlin stared, transfixed, at his brother. Shouting for help, Caramon turned slowly in the wind while flaming leaves fell all about him.

"Raist!" He was still yelling. "Get me—Oh—"

Caramon's next revolution brought him within sight of his astounded twin. Flushing, the blood rushing to his head, Caramon gave a sheepish grin. "Wolf snare," he said.

The forest was ablaze with brilliant orange light. The fire flickered on the big man's sword, which lay on the ground where he'd dropped it. It sparkled on Caramon's shining armor as he revolved slowly around again. It gleamed in the frantic, panic-stricken eyes of the rabbit.

Raistlin snickered.

Now it was Caramon's turn to stare in hurt astonishment at his brother. Revolving back around to face him, Caramon twisted his head, trying to see Raistlin right side up. He gave a pitiful, pleading look.

"C'mon, Raist! Get me down!"

Raistlin began to laugh silently, his shoulders heaving.

"Damn it, Raist! This isn't funny!" Caramon blustered, waving his arms. This gesture, of course, caused the snared warrior to stop revolving and begin to swing from side to side. The rabbit, on the other end of the snare, started swinging, too, pawing even more frantically at the air. Soon, the two of them were spinning in opposite directions, circling each other, entangling the ropes that held them.

"Get me down!" Caramon roared. The rabbit squealed in terror.

This was too much. Memories of their youth returned vividly to the archmage, driving away the darkness and horror that had clutched at his soul for what seemed like years unending. Once again

he was young, hopeful, filled with dreams. Once again, he was with his brother, the brother who was closer to him than any other person had ever been, would ever be. His bumbling, thick-headed, beloved brother. . . . Raistlin doubled over. Gasping for air, the mage collapsed upon the grass and laughed wildly, tears running down his cheeks.

Caramon glared at him—but this baleful look from a man being held upside down by his foot simply increased his twin's mirth. Raistlin laughed until he thought he might have hurt something inside him. The laughter felt good. For a time, it banished the darkness. Lying on the damp ground of the glade illuminated by the light of the flaming trees, Raistlin laughed harder, feeling the merriment sparkle through his body like fine wine. And then Caramon joined in, his booming bellow echoing through the forest.

Only the falling of blazing bits of tree striking the ground near him recalled Raistlin to himself. Wiping his streaming eyes, so weak from laughter he could barely stand, the mage staggered to his feet. With a flick of his hand, he brought forth the little silver dagger he wore concealed upon his wrist.

Reaching up, stretching his full height, the mage cut the rope wrapped around his brother's ankle. Caramon plunged to the ground with a curse and thudding crash.

Still chuckling to himself, the mage walked over and cut the cord that some hunter had tied around the rabbit's hind leg, catching hold of the animal in his arms. The creature was half-mad with terror, but Raistlin gently stroked its head and murmured soft words. Gradually, the animal grew calm, seeming almost to be in a trance.

"Well, we took him alive," Raistlin said, his lips twitching. He held up the rabbit. "I don't think we'll get much information out of him, however."

So red in the face he gave the impression of having tumbled into a vat of paint, Caramon sat up and began to rub a bruised shoulder.

"Very funny," he muttered, glancing up at the animal with a shamefaced grin. The flames in the tree-tops were dying, though the air was filled with smoke and, here and there, the grass was burning. Fortunately, it had been a damp, rainy autumn, so these small fires died quickly.

"Nice spell," Caramon commented, looking up into the glowing remains of the surrounding tree-tops as, swearing and groaning, he hauled himself to his feet.

"I've always liked it," Raistlin replied wryly. "Fizban taught it to me. You remember?"† Looking up into the smoldering trees, he smiled. "I think that old man would have appreciated this."

Cradling the rabbit in his arms, absently petting the soft, silken ears, Raistlin walked from the smoke-filled woods. Lulled by the mage's caressing fingers and hypnotic words, the rabbit's eyes closed. Caramon retrieved his sword from the brush where he'd dropped it and followed, limping slightly.

"Damn snare cut off my circulation." He shook his foot to try to get the blood going.

Heavy clouds had rolled in, blotting out the stars and snuffing Lunitari's flame completely. As the flames in the trees died, the woods were plunged into darkness so thick that neither brother could see the trail ahead.

"I suppose there is no need for secrecy now," Raistlin murmured. *"Shirak."* The crystal on the top of the Staff of Magius began to glow with a bright, magical brilliance.

The twins returned to their camp in silence, a companionable, comfortable silence, a silence they had not shared in years. The only sounds in the night were the restless stirring of their horses, the creak and jingle of Caramon's armor, and the soft rustle of the mage's black robes as he walked. Behind them, once, they heard a crash—the falling of a charred branch.

Reaching camp, Caramon ruefully stirred at the remains of their fire, then glanced up at the rabbit in Raistlin's arms.

"I don't suppose you'd consider that breakfast."

"I do not eat goblin flesh," Raistlin answered with a smile, placing the creature down on the trail. At the touch of the cold ground beneath its paws, the rabbit started, its eyes flared open. Staring around for an instant to get its bearings, it suddenly bolted for the shelter of the woods.

Caramon heaved a sigh, then, chuckling to himself, sat down heavily upon the ground near his bedroll. Removing his boot, he rubbed his bruised ankle.

The fireball was one of Fizban's favorite spells, though he often forgot how to cast it; see Dragons of Autumn Twilight, *Book II, Chapter 4. Fizban did indeed instruct Raistlin in the use of magic; see* Dragons of Winter Night, *Book I, Chapter 5.*

"Dulak," Raistlin whispered and the staff went dark. He laid it beside his bedroll, then laid down, drawing the blankets up around him.

With the return of darkness, the dream was there. Waiting.

Raistlin shuddered, his body suddenly convulsed with chills. Sweat covered his brow. He could not, dared not close his eyes! Yet, he was so tired . . . so exhausted. How many nights had it been since he'd slept? . . .

"Caramon," he said softly.

"Yeah," Caramon answered from the darkness.

"Caramon," Raistlin said after a moment's pause, "do . . . do you remember how, when we were children, I'd have those . . . those horrible dreams? . . ." His voice failed him for a moment. He coughed.

There was no sound from his twin.

Raistlin cleared his throat, then whispered, "And you'd guard my sleep, my brother. You kept them away. . . ."

"I remember," came a muffled, husky voice.

"Caramon," Raistlin began, but he could not finish. The pain and weariness were too much. The darkness seemed to close in, the dream crept from its hiding place.

And then there was the jingle of armor. A big, hulking shadow appeared beside him. Leather creaking, Caramon sat down beside his brother, resting his broad back against a tree trunk and laying his naked sword across his knees.

"Go to sleep, Raist," Caramon said gently. The mage felt a rough, clumsy hand pat him on the shoulder. "I'll stay up and keep watch. . . ."

Wrapping himself in his blankets, Raistlin closed his eyes. Sleep, sweet and restful, stole upon him. The last thing he remembered was a fleeting fancy of the dream approaching, reaching out its bony hands to grasp him, only to be driven back by the light from Caramon's sword.

This chapter remains one of my favorite chapters ever. It was actually suggested by Tracy, who asked rather wistfully one day, while we were working on the book, if Caramon and Raistlin didn't ever have any happy times together. This scene not only reminds us that they are brothers and that they do share a bond, but it also introduces the theme of the rabbit and presages the ending of the trilogy. —MW

CHAPTER
7

Caramon's horse shifted restlessly beneath him as the big man leaned forward in the saddle, staring down into the valley at the village. Frowning darkly, he glanced at his brother. Raistlin's face was hidden behind his black hood. A steady rain had started about dawn and now dripped dull and monotonously around them. Heavy gray clouds sagged above them, seemingly upheld by the dark, towering trees. Other than the drip of water from the leaves, there was no sound at all.

Raistlin shook his head. Then, speaking gently to his horse, he rode forward. Caramon followed, hurrying to catch up, and there was the sound of steel sliding from a scabbard.

"You will not need your sword, my brother," Raistlin said without turning.

The horses' hooves clopped through the mud of the road, their sound thudding too loudly in the

thick, rain-soaked air. Despite Raistlin's words, Caramon kept his hand upon the hilt of his sword until they rode into the outskirts of the small village. Dismounting, he handed the reins of his horse to his brother, then, cautiously, approached the same small inn Crysania had first seen.

Peering inside, he saw the table set for dinner, the broken crockery. A dog came dashing up to him hopefully, licking his hand and whimpering. Cats slunk beneath the chairs, vanishing into the shadows with a guilty, furtive air. Absently patting the dog, Caramon was about to walk inside when Raistlin called.

"I heard a horse. Over there."

Sword drawn, Caramon walked around the corner of the building. After a few moments, he returned, his weapon sheathed, his brow furrowed.

"It's hers," he reported. "Unsaddled, fed, and watered."

Nodding his hooded head as though he had expected this information, Raistlin pulled his cloak more tightly about him.

Caramon glanced uneasily about the village. Water dripped from the eaves, the door to the inn swung on rusty hinges, making a shrill squeaking sound. No light came from any of the houses, no sounds of children's laughter or women calling to each other or men complaining about the weather as they went to their work. "What is it, Raist?"

Plague and disease are still common problems in many parts of the world, but the Plague here was most likely inspired by Europe's "Black Death" in the Middle Ages.

"Plague,"† said Raistlin.

Caramon choked and instantly covered his mouth and nose with his cloak. From within the shadows of the cowl, Raistlin's mouth twisted in an ironic smile.

"Do not fear, my brother," he said, dismounting from his horse. Taking the reins, Caramon tied both animals to a post, then came to stand beside his twin. "We have a true cleric with us, have you forgotten?"

"Then where is she?" Caramon growled in a muffled voice, still keeping his face covered.

The mage's head turned, staring down the rows of silent, empty houses. "There, I should guess," he remarked finally. Caramon followed his gaze and saw a single light flickering in the window of a small house at the other end of the village.

"I'd rather be walking into a camp of ogres," Caramon muttered as he and his brother slogged through the muddy, deserted streets. His voice was gruff with a fear he could not hide. He could face with equanimity the prospect of dying with six inches of cold steel in his gut. But the thought of dying helplessly, wasted by something that could not be fought, that floated unseen upon the air, filled the big man with horror.

Raistlin did not reply. His face remained hidden. What his thoughts might have been, his brother could not guess. The two reached the end of the row of houses, the rain spattering all around them with thudding plops. They were nearing the light when Caramon happened to glance to his left.

"Name of the gods!" he whispered as he stopped abruptly and grasped his brother by the arm.

He pointed to the mass grave.

Neither spoke. With croaks of anger at their approach, the carrion birds rose into the air, black wings flapping. Caramon gagged. His face pale, he turned hurriedly away. Raistlin continued to stare at the sight a moment, his thin lips tightening into a straight line.

"Come, my brother," he said coldly, walking toward the small house again.

Glancing in at the window, hand on the hilt of his sword, Caramon sighed and, nodding his head, gave his brother a sign. Raistlin pushed gently upon the door, and it opened at his touch.

A young man lay upon a rumpled bed. His eyes were closed, his hands folded across his chest. There was a look of peace upon the still, ashen face, though the closed eyes were sunken into gaunt cheekbones and the lips were blue with the chill of death. A cleric dressed in robes that might once have been white knelt on the floor beside him, her head bowed on her folded hands. Caramon started to say something, but Raistlin checked him with a hand on his arm, shaking his hooded head, unwilling to interrupt her.

Silently, the twins stood together in the doorway, the rain dripping around them.

Crysania was with her god. Intent upon her prayers, she was unaware of the twins' entrance until, finally, the jingle and creak of Caramon's armor brought

her back to reality. Lifting her head, her dark, tousled hair falling about her shoulders, she regarded them without surprise.

Her face, though pale with weariness and sorrow, was composed. Though she had not prayed to Paladine to send them, she knew the god answered prayers of the heart as well as those spoken openly. Bowing her head once more, giving thanks, she sighed, then rose to her feet and turned to face them.

Her eyes met Raistlin's eyes, the light of the failing fire causing them to gleam even in the depths of his hood. When she spoke, her voice seemed to her to blend with the sound of the falling raindrops.

"I failed," she said.

Raistlin appeared undisturbed. He glanced at the body of the young man. "He would not believe?"

"Oh, he believed." She, too, looked down at the body. "He refused to let me heal him. His anger was . . . very great." Reaching down, she drew the sheet up over the still form. "Paladine has taken him. Now he understands, I am certain."

"He does," Raistlin remarked. "Do you?"

Crysania's head bowed, her dark hair fell around her face. She stood so still for so long that Caramon, *not* understanding, cleared his throat and shifted uneasily.

"Uh, Raist—" he began softly.

"Shh!" Raistlin whispered.

Crysania raised her head. She had not even heard Caramon. Her eyes were a deep gray now, so dark they seemed to reflect the archmage's black robes.† "I understand," she said in a firm voice. "For the first time, I understand and I see what I must do. In Istar, I saw belief in the gods lost. Paladine granted my prayer and showed me the Kingpriest's fatal weakness—pride. The god gave me to know how I might avoid that mistake. He gave me to know that, if I asked, he would answer.

"But Paladine also showed me, in Istar, how weak I was. When I left the wretched city and came here with you, I was little more than a frightened child, clinging to you in the terrible night. Now, I have regained my strength. The vision of this tragic sight has burned into my soul."

As Crysania spoke, she drew nearer Raistlin. His eyes held hers in an unblinking gaze. She saw

The symbolism in this passage is important. Crysania, a cleric who dresses in white robes now gone gray looks at Raistlin through gray eyes, reflecting his black robes. This symbolism continues throughout this scene.

herself in their flat surface. The medallion of Paladine she wore around her neck shone with a cold, white light. Her voice grew fervent, her hands clasped together tightly.

"That sight will be before my eyes," she said softly, coming to stand before the archmage, "as I walk with you through the Portal, armed with my faith,† strong in my belief that together you and I will banish darkness from the world forever!"

Reaching out, Raistlin took hold of her hands. They were numb with cold. He enclosed them in his own slender hands, warming them with his burning touch.

"We have no need to alter time!" Crysania said. "Fistandantilus was an evil man. What he did, he did for his own personal glory. But we care, you and I. *That* alone will be sufficient to change the ending. I know—my god has spoken to me!"

Slowly, smiling his thin-lipped smile, Raistlin brought Crysania's hands to his mouth and kissed them, never taking his eyes from her.

Crysania felt her cheeks flush, then caught her breath. With a choked, half-strangled sound, Caramon turned abruptly and walked out the door.

Standing in the oppressive silence, the rain beating down upon his head, Caramon heard a voice thudding at his brain with the same monotonous, dull tone as the drops spattering about him.

He seeks to become a god. He seeks to become a god!

Sick and afraid, Caramon shook his head in anguish. His interest in the army, his fascination with being a "general," his attraction to Crysania, and all the other, thousand worries had driven from his mind the real reason he had come back. Now— with Crysania's words—it returned to him, hitting him like a wave of chill sea water.

Yet all he could think of was Raistlin as he was last night. How long had it been since he'd heard his brother laugh like that? How long had it been since they'd shared that warmth, that closeness? Vividly, he remembered watching Raistlin's face as he guarded his twin's sleep. He saw the harsh lines of cunning smooth, the bitter creases around the mouth fade. The archmage looked almost young again, and Caramon remembered their childhood and young

Crysania's faith may be in the process of being shaped through conflict, trial, and adversity, but her metal is not easily forged. She still shares the Kingpriest's folly in this passage. —TRH

manhood together—those days that had been the happiest of his life.

But then came, unbidden, a hideous memory, as though his soul were taking a perverse delight in torturing and confusing him. He saw himself once more in that dark cell in Istar, seeing clearly, for the first time, his brother's vast capability for evil. He remembered his firm determination that his brother must die. He thought of Tasslehoff. . . .

But Raistlin had explained all that! He had explained things at Istar. Once again, Caramon felt himself foundering.

What if Par-Salian is wrong, what if they are all wrong? What if Raist and Crysania *could* save the world from horror and suffering like this?

"I'm just a jealous, bumbling fool," Caramon mumbled, wiping the rainwater from his face with a trembling hand. "Maybe those old wizards are all like me, all jealous of him."

The darkness deepened about him, the clouds above grew denser, changing from gray to black. The rain† beat down more heavily.

Weather is rarely accidental in great storytelling. Here, the rain is more than just setting; it is symbol.

The change in her robe color here is no accident. It signifies the changes that are taking place in her own thinking and faith. —TRH

Raistlin came out the door, Crysania with him, her hand on his arm. She was wrapped in her thick cloak, her grayish-white† hood drawn up over her head. Caramon cleared his throat.

"I'll go bring him out and put him with the others," he said gruffly, starting for the door. "Then I'll fill in the grave—"

"No, my brother," Raistlin said. "No. This sight will not be hidden in the ground." He cast back his hood, letting the rain wash over his face as he lifted his gaze to the clouds. "This sight will flare in the eyes of the gods! The smoke of their destruction will rise to heaven! The sound will resound in their ears!"

Caramon, startled at this unusual outburst, turned to look at his twin. Raistlin's thin face was nearly as gaunt and pale as the corpse's inside the small house, his voice tense with anger.

"Come with me," he said, abruptly breaking free of Crysania's hold and striding toward the center of the small village. Crysania followed, holding her hood to keep the slashing wind and rain from blowing it off. Caramon came after, more slowly.

Stopping in the middle of the muddy, rain-soaked

street, Raistlin turned to face Crysania and his brother as they came up to him.

"Get the horses, Caramon—ours and Crysania's. Lead them to those woods outside of town"—the mage pointed—"blindfold them, then return to me."

Caramon stared at him.

"Do it!" Raistlin commanded, his voice rasping.

Caramon did as he was told, leading the horses away.

"Now, stand there," Raistlin continued when his twin returned. "Do not move from that spot. Do not come close to me, my brother, no matter what happens." His gaze went to Crysania, who was standing near him, then back to his brother. "You understand, Caramon."

Caramon nodded wordlessly and, reaching out, gently took Crysania's hand.

"What is it?" she asked, holding back.

"His magic," Caramon replied.

He fell silent as Raistlin cast a sharp, imperious glance at him. Alarmed by the strange, fiercely eager expression on Raistlin's face, Crysania suddenly drew nearer Caramon, shivering. The big man, his eyes on his frail twin, put his arm around her. Standing together in the pounding rain, almost not daring to breathe lest they disturb him, they watched the archmage.

Raistlin's eyes closed. Lifting his face to the heavens, he raised his arms, palms outward, toward the lowering skies. His lips moved, but—for a moment—they could not hear him. Then, though he did not seem to raise his voice, each could begin to make out words—the spidery language of magic. He repeated the same words over and over, his soft voice rising and falling in a chant. The words never changed, but the way he spoke them, the inflection of each, varied every time he repeated the phrase.

A hush settled over the valley. Even the sound of the falling rain died in Caramon's ears. All he could hear was the soft chanting, the strange and eerie music of his brother's voice. Crysania pressed closer still, her dark eyes wide, and Caramon patted her reassuringly.

As the chanting continued, a feeling of awe crept over Caramon. He had the distinct impression that he was being drawn irresistibly toward Raistlin,

that everything in the world was being drawn toward the archmage, though—in looking fearfully around—Caramon saw that he hadn't moved from the spot. But, turning back to stare at his brother, the feeling returned even more forcibly.

Raistlin stood in the center of the world, his hands outstretched, and all sound, all light, even the air itself, seemed to rush eagerly into his grasp. The ground beneath Caramon's feet began to pulse in waves that flowed toward the archmage.

Raistlin lifted his hands higher, his voice rising ever so slightly. He paused, then he spoke each word in the chant slowly, firmly. The winds rose, the ground heaved. Caramon had the wild impression that the world was rushing in upon his brother, and he braced his feet, fearful that he, too, would be sucked into Raistlin's dark vortex.

Raistlin's fingers stabbed toward the gray, boiling heavens. The energy that he had drawn from ground and air surged through him. Silver lightning flashed from his fingers, striking the clouds. Brilliant, jagged light forked down in answer, touching the small house where the body of the young cleric lay. With a shattering explosion, a ball of blue-white flame engulfed the building.

Again Raistlin spoke and again the silver lightning shot from his fingers. Again another streak of light answered, striking the mage! This time it was Raistlin who was engulfed in red-green flame.

Crysania screamed. Struggling in Caramon's grasp, she sought to free herself. But, remembering his brother's words, Caramon held her fast, preventing her from rushing to Raistlin's side.

"Look!" he whispered hoarsely, gripping her tightly. "The flames do not touch him!"

Standing amidst the blaze, Raistlin lifted his thin arms higher, and the black robes blew around him as though he were in the center of a violent wind storm. He spoke again. Fiery fingers of flame spread out from him, lighting the darkness, ran through the wet grass, dancing on top of the water as though it were covered with oil. Raistlin stood in the center, the hub of a vast, spoked wheel of flame.

Crysania could not move. Awe and terror such as she had never before experienced paralyzed her. She held onto Caramon, but he offered her no comfort.

The two clung together like frightened children as the flames surged around them. Traveling through the streets, the fire reached the buildings and ignited them with one bursting explosion after another.

Purple, red, blue, and green, the magical fire blazed upward, lighting the heavens, taking the place of the cloud-shrouded sun. The carrion birds wheeled in fear as the tree they had occupied became a living torch.

Raistlin spoke again, one last time. With a burst of pure, white light, fire leaped down from the heavens, consuming the bodies in the mass grave.

Wind from the flames gusted about Crysania, blowing the hood from her head. The heat was intense, beating upon her face. The smoke choked her, she could not breathe. Sparks showered around her, flames flickered at her feet until it seemed that she, too, must end up part of the conflagration. But nothing touched her. She and Caramon stood safely in the midst of the blaze. And then Crysania became aware of Raistlin's gaze upon her.

From the fiery inferno in which he stood, the mage beckoned.

Crysania gasped, shrinking back against Caramon.

Raistlin beckoned again, his black robes flowing about his body, rippling with the wind of the fire storm he had created. Standing within the center of the flames, he held out his hands to Crysania.

"No!" Caramon cried, holding fast to her. But Crysania, never taking her eyes from Raistlin, gently loosened the big man's grip and walked forward.

"Come to me, Revered Daughter!" Raistlin's soft voice touched her through the chaos and she knew she was hearing it in her heart. "Come to me through the flame. Come taste the power of the gods. . . ."

The heat of the blazing fire that enveloped the archmage burned and scorched her soul. It seemed her skin must blacken and shrivel. She heard her hair crackling. Her breath was sucked from her lungs, searing them painfully. But the fire's light entranced her, the flames danced, luring her forward, even as Raistlin's soft voice urged her toward him.

"No!" Behind her, she could hear Caramon cry out, but he was nothing to her, less than the sound of her own heart beating. She reached the curtain of flame. Raistlin extended his hand, but, for an instant, she faltered, hesitating.

His hand burned! She saw it withering, the flesh black and charred.

"Come to me, Crysania. . . ." whispered his voice.

Reaching out her hand, trembling, she thrust it into the flame. For an instant, there was searing, heart-stopping pain. She cried out in horror and anguish, then Raistlin's hand closed over hers, drawing her through the blazing curtain. Involuntarily, she closed her eyes.

Cool wind soothed her. She could breathe sweet air. The only heat she felt was the warm, familiar heat from the mage's body. Opening her eyes, she saw that she stood close to him. Raising her head, she gazed up into his face . . . and felt a swift, sharp ache in her heart.

Raistlin's thin face glistened with sweat, his eyes reflected the pure, white flame of the burning bodies, his breath came fast and shallow. He seemed lost, unaware of his surroundings. And there was a look of ecstasy on his face, a look of exultation, of triumph.

"I understand," Crysania said to herself, holding onto his hands. "I understand. This is why he cannot love me. He has only one love in this life and that is his magic. To this love he will give everything, for this love he will risk everything!"

The thought was painful, but it was a pleasant kind of melancholy pain.

"Once again," she said to herself, her eyes dimming with tears, "he is my example. Too long have I let myself be preoccupied with petty thoughts of this world, of myself. He is right. Now I taste the power of the gods. I must be worthy—of them and of him!"

Raistlin closed his eyes. Crysania holding onto him, felt the magic drain from him as though his life's blood were flowing from a wound. His arms fell to his sides. The ball of flame that had enveloped them flickered and died.

With a sigh that was little more than a whisper, Raistlin sank to his knees upon the scorched ground. The rain resumed. Crysania could hear it hiss as it struck the charred remains of the still-smoldering village. Steam rose into the air, flitting among the

skeletons of the buildings, drifting down the street like ghosts of the former inhabitants.

Kneeling beside the archmage, Crysania smoothed back his brown hair† with her hand. Raistlin opened his eyes, looking at her without recognition. And in them she saw deep, undying sorrow—the look of one who has been permitted to enter a realm of deadly, perilous beauty and who now finds himself, once more, cast down into the gray, rain-swept world.

Raistlin's hair color is brown in this part of the story because he has yet to undergo his Test in the Tower of High Sorcery, where his hair will go white. —MW

The mage slumped forward, his head bowed, his arms hanging limply. Crysania looked up at Caramon as the big man hurried over.

"Are you all right?" he asked her.

"I'm all right," she whispered. "How is he?"

Together, they helped Raistlin rise to his feet. He seemed completely unaware of their very existence. Tottering with exhaustion, he sagged against his brother.

"He'll be fine. This always happens." Caramon's voice died, then he muttered, "Always happens! What I am saying? I've never seen anything like that in my life! Name of the gods"—he stared at his twin in awe—"I've never seen power like that! I didn't know! I didn't know. . . ."

Supported by Caramon's strong arm, Raistlin leaned against his twin. He began to cough, gasping for air, choking until he could barely stand. Caramon held onto him tightly. Fog and smoke swirled about their feet, the rain splashed down around them. Here and there came the crash of burning wood, the hiss of water upon flame. When the coughing fit passed, Raistlin raised his head, life and recognition returning to his eyes.

"Crysania," he said softly, "I asked you to do that because you must have implicit faith in me and in my power. If we succeed in our quest, Revered Daughter, then we will enter the Portal and we will walk with our eyes open into the Abyss—a place of horror unimaginable."

Crysania began to shiver uncontrollably as she stood before him, held mesmerized by his glittering eyes.

"You must be strong, Revered Daughter," he continued intently. "And that is the reason I brought you on this journey. I have gone through my own trials. You had to go through yours. In Istar, you faced the trials of wind and water. You came through the trial of darkness within the Tower, and now you have withstood the trial by fire. But one more trial awaits you, Crysania! One more, and you must prepare for it, as must we all."

His eyes closed wearily, he staggered. Caramon, his face grim and suddenly haggard, caught hold of his twin and, lifting him, carried him to the waiting horses.

Crysania hurried after them, her concerned gaze on Raistlin. Despite his weakness, there was a look of sublime peace and exultation on his face.

"What's wrong?" she asked.

"He sleeps," Caramon said, his voice deep and gruff, concealing some emotion she could not guess at.

Reaching the horses, Crysania stopped a moment, turning to look behind her.

Smoke rose from the charred ruins of the village. The skeletons of the buildings had collapsed into heaps of pure white ash, the trees were nothing but branched smoke drifting up to the heavens. Even as she watched, the rain beat down upon the ash, changing it to mud, washing it away. The fog blew to shreds, the smoke was swept away on the winds of the storm.

The village was gone as though it had never been.

Shivering, Crysania clutched her cloak about her and turned to Caramon, who was placing Raistlin into his saddle, shaking him, forcing him to wake up enough to ride.

"Caramon," Crysania said as the warrior came over to help her. "What did Raistlin mean—'another trial.' I saw the look on your face when he said it. You know, don't you? You understand?"

Caramon did not answer immediately. Next to them, Raistlin swayed groggily in his saddle. finally, his head bowed, the mage lapsed once more into sleep. After assisting Crysania, Caramon walked over to his own horse and mounted. Then, reaching over, he took the reins from the limp hands of his slumbering brother. They rode back up the mountain, through the rain, Caramon never once looking behind at the village.

In silence, he guided the horses up the trail. Next to him, Raistlin slumped over his mount's neck. Caramon steadied his brother with a firm, gentle hand.

"Caramon?" Crysania asked softly as they reached the summit of the mountain.†

The warrior turned to look at Crysania. Then, with a sigh, his gaze went to the south, where, far from them, lay Thorbardin. The storm clouds massed thick and dark upon the distant horizon.

"It is an old legend that, before he faced the Queen of Darkness, Huma was tested by the gods. He went through the trial of wind, the trial of fire, the trial of water. And his last test," Caramon said quietly, "was the trial of blood."

Again, this is more than just setting; it is symbol. Crysania asks her question at "the summit of the mountain." They are looking to their destination, which is wreathed in storm clouds.

SONG OF HUMA (REPRISE)†

This poem, of course, comes from the Chronicles. It is an excerpt (actually straddling two stanzas) from the much longer "Song of Huma," which can be found in the final pages of Dragons of Autumn Twilight. *This, along with the "Canticle of the Dragon" from the same volume, was my first attempt at narrative poetry for the series, and it is tricky stuff. How do you strike the balance between the lyricism and song of poetry and the straight-forward narration of fiction? In short, how do you tell a story in poetry and keep the words from getting in the way?*

In every copy of Dragons of Autumn Twilight *I have (I'm talking about the original paperback copies— not the nice ones like the hardbound Annotated Chronicles) the last several pages always seem to fall out. That may stem from the problems that naturally arise from paperback binding; it may also result from the fact that I look at those pages pretty often, determining how "The Song of Huma" might have been made better.*

I also have this dark suspicion that the pages fall out at the cosmic bequests of Gilean or Branchala, but I think that might be carrying things too far. —Michael Williams

This is one of the most beautiful phrases in the book: ". . . becoming what we can never be." To me it signifies our desire and purposeful quest for perfection. —TRH

*T*hrough cinders and blood, the harvest of dragons,
Traveled Huma, cradled by dreams of the Silver Dragon,
The Stag perpetual, a signal before him.
At last the eventual harbor, a temple so far to the east
That it lay where the east was ending.
There Paladine appeared
In a pool of stars and glory, announcing
That of all choices, one most terrible had fallen to Huma.
For Paladine knew that the heart is a nest of yearnings,
That we can travel forever toward the light, becoming
What we can never be.†

BOOK 3

Footsteps In The Sand . . .

The Army of Fistandantilus surged southward, reaching Caergoth just as the last of the leaves were blowing from the tree limbs and the chill hand of winter was getting a firm grip upon the land.

The banks of New Sea brought the army to a halt. But Caramon, knowing he was going to have to cross it, had long had his preparations underway. Turning over command of the main part of the army to his brother and the most trusted of his subordinates, Caramon led a group of his best-trained men to the shores of New Sea. Also with him were all the blacksmiths, woodwrights, and carpenters who had joined the army.

Caramon made his command post in the city of Caergoth. He had heard of the famous port city all his life—his former life. Three hundred years after the Cataclysm would find it a bustling, thriving harbor town. But now, one hundred years after the fiery mountain had struck Krynn, Caergoth was a town in confusion. Once a small farming community in the middle of the Solamnic Plain, Caergoth was still struggling with the sudden appearance of a sea at its doorstep.

Looking down from his quarters where the roads in town ended—suddenly—in a precarious drop down steep cliffs to the beaches below, Caramon thought—incongruously—of Tarsis. The Cataclysm had robbed that town of its sea, leaving its boats stranded upon the sands like dying sea birds, while here, in Caergoth, New Sea lapped on what was once plowed ground.

Caramon thought with longing of those stranded ships in Tarsis. Here, in Caergoth, there were a few boats but not nearly enough for his needs. He sent his men ranging up and down the coast for hundreds of miles, with orders to either purchase or commandeer sea-going vessels of any type, their crews with them, if possible. These they sailed to Caergoth, where the smiths and the craftsmen reoutfitted them to carry as great a load as possible

At its narrowest point, the Straits of Schallsea is about a ten-mile sea journey.

for the short journey across the Straits of Schallsea to Abanasinia.†

Daily, Caramon received reports on the build-up of the dwarven armies—how Pax Tharkas was being fortified; how the dwarves had imported slave labor (gully dwarves) to work the mines and the steel forges day and night, turning out weapons and armor; how these were being carted to Thorbardin and taken inside the mountain.

He also received reports from the emissaries of the hill dwarves and the Plainsmen. He heard about the great gathering of the tribes in Abanasinia, putting aside blood feuds to fight together for survival. He heard about the preparations of the hill dwarves, who were also forging weapons, using the same gully-dwarf slave labor as their cousins, the mountain dwarves.

He had even made discreet advances to the elves in Qualinesti. This gave Caramon an eerie feeling, for the man to whom he sent his message was none other than Solostaran, Speaker of the Suns, who had—just weeks ago—died in Caramon's own time. Raistlin had sneered at hearing of this attempt to draw the elves into the war, knowing full well what their answer would be. The archmage had, however, not been without a secret hope, nurtured in the dark hours of the night, that *this time* it might prove different. . . .

It didn't.

Caramon's men never even had a chance to speak to Solostaran. Before they could dismount from their horses, arrows zinged through the air, thudding into the ground, forming a deadly ring around each of them. Looking into the aspen woods, they could see literally hundreds of archers, each with an arrow nocked and ready. No words were spoken. The messengers left, carrying an elven arrow to Caramon in answer.

The war itself, in fact, was beginning to give Caramon an eerie feeling. Piecing together what he had heard Raistlin and Crysania discussing, it suddenly occurred to Caramon that everything he was doing had all been done before. The thought was almost as nightmarish to him as to his brother, though for vastly different reasons.

"I feel as though that iron ring I wore round my neck in Istar had been bolted back on," Caramon

muttered to himself one night as he sat in the inn at Caergoth that he had taken over for his command post. "I'm a slave again, same as I was then. Only this time it's worse, because—even when I was a slave—at least I had freedom to choose whether I was going to draw breath or not that day. I mean, if I'd wanted to die, I could have fallen on my sword and died! But now I'm not even given that choice, apparently."

It was a strange and horrifying concept for Caramon, one he dwelt on and mulled over many nights, one he knew he didn't understand. He would like to have talked it over with his brother, but Raistlin was back at the inland camp with the army and even if they had been together, Caramon was certain his twin would have refused to discuss it.

Raistlin, during this time, had been gaining in strength almost daily. Following the use of his magical spells that consumed the dead village in a blazing funeral pyre, the archmage had laid almost dead to the world for two days. Upon waking from his feverish sleep, he had announced that he was hungry. Within the next few days, he ate more solid food than he had been able to tolerate in months. The cough vanished. He rapidly regained strength and added flesh to his bones.

But he was still tormented by nightmares that not even the strongest of sleeping potions could banish.

Day and night, Raistlin pondered his problem. If only he could learn Fistandantilus's fatal mistake, he might be able to correct it!

Wild schemes came to mind. The archmage even toyed with the idea of traveling forward to his own time to research, but abandoned the idea almost immediately. If consuming a village in flame had plunged him into exhaustion for two days, the time-travel spell would prove even more wearing. And, though only a day or two might pass in the present while he recuperated, eons would flit by in the past. Finally, if he did make it back, he wouldn't have the strength needed to battle the Dark Queen.

And then, just when he had almost given up in despair, the answer came to him. . . .

I can still remember when I was a child making up fantastic stories involving the grown up world around me and how I would somehow be in a position to be a hero. I saved my fourth grade teacher with a flying saucer I build for a science-fair project—or at least did so in long moments of daydreaming.

My parents use to worry about me when I would play by myself in the basement for hours on end, making up amazing stories enacted entirely between myself and my toys. One year I had a large cardboard barrel in which I drew a space ship control panel. I would spend hours at a time flying to the stars in my basement. Such things would concern my parents, but it seems, at last, to have evolved into an almost respectable career. —TRH

Raistlin lifted the tent flap and walked out. The guard on duty started and shuffled uncomfortably. The appearance of the archmage was always unnerving, even to those of his own personal guard. No one ever heard him coming. He always seemed to materialize out of the air. The first indication of his presence was the touch of burning fingers upon a bare arm, or soft, whispered words, or the rustle of black robes.

The wizard's tent was regarded with wonder and awe though no one had ever seen anything strange emanating from it. Many, of course, watched—especially the children, who secretly hoped to see a horrible monster break free of the archmage's control and go thundering through the camp, devouring everyone in sight until *they* were able to tame it with a bit of gingerbread.†

But nothing of the kind ever happened. The arch-mage carefully nurtured and conserved his strength. Tonight would be different, Raistlin reflected with a sigh and scowl. But it couldn't be helped.

"Guard," he murmured.

"M-my lord?" the guard stammered in some confusion. The archmage rarely spoke to anyone, let alone a mere guard.

"Where is Lady Crysania?"

The guard could not suppress a curl of his lip as he answered that the "witch" was, he believed, in General Caramon's tent, having retired for the evening.

"Shall I send someone for her, my lord?" he asked Raistlin with such obvious reluctance that the mage could not help but smile, though it was hidden in the shadows of his black hood.

"No," Raistlin replied, nodding as if pleased at this information. "And my brother, have you word of him? When is his return expected?"

"General Caramon sent word that he arrives tomorrow, my lord," the guard continued in a mystified tone, certain that the mage knew this already. "We are to await his arrival here and let the supply train catch up with us at the same time. The first wagons rolled in this afternoon, my lord." A sudden thought struck the guard. "If—if you're thinking of changing these orders, my lord, I should call the Captain of the Watch—"

"No, no, nothing of the sort," Raistlin replied soothingly. "I merely wanted to make certain that I would not be disturbed this night—for anything or by anyone. Is that clear, uh—what is your name?"

"M-Michael, lordship," the guard answered. "Certainly, my lord. If such are your orders, I will carry them out."

"Good," Raistlin said. The archmage was silent for a moment, staring out into the night which was cold but bright with the light from Lunitari and the stars. Solinari, waning, was nothing but a silver scratch across the sky. More important, to Raistlin's eyes, was the moon he alone could see. Nuitari, the Black Moon, was full and round, a hole of darkness amid the stars.

Raistlin took a step nearer the guard. Casting his hood back slightly from his face, he let the light of the red moon strike his eyes. The guard, startled,

involuntarily stepped backward, but his strict training as a Knight of Solamnia made him catch himself.

Raistlin felt the man's body stiffen. He saw the reaction and smiled again. Raising a slender hand, he laid it upon the guard's armored chest.

"No one is to enter my tent for *any* reason," the archmage repeated in the soft, sibilant whisper he knew how to use so effectively. "No matter what happens! No one—Lady Crysania, my brother, you yourself . . . no one!"

"I—I understand, my lord," Michael stammered.

"You may hear or see strange things this night," Raistlin continued, his eyes holding the guard's in their entrancing gaze. "Ignore them. Any who enters this tent does so at the risk of his own life . . . *and mine!*"

"Y-yes, lord!" Michael said, swallowing. A trickle of sweat rolled down his face, though the night air was exceedingly cool for autumn.

"You are—or were—a Knight of Solamnia?" Raistlin asked abruptly.

Michael seemed uncomfortable, his gaze wavered. His mouth opened, but Raistlin shook his head. "Never mind. You do not have to tell me. Though you have shaved your mustaches, I can tell it by your face. I knew a Knight once, you see. Therefore, swear to me, by the Code and the Measure, that you will do as I ask."

"I swear, by the Code and . . . the Measure . . ." Michael whispered.

The mage nodded, apparently satisfied, and turned to reenter his tent. Michael, free of those eyes in which he saw only himself reflected, returned to his post, shivering beneath his heavy, woolen cloak. At the last moment, however, Raistlin paused, his robes rustling softly around him.

"Sir Knight," he whispered.

Michael turned.

"If anyone enters this tent," the mage said in a gentle, pleasant voice, "and disturbs my spellcasting and—if I survive—I will expect to find nothing but your corpse upon the ground. That is the only excuse I will accept for failure."

"Yes, my lord," Michael said, more firmly, though he kept his voice low. "*Est Sularas oth Mithas*. My Honor is My Life."

"Yes." Raistlin shrugged. "So it generally ends."

The archmage entered his tent, leaving Michael to stand in the darkness, waiting for the new-gods-knew-what to happen in the tent behind him. He wished his cousin, Garic, were here to share this strange and forbidding duty. But Garic was with Caramon. Michael hunched his shoulders deeper into his cloak and looked longingly out into the camp. There were bonfires, warm spiced wine, good fellowship, the sounds of laughter. Here, all was wrapped in thick, red-tinged, starlit darkness. The only sound Michael could hear was the sound of his armor jingling as he began to shake uncontrollably.

Crossing the tent floor, Raistlin came to a large, wooden chest that sat upon the floor beside his bed. Carved with magical runes, the chest was the only one of Raistlin's possessions—beside the Staff of Magius— that the mage allowed no one but himself to touch. Not that any sought to try. Not after the report of one of the guards, who had mistakenly attempted to lift it.

Raistlin had not said a word, he simply watched as the guard dropped it with a gasp.

The chest was bitterly cold to the touch, the guard reported in a shaken voice to his friends around the fire that night. Not only that, but he was overcome by a feeling of horror so great it was a wonder he didn't go mad.

Since that time, only Raistlin himself moved it, though how, no one could say. It was always present in his tent, yet no one could ever recall seeing it on any of the pack horses.

Lifting the lid of the chest, Raistlin calmly studied the contents—the nightblue-bound spellbooks, the jars and bottles and pouches of spell components, his own black-bound spellbooks, an assortment of scrolls, and several black robes folded at the bottom. There were no magical rings or pendants, such as might have been found in the possession of lesser mages. These Raistlin scorned as being fit only for weaklings.

His gaze passed quickly over all the items, including one slim, well-worn book that might have made the casual observer pause and stare, wondering that such a mundane item was kept with objects of arcane value. The title—written in

Anyone who has ever read the advertisements in old comic books will recognize the tenor of these hyperbolic titles. —TRH

flamboyant letters to attract the attention of the buyer—was *Sleight-of-Hand Techniques Designed to Amaze and Delight*!† Below that was written *Astound Your Friends*! *Trick the Gullible*! There might have been more but the rest had been worn away long ago by young, eager, loving hands.

Passing over this book that, even now, brought a thin smile of remembrance to the mage's lips, Raistlin reached down among his robes, uncovered a small box, and drew it forth. This, too, was guarded by runes carved upon its surface. Muttering magical words to nullify their effects, the mage opened the box reverently. There was only one thing inside—an ornate, silver stand. Carefully, Raistlin removed the stand and, rising to his feet, carried it to the table he had placed in the center of the tent.

Settling himself into a chair, the mage put his hand into one of the secret pockets of his robes and pulled forth a small crystal object. Swirling with colors, it resembled at first glance nothing more sinister than a child's marble. Yet, looking at the object closely, one saw that the colors trapped within were alive. They could be seen constantly moving and shifting, as though seeking escape.

Raistlin placed the marble upon the stand. It looked ludicrous perched there, much too small. And then, suddenly, as always, it was perfectly right. The marble had grown, the stand had shrunk . . . perhaps Raistlin himself had shrunk, for now the mage felt himself to be the one that appeared ludicrous.

It was a common feeling and he was accustomed to it, knowing that the dragon orb—for such was the shimmering, swirling-colored crystal globe—sought always to put its user at a disadvantage. But, long ago (no—in time to come!), Raistlin had mastered the dragon orb. He had learned to control the essence of dragonkind that inhabited it.

Relaxing his body, Raistlin closed his eyes and gave himself up to his magic. Reaching out, he placed his fingers upon the cold crystal of the dragon orb and spoke the ancient words.

"Ast bilak moiparalan/Suh akvlar tantangusar."†

The chill of the orb began to spread through his fingers, causing his very bones to ache. Gritting his teeth, Raistlin repeated the words.

"Ast bilak moiparalan/Suh akvlar tantangusar."

Once again, these follow the Indonesian grammatical structure but are made up of nonsense syllables. —TRH

The swirling colors within the orb ceased their lazy meandering and began to spin madly. Raistlin stared within the dazzling vortex, fighting the dizziness that assailed him, keeping his hands placed firmly upon the orb.

Slowly, he whispered the words again.

The colors ceased to swirl and a light glowed in the center. Raistlin blinked, then frowned. The light should have been neither black nor white, all colors yet none, symbolizing the mixture of good and evil and neutrality that bound the essence of the dragons within the orb. Such it had always been, ever since the first time he had looked within the orb and fought for its control.

But the light he saw now, though much the same as he had seen before, seemed ringed round by dark shadows. He stared at it closely, coldly, banishing any fanciful flights of imagination. His frown deepened. There *were* shadows hovering about the edges . . . shadows of . . . wings!

Out of the light came two hands. Raistlin caught hold of them—and gasped.

The hands pulled him with such strength that, totally unprepared, Raistlin nearly lost control. It was only when he felt himself being drawn into the orb by the hands within the shadowy light that he exerted his own force of will and yanked the hands back toward him.

"What is the meaning of this?" Raistlin demanded sternly. "Why do you challenge me? Long ago, I became your master."

She calls. . . . She calls and we must obey!

"Who calls who is more important than I?" Raistlin asked with a sneer, though his blood suddenly ran colder than the touch of the orb.

Our Queen! We hear her voice, moving in our dreams, disturbing our sleep. Come, master, we will take you! Come, quickly!

The Queen! Raistlin shuddered involuntarily, unable to stop himself. The hands, sensing him weakening, began to draw him in once more. Angrily, Raistlin tightened his grip on them and paused to try to sort his thoughts that swirled as madly as the colors within the orb.

The Queen! Of course, he should have foreseen this. She had entered the world—partially—and

now she moved among the evil dragons. Banished from Krynn long ago by the sacrifice of the Solamnic Knight, Huma, the dragons, both good and evil, slept in deep and secret places.

Here we see the events of Chronicles being set up, and that Legends is unique in being both a sequel and a prequel at the same time. —TRH

Leaving the good dragons† to sleep on undisturbed, the Dark Queen, Takhisis, the Five-Headed Dragon, was awaking the evil dragons, rallying them to her cause as she fought to gain control of the world.

One of the things that made Legends so much fun to write was that it was both a sequel and a prequel to Chronicles. —MW

The dragon orb, though composed of the essences of all dragons—good, evil, and neutral—would, of course, react strongly to the Queen's commands, especially as—for the present—its evil side was predominant, enhanced by the nature of its master.

Are those shadows I see the wings of dragons, or shadows of my own soul? Raistlin wondered, staring into the orb.

He did not have leisure for reflection, however. All of these thoughts flitted through his mind so rapidly that between the drawing of one breath and the releasing of it, the archmage saw his grave danger. Let him lose control for an instant, and Takhisis would claim him.

"No, my Queen," he murmured, keeping a tight grip upon the hands within the orb. "No, it will not be so easy as this."

See Dragons of Winter Night, *Book I, Chapter 10.*

To the orb he spoke softly but firmly, "I am your master still. I was the one who rescued you from Silvanesti and Lorac, the mad elven king.† I was the one who carried you safely from the Blood Sea of Istar. I am Rai—" He hesitated, swallowed the suddenly bitter taste in his mouth, then said through clenched teeth, "I am . . . Fistandantilus—Master of Past and of Present—and I command you to obey me!"

The orb's light dimmed. Raistlin felt the hands holding his own tremble and start to slip away. Anger and fear shot through him, but he suppressed these emotions instantly and kept his clasp firmly upon the hands. The trembling ceased, the hands relaxed.

We obey, master.

Raistlin dared not breathe a sigh of relief.

"Very well," he said, keeping his voice stern, a parent speaking to a chastened child (but what a dangerous child! he thought). Coldly, he continued, "I

must contact my apprentice in the Tower of High Sorcery in Palanthas. Heed my command. Carry my voice through the ethers of time. Bring my words to Dalamar."

Speak the words, master. He shall hear them as he hears the beating of his own heart, and so shall you hear his response.

Raistlin nodded. . . .

CHAPTER
2

Continual Light: *This spell . . . is as bright as full daylight and lasts until negated by magical darkness or by a dispel magic spell. [2nd Edition* ADVANCED DUNGEONS & DRAGONS *Player's* Handbook, *by David "Zeb" Cook, TSR, 1997, p. 181.]*

alamar shut the spellbook, clenching his fist in frustration. He was certain he was doing everything right, pronouncing the words with the proper inflection, repeating the chant the prescribed number of times. The components were those called for. He had seen Raistlin cast this spell a hundred times. Yet, he could not do it.

Putting his head wearily in his hands, he closed his eyes and brought memories of his *Shalafi* to mind, hearing Raistlin's soft voice, trying to remember the exact tone and rhythm, trying to think of anything he might be doing wrong.

It didn't help. Everything seemed the same! Well, thought Dalamar with a tired sigh, I must simply wait until he returns.

Standing up, the dark elf spoke a word of magic and the continual light† spell he had cast upon a crystal globe standing on the desk of Raistlin's library

winked out. No fire burned in the grate. The late spring night in Palanthas was warm and fine. Dalamar had even dared open the window a crack.

Raistlin's health at the best of times was fragile. He abhorred fresh air, preferring to sit in his study wrapped in warmth and the smells of roses and spice and decay. Ordinarily, Dalamar did not mind. But there were times, particularly in the spring, when his elven soul longed for the woodland home he had left forever.†

Standing by the window, smelling the perfume of renewed life that not even the horrors of the Shoikan Grove could keep from reaching the Tower, Dalamar let himself think, just for a moment, of Silvanesti.

Much of Dalamar's early life is told in the novel Dalamar the Dark *by Nancy Varian Berberick.*

A dark elf—one who is cast from the light. Such was Dalamar to his people. When they'd caught him wearing the Black Robes that no elf could even look upon without flinching, practicing arcane arts forbidden to one of his low rank and station,† the elven lords had bound Dalamar hand and foot, gagged his mouth, and blindfolded his eyes. Then he had been thrown in a cart and driven to the borders of his land.

Deprived of his sight, Dalamar's last memories of Silvanesti were the smells of aspen trees, blooming flowers, rich loam. It had been spring then, too, he recalled.

The Silvanesti, perhaps more than any other people of Ansalon, have a very strict, caste-oriented society. Every citizen is a member of one of various Houses. Dalamar was born into House Servitor, one of the lowest castes of Silvanesti society.

Would he go back if he could? Would he give up this to return? Did he feel any sorrow, regret? Without conscious volition, Dalamar's hand went to his breast. Beneath the black robes, he could feel the wounds in his chest. Though it had been a week since Raistlin's hand had touched him, burning five holes into his flesh, the wounds had not healed.† Nor would they ever heal, Dalamar knew with bitter certainty.

Always, the rest of his life, he would feel their pain. Whenever he stood naked, he would see them, festering scabs that no skin would cover. Such was the penalty he had paid for his treachery against his *Shalafi.*

Wounds that do not heal are common mythological symbols from many cultures down through the ages. Here, they are a constant reminder to Dalamar of his own choices and the eternal consequences they represent. —TRH

As he had told the great Par-Salian, Head of the Order, master of the Tower of High Sorcery in Wayreth—and Dalamar's master, too, of a sort, since the dark elf mage had, in reality, been a spy for the Order of Mages who feared and distrusted Raistlin

as they had feared no mortal in their history—"It was no more than I deserved."

Would he leave this dangerous place? Go back home, go back to Silvanesti?

Dalamar stared out the window with a grim, twisted smile, reminiscent of Raistlin, the *Shalafi*. Almost unwillingly, Dalamar's gaze went from the peaceful, starlit night sky back indoors, to the rows and rows of nightblue-bound spellbooks that lined the walls of the library. In his memory, he saw the wonderful, awful, beautiful, dreadful sights he had been privileged to witness as Raistlin's apprentice. He felt the stirrings of power within his soul, a pleasure that outweighed the pain.

No, he would never return. Never leave. . . .

Dalamar's musings were cut short by the sound of a silver bell. It rang only once, with a sweet, low sound. But to those living (and dead) within the Tower, it had the effect of a shattering gong splitting the air. Someone was attempting to enter! Someone had won through the perilous Shoikan Grove and was at the gates of the Tower itself!

His mind having already conjured up memories of Par-Salian, Dalamar had sudden unwelcome visions of the powerful, white-robed wizard standing on his doorstep. He could also hear in his mind what he had told the Council only nights earlier—"If any of you came and tried to enter the Tower while he was gone, I would kill you."

On the words of a spell, Dalamar disappeared from the library to reappear, within the drawing of a breath, at the Tower entrance.

But it was not a conclave of flashing-eyed wizards he faced. It was a figure dressed in blue dragon-scale armor, wearing the hideous, horned mask of a Dragon Highlord. In its gloved hand, the figure held a black jewel—a nightjewel, Dalamar saw—and behind the figure he could sense, though he could not see, the presence of a being of awesome power—a death knight.†

The Dragon Highlord was using the jewel to hold at bay several of the Tower's Guardians; their pale visages could be seen in the dark light of the night-jewel, thirsting for her living blood. Though Dalamar could not see the Highlord's face beneath the helm, he could feel the heat of her anger.

I first came across death knights in an old A&D product called the Fiend Folio. *I was looking through the book for creatures that might have some application to the* DRAGONLANCE *setting. The death knight became Lord Soth. —TRH*

"Lord Kitiara,"† Dalamar said gravely, bowing. "Forgive this rude welcome. If you had but let us know you were coming—"

Yanking off the helm, Kitiara glared at Dalamar with cold, brown eyes that reminded the apprentice forcibly of her kinship to the *Shalafi*.

"—you would have had an even more interesting reception planned for me, no doubt!" she snarled with an angry toss of her dark, curly hair. "I come and go where I please, especially to pay a visit to my brother!" Her voice literally shook with rage. "I made my way through those god-cursed trees of yours out there, then I'm attacked at his front door!" Her hand drew her sword. She took a step forward. "By the gods, I should teach you a lesson, elven slime—"

"I repeat my apologies," Dalamar said calmly, but there was a glint in his slanted eyes that made Kit hesitate in her reckless act.

Like most warriors, Kitiara tended to regard magic-users as weaklings who spent time reading books that could be put to better use wielding cold steel. Oh, they could produce some flashy results, no doubt, but when put to the test, she would much rather rely on her sword and her skill than weird words and bat dung.

Thus she pictured Raistlin, her half-brother, in her mind, and this was how she pictured his apprentice— with the added mark against Dalamar that he was only an elf—a race noted for its weakness.†

But Kitiara was, in another respect, different from most warriors—the main reason she had outlived all who opposed her. She was skilled at assessing her opponents. One look at Dalamar's cool eyes and composed stature—in the face of her anger— and Kitiara wondered if she might not have encountered a foe worthy of her.

She didn't understand him, not yet—not by any means. But she saw and recognized the danger in this man and, even as she made a note to be wary of it and to use it, if possible, she found herself attracted to it. The fact that it went with such handsome features (he didn't look at all elvish, now that she thought of it) and such a strong, muscular body (whose frame admirably filled out the black robes), made it suddenly occur to her that she

At this time in Krynn, society was highly male dominated. Knowing Kitiara as I do, she would have taken the "Lord" appellation—and wryly comment in the next breath that she was certainly no lady! There is some precedent in history for this. Hatchepsut ruled the Eighteenth Dynasty in Egypt not as a queen but as a king, wearing the clothes of a man and even sporting the false beard that was a symbol of a king of Egypt. It is one of the great ironies of antiquity that the man who is considered most responsible for trying to erase all memory and images of Hatchepsut's existence should find his own monument now in Central Park in New York City and that it is erroneously known as "Cleopatra's Obelisk." —TRH

Another slight nod to the AD&D rules. In the game, each race has unique benefits and drawbacks, and the elves were stuck with a penalty to their Constitution (health, well-being, physical endurance, etc.).

might accomplish more by being friendly than intimidating. Certainly, she thought, her eyes lingering on the elf's chest, where the black robes had parted slightly and she could see bronze skin beneath, it might be much more entertaining.

Thrusting her sword back in its sheath, Kitiara continued her step forward, only now the light that had flashed on the blade flashed in her eyes.

"Forgive me, Dalamar—that's your name, isn't it?" Her scowl melted into the crooked, charming smile that had won so many. "That damned Grove unnerves me. You are right. I should have notified my brother I was coming, but I acted on impulse." She stood close to Dalamar now, very close. Looking up into his face, hidden as it was by the shadows of his hood, she added, "I . . . often act on impulse."

With a gesture, Dalamar dismissed the Guardians. Then the young elf regarded the woman before him with a smile of charm that rivaled her own.

Seeing his smile, Kitiara held out her gloved hand. "Forgiven?"

Dalamar's smile deepened, but he only said, "Remove your glove, lord."

Kitiara started and, for an instant, the brown eyes dilated dangerously. But Dalamar continued to smile at her. Shrugging, Kitiara jerked one by one at the fingers of the leather glove, baring her hand.

"There," she said, her voice tinged with scorn, "you see that I hold no concealed weapon."

"Oh, I already knew that," Dalamar replied, now taking the hand in his own. His eyes still on hers, the dark elf drew her hand up to his lips and kissed it lingeringly. "Would you have had me deny myself this pleasure?"

His lips were warm, his hands strong, and Kitiara felt the blood surge through her body at his touch. But she saw in his eyes that he knew her game and she saw, too, that it was one he played himself. Her respect rose, as did her guard. Truly a foe worthy of her attention—her undivided attention.

Slipping her hand from his grasp, Kitiara put it behind her back with a playful female gesture that contrasted oddly with her armor and her manlike, warrior stance. It was a gesture designed to attract and confuse, and she saw from the elf's slightly flushed features that it had succeeded.

"Perhaps I have concealed weapons beneath my armor you should search for sometime," she said with a mocking grin.

"On the contrary," Dalamar returned, folding his hands in his black robes, "your weapons seem to me to be in plain sight. Were I to search you, lord, I would seek out that which the armor guards and which, though many men have penetrated, none has yet touched." The elven eyes laughed.

Kitiara caught her breath. Tantalized by his words, remembering still the feel of those warm lips upon her skin, she took another step forward, tilting her face to the man's.

Coolly, without seeming aware of his action, Dalamar made a graceful move to one side, slightly turning away from Kitiara. Expecting to be caught up in the man's arms, Kit was, instead, thrown off balance. Awkwardly, she stumbled.

Recovering her balance with feline skill, she whirled to face him, her face flushed with embarrassment and fury. Kitiara had killed men for less than mocking her like this. But she was disconcerted to see that he was, apparently, totally unaware of what he had done. Or was he? His face was carefully devoid of all expression. He was talking about her brother. No, he had done that on purpose. He would pay. . . .

Kit knew her opponent now, conceded his skill. Characteristically, she did not waste time berating herself for her mistake. She had left herself open, she had taken a wound. Now, she was prepared.

"—I deeply regret that the *Shalafi* is not here," Dalamar was saying. "I am certain that your brother will be sorry to learn he has missed you."

"Not here?" Kit demanded, her attention caught instantly. "Why, where is he? Where would he go?"

"I am certain he told you," Dalamar said with feigned surprise. "He has gone back to the past to seek the wisdom of Fistandantilus and from thence to discover the Portal through which he will—"

"You mean—he went anyway! Without the cleric?" Suddenly Kit remembered that no one was supposed to have known that she had sent Lord Soth to kill Crysania in order to stop her brother's insane notion of challenging the Dark Queen. Biting her lip, she glanced behind her at the death knight.

Dalamar followed her gaze, smiling, seeing every thought beneath that lovely, curling hair. "Oh, you knew about the attack on Lady Crysania?" he asked innocently.

Kit scowled. "You know damn well I knew about the attack! And so does my brother. He's not an idiot, if he is a fool."

She spun around on her heel. "You told me the woman was dead!"

"She was," intoned Lord Soth, the death knight, materializing out of the shadows to stand before her, his orange eyes flaring in their invisible sockets. "No human could survive my assault." The orange eyes turned their undying gaze to the dark elf. "And your master could not have saved her."

"No," Dalamar agreed, "but *her* master could and did. Paladine cast a counter-spell upon his cleric, drawing her soul to him, though he left the shell of her body behind. The *Shalafi's* twin, your half-brother, Caramon, lord"—Dalamar bowed to the infuriated Kitiara—"took the woman to the Tower of High Sorcery where the mages sent her back to the only cleric powerful enough to save her—the Kingpriest of Istar."

"Imbeciles!" Kitiara snarled, her face going livid. "They sent her back to him! That's just what Raistlin wanted!"

"They knew that," Dalamar said softly. "I told them—"

"*You* told them?" Kitiara gasped.

"There are matters I should explain to you," Dalamar said. "This may take some time. At least let us be comfortable. Will you come to my chambers?"

He extended his arm. Kitiara hesitated, then laid her hand upon his forearm. Catching hold of her around her waist, he pulled her close to his body. Startled, Kitiara tried to pull away, but she didn't try very hard. Dalamar held her with a grip both strong and firm.

"In order for the spell to transport us," he said coolly, "you need to stand as close to me as possible."

"I'm quite capable of walking," Kit returned. "I have little use for magic!"

But, even as she spoke, her eyes looked into his, her body pressed against his hard, well-muscled body with sensuous abandon.

"Very well," Dalamar shrugged and suddenly vanished.

Looking around, startled, Kit heard his voice. "Up the spiral staircase, lord. After the five hundred and thirty-ninth step, turn left."

"And so you see," Dalamar said, "I have as great a stake in this as do you. I have been sent, by the Conclave of all three Orders—the Black, the White, and the Red—to stop this appalling thing from happening."

The two relaxed in the dark elf's private, sumptuously appointed quarters within the Tower. The remains of an elegant repast had been whisked away by a graceful gesture of the elf's hand. Now, they sat before a fire that had been lit more for the sake of its light than its warmth on this spring night. The dancing flames seemed more conducive to conversation. . . .

"Then why *didn't* you stop him?" Kit demanded angrily, setting her golden goblet down with a sharp clinking sound. "What's so difficult about that?" Making a gesture with her hand, she added words to suit her action. "A knife in the back. Quick, simple." Giving Dalamar a look of scorn, she sneered. "Or are you above that, you mages?"

"Not above it," Dalamar said, regarding Kitiara intently. "There are subtler means we of the Black Robes generally use to rid ourselves of our enemies. But not against *him*, lord. Not your brother."

Dalamar shivered slightly and drank his wine with undue haste.

"Bah!" Kitiara snorted.

"No, listen to me and understand, Kitiara," Dalamar said softly. "You do not know your brother. You do not know him and, what is worse, *you do not fear him*! That will lead to your doom."

"Fear him? That skinny, hacking wretch? You're not serious—" Kitiara began, laughing. But her laughter died. She leaned forward. "You *are* serious. I can see it in your eyes!"

Dalamar smiled grimly. "I fear him as I fear nothing in this world—including death." Reaching up, the dark elf grasped the seam of his black robes and ripped it open, revealing the wounds on his chest.

Kitiara, mystified, looked at the wounds, then looked up at the dark elf's pale face. "What weapon made those? I don't recog—"

"His hand," Dalamar said without emotion. "The mark of his five fingers. This was his message to Par-Salian and the Conclave when he commanded me to give them his regards."

Kit had seen many terrible sights—men disemboweled before her eyes, heads hacked off, torture sessions in the dungeons beneath the mountains known as the Lords of Doom.† But, seeing those oozing sores and seeing, in her mind, her brother's slender fingers burning into the dark elf's flesh, she could not repress a shudder.

Sinking back in her chair, Kit went over carefully in her mind everything Dalamar had told her, and she began to think that, perhaps, she *had* underestimated Raistlin. Her face grave, she sipped her wine.

"And so he plans to enter the Portal," she said to Dalamar slowly, trying to readjust her thinking along these new and startling lines. "He will enter the Portal with the cleric. He will find himself in the Abyss. Then what? Surely he knows he cannot fight the Dark Queen on her own plane!"

"Of course he knows," Dalamar said. "He is strong, but—there—she is stronger. And so he intends to lure her out, to force her to enter this world. Here, he believes, he can destroy her."

"Mad!" Kitiara whispered with barely enough breath to say the word. "He is mad!" She hastily set her wine goblet down, seeing the liquid slopping over her shaking hand. "He has seen her in this plane when she was but a shadow, when she was blocked from entering completely. He cannot imagine what she would be like—!"

Rising to her feet, Kit nervously crossed the soft carpet with its muted images of trees and flowers so beloved of the elves. Feeling suddenly chilled, she stood before the fire. Dalamar came to stand beside her, his black robes rustling. Even as Kit spoke, absorbed in her own thoughts and fears, she was conscious of the elf's warm body near hers.

"What do your mages think will happen?" she asked abruptly. "Who will win, if he succeeds in this insane plan? Does he have a chance?"

The Lords of Doom are three active volcanoes surrounding the city of Sanction, and they often play a large part in the defense of that city, as seen in the novels The Clandestine Circle *by Mary H. Herbert and the* War of Souls *trilogy by Margaret Weis and Tracy Hickman.*

Dalamar shrugged and, moving a step nearer, put his hands on Kitiara's slender neck. His fingers softly caressed her smooth skin. The sensation was delicious. Kitiara closed her eyes, drawing a deep, shivering breath.

"The mages do not know," Dalamar said softly, bending down to kiss Kitiara just below her ear. Stretching like a cat, she arched her body back against his.

"Here he would be in his element," Dalamar continued, "the Queen would be weakened. But she certainly would not be easily defeated. Some think the magical battle between the two could well destroy the world."

Lifting her hand, Kitiara ran it through the elf's thick, silken hair, drawing his eager lips to her throat. "But . . . does he have a chance?" she persisted in a husky whisper.

Dalamar paused, then drew back away from her. His hands still on her shoulders, he turned Kitiara around to face him. Looking into her eyes, he saw what she was thinking. "Of course. There's always a chance."

"And what is it you will do, if he succeeds in entering the Portal?" Kitiara's hands rested lightly on Dalamar's chest, where her half-brother had left his terrible mark. Her eyes, looking into the elf's, were luminous with passion that almost, but not quite, hid her calculating mind.

"I am to stop him from returning to this world," Dalamar said. "I am to block the Portal so that he cannot come through." His hand traced her crooked, curving lips.

"What will be your reward for so dangerous an assignment?" She pressed closer, biting playfully at his fingertips.

"I will be Master of the Tower, then," he answered. "And the next head of the Order of Black Robes. Why?"

"I could help you," Kitiara said with a sigh, moving her fingers over Dalamar's chest and up over his shoulders, kneading her hands into his flesh like a cat's paws. Almost convulsively, Dalamar's hands tightened around her, drawing her nearer still.

"I could help," Kitiara repeated in a fierce whisper. "You cannot fight him alone."

Surely, Kitiara is just toying with Dalamar here. I've been to a number of fantasy conventions over the years and seen more than enough women in chainmail bikinis. Not only am I certain that it is uncomfortable in the extreme and impractical for battle, but it must surely leave an odd pattern behind when removed. —TRH

As I stated in The Annotated Chronicles I love "boot scenes." I recently watched an old "Dick Van Dyke" TV episode from the 1960s in which Laura Petrie gets her toe stuck in the faucet of a bath and can't reach the door to unlock it for her husband. The background material (thank you, DVD!) told the story of how the actress, Mary Tyler Moore, was at first terribly upset about the script. That was supposed to be an episode highlighting her character, and here she was spending most of her time off camera, calling out her lines behind a locked bathroom door. Carl Reiner, who wrote the episode, pointed out to her that if they took the camera into the bathroom, they could only show Ms. Moore from the shoulders up, but if they shot it the way the script was written . . . Well, every man in the United States would spend the half hour imagining what Mary Tyler Moore looked like naked in the bath. He was right. Not only was that episode an instant classic,

"Ah, my dear"—Dalamar regarded her with a wry, sardonic smile—"who would you help—me or him?"

"Now that," said Kitiara, slipping her hands beneath the tear in the fabric of the dark elf's black robes, "would depend entirely upon who's winning!"

Dalamar's smile broadened, his lips brushed her chin. He whispered into her ear, "Just so we understand each, lord."

"Oh, we understand each other," Kitiara said, sighing with pleasure. "And now, enough of my brother. There is something I would ask. Something I have long been curious about. What do magic-users wear beneath their robes, dark elf?"

"Very little," Dalamar murmured. "And what do warrior women wear beneath their armor?"

"Nothing."†

Kitiara was gone.†

Dalamar lay, half-awake and half-asleep, in his bed. Upon his pillow, he could still smell the fragrance of her hair—perfume and steel—a strange, intoxicating mixture not unlike Kitiara herself.

The dark elf stretched luxuriously, grinning. She would betray him, he had no doubt about that. And she knew he would destroy her in a second, if necessary, to succeed in his purpose. Neither found the knowledge bitter. Indeed, it added an odd spice to their lovemaking.

Closing his eyes, letting sleep drift over him, Dalamar heard, through his open window, the sound of dragonwings spreading for flight. He imagined her, seated upon her blue dragon, the dragonhelm glinting in the moonlight. . . .

Dalamar!

The dark elf started and sat up. He was wide awake. Fear coursed through his body. Trembling at the sound of that familiar voice, he glanced about the room.

"*Shalafi?*" He spoke hesitantly. There was no one there. Dalamar put his hand to his head. "A dream," he muttered.

Dalamar!

The voice again, this time unmistakable. Dalamar looked around helplessly, his fear increasing. It was completely unlike Raistlin to play games. The

archmage had cast the time-travel spell. He had journeyed back in time. He had been gone a week and was not expected to return for many more. Yet Dalamar knew that voice as he knew the sound of his own heartbeat!

"*Shalafi*, I hear you," Dalamar said, trying to keep his tone firm. "Yet I cannot see you. Where—"

I am, as you surmise, back in time, apprentice. I speak to you through the dragon orb. I have an assignment for you. Listen to me carefully and follow my instructions exactly. Act at once. No time must be lost. Every second is precious. . . .

Closing his eyes that he might concentrate, Dalamar heard the voice clearly, yet he also heard sounds of laughter floating in through the open window. A festival of some sort, designed to honor spring, was beginning. Outside the gates of Old City, bonfires burned, young people exchanged flowers in the light and kisses in the dark. The air was sweet with rejoicing and love and the smell of spring blooming roses.

But then Raistlin began speaking and Dalamar heeded none of these. He forgot Kitiara. He forgot love. He forgot springtime. Listening, questioning, understanding, his entire body tingled with the voice of his *Shalafi*.

but there are people to this day who swear they saw Mary Tyler Moore naked in that bathtub.

A picture may be worth a thousand words, but imagination beats them both a thousand fold. Gratuitous description detracts from the experience. Give me a boot scene every time. —TRH

CHAPTER 3

Bertrem padded softly through the halls of the Great Library of Palanthas. His Aesthetics' robes whispered about his ankles, their rustle keeping time to the tune Bertrem hummed as he went along. He had been watching the spring festival from the windows of the Great Library and now, as he returned to his work among the thousands and thousands of books and scrolls housed within the Library, the melody of one of the songs lingered in his head.

"Ta-tum, ta-tum," Bertrem sang in a thin, off-key voice, pitched low so as not to disturb the echoes of the vast, vaulted halls of the Great Library.

The echoes were all that could be disturbed by Bertrem's singing, the Library itself being closed and locked for the night. Most of the other Aesthetics—members of the order whose lives were spent in study and maintenance of the Great Library's collection of

knowledge gathered from the beginning of Krynn's time—were either sleeping or absorbed in their own works.

"Ta-tum, ta-tum. My lover's eyes are the eyes of the doe. Ta-tum, ta-tum. And I am the hunter, closing in . . ." Bertrem even indulged in an impromptu dance step.

"Ta-tum, ta-tum. I lift my bow and draw my arrow—" Bertrem skipped around a corner. "I loose the shaft. It flies to my lover's heart and—Ho, there! Who are you?"

Bertrem's own heart leaped into his throat, very nearly strangling the Aesthetic as he was suddenly confronted with a tall, black-robed and hooded figure standing in the center of the dimly lit marble hall.

The figure did not answer. It simply stared at him in silence.

Gathering his wits and his courage and his robes about him, Bertrem glared at the intruder.

"What business have you here? The Library's closed! Yes, even to those of the Black Robes." The Aesthetic frowned and waved a pudgy hand. "Be gone. Return in the morning, and use the front door, like everyone else."

"Ah, but I am not everyone else," said the figure, and Bertrem started, for he detected an elvish accent though the words were Solamnic. "As for doors, they are for those without the power to pass through walls. I have that power, as I have the power to do other things, many not so pleasant."

Bertrem shuddered. This smooth, cool elven voice did not make idle threats.

"You are a dark elf," Bertrem said accusingly, his brain scrambling about, trying to think what to do. Should he raise the alarm? Yell for help?

"Yes." The figure removed his black hood so that the magical light imprisoned in the globes hanging from the ceiling—a gift from the magic-users to Astinus given during the Age of Dreams—fell upon his elven features. "My name is Dalamar. I serve—

"Raistlin Majere!" Bertrem gasped. He glanced about uneasily, expecting the black-robed archmage to leap out at him any moment.

Dalamar smiled. The elven features were delicate, handsome. But there was a cold, single-minded purposefulness about them that chilled Bertrem. All

thoughts of calling for help vanished from the Aesthetic's mind.

"Wha-what do you want?" he stammered.

"It is what my master wants," Dalamar corrected. "Do not be frightened. I am here seeking knowledge, nothing more. If you aid me, I will be gone as swiftly and silently as I have come."

If I don't aid him. . . . Bertrem shivered from head to toe. "I will do what I can, magus,"† the Aesthetic faltered, "but you should really talk to. . . ."

"Me," came a voice out of the shadows.

Bertrem nearly fainted in relief.

"Astinus!" he babbled, pointing at Dalamar, "this . . . he . . . I didn't let him . . . appeared . . . Raistlin Majere . . ."

"Yes, Bertrem,"† Astinus said soothingly. Coming forward, he patted the Aesthetic on the arm. "I know everything that has transpired." Dalamar had not moved, nor even indicated that he was aware of Astinus's presence. "Return to your studies, Bertrem," Astinus continued, his deep baritone echoing through the quiet hallways. "I will handle this matter."

"Yes, Master!" Bertrem backed thankfully down the hall, his robes fluttering about him, his gaze on the dark elf, who had still neither moved nor spoken. Reaching the corner, Bertrem vanished around it precipitously, and Astinus could hear, by the sounds of his flapping sandals, that he was running down the hallway.

The head of the Great Library of Palanthas smiled, but only inwardly. To the eyes of the dark elf watching him, the man's calm, ageless face reflected no more emotion than the marble walls about them.

"Come this way, young mage," Astinus said, turning abruptly and starting off down the hall with a quick, strong stride that belied his middle-aged appearance.

Caught by surprise, Dalamar hesitated, then— seeing he was being left behind—hurried to catch up.

"How do you know what I seek?" the dark elf demanded.

"I am a chronicler of history," Astinus replied imperturbably "Even as we speak and walk, events transpire around us and I am aware of them. I hear

The derivation of magus is from magi, *meaning "wise man." —TRH*

One of my favorite authors, Stephen Leacock, wrote a wonderful piece about Sherlock Holmes-style detective stories. In it, he identified a character type he called "the Dumb Nut." This character, he says, is so dense and so stupid that he purposefully exceeds even the lowest intelligence of anyone who might read the story. Mr. Leacock claims that Dr. Watson is one of these Dumb Nuts. The point of the Dumb Nut in the story is so that the Genius character can explain his brilliance—using small words and pictures if necessary—to the Dumb Nut, and through him to the audience. The reader can then feel secure that it isn't them who needs this information but this Dumb Nut who really needs the talking to. By this device the Genius can reveal and explain any necessary information to the audience without offending any of them.

Bertrem is, I fear, a Dumb Nut to the Genius Astinus. —TRH

every word spoken, I see every deed committed, no matter how mundane, how good, how evil. Thus I have watched throughout history. As I was the first, so shall I be the last.† Now, this way."

Astinus made a sharp turn to his left. As he did so, he lifted a glowing globe of light from its stand and carried it with him in his hand. By the light, Dalamar could see long rows of books standing on wooden shelves. He could tell by their smooth leather binding that they were old. But they were in excellent condition. The Aesthetics kept them dusted and, when necessary, rebound those particularly worn.

While this certainly has resonance with the concept of Alpha and Omega (see Revelation 1:8, 21:6, 22:13), Astinus is primarily referring here to his role to chronicle all of Krynn's history. —TRH

"Here is what you want"—Astinus gestured—"the Dwarfgate Wars."

Dalamar stared. "All these?" He gazed down a seemingly endless row of books, a feeling of despair slowly creeping over him.

"Yes," Astinus replied coldly, "and the next row of books as well."

"I—I . . ." Dalamar was completely at a loss. Surely Raistlin had not guessed the enormity of this task. Surely he couldn't expect him to devour the contents of these hundreds of volumes within the specified time limit. Dalamar had never felt so powerless and helpless before in his life. Flushing angrily, he sensed Astinus's icelike gaze upon him.

"Perhaps I can help," the historian said placidly. Reaching up, without even reading the spine, Astinus removed one volume from the shelf. Opening it, he flipped quickly through the thin, brittle pages, his eyes scanning the row after row of neat precisely written, black-inked letters.

"Ah, here it is." Drawing an ivory marker from a pocket of his robes, Astinus laid it across a page in the book, shut it carefully, then handed the book to Dalamar. "Take this with you. Give him the information he seeks. And tell him this—'The wind blows. The footsteps in the sand will be erased, but only after he has trod them.' "

The historian bowed gravely to the dark elf, then walked past him, down the row of books to reach the corridor again. Once there, he stopped and turned to face Dalamar, who was standing, staring, clutching the book Astinus had thrust into his hands.

"Oh, young mage. You needn't come back here again. The book will return of its own accord when you are finished. I cannot have you frightening the Aesthetics. Poor Bertrem will have undoubtedly taken to his bed. Give your *Shalafi* my greetings."

Astinus bowed again and disappeared into the shadows.

Dalamar remained standing, pondering, listening to the historian's slow, firm step fade down the hallway. Shrugging, the dark elf spoke a word of magic and returned to the Tower of High Sorcery.

"What Astinus gave me is his own commentary on the Dwarfgate Wars, *Shalafi*. It is drawn from the ancient texts he wrote—"

Astinus would know what I need. Proceed.

"Yes, *Shalafi*. This begins the marked passage—

" 'And the great archmage, Fistandantilus, used the dragon orb to call forward in time to his apprentice, instructing him to go the Great Library at Palanthas and read in the books of history there to see if the result of his great undertaking would prove successful.' " Dalamar's voice faltered as he read this and eventually died completely as he re-read this amazing statement.

Continue! came his *Shalafi's* voice, and though it resounded more in his mind than his ears, Dalamar did not miss the note of bitter anger. Hurriedly tearing his gaze from the paragraph, written hundreds of years previously, yet accurately reflecting the mission he had just undertaken, Dalamar continued.

"'It is important here to note this: the *Chronicles* as they existed *at that point in time* indicate—'

"That part is underscored, *Shalafi*," Dalamar interrupted himself.

What part?

" '—at that point in time' is underscored."

Raistlin did not reply, and Dalamar, momentarily losing his place, found it and hastened on.

"—'indicated that the undertaking would have been successful. Fistandantilus, along with the cleric, Denubis, should have been able, from all indications that the great archmage saw, to safely enter the Portal. What might have happened in the Abyss, of course, is unknown, since the actual historical events transpired differently.

" 'Thus, believing firmly that his ultimate goal of entering the Portal and challenging the Queen of Darkness was within his reach, Fistandantilus pursued the Dwarfgate Wars with renewed vigor. Pax Tharkas fell to the armies of the hill dwarves and the Plainsmen. (See *Chronicles* Volume 126, Book 6, pages 589-700.) Led by Fistandantilus's great general, Pheragas—the former slave from Northern Ergoth whom the wizard had purchased and trained as a gladiator in the Games at Istar—the Army of Fistandantilus drove back the forces of King Duncan, forcing the dwarves to retreat to the mountain fastness of Thorbardin.

" 'Little did Fistandantilus care for this war. It simply served to further his own ends. Finding the Portal beneath the towering mountain fortress known as Zhaman, he established his headquarters there and began the final preparations that would give him the power to enter the forbidden gates, leaving his general to fight the war.

" 'What happened† at this point is beyond even me to relate with accuracy, since the magical forces at work here were so powerful it obscured my vision.

" 'General Pheragas was killed fighting the Dewar, the dark dwarves of Thorbardin. At his death, the Army of Fistandantilus crumbled. The mountain dwarves swarmed out of Thorbardin toward the fortress of Zhaman.

" 'During the fighting, aware that the battle was lost and that they had little time, Fistandantilus and Denubis hastened to the Portal. Here the great wizard began to cast his spell.

" 'At the same instant, a gnome, being held prisoner by the dwarves of Thorbardin, activated a time-traveling device he had constructed in an effort to escape his confinement. Contrary to every recorded instance in the history of Krynn, this gnomish device actually worked. It worked quite well, in fact.

" 'I can only speculate from this point on, but it seems probable that the gnome's device interacted somehow with the delicate and powerful magical spells being woven by Fistandantilus. The result we know all too clearly.

" 'A blast occurred of such magnitude that the Plains of Dergoth were utterly destroyed. Both armies were almost completely wiped out. The towering

This point in history is a nexus of various possible futures, the outcome of only one of which is the history that Astinus is experiencing. This begs the question of which timeline is the optimum timeline and whether the High God is primarily interested only in the optimum outcome. See Appendix B. —TRH

mountain fortress of Zhaman shattered and fell in upon itself, creating the hill now called Skullcap.

" 'The unfortunate Denubis died in the blast. Fistandantilus should have died as well, but his magic was so great that he was able to cling to some portion of life, though his spirit was forced to exist upon another plane until it found the body of a young magic-user named Raistlin Majere. . . .' "

Enough!

"Yes, *Shalafi*," Dalamar murmured.

And then Raistlin's voice was gone.

Dalamar, sitting in the study, knew he was alone. Shivering violently, he was completely overawed and amazed by what he had just read. Seeking to make some meaning of it, the dark elf sat in the chair behind the desk—Raistlin's desk—lost in thought until night's shadows withdrew and gray dawn lit the sky.

A tremor of excitement made Raistlin's thin body quiver. His thoughts were confused, he would need a period of cool study and reflection to make absolutely certain of what he had discovered. One phrase shone with dazzling brilliance in his mind—*the undertaking would have been successful!*

The undertaking would have been successful!

Raistlin sucked in his breath with a gasp, realizing at that point only that he had ceased breathing. His hands upon the dragon orb's cold surface shook. Exultation swept over him. He laughed the strange, rare laughter of his, for the footsteps he saw in his dream led to a scaffold no longer, but to a door of platinum,† decorated with the symbols of the Five-Headed Dragon. At *his* command, it would open. He had simply to find and destroy this gnome—

Raistlin felt a sharp tug on his hands.

"Stop!" he ordered, cursing himself for losing control.

But the orb did not obey his command. Too late, Raistlin realized he was being drawn inside. . . .

The hands had undergone a change, he saw as they pulled him closer and closer. They had been unrecognizable before—neither human nor elven, young nor old. But now they were the hands of a female, soft, supple, with smooth white skin and the grip of death.†

Gold, by itself, is such a soft metal and not terribly practical in non-technological societies. However, this platinum, I must confess, most likely came out of AD&D.
—TRH

The Temptress/Temptor is a character archetype throughout the world. Dramatica theory identifies this character type as a "Contagonist," an archetype that exists opposite the "Guardian" character and whose function is to dissuade, influence, and lure the Hero away from the goal.
—TRH

Sweating, fighting down the hot surge of panic that threatened to destroy him, Raistlin summoned all his strength—both physical and mental—and fought the will behind the hands.

Closer they drew him, nearer and nearer. He could see the face now—a woman's face, beautiful, dark-eyed; speaking words of seduction that his body reacted to with passion even as his soul recoiled in loathing.

Nearer and nearer. . . .

Desperately, Raistlin struggled to pull away, to break the grip that seemed so gentle yet was stronger than the bonds of his life force. Deep he delved into his soul, searching the hidden parts— but for what, he little knew. Some part of him, somewhere, existed that would save him. . . .

An image of a lovely, white-robed cleric wearing the medallion of Paladine emerged. She shone in the darkness and, for a moment, the hands' grasp loosened—but only for a moment. Raistlin heard a woman's sultry laughter. The vision shattered.

"My brother!" Raistlin called through parched lips, and an image of Caramon came forward. Dressed in golden armor, his sword flashing in his hands, he stood in front of his twin, guarding him. But the warrior had not taken a step before he was cut down—from behind.

Nearer and nearer. . . .

Raistlin's head slumped forward, he was rapidly losing strength and consciousness. And then, unbidden, from the innermost recesses of his soul, came a lone figure. It was not robed in white, it carried no gleaming sword. It was small and grubby and its face was streaked with tears.

In its hand, it held only a dead . . . very dead . . . rat.

Caramon arrived back in camp just as the first rays of dawn were spreading through the sky. He had ridden all night and was stiff, tired, and unbelievably hungry.

Fond thoughts of his breakfast and his bed had been comforting him for the last hour, and his face broke into a grin as the camp came into sight. He was about to put the spurs to his weary horse when, looking ahead into the camp itself, the big man

reined in his horse and brought his escort to a halt with an upraised hand.

"What's going on?" he asked in alarm, all thoughts of food vanishing.

Garic, riding up beside him, shook his head, mystified.

Where there should have been lines of smoke rising from morning cooking fires and the disgruntled snorts of men being roused from a night's sleep, the camp resembled a beehive after a bear's feast. No cooking fires were lit, people ran about in apparent aimlessness or stood clustered together in groups that buzzed with excitement.

Then someone caught sight of Caramon and let out a yell. The crowd came together and surged forward. Instantly, Garic shouted and, within moments, he and his men had galloped up to form a protective shield of armor-clad bodies around their general.

It was the first time Caramon had seen such a display of loyalty and affection from his men and, for a moment, he was so overcome he could not speak. Then, gruffly clearing his throat, he ordered them aside.

"It's not a mutiny," he growled, riding forward as his men reluctantly parted to let him pass. "Look! No one's armed. Half of 'em are women and children. But—" he grinned at them—"thanks for the thought."

His gaze went particularly to the young knight, Garic, who flushed with pleasure even as he kept his hand on his sword hilt.

By this time, the outer fringes of the crowd had reached Caramon. Hands grasped his bridle, startling his horse, who—thinking this was battle—pricked its ears dangerously, ready to lash out with its hooves as it had been trained.

"Stand back!" Caramon roared, barely holding the animal in check. "Stand back! Have you all gone mad? You look like just what you are—a bunch of farmers! Stand back, I say! Did your chickens all get loose? What's the meaning of this? Where are my officers?"

"Here, sir," came a voice of one of the captains. Red-faced, embarrassed, and angry, the man shoved his way through the crowd. Chagrined at the reprimand

from their commander, the men calmed down and the shouting died to a few mutterings as a group of guards, arriving with the captain, began to try to break up the mob.

"Begging the general's pardon for all this, sir," the captain said as Caramon dismounted and patted his horse's neck soothingly. The animal stood still under Caramon's touch, though its eyes rolled and its ears still twitched.

The captain was an older man, not a Knight but a mercenary of thirty years' experience. His face was seamed with scars, he was missing part of his left hand from a slashing sword blow, and he walked with a pronounced limp. This morning, the scarred face was flushed with shame as he faced his young general's stern gaze.

"The scouts sent word of yer comin', sir, but afore I could get to you, this pack o' wild dogs"—he glowered at the retreating men—"lit out for you like you was a bitch in heat. Beggin' the general's pardon," he muttered again, "and meanin' no disrespect."

Caramon kept his face carefully composed. "What's happened?" he asked, leading his tired horse into camp at a walk. The captain did not answer right away but cast a significant glance at Caramon's escort.

Caramon understood. "Go on ahead, men," he said, waving his hand. "Garic, see to my quarters."

When he and the captain were alone—or as alone as possible in the crowded camp where everyone was staring at them in eager curiosity—Caramon turned to question the man with a glance.

The old mercenary said just two words: "The wizard."

Reaching Raistlin's tent, Caramon saw with a sinking heart the ring of armed guards surrounding it, keeping back onlookers. There were audible sighs of relief at the sight of Caramon, and many remarks of, "General's here now. He'll take care of things," much nodding of heads, and some scattered applause.

Encouraged by a few oaths from the captain, the crowd opened up an aisle for Caramon to walk through. The armed guards stepped aside as he passed, then quickly closed ranks again. Pushing

and shoving, the crowd peered over the guards, straining to see. The captain having refused to tell him what was going on, Caramon would not have been surprised to find anything from a dragon sitting atop his brother's tent to the whole thing surrounded by green and purple flame.

Instead, he saw one young man standing guard and Lady Crysania pacing in front of the closed tent flap. Caramon stared at the young man curiously, thinking he recognized him.

"Garic's cousin," he said hesitantly, trying to remember the name. "Michael, isn't it?"

"Yes, general," the young Knight said. Drawing himself up straight, he attempted a salute. But it was a feeble attempt. The young man's face was pale and haggard, his eyes red-rimmed. He was clearly about to drop from exhaustion, but he held his spear before him, grimly barring the way into the tent.

Hearing Caramon's voice, Crysania looked up.

"Thank Paladine!" she said fervently.

One look at her pale face and sunken gray eyes, and Caramon shivered in the bright morning sunlight.

"Get rid of them!" he ordered the captain, who immediately began to issue orders to his men. Soon, with much swearing and grumbling, the crowd started to break up, most figuring the excitement was over now anyway.

"Caramon, listen to me!" Crysania laid her hand on his arm. "This—"

But Caramon shrugged off Crysania's hand. Ignoring her attempts to speak, he started to push past Michael. The young knight raised his spear, blocking his path.

"Out of my way!" Caramon ordered, startled.

"I am sorry, sir," Michael said in firm tones, though his lips trembled, "but Fistandantilus told me *no one* was to pass."

"You see," said Crysania in exasperation as Caramon fell back a pace, staring at Michael in perplexed anger. "I tried to tell you, if you'd only listened! It's been like this all night, and I *know* something dreadful's happened inside! But Raistlin made him take an oath—by the Code and the Rules or some such thing—"

"Measure," Caramon muttered, shaking his head. "The Code and the Measure." He frowned,

thinking of Sturm. "A code no knight will break on pain of death."

"But this is insane!" Crysania cried. Her voice broke. She covered her face with her hand a moment. Caramon put his arm around her hesitantly, fearing a reprimand, but she leaned against him gratefully.

"Oh, Caramon, I've been so frightened!" she murmured. "It was awful. I woke out of a sound sleep, hearing Raistlin screaming my name. I ran over here—There were flashes of light inside his tent. He was shrieking incoherent words, then I heard him call your name . . . and then he began to moan in despair. I tried to get in but . . ." She made a weak gesture toward Michael, who stood staring straight ahead. "And then his voice began to . . . to fade! It was awful, as though he were being sucked away somehow!"

"Then what happened?"

Crysania paused. Then, hesitantly, "He . . . he said something else. I could barely hear it. The lights went out. There was a sharp crack and . . . everything was still, horribly still!" She closed her eyes, shuddering.

"What did he say? Could you understand?"

"That's the strange part." Crysania raised her head, looking at him in confusion. "It sounded like . . . Bupu."†

"Bupu!" Caramon repeated in astonishment. "Are you sure?"

She nodded.

"Why would he call out the name of a gully dwarf?" Caramon demanded.

"I haven't any idea." Crysania sighed wearily, brushing her hair back out of her eyes. "I've wondered the same thing. Except—wasn't that the gully dwarf who told Par-Salian how kind Raistlin had been to her?"

Caramon shook his head. He would worry about gully dwarves later. Now, his immediate problem was Michael. Vivid memories of Sturm came back to him. How many times had he seen that look on the knight's face? An oath by the Code and the Measure—

Damn Raistlin!

Michael would stand at his post now until he dropped and then, when he awoke to find he had

First introduced in Dragons of Autumn Twilight, Book I, Chapter 17.

Charm Person or Mammal, *a 2nd Level Priest Spell: This spell affects any single person or mammal it is cast upon. The creature then regards the caster as a trusted friend and ally to be heeded and protected. [2nd Edition* ADVANCED DUNGEONS & DRAGONS *Player's Handbook, by David "Zeb" Cook, TSR, 1997, p. 258, 259.]*

failed, he'd kill himself. There had to be some way around this—around him! Caramon glanced at Crysania. She could use her clerical powers to spellbind† the young man. . . .

Caramon shook his head. That would have the entire camp ready to burn her at the stake! Damn Raistlin! Damn clerics! Damn the Knights of Solamnia and damn their Code and their Measure!

Heaving a sigh, he walked up to Michael. The young man raised his spear threateningly, but Caramon only lifted his hands high, to show they were empty.

He cleared his throat, knowing what he wanted to say, yet uncertain how to begin. And then as he thought about Sturm, suddenly he could see the Knight's face once again, so clearly that he marveled. But it was not as he had seen it in life—stern, noble, cold. And then Caramon knew—he was seeing Sturm's face in death! Marks of terrible suffering and pain had smoothed away the harsh lines of pride and inflexibility. There was compassion and understanding in the dark, haunted eyes and—it seemed to Caramon—that the Knight smiled on him sadly.

For a moment, Caramon was so startled by this vision that he could say nothing, only stare. But the image vanished, leaving in its place only the face of a young Knight, grim, frightened, exhausted—determined. . . .

"Michael," Caramon said, keeping his hands raised, "I had a friend once, a Knight of Solamnia. He—he's dead now. He died in a war far from here when—But that doesn't matter. Stur—my friend was like you. He believed in the Code and . . . and the Measure. He was ready to give his life for them. But, at the end, he found out there was something more important than the Code and the Measure, something that the Code and the Measure had forgotten."

Michael's face hardened stubbornly. He gripped his spear tighter.

"Life itself," Caramon said softly.

He saw a flicker in the Knight's red-rimmed eyes, a flicker that was drowned by a shimmer of tears. Angrily, Michael blinked them away, the look of firm resolution returning, though—it seemed to Caramon—it was now mingled with a look of desperation.

Caramon caught hold of that desperation, driving his words home as if they were the point of a sword seeking his enemy's heart. "*Life,* Michael. That's all there is. That's all we have. Not just our lives, but the lives of everyone on this world. It's what the Code and the Measure were designed to protect, but somewhere along the line that got all twisted around and the Code and the Measure became more important than life."†

Slowly, still keeping his hands raised, he took a step toward the young man.

"I'm not asking you to leave your post for any treacherous reason. And you and I both know you're not leaving it from cowardice." Caramon shook his head. "The gods know what you must have seen and heard tonight. I'm asking you to leave it out of compassion. My brother's inside there, maybe dying, maybe dead. When he made you swear that oath, he couldn't have foreseen this happening. I must go to him. Let me pass, Michael. There is nothing dishonorable in that."

Michael stood stiffly, his eyes straight ahead. And then, his face crumpled. His shoulders slumped, and the spear fell from his nerveless hand. Reaching out, Caramon caught the young man in his big arms and held him close. A shuddering sob tore through the young man's body. Caramon patted his shoulder awkwardly.

"Here, one of you"—he looked around—"find Garic—Ah, there you are," he said in relief as the young Knight came running over. "Take your cousin back to the fire. Get some hot food inside him, then see that he sleeps. You there—" he motioned to another guard—"take over here."

As Garic led his cousin away, Crysania started to enter the tent, but Caramon stopped her. "Better let me go first, lady," he said.

Expecting an argument, he was surprised to see her meekly step aside. Caramon had his hand on the tent flap when he felt her hand upon his arm.

Startled, he turned.

"You are as wise as Elistan, Caramon," she said, regarding him intently. "I could have said those words to the young man. Why didn't I?"

Caramon flushed. "I—I just understood him, that's all," he muttered.

Caramon may not have always been smart, but he has always been wise. — TRH

We come to learn more about Caramon in this book, and we realize that he is not stupid. He is actually very intelligent. He thinks things through thoroughly before making up his mind, and that sometimes makes him seem slow or sluggish. Caramon has to develop both self-confidence and self-esteem in these books. In essence, he goes on a quest to find himself, to learn to live his life without being dependent on his brother. —MW

"I didn't *want* to understand him." Crysania, her face pale, bit her lip. "I just wanted him to obey me."

"Look, lady," Caramon said grimly, "you can do your soul-searching later. Right now, I need your help!"†

"Yes, of course." The firm, self-confident look returned to Crysania's face. Without hesitation, she followed Caramon into Raistlin's tent.

Much of Caramon's wisdom stems from his natural practicality: first things first.

Mindful of the guard outside, and any other curious eyes, Caramon shut the tent flap quickly. It was dark and still inside; so dark that at first neither could make out anything in the shadows. Standing near the entrance, waiting until their eyes grew accustomed to the dimness, Crysania clutched at Caramon suddenly.

"I can hear him breathing!" she said in relief.

Caramon nodded and moved forward slowly. The brightening day was driving night from the tent, and he could see more clearly with each step he took.

"There," he said. He hurriedly kicked aside a camp stool that blocked his way. "Raist!" he called softly as he knelt down.

The archmage was lying on the floor. His face was ashen, his thin lips blue. His breathing was shallow and irregular, but he was breathing. Lifting his twin carefully, Caramon carried him to his bed. In the dim light, he could see a faint smile on Raistlin's lips, as though he were lost in a pleasant dream.

"I think he's just sleeping now," Caramon said in a mystified voice to Crysania, who was covering Raistlin with a blanket. "But something's happened. That's obvious." He looked around the tent in the brightening light. "I wonder—Name of the gods!"

Crysania looked up, glancing over her shoulder.

The poles of the tent were scorched and blackened, the material itself was charred and, in some places, appeared to have melted. It looked as though it had been swept by fire, yet incongruously, it remained standing and did not appear to have been seriously damaged. It was the object on the table, however, that had brought the exclamation from Caramon.

"The dragon orb!" he whispered in awe.

Made by the mages of all three Robes long ago, filled with the essence of good, evil, and neutral dragons, powerful enough to span the banks of

time, the crystal orb still stood upon the table, resting on the silver stand Raistlin had made for it.

Once it had been an object of magical, enchanting light.

Now it was a thing of darkness, lifeless, a crack running down its center. Now—"It's broken," Caramon said in a quiet voice.

CHAPTER 4

The Army of Fistandantilus sailed across the Straits of Schallsea in a ramshackle fleet made up of many fishing boats, row boats, crude rafts, and gaudily decorated pleasure boats. Though the distance was not great, it took over a week to get the people, the animals, and the supplies transported.

By the time Caramon was ready to make the crossing, the army had grown to such an extent that there were not enough boats to ferry everyone across at once. Many craft had to make several trips back and forth. The largest boats were used to carry livestock. Converted into floating barns, they had stalls for the horses and the scrawny cattle and pens for the pigs.

Things went smoothly, for the most part, though Caramon got only about three hours of sleep each night, so busy was he with the problems that everyone

was sure only he could solve—everything from seasick cattle to a chest-load of swords that was accidentally dropped overboard and had to be retrieved. Then, just when the end was in sight and nearly everyone was across, a storm came up. Whipping the seas to froth, it wrecked two boats that slipped from their moorings and prevented anyone from crossing for two days. But, eventually, everyone made it in relatively good shape, with only a few cases of seasickness, one child tumbling overboard (rescued), and a horse that broke its leg kicking down its stall in a panic (killed and butchered).†

Horse meat, it must be pointed out, is not a traditional food of choice in this part of Krynn. It's just that there is not much else left to eat at this point in history. —TRH

Upon landing on the shores of Abanasinia, the army was met by the chief of the Plainsmen—the tribes of barbarians inhabiting the northern plains of Abanasinia who were eager to gain the fabled gold of Thorbardin—and also by representatives from the hill dwarves. When he met with the representative of the hill dwarves, Caramon experienced a profound shock that unnerved him for days.

"Reghar Fireforge and party," announced Garic from the entrance to the tent. Standing aside, the knight allowed a group of three dwarves to enter.

That name ringing in his ears, Caramon stared at the first dwarf in disbelief. Raistlin's thin fingers closed painfully over his arm.

"Not a word!" breathed the archmage.

"But he—he looks . . . and the name!" Caramon stammered in a low voice.

"Of course," Raistlin said matter-of-factly, "this is Flint's grandfather."

Flint's grandfather! Flint Fireforge—his old friend. The old dwarf who had died in Tanis's arms at Godshome, the old dwarf—so gruff and irascible, yet so tender-hearted, the dwarf who had seemed ancient to Caramon. He had not even been born yet! This was his grandfather.

Suddenly the full scope of where he was and what he was doing struck Caramon a physical blow. Before this, he might have been adventuring in his own time. He knew then that he hadn't really been taking any of this seriously. Even Raistlin "sending" him home had seemed as simple as the archmage putting him on a boat and bidding him farewell. Talk of "altering" time he'd put out of his

mind. It confused him, seeming to go round in a closed, endless circle.

Carmon felt hot, then cold. Flint hadn't been born yet. Tanis didn't exist, Tika didn't exist. *He, himself, didn't exist!*† No! It was too implausible! It couldn't be!

The tent tilted before Caramon's eyes. He was more than half afraid he might be sick. Fortunately, Raistlin saw the pallor of his brother's face. Knowing intuitively what his twin's brain was trying to assimilate, the mage rose to his feet and, moving gracefully in front of his momentarily befuddled brother, spoke suitable words of welcome to the dwarves. But, as Raistlin did so, he shot a dark, penetrating glance at Caramon, reminding him sternly of his duty.

Pulling himself together, Caramon was able to thrust the disturbing and confusing thoughts from his mind, telling himself he would deal with them later in peace and quiet. He'd been doing that a lot lately. Unfortunately, the peace and quiet time never seemed to come about . . . .

Getting to his feet, Caramon was even able to shake hands calmly with the sturdy, gray-bearded dwarf.

"Little did I ever think," Reghar said bluntly, sitting down in the chair offered him and accepting a mug of ale, which he quaffed at one gulp, "that I'd be making deals with humans and wizards, especially against my own flesh and blood." He scowled into the empty mug. Caramon, with a gesture, had the lad who attended him refill it.

Reghar, still with the same scowl, waited for the foam to settle. Then, sighing, he raised it to Caramon, who had returned to his chair. "*Durth Zamish och Durth Tabor.* Strange times makes strange brothers."

"You can say that again," Caramon muttered with a glance at Raistlin. The general lifted his glass of water† and drank it. Raistlin—out of politeness—moistened his lips from a glass of wine, then set it down.

"We will meet in the morning to discuss our plans," Caramon said. "The chief of the Plainsmen will be here then, too." Reghar's scowl deepened, and Caramon sighed inwardly, foreseeing trouble. But he continued in a hearty, cheerful tone. "Let's dine together tonight, to seal our alliance."

Yet Caramon is here, back in the stream of time. He is a part of what is happening in the here and now. See Appendix B. —TRH

The question of Caramon's alcoholism was an important aspect of this book. Caramon is trying not to fall off the wagon. —TRH

At this, Reghar rose to his feet. "I may have to fight with the barbarians," he growled. "But, by Reorx's beard, I don't have to eat with them—or you either!"

Caramon stood up again. Dressed in his best ceremonial armor (more gifts from the knights), he was an imposing sight. The dwarf squinted up at the warrior.

"You're a big one, ain't you?" he said. Snorting, he shook his head dubiously. "I mistrust there's more muscle in your head than brain."

Caramon could not help smiling, though his heart ached. It sounded so much like Flint talking!

But Raistlin did not smile.

"My brother has an excellent mind for military matters," the mage said coldly and unexpectedly. "When we left Palanthas, there were but three of us. It is due to General Caramon's skill and quick thinking that we are able to bring this mighty army to your shores. I think you would find it well to accept his leadership."

Reghar snorted again, peering at Raistlin keenly from beneath his bushy gray, overhanging eyebrows. His heavy armor clanging and rattling about him, the dwarf turned and started to stump out of the tent, then he paused.

"Three of you, from Palanthas? And now—this?" His piercing, dark-eyed gaze went to Caramon, his hand made a sweeping gesture, encompassing the tent, the knights in the shining armor who stood guard outdoors, the hundreds of men he had seen working together to unload supplies from the ships, other men practicing their fighting techniques, the row after row of cooking fires . . . .

Overwhelmed and astounded by his brother's unaccustomed praise, Caramon couldn't answer. But he managed to nod.

The dwarf snorted again, but there was a glint of grudging admiration in his eyes as he clanked and rattled his way out of the tent.

Reghar suddenly poked his head back inside. "I'll be at yer dinner," he snarled ungraciously, then stomped off.

"I, too, must be leaving, my brother," Raistlin said absently as he rose to his feet and walked toward the tent entrance. His hands folded in his black robes, he was lost in thought when he felt a touch on his arm. Irritated at the disturbance, he glanced at his brother.

"Well?"

"I—I just want to say . . . thank you." Caramon swallowed, then continued huskily. "For what you said. You—you never said . . . anything like that about me . . . before."

Raistlin smiled. There was no light in his eyes from that thin-lipped smile, but Caramon was too flushed and pleased to notice.

"It is only the simple truth, my brother," Raistlin replied, shrugging. "And it helped accomplish our objective, since we need these dwarves as our allies. I have often told you that you have hidden resources if you would only take the time and trouble to develop them. We *are* twins after all," the mage added sardonically. "I did not think we could be so unlike as you had convinced yourself."

The mage started to leave again but once more felt his brother's hand on his arm. Checking an impatient sigh, Raistlin turned.

"I wanted to kill you back in Istar, Raistlin—" Caramon paused, licking his lips—"and . . . and I think I had cause. At least, from what I knew then. Now, I'm not so certain." He sighed, looking down at his feet, then raising his flushed face. "I—I'd like to think that you did this—that you put the mages in a position where they had to send me back in time—to help me learn this lesson. That may not be the reason," Caramon hastened to add, seeing his brother's lips compress and the cold eyes grow colder, "and I'm sure it isn't—at least all of it. You are doing this for yourself, I know that. But—I think, somewhere, some part of you cares, just a little. Some part of you saw I was in trouble and you wanted to help."

Raistlin regarded his brother with amusement. Then he shrugged again. "Very well, Caramon. If this romantic notion of yours will help you fight better, if it will help you plan your strategies better, if it will aid your thinking, and—above all—if it will let me get out of this tent and back to my work, then—by all means—cradle it to your breast! It matters little to me."

Withdrawing his arm from his brother's grasp, the mage stalked to the entrance to the tent. Here he

hesitated. Half-turning his hooded head, he spoke in a low voice, his words exasperated, yet tinged with a certain sadness.

"You never did understand me, Caramon."

Then he left, his black robes rustling around his ankles as he walked.

The banquet that evening was held outdoors. Its beginnings were less than propitious.

The food was set on long tables of wood, hastily constructed from the rafts that had been used to cross the straits. Reghar arrived with a large escort, about forty dwarves. Darknight, Chief of the Plainsmen, who—with his grim face and tall, proud stance, reminded Caramon forcibly of Riverwind—brought with him forty warriors. In turn, Caramon chose forty of his men whom he knew (or at least hoped) could be trusted and could hold their liquor.

Caramon had figured that, when the groups filed in, the dwarves would sit by themselves, the Plainsmen by themselves, and so forth. No amount of talking would get them to mingle. Sure enough, after each group had arrived, all stood staring at each other in grim silence; the dwarves gathered around their leader, the Plainsmen around theirs, while Caramon's men looked on uncertainly.

Caramon came to stand before them. He had dressed with care, wearing his golden armor and helmet from the gladiatorial games, plus some new armor he'd had made to match. With his bronze skin, his matchless physique, his strong, handsome face, he was a commanding presence and even the dour dwarves exchanged looks of reluctant approval.

Caramon raised his hands.

"Greetings to my guests!" he called in his loud, booming baritone. "Welcome. This is a dinner of fellowship, to mark alliance and newfound friendship among our races—"

At this there were muttered, scoffing words and snorts of derision. One of the dwarves even spat upon the ground, causing several Plainsmen to grip their bows and take a step forward—this being considered a dreadful insult among Plainspeople. Their chief stopped them, and, coolly ignoring the interruption, Caramon continued.

The sharing of a meal is considered sacred by many cultures of the world.

"We are going to be fighting together, perhaps dying together. Therefore, let us start our meeting this first night by sitting together and sharing bread and drink like brothers.† I know that you are reluctant to be parted from your kinsmen and friends, but I want you to make new friends. And so, to help us get acquainted, I have decided we should play a little game."

At this, the dwarves' eyes opened wide, beards wagged, and low mutterings rumbled through the air like thunder. No grown dwarf ever played games! (Certain recreational activities such as "Stone Strike" and "Hammer Throw" were considered sports.) Darknight and his men brightened, however; the Plainsmen lived for games and contests, these being considered almost as much fun as making war on neighboring tribes.

Waving his arm, Caramon gestured to a new, huge, cone-shaped tent that stood behind the tables and had been the object of many curious, suspicious stares from dwarves and Plainsmen alike. Standing over twenty feet tall, it was topped by Caramon's banner. The silken flag with the nine-pointed star fluttered in the evening wind, illuminated by the great bonfire burning nearby.

As all stared at the tent, Caramon reached out and, with a yank of his strong hand, pulled on a rope. Instantly, the canvas sides of the tent fell to the ground and, at a signal from Caramon, were dragged away by several grinning young boys.

"What nonsense is this?" Reghar growled, fingering his axe.

A single heavy post stood in a sea of black, oozing mud. The post's shaft had been planed smooth and gleamed in the firelight. Near the top of the post was a round platform made of solid wood, except for several irregularly shaped holes that had been cut into it.

But it was not the sight of the pole or the platform or the mud that brought forth sudden exclamations of wonder and excitement† from dwarves and humans alike. It was the sight of what was embedded in the wood at the very top of the post. Shining in the firelight, their crossed handles flashing, were a sword and a battle-axe. But these were not the crude iron weapons many carried. These were of the finest

wrought steel, their exquisite workmanship apparent to those who stood twenty feet below, staring up at them.

"Reorx's beard!" Reghar drew a deep, quivering breath. "Yon axe is worth the price of our village! I'd trade fifty years of my life for a weapon such as that!"

Darknight, staring at the sword, blinked his eyes rapidly as swift tears of longing caused the weapon to blur in his vision.

Caramon smiled. "These weapons are yours!" he announced.

Darknight and Reghar both stared at him, their faces registering blank astonishment.

"*If—*" Caramon continued, "you can get them down!"

A vast hubbub of voices broke out among both dwarves and men. Immediately, everyone broke into a run for the pit, forcing Caramon to shout over the turmoil.

"Reghar and Darknight—each of you may choose nine warriors to help you! The first to gain the prizes wins them for his own!"

Darknight needed no urging. Without bothering to get help, he leaped into the mud and began to wade toward the post. But with each step, he sank farther and farther, the mud growing deeper and deeper as he neared his objective. By the time he reached the post, he had sunk past his knees in the sticky substance.

Reghar—more cautious—took time to observe his opponent. Calling on nine of his stoutest men to help, the dwarven leader and his men stepped into the mud. The entire contingent promptly vanished, their heavy armor causing them to sink almost immediately. Their fellows helped drag them out. Last to emerge was Reghar.

Swearing an oath to every god he could think of, the dwarf wrung mud out of his beard, then, scowling, proceeded to strip off his armor. Holding his axe high over his head, he waded back into the mud, not even waiting for his escort.

Darknight had reached the pole. Right at the base, the mud wasn't so deep—there was firm ground below it. Grasping the pole with his arms, the chieftain dragged himself up out of the mud and wrapped his legs around it. He moved up

Tracy came up with the idea for this game. Again, it is meant to show Caramon's thoughtful and deft handling of the situation. —MW

about three feet, grinning broadly at his tribesmen who cheered him on.† Then, suddenly, he began to slide back down. Gritting his teeth, he strove desperately to hang on, but it was useless. At last, the great chieftain slid slowly down to the base, amid howls of dwarven derision. Sitting in the mud, he glared grimly at the pole. It had been greased with animal fat.

More swimming that walking, Reghar at last reached the base of the pole. He was waist-deep in mud by that time, but the dwarf's great strength kept him going.

"Stand aside," he growled to the frustrated Plainsman. "Use your brains! If we can't go up, we'll bring the prize down to us!"

A grin of triumph on his mud-splattered, bearded face, Reghar drew back his axe and aimed a mighty blow at the pole.

Grinning to himself, Caramon winced in anticipation.

There was a tremendous ringing sound. The dwarf's axe rebounded off the pole as if it had struck the side of a mountain—the pole had been hewn from the thick trunk of an ironwood tree. As the reverberating axe flew from the dwarf's stinging hands, the force of the blow sent Reghar sprawling on his back in the mud. Now it was the Plainsmen's turn to laugh—none louder than their mud-covered chief.

Glaring at each other, dwarf and human tensed. The laughter died, replaced by angry mutterings. Caramon held his breath. Then Reghar's eyes went to the notched axe that was slowly sinking into the ooze. He glanced up at the beautiful axe, its steel flashing in the firelight, and—with a growl, turned to face his men.

Reghar's escort, now stripped of their armor, had waded out to him by now. Shouting and gesturing, Reghar motioned them to line up at the base of the slick pole. Then the dwarves began to form a pyramid. Three stood at the bottom, two climbed upon their backs, then another. The bottom row sank into mud past their waists but, eventually finding the firm ground at the bottom, stood fast.

Darknight watched for a moment in grim silence, then he called to nine of his warriors. Within moments,

the humans were forming their own pyramid. Being shorter, the dwarves were forced to make their pyramid smaller at the base and extend it up by single dwarves to reach the top. Reghar himself made the final ascent. Teetering on the pinnacle as the dwarves swayed and groaned beneath him, his arms strained to reach the platform—but he wasn't tall enough.

Darknight, climbing over the backs of his own men, easily reached the underside of the platform. Then, laughing at the scowl on Reghar's mud-covered face, the chieftain tried to pull himself through one of the odd-shaped openings.

He couldn't fit.

Squeezing, swearing, holding his breath was no help. The human could not force even his wiry-framed body through the small hole. At that moment, Reghar made a leap for the platform. . . .

And missed.

The dwarf sailed through the air, landing with a splat in the mud below, while the force of his jump caused the entire dwarven pyramid to topple, sending dwarves everywhere.

This time, though, the humans didn't laugh. Staring down at Reghar, Darknight suddenly jumped down into the mud himself. Landing next to the dwarf, he grabbed hold of him and dragged him to the surface of the ooze.

Both were, by this time, almost indistinguishable, covered head to foot with the black goop. They stood, staring at each other.

"You know," said Reghar, wiping mud from his eyes, "that I'm the only one who can fit through that hole."

"And you know," said Darknight through clenched teeth, "that I'm the only who can get you up there."

The dwarf grabbed the Plainsman's hand. The two moved quickly over to the human pyramid. Darknight climbed first, providing the last link to the top. Everyone cheered as Reghar climbed up onto the human's shoulders and easily squirmed through the hole.

Scrambling up onto the platform, the dwarf grasped the hilt of the sword and the handle of the axe and raised them triumphantly over his head.

The crowd fell silent. Once again, human and dwarf eyed each other suspiciously.

This is it! Caramon thought. How much of Flint did I see in you, Reghar? How much of Riverwind in you, Darknight? So much depends on this!

Reghar looked down through the hole at the stern face of the Plainsman. "This axe, which must have been forged by Reorx himself, I owe to you, Plainsman. I will be honored to fight by your side. And, if you're going to fight with me, you need a decent weapon!"

Amid cheers from the entire camp, he handed the great, gleaming sword down through the hole to Darknight.

The banquet lasted well into the night. The field rang with laughter and shouts and good-natured oaths sworn in dwarven and tribal tongues as well as Solamnic and Common.

It was easy for Raistlin to slip away. In the excitement, no one missed the silent, cynical archmage.

Walking back to his tent, which Caramon had refurbished for him, Raistlin kept to the shadows. In his black robes, he was nothing more than a glimpse of movement seen from the corner of the eye.

He avoided Crysania's tent. She was standing in the entryway, watching the fun with a wistful expression on her face. She dared not join them, knowing that the presence of the "witch" would harm Caramon immensely.

How ironic, thought Raistlin, that a black-robed

wizard is tolerated in this time, while a cleric of Paladine is scorned and reviled.

Treading softly in his leather boots across the field where the army camped, barely even leaving footprints in the damp grass, Raistlin found a grim sort of amusement in this. Glancing up at the constellations in the sky, he regarded both the Platinum Dragon and the Five-Headed Dragon opposite with a slight sneer.

The knowledge that Fistandantilus might have succeeded if it had not been for the unforeseen intervention of some wretched gnome had brought dark joy to Raistlin's being. By all his calculations, the gnome was the key factor. The gnome had altered time, apparently, though just how he had done that was unclear. Still, Raistlin figured that all he had to do was to get to the mountain fortress of Zhaman, then, from there, it would be simple indeed to make his way into Thorbardin, discover this gnome, and render him harmless.

Time—which had been altered previously—would return to its proper flow. Where Fistandantilus had failed, *he* would succeed.

Therefore, even as Fistandantilus had done before him, Raistlin now gave the war effort his undivided interest and attention to make certain that he would be able to reach Zhaman. He and Caramon spent long hours poring over old maps, studying the fortifications, comparing what they remembered from their journeys in these lands in a time yet to come and trying to guess what changes might have occurred.

The key to winning the battle was the taking of Pax Tharkas.

And that, Caramon had said more than once with a heavy sigh, seemed well-nigh impossible.

"Duncan's bound to have it heavily manned," Caramon argued, his finger resting on the spot on the map that marked the great fort. "You remember what it's like, Raist. You remember how it's built, between those two sky-high mountain peaks! Those blasted dwarves can hold out there for years! Close the gates, drop the rocks from that mechanism,† and we're stuck. It took silver dragons to lift those rocks, as I recall," the big man added gloomily.

"Go around it," Raistlin suggested.

"The chain leads to the mechanism itself," Gilthanas answered. "As to how it worked, you must ask the dwarf for I am unfamiliar with engineering. But if this chain is released from its moorings"—he pointed to the iron bracket in the floor—"massive blocks of granite drop down behind the gates of the fortress. Then no force on Krynn can open them." [Dragons of Autumn Twilight, Book II, Chapter 10]

Caramon shook his head. "Where?" His finger moved west. "Qualinesti on one side. The elves'd cut us to meat and hang us up to dry." He moved east. "This way's either sea or mountain. We don't have boats enough to go by sea and, look"—he moved his finger down—"if we land here, to the south, in that desert, we're stuck right in the middle—both flanks exposed—Pax Tharkas to the north, Thorbardin to the south."

The big man paced the room, pausing occasionally to glare at the map in irritation.

Raistlin yawned, then stood up, resting his hand lightly on Caramon's arm. "Remember this, my brother," he said softly, "Pax Tharkas *did* fall!"

Caramon's face darkened. "Yeah," he muttered, angry at being reminded of the fact that this was all just some vast game he seemed to be playing. "I don't suppose you remember how?"

"No." Raistlin shook his head. "But it will fall. . . ."

He paused, then repeated quietly, "It *will* fall!"

Out of the forest, wary of the lights of lodge and campfire and even moon and stars, crept three dark, squat figures. They hesitated on the outskirts of the camp, as though uncertain of their destination. Finally, one pointed, muttering something. The other two nodded and, now moving rapidly, they hurried through the darkness.

Quickly they moved, but not quietly. No dwarf could ever move quietly,† and these seemed noisier than usual. They creaked and rattled and stepped on every brittle twig, muttering curses as they blundered along.

Raistlin, awaiting them in the darkness of his tent, heard them coming from far off and shook his head. But he had reckoned on this in his plans, thus he had arranged this meeting when the noise and hilarity of the banquet would provide suitable cover.

"Enter," he said wryly as the clumping and stomping of ironshod feet halted just outside the tent flap.

There was a pause, accompanied by heavy breathing and a muttered exclamation, no one wanting to be the first to touch the tent. This was answered by a snarling oath. The tent flap was yanked open with a violence that nearly tore the strong fabric and a

It has become a standard in many fantasy books that while the elves are lithe and graceful, the dwarves are loud, gruff, and boisterous.

dwarf entered, apparently the leader, for he advanced with a bold swagger while the other two, who came after him, were nervous and cringing.

The lead dwarf advanced toward the table in the center of the tent, moving swiftly though it was pitch dark. After years of living underground, the Dewar† had developed excellent night vision. Some, it was rumored, even had the gift of elvensight that allowed them to see the glow of living beings in the darkness.

But, good though the dwarf's eyes were, he could make out nothing at all about the black-robed figure that sat facing him across the desk. It was as though, looking into deepest night, he saw something darker—like a vast chasm suddenly yawning at his feet. This Dewar was strong and fearless, reckless even; his father had died a raving lunatic. But the dark dwarf found he could not repress a slight shiver that started at the back of his neck and tingled down the length of his spine.

He sat down. "You two," he said in dwarven to those with him, "watch the entrance."

They nodded and retreated quickly, only too glad to leave the vicinity of the black-robed figure and crouch beside the opening, peering out into the shadows. A sudden flare of light made them start up in alarm, however. Their leader raised his arm with a vicious oath, shielding his eyes.

"No light . . . no light!" he cried in crude Common. Then his tongue clove to the roof of his mouth and for a moment all he could make were garbled noises. For the light came, not from torch or candle, but from a flame that burned in the palm of the mage's cupped hand.

All dwarves are, by nature, suspicious and distrustful of magic.† Uneducated, given to superstition, the Dewar were terrified of it and thus even this simple trick that nearly any street illusionist could perform caused the dwarf to suck in his breath in fear.

"I see those I deal with," Raistlin said in a soft, whispering voice. "Do not fear, this light will not be detected from outside or, if it is, anyone passing will assume I am studying."

Slowly, the Dewar lowered his arm, blinking his eyes painfully in the brightness of the light. His

---

"Daegar ("Deepest"): During the Age of Dreams, the Daegar were a noble clan who fought on the side of the Hylar and their cousins, the Daewar. After joining sides with rebel Theiwar, the Daegar were banished into the deep undermountain. By the middle of the Age of Might, the Daegar intermarried with the Theiwar and became like them. The other clans often call the Daegar "Dewar" (a corrupted combination of Daegar and Theiwar) because they sacrificed the purity of their clan to become dark dwarves." [DRAGONLANCE Campaign Setting, Wizards of the Coast, Inc., 2003, p. 14.]

"By nature, dwarves are nonmagical and never use magical spells." [2nd Edition ADVANCED DUNGEONS & DRAGONS Player's Handbook, by David "Zeb" Cook, TSR, 1997, p. 28.]
This is a departure from the traditional dwarves of myth and legend. Particularly in Teutonic mythology, the dwarves were very magical creatures, and even in Tolkien, dwarves were proficient in the crafting of "magical" items.

two associates seated themselves again, even nearer the entrance this time. This Dewar leader was the same one who had attended Duncan's council meeting. Though his face was stamped with the half-mad, half-calculating cruelty that marked most of his race, there was a glimmer of rational intelligence in his dark eyes that made him particularly dangerous.

These eyes were now assessing the mage across from him, even as the mage assessed him. The Dewar was impressed. He had about as much use for humans as most dwarves. A human magic-user was doubly suspect. But the Dewar was a shrewd judge of character, and he saw in the mage's thin lips, gaunt face, and cold eyes a ruthless desire for power that he could both trust and understand.

"You . . . Fistandantilus?" the Dewar growled roughly.

"I am." The mage closed his hand and the flame vanished, leaving them once more in the darkness—for which the dwarf, at least, was relieved. "And I speak dwarven, so we may converse in your language. I would prefer that, in fact, so that there can be no chance of misunderstanding."

"Well and good." The Dewar leaned forward. "I am Argat, thane of my clan. I receive your message. We are interested. But we must know more."

"Meaning 'what's in it for us?'" Raistlin said in a mocking voice. Extending his slender hand, he pointed to a corner of his tent.

Looking in the direction indicated, Argat saw nothing. Then an object in one corner of the tent began to glow, softly at first, then with increasing brilliance. Argat once again sucked in his breath, but this time in wonder and disbelief rather than fear.

Suddenly, he cast Raistlin a sharp, suspicious glance.

"By all means, go examine it for yourself," Raistlin said with a shrug. "You may take it with you tonight, in fact . . . if we come to terms."

But Argat was already out of his chair, stumbling over to the corner of the tent. Falling to his knees, he plunged his hands into the coffer of steel coins† that shone with a bright, magical gleam. For long moments, he could do nothing but stare at the wealth with glittering eyes, letting the coins run

It was my idea to make steel the metal of value in this world—a decision that had mixed results. I considered gold too soft a metal to be of much use and thought that in a warrior state, steel would have a more intrinsic value. —TRH

through his fingers. Then, with a shuddering sigh, he stood up and came back to his seat.

"You have plan?"

Raistlin nodded. The magical glow of the coins faded, but there was still a faint glimmer that continually drew the dwarf's gaze.

"Spies tell us," said Raistlin, "that Duncan plans to meet our army on the plains in front of Pax Tharkas, intending to defeat us there or, if unable to do so, at least inflict heavy casualties. If we are winning, he will withdraw his forces back into the fortress, close the gates and operate the mechanism that drops thousands of tons of rocks down to block those gates.

"With the stores of food and weapons he has cached there, he can wait until we either give up and retreat or until his own reinforcements arrive from Thorbardin to pen us up in the valley. Am I correct?"

Argat ran his fingers through his black beard. Drawing out his knife, he flipped it into the air and caught it deftly. Glancing at the mage, he stopped suddenly, spreading his hands wide.

"I sorry. A nervous habit," he said, grinning wickedly. "I hope I not alarm you. If it make you uneasy, I can—"

"If it makes me uneasy, I can deal with it," Raistlin observed mildly. "Go ahead." He gestured. "Try it."

Shrugging, but feeling uncomfortable under the gaze of those strange eyes that he could sense but could not see within the shadows of the black hood, Argat tossed the knife into the air—

A slender, white hand snaked out of the darkness, snatched the knife by the hilt, and deftly plunged the sharp blade into the table between them.

Argat's eyes glinted. "Magic," he growled.

"Skill," said Raistlin coldly. "Now, are we going to continue this discussion or play games that I excelled at in my childhood?"

"Your information accurate," muttered Argat, sheathing his knife. "That Duncan's plan."

"Good. *My* plan is quite simple. Duncan will be inside the fortress itself. He will not take the field. He will give the command to shut the gates."

Raistlin sank back into his chair, the tips of his long fingers came together. "When that command comes, the gates will not shut."

"That easy?" Argat sneered.

"That easy." Raistlin spread his hands. "Those who would shut them die. All you must do is hold the gates open for minutes only, until we have time to storm them. Pax Tharkas will fall. Your people lay down their arms and offer to join up with us."

"Easy, but for one flaw," Argat said, eyeing Raistlin shrewdly. "Our homes, families, in Thorbardin. What become of them if we turn traitor?"

"Nothing," Raistlin said. Reaching into a pouch at his side, the mage pulled forth a rolled scroll tied with black ribbon. "You will have this delivered to Duncan." Handing it to Argat, he motioned. "Read it."

Frowning, still regarding Raistlin with suspicion, the dwarf took the roll, untied it, and—carrying it over near the chest of coins—read it by their faint, magical glow.

He looked up at Raistlin, astonished. "This . . . this in language of my people!"

Raistlin nodded, somewhat impatiently. "Of course, what did you expect? Duncan would not believe it otherwise."

"But"—Argat gaped—"that language is secret, known only to the Dewar and a few others, such as Duncan, king—"

"Read!" Raistlin gestured irritably. "I haven't got all night."

Muttering an oath to Reorx, the dwarf read the scroll. It took him long moments, though the words were few. Stroking his thick, tangled beard, he pondered. Then, rising, he rolled the scroll back up and held it in his hand, tapping it slowly in his palm.

"You're right. This solve everything." He sat back down, his dark eyes, fixed on the mage, narrowing. "But I want something else give to Duncan. Not just scroll. Something . . . impressive."

"What does your kind consider 'impressive'?" Raistlin asked his lip curling. "A few dozen hacked-up bodies—"

Argat grinned. "The head of your general."

There was a long silence. Not a rustle, not a whisper of cloth betrayed Raistlin's thoughts. He even seemed to stop breathing. The silence lasted until it seemed to Argat to become a living entity itself, so powerful was it.

The dwarf shivered, then scowled. No, he would stick to this demand. Duncan would be forced to proclaim him a hero, like that bastard Kharas.

"Agreed." Raistlin's voice was level, without tone or emotion. But, as he spoke, he leaned over the table. Sensing the archmage gliding closer, Argat pulled back. He could see the glittering eyes now, and their deep, black chilling depths pierced him to the very core of his being.

"Agreed," the mage repeated. "See that you keep your part of the bargain."

Gulping, Argat gave a sickly smile. "You not called the Dark One without reason, are you, my friend?" he said, attempting a laugh as he rose to his feet, thrusting the scroll in his belt.

Raistlin did not answer, indicating he had heard only by a rustle of his hood. Shrugging, Argat turned and motioned to his companions, making a commanding gesture at the chest in the corner. Hurrying over, the two shut it and locked it with a key Raistlin drew out of the folds of his robes and silently handed to them. Though dwarves are accustomed to carrying heavy burdens with ease, the two grunted slightly as they lifted the chest. Argat's eyes shone with pleasure.

The two dwarves preceded their leader from the tent. Bearing their burden between them, they hurried off to the safe shadows of the forest. Argat watched them, then turned back to face the mage, who was, once more, a pool of blackness within blackness.

"Do not worry, friend. We not fail you."

"No, friend," said Raistlin softly. "You won't."

Argat started, not liking the mage's tone.

"You see, Argat, that money has been cursed. If you double-cross me, you and anyone else who has touched that money will see the skin of your hands turn black and begin to rot away. And when your hands are a bleeding mass of stinking flesh, the skin of your arms and your legs will blacken. And, slowly, as you watch helplessly, the curse will spread over your entire body. When you can no longer stand on your decaying feet, you will drop over dead."

Argat made a strangled, inarticulate sound. "You— you're lying!" he managed to snarl.

Raistlin said nothing. He might very well have disappeared from the tent for all Argat knew. The

dwarf couldn't see the mage or even sense his presence. What he did hear were shouts of laughter from the lodge as the door burst open. Light streamed out, dwarves and men staggered out into the night air.

Cursing under his breath, Argat hurried off.

But, as he ran, he wiped his hands frantically upon his trousers.†

Notice how the conflict is set up. We met Duncan in an earlier chapter and saw that he was a good and noble king. The Plainsmen and hill dwarves also have their virtues. But Raistlin is dealing with some truly vile characters in the Dewar. The set-up is two opposing factions, neither of which is completely in the right or in the wrong.

Fantasy is a medium of ethics. It is one of the things I like about writing in the fantasy genre. However, the conflict that is set up here at the Dwarfgate Wars is not a clear-cut issue of good guys against bad guys. Both sides see their cause as just. Both sides have villains pushing their own agendas. This, I think, is a more accurate reflection of the ethical question we face in this twenty-first century. That the questions are complex, however, in no way excuses us from the ethics of our actions. That is the journey that Crysania, Raistlin, and Caramon are all exploring.
—TRH

CHAPTER 6

awn. Krynn's sun crept up from behind the mountains slowly, almost as if it knew what ghastly sights it would shed its light upon this day. But time could not be stopped. Finally appearing over the mountains peaks, the sun was greeted with cheers and the clashing of sword against shield by those who were, perhaps, looking upon dawn for the last time in their lives.

Among those who cheered was Duncan, King of the Mountain Dwarves. Standing atop the battlements of the great fortress of Pax Tharkas, surrounded by his generals, Duncan heard the deep, hoarse voices of his men swelling up around him and he smiled with satisfaction. This would be a glorious day.

Only one dwarf was not cheering. Duncan didn't even have to look at him to be aware of the silence

that thundered in his heart as loudly as the cheers thundered in his ears.

Standing apart from the others was Kharas, hero of the dwarves. Tall, splendid in his shining armor, his great hammer clasped in his large hands, he stood staring at the sunrise and, if anyone had looked, they would have seen tears trickling down his face.

But no one looked. Everyone's gaze carefully avoided Kharas. Not because he wept, though tears are considered a childish weakness by dwarves. No, it was not because Kharas wept that everyone keep their eyes averted from him. It was because, when his tears fell, they trickled unimpeded, down a bare face.

Kharas had shaved his beard.

Even as Duncan's eyes swept the plains before Pax Tharkas, even as his mind took in the disposition of the enemy, spreading out upon the barren plains, their spear tips glittering in the light of the sun, the Thane could still feel the boundless shock that had overwhelmed his soul that morning when he had seen Kharas take his place upon the battlements, bare-faced. In his hands, the dwarf held the long, curling tresses of his luxurious beard and, as they watched in horror, Kharas hurled them out over the battlements.

A beard is a dwarf's birthright, his pride, his family's pride. In deep grief, a dwarf will go through the mourning time without combing his beard, but there is only one thing that will cause a dwarf to shave his beard. And that is shame. It is the mark of disgrace—the punishment for murder, the punishment for stealing, the punishment for cowardice, the punishment for desertion.

"Why?" was all that the stunned Duncan could think of to ask.

Staring out over the mountains, Kharas answered in a voice that split and cracked like rock. "I fight this battle because you order me to fight, Thane. I pledged you my loyalty and I am honor-bound to obey that pledge. But, as I fight, I want all to know that I find no honor in killing my kinsmen, nor even humans who have, more than once, fought at my side. Let all know, Kharas goes forward this day in shame."

"A fine figure you will look to those you lead!" Duncan responded bitterly.

But Kharas shut his mouth and would say no more.

"Thane!" Several men called at once, diverting Duncan's attention back to the plains. But he, too, had seen the four figures, tiny as toys from this distance, detach themselves from the army and ride toward Pax Tharkas. Three of the figures carried fluttering flags. The fourth carried only a staff from which beamed a clear, bright light that could be seen in the growing daylight, even at this distance.

Two of the standards Duncan recognized, of course. The banner of the hill dwarves, with its all-too-familiar symbol of anvil and hammer, was repeated in different colors on Duncan's own banner. The banner of the Plainsmen he had never seen before, but he knew it at once. It suited them—the symbol of the wind sweeping over prairie grass. The third banner, he presumed, must belong to this upstart general who had ridden out of nowhere.

"Humpf!" Duncan snorted, eyeing the banner with its symbol of the nine-pointed star with scorn. "From all we've heard, he should be carrying a banner with the sign of the Thieves' Guild upon it, coupled with a mooing cow!"

The generals laughed.

"Or dead roses," suggested one. "I hear many renegade Knights of Solamnia ride among his thieves and farmers."

The four figures galloped across the plain, their standards fluttering behind, their horses' hooves puffing up clouds of dust.

"The fourth one, in black robes, would be the wizard, Fistandantilus?" Duncan asked gruffly, his heavy brows nearly obliterating his eyes in a frown. Dwarves have no talent for magic and therefore despise and distrust it above all things.

"Yes, Thane," responded a general.

"Of all of them, I fear him the most," Duncan muttered in dark tones.

"Bah!" An old general stroked his long beard complacently. "You need not fear this wizard. Our spies tell us his health is poor. He uses his magic rarely, if at all, spending most of his time skulking in his tent. Besides, it would take an army of wizards as powerful as he to take this fortress by magic."

"I suppose you're right," Duncan said, reaching up to stroke his own beard. Catching a glimpse of Kharas out of the corner of his eye, he halted his hand, suddenly uncomfortable, and abruptly clasped his hands behind his back. "Still, keep your eyes on him" He raised his voice. "You sharpshooters—a bag of gold to the one whose arrow lodges in the wizard's ribs!"

There was a resounding cheer that hushed immediately as the four came to a halt before the fortress. The leader, the general, raised his hand palm outward in the ancient gesture of parley. Striding across the battlements and clambering up onto a block of stone that had been placed there for this very purpose, Duncan placed his hands on his hips, spread his legs, and stared down grimly.

"We would talk!" General Caramon shouted from below. His voice boomed and echoed among the walls of the steep mountains that flanked the fortress.

"All has been said!" Duncan returned, the dwarf's voice sounding nearly as powerful, though he was about one-fourth the size of the big human.

"We give you one last chance! Restore to your kinsmen what you know to be rightfully theirs! Return to these humans what you have taken from them. Share your vast wealth. After all, the dead cannot spend it!"

"No, but you living would find a way, wouldn't you?" Duncan boomed back, sneering. "What we have, we earned by honest toil, working in our homes beneath the mountains, not roaming the land in the company of savage barbarians. Here is our answer!"

Duncan raised his hand. Sharpshooters, ready and waiting, drew back the strings of their bows. Duncan's hand fell, and a hundred arrows whizzed through the air. The dwarves on the battlements began to laugh, hoping to see the four turn their horses and ride madly for their lives.

But the laughter died on their lips. The figures did not move as the arrows arced toward them. The black-robed wizard raised his hand. Simultaneously, the tip of each arrow burst into flame, the shaft became smoke and, within moments, all dwindled away to nothing in the bright morning air.

"And there is our answer!" The general's stern, cold voice drifted upwards. Turning his horse, he galloped back to his armies, flanked by the black-robed wizard, the hill dwarf, and the Plainsman.

Hearing his men muttering among themselves and seeing them cast dour, dubious looks at each other, Duncan firmly squelched his own momentary doubt and turned to face them, his beard quivering with rage.

"What is this?" he demanded angrily. "Are you frightened by the tricks of some street illusionist? What am I leading, an army of men—or of children?"

Seeing heads lower and faces flush in embarrassment, Duncan climbed down from his vantage point. Striding across to the other side of the battlements, he looked down into the vast courtyard of the mighty fortress that was formed, not by man-made walls, but by the natural walls of the mountains themselves. Caves lined the sides. Ordinarily, smoke and the sounds of metal being mined and forged into steel would have poured forth from their gaping mouths. But the mines were shut down today, as were the forges.

This morning, the courtyard teemed with dwarves. Dressed in their heavy armor, they bore shields and axes and hammers, favored weapons of the infantry. All heads raised when Duncan appeared and the cheering that had momentarily died began again.

"It is war!" Duncan shouted above the noise, raising his hands.

The cheering increased, then stopped. After a moment's silence, the deep dwarven voices raised in song.

> *Under the hills the heart of the axe*
> *Arises from cinders the still core of the fire,*
> *Heated and hammered the handle an afterthought,*
> *For the hills are forging the first breath of war.*
> *The soldier's heart sires and brothers*
> *The battlefield.*
> *Come back in glory*
> *Or on your shield.*
>
> *Out of the mountains in the midst of the air,*
> *The axes are dreaming dreaming of rock,*
> *Of metal alive through the ages of ore,*

Stone on metal metal on stone.
The soldier's heart contains and dreams
The battlefield.
Come back in glory
Or on your shield.

Red of iron imagined from the vein,
Green of brass green of copper
Sparked in the fire the forge of the world,
Consuming in its dream as it dives into bone.
The soldier's heart lies down, completes
The battlefield.
Come back in glory
Or on your shield.†

His blood stirred by the song, Duncan felt his doubts vanish as the arrows had vanished in the still air. His generals were already descending from the battlements, hurrying to take up their positions. Only one remained, Argat, general of the Dewar. Kharas remained, too. Duncan looked over at Kharas now, and opened his mouth to speak.

But the hero of the dwarves simply regarded his king with a dark, haunted gaze, then, bowing toward his thane, turned and followed after the others to take his place as one of the leaders of the infantry.

Duncan glared at him angrily. "May Reorx send his beard up in flames!" he muttered as he started to follow. He would be present when the great gates swung open and his army marched out into the plains. "Who does he think he is? My own sons would not act so to me! This must not go on. After the battle, he will be put in his place."

Grumbling to himself, Duncan was nearly to the stairs leading downward when he felt a hand upon his arm. Looking up, he saw Argat.

"I ask you, King," said the dwarf in his crude language, "to think again. Our plan is good one. Abandon worthless hunk of rock. Let them have it." He gestured toward the armies out in the plains. "They not fortify it. When we retreat back to Thorbardin, they chase after us into the plains. Then we retake Pax Tharkas and—*bam*"—the dark dwarf clapped his hands shut—"we have them! Caught between Pax Tharkas on north and Thorbardin on south."

This song is a variation on the Middle English "bob and wheel" stanza. Basically, the longer lines are held together by alliteration, and the short lines that mark the end of each stanza are the more familiar metrical rhyme that is part of the tradition of English poetry. I wanted something for the dwarves that would feel different from the other styles of poetry in the book—to mark the distinction between their culture and that of, say, the men or elves. The "come back in glory/or on your shield" lines, however, echo a sentiment that is not Middle English but Spartan. Somewhere or other, I read that Spartan mothers said this to their sons departing for battle.
—Michael Williams

Duncan stared coldly at the Dewar. Argat had presented this strategy at the War Council, and Duncan had wondered at the time how he had come up with it. The Dewar generally took little interest in military matters, caring about only one thing—their share of the spoils. Was it Kharas, trying once again to get out of fighting?

Duncan angrily shook off the Dewar's arm. "Pax Tharkas will never fall!" he said. "Your strategy is the strategy of the coward. I will give up nothing to these rabble, not one copper piece, not one pebble of ground! I'd sooner die here!"

Stomping away, Duncan clattered down the stairs, his beard bristling in his wrath.

Watching him go, Argat's lip twisted in a sneer. "Perhaps you would die upon this wretched rock, Duncan King. But not Argat." Turning to two Dewar who had been standing in the shadows of a recessed corner, the dark dwarf nodded his head twice. The dwarves nodded in return, then quickly hurried away.

Standing upon the battlements, Argat watched as the sun climbed higher in the sky. Preoccupied, he began to absentmindedly rub his hands upon his leather armor as though trying to clean them.

The Highgug was not certain, but he had the feeling something was wrong.

Though not terribly perceptive, and understanding little of the complex tactics and strategies of warfare, it occurred to the Highgug nevertheless that dwarves returning victorious from the field of battle did not come staggering into the fortress covered with blood and fall down dead at his feet.

One or two, he might have considered the fortunes of war, but the number of dwarves doing this sort of thing seemed to be increasing at a truly alarming rate. The Highgug decided to see if he could find out what was going on.

He took two steps forward, then, hearing the most dreadful commotion behind him, came to a sudden halt. Heaving a heavy sigh, the Highgug turned around. He had forgotten his company.

"No, no, no!" the Highgug shouted angrily, waving his arms in the air. "How many time I tell you?— Stay Here! Stay Here! King tell Highgug—'You gugs Stay Here.' That mean Stay Here! You got that?"

The Highgug fixed his company with a stern eye,
causing those still on their feet and able to meet the
gaze of that eye (the other was missing) to tremble in
shame. Those gully dwarves in the company who had
stumbled over their pikes, those who had dropped
their pikes, those who had, in the confusion, accidentally stabbed a neighbor with a pike, those who
were lying prone on the ground, and those who had
gotten turned around completely and were now
stalwartly facing the rear, heard their commander's
voice and quailed.

"Look, gulphfunger slimers," snarled the Highgug, breathing noisily, "I go find out what go on. It
not seem right, everyone coming back into fort like
this. No singing—only bleeding. This not the way
king tell Highgug things work out. So I Go. You
Stay Here. Got that? Repeat."

"I Go," echoed his troops obediently. "You Stay
Here."

The Highgug tore at his beard. "No! *I* Go! *You*—
Oh, never mind!" Stalking off in a rage, he heard
behind him—once again—the clattering of falling
pikes hitting the ground.

Perhaps fortunately, the Highgug did not have far
to go. Otherwise, when he returned, he would have
found about half of his command dead, skewered on
the ends of their own pikes. As it was, he was able to
discover what he needed to know and return to his
troops before they had inadvertently killed more
than half a dozen or so.

The Highgug had taken only about twenty steps
when he rounded a corner and very nearly ran into
Duncan, his king. Duncan did not notice him, his
back being turned. The king was engrossed in a
conversation with Kharas and several commanding
officers. Taking a hasty step backwards, the Highgug looked and listened anxiously.

Unlike many of the dwarves who had returned
from the field of battle, whose heavy plate mail was
so dented it looked like they had tumbled down a
rocky mountainside, Kharas's armor was dented
only here and there. The hero's hands and arms
were bloodied to the elbows, but it was the enemy's
blood, not his own that he wore. Few there were
who could withstand the mighty swings of the
hammer he carried. Countless were the dead that

fell by Kharas's hand, though many wondered, in their last moments, why the tall dwarf sobbed bitterly as he dealt the killing blow.

Kharas was not crying now, however. His tears were gone, completely dry. He was arguing with his king.

"We are beaten on the field, Thane," he said sternly. "General Ironhand was right to order the retreat. If you would hold Pax Tharkas, we must fall back and shut the gates as we had planned. Remember, this was not a moment that was unforeseen, Thane."

"But a moment of shame, nonetheless," Duncan growled with a bitter oath. "Beaten by a pack of thieves and farmers!"

"That pack of thieves and farmers has been well-trained, Thane," Kharas said solemnly, the generals nodding grudging agreement to his words. "The Plainsmen glory in battle and our own kinsmen fight with the courage with which they are born. And then comes sweeping down from the hills the Knights of Solamnia on their horses."

"You must give the command, Thane!" one of the generals said. "Or prepare to die where we stand."

"Close the god-cursed gates, then!" Duncan shouted in a rage. "But do not drop the mechanism. Not until the last possible moment. There may be no need. It will cost them dearly to try to breach the gates, and I want to be able to get out again without having to clear away tons of rock."

"Close the gates, close the gates!" rang out many voices.

Everyone in the courtyard, the living, the wounded, even the dying, turned their heads to see the massive gates swing shut. The Highgug was among these, staring in awe. He had heard of these great gates—how they moved silently on gigantic, oiled hinges that worked so smoothly only two dwarves on each side were needed to pull them shut. The Highgug was somewhat disappointed to hear that the mechanism was not going to be operated. The sight of tons of rock tumbling down to block the gates was one he was sorry to miss.

Still, this should be quite entertaining. . . .

The Highgug caught his breath at the next sight, very nearly strangling himself. Looking at the gate, he could see beyond it, and what he saw was paralyzing.

A vast army was racing toward him. And it was not *his* army!

Which meant it must be the enemy, he decided after a moment's deep thought, there being—as far as he knew—only two sides to this conflict—his and theirs.

The noonday sun shone brightly upon the armor of the Knights of Solamnia, it flashed upon their shields and glittered upon their drawn swords. Farther behind them came the infantry at a run. The Army of Fistandantilus was dashing for the fortress, hoping to reach it before the gates could be closed and blocked. Those few mountain dwarves brave enough to stand in their way were cut down by flashing steel and trampling hoof.

The enemy was getting closer and closer. The Highgug swallowed nervously. He didn't know much about military maneuvers, but it did seem to him that this would be an excellent time for the gates to shut. It seemed that the generals thought so too, for they were now all running in that direction, yelling and screaming.

"In the name of Reorx, what's taking them—" Duncan began.

Suddenly, Kharas's face grew pale.

"Duncan," he said quietly, "we have been betrayed. You must leave at once."

"Wh-what?" Duncan stammered in bewilderment. Standing on his toes, he tried in vain to see over the crowd milling about in the courtyard. "Betrayed! How—"

"The Dewar, my Thane," Kharas said, able, with his unusual height, to see what was transpiring. "They have murdered the gate wardens, apparently, and are now fighting to keep the gates open."

"Slay them!" Duncan's mouth frothed in his anger, saliva dribbled down his beard. "Slay every one of them!" The dwarven king drew his own sword and leaped forward. "I'll personally—"

"No, Thane!" Kharas caught hold of him, dragging him back. "It is too late! Come, we must get to the griffons!† You must go back to Thorbardin, my king!"

But Duncan was beyond all reason. He fought Kharas viciously. Finally, the younger dwarf, with a grim face, doubled his great fist and punched his

In the DRAGONLANCE setting, griffon riders are most often associated with the elves, particularly the Silvanesti, but here we see that in ages past, the dwarves used them as well.

king squarely on the jaw. Duncan stumbled backward, reeling from the blow but not down.

"I'll have your head for this!" the king swore, grasping feebly for his sword hilt. One more blow from Kharas finished the job, however. Duncan sprawled onto the ground and lay there quietly.

With a grieving face, Kharas bent down, lifted his king, plate-mail armor and all, and—with a grunt—heaved the stout dwarf over his shoulder. Calling for some of those still able to stand and fight to cover him, Kharas hurried off toward where the griffons waited, the comatose king hanging, arms dangling, over his shoulder.

The Highgug stared at the approaching army in horrified fascination. Over and over echoed in his mind Duncan's last command to him—"You Stay Here."

Turning around, running back to his troop, that was exactly what the Highgug intended to do.

Although gully dwarves have a well-deserved reputation for being the most cowardly race living upon Krynn, they can—when driven into a corner—fight with a ferocity that generally amazes an enemy.

Most armies, however, use gully dwarves only in support positions, keeping them as far to the rear as possible since it is almost even odds that a regiment of gully dwarves will inflict as much damage to its own side as it will ever succeed in doing to an enemy.

Thus Duncan had posted the only detachment of gully dwarves currently residing in Pax Tharkas—they were former mine workers—in the center of the courtyard and told them to stay there, figuring this would be the best way to keep them out of mischief. He had given them pikes, in the unlikely event that the enemy would crash through the gates with a cavalry charge.

But that was what was happening. Seeing the Army of Fistandantilus closing in upon them, knowing that they were trapped and defeated, all the dwarves in Pax Tharkas were thrown into confusion.

A few kept their heads. The sharpshooters on the battlements were raining arrows into the advancing foe, slowing them somewhat. Several commanders

were gathering their regiments, preparing to fight as they retreated to the mountains. But most were just fleeing, running for their lives to the safety of the surrounding hills.

And soon only one group stood in the path of the approaching army—the gully dwarves.

"This is it," the Highgug called hastily to his men as he came huffing and puffing back. His face was white beneath the dirt, but he was calm and composed. He had been told to Stay Here and, by Reorx's beard, he was going to Stay Here.

However, seeing that most of his men were starting to edge away, their eyes wide at the sight of the thundering horses which could now be seen approaching the open gates, the Highgug decided this called for a little morale boost.

Having drilled them for just such an occasion, the Highgug had also taught his troops a war chant and was quite proud of it. Unfortunately, they'd never yet got it right.

"Now," he shouted, "what you give me?"

"Death!" his men all shouted cheerfully with one voice.

The Highgug cringed. "No, no, no!" he yelled in exasperation, stomping on the ground. His men looked at each other, chagrined.

"I tell you, gulphbludders—it's—"

"Undying loyalty!" cried one suddenly in triumph.

The others scowled at him, muttering "brown nose." One jealous neighbor even poked him in the back with a pike. Fortunately, it was the butt end (he was holding it upside down) or serious damage might have been incurred.

"That's it," said the Highgug, trying not to notice that the sound of hoofbeats was getting louder and louder behind him. "Now, we try again. What you give me?"

"Un-undy . . . dying loy . . . loy . . . alty." This was rather straggled-sounding, many stumbling over the difficult words. It certainly seemed to lack the ring (or the enthusiasm) of the first.

A hand shot up in the back.

"Well, what is it, Gug Snug?" snarled the Highgug.

"Us got to give . . . undying . . . loyal . . . ty when dead?"

The Highgug glared at him with his one good eye.

"No, you phungerwhoop," he snapped, gritting his teeth. "Death or undying loyalty. Whichever come first."

The gully dwarves grinned, immensely cheered by this.

The Highgug, shaking his head and muttering, turned around to face the enemy. "Set pikes!" he shouted.

That was a mistake and he knew it as soon as he said it, hearing the vast turmoil and confusion and swearing (and a few groans of pain) behind him.

But, by that time, it didn't matter. . . .

The sun set in a blood-red haze, sinking down into the silent forests of Qualinesti.

All was quiet in Pax Tharkas, the mighty, impregnable fortress having fallen shortly after midday. The afternoon had been spent in skirmishes with pockets of dwarves, who were retreating, fighting, back into the mountains. Many had escaped, the charge of the knights having been effectively held up by a small group of pikesmen, who had stood their ground when the gates were breached, stubbornly refusing to budge.

Kharas, carrying the unconscious king in his arms, flew by griffon back to Thorbardin, accompanied by those of Duncan's officers still alive.

The remainder of the army of the mountain dwarves, at home in the caves and rocks of the snow-covered passes, were making their way back to Thorbardin. The Dewar who had betrayed their kinsmen were drinking Duncan's captured ale and boasting of their deeds, while most of Caramon's army regarded them with disgust.

Tonight, as the sun set, the courtyard was filled with dwarves and humans celebrating their victory, and by officers trying in vain to stem the tide of drunkenness that was threatening to wash everyone under. Shouting, bullying, and smashing a few heads together, they managed to drag off enough to post the watch and form burial squads.

Crysania had passed her trial by blood. Though she had been kept well away from the battle by a watchful Caramon, she had—once they entered the fort—managed to elude him. Now, cloaked and

hooded, she moved among the wounded, surreptitiously healing those she could without drawing unwanted attention to herself. And, in later years, those who survived would tell stories to their grandchildren, claiming that they had seen a white-robed figure bearing a shining light around her neck, who laid her gentle hands upon them and took away their pain.

Caramon was, meanwhile, meeting with officers in a room in Pax Tharkas, planning their strategy, though the big man was so exhausted he could barely think straight.

Thus, few saw the single, black-robed figure entering the open gates of Pax Tharkas. It rode upon a restive black horse that shied at the smell of blood. Pausing, the figure spoke a few words to his mount, seeming to soothe the animal. Those that did see the figure paused for a moment in terror, many having the fevered (or drunken) impression that it was Death in person,† come to collect the unburied.

Then someone muttered, "the wizard," and they turned away, laughing shakily or breathing a sigh of relief.

His eyes obscured by the depths of his black hood, yet intently observing all around him, Raistlin rode forward until he came to the most remarkable sight on the entire field of battle—the bodies of a hundred or more gully dwarves, lying (for the most part) in even rows, rank upon rank. Most still held their pikes (many upside down) clutched tightly in their dead hands. There were also lying among them, though, a few horses that had been injured (generally accidentally) by the wild stabs and slashings of the desperate gully dwarves. More than one animal, when hauled off, was noted to have teeth marks sunk into its forelegs. At the end, the gully dwarves had dropped the useless pikes to fight as they knew best—with tooth and nail.

"This wasn't in the histories," Raistlin murmured to himself, staring down at the wretched little bodies, his brow furrowed. His eyes flashed. "Perhaps," he breathed, "this means time has already been altered?"

For long moments he sat there, pondering. Then suddenly he understood.

Since death is common to all people, it is only natural that all cultures should have a personification of death in their mythos. —TRH

None saw Raistlin's face, hidden as it was by his hood, or they would have noted a swift, sudden spasm of sorrow and anger pass across it.

"No," he said to himself bitterly, "the pitiful sacrifice of these poor creatures was left out of the histories not because it did not happen. It was left out simply because—"

He paused, staring grimly down at the small broken bodies. "No one cared. . . ."†

Yet Raistlin obviously does care. Despite his many faults, there is no question that Raistlin has great sympathy for the weak and downtrodden.

Chapter 7

"I must see the general!"

The voice pierced through the soft, warm cloud of sleep that wrapped Caramon like the down-filled comforter on the bed†—the first real bed he'd slept in for months.

"Go 'way," mumbled Caramon and heard Garic say the same thing, or close enough. . . .

"Impossible. The general is sleeping. He's not to be disturbed."

"I must see him. It's urgent!"

"He hasn't slept in almost forty-eight hours—"

"I know! But—"

The voices dropped. Good, Caramon thought, now I can go back to sleep. But he found, unfortunately, that the lowered voices only made him more wakeful. Something was wrong, he knew it. With a groan, he rolled over, dragging the pillow on top his

Unless the dwarves have some special accommodation for visiting humans, Caramon is going to feel a little cramped in this dwarven bed! —TRH

723

head. Every muscle in his body ached; he had been on horseback almost eighteen hours without rest. Surely Garic could handle it. . . .

The door to his room opened softly.

Caramon squeezed his eyes shut, burrowing farther down into the feather bed. It occurred to him as he did so that, a couple of hundred years from now, Verminaard, the evil Dragon Highlord, would sleep in this very same bed. Had someone wakened him like this, that morning the Heroes had freed the slaves of Pax Tharkas?. . .†

"General," said Garic's soft voice. "Caramon."

There was a muttered oath from the pillow.

Perhaps, when I leave, I'll put a frog in the bed, Caramon thought viciously. It would be nice and stiff in two hundred years. . . .

"General," Garic persisted, "I'm sorry to wake you, sir, but you're needed in the courtyard at once."

"What for?" growled Caramon, throwing off the blankets and sitting up, wincing at the soreness in his thighs and back. Rubbing his eyes, he glared at Garic.

"The army, sir. It's leaving."

Caramon stared at him. "What? You're crazy."

"No, s-sir," said a young soldier, who had crept in after Garic and now stood behind him, his eyes wide with awe at being in the presence of his commanding officer—despite the fact that the officer was naked and only half-awake. "They— they're gathering in the courtyard, n-now, sir. . . . The dwarves and the Plainsmen and . . . and some of ours."

"Not the Knights," Garic added quickly.

"Well . . . well . . ." Caramon stammered, then waved his hand. "Tell them to disperse, damn it! This is nonsense." He swore. "Name of the gods, three-fourths of them were dead drunk last night!"

"They're sober enough this morning, sir. And I think you should come," Garic said softly. "Your brother is leading them."

"What's the meaning of this?" Caramon demanded, his breath puffing white in the chill air. It was the coldest morning of the fall. A thin coat of frost covered the stones of Pax Tharkas, mercifully obliterating the red stains of battle. Wrapped in a thick cloak,

After the dragonarmies conquered Solace, Haven, and Gateway during the War of the Lance, the inhabitants were carried away as slaves to Pax Tharkas. The freeing of the slaves is in the latter half of Dragons of Autumn Twilight.

dressed only in leather breeches and boots that he had hastily thrown on, Caramon glanced about the courtyard. It was crowded with dwarves and men, all standing quietly, grimly, in ranks, waiting for the order to march.

Caramon's stern gaze fixed itself on Reghar Fireforge, then shifted to Darknight, chief of the Plainsmen.

"We went over this yesterday," Caramon said. His voice taut with barely contained anger, he came to stand in front of Reghar. "It'll take another two days for our supply wagons to catch up. There's not enough food left here for the march, you told me that yourself last night. And you won't find so much as a rabbit on the Plains of Dergoth—"

"*We* don't mind missing a few meals," grunted Reghar, the emphasis on the "we" leaving no doubt as to his meaning. Caramon's love of his dinner was well-known.

This did nothing to improve the general's humor. Caramon's face flushed. "What about weapons, you long-bearded fool?" he snapped. "What about fresh water, shelter, food for the horses?"

"We won't be in the Plains that long," Reghar returned, his eyes flashing. "The mountain dwarves, Reorx curse their stone hearts, are in confusion. We must strike now, before they can get their forces back together."

"We went over this last night!" Caramon shouted in exasperation. "This was just a *part* of their force we faced here. Duncan's got another whole damn army waiting for you beneath the mountain!"

"Perhaps. Perhaps not," Reghar snarled surlily, staring southward and folding his arms in front of him. "At any rate, we've changed our minds. We're marching today—with or without you."

Caramon glanced at Darknight, who had remained silent throughout this conversation. The chief of the Plainsmen only nodded, once. His men, standing behind him, were stern and quiet, though—here and there—Caramon saw a few green-tinged faces and knew that many had not fully recovered from last night's celebration.

Finally, Caramon's gaze shifted to a black-robed figure seated on a black horse. Though the figure's eyes were shadowed by his black hood, Caramon

had felt their intense, amused gaze ever since he walked out of the door of the gigantic fortress.

Turning abruptly away from the dwarf, Caramon stalked over to Raistlin. He was not surprised to find Lady Crysania on her horse, muffled in a thick cloak. As he drew nearer, he noticed that the bottom of the cleric's cloak was stained dark with blood. Her face, barely visible above a scarf she had wound around her neck and chin, was pale but composed. He wondered briefly where she had been and what she had been doing during the long night. His thoughts were centered, however, on his twin.

"This is your doing," he said in a low voice, approaching Raistlin and laying his hand upon the horse's neck.

Raistlin nodded complacently, leaning forward over the pommel of the saddle to talk to his brother. Caramon could see his face, cold and white as the frost on the pavement beneath their feet.

"What's the idea?" Caramon demanded, still in the same low voice, "What's this all about? You know we can't march without supplies!"

"You're playing this much too safely, my brother," said Raistlin. He shrugged and added, "The supply trains will catch up with us. As for weapons, the men have picked up extra ones here after the battle. Reghar is right—we must strike quickly, before Duncan can get organized."

"You should have discussed this with me!" Caramon growled, clenching his fist. "*I* am in command!"

Raistlin looked away, shifting slightly in his saddle. Caramon, standing near him, felt his brother's body shiver beneath the black robes. "There wasn't time," the archmage said after a moment. "I had a dream last night, my brother. *She* came to me—my Queen . . . Takhisis. . . . It is imperative that I reach Zhaman as soon as possible."

Caramon gazed at his brother in silent, sudden understanding. "They mean nothing to you!" he said softly, gesturing to the men and dwarves standing, waiting behind him. "You're interested in one thing only, reaching your precious Portal!" His bitter gaze shifted to Crysania, who regarded him calmly, though her gray eyes were dark and shadowed from a sleepless, horror-filled night spent among the wounded and dying. "You, too? You support him in this?"

"The trial of blood, Caramon," she said softly. "It must be stopped—forever. I have seen the ultimate evil mankind can inflict upon itself."

"I wonder!" Caramon muttered, glancing at his twin.

Reaching up with his slender hands, Raistlin slowly drew back the folds of his hood, leaving his eyes visible. Caramon recoiled, seeing himself reflected in the flat surface, seeing his face—haggard, unshaven, his hair uncombed, fluttering raggedly in the wind. And then, as Raistlin stared at him, holding him in an intense gaze as a snake charms a bird, words came into Caramon's mind.

You know me well my brother. The blood that flows in our veins speaks louder than words sometimes. Yes, you are right. I care nothing for this war. I have fought it for one purpose only, and that is to reach the Portal. These fools will carry me that far. Beyond that, what does it matter to me whether we win or lose?

I have allowed you to play general, Caramon, since you seemed to enjoy your little game. You are, in fact, surprisingly good at it. You have served my purpose adequately. You will serve me still. You will lead the army to Zhaman. When Lady Crysania and I are safely there, I will send you home. Remember this, my brother— the battle on the Plains of Dergoth was lost! You cannot change that!

"I don't believe you!" Caramon said thickly, staring at Raistlin with wild eyes. "You wouldn't ride to your own death! You must know something! You—"

Caramon choked, half-strangled. Raistlin drew nearer to him, seeming to suck the words out of his throat.

My counsel is my own to keep! What I know or do not know does not concern you, so do not tax your brain with fruitless speculation.

"I'll tell them," Caramon said forcing the words out through clenched teeth. "I'll tell them the truth!"

Tell them what? That you have seen the future? That they are doomed? Seeing the struggle in Caramon's anguish-filled face, Raistlin smiled. *I think not, my brother. And now, if you ever want to return to your home again, I suggest you go upstairs, put on your armor, and lead your army.*

The archmage lifted his hands and pulled his hood down low over his eyes again. Caramon drew in his breath with a gasp, as though someone had dashed cold water in his face. For a moment, he could only stand staring at his twin, shivering with a rage that nearly overpowered him.

All he could think of, at that moment, was Raistlin . . . laughing with him by the tree . . . Raistlin holding the rabbit . . . That camaraderie between them had been real. He would swear it! And yet, this, too, was real. Real and cold and sharp as the blade of a knife shining in the clear light of morning.

And, slowly, the light from that knife blade began to penetrate the clouds of confusion in Caramon's mind, severing another of the ties that bound him to his brother.

The knife moved slowly. There were many ties to cut.

The first gave in the blood-soaked arena at Istar, Caramon realized. And he felt another part as he stared at his brother in the frost-rimed courtyard of Pax Tharkas.

"It seems I have no choice," he said, tears of anger and pain blurring the image of his brother in his sight.

"None," Raistlin replied. Grasping the reins, he made ready to ride off. "There are things I must attend to. Lady Crysania will ride with you, of course, in the vanguard. Do not wait for me. I will ride behind for a time."

And so I'm dismissed, Caramon said to himself. Watching his brother ride away, he felt no anger anymore, just a dull, gnawing ache. An amputated limb left behind such phantom pain, so he had heard once. . . .

Turning on his heel, feeling more than hearing the heavy silence that had settled over the courtyard, the general walked alone to his quarters and slowly began to put on his armor.

When Caramon returned, dressed in his familiar golden armor, his cape fluttering in the wind, the dwarves and Plainsmen and the men of his own army raised their voices in a resounding cheer.

Not only did they truly admire and respect the big man, but all credited him with the brilliant strategy that had brought them victory the day before. General Caramon was lucky, it was said, blessed by

some god. After all, wasn't it luck that had kept the dwarves from closing the gates?

Most had felt uncomfortable when it was rumored they might be riding off without him. There had been many dark glances cast at the black-robed wizard, but who dared voice disapproval?

The cheers were immensely comforting to Caramon and, for a moment, he could say nothing. Then, finding his voice, he gruffly issued orders as he made ready to ride.

With a gesture, Caramon called one of the young Knights forward.

"Michael, I'm leaving you here in Pax Tharkas, in command," he said, pulling on a pair of gloves. The young Knight flushed with pleasure at this unexpected honor, even as he glanced behind at the hole his leaving made in the ranks.

"Sir, I'm only a low-ranking—Surely, someone more qualified—"

Smiling at him sadly, Caramon shook his head. "I know your qualifications, Michael. Remember? You were ready to die to fulfill a command, and you found the compassion to disobey. It won't be easy, but do the best you can. The women and children will stay here, of course. And I'll send back any wounded. When the supply trains arrive, see that they're sent on as quickly as possible." He shook his head. "Not that it is likely to be soon enough," he muttered. Sighing, he added, "You can probably hold out the winter here, if you have to. No matter what happens to us. . . ."

Seeing the Knights glance at each other, their faces puzzled and worried, Caramon abruptly bit off his words. No, his bitter foreknowledge must not be allowed to show. Feigning cheerfulness, therefore, he clapped Michael upon the shoulder, added something brave and inane, then mounted his horse amidst wild yelling.

The yells increased as the standard-bearer raised the army's standard. Caramon's banner with its nine-pointed star gleamed brightly in the sun. His Knights formed ranks behind him. Crysania came up to ride with them, the Knights parting, with their usual chivalry, to let her take her place. Though the Knights had no more use for the witch than anyone else in camp, she was a woman,† after all, and the

This comment seems to suggest that during this time period the Solamnic Knights held very chivalric views on women. These would change over the years, so that by the time of the War of Souls, women could even join the Knighthood. Caramon's own granddaughter, Linsha, would one day become a Knight of the Rose.

Code required them to protect and defend her with their lives.

"Open the gates!" Caramon shouted.

Pushed by eager hands, the gates swung open. Casting a final glance around to see that all was in readiness, Caramon's eyes suddenly encountered those of his twin.

Raistlin sat upon his black horse within the shadows of the great gates. He did not move nor speak. He simply sat, watching, waiting.

For as long as it took to draw a shared, simultaneous breath, the twins regarded each other intently, then Caramon turned his face away.

Reaching over, he grabbed his standard from his bearer. Holding it high over his head, he cried out one word, "Thorbardin!" The morning sun, just rising above the peaks, burned golden on Caramon's armor. It sparkled golden on the threads of the banner's star, glittered golden on the spear tips of the long ranks behind him.

"Thorbardin!" he cried once again and, spurring his horse, he galloped out of the gates.

"Thorbardin!" His cry was echoed by thunderous yells and the clashing of sword against shield. The dwarves began their familiar, eerie, deep-throated chant, "Stone and metal, metal and stone, stone and metal, metal and stone," stomping their iron-shod feet to it in stirring rhythm as they marched out of the fort in rigid lines.

They were followed by the Plainsmen, who moved in less orderly fashion. Wrapped in their fur cloaks against the chill, they walked in leisurely fashion, sharpening weapons, tying feathers in their hair, or painting strange symbols on their faces. Soon, growing tired of the rigid order, they would drift off the road to travel in their accustomed hunting packs. After the barbarians came Caramon's troop of farmers and thieves, more than a few of them staggering from the after-effects of last night's victory party. And finally, bringing up the rear, were their new allies, the Dewar.

Argat tried to catch Raistlin's eye as he and his men trooped out, but the wizard sat wrapped in black upon his black horse, his face hidden in darkness. The only flesh and blood part of him visible were the slender, white hands, holding the horse's reins.

Raistlin's eyes were not on the Dewar, nor on the army marching past him. They were on the gleaming golden figure riding at the army's head. And it would have taken a sharper eye than the Dewar's to note that the wizard's hands gripped the reins with an unnatural tightness or that the black robes shivered, for just a moment, as if with a soft sigh.

The Dewar marched out, and the courtyard was empty except for the camp followers. The women wiped away their tears and, chatting among themselves, returned to their tasks. The children clambered up onto the walls to cheer the army as long as it was in sight. The gates to Pax Tharkas swung shut at last, sliding smoothly and silently upon their oiled hinges.

Standing on the battlements alone, Michael watched the great army surge southward, their spear tips shining in the morning sun, their warm breath sending up puffs of mist, the chanting of the dwarves echoing through the mountains.

Behind them rode a single, solitary figure, cloaked in black. Looking at the figure, Michael felt cheered. It seemed a good omen. Death now rode behind the army, instead of in front.

The sun shone upon the opening of the gates of Pax Tharkas; it set upon the closing of the gates of the great mountain fastness of Thorbardin. As the water-controlled mechanism that operated the gates groaned and wheezed, part of the mountain itself appeared to slide into place upon command. When shut and sealed, in fact, the gates were impossible to tell from the face of the rock of the mountain itself, so cunning was the craftsmanship of the dwarves who had spent years constructing them.

The shutting of the gates meant war. News of the marching of the Army of Fistandantilus had been reported, carried by spies upon the swift wings of griffons. Now the mountain fastness was alive with activity. Sparks flew in the weapons makers' shops. Armorers fell asleep, hammers in their hands. The taverns doubled their business overnight as everyone came to boast of the great deeds they would accomplish on the field of battle.

Only one part of the huge kingdom beneath the ground was quiet, and it was to this place that the hero

of the dwarves turned his heavy footsteps two days after Caramon's army had left Pax Tharkas.

Entering the great Hall of Audience of the King of the Mountain Dwarves, Kharas heard his boots ring hollowly in the bowl-shaped chamber that was carved of the stone of the mountain itself. The chamber was empty now, save for several dwarves seated at the front on a stone dais.

Kharas passed the long rows of stone benches where, last night, thousands of dwarves had roared approval as their king declared war upon their kinsmen.

Today was a War Meeting of the Council of Thanes.† As such, it did not require the presence of the citizenry, so Kharas was somewhat startled to find himself invited. The hero was in disgrace—everyone knew it. There was speculation, even, that Duncan might have Kharas exiled.

Kharas noted, as he drew near, that Duncan was regarding him with an unfriendly eye, but this may have had something to do with the fact that the king's eye and left cheekbone above his beard were undeniably black and swollen—a result of the blow Kharas had inflicted.

"Oh, get up, Kharas," Duncan snapped as the tall, beardless dwarf bowed low before him.

"Not until you have forgiven me, Thane," Kharas said, retaining his position.

"Forgiven you for what—knocking some sense into a foolish old dwarf?" Duncan smiled wryly. "No, you're not forgiven for that. You are thanked." The king rubbed his jaw. " 'Duty is painful,'† goes the proverb. Now I understand. But enough of that."

Seeing Kharas straighten, Duncan held out a scroll of parchment. "I asked you here for another reason. Read this."

Puzzled, Kharas examined the scroll. It was tied with black ribbon but was not sealed. Glancing at the other thanes, who were all assembled, each in his own stone chair sitting somewhat lower than the king's, Kharas's gaze went to one chair in particular—a vacant chair, the chair of Argat, Thane of the Dewar. Frowning, Kharas unrolled the scroll and read aloud, stumbling over the crude language of the Dewar.

Duncan, of the Dwarves of Thorbardin, King.

Greetings from those you now call traitor.

This scroll is deliver to you from us who know that you will punish Dewar under the mountain for what we did at Pax Tharkas. If this scroll is deliver to you at all, it mean that we succeed in keeping the gates open.

You scorn our plan in Council. Perhaps now you see wisdom. The enemy is led by the wizard now. Wizard is friend of ours. He make army march for the Plains of Dergoth. We march with them, friend with them. When the hour to come, those you call traitor will strike. We will attack the enemy from within and drive them under your axe-blades.

If you to have doubt of our loyalty, hold our people hostage beneath the mountain until such time we return. We promise great gift we deliver to you as proof loyalty.

Argat, of the Dewar, Thane

Kharas read the scroll through twice, and his frown did not ease. If anything, it grew darker.

"Well?" demanded Duncan.

"I have nothing to do with traitors," Kharas said, rolling up the scroll and handing it back in disgust.

"But if they are sincere," Duncan pursued, "this could give us a great victory!"

Kharas raised his eyes to meet those of his king, who sat on the dais above him. "If, at this moment, Thane, I could talk to our enemy's general, this Caramon Majere, who—by all accounts—is a fair and honorable man, I would tell him exactly what peril threatens him, even if it meant that we ourselves would go down in defeat."

The other thanes snorted or grumbled.

"You should have been a Knight of Solamnia!" one muttered, a statement not intended as a compliment.

Duncan cast them all a stern glance, and they fell into a sulking silence.

"Kharas," Duncan said patiently, "we know how you feel about honor, and we applaud you for that. But honor will not feed the children of those who may die in this battle, nor will it keep our kinsmen from picking clean our bones if we ourselves fall. No," Duncan continued, his voice growing stern and deep, "there is a time for honor and a time when one

must do what he must."† Once again, he rubbed his jaw. "You yourself showed me that."

Kharas's face grew grim. Absent-mindedly raising a hand to stroke the flowing beard that was no longer there, he dropped his hand uncomfortably and, flushing, stared down at his feet.

"Our scouts have verified this report," Duncan continued. "The army has marched."

Kharas looked up, scowling. "l don't believe it!" he said. "I didn't believe it when I heard it! They have left Pax Tharkas? Before their supply wagons got through? It must be true then, the wizard must be in charge. No general would make that mistake—"

"They will be on the Plains within the next two days. Their objective is, according to our spies, the fortress of Zhaman, where they plan to set up headquarters. We have a small garrison there that will make a token defense and then retreat, hopefully drawing them out into the open."

"Zhaman," Kharas muttered, scratching his jaw since he could no longer tug at his beard. Abruptly, he took a step forward, his face now eager. "Thane, if I can present a plan that will end this war with a minimum of bloodshed, will you listen to it and allow me to try?"

"I'll listen," said Duncan dubiously, his face setting into rigid lines.

"Give me a hand-picked squadron of men, Thane, and I will undertake to kill this wizard, this Fistandantilus. When he is dead, I will show this scroll to his general and to our kinsmen. They will see that they have been betrayed. They will see the might of our army lined up against them. They must surely surrender!"

"And what are we to do with them if they *do* surrender?" Duncan snapped irritably, though he was going over the plan in his mind even as he spoke. The other thanes had ceased muttering into their beards and were looking at each other, heavy brows knotting over their eyes.

"Give them Pax Tharkas, Thane," Kharas said, his eagerness growing. "Those who want to live there, of course. Our kinsmen will, undoubtedly, return to their homes. We could make a few concessions to them—very few," he added hastily, seeing Duncan's face darken. "That would be arranged with the

surrender terms. But there would be shelter and protection for the humans and our kinsmen during the winter—they could work in the mines. . . ."

"The plan has possibilities," Duncan muttered thoughtfully. "Once you're in the desert, you could hide in the Mounds—"

He fell silent, pondering. Then he slowly shook his head. "But it is a dangerous course, Kharas. And all may be for nought. Even if you succeed in killing the Dark One—and I remind you that he is said to be a wizard of great power—there is every possibility you will be killed before you can talk to this General Majere. Rumor has it he is the wizard's twin brother!"

Kharas smiled wearily, his hand still on his smooth-shaven jaw. "That is a risk I will take gladly, Thane, if means that no more of my kinsmen will die at my hands."

Duncan glared at him, then, rubbing his swollen jaw, he heaved a sigh. "Very well," he said. "You have our leave. Choose your men with care. When will you go?"

"Tonight, Thane, with your permission."

"The gates of the mountain will open to you, then they will close. Whether they open again to admit you victorious or to disgorge the armed might of the mountain dwarves will be dependent upon you, Kharas. May Reorx's flame shine on your hammer."

Bowing, Kharas turned and walked from the hall, his step swifter and more vigorous than it had been when he arrived.

"There goes one we can ill afford to lose," said one of the thanes, his eyes on the retreating figure of the tall, beardless dwarf.

"He was lost to us from the beginning," Duncan snapped harshly. But his face was haggard and lined with grief as he muttered, "Now, we must plan for war."

*The reader will note that in Chronicles we wrote titles for every chapter but did not do so in Legends. The main reason the chapter titles were discontinued was that we discovered it sometimes took more time to write the titles than it did the chapter, because we had to make them intriguing yet be careful not to give anything away.
—MW*

"No water again," Caramon said quietly.

Reghar scowled. Though the general's voice was carefully expressionless, the dwarf knew that he was being held accountable. Realizing that he was, in large part, to blame, didn't help matters. The only feeling more wretched and unbearable than guilt is the feeling of well-deserved guilt.

"There'll be another water hole within half a day's march," Reghar growled, his face setting into granite. "They were all over the place in the old days, like pock marks."

The dwarf waved an arm. Caramon glanced around. As far as the eye could see there was nothing—not tree, not bird, not even scrubby bushes. Nothing but endless miles of sand, dotted here and there with strange, domed mounds. Far off in the distance, the dark shadows of the mountains of Thorbardin

hovered before his eyes like the lingering remembrance of a bad dream.

The Army of Fistandantilus was losing before the battle even started.

After days of forced marching, they had finally come out of the mountain pass from Pax Tharkas and were now upon the Plains of Dergoth. Their supplies had not caught up with them and, because of the rapid pace at which they were moving, it looked as if it might be more than a week before the lumbering wagons found them.

Raistlin pressed the need for haste upon the commanders of the armies and, though Caramon opposed his brother openly, Reghar supported the archmage and managed to sway the Plainsmen to their side as well. Once again, Caramon had little choice but to go along. And so the army rose before dawn, marched with only a brief rest at midday, and continued until twilight when they stopped to make camp while there was still light enough to see.

It did not seem like an army of victors. Gone were the comradeship, the jokes, the laughter, the games of evening. Gone was the singing by day; even the dwarves ceased their stirring chant, preferring to keep their breath for breathing as they marched mile after weary mile. At night, the men slumped down practically where they stood, ate their meager rations, and then fell immediately into exhausted sleep until kicked and prodded by the sergeants to begin another day.

Spirits were low. There were grumblings and complaints, especially as the food dwindled. This had not been a problem in the mountains. Game had been plentiful. But once on the Plains, as Caramon had foretold, the only living things they saw were each other. They lived on hard-baked, unleavened bread and strips of dried meat rationed out twice per day—morning and night. And Caramon knew that if the supply wagons didn't catch up with them soon, even this small amount would be cut in half.

But the general had other concerns besides food, both of which were more critical. One was a lack of fresh water. Though Reghar had told him confidently that there were water holes in the Plains, the first two they discovered were dry. Then—and only then—had the old dwarf dourly admitted that the

last time he'd set eyes on these Plains was in the days before the Cataclysm. Caramon's other problem was the rapidly deteriorating relationships between the allies.

Always threadbare at best, the alliance was now splitting apart at the seams. The humans from the north blamed their current problems on the dwarves and the Plainsmen since they had supported the wizard.

The Plainsmen, for their part, had never been in the mountains before. They discovered that fighting and living in mountainous terrain was cold and snowy and, as the chief put it crudely to Caramon, "it is either too *up* or too *down*."

Now, seeing the gigantic mountains of Thorbardin looming on the southern horizon, the Plainsmen were beginning to think that all the gold and steel in the world wasn't as beautiful as the golden, *flat* grasslands of their home. More than once Caramon saw their dark eyes turn northward, and he knew that one morning he would awaken and find they had gone.

The dwarves, for their part, viewed the humans as cowardly weaklings who ran crying home to mama the minute things got a little tough. Thus they treated the lack of food and water as a petty annoyance. The dwarf who even dared *hint* he was thirsty was immediately set upon by his fellows.

Caramon thought of this and he thought of his numerous other problems as he stood in the middle of the desert that evening, kicking at the sand with the toe of his boot.

Then, raising his eyes, Caramon's gaze rested on Reghar. Thinking Caramon was not watching him, the old dwarf lost his rocky sternness—his shoulders slumped, and he sighed wearily. His resemblance to Flint was painful in its intensity. Ashamed of his anger, knowing it was directed more at himself than anyone else, Caramon did what he could to make amends.

"Don't worry. We've enough water to last the night. Surely we'll come on a water hole tomorrow, don't you think?" he said, patting Reghar clumsily on the back. The old dwarf glanced up at Caramon, startled and instantly suspicious, fearing he might be the butt of some joke.

But, seeing Caramon's tired face smiling at him cheerfully, Reghar relaxed. "Aye," the dwarf said with a grudging smile in return. "Tomorrow for sure."

Turning from the dry water hole, the two made their way back to camp.

Night came early to the Plains of Dergoth. The sun dropped behind the mountains rapidly, as though sick of the sight of the vast, barren desert wasteland. Few campfires glowed; most of the men were too tired to bother lighting them, and there wasn't any food to cook anyway. Huddling together in their separate groups, the hill dwarves, the northerners, and the Plainsmen regarded each other suspiciously. Everyone, of course, shunned the Dewar.

Caramon, glancing up, saw his own tent, sitting apart from them all, as though he had simply written them off.

An old Krynnish legend told of a man who had once committed a deed so heinous that the gods themselves gathered to inflict his punishment. When they announced that, henceforth, the man was to have the ability to see into the future, the man laughed, thinking he had outwitted the gods. The man had, however, died a tortured death—something Caramon had never been able to understand.

But now he understood, and his soul ached. Truly, no greater punishment could be inflicted upon any mortal. For, by seeing into the future and knowing what the outcome will be, man's greatest gift—hope—is taken away.

Up until now, Caramon had hoped. He had believed Raistlin would come up with a plan. He had believed his brother wouldn't let this happen. Raistlin *couldn't* let this happen. But now, knowing that Raistlin truly didn't care what became of these men and dwarves and the families they had left behind, Caramon's hope died. They were doomed. There was nothing he could do to prevent what had happened before from happening again.

Knowing this and knowing the pain that this must inevitably cost him, Caramon began to unconsciously distance himself from those he had come to care about. He began to think about home.

Home! Almost forgotten, even purposefully shoved to the back of his mind, memories of his

home now flooded over him with such vivid clarity—once he let them—that sometimes, in the long, lonely evenings, he stared into a fire he could not see for his tears.

It was the one thought that kept Caramon going. As he led his army closer and closer to their defeat, each step led him closer to Tika, closer to home. . . .

"Look out there!" Reghar grabbed hold of him, shaking him from his reverie. Caramon blinked and looked up just before he stumbled into one of the strange mounds that dotted the Plains.

"What are these confounded contrivances anyway?" Caramon grumbled, glaring at it. "Some type of animal dwelling? I've heard tell of squirrels without tails† who live in homes like these upon the great flatlands of Estwilde." He eyed the structure that was nearly three feet tall and just as wide, and shook his head. "But I'd hate to meet up with the squirrel who built this!"

"Bah! Squirrel indeed!" Reghar scoffed. "Dwarves built these! Can't you tell? Look at the workmanship." He ran his hand lovingly over the smooth-sided dome. "Since when did Nature do such a perfect job?"

Caramon snorted. "Dwarves! But—why? What for? Not even dwarves love work so much that they do it for their health! Why waste time building mounds in a desert?"

"Observation posts," Reghar said succinctly.

"Observation?" Caramon grinned. "What do they observe? Snakes?"

"The land, the sky, armies—like ours." Reghar stamped his foot, raising a cloud of dust. "Hear that?"

"Hear what?"

"That." Reghar stamped again. "Hollow."

Caramon's brow cleared. "Tunnels!" His eyes opened wide. Looking around the desert at mound after mound rising up out of the flatlands, he whistled softly.

"Miles of 'em!" Reghar said, nodding his head. "Built so long ago that they were old to my great-grandfather. Of course"—the dwarf sighed—"most of them haven't been used in that long either. Legend had it that there were once fortresses between here and Pax Tharkas, connecting up with the Kharolis Mountains. A dwarf could walk from Pax Tharkas

Sounds like groundhogs to me. —TRH

to Thorbardin without ever once seeing the sun, if the old tales be true.

"The fortresses are gone now. And many of the tunnels, in all likelihood. The Cataclysm wrecked most of 'em. Still," Reghar continued cheerfully, as he and Caramon resumed walking, "I wouldn't be surprised if Duncan hadn't a few spies down there, skulking about like rats."

"Above or below, they'll see us coming from a long way off," Caramon muttered, his gaze scanning the flat, empty land.

"Aye," Reghar said stoutly, "and much good it will do them."

Caramon did not answer, and the two kept going, the big man returning alone to his tent and the dwarf returning to the encampment of his people.

In one of the mounds, not far from Caramon's tent, eyes *were* watching the army, watching its every move. But those eyes weren't interested in the army itself. They were interested in three people, three people only. . . .

"Not long now," Kharas said. He was peering out through slits so cunningly carved into the rock that they allowed those in the mound to look out but prevented anyone looking at the outside of the mound from seeing in. "How far do you make the distance?"

This to a dwarf of ancient, scruffy appearance, who glanced out the slits once in a bored fashion, then glanced down the length of the tunnel. "Two hundred, fifty-three steps. Bring you smack up in the center," he said without hesitation.

Kharas looked back out onto the Plains to where the general's large tent sat apart from the campfires of his men. It seemed marvelous to Kharas that the old dwarf could judge the distance so accurately. The hero might have expressed doubts, had it been anyone but Smasher. But the elderly thief who had been brought out of retirement expressly for this mission had too great a reputation for performing remarkable feats—a reputation that almost equaled Kharas's own.

"The sun is setting," Kharas reported, rather unnecessarily since the lengthening shadows could be seen slanting against the rock walls of the tunnel behind him. "The general returns. He is entering his tent." Kharas frowned. "By Reorx's beard, I hope he doesn't decide to change his habits tonight."

"He won't," Smasher said. Crouched comfortably in a corner, he spoke with the calm certainty of one who had (in former days) earned a living by watching† the comings and—more particularly—the goings of his fellows. "First two things you learn when yer breakin' house—everyone has a routine and no one likes change.† Weather's fine, there've been no startlements, nothin' out there 'cept sand an' more sand. No, he won't change."

Kharas frowned, not liking this reminder of the dwarf's lawless past. Well aware of his own limitations, Kharas had chosen Smasher for this mission because they needed someone skilled in stealth, skilled in moving swiftly and silently, skilled in attacking by night, and escaping into the darkness.

But Kharas, who had been admired by the Knights of Solamnia for his honor, suffered pangs of conscience nonetheless. He soothed his soul by reminding himself that Smasher had, long ago, paid for his misdeeds and had even performed several services for his king that made him, if not a completely reputable character, at least a minor hero.

Besides, Kharas said to himself, think of the lives we will save.

Even as he thought this, he breathed a sigh of relief. "You are right, Smasher. Here comes the wizard from his tent and here comes the witch from hers."

Grasping the handle of his hammer strapped securely to his belt with one hand, Kharas used the other hand to shift a shortsword he had tucked into his belt into a slightly more comfortable position. Finally, he reached into a pouch, drew out a piece of rolled parchment, and with a thoughtful, solemn expression on his beardless face, tucked it into a safe pocket in his leather armor.

Turning to the four dwarves who stood behind him, he said, "Remember, do not harm the woman or the general any more than is necessary to subdue them. But—the wizard must die, and he must die quickly, for he is the most dangerous."

Smasher grinned and settled back more comfortably. He would not be going along. Too old. That would have insulted him once, but he was of an age

Dwarves, it appears, are noisy by nature. This requires that they use a good deal more planning when attempting stealth. —TRH

We had made the acquaintance of an FBI agent, who frequently came to Gen Con, and he was our reference for the habits of criminals. —MW

now where it came as a compliment. Besides, his knees creaked alarmingly.

"Let them settle in," the old thief advised. "Let them start their evening meal, relax. Then"—drawing his hand across his throat, he chortled—"two hundred and fifty-three steps. . . ."

Standing guard duty outside the general's tent, Garic listened to the silence within. It was more disturbing and seemed to echo louder than the most violent quarrel.

Glancing inside through the tent flap opening, he saw the three sitting together as they did every night, quiet, muttering only occasionally, each one apparently wrapped in his or her own concerns.

The wizard was deeply involved in his studies. Rumor had it that he was planning some great, powerful spells that would blow the gates of Thorbardin wide open. As for the witch, who knew what she was thinking? Garic was thankful, at least, that Caramon was keeping an eye on her.

There had been some weird rumors about the witch among the men. Rumors of miracles performed at Pax Tharkas, of the dead returning to life at her touch, of limbs growing back onto bloody stumps. Garic discounted these, of course. Still, there was something about her these days that made the young man wonder if his first impressions had been correct.

Garic shifted restlessly in the cold wind that swept over the desert. Of the three in the tent, he worried most about his general. Over the past months, the young knight had come to revere and idolize Caramon. Observing him closely, trying to be as much like him as possible, Garic noticed Caramon's obvious depression and unhappiness which the big man thought he was doing quite well at hiding. For Garic, Caramon had taken the place of the family he had lost, and now the young Knight brooded over Caramon's sorrow as he would have brooded about an older brother.

"It's those blasted dark dwarves," Garic muttered out loud, stomping his feet to keep them from going numb. "I don't trust 'em, that's for certain. I'd send them packing, and I'll bet the general would, too, if it weren't for his bro—"

Garic stopped, holding his breath, listening. Nothing. But he could have sworn. . . .

Hand on the hilt of his sword, the young Knight stared out into the desert. Though hot by day, it was a cold and forbidding place at night. Off in the distance, he saw the campfires. Here and there, he could see the shadows of men passing by.

Then he heard it again. A sound behind him. Directly behind him. The sound of heavy, iron-shod boots. . . .

"What was that?" Caramon asked, lifting his head.

"The wind," Crysania muttered, glancing at the tent and shivering, watching as the fabric rippled and breathed like a living thing. "It blows incessantly in this horrid place."

Caramon half-rose, hand on his sword hilt. "It wasn't the wind."

Raistlin glanced up at his brother. "Oh, sit down!" he snarled softly in irritation, "and finish your dinner so that we can end this. I must return to my studies."

The archmage was going over a particularly difficult spell chant in his mind. He had been wrestling with it for days, trying to discover the correct voice inflection and pronunciation needed to unlock the secrets of the words.† So far, they had eluded his grasp and made little sense.

Shoving his still-full plate aside, Raistlin started to stand—

—when the world literally gave way beneath his feet.

As though he were on the deck of a ship sliding down a steep wave, the sandy ground canted away from under foot. Staring down in amazement, the archmage saw a vast hole opening up before him. One of the poles that held up the tent slipped and toppled into it, causing the tent to sag. A lantern hanging from the supports swung wildly, shadows pitching and leaping around like demons.

Instinctively, Raistlin caught hold of the table and managed to save himself from falling into the rapidly widening hole. But, even as he did so, he saw figures crawling up through the hole—squat, bearded figures. For an instant, the wildly dancing light flashed off steel blades, shone in dark, grim eyes. Then the figures were plunged in shadows.

In AD&D, magic-users cast spells by reciting the words, using various components, and making all the proper hand motions. I often wondered: if that's all there is to it, why couldn't a 2nd level magic-user simply get the 12th level magic-user's spellbook and cast all his spells? Here, we find out why. Magic is an art, a science, and the more advanced the spells, the more difficult the casting.

"Caramon!" Raistlin shouted, but he could tell by the sounds behind him—a vicious oath and the rattle of a steel sword sliding from its scabbard—that Caramon was well aware of the danger.

Raistlin heard, too, a strong, feminine voice calling on the name of Paladine, and saw the glimmering outline of pure, white light, but he had no time to worry about Crysania. A huge dwarven warhammer, seemingly wielded by the darkness itself, flashed in the lantern light, aiming right at the mage's head.

Speaking the first spell that came to his mind, Raistlin saw with satisfaction an invisible force pluck the hammer from the dwarf's hand. By his command, the magical force carried the hammer through the darkness to drop it with a thud in the corner of the tent.

At first numbed by the unexpectedness of the attack, Raistlin's mind was now active and working. Once the initial shock had passed, the mage saw this as simply another irritating interruption to his studies. Planning to end it quickly, the archmage turned his attention to his enemy, who stood before him, regarding him with eyes that were unafraid.

Feeling no fear himself, calm in the knowledge that nothing could kill him since he was protected by time,† Raistlin called upon his magic in cool, unhurried fashion.

He felt it coiling and gathering within his body, felt the ecstasy course through him with a sensual pleasure. This would be a pleasant diversion from his studies, he decided. An interesting exercise . . . Stretching out his hands, he began to pronounce the words that would send bolts of blue lightning sizzling through his enemy's writhing body. Then he was interrupted.

With the suddenness of a thunder clap, two figures appeared before him, leaping out of the darkness at him as though they had dropped from a star.

Tumbling at the mage's feet, one of the figures stared up at him in wild excitement.

"Oh, look! It's Raistlin! We made it, Gnimsh! We made it! Hey, Raistlin! Bet you're surprised to see me, huh? And, oh, have I got the most wonderful story to tell you! You see, I was dead. Well, I wasn't actually, but—"

"Tasslehoff!" Raistlin gasped.

Raistlin believes that he is protected because the history that he knows tells him that he will survive. However . . . (see next page)

Thoughts sizzled in Raistlin's mind as the lightning might have sizzled from his fingertips.

The first—a kender! Time could be altered!

The second—Time *can* be altered. . . .

The third—I can die!†

. . . the kender has changed all that. Raistlin is very much in danger here. —TRH

The shock of these thoughts jolted through Raistlin's body, burning away the coolness and calmness so necessary to the magic-user for casting his complex spells.

As both the unlooked-for solution to his problem and the frightful realization of what it might cost him penetrated his brain, Raistlin lost control. The words of the spell slipped from his mind. But his enemy still advanced.

Reacting instinctively, his hand shaking, Raistlin jerked his wrist, bringing into his palm the small silver dagger he carried with him.

But it was too late . . . and too little.

CHAPTER 9

haras's concentration was completely centered on the man he had vowed to kill. Reacting with the trained single-mindedness of the military mindset, he paid no attention to the startling appearance of the two apparitions, thinking them, perhaps, nothing more than beings conjured up by the archmage.

Kharas saw, at the same time, the wizard's glittering eyes go blank. He saw Raistlin's mouth—opened to recite deadly words—hang flaccid and loose, and the dwarf knew that for a few seconds at least, his enemy was at his mercy.

Lunging forward, Kharas drove his shortsword through the black, flowing robes and had the satisfaction of feeling it hit home.

Closing with the stricken mage, he drove the blade deeper and deeper into the human's slender body. The man's strange, burning heat enveloped him like

a blazing inferno. A hatred and an anger so intense struck Kharas a physical blow, knocking him backward and slamming him into the ground.

But the wizard was wounded—mortally. That much Kharas knew. Staring up from where he lay, looking into those searing, baleful eyes, Kharas saw them burn with fury, but he saw them fill with pain as well. And he saw—by the leaping, swaying light of the lantern—the hilt of his shortsword sticking out of the mage's gut. He saw the wizard's slender hands curl around it, he heard him scream in terrible agony. He knew he had no reason to fear. The wizard could harm him no longer.

Stumbling to his feet, Kharas reached out his hand and jerked the sword free. Crying out in bitter anguish, his hands deluged in his own blood, the wizard pitched forward onto the ground and lay still.

Kharas had time to look around then. His men were fighting a pitched battle with the general who, hearing his brother scream, was livid with fear and anger. The witch was nowhere to be seen, the eerie white light that had shone from her was gone, lost in the darkness.

Hearing a strangled sound from his left, Kharas turned to see the two apparitions the archmage had summoned staring down in stunned horror at the wizard's body. Getting a good look at them, Kharas was startled to see that these demons conjured from the nether planes were nothing more sinister than a kender in bright blue leggings and a balding gnome in a leather apron.

Kharas didn't have time to ponder this phenomenon. He had accomplished what he came for, at least he had almost. He knew he could never talk to the general, not now. His main concern was getting his men out safely. Running across the tent, Kharas picked up his warhammer and, yelling to his men in dwarven to get out of his way, flung it straight at Caramon.

The hammer struck the man a glancing blow on the head, knocking him out but not killing him. Caramon dropped like a felled ox and, suddenly, the tent was deathly silent.

It had all taken just a few short minutes.

Glancing through the tent flap, Kharas saw the young Knight who stood guard lying senseless upon

the ground. There was no sign that anyone sitting around those far-off fires had heard or seen anything unusual.

Reaching up, the dwarf stopped the lantern from swinging and looked around. The wizard lay in a pool of his own blood. The general lay near him, his hand reaching out for his brother as though that had been his last thought before he lost consciousness. In a corner lay the witch, on her back, her eyes closed.

Seeing blood on her robes, Kharas glared sternly at his men. One of them shook his head.

"I'm sorry, Kharas," the dwarf said, looking down at her and shivering. "But—the light from her was so bright! It split my head open. All I could think of was to stop it. I—I wouldn't have been able to, but then the wizard screamed and she cried out, and her light wavered. I hit her, then, but not very hard. She's not hurt badly."

"All right." Kharas nodded. "Let's go." Retrieving his hammer, the dwarf looked down at the general lying at his feet. "I'm sorry," he said, fishing out the little bit of parchment and tucking it into the man's outstretched hand. "Maybe, sometime, I can explain it to you." Rising, he looked around. "Everyone all right? Then let's get out of here."

His men hurried to the tunnel entrance.

"What about these two?" one asked, stopping by the kender and the gnome.

"Take them," Kharas said sharply. "We can't leave them here, they'll raise the alarm."

For the first time, the kender seemed to come to life.

"No!" he cried, looking at Kharas with pleading, horrified eyes. "You can't take us! We just got here! We've found Caramon and now we can go home! No, please!"

"Take them!" Kharas ordered sternly.

"No!" the kender wailed, struggling in his captor's arms. "No, please, you don't understand. We were in the Abyss and we escaped—"

"Gag him," Kharas growled, peering down into the tunnel beneath the tent to see that all was well. Motioning for them to hurry, he knelt beside the hole in the ground.

His men descended into the tunnel, dragging the gagged kender, who was still putting up such a

fight—kicking with his legs and clawing at them—
that they were finally forced to stop and truss him
up like a chicken before they could haul him away.
They had nothing to worry about with their other
captive, however. The poor gnome was so horrified
that he had lapsed into a state of shock. Staring around
helplessly, his mouth gaping wide open, he quietly
did whatever he was told.

Kharas was the last to leave. Before jumping
down into the tunnel, he took a final glance about
the tent.

The lantern hung quite still now, shedding its soft,
glowing light upon a scene from a nightmare. Tables
were smashed, chairs were overturned, food was
scattered everywhere. A thin trail of blood ran from
beneath the body of the black-robed magic-user.
Forming a pool at the lip of the hole, the blood began
to drip, slowly, down into the tunnel.

Leaping into the hole, Kharas ran a safe distance
down the tunnel, then stopped. Grabbing up the end
of a length of rope lying on the tunnel floor, he gave
the rope a sharp yank. The opposite end of the rope
was tied to one of the support beams right beneath
the general's tent. The jerk on the rope brought the
beam tumbling down. There was a low rumble. Then,
in the distance, he could see stone falling, and his
vision was obscured by a thick cloud of dust.

The tunnel now safely blocked behind him, Kharas
turned and hurried after his men.

"General—"

Caramon was on his feet, his big hands reaching
out for the throat of his enemy, a snarl contorting
his face.

Startled, Garic stumbled backward.

"General!" he cried. "Caramon! It's me!"

Sudden, stabbing pain and the sound of Garic's
familiar voice penetrated Caramon's brain. With a
moan, he clasped his head in his hands and staggered. Garic caught him as he fell, lowering him
safely into a chair.

"My brother?" Caramon said thickly.

"Caramon—I—" Garic swallowed.

"My brother!" Caramon rasped, clenching his fist.

"We took him to his tent," Garic replied softly.
"The wound is—"

"What? The wound is what?" Caramon snarled impatiently, raising his head and staring at Garic with blood-shot, pain-filled eyes.

Garic opened his mouth, closed it, then shook his head. "M-my father told me about wounds like it," he mumbled. "Men lingering for days in dreadful agony. . . ."

"You mean it's a belly wound," Caramon said.

Garic nodded and then covered his face with his hand. Caramon, looking at him closely, saw that the young man was deathly white. Sighing, closing his eyes, Caramon braced himself for the dizziness and nausea he knew would assail him when he stood up again. Then, grimly, he rose to his feet. The darkness whirled and heaved around him. He made himself stand steadily and, when it had settled, opened his eyes.

"How are you?" he asked Garic, looking intently at the young Knight.

"I'm all right," Garic answered, and his face flushed with shame. "Th-they took me . . . from behind."

"Yeah." Caramon saw the matted blood in the young man's hair. "It happens. Don't worry about it." The big warrior smiled without mirth. "They took me from the front."

Garic nodded again, but it was obvious from the expression on his face that this defeat preyed on his mind.

He'll go over it, Caramon thought wearily. We all have to face it sooner or later.

"I'll see my brother now," he said, starting out of the tent with uneven steps. Then he stopped. "Lady Crysania?"

"Asleep. Knife wound glanced off her . . . uh . . . ribs. I—We dressed it . . . as well as we could. We had to . . . rip open her robes." Garic's flush deepened. "And we gave her some brandy to drink. . . ."

"Does she know about Raist—Fistandantilus?"

"The wizard forbade it."

Caramon raised his eyebrows, then frowned. Glancing around at the wrecked tent, he saw the trail of blood on the trampled dirt floor. Drawing a deep breath, he opened the tent flap and walked unsteadily outside, Garic following.

"The army?"

"They know. The word spread." Garic spread his hands helplessly. "There was so much to do. We tried to go after the dwarves—"

"Bah!" Caramon snorted, wincing as pain shot through his head. "They would have collapsed the tunnel."

"Yes. We tried digging, but you might as well dig up the whole damn desert," Garic said bitterly.

"What about the army?" Caramon persisted, pausing outside Raistlin's tent. Inside, he could hear a low moaning sound.

"The men are upset," Garic said with a sigh. "Talking, confused. I don't know."

Caramon understood. He glanced into the darkness of his brother's tent. "I'll go in alone. Thank you for all you've done, Garic," he added gently. "Now, go get some rest before you pass out. I'm going to need you later on, and you'll be no help to me sick."

"Yes, sir," Garic said. He started to stagger off, then stopped, turning back. Reaching beneath the breastplate of his armor, he withdrew a blood-soaked bit of parchment. "We—we found this . . . in your hand, sir. The handwriting's dwarven. . . ."

Caramon looked at it, opened it, read it, then rolled it back up without comment, tucking it into his belt.

Guards surrounded the tents now. Gesturing to one, Caramon waited until he saw Garic being helped to his bed. Then, bracing himself, he stepped into Raistlin's tent.

A candle burned on a table, near a spellbook that had been left open—the archmage had obviously been expecting to return to his studies soon after dinner. A middle-aged, battle-scarred dwarf—Caramon recognized him as one of Reghar's staff—crouched in the shadows near the bed. A guard beside the entrance saluted when Caramon entered.

"Wait outside," Caramon ordered, and the guard left.

"He won't let us touch 'im," the dwarf said laconically, nodding toward Raistlin. "Wound's gotta be dressed. Won't help much, of course. But it might hold some of 'im inside for a bit."

"I'll tend to him," Caramon said harshly.

Hands on his knees, the dwarf shoved himself up. Hesitating, he cleared his throat as if wondering

whether or not to speak. Decision made, he squinted up at Caramon with shrewd, bright eyes.

"Reghar said I was to tell you. If you want me to do it . . . you know—end it quick, I've done it afore. Sort of a knack I've got. I'm a butcher by trade, you see—"

"Get out."

The dwarf shrugged. "As you say. Up to you. If it was my brother, though—"

"Get out!" Caramon repeated softly. He did not look at the dwarf as he left, nor even hear the sounds of his heavy boots. All his senses were concentrated on his twin.

Raistlin lay on his bed, still dressed, his hands clenched over the horrible wound. Stained black with blood, the mage's robes and flesh were gummed together in a ghastly mass. And he was in agony. Rolling involuntarily back and forth upon the bed, every breath the mage exhaled was a low, incoherent moan of pain. Every breath he drew in was bubbling torture.

But to Caramon, the most awful sight of all was his brother's glittering eyes, staring at him, aware of him, as he moved nearer the bed. Raistlin was conscious.

Kneeling down beside his brother's bed, Caramon laid a hand upon his twin's feverish head. "Why didn't you let them send for Crysania?" he asked softly.

Raistlin grimaced. Gritting his teeth, he forced the words out through blood-stained lips. "Paladine . . . will . . . not . . . heal . . . me!" The last was a gasp, ending in a strangled scream.

Caramon stared at him, confused. "But—you're dying! You *can't* die! You said—"

Raistlin's eyes rolled, his head tossed. Blood trickled from his mouth. "Time . . . altered. . . . All . . . changed!"

"But—"

"Leave me! Let me die!" Raistlin shrieked in anger and pain, his body writhing.

Caramon shuddered. He tried to look upon his brother with pity, but the face, gaunt and twisted in suffering, was not a face he knew.

The mask of wisdom and intelligence had been stripped away, revealing the splintered lines of pride, ambition, avarice, and unfeeling cruelty beneath. It

was as if Caramon, seeing a face he had known always, were seeing his twin for the first time.

Perhaps, Caramon thought, Dalamar saw this face in the Tower of High Sorcery as Raistlin burned holes in his flesh with his bare hands. Perhaps Fistandantilus, too, saw the face as he died. . . .

Repulsed, his very soul shaken with horror, Caramon tore his gaze from that hideous, skull-like visage and, hardening his own expression, reached out his hand. "At least let me dress the wound."

Raistlin shook his head vehemently. A blood-covered hand wrenched itself free from holding his very life inside him to clutch at Caramon's arm. "No! End it! I have failed. The gods are laughing. I can't . . . bear . . ."

Caramon stared at him. Suddenly, irrationally, anger took hold of the big man—anger that rose from years of sarcastic gibes and thankless servitude. Anger that had seen friends die because of this man. Anger that had seen himself nearly destroyed. Anger that had seen love devoured, love denied. Reaching out his hand, Caramon grasped hold of the black robes and jerked his brother's head up off the pillow.

"No, by the gods," Caramon shouted with a voice that literally shook with rage. "No, you will not die! Do you hear me?" His eyes narrowed. "You will not die, *my brother*! All your life, you have lived only for yourself. Now, even in your death, you seek the easy way out—for you! You'd leave me trapped here without a second's thought. You'd leave Crysania! No, brother! You *will* live, damn you! You'll live to send me back home. What you do with yourself after that is your concern."

Raistlin looked at Caramon and, despite his pain, a gruesome parody of a smile touched his lips. It almost seemed he might have laughed, but a bubble of blood burst in his mouth instead. Caramon loosened his hold of his brother's robes, almost but not quite, hurling him backward. Raistlin collapsed back upon the pillow. His burning eyes devoured Caramon. At that moment the only life in them was bitter hatred and rage.

"I'm going to tell Crysania," Caramon said grimly, rising to his feet, ignoring Raistlin's glare of fury. "At least she must have the chance to try to heal you.

Yes, if looks could kill, I know I'd be dead right now. But, listen to me, Raistlin or Fistandantilus or whoever you are—if it is Paladine's will that you die before you can commit greater harm in this world, then so be it. I'll accept that fate and so will Crysania. But if it is his will that you live, we'll accept that, too—and so will you!"

Raistlin, his strength nearly spent, kept hold of his bloody clasp around Caramon's arm, clutching at him with fingers already seeming to stiffen in death.

Firmly, his lips pressed together, Caramon detached his brother's hand. Rising to his feet, he left his brother's bedside hearing, behind him, a ragged moan of agonized torment. Caramon hesitated, that moan going straight to his heart. Then he thought of Tika, he thought of home. . . .

Caramon kept walking. Stepping outside into the night, heading quickly for Crysania's tent, the big warrior glanced to one side and saw the dwarf, standing nonchalantly in the shadows, whittling a piece of wood with a sharp knife.

Reaching into his armor, Caramon withdrew the piece of parchment. He had no need to reread it. The words were few and simple.

The wizard has betrayed you and the army. Send a messenger to Thorbardin to learn the truth.

Caramon tossed the parchment upon the ground.

What a cruel joke!

What a cruel and twisted joke!

Through the hideous torment of his pain, Raistlin could hear the laughter of the gods. To offer him salvation with one hand and snatch it away with the other! How they must revel in his defeat!

Raistlin's tortured body twisted in spasms and so did his soul, writhing in impotent rage, burning with the knowledge that he had failed.

Weak and puny human! he heard the voices of the gods shout. Thus do we remind you of your mortality!

He would not face Paladine's triumph. To see the god sneering at him, glorying in his downfall—no! Better to die swiftly, let his soul seek what dark refuge it could find. But that bastard brother of his, that other half of him, the half he envied and despised, the half he should have been—by rights. To deny him this . . . this last blessed solace. . . .

Pain convulsed his body. "Caramon!" Raistlin cried alone into the darkness. "Caramon, I need you! Caramon, don't leave me!" He sobbed, clutching his stomach, curling up in a tight ball. "Don't leave me . . . to face this . . . alone!"

And then his mind lost the thread of its consciousness. Visions came to the mage as his life spilled out from between his fingers. Dark dragon wings, a broken dragon orb . . . Tasslehoff . . . a gnome . . .

My salvation . . .

My death . . .

Bright, white light, pure and cold and sharp as a sword, pierced the mage's mind. Cringing, he tried to escape, tried to submerge himself in warm and soothing darkness. He could hear himself begging with Caramon to kill him and end the pain, end the bright and stabbing light.

Raistlin heard himself say those words, but he had no knowledge of himself speaking. He knew he spoke only because, in the reflection of the bright, pure light, he saw his brother turn away from him.

The light shone more brightly and it became a face of light, a beautiful, calm, pure face with dark, cool, gray eyes. Cold hands touched his burning skin.

"Let me heal you."

The light hurt, worse than the pain of steel. Screaming, twisting, Raistlin tried to escape, but the hands held him firmly.

"Let me heal you."

"Get . . . away! . . ."†

"Let me heal you!"

Weariness, a vast weariness, came over Raistlin. He was tired of fighting—fighting the pain, fighting the ridicule, fighting the torment he'd lived with all his life.

Very well. Let the god laugh. He's earned it, after all, Raistlin thought bitterly. Let him refuse to heal me. And then I'll rest in the darkness. . . . the soothing darkness. . . .

Shutting his eyes, shutting them tightly against the light, Raistlin waited for the laughter—

—and saw,† suddenly, the face of the god.

Raistlin believes it would be weakness to be in debt to anyone—especially Paladine. —TRH

Raistlin gets to stare into the divine, but we are left to imagine the great, glorious, and terrible things he sees. Better for us to imagine it, for our imagination is more powerful than words here. —TRH

Caramon stood outside in the shadows of his brother's tent, his aching head in his hands. Raistlin's tortured pleas for death cut through him. Finally, he could stand it no longer. The cleric had obviously failed. Grasping the hilt of his sword, Caramon entered the tent and walked toward the bed.

At that moment, Raistlin's cries ceased.

Lady Crysania slumped forward over his body, her head falling onto the mage's chest.

He's dead! Caramon thought. Raistlin's dead.

Staring at his brother's face, he did not feel grief. Instead, he felt a kind of horror stealing over him at the sight, thinking, What a grotesque mask for death to wear!

Raistlin's face was rigid as a corpse's, his mouth gaped open, no sound came from it. The skin was livid. The sightless eyes, fixed in the sunken cheeks, stared straight before him.

Taking a step nearer, so numb he was unable to feel grief or sorrow or relief, Caramon looked closer at that strange expression on the dead man's face and then realized, with a riveting shock, that Raistlin was *not* dead! The wide, fixed eyes stared at this world sightlessly, but that was only because they were seeing another.

A whimpering cry shook the mage's body, more dreadful to hear than his screams of agony. His head moved slightly, his lips parted, his throat worked but made no sound.

And then Raistlin's eyes closed. His head lolled to one side, the writhing muscles relaxed. The look of pain faded, leaving his face drawn, pallid. He drew a deep breath, let it out with a sigh, drew another. . . .

Jolted by what he had seen, uncertain whether he should feel thankful or only more deeply grieved to know his brother lived, Caramon watched life return to his twin's torn and bleeding body.

Slowly shaking off the paralyzed feeling that comes sometimes to one awakened suddenly from a deep sleep, Caramon knelt beside Crysania and, grasping her gently, helped her stand. She stared at him, blinking, without recognition. Then her gaze shifted immediately to Raistlin. A smile crossed her face. Closing her eyes, she murmured a prayer of thankfulness. Then, pressing her hand to her side,

she sagged against Caramon. There was fresh blood visible on her white robes.

"You should heal yourself," Caramon said, helping her from the tent, his strong arm supporting her faltering footsteps.

She looked up at him and, though weak, her face was beautiful in its calm triumph.

"Perhaps tomorrow," she answered softly. "This night, a greater victory is mine. Don't you see? This is the answer to my prayers."

Looking at her peaceful, serene beauty, Caramon felt tears come to his eyes.

"So this is your answer?" he asked gruffly, glancing out over the camp. The fires had burned down to heaps of ash and coal. Out of the corner of his eye, Caramon saw someone go running off, and he knew that the news would be quickly spread that the wizard and the witch, between them, had somehow managed to restore the dead to life.

Caramon felt bile rise in his mouth. He could picture the talk, the excitement, the questions, the speculations, the dark looks and shaking heads, and his soul shrank from it. He wanted only to go to bed and sleep and forget everything.

But Crysania was talking. "This is your answer, too, Caramon," she said fervently. "This is the sign from the gods we have both sought." Stopping, she turned to face him, looking up at him earnestly. "Are you still as blind as you were in the Tower? Don't you yet believe? We placed the matter in Paladine's hands and the god has spoken. Raistlin was meant to live. He was meant to do this great deed. Together, he and I and you, if you will join us, will fight and overcome evil as I have fought and overcome death this night!"

Caramon stared at her. Then his head bowed, his shoulders slumped. I don't want to fight evil, he thought wearily. I just want to go home.† Is that too much to ask?

Lifting his hand, he began to rub his throbbing temple. And then he stopped, seeing in the slowly brightening light of dawn the marks of his brother's bloody fingers still upon his arm. "I'm posting a guard inside your tent," he said harshly. "Get some sleep. . . ."

He turned away.

One of the reasons I believe that Legends has had such a profound impact on people is that neither its heroes nor its villains follow the classic pattern. Caramon does not want to save the world from evil. He simply wants to go back home. Crysania is blinded by ambition and her own idealism. She does good but for the wrong reasons. Turning that around, the villain, Raistlin, commits evil acts, but for (sometimes) very good reasons. Thus this becomes a tale not of heroes but of humanity.
—MW

The classic Hero's Journey, as defined by Campbell, has the hero leaving the safety of his tribal home and entering the place of great mystery and power. After his adventures and growth in that realm, the hero returns home, himself changed. The longing for home has resonated through our adventure tales since Odysseus and beyond. —TRH

"Caramon," Crysania called.

"What?" He stopped with a sigh.

"You will feel better in the morning. I will pray for you tonight. Good night, my friend. Remember to thank Paladine for his grace in granting your brother his life."

"Yeah, sure," Caramon mumbled. Feeling uncomfortable, his headache growing worse, and knowing that he was soon going to be violently sick, he left Crysania and stumbled back to his tent.

Here, by himself, in the darkness, he was sick, retching in a corner until he no longer had anything left to bring up. Then, falling down upon his bed, he gave himself up at last to pain and to exhaustion.

But as the darkness closed mercifully over him, he remembered Crysania's words—"thank Paladine for your brother's life."

The memory of Raistlin's stricken face floated before Caramon, and the prayer stuck in his throat.

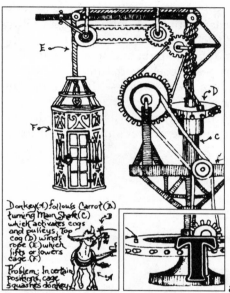

Donkey (A) follows Carrot (B) turning Main Shaft (C) which activates cogs and pulleys. Top cog (D) winds rope (E) which lifts or lowers cage. (F)

Problem: In certain positions, cage squashes donkey.

apping lightly on the guest stone that stood outside Duncan's dwelling, Kharas waited nervously for the answer. It came soon. The door opened, and there stood his king.

"Enter and welcome, Kharas," Duncan said, reaching out and pulling the dwarf.

Flushing in embarrassment, Kharas stepped inside his king's dwelling place. Smiling at him kindly, to put him at ease, Duncan led the way through his house to his private study.

Built far underground, in the heart of the mountain kingdom, Duncan's home was a complex maze of rooms and tunnels filled with the heavy, dark, solid wood furniture that dwarves admire. Though larger and roomier than most homes in Thorbardin, in all other respects Duncan's dwelling was almost exactly like the dwelling of every other dwarf. It

would have been considered the height of bad taste had it been otherwise. Just because Duncan was king didn't give him the right to put on airs.† So, though he kept a staff of servants, he answered his own door and served his guests with his own hands. A widower, he lived in the house with his two sons, who were still unmarried, both being young (only eighty or so).

This is a cultural contrast to the elves, who are far more formal in their caste system. —TRH

The study Kharas entered was obviously Duncan's favorite room. Battle-axes and shields decorated the walls, along with a fine assortment of captured hobgoblin swords with their curved blades, a minotaur trident won by some distant ancestor, and, of course, hammers and chisels and stone-working tools.

Duncan made his guest comfortable with true dwarvish hospitality, offering him the best chair, pouring out the ale, and stirring up the fire. Kharas had been here before, of course; many times, in fact. But now he felt uncomfortable and ill at ease, as though he had entered the house of a stranger. Perhaps it was because Duncan, though he treated his friend with his usual courtesy, occasionally regarded the beardless dwarf with an odd, penetrating gaze.

Noticing this unusual look in Duncan's eyes, Kharas found it impossible to relax and sat fidgeting in his chair, nervously wiping the foam from his mouth with the back of his hand while waiting for the formalities to end.

They did, quickly. Pouring himself a mug of ale, Duncan drained it at a sitting. Then, placing the mug on the table by his arm, he stroked his beard, staring at Kharas with a dark, somber expression.

"Kharas," he said finally, "you told us the wizard was dead."

"Yes, Thane," Kharas replied, startled. "It was a mortal blow I struck him. No man could have survived—"

"He did," Duncan replied shortly.

Kharas scowled. "Are you accusing me—"

Now it was Duncan who flushed. "No, my friend! Far be it. I am certain that, whatever may have happened, you truly believed you killed him." Duncan sighed heavily. "But our scouts report seeing him in camp. He was wounded, apparently. At least, he could no longer ride. The army moved on to

Zhaman, however, carrying the wizard with them in a cart."

"Thane!" Kharas protested, his face flushing in anger. "I swear to you! His blood washed over my hands! I yanked the sword from his body. By Reorx!" The dwarf shuddered. "I saw the death look in his eyes!"

"I don't doubt you, son!" Duncan said earnestly, reaching out to pat the young hero's shoulder. "I never heard of anyone surviving a wound such as you described—except in the old days, of course, when clerics still walked the land."

Like all other true clerics, dwarven clerics had also vanished right before the Cataclysm. Unlike other races on Krynn, the dwarves, however, never abandoned their belief in their ancient god,† Reorx, the Forger of the World. Although the dwarves were upset with Reorx for causing the Cataclysm, their belief in their god was too deeply ingrained and too much a part of their culture simply to toss out after one minor infraction on the god's part. Still, they were angered enough to no longer worship him openly.

"Have you any idea how this might have happened?" Duncan asked, frowning.

"No, Thane," Kharas said heavily. "But I did wonder why we hadn't received a reply from General Caramon." He pondered. "Has anyone questioned those two prisoners we brought back? They might know something."

"A kender and a gnome?" Duncan snorted. "Bah! What could either of those two possibly know?† Besides, there is no need to question them. I am not particularly interested in the wizard anyway. In fact, the reason I called you here to tell you this news, Kharas, was to insist that now you forget this talk of peace and concentrate on the war."

"There is more to those two than beards, Thane," Kharas muttered, quoting an old expression. It was obvious he hadn't heard a word. "I think you should—"

"I know what you think," Duncan said grimly. "Apparitions, conjured up by the wizard. And I tell you that's ridiculous! What self-respecting wizard would ever conjure up a kender? No, they're servants or something, most likely. It was dark and confused in there. You said so yourself."

The dwarves have a very pragmatic view of their religion, which I believe is based on the familial relationship with their god, Reorx. The dwarves know that families can have internal upheavals that take their toll, but they also know that the family is the bedrock of their society and should be respected. Thus I think the dwarves view Reorx as an eccentric, sometimes dotty, but always extremely powerful uncle, who has done something bad—and they're all furious with him—but they're not about to abandon him. —MW

It is the overlooked, humble, and small individuals that make a difference. Frodo and Samwise were insignificant and missed, despite the burden they carried. This kender and this gnome likewise. —TRH

"I'm not sure," Kharas replied, his voice soft. "If you had seen the mage's face when he looked at them! It was the face of one who walks the plains and suddenly sees a coffer of gold and jewels lying in the sand at his feet. Give me leave, Thane," Kharas said eagerly. "Let me bring them before you. Talk to them, that's all I ask!"

Duncan heaved a vast sigh, glaring at Kharas gloomily.

"Very well," he snapped. "I don't suppose it can hurt. But"—Duncan studied Kharas shrewdly—"if this proves to be nothing, will you promise me to give up this wild notion and concentrate on the business of war? It will be a hard fight, son," Duncan added more gently, seeing the look of true grief on his young hero's beardless face. "We need you, Kharas."

"Aye, Thane," Kharas said steadily. "I'll agree. If this proves to be nothing."

With a gruff nod, Duncan yelled for his guards and stumped out of the house, followed more slowly by a thoughtful Kharas.

Traversing the vast underground dwarven kingdom, winding down streets here and up streets there, crossing the Urkhan Sea† by boat, they eventually came to the first level of the dungeons. Here were held prisoners who had committed minor crimes and infractions—debtors, a young dwarf who had spoken disrespectfully to an elder, poachers, and several drunks, sleeping off overnight revels. Here, too, were held the kender and the gnome.

At least, they had been—last night.

"It all comes," said Tasslehoff Burrfoot as the dwarven guard prodded him along, "of not having a map."

"I thought you said you'd been here before," Gnimsh grumbled peevishly.

"Not *before*," Tas corrected. "*After*. Or maybe *later* would be a better word. About two hundred years later, as near as I can figure. It's quite a fascinating story, actually. I came here with some friends of mine. Let's see . . . that was right after Goldmoon and Riverwind were married† and before we went to Tarsis. Or was it after we went to Tarsis?"† Tas pondered. "No, it couldn't have been, because Tarsis was where the building fell on me† and—"

"When the Daewar explorer Urkhan stumbled upon the great network of caverns below Cloudseeker Peak, and gave his name to the great underground lake at its center, he knew that he had found a natural wonder unequalled anywhere else upon Krynn." [DWARVEN KINGDOMS OF KRYNN Boxed Set, A World in Stone, by Douglas Niles, TSR, Inc., 1993, p. 55]

Riverwind and Goldmoon were married in the very last chapter of Dragons of Autumn Twilight, *appropriately named "The Wedding."*

The Companions' adventures in Tarsis are found in Dragons of Winter Night.

Tas told this story to Flint in Dragons of Winter Night, Book II, Chapter 1.

"I'veheardthatstory!" Gnimsh snapped.

"What?" Tas blinked.

"I've . . . heard . . . it!" Gnimsh shouted loudly. His thin, gnomish voice echoed in the underground chamber, causing several passersby to glare at him sternly. Their faces grim, the dwarven guards hurried their recaptured prisoners along.

"Oh," Tas said, crestfallen. Then the kender cheered up. "But the king hasn't and we're being taken to see him. He'll probably be quite interested. . . ."

"You said we weren't supposed to say anything about coming from the future," Gnimsh said in a loud whisper, his long leather apron flapping about his feet. "We're supposed to act like we belong here, remember?"

"That was when I thought everything would go right," Tas said with a sigh. "And everything was going right. The device worked, we escaped from the Abyss—"

"They let us escape—" Gnimsh pointed out.

"Well, whatever," Tas said, irritated at the reminder. "Anyway, we *got out*, which is all that counts. And the magical device worked, just like you said"—Gnimsh smiled happily and nodded—"and we found Caramon. Just like you said—the device was cali-cala-whatever to return to him—"

"Calibrated," Gnimsh interrupted.

"—but then"—Tas chewed nervously on the end of his topknot of hair—"everything went all wrong, somehow. Raistlin stabbed, maybe dead. The dwarves hauling us off without ever giving me a chance to tell them they were making a serious mistake."

The kender trudged along, pondering deeply. Finally, he shook his head. "I've thought it over, Gnimsh. I know it's a desperate act and one I wouldn't ordinarily resort to, but I don't think we have any choice. The situation has gotten completely out of hand." Tas heaved a solemn sigh. "I think we should tell the truth."

Gnimsh appeared extremely alarmed at this drastic action, so alarmed, in fact, that he tripped over his apron and fell flat on the ground. The guards, neither of whom spoke Common, hauled him to his feet and dragged the gnome the rest of way, coming at last to a halt before a great, wooden door. Here other guards, eyeing the kender and the gnome

with disgust, shoved on the doors, slowly pushing them open.

"Oh, I've been here!" Tas said suddenly. "Now I know where we are."

"That's a big help," Gnimsh muttered.

"The Hall of Audience," Tas continued. "The last time we were here, Tanis got sick. He's an elf, you know. Well, half an elf, anyway, and he hated living underground." The kender sighed again. "I wish Tanis was here now. He'd know what to do. I wish *someone* wise was here now."

The guards shoved them inside the great hall. "At least," Tas said to Gnimsh softly, "we're not alone. At least we've got each other."

"Tasslehoff Burrfoot," said the kender, bowing before the king of the dwarves, then bowing again to each of the thanes seated in the stone seats behind and on a lower level than Duncan's throne. "And this is—"

The gnome pushed forward eagerly. "Gnimsh-mari—"

"Gnimsh!" Tas said loudly, stepping on the gnome's foot as Gnimsh paused for breath. "Let me do the talking!" the kender scolded in an audible whisper.

Scowling, Gnimsh lapsed into hurt silence as Tas looked around the hall brightly.

"Gee, you're not planning a lot in the way of renovation the next two hundred years, are you? It's going to look just about the same. Except I seem to remember that crack there—no, over there. Yes, that one. It's going to get quite a bit bigger in the future. You might want to—"

"Where do you come from, kender?" Duncan growled.

"Solace," said Tas, remembering he was telling the truth. "Oh, don't worry if you've never heard of it. It doesn't exist yet.† They hadn't heard of it in Istar, either, but that didn't matter so much because no one cared about anything in Istar that wasn't there. In Istar, I mean. Solace is north of Haven, which isn't there either but will be sooner than Solace, if you take my meaning."

Duncan, leaning forward, glowered at Tas alarmingly from beneath his thick eyebrows. "You're lying."

† *Solace does not exist in this time. How then, in* Time of the Twins, *did Arack know the name when he asked Caramon, "...are they all as dumb as you in Solace?" Of course, Arack himself knew of no such place, for as Tas says, it did not yet exist. Arack was simply repeating what he had heard Caramon speak of.*

"I am not!" Tas said indignantly. "We came here using a magical device that I had borrowed—sort of—from a friend. It worked fine when I had it, but then I accidentally broke it. Well, actually that wasn't my fault. But that's another story. At any rate, I survived the Cataclysm and ended up in the Abyss. *Not* a nice place. Anyway, I met Gnimsh in the Abyss and he fixed it. The device, I mean, not the Abyss. He's really a wonderful fellow," Tas continued confidentially, patting Gnimsh on the shoulder. "He's a gnome, all right, but his inventions work."

"So—you *are* from the Abyss!" Kharas said sternly. "You admit it! Apparitions from the Realms of Darkness! The black-robed wizard conjured you, and you came at his bidding."

This startling accusation actually rendered the kender speechless.

"Wh-wh"—Tas sputtered for a moment incoherently, then found his voice—"I've never been so insulted! Except perhaps when the guard in Istar referred to me as a—a cut-cutpur—well, never mind. To say nothing of the fact that if Raistlin was going to conjure up anything, I certainly don't think it would be us. Which reminds me!" Tas glared back sternly at Kharas. "Why did you go and kill him like that? I mean, maybe he *wasn't* what you might call a really nice person. And maybe he *did* try to kill me by making me break the magical device and then leaving me behind in Istar for the gods to drop a fiery mountain on. But"—Tas sighed wistfully—"he was certainly one of the most *interesting* people I've ever known."

"Your wizard isn't dead, as you well know, apparition!" Duncan growled.

"Look, I'm not an appari—Not dead?" Tas's face lit up. "Truly? Even after you stabbed him like that and all the blood and everything and—Oh! I know how! Crysania! Of course! Lady Crysania!"

"Ah, the witch!" Kharas said softly, almost to himself as the thanes began to mutter among themselves.

"Well, she is kind of cold and impersonal sometimes," Tas said, shocked, "but I certainly don't think that gives you any right to call her names! She's a cleric of Paladine, after all."

"Cleric!" The thanes began to laugh.

"There's your answer," Duncan said to Kharas, ignoring the kender. "Witchcraft."

"You are right, of course, Thane," Kharas said, frowning, "but—"

"Look," Tas begged, "if you'd just let me go! I keep trying to tell you dwarves. This is all a dreadful mistake! I've got to get to Caramon!"

That caused a reaction. The thanes immediately hushed.

"You know General Caramon?" Kharas asked dubiously.

"General?" Tas repeated. "Wow! Won't Tanis be surprised to hear that? General Caramon! Tika would laugh. . . . Uh, of course I know Cara— General Caramon," Tas continued hurriedly, seeing Duncan's eyebrows coming together again. "He's my best friend. And if you'll only listen to what I'm trying to tell you, Gnimsh and I came here with the magical device to find Caramon and take him home. He doesn't want to be here, I'm sure. You see, Gnimsh fixed the device so that it will take more than one person—"

"Take him home where?" Duncan growled. "The Abyss? Perhaps the wizard conjured him up, too!"

"No!" Tas snapped, beginning to lose patience. "Take him home to Solace, of course. And Raistlin, too, if he wants to go. I can't imagine what they're doing here, in fact. Raistlin couldn't stand Thorbardin the last time we were here, which will be in about two hundred years. He spent the whole time coughing and complaining about the damp. Flint said—Flint Fireforge, that is, an old friend of mine—"

"Fireforge!" Duncan actually jumped up from his throne, glaring at the kender. "You're a friend of Fireforge?"

"Well, you needn't get so worked up," Tas said, somewhat startled. "Flint had his faults, of course— always grumbling and accusing people of stealing things when I was *truly* intending to put that bracelet right back where I found it, but that doesn't mean you—"

"Fireforge," Duncan said grimly, "is the leader of our enemies. Or didn't you know that?"

"No," said Tas with interest, "I didn't. Oh, but I'm sure it couldn't be the same Fireforge," he

added after some thought. "Flint won't be born for at least another fifty years. Maybe it's his father. Raistlin says—"

"Raistlin? Who is this Raistlin?" Duncan demanded.

Tasslehoff fixed the dwarf with a stern eye. "You're not paying attention. Raistlin is the wizard. The one you killed—Er, the one you didn't kill. The one you thought you killed but didn't."

"His name isn't Raistlin. It's Fistandantilus!" Duncan snorted. Then, his face grim, the dwarven king resumed his seat. "So," he said, looking at the kender from beneath his bushy eyebrows, "you're planning to take this wizard who was healed by a cleric when there are no clerics in this world and a general you claim is your best friend back to a place that doesn't exist to meet our enemy who hasn't been born yet using a device, built by a gnome, which actually works?"

"Right!" cried Tas triumphantly. "You see there! Look what you can learn when you just listen!"

Gnimsh nodded emphatically.

"Guards! Take them away!" Duncan snarled. Spinning around on his heel, he looked at Kharas coldly. "You gave me your word. I'll expect to see you in the War Council room in ten minutes."

"But, Thane! If he truly knows General Caramon—"

"Enough!" Duncan was in a rage. "War is coming, Kharas. All your honor and all your noble yammering about slaying kinsmen can't stop it! And you will be out there on the field of battle or you can take your face that shames us all and hide it in the dungeons along with the rest of the traitors to our people—the Dewar! Which will it be?"

"I serve you, of course, Thane," Kharas said, his face rigid. "I have pledged my life."

"See you remember that!" Duncan snapped. "And to keep your thoughts from wandering, I am ordering that you be confined to your quarters except to attend the War Council meetings and that, further, these two"—he waved at Tas and Gnimsh—"are to be imprisoned and their whereabouts kept secret until after the war has ended. Death come upon the head of any who defy this command."

The thanes glanced at each other, nodding approvingly, though one muttered that it was too late. The guards grabbed hold of Gnimsh and Tas, the kender still protesting volubly as they led him away.

"I was telling the truth," he wailed. "You've got to believe me! I know it sounds funny, but, you see, I—I'm not quite used to—uh—telling the truth! But give me a while. I'm sure I'll get the hang of it someday. . . ."

Tasslehoff wouldn't have believed it was possible to go down so far beneath the surface of the world as the guards were taking them if his own feet hadn't walked it. He remembered once Flint telling him once that Reorx lived down here, forging the world with his great hammer.

"A nice, cheerful sort of person *he* must be," Tas grumbled, shivering in the cold until his teeth chattered. "At least if Reorx was forging the world, you'd think it'd be warmer."

"Trustdwarves," muttered Gnimsh.

"What?" It seemed to the kender that he'd spent the last half of his life beginning every sentence he spoke to the gnome with "what?"

"I said trust dwarves!" Gnimsh returned loudly. "Instead of building their homes in active volcanoes, which, though slightly unstable, provide an excellent source of heat, they build theirs in old dead mountains." He shook his wispy-haired head. "Hard to believe we're cousins."

Tas didn't answer, being preoccupied with other matters—like how do we get out of this one, where do we go if we do get out, and when are they likely to serve dinner? There seeming to be no immediate answers to any of these (including dinner), the kender lapsed into a gloomy silence.

Oh, there was one rather exciting moment—when they were lowered down a narrow rocky tunnel that had been bored straight down into the mountain. The device they used to lower people down this tunnel was called a "lift" by the gnomes, according to Gnimsh. ("Isn't 'lift' an inappropriate name for it when it's going *down*?" Tas pointed out, but the gnome ignored him.)

Since no immediate solution to his problems appeared forthcoming, Tas decided not to waste his time in this interesting place moping about. He therefore enjoyed the journey in the lift thoroughly, though it was rather uncomfortable in spots when the rickety, wooden device—operated by muscular

dwarves pulling on huge lengths of rope—bumped against the side of the rocky tunnel as it was being lowered, jouncing the occupants about and inflicting numerous cuts and bruises on those inside.

This proved highly entertaining, especially as the dwarven guards accompanying Tas and Gnimsh shook their fists, swearing roundly in dwarven at the operators up above them.

As for the gnome, Gnimsh was plunged into a state of excitement impossible to believe. Whipping out a stub of charcoal and borrowing one of Tas's handkerchiefs, he plopped himself down on the floor of the lift and immediately began to draw plans for a New Improved Lift.

"Pulleyscablessteam," he yammered to himself happily, busily sketching what looked to Tas like a giant lobster trap on wheels. "Updownupdown. Whatfloor? Steptotherear. Capacity:thirtytwo. Stuck? Alarms! Bellswhistleshorns."

When they eventually reached ground level, Tas tried to watch carefully to see where they were going (so that they could leave, even if he didn't have a map), but Gnimsh was hanging onto him, pointing to his sketch and explaining it to him in detail.

"Yes, Gnimsh. Isn't that interesting?" Tas said, only half-listening to the gnome as his heart sank even lower than where they were standing. "Soothing music by a piper in the corner? Yes, Gnimsh, that's a great idea."

Gazing around as their guards prodded them forward, Tas sighed. Not only did this place look as boring as the Abyss, it had the added disadvantage of smelling even worse. Row after row of large, crude prison cells lined the rocky walls. Lit by torches that smoked in the foul, thin air, the cells were filled to capacity with dwarves.

Tas gazed at them in growing confusion as they walked down the narrow aisle between cell blocks. These dwarves didn't look like criminals. There were males, females, even children crammed inside the cells. Crouched on filthy blankets, huddled on battered stools, they stared glumly out from behind the bars.

"Hey!" Tas said, tugging at the sleeve of a guard. The kender spoke some dwarven, having picked it up from Flint. "What is all this?" he asked, waving

his hand. "Why are all these people in here?" (At least that's what he hoped he said. There was every possibility he might have inadvertently asked the way to the nearest alehouse.)

But the guard, glowering at him, only said, "Dewar."

CHAPTER II

"Dewar?" Tas repeated blankly.

The guard, however, refused to elaborate but prodded Tas on ahead with a vicious shove. Tas stumbled, then kept walking, glancing about, trying to figure out what was going on. Gnimsh, meanwhile, apparently seized by another fit of inspiration, was going on about "hydraulics."

Tas pondered. Dewar, he thought, trying to remember where he'd heard that word. Suddenly, he came up with the answer.

"The dark dwarves!" he said. "Of course! I remember! They fought for the Dragon Highlord. But, they didn't live down here the last time—or I suppose it will be the next time—we were here. Or will come here. Drat, what a muddle. Surely they don't live in prison cells, though. Hey"—Tas tapped the dwarf again—"what did they do! I mean, to get thrown in jail?"

"Traitors!" the dwarf snapped. Reaching a cell at the far end of the aisle, he drew out a key, inserted it into the lock, and swung the door open.

Peering inside, Tas saw about twenty or thirty Dewar crowded into the cell. Some lay lethargically on the floor, others sat against the wall, sleeping. One group, crouched together off in a corner, were talking in low voices when the guard arrived. They quit immediately as soon as the cell door opened. There were no women or children in this cell, only males; and they regarded Tas, the gnome, and the guard with dark, hate-filled eyes.

Tas grabbed Gnimsh just as the gnome—still yammering about people getting stuck between floors—was just about to walk absentmindedly into the cell.

"Well, well," Tas said to the dwarven guard as he dragged Gnimsh back to stand beside him, "this tour was quite—er—entertaining. Now, if you'll just take us back to our cells, which were, I must say, *very nice* cells—so light and airy and roomy—I think I can safely promise that my partner and I won't be taking any more unauthorized excursions into your city, though it *is* an extremely interesting place and I'd like to see more of it. I—"

But the dwarf, with a rough shove of his hand, pushed the kender into the cell, sending him sprawling.

"I wish you'd make up your mind," Gnimsh snapped irritably, stumbling inside after Tas. "Are we going in or out?"

"I guess we're in," Tas said ruefully, sitting up and looking doubtfully at the Dewar, who were staring back in silence. The guards' heavy boots could be heard stumping back up the corridor, accompanied by shouted obscenities and threats from the surrounding cells.

"Hello," Tas said, smiling in friendly fashion, but *not* offering to shake hands. "I'm Tasslehoff Burrfoot and this is my friend, Gnimsh, and it looks like we're going to be cellmates, doesn't it now? So, what's your names? Er, now, I say, that isn't very nice. . . ."

Tas drew himself up, glaring sternly at one of the Dewar, who had risen to his feet and was approaching them.

A tall dwarf, his face was nearly invisible beneath a thick matting of tangled hair and beard. He grinned suddenly. There was a flash of steel and a large knife appeared in his hand. Shuffling forward, he advanced upon the kender, who retreated as far as possible into a corner, dragging Gnimsh with him.

"Who*are*thesepeople?" Gnimsh squeaked in alarm, having finally taken note of their dismal surroundings.

Before Tas could answer, the Dewar had the kender by the neck and was holding the knife to his throat.

This is it! Tas thought with regret. I'm dead this time for sure. Flint will get a chuckle out of this one!

But the dark dwarf's knife inched right past Tas's face. Reaching his shoulder, the dark dwarf expertly cut through the straps of Tas's pouches, sending them and their contents tumbling to the floor.

Instantly, chaos broke out in the cell as the Dewar leaped for them. The dwarf with the knife grabbed as many as he could, slashing and hacking at his fellows, trying to drive them back. Everything vanished within seconds.

Clutching the kender's belongings, the Dewar immediately sat down and began rummaging through them. The dark dwarf with the knife had managed to make the richest haul. Clutching his booty to his chest, he returned to a place against the back of the cell, where he and his friends immediately began to shake the contents of the pouches onto the floor.

Gasping in relief, Tas sank down to the cold, stone floor. But it was a worried sigh of relief, nonetheless, for Tas figured that when the pouches had lost their appeal, the Dewar would get the bright idea of searching *them* next.

"And we'll certainly be a lot easier to search if we're corpses," he muttered to himself. That led, however, to a sudden thought.

"Gnimsh!" he whispered urgently. "The magical device! Where is it?"

Gnimsh, blinking, patted one pocket in his leather apron and shook his head. Patting another, he pulled out a T-square and a bit of charcoal. He examined these carefully for a moment then, seeing

that neither was the magical device, stuffed them back into his pockets. Tas was seriously considering throttling him when, with a triumphant smile, the gnome reached into his boot and pulled out the magical device.

During their last incarceration, Gnimsh had managed to make the device collapse again. Now it had resumed the size and shape of a rather ordinary, nondescript pendant instead of the intricate and beautiful sceptre that it resembled when fully extended.

"Keep it hidden!" Tas warned. Glancing at the Dewar, he saw that they were absorbed in fighting over what they'd found in his pouches. "Gnimsh," he whispered, "this thing worked to get us out of the Abyss and you said it was cali-calo-caliwhatever'd to go straight to Caramon, since he was the one Par-Salian gave it to. Now, I really don't want it to take us anywhere in *time* again, but do you think it would work for, say, just a short hop? If Caramon is general of that army, he can't be far from here."

"That's a great idea!" Gnimsh's eyes began to shine. "Just a minute, let me think. . . ."

But they were too late. Tas felt a touch on his shoulder. His heart leaping into his throat, the kender whirled around with what he hoped was the Grim Expression of a Hardened Killer on his face. Apparently it was for the Dewar who had touched him stumbled back in terror hurriedly flinging his hands up for protection.

Noting that this was a youngish-appearing dwarf with a halfway sane look in his eye, Tasslehoff sighed and relaxed, while the Dewar, seeing that the kender wasn't going to eat him alive, quit shaking and looked at him hopefully.

"What is it?" Tas asked in dwarven. "What do you want?"

"Come. You come." The Dewar made a beckoning gesture. Then, seeing Tas frown, he pointed, then beckoned again, hedging back farther into the cell.

Tas rose cautiously to his feet. "Stay here, Gnimsh," he said. But the gnome wasn't listening. Muttering happily to himself, Gnimsh was occupied with twisting and turning little somethings on the device.

Curious, Tas crept after the Dewar. Maybe this fellow had discovered the way out. Maybe he'd been digging a tunnel . . . .

The Dewar, still motioning, led the kender to the center of the cell. Here, he stopped and pointed. "Help?" he said hopefully.

Tas, looking down, didn't see a tunnel. What he saw was a Dewar lying on a blanket. The dwarf's face was covered with sweat, his hair and beard were soaking wet. His eyes were closed and his body jerked and twitched spasmodically. At the sight, Tas began to shiver. He glanced around the cell. Then, his gaze coming back to the young Dewar, he regretfully shook his head.

"No," Tas said gently, "I'm sorry. There's . . . nothing I can do. I—I'm sorry." He shrugged helplessly.

The Dewar seemed to understand, for he sank back down beside the sick dwarf, his head bowed disconsolately.

Tas crept back to where Gnimsh was sitting, feeling all numb inside. Slumping down into the corner, he stared into the dark cell, seeing and hearing what he should have seen and heard right away—the wild, incoherent ramblings, cries of pain, cries for water and, here and there, the awful silence of those who lay very, very still.

"Gnimsh," Tas said quietly, "these dwarves are sick. Really sick. I've seen it before in days to come. These dwarves have the plague."

Gnimsh's eyes widened. He almost dropped the magical device.

"Gnimsh," said Tas, trying to speak calmly, "we've got to get out of here fast! The way I see it, the only choices we have down here are dying by knifepoint—which, while undoubtedly interesting, does have its drawbacks, or dying rather slowly and boringly of the plague."

"I think it will work," Gnimsh said, dubiously eyeing the magical device. "Of course, it might take us right back to the Abyss—"

"Not really a *bad* place," Tas said, slowly rising to his feet and helping Gnimsh to his. "Takes a bit getting used to, and I don't suppose *they'd* be wildly happy to see us again, but I think it's definitely worth a try."

"Very well, just let me make an adjustment—"

"Do not touch it!"

The familiar voice came from the shadows and was so stern and commanding that Gnimsh froze in his tracks, his hand clutching the device.

"Raistlin!" cried Tas, staring about wildly. "Raistlin! We're here! We're here!"

"I know where you are," the archmage said coldly, materializing out of the smoky air to stand before them in the cell.

His sudden appearance brought gasps and screams and cries from the Dewar. The one in the corner with the knife snaked to his feet and lunged forward.

"Raistlin, look ou—" Tas shrieked.

Raistlin turned. He did not speak. He did not raise his hand. He simply stared at the dark dwarf. The Dewar's face went ashen. Dropping the knife from nerveless fingers, he shrank back and attempted to hide himself in the shadows. Before turning back to the kender, Raistlin cast a glance around the cell. Silence fell instantly. Even those who were delirious hushed.

Satisfied, Raistlin turned back to Tas.

"—out," Tas finished lamely. Then the kender's face brightened. He clapped his hands. "Oh, Raistlin! It's so good to see you! You're looking really well, too. Especially for having a—er—sword stuck in your—uh—Well, never mind that. And you came to rescue us, didn't you? That's splendid! I—"

"Enough driveling!" Raistlin said coolly. Reaching out a hand, he grabbed Tas and jerked him close. "Now, tell me—where did you come from?"

Tas faltered, staring up into Raistlin's eyes. "I—I'm not sure you're going to believe this. No one else does. But it's the truth, I swear it!"

"Just tell me!" Raistlin snarled, his hand deftly twisting Tasslehoff's collar.

"Right!" Tas gulped and squirmed. "Uh, remember—it helps if you let me breathe occasionally. Now, let's see. I tried to stop the Cataclysm and the device broke. I—I'm sure you didn't mean to," Tas stammered, "but you—uh—seem to have given me the wrong instructions. . . ."

"I did. Mean to, that is," Raistlin said grimly. "Go on."

"I'd like to, but it's . . . hard to talk without air. . . ."

Raistlin loosened his hold on the kender slightly. Tas drew a deep breath. "Good! Where was I? Oh, yes. I followed Lady Crysania down, down, down into the very bottom part of the Temple in Istar, when it was falling apart, you know? And I saw her go into this room and I knew she must be going to see you, because she said your name, and I was hoping you'd fix the device—"

"Be quick!"

"R-right." Speeding up as much as possible, Tas became nearly incomprehensible. "And then there was a thud behind me and it was Caramon, only he didn't see me, and everything went dark, and when I woke up, you were gone, and I looked up in time to see the gods throw the fiery mountain—" Tas drew a breath. "Now *that* was something. Would you like to hear about—No? Well, some other time.

"I—I guess I must have gone back to sleep again, because I woke up and everything was quiet. I thought I must be dead only I wasn't. I was in the Abyss, where the Temple went after the Cataclysm."

"The Abyss!" Raistlin breathed. His hand trembled.

"*Not* a nice place," Tas said solemnly. "Despite what I said earlier. I met the Queen—" The kender shivered.† "I—I don't think I want to talk about that now, if you don't mind." He held out a trembling hand. "But there's her mark, those five little white spots . . . anyway, she said I had to stay down there forever, be-because now she could change history and win the war. And I didn't mean to"—Tas stared pleadingly at Raistlin—"I just wanted to help Caramon. But then, while I was down in the Abyss, I found Gnimsh—"

"The gnome," Raistlin said softly, his eyes on Gnimsh, who was staring at the magic-user in amazement, not daring to move.

"Yes." Tas twisted his head to smile at his friend. "He'd built a time-traveling device that worked—actually worked, think of that! And, whoosh! Here we are!"

"You escaped the Abyss?" Raistlin turned his mirrorlike gaze on the kender.

Tas squirmed uncomfortably. Those last few moments haunted his dreams at night, and kender

To frighten those who are without fear must be frightful indeed! The kender's fearlessness has not been overestimated. Rather, the power of the Dark Queen is that much greater. —TRH

rarely dreamed.† "Uh, sure," he said, smiling up at the archmage in what he hoped was a disarming manner.

It was apparently wasted, however. Raistlin, preoccupied, was regarding the gnome with an expression that suddenly made Tas go cold all over.

"You said the device broke?" Raistlin said softly.

"Yes," Tas swallowed. Feeling Raistlin's hold on him slacken, seeing the mage lost in thought, Tas wriggled slightly, endeavoring to free himself from the mage's grasp. To his surprise, Raistlin let him go, releasing his grip so suddenly that Tas nearly tumbled over backward.

"The device was broken," Raistlin murmured. Suddenly, he stared at Tas intently. "Then—who fixed it?" The archmage's voice was little more than a whisper.

Edging away from Raistlin, Tas hedged. "I—I hope the mages won't be angry. Gnimsh didn't actually *fix* it. You'll tell Par-Salian, won't you, Raistlin? I wouldn't want to get into trouble—well, any *more* trouble with him than I'm in already. We didn't do anything to the device, not really. Gnimsh just—uh—sort of put it back together—the way it was, so that it worked "

"He reassembled it?" Raistlin persisted, that same, strange expression in his eyes.

"Y-yes." With a weak grin, Tas scrambled back to poke Gnimsh in the ribs just as the gnome was about to speak. "Re . . . assembled. That's the word, all right. Reassembled."

"But, Tas—" Gnimsh began loudly. "Don't you remember what happened? I—"

"Just shut up!" Tas whispered. "And let me do the talking. We're in a lot of trouble here! Mages don't like having their devices messed with, even if you did make it better! I'm sure I can make Par-Salian understand that, when I see him. He'll undoubtedly be pleased that you fixed it. After all, it must have been rather bothersome for them, what with the device only transporting one person at a time and all that. I'm sure Par-Salian will see it that way, but I'd rather be the one to tell him—if you take my meaning. Raistlin's kind of . . . well, jumpy about things like that. I don't think he'd understand and, believe me"—with a glance at the mage and a gulp—"this isn't the time to try to explain."

Kender dream, of course, but I doubt that they remember their dreams, for usually recalling a dream requires pretty intense concentration. A kender would probably remember a nightmare if it woke him up, but he'd undoubtedly forget it the moment something more interesting came up. —MW

I believe that kender do, in fact, dream, but they do not remember them. On the other hand, being truly innocent, perhaps they have less to work out in their dreams than we do. —TRH

Gnimsh, glancing dubiously at Raistlin, shivered and crowded closer to Tas.

"He's looking at me like he's going to turn me inside out!" the gnome muttered nervously.

"That's how he looks at everyone," Tas whispered back. "You'll get used to it."

No one spoke. In the crowded cell, one of the sick dwarves moaned and cried out in delirium. Tas glanced over at them uneasily, then looked at Raistlin. The magic-user was once again staring at the gnome, that strange, grim, preoccupied look on his pale face.

"Uh, that's really all I can tell you now, Raistlin," Tas said loudly, with another nervous glance at the sick dwarves. "Could we go now? Will you swoosh us out of here the way you used to in Istar? That was great fun and—"

"Give me the device," Raistlin said, holding out his hand.

For some reason—perhaps it was that look in the mage's eye, or perhaps it was the cold dampness of the underground dungeons—Tas began to shiver. Gnimsh, holding the device in his hand, looked at Tas questioningly.

"Uh, would you mind if we just sort of kept it awhile?" Tas began. "I won't lose it—"

"Give me the device." Raistlin's voice was soft.

Tas swallowed again. There was a funny taste in his mouth. "You—you better give it to him, Gnimsh."

The gnome, blinking in a befuddled manner and obviously trying to figure out what was going on, only stared at Tas questioningly.

"It—it'll be all right," Tas said, trying to smile, though his face had suddenly gone all stiff. "Raist-Raistlin's a friend of mine, you see. He'll keep it safe. . . ."

Shrugging, Gnimsh turned and, taking a few shuffling steps forward, held out the device in his palm. The pendant looked plain and uninteresting in the dim torchlight. Stretching forth his hand, Raistlin slowly and carefully took hold of the device. He studied it closely, then slipped it into one of the secret pockets in his black robes.

"Come to me, Tas," Raistlin said in a gentle voice, beckoning to him.

Gnimsh was still standing in front of Raistlin, staring disconsolately at the pocket into which the device had disappeared. Catching hold of the gnome by the strings of his leather apron, Tas dragged Gnimsh back away from the mage. Then, clasping Gnimsh by the hand, Tas looked up.

"We're ready, Raistlin," he said brightly. "Whoosh away! Gee, won't Caramon be surprised—"

"I said—come here, Tas," Raistlin repeated in that soft, expressionless voice. His eyes were on the gnome.

"Oh, Raistlin, you're not going to leave him here, are you?" Tas wailed. Dropping Gnimsh's hand, he took a step forward. "Because, if you are, I'd just as soon stay. I mean, he'll never get out of this by himself. And he's got this wonderful idea for a mechanical lift—"

Raistlin's hand snaked out, caught hold of Tas by the arm, and yanked him over to stand beside him. "No, I'm not going to leave him here, Tas."

"You see? He's going to whoosh us back to Caramon. The magic's great fun," Tas began, twisting around to face Gnimsh and trying to grin, though the mage's strong fingers were hurting him most dreadfully. But at the sight of Gnimsh's face, Tas's grin vanished. He started to go back to his friend, but Raistlin held him fast.

The gnome was standing all by himself, looking thoroughly confused and pathetic, still clutching Tas's handkerchief in his hand.

Tas squirmed. "Oh, Gnimsh, please. It'll be all right. I told you, Raistlin's my fri—"

Raising one hand, holding Tas by the collar with the other, the archmage pointed a finger at the gnome. Raistlin's soft voice began to chant, "*Ast kiranann kair—*"

Horror broke over Tas. He had heard those words of magic before. . . .

"No!" he shrieked in anguish. Whirling, he looked up into Raistlin's eyes. "No!" he screamed again, hurling himself bodily at the mage, beating at him with his small hands.

"—*Gardurm Soth-arn/Suh kali Jalaran!*" Raistlin finished calmly.

Tas, his hands still grasping Raistlin's black robes, heard the air begin to crackle and sizzle. Turning

with an incoherent cry, the kender watched bolts of flame shoot from the mage's fingers straight into the gnome. The magical lightning struck Gnimsh in the chest. The terrible energy lifted the gnome's small body and flung it backward, slamming it into the stone wall behind.

Gnimsh crumpled to the floor without so much as a cry. Smoke rose from his leather apron. There was the sweet, sickening smell of burning flesh. The hand holding the kender's handkerchief twitched, and then was still.

Tas couldn't move. His hands still entangled in Raistlin's robes, he stood, staring.

"Come along, Tas," Raistlin said.

Turning, Tas looked up at Raistlin. "No," he whispered, trembling, trying to free himself from Raistlin's strong grip. Then he cried out in agony. "You murdered him! Why? He was my friend!"

"My reasons are my own," Raistlin said, holding onto the writhing kender firmly. "Now you are coming with me."

"No, I'm not!" Tas cried, struggling frantically. "You're not interesting or exciting—you're evil— like the Abyss! You're horrible and ugly, and I won't go anywhere with you! Ever! Let me go! Let me go!"

Blinded by tears, kicking and screaming and flailing out with his clenched fists, Tas struck at Raistlin in a frenzy.

Coming out of their terror, the Dewar in the cell began shouting in panic, arousing the attention of dwarves in the other cells. Shrieking and yelling, other Dewar crowded close against the bars, trying to see what was going on.

Pandemonium broke out. Above the cries and shouts could be heard the deep voices of the guards, yelling something in dwarven.

His face cold and grim, Raistlin laid a hand on Tasslehoff's forehead and spoke swift, soft words. The kender's body relaxed instantly. Catching him before he fell to the floor, Raistlin spoke again, and the two of them disappeared, leaving the stunned Dewar to stand, gaping, staring at the vacant space on the floor and the body of the dead gnome, lying huddled in the corner.

An hour later Kharas, having escaped his own confinement with ease, made his way to the cellblock where the Dewar clans were being held captive.

Grimly, Kharas stalked down the aisles.

"What's going on?" he asked a guard. "It seems awfully quiet."

"Ah, some sort of riot a while back," the guard muttered. "We never could figure out what the matter was."

Kharas glanced around sharply. The Dewar stared back at him not with hatred but with suspicion, even fear.

Growing more worried as he went along, sensing that something frightful had occurred, the dwarf quickened his pace. Reaching the last cell, he looked inside.

At the sight of Kharas, those Dewar who could move leaped to their feet and backed into the farthest corner possible. There they huddled together, muttering and pointing at the front corner of the cell.

Looking over, Kharas frowned. The body of the gnome lay limply on the floor.

Casting a furious glance at the stunned guard, Kharas turned his gaze upon the Dewar.

"Who did this?" he demanded. "And where's the kender?"

To Kharas's amazement, the Dewar—instead of sullenly denying the crime—immediately surged forward, all of them babbling at once. With an angry, slashing hand motion, Kharas silenced them. "You, there"—he pointed at one of the Dewar, who was still holding onto Tas's pouches—"where did you get that pouch? What happened? Who did this? Where is the kender?"

As the Dewar shambled forward, Kharas looked into the dark dwarf's eyes. And he saw, to his horror, that any sanity the dark dwarf might once have possessed was now completely gone.

"I saw 'im," the Dewar said, grinning. "I saw 'im. In 'is black robes and all. He come for the gnome. An' 'e come for the kender. An' e's comin' fer us nex'!"

The dark dwarf laughed horribly. "Us nex'!" he repeated.

"Who?" Kharas asked sternly. "Saw who? Who came for the kender?"

"Why, hisself!" whispered the Dewar, turning to gaze upon the gnome with wild, staring eyes. "Death . . ."

CHAPTER 12

o one had set foot inside the magical fortress of Zhamant for centuries. The dwarves viewed it with suspicion and distrust for several reasons. One, it had belonged to wizards. Two, its stonework was not dwarven, nor was it even natural. The fortress had been raised—so legend told—up out of the ground by magic, and it was magic that still held it together.

"*Has* to be magic," Reghar grumbled to Caramon, giving the tall thin spires of the fortress a scathing glance. "Otherwise, it would have toppled over long ago."

The hill dwarves, refusing to a dwarf to stick so much as the tip of their beards inside the fortress, set up camp outside, on the plains. The Plainsmen did likewise. Not so much from fear of the magical building—though they looked at it askance and whispered about it in their own

Sites that have mysterious, ancient origins are common in myth and legend. Stonehenge, for example, was said to have been raised by giants—or Merlin or Japheth, depending on the tale you read. Krynn, it seems, has similar myths and legends.

language—but from the fact that they felt uneasy in any building.

The humans, scoffing at these superstitions, entered the ancient fortress, laughing loudly about spooks and haunts. They stayed one night. The next morning found them setting up camp in the open, muttering about fresh air and sleeping better beneath the stars.

"What went on here?" Caramon asked his brother uneasily as they walked through the fortress on their arrival. "You said it wasn't a Tower of High Sorcery, yet it's obviously magical. Wizards built it. And"—the big man shivered—"there's a strange feeling about it†—not eerie, like the Towers. But a feeling of . . . of—" He floundered.

"Of violence," Raistlin murmured, his darting, penetrating gaze encompassing all the objects around him, "of violence and of death, my brother. For this was a place of experimentation. The mages built this fortress far away from civilized lands for one reason—and that was that they knew the magic conjured here might well escape their control. And so it did—often. But here, too, emerged great things—magics that helped the world."†

"Why was it abandoned?" Lady Crysania asked, drawing her fur cloak around her shoulders more tightly. The air that flowed through the narrow stone hallways was chill and smelled of dust and stone.

Raistlin was silent for long moments, frowning. Slowly, quietly, they made their way through the twisting halls. Lady Crysania's soft leather boots made no sound as she walked, Caramon's heavy booted footsteps echoed through the empty chambers, Raistlin's rustling robes whispered through the corridors, the Staff of Magius upon which he leaned thumping softly on the floor. As quiet as they were, they could almost have been the ghosts of themselves, moving through the hallways. When Raistlin spoke, his voice made both Caramon and Crysania start.

"Though there have always been the three Robes—good, neutral, and evil—among the magic-users, we have, unfortunately, not always maintained the balance," Raistlin said. "As people turned against us, the White Robes withdrew into their Towers, advocating peace. The Black Robes,

The idea that buildings or houses or even land can hold some sort of memory or "feeling" of past happenings (good and bad) runs throughout many great stories. Stephen King actually played with this idea a lot in his early books—the Marsten house from 'Salem's Lot and the Overlook Hotel from The Shining.

Wizards are very much the fantasy equivalent of scientists. —TRH

786

however, sought—at first—to strike back. They took over this fortress and used it in experiments to create armies." He paused. "Experiments that were not successful at that time, but which led to the creation of draconians in our own age.

"With this failure, the mages realized the hopelessness of their situation. They abandoned Zhaman, joining with their fellows in what became known as the Lost Battles."†

"You seem to know your way around here," Caramon observed.

Raistlin glanced sharply at his brother, but Caramon's face was smooth, guileless—though there was, perhaps, a strange, shadowed look in his brown eyes.

"Do you not yet understand, my brother?" Raistlin said harshly, coming to a stop in a drafty, dark corridor. "I have never been here, yet I have walked these halls. The room I sleep in I have slept in many nights before, though I have yet to spend a night in this fortress. I am a stranger here, yet I know the location of every room, from those rooms of meditation and study at the top to the banquet halls on the first level."

Caramon stopped, too. Slowly he looked around him, staring up at the dusty ceiling, gazing down the empty hallways where sunlight filtered through carved windows to lie in square tiles upon the stone floors. His gaze finally came back to meet that of his twin.

"Then, Fistandantilus," he said, his voice heavy, "you know that this is also going to be your tomb."

For an instant, Caramon saw a tiny crack in the glass of Raistlin's eyes, he saw—not anger—but amusement, triumph. Then the bright mirrors returned. Caramon saw only himself reflected there, standing in a patch of weak, winter sunlight.

Crysania moved next to Raistlin. She put her hands over his arm as he leaned upon his staff and regarded Caramon with cold, gray eyes. "The gods are with us," she said. "They were not with Fistandantilus. Your brother is strong in his art, I am strong in my faith. We will not fail!"

Still looking at Caramon, still keeping his twin's reflection in the glistening orbs of his eyes, Raistlin smiled. "Yes," he whispered, and there was a slight hiss to his words, "truly, the gods are with us!"

"Prior to the Cataclysm, Lunitari was distressed by the growing influence of the Kingpriest of Istar, and did what she could to limit the spread of his power. Her followers worked to save magic and fought the Lost Battles, which ended with the destruction of two Towers of High Sorcery. After an uneasy truce was brokered with the church of Istar, Lunitari's followers salvaged any remaining magical artifacts and withdrew to the Tower of Wayreth. Unlike the other clerics of other gods, Lunitari's followers didn't depart the world on the Night of Doom, nor did her gift of neutral magic vanish after the fiery mountain struck Istar. Mages of all orders found themselves reviled and distrusted after the Cataclysm, and many remained withdrawn from the world."
[DRAGONLANCE Campaign Setting, Wizards of the Coast, Inc., 2003, p. 257.]

Upon the first level of the great, magical fortress of Zhaman were huge, stone-carved halls that had—in past days—been places of meeting and celebration. There were also, on the first level, rooms that had once been filled with books, designed for quiet study and meditation. At the back end were kitchens and storage rooms, long unused and covered by the dust of years.

On the upper levels were large bedrooms filled with quaint, old-fashioned furniture, the beds covered with linens preserved through the years by the dryness of the desert air. Caramon, Lady Crysania, and the officers of Caramon's staff slept in these rooms. If they did not sleep soundly, if they woke up sometimes during the night thinking they had heard voices chanting strange words or glimpsing wisps of ghostly figures fluttering through the moonlit darkness, no one mentioned these in the daylight.

But after a few nights, these things were forgotten, swallowed up in larger worries about supplies, fights breaking out between humans and dwarves, reports from spies that the dwarves of Thorbardin were massing a huge, well-armed force.

There was also in Zhaman, on the first level, a corridor that appeared to be a mistake. Anyone venturing into it discovered that it wandered off from a short hallway and ended abruptly in a blank wall. It looked for all the world as if the builder had thrown down his tools in disgust, calling it quits.†

Detail calls attention to an item or device. It also slows the pace somewhat and, when done right, raises dramatic tension.
—TRH

But the corridor was not a mistake. When the proper hands were laid upon that blank wall, when the proper words were spoken, when the proper runes were traced in the dust of the wall itself, then a door appeared, leading to a great staircase cut from the granite foundation of Zhaman.

Down, down the staircase, down into darkness, down—it seemed—into the very core of the world, the proper person could descend. Down into the dungeons of Zhaman. . . .

"One more time." The voice was soft, patient, and it dove and twisted at Tasslehoff like a snake. Writhing around him, it sank its curved teeth into his flesh, sucking out his life.

"We will go over it again. Tell me about the Abyss," said the voice. "Everything you remember.

How you entered. What the landscape is like. Who and what you saw. The Queen herself, how she looked, her words. . . ."

"I'm trying, Raistlin, truly!" Tasslehoff whimpered. "But . . . we've gone over it and over it these last couple of days. I can't think of anything else! And, my head's hot and my feet and my hands are cold and . . . the room's spinning 'round and 'round. If—if you'd make it stop spinning, Raistlin, I think I might be able to recall . . ."

Feeling Raistlin's hand on his chest, Tas shrank down into the bed. "No!" he moaned, trying desperately to wriggle away. "I'll be good, Raistlin! I'll remember. Don't hurt me, not like poor Gnimsh!"

But the archmage's hand only rested lightly on the kender's chest for an instant, then went to his forehead. Tas's skin burned, but the touch of that hand burned worse.

"Lie still," Raistlin commanded. Then, lifting Tas up by the arms, Raistlin stared intently into the kender's sunken eyes.

Finally, Raistlin dropped Tas back down into the bed and, muttering a bitter curse, rose to his feet.

Lying upon a sweat-soaked pillow, Tas saw the black-robed figure hover over him an instant, then, with a flutter and swirl of robes, it turned and stalked out of the room. Tas tried to lift his head to see where Raistlin was going, but the effort was too much. He fell back limply.

Why am I so weak? he wondered. What's wrong? I want to sleep. Maybe I'll quit hurting then. Tas closed his eyes. But they flew open again as if he had wires attached to his hair. No, I can't sleep! he thought fearfully. There are things out there in the darkness, horrible things, just waiting for me to sleep! I've seen them, they're out there! They're going to leap out and—

As if from a great distance, he heard Raistlin's voice, talking to someone. Peering around, trying desperately to keep sleep away from him, Tas decided to concentrate on Raistlin. Maybe I'll find out something, he thought drearily. Maybe I'll find out what's the matter with me.

Looking over, he saw the black-robed figure talking to a squat, dark figure. Sure enough, they were discussing him. Tas tried to listen, but his mind kept doing strange things—going off to play somewhere without inviting his body along. So Tas couldn't be certain if he was hearing what he was hearing or dreaming it.

"Give him some more of the potion. That should keep him quiet," a voice that sounded like Raistlin's said to the short, dark figure. "There's little chance anyone will hear him down here, but I can't risk it."

The short, dark figure said something. Tas closed his eyes and let the cool waters of a blue, blue lake—Crystalmir Lake†—lap over his burning skin. Maybe his mind had decided to take his body along after all.

"When I am gone," Raistlin's voice came up out of the water, "lock the door after me and extinguish the light. My brother has grown suspicious of late. Should he discover the magical door, he will undoubtedly come down here. He must find nothing. All these cells should appear empty."

The figure muttered, and the door squeaked on its hinges.

The water of Crystalmir suddenly began to boil around Tas. Tentacles snaked up out of it, grasping for him. His eyes flew open. "Raistlin!" he begged. "Don't leave me. Help me!"

But the door banged shut. The short, dark figure shuffled over to Tas's bedside. Staring at it with a kind of dreamlike horror, Tas saw that it was a dwarf. He smiled.

"Flint?" he murmured through parched, cracked lips. "No! Arack!" He tried to run, but the tentacles in the water were reaching out for his feet.

"Raistlin!" he screamed, frantically trying to scramble backward. But his feet wouldn't move. Something grabbed hold of him! The tentacles! Tas fought, shrieking in panic.

"Shut up, you bastard. Drink this." The tentacles gripped him by the topknot and shoved a cup to his lips. "Drink, or I'll pull your hair out by the roots!"

Choking, staring at the figure wildly, Tas took a sip. The liquid was bitter but cool and soothing. He was thirsty, so thirsty! Sobbing, Tas grabbed the cup away from the dwarf and gulped it down. Then he lay back on his pillow. Within moments,

"The lake lay in the midst of a mountain bowl known as Solace Vale. Sentinel Peaks, a branch of the Kharolis Mountains, partially encircled the vale to the east, west, and south. To the north the land was relatively flat, with a patchwork of farmlands known as the Northfields." [The Atlas of the DRAGONLANCE World, *by Karen Wynn Fonstad, TSR, Inc., 1987, p. 13.*]

the tentacles slipped away, the pain in his limbs left him, and the clear, sweet waters of Crystalmir closed over his head.

Crysania came out of a dream with the distinct impression that someone had called her name. Though she could not remember hearing a sound, the feeling was so strong and intense that she was immediately wide awake, sitting up in bed, before she was truly aware of what it was that had awakened her. Had it been a part of the dream? No. The impression remained and grew stronger.

Someone was in the room with her! She glanced about swiftly. Solinari's light, coming through a small corner at the far end of the room, did little to illuminate it. She could see nothing, but she heard movement. Crysania opened her mouth to call the guard. . . .

And felt a hand upon her lips. Then Raistlin materialized out of night's darkness, sitting on her bed.

"Forgive me for frightening you, Revered Daughter," he said in a soft whisper, barely above a breath. "I need your help and I do not wish to attract the attention of the guards." Slowly, he removed his hand.

"I wasn't frightened," Crysania protested. He smiled, and she flushed. He was so near her that he could feel her trembling. "You just . . . startled me, that's all. I was dreaming. You seemed a part of the dream."

"To be sure," Raistlin replied quietly. "The Portal is here, and thus we are very near the gods."

It isn't the nearness of the gods that is making me tremble, Crysania thought with a quivering sigh, feeling the burning warmth of the body beside hers, smelling his mysterious, intoxicating fragrance. Angrily, she moved away from him, firmly suppressing her desires and longings. *He is above such things.* Would she show herself weaker?

She returned to the subject abruptly. "You said you needed my help. Why?" Sudden fear gripped her. Reaching out impulsively, she grasped his hand. "You are well, aren't you? Your wound—?"

A swift spasm of pain crossed Raistlin's face, then his expression grew bitter and hard. "No, I am well," he said curtly.

"Thanks be to Paladine," Crysania said, smiling, letting her hand linger in his.

Raistlin's eyes grew narrow. "The god has no thanks of mine!" he muttered. The hand holding hers clenched, hurting her.

Crysania shivered. It seemed for an instant as if the burning heat of the mage's body so near hers was drawing out her own, leaving her chilled. She tried to remove her hand from his, but Raistlin, brought out of his bitter reverie by her movement, turned to look at her.

"Forgive me, Revered Daughter," he said, releasing her. "The pain was unendurable. I prayed for death. It was denied me."

"You know the reason," Crysania said, her fear lost in her compassion. Her hand hesitated a moment, then dropped to the coverlet near his trembling hand, yet not touching him.

"Yes, and I accept it. Still, I cannot forgive him. But that is between your god and myself," Raistlin said reprovingly.

Crysania bit her lip. "I accept my rebuke. It was deserved." She was silent a moment. Raistlin, too, was not inclined to speak, the lines in his face deepening.

"You told Caramon that the gods were with us. So, then, you have communed with my god . . . with Paladine?" Crysania ventured to ask hesitantly.

"Of course," Raistlin smiled his twisted smile. "Does that surprise you?"

Crysania sighed. Her head drooped, the dark hair falling around her shoulders. The faint moonlight in the room made her black hair glimmer with a soft, blue radiance, made her skin gleam purest white. Her perfume filled the room, filled the night. She felt a touch upon her hair. Lifting her head, she saw Raistlin's eyes burn with a passion that came from a source deep within, a source that had nothing to do with magic. Crysania caught her breath, but at that moment Raistlin stood up and walked away.

Crysania sighed. "So, you have communed with both the gods, then?" she asked wistfully.

Raistlin half-turned. "I have communed with all three," he replied of offhandedly.

"Three?" She was startled. "Gilean?"

"Who is Astinus but Gilean's mouthpiece?" Raistlin said scornfully. "If, indeed, he is not Gilean himself,

as some have speculated. But, this must be nothing new to you—"

"I have never talked to the Dark Queen," Crysania said.

"Haven't you?" Raistlin asked with a penetrating look that shook the cleric to the core of her soul. "Does she not know of your heart's desire? Hasn't she offered it to you?"

Looking into his eyes, aware of his nearness, feeling desire sweep over her, Crysania could not reply. Then, as he continued to watch her, she swallowed and shook her head. "If she has," she answered in almost inaudible tones, "she has given it with one hand and denied it to me with the other."

Crysania heard the black robes rustle as if the mage had started. His face, visible in the moonlight, was, for an instant, worried and thoughtful. Then it smoothed.

"I did not come here to discuss theology," Raistlin said with a slight sneer. "I have another, more immediate worry."

"Of course." Crysania flushed, nervously brushing her tangled hair out of her face. "Once again, I apologize. You needed me, you said—"

"Tasslehoff is here."

"Tasslehoff?" Crysania repeated in blank amazement.

"Yes, and he is very ill. Near death, in fact. I need your healing skills."

"But, I don't understand. Why—How did he come to be here?" Crysania stammered, bewildered. "You said he had returned to our own time."

"So I believed," Raistlin replied gravely. "But, apparently, I was mistaken. The magical device brought him here, to this time. He has been wandering the world in the manner of kender, enjoying himself thoroughly. Eventually, hearing of the war, he arrived here to share in the adventure. Unfortunately, he has, in his wanderings, contracted the plague."

"This is terrible! Of course I'll come." Catching up her fur cloak from the end of her bed, she wrapped it around her shoulders, noticing, as she did so, that Raistlin turned away from her. Staring out the window, into the silver moonlight, she saw the muscles of his jaw tighten, as if with some inner struggle.

"I am ready," Crysania said in smooth, businesslike tones, fastening her cloak. Raistlin turned back and extended his hand to her. Crysania looked at him, puzzled.

"We must travel the pathways of the night," he said quietly. "As I told you, I do not want to alert the guards."

"But why not?" she said. "What difference—"

"What will I tell my brother?"

Crysania paused. "I see. . . ."

"You understand my dilemma?" Raistlin asked, regarding her intently. "If I tell him, it will be a worry to him, at a time he can ill afford to add burdens to those he already carries. Tas has broken the magical device. That will upset Caramon, too, even though he is aware I plan to send him home. But—I should tell him the kender is here."

"Caramon *has* looked worried and unhappy these past few days," Crysania said thoughtfully, concern in her voice.

"The war is not going well," Raistlin informed her bluntly. "The army is crumbling around him. The Plainsmen talk every day of leaving. They may be gone now, for all we know. The dwarves under Fireforge are an untrustworthy lot, pressuring Caramon into striking before he is ready. The supply wagons have vanished, no one knows what has become of them. His own army is restless, upset. On top of all this, to have a kender roaming about, chattering aimlessly, distracting him . . ."

Raistlin sighed. "Still, I cannot—in honor—keep this from him."

Crysania's lips tightened. "No, Raistlin. I do not think it would be wise to tell him." Seeing Raistlin look dubious, she continued earnestly. "There is nothing Caramon can do. If the kender is truly ill, as you suspect, I can heal him, but he will be weak for several days. It would only be an added worry to your brother. Caramon plans to march in a few days' time. We will tend the kender, then have him completely recovered, ready to meet his friend on the field if such is his desire."

The archmage sighed again, in reluctance and doubt. Then, he shrugged. "Very well, Revered Daughter," he said. "I will be guided by you in this.

Your words are wise. We will not tell Caramon that the kender has returned."

He moved close to her; and Crysania, looking up at him caught a strange smile upon his face, a smile that—for just this once—was reflected in his glittering eyes. Startled, upset without quite knowing why, she drew back, but he put his arm around her, enveloping her in the soft folds of his black sleeves, holding her close.

Closing her eyes, she forgot that smile. Nestling close, wrapped in his warmth, she listened to his rapid heartbeat . . . .

Murmuring the words of magic, he transformed them both into nothingness. Their shadows seemed to hover for an instant in the moonlight, then these, too, vanished with a whisper.

"You are keeping him here? In the dungeons?" Crysania asked, shivering in the chill, dank air.

"*Shirak.* "Raistlin caused the crystal atop the Staff of Magius to fill the room with soft light. "He lies over there," the mage said, pointing.

A crude bed stood up against one wall. Giving Raistlin a reproachful glance, Crysania hurried to the bedside. As the cleric knelt beside the kender and laid her hand on his feverish forehead, Tas cried out. His eyes flared open, but he stared at her unseeing. Raistlin, following more slowly, gestured to a dark dwarf who was crouched in a corner. "Leave us," the mage motioned, then came to stand by the bedside. Behind him, he heard the door to the cell close.

"How can you keep him locked up in the darkness like this?" Crysania demanded.

"Have you ever treated plague victims before, Lady Crysania?" Raistlin asked in an odd tone.

Startled, she looked up at him, then flushed and averted her eyes.

Smiling bitterly, Raistlin answered his own question. "No, of course not. The plague never came to Palanthas. It never struck the beautiful, the wealthy. . . ." He made no effort to hide his contempt,† and Crysania felt her skin burn as though she were the one with the fever.

"Well, it came to us," Raistlin continued. "It swept through the poorer sections of Haven. Of

Yet more confirmation that Raistlin disdains, more than anything, the "high and mighty" of the world. Despite his thirst for power, he hates those who have power and is the one character who consistently shows compassion, pity, and even affection for gully dwarves and the other downtrodden of the world.

course, there were no healers. Nor were there even many who would stay to care for those who were afflicted. Even their own family members fled them. Poor, pathetic souls. I did what I could, tending them with the herb skill I had acquired. If I could not cure them, at least I could ease their pain. My Master disapproved." Raistlin spoke in an undertone, and Crysania realized that he had forgotten her presence. "So did Caramon—fearing for my health, he said. Bah!" Raistlin laughed without mirth. "He feared for himself. The thought of the plague frightens him more than an army of goblins. But how could I turn my back on them? They had no one . . . no one. Wretched, dying . . . dying alone."

Staring at him dumbly, Crysania felt tears sting her eyes. Raistlin did not see her. In his mind, he was back in those stinking little hovels that huddled on the outskirts of town as though they had run there to hide. He saw himself moving among the sick in his red robes, forcing the bitter medicine down their throats, holding the dying in his arms, easing their last moments. He worked among the sick grimly, asking for no thanks, expecting none. His face—the last human face many would see— expressed neither compassion nor caring. Yet the dying found comfort. Here was one who understood, here was one who lived with pain daily, here was one who had looked upon death and was not afraid. . . .

Raistlin tended the plague victims. He did what he felt he had to do at the risk of his own life, but why? For a reason he had yet to understand. A reason, perhaps, forgotten. . . .

"At any rate"—Raistlin returned to the present— "I discovered that light hurt their eyes. Those who recovered were occasionally stricken blind by—"

A terrified shriek from the kender interrupted him.

Tasslehoff was staring at him wildly. "Please, Raistlin! I'm trying to remember! Don't take me back to the Dark Queen—"

"Hush, Tas," Crysania said softly, gripping the kender with both hands as Tas seemed to be trying, literally, to climb into the wall behind him. "Calm down, Tas. It is Lady Crysania. Do you know me? I'm going to help you."

Tas transferred his wide-eyed, feverish gaze to the cleric, regarding her blankly for a moment. Then, with a sob, he clutched at her. "Don't let him take me back to the Abyss, Crysania! Don't let him take you! It's horrible, horrible. We'll all die, die like poor Gnimsh. The Dark Queen told me!"

"He's raving," Crysania murmured, trying to disengage Tas's clinging hands and force him to lie back down. "What strange delusions. Is this common with plague victims?"

"Yes," Raistlin replied. Regarding Tas intently, the mage knelt by the bedside. "Sometimes it's best to humor them. It may calm him. Tasslehoff—"

Raistlin laid his hand upon the kender's chest. Instantly, Tas collapsed back onto the bed, shrinking away from the mage, shivering and staring at him in horror. "I'll be good, Raistlin." He whimpered. "Don't hurt me, not like poor Gnimsh. Lightning, lightning!"

"Tas," said Raistlin firmly, with a hint of anger and exasperation in his voice that caused Crysania to glance over at him reprovingly.

But, seeing only a look of cool concern on his face, she supposed she must have mistaken his tone. Closing her eyes, she touched the medallion of Paladine she wore around her neck and began to murmur a healing prayer.

"I'm not going to hurt you, Tas. Shhh, lie still." Seeing Crysania lost in her communion with her god, Raistlin hissed, "Tell me, Tas. Tell me what the Dark Queen said."

The kender's face lost its bright, feverish flush as Crysania's soft words flowed over him, sweeter and cooler than the waters of his delirious imaginings. The diminishing fever left Tas's face a ghastly, ashen color. A faint glimmering of sense returned to his eyes. But he never took his gaze from Raistlin.

"She told me . . . before we left. . . ." Tas choked.

"Left?" Raistlin leaned forward. "I thought you said you escaped!"

Tas blanched, licking his dry, cracked lips. He tried to tear his gaze away from the mage, but Raistlin's eyes, glittering in the light of the staff, held the kender fast, draining the truth from him. Tas swallowed. His throat hurt.

"Water," he pleaded.

"When you've told me!" Raistlin snarled with a glance at Crysania, who was still kneeling, her head in her hands, praying to Paladine.

Tas gulped painfully. "I . . . I thought we were . . . escaping. We used th-the device and began . . . to rise. I saw . . . the Abyss, the plane, flat, empty, fall away beneath m-my feet. And"—Tas shuddered—"it wasn't empty anymore! There . . . there were shadows and—" He tossed his head, moaning. "Oh, Raistlin, don't make me remember! Don't make me go back there!"

"Hush!" Raistlin whispered, covering Tas's mouth with his hand. Crysania glanced up in concern, only to see Raistlin tenderly stroking the kender's cheek. Seeing Tas's terrified expression and pale face, Crysania frowned and shook her head.

"He is better," she said. "He will not die. But dark shadows hover around him, preventing Paladine's healing light from restoring him fully. They are the shadows of these feverish ramblings. Can you make anything from them?" Her feathery brows came together. "Whatever it is seems very real to him. It must have been something dreadful to have unnerved a kender like this."

"Perhaps, lady, if you left, he would feel more comfortable talking to me," Raistlin suggested mildly. "We are such old friends."

"True," Crysania smiled, starting to rise to her feet. To her amazement, Tas grabbed her hands.

"Don't leave me with him, lady!" He gasped. "He killed Gnimsh! Poor Gnimsh. I saw him di-die!" Tas began to weep. "Burning lightning . . ."

"There, there, Tas," Crysania said soothingly, gently but firmly forcing the kender to lie back down. "No one's going to hurt you. Whoever killed this—uh—Gnimsh can't harm you now. You're with your friends. Isn't he, Raistlin?"

"My magic is powerful," Raistlin said softly. "Remember that, Tasslehoff. Remember the power of my magic."

"Yes, Raistlin," Tas replied, lying quite still, pinned by the mage's fixed and staring gaze.

"I think it would be wise if you remained behind to talk to him," Crysania said in an undertone. "These dark fears will prey on him and hinder the

healing process. I will return to my room on my own, with Paladine's help."

"So we agree not to tell Caramon?" Raistlin glanced at Crysania out of the corner of his eye.

"Yes," Crysania said firmly. "This would only worry him unnecessarily." She looked back at her patient. "I will return in the morning, Tasslehoff. Talk to Raistlin. Unburden your soul. Then sleep." Laying her cool hand upon Tas's sweat-covered forehead, she added, "May Paladine be with you."

"Caramon?" Tas said hopefully. "Did you say Caramon? Is he here?"

"Yes, and when you've slept and eaten and rested, I'll take you to him."

"Couldn't I see him now!" Tas cried eagerly, then he cast a fearful sideways glance at Raistlin. "If—if it wouldn't be too much trouble, that is. . . ."

"He's very busy." Raistlin said coldly. "He is a general now, Tasslehoff. He has armies to command, a war to fight. He has no time for kenders."

"No, I—I suppose not," Tas said with a small sigh, lying back on his pillow, his eyes still on Raistlin.

With a final, soft pat on his head, Crysania stood up. Holding the medallion of Paladine in her hand, she whispered a prayer and was gone, vanishing into the night.

"And now, Tasslehoff," Raistlin said in a soft voice that made Tas tremble, "we are alone." With his strong hands, the mage pulled the blankets up over the kender's body and straightened the pillow beneath his head. "There, are you comfortable?"

Tas couldn't speak. He could only stare at the archmage in growing horror.

Raistlin sat down on the bed beside him. Putting one slender hand upon Tas's forehead, he idly caressed the kender's skin and smoothed back his damp hair.

"Do you remember Dalamar, my apprentice, Tas?" Raistlin asked conversationally. "You saw him, I believe at the Tower of High Sorcery, am I correct?" Raistlin's fingers were light as the feet of spiders upon Tas's face. "Do you recall, at one point, Dalamar tore open his black robes, exhibiting five wounds upon his chest? Yes, I see you recall that. It was his punishment, Tas. Punishment for hiding things from me." Raistlin's fingers stopped crawling about the

kender's skin and remained in one place, exerting a slight pressure on Tas's forehead.

Tas shivered, biting his tongue to keep from crying out. "I—I remember, Raistlin."

"An interesting experience, don't you think?" Raistlin said offhandedly. "I can burn through your flesh with a touch, as I might burn through, say"—he shrugged—"butter with a hot knife. Kender are fond of interesting experiences, I believe."

"Not—not quite *that* interesting," Tas whispered miserably. "I'll tell you, Raistlin! I'll tell you everything that—that happened." He closed his eyes a moment, then began to talk, his entire body quivering with the remembered terror. "We—we seemed not to rise up out of the Abyss so much as . . . as the Abyss dropped away beneath us! And then, like I said, I saw it wasn't empty. I could see shadows and I thought . . . I thought they were valleys and mountains . . . ."

Tas's eyes flared open. He stared at the mage in awe. "It wasn't! Those shadows were *her* eyes, Raistlin! And the hills and valleys were *her* nose and mouth. We were rising up out of her face! She looked at me with eyes that were bright and gleamed with fire, and she opened her mouth and I—I thought she was going to swallow us! But we only rose higher and higher and she fell away beneath us, swirling, and then she looked at me and she said . . . she said. . . ."

"What did she say?" Raistlin demanded. "The message was to me! It must have been! *That* was why she sent you! What did the Queen say?"

Tas's voice grew hushed. "She said, 'Come home . . .' "

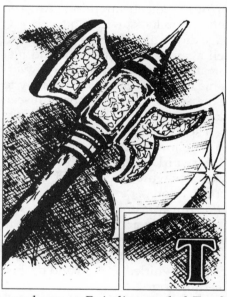

Chapter 13

The effect of his words upon Raistlin startled Tasslehoff just about as much as anything had ever startled him in his entire life. Tas had seen Raistlin angry before. He had seen him pleased, he had seen him commit murder, he had seen the mage's face when Kharas, the dwarven hero, drove his sword blade into the mage's flesh.

But he had never seen an expression on it like this.

Raistlin's face went ashen, so white Tas thought for a wild moment that the mage had died, perhaps been struck dead on the spot. The mirrorlike eyes seemed to shatter; Tas saw himself reflected in tiny, splintered shards of the mage's vision. Then he saw the eyes lose all recognition, go completely blank, staring ahead sightlessly.

The hand that rested upon Tas's head began to tremble violently. And, as the kender watched in astonishment, he saw Raistlin seem to shrivel up before him. His face aged perceptively. When he rose to his feet, still staring unseeing around him, the mage's entire body shook.

"Raistlin?" Tas asked nervously, glad to have the mage's attention off him but bewildered by his strange appearance. The kender sat up weakly. The terrible dizziness had gone, along with the weird, unfamiliar feeling of fear. He felt almost like himself again.

"Raistlin . . . I didn't mean anything. Are *you* going to be sick now? You look awfully queer—"

But the archmage didn't answer. Staggering backward, Raistlin fell against the stone wall and just stood there, his breathing rapid and shallow. Covering his face with his hand, he fought desperately to regain control of himself, a fight with some unseen opponent that was yet as visible to Tas as if the mage had been fighting a spectre.

Then, with a low, hollow cry of rage and anguish, Raistlin lurched forward. Gripping the Staff of Magius, his black robes whipping around him, he fled through the open door.

Staring after Raistlin in astonishment, Tas saw him hurtle past the dark dwarf standing guard in the doorway. The dwarf took one look at the mage's cadaverous face as Raistlin ran blindly past him, and, with a wild shriek, whirled around and dashed off in the opposite direction.

So amazing was all this that it took Tas a few moments to realize he wasn't a prisoner anymore.

"You know," the kender said to himself, putting his hand on his forehead, "Crysania was right. I *do* feel better now that I've gotten that off my mind. It didn't do much for Raistlin, unfortunately, but then I don't care about that. Well, much." Tas sighed. "I'll never understand why he killed poor Gnimsh. Maybe I'll have a chance to ask him someday.

"But, now"—the kender glanced around—"the first thing to do is find Caramon and tell him I've got the magical device and we can go home. I never thought I'd say this," Tas said wistfully, swinging his feet to the floor, "but home sounds *awfully* nice right now!"

He was going to stand up, but his legs apparently

preferred to be back in bed because Tas suddenly found himself sitting down again.

"This won't do!" Tas said,† glaring at the offending parts of his body. "You're nowhere without me! Just remember that! I'm boss and when I say move—you'll move! Now, I'm going to stand up again," Tas warned his legs sternly. "And I expect some cooperation."

This speech had some effect. His legs behaved a bit better this time and the kender, though still somewhat wobbly, managed to make his way across the dark room toward the torchlit corridor he could see beyond the door.

Reaching it, he peeped cautiously up and down the hall, but no one was in sight. Creeping out into corridor, he saw nothing but dark, closed-up cells like the one he'd been in—and a staircase at one end, leading up. Looking down the other end, he saw nothing but dark shadows.

"I wonder where I am?" Tas made his way down the corridor toward the staircase—that being, as far as he could tell, the only way up. "Oh, well!"—the kender reflected philosophically—"I don't suppose it matters. One *good* thing about having been in the Abyss is that every place else, no matter how dismal, looks congenial by comparison."†

He had to stop a moment for a brief argument with his legs—they still seemed much inclined to return to bed—but this momentary weakness passed, and the kender reached the bottom of the staircase. Listening, he could hear voices.

"Drat," he muttered, coming to a halt and ducking back into the shadows. "Someone's up there. Guards, I suppose. Sounds like dwarves. Those whatcha'ma call-ems—Dewar." Tas stood, quietly, trying to make out what the deep voices were saying. "You'd think they could speak a civilized language," he snapped irritably. "One a fellow could understand. They sound excited, though."

Curiosity finally getting the better of him, Tas crept up the first flight of stone steps and peered around the corner. He ducked back quickly with a sigh. "Two of 'em. Both blocking the stair. And there's no way around them."

His pouches with his tools and weapons were gone, left behind in the mountain dungeon of

I believe that Tasslehoff speaks to himself so much because first of all, he finds his own conversation more interesting than the conversation of those around him and secondly, those around him quickly tire of his conversation.
—TRH

Tas, the eternal optimist, manages to see good in almost anything.

Thorbardin. But he still had his knife. "Not that it will do much good against *those.*" Tas reflected, envisioning once again the huge battle-axes he'd seen the dwarves holding.

He waited a few more moments, hoping the dwarves would leave. They certainly seemed worked up, but they also appeared rooted to the spot.

"I can't stay here all night or day, whichever it is," the kender grumbled. "Well, as dad said, 'always try talk before the lockpick.' The very *worst* they could do to me, I suppose—not counting killing me, of course—would be to lock me back up. And, if I'm any judge of locks, I could probably be out again in about half-an-hour." He began to climb the stairs. "Was it dad who said that," he pondered as he climbed, "or Uncle Trapspringer?"†

Rounding the corner, he confronted two Dewar, who appeared considerably startled to see him. "Hello!" the kender said cheerfully. "My name is Tasslehoff Burrfoot." He extended a hand. "And your names are? Oh, you're not going to tell me. Well, that's all right. I probably couldn't pronounce them anyway. Say, I'm a prisoner and I'm looking for the fellow who was keeping me locked up in that cell back there. You probably know him—a black-robed magic-user. He was interrogating me, when something I said took him by surprise, I think, because he had a sort of a fit and ran out of the room. And he forgot to lock the door behind him. Did either of you see which way he—Well!" Tas blinked. "How rude."

This in response to the actions of the Dewar who, after regarding the kender with growing looks of alarm on their faces, shouted one word, turned, and bolted.

"*Antarax,*"† Tas repeated, looking after them, puzzled. "Let's see. That sounds like dwarven for . . . for . . . Oh, of course! Burning death. Ah—they think I've still got the plague! Mmmmm, that's handy. Or is it?"

The kender found himself alone in another long corridor, every bit as bleak and dismal as the one he'd just left. "I still don't know where I am, and no one seems inclined to tell me. The only way out is that staircase down there and those two are

For years, Uncle Trapspringer was relegated to kender folklore. However, he was finally given his own story in Tales of Uncle Trapspringer *by Dixie Lee McKeone.*

Antarax is most likely a play on the word "anthrax." One of the most difficult things writers do is constantly coming up with fantasy names for things, so sometimes we just borrow from real language. —TRH

heading for it so I guess the best thing to do is just tag along. Caramon's bound to be around here somewhere."

But Tas's legs, which had already registered a protest against walking, informed the kender in no uncertain terms that running was out of the question. He stumbled along as fast as possible after the dwarves, but they had dashed up the stairs and were out of sight by the time he had made it halfway down the corridor. Puffing along, feeling a bit dizzy but determined to find Caramon, Tas climbed the stairs after them. As he rounded a corner, he came to a sudden halt.

"Oops," he said, and hurriedly ducked into the shadows. Clapping a hand over mouth, he severely reprimanded himself. "Shut up, Burrfoot! It's the whole Dewar army."

It certainly seemed like it. The two he had been following had met up with about twenty other dwarves. Crouching in the shadows, Tas could hear them yelping excitedly, and he expected them to come tromping down after him any moment . . . . But nothing happened.

He waited, listening to the conversation, then, risking a peep, he saw that some of the dwarves present didn't look like Dewar. They were clean, their beards were brushed, and they were dressed in bright armor. And they didn't appear pleased. They glared grimly at one of the Dewar, as though they'd just as soon skin him as not.

"Mountain dwarves!" Tas muttered to himself in astonishment, recognizing the armor. "And, from what Raistlin said, *they're* the enemy. Which means they're supposed to be in their mountain, not in ours. Provided we're in a mountain, of course, which I'm beginning to think likely from the looks of it. But, I wonder—"

As one of the mountain dwarves began speaking, Tas brightened. "Finally, someone who knows how to talk!" The kender sighed in relief. Because of the mixture of races, the dwarf was speaking a crude version of Common and dwarven.

The gist of the conversation, as near as Tas could follow, was that the mountain dwarf didn't give a cracked stone about a crazed wizard or a wandering, plague-ridden kender.

"We came here to get the head of this General Caramon," the mountain dwarf growled. "You said that the wizard promised it would be arranged. If it is, we can dispense with the wizard. I'd just as soon not deal with a Black Robe anyway. And now answer me this, Argat. Are your people ready to attack the army from within? Are you prepared to kill this general? Or was this just a trick? If so, you will find it will go hard with your people back in Thorbardin."

"It no trick!" Argat growled, his fist clenching. "We ready to move. The general is in the War Room. The wizard said he make sure him alone with just bodyguard. Our people get the hill dwarves to attack. When *you* keep your part bargain, when scouts give signal that great gates to Thorbardin are open—"

"The signal is sounding, even as we speak," the mountain dwarf snapped. "If we were above ground level, you could hear the trumpets. The army rides forth!"

"Then we go!" Argat said. Bowing, he added with a sneer, "If your lordship dares, come with us—we take General Caramon's head right now!"

"I will join you," the mountain dwarf said coldly, "if only to make certain you plot no further treachery."

What else the two said was lost on Tas, who leaned back against the wall. His legs had gone all prickly-feeling, and there was a buzzing noise in his ears.

"Caramon," he whispered, clutching at his head, trying to think. "They're going to kill him! And Raistlin's done this!" Tas shuddered. "Poor Caramon. His own twin. If he knew that, it would probably just kill him dead on the spot. The dwarves wouldn't need axes."

Suddenly, the kender's head snapped up. "Tasslehoff Burrfoot!" he said angrily. "What are you doing—standing around like a gully dwarf with one foot in the mud. You've got to save him! You promised Tika you'd take care of him, after all."

"Save him? How, you doorknob?" boomed a voice inside of him that sounded suspiciously like Flint's. "There must be twenty dwarves! And you armed with that rabbit-killer!"†

Tas's blade was named "Rabbit-slayer" after Caramon told him disparagingly that the blade was good only for killing rabbits. Also, the image of the rabbit that runs throughout the story returns here. —MW

"I'll think of something," Tas retorted. "So just keep sitting under your tree."

There was a snorting sound. Resolutely ignoring it, the kender stood up tall and straight, pulled out his little knife, and crept quietly—as only kender can—down the corridor.

This seems to indicate that magic is a matter of birthright or genetics. I'm not aware that this concept ever found its way into general thought within the DRAGONLANCE setting. —TRH

I have always equated magic in Krynn with artistic talent. I believe that there are many talented artists, but very few great ones. The talented artist can gain magic by diligent work and study. The great artist has the magic present in his or her blood at birth. In other words, there are many composers, but only one Mozart. —MW

She had the dark, curly hair and the crooked smile that men would later find so charming in her daughter. She had the simple, guileless honesty that would characterize one of her sons and she had a gift—a rare and wonderful power—that she would pass on to the other.

She had magic in her blood,† as did her son. But she was weak—weak-willed, weak-spirited. Thus she let the magic control her, and thus, finally, she died.

Neither the strong-souled Kitiara nor the physically strong Caramon was much affected by their mother's death. Kitiara hated her mother with bitter jealousy, while Caramon, though he cared about his mother, was far closer to his frail twin. Besides, his mother's weird ramblings and mystical trances made her a complete enigma to the young warrior.

But her death devastated Raistlin. The only one of her children who truly understood her, he pitied her for her weakness, even as he despised her for it. And he was furious at her for dying, furious at her for leaving him alone in this world, alone with the gift. He was angry and, deep within, he was filled with fear, for Raistlin saw in her his own doom.†

Following the death of her father, his mother had gone into a grief-stricken trance from which she never emerged. Raistlin had been helpless. He could do nothing but watch her dwindle away. Refusing food, she drifted, lost, onto magical planes only she could see. And the mage—her son—was shaken to his very core.

This paragraph sums up much of Raistlin's character. His greatest motivation—in fact the one above all others that so drives his lust for power—is his pity for weakness. Here we learn that this is tied up with Raistlin's relationship with his mother.

He sat up with her on that last night. Holding her wasted hand in his, he watched as her sunken, feverish eyes stared at wonders conjured up by magic gone berserk.

That night, Raistlin vowed deep within his soul that no one and nothing would ever have the power to manipulate him like this—not his twin brother, not his sister, not the magic, not the gods. He and he alone would be the guiding force of his life.

He vowed this, swearing it with a bitter, binding oath. But he was a boy still—a boy left alone in darkness as he sat there with his mother the night she died. He watched her draw her last, shuddering breath. Holding her thin hand with its delicate fingers (so like his own!), he pleaded softly through his tears, "Mother, come home . . . . Come home!"

Now at Zhaman he heard these words again, challenging him, mocking him, daring him. They rang in his ears, reverberated in his brain with wild, discordant clangings. His head bursting with pain, he stumbled into a wall.

Raistlin had once seen Lord Ariakas torture a captured knight by locking the man inside a bell tower. The dark clerics rang the bells of praise to their Queen that night—all night. The next morning, the man had been found dead—a look of horror upon his face so profound and awful that even those steeped in cruelty were quick to dispose of the corpse.

Raistlin felt as if he were imprisoned within his own bell tower, his own words ringing his doom in his skull. Reeling, clutching his head, he tried desperately to blot out the sound.

"Come home . . . come home. . . ."

Dizzy and blinded by the pain, the mage sought to outrun it. He staggered about with no clear idea of where he was, searching only for escape. His numb feet lost their footing. Tripping over the hem of his black robe, he fell to his knees.

An object leaped from a pocket in his robes and rolled out onto the stone floor. Seeing it, Raistlin gasped in fear and anger. It was another mark of his failure—the dragon orb, cracked, darkened, useless. Frantically he grabbed for it, but it skittered like a marble across the flagstone, eluding his clawing grasp.

Desperate, he crawled after it and, finally, it rolled to a stop. With a snarl, Raistlin started to take hold of it, then halted. Lifting his head, his eyes opened wide. He saw where he was, and he shrank back, trembling.

Before him loomed the Great Portal.

It was exactly like the one in the Tower of High Sorcery in Palanthas. A huge oval door standing upon a raised dais, it was ornamented and guarded by the heads of five dragons. Their sinuous necks snaking up from the floor, the five heads faced inward, five mouths open, screaming silent tribute to their Queen.

In the Tower at Palanthas, the door to the Portal was closed. None could open it except from within the Abyss itself, coming the opposite direction—an egress from a place none ever left. This door, too, was closed, but there were two who could enter— a White-Robed Cleric of Infinite Goodness and a Black-Robed Archmage of Infinite Evil. It was an unlikely combination.† Thus the great wizards hoped to seal forever this terrible entrance onto an immortal plane.

An ordinary mortal, looking into that Portal, could see nothing but stark, chill darkness.

But Raistlin was no longer ordinary. Drawing nearer and nearer his goddess, bending his energies and his studies toward this one object, the archmage was now in a state suspended between both worlds. Looking into the closed door, *he* could almost penetrate that darkness! It wavered in his vision. Wrenching his gaze from it, he turned his attention back to retrieving the dragon orb.

The light and the dark, the good and the evil in combination, and the balance between them is, once again, at the heart of the DRAGONLANCE setting's mythology. This combination directly reflects those qualities. —TRH

How did it escape me? he wondered angrily. He kept the orb in a bag hidden deep within a secret pocket of his robes. But then he sneered at himself, for he knew the answer. Each dragon orb was endowed with a strong sense of self-preservation.† The one at Istar had escaped the Cataclysm by tricking the elven king, Lorac, into stealing it and taking it into Silvanesti. When the orb could no longer use the insane Lorac, it had attached itself to Raistlin. It had sustained Raistlin's life when he was dying in Astinus's library. It had conspired with Fistandantilus to take the young man to the Queen of Darkness. Now, sensing the greatest danger of its existence, it was trying to flee him.

Not unlike Sauron's Ring in The Lord of the Rings.

He would not allow it! Reaching out, his hand closed firmly over the dragon orb.

There was a shriek. . . .

The Portal opened.

Raistlin looked up. It had not opened to admit him. No, it had opened to warn him—to show him the penalty of failure.

Prostrate upon his knees, clutching the orb to his chest, Raistlin felt the presence and the majesty of Takhisis, Queen of Darkness rise up before him. Awe-stricken, he cowered, trembling, at the Dark Queen's feet.

This is your doom! Her words hissed in his mind. *Your mother's fate will be your own. Swallowed by your magic, you will be held forever spellbound without even the sweet consolation of death to end your suffering!*

Raistlin collapsed. He felt his body shrivel. Thus he had seen the withered body of Fistandantilus shrivel at the touch of the bloodstone.

His head resting on the stone floor as it rested upon the executioner's block of his nightmare, the mage was about to admit defeat. . . .

But there was a core of strength within Raistlin. Long ago, Par-Salian, head of the Order of White Robes, had been given a task by the gods. They needed a magic-user strong enough to help defeat the growing evil of the Queen of Darkness. Par-Salian had searched long and had at last chosen Raistlin. For he had seen within the young mage this inner core of strength. It had been a cold, shapeless mass of iron when Raistlin was young. But

Par-Salian hoped that the white-hot fire of suffering, pain, war, and ambition would forge that mass into finest tempered steel.

Raistlin lifted his head from the cold stone.

The heat of the Queen's fury beat around him. Sweat poured from his body. He could not breathe as fire seared his lungs. She tormented him, mocked him with his own words, his own visions. She laughed at him, as so many had laughed at him before. And yet, even as his body shivered with a fear unlike any he had ever known, Raistlin's soul began to exult.

Puzzled, he tried to analyze it. He sought to regain control and, after an exertion that left him weak and shaking, he banished the ringing sounds of his mother's voice from his ears. He closed his eyes to his Queen's mocking smile.

Darkness enveloped him and he saw, in the cool, sweet darkness, his Queen's fear.

She was afraid . . . afraid of him!

Slowly, Raistlin rose to his feet. Hot winds blew from the Portal, billowing the black robes around him until he seemed enveloped in thunderclouds. He could look directly into the Portal now. His eyes narrowed. He regarded the dread door with a grim, twisted smile. Then, lifting his hand, Raistlin hurled the dragon orb into the Portal.

Hitting that invisible wall, the orb shattered. There was an almost imperceptible scream. Dark, shadowy wings fluttered around the mage's head, then, with a wail, the wings dissolved into smoke and were blown away.

Strength coursed through Raistlin's body, strength such as he had never known. The knowledge of his enemy's weakness affected him like an intoxicating liquor. He felt the magic flow from his mind into his heart and from there to his veins. The accumulated, combined power of centuries of learning was his— his and Fistandantilus's!

And then he heard it, the clear, clarion call of a trumpet, its music cold as the air from the snow-covered mountains of the dwarven homelands in the distance. Pure and crisp, the trumpet call echoed in his mind, driving out the distracting voices, calling him into darkness, giving him a power over death itself.

Raistlin paused. He hadn't intended to enter the Portal this soon. He would have like to have waited just a little longer. But now would do, if necessary. The kender's arrival meant time could be altered. The death of the gnome insured there would be no interference from the magical device— the interference that had proved the death of Fistandantilus.

The time had come.

Raistlin gave the Portal a last, lingering glance. Then, with a bow to his Queen, he turned and strode purposefully away up the corridor.

Crysania knelt in prayer in her room.

She had started to go back to bed after her return from the kender, but a strange feeling of foreboding filled her. There was a breathlessness in the air. A sense of waiting made her pause. Sleep would not come. She was alert, awake, more awake than she had ever been in her entire life.

The sky was filled with light—the cold fire of the stars burning in the darkness; the silver moon, Solinari, shining like a dagger. She could see every object in her room with an uncanny clarity, Each seemed alive, watching, waiting with her.

Transfixed, she stared at the stars, tracing the lines of the constellations—Gilean, the Book, the Scales of Balance; Takhisis, the Queen of Darkness, the Dragon of Many Colors and of None; Paladine, the Valiant Warrior, the Platinum Dragon. The moons—Solinari, God's Eye; Lunitari, Night Candle. Beyond them, ranged about the skies, the lesser gods, and among them, the planets.

And, somewhere, the Black Moon—the moon only his eyes could see.

Standing, staring into the night, Crysania's fingers grew cold as she rested them upon the chill stone. She realized she was shivering and she turned around, telling herself it was time to sleep. . . .

But there was still that tremulous intake of breath about the night. "Wait," it whispered. "Wait. . . ."

And then she heard the trumpet. Pure and crisp, its music pierced her heart, crying a paean of victory that thrilled her blood.

At that moment, the door to her room opened.

She was not surprised to see him. It was as if she

had been expecting his arrival, and she turned, calmly, to face him.

Raistlin stood silhouetted in the doorway, outlined against the light of torches blazing in the corridor and outlined as well by his own light which welled darkly from beneath his robes, an unholy light that came from within.

Drawn by some strange force, Crysania looked back into the heavens and saw, gleaming with that same dark light, Nuitari—the Black Moon.

For a moment, she closed her eyes, overwhelmed by the dizzying rush of blood, the beating of her heart. Then, feeling herself grow strong, she opened them again to find Raistlin standing before her.

She caught her breath. She had seen him in the ecstasy of his magic, she had seen him battling defeat and death. Now she saw him in the fullness of his strength, in the majesty of his dark power. Ancient wisdom and intelligence were etched into his face, a face that she barely recognized as his own.

"It is time, Crysania," he said, extending his hands.

She took hold of his hands. Her fingers were chilled, his touch burned them. "I am afraid," she whispered.

He drew her near.

"You have no need to be afraid," he said. "Your god is with you. I see that clearly. It is my goddess who is afraid, Crysania. I sense her fear! Together, you and I will cross the borders of time and enter the realm of death. Together, we will battle the Darkness. Together, we will bring Takhisis to her knees!"†

His hands caught her close to his breast, his arms embraced her. His lips closed over hers, stealing her breath with his kiss.

Crysania closed her eyes and let the magical fire, the fire that consumed the bodies of the dead, consume her body, consume the cold, frightened, white-robed shell she had been hiding in all these years.

He drew back, tracing her mouth with his hand, raising her chin so that she could look into his eyes. And there, reflected in the mirror of his soul, she saw herself, glowing with a flaming aura of radiant, pure, white light. She saw herself beautiful, beloved, worshipped. She saw herself bringing truth and justice to the world, banishing forever sorrow and fear and despair.

Raistlin is using Crysania badly, playing directly to her fault (and to the fault of the Kingpriest). Raistlin certainly intends to defeat the god of evil, but what he is not telling Crysania is that he intends to replace her—and all the gods for that matter. —TRH

"Blessed be to Paladine," Crysania whispered.

"Blessed be," Raistlin replied. "Once again, I give you a charm. As I protected you through Shoikan Grove, so you shall be guarded when we pass through the Portal."

She trembled. Drawing her near, holding her close one last time, he pressed his lips upon her forehead. Pain shot through her body and seared her heart. She flinched but did not cry out. He smiled at her.

"Come."

On the whispered words of a winged spell, they left the room to the night, just as the red rays of Lunitari spilled into the darkness—blood drawn from Solinari's† glittering knife.

Here, once more, all three symbols are present—good, evil, and neutrality. This is a sign of the culmination of the plan. —TRH

CHAPTER 15

The supply wagons?" Caramon asked in even, measured tones—the tones of one who already knows the answer.

"No word, sir," replied Garic, avoiding Caramon's steady gaze. "But . . . but we expect them—"

"They won't be coming. They've been ambushed. You know that." Caramon smiled wearily.

"At least we've found water," Garic said lamely, making a valiant effort to sound cheerful, which failed miserably. Keeping his gaze fixed on the map spread on the table before him, he nervously drew a small circle around a tiny green dot on the parchment.

Caramon snorted. "A hole that is emptied by midday. Oh, sure, it fills again at night, but my own sweat tastes better. Blasted stuff must be tainted by sea water."

"Still, it's drinkable. We're rationing, of course,

and I've set guards around it. But it doesn't look like it's going to run dry."

"Oh, well. There won't be men enough left to drink it to worry about it after a while," Caramon said, running his hand through his curly hair with a sigh. It was hot in the room, hot and stuffy. Some overzealous servant had tossed wood onto the fire before Caramon, accustomed to living outdoors, could stop him. The big man had thrown open a window to let the fresh, crisp air inside, but the blaze roaring at his back was toasting him nicely nonetheless. "What's the desertion count today?"

Garic cleared his throat. "About—about one hundred, sir," he said reluctantly.

"Where'd they go? Pax Tharkas?"

"Yes, sir. So we believe."

"What else?" Caramon asked grimly, his eyes studying Garic's face. "You're keeping something back."

The young knight flushed. Garic had a passing wish, at this moment, that lying was not against every code of honor he held dear. As he would have given his life to spare this man pain, so he would almost have lied. He hesitated, then—looking at Caramon—he saw it wasn't necessary. The general knew already.

Caramon nodded slowly. "The Plainsmen?"

Garic looked down at the maps.

"All of them?"

"Yes, sir."

Caramon's eyes closed. Sighing softly, he picked up one of the small wooden figures that had been spread out on the map to represent the placement and disposition of his troops. Rolling it around in his fingers, he grew thoughtful. Then, suddenly, with a bitter curse, he turned and heaved the figurine into the fire. After a moment, he let his aching head sink into his hands.

"I don't suppose I blame Darknight. It won't be easy for him and his men, even now. The mountain dwarves undoubtedly hold the mountain passes behind us—that's what happened to the supply wagons. He'll have to fight his way home. May the gods go with him."

Caramon was silent a moment, then his fists clenched. "Damn my brother," he cursed. "Damn him!"

Garic shifted nervously. His gaze darted about the room, fearful that the black-robed figure might materialize from the shadows.

"Well," Caramon said, straightening and studying the maps once again, "this isn't getting us anywhere. Now, our only hope—as I see it—is to keep what's left of our army here in the plains. We've got to draw the dwarves out, force them to fight in the open so we can utilize our cavalry. We'll never win our way into the mountain," he added, a note of bitterness creeping into his voice, "but at least we can retreat with a hope of winning back to Pax Tharkas with our forces still intact. Once there, we can fortify it and—"

"General." One of the guards at the door entered the room, flushing at having to interrupt. "Begging your pardon, sir, but a messenger's arrived."

"Send him in."

A young man entered the room. Covered with dust, his cheeks red from the cold, he cast the blazing fire a longing glance but stepped forward first to deliver his message.

"No, go on, warm yourself," Caramon said, waving the man over to the fireplace. "I'm glad someone can appreciate it. I have a feeling your news is going to be foul to the taste anyway."

"Thank you, sir," the man said gratefully. Standing near the blaze, he spread his hands out to the warmth. "My news is this—the hill dwarves have gone."

"Gone?" Caramon repeated in blank astonishment, rising to his feet. "Gone where? Surely not back—"

"They march on Thorbardin." The messenger hesitated. "And, sir, the Knights went with them."

"That's insane!" Caramon's fist crashed down upon the table, sending the wooden markers flying through the air, the maps rolling off the edges. His face grew grim. "My brother."

"No, sir. It was apparently the Dewar. I was instructed to give you this." Drawing a scroll from his pouch, he handed it to Caramon, who quickly opened it.

General Caramon,

I have just learned from Dewar spies that the gates to the mountain will open when the trumpet sounds. We

*plan to steal a march on them. Rising at dawn, we will
reach there by nightfall. I am sorry there wasn't time to
inform you of this. Rest assured, you will receive what
share of the spoils you are due, even if you arrive late.
Reorx's light shine on your axes.*

Reghar Fireforge

Caramon's mind went back to the piece of blood-
stained parchment he'd held in his hand not long
ago. *The wizard has betrayed you. . . .*

"Dewar," Caramon scowled. "Dewar spies. Spies
all right, but not for us! Traitors all right, but not to
their own people!"

"A trap!" Garic said, rising to his feet as well.

"And we fell into it like a bunch of damn rabbits,"
Caramon muttered, thinking of another rabbit in a
trap; seeing, in his mind's eyes, his brother setting it
free. "Pax Tharkas falls. No great loss. It can always
be retaken—especially if the defenders are dead.
Our people deserting in droves, the Plainsmen leaving. And now the hill dwarves marching to Thorbardin, the Dewar marching with them. And, when
the trumpet sounds—"

The clear, clarion call of a trumpet rang out. Caramon started. Was he hearing it or was it a dream,
borne on the wings of a terrible vision? He could
almost see it being played out before his eyes—the
Dewar, slowly, imperceptibly spreading out among
the hill dwarves, infiltrating their ranks. Hand
creeping to axe, hammer . . .

Most of Reghar's people would never know what
hit them, would never have a chance to strike.

Caramon could hear the shouts, the thudding of
iron-shod boots, the clash of weapons, and the
harsh, discordant cries of deep voices. It was real, so
very real. . . .

Lost in his vision, Caramon only dimly became
aware of the sudden pallor of Garic's face. Drawing
his sword, the young Knight sprang toward the door
with a shout that jolted Caramon back to reality.
Whirling, he saw a black tide of dark dwarves surging outside the door. There was a flash of steel.

"Ambush!" Garic yelled.

"Fall back!" Caramon thundered. "Don't go out
there! The Knights are gone—we're the only ones

here! Stay inside the room. Bolt the door." Leaping after Garic, he grabbed the Knight and hurled him back. "You guards, retreat!" he yelled to the two who were still standing outside the door and who were now battling for their lives.

Caramon gripped the arm of one of the guards to drag him into the room, bringing his sword down upon the head of an attacking Dewar at the same time. The dwarf's helm shattered. Blood spattered over Caramon, but he paid no attention. Shoving the guard behind him, Caramon hurled himself bodily at the horde of dark dwarves packed into the corridor, his sword slashing a bloody swath through them.

"Fall back, you fool!" he shouted over his shoulder at the second guard, who hesitated only a moment, then did as ordered. Caramon's ferocious charge had the intended effect of catching the Dewar off-balance—they stumbled backward in momentary panic at the sight of his battle-rage. But, that was all the panic was—momentary. Already Caramon could see them starting to recover their wits and their courage.

"General! Look out!" shouted Garic, standing in the doorway, his sword still in hand. Turning, Caramon headed back for the safety of the map room. But his foot slipped on the blood-covered stones and the big man fell, wrenching his knee painfully.

With a wild howl, the Dewar leaped on him.

"Get inside! Bolt the door, you—" The rest of Caramon's words were lost as he disappeared beneath a seething mass of dwarves.

"Caramon!"

Sick at heart, cursing himself for hanging back, Garic jumped into the fray. A hammer blow crashed into his arm, and he heard the bone crunch. His left hand went oddly limp. Well, he thought, oblivious to the pain, at least it wasn't my sword arm. His blade swung, a dark dwarf fell headless. An axe blade whined, but its wielder missed his mark. The dwarf was cut down from behind by one of the guards at the door.

Though unable to stand, Caramon still fought. A kick from his uninjured leg sent two dwarves reeling backward to crash into their fellows. Twisting onto his side, the big man smashed the hilt of his sword

through the face of another dwarf, splashing blood up to his elbows. Then, in the return stroke, he thrust the blade through the guts of another. Garic's charge spared his life for an instant, but it seemed it was an instant only.

"Caramon! Above you!" shrieked Garic, battling viciously.

Rolling onto his back, Caramon looked up to see Argat standing over him, his axe raised. Caramon lifted his sword, but at that moment four dark dwarves leaped on him, pinning him to the floor.

Almost weeping in rage, heedless of the weapons flashing around him, Garic tried desperately to save Caramon. But there were too many dwarves between him and his general. Already, the Dewar's axe blade was falling. . . .

The axe fell—but it fell from nerveless hands. Garic saw Argat's eyes open wide in profound astonishment. The dwarf's axe fell to the blood-slick stones with a ringing clatter as the dark dwarf himself toppled over on top of Caramon. Staring at Argat's corpse, Garic saw a small knife sticking out of the back of the dwarf's neck.

He looked up to see the dark dwarf's killer and gasped in astonishment.

Standing over the body of the dead traitor was, of all things, a kender.

Garic blinked, thinking perhaps the fear and pain had done something strange to his mind, causing him to see phantoms. But there wasn't time to try to figure out this astounding occurrence. The young Knight had finally managed to reach his general's side. Behind him, he could hear the guards shouting and driving back the Dewar who, seeing their leader fall, had suddenly lost a great deal of their enthusiasm for a fight that was supposed to have been an easy slaughter.

The four dwarves who were holding Caramon stumbled back hastily as the big man struggled out from beneath Argat's body. Reaching down, Garic jerked the dead dwarf up by the back of his armor and tossed the body to one side, then hauled Caramon to his feet. The big man staggered, groaning, as his crippled knee gave way under his weight.

"Help us!" Garic cried unnecessarily to the guards, who were already by his side. Half-dragging and

half-carrying Caramon, they assisted the limping man into the map room.

Turning to follow, Garic cast a quick glance around the corridor. The dark dwarves were eyeing him uncertainly. He caught a glimpse of other dwarves behind them—mountain dwarves, his mind registered.

And there, seemingly rooted to the spot, was the strange kender who had come out of nowhere, apparently, to save Caramon's life. The kender's face ashen, there was a green look about his lips. Not knowing what else to do, Garic wrapped his good arm around the kender's waist and, lifting him off his feet, hauled him back into the map room. As soon as he was inside, the guards slammed and bolted the door.

Caramon's face was covered with blood and sweat, but he grinned at Garic. Then he assumed a stern look.

"You damn fool knight," he growled. "I gave you a direct order and you disobeyed! I ought to—"

But his voice broke off as the kender, wriggling in Garic's grasp, raised his head.

"Tas," whispered Caramon, stunned.

"Hello, Caramon," Tas said weakly. "I—I'm awfully glad to see you again. I've got lots to tell you and it's very important and I really should tell you now but I . . . I think . . . I'm going . . . to faint."

"And so that's it," Tas said softly, his eyes dim with tears as he looked into Caramon's pale, expressionless face. "He lied to me about how to work the magical device. When I tried, it came apart in my hands. I *did* get to see the fiery mountain fall," he added, "and that was *almost* worth all the trouble. It might have even been worth dying to see. I'm not sure, since I haven't died yet, although I thought for a while I had. It certainly *wouldn't* be worth it, though, if I had to spend the Afterlife in the Abyss, which is *not* a nice place. I can't imagine why he wants to go there."

Tas sighed. "But, anyway, I could forgive him for that"—the kender's voice hardened and his small jaw set firmly—"but not for what he did to poor Gnimsh and what he tried to do to you—"

Tasslehoff bit his tongue. He hadn't meant to say that.

Caramon looked at him. "Go on, Tas," he said. "Tried to do to me?"

"N-nothing," Tas stammered, giving Caramon a sickly smile. "Just my rambling. You know me."

"What *did* he try to do?" Caramon smiled bitterly. "I didn't suppose there was anything left he *could* do to me."

"Have you killed," Tas muttered.

"Ah, yes." Caramon's expression did not change. "Of course. So *that's* what the dwarf's message meant."

"He gave you to—to the Dewar," Tas said miserably. "They were going to take your head back to King Duncan. Raistlin sent away all the Knights in the castle, telling them you'd ordered them off to Thorbardin." Tas waved his hand at Garic and the two guards. "He told the Dewar you'd have only your bodyguards "

Caramon said nothing. He felt nothing—neither pain nor anger, nor surprise. He was empty. Then a great surge of longing for his home, for Tika, for his friends, for Tanis, Laurana, for Riverwind and Gold-moon, rushed in to fill up that vast emptiness.

As if reading his thoughts, Tas rested his small head on Caramon's shoulder. "Can we go back to our own time now?" he said, looking up at Caramon wistfully. "I'm awfully tired. Say, do you think I could stay with you and Tika for a while? Just until I'm better. I wouldn't be a bother—I promise. . . ."

His eyes dim with tears, Caramon put his arm around the kender and held him close. "As long as you want, Tas," he said. Smiling sadly, he stared into the flames. "I'll finish the house. It won't take more than a couple of months. Then we'll go visit Tanis and Laurana. I promised Tika we'd do that. I promised her a long time ago, but I never seemed to get there. Tika always wanted to see Palanthas, you know. And maybe all of us could go to Sturm's tomb. I never did get a chance to tell him good-bye."

"And we can visit Elistan, and—Oh!" Tas's face grew alarmed. "Crysania! Lady Crysania! I tried to tell her about Raistlin, but she doesn't believe me. We can't leave her!" He leaped to his feet, wringing his hands. "We can't let him take her to that horrible place!"

Caramon shook his head. "We'll try to talk to her again, Tas. I don't think she'll listen, but at least we can try." He heaved himself up painfully. "They'll be at the Portal now. Raistlin can't wait much longer. The fortress will fall to the mountain dwarves soon.

"Garic," he said, limping over to where the Knight sat. "How's it going?"

One of the other Knights had just finished setting Garic's broken arm. They were tying it up in a rude sling, binding it to his side so that it was immobile. The young man looked up at Caramon, gritting his teeth with the pain but managing a smile nonetheless.

"I'll be fine, sir," he said weakly. "Don't worry."

Smiling, Caramon drew up a chair next to him. "Feel like traveling?"

"Of course, sir."

"Good. Actually, I guess you don't have much choice. This place will be overrun soon. You've got to try to go out now." Caramon rubbed his chin. "Reghar told me there were tunnels running beneath the plains, tunnels that lead from Pax Tharkas to Thorbardin. My advice is to find these. That shouldn't be too difficult. Those mounds out there lead down to them. You should be able to use the tunnels to at least get out of here safely."

Garic did not answer. Glancing at the other two guards, he said quietly, "You say 'your advice,' sir. What about you? Aren't you coming with us?"

Caramon cleared his throat and started to answer, but he couldn't talk. He stared down at his feet. This was a moment he had been dreading and, now that it was here, the speech he had carefully prepared blew out of his head like a leaf in the wind.

"No, Garic," he said finally, "I'm not." Seeing the Knight's eyes flash and guessing what he was thinking, the big man raised his hand. "No, I'm not going to do anything so foolish as to throw my life away on some noble, stupid cause—like rescuing my commanding officer!"

Garic flushed in embarrassment as Caramon grinned at him.

"No," the big man continued more somberly, "I'm not a Knight, thank the gods. I have enough sense to run when I'm beaten. And right now"—he couldn't

help but sigh—"I'm beaten." He ran his hand through his hair. "I can't explain this so that you'll understand it. I'm not sure I understand, not fully. But—let's just say that the kender and I have a magical way home."

Garic glanced from one to the other. "Not your brother!" he said, frowning darkly.

"No," Caramon answered, "not my brother. Here, he and I part company. He has his own life to live and—I finally see—I have mine." He put his hand on Garic's shoulder. "Go to Pax Tharkas. You and Michael do what you can to help those who make it there safely survive the winter."

"But—"

"That's an order, Sir Knight," Caramon said harshly.

"Yes, sir." Garic averted his face, his hand brushing quickly across his eyes.

Caramon, his own face growing gentle, put his arm around the young man. "Paladine be with you,† Garic," he said, clasping him close. He looked at the others. "May he be with all of you."

Garic looked up at him in astonishment, tears glistening on his cheeks. "Paladine?" he said bitterly. "The god who deserted us?"

"Don't lose your faith, Garic." Caramon admonished, rising to his feet with a pain-filled grimace. "Even if you can't believe in the god, put your trust in your heart. Listen to its voice above the Code and the Measure. And, someday, you'll understand."

"Yes, sir," Garic murmured. "And . . . may whatever gods you believe in be with you, too, sir."

"I guess they have been," Caramon said, smiling ruefully, "all my life. I've just been too damn thickheaded to listen. Now, you better be off."

One by one, he bade the other young Knights farewell, feigning to ignore their manful attempts to hide their tears. He was truly touched by their sorrow at parting—a sorrow he shared to such an extent that he could have broken down and wept like a child himself.

Cautiously, the Knights opened the door and peered out into the corridor. It was empty, except for the corpses. The Dewar were gone. But Caramon had no doubt this lull would last only long enough for them to regroup. Perhaps they were waiting until

A similar blessing—"The Lord be with you"—has been part of Christian liturgy for hundreds of years. George Lucas took this and turned it into "May the force be with you."

reinforcements arrived. Then they would attack the map room and finish off these humans.

Sword in hand, Garic led his Knights out into the blood-spattered corridor, planning to follow Tas's somewhat confused directions on how to reach the lower levels of the magical fortress. (Tas had offered to draw them a map, but Caramon said there wasn't time.)

When the Knights were gone, and the last echoes of their footfalls had died away, Tas and Caramon set off in the opposite direction. Before they went, Tas retrieved his knife from Argat's body.

"And you said once that a knife like this would be good only for killing vicious rabbits," Tas said proudly, wiping the blood from the blade before thrusting it into his belt.

"Don't mention rabbits," Caramon said in such an odd, tight voice that Tas looked at him and was startled to see his face go deathly pale.

CHAPTER 16

This was his moment. The moment he had been born to face. The moment for which he had endured the pain, the humiliation, the anguish of his life. The moment for which he had studied, fought, sacrificed . . . killed.

He savored it, letting the power flow over him and through him, letting it surround him, lift him. No other sounds, no other objects, nothing in this world existed for him this moment now save the Portal and the magic.

But even as he exulted in the moment, his mind was intent upon his work. His eyes studied the Portal, studied every detail intently—although it was not really necessary. He had seen it myriad times in dreams both sleeping and waking. The spells to open it were simple, nothing elaborate or complex. Each of the five dragon heads surrounding and guarding the Portal must be propitiated with the

correct phrase. Each must be spoken to in the proper order. But, once that was done and the White-Robed Cleric had exhorted Paladine to intercede and hold the Portal open, they would enter. It would close behind them.

And he would face his greatest challenge.

The thought excited him. His rapidly beating heart sent blood surging through his veins, throbbing in his temples, pulsing in his throat. Looking at Crysania, he nodded. It was time.

The cleric, her own face flushed with heightened excitement, her eyes already shimmering with the luster of the ecstasy of her prayers, took her place directly inside the Portal, facing Raistlin. This move required that she place utter, complete, unwavering confidence in him. For one wrong syllable spoken, the wrong breath drawn at the wrong moment, the slightest slip of the tongue or hand gesture would be fatal to her, to himself.

Thus had the ancients†—devising ways to guard this dread gate that they, because of their folly,† could not shut—sought to protect it. For a wizard of the Black Robes—who had committed the heinous deeds they knew *must* be committed to arrive at this point, and a Cleric of Paladine—pure of faith and soul—to put implicit trust in each other was a ludicrous supposition.

Yet, it had happened once: bound by the false charm of the one and the loss of faith of the other, Fistandantilus and Denubis had reached this point. And it would happen again, it seemed, with two bound by something that the ancients, for all their wisdom, had not foreseen—a strange, unhallowed love.†

Stepping into the Portal, looking at Raistlin for the last time upon this world, Crysania smiled at him. He smiled back, even as the words for the first spell were forming in his mind.

Crysania raised her arms. Her eyes stared beyond Raistlin now, stared into the brilliant, beautiful realms where dwelt her god. She had heard the last words of the Kingpriest, she knew the mistake he had made—a mistake of pride, demanding of the god in his arrogance what he should have requested in humility.

At that moment Crysania had come to understand why the gods had—in their righteous anger—

Before either Chronicles or Legends were written, there already existed an extensive background for the world. It included maps of Ansalon both before and after the Cataclysm and a historical timeline that went back three thousand years. All of this, I felt, was important so that the story would "have roots." The people and their cultures needed to come from somewhere, to have legends and heroes and a past all their own. I think it was this detail that gave the story such a rich feeling of depth. —TRH

Their folly lay in thinking that they could find a way to have a human relationship with a god, something that is impossible, for no human can comprehend the mind of a god. —MW

Their love is "unhallowed" because it is a destructive love. It is codependent, feeding on the weaknesses in each other. Love should be ennobling, supportive, and constructive. If not, then I would think of it as "unhallowed." —TRH

inflicted destruction upon the world. And she had known in her heart that Paladine would answer *her* prayers, as he had not answered those of the King-priest. This was Raistlin's moment of greatness. It was also her own.

Like the holy Knight Huma, she had been through her trials. Trials of fire, darkness, death, and blood. She was ready. She was prepared.

"Paladine, Platinum Dragon, your faithful servant comes before you and begs that you shed your blessing upon her. Her eyes are open to your light. At last, she understands what you have, in your wisdom, been trying to teach her. Hear her prayer, Radiant One. Be with her. Open this Portal so that she may enter and go forward bearing your torch. Walk with her as she strives to banish the darkness forever!"

Raistlin held his breath. All depended on this! Had he been right about her? Did she possess the strength, the wisdom, the faith? Was she truly Paladine's chosen? . . .

A pure and holy light began to glimmer from Crysania. Her dark hair shimmered, her white robes shone like sunlit clouds, her eyes gleamed like the silver moon. Her beauty at this moment was sublime.

"Thank you for granting my prayer, God of Light," Crysania murmured, bowing her head. Tears sparkled like stars upon her pale face. "I will be worthy of you!"

Watching her, enchanted by her beauty, Raistlin forgot his great goal. He could only stare at her, entranced. Even the thoughts of his magic—for a heartbeat—fled.

Then he exulted. Nothing! Nothing could stop him now . . . .

"Oh, Caramon!" whispered Tasslehoff in awe.

"We're too late," Caramon said.

The two, having made their way through the dungeons to the very bottom level of the magical fortress, came to a sudden halt—their eyes on Crysania. Enveloped in a halo of silver light, she stood in the center of the Portal, her arms outstretched, her face lifted to the heavens. Her unearthly beauty pierced Caramon's heart.

"Too late? No!" Tas cried in anguish. "We can't be!"

"Look, Tas," Caramon said sadly. "Look at her eyes. She's blind. Blind! Just as blind as I was in the Tower of High Sorcery. She cannot see through the light. . . ."

"We've got to *try* to talk to her, Caramon!" Tas clutched at him frantically. "We can't let her go. It—it's my fault! I'm the one who told her about Bupu! She might not have come if it hadn't been for me! I'll talk to her!"

The kender leaped forward, waving his arms. But he was jerked back suddenly by Caramon, who caught hold of him by his tassel of hair. Tas yelped in pain and protest, and—at the sound—Raistlin turned.

The archmage stared over at his twin and the kender for an instant without seeming to recognize them. Then recognition dawned in his eyes. It was not pleasant.

"Hush, Tas," Caramon whispered. "It's not your fault. Now, stay put!" Caramon thrust the kender behind a thick, granite pillar. "Stay there," the big man ordered. "Keep the pendant safe—and yourself, too."

Tas's mouth opened to argue. Then he saw Caramon's face and, looking down the corridor, he saw Raistlin. Something came over the kender. He felt as he had in the Abyss†—wretched and frightened. "Yes, Caramon," he said softly. "I'll stay here. I—I promise. . . ."

Leaning against the pillar, shivering, Tas could see in his mind poor Gnimsh lying crumpled on the cell floor.

Giving the kender a final, warning glance, Caramon turned and limped down the corridor toward where his brother stood.

Gripping the Staff of Magius in his hand, Raistlin watched him warily. "So you survived," he commented.

"Thanks to the gods, not you," Caramon replied.

"Thanks to *one* god,† my dear brother," Raistlin said with a slight, twisted smile. "The Queen of Darkness. She sent the kender back here, and it was he, I presume, who altered time, allowing your life to be spared. Does it gall you, Caramon, to know you owe your life to the Dark Queen?"

The feeling Tas is experiencing does, indeed, come from the Abyss—the only thing that could possibly frighten him.
—TRH

This presages the War of Souls. Again, here we see the seeds of that tale.
—TRH

"Does it gall you to know you owe her your soul?"

Raistlin's eyes flashed, their mirrorlike surface cracking for just an instant. Then, with a sardonic smile, he turned away. Facing the Portal, he lifted his right hand and held it palm out, his gaze upon the dragon's head at the lower right of the oval-shaped entrance.

"*Black Dragon.*" His voice was soft, caressing. "*From darkness to darkness/My voice echoes in the emptiness.*"

As Raistlin spoke these words, an aura of darkness began to form around Crysania, an aura of light as black as the nightjewel, as black as the light of the dark moon. . . .

Raistlin felt Caramon's hand close over his arm. Angrily, he tried to shake off his brother's grasp, but Caramon's grip was strong.

"Take us home, Raistlin. . . ."

Raistlin turned and stared, his anger forgotten in his astonishment. "What?" His voice cracked.

"Take us home," Caramon repeated steadily.

Raistlin laughed contemptuously.

"You are such a weak, sniveling fool, Caramon!" he snarled. Irritably he tried to shake off his twin's grip. He might as well have tried to shake off death. "Surely you must know by now what I have done! The kender must have told you about the gnome, You know I betrayed you. I would have left you for dead in this wretched place. And still you cling to me!"

"I'm clinging to you because the waters are closing over your head, Raistlin," Caramon said.

His gaze went down to his own, strong, sunburned hand holding his brother's thin wrist, its bones as fragile as the bones of a bird, its skin white, almost transparent. Caramon fancied he could see the blood pulse in the blue veins.

"My hand upon your arm. That's all we have." Caramon paused and drew a deep breath. Then, his voice deep with sorrow, he continued, "Nothing can erase what you have done, Raist. It can never be the same between us. My eyes have been opened. I now see you for what you are."

"And yet you beg me to come with you!" Raistlin sneered.

"I could learn to live with the knowledge of what you are and what you have done." Looking intently

into his brother's eyes Caramon said softly, "But you have to live with yourself, Raistlin. And there are times in the night when that must be damn near unbearable."

Raistlin did not respond. His face was a mask, impenetrable, unreadable.

Caramon swallowed a huskiness in his throat. His grip on his twin's arm tightened. "Think of this, though. You *have* done good in your life, Raistlin—maybe better than most of us. Oh, I've helped people. It's easy to help someone when that help is appreciated. But you helped those who only threw it back in your face. You helped those who didn't deserve it. You helped even when you knew it was hopeless, thankless." Caramon's hand trembled. "There's still good you could do† . . . to make up for the evil. Leave this. Come home."

Come home . . . come home. . . .†

Raistlin closed his eyes, the ache in his heart almost unendurable. His left hand stirred, lifted. Its delicate fingers hovered near his brother's hand, touching it for an instant with a touch as soft as the feet of a spider. On the edges of reality, he could hear Crysania's soft voice, praying to Paladine. The lovely white light flickered upon his eyelids.

Come home. . . .

When Raistlin spoke next, his voice was soft as his touch.

"The dark crimes that stain my soul, brother, you cannot begin to imagine. If you knew, you would turn from me in horror and in loathing." He sighed, shivering slightly. "And, you are right. Sometimes, in the night, even I turn from myself."

Opening his eyes, Raistlin stared fixedly into his brother's. "But, know this, Caramon—I committed those crimes intentionally, willingly. Know this, too—there are darker crimes before me, and I will commit them, intentionally, willingly. . . ." His gaze went to Crysania, standing unseeing in the Portal, lost in her prayers, shimmering with beauty and power.

Caramon looked at her and his face grew grim.

Raistlin, watching, smiled. "Yes, my brother. She will enter the Abyss with me. She will go before me and fight my battles. She will face dark clerics, dark magic-users, spirits of the dead doomed to wander

I hear a little of Luke Skywalker's voice in this sentence. On the other hand, Margaret so hated The Return of the Jedi that I once rewrote the ending for her. —TRH

As I mentioned before, coming home is part of the Hero's Journey as defined by Campbell. Raist is confronted with this repeatedly and the sound of "Come home" reverberates through these chapters. The question before Raistlin is: Which home? He makes his decision at last, forever closing the door on his brother. —TRH

in that cursed land, plus the unbelievable torments that my Queen can devise. All these will wound her in body, devour her mind, and shred her soul. Finally, when she can endure no more, she will slump to the ground to lie at my feet . . . bleeding, wretched, dying.

"She will, with her last strength, hold out her hand to me for comfort. She will not ask me to save her. She is too strong for that. She will give her life for me willingly, gladly. All she will ask is that I stay with her as she dies."

Raistlin drew a deep breath, then shrugged. "But I will walk past her, Caramon. l will walk past her without a look, without a word. Why? Because I will need her no longer.† I will continue forward toward my goal, and my strength will grow even as the blood flows from her pierced heart."

Half-turning, once again he raised his left hand, palm outward. Looking at the head of the dragon upon the top of the Portal, he softly said the second chant. *"White Dragon. From this world to the next/My voice cries with life."*

Caramon's gaze was on the Portal, on Crysania, his mind swamped by horror and revulsion. Still he held onto his brother. Still he thought to make one last plea. Then he felt the thin arm beneath his hand make a sharp, twisting motion. There was a flash, a swift movement, and the gleaming blade of a silver dagger pressed against the flesh of his throat, right where his life's blood pulsed in his neck.

"Let go of me, my brother," Raistlin said.

And though he did not strike with the dagger, it drew blood anyway; drew blood not from flesh but from soul. Quickly and cleanly, it sliced through the last spiritual tie between the twins. Caramon winced slightly at the swift, sharp pain in his heart.

But the pain did not endure. The tie was severed. Free at last, Caramon released his twin's arm without a word.

Turning, he started to limp back to where Tas waited, still hidden behind the pillar.

"One final hint of caution, my brother," Raistlin said coldly, returning the dagger to the thong he wore on his wrist.

Caramon did not respond, he neither stopped walking nor turned around.

*Raistlin has finally gone over the edge. He now exhibits the traits of a sociopath that, I think, he has long fought but to which he now surrenders.
—TRH*

"Be wary of that magical time device," Raistlin continued with a sneer. "Her Dark Majesty repaired it. It was she who sent the kender back. If you use it, you could find yourselves in a most unpleasant place!"

"Oh, but she didn't fix it!" Tas cried, popping out from behind the pillar. "Gnimsh did. Gnimsh fixed it! Gnimsh, my friend. The gnome that you murdered! I—"

"Use it then," Raistlin said coldly. "Take him and yourself out of here, Caramon. But remember I warned you."

Caramon caught hold of the angry kender. "Easy, Tas. That's enough. It doesn't matter now."

Turning around, Caramon faced his twin. Though the warrior's face was drawn with pain and weariness, his expression was one of peace and calm, one who knows himself at last. Stroking Tas's topknot of hair soothingly with his hand, he said, "Come on, Tas. Let's go home. Farewell, my brother."

Raistlin didn't hear. Facing the Portal, he was once again lost in his magic. But, out of the corner of his eye, even as he began the third chant, Raistlin saw his twin take the pendant from Tas and began the manipulations that would transfer its shape from pendant to the magical time-travel device.

Let them go. Good riddance! Raistlin thought. Finally, I am free of that great hulking idiot!

Looking back at the Portal, Raistlin smiled. A circle of cold light, like the harsh glare of the sun upon snow, surrounded Crysania. The archmage's behest to the White Dragon had been heard.

Raising his hand, facing the third dragon's head in the lower left part of the Portal, Raistlin recited its chant.

"Red Dragon. From darkness to darkness I shout/ Beneath my feet all is made firm."

Red lines shot from Crysania's body through the white light, through the black aura. Red and burning as blood, they spanned the gap from Raistlin to the Portal—a bridge to beyond.

Raistlin raised his voice. Turning to the right, he called to the fourth dragon. *"Blue Dragon. Time that flows/Hold in your course."*

Blue streams of light flowed over Crysania, then began to swirl. As though floating in water, she leaned her head back, her arms extended, her robes

drifting about her in the whirling flashes of light, her hair drifting black upon the currents of time.

Raistlin felt the Portal shiver. The magical field was starting to activate and respond to his commands! His soul quivered in a joy that Crysania shared. Her eyes glistened with rapturous tears, her lips parted in a sweet sigh. Her hands spread and, at her touch, the Portal opened!

Raistlin's breath caught in his throat. The surge of power and ecstasy that coursed through his body nearly choked him. He could see through the Portal now. He could see glimpses of the plane beyond, the plane forbidden to mortal men.

From somewhere, dimly heard, came his brother's voice activating the magical device—"Thy time is thy own, though across it you travel . . . Grasp firmly the beginning and the end . . . destiny be over your head. . . ."

Home. *Come home. . . .*

Raistlin began the fifth chant. *"Green Dragon. Because by fate even the gods are cast down/Weep ye all with me."*

Raistlin's voice cracked, faltered. Something was wrong! The magic pulsing through his body slowed, turned sluggish. He stammered out the last few words, but each breath was an effort. His heart ceased to beat for an instant, then started again with a great leap that shook his frail frame.

Shocked and confused, Raistlin stared frantically at the Portal. Had the final spell worked? No! The light around Crysania was beginning to waver. The field was shifting!

Desperately, Raistlin cried the words of the last chant again. But his voice cracked, snapping back on him like a whip, stinging him. What was happening? He could feel the magic slither from his grasp. He was losing control. . . .

Come home. . . .

His Queen's voice laughing, mocking. His brother's voice pleading, sorrowful. . . . And then, another voice—a shrill kender voice—only half-heard, lost in his greater affairs. Now it flashed through his brain with a blinding light.

Gnimsh fixed it. . . . The gnome, my friend . . .

As the dwarf's blade had penetrated Raistlin's shrinking flesh, so now the remembered words of Astinus's *Chronicles* stabbed his soul:

At the same instant a gnome, being held prisoner by the dwarves of Thorbardin, activated a time-traveling device. . . . The gnome's device interacted somehow with the delicate and powerful magical spells being woven by Fistandantilus. . . . A blast occurred of such magnitude that the Plains of Dergoth were utterly destroyed. . . .

Raistlin clenched his fists in anger. Killing the gnome had been useless! The wretched creature had tampered with the device *before* his death. History would repeat itself! Footsteps in the sand. . . .

Looking into the Portal, Raistlin saw the executioner step out from it. He saw his own hand lift his own black hood, he saw the flash of the axe blade descending, his own hands bringing it down upon his own neck!

The magical field began to shift violently. The dragon heads surrounding the Portal shrieked in triumph. A spasm of pain and terror twisted Crysania's face. Looking into her eyes, Raistlin saw the same look he had seen in his mother's eyes as they stared unseeing into a far-distant plane.

Come home. . . .

Within the Portal itself, the swirling lights began to whirl madly. Spinning out of control, they rose up around the limp body of the cleric as the magical flames had risen around her in the plague town. Crysania cried out in pain. Her flesh began to wither in the beautiful, deadly fire of uncontrolled magic.

Half-blinded by the brilliance, tears ran from Raistlin's eyes as he stared into the swirling vortex. And then he saw—the Portal was closing.

Hurling his magical staff to the floor, Raistlin unleashed his rage in a bitter, incoherent scream of fury.

Out of the Portal, in answer, came lilting, mocking laughter.

Come home. . . .

A feeling of calmness stole over Raistlin—the cold calm of despair. He had failed. But *She* would never see him grovel. If he must die, he would die within his magic. . . .

He lifted his head. He rose to his feet. Using all of his great powers—powers of the ancients, powers of his own, powers he had no idea he possessed, powers that rose from somewhere dark and hidden even from himself—Raistlin raised his

arms and his voice screamed out once again. But this time it was not an incoherent shriek of frustrated helplessness. This time, his words were clear. This time he shouted words of command— words of command that had never been uttered upon this world before.

This time his words were heard and understood.

The field held. *He* held it! He could feel himself holding onto it. At his command, the Portal shivered and ceased to close.

Raistlin drew a deep, shuddering breath. Then, out of the corner of his eye, somewhere to his right, he saw a flash. The magical time-travel device had been activated!

The field jumped and surged wildly. As the device's magic grew and spread, its powerful vibrations caused the very rocks of the fortress to begin to sing. In a devastating wave, their songs surged around Raistlin. The dragons' shrieking answered in anger. The ageless voices of the rocks and the timeless voices of the dragons fought, flowed together, and finally combined in a discordant, mind-shattering cacophony.

The sound was deafening, ear-splitting. The force of the two powerful spells sundered the ground. The earth beneath Raistlin's feet shuddered. The singing rocks split wide open. The metallic dragons' heads cracked. . . .

The Portal itself began to crumble.

Raistlin fell to his knees. The magical field was tearing loose, splitting apart like the bones of the world itself. It was breaking, splintering and, because Raistlin still held onto it, it began to tear him apart as well.

Pain shot through his head. His body convulsed. He writhed in agony.

It was a terrible choice he faced. Let go, and he would fall, fall to his doom, fall into a nothingness to which the most abject darkness was preferable. And yet, if he held it, he knew he would be ripped apart, his body dismembered by the forces of magic he had generated and could no longer control.

His muscles ripped from his bones, sinews shredding, tendons snapping.

"Caramon!" Raistlin moaned, but Caramon and Tas had vanished. The magical device, repaired by the

one gnome whose inventions worked, had, indeed, worked. They were gone. There was no help.

Raistlin had seconds to live, moments to act. Yet the pain was so excruciating that he could not think.

His joints were being wrested from their sockets, his eyes plucked from his face, his heart torn from his body, his brain sucked from his skull.

He could hear himself screaming and he knew it was his death cry. Still he fought on, as he had fought all his life.

I . . . will . . . control. . . .

The words came from his mouth, stained with his blood. . . .

I will control. . . .

Reaching out, his hand closed over the Staff of Magius.

I will!

And then he was hurtling forward into a blinding, swirling, crashing wave of many-colored lights—

Come home . . . come home. . . .

ACKNOWLEDGMENTS

There are many people whose interest in and work on the DRAGONLANCE books and modules have made the series the success it is today. We deeply appreciate their help and support.

Members of the DRAGONLANCE Design Team: Harold Johnson, Laura Hickman, Douglas Niles, Jeff Grubb, Michael Dobson, Michael Breault, Bruce Heard, Roger E. Moore.

Songs and Poems: Michael Williams

Original Cover Artwork: Larry Elmore

Original Interior Artwork: Valerie A. Valusek

Design: Ruth Hoyer

Maps: Steve Sullivan

Editor: Jean Blashfield Black

Valuable assistance and advice: Patrick L. Price, Dezra and Terry Phillips, John "Dalamar" Walker, Carolyn Vanderbilt, Bill Larson, Janet and Gary Pack

1987 DRAGONLANCE Calendar Artists: Clyde Caldwell, Larry Elmore, Keith Parkinson, Jeff Easley

And, finally, we want to thank all of you who have taken the time to write to us. We appreciate it very much.

—Margaret Weis and Tracy Hickman
1986

Volume 3

Test of the Twins

BOOK 1

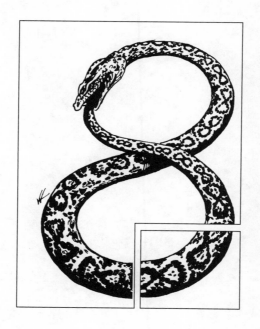

DEDICATION

To my brother, Gerry Hickman, who taught me
what a brother *should* be.
—Tracy Hickman

To Tracy
With heartfelt thanks for inviting me
into your world.
—Margaret Weis

The Hammer of the Gods

Like sharp steel, the clarion call of a trumpet split the autumn air as the armies of the dwarves of Thorbardin rode down into the Plains of Dergoth to meet their foe—their kinsmen. Centuries of hatred and misunderstanding† between the hill dwarves and their mountain cousins poured red upon the plains that day. Victory became meaningless—an objective no one sought. To avenge wrongs committed long ago by grandfathers long since dead was the aim of both sides. To kill and kill and kill again—this was the Dwarfgate War.

True to his word, the dwarven hero, Kharas, fought for his King Beneath the Mountain. Clean-shaven, his beard sacrificed to shame that he must fight those he called kin, Kharas was at the vanguard of the army, weeping even as he killed. But as he fought, he suddenly came to see that the word *victory* had become twisted to mean annihilation. He saw the standards of both armies fall, lying trampled and forgotten upon the bloody plain as the madness of revenge engulfed both armies in a fearsome red wave. And when he saw that no matter who won there would be no victor, Kharas threw down his Hammer—the Hammer forged with the help of Reorx, god of the dwarves—and left the field.

Many were the voices that shrieked "coward." If Kharas heard, he paid them no heed. He knew his worth in his own heart, he knew it better than any. Wiping the bitter tears from his eyes, washing the blood of his kinsmen from his hands, Kharas searched among the dead until he found the bodies of King Duncan's two beloved sons. Throwing the hacked and mutilated corpses of the young dwarves over the back of a horse, Kharas left the Plains of Dergoth, returning to Thorbardin with his burden.

Kharas rode far, but not far enough to escape the sound of hoarse voices crying for revenge, the clash of steel, the screams of the dying. He did not look back. He had the feeling he would hear those voices to the end of his days.

I always hope that people will think about real-world problems when reading our novels. I like to use fantasy as a means to talk about problems people are facing now. I don't necessarily provide answers, but I want people to consider the questions. —MW

The dwarven hero was just riding into the first foothills of the Kharolis Mountains when he heard an eerie rumbling sound begin. Kharas's horse shied nervously. The dwarf checked it and stopped to soothe the animal. As he did so, he looked around uneasily. What was it? It was no sound of war, no sound of nature.

Kharas turned. The sound came from behind him, from the lands he had just left, lands where his kinsmen were still slaughtering each other in the name of justice. The sound increased in magnitude, becoming a low, dull, booming sound that grew louder and louder. Kharas almost imagined he could see the sound, coming closer and closer. The dwarven hero shuddered and lowered his head as the dreadful roar came nearer, thundering across the Plains.

It is Reorx, he thought in grief and horror. It is the voice of the angry god. We are doomed.

One of the problems facing a modern fantasy writer is how to avoid anachronisms—phrases that are out of place in time. My favorite example of this was from J. R. R. Tolkien's The Lord of the Rings *(hardback collector's edition pg. 36) as the fireworks were being described at Bilbo's Party. "Out flew a red-golden dragon . . . and he whizzed three times over the heads of the crowd. . . . The dragon passed like an express train. . . ." Now, how would hobbits know what an express train sounded like? Some have jokingly remarked that this may explain the economy of the Shire. Here in the text, Kharas experiences something akin to the frontal shock wave of a nuclear blast, but we explain it in terms more believable in his time period. —TRH*

The sound hit Kharas, along with a shock† wave—a blast of heat and scorching, foul-smelling wind that nearly blew him from the saddle. Clouds of sand and dust and ash enveloped him, turning day into a horrible, perverted night. Trees around him bent and twisted, his horses screamed in terror and nearly bolted. For a moment, it was all Kharas could do to retain control of the panic-stricken animals.

Blinded by the stinging dustcloud, choking and coughing, Kharas covered his mouth and tried—as best he could in the strange darkness—to cover the eyes of the horses as well. How long he stood in that cloud of sand and ash and hot wind, he could not remember. But, as suddenly as it came, it passed.

The sand and dust settled. The trees straightened. The horses grew calm. The cloud drifted past on the gentler winds of autumn, leaving behind a silence more dreadful than the thunderous noise.

Filled with dreadful foreboding, Kharas urged his tired horses on as fast as he could and rode up into the hills, seeking desperately for some vantage site. Finally, he found it—an out-cropping of rock. Tying the pack animals with their sorrowful burden to a tree, Kharas rode his horse out onto the rock and looked out over the Plains of Dergoth. Stopping, he stared down below him in awe.

Nothing living stirred. In fact, there was nothing there at all; nothing except blackened, blasted sand and rock.

Both armies were completely wiped out. So devastating was the explosion that not even corpses remained upon the ash-covered Plain. Even the very face of the land itself had changed. Kharas's horrified gaze went to where the magical fortress of Zhaman had once stood, its tall, graceful spires ruling the Plains. It, too, had been destroyed—but not totally. The fortress had collapsed in upon itself and now—most horribly—its ruins resembled a human skull sitting, grinning, upon the barren Plain of Death.

"Reorx, Father, Forger, forgive us," murmured Kharas, tears blurring his vision. Then, his head bowed in grief, the dwarven hero left the site, returning to Thorbardin.

The dwarves would believe—for so Kharas himself would report—that the destruction of both armies on the Plains of Dergoth was brought about by Reorx. That the god had, in his anger, hurled his hammer down upon the land, smiting his children.

But the Chronicles of Astinus truly record what happened upon the Plains of Dergoth that day:

Now† at the height of his magical powers, the archmage, Raistlin, known also as Fistandantilus, and the White-robed cleric of Paladine, Crysania, sought entry into the Portal that leads to the Abyss, there to challenge and fight the Queen of Darkness.

Dark crimes of his own this archmage had committed to reach this point—the pinnacle of his ambition. The Black Robes he wore were stained with blood; some of it his own. Yet this man knew the human heart. He knew how to wrench it and twist it and make those who should have reviled him and spurned him come to admire him instead. Such a one was Lady Crysania, of the House of Tarinius. A Revered Daughter of the church, she possessed one fatal flaw in the white marble of her soul. And that flaw Raistlin found and widened so that the crack would spread throughout her being and eventually reach her heart. . . .

Crysania followed him to the dread Portal. Here she called upon her god and Paladine answered, for, truly, she was his chosen. Raistlin called upon his magic and

Being younger authors at the time, I remember there being some concern about our readers remembering where the last book left off. Hence, this recap. —TRH

*he was successful, for no wizard had yet lived as powerful
as this young man.*

The Portal opened.

*Raistlin started to enter, but a magical, time-traveling
device being operated by the mage's twin brother, Caramon, and the kender, Tasslehoff Burrfoot, interfered
with the archmage's powerful spell. The field of magic
was disrupted . . .*

. . . with disastrous and unforeseen consequences.

CHAPTER
I

"Oops," said Tasslehoff Burrfoot.

Caramon fixed the kender with a stern eye.

"It's not my fault! Really, Caramon!" Tas protested.

But, even as he spoke, the kender's gaze went to their surroundings, then he glanced up at Caramon, then back to their surroundings again. Tas's lower lip began to tremble and he reached for his handkerchief, just in case he felt a snuffle coming. But his handkerchief wasn't there, his pouches weren't there. Tas sighed. In the excitement of the moment, he'd forgotten—they'd all been left behind in the dungeons of Thorbardin.

And it had been a truly exciting moment. One minute he and Caramon had been standing in the magical fortress of Zhaman, activating the magical time-traveling device; the next minute Raistlin had begun working *his* magic and, before Tas knew it,

there had been a terrible commotion—stones singing and rocks cracking and a horrible feeling of being pulled in six different directions at once and then—WHOOSH—here they were.

Wherever here was. And, wherever it was, it certainly didn't seem to be where it was supposed to be.

He and Caramon were on a mountain trail, near a large boulder, standing ankle-deep in slick ash-gray mud† that completely covered the face of the land below them for as far as Tas could see. Here and there, jagged ends of broken rock jutted from the soft flesh of the ash covering. There were no signs of life. Nothing could be alive in that desolation. No trees remained standing; only fire-blackened stumps poked through the thick mud. As far as the eye could see, clear to the horizon, in every direction, there was nothing but complete and total devastation.

The sky itself offered no relief. Above them, it was gray and empty. To the west, however, it was a strange violet color, boiling with weird, luminous clouds laced with lightning of brilliant blue. Other than the distant rumble of thunder, there was no sound . . . no movement . . . nothing.

Caramon drew a deep breath and rubbed his hand across his face. The heat was intense and, already, even though they had been standing in this place only a few minutes, his sweaty skin was coated with a fine film of gray ash.

"Where are we?" he asked in even, measured tones.

"I—I'm sure I haven't any idea, Caramon," Tas said. Then, after a pause, "Have you?"

"*I* did everything the way you told me to," Caramon replied, his voice ominously calm. "You said Gnimsh said that all we had to do was *think* of where we wanted to go and there we'd be. I know *I* was thinking of Solace—"

"I was too!" Tas cried. Then, seeing Caramon glare at him, the kender faltered. "At least I was thinking of it *most* of the time . . . ."

"*Most* of the time?" Caramon asked in a dreadfully calm voice.

"Well"—Tas gulped—"I—I did th-think once, just for an instant, mind you, about how—er—how

While I was a missionary in Indonesia, my companions and I took a day trip high into the mountains of eastern Java. After a chill hike, we were surprised to be standing at the top of an incredible cliff that rimmed a sea of ash below. This was an ancient caldera of Mount Bromo. The image of that "sand sea" has never left me.
—TRH

much fun and interesting and, well, unique, it would be to—uh—visit a—uuh . . . um. . . ."

"Um what?" Caramon demanded.

"A . . . mmmmmm."

"A what?"

"Mmmmm," Tas mumbled.

Caramon sucked in his breath.

"A moon!" Tas said quickly.

"Moon!" repeated Caramon incredulously. "Which moon?" he asked after a moment, glancing around.

"Oh"—Tas shrugged—"any of the three. I suppose one's as good as another. Quite similar, I should imagine. Except, of course, that Solinari would have all glittering silver rocks and Lunitari all bright red rocks, and I guess the other one would be all black, though I can't say for sure, never having seen—"

Caramon growled at this point, and Tas decided it might be best to hold his tongue. He did, too, for about three minutes during which time Caramon continued to look around at their surroundings with a solemn face. But it would have taken more holding than the kender had inside him (or a sharp knife) to keep his tongue from talking longer than that.

"Caramon," he blurted out, "do—do you think we actually *did* it? Went to a—uh—moon, that is? I mean, this certainly doesn't look like anyplace I've ever been before. Not that these rocks are silver or red or even black. They're more of a rock color, but—"

"I wouldn't doubt it," Caramon said gloomily. "After all, you did take us to a seaport city that was sitting squarely in the middle of a desert—"†

"That wasn't my fault† either!" Tas said indignantly. "Why even Tanis said—"

"Still"—Caramon's face creased in puzzlement—"this place certainly *looks* strange, but it *seems* familiar somehow."

"You're right," said Tas after a moment, staring around again at the bleak, ash-choked landscape. "It does remind me of somewhere, now that you mention it. Only"—the kender shivered—"I don't recall ever having been anyplace quite this awful . . . except the Abyss," he added, but he said it under his breath.

Caramon is referring to the city of Tarsis in the Plains of Dust, where the Companions spent some time in Dragons of Winter Night.

Tas has a point here. As a great collector of maps, some of Tas's collection tends to be rather outdated. Tarsis was indeed a seaport city prior to the Cataclysm, but when the continent of Ansalon was changed, the city ended up in the middle of a desert.

The boiling clouds surged nearer and nearer as the two spoke, casting a further pall over the barren land. A hot wind sprang up, and a fine rain began to fall, mingling with the ash drifting through the air. Tas was just about to comment on the slimy quality of the rain when suddenly, without warning, the world blew up.

At least that was Tas's first impression. Brilliant, blinding light, a sizzling sound, a crack, a boom that shook the ground, and Tasslehoff found himself sitting in the gray mud, staring stupidly at a gigantic hole that had been blasted in the rock not a hundred feet away from him.

"Name of the gods!" Caramon gasped. Reaching down, he dragged Tas to his feet. "Are you all right?"

"I—I think so," said Tas, somewhat shaken. As he watched, lightning streaked again from the cloud to ground, sending rock and ash hurtling through the air. *"My!* That certainly was an interesting experience. Though nothing I'd care to repeat right away," he added hastily, fearful that the sky, which was growing darker and darker by the minute, might decide to treat him to that interesting experience all over again.

"Wherever we are, we better get off this high ground," Caramon muttered. "At least there's a trail. It must lead somewhere."

Glancing down the mud-choked trail into the equally mud-choked valley below, Tas had the fleeting thought that Somewhere was likely to be every bit as gray and yucky as Here, but, after a glimpse of Caramon's grim face, the kender quickly decided to keep his thoughts to himself.

As they slogged down the trail through the thick mud, the hot wind blew harder, driving specks of blackened wood and cinders and ash into their flesh. Lightning danced among the trees, making them burst into balls of bright green or blue flame. The ground shook with the concussive roar of the thunder. And still, the storm clouds massed on the horizon. Caramon hurried their pace.

As they labored down the hillside they entered what must once have been, Tas imagined, a beautiful valley. At one time, he guessed, the trees here must have been ablaze with autumn oranges and golds, or misty green in the spring.

Here and there, he saw spirals of smoke curling up, only to be whipped away immediately by the storm wind. Undoubtedly from more lightning strikes, he thought. But, in an odd sort of way, that reminded him of something, too. Like Caramon, he was becoming increasingly convinced that he knew this place.

Wading through the mud, trying to ignore what the icky stuff was doing to his green shoes and bright blue leggings, Tas decided to try an old kender trick To Use When Lost. Closing his eyes and blotting everything from his mind, he ordered his brain to provide him with a picture of the landscape before him. The rather interesting kender logic behind this being that since it was likely that some kender in Tasslehoff's family had undoubtedly been to this place before, the memory was somehow passed on to his or her descendants. While this was never scientifically verified (the gnomes are working on it, having referred it to committee), it certainly is true that— to this day—no kender has ever been reported lost on Krynn.

At any rate, Tas, standing shin-deep in mud, closed his eyes and tried to conjure up a picture of his sur- roundings. One came to him, so vivid in its clarity that he was rather startled—certainly his ancestors' mental maps had never been so perfect. There were trees—giant trees—there were mountains on the horizon, there was a lake. . . .

Opening his eyes, Tas gasped. There was a lake! He hadn't noticed it before, probably because it was the same gray, sludge color as the ash-covered ground. Was there water there, still? Or was it filled with mud?

I wonder, Tas mused, if Uncle Trapspringer ever visited a moon.† If so, that would account for the fact that I recognize this place. But surely he would have told someone. . . . Perhaps he would have if the goblins hadn't eaten him before he had the chance. Speaking of food, that reminds me . . .

"Caramon," Tas shouted over the rising wind and the boom of the thunder. "Did you bring along any water? I didn't. Nor any food, either. I didn't sup- pose we'd need any, what with going back home and all. But—"

As far as anyone knows, Uncle Trapspringer never visited a moon, but Kitiara and Sturm did, in the novel Darkness and Light, *by Paul B. Thompson and Tonya C. Cook.*

Tas suddenly saw something that drove thoughts of food and water and Uncle Trapspringer from his mind.

"Oh, Caramon!" Tas clutched at the big warrior, pointing. "Look, do you suppose *that's* the sun?"

"What else would it be?" Caramon snapped gruffly, his gaze on a watery, greenish-yellow disk that had appeared through a rift in the storm clouds. "And, no, I didn't bring any water. So just keep quiet about it, huh?"

"Well, you needn't be ru—" Tas began. Then he saw Caramon's face and quickly hushed.

They had come to a halt, slipping in the mud, halfway down the trail. The hot wind blew about them, sending Tas's topknot streaming out from his head like a banner and whipping Caramon's cloak out. The big warrior was staring at the lake—the same lake Tas had noticed. Caramon's face was pale, his eyes troubled. After a moment, he began walking again, trudging grimly down the trail. With a sigh, Tas squished along after him. He had reached a decision.

"Caramon," he said, "let's get out of here. Let's leave this place. Even if it *is* a moon like Uncle Trapspringer must have visited before the goblins ate him, it isn't much fun. The moon, I mean, not being eaten by goblins which I suppose wouldn't be much fun either, come to think of it. To tell you the truth, this moon's just about as boring as the Abyss and it certainly smells as bad. Besides, there I wasn't thirsty. . . . Not that I'm thirsty now," he added hastily, remembering too late that he wasn't supposed to talk about it, "but my tongue's sort of dried out, if you know what I mean, which makes it hard to talk. We've got the magical device." He held the jewel-encrusted sceptre-shaped object up in his hand, just in case Caramon had forgotten in the last half-hour what it looked like. "And I *promise* . . . I solemnly vow . . . that I'll think of Solace with *all* my brain this time, Caramon. I—Caramon?"

"Hush, Tas," Caramon said.

They had reached the valley floor, where the mud was ankle-deep on Caramon, which made it about shin-deep on Tas. Caramon had begun to limp again from when he'd fallen and wrenched his knee back

in the magical fortress of Zhaman. Now, in addition to worry, there was a look of pain on his face.

There was another look, too. A look that made Tas feel all prickly inside—a look of true fear. Tas, startled, glanced about quickly, wondering what Caramon saw. It seemed pretty much the same at the bottom as it had at the top, he thought—gray and yucky and horrible. Nothing had changed, except that it was growing darker. The storm clouds had obliterated the sun again, rather to Tas's relief, since it was an unwholesome-looking sun that made the bleak, gray landscape appear worse than ever. The rain was falling harder as the storm clouds drew nearer. Other than that, there certainly didn't appear to be anything frightening.

The kender tried his best to keep silent, but the words just sort of leaped out of his mouth before he could stop them.

"What's the matter, Caramon? I don't see anything. Is your knee bothering you? I—"

"Be quiet, Tas!" Caramon ordered in a strained, tight voice. He was staring around him, his eyes wide, his hands clenching and unclenching nervously.

Tas sighed and clapped his hand over his mouth to bottle up the words, determined to keep quiet if it killed him. When he was quiet, it suddenly occurred to him that it was so *very* quiet around here. There was no sound at all when the thunder wasn't thundering, not even the usual sounds he was used to hearing when it rained—water dripping from tree leaves and plopping onto the ground, the wind rustling in the branches, birds singing their rain songs, complaining about their wet feathers. . . .

Tas had a strange, quaking feeling inside. He looked at the stumps of the burned trees more closely. Even burned, they were huge, easily the largest trees he had ever seen in his life except for—

Tas gulped. Leaves, autumn colors, the smoke of cooking fires curling up from the valley, the lake— blue and smooth as crystal . . .

Blinking, he rubbed his eyes to clear them of the gummy film of mud and rain. He stared around him, looking back up at the trail, at that huge boulder. . . . He stared at the lake that he could see quite clearly through the burned tree stumps. He stared at the

mountains with their sharp, jagged peaks. It wasn't Uncle Trapspringer who'd been here before. . . . "Oh, Caramon!" he whispered in horror.

Chapter 2

hat is it?" Caramon turned, looking at Tas so strangely that the kender felt his inside prickly feeling spread to his outside. Little bumps appeared all up and down his arms.

"N-nothing," Tas stammered. "Just my imagination. Caramon," he added urgently, "let's leave! Right now. We can go anywhere we want to! We can go back in time to when we were all together, to when we were all happy! We can go back to when Flint and Sturm were alive, to when Raistlin still wore the red robes and Tika—"

"Shut up, Tas," snapped Caramon warningly, his words accented by a flash of lightning that made even the kender flinch.

The wind was rising, whistling through the dead tree stumps with an eerie sound, like someone drawing a shivering breath through clenched teeth. The warm, slimy rain had ceased. The clouds

above them swirled past, revealing the pale sun shimmering in the gray sky. But on the horizon, the clouds continued to mass, continued to grow blacker and blacker.

Multicolored lightning flickered among them, giving them a distant, deadly beauty.

Caramon started walking along the muddy trail, gritting his teeth against the pain of his injured leg. But Tas, looking down that trail that he now knew so well—even though it was appallingly different— could see to where it rounded a bend. Knowing what lay beyond that bend, he stood where he was, planted firmly in the middle of the road, staring at Caramon's back.

After a few moments of unusual silence, Caramon realized something was wrong and glanced around. He stopped, his face drawn with pain and fatigue.

"C'mon, Tas!" he said irritably.

Twisting his topknot of hair around his finger, Tas shook his head.

Caramon glared at him.

Tas finally burst out, "Those are vallenwood trees, Caramon!"

The big man's stern expression softened. "I know, Tas," he said wearily. "This is Solace."

"No, it isn't!" Tas cried. "It—it's just some place that has vallenwoods! There must be lots of places that have vallenwoods—"

"And are there lots of places that have Crystalmir Lake, Tas, or the Kharolis Mountains or that boulder up where you and I've both seen Flint sitting, carving his wood, or this road that leads to the—"

"You don't know!" Tas yelled angrily. "It's possible!" Suddenly, he ran forward, or he tried to run forward, dragging his feet through the oozing, clinging mud as fast as possible. Stumbling into Caramon, he grabbed the big man's hand and tugged on it. "Let's go! Let's get out of here!" Once again, he held up the time-traveling device. "We—we can go back to Tarsis! Where the dragons toppled a building down on top of me!† That was a fun time, very interesting. Remember?" His shrill voice screeched through the burned-out trees.

Reaching out, his face grim, Caramon grabbed the magical device from the kender's hand. Ignoring Tas's frantic protests, he took the device and began

Tas relates this story in Dragons of Winter Night, *Book II, Chapter 1.*

twisting and turning the jewels, gradually transforming it from a sparkling sceptre into a plain, nondescript pendant. Tas watched him miserably.

"Why won't we go, Caramon? This place is horrible. We don't have any food or water and, from
what I've seen, there's not much likelihood of us
finding either. Plus, we're liable to get blasted right
out of our shoes if one of those lightning bolts hits
us, and that storm's getting closer and closer and
you *know* this isn't Solace—"

"I *don't* know, Tas," Caramon said quietly. "But
I'm going to find out. What's the matter? Aren't you
curious? Since when did a kender ever turn down
the chance for an adventure?" He began to limp
down the trail again.

"I'm just as curious as the next kender," Tas
mumbled, hanging his head and trudging along after
Caramon. "But it's one thing to be curious about
some place you've never been before, and quite
another to be curious about home. You're not *supposed*
to be curious about home! Home isn't supposed to
change. It just stays there, waiting for you to come
back. Home† is someplace you say 'My, this looks
just like it did when I left!' not 'My, this looks like six
million dragons flew in and wrecked the joint!'
Home is *not* a place for adventures, Caramon!"

Tas peered up into Caramon's face to see if his
argument had made any impression. If it had, it
didn't show. There was a look of stern resolution on
the pain-filled face that rather surprised Tas, surprised and startled him as well.

Caramon's changed, Tas realized suddenly. And it
isn't just from giving up dwarf spirits. There's something different about him—he's more serious and . . .
well, responsible-looking, I guess. But there's something else. Tas pondered. Pride, he decided after
minute of profound reflection. Pride in himself,
pride and determination.

This isn't a Caramon who will give in easily, Tas
thought with a sinking heart. This isn't a Caramon
who needs a kender to keep him out of mischief and
taverns. Tas sighed bleakly. He rather missed that
old Caramon.

They came to the bend in the road. Each recognized
it, though neither said anything—Caramon, because
there wasn't anything to be said, and Tas, because he

*The quest for home is an
essential part of the hero's
journey. Not only the
return itself but the
recognition that one cannot
return to the same home
one left is a crucial part of
the journey. The hero, so
changed by his experience,
returns to find that
home—in his or her eyes—
seems vastly different than
he expected. Frodo returns
to the Shire and finds it
drastically changed, and
that he no longer fits in.
Reentry, as Campbell puts
it, is often the hardest task
a hero has to face. —TRH*

was steadfastly refusing to admit he recognized it. But both found their footsteps dragging.

Once, travelers coming around that bend would have seen the Inn of the Last Home, gleaming with light. They would have smelled Otik's spiced potatoes, heard the sounds of laughter and song drift from the door every time it opened to admit the wanderer or regular from Solace. Both Caramon and Tas stopped, by unspoken agreement, before they rounded that corner.

Still they said nothing, but each looked around him at the desolation, at the burned and blasted tree stumps, at the ash-covered ground, at the blackened rocks. In their ears rang a silence louder and more frightening than the booming thunder. Because both knew that they should have heard Solace, even if they couldn't see it yet. They should have heard the sounds of the town—the sounds of the smithy, the sounds of market day, the sounds of hawkers and children and merchants, the sounds of the Inn.

But there was nothing, only silence. And, far off in the distance, the ominous rumble of thunder.

Finally, Caramon sighed. "Let's go," he said, and hobbled forward.

Tas followed more slowly, his shoes so caked with mud that he felt as if he were wearing iron-shod dwarf boots. But his shoes weren't nearly as heavy as his heart. Over and over he muttered to himself, "This isn't Solace, this isn't Solace, this isn't Solace," until it began to sound like one of Raistlin's magical incantations.

Rounding the bend, Tas fearfully raised his eyes—
—and heaved a vast sigh of relief.

"What did I tell you, Caramon?" he cried over the wailing of the wind. "Look, nothing there, nothing there at all. No Inn, no town, nothing." He slipped his small hand into Caramon's large one and tried to pull him backward. "Now, let's go. I've got an idea. We can go back to the time when Fizban made the golden span come out of the sky—"

But Caramon, shaking off the kender, was limping ahead, his face grim. Coming to a halt, he stared down at the ground. "What's this then, Tas?" he demanded in a voice taut with fear.

Chewing nervously on the end of his topknot, the

kender came up to stand beside Caramon. "What's what?" he asked stubbornly.

Caramon pointed.

Tas sniffed. "So, it's a big cleared-off space on the ground. All right, maybe something was there. Maybe a big building was there. But it isn't there now, so why worry about it? I— Oh, Caramon!"

The big man's injured knee suddenly gave way. He staggered, and would have fallen if Tas hadn't propped him up. With Tas's help, Caramon made his way over to the stump of what had been an unusually large vallenwood, on the edge of the empty patch of mud-covered ground. Leaning against it, his face pale with pain and dripping with sweat, Caramon rubbed his injured knee.

"What can I do to help?" Tas asked anxiously, wringing his hands. "I know! I'll find you a crutch! There must be lots of broken branches lying about. I'll go look."

Caramon said nothing, only nodded wearily.

Tas dashed off, his sharp eyes scouring the gray, slimy ground, rather glad to have something to do and not to have to answer questions about stupid cleared-off spaces. He soon found what he was look-ing for—the end of a tree branch sticking up through the mud. Catching hold of it, the kender gave it a yank. His hands slipped off the wet branch, sending him toppling over backward. Getting up, staring ruefully at the gunk on his blue leggings, the kender tried unsuccessfully to wipe it off. Then he sighed and grimly took hold of the branch again. This time, he felt it give a little.

"I've almost got it, Caramon!" he reported. "I—"

A most unkenderlike shriek rose above the scream-ing wind. Caramon looked up in alarm to see Tas's topknot disappearing into a vast sink hole that had apparently opened up beneath his feet.

"I'm coming, Tas!" Caramon called, stumbling forward. "Hang on!"

But he halted at the sight of Tas crawling back out of the hole. The kender's face was like nothing Cara-mon had ever seen. It was ashen, the lips white, the eyes wide and staring.

"Don't come any closer, Caramon," Tas whispered, gesturing him away with a small, muddy hand. "Please, stay back!"

But it was too late. Caramon had reached the edge of the hole and was staring down. Tas, crouched beside him on the ground, began to shake and sob. "They're all dead," he whimpered. "All dead." Burying his face in his arms, he rocked back and forth, weeping bitterly.

At the bottom of the rock-lined hole that had been covered by a thick layer of mud lay bodies, piles of bodies, bodies of men, women, children. Preserved by the mud, some were still pitifully recognizable— or so it seemed to Caramon's feverish gaze. His thoughts went to the last mass grave he had seen— the plague village Crysania had found. He remembered his brother's angry, grief-stricken face. He remembered Raistlin calling down the lightning, burning everything, burning the village to ash.†

Caramon is remembering events from War of the Twins, *Book II, Chapter 7.*

Gritting his teeth, Caramon forced himself to look into that grave—forced himself to look for a mass of red curls. . . .

He turned away with a shuddering sob of relief, then, looking around wildly, he began to run back toward the Inn. "Tika!" he screamed.

Tas raised his head, springing up in alarm. "Caramon!" he cried, slipped in the mud, and fell.

"Tika!" Caramon yelled hoarsely above the howl of the wind and the distant thunder. Apparently oblivious to the pain of his injured leg, he staggered down a wide, clear area, free of tree stumps—the road leading past the Inn, Tas's mind registered, though he didn't think it clearly. Getting to his feet again, the kender hurried after Caramon, but the big man was making rapid headway, staggering through the mud, his fear and hope giving him strength.

Tas soon lost sight of him amid the blackened stumps, but he could hear his voice, still calling Tika's name. Now Tas knew where the big man was headed. His footsteps slowed. His head ached with the heat and the foul smells of the place, his heart ached with what he had just seen. Dragging his heavy, mud-caked shoes, fearful of what he would find ahead, the kender stumbled on.

Sure enough, there was Caramon, standing in a barren space next to another vallenwood stump. In his hand, he held something, staring at it with the look of one who is, at last, defeated.

Mud-covered, bedraggled, heartsick, the kender went to stand before him. "What?" he asked through trembling lips, pointing to the object in the big man's hand.

"A hammer," Caramon said in a choked voice. "*My* hammer."

Tas looked at it. It was a hammer, all right. Or at least appeared to have been one. The wooden handle had been burned about three-fourths of the way off. All that was left was a charred bit of wood and the metal head, blackened with flame.

"How—how can you be sure?" he faltered, still fighting, still refusing to believe.

"I'm sure," Caramon said bitterly. "Look at this." The handle wiggled, the head wobbled when he touched it. "I made it when I was—was still drinking." He wiped his eyes with his hand. "It isn't made very well. The head used to come off about half the time. But then"—he choked—"I never did much work with it anyway."

Weakened from the running, Caramon's injured leg suddenly gave out. This time, he didn't even try to catch himself, but just slumped down into the mud. Sitting in the clear patch of ground that had once been his home, he clutched the hammer in his hand and began to cry.

Tas turned his head away. The big man's grief was sacred, too private a thing for even his eyes. Ignoring his own tears, which were trickling past his nose, Tas stared around bleakly. He had never felt so helpless, so lost and alone. *What had happened? What had gone wrong?* Surely there must be a clue, an answer.

"I—I'm going to look around," he mumbled to Caramon, who didn't hear him.

With a sigh, Tas trudged off. He knew where he was now, of course. He could refuse to admit it no longer. Caramon's house had been located near the center of town, close to the Inn. Tas continued walking along what had once been a street running between rows of houses. Even though there was nothing left now—not the houses, not the street, not the vallenwoods that held the houses—he knew exactly where he was. He wished he didn't. Here and there he saw branches poking up out of the mud, and he shivered. For there was nothing else. Nothing except . . .

"Caramon!" Tas called, thankful to have something to investigate and to, hopefully, take Caramon's mind off his sorrow. "Caramon, I think you should come see this!"

But the big man continued to ignore him, so Tas went off to examine the object by himself. Standing at the very end of the street, in what had once been a small park, was a stone obelisk. Tas remembered the park, but he didn't remember the obelisk. It hadn't been there the last time he'd been in Solace, he realized, examining it.

Tall, crudely carved, it had, nevertheless, survived the ravages of fire and wind and storm. Its surface was blackened and charred but, Tas saw as he neared it, there were letters carved into it, letters that, once he had cleaned away the muck, he thought he could read.

Tas brushed away the soot and muddy film covering the stone, stared at it for a long moment, then called out softly, "Caramon."

The odd note in the kender's voice penetrated Caramon's haze of grief. He lifted his head. Seeing the strange obelisk and seeing Tas's unusually serious face, the big man painfully heaved himself up and limped toward it.

"What is it?" he asked.

Tas couldn't answer, he could only shake his head and point.

Caramon came around to the front and stood, silently reading the roughly carved letters and unfinished inscription.

Hero of the Lance

Tika Waylan Majere

Death Year 358

Your life's tree felled too soon.
I fear, lest in my hands the axe be found.

"I—I'm sorry, Caramon," Tas murmured, slipping his hand into the big man's limp, nerveless fingers.

Caramon's head bowed. Putting his hand on the obelisk, he stroked its cold, wet surface as the wind whipped around them. A few raindrops splattered

against the stone. "She died alone," he said. Doubling his fist, he bashed it into the rock, cutting his flesh on the sharp edges. "I left her alone! I should have been here! Damn it, I should have been here!"

His shoulders began to heave with sobs. Tas, looking over at the storm clouds and realizing that they were moving again, and coming closer, held Caramon's hand tightly.

"I don't think there would have been anything you could have done, Caramon, if you had been here—" the kender began earnestly.

Suddenly, he bit his words off, nearly biting his tongue in the process. Withdrawing his hand from Caramon's—the big man never even noticed—the kender knelt down in the mud. His quick eyes had caught sight of something shining in the sickly rays of the pale sun. Reaching down with a trembling hand, Tas hurriedly scooped away the muck.

"Name of the gods," he said in awe, leaning back on his heels. "Caramon, you *were* here!"

"What?" he growled.

Tas pointed.

Lifting his head, Caramon turned and looked down.

There, at his feet, lay his own corpse.

This is a chapter of consequence, of wrong choices and their direct effects on the home to which the heroes are struggling to return. Here Caramon graphically faces down the consequences should he fail. —TRH

CHAPTER
3

At least it ap-
peared to be Caramon's corpse. It was wearing the
armor he had acquired in Solamnia—armor he had
worn during the Dwarfgate War, armor he had been
wearing when he and Tas left Zhaman, armor he
was wearing now. . . .

But, beyond that, there was nothing specific that
identified the body. Unlike the bodies Tas had discovered that had been preserved beneath layers of
mud, this corpse lay relatively close to the surface and
had decomposed. All that was left was the skeleton
of what had obviously been a large man lying at the
foot of the obelisk. One hand, holding a chisel, rested
directly beneath the stone monument as if his final
act had been to carve out that last dreadful phrase.

There was no sign of what had killed him.

"What's going on, Caramon?" Tas asked in a quivering voice. "If that's you and you're dead, how can

you be here at the same time?" A sudden thought occurred to him. "Oh, no! What if you're *not* here!" He clutched at his topknot, twisting it round and round. "If you're *not* here, then I've made you up. My!" Tas gulped. "I never knew I had such a vivid imagination. You certainly *look* real." Reaching out a trembling hand, he touched Caramon. "You *feel* real and, if you don't mind my saying so, you even smell real!"† Tas wrung his hands. "Caramon! I'm going crazy," he cried wildly. "Like one of those dark dwarves in Thorbardin!"

"No, Tas," Caramon muttered. "This is real. All too real." He stared at the corpse, then at the obelisk that was now barely visible in the rapidly fading light. "And it's starting to make sense. If only I could—" He paused, staring intently at the obelisk. "That's it! Tas, look at the date on the monument!"

With a sigh, Tas lifted his head. "358," he read in a dull voice. Then his eyes opened wide. "358?" he repeated. "Caramon—it was 356 when we left Solace!"

"We've come too far, Tas," Caramon murmured in awe. "We've come into our own future."

Tasslehoff's humor is important in this horrific scene. Humor and horror are very much intertwined thematicallly. Terror is at its most effective when it is counterbalanced with levity. Without this contrast, the horror becomes numbingly boring. —TRH

The boiling black clouds they had been watching mass along the horizon like an army gathering its full strength for the attack surged in just before nightfall, mercifully obliterating the final few moments of the shrunken sun's existence.

The storm struck swiftly and with unbelievable fury. A blast of hot wind blew Tas off his feet and slammed Caramon back against the obelisk. Then the rain hit, pelting them with drops like molten lead. Hail beat on their heads, battering and bruising flesh.

More dreadful, though, than wind or rain was the deadly, multicolored lightning that leaped from cloud to ground, striking the tree stumps, shattering them into brilliant balls of flame visible for miles. The booming rumble of thunder was constant, shaking the very ground, numbing the senses.

Desperately trying to find shelter from the storm's violence, Tas and Caramon huddled beneath a fallen vallenwood, crouching in a hole Caramon dug in the gray, oozing mud. From this scant cover, they watched in disbelief as the storm wreaked further destruction upon the already dead land. Fires swept the sides of the mountains; they could smell the stench of burning wood. Lightning struck near, exploding trees, sending great chunks of ground flying. Thunder hit their ears with concussive force.

The only blessing the storm offered was rainwater. Caramon left his helmet out, upturned, and almost immediately collected water enough to drink. But it tasted horrible—like rotten eggs,† Tas shouted, holding his nose as he drank—and it did little to ease their thirst.

After crossing the sand sea at Mount Bromo on Java, my companions and I climbed the cone of the volcano and stared down into the open maw of the beast. It was not active, of course, but we could still smell the sulfur fumes drifting up in the smoke from below. —TRH

Neither mentioned, though both thought of it, that they had no way to store water, nor was there anything to eat.

Feeling more like himself since he now knew where he was and when he was (if not exactly why he was or how he got here), Tasslehoff even enjoyed the storm for the first hour or so.

"I've never seen lightning that color," he shouted above the booming thunder, and he watched it with rapt interest. "It's as good as a street illusionist's show!" But he soon grew bored with the spectacle.

"After all," he yelled, "even watching trees get blasted right out of the ground loses something after about the fiftieth time you've seen it. If you won't be lonely, Caramon," he added with a jaw-cracking yawn, "I think I'll take a little nap. You don't mind keeping watch, do you?"

Caramon shook his head, about to reply when a shattering blast made him start. A tree stump not a hundred feet from them disappeared in a bluegreen ball of flame.

That could have been us, he thought, staring at the smoldering ashes, his nose wrinkling at the smell of sulfur. We could be next! A wild desire to run came into his head, a desire so strong that his muscles twitched and he had to force himself to stay where he was.

It's certain death out there. At least here, in this hole, we're below ground level. But, even as he watched, he saw lightning blow a gigantic hole in the ground itself, and he smiled bitterly. No, nowhere was safe. We'll just have to ride it out and trust in the gods.

He glanced over at Tas, prepared to say something comforting to the kender. The words died on

his lips. Sighing, he shook his head. Some things never changed—kender among them. Curled up in a ball, completely oblivious to the horrors raging around him, Tas was sound asleep.

Caramon crouched down farther into the hole, his eyes on the churning, lightning-laced clouds above him. To take his mind off his fear, he began to try to sort out what had happened, how they had landed in this predicament. Closing his eyes to the blinding lightning, he saw—once again—his twin standing before the dread Portal. He could hear Raistlin's voice, calling on the five dragon's heads that guarded the Portal to open it and permit his entry into the Abyss. He saw Crysania, cleric of Paladine, praying to her god, lost in the ecstasy of her faith, blind to his brother's evil.

Caramon shuddered, hearing Raistlin's words as clearly as if the archmage were standing beside him.

She will enter the Abyss with me. She will go before me and fight my battles. She will face dark clerics, dark magic-users, spirits of the dead doomed to wander in that cursed land, plus the unbelievable torments that my Queen can devise. All these will wound her in body, devour her mind, and shred her soul. Finally, when she can endure no more, she will slump to the ground to lie at my feet . . . bleeding, wretched, dying.

She will, with her last strength, hold out her hand to me for comfort. She will not ask me to save her. She is too strong for that. She will give her life for me willingly, gladly. All she will ask is that I stay with her as she dies. . . .

But I will walk past her without a look, without a word. Why? Because I will need her no longer. . . .

It was after hearing these words that Caramon had understood at last that his brother was past redemption. And so he had left him.

Let him go into the Abyss, Caramon had thought bitterly. Let him challenge the Dark Queen. Let him become a god. It doesn't matter to me. I don't care what happens to him any longer. I am finally free of him—as he is free of me.

Caramon and Tas had activated the magical device, reciting the rhyme Par-Salian had taught the big man. He had heard the stones singing, just as he had heard them sing during the two other times he had been present at the casting of the time-travel spell.

But then, something had happened. Something that was different. Now that he had time to think and consider, he remembered wondering in sudden panic if something was wrong, but he couldn't think what.

Not that I could have done anything about it anyway, he thought bitterly. I never understood magic—never trusted it either, for that matter.

Another nearby lightning strike shattered his concentration and even caused Tas to jump in his sleep. Muttering in irritation, the kender covered his eyes with his hands and slept on, looking like a dormouse curled up in its burrow.

With a sigh, Caramon forced his thoughts away from storms and dormice back to those last few moments when the magical spell had been activated.

I remember feeling pulled, he realized suddenly, pulled out of shape, as if some force were trying to drag me one way while another was tugging at me from the opposite direction. What was Raistlin doing then? Caramon struggled to recall. A dim image of his brother came to his mind. He saw Raistlin, his face twisted in horror, staring at the Portal in shock. He saw Crysania, standing in the Portal, but she was no longer praying to her god. Her body seemed wracked by pain, her eyes were wide with terror.

Caramon shivered and licked his lips. The bitter-tasting water had left some kind of film behind that made his mouth taste as if he'd been chewing on rusty nails. Spitting, he wiped his mouth with his hand and leaned back wearily. Another blast made him flinch. And so did the answer.

His brother had failed.

The same thing had happened to Raistlin that had happened to Fistandantilus. He had lost control of the magic. The magical field of the time-travel device had undoubtedly disrupted the spell he was casting. That was the only probable explanation—

Caramon frowned. No, surely Raistlin must have foreseen the possibility of that happening. If so, he would have stopped them from using the device, killed them just as he had killed Tas's friend, the gnome.

Shaking his head to clear it, Caramon started over,† working through the problem much as he had worked through the hated ciphering his mother'd

---

Caramon was always very intelligent. He is the type who likes to consider all the angles before acting, and so he seems to be slow-witted when, in fact, he is just a slow thinker. His twin, on the other hand, has a lightning fast intelligence, and thus Raistlin always appeared to be the smarter of the two brothers. One reason Raistlin forces Caramon to undergo these trials is to prove to Caramon that he really is smarter than he gives himself credit for.
—MW

Many people think of Caramon as somehow mentally handicapped. Such is not the case. Caramon thinks deliberately, considering questions carefully before proceeding. This is in sharp contract to this brother. —TRH

taught him when he was a child. The magical field had been disrupted, that much was obvious. It had thrown him and the kender too far forward in time, sending them into their future.

Which means, I suppose, that all I have to do is activate the device and it will take us back to the present, back to Tika, back to Solace. . . .

Opening his eyes, he looked around. But would they face this same future when they returned?

Caramon shivered. He was soaked through from the torrential rain. The night was growing chill, but it wasn't the cold that was tormenting him. He knew what it was to live knowing what was going to happen in the future. He knew what it was to live without hope. How could he go back and face Tika and his friends, knowing that this awaited them? He thought of the corpse beneath the monument. How could he go back knowing what awaited him?

If that had *been* him. He remembered the last conversation between himself and his brother. Tas had altered time—so Raistlin had said. Because kender, dwarves, and gnomes were races created by accident, not design, they were not in the flow of time as were the human, elf, and ogre races. Thus kender were prohibited from traveling back in time because they had the power to alter it.

But Tas had been send back by accident, leaping into the magical field just as Par-Salian, head of the Tower of High Sorcery, was casting the spell to send back Caramon and Crysania. Tas had altered time. Therefore, Raistlin knew he wasn't locked into the doom of Fistandantilus. He had the power to change the outcome. Where Fistandantilus had died, Raistlin might live.

Caramon's shoulders slumped. He felt suddenly sick and dizzy. What did it mean? What was he doing here? How could he be dead and alive at the same time? Was that even his corpse? Since Tas had altered time, it could be someone else. But—most importantly—what had happened to Solace?

"Did Raistlin cause this?" Caramon muttered to himself, just to hear the sound of his voice amid the flashing light and concussive blasts. "Does this have something to do with him? Did this happen because he failed or—"

Caramon caught his breath. Beside him, Tas stirred in his sleep and whimpered and cried out. Caramon patted him absently. "A bad dream," he said, feeling the kender's small body twitch beneath his hand. "A bad dream, Tas. Go back to sleep."

Tas rolled over, pressing his small body close against Caramon's, his hands still covering his eyes. Caramon continued to pat him soothingly.

A bad dream. He wished that were all this was. He wished, most desperately, that he would wake up in his own bed, his head pounding from drinking too much. He wished he could hear Tika slamming plates around in the kitchen, cursing him for being a lazy, drunken bum even while she fixed his favorite breakfast. He wished that he could have gone on in that wretched, spirit-soaked existence because then he would have died, died without knowing. . . .

Oh, please let it be a dream! Caramon prayed, lowering his head to his knees and feeling bitter tears creep beneath his closed eyelids.

He sat there, no longer even affected by the storm, crushed by the weight of his sudden understanding. Tas sighed and shivered, but continued to sleep quietly. Caramon did not move. He did not sleep. He couldn't. The dream he walked in was a waking dream, a waking nightmare. He needed only one thing to confirm the knowledge that he knew, in his heart, needed no confirmation.

The storm passed gradually, moving on to the south. Caramon could literally feel it go, the thunder walking the land like the feet of giants. When it was ended, the silence rang in his ears louder than the blasts of the lightning. The sky would be clear now, he knew. Clear until the next storm. He would see the moons, the stars. . . .

The stars . . .

He had only to raise his head and look up into the sky, the clear sky, and he would know.

For another moment he sat there, willing the smell of spiced potatoes to come to him, willing Tika's laughter to banish the silence, willing a drunken aching in his head to replace the terrible ache in his heart.

But there was nothing. Only the silence of this dead, barren land, broken by the distant, faraway rumble of thunder.

With a small sigh, barely audible even to himself, Caramon raised his head and looked up into the heavens.

He swallowed the bitter saliva in his mouth, nearly choking. Tears stung his eyes, but he blinked them back so that he could see clearly.

There it was—the confirmation of his fears, the sealing of his doom.

A new constellation† in the sky.

An hourglass. . . .

"What does it mean?" asked Tas, rubbing his eyes and staring sleepily up at the stars, only half awake.

"It means Raistlin succeeded," Caramon answered with an odd mixture of fear, sorrow, and pride in his voice. "It means he entered the Abyss and challenged the Queen of Darkness and— defeated her!"

"Not defeated her, Caramon," said Tas, studying the sky intently and pointing. "There's *her* constellation, but it's in the wrong place. It's over there when it should be over here. And there's Paladine." He sighed. "Poor Fizban. I wonder if he had to fight Raistlin. I don't think he'd like that. I always had the feeling that he understood Raistlin, perhaps better than any of the rest of us."

"So maybe the battle is still going on," Caramon mused. "Perhaps that's the reason for the storms." He was silent for a moment, staring up at the glittering shape of the hourglass. In his mind, he could see his brother's eyes as they had been when he emerged—so long ago—from the terrible test in the Tower of High Sorcery—the pupils of the eyes had become the shape of hourglasses.

"Thus, Raistlin, you will see time as it changes all things," Par-Salian had told him. "Thus, hopefully, you will gain compassion for those around you."

But it hadn't worked.

"Raistlin won," Caramon said with a soft sigh. "He's what he wanted to be—a god. And now he rules over a dead world"

"Dead world?" Tas said in alarm. "D-do you mean the whole world's like *this*? Everything in Krynn— Palanthas and Haven and Qualinesti? K-kender-more? Everything?"

The link between the constellations and the gods of Krynn took place very early in our development of the world. It is not really any form of astrology. The constellations of Krynn are much more direct symbols of the gods rather than portents of the future. The inference here is that all the gods of Krynn have been defeated and replaced by a single symbol of Raistlin. —TRH

"Look around," Caramon said bleakly. "What do you think? Have you seen any other living being since we've been here?" He waved a hand that was barely visible by the pale light of Solinari, visible now that the clouds were gone, shining like a staring eye in the sky. "You watched the fire sweep the mountainside. I can see the lightning now, on the horizon." He pointed east. "And there, another storm coming. No, Tas. Nothing can live through this. We'll be dead ourselves before long—either blown to bits or—"

"Or . . . or something else . . ." Tas said miserably. "I—I really don't feel good, Caramon. And it—it's either the water or I'm getting the plague again." His face twisting in pain, he put his hand on his stomach. "I'm beginning to feel all funny inside, like I swallowed a snake."

"The water," said Caramon with a grimace. "I'm feeling it, too. Probably some kind of poison from those clouds."

"Are—are we just going to die here then, Caramon?" Tas asked after a minute of silent contemplation. "Because, if we are, I really think I'd like to go over and lie down next to Tika, if you don't mind. It—it would make me feel more at home. Until I got to Flint and his tree." Sighing, he rested his head against Caramon's strong arm. "I'll certainly have a lot to tell Flint, won't I, Caramon? All about the Cataclysm and the fiery mountain and me saving your life and Raistlin becoming a god. I'll bet he won't believe that part. But maybe you'll be there with me, Caramon, and you can tell him I'm truly not, well—er—exaggerating."

"Dying would certainly be easy," Caramon murmured, looking wistfully over in the direction of the obelisk.

Lunitari was rising now, its blood-red light blending with the deathly white light of Solinari to shed an eerie purplish radiance down upon the ash-covered land. The stone obelisk, wet with rain, glistened in the moonlight, its crudely carved black letters starkly visible against the pallid surface.

"It would be easy to die," Caramon repeated, more to himself than to Tas. "It would be easy to lie down and let the darkness take me." Then, gritting his teeth, he staggered to his feet. "Funny," he added

as he drew his sword and began to hack a branch off the fallen vallenwood they had been using as shelter. "Raist asked me that once. 'Would you follow me into darkness?' he said."

"What are you doing?" Tas asked, staring at Caramon curiously.

But Caramon didn't answer. He just kept hacking away at the tree branch.

"You're making a crutch!" Tas said, then jumped to his feet in sudden alarm. "Caramon! You can't be thinking that! That—that's crazy! *I* remember when Raistlin asked you that question and I remember his answer when you told him yes! He said it would be the death of you, Caramon! As strong as you are, it would kill you!"

Caramon still did not reply. Wet wood flew as he sawed at the tree branch. Occasionally he glanced behind him at the new storm clouds that were approaching, slowly obliterating the constellations and creeping toward the moons.

"Caramon!" Tas grabbed the big man's arm. "Even if you went . . . there"—the kender found he couldn't speak the name—"what would you do?"

"Something I should have done a long time ago," Caramon said resolutely.

CHAPTER 4

"Y ou're going after him, aren't you?" Tas cried, scrambling out of the hole—a move which, more or less, put him at eye-level with Caramon, who was still chopping away at the branch. "That's crazy, just crazy! How will you get there?" A sudden thought struck him. "Where is *there* anyway? You don't even know where you're going! You don't know where *he* is!"

"I have a way to get there," Caramon said coolly, putting his sword back in its sheath. Taking the branch in his strong hands, he bent and twisted it and finally succeeded in breaking it off. "Lend me your knife," he muttered to Tas.

The kender handed it over with a sigh, starting to continue his protest as Caramon trimmed off small twigs, but the big man interrupted him.

"I have the magical device. As for where *there* is"—he eyed Tas sternly—"*you* know that!"

"The—the Abyss?" Tas faltered.

A dull boom of thunder made them both look apprehensively at the approaching storm, then Caramon returned to his work with renewed vigor while Tas returned to his argument. "The magical device got Gnimsh and me *out* of there, Caramon, but I'm positive it won't get you *in*. You don't want to go there anyway," the kender added resolutely. "It is *not* a nice place."

"Maybe it can't get me in," Caramon began, then motioned Tas over to him. "Let's see if this crutch I've made works before another storm hits. We'll walk over to Tika's—the obelisk."

Slashing off a part of his muddy wet cloak with his sword, the warrior bundled it over the top of the branch, tucked it under his arm and leaned his weight on it experimentally. The crude crutch sank into the mud several inches. Caramon yanked it out and took another step. It sank again, but he managed to move forward at least a little and keep his weight off his injured knee. Tas came over to help him walk and, hobbling along slowly, they inched their way across the wet, slimy ground.

Where are we going? Tas longed to ask, but he was afraid to hear the answer. For once, he didn't find it hard to keep quiet. Unfortunately, Caramon seemed to *hear* his thoughts, for he answered his unspoken question.

"Maybe that device can't get me into the Abyss," Caramon repeated, breathing heavily, "but I know someone who can. The device'll take us to him."

"Who?" the kender asked dubiously.

"Par-Salian. He'll be able to tell us what has happened. He'll be able to send me . . . wherever I need to go."

"Par-Salian?" Tas looked almost as alarmed as if Caramon had said the Queen of Darkness herself. "That's even crazier!" he started to say, only he was suddenly violently sick instead. Caramon paused to wait for him, looking pale and ill in the moonlight himself.

Convinced that he had thrown up everything inside him from his topknot down to his socks, Tas felt a little better. Nodding at Caramon, too tired to talk just yet, he managed to stagger on.

Trudging through the slime and the mud, they reached the obelisk. Both slumped down on the ground and leaned against it, exhausted by the exertion even that short journey of only twenty or so paces had cost them. The hot wind was rising again, the sound of thunder getting nearer. Sweat covered Tas's face and he had a green tinge around his lips, but he managed nonetheless, to smile at Caramon with what he hoped was innocent appeal.

"Us going to see Par-Salian?" he said offhandedly, mopping his face with his topknot. "Oh, I don't think that would be a good idea at all. You're in no shape to walk all that way. We don't have any water or food and—"

"I'm not going to walk." Caramon took the pendant out of his pocket and begin the transformation process that would turn it into a beautiful, jeweled sceptre.

Seeing this and gulping slightly, Tas continued on talking more rapidly.

"I'm certain Par-Salian is—uh—is . . . busy. Busy! That's it!" He gave a ghastly grin. "Much too busy to see us now. Probably lots of things to do, what with all this chaos going on around him. So let's just forget this and go back to someplace in time where we had fun. How about when Raistlin put the charm spell on Bupu and she fell in love with him?† That was really funny! That disgusting gully dwarf following him around. . . ."

This happened in Dragons of Autumn Twilight, *Book I, Chapter 17.*

Caramon didn't reply. Tas twisted the end of his topknot around his finger.

"Dead," he said suddenly, heaving a mournful sigh. "Poor Par-Salian. Probably dead as a doorknob. After all," the kender pointed out cheerfully, "he was *old* when we saw him back in 356. He didn't look at all well then, either. This must have been a real shock to him—Raistlin becoming a god and all. Probably too much for his heart. Bam—he probably just keeled right over."

Tas peeped up at Caramon. There was a slight smile on the big man's lips, but he said nothing, just kept turning and twisting the pieces of the pendant. A bright flash of lightning made him start. He glanced at the storm, his smile vanishing.

"I'll bet the Tower of High Sorcery's not even there anymore!" Tas cried in desperation. "If what

you say is right and the whole world is . . . is like this"—he waved his small hand as the foul-smelling rain began to fall—"then the Tower must have been one of the first places to go! Struck by lightning! Blooey! After all, the Tower's much taller than most trees I've seen—"

"The Tower'll be there," Caramon said grimly, making the final adjustment to the magical device. He held it up. Its jewels caught the rays of Solinari and, for an instant, gleamed with radiance. Then the storm clouds swept over the moon, devouring it. The darkness was now intense, split only by the brilliant, beautiful, deadly lightning.

Gritting his teeth against the pain, Caramon grabbed his crutch and struggled to his feet. Tas followed more slowly, gazing at Caramon miserably.

"You see, Tas, I've come to know Raistlin," Caramon continued, ignoring the kender's woebegone expression. "Too late, maybe, but I know him now. He hated that Tower, just as he hated those mages for what they did to him there. But even as he hates it, he loves it all the same†—because it is part of his Art, Tas. And his Art, his magic, means more to him than life itself. No, the Tower will be there."

Lifting the device in his hands, Caramon began the chant, "'Thy time is thine own. Though across it you travel—'"

But he was interrupted.

"Oh, Caramon!" Tas wailed, clutching at him. "Don't take me back to Par-Salian! He'll do something *awful* to me! I know it! He might turn me into a—a bat!" Tas paused. "And, while I suppose it might be interesting being a bat, I'm not certain I could get used to sleeping upside down, hanging by my feet. And I *am* rather fond of being a kender, now that I think of it, and—"

"What are you talking about?" Caramon glared at him, then glanced up at the storm clouds. The rain was increasing in fury, the lightning striking nearer.

"Par-Salian!" cried Tas frantically. "I—I messed up his magical time-traveling spell! I went when I wasn't supposed to! And then I stol—er—found a magical ring† that someone had left lying about and it turned me into a mouse! I'm certain he must be rather peeved over that! And then I—I broke the magical device, Caramon. Remember? Well, it

Addiction is another central theme in Legends. Caramon understands his brother better now because he understands that they are both addicts of a kind. Caramon is a recovering alcoholic, and Raistlin is consumed by his own magic. —TRH

See Time of the Twins, Book I, Chapter 15.

wasn't exactly my fault, Raistlin made me break it! But a really strict person might take the unfortunate attitude that if I had left it alone in the first place—like I knew I was supposed to—then that wouldn't have happened. And Par-Salian seems an *awfully* strict sort of person, don't you think? And while I *did* have Gnimsh fix it, he didn't fix it quite right, you know—"

"Tasslehoff," said Caramon tiredly, "shut up."

"Yes, Caramon," Tas said meekly, with a snuffle.

Caramon looked at the small dejected figure reflected in the bright lightning and sighed. "Look, Tas, I won't let Par-Salian do anything to you. I promise. He'll have to turn *me* into a bat first."

"Truly?" asked Tas anxiously.

"My word," said Caramon, his eyes on the storm. "Now, give me your hand and let's get out of here."

"Sure," said Tas cheerfully, slipping his small hand into Caramon's large one.

"And Tas . . ."

"Yes, Caramon?"

"This time—think of the Tower of High Sorcery in Wayreth! No moons!"

"Yes, Caramon," Tas said with a profound sigh. Then he smiled again. "You know," he said to himself as Caramon began to recite the chant again, "I'll bet Caramon would make a whopping big bat—"

They found themselves standing at the edge of a forest.

"It's not my fault, Caramon!" Tas said quickly. "I thought about the Tower with all my heart and soul. I'm certain I never thought once about a forest."

Caramon stared intently into the woods. It was still night, but the sky was clear, though storm clouds were visible on the horizon. Lunitari† burned a dull, smoldering red. Solinari was dropping down into the storm. And above them, the starry hourglass.

"Well, we're in the right time period. But where in the name of the gods are we?" Caramon muttered, leaning on his crutch and glaring at the magical device irritably. His gaze went back to the shadowy trees, their trunks visible in the garish moonlight. Suddenly, his expression cleared. "It's all right, Tas," he said in relief. "Don't you recognize this? It's

There are a number of different opinions about whether the moons of Krynn are only symbols of the gods or the actual gods themselves. I have always seen them as symbols of the power that magic taps rather than actual deities.
—TRH

Wayreth Forest—the magical forest that stands guard around the Tower of High Sorcery!"

"Are you sure?" Tas asked doubtfully. "It certainly doesn't look the same as the last time I saw it. Then it was all ugly, with dead trees lurking about, staring at me, and when I tried to go inside it wouldn't let me and when I tried to leave it wouldn't let me and—"

"This is it," Caramon muttered, folding the sceptre back into its nondescript pendant shape again.

"Then what happened to it?"

"The same thing that happened to the rest of the world, Tas," Caramon replied, carefully slipping the pendant back into the leather pouch.

Tas's thoughts went back to the last time he had seen the magical Forest of Wayreth. Set to guard the Tower of High Sorcery from unwelcome intruders, the Forest was a strange and eerie place. For one thing, a person didn't find the magical forest—it found you. And the first time it had found Tas and Caramon was right after Lord Soth had cast the death spell on Lady Crysania. Tas had wakened from a sound sleep to discover the Forest standing where no forest had been the night before!

The trees then had appeared to be dead. Their limbs were bare and twisted, a chill mist flowed from beneath their trunks. Inside dwelt dark and shadowy shapes. But the trees hadn't been dead. In fact, they had the uncanny habit of *following* a person. Tas remembered trying to walk away from the Forest, only to continually find himself—no matter what direction he traveled—always walking into it.

That had been spooky enough, but when Caramon walked into the Forest, it had changed dramatically. The dead trees began to grow, turning into vallenwoods! The Forest was transformed from a dark and forbidding wood filled with death into a beautiful green and golden forest of life. Birds sang sweetly in the branches of the vallenwoods, inviting them inside.

And now the Forest had changed again. Tas stared at it, puzzled. It seemed to be both forests he remembered—yet neither of them. The trees appeared dead, their twisted limbs were stark and bare. But, as he watched, he thought he saw them move in a

manner that seemed very much alive! Reaching out, like grasping arms. . . .

Turning his back on the spooky Forest of Wayreth, Tas investigated his surroundings. All else was exactly as it had been in Solace. No other trees stood at all—living or dead. He was surrounded by nothing but blackened, blasted stumps. The ground was covered with the same slimy, gray mud. For as far as he could see, in fact, there was nothing but desolation and death. . . .

"Caramon," Tas cried suddenly, pointing.

Caramon glanced over. Beside one of the stumps lay a huddled figure.

"A person!" Tas cried in wild excitement. "Someone else is here!"

"Tas!" Caramon called out warningly, but before he could stop him, the kender was dashing over.

"Hey!" he yelled. "Hullo! Are you asleep? Wake up." Reaching down, he shook the figure, only to have it roll over at his touch, lying stiff and rigid.

"Oh!" Tas took a step backward, then stopped. "Oh, Caramon," he said softly. "It's Bupu!"†

This is the gully dwarf whom Raistlin first met back in Dragons of Autumn Twilight, *Book I, Chapter 17. Raistlin has always had a soft spot in his heart for the gully dwarf, and she therefore symbolizes Raistlin's compassion for the weak and downtrodden of the world. The fact that Caramon and Tas have found her dead, speaks volumes. . . .*

Once, long ago, Raistlin had befriended the gully dwarf. Now she stared up at the starlit sky with empty, sightless eyes. Dressed in filthy, ragged clothing, her small body was pitifully thin, her grubby face wasted and gaunt. Around her neck was a leather thong. Attached to the end of the thong was a stiff, dead lizard. In one hand, she clutched a dead rat, in the other she held a dried-up chicken leg. As death approached, she had summoned up all the magic she possessed, Tas thought sadly, but it hadn't helped.

"She hasn't been dead long," Caramon said. Limping over, he knelt down painfully beside the shabby little corpse. "Looks like she starved to death." He reached out his hand and gently closed the staring eyes. Then he shook his head. "I wonder how she came to live this long? The bodies we saw back in Solace must have been dead months, at least."

"Maybe Raistlin protected her," Tasslehoff said before he thought.

Caramon scowled. "Bah! It's just coincidence, that's all," he said harshly. "You know gully dwarves, Tas. They can live on anything. My guess is that they were the last creatures to survive. Bupu, being the smartest of the lot, just managed to survive longer

than the rest. But—in the end, even a gully dwarf would perish in this god-cursed land." He shrugged. "Here, help me stand."

"What—what are we going to do with her, Caramon?" Tas asked bleakly. "Are—are we just going to leave her?"

"What else can we do?" Caramon muttered gruffly. The sight of the gully dwarf and the nearness of the Forest were bringing back painful, unwelcome memories. "Would you want to be buried in that mud?" He shivered and glanced about. The storm clouds were rushing closer; he could see the lightning streaking down to the ground and hear the roar of the thunder. "Besides, we don't have much time, not the way those clouds are moving in."

Tas continued to stare at him sorrowfully.

"There's nothing left alive to bother her anyway, Tas," he snapped irritably. Then, seeing the grieved expression on the kender's face, Caramon slowly removed his own cloak and carefully spread it over the emaciated corpse. "We better get going," he said.

"Good-bye, Bupu," Tas said softly. Patting the stiff little hand that was tightly clutching the dead rat, he started to pull the corner of the cloak over it when he saw something flash in Lunitari's red light. Tas caught his breath, thinking he recognized the object. Carefully, he pried the gully dwarf's death-stiffened fingers apart. The dead rat fell to the ground and—with it—an emerald.

Tas picked up the jewel. In his mind, he was back to . . . where had it been? Xak Tsaroth?†

They had been in a sewer pipe hiding from draconian troops. Raistlin had been seized by a fit of coughing. . . .

Bupu† gazed at him anxiously, then thrust her small hand into her bag, fished around for several moments, and came up with an object that she held up to the light. She squinted at it then sighed and shook her head. "This not what I want," she mumbled.

Tasslehoff, catching sight of a brilliant, colorful flash, crept closer. "What is it?" he asked, even though he knew the answer. Raistlin, too, was staring at the object with wide glittering eyes.

Bupu shrugged. "Pretty rock," she said without interest, searching through the bag once more.

"An emerald!" Raistlin wheezed.

You may have to blame my interest in the Russian and Eastern languages for some of the names in Ansalon. I was enchanted by the Russian use of the ts sound. —TRH

Tas is remembering events that occurred in Dragons of Autumn Twilight, Book I, Chapter 18.

Bupu glanced up. "You like?" she asked Raistlin.

"Very much!" The mage gasped.

"You keep." Bupu put the jewel in the mage's hand. Then, with a cry of triumph, she brought out what she had been searching for. Tas, leaning up close to see the new wonder, drew back in disgust. It was a dead—very dead— lizard. There was a piece of chewed-on leather tied around the lizard's stiff tail. Bupu held it toward Raistlin.

"You wear around neck," she said. "Cure cough."

"So Raistlin *was* here," Tas murmured. "He gave this to her, he must have! But why? A charm . . . a gift? . . ." Shaking his head, the kender sighed and stood up. "Caramon—" he began, then he saw the big man standing, staring into the Forest of Wayreth. He saw Caramon's pale face and he guessed what he must be thinking, remembering.

Tasslehoff slipped the emerald into a pocket.

The Forest of Wayreth seemed as dead and desolate as the rest of the world around them. But, to Caramon, it was alive with memories. Nervously he stared at the strange trees, their wet trunks and decaying limbs seeming to glisten with blood in Lunitari's light.

"I was frightened the first time I came here," Caramon said to himself, his hand on the hilt of his sword. "I wouldn't have gone in at all if it hadn't been for Raistlin. I was even more frightened the second time, when we brought Lady Crysania here to try to find help for her. I wouldn't have gone in then for any reason except those birds lured me with their sweet song." He smiled grimly. " 'Easeful the forest. Easeful the mansions perfected. Where we grow and decay no longer,' they sang. I thought they promised help. I thought they promised me all the answers. But I see now what the song meant. Death, that is the only perfect mansion, the only dwelling place where we grow and decay no longer!"

Staring into the woods, Caramon shivered, despite the oppressive heat of the night air. "I'm more frightened of it this time than ever before," he muttered. "Something's wrong in there." A brilliant flash lit up sky and ground with the brightness of day, followed by a dull boom and the splash of rain upon his cheek. "But at least it's still standing," he said. "Its magic must be strong—to survive the storm." His stomach wrenched painfully. Reminded of his thirst, he

licked his dry, parched lips. " 'Easeful the forest,' "
he muttered.

"What did you say?" asked Tas, coming up beside
him.

"I said as good one death as another," Caramon
answered, shrugging.

"You know, I've died three times," said Tas
solemnly. "The first was in Tarsis, where the dragons
knocked a building down on top of me.† The second
was in Neraka, where I was poisoned by a trap† and
Raistlin saved me. And the last was when the gods
dropped a fiery mountain on me.† And, all in all"—
he pondered a moment—"I think I could say that
was a fair statement. One death *is* just about the
same as another. You see, the poison hurt a great
deal, but it was over pretty quickly. While the building, on the other hand—"

"C'mon"—Caramon grinned wearily—"save it to
tell Flint." He drew his sword. "Ready?"

"Ready," answered Tas stoutly. " 'Always save
the best for last,' my father used to say. Although"—
the kender paused—"I think he meant that in reference to dinner, not to dying. But perhaps it has the
same significance."

Drawing his own small knife, Tas followed Caramon into the enchanted Forest of Wayreth.

See Dragons of Winter
Night, *Book II, Chapter 1.*

See Dragons of Spring
Dawning, *Book III,
Chapter 9.*

See Time of the Twins,
Book II, Chapter 19.

CHAPTER
5

The darkness swallowed them. Light from neither moon nor stars could penetrate the night of the Forest of Wayreth. Even the brilliance of the deadly, magical lightning was lost here. And though the booming of the thunder could be heard, it seemed nothing but a distant echo of itself. Behind them, Caramon could hear, too, the drumming of the rain and the pelting of the hail. In the Forest, it was dry. Only the trees that stood on the outer fringes were affected by the rain.

"Well, this is a relief!" said Tasslehoff cheerfully. "Now, if we just had some light. I—"

His voice was cut off with a choking gurgle. Caramon heard a thud and creaking wood and a sound like something being dragged along the ground.

"Tas?" he called.

"Caramon!" Tas cried. "It's a tree! A tree's got me! Help, Caramon! Help!"

"Is this a joke, Tas?" Caramon asked sternly. "Because it's not funny—"

"No!" Tas screamed. "It's got me and it's dragging me off somewhere!"

"What . . . where?" Caramon yelled. "I can't see in this damn darkness? Tas?"

"Here! Here!" Tas screamed wildly. "It's got hold of my foot and it's trying to tear me in two!"

"Keep yelling, Tas!" Caramon cried, stumbling about in the rustling blackness. "I think I'm close—"

A huge tree limb† bashed Caramon in the chest, knocking him to the ground and slamming his breath from his body. He lay there, trying to draw in air, when he heard a creaking to his right. As he slashed at it blindly with his sword, he rolled away. Something heavy crashed right where he'd been lying. He staggered to his feet, but another limb struck him in the small of his back, sending him sprawling face first onto the barren floor of the Forest.

A nod to Tolkien's Old Man Willow here. —MW

The blow to the back caught him in the kidneys, making him gasp in pain. He tried to struggle back up, but his knee throbbed painfully, his head spun. He couldn't hear Tas anymore. He couldn't hear anything except the creaking, rustling sounds of the trees closing in on him. Something scraped along his arm. Caramon flinched and crawled out of its reach, only to feel something grab his foot. Desperately he hacked at it with his sword. Flying wood chips stung his leg, but apparently did no harm to his attacker.

The strength of centuries was in the tree's† massive limbs. Magic gave it thought and purpose. Caramon had trespassed on land it guarded, land forbidden to the uninvited. It was going to kill him, he knew.

Intelligent and sometimes malevolent trees seem to be a staple of fantasy—from Tolkien's Ents, to the apple trees next to the yellow brick road, to the Whomping Willow of Harry Potter. If you find yourself in the woods of a fantasy setting, I suggest you make for open ground! —TRH

Another tree limb caught hold of Caramon's thick thigh. Branches clutched at his arms, seeking a firm grip. Within seconds, he would be ripped apart. . . . He heard Tas cry out in pain. . . .

Raising his voice, Caramon shouted desperately, "I am Caramon Majere, brother of Raistlin Majere! I must speak to Par-Salian or whoever is Master of the Tower now!"

There was a moment's silence, a moment's hesitation. Caramon felt the will of the trees waver, the branches loosen their grip ever so slightly.

"Par-Salian, are you there? Par-Salian, you know me! I am *his* twin. I am your only hope!"

"Caramon?" came a quavering voice.

"Hush, Tas!" Caramon hissed.

The silence was as thick as the darkness. And then, slowly, he felt the branches release him. He heard the creaking and rustling sounds again, only this time they were moving slowly away from him. Gasping in relief, weak from fear and the pain and the growing sickness inside him, Caramon lay his head on his arm, trying to catch his breath.

"Tas, are you all right?" he managed to call out.

"Yes, Caramon," came the kender's voice beside him. Reaching out his hand, Caramon caught hold of the kender and pulled him close.

Though he heard the sounds of movement in the darkness and knew the trees were withdrawing, he also had the feeling the trees were watching his every move, listening to every word. Slowly and cautiously, he sheathed his sword.

"I am truly thankful you thought of telling Par-Salian who you are, Caramon," Tas said, panting for breath. "I was just imagining trying to explain to Flint how I'd been murdered by a tree. I'm not certain whether or not you're allowed to laugh in the Afterlife, but I'll bet he would have roared—"

"Shhhh," Caramon said weakly.

Tas paused, then whispered, "Are you all right?"

"Yeah, just let me catch my breath. I've lost my crutch."

"It's over here. I fell over it." Tas crawled off and returned moments later, dragging the padded tree branch. "Here." He helped Caramon stagger to his feet.

"Caramon," he asked after a moment, "how long do you think it will take us to get to the Tower? I— I'm awfully thirsty and, while my insides are a little better since I was sick a while back, I still get queer squirmy feelings in my stomach sometimes."

"I don't know, Tas," Caramon sighed. "I can't see a damn thing in this darkness. I don't know where we're going or what's the right way or how we're going to manage to walk without running smack into something—"

The rustling sounds suddenly started again, as though a storm wind were tossing the branches of the trees. Caramon tensed and even Tas stiffened in alarm as they heard the trees start to close in around

them once more. Tas and Caramon stood helpless in the darkness as the trees came nearer and nearer. Branches touched their skin and dead leaves brushed their hair, whispering strange words in their ears. Caramon's shaking hand closed over his sword hilt, though he knew it would do little good. But then, when the trees were pressed close around them, the movement and the whispering ceased. The trees were silent once more.

Reaching out his hand, Caramon touched solid trunks to his right and his left. He could feel them massed behind him. An idea occurred to him. He stretched his arm out into the darkness and felt around ahead of him. All was clear.

"Keep close to me, Tas," he ordered and, for once in his life, the kender didn't argue. Together, they walked forward into the opening provided by the trees.

At first they moved cautiously, fearful of stumbling over a root or a fallen branch or becoming entangled in brush or tumbling into a hole. But gradually they came to realize that the forest floor was smooth and dry, cleared of all obstacles, free from undergrowth. They had no idea where they were going. They walked in absolute darkness, kept to some irreversible path only by the trees that parted before them and closed in after them. Any deviation from the set path brought them into a wall of trunks and tangled branches and dead, whispering leaves.

The heat was oppressive. No wind blew, no rain fell. Their thirst, lost in their fear, returned to plague them. Wiping the sweat from his face, Caramon wondered at the strange, intense heat, for it was much greater here than outside the Forest. It seemed as if the heat were being generated by the Forest itself. The Forest was more alive than he had noticed the last two times he had been here. It was certainly more alive than the world outside. Amid the rustling of the trees, he could hear—or thought he heard—movements of animals or the rush of birds' wings, and sometimes he caught a glimpse of eyes shining in the darkness. But being among living beings once more brought no sense of comfort to Caramon. He felt their hatred and their anger and, even as he felt it, he realized that it wasn't directed against him. It was directed against itself.†

These creatures represent the failure of neutrality (their failure to maintain the status quo). —TRH

And then he heard the birds' songs again, as he had heard them the last time he'd entered this eerie place. High and sweet and pure, rising above death and darkness and defeat, rose the song of a lark.† Caramon stopped to listen, tears stinging his eyes at the beauty of the song, feeling his heart's pain ease.

One of my favorite pieces of classical music is "The Lark Ascending" by Vaughan Williams.
—MW

This lark brings us hope. Once again we see the need and use of contrast to bring definition and focus to the story. —TRH

"Like to the lark at break of day arising
*   From sullen earth, sings hymns at heaven's gate"*
*   —Shakespeare's 29th Sonnet*

> *The light in the eastern skies*
> *Is still and always morning,*
> *It alters the renewing air*
> *Into belief and yearning.*
>
> *And larks† rise up like angels,*
> *Like angels larks ascend*
> *From sunlit grass as bright as gems*
> *Into the cradling wind.*

But even as the lark's song pierced his heart with its sweetness, a harsh cackle made him cringe. Black wings fluttered around him, and his soul was filled with shadows.

> *The plain light in the east*
> *Contrives out of the dark*
> *The machinery of day,*
> *The diminished song of the lark.*
>
> *But ravens ride the night*
> *And the darkness west,*
> *The wingbeat of their hearts*
> *Large in a buried nest.*

"What does it mean, Caramon?" Tas asked in awe as they continued to grope their way through the Forest, guided, always, by the angry trees.

The answer to his question came, not from Caramon, but from other voices, mellow, deep, sad with the ancient wisdom of the owl.†

This song utilizes the images of a lark, a raven, and an owl. These three represent the three founding concepts of the DRAGONLANCE setting: good, evil, and chaos. —TRH

> *Through night the seasons ride into the dark,*
> *The years surrender in the changing lights,*
> *The breath turns vacant on the dusk or dawn*
> *Between the abstract days and nights.*
> *For there is always corpselight in the fields*
> *And corposants above the slaughterhouse,*

And at deep noon the shadowy vallenwoods
Are bright at the topmost boughs.†

"It means the magic is out of control," Caramon said softly. "Whatever will holds this Forest in check is just barely hanging on." He shivered. "I wonder what we'll find when we get to the Tower."

"*If* we get to the Tower," Tas muttered. "How do we know that these awful, old trees aren't leading us to the edge of a tall cliff?"

Caramon stopped, panting for breath in the terrible heat. The crude crutch dug painfully into his armpit. With his weight off of it, his knee had begun to stiffen. His leg was inflamed and swollen, and he knew he could not go on much longer. He, too, had been sick, purging his system of the poison, and now he felt somewhat better. But thirst was a torment. And, as Tas reminded him, he had no idea where these trees were leading them.

Raising his voice, his throat parched, Caramon cried out harshly, "Par-Salian! Answer me or I'll go no farther! Answer me!"

The trees broke out in a clamor, branches shaking and stirring as if in a high wind, though no breeze cooled Caramon's feverish skin. The birds' voices rose in a fearful cacophony, intermingling, overlapping, twisting their songs into horrible, unlovely melodies that filled the mind with terror and foreboding.

Even Tas was a bit startled by this, creeping closer to Caramon (in case the big man needed comfort), but Caramon stood resolutely, staring into the endless night, ignoring the turmoil around him.

"Par-Salian!" he called once more.

Then he heard his answer—a thin, high-pitched scream.

At the dreadful sound, Caramon's skin crawled. The scream pierced through the darkness and the heat. It rose above the strange singing of the birds and drowned out the clashing of the trees. It seemed to Caramon as if all the horror and sorrow of the dying world had been sucked up and released at last in that fearful cry.

"Name of the gods!" Tas breathed in awe, catching hold of Caramon's hand (in case the big man should feel frightened).† "What's happening?"

These are, again, "companion poems"—this time, three instead of the customary two. It's pretty evident how they work: the songs of the lark and raven establish an antithesis, an opposition, and then the owl's song drops down somewhere in between. Caramon says that "the magic is out of control," but the poetry's metrical regularity and rhyme scheme should set up the other opposition: that even when it appears that everything is out of control, there are some kinds of order at work, shaping things toward a design.

The philosophy behind most companion poems that I've read is not only that the universe is ordered but that it's pretty much a balanced place as well. I don't claim to be a philosopher by any means—I aced Philosophy 101 in college, but that's as metaphysical as I ever got. The universe doesn't seem that balanced to me, but fictional worlds often are, and if you ever read any of Tracy's reflections on Krynn, you'll find that the concept of balance underlies his musings on the way things are. So this type of poem makes a kind of provisional fit to the whole vision of the novels.
—Michael Williams

Kender aren't supposed to know fear and generally they don't, but this situation is so terrifying that it even manages to frighten the kender. (Although Tas would be the last to admit it!)
—MW

Caramon didn't answer. He could feel the anger in the Forest grow more intense, mingled now with an overwhelming fear and sadness. The trees seemed to be prodding them ahead, crowding them, urging them on. The screaming continued for as long as it might take a man to use up his breath, then it quit for the space of a man drawing air into his lungs, then it began again. Caramon felt the sweat chill on his body.

He kept walking, Tas close by his side. They made slow progress, made worse by the fact that they had no idea if they were making progress at all, since they could not see their destination nor even know if they were headed in the right direction. The only guide they had to the Tower was that shrill, inhuman scream.

On and on they stumbled and, though Tas helped as best he could, each step for Caramon was agony. The pain of his injuries took possession of him and soon he lost all conception of time. He forgot why they had come or even where they were going. To stagger ahead, one step at a time through the darkness that had become a darkness of the mind and soul, was Caramon's only thought.

He kept walking—
and walking—
and walking—
one step, one step, one step . . .

And all the time, shrilling in his ears, that horrible, undying scream . . .

"Caramon!"

The voice penetrated his weary, pain-numbed brain. He had a feeling he had been hearing it for some time now, above the scream, but—if so—it hadn't pierced the fog of blackness that enshrouded him.

"What?" he mumbled, and now he became aware that hands were grasping him, shaking him. He raised his head and looked around. "What?" he asked again, struggling to regain his grasp of reality. "Tas?"

"Look, Caramon!" The kender's voice came to him through a haze, and he shook his head, desperately, to clear away the fog in his brain.

And he realized he could see. It was light—moonlight! Blinking his eyes, he stared around. "The Forest?"

"Behind us," Tas whispered, as though talking about it might suddenly bring it back. "It's brought us somewhere, at least. I'm just not certain where. Look around. Do you remember this?"

Caramon looked. The shadow of the Forest was gone. He and Tas were standing in a clearing. Swiftly, fearfully, he glanced around.

At his feet yawned a dark chasm.

Behind them, the Forest waited. Caramon did not have to turn to see it, he knew it was there, just as he knew that they would never reenter it and get out alive. It had led them this far, here it would leave them. But where was here? The trees were behind them, but ahead of them lay nothing—just a vast, dark void. They might have been standing on the very edge of a cliff, as Tas had said.

Storm clouds darkened the horizon, but—for the time being—none seemed close. Up above, he could see the moons and stars in the sky. Lunitari burned a fiery red, Solinari's silver light glowed with a radiant brilliance Caramon had never seen before. And now, perhaps because of the stark contrast between darkness and light, he could see Nuitari†— the black moon, the moon that had been visible only to his brother's eyes. Around the moons, the stars shone fiercely, none brighter than the strange hourglass constellation.

Caramon can see Nuitari because evil is ascendant and predominant in the world. The balance has been destroyed. —MW

The only sounds he could hear were the angry mutterings of the Forest behind him and, ahead of him, that shrill, horrible scream.

They had no choice, Caramon thought wearily. There was no turning back. The Forest would not permit that. And what was death anyhow except an end to this pain, this thirst, this bitter aching in his heart.

"Stay here, Tas," he began, trying to disengage the kender's small hand as he prepared to step forward into the darkness. "I'm going to go ahead a little way and scout—"

"Oh, no!" Tas cried. "You're not going anywhere without me!" The kender's hand gripped his even more firmly. "Why, just look at all the trouble you got into by yourself in the dwarf wars!" he added, trying to get rid of an annoying choking feeling in his throat. "And when I *did* get there, I had to save your life." Tas looked down into the darkness that

The moons being so ordered shows the fall of neutrality as the heavens are ordered. It is a powerful symbol that the universe is being forced to conform to Raistlin's will and tearing itself apart in the process. —TRH

lay at their feet, then he gritted his teeth resolutely and raised his gaze to meet that of the big man. "I—I think it would be awfully lonely in—in the Afterlife without you and, besides, I can just hear Flint—'Well, you doorknob, what have you gone and done *this* time? Managed to lose that great hulking hunk of lard, did you? It figures. Now, I suppose *I'll* have to leave my nice soft seat here under this tree and set off in search of the muscle-bound idiot. Never did know when to come in out of the rain—' "

"Very well, Tas," Caramon interrupted with a smile, having a sudden vision of the crotchety old dwarf. "It would never do to disturb Flint. I'd never hear the end of it."

"Besides," Tas went on, feeling more cheerful, "why would they bring us all this way just to dump us in a pit?"

"Why, indeed?" Caramon said, reflecting. Gripping his crutch, feeling more confident, he took a step into the darkness, Tas following along behind.

"Unless," the kender added with a gulp, "Par-Salian's still mad at me. . . ."

CHAPTER 6

The Tower† of
High Sorcery loomed before them—a thing of darkness, silhouetted against the light of moon and stars,
looking as though it had been created out of the night
itself. For centuries it had stood, a bastion of magic,
the repository of the books and artifacts of the Art,
collected over the years.

Here the mages had come when they were driven
from the Tower of High Sorcery in Palanthas by the
Kingpriest, here they brought with them those
most valued objects, saved from the attacking mobs.
Here they dwelt in peace, guarded by the Forest of
Wayreth. Young apprentice magic-users took the
Test here, the grueling Test that meant death to those
who failed it.

Here Raistlin had come and lost his soul to Fistandantilus. Here Caramon had been forced to watch as
Raistlin murdered an illusion of his twin brother.†

*The Tower is a powerful
symbol. Besides Rapunzel
and the wizards' towers of
fairy tales, there is
Tolkien's Barad-dûr and
Orthanc, Stoker's Castle
Dracula, and Robert
Browning's Dark Tower,
which inspired Stephen
King's Dark Tower series.*

*These events are alluded to
throughout the Chronicles,
since they define so much
of Raistlin and Caramon's
characters. The events
themselves were told in*
The Soulforge *by
Margaret Weis.*

Here Caramon and Tas had returned with the gully dwarf, Bupu, bearing the comatose body of Lady Crysania. Here they had attended a Conclave of the Three Robes—Black, Red, and White. Here they had learned Raistlin's ambition—to challenge the Queen of Darkness. Here they had met his apprentice and spy for the Conclave—Dalamar. Here the great archmage Par-Salian had cast a time-travel spell on Caramon and Lady Crysania, sending them back to Istar before the mountain fell.

Here, Tasslehoff had inadvertently upset the spell by jumping in to go with Caramon. Thus, the presence of the kender—forbidden by all the laws of magic—allowed time to be altered.

Now Caramon and Tas had returned—to find what?

Caramon stared at the Tower, his heart heavy with foreboding and dread. His courage failed him. He could not enter, not with the sound of that pitiful, persistent screaming echoing in his ears. Better to go back, better to face quick death in the Forest. Besides, he had forgotten the gates. Made of silver and of gold, they still stood, steadfastly blocking his way into the Tower. Thin as cobweb they seemed, looking like black streaks painted down the starlit sky. A touch of a kender's hand might have opened them. Yet magical spells were wound about them, spells so powerful an army of ogres could have hurled itself against those fragile-seeming gates without effect.

Still the screaming, louder now and nearer. So near, in fact, that it might have come from—

Caramon took another step forward, his brow creased in a frown. As he did so, the gate came clearly into view.

And revealed the source of the screaming. . . .

The gates were not shut, nor were they locked. One gate stood fast, as if still spellbound. But the other had broken, and now it swung by one hinge, back and forth, back and forth in the hot, unceasing wind. And, as it blew back and forth slowly in the breeze, it gave forth a shrill, high-pitched shriek.

"It's not locked," said Tas in disappointment. His small hand had already been reaching for his lock-picking tools.

"No," said Caramon, staring up at the squeaking hinge. "And there's the voice we heard—the voice of rusty metal." He supposed he should have been relieved, but it only deepened the mystery. "If it wasn't Par-Salian or someone up there"—his eyes went to the Tower that stood, black and apparently empty before them—"who got us through the Forest, then who was it?"

"Maybe no one," Tas said hopefully. "If no one's here, Caramon, can we leave?"

"There has to be someone," Caramon muttered. "Something made those trees let us pass."

Tas sighed, his head drooping. Caramon could see him in the moonlight, his small face pale and covered with grime. There were dark shadows beneath his eyes, his lower lip quivered, and a tear was sneaking down one side of his small nose.

Caramon patted him on the shoulder. "Just a little longer," he said gently. "Hold out just a little longer, please, Tas?"

Looking up quickly, swallowing that traitor tear and its partner that had just dripped into his mouth, Tas grinned cheerfully. "Sure, Caramon," he said. Not even the fact that his throat was aching and parched with thirst could keep him from adding, "You know me—always ready for adventure. There's bound to be lots of magical, wonderful things in there, don't you think?" he added, glancing at the silent Tower. "Things no one would miss. Not magical rings, of course. I'm finished with magical rings. First one lands me in a wizard's castle where I met a truly wicked demon, then the next turns me into a mouse. I—"

Letting Tas prattle on, glad that the kender was apparently feeling back to normal, Caramon hobbled forward and put his hand upon the swinging gate to shove it to one side. To his amazement, it broke off—the weakened hinge finally giving way. The gate clattered to the gray paving stone beneath it with a clang that made both Tas and Caramon cringe. The echoes bounded off the black, polished walls of the Tower, resounding through the hot night and shattering the stillness.

"Well, now they know we're here," said Tas.

Caramon's hand once again closed over his sword hilt, but he did not draw it. The echoes faded. Silence

closed in. Nothing happened. No one came. No voice spoke.

Tas turned to help Caramon limp ahead. "At least we won't have to listen to that awful sound anymore," he said, stepping over the broken gate. "I don't mind saying so now, but that shriek was beginning to get on my nerves. It certainly sounded very ungate-like, if you know what I mean. It sounded just like . . . just like . . ."

"Like that," Caramon whispered.

The scream split the air, shattering the moonlit darkness, only this time it was different. There were words in this scream—words that could be heard, if not defined.

Turning his head involuntary, though he knew what he would see, Caramon stared back at the gate. It lay on the stones, dead, lifeless.

"Caramon," said Tas, swallowing, "it—it's coming from there—the Tower. . . ."

"End it!" screamed Par-Salian. "End this torment! Do not force me to endure more!"

How much did you force me to endure, O Great One of the White Robes? came a soft, sneering voice into Par-Salian's mind. The wizard writhed in agony, but the voice persisted, relentless, flaying his soul like a scourge. *You brought me here and gave me up to* him— Fistandantilus! *You sat and watched as he wrenched the lifeforce from me, draining it so that he might live upon this plane.*

"It was you who made the bargain," Par-Salian cried, his ancient voice carrying through the empty hallways of the Tower. "You could have refused him—"

And what? Died honorably? The voice laughed. *What kind of choice is that? I wanted to live! To grow in my Art! And I did live. And you, in your bitterness, gave me these hourglass eyes†—these eyes that saw nothing but death and decay all around me. Now, you look, Par-Salian! What do you see around you? Nothing but death. . . . Death and decay . . . So we are even.*

Par-Salian moaned. The voice continued, mercilessly, pitilessly.

Even, yes. And now I will grind you into dust. For, in your last tortured moments, Par-Salian, you will witness my triumph. Already my constellation shines in the sky.

Raistlin's hourglass eyes were first established in a committee. We had a group of game designers together trying to come up with the "quintessential dungeon group" around which we would form our adventures. Someone suggested (I think it was Harold Johnson) that the fighter and the mage be twin brothers, that one be enormous and the other sickly. "And he has hourglass pupils," he added. It sounded cool, and no one bothered to question why he would have hourglass pupils. It was not until Margaret confronted writing about Raistlin that we questioned why and made it an integral part of Raistlin's destiny. —TRH

The Queen dwindles. Soon she will fade and be gone forever. My final foe,† Paladine, waits for me now. I see him approach. But he is no challenge—an old man, bent, his face grieved and filled with the sorrow that will prove his undoing. For he is weak, weak and hurt beyond healing, as was Crysania, his poor cleric, who died upon the shifting planes of the Abyss. You will watch me destroy him, Par-Salian, and when that battle is ended, when the constellation of the Platinum Dragon plummets from the sky, when Solinari's light is extinguished, when you have seen and acknowledged the power of the Black Moon and paid homage to the new and only god—to me—then you will be released, Par-Salian, to find what solace you can in death!

Astinus of Palanthas recorded the words as he had recorded Par-Salian's scream, writing the crisp, black, bold letters in slow, unhurried style. He sat before the great Portal in the Tower of High Sorcery, staring into the Portal's shadowy depths, seeing within those depths a figure blacker even than the darkness around him. All that was visible were two golden eyes, their pupils the shape of hourglasses, staring back at him and at the white-robed wizard trapped next to him.

For Par-Salian was a prisoner in his own Tower. From the waist up, he was living man—his white hair flowing about his shoulders, his white robes covering a body thin and emaciated, his dark eyes fixed upon the Portal. The sights he had seen had been dreadful and had, long ago, nearly destroyed his sanity. But he could not withdraw his gaze. From the waist up, Par-Salian was living man. From the waist down—he was a marble pillar.† Cursed by Raistlin, Par-Salian was forced to stand in the topmost room of his Tower and watch—in bitter agony—the end of the world.

Next to him sat Astinus—Historian of the World, Chronicler, writing this last chapter of Krynn's brief, shining history. Palanthas the Beautiful, where Astinus had lived and where the Great Library had stood, was now nothing but a heap of ash and charred bodies. Astinus had come to this, the last place standing upon Krynn, to witness and record the world's final, terrifying hours. When all was finished, he would take the closed book† and lay it upon the altar of Gilean, God of Neutrality. And that would be the end.

A reflection of John Milton's Satan, who decided it was better to rule hell than serve in heaven. —MW

Raistlin certainly would agree with Milton's Satan from Paradise Lost: *" 'Tis better to rule in Hell than to serve in Heaven." It is, to a great extent, the driving motivation underlying all that Raistlin is doing. —TRH*

There is a great mythic quality to this scene—mythic and cruel. —TRH

Astinus's book resembles the Book of Life (Psalm 69:28; Philippians 4:3; Revelation 3:5, 13:8, 17:8, and chapters 20-22) kept in heaven as well as the seven seals of the book of Revelation. —TRH

Sensing the black-robed figure within the Portal turning its gaze upon him, when he came to the end of a sentence, Astinus raised his eyes to meet the figure's golden ones.

As you were first, Astinus, said the figure, *so shall you be last. When you have recorded my ultimate victory, the book will be closed. I will rule unchallenged.*

"True, you will rule unchallenged. You will rule a dead world. A world your magic destroyed. You will rule alone. And you will *be* alone, alone in the formless, eternal void," Astinus replied coolly, writing even as he spoke. Beside him, Par-Salian moaned and tore at his white hair.

Seeing as he saw everything—without seeming to see—Astinus watched the black-robed figure's hands clench. *That is a lie, old friend! I will create! New worlds will be mine. New peoples I will produce— new races who will worship me!*

This reflects Tracy's underlying philosophy in the creation of the DRAGONLANCE *saga. —MW*

"Evil cannot create,"† Astinus remarked, "it can only destroy. It turns in upon itself, gnawing itself. Already, you feel it eating away at you. Already, you can feel your soul shrivel. Look into Paladine's face, Raistlin. Look into it as you looked into it once, back on the Plains of Dergoth, when you lay dying of the dwarf's sword wound and Lady Crysania laid healing hands upon you. You saw the grief and sorrow of the god then as you see it now, Raistlin. And you knew then, as you know now but refuse to admit, that Paladine grieves, not for himself, but for you.

One of the pillars of the DRAGONLANCE *saga, spoken now quite clearly. —TRH*

"Easy will it be for us to slip back into our dreamless sleep. For you, Raistlin, there will be no sleep. Only an endless waking, endless listening for sounds that will never come, endless staring into a void that holds neither light nor darkness, endless shrieking words that no one will hear, no one will answer, endless plotting and scheming that will bear no fruit as you turn round and round upon yourself.† Finally, in your madness and desperation, you will grab the tail of your existence and, like a starving snake, devour yourself whole in an effort to find food for your soul.

Here we get a glimpse of the cosmology underlying the DRAGONLANCE *setting. The symbol of a snake eating its own tale has Hindu origins but in this case is a metaphor for the "damnation" of souls into a non-progressive round. It is better understood in the light of the broader cosmology that is set out in the War of Souls. Raistlin, who does not understand this broader cosmology, could not foresee the results of his actions. —TRH*

"But you will find nothing but emptiness. And you will continue to exist forever within this emptiness— a tiny spot of nothing, sucking in everything around itself to feed your endless hunger. . . ."

The Portal shimmered. Astinus quickly looked up from his writing, feeling the will behind those golden eyes waver. Staring past the mirrorlike surface, looking deep into their depths, he saw—for the space of a heartbeat—the very torment and torture he had described. He saw a soul, frightened, alone, caught in its own trap, seeking escape. For the first time in his existence, compassion touched Astinus. His hand marking his place in his book, he half-rose from his seat, his other hand reaching into the Portal. . . .

Then, laughter . . . eerie, mocking, bitter laughter— laughter not at him, but at the one who laughed.

The black-robed figure within the Portal was gone.

With a sigh, Astinus resumed his seat and, almost at the same instant, magical lightning flickered inside the Portal. It was answered by flaring, white light—the final meeting of Paladine and the young man who had defeated the Queen of Darkness and taken her place.

Lighting flickered outside, too, stabbing the eyes of the two men watching with blinding brilliance. Thunder crashed, the stones of the Tower trembled, the foundations of the Tower shook. Wind howled, its wail drowning out Par-Salian's moaning.

Lifting a drawn, haggard face, the ancient wizard twisted his head to stare out the windows with an expression of horror. "This is the end," he murmured, his gnarled, wasted hands plucking feebly at the air. "The end of all things."

"Yes," said Astinus, frowning in annoyance as a sudden lurching of the Tower caused him to make an error. He gripped his book more firmly, his eyes on the Portal, writing, recording the last battle as it occurred.

Within a matter of moments, all was over. The white light flickered briefly, beautifully, for one instant. Then it died.

Within the Portal, all was darkness.

Par-Salian wept. His tears fell down upon the stone floor and, at their touch, the Tower shook like a living thing, as if it, too, foresaw its doom and was quaking in horror.

Ignoring the falling stones and the heaving of the rocks, Astinus coolly penned the final words.

As of Fourthday, Fifthmonth, Year 358, the world ends.
Then, with a sigh, Astinus started to close the book.
A hand slammed down across the pages.
"No," said a firm voice, "it will not end here."

Astinus's hands trembled, his pen dropped a blot of ink upon the paper, obliterating the last words.

"Caramon . . . Caramon Majere!" Par-Salian cried, pitifully reaching out to the man with feeble hands. "It was you I heard in the Forest!"

"Did you doubt me?" Caramon growled. Though shocked and horrified by the sight of the wretched wizard and his torment, Caramon found it difficult to feel any compassion for the archmage. Looking at Par-Salian, seeing his lower half turned to marble, Caramon recalled all too clearly his twin's torment in the Tower, his own torment upon being sent back to Istar with Crysania.

"No, not doubted you!" Par-Salian wrung his hands. "I doubted my own sanity! Can't you understand? How can you be here? How could you have survived the magical battles that destroyed the world?"

"He didn't," Astinus said sternly. Having regained his composure, he placed the open book down on the floor at his feet and stood up.† Glowering at Caramon, he pointed an accusing finger. "What trick is this? You died! What is the meaning—"

Without speaking a word, Caramon dragged Tasslehoff out from behind him. Deeply impressed by the solemnity and seriousness of the occasion, Tas huddled next to Caramon, his wide eyes fixed upon Par-Salian with a pleading gaze.

"Do—do you want me to explain, Caramon?" Tas asked in a small, polite voice, barely audible over the thunder. "I—I really feel like I should tell *why* I disrupted the time-travel spell, and then there's how Raistlin gave me the wrong instructions and made me break the magical device, even though part of that was my fault, I suppose, and how I ended up in the Abyss where I met poor Gnimsh." Tas's eyes filled with tears. "And how Raistlin killed him—"

"All this is known to me," Astinus interrupted. "So you were able to come here because of the kender. Our time is short. What is it you intend, Caramon Majere?"

*This is the only time I know of that Astinus set aside his chronicling.
—TRH*

The big man turned his gaze to Par-Salian. "I bear you no love, wizard. In that, I am at one with my twin. Perhaps you had your reasons for what you did to me and to Lady Crysania back there in Istar. If so"—Caramon raised a hand to stop Par-Salian who, it seems, would have spoken—"if so, then you are the one who lives with them, not me. For now, know that I have it in my power to alter time. As Raistlin himself told me, because of the kender, we can change what has happened.

"I have the magical device. I can travel back to any point in time. Tell me when, tell me what happened that led to this destruction, and I will undertake to prevent it, if I can."

Caramon's gaze went from Par-Salian to Astinus. The historian shook his head. "Do not look to me, Caramon Majere. I am neutral in this as in all things. I can give you no help. I can only give you this warning: You may go back, but you may find you change nothing. A pebble in a swiftly flowing river, that is all you may be."

Caramon nodded. "If that is all, then at least I will die knowing that I tried to make up for my failure."

Astinus regarded Caramon with a keen, penetrating glance. "What failure is that you speak of, Warrior? You risked your life going back after your brother. You did your best, you endeavored to convince him that this path of darkness he walked would lead only to his own doom." Astinus gestured toward the Portal. "You heard me speak to him? You know what he faces?"

Wordlessly, Caramon nodded again, his face pale and anguished.

"Then tell me," Astinus said coolly.

The Tower shuddered. Wind battered the walls, lightning turned the waning night of the world into a garish, blinding day. The small, bare tower room in which they stood shook and trembled. Though they were alone within it, Caramon thought he could hear sounds of weeping, and he slowly came to realize it was the stones of the Tower itself. He glanced about uneasily.

"You have time," Astinus said. Sitting back down on his stool, he picked up the book. But he did not close it. "Not long, perhaps, but time, still. Wherein did you fail?"

Caramon drew a shaking breath. Then his brows came together. Scowling in anger, his gaze went to Par-Salian. "A trick, wasn't it, wizard? A trick to get me to do what you mages could not—stop Raistlin in his dreadful ambition. But you failed. You sent Crysania back to die because you feared her. But her will, her love was stronger than you supposed. She lived and, blinded by her love and her own ambition, she followed Raistlin into the Abyss." Caramon glowered. "I don't understand Paladine's purpose in granting her prayers, in giving her the power to go there—"

"It is not for you to understand the ways of the gods, Caramon Majere," Astinus interrupted coldly. "Who are you to judge them? It may be that they fail, too, sometimes. Or that they choose to risk the best they have in hopes that it will be still better."

"Be that as it may," Caramon continued, his face dark and troubled, "the mages sent Crysania back and thereby gave my brother one of the keys he needed to enter the Portal. They failed. The gods failed.† And I failed." Caramon ran a trembling hand through his hair.

"I thought I could convince Raistlin with words to turn back from this deadly path he walked. I should have known better." The big man laughed bitterly. "What poor words of mine ever affected him? When he stood before the Portal, preparing to enter the Abyss, telling me what he intended, I left him. It was all so easy. I simply turned my back and walked away."

"Bah!" Astinus snorted. "What would you have done? He was strong then, more powerful than any of us can begin to imagine. He held the magical field together by his force of will and his strength alone. You could not have killed him—"

"No," said Caramon, his gaze shifting away from those in the room, staring out into the storm that raged ever more fiercely, "but I could have followed him—followed him into darkness—even if it meant my death. To show him that I was willing to sacrifice for love what he was willing to sacrifice for his magic and his ambition." Caramon turned his gaze upon those in the room. "Then he would have respected me. Then he might have listened. And so I will go back. I will enter the Abyss"—he

Caramon here is referring to the only gods of which he knows—the pantheon. The concept of the High God was in the DRAGONLANCE *setting from the beginning. Being a Christian as well as a student of mythology, I wanted a cosmology that reflected my beliefs but which also allowed for a diverse pantheon for our fantasy world. Thus the gods of Krynn are very much like the mythic gods of Greece and Rome—often flawed, quarrelsome, and passionate. They have been the only gods known to the people of Krynn, the High God never having been revealed, let alone worshipped. The gods of Krynn then acted both as intermediaries and independently toward their own ends, with little or no interference by the High God. These concepts became important in War of Souls and were brought out more fully there, but they have always been an integral, if behind the scenes part, of the foundation of the* DRAGONLANCE *setting.*
—TRH

ignored Tasslehoff's cry of horror—"and there I will do what must be done."

"What must be done," Par-Salian repeated feverishly. "You do not realize what that means! Dalamar—"

A blazing, blinding bolt of lightning exploded within the room, slamming those within back against the stone walls. No one could see or hear anything as the thunder crashed over them. Then above the blast of thunder rose a tortured cry.

Shaken by that strangled, pain-filled scream, Caramon opened his eyes, only to wish they had been shut forever before seeing such a grisly sight.

Par-Salian had turned from a pillar of marble to a pillar of flame! Caught in Raistlin's spell, the wizard was helpless. He could do nothing but scream as the flames slowly crept up his immobile body.

Unnerved, Tasslehoff covered his face with his hands and cowered, whimpering, in a corner. Astinus rose from where he had been hurled to the floor, his hands going immediately to the book he still held. He started to write, but his hand fell limp, the pen slipped from his fingers. Once more, he began to close the cover . . .

"No!" Caramon cried. Reaching out, he laid his hands upon the pages.

Astinus looked at him, and Caramon faltered beneath the gaze of those deathless eyes. His hands shook, but they remained pressed firmly across the white parchment of the leather-bound volume. The dying wizard wailed in dreadful agony.

Astinus released the open book.

"Hold this," Caramon ordered, closing the precious volume and thrusting it into Tasslehoff's hands. Nodding numbly, the kender wrapped his arms around the book, which was almost as big as he was, and remained, crouched in his corner, staring around him in horror as Caramon lurched across the room toward the dying wizard.

"No!" shrieked Par-Salian. "Do not come near me!" His white, flowing hair and long beard crackled, his skin bubbled and sizzled, the terrible cloying stench of burning flesh mingling with the smell of sulfur.

"Tell me!" cried Caramon, raising his arm against the heat, getting as near the mage as he could. "Tell me, Par-Salian! What must I do? How can I prevent this?"

The wizard's eyes were melting. His mouth was a gaping hole in the black formless mass that was his face. But his dying words struck Caramon like another bolt of lightning, to be burned into his mind forever.

"Raistlin must not be allowed to leave the Abyss!"

BOOK 2

The Knight of the Black Rose

Lord Soth sat upon the crumbling, fire-blackened throne in the blasted, desolate ruins of Dargaard Keep.† His orange eyes flamed in their unseen sockets, the only visible sign of the cursed life that burned within the charred armor of a Knight of Solamnia.

Soth sat alone.†

The death knight had dismissed his attendants—former knights, like himself, who had remained loyal to him in life and so were cursed to remain loyal to him in death. He had also sent away the banshees, the elven women who had played a role in his downfall and who were now doomed to spend their lives in his service. For hundreds of years, ever since that terrible night of his death, Lord Soth had commanded these unfortunate women to relive that doom with him. Every night, as he sat upon his ruined throne, he forced them to serenade him with a song that related the story of his disgrace and their own.

That song brought bitter pain to Soth, but he welcomed the pain. It was ten times better than the nothingness† that pervaded his unholy life-in-death at all other times. But tonight he did not listen to the song. He listened, instead, to his story as it whispered like the bitter night wind through the eaves of the crumbling keep.

"Once, long ago,† I was a Lord Knight of Solamnia. I was everything then—handsome, charming, brave, married to a woman of fortune, if not of beauty. My knights were devoted to me. Yes, men envied me—Lord Soth of Dargaard Keep.

"The spring before the Cataclysm, I left Dargaard Keep and rode to Palanthas with my retinue. A Knights' Council was being held, my presence was required. I cared little for the Council meeting—it would drag on with endless arguments over insignificant rules. But there would be drinking, good fellowship, tales of battle and adventure. *That* was why I went.

Names need to be evocative of something. Dargaard is meaningless as a word, but it evokes the concept of "dark guard" in English-speaking readers. —TRH

Lord Soth is a tragic figure. Tragic figures often cause their own doom. Soth is a victim of cosmic justice, brought down on his own head. His torment is that he knows this. —TRH

Lord Soth is the example of the end result of evil's self-consuming nature— a life consumed until it is meaningless. —TRH

Soth's background came entirely from me—or maybe it is better to say that it came from Soth, since he made himself so forcefully known to me! —TRH

"We rode slowly, taking our time, our days filled with song and jesting. At night we'd stay in inns when we could, sleep beneath the stars when we could not. The weather was fine, it was a mild spring. The sunshine was warm upon us, the evening breeze cooled us. I was thirty-two years old that spring. Everything was going well with my life. I do not recall ever being happier.

"And then, one night—curse the silver moon that shone upon it—we were camped in the wilderness. A cry cut through the darkness, rousing us from our slumbers. It was a woman's cry, then we heard many women's voices, mingled with the harsh shouts of ogres.

"Grabbing our weapons, we rushed to battle. It was an easy victory; only a roving band of robbers. Most fled at our approach, but the leader, either more daring or more drunken than the rest, refused to be deprived of his spoils. Personally, I didn't blame him. He'd captured a lovely young elf-maiden. Her beauty in the moonlight was radiant, her fear only enhanced her fragile loveliness. Alone, I challenged him. We fought, and I was the victor. And it was my reward—ah, what bitter-sweet reward—to carry the fainting elfmaid in my arms back to her companions.

"I can still see her fine, golden hair shining in the moonlight. I can see her eyes when she wakened, looking into mine, and I can see even now—as I saw then—her love for me dawn in them. And she saw—in my eyes—the admiration I could not hide. Thoughts of my wife, of my honor, of my castle— everything fled as I gazed upon her beautiful face.

"She thanked me; how shyly she spoke. I returned her to the elven women—a group of clerics they were, traveling to Palanthas and thence to Istar on a pilgrimage. She was just an acolyte. It was on this journey that she was to be made a Revered Daughter of Paladine. I left her and the women, returning with my men to my camp. I tried to sleep, but I could still feel that lithe, young body in my arms. Never had I been so consumed with passion for a woman.

"When I did sleep, my dreams were sweet torture. When I awoke, the thought that we must part was like a knife in my heart. Rising early, I returned to the elven camp. Making up a tale of roving bands of

goblins between here and Palanthas, I easily convinced the elven women that they needed my protection. My men were not averse to such pleasant companions, and so we traveled with them. But this did not ease my pain. Rather, it intensified it. Day after day I watched her, riding near me—but not near enough. Night after night I slept alone—my thoughts in turmoil.

"I wanted her,† wanted her more than anything I had ever wanted in this world. And yet, I was a Knight, sworn by the strictest vows to uphold the Code and the Measure, sworn by holy vows to remain true to my wife, sworn by the vows of a commander to lead my men to honor. Long I fought with myself and, at last, I believed I had conquered. Tomorrow, I will leave, I said, feeling peace steal over me.

Soth's tragedy has its roots in the story of David and Bathsheba from the Bible.
—TRH

"I truly intended to leave, and I would have. But, curse the fates, I went upon a hunting expedition in the woods and there, far from camp, I met her. She had been sent to gather herbs.

"She was alone. I was alone. Our companions were far away. The love that I had seen in her eyes shone there still. She had loosened her hair, it fell to her feet in a golden cloud. My honor, my resolve, were destroyed in an instant, burned up by the flame of desire that swept over me. She was easy to seduce, poor thing. One kiss, then another. Then drawing her down beside me on the new grass, my hands caressing, my mouth stopping her protests, and . . . after I had made her mine . . . kissing away her tears.

"That night, she came to me again, in my tent. I was lost in bliss. I promised her marriage, of course. What else could I do? At first, I didn't mean it. How could I? I had a wife, a wealthy wife. I needed her money. My expenses were high. But then one night, when I held the elf maid in my arms, I knew I could never give her up. I made arrangements to have my wife permanently removed. . . .

"We continued our journey. By this time, the elven women had begun to suspect. How not? It was hard for us to hide our secret smiles during the day, difficult to avoid every opportunity to be together.

"We were, of necessity, separated when we reached Palanthas. The elven women went to stay in one of

the fine houses that the Kingpriest used when he visited the city. My men and I went to our lodgings. I was confident, however, that she would find a way to come to me since I could not go to her. The first night passed, I was not much worried. But then a second and a third, and no word.

"Finally, a knock on my door. But it was not her. It was the head of the Knights of Solamnia, accompanied by the heads of each of the three Orders of Knights. I knew then, when I saw them, what must have happened. She had discovered the truth and betrayed me.

"As it was, it was not she who betrayed me, but the elven women. My lover had fallen ill and, when they came to treat her, they discovered that she was carrying my child. She had told no one, not even me. They told her I was married and, worse still, word arrived in Palanthas at the same time that my wife had 'mysteriously' disappeared.

"I was arrested. Dragged through the streets of Palanthas in public humiliation, I was the object of the vulgars' crude jokes and vile names. They enjoyed nothing more than seeing a Knight fall to their level. I swore that, someday, I would have my revenge upon them and their fine city. But that seemed hopeless. My trial was swift. I was sentenced to die—a traitor to the Knighthood. Stripped of my lands and my title, I would be executed by having my throat slit with my own sword. I accepted my death. I even looked forward to it, thinking still that she had cast me off.

"But, the night before I was to die, my loyal men freed me from my prison. She was with them. She told me everything, she told me she carried my child.

"The elven women had forgiven her, she said, and, though she could never now become a Revered Daughter of Paladine, she might still live among her people—though her disgrace would follow her to the end of her days. But she could not bear the thought of leaving without telling me good-bye. She loved me, that much was plain. But I could tell that the tales she had heard worried her.

"I made up some lie about my wife that she believed. She would have believed dark was light if I'd told her. Her mind at ease, she agreed to run

away with me. I know now that this was why she had come in the first place. My men accompanying us, we fled back to Dargaard Keep.

"It was a difficult journey, pursued constantly by the other Knights, but we arrived, finally, and entrenched ourselves within the castle. It was an easy position to defend—perched as it was high upon sheer cliffs. We had large stores of provisions and we could easily hold out during the winter that was fast approaching.

"I should have been pleased with myself, with life, with my new bride—what a mockery that marriage ceremony was! But I was tormented by guilt and, what was worse, the loss of my honor. I realized that I had escaped one prison only to find myself in another—another of my own choosing. I had escaped death only to live a dark and wretched life. I grew moody, morose. I was always quick to anger, quick to strike, and now it was worse. The servants fled, after I'd beaten several. My men took to avoiding me. And then, one night, I struck her—*her*, the only person in this world who could give me even a shred of comfort.

"Looking into her tear-filled eyes, I saw the monster I had become. Taking her in my arms, I begged forgiveness. Her lovely hair fell around me. I could feel my child kicking in her womb. Kneeling there, together, we prayed to Paladine. I would do anything, I told the god, to restore my honor. I asked only that my son or daughter never grow up to know my shame.

"And Paladine answered. He told me of the Kingpriest, and what arrogant demands the foolish man planned to make of the gods. He told me that the world itself would feel the anger of the gods unless— as Huma had done before me—one man was willing to sacrifice himself for the sake of the innocent.

"Paladine's light shone around me. My tormented soul was filled with peace. What small sacrifice it seemed to me to give my life so that my child should be raised in honor and the world could be saved. I rode to Istar, fully intent upon stopping the Kingpriest, knowing that Paladine was with me.

"But another rode beside me, too, on that journey— the Queen of Darkness. So does she wage constant war for the souls she delights in holding in thrall.

What did she use to defeat me? Those very same elven women—clerics of the god whose mission I rode upon.

"These women had long since forgotten the name of Paladine. Like the Kingpriest, they were wrapped in their own righteousness and could see nothing through their veils of goodness. Filled with my own self-righteousness, I let them know what I intended. Their fear was great. They did not believe the gods would punish the world. They saw a day when only the good (meaning the elves) would live upon Krynn.

"They had to stop me. And they were successful.

"The Queen is wise. She knows the dark regions of a man's heart. I would have ridden down an army, if it had stood in my way. But the soft words of those elven women worked in my blood like poison. How clever it was for the elfmaid to have been rid of me so easily, they said. Now she had my castle, my wealth, all to herself, without the inconvenience of a human husband. Was I even certain the baby was mine? She had been seen in the company of one of my young followers. Where did she go when she left my tent in the night?

"They never once lied.† They never once said anything against her directly. But their questions ate at my soul, gnawing at me. I remembered words, incidents, looks. I was certain I'd been betrayed. I would catch them together! I would kill him! I would make her suffer!

"I turned my back upon Istar.

"Arriving home, I battered down the doors of my castle. My wife, alarmed, came to meet me, holding her infant son in her arms. There was a look of despair upon her face—I took it for an admission of guilt. I cursed her, I cursed her child. And, at that moment, the fiery mountain struck Ansalon.

"The stars fell from the sky. The ground shook and split asunder. A chandelier, lit with a hundred candles, fell from the ceiling. In an instant my wife was engulfed with flame. She knew she was dying, but she held out her babe to me to rescue from the fire that was consuming her. I hesitated, then, jealous rage still filling my heart, I turned away.

"With her dying breath, she called down the wrath of the gods upon me. 'You will die this night in fire,'

I have always believed that carefully controlled truth is one of evil's greatest weapons. We are free to think and act for ourselves—it is the agency that God gives to all men—but we can only make decisions based on what we know. At the heart of evil is always a lie—but cloaked in enough partial truths it can often go unnoticed or ignored. —TRH

she cried, 'even as your son and I die. But you will live eternally in darkness. You will live one life for every life that your folly has brought to an end this night!' She perished.

"The flames spread. My castle was soon ablaze. Nothing we tried would put out that strange fire. It burned even rock. My men tried to flee. But, as I watched, they, too, burst into flame. There was no one, no one left alive except myself upon that mountain. I stood in the great hall, alone, surrounded on all sides by fire that did not yet touch me. But, as I stood there, I saw it closing in upon me, coming closer . . . closer. . . .

"I died slowly, in unbearable agony. When death finally came, it brought no relief. For I closed my eyes only to open them again, looking into a world of emptiness and bleak despair and eternal torment. Night after night, for endless years, I have sat upon this throne and listened to those elven women sing my story.

"But that ended, it ended with you, Kitiara. . . .

"When the Dark Queen called upon me to aid her in the war, I told her I would serve the first Dragon Highlord who had courage enough to spend the night in Dargaard Keep. There was only one—you, my beauty. You, Kitiara. I admired you for that, I admired you for your courage, your skill, your ruthless determination. In you, I see myself. I see what I might have become.

"I helped you murder the other Highlords† when we fled Neraka in the turmoil following the Queen's defeat, I helped you reach Sanction, and there I helped you establish your power once again upon this continent. I helped you when you tried to thwart your brother, Raistlin's, plans for challenging the Queen of Darkness. No, I wasn't surprised he outwitted you. Of all the living I have ever met, he is the only one I fear.

"I have even been amused by your love affairs, my Kitiara. We dead cannot feel lust. That is a passion of the blood and no blood flows in these icy limbs. I watched you twist that weakling, Tanis Half-Elven, inside out, and I enjoyed it every bit as much as you did.

"But now, Kitiara, what have you become? The mistress has become the slave. And for what—an elf!

Here, Soth is recounting events that occurred after the War of the Lance.

Oh, I have seen your eyes burn when you speak his name. I've seen your hands tremble when you hold his letters. You think of him when you should be planning war. Even your generals can no longer claim your attention.

"No, we dead cannot feel lust. But we can feel hatred, we can feel envy, we can feel jealousy and possession.

"I could kill Dalamar—the dark elf apprentice is good, but he is no match for me. His master? Raistlin? Ah, now that would be a different story.

"My Queen in your dark Abyss—beware Raistlin! In him, you face your greatest challenge, and you must—in the end—face it alone. I cannot help you on that plane, Dark Majesty, but perhaps I can aid you on this one.

"Yes, Dalamar, I could kill you. But I have known what it is to die, and death is a shabby, paltry thing. Its pain is agony, but soon over. What greater pain to linger on and on in the world of the living, smelling their warm blood, seeing their soft flesh, and knowing that it can never, never be yours again. But you will come to know, all too well, dark elf. . . .

"As for you, Kitiara, know this—I would endure this pain, I would live out another century of tortured existence rather than see you again in the arms of a living man!"

The death knight brooded and plotted, his mind twisting and turning like the thorny branches of the black roses that overran his castle. The skeletal warriors paced the ruined battlements, each hovering near the place where he had met his death. The elven women wrung their fleshless hands and moaned in bitter sorrow at their fate.

Soth heard nothing, was aware of nothing. He sat upon his blackened throne, staring unseeing at a dark, charred splotch upon the stone floor—a splotch that he had sought for years with all the power of his magic to obliterate—and still it remained, a splotch in the shape of a woman. . . .

And then, at last, the unseen lips smiled, and the flame of the orange eyes burned bright in their endless night.

"You, Kitiara—you will be mine—forever. . . ."

The carriage rumbled to a stop. The horses snorted and shook themselves, jingling the harness, thudding their hooves against the smooth paving stones, as if eager to get this journey over with and return to their comfortable stables.

A head poked in the carriage window.

"Good morning, sir. Welcome to Palanthas. Please state your name and business." This delivered in a bright, official voice by a bright, official young man who must have just come on duty. Peering into the carriage, the guard blinked his eyes, trying to adjust them to the cool shadows of the coach's interior. The late spring sun shone as brightly as the young man's face, probably because it, too, had just recently come on duty.

"My name is Tanis Half-Elven," said the man inside the carriage, "and I am here by invitation to

Tanis's celebrity status
apparently is quite
elevated to be so quickly
recognized. Perhaps he
should consider endorsing
some Palanthian ale
products or combat boots?
The royalties alone . . .
—TRH

"As his name implies, the
family of Amothus
Palanthas has ruled the city
of Palanthas for hundreds
of years. Rulership of
Palanthas was always
passed on to the eldest son,
while the younger sons
generally served in the
Knights of Solamnia.
Amothus is an only child,
however, and is
unmarried—a situation
that many mothers of
daughters in Palanthas
hope to remedy. In his
early forties, Amothus is
much like the people of
Palanthas themselves—
appearing weak, shallow,
and foppish, but with a
core of steel beneath."
[DRAGONLANCE
Adventures, by Tracy
Hickman and Margaret
Weis, TSR, Inc., 1987,
p. 110.]

"Many of the cities of
Ansalon have been
devastated by the war [of
the Lance]. Only
Palanthas, of all the great
cities, escaped damage.
Because of this good
fortune, Palanthas is now
the center of civilization
upon Krynn. The Knights
of Solamnia have set up
their central headquarters
there, and the Port of
Palanthas still receives
ships from all corners of
Ansalon." [DRAGONLANCE
Adventures, by Tracy

see Revered Son Elistan. I've got a letter here. If
you'll wait half a moment, I'll—"

"Lord Tanis!" The face outlined by the carriage
window turned as crimson as the ridiculously frogged
and epauletted uniform he wore. "I beg your pardon,
sir. I—I didn't recognize . . . that is, I couldn't see or
I'm sure I would have recognized—"†

"Damn it, man," Tanis responded irritably, "don't
apologize for doing your job. Here's the letter—"

"I won't, sir. That is, I will, sir. Apologize, that is.
Dreadfully sorry, sir. The letter? That really won't be
necessary, sir."

Stammering, the guard saluted, cracked his head
smartly on the top of the carriage window, caught
the lacy sleeve of his cuff on the door, saluted again,
and finally staggered back to his post looking as if he
had just emerged from a fight with hobgoblins.

Grinning to himself, but a rueful grin at that,
Tanis leaned back as the carriage continued on its
way through the gates of the Old City Wall. The
guard was his idea. It had taken a great deal of
argument and persuasion on Tanis's part to convince Lord Amothus† of Palanthas that the city
gates should actually not only be shut but guarded
as well.

"But people might not feel welcome. They might
be offended," Amothus had protested faintly. "And,
after all, the war *is* over."

Tanis sighed again. When would they learn?
Never, he supposed gloomily, staring out the
window into the city that, more than any other on
the continent of Ansalon, epitomized the complacency into which the world had fallen since the end
of the War of the Lance two years ago.† Two years
ago this spring, in fact.

That brought still another sigh from Tanis. Damn!
He had forgotten! War End's Day! When was that?
Two weeks? Three? He would have to put on that
silly costume—the ceremonial armor of a Knight of
Solamnia, the elven regalia, the dwarven trappings.
There'd be dinners of rich food that kept him awake
half the night, speeches that put him to sleep after
dinner, and Laurana. . . .

Tanis gasped. Laurana! *She'd* remembered! Of
course! How could he have been so thick-headed?
They'd just returned home to Solanthus a few weeks

In order to tell a bigger story, Matt Stawicki was permitted some
liberties with the climax in his recover of *Test of the Twins*.

ago after attending Solostaran's funeral in Qualinesti— and after he'd made an unsuccessful trip back to Solace in search of Lady Crysania—when a letter arrived for Laurana in flowing elven script:

Hickman and Margaret Weis, TSR, Inc., 1987, p. 105.]

"Your Presence Urgently Required in Silvanesti!"

"I'll be back in four weeks, my dear," she'd said, kissing him tenderly. Yet there had been laughter in her eyes, those lovely eyes!

She'd left him! Left him behind to attend those blasted ceremonies! And she would be back in the elven homeland which, though still struggling to escape the horrors inflicted upon it by Lorac's nightmare, was infinitely preferable to an evening with Lord Amothus. . . .

It suddenly occurred to Tanis what he had been thinking. A mental memory of Silvanesti came to mind—with its hideously tortured trees weeping blood, the twisted, tormented faces of long dead elven warriors staring out from the shadows. A mental image of one of Lord Amothus's dinner parties rose in comparison—

Tanis began to laugh. He'd take the undead warriors any day!

As for Laurana, well, he couldn't blame her. These ceremonies were hard enough on him—but Laurana was the Palanthians' darling, their Golden General, the one who had saved their beautiful city from the ravages of the war. There was nothing they wouldn't do for her, except leave her some time to herself. The last War's End Day celebration, Tanis had carried his wife home in his arms, more exhausted than she had been after three straight days of battle.

He envisioned her in Silvanesti, working to replant the flowers, working to soothe the dreams of the tortured trees and slowly nurse them back to life, visiting with Alhana Starbreeze, now her sister-in-law, who would be back in Silvanesti as well—but without her new husband, Porthios. Theirs was, so far, a chill, loveless marriage and Tanis wondered, briefly, if Alhana might not be seeking the haven of Silvanesti for the same reason. War's End Day must be difficult for Alhana, too. His thoughts went to Sturm Brightblade—the knight Alhana had loved, who was lying dead in the High Clerist's Tower† and, from there, Tanis's memories wandered to other friends . . . and enemies.

See Dragons of Winter Night, *Book III, Chapter 13.*

As if conjured up by those memories, a dark shadow swept over the carriage. Tanis looked out the window. Down a long, empty, deserted street, he caught a glimpse of a patch of blackness—Shoikan Grove, the guardian forest of Raistlin's Tower of High Sorcery.

Even from this distance, Tanis could feel the chill that flowed from those trees, a chill that froze the heart and the soul. His gaze went to the Tower, rising up above the beautiful buildings of Palanthas like a black iron spike driven through the city's white breast.

His thoughts went to the letter that had brought him to Palanthas. Glancing down at it, he read the words over:

Tanis Half-Elven,

We must meet with you immediately. Gravest emergency. The Temple of Paladine, Afterwatch Rising 12, Fourthday, Year 356.

That was all. No signature. He knew only that Fourthday was today and, having received the missive only two days ago, he had been forced to travel day and night to reach Palanthas on time. The note's language was elven, the handwriting was elven, also. Not unusual. Elistan had many elven clerics, but why hadn't he signed it? If, indeed, it came from Elistan. Yet, who else could so casually issue such an invitation to the Temple of Paladine?

Shrugging to himself—remembering that he had asked himself these same questions more than once and had never come to a satisfactory conclusion—Tanis tucked the letter back inside his pouch. His gaze went, unwillingly, to the Tower of High Sorcery.

"I'll wager it has something to do with *you*, old friend," he murmured to himself, frowning and thinking, once again, of the strange disappearance of the cleric, Lady Crysania.

The carriage rolled to a halt again, jolting Tanis from his dark thoughts. He looked out the window, catching a glimpse of the Temple, but forcing himself to sit patiently in his seat until the footman came to open the door for him. He smiled to himself. He could almost see† Laurana, sitting across from him,

Thoughts of home are a recurring theme in Legends. —TRH

glaring at him, daring him to make a move for the door handle. It had taken her many months to break Tanis of his old impetuous habit of flinging open the door, knocking the footman to one side, and proceeding on his way without a thought for the driver, the carriage, the horses, anything.

It had now become a private joke between them. Tanis loved watching Laurana's eyes narrow in mock alarm as his hand strayed teasingly near the door handle. But that only reminded him how much he missed her. Where was that damn footman anyway? By the gods, he was alone, he'd do it *his* way for a change—

The door flew open. The footman fumbled with the step that folded down from the floor. "Oh, forget that," Tanis snapped impatiently, hopping to the ground. Ignoring the footman's faint look of outraged sensibility, Tanis drew in a deep breath, glad to have escaped—finally—from the stuffy confines of the carriage.

He gazed around, letting the wonderful feeling of peace and well-being that radiated from the Temple of Paladine seep into his soul. No forest guarded this holy place. Vast, open lawns of green grass as soft and smooth as velvet invited the traveler to walk upon it, sit upon it, rest upon it. Gardens of bright-colored flowers delighted the eye, their perfume filling the air with sweetness. Here and there, groves of carefully pruned shade trees offered a haven from glaring sunlight. Fountains poured forth pure cool water. White-robed clerics walked in the gardens, their heads bent together in solemn discussion.

Rising from the frame of the gardens and the shady groves and the carpet of grass, the Temple of Paladine glowed softly in the morning sunlight. Made of white marble, it was a plain, unadorned† structure that added to the impression of peace and tranquillity that prevailed all around it.

There were gates, but no guards. All were invited to enter, and many did so. It was a haven for the sorrowful, the weary, the unhappy. As Tanis started to make his way across the well-kept lawn, he saw many people sitting or lying upon the grass, a look of peace upon faces that, from the marks of care and weariness, had not often known such comfort.

The Temple of Paladine here in Palanthas is in stark contrast to the overly ornate temple we saw in Istar. The contrast is deliberate—evidence of a simple faith that needs no adornment. —TRH

Tanis had taken only a few steps when he remembered—with another sigh—the carriage. Stopping, he turned. "Wait for me," he was about to say when a figure emerged from the shadows of a grove of aspens that stood at the very edge of the Temple property.

"Tanis Half-Elven?" inquired the figure.

As the figure walked into the light, Tanis started. It was dressed in black robes. Numerous pouches and other spellcasting devices hung from its belt, runes of silver were embroidered upon the sleeves and the hood of its black cloak. *Raistlin!* Tanis thought instantly, having had the archmage in his mind only moments before.

But no. Tanis breathed easier. This magic-user was taller than Raistlin by at least a head and shoulders. His body was straight and well-formed, even muscular, his step youthful and vigorous. Besides, now that Tanis was paying attention, he realized that the voice was firm and deep—not like Raistlin's soft, unsettling whisper.

And, if it were not too odd, Tanis would have sworn he had heard the man speak with an elven accent.

"I am Tanis Half-Elven," he said, somewhat belatedly.

Though he could not see the figure's face, hidden as it was by the shadows of its black hood, he had the impression the man smiled.

"I thought I recognized you. You have often been described to me. You may dismiss your carriage. It will not be needed. You will be spending many days, possibly even weeks, here in Palanthas."

The man was speaking elven! Silvanesti Elven! Tanis was, for a moment, so startled that he could only stare. The driver of the carriage cleared his throat at that moment. It had been a long, hard journey and there were fine inns in Palanthas with ale that was legendary all over Ansalon. . . .

But Tanis wasn't going to dismiss his equipage on the word of a black-robed mage. He opened his mouth to question him further when the magic-user withdrew his hands from the sleeves of his robes, where he'd kept them folded, and made a swift, negating motion with one, even as he made a motion of invitation with the other.

"Please," he said in elven again, "won't you walk with me? For I am bound for the same place you go. Elistan expects us."

Us! Tanis's mind fumbled about in confusion. Since when did Elistan invite black-robed magic-users to the Temple of Paladine? And since when did black-robed magic-users voluntarily set foot upon these sacred grounds!

Well, the only way to find out, obviously, was to accompany this strange person and save his questions until they were alone. Somewhat confusedly, therefore, Tanis gave his instructions to the coachman. The black-robed figure stood in silence beside him, watching the carriage depart. Then Tanis turned to him.

"You have the advantage of me, sir," the half-elf said in halting Silvanesti, a language that was purer elven than the Qualinesti† he'd been raised to speak.

The figure bowed, then cast aside his hood so that the morning light fell upon his face. "I am Dalamar," he said, returning his hands to the sleeves of his robe. Few there were upon Krynn who would shake hands with a black-robed mage.

"A dark elf!" Tanis said in astonishment, speaking before he thought. He flushed. "I'm sorry," he said awkwardly. "It's just that I've never met—"

"One of my kind?" Dalamar finished smoothly, a faint smile upon his cold, handsome, expressionless elven features. "No, I don't suppose you would have. We who are 'cast from the light,' as they say, do not often venture onto the sunlit planes of existence." His smile grew warmer, suddenly, and Tanis saw a wistful look in the dark elf's eyes as their gaze went to the grove of aspens where he had been standing. "Sometimes, though, even we grow homesick."

Tanis's gaze, too, went to the aspens—of all trees most beloved of the elves. He smiled, too, feeling much more at ease. Tanis had walked his own dark roads, and had come very near tumbling into several yawning chasms. He could understand.

"The hour for my appointment draws near," he said. "And, from what you said, I gather that you are somehow involved in this. Perhaps we should continue—"

"Certainly." Dalamar seemed to recollect himself. He followed Tanis onto the green lawn without hesitation. Tanis, turning, was considerably startled,

While a missionary, I learned that the Indonesian language—and indeed many languages throughout the world—has different forms depending upon the class or rank you are addressing. Moreover, languages are living things that evolve over time to fit the needs of their populace. The Silvanesti elves take great pride in the "superiority" of their culture and go to great lengths to keep things untouched by such troublesome things as "evolution." The Qualinesti history, however, suggested that their language would adapt somewhat, as they themselves were forced to adapt. Thus the language differences between them. A trip around England with numerous encounters with people in London, the Midlands, and Liverpool will, I think, aptly demonstrate how a single language can be so different by location and yet still be the same.
—TRH

therefore, to see a swift spasm of pain contort the elf's delicate features and to see him flinch, visibly.

"What is it?" Tanis stopped. "Are you unwell? Can I help—"

Dalamar forced his pain-filled features into a twisted smile. "No, Half-Elven," he said. "There is nothing you can do to help. Nor am I unwell. Much worse would you look, if you stepped into the Shoikan Grove that guards *my* dwelling place."

Tanis nodded in understanding, then, almost unwillingly, glanced into the distance at the dark, grim Tower that loomed over Palanthas. As he looked at it, a strange impression came over him. He looked back at the plain white Temple, then over again at the Tower. Seeing them together, it was as if he were seeing each for the first time. Both looked more complete, finished, whole, than they had when viewed separately and apart. This was only a fleeting impression and one he did not even think about until later. Now, he could only think of one thing—

"Then you live there? With Rai—With him?" Try as he might, Tanis knew he could not speak the arch-mage's name without bitter anger, and so he avoided it altogether.

"He is my *Shalafi*," answered Dalamar in a pain-tightened voice.

"So you are his apprentice," Tanis responded, recognizing the elven word for *Master*. He frowned. "Then what are you doing here? Did he send you?" If so, thought the half-elf, I will leave this place, if I have to walk back to Solanthas.

"No," Dalamar replied, his face draining of all color. "But it is of him we will speak." The dark elf cast his hood over his head. When he spoke, it was obviously with intense effort. "And now, I must beg of you to move swiftly. I have a charm, given me by Elistan, that will help me through this trial. But it is not one I care to prolong."

Elistan† giving charms to black-robed magic-users? Raistlin's apprentice? Absolutely mystified, Tanis agreeably quickened his steps.

"Tanis, my friend!"

Elistan, cleric of Paladine and head of the church on the continent of Ansalon, reached out his hand to

Once again, we have resonance with the foundation themes of the DRAGONLANCE setting. Elistan is Good, Dalamar represents Evil, and Astinus is our Neutral. Tanis's role in this is to be the deciding factor in the center of the three poles— and once again, we see the theme restated. —TRH

the half-elf. Tanis clasped the man's hand warmly, trying not to notice how wasted and feeble was the cleric's once strong, firm grip. Tanis also fought to control his face, endeavoring to keep the feelings of shock and pity from registering on his features as he stared down at the frail, almost skeletal, figure resting in a bed, propped up by pillows.

"Elistan—" Tanis began warmly.

One of the white-robed clerics hovering near their leader glanced up at the half-elf and frowned.

"That is, R-revered Son"—Tanis stumbled over the formal title— "you are looking well."

"And you, Tanis Half-Elven, have degenerated into a liar," Elistan remarked, smiling at the pained expression Tanis tried desperately to keep off his face.

Elistan patted Tanis's sun-browned hand with his thin, white fingers. "And don't fool with that 'Revered Son' nonsense. Yes, I know it's only proper and correct, Garad, but this man knew me when I was a slave in the mines of Pax Tharkas.† Now, go along, all of you," he said to the hovering clerics. "Bring what we have to make our guests comfortable."

See Dragons of Autumn Twilight, *Book II, Chapter 12.*

His gaze went to the dark elf who had collapsed into a chair near the fire that burned in Elistan's private chambers. "Dalamar," Elistan said gently, "this journey cannot have been an easy one for you. I am indebted to you that you have made it. But, here in my quarters you can, I believe, find ease. What will you take?"

"Wine," the dark elf managed to reply through lips that were stiff and ashen. Tanis saw the elf's hands tremble on the arm of the chair.

"Bring wine and food for our guests." Elistan told the clerics who were filing out of the room, many casting glances of disapproval at the black-robed mage. "Escort Astinus here at once, upon his arrival, then see that we are not disturbed."

"Astinus?" Tanis gaped. "Astinus, the Chronicler?"

"Yes, Half-Elven," Elistan smiled once again. "Dying lends one special significance. 'They stand in line to see me, who once would not have glanced my way.' Isn't that how the old man's poem went? There now, Half-Elven. The air is cleared. Yes, I know I am dying. I have known for a long time. My months dwindle to weeks. Come, Tanis. You have seen men die before. What was it you told me the Forestmaster

This occurred in Dragons of Autumn Twilight, Book II, Chapter 11.

said to you in Darken Wood—'we do not mourn the loss of those who die fulfilling their destinies.'† My life has been fulfilled, Tanis—much more than I could ever have imagined." Elistan glanced out the window, out to the spacious lawns, the flowering gardens, and—far in the distance—the dark Tower of High Sorcery.

"It was given me to bring hope back to the world, Half-Elven," Elistan said softly. "Hope and healing. What man can say more? I leave knowing that the church has been firmly established once again. There are clerics among all the races now. Yes, even kender." Elistan, smiling, ran a hand through his white hair. "Ah," he sighed, "what a trying time *that* was for our faith, Tanis! We are still unable to determine exactly what all is missing. But they are a good-hearted, good-souled people. Whenever I started to lose patience, I thought of Fizban—Paladine, as he revealed† himself to us—and the special love he bore your little friend, Tasslehoff."

The old man Fizban revealed that he was actually the god Paladine in Dragons of Spring Dawning, Book III, Chapter 14.

Tanis's face darkened at the mention of the kender's name, and it seemed to him that Dalamar looked up, briefly, from where he had been staring into the dancing flames. But Elistan did not notice.

"My only regret is that I leave no one truly capable of taking over after me," Elistan shook his head. "Garad is a good man. Too good. I see the makings of another Kingpriest in him. But he doesn't understand yet that the balance† must be maintained, that we are all needed to make up this world. Is that not so, Dalamar?"

This, too, is a restatement of the DRAGONLANCE saga's underlying themes. —TRH

To Tanis's surprise, the dark elf nodded his head. He had cast his hood aside and had been able to drink some of the red wine the clerics brought to him. Color had returned to his face, and his hands trembled no longer. "You are wise, Elistan," the mage said softly. "I wish others were as enlightened."

"Perhaps it is not wisdom so much as the ability to see things from all sides,† not just one," Elistan turned to Tanis. "You, Tanis, my friend. Did you not notice and appreciate the view as you came?" He gestured feebly to the window, through which the Tower of High Sorcery was plainly visible.

Elistan is pointing out to Tanis that good and evil must exist in the world in order for the world to progress. Elistan understands the need for the balance and so, too, does Dalamar. Crysania, on the other hand, has yet to learn this. —MW

"I'm not certain I know what you mean." Tanis hedged, uncomfortable as always about sharing his feelings.

"Yes, you do, Half-Elven," Elistan said with a return of his old crispness. "You looked at the Tower and you looked at the Temple and you thought how right it was they should be so near. Oh, there were many who argued long against this site for the Temple. Garad and, of course, Lady Crysania—"

At the mention of that name, Dalamar choked, coughed, and set the wine glass down hurriedly. Tanis stood up, unconsciously beginning to pace the room—as was his custom—when, realizing that this might disturb the dying man, he sat back down again, shifting uncomfortably in his chair.

"Has there been word of her?" he asked in a low voice.

"I am sorry, Tanis," Elistan said gently, "I did not mean to distress you. Truly, you must stop blaming yourself. What she did, she chose to do of her own free will. Nor would I have had it otherwise. You could not have stopped her, nor saved her from her fate—whatever that may be. No, there has been no word of her."

"Yes, there has," Dalamar said in a cold, emotionless voice that drew the immediate attention of both men in the room. "That is one reason I called you together."

"*You* called!" Tanis repeated, standing up again. "I thought Elistan asked us here. Is your *Shalafi* behind this? Is he responsible for this woman's disappearance?" He advanced a step, his face beneath his reddish beard flushed. Dalamar rose to his feet, his eyes glittering dangerously, his hand stealing almost imperceptibly to one of the pouches he wore upon his belt. "Because, by the gods, if he has harmed her, I'll twist his golden neck—"

"Astinus of Palanthas," announced a cleric from the doorway.

The historian stood within the doorway. His ageless face bore no expression as his gray-eyed gaze swept the room, taking in everything, everyone with a minute attention to the detail that his pen would soon record. It went from the flushed and angry face of Tanis, to the proud, defiant face of the elf, to the weary, patient face of the dying cleric.

"Let me guess," Astinus remarked, imperturbably entering and taking a seat. Setting a huge book down upon a table, he opened it to a blank page,

drew a quill pen from a wooden case he carried with him, carefully examined the tip, then looked up. "Ink, friend," he said to a startled cleric, who—after a nod from Elistan—left the room hurriedly. Then the historian continued his original sentence. "Let me guess. You were discussing Raistlin Majere."

"It is true," Dalamar said. "I called you here."

The dark elf had resumed his seat by the fire. Tanis, still scowling, went back to his place near Elistan. The cleric, Garad, returning with Astinus's ink, asked if they wanted anything else. The reply being negative, he left, sternly adding, for the benefit of those in the room, that Elistan was unwell and should not be long disturbed.

"I called you here, together," Dalamar repeated, his gaze upon the fire. Then he raised his eyes, looking directly at Tanis. "You come at some small inconvenience. But *I* come, knowing that I will suffer the torment all of my faith feel trodding upon this holy ground. But it is imperative that I speak to you, all of you, together. I knew Elistan could not come to me. I knew Tanis Half-Elven *would* not come to me. And so I had no choice but to—"

"Proceed," Astinus said in his deep, cool voice. "The world passes as we sit here. You have called us here together. That is established. For what reason?"

Dalamar was silent for a moment, his gaze going back once again to the fire. When he spoke, he did not look up.

"Our worst fears are realized," he said softly. "He has been successful."†

Councils of the Wise are an archetype in fantasy and mythology. These wise beings represent the guardians of the gates to adventure. Yet while they debate, the focus of their discussions always comes down to the Hero in their midst and the journey he must undertake. —TRH

CHAPTER 2

Come home. . . .

The voice lingered in his memory. Someone kneeling beside the pool of his mind, dropping words into the calm, clear surface. Ripples of consciousness disturbed him, woke him from his peaceful, restful sleep.

"Come home. . . . My son, come home."

Opening his eyes, Raistlin looked into the face of his mother.

Smiling, she reached out her hand and stroked back the wispy, white hair that fell down across his forehead. "My poor son," she murmured, her dark eyes soft with grief and pity and love. "What they did to you! I watched. I've watched for so long now. And I've wept. Yes, my son, even the dead weep. It is the only comfort we have. But all that is over now. You are with me. Here you can rest. . . ."

Raistlin struggled to sit up. Looking down at himself, he saw—to his horror—that he was covered with blood. Yet he felt no pain, there seemed to be no wound. He found it hard to take a breath, and he gasped for air.

"Here, let me help you," his mother said. She began to loosen the silken cord he wore around his waist, the cord from which hung his pouches, his precious spell components. Reflexively, Raistlin thrust her hand aside. His breath came easier. He looked around.

"What happened? Where am I?" He was vastly confused. Memories of his childhood came to him. Memories of *two* childhoods came to him! His . . . and someone else's! He looked at his mother, and she was someone he knew and she was a stranger.

"What happened?" he repeated irritably, beating back the surging memories that threatened to overthrow his grasp on sanity.

"You have died, my son," his mother said gently. "And now you are here with me."

"*Died!*' Raistlin repeated, aghast.

Frantically he sorted through the memories. He recalled being near death. . . . How was it that he had failed? He put his hand to his forehead and felt . . . flesh, bone, warmth . . . And then he remembered. . . .

The Portal!

"No," he cried angrily, glaring at his mother. "That's impossible."

"You lost control of the magic, my son," his mother said, reaching out her hand to touch Raistlin again. He drew away from her. With the slight, sad smile— a smile he remembered so well—she let her hand drop back in her lap. "The field shifted, the forces tore you apart. There was a terrible explosion, it leveled the Plains of Dergoth. The magical fortress of Zhaman collapsed." His mother's voice shook. "The sight of your suffering was almost more than I could bear."

"I remember," Raistlin whispered, putting his hands to his head. "I remember the pain . . . but . . ."

He remembered something else, too—brilliant bursts of multicolored lights, he remembered a feeling of exultation and ecstasy welling up in his soul, he remembered the dragon's heads that guarded the

Portal screaming in fury, he remembered wrapping his arms around Crysania.

Standing up, Raistlin looked around. He was on flat, level ground—a desert of some sort. In the distance he could see mountains. They looked familiar— of course! Thorbardin! The dwarven kingdom. He turned. There were the ruins of the fortress, looking like a skull devouring the land in its eternally grinning mouth. So, he was on the Plains of Dergoth. He recognized the landscape. But, even as he recognized it, it seemed strange to him. Everything was tinged with red, as though he were seeing all objects through blood-dimmed eyes. And, though objects looked the same as he remembered them, they were strange to him as well.

Skullcap he had seen during the War of the Lance. He didn't remember it grinning in that obscene way. The mountains, too, were sharp and clearly defined against the sky. The sky! Raistlin drew in a breath. It was empty! Swiftly he looked in all directions. No, there was no sun, yet it was not night. There were no moons, no stars; and it was such a strange color—a kind of muted pink, the reflection of a sunset.

He looked down at the woman kneeling on the ground before him.

Raistlin smiled, his thin lips pressed together grimly.

"No," he said, and this time his voice was firm and confident. "No, I did *not* die! I succeeded." He gestured. "This is proof of my success. I recognize this place. The kender described it to me. He said it was all places he had ever been. This is where I entered the Portal, and now I stand in the Abyss."†

Leaning down, Raistlin grabbed the woman by the arm, dragging her to her feet. "Fiend, apparition! Where is Crysania? Tell me, whoever or whatever you are! Tell me, or by the gods I'll—"

"Raistlin! Stop, you're hurting me!"

Raistlin started, staring. It was Crysania who spoke, Crysania whose arm he held! Shaken, he loosed his grip but, within instants, he was master of himself again. She tried to pull free, but he held her firmly, drawing her near.

"Crysania?" he questioned, studying her intently.

She looked up at him, puzzled. "Yes," she faltered. "What's wrong, Raistlin? You've been talking so strangely."

The Abyss, in my mind, was always the reflection of our own guilt and flaws made real to us. —TRH

The archmage tightened his grip. Crysania cried out. Yes, the pain in her eyes was real, so was the fear.

Smiling, sighing, Raistlin put his arms around her, pressing her close against his body. She was flesh, warmth, perfume, beating heart. . . .

"Oh, Raistlin!" She nestled close to him. "I was so frightened. This terrible place. I was all alone."

His hand tangled in her black hair. The softness and fragrance of her body intoxicated him, filling him with desire. She moved against him, tilting her head back. Her lips were soft, eager. She trembled in his arms. Raistlin looked down at her—

—and stared into eyes of flame.

So, you have come home at last, my mage!

Sultry laughter burned his mind, even as the lithe body in his arms writhed and twisted . . . he clasped one neck of a five-headed dragon . . . acid dripped from the gaping jaws above him . . . fire roared around him . . . sulfurous fumes choked him. The head snaked down. . . .

Desperately, furiously, Raistlin called upon his magic. Yet, even as he formed the words of the defensive spell chant in his mind, he felt a twinge of doubt. Perhaps the magic won't work! I am weak, the journey through the Portal has drained my strength. Fear, sharp and slender as the blade of a dagger, pierced his soul. The words to the chant slipped from his mind. Panic flooded his body. The Queen! She is doing this! *Ast takar ist* . . . No! That isn't right! He heard laughter, victorious laughter. . . .

Bright white light blinded him. He was falling, falling, falling endlessly, spiraling down from darkness into day.

Opening his eyes, Raistlin looked into Crysania's face.

Her face, but it was not the face he remembered. It was aging, dying, even as he watched. In her hand, she held the platinum medallion of Paladine. Its pure white radiance shone brightly in the eerie pinkish light around them.

Raistlin closed his eyes to blot out the sight of the cleric's aging face, summoning back memories of how it looked in the past—delicate, beautiful, alive with love and passion. Her voice came to him, cool, firm.

"I very nearly lost you."

Reaching up, but without opening his eyes, he grabbed hold of the cleric's arms, clinging to her desperately. "What do I look like? Tell me! I've changed, haven't I?"

"You are as you were when I first met you in the Great Library," Crysania said, her voice still firm, too firm—tight, tense.

Yes, thought Raistlin, I am as I was. Which means I have returned to the present. He felt the old frailty, the old weakness, the burning pain in his chest, and with it the choking huskiness of the cough, as though cobwebs were being spun in his lungs. He had but to look, he knew, and he would see the gold-tinged skin, the white hair, the hourglass eyes. . . .

Shoving Crysania away, he rolled over onto his stomach, clenching his fists in fury, sobbing in anger and fear.

"Raistlin!" True terror was in Crysania's voice now. "What is it? Raistlin, where are we? What's wrong?"

"I succeeded," he snarled. Opening his eyes, he saw her face, withering in his sight. "I succeeded. We are in the Abyss."

Her eyes opened wide, her lips parted. Fear mingled with joy.

Raistlin smiled bitterly. "And my magic is gone."

Startled, Crysania stared at him. "I don't understand—"

Twisting in agony, Raistlin screamed at her. *"My magic is gone!* I am weak, helpless, here—in her realm!" Suddenly, recollecting that *she* might be listening, watching, enjoying, Raistlin froze. His scream died in the blood-tinged froth upon his lips. He looked about, warily.

"But, no, you haven't defeated me!" he whispered. His hand closed over the Staff of Magius, lying at his side. Leaning upon it heavily, he struggled to his feet. Crysania gently put her strong arm around him, helping him stand.

"No," he murmured, staring into the vastness of the empty Plains, into the pink, empty sky, "I know where you are! I sense it! You are in Godshome. I know the lay of the land. I know how to move about, the kender gave me the key in his feverish

ramblings. The land below mirrors the land above. I will seek you out, though the journey be long and treacherous.

"Yes!"—he looked all around him—"I feel you probing my mind, reading my thoughts, anticipating all I say and do. You think it will be easy to defeat me! But I sense your confusion, too. There is one with me whose mind you cannot touch! She defends and protects me, do you not, Crysania?"

"Yes, Raistlin," Crysania replied softly, supporting the archmage.

Raistlin took a step, another, and another. He leaned upon Crysania, he leaned upon his staff. And still, each step was an effort, each breath he drew burned. When he looked about this world, all he saw was emptiness.

Inside him, all was emptiness. His magic was gone.

Raistlin stumbled. Crysania caught him and held onto him, clasping him close, tears running down her cheeks.

He could hear laughter. . . .

Maybe I should give up now! he thought in bitter despair. I am tired, so very tired. And without my magic, what am I?

Nothing. Nothing but a weak, wretched child. . . .

Chapter 3

For long moments after Dalamar's pronouncement, there was silence in the room. Then the silence was broken by the scratching of a pen as Astinus recorded the dark elf's words in his great book.

"May Paladine have mercy," Elistan murmured. "Is she with him?"

"Of course," Dalamar snapped irritably, revealing a nervousness that all the skills of his Art could not hide. "How else do you think he succeeded? The Portal is locked to all except the combined forces of a Black-Robed wizard of such powers as his and a White-Robed cleric of such faith as hers."

Tanis glanced from one to the other, confused. "Look," he said angrily, "I don't understand. What's going on? Who are you talking about? Raistlin? What's he done? Does it have something to do with

Dalamar admires Raistlin, but he also sees quite clearly that Raistlin is a danger both to the world and to himself. Dalamar is a man of faith. He believes in the gods, and he honors them. Dalamar is one of the few characters in the books who understands and is comfortable with himself. He knows his limits; he knows his strengths. He believes in himself, rarely doubting or questioning what he must do and, in this, he has a lot to teach Caramon. —MW

Crysania? And what about Caramon? He's vanished, too. Along with Tas! I—"

"Get a grip on the impatient human half of your nature, Half-Elven," Astinus remarked, still writing in firm, black strokes. "And you, Dark Elf, begin at the beginning instead of in the middle."

"Or the end, as the case may be," Elistan remarked in a low voice.

Moistening his lips with the wine, Dalamar—his gaze still on the fire—related the strange tale that Tanis, up until now, had only known in part. Much the half-elf could have guessed, much astounded him, much filled him with horror.

"Lady Crysania was captivated by Raistlin. And, if the truth be told, he was attracted to her, I believe. Who can tell with him? Ice water is too hot to run in *his* veins. Who knows how long he has plotted this, dreamed of this? But, at last, he was ready. He planned a journey, back in time, to seek the one thing he lacked—the knowledge of the greatest wizard who has ever lived—Fistandantilus.

"He set a trap for Lady Crysania, planning to lure her back in time with him, as well as his twin brother—"

"Caramon?" asked Tanis in astonishment.

Dalamar ignored him. "But something unforeseen occurred. The *Shalafi's* half-sister, Kitiara, a Dragon Highlord. . . ."

Blood pounded in Tanis's head, dimming his vision and obscuring his hearing. He felt that same blood pulse in his face. He had the feeling his skin might be burning to the touch, so hot was it.

Kitiara!

She stood before him,† dark eyes flashing, dark hair curling about her face, her lips slightly parted in that charming, crooked smile, the light gleaming off her armor. . . .

She looked down on him from the back of her blue dragon, surrounded by her minions, lordly and powerful, strong and ruthless. . . .

She lay in his arms, languishing, loving, laughing. . . .

Tanis sensed, though he could not see, Elistan's sympathetic but pitying gaze. He shrank from the stern, knowing look of Astinus. Wrapped up in his own guilt, his own shame, his own wretchedness,

The Temptress is another archetype. In Dramatic story theory, this archetype is called the Contagonist. The Contagonist sits opposite the Guardian and tries to manipulate either the Antagonist or the Hero—or both—in order to prevent the Hero from completing his journey. This character is an essential part of the complete argument of the story. —TRH

Tanis did not notice that Dalamar, too, was having trouble with *his* countenance which was pale, rather than flushed. He did not hear the dark elf's voice quiver when he spoke the woman's name.

After a struggle, Tanis regained control of himself and was able to continue listening. But he felt, once again, that old pain in his heart, the pain he had thought forever vanished. He was happy with Laurana. He loved her more deeply and tenderly than he had supposed it possible for a man to love a woman. He was at peace with himself. His life was rich, full. And now he was astonished to discover the darkness still inside of him, the darkness he thought he had banished forever.†

"At Kitiara's command, the death knight, Lord Soth, cast a spell upon Lady Crysania, a spell that should have killed her. But Paladine interceded. He took her soul to dwell with him, leaving the shell of her body behind. I thought the *Shalafi* was defeated. But, no. He turned this betrayal of his sister's into an advantage. His twin brother, Caramon, and the kender, Tasslehoff, took Lady Crysania to the Tower of High Sorcery in Wayreth, hoping that the mages would be able to cure her. They could not, of course, as Raistlin well knew. They could only send her back in time to the one period in the history of Krynn when there lived a Kingpriest powerful enough to call upon Paladine to restore the woman's soul to her body. And this, of course, was exactly what Raistlin wanted."

Dalamar's fist clenched. "I told the mages so! Fools! I told them they were playing right into his hands."

"*You* told them?" Tanis felt master of himself enough now to ask this question. "You betrayed him, your *Shalafi*?" He snorted in disbelief.

"It is a dangerous game I play, Half-Elven." Dalamar looked at him now, his eyes alight from within, like the burning embers of the fire. "I am a spy,† sent by the Conclave of Mages to watch Raistlin's every move. Yes, you may well look astonished. They fear him—all of the Orders fear him, the White, the Red, the Black. Most especially the Black, for we know what our fate will be should he rise to power."

As Tanis† stared, the dark elf lifted his hand and slowly parted the front closure of his black robes,

Even though Tanis loves Laurana, he still has feelings for Kitiara. G.K. Chesterton wrote, "The first two facts which a healthy boy or girl feels about sex are these: first that it is beautiful and then that it is dangerous." [Illustrated London News 1/9/09.] Tanis is torn between Laurana, who is beautiful, and Kitiara, who is dangerous.

Much of this is expanded in Dalamar the Dark *by Nancy Varian Berberick.*

Tanis very much represents us in the story when he is present. He is a flawed man with a past of checkered experiences. He is a good man who has, in the past, given in to temptations. We, as readers, recognize our own struggles in him and identify with him. —TRH

laying bare his breast. Five oozing wounds marred the surface of the dark elf's smooth skin. "The mark of his hand," Dalamar said in an expressionless tone. "My reward for my treachery."

Tanis could see Raistlin laying those thin, golden fingers upon the young dark elf's chest, he could see Raistlin's face—without feeling, without malice, without cruelty, without any touch of humanity whatsoever—and he could see those fingers burn through the flesh of his victim. Shaking his head, feeling sickened, Tanis sank back in his chair, his gaze on the floor.

"But they would not listen to me," Dalamar continued. "They grasped at straws. As Raistlin had foreseen, their greatest hope lay in their greatest fear. They decided to send Lady Crysania back in time, ostensibly so that the Kingpriest could aid her. That is what they told Caramon, for they knew he would not go otherwise. But, in reality, they sent her back to die or to at least disappear as did all other clerics before the Cataclysm. And they hoped that Caramon, when he went back into time and learned the truth about his twin—learned that Raistlin was, in reality, Fistandantilus—that he would be forced to kill his brother."

"Caramon?" Tanis laughed bitterly, then scowled again in anger. "How could they do such a thing? The man is sick! The only thing Caramon can kill now is a bottle of dwarf spirits! Raistlin's already destroyed him. Why didn't they—"

Catching Astinus's irritated glance, Tanis subsided. His mind reeled in turmoil. None of this made sense! He looked over at Elistan. The cleric must have known much of this already. There was no look of shock or surprise on his face—even when he heard that the mages had sent Crysania back to die. There was only an expression of deep sorrow.

Dalamar was continuing. "But the kender, Tasslehoff Burrfoot, disrupted Par-Salian's spell and accidentally traveled back in time with Caramon. The introduction of a kender into the flow of time made it possible for time to be altered. What happened back there, in Istar, we can only surmise. What we do know is that Crysania did *not* die. Caramon did *not* kill his brother. And Raistlin was successful in obtaining the knowledge of Fistandantilus. Taking

Crysania and Caramon with him, he moved forward in time to the one period when he would possess, in Crysania, the only true cleric in the land. He traveled to the one period in our history when the Queen of Darkness would be most vulnerable and unable to stop him.

"As Fistandantilus did before him, Raistlin fought the Dwarfgate War, and so obtained access to the Portal that stood, then, in the magical fortress of Zhaman. If history had repeated itself, Raistlin should have died at that Portal, for thus did Fistandantilus meet his doom."

"We counted on this," Elistan murmured, his hands plucking feebly at the bedclothes that covered him. "Par-Salian said that there was no way Raistlin could change history—"

"That wretched kender!" Dalamar snarled. "Par-Salian should have known, he should have realized the miserable creature would do exactly what he did—leap at a chance for some new adventure! He should have taken our advice and smothered the little bastard—"

"Tell me what's happened to Tasslehoff and Caramon," Tanis interrupted coldly. "I don't care what's become of Raistlin or—and I apologize, Elistan—Lady Crysania. She was blinded by her own goodness. I am sorry for her, but she refused to open her eyes and see the truth. I care about my friends. What has become of them?"

"We do not know," Dalamar said. He shrugged. "But if I were you, I would not look to see them again in this life, Half-Elven. . . .They would be of little use to the *Shalafi*."

"Then you have told me all I need to hear," Tanis said, rising, his voice taut with grief and fury. "If it's the last thing I do, I'll seek out Raistlin and I'll—"

"Sit down, Half-Elven," Dalamar said. He did not raise his voice, but there was a dangerous glint in his eyes that made Tanis's hand reach for the hilt of his sword, only to remember that—since he was visiting the Temple of Paladine—he had not worn it. More furious still, not trusting himself to speak, Tanis bowed to Elistan, then to Astinus, and started for the door.

"You *will* care what becomes of Raistlin, Tanis Half-Elven," Dalamar's smooth voice intercepted

Good and Evil both speak out here, yet Neutrality remains silent. This resonates back to the beginning of the book where Caramon had his vision of the fallen future. Neutrality was cursing itself for its silence. —TRH

him, "because it affects you. It affects all of us. Do I speak truly, Revered Son?"

"He does, Tanis," Elistan said. "I understand your feelings, but you must put them aside!"

Astinus said nothing,† the scratching of his pen was the only indication that the man was in the room. Tanis clenched his fists, then, with a vicious oath that caused even Astinus to glance up, the half-elf turned to Dalamar. "Very well, then. What could Raistlin possibly do that would further hurt and injure and destroy those around him?"

"I said when I began that our worst fears were realized," Dalamar replied, his slanted, elven eyes looking into the slightly slanted eyes of the half-elf.

"Yes," snapped Tanis impatiently, still standing.

Dalamar paused dramatically. Astinus, looking up again, raised his gray eyebrows in mild annoyance.

"Raistlin has entered the Abyss. He and Lady Crysania will challenge the Queen of Darkness."

Tanis stared at Dalamar in disbelief. Then he burst out laughing. "Well," he said, shrugging, "it seems I have little to worry about. The mage has sealed his own doom."

But Tanis's laughter fell flat. Dalamar regarded him with cool, cynical amusement, as if he might have expected this absurd response from a half-human. Astinus snorted and kept writing. Elistan's frail shoulders slumped. Closing his eyes, he leaned back against his pillows.

Tanis stared at all of them. "You can't consider this a serious threat!" he demanded. "By the gods, I have stood before the Queen of Darkness! I have felt her power and her majesty—and that was when she was only partially in this plane of existence." The half-elf shuddered involuntarily. "I can't imagine what it would be like to meet her on her own . . . her own . . ."

The gods of Krynn, as I have noted before, were always, in my mind, a pantheon of "middle management"—interceders between the races of mortality and the High God. This, in many ways, mirrors the gods of classical Greece, complete with their passions and fallibilities. —TRH

"You are not alone, Tanis," said Elistan wearily. "I, too, have conversed with the Dark Queen."† He opened his eyes, smiling wanly. "Does that surprise you? I have had my trials and temptations as have all men."

"Once only has she come to me." Dalamar's face paled, and there was fear in his eyes. He licked his lips. "And that was to bring me these tidings."

Astinus said nothing, but he had ceased to write.

Rock itself was more expressive than the historian's face.

Tanis shook his head in wonder. "You've met the Queen, Elistan? You acknowledge her power? Yet you still think that a frail and sickly wizard and an old-maid cleric can somehow do her harm?"

Elistan's eyes flashed, his lips tightened, and Tanis knew he had gone too far. Flushing, he scratched his beard and started to apologize, then stubbornly snapped his mouth shut. "It just doesn't make sense," he mumbled, walking back and throwing himself down in his chair.

"Well, how in the Abyss do we stop him?" Realizing what he'd said, Tanis's flush deepened. "I'm sorry," he muttered. "I don't mean to make this a joke. Everything I'm saying seems to be coming out wrong. But, damn it, I don't understand! Are we supposed to stop Raistlin or cheer him on?"

"You cannot stop him." Dalamar interposed coolly as Elistan seemed about to speak. "That we mages alone can do. Our plans for this have been underway for many weeks now, ever since we first learned of this threat. You see, Half-Elven, what you have said is—in part—correct. Raistlin knows, we all know, that he cannot defeat the Queen of Darkness on her own plane of existence. Therefore, it is his plan to draw her out, to bring her back through the Portal and into the world—"

Tanis felt as if he had been punched hard in the stomach. For a moment, he could not draw a breath. "That's madness," he managed to gasp finally, his hands curling over the armrests of his chair, his knuckles turning white with the strain. "We barely defeated her at Nerakat as it was! He's going to bring her back into the world?"

The Companions defeated Takhisis in the latter chapters of Dragons of Spring Dawning.

"Unless he can be stopped," Dalamar continued, "which is my duty, as I have said."

"So what are we supposed to do?" Tanis demanded, leaning forward. "Why have you brought us here? Are we to sit around and watch? I—"

"Patience, Tanis!" Elistan interrupted. "You are nervous and afraid. We all share these feelings."

With the exception of that granite-hearted historian over there, Tanis thought bitterly—

"But nothing will be gained by rash acts or wild words." Elistan looked over at the dark elf and his

voice grew softer. "I believe that we have not yet heard the worst, is that true, Dalamar?"

"Yes, Revered Son," Dalamar said, and Tanis was surprised to see a trace of emotion flicker in the elf's slanted eyes. "I have received word that Dragon Highlord Kitiara"—the elf choked slightly, cleared his throat, and continued speaking more firmly— "Kitiara is planning a full-scale assault on Palanthas."

Tanis sank back in his chair. His first thought was one of bitter, cynical amusement—I told you so,† Lord Amothus. I told you so, Porthios. I told you, all of you who want to crawl back into your nice, warm little nests and pretend the war never happened. His second thoughts were more sobering. Memories returned—the city of Tarsis in flames, the dragonarmies taking over Solace,† the pain, the suffering . . . death.

Elistan was saying something, but Tanis couldn't hear. He leaned back, closing his eyes, trying to think. He remembered Dalamar talking about Kitiara, but what was it he had said? It drifted on the fringes of his consciousness. He had been thinking about Kit. He hadn't been paying attention. The words were vague. . . .

"Wait!" Tanis sat up, suddenly remembering. "You said Kitiara was furious with Raistlin. You said she was just as frightened of the Queen reentering the world as we are. That was why she ordered Soth to kill Crysania. If that's true, *why* is she attacking Palanthas? That doesn't make sense! She grows in strength daily in Sanction. The evil dragons have congregated there and we have reports that the draconians who were scattered after the war have also been regrouping under her command. But Sanction is a long way from Palanthas. The lands of the Knights of Solamnia lie in between. The good dragons will rise up and fight if the evil ones take to the skies again. Why? Why would she risk all she has gained? And for what—"

"You know Lord Kitiara I believe, Half-Elven?" Dalamar interrupted.

Tanis choked, coughed, and muttered something.

"I beg your pardon?"

"Yes, damn it, I know her!" Tanis snapped, caught Elistan's glance, and sank back into his chair once again, feeling his skin burn.

The situation here in some ways harkens back to Patton's desire to continue the war in Europe by moving his armies against the Soviets or MacArthur's desire to continue north against the Chinese in Korea. I think, however, that the intention of the text here is more gentle, that the sacrifices made in such conflicts are all too often forgotten by those who reap the benefits of the peace. My youth was colored by Viet Nam, and I always try to make a point of shaking a veteran's hand and thanking him for his service. —TRH

The dragonarmies conquered Solace in Dragons of Autumn Twilight, *Book II, Chapter 1.*

"You are right," Dalamar said smoothly, a glint of amusement in his light, elven eyes. "When Kitiara first heard about Raistlin's plan, she was frightened. Not for him, of course, but for fear that he would bring the wrath of the Dark Queen down upon her. But"—Dalamar shrugged—"this was when Kitiara believed Raistlin must lose. Now, it seems, she thinks he has a chance to win. And Kit will always try to be on the winning side. She plans to conquer Palanthas and be prepared to greet the wizard as he passes through the Portal. Kit will offer the might of her armies to her brother. If he is strong enough—and by this time, he should be—he can easily convert the evil creatures from their allegiance to the Dark Queen to serving *his* cause."

"Kit?" It was Tanis's turn to look amused. Dalamar sneered slightly.

"Oh, yes, Half-Elven. I know Kitiara every bit as well as you do."

But the sarcastic tone in the dark elf's voice faltered, twisting unconsciously to one of bitterness. His slender hands clenched. Tanis nodded in sudden understanding, feeling, oddly enough, a strange kind of sympathy for the young elf.

"So she has betrayed you, too," Tanis murmured softly. "She pledged you her support. She said she would be there, stand beside you. When Raistlin returned, she would fight at your side."

Dalamar rose to his feet, his black robes rustling around him. "I never trusted her," he said coldly, but he turned his back upon them and stared intently into the flames, keeping his face averted. "I knew what treachery she was capable of committing, none better. This came as no surprise."

But Tanis saw the hand that gripped the mantelpiece turn white.

"Who told you this?" Astinus asked abruptly. Tanis started. He had almost forgotten the historian's presence. "Surely not the Dark Queen. She would not care about this."

"No, no." Dalamar appeared confused for a moment. His thoughts had obviously been far away. Sighing, he looked up at them once more. "Lord Soth, the death knight, told me."

"Soth?" Tanis felt himself losing his grip on reality.

Frantically his brain scrambled for a handhold. Mages spying on mages. Clerics of light aligned with wizards of darkness. Dark trusting light, turning against darkness. Light turning to the dark. . . .

"Soth has pledged allegiance to Kitiara!" Tanis said in confusion. "Why would he betray her?"

Turning from the fire, Dalamar looked into Tanis's eyes. For the span of a heartbeat, there was a bond between the two, a bond forged by a shared understanding, a shared misery, a shared torment, a shared passion. And, suddenly, Tanis understood, and his soul shriveled in horror.

Kitiara has betrayed all the men in her life. Now they are allying to take her down. Once again, evil feeds on itself. —TRH

"He wants her dead,"† Dalamar replied.

CHAPTER 4

The young boy†
walked down the streets of Solace. He was not a
comely boy, and he knew it—as he knew so much
about himself that is not often given children to
know. But then, he spent a great deal of time with
himself, precisely because he was not comely and
because he knew too much.

He was not walking alone today, however. His twin
brother, Caramon, was with him. Raistlin scowled,
scuffing through the dust of the village street, watching it rise in clouds about him. He may not have been
walking alone, but in a way he was more alone with
Caramon than without him. Everyone called out
greetings to his likeable, handsome twin. No one said
a word to him. Everyone yelled for Caramon to come
join their games. No one invited Raistlin. Girls looked
at Caramon out of the corners of their eyes in that special way girls had. Girls never even noticed Raistlin.

*We see the innocence of
youth here in this vision
from Raistlin's past. While
Raistlin has become a
monster, he certainly was
not born one. He became
one through the choices
that he made in life. So it is
with all monsters in our
real world. —TRH*

"Hey, Caramon, wanna play King of the Castle?" a voice yelled.

"You want to, Raist?" Caramon asked, his face lighting up eagerly. Strong and athletic, Caramon enjoyed the rough, strenuous game. But Raistlin knew that if he played he would soon start to feel weak and dizzy. He knew, too, that the other boys would argue about whose team *had* to take him.

"No. You go ahead, though."

Caramon's face fell. Then, shrugging, he said, "Oh, that's all right, Raist. I'd rather stay with you."

Raistlin felt his throat tighten, his stomach clenched. "No, Caramon," he repeated softly, "it's all right. Go ahead and play."

"You don't look like you're feeling good, Raist," Caramon said. "It's no big deal. Really. C'mon, show me that new magic trick you learned—the one with the coins—"

"Don't treat me like this!" Raistlin heard himself screaming. "I don't need you! I don't want you around! Go ahead! Go play with those fools! You're all a pack of fools together! I don't need any of you!"

Caramon's† face crumbled. Raistlin had the feeling he'd just kicked a dog. The feeling only made him angrier. He turned away.

"Sure, Raist, if that's what you want," Caramon mumbled.

Glancing over his shoulder, Raistlin saw his twin run off after the others. With a sigh, trying to ignore the shouts of laughter and greeting, Raistlin sat down in a shady place† and, drawing one of his spellbooks from his pack, began to study. Soon, the lure of the magic drew him away from the dirt and the laughter and the hurt eyes of his twin. It led him into an enchanted land where *he* commanded the elements, *he* controlled reality. . . .

The spellbook tumbled from his hands, landing in the dust at his feet. Raistlin looked up, startled. Two boys stood above him. One held a stick in his hand. He poked the book with it, then, lifting the stick, he poked Raistlin, hard, in the chest.

You are bugs, Raistlin told the boys silently. Insects. You mean nothing to me. Less than nothing. Ignoring the pain in his chest, ignoring the insect life standing before him, Raistlin reached out his hand for his book. The boy stepped on his fingers.

Caramon's love for his brother is genuine and selfless. Indeed, their relationship reminds me of one that I had in my youth—an unhealthy one for both the girl and myself. I gave, she took but did not know how to give back. For me, this has always been at the heart of Caramon's relationship with his brother: always loving, giving selflessly, and painfully wondering all the while why his brother could not love or give back selflessly to him. —TRH

I, too, was somewhat of a recluse as a child. I preferred my books, games, and imagination to sports or outdoor activities. I identify very closely with this in Raistlin—as many of us do. —TRH

Frightened, but now more angry than afraid, Raistlin rose to his feet. His hands were his livelihood. With them, he manipulated the fragile spell components, with them he traced the delicate arcane symbols of his Art in the air.

"Leave me alone," he said coldly, and such was the way he spoke and the look in his eye that, for an instant, the two boys were taken aback. But now a crowd had gathered. The other boys left their game, coming to watch the fun. Aware that others were watching, the boy with the stick refused to let this skinny, whining, sniveling bookworm have the better of him.

"What're ya going to do?" the boy sneered. "Turn me into a frog?"

There was laughter. The words to a spell formed in Raistlin's mind. It was not a spell he was supposed to have learned yet, it was an offensive spell, a hurting spell, a spell to use when true danger threatened. His Master would be furious. Raistlin smiled a thin-lipped smile. At the sight of that smile and the look in Raistlin's eyes, one of the boys edged backward.

"Let's go," he muttered to his companion.

But the other boy stood his ground. Behind him, Raistlin could see his twin standing among the crowd, a look of anger on his face.

Raistlin began to speak the words—

—and then he froze. No! Something was wrong! He had forgotten! His magic wouldn't work! Not here! The words came out as gibberish, they made no sense. Nothing happened! The boys laughed. The boy with the stick raised it and shoved it into Raistlin's stomach, knocking him to the ground, driving the breath from his body.

He was on his hand and knees, gasping for air. Somebody kicked him. He felt the stick break over his back. Somebody else kicked him. He was rolling on the ground now, choking in the dust, his thin arms trying desperately to cover his head. Kicks and blows rained in on him.

"Caramon!" he cried. "Caramon, help me!"

But there was only a deep, stern voice in answer. "You don't need me, remember."

A rock struck him in the head, hurting him terribly. And he knew, although he couldn't see, that it was

Caramon who had thrown it. He was losing consciousness. Hands were dragging him along the dusty road, they were hauling him to a pit of vast darkness and cold, icy cold. They would hurl him down there and he would fall, endlessly, through the darkness and the cold and he would never, never hit the bottom, for there was no bottom. . . .

Crysania stared around. Where was she? Where was Raistlin? He had been with her only moments before, leaning weakly on her arm. And then, suddenly, he had vanished and she had found herself alone, walking in a strange village.

Or was it strange? She seemed to recall having been here once, or at least someplace like this. Tall vallenwoods surrounded her. The houses of the town were built in the trees. There was an inn in a tree. She saw a signpost.

Solace.

How strange, she marveled, looking around. It was Solace, all right. She had been here recently, with Tanis Half-Elven, looking for Caramon. But *this* Solace was different. Everything seemed tinged with red and just a tiny bit distorted. She kept wanting to rub her eyes to clear them.

"Raistlin!" she called.

There was no answer. The people passing by acted as if they neither heard her nor saw her. "Raistlin!" she cried, starting to panic. What had happened to him? Where had he gone? Had the Dark Queen—

She heard a commotion, children shouting and yelling and, above the noise, a thin, high-pitched scream for help.

Turning, Crysania saw a crowd of children gathered around a form huddled on the ground. She saw fists flailing and feet kicking, she saw a stick raised and then brought down, hard. Again, that high-pitched scream. Crysania glanced at the people around her, but they seemed unaware of anything unusual occurring.

Gathering her white robes in her hand, Crysania ran toward the children. She saw, as she drew nearer, that the figure in the center of the circle was a child! A young boy! They were killing him, she realized in sudden horror! Reaching the crowd, she grabbed

hold of one of the children to pull him away. At the touch of her hand, the child whirled to face her. Crysania fell back, alarmed.

The child's face was white, cadaverous, skull-like.† Its skin stretched taut over the bones, its lips were tinged with violet. It bared its teeth at her, and the teeth were black and rotting. The child lashed out at her with its hand. Long nails ripped her skin, sending a stinging, paralyzing pain through her. Gasping, she let go, and the child—with a grin of perverted pleasure on its face—turned back to torment the boy on the ground.

This nightmare quality is reminiscent of the dark dreams woven into reality by King Lorac in Dragons of Winter Night. *—TRH*

Staring at the bleeding marks upon her arm, dizzy and weak from the pain, Crysania heard the boy cry out again.

"Paladine, help me," she prayed. "Give me strength."

Resolutely, she grabbed hold of one of the demon children and hurled it aside, and then she grabbed another. Managing to reach the boy upon the ground, she shielded his bleeding, unconscious body with her own, trying desperately all the while to drive the children away.

Again and again, she felt the long nails tear her skin, the poison course through her body. But soon she noticed that, once they touched her, the children drew back, in pain themselves. Finally, sullen expressions on their nightmarish faces, they withdrew, leaving her—bleeding and sick—alone with their victim.

Gently, she turned the bruised body of the young boy over. Smoothing back the brown hair, she looked at his face. Her hands began to shake. There was no mistaking that delicate facial structure, the fragile bones, the jutting chin.

"Raistlin!" she whispered, holding his small hand in her own.

The boy opened his eyes. . . .

The man, dressed in black robes, sat up.

Crysania stared at him as he looked grimly around.

"What is happening?" she asked, shivering, feeling the effects of the poison spreading through her body.

Raistlin nodded to himself. "This is how she torments me," he said softly. "This is how she fights me, striking at me where she knows I am weakest."†

I worry about over-analyzing Raistlin in these annotations for fear that it will take away your appreciation of the story or his powerful, tragic character. Nevertheless, Raistlin here says to me that the most painful thing for him is the experience of fully knowing the innocent that he once was and knowing what he has become. —TRH

The golden, hourglass eyes turned to Crysania, the thin lips smiled. "You fought for me. You defeated her." He drew her near, enfolding her in his black robes, holding her close. "There, rest a while. The pain will pass, and then we will travel on."

Still shivering, Crysania laid her head on the arch-mage's breast, hearing his breath wheeze and rattle in his lungs, smelling that sweet, faint fragrance of rose petals and death. . . .†

Are Raistlin and Crysania experiencing illusions, dreams, or reality? There is no difference in the Abyss. —TRH

CHAPTER 5

nd so this is what comes of his courageous words and promises," said Kitiara in a low voice.

"Did you really expect otherwise?" asked Lord Soth.† The words, accompanied with a shrug of the ancient armor, sounded nonchalant, almost rhetorical. But there was an edge to them that made Kitiara glance sharply at the death knight.

Seeing him staring at her, his orange eyes burning with a strange intensity, Kitiara flushed. Realization that she was revealing more emotion than she intended made her angry, her flush deepened. She turned from Soth abruptly.

Walking across the room, which was furnished with an odd mixture of armor, weaponry, perfumed silken sheets, and thick fur rugs, Kitiara clasped the folds of her filmy nightdress together across her breasts with a shaking hand. It was a gesture

Lord Soth and his banshee followers sprang to life one day in my cubicle at TSR. I was designing a battle using Douglas Niles's excellent AD&D miniatures rules (then known as BATTLESYSTEM). It was to be an important supplemental part of the DRAGONLANCE D&D module, "Dragons of War," written by Laura Curtis and myself. In the middle of designing component units for the siege of the High Clerist's Tower, Lord Soth suddenly appeared on my imagined battlefield with his chariots of banshees behind him. In that rush of a moment, I knew his entire history, why he had fallen to this undead state, and what the banshees had to do with the tragic tale. I was so excited that I immediately ran over to Margaret's cubicle to tell her all about him. He instantly shoved his way into our text, and we have been trying to keep him at bay ever since. —TRH

951

that accomplished little in the way of modesty, and Kitiara knew it, even as she wondered why she made it. Certainly she had never been concerned with modesty before, especially around a creature who had fallen into a heap of ash three hundred years ago. But she suddenly felt uncomfortable under the gaze of those blazing eyes, staring at her from a nonexistent face. She felt naked and exposed.

"No, of course not," Kitiara replied coldly.

"He is, after all, a dark elf." Soth went on in the same even, almost bored tones. "And he makes no secret of the fact that he fears your brother more than death itself. So is it any wonder that he chooses now to fight on Raistlin's side rather than the side of a bunch of feeble old wizards who are quaking in their boots?"

"But he stood to gain so much!" Kitiara argued, trying her best to match her tone to Soth's. Shivering, she picked up a fur nightrobe that lay across the end of her bed and flung it around her shoulders. "They promised him the leadership of the Black Robes. He was certain to take Par-Salian's place after that as Head of the Conclave—undisputed master of magic on Krynn."

And you would have known other rewards, as well, Dark Elf, Kitiara added silently, pouring herself a glass of red wine. Once that insane brother of mine is defeated, no one will be able to stop you. What of *our* plans? You ruling with the staff, I with the sword. We could have brought the Knights to their knees! Driven the elves from their homeland—your homeland! You would have gone back in triumph, my darling, and I would have been at your side!

The wine glass slipped from her hand. She tried to catch it—Her grasp was too hasty, her grip too strong. The fragile glass shattered in her hand, cutting into her flesh. Blood mingled with the wine that dripped onto the carpet.

Battle scars traced over Kitiara's body like the hands of her lovers. She had borne her wounds without flinching, most without a murmur. But now her eyes flooded with tears. The pain seemed unbearable.

A wash bowl stood near. Kitiara plunged her hand into the cold water, biting her lip to keep from crying out. The water turned red instantly.

"Fetch one of the clerics!" she snarled at Lord Soth, who had remained standing, staring at her with his flickering eyes.

Walking to the door, the death knight called a servant who left immediately. Cursing beneath her breath, blinking back her tears, Kitiara grabbed a towel and wound it around her hand. By the time the cleric arrived, stumbling over his black robes in his haste, the towel was soaked through with blood, and Kitiara's face was ashen beneath her tanned skin.

The medallion of the Five-Headed Dragon brushed against Kit's hand as the cleric bent over it, muttering prayers to the Queen of Darkness. Soon the wounded flesh closed,† the bleeding stopped.

In the DRAGONLANCE *setting, clerics have the power to heal wounds. This is another holdover from the AD&D rules.*

"The cuts were not deep. There should be no lasting harm," the cleric said soothingly.

"A good thing for you!" Kitiara snapped, still fighting the unreasonable faintness that assailed her. "That is my sword hand!"

"You will wield a blade with your accustomed ease and skill, I assure your lordship," the cleric replied. "Will there be—"

"No! Get out!"

"My lord." The cleric bowed—"Sir Knight"—and left the room.

Unwilling to meet the gaze of Soth's flaming eyes, Kitiara kept her head turned away from the death knight, scowling at the vanishing, fluttering robes of the cleric.

"What fools! I detest keeping them around. Still, I suppose they come in handy now and then." Though it seemed perfectly healed, her hand still hurt. *All in my mind,* she told herself bitterly. "Well, what do you propose I do about . . . about the dark elf?" Before Soth could answer, however, Kitiara was on her feet, yelling for the servant.

"Clean that mess up. And bring me another glass." She struck the cowering man across the face. "One of the golden goblets this time. You know I detest these fragile elf-made things! Get them out of my sight! Throw them away!"

"Throw them away!" The servant ventured a protest. "But they are valuable, Lord. They came from the Tower of High Sorcery in Palanthas, a gift from—"

"I said get rid of them!" Grabbing them up, Kitiara flung them, one by one, against the wall of her room. The servant cringed, ducking as the glass flew over his head, smashing against the stone. When the last one left her fingers, she sat down into a chair in a corner and stared straight ahead, neither moving nor speaking.

The servant hastily swept up the broken glass, emptied the bloody water in the wash bowl, and departed. When he returned with the wine, Kitiara had still not moved. Neither had Lord Soth. The death knight remained standing in the center of the room, his eyes glowing in the gathering gloom of night.

"Shall I light the candles, Lord?" the servant asked softly, setting down the wine bottle and a golden goblet.

"Get out," Kitiara said, through stiff lips.

The servant bowed and left, closing the door behind him.

Moving with unheard steps, the death knight walked across the room. Coming to stand next to the still unmoving, seemingly unseeing Kitiara, he laid his hand upon her shoulder. She flinched at the touch of the invisible fingers, their cold piercing her heart. But she did not withdraw.

"Well," she said again, staring into the room whose only source of light now came from the flaming eyes of the death knight, "I asked you a question. What do we do to stop Dalamar and my brother in this madness? What do we do before the Dark Queen destroys us all?"

"You must attack Palanthas," said Lord Soth.

"I believe it can be done!" Kitiara murmured, thoughtfully tapping the hilt of her dagger against her thigh.

"Truly ingenious, my lord," said the commander of her forces with undisguised and unfeigned admiration in his voice.

The commander—a human near forty years of age—had scratched and clawed and murdered his way up through the ranks to attain his current position, General of the Dragonarmies. Stooped and ill-favored, disfigured by a scar that slashed across his face, the commander had never tasted the favors

enjoyed in the past by so many of Kitiara's other captains. But he was not without hope. Glancing over at her, he saw her face—unusually cold and stern these past few days—brighten with pleasure at his praise. She even deigned to smile at him— that crooked smile she knew how to use so well. The commander's heart beat faster.

"It is good to see you have not lost your touch," said Lord Soth, his hollow voice echoing through the map room.

The commander shuddered. He should be used to the death knight by now. The Dark Queen knew, he'd fought enough battles with him and his troop of skeletal warriors. But the chill of the grave surrounded the knight as his black cloak shrouded his charred and blood-stained armor.

How does she stand him? the commander wondered. They say he even haunts her bedchambers! The thought made the commander's heartbeat rapidly return to normal. Perhaps, after all, the slave women weren't so bad. At least when one was alone with them in the dark, one was *alone* in the dark!

"Of course, I have not lost my touch!" Kitiara returned with such fierce anger that the commander looked about uneasily, hurriedly manufacturing some excuse to leave. Fortunately, with the entire city of Sanction preparing for war, excuses were not hard to find.

"If you have no further need of me, my lord," the commander said, bowing, "I must check on the work of the armory. There is much to be done, and not much time in which to do it."

"Yes, go ahead," Kitiara muttered absently, her eyes on the huge map that was inlaid in tile upon the floor beneath her feet. Turning, the commander started to leave, his broadsword clanking against his armor. At the door, however, his lord's voice stopped him.

"Commander?"

He turned. "My lord?"

Kitiara started to say something, stopped, bit her lip, then continued, "I—I was wondering if you would join me for dinner this evening." She shrugged. "But, it is late to be asking. I presume you have made plans."

The commander hesitated, confused. His palms began to sweat. "As a matter of fact, lord, I *do* have a prior commitment, but that could easily be changed—"

"No," Kitiara said, a look of relief crossing her face. "No, that won't be necessary. Some other night. You are dismissed."

The commander, still puzzled, turned slowly and started once again to leave the room. As he did so, he caught a glimpse of the orange, burning eyes of the death knight, staring straight through him.

Now he would have to come up with a dinner engagement, he thought as he hurried down the hall. Easy enough. And he would send for one of the slave girls tonight—his favorite. . . .

"You should relax. Treat yourself to an evening of pleasure," Lord Soth said as the commander's footsteps faded away down the corridor of Kitiara's military headquarters.

"There is much to be done, and little time to do it," Kitiara replied, pretending to be totally absorbed in the map beneath her feet. She stood upon the place marked "Sanction," looking into the far north-western corner of the room where Palanthas nestled in the cleft of its protective mountains.

Following her gaze, Soth slowly paced the distance, coming to a halt at the only pass through the rugged mountains, a place marked "High Clerist's Tower."

"The Knights will try to stop you here, of course," Soth said. "Where they stopped you during the last war."†

Soth is recalling events that occurred in the latter chapters of Dragons of Winter Night.

Kitiara grinned, shook out her curly hair, and walked toward Soth. The lithe swagger was back in her step. "Now, won't that be a sight? All the pretty Knights, lined up in a row." Suddenly, feeling better than she had in months, Kitiara began to laugh. "You know, the looks on their faces when they see what we have in store for them will be almost worth waging the entire campaign."

Standing on the High Clerist's Tower, she ground it beneath her heel, then took a few quick steps to stand next to Palanthas.

"At last," she murmured, "the fine, fancy lady will feel the sword of war slit open her soft, ripe flesh." Smiling, she turned back to face Lord Soth.

"I think I will have the commander to dinner tonight after all. Send for him." Soth bowed his acquiescence, the orange eyes flaming with amusement. "We have many military matters to discuss," Kitiara laughed again, starting to unbuckle the straps of her armor. "Matters of unguarded flanks, breaching walls, thrust, and penetration. . . ."

"Now, calm down, Tanis," said Lord Gunthar good-naturedly. "You are overwrought."

Tanis Half-Elven muttered something.

"What was that?" Gunthar turned around, holding in his hand a mug of his finest ale (drawn from the barrel in the dark corner by the cellar stairs). He handed the ale to Tanis.

"I said you're damn right I'm overwrought!" the half-elf snapped, which wasn't what he had said at all, but was certainly more appropriate when talking to the head of the Knights of Solamnia than what he had actually spoken.

Lord Gunthar uth† Wistan stroked his long mustaches—the ages-old symbol of the Knights and one that was currently much in fashion—hiding his smile. He had heard, of course, what Tanis originally said. Gunthar shook his head. Why hadn't this matter been brought straight to the military? Now, as well as preparing for this minor flare-up of undoubtedly frustrated enemy forces, he had also to deal with black-robed wizards' apprentices, white-robed clerics, nervous heroes, and a librarian! Gunthar sighed and tugged at his mustaches gloomily. All he needed now was a kender. . . .

The uth in some Solamnic names (especially from Ergoth) is analogous to both the Gaelic mac and the Welsh ap of my own ancestry. It is a linking patronymic that might roughly be translated as "of." —TRH

"Tanis, my friend, sit down. Warm yourself by the fire. You've had a long journey, and it's cold for late spring. The sailors say something about prevailing winds or some such nonsense. I trust your trip was a good one? I don't mind telling you, I prefer griffons to dragons—"

"Lord Gunthar," Tanis said tensely, remaining standing, "I did not fly all the way to Sancrist† to discuss the prevailing winds nor the merits of griffons over dragons! We are in danger! Not only Palanthas, but the world! If Raistlin succeeds—" Tanis's fist clenched. Words failed him.

Filling his own mug from the pitcher that Wills, his old retainer, had brought up from the cellar,

I have always preferred to set scenes up with dialogue when possible. I think dialogue is far more interesting and carries a better voice than direct prose. —TRH

Gunthar walked over to stand beside the half-elf. Putting his hand on Tanis's shoulder, he turned the man to face him.

"Sturm Brightblade spoke highly of you, Tanis. You and Laurana were the closest friends he had."

Tanis bowed his head at these words. Even now, more than two years since Sturm's death,† he could not think of the loss of his friend without sorrow.

Sturm Brightblade died in Dragons of Winter Night, *Book III, Chapter 13.*

"I would have esteemed you on that recommendation alone, for I loved and respected Sturm like one of my own sons," Lord Gunthar continued earnestly. "But I have come to admire and like you myself, Tanis. Your bravery in battle was unquestioned, your honor, your nobility worthy of a Knight." Tanis shook his head irritably at this talk of honor and nobility, but Gunthar did not notice. "Those honors accorded you at the end of the war you more than merited. Your work since the war's end has been outstanding. You and Laurana have brought together nations that have been separated for centuries. Porthios has signed the treaty and, once the dwarves of Thorbardin have chosen a new king, they will sign as well."

"Thank you, Lord Gunthar," Tanis said, holding his mug of untouched ale in his hand and staring fixedly into the fire. "Thank you for your praise. I wish I felt I had earned it. Now, if you'll tell me where this trail of sugar is leading—"

"I see you are far more human than you are elven," Gunthar said, with a slight smile. "Very well, Tanis. I will skip the elven amenities and get right to the point. I think your past experiences have made you jumpy—you and Elistan both. Let's be honest, my friend. You are not a warrior. You were never trained as such. You stumbled into this last war by accident. Now, come with me. I want to show you something. Come, come . . ."

I may have come up with these Orders, although I certainly do not remember doing so. I believe the Rose came from the War of the Roses, as well as being a symbol of passion. Because these are Orders of a knighthood, Sword and Crown seemed logical extensions. —TRH

Tanis set his full mug down upon the mantelpiece and allowed himself to be led by Gunthar's strong hand. They walked across the room that was filled with the solid, plain, but comfortable furniture preferred by the Knights. This was Gunthar's war room, shields and swords were mounted on the walls, along with the banners of the three Orders of Knights†—the Rose, the Sword, and the Crown. Trophies of battles fought through the years gleamed

from the cases where they were carefully preserved. In an honored place, spanning the entire length of the wall, was a dragonlance—the first one Theros Ironfeld had forged. Ranged around it were various goblin swords, a wicked saw-toothed blade of a draconian, a huge, double-bladed ogre sword, and a broken sword that had belonged to the ill-fated Knight, Derek Crownguard.†

It was an impressive array, testifying to a lifetime of honored service in the Knights. Gunthar walked past it without a glance, however, heading for a corner of the room where a large table stood. Rolled-up maps were stuffed neatly into small compartments beneath the table, each compartment carefully labeled. After studying them for a moment, Gunthar reached down, pulled out a map, and spread it out upon the table's surface. He motioned Tanis nearer. The half-elf came closer, scratching his beard, and trying to look interested.

Derek Crownguard was a Knight of Solamnia who aided the Companions during the War of the Lance. He died, along with his troops, at the Battle of the Tower of the High Clerist in Dragons of Winter Night.

Gunthar rubbed his hands with satisfaction. He was in his element now. "It's a matter of logistics, Tanis. Pure and simple. Look, here are the Dragon Highlord's armies, bottled up in Sanction. Now I admit the Highlord is strong, she has a vast number of draconians, goblins, and humans who would like nothing better than to see the war start up again. And I also admit that our spies have reported increased activity in Sanction. The Highlord is up to something. But attacking Palanthas! Name of the Abyss, Tanis, look at the amount of territory she'd have to cover! And most of it controlled by the Knights! And even if she had the manpower to fight her way through, look how long she'd have to extend her supply lines! It would take her entire army just to guard her lines. We could cut them easily, any number of places."

Gunthar pulled on his mustaches again. "Tanis, if there was one Highlord in that army I came to respect, it was Kitiara. She is ruthless and ambitious, but she is also intelligent, and she is certainly not given to taking unnecessary risks. She has waited two years, building up her armies, fortifying herself in a place she knows we dare not attack. She has gained too much to throw it away on a wild scheme like this."

"Suppose this isn't her plan," Tanis muttered.

"What other plan could she possibly have?" Gunthar asked patiently.

"I don't know," Tanis snapped. "You say you respect her, but do you respect her enough? Do you fear her enough? I know her, and I have a feeling that she has something in mind. . . ." His voice trailed off, he scowled down at the map.

Gunthar kept quiet. He'd heard strange rumors about Tanis Half-Elven and this Kitiara. He didn't believe them, of course, but felt it better not to pursue the subject of the depth of the half-elf's knowledge of this woman further.

"You don't believe this, do you?" Tanis asked abruptly. "Any of it?"

Shifting uncomfortably, Gunthar smoothed both his long, gray mustaches and, bending down, began to roll up the map, using extreme care. "Tanis, my son, you know I respect you—"

"We've been through that."

Gunthar ignored the interruption. "And you know that there is no one in this world I hold in deeper reverence than Elistan. But when you two bring me a tale told to you by one of the Black Robes—and a dark elf at that—a tale about this wizard, Raistlin, entering the Abyss and challenging† the Queen of Darkness! Well, I'm sorry, Tanis. I am not a young man anymore by any means. I've seen many strange things in my life. But this sounds like a child's bedtime story!"

"So they said of dragons," Tanis murmured, his face flushing beneath his beard. He stood, head bowed, for a moment, then, scratching his beard, he looked at Gunthar intently. "My lord, I watched Raistlin grow up. I have traveled with him, seen him, fought both with him and against him. I *know* what this man is capable of!" Tanis grasped Gunthar's arm with his hand. "If you will not accept my counsel, then accept Elistan's! We need you, Lord Gunthar! We need you, we need the Knights. You must reinforce the High Clerist's Tower. We have little time. Dalamar tells us that time has no meaning on the planes of the Dark Queen's existence. Raistlin might fight her for months or even years there, but that would seem only days to us. Dalamar believes his master's return is imminent. I believe him, and so does Elistan. Why do we believe

It is archetypical in the hero's journey that the guardians—the great powers over us who are supposed to take care of such things—are blind to the dangers involved. If they were not, there would be no hero's journey to take, for the parent/guardian figure would just take care of the problem for us. Guardians in the grand argument story of Dramatica are therefore of necessity weak and less than all powerful—either through fact or, as in this case, choice. —TRH

him, Lord Gunthar? Because Dalamar is frightened. He is afraid—and so are we.

"Your spies say there is unusual activity in Sanction. Surely, that is evidence enough! Believe me, Lord Gunthar, Kitiara will come to her brother's aid. She knows he will set her up as ruler of the world if he succeeds. And she is gambler enough to risk everything for that chance! Please, Lord Gunthar, if you won't listen to me, at least come to Palanthas! Talk to Elistan!"

Lord Gunthar studied the man before him carefully. The leader of the Knights had risen to his position because he was, basically, a just and honest man. He was also a keen judge of character. He had liked and admired the half-elf since meeting him after the end of the war. But he had never been able to get close to him. There was something about Tanis, a reserved, withdrawn air that permitted few to cross the invisible barriers he set up.

Looking at him now, Gunthar felt suddenly closer than he had ever come before. He saw wisdom in the slightly slanted eyes, wisdom that had not come easily, wisdom that came through inner pain and suffering. He saw fear, the fear of one whose courage is so much a part of him that he readily admits he is afraid. He saw in him a leader of men. Not one who merely waves a sword and leads a charge in battle, but a leader who leads quietly, by drawing the best out of people, by helping them achieve things they never knew were in them.

And, at last, Gunthar understood something he had never been able to fathom. He knew now why Sturm Brightblade, whose lineage went back unsullied through generations, had chosen to follow this bastard half-elf, who—if rumors were true—was the product of a brutal rape. He knew now why Laurana, an elven princess and one of the strongest, most beautiful women he had ever known, had risked everything—even her life—for love of this man.

"Very well, Tanis." Lord Gunthar's stern face relaxed, the cool, polite tones of his voice grew warmer. "I will return to Palanthas with you. I will mobilize the Knights and set up our defenses at the High Clerist's Tower. As I said, our spies did inform us that there is unusual activity going on in

Sanction. It won't hurt the Knights to turn out. Been a long time since we've had field drill."

Decision made, Lord Gunthar immediately proceeded to turn the household upside down, shouting for Wills, his retainer, shouting for his armor to be brought, his sword sharpened, his griffon readied. Soon servants were flying here and there, his lady-wife came in, looking resigned, and insisted that he pack his heavy, fur-lined cloak even though it *was* near Spring Dawning celebration.

Forgotten in the confusion, Tanis walked back to the fireplace, picked up his mug of ale, and sat down to enjoy it. But, after all, he did not taste it. Staring into the flames, he saw, once again, a charming, crooked smile, dark curly hair. . . .

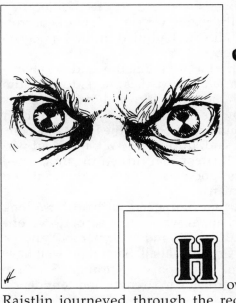

CHAPTER
6

How long she and Raistlin journeyed through the red-tinged, distorted land of the Abyss, Crysania had no idea. Time ceased to have any meaning or relevance. Sometimes it seemed they had been here only a few seconds, sometimes she knew she had been walking the strange, shifting terrain for weary years. She had healed herself of the poison, but she felt weak, drained. The scratches on her arms would not close. She wrapped fresh bandages about them each day. By night, they were soaked through with blood.

She was hungry, but it was not a hunger that required food to sustain life so much as a hunger to taste a strawberry, or a mouthful of warm, fresh-baked bread, or a sprig of mint. She did not feel thirst either,† and yet she dreamed of clear running water and bubbling wine and the sharp, pungent

One's needs are never lacking in the abyss, but the wants are never satisfied. —TRH

Needs are satisfied in the Abyss, but what is lacking are the small things that make life pleasurable and that we so often take for granted until we don't have them anymore. —MW

aroma of tarbean tea. In this land, all the water was tinged reddish brown and smelled of blood.

Yet, they made progress. At least so Raistlin said. He seemed to gain in strength as Crysania grew weaker. Now it was he who helped her walk sometimes. It was he who pushed them onward without rest, passing through town after town, always nearing, he said, Godshome. The mirror-image villages of this land below blurred together in Crysania's mind—Que-shu, Xak Tsaroth. They crossed the Abyss's New Sea—a dreadful journey. Looking into the water, Crysania saw the horror-filled faces of all who had died in the Cataclysm staring up at her.

They landed at a place Raistlin said was Sanction. Crysania felt her weakest here, for Raistlin told her it was the center of worship for the Dark Queen's followers. Her Temples were built far below the mountains known as the Lords of Doom. Here, Raistlin said, during the War, they had performed the evil rites† that turned the unhatched children of the good dragons into the foul and twisted draconians.

Draconians were made from the eggs of good dragons, in rites performed by an evil cleric, an evil mage, and a red dragon.

Nothing further happened to them for a long while—or perhaps it was only a second. No one looked twice at Raistlin in his black robes and no one looked at Crysania at all. She might well have been invisible. They passed through Sanction easily, Raistlin growing in strength and confidence. He told Crysania they were very close now. Godshome was located somewhere to the north in Khalkist Mountains.†

Godshome is about seventy-five miles north of Sanction, through mountainous territory, though the rules of distance and time may be subject to change in the Abyss.

How he could tell any direction at all in this weird and awful land was beyond Crysania—there was nothing to guide them, no sun, no moons, no stars. It was never really night and never truly day, just some sort of dreary, reddish in-between. She was thinking of this, trudging wearily beside Raistlin, not watching where they were going since it all looked the same anyway, when, suddenly, the archmage came to a halt. Hearing his sharp intake of breath, feeling him stiffen, Crysania looked up in swift alarm.

A middle-aged man dressed in the white robes of a teacher was walking down the road toward them. . . .

"Repeat the words after me, remembering to give them the proper inflection." Slowly he said the words. Slowly the class repeated them. All except one.

"Raistlin!"

The class fell silent.

"Master?" Raistlin did not bother to conceal the sneer in his voice as he said the word.

"I didn't see your lips moving."

"Perhaps that is because they were not moving, Master," Raistlin replied.

If someone else in the class of young magic-users had made such a remark, the pupils would have snickered. But they knew Raistlin felt the same scorn for them that he felt for the Master, and so they glowered at him and shifted uncomfortably.

"You know the spell, do you, apprentice?"

"Certainly I know the spell," Raistlin snapped. "I knew it when I was six! When did you learn it? Last night?"

The Master glared, his face purpled with rage. "You have gone too far this time, apprentice! You have insulted me once too often!"

The classroom faded before Raistlin's eyes, melting away. Only the Master remained and, as Raistlin watched, his old teacher's white robes turned to black! His stupid, paunchy face twisted into a malevolent, crafty face of evil. A bloodstone pendant appeared, hanging around his neck.

"Fistandantilus!" Raistlin gasped.

"Again we meet, apprentice. But now, where is your magic?" The wizard laughed. Reaching up a withered hand, he began fingering the bloodstone pendant.

Panic swept over Raistlin. Where *was* his magic? Gone! His hands shook. The words of spells tumbled into his mind; only to slip away before he could grasp hold of them. A ball of flame appeared in Fistandantilus's hands. Raistlin choked on his fear.

The Staff! he thought suddenly. The Staff of Magius. Surely its magic will not be affected! Raising the staff, holding it before him, he called upon it to protect him. But the staff began to twist and writhe in Raistlin's hand. "No!" he cried in terror and anger. "Obey my command! Obey!"

The staff coiled itself around his arm and it was no longer a staff at all, but a huge snake. Glistening fangs sank into his flesh.

Screaming, Raistlin dropped to his knees, trying desperately to free himself from the staff's poisonous bite. But, battling one enemy, he had forgotten the other. Hearing the spidery words of magic being chanted, he looked up fearfully. Fistandantilus was gone, but in his place stood a drow—a dark elf. The dark elf Raistlin had fought in his final battle of the Test. And then the dark elf was Dalamar, hurling a fireball at him, and then the fireball became a sword, driven into his flesh by a beardless dwarf.†

A beardless dwarf is a cursed dwarf, though I do not know to which particular dwarf this alludes. —TRH

Flames burst around him, steel pierced his body, fangs dug into his skin. He was sinking, sinking into the blackness, when he was bathed in white light and wrapped in white robes and held close to a soft, warm breast. . . .

And he smiled, for he knew by the flinching of the body shielding his and the low cries of anguish, that the weapons were striking her, not him.

"**L**ord Gunthar!" said Amothus, Lord of Palanthas, rising to his feet. "An unexpected pleasure. And you, too, Tanis Half-Elven. I assume you're both here to plan the War's End celebration. I'm so glad. Now we can get started on it *early* this year. I, that is, the committee and I believe—"

"Nonsense," said Lord Gunthar crisply, walking about Amothus's audience chamber and staring at it with a critical eye, already calculating—in his mind—what it would take to fortify it if necessary. "We're here to discuss the defense of the city."

Lord Amothus blinked at the Knight, who was peering out the windows and muttering to himself. Once he turned and snapped, "Too much glass,"† which statement increased the lord's confusion to such an extent that he could only stammer an apology and then stand helplessly in the center of the room.

Glass, while uncommon in the Middle Ages and a sign of great wealth, is nevertheless common here in Palanthas. —TRH

967

"Are we under attack?" he ventured to ask hesitantly, after a few more moments of Gunthar's reconnaissance.

Lord Gunthar cast Tanis a sharp look. With a sigh, Tanis politely reminded Lord Amothus of the warning the dark elf, Dalamar, had brought them—the probability that the Dragon Highlord, Kitiara, planned to try to enter Palanthas in order to aid her brother, Raistlin, Master of the Tower of High Sorcery, in his fight against the Queen of Darkness.

"Oh, yes!" Lord Amothus's face cleared. He waved a delicate, deprecating hand, as though brushing away gnats. "But I don't believe you need be concerned about Palanthas, Lord Gunthar. The High Clerist's Tower—"

"—is being manned. I'm doubling the strength of our forces there. That's where the major assault will come, of course. No other way into Palanthas except by sea to the north, and we rule the seas. No, it will come overland. Should matters go wrong, though, Amothus, I want Palanthas ready to defend herself. Now—"

Having mounted the horse of action, so to speak, Gunthar charged ahead. Completely riding over Lord Amothus's murmured remonstration that perhaps he should discuss this with his generals, Gunthar galloped on, and soon left Amothus choking in the dust of troop disbursements, supply requisitions, armorment caches, and the like. Amothus gave himself for lost. Sitting down, he assumed an expression of polite interest, and immediately began to think about something else. It was all nonsense anyway. Palanthas had never been touched in battle. Armies had to get past the High Clerist's Tower† first and none—not even the great dragon armies of the last war—had been able to do that.

The placement of the High Clerist's Tower is one of military strategy. The mountains surrounding its guarded cleft are otherwise impassable and would require an army approaching the Palanthian lands to the north to divert either many hundreds of miles east or even farther to the south. —TRH

Tanis, watching all of this, and knowing well what Amothus was thinking, smiled grimly to himself and was just beginning to wonder how he, too, might escape the onslaught when there was a soft knock upon the great, ornately carved, gilt doors. With the look of one who hears the trumpets of the rescuing division, Amothus sprang to his feet, but before he could say a word, the doors opened and an elderly servant entered.

Charlest had been in the service of the royal house of Palanthas for well over half a century. They could not get along without him, and he knew it. He knew everything—from the exact count of the number of wine bottles in the cellar, to which elves should be seated next to which at dinner, to when the linen had been aired last. Though always dignified and deferential, there was a look upon his face which implied that when he died, he expected the royal house to crumble down about its master's ears.

"I am sorry to disturb you, my lord," Charles began.

"*Quite* all right!" Lord Amothus cried, beaming with pleasure. "Quite all right. Please—"

"But there is an urgent message for Tanis Half-Elven," finished Charles imperturbably, with only the slightest hint of rebuke to his master for interrupting him.

"Oh," Lord Amothus looked blank and extremely disappointed. "Tanis Half-Elven?"

"Yes, my lord," Charles replied.

"Not for me?" Amothus ventured, seeing the rescuing division vanish over the horizon.

"No, my lord."

Amothus sighed. "Very well. Thank you, Charles. Tanis, I suppose you had better—"

But Tanis was already halfway across the room.

"What is it? Not from Laurana—"

"This way, please, my lord," Charles said, ushering Tanis out the door. At a glance from Charles, the half-elf remembered just in time to turn and bow to Lords Amothus and Gunthar. The knight smiled and waved his hand. Lord Amothus could not refrain from casting Tanis an envious glance, then sank back down to listen to a list of equipment necessary for the boiling of oil.

Charles carefully and slowly shut the doors behind him.

"What is it?" Tanis asked, following the servant down the hall. "Didn't the messenger say anything else?"

"Yes, my lord." Charles's face softened into an expression of gentle sorrow. "I was not to reveal this unless it became absolutely necessary to free you from your engagement. Revered Son, Elistan, is dying. He is not expected to live through the night."

Charles seemed to be the perfect name for this character, because he is so pragmatic and not fantastical. —MW

Names give us a feeling for a place we are visiting. Every now and then, it is comforting—and grounding—to come across the familiar amid all the strange-sounding names in fantasy. —TRH

The Temple lawns were peaceful and serene in the fading light of day. The sun was setting, not with fiery splendor, but with a soft, pearlized radiance, filling the sky with a rainbow of gentle color like that of an inverted sea shell. Tanis, expecting to find crowds of people standing about, waiting for news, while white-robed clerics ran here and there in confusion, was startled to see that all was calm and orderly. People rested on the lawn as usual, white-robed clerics strolled beside the flower beds, talking together in low voices or, if alone, appearing lost in silent meditation.

Perhaps the messenger was wrong or misinformed, Tanis thought. But then, as he hurried across the velvety green grass, he passed a young cleric. She looked up at him, and he saw her eyes were red and swollen with weeping. But she smiled at him, nonetheless, wiping away traces of her grief as she went on her way.

And then Tanis remembered that neither Lord Amothus, ruler of Palanthas, nor Lord Gunthar, head of the Knights of Solamnia, had been informed. The half-elf smiled sadly in sudden understanding. Elistan was dying as he had lived—with quiet dignity.

A young acolyte met Tanis at the Temple door.

"Enter and welcome, Tanis Half-Elven," the young man said softly. "You are expected. Come this way."

Cool shadows washed over Tanis. Inside the Temple, the signs of grieving were clear. An elven harpist played sweet music, clerics stood together, arms around each other, sharing solace in their hour of trial. Tanis's own eyes filled with tears.

"We are grateful that you returned in time," the acolyte continued, leading Tanis deeper into the inner confines of the quiet Temple. "We feared you might not. We left word where we could, but only with those we knew we could count upon to keep the secret of our great sorrow. It is Elistan's wish that he be allowed to die quietly and peacefully."

The half-elf nodded brusquely, glad his beard hid his tears. Not that he was ashamed of them. Elves revere life above all things, holding it to be the most sacred of the gifts from the gods. Elves do not hide their feelings, as do humans. But Tanis feared the sight of his grief might upset Elistan. He knew the good man's one regret in dying lay in the knowledge that

his death would bring such bitter sorrow to those left behind.

Tanis and his guide passed through an inner chamber where stood Garad and other Revered Sons and Daughters, heads bowed, speaking words of comfort to each other. Beyond them, a door was shut. Everyone's glance strayed to that door, and Tanis had no doubt who lay beyond it.

Looking up on hearing Tanis enter, Garad himself crossed the room to greet the half-elf.

"We are so glad you could come," the older elf said cordially. He was Silvanesti, Tanis recognized, and must have been one of the first of the elven converts to the religion that they had, long ago, forgotten. "We feared you might not return in time."

"This must have been sudden," Tanis murmured, uncomfortably aware that his sword—which he had forgotten to take off—was clanking, sounding loud and harsh in such peaceful, sorrowful surroundings. He clapped his hand over it.

"Yes, he was taken gravely ill the night you left," Garad sighed. "I do not know what was said in that room, but the shock was great. He has been in terrible pain. Nothing we could do would help him. Finally, Dalamar, the wizard's apprentice"—Garad could not help but frown—"came to the Temple. He brought with him a potion that would, he said, ease pain. How he came to know of what was transpiring, I cannot guess. Strange things happen in that place." He glanced out the window to where the Tower stood, a dark shadow, defiantly denying the sun's bright light.

"You let him in?" Tanis asked, startled.

"I would have refused," Garad said grimly. "But Elistan gave orders that he should be allowed entry. And, I must admit, his potion worked. The pain left our master, and he will be granted the right to die in peace."

"And Dalamar?"

"He is within. He has neither moved nor spoken since he came, but sits silently in a corner. Yet, his presence seems to comfort Elistan, and so we permit him to stay."

I'd like to see you try to make him leave, Tanis thought privately, but said nothing. The door opened. People looked up fearfully, but it was only the acolyte

who had knocked softly and who was conferring with someone on the other side. Turning, he beckoned to Tanis.

The half-elf entered the small, plainly furnished room, trying to move softly, as did the clerics with their whispering robes and padded slippers. But his sword rattled, his boots clomped, the buckles of his leather armor jingled. He sounded, to his ears, like an army of dwarves. His face burning, he tried to remedy matters by walking on tiptoe. Elistan, turning his head feebly upon the pillow, looked over at the half-elf and began to laugh.

"One would think, my friend, that you were coming to rob me," Elistan remarked, lifting a wasted hand and holding it out to Tanis.

The half-elf tried to smile. He heard the door shut softly behind him and he was aware of a shadowy figure darkening one corner of the room. But he ignored all this. Kneeling beside the bed of the man he had helped rescue from the mines of Pax Tharkas,† the man whose gentle influence had played such an important role in his life and in Laurana's, Tanis took the dying man's hand and held it firmly.

Tanis and the Companions rescued Elistan—as well as many other captives—from Pax Tharkas in the latter chapters of Dragons of Autumn Twilight.

"Would that I were able to fight this enemy for you, Elistan," Tanis said, looking at the shrunken white hand clasped in his own strong, tanned one.

"Not an enemy, Tanis, not an enemy. An old friend is coming for me." He withdrew his hand gently from Tanis's grasp, then patted the half-elf's arm. "No, you don't understand. But you will, someday, I promise. And now, I did not call you here to burden you with saying good-bye. I have a commission to give to you, my friend." He motioned. The young acolyte came forward, bearing a wooden box, and gave it into Elistan's hands. Then, he retired, returning to stand silently beside the door.

The dark figure in the corner did not move.

Lifting the lid of the box, Elistan removed a folded piece of pure white parchment. Taking Tanis's hand, he placed the parchment in the half-elf's palm, then closed his fingers over it.

"Give this to Crysania," he said softly. "If she survives, she is to be the next head of the church." Seeing the dubious, disapproving expression come onto Tanis's face, Elistan smiled. "My friend, you have walked in darkness—none know that better than I.

We came near losing you, Tanis. But you endured the night and faced the daylight, strengthened by the knowledge that you had gained. This is what I hope for Crysania. She is strong in her faith, but, as you yourself noted, she lacks warmth, compassion, humanity. She had to see with her own eyes the lessons that the fall of the Kingpriest taught us. She had to be hurt, Tanis, and hurt deeply, before she would be able to react with compassion to the hurt of others. Above all, Tanis, she had to love."†

Elistan closed his eyes, his face, drawn with suffering, filled with grief. "I would have chosen differently for her, my friend, had I been able. I saw the road she walked. But, who questions the ways of the gods? Certainly not I. Although"—opening his eyes, he looked up at Tanis, and the half-elf saw a glint of anger in them—"I might argue with them a bit."

Tanis heard, behind him, the soft step of the acolyte. Elistan nodded. "Yes, I know. They fear that visitors tire me. They do, but I will find rest soon enough." The cleric closed his eyes, smiling. "Yes, I will rest. My old friend is coming to walk with me, to guide my feeble steps."

Rising to his feet, Tanis cast a questioning glance at the acolyte, who shook his head.

"We do not know of whom he speaks," the young cleric murmured. "He has talked of little else but this old friend. We thought, perhaps, it might be you—"

But Elistan's voice rose clearly from his bed. "Farewell, Tanis Half-Elven. Give my love to Laurana. Garad and the others"—he nodded toward the doorway—"know of my wishes in this matter of the succession. They know that I have entrusted this to you. They will help you all they can. Good-bye, Tanis. May Paladine's blessing be with you."

Tanis could say nothing. Reaching down, he pressed the cleric's hand, nodded, struggled to speak, and at last gave up. Turning abruptly, he walked past the dark and silent figure in the corner and left the room, his vision blinded by tears.

Garad accompanied him to the front entrance of the Temple. "I know what Elistan has charged you with," the cleric said, "and, believe me, I hope with

"You cannot love a thing without wanting to fight for it. You cannot fight without something to fight for. To love a thing without wishing to fight for it is not love at all; it is lust." [Appreciations and Criticisms of the Works of Charles Dickens, G.K. Chesterton, London, J. M. Dent & sons, Ltd, 1911.]

all my heart his wishes come to pass. Lady Crysania is, I understand, on some sort of pilgrimage that could prove very dangerous?"

"Yes," was all Tanis could trust himself to answer.

Garad sighed. "May Paladine be with her. We are praying for her. She is a strong woman. The church needs such youth and such strength if it is to grow. If you need any help, Tanis, please know that you can call upon us."

The half-elf could only mutter a polite reply. Bowing, Garad hurried back to be with his dying master. Tanis paused a moment near the doorway in an effort to regain control of himself before stepping outside. As he stood there, thinking over Elistan's words, he became aware of an argument being carried on near the Temple door.

"I am sorry, sir, but I cannot permit you to go inside," a young acolyte was saying firmly.

"But I tell you I'm here to see Elistan," returned a querulous, crotchety voice.

Tanis closed his eyes, leaning against the wall. He knew that voice. Memories washed over him with an intensity so painful that, for a moment, he could neither move nor speak.

"Perhaps, if you gave me your name," the acolyte said patiently, "I could ask him—"

"I am—The name is—" The voice hesitated, sounding a bit bewildered, then muttered. "I knew it yesterday . . ."

Tanis heard the sound of a wooden staff thumping irritably against the Temple steps. The voice raised shrilly. "I am a very important person, young man. And I'm not accustomed to being treated with such impertinence. Now get out of my way before you force me to do something I'll regret. I mean, you'll regret. Well, one of us will regret it."

"I'm terribly sorry, sir," the acolyte repeated, his patience obviously wearing thin, "but without a name I cannot allow—"

There was the sound of a brief scuffle, then silence, then Tanis heard a truly ominous sound—the sound of pages being turned. Smiling through his tears, the half-elf walked to the door. Looking outside, he saw an old wizard standing on the Temple stairs. Dressed in mouse-colored robes, his misshapen wizard's hat appearing ready to topple from his head at the

slightest opportunity, the ancient wizard was a most disreputable sight.† He had leaned the plain wooden staff he carried against the Temple wall and now, ignoring the flushed and indignant acolyte, the wizard was flipping through the pages of his spellbook, muttering "Fireball . . . Fireball. How does that dratted spell go? . . ."†

Gently, Tanis placed his hand upon the acolyte's shoulder. "He truly is an important person," the half-elf said softly. "You can let him in. I'll take full responsibility."

"He is?" The acolyte looked dubious.

At the sound of Tanis's voice, the wizard raised his head and glanced about. "Eh? Important person? Where?" Seeing Tanis, he started. "Oh, there! How do you do, sir?" He started to extend his hand, became entangled in his robes, and dropped his spellbook on his foot. Bending down to pick it up, he knocked over his staff, sending it down the steps with a clatter. In the confusion, his hat tumbled off. It took Tanis and the acolyte both to get the old man back together again.

"Ouch, my toe! Confound it! Lost my place. Stupid staff! Where's my hat?"

Eventually, however, he was more or less intact. Stuffing the spellbook back in a pouch, he planted his hat firmly on his head. (Having attempted, at first, to do those two things in reverse order.) Unfortunately, the hat immediately slipped down, covering his eyes.

"Struck blind, by the gods!" the old wizard stated in awe, groping about with his hands.

This matter was soon remedied. The young acolyte—with an even more dubious glance at Tanis— gently pushed the wizard's hat to the back of his white-haired head. Glaring at the acolyte irritably, the old wizard turned to Tanis. "Important person? Yes, so you are . . . I think. Have we met before?"

"Indeed, yes," Tanis replied. "But *you* are the important person I was referring to, Fizban."

"I am?" The old wizard seemed staggered for a moment. Then, with a humpf, he glared again at the young cleric. "Well, of course. Told you so! Stand aside, stand aside," he ordered the acolyte irritably.

Entering the Temple door, the old man turned to look at Tanis from beneath the brim of the battered

Fizban's fumbling, I believe, is an outward parable apparent for all who see him—an unconscious reflection of the fact that while he is their shepherd/guardian, he will not solve their problems for them. He appears weak so that others will depend upon themselves rather than his god-like powers. Indeed, it is a message that he will not use such powers should it interfere with their agency of choice.
—TRH

"The wizard points his finger and speaks the range (distance and height) at which the fireball is to burst. A streak flashes from the pointing digit and, unless it impacts upon a material body or solid barrier prior to attaining the prescribed range, blossoms into the fireball (an early impact results in early detonation). The material component of this spell is a tiny ball of bat guano and sulphur." [2ⁿᵈ Edition ADVANCED DUNGEONS & DRAGONS Player's Handbook, *by David "Zeb" Cook, TSR, 1997, p. 192.]*

hat. Pausing, he laid his hand on the half-elf's arm. The befuddled look left the old wizard's face. He stared at Tanis intently.

"You have never faced a darker hour, Half-Elven," the old wizard said gravely. "There is hope, but love must triumph."

With that, he toddled off and, almost immediately, blundered into a closet. Two clerics came to his rescue, and guided him on.

"Who *is* he?" the young acolyte asked, staring, perplexed, after the old wizard.

"A friend of Elistan's," Tanis murmured. "A very old friend."

As he left the Temple, Tanis heard a voice wail, "My hat!"

CHAPTER 8

"Crysania. . . ."

There was no reply, only a low moaning sound.

"Shh. It's all right. You have been hurt, but the enemy is gone. Drink this, it will ease the pain."

Taking some herbs from a pouch, Raistlin mixed them in a mug of steaming water and, lifting Crysania from the bed of blood-soaked leaves upon which she lay, he held the mug to her lips. As she drank it, her face smoothed, her eyes opened.

"Yes," she murmured, leaning against him. "That is better."

"Now," continued Raistlin smoothly, "you must pray to Paladine to heal you, Revered Daughter. We have to keep going."

"I—I don't know, Raistlin. I'm so weak and—and Paladine seems so far away!"

"Pray to Paladine?" said a stern voice. "You blaspheme, Black Robe!"

Frowning, annoyed, Raistlin glanced up. His eyes widened. "Sturm!" he gasped.

But the young knight did not hear him. He was staring at Crysania, watching in awe as the wounds upon her body closed, though they did not heal completely. "Witches!" cried the knight, drawing his sword. "Witches!"

"Witches!" Crysania raised her head. "No, Sir Knight. We are not witches. I am a cleric, a cleric of Paladine! Look at the medallion I wear!"

"You lie!" Sturm said fiercely. "There are no clerics! They vanished in the Cataclysm. And, if you were, what would you be doing in the company of this dark one of evil?"

"Sturm! It's me, Raistlin!" The archmage rose to his feet. "Look at me! Don't you recognize me?"

The young knight turned his sword upon the mage, its point at Raistlin's throat. "I do not know by what sorcerous ways you have conjured up my name, Black Robe, but, speak it once more and it will go badly for you. We deal shortly with witches in Solace."

"As you are a virtuous and holy knight, bound by vows of chivalry and obedience, I beg you for justice," Crysania said, rising to her feet slowly, with Raistlin's help.

The young man's stern face smoothed. He bowed, and sheathed his sword, but not without a sideways glance at Raistlin. "You speak truly, madam. I am bound by such vows and I will grant you justice."

Even as he spoke, the bed of leaves became a wooden floor; the trees—benches; the sky above— a ceiling; the road—an aisle between the benches. We are in a Hall of Judgment, Raistlin saw, momentarily dizzied by the sudden change. His arm around Crysania still, he helped her to sit down at a small table that stood in the center of the room. Before them loomed a podium. Glancing behind them, Raistlin saw that the room was packed with people, all watching with interest and enjoyment.

He stared. He knew these people! There was Otik, the owner of the Inn of the Last Home, eating a plateful of spiced potatoes. There was Tika, her red curls bouncing, pointing at Crysania and saying

something and laughing. And Kitiara! Lounging against the doorway, surrounded by admiring young men, her hand on the hilt of her sword, she looked over at Raistlin and winked.

Raistlin glanced about feverishly. His father,† a poor woodcutter, sat in a corner, his shoulders bent, that perpetual look of worry and care on his face. Laurana sat apart, her cool elven beauty shining like a bright star in the darkest night.

Beside him, Crysania cried out, "Elistan!" Rising to her feet, she stretched out her hand, but the cleric only looked at her sadly and sternly and shook his head.

"Rise and do honor!" rang out a voice.

With much shuffling of feet and scraping of the benches, everyone in the Hall of Judgment stood up. A respectful silence descended upon the crowd as the judge entered. Dressed in the gray robes of Gilean, God of Neutrality, the judge took his place behind the podium and turned to face the accused.

"Tanis!" Raistlin cried, taking a step forward.

But the bearded half-elf only frowned at this unseemly conduct while a grumbling old dwarf—the bailiff—stumped over and prodded Raistlin in the side with the butt-end of his battle-axe. "Sit down, witch, and don't speak unless you're spoken to."

"Flint?" Raistlin grabbed the dwarf by the arm. "Don't you know me?"

"And don't touch the bailiff!" Flint roared, incensed, jerking his arm away. "Humpf," he grumbled as he stalked back to take his place beside the judge. "No respect for my age or my station. You'd think I was a sack of meal to be handled by everyone—"

"That will do, Flint," said Tanis, sternly eyeing Raistlin and Crysania. "Now, who brings the charges against these two?"

"I do," said a knight in shining armor, rising to his feet.

"Very well, Sturm Brightblade," Tanis said, "you will have a chance to present your charges. And who defends these two?"

Raistlin started to rise and reply, but he was interrupted.

"Me! Here, Tanis—uh, your honorship! Me, over here! Wait. I—I seem to be stuck. . . ."

Gilon Majere, Raistlin and Caramon's father, died when the brothers were still boys.

"It was the first time death had come so close to Raistlin. He felt it as a physical presence, passing among them, dark wings spreading over them. He felt small and insignificant, naked and vulnerable.

"So sudden. An hour ago Gilon had walked among the trees, thinking of nothing more important than what he might enjoy for dinner that night.

"So dark. Endless darkness, eternal. It was not the absence of light that was as frightening as the absence of thought, of knowledge, of comprehension. Our lives, the lives of the living, will go on. The sun shines, the moons rise, and we will laugh and talk, and he will know nothing, feel nothing. Nothing.

"So final. It will come to us all. It will come to me.

"Raistlin thought he should be grieved or sorrowful for his father, but all he felt was sorrow for himself, grief for his own mortality."

[The Soulforge, by Margaret Weis, p. 114]

Laughter filled the Hall of Judgment, the crowd turning and staring at a kender, loaded down with books, struggling to get through the doorway. Grinning, Kitiara reached out, grabbed him by his topknot of hair, and yanked him through the door, tossing him unceremoniously onto the floor. Books scattered everywhere, and the crowd roared with laughter. Unfazed, the kender picked himself up, dusted himself off, and, tripping over the books, managed eventually to make it up to the front.

"I'm Tasslehoff Burrfoot," the kender said, holding out his small hand for Raistlin to shake. The archmage stared at Tas in amazement and did not move. With a shrug, Tas looked at his hand, sighed, and then, turning, started toward the judge. "Hi, my name's Tasslehoff Burrfoot—"

"Sit down!" roared the dwarf. "You don't shake hands with the judge, you doorknob!"

"Well," said Tas indignantly. "I think I might if I liked. I'm only being polite, after all, something you dwarves know nothing about. I—"

"Sit down and shut up!" shouted the dwarf, thudding the butt-end of the axe on the floor.

His topknot bouncing, the kender turned and meekly made his way over to sit beside Raistlin. But, before sitting, he faced the audience and mimicked the dwarf's dour look so well that the crowd howled with glee, making the dwarf angrier than ever. But this time the judge intervened.

"Silence," called Tanis sternly, and the crowd hushed.

Tas plopped himself down beside Raistlin. Feeling a soft touch brush against him, the mage glared down at the kender and held out his hand.

"Give that back!" he demanded.

"What back? Oh, this? Is that yours? You must have dropped it," Tas said innocently, handing over one of Raistlin's spell component pouches. "I found it on the floor—"

Snatching it from the kender, Raistlin attached it once more to the cord he wore around his waist.

"You might at least have said thank you," Tas remarked in a shrill whisper, then subsided as he caught the stern gaze of the judge.

"What are the charges against these two?" Tanis asked.

Sturm Brightblade came to the front of the room. There was some scattered applause. The young knight with his high standards of honor and melancholy mien was apparently well-liked.

"I found these two in the wilderness, your honor. The Black Robed one spoke the name of Paladine"— there was angry mutterings from the crowd—"and, even as I watched, he brewed up some foul concoction and gave it to the woman to drink. She was badly hurt when I first saw them. Blood covered her robes, and her face was burned and scarred as if she had been in a fire. But when she drank that witch's brew, she was healed!"

"No!" cried Crysania, rising unsteadily to her feet. "That is wrong. The potion Raistlin gave me simply eased the pain. It was my prayers that healed me! I am a cleric of Paladine—"

"Pardon us, your honor," yelled the kender, leaping to his feet. "My client didn't mean to say she was a cleric of Paladine. *Performing a pantomime.* That's what she meant to say. Yes, that's it," Tas giggled. "Just having a little fun to lighten the journey. It's a game they play all the time. Hah, hah." Turning to Crysania, the kender frowned and said in a whisper that was audible to everyone in the room, "What *are* you doing? How can I possibly get you off if you go around telling the truth like that! I simply won't put up with it!"

"Quiet!" roared the dwarf.

The kender whirled around. "And I'm getting a bit tired of you, too, Flint!" he shouted. "Quit pounding that axe on the floor or I'll wrap it around your neck."

The room dissolved into laughter, and even the judge grinned.

Crysania sank back down beside Raistlin, her face deathly pale. "What is this mockery?" she murmured fearfully.

"I don't know, but I'm going to put an end to it." Raistlin rose to his feet.

"Silence, all of you." His soft, whispering voice brought immediate quiet to the room. "This lady *is* a holy cleric of Paladine! I am a wizard of the Black Robes, skilled in the arts of magic—"

"Oh, do something magic!" the kender cried, jumping to his feet again. "Whoosh me into a duck pond—"

"Sit down!" yelled the dwarf.

"Set the dwarf's beard on fire!" Tasslehoff laughed.

There was a round of applause for this suggestion.

"Yes, show us some magic, wizard." Tanis called out over the hilarity in the Hall.

Everyone hushed, and then the crowd began to murmur, "Yes, wizard, show us some magic. Do some magic, wizard!" Kitiara's voice rang out above the others, strong and powerful. "Perform some magic, frail and sickly wretch, if you can!"

Raistlin's tongue clove to the roof of his mouth. Crysania was staring at him, hope and terror in her gaze. His hands trembled. He caught up the Staff of Magius, which stood at his side, but, remembering what it had done to him, he dared not use it.

Drawing himself up, he cast a look of scorn upon the people around him. "Hah! I do not need to prove myself to such as you—"

"I really think it might be a good idea," Tas muttered, tugging at Raistlin's robe.

"You see!" shouted Sturm. "The witch cannot! I demand judgment!"

"Judgment! Judgment!" chanted the crowd. "Burn the witches! Burn their bodies! Save their souls!"

"Well, wizard?" Tanis asked sternly. "Can you prove you are what you claim?"

Spell words slithered from his grasp. Crysania's hands clutched at him. The noise deafened him. He couldn't think! He wanted to be alone, away from the laughing mouths and pleading, terror-filled eyes. "I—" He faltered, and bowed his head.

"Burn them."

Rough hands caught hold of Raistlin. The courtyard disappeared before his eyes. He struggled, but it was useless. The man who held him was big and strong, with a face that might once have been jovial but was now serious and intent.

"Caramon! Brother!" Raistlin cried, twisting in the big man's grasp to look into his twin's face.

But Caramon ignored him. Gripping Raistlin firmly, he dragged the frail mage up a hill. Raistlin looked around. Before him, on the top of the hill, he saw two tall, wooden stakes that had been driven into the ground. At the foot of each stake,

the townspeople—his friends, his neighbors—were gleefully tossing great armloads of dry tinder onto a mound.

"Where's Crysania?" he asked his brother, hoping she might have escaped and could now return to help him. Then Raistlin caught a glimpse of white robes. Elistan was binding her to a stake. She fought, trying to escape his grasp, but she was weakened from her suffering. At last, she gave up. Weeping in fear and despair, she slumped against the stake as they tied her hands behind it and bound her feet to the base.

Her dark hair fell over the smooth bare shoulders as she wept. Her wounds had opened, blood staining her robes red. Raistlin thought he heard her cry out to Paladine, but, if she did, the words could not be heard above the howling of the mob. Her faith was weakening even as she herself weakened.

Tanis advanced, a flaming torch in his hand. He turned to look at Raistlin.

"Witness her fate and see your own, witch!" the half-elf shouted.

"No!" Raistlin struggled, but Caramon held him fast.

Leaning down, Tanis thrust the blazing torch into the oil-soaked, drying tinder. It caught. The fire spread quickly, soon engulfing Crysania's white robes. Raistlin heard her anguished scream above the roar of the flame. She managed to raise her head, seeking for one final look at Raistlin. Seeing the pain and terror in her eyes, yet, seeing, too, love for him, Raistlin's heart burned with a fire hotter than any man could create.

"They want magic! I'll give them magic!" And, before he thought, he shoved the startled Caramon away and, breaking free, raised his arms to the heavens.

And, at that moment, the words of magic entered his soul, never to leave again.

Lightning streaked from his fingertips, striking the clouds in the red-tinged sky. The clouds answered with lightning, streaking down, striking the ground before the mage's feet.

Raistlin turned in fury upon the crowd—but the people had vanished, disappeared as though they had never existed.

"Ah, my Queen!" Laughter bubbled on his lips. Joy shot through his soul as the ecstasy of his magic burned in his blood. And, at last, he understood. He perceived his great folly and he saw his great chance.

He had been deceived—by himself! Tas had given him the clue at Zhaman, but he had not bothered to think it through. *I thought of something in my mind,* the kender said, *and there it was! When I wanted to go somewhere, all I had to do was think about it, and either it came to me or I went to it, I'm not sure. It was all the cities I have ever been in and yet none.* So the kender had told him.

I assumed the Abyss was a reflection of the world, Raistlin realized. *And thus I journeyed through it. It isn't, however. It is nothing more than a reflection of my mind! All I have been doing is traveling through my own mind!*

The Queen is in Godshome because that is where I perceived her to be. And Godshome is as far away or as near as I choose! My magic did not work because I doubted it, not because she prevented it from working. I have come close to defeating myself! Ah, but now I know, my Queen! Now I know and now I can triumph! For Godshome is just a step away and it is only another step to the Portal. . . .

"Raistlin!"

The voice was low, agonized, weary, spent. Raistlin turned his head. The crowd had vanished because it had never existed. It had been his creation. The village, the land, the continent, everything he had imagined was gone. He stood upon flat, undulating nothingness. Sky and ground were impossible to tell apart, both were the same eerie, burning pink. A faint horizon line was like a knife slit across the land.

But one object had not vanished—the wooden stake. Surrounded by charred wood, it stood outlined against the pink sky, thrusting up from the nothingness below. A figure lay below it. The figure might once have worn white robes, but these were now burnt black. The smell of burned flesh was strong.

Raistlin drew closer. Kneeling down upon the still-warm ashes, he turned the figure over.

"Crysania," he murmured.

"Raistlin?" Her face was horribly burned, sightless eyes stared into the emptiness around her, she reached out a hand that was little more than a blackened claw. "Raistlin?" She moaned in agony.

His hand closed over hers. "I can't see!" she whimpered. "All is darkness! Is that you?"

"Yes," he said.

"Raistlin, I've failed—"

"No, Crysania, you have not," he said, his voice cool and even. "I am unharmed. My magic is strong now, stronger than it has ever been before in any of the times I have lived. I will go forward, now, and defeat the Dark Queen."

The cracked and blistered lips parted in a smile. The hand holding Raistlin's tightened its feeble grasp. "Then my prayers have been granted." She choked, a spasm of pain twisted her body. When she could draw breath, she whispered something. Raistlin bent close to hear. "I am dying, Raistlin. I am weakened past endurance. Soon, Paladine will take me to him. Stay with me, Raistlin. Stay with me while I die. . . ."

Raistlin gazed down at the remains of the wretched woman before him. Holding her hand, he had a sudden vision of her as he had seen her in the forest near Caergoth the one time he had come close to losing control and making her his own†—her white skin, her silken hair, her shining eyes. He remembered the love in those eyes, he remembered holding her close in his arms, he remembered kissing the smooth skin. . . .

See War of the Twins, *Book II, Chapter 3.*

One by one, Raistlin burned those memories in his mind, setting fire to them with his magic, watching them turn to ash and blow away in smoke.

Reaching out his other hand, he freed himself from her clinging grasp.

"Raistlin!" she cried, her hand clutching out at the empty air in terror.

"You have served my purpose, Revered Daughter," Raistlin said, his voice as smooth and cold as the silver blade of the dagger he wore at his wrist. "Time presses. Even now come those to the Portal at Palanthas who will try to stop me. I must challenge the Queen, fight my final battle with her minions. Then, when I have won, I must return to

the Portal and enter it before anyone has a chance to stop me."

"Raistlin, don't leave me! Please don't leave me alone in the darkness!"

Leaning upon the Staff of Magius, which now gleamed with a bright, radiant light, Raistlin rose to his feet. "Farewell, Revered Daughter," he said in a soft, hissing whisper. "I need you no longer."

Crysania heard the rustle of his black robes as he walked away. She heard the soft thud of the Staff of Magius. Through the choking, acrid smell of smoke and burned flesh, she caught the faintest scent of rose petals. . . .

And then, there was only silence. She knew he was gone.

She was alone, her life dwindling through her veins as her illusions slowly dwindled from her mind.

"The next time you will see, Crysania, is when you are blinded by darkness . . . darkness unending."†

So spoke Loralon, the elven cleric, at the fall of Istar. Crysania would have cried, but the fire had burned away her tears and their source.

"I see now," she whispered into the darkness. "I see so clearly! I have deceived myself! I've been nothing to him—nothing but his gamepiece to move about the board of his great game as he chose. And even as he used me—so I used him!" She moaned. "I used him to further *my* pride, *my* ambition! My darkness only deepened his own! He is lost, and I have led him to his downfall. For if he does defeat the Dark Queen, it will be but to take her place!"

Staring up at the heavens she could not see, Crysania screamed in agony. "I have done this, Paladine! I have brought this harm upon myself, upon the world! But, oh, my god, what greater harm have I brought upon *him*?"†

Lying there, in the eternal darkness, Crysania's heart wept the tears her eyes could not. "I love you, Raistlin," she murmured. "I could never tell you. I could never admit it to myself." She tossed her head, gripped by a pain that seared her more deeply than the flames. "What might have changed, if I had?"

The pain eased. She seemed to be slipping away, losing her grasp upon consciousness.

Crysania is remembering events found in Time of the Twins, *Book II, Chapter 16.*

Crysania realizes at last that she has been an enabler to Raistlin's faults rather than a redeemer. Like Raistlin, the Dark Queen's greatest weakness is the full realization of her mistake. —TRH

"Good," she thought wearily, "I am dying. Let death come swiftly, then, and end my bitter torment."

She drew a breath. "Paladine, forgive me," she murmured.

Another breath. "Raistlin . . ."

Another, softer breath. " . . . forgive . . ."

CRYSANIA'S SONG†

W ater from dust, and dust rising out of the
water
Continents forming, abstract as color or light
To the vanished eye, to the touch of Paladine's
daughter
Who knows with a touch that the robe is white,
Out of that water a country is rising, impossible
When first imagined in prayer,
And the sun and the seas and the stars invisible
As gods in a code of air.

Dust from the water, and water arising from dust,
And the robe containing all colors assumed into
white,
Into memory, into countries assumed in the trust
Of ever returning color and light,
Out of that dust arises a wellspring of tears
To nourish the work of our hands
In forever approaching country of yearning
and years,
In due and immanent lands.†

988

CHAPTER 9

anis stood outside the Temple, thinking about the old wizard's words. Then he snorted.† *Love must triumph!*

Brushing away his tears, Tanis shook his head bitterly. Fizban's magic wasn't going to work this time. Love didn't even have a bit part in this play. Raistlin had long ago twisted and used his twin's love to his own ends, finally crushing Caramon into a sodden mass of blubbery flesh and dwarf spirits. Marble had more capacity to love than did the marble maiden, Crysania. And, as for Kitiara. . . . Had she ever loved?

Tanis scowled. He hadn't meant to think of her, not again. But an attempt to shove the memories of her back into the dark closet of his soul only made the light seem to shine upon them more brightly. He caught himself going back to the time they'd first met, in the wilderness near Solace. Discovering a

There are eight character archetypes in the Dramatica theory of story. The qualities of all eight must be found in the characters of a grand argument story for the argument to be complete. It seems that we are seeing the qualities of the Skeptic here in Tanis. —TRH

young woman fighting for her life against goblins, Tanis had raced to the rescue—only to have the young woman turn upon him in anger, accusing him of spoiling her fun!

Tanis was captivated. Up until then, his only love interest had been a delicate elven maiden, Laurana. But that had been a childish romance. He and Laurana had grown up together, her father having taken in the bastard half-elf out of charity when his mother died in childbirth. It was, in fact, partly because of Laurana's girlish infatuation with Tanis—a love her father would never have approved—that the half-elf left his elven homeland and traveled into the world with old Flint, the dwarven metalsmith.

Certainly Tanis had never met a woman like Kitiara—bold, courageous, lovely, sensual. She made no secret of the fact that she found the half-elf attractive on that first meeting. A playful battle between them ended in a night of passion beneath Kitiara's fur blankets. After that, the two had often been together, traveling by themselves or in the company of their friends, Sturm Brightblade, and Kitiara's half-brothers, Caramon and his frail twin, Raistlin.

Hearing himself sigh, Tanis shook his head angrily. No! Grasping the thoughts, he hurled them back into the darkness, shut and locked the door. Kitiara had never loved him. She had been amused by him, that was all. He had kept her entertained. When a chance came to gain what she truly wanted—power—she had left him without a second thought. But, even as he turned the key in the lock of his soul, Tanis heard, once again, Kitiara's voice. He heard the words she had spoken the night of the downfall of the Queen of Darkness, the night Kitiara had helped him and Laurana escape.†

Tanis is recalling events found in Dragons of Spring Dawning, *Book III, Chapter 13.*

"Farewell, Half-Elven. Remember, I do this for love of you!"

A dark figure, like the embodiment of his own shadow, appeared beside Tanis. The half-elf started in a sudden, unreasonable fear that he had, perhaps, conjured up an image from his own subconscious. But the figure spoke a word of greeting, and Tanis realized it was flesh and blood. He sighed in relief, then hoped the dark elf had not noticed how abstracted his thoughts had been. He was more than half afraid, in fact, that Dalamar might have

guessed them. Clearing his throat gruffly, the half-elf glanced at the black-robed mage.

"Is Elistan dead?" said Dalamar coldly. "No, not yet. But I sensed the approach of one whose presence I would find most uncomfortable, and so, seeing that my services were no longer necessary, I left."

Stopping on the lawn, Tanis turned to face the dark elf. Dalamar had not drawn up his black hood, and his features were plainly visible in the peaceful twilight. "Why did you do it?" Tanis demanded.

The dark elf stopped walking as well, looking at Tanis with a slight smile. "Do what?"

"Come here, to Elistan! Ease his pain." Tanis waved a hand. "From what I saw last time, setting foot on this ground makes you suffer the torments of the damned." His face became grim. "I cannot believe a pupil of Raistlin's could care so much about anyone!"

"No," Dalamar replied smoothly, "Raistlin's pupil personally didn't give a cracked iron piece what became of the cleric. But Raistlin's pupil is honorable. He was taught to pay his debts, taught to be beholden to no one. Does that accord with what you know of my *Shalafi*?"

"Yes," Tanis admitted grudgingly, "but—"

"I was repaying a debt, nothing more," Dalamar said. As he resumed his walk across the lawn, Tanis saw a look of pain upon his face. The dark elf obviously wanted to leave this place as quickly as possible. Tanis had some trouble keeping pace with him. "You see," Dalamar continued, "Elistan came once to the Tower of High Sorcery to help my *Shalafi*."

"Raistlin?" Tanis stopped again, stunned. Dalamar did not halt, however, and Tanis was forced to hurry after him.

"Yes," the dark elf was saying, as if caring little whether Tanis heard him or not, "no one knows this, not even Raistlin. The *Shalafi* grew ill once about a year ago, terribly ill. I was alone, frightened. I know nothing of sickness. In desperation, I sent for Elistan. He came."

"Did . . . did he . . . *heal* Raistlin?" Tanis asked in awe.

"No." Dalamar shook his head, his long black hair falling down around his shoulders. "Raistlin's malady is beyond the healing arts, a sacrifice made

for his magic. But Elistan was able to ease the *Sha-lafi's* pain and give him rest. And so, I have done nothing more than discharge my debt."

"Do you . . . care about Raistlin as much as this?" Tanis asked hesitantly.

"What is this talk of caring, half-elf?" Dalamar snapped impatiently. They were near the edge of the lawn. Evening's shadows spread across it like soothing fingers, gently reaching out to close the eyes of the weary. "Like Raistlin, I care for one thing only—and that is the Art and the power that it gives. For that, I gave up my people, my homeland, my her-itage.† For that, I have been cast in darkness. Raistlin is the *Shalafi*, my teacher, my master. He is skilled in the Art, one of the most skilled who has ever lived. When I volunteered to the Conclave to spy upon him, I knew I might well sacrifice my life. But how little was that price to pay for the chance of study-ing with one so gifted! How could I afford to lose him? Even now, when I think of what I must do to him, when I think of the knowledge he has gained that will be lost when he dies, I almost—"

"Almost what?" Tanis said sharply, in sudden fear. "Almost let him through the Portal? Can you truly stop him, when he comes back, Dalamar? *Will* you stop him?"

They had reached the end of the Temple grounds. Soft darkness blanketed the land. The night was warm and filled with the smells of new life. Here and there among the aspen trees, a bird chirped sleepily. In the city, lighted candles were set in the windows to guide loved ones home. Solinari glim-mered on the horizon, as though the gods had lit their own candle to brighten the night. Tanis's eyes were drawn to the one patch of chill blackness in the warm, perfumed evening. The Tower of High Sorcery stood dark and forbidding. No candles flick-ered in its windows. He wondered, briefly, who or what waited within that blackness to welcome the young apprentice home.

"Let me tell you of the Portals, Half-Elven," Dala-mar replied. "I will tell you as my *Shalafi* told me." His gaze followed Tanis's, going to the very topmost room in Tower. When he spoke, his voice was hushed. "There is a corner in that laboratory where stands a doorway, a doorway without a lock. Five dragon's

Dalamar's life story is told in Dalamar the Dark *by Nancy Varian Berberick.*

heads made of metal surround it. Look within it, you will see nothing—simply a void. The dragon's heads are cold and still. That is the Portal. Another exists beside this one—it stands in the Tower of High Sorcery at Wayreth. The only other one, as far as we know, was in Istar and it was destroyed in the Cataclysm. The one in Palanthas was originally moved to the magical fortress in Zhaman to protect it when the mobs of the Kingpriest tried to take over the Tower here. It moved again when Fistandantilus destroyed Zhaman, returning to Palanthas. Created long ago by mages who desired faster communication with each other, it led them too far—it led them onto other planes."

"The Abyss," Tanis murmured.

"Yes. Too late the mages realized what a perilous gate they had devised. For if someone from this plane entered the Abyss and returned through the Portal, the Queen would have the entrance into the world she has long sought. Thus with the help of the holy clerics of Paladine, they insured—so they thought—that none could ever use the Portals. Only one of the most profound evil, who had committed his very soul to darkness, could hope to gain the knowledge necessary to open that dread doorway. And only one of goodness and purity, with absolute trust in the one person upon this world who could never merit trust, could hold the doorway open."

"Raistlin and Crysania."

Dalamar smiled cynically. "In their infinite wisdom, those dried-up old mages and clerics never foresaw that love would overthrow their grand design. So, you see, Half-Elven, when Raistlin attempts to reenter the Portal from the Abyss, I must stop him. For the Queen will be right behind him."

None of this explanation did much to ease Tanis's doubts. Certainly the dark elf appeared cognizant of the grave danger. Certainly he appeared calm, confident. . . . "But can *you* stop him?" Tanis persisted, his gaze going—without meaning to—to the dark elf's chest where he had seen those five holes burned into his smooth skin.

Noticing Tanis's look, Dalamar's hand went involuntarily to his chest. His eyes grew dark and haunted. "I know my own limitations, Half-Elven,"

he said softly. Then, he smiled and shrugged. "I will be honest with you. If my *Shalafi* were in the full strength of his power when he tried to come through the Portal, then, no, I could not stop him. No one could. But Raistlin will not be. He will already have expended much of his power in destroying the Queen's minions and forcing her to face him alone. He will be weak and injured. His only hope—to draw the Dark Queen out here onto *his* plane. Here he can regain strength, here *she* will be the weaker of the two. And thus, yes, because he will be injured, I can stop him. And, yes, I *will* stop him!"

Noticing Tanis still looked dubious, Dalamar's smile twisted. "You see, Half-Elven," he said coolly, "I have been offered enough to make it worth my while." With that, he bowed, and—murmuring the words of a spell—vanished.

But as he left, Tanis heard Dalamar's soft, elven voice speak through the night. "You have looked upon the sun for the last time, Half-Elven. Raistlin and the Dark Queen have met. Takhisis now gathers her minions. The battle begins. Tomorrow, there will be no dawn."

If, as the book progresses, you find the annotations thinning out, it may well be because we, too, are enjoying the book along with you. I despise people who talk through movies, but I especially loathe them when they speak through the climax of a film. I worry about spoiling your fun as we experience the book together. —TRH

CHAPTER
10

And so, Raistlin, we meet again.

"My Queen."

You bow before me, wizard?

"This one last time, I do you homage."

And I bow to you, Raistlin.

"You do me too much honor, Majesty."

On the contrary, I have watched your gameplay† with the keenest pleasure. For every move of mine, you had a counter move. More than once, you risked all you had to win a single turn. You have proved yourself a skilled player, and our game has brought me much amusement. But now it comes to the end, my worthy opponent. You have one game-piece left upon the board—yourself. Ranged against you is th full might of my dark legions. But, because I have found pleasure in you, Raistlin, I will grant you one favor.

Return to your cleric. She lies dying, alone, in such torment of mind and body as only I can inflict. Return to

As we were working at a game company at the time, should it be surprising that Takhisis should view this contest as a game? —TRH

her. Kneel down beside her. Take her in your arms and hold her close. The mantle of death will fall upon you both. Gently it will cover you, and you will drift into the darkness and find eternal rest.

"My Queen . . ."

You shake your head.

"Takhisis, Great Queen, truly I thank you for this gracious offer. But I play this game—as you call it— to win. And I will play it to the end."

And it will be a bitter end—for you! I have given you the chance your skill and daring earned for you. You would spurn it?

"Your Majesty is too gracious. I am unworthy of such attention. . . ."

And now you mock me! Smile your twisted smile while you can, mage, for when you slip, when you fall, when you make that one, small mistake—I will lay my hands upon you. My nails will sink into your flesh, and you will beg for death. But it will not come. The days are eons long here, Raistlin Majere. And every day, I will come to see you in your prison—the prison of your mind. And, since you have provided me with amusement, you will continue to provide me with amusement. You will be tortured in mind and in body. At the end of each day, you will die from the pain. At the beginning of each night, I will bring you back to life. You will not be able to sleep, but will lie awake in shivering anticipation of the day to come. In the morning, my face will be the first sight you see.†

This is very much a reference to Promethian Justice. —TRH

What? You grow pale, mage. Your frail body trembles, your hands shake. Your eyes grow wide with fear. Prostrate yourself before me! Beg my forgiveness! . . .

"My Queen . . ."

What, not yet on your knees?

"My Queen . . . it is your move."

CHAPTER
II

Blasted overcast! If it's going to storm, I wish it would do it and be done with it," muttered Lord Gunthar.

Prevailing winds, Tanis thought sarcastically, but he kept his thoughts to himself. He also kept Dalamar's words to himself, knowing that Lord Gunthar would never believe them. The half-elf was nervous and on edge. He was finding it difficult to be patient with the seemingly complacent knight. Part of it was the strange-looking sky. That morning, as Dalamar had predicted, there came no dawn. Instead, purplish blue clouds, tinged with green and flickering with eerie, multicolored lightning, appeared, boiling and churning above them. There was no wind. No rain fell. The day grew hot and oppressive. Walking their rounds upon the battlements of the High Clerist's Tower, the knights in their heavy plate-mail armor wiped sweat from their brows and muttered about spring storms.

Only two hours ago, Tanis had been in Palanthas, tossing and turning on the silk sheets of the bed in Lord Amothus's guest room, pondering Dalamar's cryptic final words. The half-elf had been up most of the night, thinking about them, and thinking, too, of Elistan.

Word had come to the palace near midnight that the cleric of Paladine had passed from this world into another, brighter realm of existence.† He had died peacefully, his head cradled in the arms of a befuddled, kindly old wizard who had appeared mysteriously and left just as mysteriously. Worrying about Dalamar's warning, grieving for Elistan, and thinking he had seen too many die, Tanis had just dropped into an exhausted sleep when a messenger arrived for him.

The message was short and terse:

Your presence required immediately. High Clerist's Tower—Lord Gunthar uth Wistan.

Splashing cold water into his face, rebuffing the attempts of one of Lord Amothus's servants to help buckle him into his leather armor, Tanis dressed and stumbled out of the Palace, politely refusing Charles's offer of breakfast. Outside waited a young bronze dragon, who introduced himself as Fireflash, his secret dragon name being Khirsah.

"I am acquainted with two friends of yours, Tanis Half-Elven," the young dragon said as his strong wings carried them easily over the walls of the sleeping city. "I had the honor to fight in the Battle of the Vingaard Mountains, carrying† the dwarf, Flint Fireforge, and the kender, Tasslehoff Burrfoot, into the fray."

"Flint's dead,"† Tanis said heavily, rubbing his eyes. He'd seen too many die.

"So I heard," the young dragon replied respectfully. "I was sorry to hear it. Yet, he led a rich, full life. Death to such a one comes as the final honor."

Sure, Tanis thought tiredly. And what of Tasslehoff? Happy, good-natured, good-hearted kender, asking nothing more of life than adventure and a pouch full of wonders? If it was true—if Raistlin had killed him, as Dalamar had intimated—what honor was there in his death? And Caramon, poor drunken Caramon—did death at the hands of his twin come as the final honor or was it the final stab of the knife to end his misery?

From the perspective of the inhabitants of Ansalon the gods are a pantheon, and each of their belief systems varies regarding their theological origins, purposes, rites, ceremonies, and the afterlife. This is right considering that none of the religions extant on Krynn at the time of these events had a clear picture of the total cosmology of Krynn. The beliefs here reflect those of the followers of Paladine. Other races and sects had different beliefs and, of course, gods. A more complete understanding of the cosmology of creation would not be known in Krynn until the Fifth Age—after the War of Souls. —TRH

This occurred in Dragons of Spring Dawning, *Book I, Chapter 9.*

The death of Flint Fireforge can be found in Dragons of Spring Dawning, *Book III, Chapter 3.*

Brooding, Tanis fell asleep upon the dragon's back, awaking only when Khirsah landed in the courtyard of the High Clerist's Tower. Looking around grimly, Tanis's spirits did not rise. He had ridden with death only to arrive with death, for here Sturm was buried†—another final honor.

Thus, Tanis was in no good humor when he was ushered into the Lord Gunthar's chambers, high in one of the tall spires of the High Clerist's Tower. It commanded an excellent view of sky and land. Staring out the window, watching the clouds with a growing feeling of ominous foreboding, Tanis only gradually became aware that Lord Gunthar had entered and was talking to him.

Sturm's funeral occurred in the very last chapter of Dragons of Spring Dawning, *appropriately named "The Funeral."*

"I beg your pardon, lord," he said, turning around.

"Tarbean tea?" Lord Gunthar said, holding up a steaming mug of the bitter-tasting drink.

"Yes, thank you," Tanis accepted it and gulped it down, welcoming the warmth spreading through his body, ignoring the fact that he had burned his tongue.

Coming over to stand next to Tanis and stare out the window at the storm, Lord Gunthar sipped his tea with a calm that made the half-elf want to rip off the knight's mustaches.

Why did you send for me? Tanis fumed. But he knew that the knight would insist upon fulfilling the ages-old ritual of politeness before coming to the point.

"You heard about Elistan?" Tanis asked finally.

Gunthar nodded. "Yes, we heard early this morning. The knights will hold a ceremony in his honor here at the Tower . . . if we are permitted."

Tanis choked upon his tea and hastily swallowed. Only one thing would prevent the knights from holding a ceremony in honor of a cleric of their god, Paladine—war. "Permitted? Have you had some word, then? News from Sanction? What do the spies—"

"Our spies have been murdered," Lord Gunthar said evenly.

Tanis turned from the window. "What? How—"

"Their mutilated bodies were carried to the fortress of Solanthas by black dragons and were dropped into the courtyard last evening. Then came this strange storm—perfect cover for dragons and . . ." Lord Gunthar fell silent, staring out the window, frowning.

"Dragons and what?" Tanis demanded. A possibility was beginning to form in his mind. Hot tea sloshed over his shaking hand. Hastily, he set the cup down on the window ledge.

Gunthar tugged at his mustaches, his frown deepened. "Strange reports have come to us, first from Solanthas, then Vingaard."

"What reports. Have they seen something? What?"

"They've *seen* nothing. It's what they've heard. Strange sounds, coming from the clouds—or perhaps even from above the clouds."

Tanis's mind went back to Riverwind's description of the Siege of Kalaman. "Dragons?"

Gunthar shook his head. "Voices, laughter, doors opening and slamming, rumblings, creakings. . . ."

"I knew it!" Tanis's clenched fist smote the window ledge. "I knew Kitiara had a plan! Of course! This has to be it!" Gloomily, he stared out into the churning clouds. "A flying citadel!"†

Beside him, Gunthar sighed heavily. "I told you I respected this Dragon Highlord, Tanis. Apparently, I did not respect her enough. In one fell swoop, she has solved her problems of troop movements and logistics. She has no need for supply lines, she carries her supplies with her. The High Clerist's Tower was designed to defend against ground attack. I have no idea how long we can hold out against a flying citadel.† At Kalaman, draconians jumped from the citadel, floating down upon their wings, carrying death into the streets. Black-robed magic-users hurled down balls of flame, and with her, of course, are the evil dragons.

"Not that I have any doubts the knights can hold the fortress against the citadel, of course," Gunthar added sternly. "But it will be a much stiffer battle than I had at first anticipated. I've readjusted our strategy. Kalaman survived a citadel's attack by waiting until most of its troops had been dropped, then good dragons carrying men-at-arms on their backs flew up and took control of the citadel. We'll leave most of the Knights here in the fortress, of course, to fight the draconians who will drop down upon us. I have about a hundred standing by with bronze dragons ready to fly up† and begin the assault on the flying citadel itself."

It made sense, Tanis admitted to himself. That much of the battle of Kalaman Riverwind had told

It is hard to say where this idea came from, but I certainly remember being influenced here by certain rock album covers from the '60s and '70s. —TRH

The feared flying citadels of the dragonarmies later became the focus of an entire DRAGONLANCE novel in Richard Knaak's The Citadel.

The dream of flight is common throughout history and mythology in all cultures of the world. That the DRAGONLANCE saga had such extensive aerial combat certainly made the world stand out. I personally was enamored with flight from a very early age. I earned my private glider pilot's license when I was seventeen and soloed in power planes not long after that. Those experiences all translated into the DRAGONLANCE setting. Aerial combat, incidentally, drastically affects land battles in fantasy worlds, and we tried to evolve that in the books. —TRH

him. But Tanis also knew that Kalaman had been unable to hold the citadel. They had simply driven it back. Kitiara's troops, giving up the battle of Kalaman, had been able to easily recapture their citadel and fly it back to Sanction where Kit had, apparently, once more put it to good use.

He was about to point this out to Lord Gunthar when he was interrupted.

"We expect the citadel to attack us almost any moment," Gunthar said, calmly staring out the window. "In fact—"

Tanis gripped Gunthar's arm. "There!" He pointed.

Gunthar nodded. Turning to an orderly by the door, he said, "Sound the alarm!"

Trumpets pealed, drums beat. The knights took their places upon the battlements of the High Clerist's Tower with orderly efficiency. "We've been on alert most of the night," Gunthar added unnecessarily.

So disciplined were the knights that no one spoke or cried out when the flying fortress dropped down from the cover of the storm clouds and floated into view. The captains walked their rounds, issuing quiet commands. Trumpets blared their defiance. Occasionally Tanis heard the clinking of armor as, here and there, a knight shifted nervously in place. And then, high above, he heard the beating of dragon wings as several flights of bronze dragons—led by Khirsah—took to the skies from the Tower.

"I am thankful you persuaded me to fortify the High Clerist's Tower, Tanis," Gunthar said, still speaking with elaborate calm. "As it was, I was able to call upon only those knights I could muster at practically a moment's notice. Still, there are well over two thousand here. We are well-provisioned. Yes," he repeated again, "we can hold the Tower—even against a citadel, I have no doubt. Kitiara could not have more than a thousand troops in that thing. . . ."

Tanis wished sourly that Gunthar would quit emphasizing that. It was beginning to sound as if the knight were trying to convince himself. Staring at the citadel as it came nearer and nearer, some inner voice was shouting at him, pummeling him, screaming that something wasn't right. . . .

And yet he couldn't move. He couldn't think. The flying citadel was now plainly visible, having

dropped down completely out of the clouds. The fortress absorbed his entire attention. He recalled the first time he had seen it at Kalaman, recalled the riveting shock of the sight, at once horrifying and awe-inspiring. As before, he could only stand and stare.

Working in the depths of the dark temples of the city of Sanction, under the supervision of Lord Ariakas—the commander of the dragonarmies whose evil genius had nearly led to the victory of his Dark Queen—black-robed magic-users and dark clerics had managed to magically rip a castle from its foundations and send it up into the skies. The flying citadels had attacked several towns during the war, the last being Kalaman in the war's final days. It had nearly defeated the walled city that had been well-fortified and expecting assault.

Drifting upon clouds of dark magic, illuminated by flashes of blinding multicolored lightning, the flying citadel came nearer and nearer. Tanis could see the lights in the windows of its three towers, he could hear the sounds that were ordinary when heard upon land but seemed sinister and appalling heard coming from the skies—sounds of voices calling orders, weapons clashing. He could continue to hear, so he thought, the chants of the black-robed magic-users preparing to cast their powerful spells. He could see the evil dragons flying about the citadel in lazy circles. As the flying citadel drew nearer still, he could see a crumbling courtyard on one side of the fortress, its broken walls lying in ruins from where it had been dragged out of its foundation.

Tanis watched in helpless fascination, and still that inner voice spoke to him. Two thousand knights! Gathered at the last moment and so ill-prepared! Only a few flights of dragons. Certainly the High Clerist's Tower might hold out, but the cost would be high. Still, they just needed to hold a few days. By that time, Raistlin would have been defeated. Kitiara would have no more need to try to attack Palanthas. By that time, too, more knights would have reached the High Clerist's Tower, along with more good dragons. Perhaps they could defeat her here, finally, once and for all.

She had broken the uneasy truce that had existed between the Dragon Highlord and the free people of Ansalon. She had left the haven of Sanction, she had

come out into the open. This was their opportunity. They could defeat her, capture her perhaps. Tanis's throat constricted painfully. Would Kitiara let herself be taken alive? No. Of course not. His hand closed over the hilt of his sword. He'd be there when the knights tried to take the citadel. Perhaps *he* could persuade her to give herself up. He would see that she was treated justly, as an honorable enemy—

He could see her so clearly in his mind! Standing defiantly, surrounded by her enemies, prepared to sell her life dearly. And then she would look over, she would see him. Perhaps those glittering, hard dark eyes would soften, perhaps she would drop her sword and hold out her hands—

What *was* he thinking about! Tanis shook his head. He was daydreaming like a moon-struck youth. Still, he'd make certain he was with the knights. . . .

Hearing a commotion down on the battlements below, Tanis looked hastily outside, although he really had no need. He knew what was happening— dragonfear.† More destructive than arrows, the fear generated by the evil dragons, whose black wings and blue could now be seen against the clouds, struck the knights as they stood waiting upon the battlements. Older knights, veterans of the War of the Lance, held their ground, grimly clutching their weapons, fighting the terror that filled their hearts. But younger knights, who were facing their first dragons in battle, blenched and cowered, some shaming themselves by crying out or turning from the awesome sight before them.

This entire "dragonfear" element makes me hear the dice rolling somewhere. It came from the AD&D Monster Manual, and I have never been all that clear on how it works beyond that it is "magic."
—TRH

Seeing some of these fear-stricken young knights on the battlements below him, Tanis gritted his teeth. He, too, felt the sickening fear sweep over him, felt his stomach clench and the bile rise to his mouth. Glancing over at Lord Gunthar, he saw the knight's expression harden, and he knew he experienced the same thing.

Looking up, Tanis could see the bronze dragons who served the Knights of Solamnia flying in formation, waiting above the Tower. They would not attack until attacked—such were terms of the truce that had existed between the good dragons and the evil ones since the end of the war. But Tanis saw Khirsah, the leader, toss his head proudly, his sharp talons flaring in the reflected glare of the lightning.

There was no doubt in the dragon's mind at least, that battle would soon be joined.

Still, that inner voice nagged at Tanis. All too simple, all too easy. Kitiara was up to something. . . .

The citadel flew closer and closer. It looked like the home of some foul colony of insects, Tanis thought grimly. Draconians literally covered the thing! Clinging to every available inch of space, their short, stubby wings extended, they hung from the walls and the foundation, they perched upon the battlements and dangled from the spires. Their leering, reptilian faces were visible in the windows and peered from doorways. Such awed silence reigned in the High Clerist's Tower (except for the occasional harsh weeping of some knight, overcome by fear) that there could be heard from the citadel above the rustling of the creatures' wings and, over that, faint sounds of chanting—the mingled voices of the wizards and clerics whose evil power kept the terrible device afloat.

Nearer and nearer it came, and the knights tensed. Quiet orders rang out, swords slid from scabbards, spears were set, archers nocked their arrows, buckets of water stood filled and ready to douse fires, divisions assembled within the courtyard to fight those draconians who would leap down and attack from the skies.

Above, Khirsah aligned his dragons in battle formation, breaking them into groups of twos and threes, hovering, poised to descend upon the enemy like bronze lightning.

"I am needed below," Gunthar said. Picking up his helm, he put it on and strode out the door of his headquarters to take his place at the observation tower, his officers and aides accompanying him.

But Tanis did not leave, nor even answer Gunthar's belated invitation to come with them. The voice inside him was growing louder, more insistent. Shutting his eyes, he turned from the window. Blocking out the debilitating dragonfear, blotting out the sight of that grim fortress of death, he fought to concentrate on the voice within.

And finally, he heard it.

"Name of the gods, no!" he whispered. "How stupid! How blind we've been! We've played right into her hands!"

Suddenly Kitiara's plan was clear. She might have been standing there with him, explaining it to him in detail. His chest tight with fear, he opened his eyes and leaped toward the window. His fist slammed into the carved stone ledge, cutting him. He knocked the tea mug to the floor, where it shattered. But he noticed neither the blood that flowed from his injured hand nor the spilled tea. Staring up into the eerie, cloud-darkened sky, he watched the floating citadel come nearer and nearer, draw closer and closer.

It was within long-bow-shot range.

It was within spear range.

Looking up, nearly blinded by the lightning, Tanis could see the details on the armor of the draconians, he could see the grinning faces of the mercenary humans who fought in the ranks, he could see the shining scales of the dragons flying overhead.

And then, it was gone.

Not an arrow had flown, not a spell had been cast. Khirsah and the bronze dragons circled uneasily, eyeing their evil cousins with fury, yet constrained by their oaths not to attack those who had not attacked them first. The knights stood upon the battlements, craning their necks to watch the huge, awesome creation fly over them, skimming the topmost spire of the High Clerist's Tower as it went, sending a few stones tumbling down to crash into the courtyard below.

Swearing beneath his breath, Tanis ran for the door, slamming into Gunthar as the knight, a perplexed look upon his face, was coming inside.

"I can't understand," Gunthar was saying to his aides. "Why didn't she attack us? What is she doing?"

"She's attacking the city directly, man!" Tanis gripped Gunthar by the arms, practically shaking him. "It's what Dalamar said all along! Kitiara's plan is to attack Palanthas! She's not going to fool with us and now she doesn't have to! She's going over the High Clerist's Tower!"

Gunthar's eyes, barely visible beneath the slits of his helm, narrowed. "That's insane," he said coldly, tugging on his mustache. Finally, irritably, he yanked his helm off. "Name of the gods, Half-Elven, what kind of military strategy's that? It leaves the rear of her army unguarded! Even if she takes Palanthas,

she hasn't got strength enough to hold it. She'll be caught between the walls of the city and us. No! She has to finish us here, then attack the city! Otherwise we'll destroy her easily. There's no escape for her!"

Gunthar turned to his aides. "Perhaps this is a feint, to throw us off-guard. Better prepare for the citadel to strike from the opposite direction—"

"Listen to me!" Tanis raved. "This isn't a feint. She's going to Palanthas! And by the time you and the knights get to the city, her brother will have returned through the Portal! And she'll be waiting for him, with the city under her control!"

"Nonsense!" Gunthar scowled. "She can't take Palanthas that quickly. The good dragons will rise up to fight—Damn it, Tanis, even if the Palanthians aren't such great soldiers, they can hold her off through sheer numbers alone!" He snorted. "The knights can march at once. We'll be there within four days."

"You've forgotten one thing," Tanis snapped, firmly but politely shoving his way past the knight. Turning on his heel, he called out, "We've all forgotten one thing—the element that makes this battle even—Lord Soth!"

CHAPTER
12

ropelled by his
powerful hind legs, Khirsah leaped into the air and
soared over the walls of the High Clerist's Tower
with graceful ease. The dragon's strong wing strokes
soon caused himself and his rider to overtake the
slowly moving citadel. And yet, noted Tanis grimly,
the fortress is moving rapidly enough to arrive in
Palanthas by dawn tomorrow.

"Not too close," he cautioned Khirsah.

A black dragon flew over, circling overhead in
large, lazy spirals to keep an eye on them. Other blacks
hovered in the distance and, now that he was on the
same level as the citadel, Tanis could see the blue
dragons as well, flying around the gray turrets of the
floating castle. One particularly large blue dragon
Tanis recognized as Kitiara's† own mount, Skie.†

Where is Kit? Tanis wondered, trying unsuccessfully to peer into the windows, crowded with milling

*As I may have mentioned
before, names are evocative,
and their sound should
remind you of something.
Kitiara sounds feline to
me. The problem is,
however, that such nuances
are difficult to translate
into other cultures or
languages. —TRH*

*Kitiara's dragon, Skie,
would play a large and
rather infamous part
many years later in the
Age of Mortals. Changing
his name to Khellendros,
he became one of the
dragon overlords who
ruled over portions of
Ansalon for years.*

draconians, who were pointing at him and jeering. He had a sudden fear she might recognize him, if she were watching, and he pulled his cloak hood over his head. Then, smiling ruefully, he scratched his beard. At this distance, Kit would see nothing more than a lone rider on dragonback, probably a messenger for the knights.

He could picture clearly what would be occurring within the citadel.

"We could shoot him from the skies, Lord Kitiara," one of her commanders would say.

Kitiara's remembered laughter rang in Tanis's ears. "No, let him carry the news to Palanthas, tell them what to expect. Give them time to sweat."

Time to sweat. Tanis wiped his face. Even in the chill air above the mountains, the shirt beneath his leather tunic and armor was damp and clammy. He shivered with the cold and pulled his cloak more closely about him. His muscles ached; he was accustomed to riding in carriages, not on dragons, and he briefly thought with longing of his warm carriage. Then he sneered at himself. Shaking his head to clear it (why should missing one night's sleep affect him so?), he forced his mind from his discomfort to the impossible problem confronting him.

Khirsah was trying his best to ignore the black dragon still hovering near them. The bronze increased his speed, and eventually the black, who had been sent simply to keep an eye on them, turned back. The citadel was left far behind, drifting effortlessly above mountain peaks that would have stopped an army dead.

Tanis tried to make plans, but everything he thought of doing involved doing something more important first until he felt like one of those trained mice in a fair who runs round and round upon the little wheel, getting nowhere in a tremendous hurry. At least Lord Gunthar had actually bullied and badgered Amothus's generals (an honorary title in Palanthas, granted for outstanding community service; not one general now serving had actually been in a battle) into mobilizing the local militia.† Unfortunately, the mobilization had been regarded as merely an excuse for a holiday.

Gunthar and his knights had stood around, laughing and nudging each other as they watched

The Palanthian Militia doesn't sound too great here. They are certainly untested. This book was written in the 1980s when this could, by and large, have been said about the United States Military.
—TRH

the civilian soldiers stumble through the drills. Following this, Lord Amothus had made a two-hour speech, the militia—proud of its heroics—had drunk itself into a stupor, and everyone had enjoyed himself immensely.

Picturing in his mind the chubby tavern owners, the perspiring merchants, the dapper tailors and the ham-fisted smithies tripping over their weapons and each other, following orders that were never given, not following those that were, Tanis could have wept from sheer frustration. This, he thought grimly, is what will face a death knight and his army of skeletal warriors at the gates of Palanthas tomorrow.

"Where's Lord Amothus?" Tanis demanded, shoving his way inside the huge doors of the palace before they were open, nearly bowling over an astonished footman.

"A-asleep, sir," the footman began, "it's only midmorning—"

"Get him up. Who's in charge of the Knights?"

The footman, eyes wide, stammered.

"Damn it!" Tanis snarled. "Who's the highest ranking knight, dim-wit!"

"That would be Sir Markham, sir, Knight of the Rose," said Charles in his calm, dignified voice, emerging from one of the antechambers. "Shall I send—"

"Yes!" shouted Tanis, then, seeing everyone in the great entry hall of the palace staring at him as if he were a madman, and remembering that panic would certainly not help the situation, the half-elf put his hand over his eyes, drew a calming breath, and made himself talk rationally.

"Yes," he repeated in a quiet voice, "send for Sir Markham and for the mage, Dalamar, too."

This last request seemed to confound even Charles. He considered it a moment, then, a pained expression on his face, he ventured to protest, "I am extremely sorry, my lord, but I have no way to way to send a message to—to the Tower of High Sorcery. No living being can set foot in that accursed grove of trees, not even kender!"

"Damn!" Tanis fumed. "I *have* to talk to him!" Ideas raced through his mind. "Surely you've got

goblin prisoners? One of their kind could get through the Grove. Get one of the creatures, promise it freedom, money, half the kingdom, Amothus himself, anything! Just get it inside that blasted Grove—"

"That will be unnecessary, Half-Elven," said a smooth voice. A black-robed figure materialized within the hallway of the palace, startling Tanis, traumatizing the footmen, and even causing Charles to raise his eyebrows.

"You *are* powerful," Tanis remarked, drawing near the dark elf magic-user. Charles was issuing orders to various servants, sending one to awaken Lord Amothus and another to locate Sir Markham. "I need to talk to you privately. Come in here."

Following Tanis, Dalamar smiled coolly. "I wish I could accept the compliment, Half-Elven, but it was simply through observation that I discerned your arrival, not any magical mind-reading. From the laboratory window, I saw the bronze dragon land in the palace courtyard. I saw you dismount and enter the palace. I have need to talk to you as much as you to me. Therefore, I am here."

Tanis shut the door. "Quickly, before the others come. You know what is headed this way?"

"I knew last night. I sent word to you, but you had already left," Dalamar's smile twisted. "My spies fly on swift wings."

"If they fly on wings at all," Tanis muttered. With a sigh, he scratched his beard, then, raising his head, looked at Dalamar intently. The dark elf stood, hands folded in his black robes, calm and collected. The young elf certainly appeared to be someone who could be relied upon to perform with cool courage in a tight spot. Unfortunately, just who he would perform for was open to doubt.

Tanis rubbed his forehead. How confusing this was! How much easier it had been back in the old days—he sounded like someone's grandfather!—when good and evil had been clearly defined and everyone knew which side they were fighting for or against. Now, he was allied with evil fighting against evil. How was that possible? *Evil turns in upon itself,* so Elistan read from the Disks of Mishakal. Shaking his head angrily, Tanis realized he was wasting time. He had to trust this Dalamar—at least, he had to trust to his ambition.

"Is there any way to stop Lord Soth?"

Dalamar nodded slowly. "You are quick-thinking, Half-Elven. So you believe, too, that the death knight will attack Palanthas?"

"It's obvious, isn't it?" Tanis snapped. "That *has* to be Kit's plan. It's what equalizes the odds."

The dark elf shrugged. "To answer your question, no, there is nothing that can be done. Not now, at any rate."

"You? Can you stop him?"

"I dare not leave my post beside the Portal. I came this time because I know Raistlin is still far from it. But every breath we draw brings him nearer. This will be my last chance to leave the Tower. That was why I came to talk to you—to warn you. There is little time."

"He's winning!" Tanis stared at Dalamar incredulously.

"You have always underestimated him," Dalamar said with a sneer. "I told you, he is now strong, powerful, the greatest wizard who has ever lived. Of course, he is winning! But at what cost . . . at what great cost."

Tanis frowned. He didn't like the note of pride he heard in Dalamar's voice when he talked about Raistlin. That certainly didn't sound like an apprentice who was prepared to kill his *Shalafi* if need arose.

"But, to return to Lord Soth," said Dalamar coldly, seeing more of Tanis's thoughts on the half-elf's face than Tanis had intended. "When I first realized that he would undoubtedly use this opportunity to take his own revenge upon a city and a people he has long hated—if one believes the old legends† about his downfall—I contacted the Tower of High Sorcery in Wayreth Forest—"

"Of course!" Tanis gasped in relief. "Par-Salian! The Conclave. They could—"

"There was no answer to my message," Dalamar continued, ignoring the interruption. "Something strange is transpiring there. I do not know what. My messenger found the way barred and, for one of his—shall we say—light and airy nature,† that is not easy."

"But—"

"Oh"—Dalamar shrugged his black-robed shoulders—"I will continue to try. But we cannot

The Cataclysm spread chaos throughout Ansalon, and many histories were lost. The true account of Soth's background is still passed down as legend by the people of Ansalon, but very few know the truth.

Dalamar is hinting that this spirit form should have been able to pass.
—TRH

count on them, and they are the only magic-users powerful enough to stop a death knight."

"The clerics of Paladine—"

"—are new in their faith. In Huma's day, it was said the truly powerful clerics could call down Paladine's aid and use certain holy words against death knights, but—if so—there are none now on Krynn who have that power."

Tanis pondered a moment.

"Kit's destination will be the Tower of High Sorcery to meet and help her brother, right?"

"And try to stop me," Dalamar said in a tight voice, his face paling.

"Can Kitiara get through the Shoikan Grove?"

Dalamar shrugged again, but his cool manner was, Tanis noticed, suddenly tense and forced. "The Grove is under my control. It will keep out all creatures, living and dead." Dalamar smiled again, but this time, without mirth. "Your goblin, by the way, wouldn't have lasted five seconds. However, Kitiara had a charm, given her by Raistlin. If she has it still, and the courage to use it, and if Lord Soth is with her, yes, she might get through. Once inside, however, she must face the Tower's guardians, no less formidable than those in the Grove. Still, that is my concern—not yours—"

"Too much is your concern!" Tanis snapped. "Give *me* a charm! Let me inside the Tower! I can deal with her—"

"Oh, yes." Dalamar returned, amused, "I know how well you dealt with her in the past. Listen, Half-Elven, you will have all you can handle trying to keep control of the city. Besides, you have forgotten one thing—Soth's true purpose in this. He wants Kitiara dead. He wants her for himself. He told me as much. Of course, he must make it look good. If he can accomplish her death and avenge himself upon Palanthas, he will have succeeded in his objective. He couldn't care less about Raistlin."

Feeling suddenly chilled to the very soul, Tanis could not reply. He had, indeed, forgotten Soth's objective. The half-elf shuddered. Kitiara had done much that was evil. Sturm had died upon the end of her spear, countless had died by her commands, countless more had suffered and still suffered. But did she deserve this? An endless life of cold and

dark torment, bound forever in some type of unholy marriage to this creature of the Abyss?

A curtain of darkness shrouded Tanis's vision. Dizzy, weak, he saw himself teetering on the brink of a yawning chasm and felt himself falling. . . .

There was a dim sensation of being enfolded in soft black cloth, he felt strong hands supporting him, guiding him. . . .

Then nothing.

The cool, smooth rim of a glass touched Tanis's lips, brandy stung his tongue and warmed his throat. Groggily, he looked up to see Charles hovering over him.

"You have ridden far, without food or drink, so the dark elf tells me." Behind Charles floated the pale anxious face of Lord Amothus. Wrapped in a white dressing robe, he looked very much like a distraught ghost.

"Yes," Tanis muttered, pushing the glass away from him and trying to rise. Feeling the room sway beneath his feet, however, he decided he better remain seated. "You are right—I had better have something to eat." He glanced around for the dark elf. "Where is Dalamar?"

Charles's face grew stern. "Who knows, my lord? Fled back to his dark abode, I suppose. He said his business with you was concluded. I will, with your leave, my lord, have the cook prepare you breakfast." Bowing, Charles withdrew, first standing aside to allow young Sir Markham to enter.

"Have you breakfasted, Sir Markham?" Lord Amothus asked hesitantly, not at all certain what was going on and decidedly flustered by the fact that a dark elf magic-user felt free to simply appear and disappear in his household. "No? Then we will have quite a threesome. How do you prefer your eggs?"

Perhaps we shouldn't be discussing eggs right now, m'lord." Sir Markham said, glancing at Tanis with a slight smile. The half-elf's brows had knit together alarmingly and his disheveled and exhausted appearance showed that some dire news was at hand.

Amothus sighed, and Tanis saw that the lord had simply been trying to postpone the inevitable.

"I have returned this morning from the High Clerist's Tower—" he began.

"Ah," Sir Markham interrupted, seating himself negligently in a chair and helping himself to a glass of brandy. "I received a message from Lord Gunthar that he expected to engage the enemy this morning. How goes the battle?" Markham was a wealthy young nobleman, handsome, good-natured, carefree, and easy-going. He had distinguished himself in the War of the Lance, fighting under Laurana's command, and had been made a Knight of the Rose. But Tanis remembered Laurana telling him that the young man's bravery was nonchalant—almost casual—and totally undependable. ("I always had the feeling," Laurana said thoughtfully, "that he fought in the battle simply because there was nothing more interesting to do at the time.")†

A nod to Dorothy Sayers's Lord Peter Wimsey here. —MW

Remembering her assessment of the young knight, and hearing his cheerful, unconcerned tone, Tanis frowned.

"There wasn't one," he said abruptly. An almost comic look of hope and relief dawned in Lord Amothus's face. At the sight, Tanis nearly laughed, but—fearing it would be hysterical laughter—he managed to control himself. He glanced at Sir Markham, who had raised an eyebrow.

"No battle? Then the enemy didn't come—"

"Oh, they came," Tanis said bitterly, "came and went. Right by." He gestured in the air. "Whoosh."

"Whoosh?" Amothus turned pale. "I don't understand."

"A flying citadel!"

"Name of the Abyss!" Sir Markham let out a low whistle. "A flying citadel." He grew thoughtful, his hand absently smoothing his elegant riding clothes. "They didn't attack the High Clerist's Tower. They're flying over the mountains. That means—"

"They plan to throw everything they have at Palanthas," Tanis finished.

"But, I don't understand!" Lord Amothus looked bewildered. "The knights didn't stop them?"

"It would have been impossible, m'lord," Sir Markham said with a negligent shrug. "The only way to attack a flying citadel that stands a chance of succeeding is with flights of dragons."

"And by terms of the surrender treaty, the good dragons will not attack unless first attacked. All we had at the High Clerist's Tower was one flight of bronzes. It will take far greater numbers than that—silver and golden dragons, as well—to stop the citadel," Tanis said wearily.

Leaning back in his chair, Sir Markham pondered. "There are a few silver dragons in the area who will, of course, immediately rise up when the evil dragons are sighted. But there are not many. Perhaps more could be sent for—"

"The citadel is not our gravest danger," Tanis said. Closing his eyes, he tried to stop the room from spinning. What was the matter with him? Getting old, he supposed. Too old for this.

"It isn't?" Lord Amothus appeared to be on the verge of collapse from this additional blow but—nobleman that he was—he was doing his best to regain his shattered composure.

"Most assuredly Lord Soth rides with Highlord Kitiara."

"A death knight!" Sir Markham murmured with a slight smile. Lord Amothus paled so visibly that Charles, returning with the food, set it down at once and hurried to his master's side.

"Thank you, Charles," Amothus said in a stiff, unnatural voice. "A little brandy, perhaps."

"A lot of brandy would be more to the point," Sir Markham said gaily, draining his glass. "Might as well get good and roaring drunk. Not much use staying sober. Not against a death knight and his legions. . . ." The young knight's voice trailed off.

"You gentlemen should eat now," Charles said firmly, having made his master more comfortable. A sip of brandy brought some color back to Amothus's face. The smell of the food made Tanis realize that he was hungry, and so he did not protest when Charles, bustling about efficiently, brought over a table and served the meal.

"Wh-what does it all mean?" Lord Amothus faltered, spreading his napkin on his lap automatically. "I—I've heard of this death knight before. My great-great-great grandfather was one of the nobles who witnessed Soth's trial in Palanthas. And this Soth was the one who kidnapped Laurana,† wasn't he, Tanis?"

Soth captured Laurana in Dragons of Spring Dawning, Book II, Chapter 3.

The half-elf's face darkened. He did not reply.

Amothus raised his hands appealingly. "But what can he do against a city?"

Still no one replied. There was, however, no need. Amothus looked from the grim, exhausted face of the half-elf to the young knight, who was smiling bitterly as he methodically stabbed tiny holes in the lace tablecloth with his knife. The lord had his answer.

Rising to his feet, his breakfast untouched, his napkin slipping unnoticed from his lap to the floor, Amothus walked across the sumptuously appointed room to stand before a tall window made of hand-cut glass, crafted in an intricate design. A large oval pane in the center framed a view of the beautiful city of Palanthas. The sky above it was dark and filled with the strange, churning clouds. But the storm above only seemed to intensify the beauty and apparent serenity of the city below.

Lord Amothus stood there, his hand resting upon a satin curtain, looking out into the city. It was market day. People passed the palace on their way to the market square, chatting together about the ominous sky, carrying their baskets, scolding their playful children.

"I know what you're thinking, Tanis," Amothus said finally, a break in his voice. "You're thinking of Tarsis and Solace and Silvanesti and Kalaman. You're thinking of your friend who died at the High Clerist's Tower. You're thinking of all those who died and suffered in the last war while we in Palanthas remained untouched, unaffected."

Still Tanis did not respond. He ate in silence.

"And you, Sir Markham—" Amothus sighed. "I heard you and your knights laughing the other day. I heard the comments about the people of Palanthas carrying their money bags into battle, planning to defeat the enemy by tossing coins and yelling, 'Go away! Go away.' "

"Against Lord Soth, that will do quite as well as swords!" With a shrug and a short, sardonic laugh, Markham held out his brandy snifter for Charles to refill.

Amothus rested his head against the window pane. "We never thought war would come to us! It never has! Through all the Ages, Palanthas has

remained a city of peace, a city of beauty and light. The gods spared us, even during the Cataclysm. And now, now that there is peace in the world, *this* comes to us!" He turned around, his pale face drawn and anguished. "Why? I don't understand?"†

Tanis shoved his plate away. Leaning back, he stretched, trying to ease the cramps in his muscles. I *am* getting old, he thought, old and soft. I miss my sleep at night. I miss a meal and grow faint. I miss days long past. I miss friends long gone. And I'm sick and tired of seeing people die in some stupid, senseless war! Heaving a sigh, he rubbed his bleary eyes and then, resting his elbows on the table, let his head sink into his hands.

"You talk of peace. What peace?" he asked. "We've been behaving like children in a house where mother and father have fought constantly for days and now, at last, they're quiet and civil. We smile a lot and try to be merry and eat all our vegetables and tiptoe around, scared of making a sound. Because we know, if we do, the fighting will start all over again. And we call this peace!" Tanis laughed bitterly. "Speak one false word, my lord, and Porthios will have the elves on your neck. Stroke your beard the wrong way, and the dwarves will bar the gates to the mountain once again."

Glancing over at Lord Amothus, Tanis saw the man's head bow, he saw the delicate hand brush his eyes, his shoulders slump. Tanis's anger dwindled. Who was he angry at anyway? Fate? The gods?

Rising tiredly to his feet, Tanis walked over to stand at the, window, looking out over the peaceful, beautiful, doomed city,

"I don't have the answer, my lord," he said quietly. "If I did, I'd have a Temple built to me and a whole string of clerics following me about, I suppose. All I know is that we can't give up. We've got to keep trying."

"Another brandy, Charles," said Sir Markham, holding out his glass once again. "A pledge, gentlemen." He raised his glass.

"Here's to trying. . . . Rhymes with dying."

This paragraph has startling meaning for people of the United States since September 11, 2001. It also mirrors the hurt and confusion that we felt and that is still a deep wound in our souls. It is chilling to read these words now, written years before we would understand them with such terrible reality.
—TRH

CHAPTER 13

There came a soft knock at the door. Absorbed in his work, Tanis started. "Yes, what is it?" he called.

The door opened. "It is Charles, my lord. You asked that I call you during the changing of the watch."

Turning his head, Tanis glanced out the window. He had opened it to let in some air. But the spring night was warm and sultry and no breeze stirred. The sky was dark except for the occasional streaks of the eerie pink-tinged lightning that flashed from cloud to cloud. Now that his attention was drawn to it, he could hear the chimes striking Deepwatch, he could hear the voices of the guards newly arrived on duty, he could hear the measured tread of those departing for their rest.

Their rest would be short-lived.

"Thank you, Charles," Tanis said. "Step in for a moment, will you?"

"Certainly, my lord."

The servant entered, gently closing the door behind him. Tanis stared for a moment longer at the paper on the desk.

Then, his lips tightening in resolve, he wrote two more lines in a firm, elven hand. Sprinkling sand upon the ink to dry it, he began to reread the letter carefully. But his eyes misted over and the handwriting blurred in his vision. Finally, giving up, he signed his name, rolled up the parchment, and sat holding it in his hand.

"Sir," said Charles, "are you quite well?"

"Charles . . ." began Tanis, twisting a ring of steel and gold that he wore upon his finger. His voice died.

"My lord?" Charles prompted.

"This is a letter to my wife, Charles," Tanis continued in a low voice, not looking at the servant. "She is in Silvanesti. This needs to get out tonight, before—"

"I quite understand, sir," Charles said, stepping forward and taking charge of the letter.

Tanis flushed guiltily. "I know there are much more important documents than this that need to be going out—dispatches to the knights, and such—but—"

"I have just the messenger, my lord. He is elven, from Silvanesti, in fact. He is loyal and, to be quite honest, sir, will be more than pleased to leave the city on some honorable assignment."

"Thank you, Charles." Tanis sighed and ran his hand through his hair. "If something were to happen, I want her to know—"

"Of course you do, my lord. Perfectly understandable. Do not give it another thought. Your seal, perhaps, however?"

"Oh, yes, certainly." Removing the ring, Tanis pressed it into the hot wax that Charles dripped onto the parchment, imprinting in the sealing wax the image of an aspen leaf.

"Lord Gunthar has arrived, my lord. He is meeting with Lord Markham right now."

"Lord Gunthar!" Tanis's brow cleared. "Excellent. Am I—"

"They asked to meet with you, if it is convenient, my lord," Charles said imperturbably.

"Oh, it's quite convenient," Tanis said, rising to his feet. "I don't suppose there's been any sign of the cita—"

"Not yet, my lord. You will find the lords in the summer breakfast parlor—now, officially, the war room."

"Thank you, Charles," Tanis said, amazed that he had, at last, managed to complete a sentence.

"Will there be anything else, my lord?"

"No, thank you. I know the—"

"Very good, my lord." Bowing, letter in hand, Charles held the door for Tanis, then locked it behind him. After waiting a moment to see if Tanis might have any last minute desires, he bowed again and departed.

His mind still on his letter, Tanis stood alone, thankful for the shadowy stillness of the dimly lit corridor. Then, drawing a shaking breath, he walked firmly off in search of the morning breakfast parlor—now the war room.

Tanis had his hand on the doorknob and was just about to enter the room when he caught a glimpse of movement out of the corner of his eye. Turning his head, he saw a figure of darkness materialize out of the air.

"Dalamar?" Tanis said in astonishment, leaving the unopened door to the war room and walking down the hallway toward the dark elf. "I thought—"

"Tanis. You are the one I seek."

"Do you have news?"

"None that you will like to hear," Dalamar said, shrugging. "I cannot stay long, our fate teeters on the edge of a knife's blade. But I brought you this." Reaching into a black velvet pouch hanging at his side, he took out a silver bracelet and held it out to Tanis.

Taking hold of the bracelet in his hand, Tanis examined it curiously. The bracelet was about four inches in width, made of solid silver. From its width and weight, Tanis guessed, it had been designed to fit on a man's wrist. Slightly tarnished, it was set with black stones whose polished surfaces gleamed in the flickering torchlight of the corridor. And it came from the Tower of High Sorcery.

Tanis held it gingerly. "Is it—" he hesitated, not sure he wanted to know.

"Magical? Yes," Dalamar replied.

"Raistlin's?" Tanis frowned.

"No." Dalamar smiled sardonically. "The *Shalafi* needs no such magical defenses as these. It is part of the collection of such objects in the Tower. This† is very old, undoubtedly dating back to the time of Huma."

"What will it do?" Tanis studied the bracelet dubiously, still frowning.

"It makes the one wearing it resistant to magic."

Tanis raised his head. "Lord Soth's magic?"

"Any magic. But, yes, it will protect the wearer from the death knight's power words—'kill,' 'stun,' 'blind.' It will keep the wearer from feeling the effects of the fear he generates. And it will protect the wearer from both his spells of fire and of ice."†

Tanis stared at Dalamar intently. "This is truly a valuable gift! It gives us a chance."

"The wearer may thank me when and if he returns alive!" Dalamar folded his hands within his sleeves. "Even without his magic, Lord Soth is a formidable opponent, not to mention those who follow him, who are sworn to his service with oaths death itself could not erase. Yes, Half-Elven, thank me *when* you return."

"Me?" Tanis said in astonishment. "But—I haven't wielded a sword in over two years!" He stared at Dalamar intently, suddenly suspicious. "Why me?"

Dalamar's smile widened. The slanted eyes glinted in amusement. "Give it to one of the knights, half-elf. Let one of them hold it. You will understand. Remember—it came from a place of darkness. It knows one of its own."

"Wait!" Seeing the dark elf prepared to leave, Tanis caught hold of Dalamar's black-robed arm. "Just one more second. You said there was news—"

"It is not your concern."

"Tell me."

Dalamar paused, his brows came together in irritation at this delay. Tanis felt the young elf's arm tense. He's frightened, Tanis realized suddenly. But even as this thought crossed his mind, he saw Dalamar regain control of himself. The handsome features grew calm, expressionless.

"The cleric, Lady Crysania, has been mortally wounded. She managed to protect Raistlin, however.

In science-fiction or spy stories, the hero is often given a talisman/device whose advanced properties assist him in his quest, while in fantasy, it seems that it is always an item from the past that has greater power than the present objects. Both are hopeful expressions that look for answers in a time different than our own. We often refer to "the good old days" as though they were, somehow, better than our own, or we look toward a future that is better than our present time. Life, however, is what happens in the now, and we can only affect the future or past by what we do in the present moment. —TRH

These are all references to the magic attacks of which death knights are capable in the AD&D rules.

He is uninjured and has gone on to find the Queen. So Her Dark Majesty tells me."

Tanis felt his throat constrict. "What about Crysania?" he said harshly. "Did he just leave her to die?"

"Of course." Dalamar appeared faintly surprised at the question. "She can be of no more use to him."

Looking down at the bracelet in his hand, Tanis longed to hurl it into the gleaming teeth of the dark elf. But, in time, he remembered that he could not afford the luxury of anger. What an insane, twisted situation! Incongruously, he remembered Elistan going to the Tower, bringing comfort to the archmage . . .

Turning on his heel, Tanis stalked angrily away. But he gripped the bracelet tightly in his hand.

"The magic is activated when you put it on." Dalamar's soft voice floated through Tanis's haze of fury. He could have sworn the dark elf was laughing.

"What's the matter, Tanis?" Lord Gunthar asked as the half-elf came into the war room. "My dear fellow, you're pale as death. . . ."

"Nothing. I—I just heard some disturbing news. I'll be all right." Tanis drew a deep breath, then glanced at the knights. "You don't look any too good yourselves."

"Another pledge?" Sir Markham said, raising his brandy snifter.

Lord Gunthar gave him a stern, disapproving glance, which the young knight ignored as he casually quaffed his drink in a gulp.

"The citadel has been sighted. It crossed the mountains. It will be here at dawn."

Tanis nodded. "About what I had figured." He scratched his beard, then wearily rubbed his eyes. Casting a glance at the brandy bottle, he shook his head. No, it would probably just send him straight to sleep.

"What's that you're holding?" Gunthar asked, reaching out his hand to take the bracelet. "Some sort of elven good-luck charm?"

"I wouldn't touch—" Tanis began.

"Damnation!" Gunthar gasped, snatching his hand back. The bracelet dropped to the floor, landing on a plush, hand-woven rug. The knight wrung his hand in pain.

Bending down, Tanis picked up the bracelet. Gunthar watched him with disbelieving eyes. Sir Markham was choking back laughter.

"The mage, Dalamar, brought it to us. It's from the Tower of High Sorcery," Tanis said, ignoring Lord Gunthar's scowl. "It will protect the wearer from the effects of magic—the one thing that will give someone a chance of getting near Lord Soth."

"Someone!" Gunthar repeated. He stared down at his hand. The fingers where he had touched the bracelet were burned. "Not only that, but it sent a jolt through me that nearly stopped my heart! Who in the name of the Abyss can wear such a thing?"

"I can, for one," Tanis returned. *It came from a place of darkness. It knows one of its own.* "It has something to do with you knights and holy vows to Paladine," he muttered, feeling his face flush.

"Bury it!" Lord Gunthar growled. "We do not need such help as those of the Black Robes would give us!"

"It seems to me we can use all the help we can get, my lord!" Tanis snapped. "I would also remind you that, odd as it may seem, we're all on the same side! And now, Sir Markham, what of the plans for defending the city?"

Slipping the bracelet into a pouch, affecting not to notice Lord Gunthar's glare, Tanis turned to Sir Markham who, though rather startled at this sudden call, quickly rode to Tanis's rescue with his report.

The Knights of Solamnia were marching from the High Clerist's Tower. It would be days, at least, before they could reach Palanthas. He had sent a messenger to alert the good dragons, but it seemed unlikely that they, too, could reach Palanthas in time.

The city itself was on the alert. In a brief, spare speech, Lord Amothus had told the citizens what faced them. There had been no panic, a fact Gunthar found hard to believe. Oh, a few of the wealthy had tried to bribe ships' captains to take them out, but the captains had, to a man, refused to sail into the seas under the threat of such ominous-looking storm clouds. The gates to Old City were opened. Those who wanted to flee the city and risk going out in the wilderness had, of course, been allowed to go. Not many took the chance. In Palanthas, at least the city walls and the knights afforded protection.

Personally, Tanis thought that if the citizens had known what horrors they faced, they would have taken their chances. As it was, however, the women put aside their rich clothing and began filling every available container with water to have available to fight fires. Those who lived in New City (not protected by walls) were evacuated into Old City, whose walls were being fortified as best they could in the little time that remained. Children were bedded down in wine cellars and storm shelters. Merchants opened shops, handing out needed supplies. Armorers gave out weapons, and the forges were still burning, late into the night, for mending swords, shields, and armor.

Looking out over the city, Tanis saw lights in most homes—people preparing for a morning that he knew from experience could never be prepared for.

With a sigh, thinking of his letter to Laurana, he made his bitter decision. But he knew it would entail argument. He needed to lay the groundwork. Turning abruptly, he interrupted Markham. "What do you guess will be their plan of attack?" he asked Lord Gunthar.

"I think that's fairly simple." Gunthar tugged at his mustaches. "They'll do what they did at Kalaman. Bring the citadel as close as they can get. At Kalaman that wasn't very close. The dragons held them back. But"—he shrugged—"we don't have near the numbers of dragons they did. Once the citadel is over the walls, the draconians will drop from it and try to take the city from within. The evil dragons will attack—"

"And Lord Soth will sweep through the gates," Tanis finished.

"The knights should at least get here in time to keep him from looting our corpses," Sir Markham said, draining his snifter again.

"And Kitiara," Tanis mused, "will be trying to reach the Tower of High Sorcery. Dalamar says no living being can get through Shoikan Grove, but he also said Kit had a charm, given to her by Raistlin. She might wait for Soth before going, figuring he can help her, as well."

"If the Tower is her objective," Gunthar said with emphasis on the *if*. It was obvious he still believed little of the tale about Raistlin. "My guess is that she

will use the battle as cover to fly her dragon over the walls and land as near the Tower as possible. Maybe we could post knights around the Grove to try to stop her—"

"They couldn't get close enough," Sir Markham interrupted, adding a belated, "m'lord. The Grove has an unnerving effect on anyone coming within miles of it."

"Besides, we'll need the knights to deal with Soth's legions," Tanis said. He drew a deep breath. " . . . I have a plan, if I may be allowed to propose it?"

"By all means, Half-Elven."

"You believe that the citadel will attack from above and Lord Soth will come through the front gates, creating a diversion that will give Kit her chance to reach the Tower. Right?"

Gunthar nodded.

"Then, mount what knights we can upon bronze dragons. Let me have Fireflash. Since the bracelet gives me the best defense against Soth, I'll take him. The rest of the knights can concentrate on his followers. I have a private score to settle with Soth anyway," Tanis added, seeing Gunthar already shaking his head.

"Absolutely not. You did very well in the last war, but you've never been trained! To go up against a Knight of Solamnia—"

"Even a dead Knight of Solamnia!" Sir Markham struck in, with a drunken giggle.

Gunthar's mustaches quivered in anger, but he contained himself and continued coldly, "—a trained knight, as Soth is trained, and you must fall—bracelet or no bracelet."

"Without the bracelet, however, my lord, training in swordmanship will matter very little." Sir Markham pointed out, drinking another brandy. "A chap who can point at you and say 'die' has the distinct advantage."

"Please, sir," Tanis intervened, "I admit that my formal training has been limited, but my years wearing a sword outnumber yours, my lord, by almost two to one. My elven blood—"

"To the Abyss with your elven blood," Gunthar muttered, glaring at Sir Markham, who was resolutely ignoring his superior, and lifting the brandy bottle again.

"I will, if I am forced, pull rank, my lord," Tanis said quietly.

Gunthar's face reddened. "Damn it, that was honorary!"

Tanis smiled. "The Code makes no such distinction. Honorary or not, I am a Knight of the Rose, and my age—well over one hundred, my lord—gives me seniority."

Sir Markham was laughing. "Oh, for the gods' sake, Gunthar, give him your permission to die. What the Abyss difference does it make anyway?"

"He's drunk," Gunthar muttered, casting a scathing glance at Sir Markham.

"He's young," Tanis replied. "Well, my lord?"

Lord Gunthar's eyes flashed in anger. As he glared at the half-elf, sharp words of reproval came to his lips. But they were never uttered. Gunthar knew—none better—that the one who faced Soth was placing himself in a situation of almost certain death—magical bracelet or no magical bracelet. He had first assumed Tanis was either too naive or too foolhardy to recognize this. Looking into the half-elf's dark, shadowed eyes, he realized that, once again, he had misjudged him.

Swallowing his words with a gruff cough, Lord Gunthar made a gesture at Sir Markham. "See if you can get him sobered up, Half-Elven. Then I suppose you had better get yourself into position. I'll have the knights waiting."

"Thank you, my lord," Tanis murmured.

"And may the gods go with you," Gunthar added in a low, choked voice. Gripping Tanis by the hand, he turned and stalked out of the room.

Tanis glanced over at Sir Markham, who was staring intently into the empty brandy bottle with a wry smile. He's not as drunk as he's letting on, Tanis decided. Or as he wishes he could be.

Turning from the young knight, the half-elf walked over to the window. Looking out, he waited for the dawn.

Laurana

My beloved wife, when we parted a week ago, we little thought this parting might be for a long, long time. We have been kept apart so much of our lives But I must admit, I cannot grieve that we are separated now. It comforts me to know that you are safe, although if Raistlin succeeds in his designs, I fear there will be no safe havens left anywhere upon Krynn.

I must be honest, my dearest. I see no hope that any of us can survive. I face without fear the knowledge that I shall probably die—I believe I can honestly say that. But I cannot face it without bitter anger. The last war, I could afford bravery. I had nothing, so had nothing to lose. But I have never wanted so much to live as I do now. I am like a miser, coveting the joy and happiness we have found, loath to give it up. I think of our plans, the children we hope for. I think of you, my beloved, and what grief my death must bring, and I cannot see this page for the tears of sorrow and fury that I cry.

I can only ask you to let this consolation be yours as it is mine—this parting will be our last. The world can never separate us again. I will wait for you, Laurana, in that realm where time itself dies.

And one evening, in that realm of eterna spring, eternal twilight, I will look down the path and see you walking toward me. I can see you so clearly, my beloved. The last rays of the setting sun shining upon your golden hair, your eyes bright with the love that fills my own heart.

You will come to me.

I will fold you in my arms.

We will close our eyes and begin to dream our eternal dream.†

I love this letter, a soldier's heart poured out to his great love. Such letters have been written with aching heart since antiquity, and sadly we are not finished writing them yet. Here in the story we get a sense of the depth of Tanis's love for Laurana and the honor of his commitment to their love.
—TRH

BOOK 3

The Return

The gate guard lounged in the dark shadows of the gatehouse of Old City. Outside, he could hear the voices of the other guards, tight and tense with excitement and fear, talking up their courage. There must be twenty of them out there, the old guard thought sourly. The night watch had been doubled, those off duty had decided to stay rather than go back home. Above him, on the wall, he could hear the slow, steady pacing of the Knights of Solamnia. High above him, occasionally, he could hear the creak and flap of a dragon's wing, or sometimes their voices, speaking to each other in the secret tongue of the dragons. These were the bronze dragons Lord Gunthar had brought from the High Clerist's Tower, keeping watch in the air as the humans kept watch upon the ground.

All around him he could hear the sounds—the sounds of impending doom.

That thought was in the gatekeeper's mind, though not in those exact words, of course—neither "impending" nor "doom" being a part of his vocabulary. But the knowledge was there, just the same. The gate guard was an old mercenary, he'd been through many of these nights. He'd been a young man like those outside, once, boasting of the great deeds he'd do in the morning. His first battle, he'd been so scared he couldn't to this day remember a thing about it.

But there'd been many battles after that. You got used to the fear. It became a part of you, just like your sword. Thinking about this battle coming up was no different. The morning would come and, if you were lucky, so would the night.

A sudden clatter of pikes and voices and a general flurry jolted the old guard out of his philosophic musings. Grumbling, but feeling a touch of the old excitement just the same, he poked his head out of the guardhouse.

"I heard something!" a young guard panted, running up, nearly out of breath. "Out—out there! Sounded like armor jingling, a whole troop!"

The other guards were peering out into the darkness. Even the Knights of Solamnia had ceased their pacing and were looking down into the broad highway that ran through the gate from New City into Old. Extra torches had been hastily added to those that already burned on the walls. They cast a bright circle of light on the ground below. But the light ended about twenty feet away, making the darkness beyond seem just that much darker. The old guard could hear the sounds now, too, but he didn't panic. He was veteran enough to know that darkness and fear can make one man sound like a regiment.

Stumping out of the gatehouse, he waved his hands, adding with a snarl, "Back to yer posts."

The younger guards, muttering, returned to their positions, but kept their weapons ready. The old guard, hand on his sword hilt, stood stolidly in the middle of the street, waiting.

Sure enough, into the light came—not a division of draconians—but one man (who might, however, have been big enough for two) and what appeared to be a kender.

The two stopped, blinking in the torchlight. The old guard sized them up. The big man wore no cloak, and the guard could see light reflecting off armor that might once have gleamed brightly but was now caked with gray mud and even blackened in places, as though he had been in a fire. The kender, too, was covered with the same type of mud—though he had apparently made some effort to brush it off his gaudy blue leggings. The big man limped when he walked, and both he and the kender gave every indication of having recently been in battle.

Odd, thought the gate guard. There's been no fighting yet, leastways none that we've heard tell of.

"Cool customers, both of 'em," the old guard muttered, noting that the big man's hand rested easily on the hilt of his sword as he looked about, taking stock of the situation. The kender was staring around with usual kender curiosity. The gate guard was slightly startled to see, however, that the kender held in his arms a large, leather-bound book. "State yer business," the gate guard said, coming forward to stand in front of the two.

"I'm Tasslehoff Burrfoot," said the kender, managing, after a brief struggle with the book, to free a

small hand. He held it out to the guard. "And this is my friend, Caramon. We're from Sol—"

"Our business depends on where we are," said the man called Caramon in a friendly voice but with a serious expression on his face that gave the gate guard pause.

"You mean you don't know where you are?" the guard asked suspiciously.

"We're not from this part of the country," the big man answered coolly. "We lost our map. Seeing the lights of the city, we naturally headed toward it."

Yeah, and I'm Lord Amothus, thought the guard. "Yer in Palanthas."

The big man glanced behind him, then back down at the guard, who barely came to his shoulder. "So that must be New City, behind us. Where are all the people? We've walked the length and breadth of the town. No sign of anyone."

"We're under alert." The guard jerked his head. "Everyone's been taken inside the walls. I guess that's all you need to know for the present. Now, what's yer business here? And how is it you don't know what's going on? The word's over half the country by now, I reckon."

The big man ran his hand across an unshaven jaw, smiling ruefully. "A full bottle of dwarf spirits kinda blots out most everything. True enough, captain?"

"True enough," growled the guard. And also true enough that this fellow's eyes were sharp and clear and filled with a fixed purpose, a firm resolve. Looking into those eyes, the guard shook his head. He'd seen them before, the eyes of a man who is going to his death, who knows it, and who has made peace with both the gods and himself.

"Will you let us inside?" the big man asked. "I guess, from the looks of things, you could use another couple of fighters."

"We can use a man yer size," the guard returned. He scowled down at the kender. "But I mistrust we should just leave 'im here for buzzard bait."

"I'm a fighter, too!" the kender protested indignantly. "Why, I saved Caramon's life once!" His face brightened. "Do you want to hear about it? It's the most wonderful story. We were in a magical fortress. Raistlin had taken me there, after he killed my fri— But never mind about that. Anyway, there

were these dark dwarves and they were attacking Caramon and he slipped and—"

"Open the gate!" the old guard shouted.

"C'mon, Tas," the big man said.

"But I just got to the best part!"

"Oh, by the way"—the big man turned around, first deftly squelching the kender with his hand—"can you tell me the date?"

"Thirdday, Fifthmonth, 356," said the guard. "Oh, and you might be wantin' a cleric to look at that leg of yours."

"Clerics," the big man murmured to himself. "That's right, I'd forgotten. There are clerics now. Thank you," he called out as he and the kender walked through the gates. The gate guard could hear the kender's voice piping up again, as he managed to free himself from the big man's hand.

"Phew! You should really wash, Caramon. I've—blooey! Drat, mud in my mouth! Now, where was I? Oh, yes, you should have let me finish! I'd just gotten to the part where you tripped in the blood and—"

Shaking his head, the gate guard looked after the two. "There's a story there," he muttered, as the big gates swung shut again, "and not even a kender could make up a better one, I'll wager."

CHAPTER
I

W hat's it say, Car-
amon?" Tas stood on tiptoe, trying to peer over the
big man's arm.

"Shh!" Caramon whispered irritably. "I'm reading." He shook his arm. "Let loose." The big man had
been leafing hurriedly through the *Chronicles* he
had taken from Astinus. But he had stopped turning
pages, and was now studying one intently.

With a sigh—after all, *he'd* carried the book!—Tas
slumped back against the wall and looked around.
They were standing beneath one of the flaming bra-
ziers that Palanthians used to light the streets at night.
It was nearly dawn, the kender guessed. The storm
clouds blocked the sunlight, but the city was taking
on a dismal gray tint. A chill fog curled up from the
bay, swirling and winding through the streets.

Though there were lights in most of the windows,
there were few people on the streets, the citizens

having been told to stay indoors, unless they were members of the militia. But Tas could see the faces of women, pressed against the glass, watching, waiting. Occasionally a man ran past them, clutching a weapon in his hand, heading for the front gate of the city. And once, a door to a dwelling right across from Tas opened. A man stepped out, a rusty sword in his hand. A woman followed, weeping. Leaning down, he kissed her tenderly, then kissed the small child she held in her arms. Then, turning away abruptly, he walked rapidly down the street. As he passed Tas, the kender saw tears flowing down his face.

"Oh, no!" Caramon muttered.

"What? What?" Tas cried, leaping up, trying to see the page Caramon was reading.

"Listen to this. 'On the morning of Thirdday, the flying citadel appeared in the air above Palanthas, accompanied by flights of blue dragons and black. And with the appearance of the citadel in the air, there came before the Gates of Old City an apparition, the sight of which caused more than one veteran of many campaigns to blanch in fear and turn his head away.

" 'For there appeared, as if created out of the darkness of the night itself, Lord Soth, Knight of the Black Rose, mounted upon a nightmare† with eyes and hooves of flame. He rode unchallenged toward the city gate, the guards fleeing before him in terror.

" 'And there he stopped.

" ' "Lord of Palanthas," the death knight called in a hollow voice that came from the realms of death, "surrender your city to Lord Kitiara. Give up to her the keys to the Tower of High Sorcery, name her ruler of Palanthas, and she will allow you to continue to live in peace. Your city will be spared destruction."

" 'Lord Amothus took his place upon the wall, looking down at the death knight. Many of those around him could not look, so shaken were they by their fear. But the lord—although pale as death himself—stood tall and straight, his words bringing back courage to those who had lost it."

" ' "Take this message to your Dragon Highlord. Palanthas has lived in peace and beauty for many centuries. But we will buy neither peace nor beauty at the price of our freedom."†

Soth is not riding upon a bad dream here. A nightmare, as most AD&D players can tell you, is an evil steed from the nether regions. It looks like a large black horse with glowing red eyes, hooves of flame, and glowing orange nostrils.

"They that can give up essential liberty to obtain a little temporary safety deserve neither liberty nor safety." [Benjamin Franklin, Historical Review of Pennsylvania, 1759.]

" ' "Then buy it at the price of your lives!" Lord Soth shouted. Out of the air, seemingly, materialized his legions—thirteen skeletal warriors, riding upon horses with eyes and hooves of flame, took their places behind him. And, behind them, standing in chariots made of human bone pulled by wyvern, appeared bansheest—the spirits of those elven women constrained by the gods to serve Soth. They held swords of ice in their hands, to hear their wailing cry alone meant death.

I first encountered banshees in Disney's Darby O'Gill and the Little People, and yes, they scarred me for life.
—TRH

" 'Raising a hand made visible only by the glove of chain steel he wore upon it, Lord Soth pointed at the gate of the city that stood closed, barring his way. He spoke a word of magic and, at that word, a dreadful cold swept over all who watched, freezing the soul more than the blood. The iron of the gate began to whiten with frost, then it changed to ice, then—at another word from Soth—the ice gate shattered.

" 'Soth's hand fell. He charged through the broken gate, his legions following.†

" 'Waiting for him on the other side of the gate, mounted upon the bronze dragon, Fireflash (his dragonish name being Khirsah), was Tanis Half-Elven, Hero of the Lance. Immediately upon sighting his opponent, the death knight sought to slay him instantly by shouting the magical power word, "Die!" Tanis Half-Elven, being protected by the silver bracelet of magic resistance, was not affected by the spell. But the bracelet that saved his life in this first attack, could help him no longer—' "

As I mentioned earlier, the banshees appeared simultaneously with Lord Soth in my work cubicle at TSR. I knew their history at once, and they were forever linked with the Death Knight thereafter.
—TRH

" 'Help him no longer!' " cried Tas, interrupting Caramon's reading. "What does that mean?"

"Shush!" Caramon hissed and went on. " '—help him no longer. The bronze dragon he rode, having no magical protection, died at Soth's command, forcing Tanis Half-Elven to fight the death knight on foot. Lord Soth dismounted to meet his opponent according to the Laws of Combat as set forth by the Knights of Solamnia, these laws binding the death knight still, even though he had long since passed beyond their jurisdiction. Tanis Half-Elven fought bravely but was no match for Lord Soth. He fell, mortally wounded, the death knight's sword in his chest—' "

"No!" Tas gasped. "No! We can't let Tanis die!" Reaching up, he tugged on Caramon's arm. "Let's go! There's still time! We can find him and warn him—"

"I can't, Tas," Caramon said quietly. "I've got to go to the Tower. I can sense Raistlin's presence drawing closer to me. I don't have time, Tas."

"You can't mean that! We can't just let Tanis die!" Tas whispered, staring at Caramon, wide-eyed.

"No, Tas, we can't," said Caramon, regarding the kender gravely. "*You're* going to save him."

The thought literally took Tasslehoff's breath away. When he finally found his voice, it was more of a squeak. "Me? But, Caramon, I'm not a warrior! Oh, I know I told the guard that I—"

"Tasslehoff Burrfoot," Caramon said sternly, "I suppose it is possible that the gods arranged this entire matter simply for your own private amusement. Possible—but I doubt it. We're part of this world, and we've got to take some responsibility for it.† I see this now. I see it very clearly." He sighed, and for a moment his face was solemn and so filled with sadness that Tas felt a choking lump rise up in his throat.

As are each of us in our own world. This is our responsibility, too. —TRH

"I know that I'm part of the world, Caramon," Tas said miserably, "and I'd gladly take as much responsibility as I think it likely I can handle. But—it's just that I'm such a *short* part of the world—if you take my meaning. And Lord Soth's such a tall and ugly part. And—"

A trumpet sounded, then another. Both Tas and Caramon fell silent, listening until the braying had died away.

"That's it, isn't it?" Tas said softly.

"Yes," Caramon replied. "You better hurry."

Closing the book, he shoved it carefully into an old knapsack Tas had managed to "acquire" when they were in the deserted New City. The kender had managed to acquire some new pouches for himself, as well, plus a few other interesting items it was probably just as well Caramon didn't know he had. Then, reaching out his hand, the big man laid it on Tas's head, smoothing back the ridiculous topknot.

"Good-bye, Tas. Thank you."

"But, Caramon!" Tas stared at him, feeling suddenly very lonely and confused. "Wh-where will you be?"

Caramon glanced up into the sky to where the Tower of High Sorcery loomed, a black rent in the

storm clouds. Lights burned in the top windows of the Tower where the laboratory—and the Portal—were located.

Tas followed his gaze, looking up at the Tower. He saw the storm clouds lowering around it, the eerie lightning play around it, toying with it. He remembered his one close-up glimpse of the Shoikan Grove—

"Oh, Caramon!" he cried, catching hold of the big man's hand. "Caramon, don't . . . wait. . . ."

"Good-bye, Tas," Caramon said, firmly detaching the clinging kender. "I've got to do this. You know what will happen if I don't. And you know what you've got to do, too. Now hurry up. The citadel's probably over the gate by now."

"But, Caramon—" Tas wailed.

"Tas, you've got to do this!" Caramon yelled, his angry voice echoing down the empty street. "Are you going to let Tanis die without trying to help him?"

Tas shrank back. He'd never seen Caramon angry before, at least, not angry at him. And in all their adventures together, Caramon had never once yelled at him. "No, Caramon," he said meekly. "It's just . . . I'm not sure what I can do. . . ."

"You'll think of something," Caramon muttered, scowling. "You always do." Turning around, he walked away, leaving Tas to stare after him disconsolately.

"G-good-bye, Caramon," he called out after the retreating figure. "I—I won't let you down."

The big man turned. When he spoke, his voice sounded funny to Tas, like maybe he was choking on something. "I know you won't, Tas, no matter what happens." With a wave, he set off again down the street.

In the distance, Tas saw the dark shadows of Shoikan Grove, the shadows no day would ever brighten, the shadows where lurked the guardians of the Tower.

Tas stood for a moment, watching Caramon until he lost him in the darkness. He *had* hoped, if the truth be told, that Caramon would suddenly change his mind, turn around and shout, "Wait, Tas! I'll come with you to save Tanis!"

But he didn't.

"Which leaves it up to me," Tas said with a sigh. "And he *yelled* at me!" Snuffling a little, he turned and trudged off in the opposite direction, toward the gate. His heart was in his mud-coated shoes, making them feel even heavier. He had absolutely no idea how he was going to go about rescuing Tanis from a death knight, and, the more he thought about it, the more unusual it seemed that Caramon would give him this responsibility.

"Still, I *did* save Caramon's life," Tas muttered. "Maybe he's coming to realize—"

Suddenly, he stopped and stood stock-still in the middle of the street.

"Caramon got rid of me!" he cried. "Tasslehoff Burrfoot, you have all the brains of a doorknob, as Flint told you many times. He got rid of me! He's going there to *die*! Sending me to rescue Tanis was just an excuse!" Distraught and unhappy, Tas stared down the street one way and up it another. "Now, what do I do?" he muttered.

He took a step toward Caramon. Then he heard a trumpet sound again, this time with a shrill, blaring note of alarm. And, rising above it, he thought he could hear a voice, shouting orders—Tanis's voice.

"But if I go to Caramon, Tanis will die!" Tas stopped. Half-turning, he took a step toward Tanis. Then he stopped again, winding his topknot into a perfect corkscrew of indecision. The kender had never felt so frustrated in his entire life.

"Both of them need me!" he wailed in agony. "How can I choose?"

Then—"I know!" His brow cleared. "That's it!"

With a great sigh of relief, Tas spun around and continued in the direction of the gate, this time at a run.

"I'll rescue Tanis," he panted as he took a short-cut through an alley, "and then I'll just come back and rescue Caramon. Tanis might even be of some help to me."

Scuttling down the alley, sending cats scattering in a panic, Tas frowned irritably. "I wonder how many heroes this makes that I've had to save," he said to himself with a sniff. "Frankly, I'm getting just a bit fed up with all of them!"

The floating citadel appeared in the skies over Palanthas just as the trumpets sounded for the

changing of the watch. The tall, crumbling spires and battlements, the towering stone walls, the lighted windows jammed with draconian troops—all could be seen quite plainly as the citadel floated downward, resting on its foundation of boiling, magical cloud.

The wall of Old City was crammed with men—townsmen, knights, mercenaries. None spoke a word. All gripped their weapons, staring upward in grim silence.

But, after all, there was one word spoken at the sight of the citadel—or several, as it were.

"Oh!" breathed Tas in awe, clasping his hands together, marveling at the sight. "Isn't it wonderful! I'd forgotten how truly magnificent and glorious the flying citadels are! I'd give anything, *anything,* to ride on one." Then, with a sigh, he shook himself. "Not now, Burrfoot," he said to himself sternly in his Flint voice. "You have work to do. Now"—he looked around—"there's the gate. There's the citadel. And there goes Lord Amothus. . . . My, he looks terrible! I've seen better looking dead people. But where's—Ah!"

A grim processional appeared, marching up the street toward Tas—a group of Solamnic Knights, walking on foot, leading their horses. There was no cheering, they did not talk. Each man's face was solemn and tense, each man knew he walked—most likely—to his death. They were led by a man whose bearded face stood out in sharp contrast to the cleanshaven, mustached faces of the knights around him. And, although he wore the armor of a Knight of the Rose, he did not wear it with the ease of the other knights.

"Tanis always hated plate-mail," Tas said, watching his friend approach. "And here he is, wearing the armor of a Knight of Solamnia. I wonder what Sturm would have thought of that! I wish Sturm was here right now!" Tas's lower lip began quivering. A tear sneaked down his nose before he could stop it. "I wish *anyone* brave and clever was here right now!"

When the Knights drew near the Gate, Tanis stopped and turned to face them, issuing orders in a low voice. The creaking sound of dragon wings came from overhead. Looking up, Tasslehoff saw Khirsah,

circling, leading a formation of other bronze drag-ons. And there was the citadel, coming closer to the wall, dropping down lower and lower.

"Sturm's not here. Caramon's not here. No one's here, Burrfoot," Tas muttered, resolutely wiping his eyes. "Once again—you're on your own. Now, what *am* I going to do?"

Wild thoughts ran through the kender's mind—everything from holding Tanis at swordpoint ("I mean it, Tanis, keep those hands in the air!") to clunking him over the head with a sharp rock ("Uh, say, Tanis, would you mind taking off your helm for a moment?"). Tas was even desperate enough to consider telling the truth ("You see, Tanis, we went back in time, then we went ahead in time, and Cara-mon got hold of this book from Astinus just as the world was coming to an end, and, in the next to the last chapter, it tells in there how you died, and—"). Suddenly, Tas saw Tanis raise his right arm. There was a flash of silver—

"That's it," said Tas, breathing a profound sigh of relief. "That's what I'll do—just what I do best. . . ."

"No matter what happens, leave me to deal with Lord Soth," Tanis said, looking grimly at the knights standing around him. "I want you to swear this, by the Code and the Measure."†

"Tanis, my lord—" began Sir Markham.

"No, I'm not going to argue, Knight. You'll stand no chance at all against him without magical protec-tion. Each one of you will be needed to fight his legions. Now, either swear this oath, or I will order you off the field. Swear!"

From beyond the closed gate, a deep, hollow voice spoke, calling out for Palanthas to surrender. The knights glanced at each other, feeling shivers of fear run through their bodies at the inhuman sound. There was a moment's silence, broken only by the creaking of dragons' wings overhead as the great creatures—bronze, silver, blue, and black—circled, eyeing each other balefully, waiting for the call to battle. Tanis's dragon, Khirsah, hovered in the air near his rider, ready to come down upon command.

And then they heard Lord Amothus's voice—brittle and tight, but strong with purpose—answering the death knight. "Take this message to your Dragon

The "Code and the Measure?" Tanis obviously is not to up on his Solamnic Knight trivia, since it is actually the "Oath and the Measure." He would have missed this question on any game show in Krynn. —TRH

Tanis means the "Oath and the Measure," of course. He's a bit rattled at this point, I think. —MW

Highlord. Palanthas has lived in peace and beauty for many centuries. But we will buy neither peace nor beauty at the price of our freedom."

"I swear," said Sir Markham softly, "by the Code and the Measure."†

"I swear," came the responses of the other knights after him.

"Thank you," Tanis said, looking at each of the young men standing before him, thinking that most wouldn't be alive much longer. . . . Thinking that he himself— Angrily, he shook his head. "Fireflash—" The words that would summon his dragon were on Tanis's lips when he heard a commotion break out at the rear of the line of knights.

"Ouch! Get off my foot, you great lummox!"

A horse whinnied. Tanis heard one of the knights cursing, then a shrill voice answering innocently, "Well, it's not my fault! Your horse *stepped* on me! Flint was right about those stupid beasts—"

The other horses, sensing battle and already affected by the tenseness of their riders, pricked their ears and snorted nervously. One danced out of line, his rider grasping at the bridle.

"Get those horses under control!" Tanis called out tensely. "What's going on—"

"Let me past! Get out of my way. What? Is that dagger yours? You must have dropped it. . . ."

Beyond the gate, Tanis heard the death knight's voice.

"You'll pay for it with your lives!"

And from the line ahead of him, another voice.

"Tanis, it's me, Tasslehoff!"

The half-elf's heart sank. He wasn't at all certain, at that moment, which voice chilled him more.

But there didn't seem to be time for thought or wonder. Glancing over his shoulder, Tanis saw the gate turn to ice, he saw it shatter. . . .

"Tanis!" Something had hold of his arm. "Oh, Tanis!" Tas clutched at him. "Tanis! You've got to come quickly and save Caramon! He's going into Shoikan Grove!"

Caramon? Caramon's dead! was Tanis's first thought. But then Tas is dead, too. What's going on? Am I going mad from fear?

Someone shouted. Looking around dazedly, Tanis saw the faces of the knights turn deathly white

Are the Knights of Solamnia putting one over on Tanis here? Swearing by "the Oath and the Measure" would have deep meaning for these Knights. Swearing by some "Code and the Measure" may have no binding meaning at all! I think Tanis is being conned! I can only hope these Knights take the message anyway— even if they all have a good laugh later about the big "Hero of the Lance" who didn't even know what the Oath and the Measure was! —TRH

beneath their helms, and he knew Lord Soth and his legions were entering the gates.

"Mount!" he called, frantically trying to pry loose the kender, who was clinging to him tenaciously. "Tas! This is no time— Get out of here, damn it!"

"Caramon's going to die!" Tas wailed. "You've got to save him, Tanis!"

"Caramon's . . . already . . . dead!" Tanis snarled.

Khirsah landed on the ground beside him, screaming a battle cry. Evil and good—the other dragons shrieked in anger, flying at each other, talons gleaming. In an instant, battle was joined. The air was filled with the flash of lightning and the smell of acid. From above, horns sounded in the floating citadel. There were cries of glee from the draconians, who began eagerly dropping down into the city, their leathery wings spread to break their fall.

And moving closer, the chill of death flowing from his fleshless body, rode Lord Soth.

But, try as he might, Tanis couldn't shake Tas loose. Finally, swearing beneath his breath, the half-elf got a grip on the writhing kender. Catching hold of Tas around the waist, so angry he was literally choking with rage—Tanis hurled the kender into a corner of a nearby alley.

"And stay there!" he roared.

"Tanis!" Tas pleaded. "You can't go out there! You're going to die. I know!"

Giving Tas a last, furious glance, Tanis turned on his heel and ran. "Fireflash!" he shouted. The dragon swooped over to him, landing on the street beside him.

"Tanis!" Tas screamed shrilly. "You can't fight Lord Soth without the bracelet!"†

It is standard in fantasy to provide the hero with some magical means of getting him out of perilous situations. I thought it would be fun to do this with Tanis, then take it away from him at the last minute. —MW

CHAPTER
2

The bracelet!
Tanis looked down at his wrist. The bracelet was
gone! Whirling, he made a lunge for the kender. But
it was too late. Tasslehoff was dashing down the
street, running as if his life depended on it. (Which,
after glimpsing Tanis's furious face, Tas figured it
probably did.)

"Tanis!" cried out Sir Markham.

Tanis turned. Lord Soth sat upon his nightmare,
framed by the shattered gates of the city of Palanthas. His flaming-eyed gaze met Tanis's and held.
Even at that distance, Tanis felt his soul shrivel with
the fear that shrouds the walking dead.

What could he do? He didn't have the bracelet.
Without it, there'd be no chance. No chance whatsoever! Thank the gods, Tanis thought in that split
second, thank the gods I'm not a knight, bound to
die with honor.

"Run!" he commanded through lips so stiff he could barely speak. "Fly! There is nothing you can do against these! Remember your oath! Retreat! Spend your lives fighting the living—"

Even as he spoke, a draconian landed in front of him, its horrible reptilian face twisted in bloodlust. Remembering just in time not to stab the thing, whose foul body would turn to stone, encasing the sword of its killers, Tanis bashed it in the face with the hilt of his weapon, kicked it in the stomach, then leaped over it as it tumbled to the ground.

Behind him, he heard the sounds of horses shrieking in terror and the clattering of hooves. He hoped the knights were obeying his last command, but he could spare no time to see. There was still a chance, if he could get hold of Tas and the magical bracelet. . . .

"The kender!" he yelled to the dragon, pointing down the street at the fleeing, fleet-footed little figure.

Khirsah understood and was off at once, the tips of his wings grazing buildings as he swooped down the broad street in pursuit, knocking stone and brick to the ground.

Tanis ran behind the dragon. He did not look around. He didn't need to. He could hear, by the agonized cries and screams, what was happening.

That morning, death rode the streets of Palanthas. Led by Lord Soth, the ghastly army swept through the gate like a chill wind, withering everything that stood in its path.

By the time Tanis caught up with the dragon, Khirsah had Tas in his teeth. Gripping the kender upside down by the seat of his blue pants, the dragon was shaking him like the most efficient of jail wardens. Tas's newly acquired pouches flew open, sending a small hailstorm of rings, spoons, a napkin holder, and a half of a cheese tumbling about the street.

But no silver bracelet.

"Where is it, Tas?" Tanis demanded angrily, longing to shake the kender himself.

"Y-you'll . . . n-nev-ver . . . f-find-d-d it-t-t-t," returned the kender, his teeth rattling in his head.

"Put him down," Tanis instructed the dragon. "Fireflash, keep watch."

The floating citadel had come to a stop at the city's walls, its magic-users and dark clerics battling the attacking silver and bronze dragons. It was difficult to see in the flashes of blinding lightning and the spreading haze of smoke, but Tanis was certain he caught a quick glimpse of a blue dragon leaving the citadel. Kitiara, he thought—but he had no time to spare worrying about her.

Khirsah dropped Tas (nearly on his head), and—spreading his wings—turned to face the southern part of the city where the enemy was grouping and where the city's defenders were valiantly holding them back.

Tanis came over to stare down at the small culprit, who was staring right back at him defiantly as he stood up.

"Tasslehoff," said Tanis, his voice quivering with suppressed rage, "this time you've gone too far. This prank may cost the lives of hundreds of innocent people. Give me the bracelet, Tas, and know this—from this moment on, our friendship ends!"

Expecting some hare-brained excuse or some sniffling apology, the half-elf was not prepared to see Tas regarding him with a pale face, trembling lips, and an air of quiet dignity.

"It's very hard to explain, Tanis, and I really don't have time. But your fighting Lord Soth wouldn't have made any difference." He looked at the half-elf earnestly. "You must believe me, Tanis. I'm telling the truth. It wouldn't have mattered. All those people who are going to die would still have died, and you would have died, too, and—what's worse—the whole world would have died. But you didn't, so maybe it won't. And now," Tas said firmly, tugging and twitching his pouches and his clothes into place, "we've got to go rescue Caramon."

Tanis stared at Tas, then, wearily, he put his hand to his head and yanked off the hot, steel helm. He had absolutely no idea what was going on. "All right, Tas," he said in exhaustion. "Tell me about Caramon. He's alive? Where is he?"

Tas's face twisted in worry. "That's just it, Tanis. He may *not* be alive. At least not much longer. He's going to try to get into the Shoikan Grove!"

"The Grove!" Tanis looked alarmed. "That's impossible!"

"I know!" Tas tugged nervously at his topknot. "But he's trying to get to the Tower of High Sorcery to stop Raistlin—"

"I see," Tanis muttered. He tossed the helm down into the street. "Or I'm beginning to, at any rate. Let's go. Which way?" Tas's face brightened. "You're coming? You believe me? Oh, Tanis! I'm so glad! You've no idea what a major responsibility it is, looking after Caramon. This way!" he cried, pointing eagerly.

"Is there anything further I can do for you, Half-Elven?" asked Khirsah, fanning his wings, his gaze going eagerly to the battle being fought overhead.

"Not unless you can enter the Grove."

Khirsah shook his head. "I am sorry, Half-Elven. Not even dragons can enter that accursed woods. I wish you good fortune, but do not expect to find your friend alive."

Wings beating, the dragon leaped into the air and soared toward the action. Shaking his head gravely, Tanis started off down the street at a rapid pace, Tasslehoff running to keep up.

"Maybe Caramon couldn't even get that far," Tas said hopefully. "I couldn't, the last time Flint and I came. And kender aren't frightened of anything!"

"You say he's trying to stop Raistlin?"

Tas nodded.

"He'll get that far," Tanis predicted gloomily.

It had taken every bit of Caramon's nerve and courage to even approach the Shoikan Grove. As it was, he was able to come closer to it than any other living mortal not bearing a charm allowing safe passage. Now he stood before those dark, silent trees, shivering and sweating and trying to make himself take one more step.

"My death lies in there," he murmured to himself, licking his dry lips. "But what difference should that make? I've faced death before, a hundred times!" Hand gripping the hilt of his sword, Caramon edged a foot forward.

"No, I will not die!" he shouted at the forest. "I cannot die. Too much depends on me. And I will not be stopped by . . . by trees!"

He edged his other foot forward.

"I have walked in darker places than this." He kept talking, defiantly. "I have walked the Forest of

Wayreth. I have walked Krynn when it was dying. I have seen the end of the world. No," he continued firmly. "This forest holds no terrors for me that I cannot overcome."

With that, Caramon strode forward and stepped into the Shoikan Grove.

He was immediately plunged into everlasting darkness. It was like being back in the Tower again, when Crysania's spell had blinded him. Only this time he was alone. Panic clutched him. There was life within that darkness! Horrible, unholy life that wasn't life at all but living death†. . . . Caramon's muscles went weak. He fell to his hands and knees, sobbing and shivering in terror.

"You're ours!" whispered soft, hissing voices. "Your blood, your warmth, your life! Ours! Ours! Come closer. Bring us your sweet blood, your warm flesh. We are cold, cold, cold beyond endurance. Come closer, come closer."

Horror overwhelmed Caramon. He had only to turn and run and he would escape. . . . "But, no," he gasped in the hissing, smothering darkness, "I must stop Raistlin! I must . . . go . . . on."

For the first time in his life, Caramon reached far down within himself and found the same indomitable will that had led his twin to overcome frailty and pain and even death itself to achieve his goal.† Gritting his teeth, unable to stand yet determined to move ahead, Caramon crawled on his hands and knees through the dirt.

It was a valiant effort, but he did not get far. Staring into the darkness, he watched in paralyzed fascination as a fleshless hand reached up through the ground. Fingers, chill and smooth as marble, closed over his hand and began dragging him down. Desperately, he tried to free himself, but other hands grasped for him, their nails tearing into his flesh. He felt himself being sucked under. The hissing voices whispered in his ears, lips of bone pressed against his flesh. The cold froze his heart.

"I have failed. . . ."

"Caramon," came a worried voice.

Caramon stirred.

"Caramon?" Then, "Tanis, he's coming around!"

"Thank the gods!"

I think that Bram Stoker's Dracula *affected my perspective on the torment of the undead more than any other work. The subsequent adventure "Ravenloft" (co-written by my wife, Laura Curtis) more fully crystallized that vision, which is reflected here. —TRH*

Caramon is very much dependent on Raistlin, a facet of their relationship that people don't often understand, for they see the frail Raistlin as being dependent on his stronger twin. In fact, Caramon uses his care for his brother as a crutch to increase his own self-worth. When this prop is withdrawn, Caramon is helpless. He can't walk on his own. He can't truly love Tika until he comes to love himself, and he can't do that until he faces the truth about his brother. Caramon has to come to understand Raistlin's selfishness, his hunger for power, his willingness to sacrifice anyone and anything to gain his goals. Once Caramon sees this darker side of Raistlin that he could never admit, he can see the darker side to his own nature. He can let go of his brother and finally stand on his own. He can finish building Tika's house. —MW

Caramon opened his eyes. Looking up, he stared into the face of the bearded half-elf, who was looking at him with an expression of relief mingled with puzzlement, amazement, and admiration.

"Tanis!" Sitting up groggily, still numb with horror, Caramon gripped his friend in his strong arms, holding him fast, sobbing in relief.

"My friend!" Tanis said, and then was prevented from saying anything more by his own tears choking him.

"Are you all right, Caramon?" Tas asked, hovering near.

The big man drew a shivering breath. "Yes," he said, putting his head into his shaking hands. "I guess so."

"That was the bravest thing I have seen any man do," Tanis said solemnly, leaning back to rest upon his heels as he stared at Caramon. "The bravest . . . and the stupidest."†

Caramon flushed. "Yeah," he muttered, "well, you know me."

"I used to," Tanis said, scratching his beard. His gaze took in the big man's splendid physique, his bronze skin, his expression of quiet, firm resolve. "Damn it, Caramon! A month ago, you passed out dead drunk at my feet! Your gut practically dragged the floor! And now—"

"I've lived years, Tanis," Caramon said, slowly getting to his feet with Tas's help. "That's all I can tell you. But, what happened? How did I get out of that horrible place?" Glancing behind him, he saw the shadows of the trees far down at the end of the street, and he could not help shuddering.

"I found you," Tanis said, rising to his feet. "They—those things—were dragging you under. You would have had an uneasy resting place there, my friend."

"How did you get in?"

"This," Tanis said, smiling and holding up a silver bracelet.

"It got you in? Then maybe—"

"No, Caramon," Tanis said, carefully tucking the bracelet back inside his belt with a sidelong glance at Tas, who was looking extremely innocent. "Its magic was barely strong enough to get me to the edge of those cursed woods. I could feel its power dwindling—"

Stupidity and bravery are sometimes hard to tell apart. G.K. Chesterton wrote: "He can only get away from death by continually stepping within an inch of it. A soldier surrounded by enemies, if he is to cut his way out, needs to combine a strong desire for living with a strange carelessness about dying. He must not merely cling to life, for then he will be a coward, and will not escape. He must not merely wait for death, for then he will be a suicide, and will not escape. He must seek his life in a spirit of furious indifference to it; he must desire life like water and yet drink death like wine." [Orthodoxy: The Romance of Faith, G.K. Chesterton, Image/Doubleday, 1990, pp. 93.]

At conventions around the country, I often enjoy running an event I call the "Killer Breakfast." It is a roleplaying parody in which I run a game consisting of about three hundred people. One of the things I always tell them is, "If you do something incredibly brave or incredibly stupid—and they are often the same thing . . ." The difference between a brave man and a stupid one is that the brave man knows it's stupid but does it anyway on behalf of a greater ideal. —TRH

Caramon's eager expression faded. "I tried our magical device, too," he said, looking at Tas. "It doesn't work either. I didn't much expect it to. It wouldn't even get us through the Forest of Wayreth. But I had to try. I—I couldn't even get it to transform itself! It nearly fell apart in my hands, so I left it alone." He was silent for a moment, then, his voice shaking with desperation, he burst out, "Tanis, I *have* to reach the Tower!" His hands clenched into fists. "I can't explain, but I've seen the future, Tanis! I must go into the Portal and stop Raistlin. I'm the only one who can!"

Startled, Tanis laid a calming hand on the big man's shoulder. "So Tas told me—sort of. But, Caramon, Dalamar's there . . . and . . . how in the name of the gods can you get inside the Portal anyway?"

"Tanis," Caramon said, looking at his friend with such a serious, firm expression that the half-elf blinked in astonishment, "you cannot understand and there is no time to explain. But you've got to believe me. I *must* get into that Tower!"

"You're right," Tanis said, after staring at Caramon in mystified wonder, "I don't understand. But I'll help you, if I can, if it's at all possible."

Caramon sighed heavily, his head drooping, his shoulders slumping. "Thank you, my friend," he said simply. "I've been so alone through all this. If it hadn't been for Tas—"

He looked over at the kender, but Tas wasn't listening. His gaze was fixed with rapt attention on the flying citadel, still hovering above the city walls. The battle was raging in the air around it, among the dragons, and on the ground below, as could be seen from the thick columns of smoke rising from the south part of the city, the sounds of screams and cries, the clash of arms, and the clattering of horses' hooves.

"I'll bet a person could fly that citadel to the Tower," Tas said, staring at it with interest. "Whoosh! Right over the Grove. After all, its magic is evil and the Grove's magic is evil and it's pretty big—the citadel, that is, not the Grove. It would probably take a lot of magic to stop it and—"

"Tas!"

The kender turned to find both Caramon and Tanis standing, staring at him.

"What?" he cried in alarm. "I didn't do it! It's not my fault—"

"If we could only get up there!" Tanis stared at the citadel.

"The magical device!" Caramon cried in excitement, fishing it out of the inner pocket of the shirt he wore beneath his armor. "This will take us there!"

"Take us where?" Tasslehoff had suddenly realized something was going on. "Take us . . ."—he followed Tanis's gaze—"there? There!" The kender's eyes shone as brightly as stars. "Really? Truly? Into the flying citadel! That's so wonderful! I'm ready. Let's go!" His gaze went to the magical device Caramon was holding in his hand. "But that only works for two people, Caramon. How will Tanis get up?"

Caramon cleared his throat uncomfortably, and comprehension dawned upon the kender.

"Oh, no!" Tas wailed. "No!"

"I'm sorry, Tas," Caramon said, his trembling hands hastily transforming the small, nondescript pendant into the brilliant, bejeweled sceptre, "but we're going to have a stiff fight on our hands to get inside that thing—"

"You *must* take me, Caramon!" Tas cried. "It was *my* idea! I can fight!" Fumbling in his belt, he drew his little knife. "I saved your life! I saved Tanis's life!"

Seeing by the expression on Caramon's face that he was going to be stubborn about this, Tas turned to Tanis and threw his arms around him pleadingly. "Take me with you! Maybe the device will work with three people. Or rather two people and a kender. I'm short. It may not notice me! Please!"

"No, Tas," Tanis said firmly. Prying the kender loose, he moved over to stand next to Caramon. Raising a warning finger, he cautioned—with a look Tas knew well. "And I mean it this time!"

Tas stood there with an expression so forlorn that Caramon's heart misgave him. "Tas," he said softly, kneeling down beside the distraught kender, "you saw what's going to happen if we fail! I need Tanis with me—I need his strength, his sword. You understand, don't you?"

Tas tried to smile, but his lower lip quivered. "Yes, Caramon, I understand. I'm sorry."

"And, after all, it *was* your idea," Caramon added solemnly, getting to his feet.

While this thought appeared to comfort the kender, it didn't do a lot for the confidence of the half-elf. "Somehow," Tanis muttered, "*that* has me worried." So did the expression on the kender's face. "Tas"— Tanis assumed his sternest air as Caramon moved to stand beside him once more—"promise me that you will find somewhere safe and *stay there* and that you'll keep out of mischief! Do you promise?"

Tas's face was the picture of inner turmoil—he bit his lip, his brows knotted together, he twisted his topknot clear up to the top of his head. Then— suddenly—his eyes widened. He smiled, and let go of his hair, which tumbled down his back. "Of course, I promise, Tanis," he said with expression of such sincere innocence that the half-elf groaned.

But there was nothing he could do about it now. Caramon was already reciting the magical chant and manipulating the device. The last glimpse Tanis had, before he vanished into the swirling mists of magic, was of Tasslehoff standing on one foot, rubbing the back of his leg with the other, and waving goodbye with a cheerful smile.

"Fireflash!" said
Tasslehoff to himself as soon as Tanis and Caramon
had vanished from his sight.

Turning, the kender ran down the street toward
the southern end of town where the fighting was
heaviest. "For," he reasoned, "that's where the dragons are probably doing their battling."

It was then that the unfortunate flaw in his
scheme occurred to Tas. "Drat!" he muttered, stopping and staring up into the sky that was filled
with dragons snarling and clawing and biting and
breathing their breath weapons at each other in
rage. "Now, how am I ever going to find him in
that mess?"

Drawing a deep, exasperated breath, the kender
promptly choked and coughed. Looking around, he
noticed that the air was getting extremely smoky
and that the sky, formerly gray with the dawn

beneath the storm clouds, was now brightening with a fiery glow.

Palanthas was burning.

"*Not* exactly a safe place to be," Tas muttered. "And Tanis told me to find a safe place. And the safest place I know is with him and Caramon and they're up there in that citadel right now, probably getting into no end of trouble, and I'm stuck here in a town that's being burned and pillaged and looted." The kender thought hard. "I know!" he said suddenly. "I'll pray to Fizban! It worked a couple of times—well, I *think* it worked. But—at any rate—it can't hurt."

Seeing a draconian patrol coming down the street and not wanting any interruption, Tas ducked down an alley where he crouched behind a refuse pile and looked up into the sky. "Fizban," he said solemnly, "this is *it*! If we don't get out of this one, then we might just as soon toss the silver down the well and move in with the chickens, as my mother used to say, and—though I'm not too certain what she had in mind—it certainly does sound dire. I need to be with Tanis and Caramon. You *know* they can't manage things without me. And to do that, I need a dragon. Now, that isn't much. I *could* have asked for a lot more—like maybe you just skipping the middle man and whooshing me up there. But I didn't. Just one dragon. That's it."

Tas waited.

Nothing happened.

Heaving an exasperated sigh, Tas eyed the sky sternly and waited some more.

Still nothing.

Tas heaved a sigh. "All right, I admit it. I'd give the contents of one pouch—maybe even two—for the chance to fly in the citadel. There, that's the truth. The rest of the truth at any rate. And I *did* always find your hat for you. . . ."

But, despite this magnanimous gesture, no dragon appeared.

Finally, Tas gave up. Realizing that the draconian patrol had passed on by, he rose up from behind the garbage heap and made his way back out of the alley onto the street.

"Well," he muttered, "I suppose you're busy, Fizban, and—"

At that instant, the ground lifted beneath Tas's feet, the air filled with broken rock and brick and debris, a sound like thunder deafened the kender, and then . . . silence.

Picking himself up, brushing the dust off his leggings, Tas peered through the smoke and rubble, trying to see what had happened. For a moment, he thought that perhaps another building had been dropped on him, like at Tarsis. But then he saw that wasn't the case.

A bronze dragon† lay on its back in the middle of the street. It was covered with blood, its wings, spread over the block, had crushed several buildings, its tail lay across several more. Its eyes were closed, there were scorch marks up and down its flanks, and it didn't appear to be breathing.

"Now *this*," said Tas irritably, staring at the dragon, "was *not* what I had in mind!"

At that moment, however, the dragon stirred. One eye flickered open and seemed to regard the kender with dazed recollection.

"Fireflash!" Tas gasped, running up one of the huge legs to look the wounded dragon in the eye. "I was looking for you! Are—are you hurt badly?"

The young dragon seemed about to try to reply when a dark shadow covered both of them. Khirsah's eyes flared open, he gave a soft snarl and tried feebly to raise his head, but the effort seemed beyond him. Looking up, Tas saw a large black dragon swooping toward them, apparently intent on finishing off his victim.

"Oh, no, you don't!" Tas muttered. "This is *my* bronze! Fizban sent him to me. Now, how does one fight a dragon?"

Stories of Huma came to the kender's mind, but they weren't much help, since he didn't have a dragonlance, or even a sword. Pulling out his small knife, he looked at it hopefully, then shook his head and shoved it back in his belt. Well, he'd have to do the best he could.

"Fireflash," he instructed the dragon as he clamored up on the creature's broad, scaled stomach. "You just lie there and keep quiet, all right? Yes, I know all about how you want to die honorably, fighting your enemy. I had a friend who was a Knight of Solamnia. But right now we can't

"Bronze dragons are inquisitive and fond of humans and demi-humans. They are fascinated by warfare and will eagerly join an army if the cause is just and the pay is good.

"Bronze dragons like to be near deep fresh or salt water. They are good swimmers and often visit the depths to cool off or to hunt for pearls or treasure from sunken ships. They prefer caves that are accessible only from the water, but their lairs are always dry—they do not lay eggs, sleep, or store treasure under water." [2nd Edition ADVANCED DUNGEONS & DRAGONS *Monstrous Manual, Stewart, Doug (ed.) et al., TSR, 1997, p. 76.]*

afford to be honorable. I have two other friends who are alive right now but who maybe won't be if you can't help me get to them. Besides, I saved your life once already this morning, although that's probably not too obvious at the moment, and you owe me this."

Whether Khirsah understood and was obeying orders or had simply lost consciousness, Tas couldn't be certain. Anyway, he didn't have time to worry about it. Standing on top of the dragon's stomach, he reached deep into one of his pouches to see what he had that might help and out came Tanis's silver bracelet.

"You wouldn't think he'd be so careless with this," Tas muttered to himself as he put it on his arm. "He must have dropped it when he was tending to Caramon. Lucky I picked it up. Now—" Raising his arm, he pointed at the black dragon, who was hovering above, its jaws gaping open, ready to spew its deadly acid on its victim.

"Just hold it!" the kender shouted. "This dragon corpse is mine! I found it. Well . . . it found me, so to speak. Nearly squashed me into the ground. So just clear out and don't ruin it with that nasty breath of yours!"

The black dragon paused, puzzled, staring down. She had, often enough, given over a prize or two to draconians and goblins, but never—that she could recollect—to a kender. She, too, had been injured in the battle and was feeling rather light-headed from loss of blood and a clout on the nose, but something told her this wasn't right. She couldn't recollect ever having met an evil kender. She had to admit, however, that there might be a first time. This one *did* wear a bracelet of undoubtedly black magic, whose power she could feel blocking her spells.

"Do you know what I can get for dragon's teeth in Sanction these days?" the kender shouted. "To say nothing of the claws. I know a wizard paying thirty steel pieces for one claw alone!"

The black dragon scowled. This was a stupid conversation. She was hurting and angry. Deciding to simply destroy this irritating kender along with her enemy, she opened her mouth . . . when she was suddenly struck from behind by another bronze. Shrieking in fury, the black forgot her prey as she

"Black dragons are abusive, quick to anger, and resent intrusions of any kind. They like dismal surroundings, heavy vegetation, and prefer darkness to daylight. Although not as intelligent as other dragons, black dragons are instinctively cunning and malevolent.

"Black dragons are found in swamps, marshes, rain forest, and jungles. They revel in a steamy environment where canopies of trees filter out most of the sunlight, swarms of insects fill the air, and stagnant moss-covered ponds lie in abundance. Black dragons are excellent swimmers and enjoy lurking in the gloomy depths of swamps and bogs. They also are graceful in flight; however they prefer to fly at night when their great forms are hidden by the darkness of the sky. Black dragons are extremely selfish, and the majority of those encountered will be alone." [2nd Edition ADVANCED DUNGEONS & DRAGONS Monstrous Manual, Stewart, Doug (ed.) et al., TSR, 1997, p. 65.]

fought for her life, clawing frantically to gain air space, the bronze following.

Heaving a vast sigh, Tas sat down on Khirsah's stomach.

"I thought we were gone for sure there," the kender muttered, pulling off the silver bracelet and stuffing it back into his pouch. He felt the dragon stir beneath him, drawing a deep breath. Sliding down the dragon's scaly side, Tas landed on the ground.

"Fireflash? Are—are you very much hurt?" How did one heal a dragon anyway? "I—I could go look for a cleric, though I suppose they're all pretty busy right now, what with the battle going on and everything—"

"No, kender," said Khirsah in a deep voice, "that will not be necessary." Opening his eyes, the dragon shook his great head and craned his long neck to look around. "You saved my life," he said, staring at the kender in some confusion.

"Twice," Tas pointed out cheerfully. "First there was this morning with Lord Soth. My friend, Caramon—you don't know him—has this book that tells what will happen in the future—or rather what *won't* happen in the future, now that we're changing it. Anyway, you and Tanis would have fought Lord Soth and you both would have died only I stole the bracelet so now you didn't. Die, that is."

"Indeed." Rolling over on his side, Khirsah extended one huge leathery wing up into the smoky air and examined it closely. It was cut and bleeding, but had not been torn. He proceeded to examine the other wing in similar fashion while Tas watched, enchanted.

"I think I would like to be a dragon," he said with a sigh.

"Of course." Khirsah slowly twisted his bronze body over to stand upon his taloned feet, first extracting his long tail from the rubble of a building it had crushed. "We are the chosen of the gods. Our life spans are so long that the lives of the elves seem as brief as the burning of a candle to us, while the lives of humans and you kender are but as falling stars. Our breath is death, our magic so powerful that only the greatest wizards outrank us."

"I know," said Tasslehoff, trying to conceal his impatience. "Now, are you certain everything works?"

Khirsah himself concealed a smile. "Yes, Tasslehoff Burrfoot," the dragon said gravely, flexing his wings, "everything, um . . . works, as you put it." He shook his head. "I am feeling a little groggy, that is all. And so, since you have saved my life, I—"

"Twice."

"Twice," the dragon amended, "I am bound to perform a service for you. What do you ask of me?"

"Take me up to the flying citadel!" Tas said, all prepared to climb up on the dragon's back. He felt himself being hoisted in the air by his shirt collar which was hooked in one of Khirsah's huge claws. "Oh, thanks for the lift. Though I could have made it on my own—"

But he was not being placed upon the dragon's back. Rather he found himself confronting Khirsah eye to eye.

"That would be extremely dangerous—if not fatal—for you, kender," Khirsah said sternly. "I cannot allow it. Let me take you to the Knights of Solamnia, who are in the High Clerist's Tower—"

"I've been to the High Clerist's Tower!" Tas wailed. "I must get to the flying citadel! You see, uh, you see—Tanis Half-Elven! You know him? He's up there, right now, and, uh—He left me here to get some important, uh, information for him and"—Tas finished in a rush—"I've got it and now I've got to get to him with it."

"Give me the information," Khirsah said. "I will convey it to him."

"N-no, no, that—uh—won't work at all," Tas stammered, thinking frantically. "It—it's—uh—in kenderspeak! And—and it can't be translated into—er—Common. You don't speak—uh—kenderspeak, do you, Fireflash?"

"Of course," the dragon was about to say. But, looking into Tasslehoff's hopeful eyes, Khirsah snorted. "Of course *not*!" he said scornfully. Slowly, carefully, he deposited the kender on his back, between his wings. "I will take you to Tanis Half-Elven, if that is your wish. There is no dragonsaddle, since we are not fighting using mounted riders, so hold onto my mane tightly."

"Yes, Fireflash," Tas shouted gleefully, settling his pouches about him and gripping the dragon's bronze mane with both small hands. A sudden thought occurred to him. "Say, Fireflash," he cried, "you won't be doing any adventuresome things up there—like rolling over upside down or diving straight for the ground—will you? Because, while they certainly are entertaining, it might be rather uncomfortable for me since I'm not strapped in or anything. . . ."

"No," Khirsah replied, smiling. "I will take you there as swiftly as possible so that I may return to the battle."

"Ready when you are!" Tas shouted, kicking Khirsah's flanks with his heels as the bronze dragon leaped into the air. Catching the wind currents, he rose up into the sky and soared over the city of Palanthas.

It was not a pleasant ride. Looking down, Tas caught his breath. Almost all of New City was in flames. Since it had been evacuated, the draconians swept through it unchallenged, systematically looting and burning. The good dragons had been able to keep the blue and black dragons from completely destroying Old City—as they had destroyed Tarsis†—and the city's defenders were holding their own against the draconians. But Lord Soth's charge had been costly. Tas could see, from his lofty vantage point, the bodies of knights and their horses scattered about the streets like tin soldiers smashed by a vengeful child. And, while he watched, he could see Soth riding on unchecked, his warriors butchering any living thing that crossed their path, the banshees' frightful wail rising above the cries of the dying.

Tas swallowed painfully. "Oh, dear," he whispered, "suppose this *is* my fault! I don't really know, after all. Caramon never got to read any farther in the book! I just supposed—No," Tas answered himself firmly, "if I hadn't save Tanis, then Caramon would have died in the Grove. I did what I had to do and, since it's such a muddle, I won't think about it, ever again."

To take his mind off his problems—and the horrible things he could see happening on the ground below—Tas looked around, peering through the

The dragonarmies destroyed Tarsis in Dragons of Winter Night, *Book I, Chapter 8.*

smoke, to see what was happening in the skies. Catching a glimpse of movement behind him, he saw a large blue dragon rising up from the streets near Shoikan Grove. "Kitiara's dragon!" Tas murmured, recognizing the splendid, deadly Skie. But the dragon had no rider, Kitiara was nowhere to be seen.

"Fireflash!" Tas called out warningly, twisting around to watch the blue dragon, who had spotted them and was changing his direction to speed toward them.

"I am aware of him," Khirsah said coolly, glancing toward Skie. "Do not worry, we are near your destination. I will deposit you, kender, then return to deal with my enemy."

Turning, Tas saw that they were indeed very near the flying citadel. All thoughts of Kitiara and blue dragons went right out of his head. The citadel was even more wonderful up close than from down below. He could see quite clearly the huge, jagged chunks of rock hanging beneath it—what had once been the bedrock on which it was built.

Magical clouds boiled about it, keeping it afloat, lightning sizzled and crackled among the towers. Studying the citadel itself, Tas saw giant cracks snaking up the sides of the stone fortress—structural damage resulting from the tremendous force necessary to rip the building from the bones of the earth. Light gleamed from the windows of the citadel's three tall towers and from the open portcullis in front, but Tas could see no outward signs of life. He had no doubt, however, that there would be all kinds of life inside!

"Where would you like to go?" Khirsah asked, a note of impatience in his voice.

"Anywhere's fine, thank you," Tas replied politely, understanding that the dragon was eager to get back to battle.

"I don't think the main entrance would be advisable," said the dragon, swerving suddenly in his flight. Banking sharply, he circled around the citadel. "I will take you to the back."

Tas would have said "thank you" again but his stomach had, for some unaccountable reason, suddenly taken a plunge for the ground while his heart leaped into his throat as the dragon's circling motion

turned them both sideways in the air. Then Khirsah leveled out and, swooping downward, landed smoothly in a deserted courtyard. Occupied for the moment with getting his insides sorted out, Tas was barely able to slide off the dragon's back and leap down into the shadows without worrying about the social amenities.

Once on the solid ground (well, sort of solid ground), however, the kender felt immensely more himself.

"Good-bye, Fireflash!" he called, waving his small hand. "Thank you! Good luck!"

But if the bronze heard him, he did not answer. Khirsah was climbing rapidly, gaining air space. Zooming up after him came Skie, his red eyes glowing with hatred. With a shrug and a small sigh, Tas left them to their battle. Turning around, he studied his surroundings.

He was standing at the back of the fortress upon half of a courtyard, the other half having apparently been left behind when the citadel was dragged from the ground. Noticing that he was, in fact, uncomfortably near the edge of the broken stone flagging, Tas hurried toward the wall of the fortress itself. He moved softly, keeping to the shadows with the unconsciously adept stealth that kender are born possessing.

Pausing, he looked around. There was a back door leading into the courtyard, but it was a huge, wooden door, banded with iron bars. And, while it *did* have a most interesting looking lock that Tas's finger itched to try, the kender figured, with a sigh, that it probably had a very interesting looking guard standing on the other side as well. He'd do much better creeping in a window, and there happened to be a lighted window, right above him.

Way above him.

"Drat!" Tas muttered. The window was at least six feet off the ground. Glancing about, Tas found a chunk of broken rock and, with much pushing and shoving, managed to maneuver it over beneath the window. Climbing up on it, he peered cautiously inside.

Two draconians lay in a heap of stone† upon the floor, their heads smashed. Another draconian lay dead near them, its head completely severed from its body. Other than the corpses, there was no one

This tells us that these were baaz draconians, the most common—and smallest and weakest—of the draconians, who turn to stone when they die.

or nothing else in the room. Standing on tiptoe, Tas poked his head inside, listening. Not too far away, he could hear the sounds of metal clashing and harsh shouts and yells and, once, a tremendous roar.

"Caramon!" said Tas. Crawling through the window, he leaped down onto the floor, pleased to notice that, as yet, the citadel was holding perfectly still and didn't seem to be going anywhere. Listening again, he could hear the familiar roaring grow louder, mingled with Tanis's swearing. "How nice of them," Tas said, nodding in satisfaction as he crept across the room. "They're waiting for me."

Emerging into a corridor with blank stone walls, Tas paused a moment to get his bearings. The sounds of battle were above him. Peering down the torchlit hall, Tas saw a staircase and headed in that direction. As a precaution, he drew his little knife, but he met no one. The corridor was empty and so were the narrow, steep stairs.

"Humpf," Tas muttered, "certainly a much *safer* place to be than the city, right now. I must remember to mention that to Tanis. Speaking of whom, where can he and Caramon be and how do I get there?"

After climbing almost straight upward for about ten minutes, Tas stopped, staring up into the torchlit darkness. He was, he realized, ascending a narrow stair sandwiched between the inner and outer walls of one of the citadel's towers. He could still hear the battle raging—now it sounded like Tanis and Caramon were right on the other side of the wall from him—but he couldn't see any way to get through to them. Frustrated—and with tired legs—he stopped to think.

I can either go back down and try another way, he reasoned, or I can keep going. Back down—while easier on the feet—is likely to be more crowded. And there must be a door up here somewhere, or else why have a stair?

That line of logic appealing to him, Tas decided to keep going up, even though it meant that the sounds of battle seemed to be below him now instead of above him. Suddenly, just as he was beginning to think that a drunken dwarf with a warped sense of humor had built this stupid staircase, he arrived at the top and found his door.

"Ah, a lock!" he said, rubbing his hands. He hadn't had a chance to pick one in a long time, and he was afraid he might be getting rusty. Examining the lock with a practiced eye, he gingerly and delicately placed his hand upon the door handle. Much to his disappointment, it opened easily.

"Oh, well," he said with a sigh, "I don't have my lockpicking tools anyway." Cautiously pushing on the door, he peeped out. There was nothing but a wooden railing in front of him. Tas shoved the door open a bit more and stepped through it to find himself standing on a narrow balcony that ran around the inside of the tower.

The sounds of fighting were much clearer, reverberating loudly against the stone. Hurrying across the wooden floor of the balcony, Tas leaned over the edge of the railing, peering down below at the source of the sounds of wood smashing and swords clanging and cries and thuds.

"Hullo, Tanis. Hullo, Caramon!" he called in excitement. "Hey, have you figured out how to fly this thing yet?"

CHAPTER
4

Trapped on another balcony several flights below the one Tas leaned over, Tanis and Caramon were fighting for their lives on the opposite side of the tower from where the kender was standing. What appeared to be a small army of draconians and goblins were crammed on the stairs below them.

The two warriors had barricaded themselves behind a huge wooden bench which they had dragged across the head of the stairs. Behind them was a door, and it looked to Tas as if they had climbed up the stairs toward the door in an effort to escape but had been stopped before they could get out.

Caramon, his arms covered with green blood up to his elbows, was bashing heads with a hunk of wood he had ripped loose from the balcony—a more effective weapon than a sword when fighting these creatures whose bodies turned to stone. Tanis's sword was

It is not wise to stab a baaz draconian, since one's sword becomes trapped in the body as the dead creature turns to stone.

notched—he had been using it as a club—and he was bleeding from several cuts through the slashed chain mail on his arms, and there was a large dent in his breastplate. As far as Tas could tell from his first fevered glance, matters appeared to be at a stalemate. The draconians couldn't get close enough to the bench to haul it out of the way or climb over it. But, the moment Caramon and Tanis left their position, it would be overrun.

"Tanis! Caramon!" Tas shouted. "Up here!"

Both men glanced around in astonishment at the sound of the kender's voice. Then Caramon, catching hold of Tanis, pointed.

"Tasslehoff!" Caramon called, his booming voice echoing in the tower chamber. "Tas! This door, behind us! It's locked! We can't get out!"

"I'll be right there," Tas called in excitement, climbing up onto the railing and preparing to leap down into the thick of things.

"No!" Tanis screamed. "Unlock it from the other side! The other side!" He pointed frantically.

"Oh," Tas said in disappointment. "Sure, no problem." He climbed back down and was just turning to his doorway when he saw the draconians on the stairs below Tanis and Caramon suddenly cease fighting, their attention apparently caught by something. There was a harsh word of command, and the draconians began shoving and pushing each other to one side, their faces breaking into fanged grins. Tanis and Caramon, startled at the lull in the battle, risked a cautious glance over the top of the bench, while Tas stared down over the railing of the balcony.

A draconian in black robes decorated with arcane runes was ascending the stairs. He held a staff in his clawed hand—a staff carved into the likeness of a striking serpent.

A Bozak† magic-user! Tas felt a sinking sensation in the pit of his stomach almost as bad as the one he'd had when the dragon came in for a landing. The draconian soldiers were sheathing their weapons, obviously figuring the battle was ending. Their wizard would handle the matter, quickly and simply.

Tas saw Tanis's hand reach into his belt . . . and come out empty. Tanis's face went white beneath his beard. His hand went to another part of his belt.

"Bozak draconians are bronze-scaled dragonmen who make use of magical talent and often lead other draconians into battle.

*"Bozaks stand between 6 and 6 1/2 feet tall, with large horn-tipped wings that rise nearly a foot higher than their shoulders. They typically eschew armor in favor of maneuverability; when they do wear armor it is only of the lightest types. Bozaks have yellow or amber eyes and light gray teeth." [*DRAGONLANCE Campaign Setting, Wizards of the Coast, Inc., 2003, P. 218.]

Nothing there. Frantically, the half-elf looked around on the floor.

"You know," said Tas to himself, "I'll bet that bracelet of magic resistance would come in handy now. Perhaps that's what he's hunting for. I guess he doesn't realize he lost it." Reaching into a pouch, he drew out the silver bracelet.

"Here it is, Tanis! Don't worry! You dropped it, but I found it!" he cried, waving it in the air.

The half-elf looked up, scowling, his eyebrows coming together in such an alarming manner that Tas hurriedly tossed the bracelet down to him. After waiting a moment to see if Tanis would thank him (he didn't), the kender sighed.

"Be there in a minute!" he yelled. Turning, he dashed back through the door and ran down the stairs.

"He certainly didn't act very grateful," Tas humpfed as he sped along. "Not a bit like the old fun-loving Tanis. I don't think being a hero agrees with him."

Behind him, muffled by the wall, he could hear the sound of harsh chanting and several explosions. Then draconian voices raised in cries of anger and disappointment.

"That bracelet will hold them off for a while," Tas muttered, "but not for long. Now, how do I get over to the other side of the tower to reach them? I guess there's no help for it but to go clear back to the bottom level."

Racing down the stairs, he reached the ground level again, ran past the room where he had entered the citadel, and continued on until he came to a corridor running at right angles to the one he was in. Hopefully, it led to the opposite side of the tower where Tanis and Caramon were trapped.

There was the sound of another explosion and, this time, the whole tower shook. Tas increased his speed. Making a sharp turn to his right, the kender hurtled around a corner.

Bam! He slammed into something squat and dark that toppled over with a "wuf."

The impact bowled Tas head over heels. He lay quite still, having the distinct impression—from the smell—that he'd been struck by a bundle of rotting garbage. Somewhat shaken, he nevertheless

managed to stagger to his feet and, gripping his little knife, prepared to defend himself against the short, dark creature which was on its feet as well.

Putting a hand to its forehead, the creature said, "Ooh," in a pained tone. Then, glancing about groggily, it saw Tas standing in front of it, looking grim and determined. Torchlight flashed off the kender's knife blade. The "ooh," turned to an "AAAAAHHH." With a groan, the smelly creature fainted dead away.

"Gully dwarf!" said Tas, his nose wrinkling in disgust. He sheathed his knife and started to leave. Then he stopped. "You know, though," he said, talking to himself, "this might come in handy." Bending down, Tas grasped the gully dwarf by a handful of rag and shook it. "Hey, wake up!"

Drawing a shuddering breath, the gully dwarf opened his eyes. Seeing a stern-looking kender crouched threateningly above him, the gully dwarf went deathly white, hurriedly closed his eyes again, and attempted to look unconscious.

Tas shook the bundle again.

With a trembling sigh, the gully dwarf opened one eye, and saw Tas was still there. There was only one thing to do—look dead. This is achieved (among gully dwarves) by holding the breath and going instantly stiff and rigid.

"C'mon," play Tas irritably, shaking the gully dwarf. "I need your help."

"You go way," the gully dwarf said in deep, sepulchral tones. "Me dead."

"You're not dead yet," Tas said in the most awful voice he could muster, "but you're going to be unless you help me!" He raised the knife.

The gully dwarf gulped and quickly sat up, rubbing his head in confusion. Then, seeing Tas, he threw his arms around the kender. "You heal! Me back from dead! You great and powerful cleric!"

"No, I'm not!" snapped Tas, considerably startled by this reaction. "Now, let loose. No, you're tangled up in the pouch. Not *that* way. . . ."

After several moments, he finally managed to divest himself of the gully dwarf. Dragging the creature to his feet, Tas glared at him sternly. "I'm trying to get to the other side of the tower. Is this the right way?"

The gully dwarf stared up and down the corridor thoughtfully, then he turned to Tas. "This right way," he said finally, pointing in the direction Tas had been heading.

"Good!" Tas started off again.

"What tower?" the gully dwarf muttered, scratching his head.

Tas stopped. Turning around, he glared at the gully dwarf, his hand straying for his knife.

"Me go with great cleric," the gully dwarf offered hurriedly. "Me guide."

"That might not be a bad idea," the kender reflected. Grabbing hold of the gully dwarf's grubby hand, Tas dragged him along. Soon they found another staircase leading up. The sounds of battle were much louder now—a fact that caused the gully dwarf's eyes to widen.

He tried to pull his hand loose. "Me been dead once," the gully dwarf cried, frantically attempting to free himself. "When you dead two times, they put you in box, throw you in big hole. Me not like that."

Although this seemed an interesting concept, Tas didn't have time to explore it. Keeping hold of the gully dwarf firmly, Tas tugged him up the stairs, the sounds of fighting on the other side of the wall getting louder every moment. As on the opposite side of the tower, the steep staircase ended at a door. Behind it, he could hear thuds and groans and Caramon's swearing. Tas tried the handle. It was locked from this side, too. The kender smiled, rubbing his hands again.

"Certainly a well-built door," he said, studying it. Leaning down, he peered through the keyhole. "I'm here!" he shouted.

"Open the"—muffled shouts—"door!" came Caramon's booming bellow.

"I'm doing the best I can!" Tas yelled back, somewhat irritably. "I don't have my tools,† you know. Well, I'll just have to improvise. You—stay here!" He grabbed hold of the gully dwarf, who was just creeping back to the stairs. Taking out his knife, he held it up threateningly. The gully dwarf collapsed in a heap.

"Me stay!" he whimpered, cowering on the floor.

Turning back to the door, Tas stuck the tip of the knife into the lock and began twisting it around

The Thieves' Tools kit was a basic staple for every AD&D thief. Though Tas isn't a thief per se—he would be quite offended at the accusation—many of the AD&D thief's traits carried over into the kender.

carefully. He thought he could almost feel the lock give when something thudded against the door. The knife jerked out of the lock.

"You're not helping!" he shouted through the door. Heaving a long-suffering sigh, Tas put the knife back in the lock again.

The gully dwarf crawled closer, staring up at Tas from the floor. "Lot *you* know. Me guess you *not* such great cleric."

"What do you mean?" Tas muttered, concentrating.

"*Knife* not open door," the gully dwarf said with vast disdain. "*Key* open door."

"I *know* a key opens the door," Tas said, glancing about in exasperation, "but I don't have—Give me that!"

Tas angrily snatched the key the gully dwarf was holding in its hand. Putting the key into the door lock, he heard it click and yanked the door open. Tanis tumbled out, practically on top of the kender, Caramon running out behind him. The big man slammed the heavy door shut, breaking off the tip of a draconian sword just entering the doorway. Leaning his back against the door, he looked down at Tas, breathing heavily.

"Lock it!" he managed to gasp.

Quickly Tas turned the key in the lock again. Behind the door, there were shouts and more thuds and the sounds of splintering wood.

"It'll hold for a while, I think," Tanis said, studying the door.

"But not long," Caramon said grimly. "Especially with that Bozak mage down there. C'mon."

"Where?" Tanis demanded, wiping sweat from his face. He was bleeding from a slash on his hand and numerous cuts on his arms, but otherwise appeared unhurt. Caramon was covered with blood, but most of it was green, so Tas assumed that it was the enemy's. "We still haven't found out where the device that flies this thing is located!"

"I'll bet he knows," Tas said, pointing to the gully dwarf. "That's why I brought him along," the kender added, rather proud of himself.

There was a tremendous crash. The door shuddered.

"Let's at least get out of here," Tanis muttered. "What's your name?" he asked the gully dwarf as they hurried back down the stairs.

"Rounce," said the gully dwarf, regarding Tanis with deep suspicion.

"Very well, Rounce," Tanis said, pausing on a shadowy landing to catch his breath, "show us the room where the device is that flies this citadel."

"The Wind Captain's Chair," Caramon added, glaring at the gully dwarf sternly. "That's what we heard one of the goblins call it."

"That secret!" Rounce said solemnly. "Me not tell! Me make promise!"

Caramon growled so fiercely that Rounce went dead white beneath the dirt on his face, and Tas, afraid he was going to faint again, hurriedly interposed. "Pooh! I'll bet he doesn't know!" Tas said, winking at Caramon.

"Me do too know!" Rounce said loftily. "And you try trick to make me tell. Me not fall for stupid trick."

Tas slumped back against the wall with a sigh. Caramon growled again, but the gully dwarf, cringing slightly, still stared at him with brave defiance. "Cross pigs not drag secret out of me!" Rounce declared, folding his filthy arms across a grease-covered, food-spattered chest.

There was a shattering crash from above, and the sound of draconian voices.

"Uh, Rounce," Tanis murmured confidentially, squatting down beside the gully dwarf, "what is it exactly that you're not supposed to tell?"

Rounce assumed a crafty look. "Me not supposed to tell that the Wind Captain's Chair in top of middle tower. *That's* what me not supposed to tell!" He scowled at Tanis viciously and raised a small, clenched fist. "And you can't make me!"

They reached the corridor leading to the room where the Wind Captain's Chair *wasn't* located (according to Rounce, who had been guiding them the entire way by saying, "This *not* door that lead to stair that lead to secret place"). They entered it cautiously, thinking that things had been just a little too quiet. They were right. About halfway down the corridor, a door burst open. Twenty draconians, followed by the Bozak magic-user, lunged out at them.

"Get behind me!" Tanis said, drawing his sword. "I've still got the bracelet—" Remembering Tas was with them, he added, "I think," and glanced hurriedly at his arm. The bracelet was still there.

"Tanis," said Caramon, drawing his sword and falling back slowly as the draconians, waiting for instructions from the Bozak, hesitated, "we're running out of time! I know! I can sense it! I've got to get to the Tower of High Sorcery! Someone's got to get up there and fly this thing!"

"One of us can't hold off this many!" Tanis returned. "That doesn't leave anyone to operate the Wind Captain—" The words died on his lips. He stared at Caramon. "Oh, you're not serious—"

"We don't have any choice," Caramon growled as the sound of chanting filled the air. He glanced back at Tasslehoff.

"No," Tanis began, "absolutely not—"

"There's no other way!" Caramon insisted.

Tanis sighed, shaking his head.

The kender, watching both of them, blinked in confusion. Then, suddenly, he understood.

"Oh, Caramon!" he breathed, clasping his hands together, barely avoiding skewering himself with his knife. "Oh, Tanis! How wonderful! I'll make you proud of me! I'll get you to the Tower! You won't be sorry! Rounce, I'm going to need your help."

Grabbing the gully dwarf by the arm, Tas raced along the corridor toward a spiral staircase Rounce was pointing out, insisting that, "This stair *not* take you to secret place!"

Designed by Lord Ariakas,† formerly head of the Dark Queen's forces during the War of the Lance, the Wind Captain's Chair that operates a floating citadel has long since passed into history as one of the most brilliant creations of Ariakas's brilliant, if dark and twisted, mind.

The Chair is located in a room specially built for it at the very top of the citadel. Climbing a narrow flight of spiral steps, the Wind Captain ascends an iron ladder leading to a trap door. Upon opening the trap door, the Captain enters a small, circular room devoid of windows. In the center of the room is a raised platform. Two pedestals, positioned about three feet apart, stand on the platform.†

At the sight of these pedestals, Tas—pulling Rounce up after him—drew in a deep breath. Made of silver, standing about four feet tall, the pedestals

Dragon Highlord Ariakas was commander of the Red Dragonarmy, the most powerful of the five armies of Takhisis, during the War of the Lance. He later proclaimed himself Emperor of Ansalon. Tanis killed him in Dragons of Spring Dawning, *Book III, Chapter 9.*

I loved flying in my youth and love it still when my friend takes me flying. I designed these control surfaces around how I thought a magical flying citadel would be controlled. —TRH

were the most beautiful things he had ever seen. Intricate designs and magical symbols were etched into their surfaces. Every tiny line was filled with gold that glittered in the torchlight streaming up from the stairway below. And, on top of each pedestal, was poised a huge globe, made of shining black crystal.

"You *not* get up on platform," Rounce said severely.

"Rounce," said Tas, climbing up onto the platform, which was about three feet off the floor, "do you know how to make this work?"

"No," said Rounce coolly, folding his arms across his chest and glaring at Tas. "Me never been here lots. Me never run errand for big boss wizard. Me never put into this room and me never told fetch whatever wizard want. Me never watch big boss wizard fly many times."

"Big boss wizard?" Tas said, frowning. He glanced hastily about the small room, peering into the shadows. "Where *is* the big boss wizard?"

"Him not down below," Rounce said stubbornly. "Him not getting ready to blow friends to tiny bits."

"Oh, that big boss wizard," Tas said in relief. Then the kender paused. "But—if he's not here—who's flying this thing?"

"We *not* flying," Rounce said, rolling his eyes. "We stand still. Boy, you some dumb cleric!"

"I see," muttered Tas to himself. "When it's standing still, the big boss wizard can leave it and go do big boss wizard things." He glanced around. "My, my," he said loudly, studying the platform, "what is it I'm not supposed to do?"

Rounce shook his head. "Me never tell. You *not* s'posed to step in two black circles on floor of platform."

"I see," said Tas, stepping into the black circles set into the floor between the pedestals. They appeared to be made of the same type of black crystal as the glass globes. From the corridor below, he heard another explosion and, again, shouts of the angry draconians. Apparently Tanis's bracelet was still fending off the wizard's magic.

"Now," said Rounce, "you not s'pose to look up at circle in ceiling."

Looking up, Tas gasped in awe. Above him, a circle the same size and diameter as the platform upon which he stood was beginning to glow with an eerie blue-white light.

"All right, Rounce," Tas said, his voice shrill with excitement, "what is it I'm not supposed to do next?"

"You not put hands on black crystal globes. You not tell globes which way we go," Rounce replied, sniffing. "Pooh. You never figure out big magic like this!"

"Tanis." Tas yelled down through the opening in the floor, "which direction is the Tower of High Sorcery from here?"

For a moment, all he could hear was the clatter of swords and a few screams. Then, Tanis's voice, sounding gradually closer as he and Caramon backed their way down the corridor, floated up. "Northwest! Almost straight northwest!"

"Right!" Planting his feet firmly in the black crystal depressions, Tas drew a shaking breath, then raised his hands to place them upon the crystal globes—

"Drat!" he cried in dismay, staring up. "I'm too short!"

Looking down at Rounce, he motioned. "I suppose your hands don't have to be on the globe and your feet don't have to be in the black circles at the same time?"

Tas had the unfortunate feeling that he already knew the answer to this, which was just as well. The question had thrown Rounce into such a state of confusion that he could only stare at Tas, his mouth gaping open.

Glaring at the gully dwarf simply because he had to have something to glare at in his frustration, Tas decided to try to jump up to touch the globes. He could reach them then, but—when his feet left the black crystal circles—the blue-white light went dim.

"Now what?" he groaned. "Caramon or Tanis could reach it easily, but they're down there and, from the sounds of things, they're not going to be coming up here for a while. What can I do? I— Rounce!" he said suddenly, "come up here!"

Rounce's eyes narrowed suspiciously. "Me not allowed," he said, starting to back away from the platform.

"Wait! Rounce! Don't leave!" Tas cried. "Look, you come help me! We'll fly this together!"

"Me!" Rounce gasped. His eyes opened round as teacups. "Fly like big boss wizard?"

"Yes, Rounce! C'mon. Just climb up, stand on my shoulders, and—"

A look of wonder came into Rounce's face. "Me," he breathed with a gusty sigh of ecstasy, "fly like big boss wizard!"

"Yes, Rounce, yes," said Tas impatiently, "now, hurry up before—before the big boss wizard catches us."

"Me hurry," Rounce said, crawling up onto the platform and from there onto Tas's shoulders, "Me hurry. Me always want to fly—"

"Here, I've got hold of your ankles. Now, ouch! Let go of my hair! You're pulling! I'm not going to drop you. No, stand up. Stand up, Rounce. Just stand up slowly. You'll be all right. See, I have your ankles. I won't let you fall. No! No! You've got to balan—"

Kender and gully dwarf tumbled over in a heap.

"Tas!" Caramon's warning voice came up the stairs.

"Just a minute! Almost got it!" Tas cried, yanking Rounce to his feet and shaking him soundly. "Now, balance, balance!"

"Balance, balance," Rounce muttered, his teeth clicking together.

Tas took his place upon the black crystal circles once again and Rounce crawled up onto his shoulders again. This time, the gully dwarf, after a few tense moments of wobbling, managed to stand up. Tas heaved a sigh. Reaching out his dirty hands, Rounce—after a few false starts—gingerly placed them upon the black crystal globes.

Immediately, a curtain of light dropped down from the glowing circle in the ceiling, forming a brilliant wall around Tas and the gully dwarf. Runes appeared on the ceiling, glowing red and violet.

And, with a heart-stopping lurch, the flying citadel began to move.

Down the stairs in the corridor below the Wind Captain's Chair, the jolt sent draconians and their magic-user crashing to the floor. Tanis fell backward against a wall, and Caramon slammed into him.

Screaming and cursing, the Bozak wizard struggled to his feet. Stepping on his own men, who littered the corridor, and completely ignoring Tanis and

Caramon, the draconian began to run toward the staircase leading up to the Wind Captain's room.

"Stop him!" Caramon growled, pushing himself away from the wall as the citadel canted to one side like a sinking ship.

"I'll try," Tanis wheezed, having had the breath knocked out of him, "but I think this bracelet is about used up."†

He made a lunge for the Bozak, but the citadel suddenly tipped in the opposite direction. Tanis missed and tumbled to the floor. The Bozak, intent only on stopping the thieves who were stealing his citadel, stumbled on toward the stairs. Drawing his dagger, Caramon hurled it at the Bozak's back. But it struck a magical, invisible barrier around the black robes and fell harmlessly to the floor.

The Bozak had just reached the bottom of the spiral stairs leading up to the Wind Captain's room, the other draconians were finally regaining their feet, and Tanis was just nearing the Bozak once again when the citadel leaped straight up into the air. The Bozak fell backward on top of Tanis, draconians went flying everywhere, and Caramon, just barely managing to keep his feet, jumped on the Bozak wizard.

The sudden gyrations of the tower broke the mage's concentration—the Bozak's protection spell failed. The draconian fought desperately with its clawed hands, but Caramon—dragging the creature off Tanis—thrust his sword into the Bozak just as the wizard began shrieking another chant.

The draconian's body dissolved instantly in a horrible yellow pool, sending clouds of foul, poisonous smoke billowing through the chamber.

"Get away!" Tanis cried, stumbling toward an open window, coughing. Leaning out, he took a deep breath of fresh air, then gasped.

"Tas!" he shouted, "we're going the wrong way! I said northwest!"

He heard the kender's shrill voice cry, "Think *northwest*, Rounce! Northwest."

"Rounce?" Caramon muttered, coughing and glancing at Tanis in sudden alarm.

"How me think of two direction same time?" demanded a voice. "You want go north or you want go west? Make up mind."

Once again I think I hear the dice rolling in the text, but it certainly is helpful at this point in the story.
—TRH

"Northwest!" cried Tas. "It's *one* direc— Oh, never mind. Look, Rounce, you think north and I'll think west. That might work."

Closing his eyes, Caramon sighed in despair and slumped against a wall.

"Tanis," he said, "Maybe you better—"

"No time," Tanis answered grimly, his sword in his hand. "Here they come."

But the draconians, thrown into confusion by the death of their leader and completely unable to comprehend what was happening to their citadel, were eyeing each other—and their enemy—askance. At that moment, the flying citadel changed direction again, heading off northwest and dropping down about twenty feet at the same time.

Turning, tripping, shoving and sliding, the draconians ran down the corridor and disappeared back through the secret way they had come.

"We're finally going in the right direction," Tanis reported, staring out the window. Joining him, Caramon saw the Tower of High Sorcery drawing nearer and nearer.

"Good! Let's see what's going on," Caramon muttered, starting to climb the stairs.

"No, wait"—Tanis stopped him—"Tas can't see, apparently. We're going to have to guide him. Besides, those draconians might come back any moment."

"I guess you're right," Caramon said, peering up the stairs dubiously.

"We should be there in a few minutes," Tanis said, leaning against the window ledge wearily. "But I think we've got time enough for you to tell me what's going on."

"It's hard to believe," said Tanis softly, looking out the window again, "even of Raistlin."

"I know," Caramon said, his voice edged with sorrow. "I didn't want to believe it, not for a long time. But when I saw him standing before the Portal and when I heard him tell what he was going to do to Crysania, I knew that the evil had finally eaten into his soul."

"You are right, you must stop him," Tanis said, reaching out to grip the big man's hand in his own. "But, Caramon, does that mean you have to go into the Abyss after him? Dalamar is in the Tower, waiting

at the Portal. Surely, the two of you together can prevent Raistlin from coming through. You don't need to enter the Portal yourself—"

"No, Tanis," Caramon said, shaking his head. "Remember—Dalamar failed to stop Raistlin the first time. Something must be going to happen to the dark elf—something that will prevent him from fulfilling his assignment." Reaching into his knapsack, Caramon pulled out the leather-bound *Chronicles*.

"Maybe we can get there in time to stop it," Tanis suggested, feeling strange talking about a future that was already described.

Turning to the page he had marked, Caramon scanned it hurriedly, then drew in his breath with a soft whistle.

"What is it?" Tanis asked, leaning over to see. Caramon hastily shut the book.

"Something happens to him, all right," the big man muttered, avoiding Tanis's eyes. "Kitiara kills him."†

The question of destiny is now laid bare for us to stare down. Can we rewrite what has been or will be written? We now know what is supposed to happen. Is it fated, or can it be changed by our own willful choice? —TRH

CHAPTER 5

Dalamar sat alone in the laboratory of the Tower of High Sorcery. The guardians of the Tower, both living and dead, stood at their posts by the entrance, waiting . . . watching.

Outside the Tower window, Dalamar could see the city of Palanthas burning. The dark elf had watched the progress of the battle from his vantage point high atop the Tower. He had seen Lord Soth enter the gate, he had seen the knights scatter and fall, he had seen the draconians swoop down from the flying citadel. All the while, up above, the dragons battled, the dragon blood falling like rain upon the city streets.

The last glimpse he had, before the rising smoke obscured his vision, showed him the flying citadel starting to drift in his direction, moving slowly and erratically, once even seeming to change its mind and head back toward the mountains. Puzzled,

Dalamar watched this for several minutes, wondering what it portended. Was this how Kitiara planned to get into the Tower?

The dark elf felt a moment of fear. Could the citadel fly over the Shoikan Grove? Yes, he realized, it might! His hand clenched. Why hadn't he foreseen that possibility? He stared out the window, cursing the smoke that increasingly blocked his vision. As he watched, the citadel changed direction again, stumbling through the skies like a drunkard searching for his dwelling.

It was once more headed for the Tower, but at a snail's pace. What was going on? Was the operator wounded? He stared at it, trying to see. And then thick, black smoke rolled past the windows, completely blotting out his vision of the citadel. The odor of burning hemp and pitch was strong. The warehouses, Dalamar thought. As he was turning from the window with a curse, his attention was caught by the sight of a brief flare of firelight coming from a building almost directly opposite him—the Temple of Paladine. He could see, even through the smoke, the glow brightening, and he could picture, in his mind, the white robed clerics, wielding mace and stick,† calling upon Paladine as they slew their enemies.

I hear more dice rolling here. Clerics in AD&D (at the time Legends was written) could only use staves and blunt weapons such as maces. —TRH

Dalamar smiled grimly, shaking his head as he walked swiftly across the room, past the great stone table with its bottles and jars and beakers. He had shoved most of these aside, making room for his spellbooks, his scrolls and magical devices. He glanced over them for the hundredth time, making certain all was in readiness, then continued on, hurrying past the shelves lined with the nightblue-bound spellbooks of Fistandantilus, past the shelves lined with Raistlin's own black-bound spellbooks. Reaching the door of the laboratory, Dalamar opened it and spoke one word into the darkness beyond.

Instantly, a pair of eyes glimmered before him, the spectral body shimmering in and out of his vision as if stirred by hot winds.

"I want guardians at the top of the Tower," Dalamar instructed.

"Where, apprentice?"

Dalamar thought. "The doorway, leading down from the Death Walk. Post them there."

The eyes flickered closed in brief acknowledgment, then vanished. Dalamar returned to the laboratory, closing the door behind him. Then he hesitated, stopped. He could lay spells of enchantment upon the door, spells that would prevent anyone from entering. This had been a common practice of Raistlin's in the laboratory when performing some delicate magical experiment in which the least interruption could prove fatal. A breath drawn at the wrong moment could mean the unleashing of magical forces that would destroy the Tower itself. Dalamar paused, his delicate fingers on the door, the words upon his lips.

Then, no, he thought. I might need help. The guardians must be free to enter in case I am not able to remove the spells. Walking back across the room, he sat down in the comfortable chair that was his favorite—the chair he'd had brought from his own quarters to help ease the weariness of his vigil.

In case I am not able to remove the spells. Sinking down into the chair's soft, velvet cushions, Dalamar thought about death, about dying. His gaze went to the Portal. It looked as it had always looked— the five dragon heads, each a different color, facing inward, their five mouths open in five silent shouts of tribute to their Dark Queen. It looked the same as always—the heads dark and frozen, the void within the Portal empty, unchanging. Or was it? Dalamar blinked. Perhaps it was his imagination, but he thought the eyes of each of the heads were beginning to glow, slightly.

The dark elf's throat tightened, his palms began to sweat and he rubbed his hands upon his robes. Death, dying. Would it come to that? His fingers brushed over the silver runes embroidered on the black fabric, runes that would block or dispel certain magical attacks. He looked at his hands, the lovely green stone of a ring of healing sparkled there—a powerful magical device. But its power could only be used once.†

Hastily, Dalamar went over in his mind Raistlin's lessons on judging whether a wound was mortal and required immediate healing or if the healing device's power should be saved.

Dalamar shuddered. He could hear the *Shalafi's* voice coldly discussing varying degrees of pain. He

Magic must have laws and limits, or it would be too powerful and become ho-hum. —MW

could feel those fingers, burning with that strange inner heat, tracing over the different portions of his anatomy, pointing out the vital areas. Reflexively, Dalamar's hand went to his breast, where the five holes Raistlin had burned into his flesh forever bled and festered. At the same time, Raistlin's eyes burned into his mind—mirrorlike, golden, flat, deadly.

Dalamar shrank back. Powerful magic surrounds me and protects me, he told himself. I am skilled in the Art, and, though not as skilled as he, the *Shalafi* will come through that Portal injured, weak, upon the point of death! It will be easy to destroy him! Dalamar's hands clenched. Then why am I literally suffocating with fear? he demanded.

A silver bell sounded, once. Startled, Dalamar rose from the chair, his fear of the imaginings of his mind replaced by a fear of something very real. And with the fear of something concrete, tangible, Dalamar's body tensed, his blood ran cool in his veins, the dark shadows in his mind vanished. He was in control.

The silver bell meant an intruder. Someone had won his way through the Shoikan Grove and was at the Tower entrance. Ordinarily, Dalamar would have left the laboratory instantly, on the words of a spell, to confront the intruder himself. But he dared not leave the Portal. Glancing back at it, the dark elf nodded to himself slowly. No, it had not been his imagination, the eyes of the dragon's heads *were* glowing. He even thought he saw the void within stir and shift, as if a ripple had passed across its surface.

No, he dared not leave. He must trust to the guardians. Walking to the door, he bent his head, listening. He thought he heard faint sounds down below—a muffled cry, a clash of steel. Then nothing but silence. He waited, holding his breath, hearing only the beating of his own heart.

Nothing else.

Dalamar sighed. The guardians must have handled the matter. Leaving the door, he crossed the laboratory to look out the window, but he could see nothing. The smoke was as thick as fog. He heard a distant rumble of thunder, or perhaps it was an explosion. Who had it been down there? he found

himself wondering. Some draconian, perhaps? Eager for more killing, more loot. One of them might have won through—

Not that it mattered, he told himself coldly. When all this was over, he would go down, examine the corpse. . . .

"Dalamar!"

Dalamar's heart leaped, both fear and hope surging through him at the sound of that voice.

"Caution, caution, my friend," he whispered to himself. "She betrayed her brother. She betrayed you. Do not trust her."

Yet he found his hands shaking as he slowly crossed the laboratory toward the door.

"Dalamar!" Her voice again, quivering with pain and terror. There was a thud against the door, the sound of a body sliding down it. "Dalamar," she called again weakly.

Dalamar's hand was on the handle. Behind him, the dragon's eyes glowed red, white, blue, green, black.†

These are, of course, the colors of the five metallic (and therefore evil) dragons in Krynn.

"Dalamar," Kitiara murmured faintly, "I—I've come . . . to help you."

Slowly, Dalamar opened the laboratory door.

Kitiara lay on the floor at his feet. At the sight of her, Dalamar drew in his breath. If she had once worn armor, it had now been torn from her body by inhuman hands. He could see the marks of their nails upon her flesh. The black, tight-fitting garment she wore beneath her armor was ripped almost to shreds, exposing her tan skin, her white breasts. Blood oozed from a ghastly wound upon one leg, her leather boots were in tatters. Yet, she looked up at him with clear eyes, eyes that were not afraid. In her hand, she held the nightjewel, the charm Raistlin had given her to protect her in the Grove.

"I was strong enough, barely," she whispered, her lips parting in the crooked smile that made Dalamar's blood burn. She raised her arms. "I've come to you. Help me stand."

Reaching down, Dalamar lifted Kitiara to her feet. She slumped against him. He could feel her body shivering and shook his head, knowing what poison worked in her blood. His arm around her, he half-carried her into the laboratory and shut the door behind them.

Her weight upon him increased, her eyes rolled back. "Oh, Dalamar," she murmured, and he saw she was going to faint. He put his arms completely around her. She leaned her head against his chest, breathing a thankful sigh of relief.

He could smell the fragrance of her hair—that strange smell, a mixture of perfume and steel. Her body trembled in his arms. His grasp around her tightened. Opening her eyes, she looked up into his. "I'm feeling better now," she whispered. Her hands slid down. . . .

Too late, Dalamar saw the brown eyes glitter. Too late, he saw the crooked smile twist. Too late he felt her hand jerk, and the quick stabbing thrust of pain as her knife entered his body.

"Well, we made it," Caramon yelled, staring down from the crumbling courtyard of the flying citadel as it floated above the tops of the dark trees of the Shoikan Grove.

"Yes, at least this far," Tanis muttered. Even from this vantage point, high above the cursed forest, he could feel the cold waves of hatred and bloodlust rising up to grasp at them as if the guardians could, even now, drag them down. Shivering, Tanis forced his gaze to where the top of the Tower of High Sorcery loomed near. "If we can get close enough," he shouted to Caramon above the rush of the wind in his ears, "we can drop down on that walkway that circles around the top."

"The Death Walk," Caramon returned grimly.

"What?"

"The Death Walk!" Caramon edged closer, watching his footing as the dark trees drifted beneath them like the waves of a black ocean. "That's where the evil mage stood when he called down the curse upon the Tower. So Raistlin told me. That's where he jumped from."

"Nice, cheerful place," Tanis muttered into his beard, staring at it grimly. Smoke rolled around them, blotting out the sight of the trees. The half-elf tried not to think about what was happening in the city. He'd already caught a glimpse of the Temple of Paladine in flames.

"You know, of course," he yelled, grabbing hold of Caramon's shoulder as the two stood on the edge

of the courtyard of the citadel, "there's every possibility Tasslehoff is going to crash right into that thing!"

"We've come this far," Caramon said softly. "The gods are with us."

Tanis blinked, wondering if he'd heard right. "That doesn't sound like the old jovial Caramon," he said with a grin.

"That Caramon's dead, Tanis," Caramon replied flatly, his eyes on the approaching Tower.

Tanis's grin softened to a sigh. "I'm sorry," was all he could think of to say, putting a clumsy hand on Caramon's shoulder.

Caramon looked at him, his eyes bright and clear. "No, Tanis," he said. "Par-Salian told me, when he sent me back in time, that I was going back to 'save a soul. Nothing more. Nothing less.'" Caramon smiled sadly. "I thought he meant Raistlin's soul. I see now he didn't. He meant my own."† The big man's body tensed. "C'mon," he said, abruptly changing the subject. "We're close enough to jump for it."

A balcony that encircled the top of Tower appeared beneath them, dimly seen through the swirling smoke. Looking down, Tanis felt his stomach shrivel. Although he knew it was impossible, it seemed that the Tower itself was lurching around beneath him, while he was standing perfectly still. It had looked so huge, as they were nearing it. Now, he might have been planning to leap out of a vallenwood to land upon the roof of a child's toy castle.

To make matters worse, the citadel continued to fly closer and closer to the Tower. The blood-red tips of the black minarets that topped it danced in Tanis's vision as the citadel lurched back and forth and bobbed up and down.

"Jump!" shouted Caramon, hurling himself into space.

An eddy of smoke swirled past Tanis, blinding him. The citadel was still moving. Suddenly, a huge, black rock column loomed right before him. It was either jump or be squashed. Frantically, Tanis jumped, hearing a horrible crunching and grinding sound right above him. He was falling into nothingness, the smoke swirled about him, and then he had one split second to brace himself as the stones of the Death Walk materialized beneath his feet.

As a young man, I heard the call in my soul to become a missionary. At nineteen, I left my home and embarked on a journey to the farthest parts of the globe. I was assigned to Java—the single-most populated Islamic nation in the world—to teach Christianity. In all that time, I feel that I only converted one person: me. Yet I have come to accept the sublime idea that this one conversion may have made that time acceptable to God. Here, Caramon expresses a similar, quiet truth. When we save our souls, we save that part of the world within our grasp and in so doing have done our part to redeem the world itself. —TRH

He landed with a jarring thud that shook every bone in his body and left him stunned and breathless. He had just sense enough to roll over onto his stomach, covering his head with his arms as showers of rock tumbled down around him.

Caramon was on his feet, roaring, "North! Due north!"

Very, very faintly, Tanis thought he heard a shrill voice screaming from the citadel above, "North! North! North! We've got to head off straight north!"

The grinding, crunching sound ceased. Raising his head cautiously, Tanis saw, through a ripple in the smoke, the flying citadel drifting off on its new tack, wobbling slightly, and heading straight for the palace of Lord Amothus.

"You all right?" Caramon helped Tanis to his feet.

"Yeah," said the half-elf shakily. He wiped blood from his mouth. "Bit my tongue. Damn, that hurts!"

"The only way down is over here," Caramon said, leading the way around the Death Walk. They came to an archway carved into the black stone of the Tower. A small wooden door stood closed and barred.

"There'll probably be guards," Tanis pointed out as Caramon, backing off, prepared to hurl his weight against the door.

"Yeah," the big man grunted. Making a short run, he threw himself forward, smashing into the door. It shivered and creaked, wood splintered along the iron bars, but it held. Rubbing his shoulder, Caramon backed off. Eyeing the door, concentrating all his strength and effort on it, he crashed into it once again. This time, it gave with a shattering boom, carrying Caramon with it.

Hurrying inside, peering around in the smoke-filled darkness, Tanis found Caramon lying on the floor, surrounded by shards of wood. The half-elf started to reach a hand down to his friend when he stopped, staring.

"Name of the Abyss!" he swore, his breath catching in his throat.

Hurriedly, Caramon got to his feet. "Yeah," he said warily. "I've run into these before."

Two pairs of disembodied eyes, glowing white with an eerie, cold light, floated before them.

"Don't let them touch you," Caramon warned in a low voice. "They drain the life from your body."

The eyes floated nearer.

Hurriedly Caramon stepped in front of Tanis, facing the eyes. "I am Caramon Majere, brother of Fistandantilus," he said softly. "You know me. You have seen me before, in times long past."

The eyes halted, Tanis could feel their chill scrutiny. Slowly, he lifted his arm. The cold light of the guardian's eyes was reflected in the silver bracelet.

"I am a friend of your master's, Dalamar," he said, trying to keep his voice firm. "He gave me this bracelet." Tanis felt, suddenly, a cold grip on his arm. He gasped in pain that seemed to bore straight to his heart. Staggering, he almost fell. Caramon caught hold of him.

"The bracelet's gone!" Tanis said through clenched teeth.

"Dalamar!" Caramon yelled, his voice booming and echoing through the chamber. "Dalamar! It is Caramon! Raistlin's brother! I've got to get into the Portal! I can stop him! Call off the guardians, Dalamar!"

"Perhaps it's too late," Tanis said, staring at the pallid eyes, which stared back at them. "Maybe Kit got here first. Perhaps he's dead. . . ."

"Then so are we," Caramon said softly.

CHAPTER 6

Shield: *When this spell is cast, an invisible barrier comes into being in front of the wizard. [2nd Edition* ADVANCED DUNGEONS & DRAGONS *Player's Handbook, by David "Zeb" Cook, TSR, 1997, p. 178.]*

amn you, Kitiara!" Dalamar gagged in pain. Staggering backward, he pressed his hand against his side, feeling his own blood flow warm through his fingers.

There was no smile of elation on Kitiara's face. Rather, there was a look of fear, for she saw that the stroke that should have killed had missed. Why? she asked herself in fury. She had slain a hundred men that way! Why should she miss now? Dropping her knife, she drew her sword, lunging forward in the same motion.

The sword whistled with the force of her stroke, but it struck against a solid wall. Sparks crackled as the metal connected with the magical shield† Dalamar had conjured up around him, and a paralyzing shock sizzled from the blade, through the handle, and up her arm. The sword fell from her nerveless hand. Gripping her arm, the astonished Kitiara stumbled to her knees.

Dalamar had time to recover from the shock of his wound. The defensive spells he had cast had been reflexive, a result of years of training. He had not really even needed to think about them. But now he stared grimly at the woman on the floor before him, who was reaching for her sword with her left hand, even as she flexed the right, trying to regain feeling in it.

The battle had just begun.

Like a cat, Kitiara† twisted to her feet, her eyes burning with battle rage and the almost sexual lust†† that consumed her when fighting. Dalamar had seen that look in someone's eyes before—in Raistlin's, when he was lost in the ecstasy of his magic. The dark elf swallowed a choking sensation in his throat and tried to banish the pain and fear from his mind, seeking to concentrate only on his spells.

"Don't make me kill you, Kitiara," he said, playing for time, feeling himself grow stronger every moment. He had to conserve that strength! It would avail him little to stop Kitiara, only to die at her brother's hands.

His first thought was to call for the guardians. But he rejected that. She had won past them once, probably using the nightjewel. Falling backward before the Dragon Highlord, Dalamar edged his way nearer the stone desk, where lay his magical devices. From the corner of his eye, he caught the gleam of gold—a magical wand. His timing must be precise, he would have to dispel the magical shield to use the wand against Kit. And he saw in Kitiara's eyes that she knew this. She was waiting for him to drop the shield, biding her time.

"You have been deceived, Kitiara," Dalamar said softly, hoping to distract her.

"By you!" She sneered. Lifting a silver, branched candlestand, she hurled it at Dalamar. It bounced harmlessly off the magical shield to fall at his feet. A curl of smoke rose from the carpet, but the small fire died almost instantly, drowned in the melting candlewax.

"By Lord Soth," Dalamar said.

"Hah!" Kitiara laughed, hurling a glass beaker against the magical shield. It broke into a thousand, glittering shards. Another candlestand followed. Kitiara had fought magic-users before. She knew

Didn't we say earlier that Kitiara has a feline feel? —TRH

The lusts of blood and sex are both consuming. The fire involved in both has often been closely related— a fact not lost on so-called "slasher" films. This is why such movies incorporate both illicit sex and gory violence closely intertwined. That Kitiara is driven by both lusts should not surprise us. It makes both all the more horrifying. —TRH

how to defeat them. Her missiles were not intended to hurt, only to weaken the mage, force him to spend his strength maintaining the shield, make him think twice about lowering it.

"Why do you suppose you found Palanthas fortified?" Dalamar continued, backing up, creeping nearer the stone table. "Had you expected that? Soth told me your plans! He told me you were going to attack Palanthas to try to help your brother! 'When Raistlin comes through the Portal, drawing the Dark Queen after him, Kitiara will be here to greet him like a loving sister!' "

Kitiara paused, her sword lowered a fraction of an inch. "Soth told you that?"

"Yes," Dalamar said, sensing with relief her hesitation and confusion. The pain of his injury had eased somewhat. He ventured a glance down at the wound. His robes had stuck to it, forming a crude bandage. The bleeding had almost stopped.

"Why?" Kitiara raised her eyebrows mockingly. "Why would Soth betray me to you, dark elf?"

"Because he wants you,† Kitiara," Dalamar said softly. "He wants you the only way he can have you. . . ."

A cold sliver of terror pierced Kitiara to her very soul. She remembered that odd edge in Soth's hollow voice. She remembered it was he who had advised her to attack Palanthas. Her rage seeping from her, Kitiara shuddered, convulsed with chills. The wounds are poisoned she realized bitterly, seeing the long scratches upon her arms and legs, feeling again the icy claws of those who made them. Poison. Lord Soth. She couldn't think. Glancing up dizzily, she saw Dalamar smile.

Angrily, she turned from him to conceal her emotions, to get hold of herself.

Keeping an eye on her, Dalamar moved nearer the stone table, his glance going to the wand he needed.

Kitiara let her shoulders slump, her head droop. She held the sword weakly in her right hand, balancing the blade with her left, feigning to be seriously hurt. All the while, she felt strength returning to her numb sword arm. Let him think he has won. I'll hear him when he attacks. At the first magical word he utters, I'll slice him in two! Her hand tightened on the sword hilt.

This scene further emphasizes the maxim often quoted — "Evil turns in on itself." Here we have Dalamar, Kitiara, Soth, Raistlin, and Takhisis all grasping for power, willing to kill and betray each other.

Listening carefully, she heard nothing. Only the soft rustle of black robes, the painful catch in the dark elf's breath. Was it true, she wondered, about Lord Soth? If it were, did it matter? Kitiara found the thought rather amusing. Men had done more than that to gain her. She was still free. She would deal with Soth later. What Dalamar said about Raistlin intrigued her more. Could he, perhaps, win?

Would he bring the Dark Queen into this plane? The thought appalled Kitiara, appalled and frightened her. "I was useful to you once, wasn't I, Dark Majesty?" she whispered. "Once, when you were weak and only a shadow upon this side of the glass. But when you are strong, what place will there be for me in this world? None! Because you hate me and you fear me even as I hate and fear you.†

"As for my sniveling worm of a brother, there will be one waiting for him—Dalamar! You belong to your *Shalafi* body and soul! You're the one who means to help, not hinder, him when he comes through the Portal! No, dear lover. I do not trust you! Dare not trust you!"

Dalamar saw Kitiara shiver, he saw the wounds upon her body turning a purplish blue. She was weakening, certainly. He had seen her face pale when he mentioned Soth, her eyes dilate for an instant with fear. Surely she must realize she had been betrayed. Surely she must now see her great folly. Not that it mattered, not now. He did not trust her, dare not trust her†. . . .

Dalamar's hand snaked backward. Grasping the wand, he swung it up, speaking the word of magic that diffused the magical shield guarding him. At that instant, Kitiara whirled around. Her sword grasped in both hands, she wielded it with all her strength. The blow would have severed Dalamar's head from his neck, had he not twisted his body to use the wand.

As it was, the blade caught him across the back of the right shoulder, plunging deep into his flesh, shattering the shoulderblade, nearly slicing his arm off. He dropped the wand with a scream, but not before it had unleashed its magical power. Lightning forked, its sizzling blast striking Kitiara in the chest, knocking her writhing body backward, slamming her to the floor.

Hate and fear are at the heart of evil's self-destructive cycle. Distrust always tears at the fabric until it is rent asunder. Love and trust, however, are very much at the heart of that which is good and are redemptive qualities. —TRH

Had Kitiara and Dalamar joined forces they might have been able to stop Raistlin, but such is not in their nature, for there is no trust between them nor even a common goal around which they might rally. Evil consumes its own purposes. —TRH

Dalamar slumped over the table, reeling from pain. Blood spurted rhythmically from his arm. He watched it dully, uncomprehending for an instant, then Raistlin's lessons in anatomy returned. That was the heartblood pouring out. He would be dead within minutes. The ring of healing was on his right hand, his injured arm. Feebly reaching across with his left, he grasped the stone and spoke the simple word that activated the magic. Then he lost consciousness, his body slipping to the floor to lie in a pool of his own blood.

"Dalamar!" A voice called his name.

Drowsily, the dark elf stirred. Pain shot through his body. He moaned and fought to sink back into the darkness. But the voice shouted again. Memory returned, and with memory came fear.

Fear brought him to consciousness. He tried to sit up, but pain tore through him, nearly making him pass out again. He could hear the broken ends of bones crunching together, his right arm and hand hung limp and lifeless at his side. The ring had stopped the bleeding. He would live, but would it be only to die at the hands of his *Shalafi*?

"Dalamar!" the voice shouted again. "It's Caramon!"

Dalamar sobbed in relief. Lifting his head—a move that required a supreme effort—he looked at the Portal. The dragon's eyes glowed brighter still, the glow even seeming to spread along their necks. The void was definitely stirring now. He could feel a hot wind upon his cheek, or perhaps it was the fever in his body.

He heard a rustling in a shadowed corner across the room, and another fear gripped Dalamar. No! It was impossible she should be alive! Gritting his teeth against the pain, he turned his head. He could see her armored body, reflecting the glow of the dragon's eyes. She lay still, unmoving in the shadows. He could smell the stench of burned flesh. But that sound . . .

Wearily, Dalamar shut his eyes. Darkness swirled in his head, threatening to drag him down. He could not rest yet! Fighting the pain, he forced himself to consciousness, wondering why Caramon didn't come. He could hear him calling again. What

was the matter? And then Dalamar remembered—
the guardians! Of course, they would never let
him pass!

"Guardians, hear my words and obey," Dalamar
began, concentrating his thoughts and energies,
murmuring the words that would help Caramon
pass the dread defenders of the Tower and enter
the chamber.

Behind Dalamar, the dragon's heads glowed
brighter yet, while before him, in the shadowed
corner, a hand reached into a blood-drenched belt
and, with its dying strength, gripped the handle of
a dagger.

"Caramon," said Tanis softly, watching the eyes
watching him, "we could leave. Go up the stairs
again. Maybe there's another way—"

"There isn't. I'm not leaving," Caramon said
stubbornly.

"Name of the gods, Caramon! You can't fight the
damn things!"

"Dalamar!" Caramon called again desperately.
"Dalamar,
I—"

As suddenly as if they had been snuffed out, the
glowing eyes vanished.

"They're gone!" said Caramon, starting forward
eagerly. But Tanis caught hold of him.

"A trick—"

"No," Caramon drew him on. "You can sense
them, even when they're not visible. And I can't
sense them anymore. Can you?"

"I sense something!" Tanis muttered.

"But it's not *them* and it's not concerned about
us," Caramon said, heading down the winding
stairs of the top of the Tower at a run. Another door
at the bottom of the steps stood open. Here, Caramon paused, peering inside the main part of the
building cautiously.

It was dark inside, as dark as if light had not yet
been created. The torches had been extinguished. No
windows permitted even the smoke-clouded light
from outside the Tower to seep into it. Tanis had a
sudden vision of stepping into that darkness and
vanishing forever, falling into the thick, devouring
evil that permeated every rock and stone. Beside

him, he could hear Caramon's breathing quicken, and feel the big man's body tense.

"Caramon—what's out there?"

"Nothing's out there. Just a long drop to the bottom. The center of the Tower's hollow. There are stairs that run around the edge of the wall, rooms branch off from the stairs. I'm standing on a narrow landing now, if I remember right. The laboratory's about two flights down from here." Caramon's voice broke. "We've got to go on! We're losing time! He's getting nearer!" Clutching at Tanis, he continued more calmly. "C'mon. Just keep close to the wall. This stairway leads down to the laboratory—"

"One false step in this blasted darkness and it won't matter to us anymore what your brother does!" Tanis said. But he knew his words were useless. Blind as he was in the smothering endless night, he could almost see Caramon's face tighten with resolve. He heard the big man take a shuffling step forward, trying to feel his way along the wall. With a sigh, Tanis prepared to follow. . . .

And then the eyes were back, staring at them.

Tanis reached for his sword—a stupid, futile gesture. But the eyes only continued to stare at them, and a voice spoke. "Come. This way."

A hand wavered in the darkness.

"We can't see, damn it!" Tanis snarled.

A ghostly light appeared, held in that wasted hand. Tanis shuddered. He preferred the darkness, after all. But he said nothing, for Caramon was hurrying ahead, running down a long winding flight of stairs. At the bottom, the eyes and the hand and the light came to halt. Before them was an open door and a room beyond. Inside the room, light shone brightly, beaming into the corridor. Caramon dashed ahead, and Tanis followed, hastily slamming the door shut behind him so that the horrible eyes wouldn't follow.

Turning, he stopped, staring around the room, and he realized, suddenly, where he was—Raistlin's laboratory. Standing numbly, pressed against the door, Tanis watched as Caramon hurried forward to kneel beside a figure huddled in a pool of blood upon the floor. Dalamar, Tanis registered, seeing the black robes. But he couldn't react, couldn't move.

The evil in the darkness outside the door had been smothering, dusty, centuries old. But the evil in here was alive; it breathed and throbbed and pulsed. Its chill flowed from the nightblue-bound spellbooks upon the shelves, its warmth rose from a new set of black-bound spellbooks, marked with hourglass runes, that stood beside them. His horrified gaze looked into beakers and saw tormented eyes staring back at him. He choked on the smells of spices and mold and fungus and roses and, somewhere, the sweet smell of burned flesh.

And then, his gaze was caught and held by glowing light radiating from a corner. The light was beautiful, yet it filled him with awe and terror, reminding him vividly of his encounter with the Dark Queen. Mesmerized, he stared at the light. It seemed to be of every color he had ever seen whirling into one. But, as he watched, horrified, fascinated, unable to look away, he saw the light separate and become distinct, forming into the five heads of a dragon.

A doorway! Tanis realized suddenly. The five heads† rose from a golden dais, forming an oval shape with their necks. Each craned inward, its mouth open in a frozen scream. Tanis looked beyond them into the void within the oval. Nothing was there, but that nothing moved. All was empty, and alive. He knew suddenly, instinctively, where the doorway led, and the knowledge chilled him.

"The Portal," said Caramon, seeing Tanis's pale face and staring eyes. "Come here, give me a hand."

"You're going in there?" Tanis whispered savagely, amazed at the big man's calm. Crossing the room, he came to stand beside his friend. "Caramon, don't be a fool!"

"I have no choice, Tanis," Caramon said, that new look of quiet decision on his face. Tanis started to argue, but Caramon turned away from him, back to the injured dark elf.

"I've seen what will happen!" he reminded Tanis.

Swallowing his words, choking on them, Tanis knelt down beside Dalamar. The dark elf had managed to drag himself to a sitting position, so that he could face the Portal. He had lapsed into unconsciousness again, but, at the sound of their voices, his eyes flared open.

Takhisis as the five-headed dragon was borrowed from the Babylonian goddess Tiamat. However, the DRAGONLANCE setting made her its own by making each head representative of the five evil breeds of dragon— red, black, blue, white, and green.

"Caramon!" He gasped, reaching out a trembling hand. *"You* must stop—"

"I know, Dalamar," Caramon said gently. "I know what I must do. But I need your help! Tell me—"

Dalamar's eyes fluttered shut, his skin was ashen. Tanis reached across Dalamar's chest to feel for the lifebeat in the young elf's neck. His hand had just touched the mage's skin when there was a ringing sound. Something jarred his arm, striking the armor and bouncing off, falling to the floor with a clatter. Looking down, Tanis saw a blood-stained dagger.

Startled, he whirled around, twisting to his feet, sword in hand.

"Kitiara!" Dalamar whispered with a feeble nod of his head.

Staring into the shadows of the laboratory, Tanis saw the body in the corner.

"Of course," Caramon murmured. *"That's* how she killed him." He lifted the dagger in his hand. "This time, Tanis, you blocked her throw."

But Tanis didn't hear. Sliding his sword back into his sheath, he crossed the room, stepping unheedingly on broken glass, kicking aside a silver candle-stand that rolled beneath his feet.

Kitiara lay on her stomach, her cheek pressed against the bloody floor, her dark hair falling across her eyes. The dagger throw had taken her last energy, it seemed. Tanis, approaching her, his emotions in turmoil, was certain she must be dead.

But the indomitable will that had carried one brother through darkness and another into light, burned still within Kitiara.

She heard footsteps . . . her enemy. . . .

Her hand grasped feebly for her sword. She raised her head, looking up with eyes fast dimming.

"Tanis?" She stared at him, puzzled, confused. Where was she? Flotsam? Were they together there again?† Of course! He had come back to her! Smiling, she raised her hand to him.

Tanis caught his breath, his stomach wrenching. As she moved, he saw a blackened hole gaping in her chest. Her flesh had been burned away, he could see white bone beneath. It was a gruesome sight, and Tanis, sickened and overwhelmed by a surge of memories, was forced to turn his head away.

Tanis joined Kitiara in Flotsam in the latter chapters of Dragons of Winter Night.

"Tanis!" she called in a cracked voice. "Come to me."

His heart filled with pity, Tanis knelt down beside her to lift her in his arms. She looked up into his face . . . and saw her death in his eyes. Fear shook her. She struggled to rise.

But the effort was too much. She collapsed.

"I'm . . . hurt," she whispered angrily. "How . . . bad?" Lifting her hand, she started to touch the wound.

Snatching off his cloak, Tanis wrapped it around Kitiara's torn body. "Rest easy, Kit," he said gently. "You'll be all right."

"You're a damn liar!" she cried, her hands clenching into fists, echoing—if she had only known it—the dying Elistan. "He's killed me! That wretched elf!" She smiled, a ghastly smile. Tanis shuddered. "But I fixed him! He can't help Raistlin now. The Dark Queen will slay him, slay them all!"

Moaning, she writhed in agony and clutched at Tanis. He held her tightly. When the pain eased, she looked up at him. "You weakling," she whispered in a tone that was part bitter scorn, part bitter regret, "we could have had the world, you and I."

"I *have* the world, Kitiara," Tanis said softly, his heart torn with revulsion and sorrow.

Angrily, she shook her head and seemed about to say more when her eyes grew wide, her gaze fixed upon something at the far end of the room.

"No!" she cried in a terror that no torture or suffering could have ever wrenched from her. "No!" Shrinking, huddling against Tanis, she whispered in a frantic, strangled voice. "Don't let him take me! Tanis, no! Keep him away! I always loved you, half-elf! Always . . . loved . . . you . . ."

Her voice faded to a gasping whisper.

Tanis looked up, alarmed. But the doorway was empty. There was no one there. Had she meant Dalamar? "Who? Kitiara! I don't understand—"

But she did not hear him. Her ears were deaf forever to mortal voices. The only voice she heard now was one she would hear forever, through all eternity.

Tanis felt the body in his arms go limp. Smoothing back the dark, curly hair, he searched her face for some sign that death had brought peace to her soul. But the expression on her face was one of horror—

her brown eyes fixed in a terrified stare, the crooked, charming smile twisted into a grimace.

Tanis glanced up at Caramon. His face pale and grave, the big man shook his head. Slowly, Tanis laid Kitiara's body back down upon the floor. Leaning over, he started to kiss the cold forehead, but he found that he couldn't. The look on the corpse's face was too grim, too ghastly.

Pulling his cloak up over Kitiara's head, Tanis remained for a moment, kneeling beside her body, surrounded by darkness. And then he heard Caramon's step, he felt a hand upon his arm. "Tanis—"

"I'm all right," the half-elf said gruffly, rising to his feet. But, in his mind, he could still hear her dying plea—

"Keep him away!"

"I'm glad you're here with me, Tanis," Caramon said.

He stood before the Portal,† staring into it intently, watching every shift and wave of the void within. Near him sat Dalamar, propped up by pillows in his chair, his face pale and drawn with pain, his arm bound in a crude sling. Tanis paced the floor restlessly. The dragon's heads now glowed so brightly it hurt the eye to look at them directly.

"Caramon," he began, "please—"

Caramon looked over at him, his same grave, calm expression unchanged.

Tanis was baffled. How could you argue with granite? He sighed. "All right. But just how are you going to get in there?" he asked abruptly.

Caramon smiled. He knew what Tanis had been about to say, and he was grateful to him for not having said it.

Tanis Half-Elven is the mirror image of Dalamar. Tanis represents the establishment of order over chaos. Tanis is the side of light, however, whereas Dalamar is the side of darkness. Dalamar wants primarily to make life better for himself, while Tanis works selflessly to make life better for others. Like Dalamar, Tanis is both a man of faith and a practical man, and both facets of his personality provide him with the strength he requires to make the difficult decisions at the end. It is therefore fitting that Tanis and Dalamar are together at the Portal of the Abyss and that although one represents light and one darkness, both are prepared to sacrifice themselves to maintain order in the world. —MW

Giving the Portal a grim look, Tanis gestured toward the opening. "From what you told me earlier, Raistlin had to study years and become this Fistandantilus and entrap Lady Crysania into going with him, and even then he barely made it!" Tanis shifted his gaze to Dalamar. "Can you enter the Portal, dark elf?"

Dalamar shook his head. "No. As you say, it takes one of great power to cross that dread threshold. I do not have such power, perhaps I never will. But, do not glower, Half-Elven. We do not waste our time. I am certain Caramon would not have undertaken this if he did not know how he could enter." Dalamar looked at the big warrior intently. "For enter he must, or we are doomed."

"When Raistlin fights the Dark Queen and her minions in the Abyss," Caramon said, his voice even and expressionless, "he will need to concentrate upon them completely, to the exclusion of all else. Isn't that true, Dalamar?"

"Most assuredly." The dark elf shivered and pulled his black robes about him closer with his good hand. "One breath, one blink, one twitch, and they will rend him limb from limb and devour him."

Caramon nodded.

How can he be so calm? Tanis wondered. And a voice within him replied, it is the calm of one who knows and accepts his fate.

"In Astinus's book," Caramon continued, "he wrote that Raistlin, knowing he would have to concentrate his magic upon fighting the Queen, opened the Portal to make sure of his escape route before he went into battle. Thus, when he arrived, he would find it ready for him to enter when he returned to this world."

"He also knew undoubtedly that he would be too weakened by that time to open it himself," Dalamar murmured. "He would need to be at the height of his strength. Yes, you are right. He will open it, and soon. And when he does, anyone with the strength and courage necessary to pass the boundary may enter."

The dark elf closed his eyes, biting his lip to keep from crying out. He had refused a potion to ease the pain. "If you fail," he had said to Caramon, "I am our last hope."

Our last hope, thought Tanis—a dark elf. This is insane! It can't be happening. Leaning against the stone table, he let his head sink into his hands. Name of the gods, he was tired! His body ached, his wounds burned and stung. He had removed the breast plate of his armor—it felt as heavy as a gravestone, slung around his neck. But as much as his body hurt, his soul hurt worse.

Memories flitted about him like the guardians of the Tower, reaching out to touch him with their cold hands. Caramon sneaking food off Flint's plate while the dwarf had his back turned. Raistlin conjuring up visions of wonder and delight for the children of Flotsam. Kitiara, laughing, throwing her arms around his neck, whispering into his ear. Tanis's heart shrank within him, the pain brought tears to his eyes. No! It was all wrong! Surely it wasn't supposed to end this way!

A book swam into his blurred vision—Caramon's book, resting upon the stone table, the last book of Astinus. Or is *that* how it was going to end? He became aware, then, of Caramon looking at him in concern. Angrily, he wiped his eyes and his face and stood up with a sigh.

But the spectres remained with him, hovering near him. Near him . . . and near the burned and broken body that lay in the corner beneath his cloak.

Human, half-elf, and dark elf watched the Portal in silence. A water clock† on the mantle kept track of time, the drops falling one by one with the regularity of a heartbeat. The tension in the room stretched until it seemed it must snap and break, whipping around the laboratory with stinging fury. Dalamar began muttering in elven. Tanis glanced at him sharply, fearing the dark elf might be delirious. The mage's face was pale, cadaverous, his eyes surrounded by deep, purple shadows had sunken into their sockets. Their gaze never shifted, they stared always into the swirling void.

Even Caramon's calm appeared to be slipping.† His big hands clenched and unclenched nervously, sweat covered his body, glistening in the light of the five heads of the dragon. He began to shiver, involuntarily. The muscles in his arms twitched and bunched spasmodically.

I have a book on ancient inventions that tells about water clocks. You can probably find info on the Internet. —MW

Teachers of writing technique often say, "Show, don't tell." Here is a perfect example of showing instead of telling. Note that the text does not tell you Caramon was scared, Dalamar terrified, and Tanis having second thoughts. The text showed their behavior, how they were acting, which gives the scene much more poignancy and allows the reader to judge what's going on.

And then Tanis felt a strange sensation creep over him. The air was still, too still. Sounds of battle raging in the city outside the Tower—sounds that he had heard without even being aware of it—suddenly ceased. Inside the Tower, too, sound hushed. The words Dalamar muttered died on his lips.

The silence blanketed them, as thick and stifling as the darkness in the corridor, as the evil within the room. The dripping of the water clock grew louder, magnified, every drop seeming to jar Tanis's bones. Dalamar's eyes jerked open, his hand twitched, nervously grasping his black robes between white-knuckled fingers.

Tanis moved closer to Caramon, only to find the big man reaching out for him.

Both spoke at once. "Caramon . . ."

"Tanis . . ."

Desperately, Caramon grasped hold of Tanis's arm. "You'll take care of Tika for me, won't you?"

"Caramon, I can't let you go in there alone!" Tanis gripped him. "I'll come—"

"No, Tanis," Caramon's voice was firm. "If I fail, Dalamar will need your help. Tell Tika good-bye, and try to explain to her, Tanis. Tell her I love her very much, so much I—" His voice broke. He couldn't go on. Tanis held onto him tightly.

"I know what to tell her, Caramon," he said, remembering a letter of good-bye of his own.

Caramon nodded, shaking the tears from his eyes and drawing a deep, quivering breath. "And say good-bye to Tas. I—I don't think he ever did understand. Not really." He managed a smile. "Of course, you'll have to get him out of that flying castle first."

"I think he knew, Caramon," Tanis said softly.

The dragon's heads began to make a shrill sound, a faint scream that seemed to come from far away.

Caramon tensed.

The screaming grew louder, nearer, and more shrill. The Portal burned with color, each head of the dragon glistened brilliantly.

"Make ready," Dalamar warned, his voice cracking.

"Good-bye, Tanis." Caramon held onto his hand tightly.

"Good-bye, Caramon."

Releasing his hold on his friend, Tanis stepped back.

The void parted. The Portal opened.

Tanis looked into it—he knew he looked into it, for he could not turn away. But he could never recall clearly what he saw. He dreamed of it, even years later. He knew he dreamed of it because he would wake in the night, drenched in sweat. But the image was always just fading from his consciousness, never to be grasped by his waking mind. And he would lie, staring into the darkness, trembling, for hours after.

But that was later. All he knew now was that he *had* to stop Caramon! But he couldn't move. He couldn't cry out. Transfixed, horror-stricken, he watched as Caramon, with a last, quiet look, turned and mounted the golden platform.

The dragons shrieked in warning, triumph, hatred. . . . Tanis didn't know. His own cry, wrenched from his body, was lost in the shrill, deafening sound.

There was a blinding, swirling, crashing wave of many-colored light.

And then it was dark.

Caramon was gone.

"May Paladine be with you," Tanis whispered, only to hear, to his discomfiture, Dalamar's cool voice, echo, "Takhisis, my Queen, go with you."

"I see him," said Dalamar, after a moment. Staring intently into the Portal, he half-rose, to see more clearly. A gasp of pain, forgotten in the excitement, escaped him. Cursing, he sank back down into the chair, his pale face covered with sweat.

Tanis ceased his restless pacing and came to stand beside Dalamar. "There," the dark elf† pointed, his breath coming from between clenched teeth.

Reluctantly, still feeling the effects of the shock that lingered from when he had first looked into the Portal, Tanis looked into it again. At first he could see nothing but a bleak and barren landscape stretching beneath a burning sky. And then he saw red-tinged light glint off bright armor. He saw a small figure standing near the front of the Portal, sword in hand, facing away from them, waiting. . . .

"How will he close it?" Tanis asked, trying to speak calmly though grief choked his voice.

"He cannot," Dalamar replied.

Here are two outcasts of elven society—one the champion of good and the other a mage of evil—standing side by side. That two who are so much alike and so very different should stand before the portal is representative of the two powers watching the outcome from afar.
—TRH

Tanis stared at him in alarm. "Then what will stop the Queen from entering again?"

"She cannot come through unless one comes through ahead of her, half-elf," Dalamar answered, somewhat irritably. "Otherwise, she would have entered long before this. Raistlin keeps it open. If he comes through it, she will follow. With his death, it will close."

"So Caramon must kill him—his brother?"

"Yes."

"And he must die as well," Tanis murmured.

"Pray that he dies!" Dalamar licked his lips. The pain was making him dizzy, nauseated. "For he cannot return through the Portal either. And though death at the hands of the Dark Queen can be very slow, very unpleasant, believe me, Half-Elven, it is far preferable to life!"

"He knew this—"

Caramon is an archetypal hero, a savior figure who sacrifices himself for the greater good. —TRH

"Yes, he knew it.† But the world will be saved, Half-Elven," Dalamar remarked cynically. Sinking back into his chair, he continued staring into the Portal, his hand alternately crumpling, then smoothing, the folds of his black, rune-covered robes.

"No, not the world, a soul," Tanis started to reply bitterly, when he heard, behind him, the laboratory door creak.

Dalamar's gaze shifted instantly. Eyes glittering, his hand moved to a spell scroll he had slipped into his belt.

"No one can enter," he said softly to Tanis, who had turned at the sound. "The guardians—"

"Cannot stop *him*," Tanis said, his gaze fixed upon the door with a look of fear that mirrored, for an instant, the look of frozen fear upon Kitiara's dead face.

Dalamar smiled grimly, and relapsed back into his chair. There was no need to look around. The chill of death flowed through the room like a foul mist.

Although Dalamar has allied himself with Tanis and Caramon, he certainly hasn't told them everything. He's still playing his own game and can't bring himself to trust his allies.

"Enter, Lord Soth," Dalamar said. "I've been expecting you."†

CHAPTER
8

Caramon was
blinded by the dazzling light that seared even
through his closed eyelids. Then darkness wrapped
around him and, when he opened his eyes, for an
instant he could not see, and he panicked, remembering the time he had been blind and lost in the
Tower of High Sorcery.

But, gradually, the darkness, too, lifted, and his
eyes became accustomed to the eerie light of his surroundings. It burned with a strange, pinkish glow,
as if the sun had just set, Tasslehoff had told him. And
the land was just as the kender had described—
vast, empty terrain beneath a vast, empty sky. Sky
and land were the same color everywhere he looked,
in every direction.

Except in one direction. Turning his head, Caramon saw the Portal, now behind him. It was the only
swatch of colors in the barren land. Framed by the

oval door of the five heads of the dragon, it seemed small and distant to him even though he knew he must be very near. Caramon fancied it looked like a picture, hung upon a wall. Though he could see Tanis and Dalamar quite clearly, they were not moving. They might well have been painted subjects, captured in arrested motion,† forced to spend their painted eternity staring into nothing.

Time seems to be very much a relative issue in the Abyss. —TRH

Firmly turning his back upon them, wondering, with a pang, if they could see him as he could see them, Caramon drew his sword from its sheath and stood, feet firmly planted on the shifting ground, waiting for his twin.

Caramon had no doubts, no doubts at all, that a battle between himself and Raistlin must end in his own death. Even weakened, Raistlin's magic would still be strong. And Caramon knew his brother well enough to know that Raistlin would never—if he could help it—allow himself to become totally vulnerable. There would always be one spell left, or—at least—the silver dagger on his wrist.

But, even though I will die, my objective will be accomplished, Caramon thought calmly. I am strong, healthy, and all it will take is one sword thrust through that thin, frail body.

He could do that much, he knew, before his brother's magic withered him as it had withered him once, long ago, in the Tower of High Sorcery. . . .

Tears stung in his eyes, ran down his throat. He swallowed them, forcing his thoughts to something else to take his mind from his fear . . . his sorrow.

Lady Crysania.

Poor woman. Caramon sighed. He hoped, for her sake, she had died quickly . . . never knowing. . . .

Caramon blinked, startled, staring ahead of him. What was happening? Where before there had been nothing to the pinkish, glowing horizon—now there was an object. It stood starkly black against the pink sky, and appeared flat, *as if it had been cut out of paper.* Tas's words came to him again. But he recognized it—a wooden stake. The kind . . . the kind they had used in the old days to burn witches!

Memories flooded back. He could see Raistlin tied to the stake, see the heaps of wood stacked about his brother, who was struggling to free himself, shrieking defiance at those whom he had attempted to

save from their own folly by exposing a charlatan cleric. But they had believed him to be a witch. "We got there just in time, Sturm and I," Caramon muttered, remembering the knight's sword flashing in the sun, its light alone driving back the superstitious peasants.

Looking closer at the stake—which seemed, of its own accord, to move closer to him—Caramon saw a figure lying at the foot. Was it Raistlin? The stake slid closer and closer—or was he walking toward it? Caramon turned his head again. The Portal was farther back, but he could still see it.

Alarmed, fearing he might be swept away, he fought to stop himself and did so, immediately. Then, he heard the kender's voice again. *All you have to do to go anywhere is think yourself there. All you have to do to have anything you want is think of it, only be careful, because the Abyss can twist and distort what you see.*

Looking at the wooden stake, Caramon thought himself there and instantly was standing right beside it. Turning once again, he glanced in the direction of the Portal and saw it, hanging like a miniature painting in between the sky and ground. Satisfied that he could return at any second, Caramon hurried toward the figure lying below the stake.

At first, he had thought it was garbed in black robes, and his heart lurched. But now he saw that it had only appeared as a black silhouette against the glowing ground. The robes it wore were white. And then he knew.

Of course, he had been thinking of her. . . .

"Crysania," he said.

She opened her eyes and turned her head toward the sound of his voice, but her eyes did not fix on him. They stared past him, and he realized she was blind.†

"Raistlin?" she whispered in a voice filled with such hope and longing that Caramon would have given anything, his life itself, to have confirmed that hope.

But, shaking his head, he knelt down and took her hand in his. "It is Caramon, Lady Crysania."

She turned her sightless eyes toward the sound of his voice, weakly clasping his hand with her own. She stared toward him, confused. "Caramon? Where are we?"

Crysania goes blind so that she can truly see. It is part of her sacrifice to her own hubris and pride. One is reminded strongly of the biblical passage, "If thine eye offend thee, pluck it out." Crysania may have lost her mortal sight, but she gained the spiritual sight that she so desperately needed—and is thereby redeemed. —TRH

"I entered the Portal, Crysania," he said.

She sighed, closing her eyes. "So you are here in the Abyss, with us. . . ."

"Yes."

"I have been a fool, Caramon," she murmured, "but I am paying for my folly. I wish . . . I wish I knew. . . . Has harm come to . . . to anyone . . . other than myself? And him?" The last word was almost inaudible.

"Lady—" Caramon didn't know how to answer.

But Crysania stopped him. She could hear the sadness in his voice. Closing her eyes, tears streaming down her cheeks, she pressed his hand against her lips. "Of course. I understand!" she whispered. "That is why you have come. I'm sorry, Caramon! So sorry!"

She began to weep. Gathering her close, Caramon held her, rocking her soothingly, like a child. He knew, then, that she was dying. He could feel her life ebbing from her body even as he held it. But what had injured her, what wounds she had suffered he could not imagine, for there was no mark upon her skin.

"There is nothing to be sorry for, my lady," he said, smoothing back the thick, shining black hair that tumbled over her deathly pale face. "You loved him. If that is your folly, then it is mine as well, and I pay for it gladly."

"If that were only true!" She moaned. "But it was my pride, my ambition, that led me here!"

"Was it, Crysania?" Caramon asked. "If so, why did Paladine grant your prayers and open the Portal for you when he refused to grant the demands of the Kingpriest? Why did he bless you with that gift if not because he saw truly what was in your heart?"

"Paladine has turned his face from me!"† she cried. Taking the medallion in her hand she tried to wrench it from her neck. But she was too weak. Her hand closed over the medallion and remained there. And, as she did so, a look of peace filled her face. "No," she said, talking softly to herself, "he is here. He holds me. I see him so clearly. . . ."

Standing up, Caramon lifted her in his arms. Her head sank back against his shoulder, she relaxed in his firm grasp. "We are going back to the Portal," he told her.

Crysania's words here mirror Christ's words on the cross. See Matthew 27:46 and Mark 15:34.

She did not answer, but she smiled. Had she heard him, or was she listening to another voice?

Facing the Portal that glimmered like a multicolored jewel in the distance, Caramon thought himself near it, and it moved rapidly forward.

Suddenly the air around him split and cracked. Lightning stabbed from the sky, lightning such as he had never seen. Thousands of purple, sizzling branches struck the ground, penning him for a spectacular instant in a prison whose bars were death. Paralyzed by the shock, he could not move. Even after the lightning vanished, he waited, cringing, for the explosive blast of thunder that must deafen him forever.

But there was only silence, silence and, far away, an agonized, piercing scream.

Crysania's eyes opened. "Raistlin," she said. Her hand tightened around the medallion.

"Yes," Caramon replied.

Tears slid down her cheeks. She closed her eyes and clung to Caramon. He moved on, toward the Portal, traveling slowly now, a disturbing, disquieting idea coming to his mind. Lady Crysania was dying, certainly. The lifebeat in her neck was weak, fluttering beneath his fingers like the heart of a baby bird. But she was not dead, not yet. Perhaps, if he could get her back through the Portal, she might live.

Could he get her through, though, without taking her through himself?

Holding her in his arms, Caramon drew nearer the Portal. Or rather, it drew nearer him, leaping up at him as he approached, growing in size, the dragon's heads staring at him with their glittering eyes, their mouths open to grasp and devour him.

He could still see through it, he could see Tanis and Dalamar—one standing, the other sitting; neither moving, both frozen in time. Could they help him? Could they take Crysania?

"Tanis!" he called out. "Dalamar!"

But if either heard him shouting, they did not react to his cries.

Gently, he lowered Lady Crysania to the shifting ground before the Portal. Caramon knew then that it was hopeless. He had known all along. He could take her back and she would live. But that would

mean Raistlin would live and escape, drawing the Queen after him, dooming the world and its people to destruction.

He sank down to the strange ground. Sitting beside Crysania, he took hold of her hand. He was glad she was here with him, in a way. He didn't feel so alone. The touch of her hand was comforting. If only he could save her. . . .

"What are you going to do to Raistlin, Caramon?" Crysania asked softly, after a moment.

"Stop him from leaving the Abyss," Caramon replied, his voice even, without expression.

She nodded in understanding, her hand holding his firmly, her sightless eyes staring up at him.

"He'll kill you, won't he?"

"Yes," Caramon answered steadily. "But not before he himself falls."

A spasm of pain contorted Crysania's face. She gripped Caramon's hand. "I'll wait for you!" She choked, her voice weakening. "I'll wait for you. When it is over, you will be my guide since I cannot see. You will take me to Paladine. You will lead me from the darkness."

Her eyes closed. Her head sank back slowly, as though she rested upon a pillow. But her hand still held Caramon's. Her breast rose and fell with her breathing. He put his fingers on her neck, her life pulsed beneath them.

He had been prepared to condemn himself to death, he was prepared to condemn his brother. It had all been so simple!

But—could he condemn her? . . .

Perhaps he still had time. . . . Perhaps he could carry her through the Portal and return. . . .

Filled with hope, Caramon rose to his feet and started to lift Crysania in his arms again. Then he caught a glimpse of movement out of the corner of his eye.

Turning, he saw Raistlin.†

These final chapters do exactly what good books should do: each chapter ends on a cliffhanger, forcing the reader to turn the page, to keep reading. The chapters also alternate between scenes for each set of characters, each setting having its own cliffhanger, which further adds to the tension.

CHAPTER 9

"Enter, Knight of the Black Rose," repeated Dalamar.

Eyes of flame stared at Tanis, who put his hand on the hilt of his sword. At the same instant, slender fingers touched his arm, making him start.

"Do not interfere, Tanis," Dalamar said softly. "He does not care about us. He comes for one thing only."

The flickering, flaming gaze passed over Tanis. Candlelight glinted on the ancient, old-fashioned, ornate armor that bore still, beneath the blackened scorch-marks and the stains of his own blood— long since turned to dust—the faint outlines of the Rose, symbol of the Knights of Solamnia. Booted feet that made no sound crossed the room. The orange eyes had found their object in the shadowed corner—the huddled form lying beneath Tanis's cloak.

Keep him away! Tanis hear Kitiara's frantic voice. *I have always loved you, half-elf!*

Lord Soth stopped and knelt beside the body. But he appeared unable to touch it, as though constrained by some unseen force. Rising to his feet, he turned, his orange eyes flaming in the empty darkness beneath the helm he wore.

"Release her to me, Tanis Half-Elven," said the hollow voice. "Your love binds her to this plane. Give her up."

Tanis, gripping his sword, took a step forward.

"He'll kill you, Tanis," Dalamar warned. "He'll slay you without hesitation. Let her go to him. After all, I think perhaps he was the only one of us who ever truly understood her."

The orange eyes flared. "Understood her? Admired her! Like I myself, she was meant to rule, destined to conquer! But she was stronger than I was. She could throw aside love that threatened to chain her down. But for a twist of fate, she would have ruled all of Ansalon!"

The hollow voice resounded in the room, startling Tanis with its passion, its hatred.

"And there she was!" The chain mail fist clenched. "Penned up in Sanction like a caged beast, making plans for a war she could not hope to win. Her courage and resolve were beginning to weaken. She had even allowed herself to become chained like a slave to a dark-elf lover! Better she should die fighting than let her life burn out like a guttered candle."

"No!" Tanis muttered, his hand clenching his sword. "No—"

Dalamar's fingers closed over his wrist. "She never loved you, Tanis," he said coldly. "She used you as she used us all, even him."† The d͟a͟ glanced toward Soth. Tanis seemed ͟ ͟ ͟ ͟ ͟speak, but Dalamar interrupted ͟"S͟h͟ used you to the end, Half-Elven. Ev͟ ͟ ͟ ͟ ͟, ͟ she reaches from beyond, hoping ͟ ͟ ͟ ͟ ͟ save her."

͟ ͟ ͟ Tanis hesitated. In his mind burned the image of her horror-filled face. The image burned, flames rose. . . .

Flames filled Tanis's vision. Staring into them, he saw a castle, once proud and noble, now black and crumbling, falling into flame. He saw a lovely, delicate

Dalamar is absolutely right about Kitiara. Kit was, in my mind, consumed by her own lusts. Like her brothers, she too was an addict—a family trait it might seem. Caramon was addicted to drink, his brother to his magic, and his sister to her own lusts for power dominance, and

It ͟ ͟ ͟ to note that of the only one survives his addiction, while the other two are consumed by them utterly. —TRH

elf maid, a little child in her arms, falling into flame. He saw warriors, running, dying, falling into flame. And out of the flame, he heard Soth's voice.

"You have life, Half-Elven. You have much to live for. There are those among the living who depend upon you. I know, because all that you have was once mine. I cast it away, choosing to live in darkness instead of light. Will you follow me? Will you throw all you have aside for one who chose, long ago, to walk the paths of night?"†

I have the world, Tanis heard his own words. Laurana's face smiled upon him.

He closed his eyes . . . Laurana's face, beautiful, wise, loving. Light shone from her golden hair, glistened in her clear, elven eyes. The light grew brighter, like a star. Purely, brilliantly, it gleamed, shining upon him with such radiance that he could no longer see in his memory the cold face beneath the cloak.

Slowly, Tanis withdrew his hand from his sword.†

Lord Soth turned. Kneeling down, he lifted the body wrapped in the cloak, now stained dark with blood, in his unseen arms. He spoke a word of magic. Tanis had a sudden vision of a dark chasm yawning at the death knight's feet. Soul-piercing cold swept through the room, the blast forcing him to avert his head, as if against a bitter wind.

When he looked, the shadowed corner was empty.

"They are gone." Dalamar's hand released his wrist. "And so is Caramon."

"Gone?" Turning unsteadily, shivering, his body drenched in chill sweat, Tanis faced the Portal once again. The burning landscape was empty.

A hollow voice echoed. *Will you throw all you have aside for one who chose, long ago, to walk the paths of night?*

Once again we see the exquisite torture of the damned being centered on a knowledge of their failings and guilt. Soth knows full well what he has done, and the knowledge of his folly is what torments him. —TRH

This is the moment when Tanis decides to let go of his past and embrace his future. He sorrows for his past, sorrows for what he has done to others, and sorrows not only for what he has done to Kitiara but also for letting a relationship remain between them. It is time for him to let her go in every way. —TRH

Lord Soth's Song†

This, of course, picks up the song from Chapter 2 of Book I in War of the Twins *and preludes (if that's a verb) it with two new verses. There is a song in* Chronicles *that is also from the perspective of Lord Soth (The editors of the first* Leaves from the Inn of the Last Home *called it "The Knight of the Black Rose.")*

The Soth songs were fun to write because Soth was so relentlessly morbid, and I am not, by nature, a morbid person. It goes back to that same principle I talked about in my comment on "Crysania's Song"—the whole idea of letting your imagination enter the perspective and thoughts of a character someone else has created and to make the song that comes out of the process seem like something the character would sing. I don't know of any other kind of writing that does exactly that, but maybe I am overlooking something quite obvious.
—Michael Williams

Set aside the buried light
Of candle, torch, and rotting wood,
And listen to the turn of night
Caught in your rising blood.

How quiet is the midnight, love,
How warm the winds where ravens fly,
Where all the changing moonlight, love,
Pales in your fading eye.

How loud your heart is calling, love,
How close the darkness at your breast,
How hectic are the rivers, love,
Drawn through your dying wrist.

And love, what heat your frail skin hides,
As pure as salt, as sweet as death,
And in the dark the red moon rides
The foxfire of your breath.

CHAPTER 10

Ahead of him, the Portal.

Behind him, the Queen. Behind him, pain, suffering . . .

Ahead of him—victory.

Leaning upon the Staff of Magius, so weak he could barely stand, Raistlin kept the image of the Portal ever in his mind. It seemed he had walked, stumbled, crawled mile after endless mile to reach it. Now he was close. He could see its glittering, beautiful colors, colors of life—the green of grass, blue of sky, white of clouds, black of night, red of blood. . . .

Blood. He looked at his hands, stained with blood, his own blood. His wounds were too numerous to count. Struck by mace, stabbed by sword, scorched by lightning, burned by fire, he had been attacked by dark clerics, dark wizards, legions of ghouls and

At this point it is not the conflict of good vs. evil that threatens Krynn, but the titanic conflict of evil vs. evil that threatens to destroy the world in its wake. Could one not say the same of our own world? —TRH

demons—all who served Her Dark Majesty.† His black robes hung about him in stained tatters. He did not draw a breath that was not wrenching agony. He had, long ago, stopped vomiting blood. And though he coughed, coughed until he could not stand but was forced to sink to his knees, retching, there was nothing there. Nothing inside him.

And, through it all, he had endured.

Exultation ran like fever through his veins. He had endured, he had survived. He lived . . . just barely. But he lived. The Queen's fury thrummed behind him. He could feel the ground and sky pulsate with it. He had defeated her best, and there were none left now to challenge him. None, except herself.

The Portal shimmered with myriad colors in his hourglass vision. Closer, closer he came. Behind him— the Queen, rage making her careless, heedless. He would escape the Abyss, she could not stop him now. A shadow crossed over him, chilling him. Looking up, he saw the fingers of a gigantic hand darkening the sky, the nails glistening blood red.

Raistlin smiled, and kept advancing. It was a shadow, nothing more. The hand that cast the shadow reached for him in vain. He was too close, and she, having counted upon her minions to stop him, was too far away. Her hand would grasp the skirts of his tattered black robes when he crossed over the threshold of the Portal, and, with his last strength, he would drag it through the door.

And then, upon his plane, who would prove the stronger?

Raistlin coughed, but even as he coughed, even as the pain tore at him, he smiled—no, grinned—a thin-lipped, bloodstained grin. He had no doubts. No doubts at all.†

Arrogance is the great chink in Raistlin's armor, even as it was his greatest strength in many ways. Its roots lay in his addiction to the power he found in magic. —TRH

Raistlin's argument resounds with an evil version of the Kingpriest's own argument. They have, in essence, made the same mistake. —TRH

Clutching his chest with one hand, the Staff of Magius with the other, Raistlin moved ahead, carefully measuring out his life to himself as he needed it, cherishing every burning breath he drew like a miser gloating over a copper piece. The coming battle would be glorious. Now it would be his turn to summon legions to fight for him.† The gods themselves would answer his call, for the Queen appearing in the world in all her might and majesty would bring down the wrath of the heavens. Moons would fall, planets shift in their orbits, stars change their courses. The

elements would do his bidding—wind, air, water, fire—all under his command.

And now, ahead of him—the Portal, the dragon's heads shrieking in impotent fury, knowing they lacked the power to stop him.

Just one more breath, one more lurching heartbeat, one more step. . . .

He lifted his hooded head, and stopped.

A figure, unseen before, obscured by a haze of pain and blood and the shadows of death, rose up before him, standing before the Portal, a gleaming sword in its hand. Raistlin, looking at it, stared for a moment in complete and total incomprehension. Then, joy surged through his shattered body.

"Caramon!"

He stretched out a trembling hand. What miracle this was, he didn't know. But his twin was here, as he had ever been here, waiting for him, waiting to fight at his side. . . .

"Caramon!" Raistlin panted. "Help me, my brother."

Exhaustion was overtaking him, pain claiming him. He was rapidly losing the power to think, to concentrate. His magic no longer sparkled through his body like quicksilver, but moved sluggishly, congealing like the blood upon his wounds.

"Caramon, come to me. I cannot walk alone—"

But Caramon did not move. He just stood there, his sword in his hand, staring at him with eyes of mingled love and sorrow, a deep, burning sorrow. A sorrow that cut through the haze of pain and exposed Raistlin's barren, empty soul. And then he knew. He knew why his twin was here.

"You block my way, brother," Raistlin said coldly.

"I know."

"Stand aside, then, if you will not help me!" Raistlin's voice, coming from his raw throat, cracked with fury.

"No."

"You fool! You will die!" This was a whisper, soft and lethal.

Caramon drew a deep breath. "Yes," he said steadily, "and this time, so will you."

The sky above them darkened. Shadows gathered around them, as if the light were slowly being sucked away. The air grew chill as the light dimmed,

but Raistlin could feel a vast, flaming heat behind him, the rage of his Queen.

Fear twisted his bowels, anger wrenched his stomach. The words of magic surged up, tasting like blood upon his lips. He started to hurl them at his twin, but he choked, coughed, and sank to his knees. Still the words were there, the magic was his to command. He would see his twin burn in flames as he had once, long ago, seen his twin's illusion burn in the Tower of High Sorcery. If only, if only he could catch his breath. . . .

The spasm passed. The words of magic seethed in his brain. He looked up, a grotesque snarl twisting his face, his hand raised. . . .

Caramon stood before him, his sword in his hand, staring at him with pity in his eyes.

Pity!† The look slammed into Raistlin with the force of a hundred swords. Yes, his twin would die, but not with that look upon his face!

Leaning upon his staff, Raistlin pulled himself to his feet. Raising his hand, he cast the black hood from his head so that his brother could see himself— doomed—reflected in his golden eyes.

"So you pity me, Caramon," he hissed. "You bumbling harebrained slob. You who are incapable of comprehending the power that I have achieved, the pain I have overcome, the victories that have been mine. You dare to pity *me*? Before I kill you— and I *will* kill you, my brother—I want you to die with the knowledge in your heart that I am going forth into the world to become a god!"

"I know, Raistlin," Caramon answered steadily. The pity did not fade from his eyes, it only deepened. "And that is why I pity you. For I have seen the future. I know the outcome."

Raistlin stared at his brother, suspecting some trick. Above him, the red-tinged sky grew darker still, but the hand that was outstretched had paused. He could feel the Queen hesitating. She had discovered Caramon's presence. Raistlin sensed *her* confusion, *her* fear. The lingering doubt that Caramon might be some apparition conjured up to stop him vanished. Raistlin drew a step nearer his brother.

"You have seen the future? How?"

"When you went through the Portal, the magical field affected the device, throwing Tas and me into the future."

Though Raistlin occasionally showed pity to others, he utterly despised it when directed toward himself. It is entirely a defense mechanism on his part. I can hear the indignant cry of a hurt little boy in his thoughts. —TRH

Raistlin devoured his brother eagerly with his eyes. "And? What will happen?"

"You will win," Caramon said simply. "You will be victorious, not only over the Queen of Darkness, but over all the gods. Your constellation alone will shine in the skies . . . for a time—"

"For a time?" Raistlin's eyes narrowed. "Tell me! What happens? Who threatens? Who deposes me?"

"You do," Caramon replied, his voice filled with sadness. "You rule over a dead world, Raistlin—a world of gray ash and smoldering ruin and bloated corpses. You are alone in those heavens, Raistlin. You try to create, but there is nothing left within you to draw upon, and so you suck life from the stars themselves until they finally burst and die. And then there is nothing around you, nothing inside you."†

"No!" Raistlin snarled. "You lie! Damn you! You lie!" Hurling the Staff of Magius from him, Raistlin lurched forward, his clawing hands catching hold of his brother. Startled, Caramon raised his sword, but it fell to the shifting ground at a word from Raistlin. The big man's grip tightened on his twin's arms convulsively. He could break me in two, Raistlin thought, sneering. But he won't. He is weak. He hesitates. He is lost. And I will know the truth!

Reaching up, Raistlin pressed his burning blood-stained hand upon his brother's forehead, dragging Caramon's visions from his mind into his own.

And Raistlin saw.

He saw the bones of the world, the stumps of trees, the gray mud and ash, the blasted rock, the rising smoke, the rotting bodies of the dead. . . .

He saw himself, suspended in the cold void, emptiness around him, emptiness within. It pressed down upon him, squeezed him. It gnawed at him, ate at him. He twisted in upon himself, desperately seeking nourishment—a drop of blood, a scrap of pain. But there was nothing there. There would never be anything there. And he would continue to twist, snaking inward, to find nothing . . . nothing . . . nothing.

Raistlin's head slumped, his hand slipped from his brother's forehead, clenching in pain. He knew this would come to pass, knew it with every fiber of his shattered body. He knew it because the

Caramon uses the greatest weapon at his disposal: the truth. We have seen earlier in the text how the knowledge of their own guilt was used to curse the damned. Here, Caramon uses the truth to bring Raistlin to a realization of his own culpability.
—TRH

emptiness was already there. It had been there, within him, for so long, so long now. Oh, it had not consumed him utterly—not yet. But he could almost see his soul, frightened, lonely, crouched in a dark and empty corner.

With a bitter cry, Raistlin shoved his brother away from him. He looked around. The shadows deepened. His Queen hesitated no longer. She was gathering her strength.

Raistlin lowered his gaze, trying to think, trying to find the anger inside him, trying to kindle the burning flame of his magic—but even that was dying. Gripped by fear, he tried to run, but he was too feeble. Taking a step, he stumbled and fell on his hands and knees. Fear shook him. He sought for help, stretching out his hand. . . .

He heard a sound, a moan, a cry. His hand closed over white cloth, he felt warm flesh!

"Bupu," Raistlin whispered. With a choked sob, he crawled forward.

The body of the gully dwarf lay before him, her face pinched and starved, her eyes wide with terror. Wretched, terrified, she shrank away from him.

"Bupu!" Raistlin cried, grasping hold of her in desperation, "Bupu, don't you remember me? You gave me a book, once. A book and an emerald."† Fishing around in one of his pouches, he pulled out the shimmering, shining green stone. "Here, Bupu. Look, 'the pretty rock.' Take it, keep it! It will protect you!"

Raistlin is reminded here of another gift and sacrifice from another time. —TRH

She reached for it, but as she did, her fingers stiffened in death.

"No!" Raistlin cried, and felt Caramon's hand upon his arm.

"Leave her alone!" Caramon cried harshly, catching hold of his twin and hurling him backward. "Haven't you done enough to her already?"

Caramon held his sword in his hand once more. Its bright light hurt Raistlin's eyes. By its light, Raistlin saw—not Bupu—but Crysania, her skin blackened and blistered, her eyes staring at him without seeing him.

Empty . . . empty. Nothing within him? Yes. . . . Something there. Something, not much, but something. His soul stretched forth its hand. His own hand reached out, touched Crysania's blistered skin. "She is not dead, not yet," he said.

"No, not yet," Caramon replied, raising his sword. "Leave her alone! Let her at least die in peace!"

"She will live, if you take her through the Portal."

"Yes, she will live," Caramon said bitterly, "and so will you, won't you, Raistlin? I take her through the Portal and you come right after us—"

"Take her."

"No!" Caramon shook his head. Though tears glimmered in his eyes, and his face was pale with grief and anguish, he stepped toward his brother, his sword ready.

Raistlin raised his hand. Caramon couldn't move, his sword hung suspended in the hot, shifting air.

"Take her, and take this as well."

Reaching out, Raistlin's frail hand closed around the Staff of Magius that lay at his side. The light from its crystal glowed clear and strong in the deepening darkness, shedding its magical glow over the three of them. Lifting the staff, Raistlin held it out to his twin.

Caramon hesitated, his brow furrowing.

"Take it!" Raistlin snapped, feeling his strength dwindling. He coughed. "Take it!" he whispered, gasping for breath. "Take it and her and yourself back through the Portal. Use the staff to close it behind you."

Caramon stared at him, uncomprehending, then his eyes narrowed.

"No, I'm not lying," Raistlin snarled. "I've lied to you before, but not now. Try it. See for yourself. Look, I release you from the enchantment. I cannot cast another spell. If you find I am lying, you may slay me. I will not be able to stop you."

Caramon's swordarm was freed. He could move it. Still holding his sword, his eyes on his twin, he reached out his other hand, hesitantly. His fingers touched the staff and he looked fearfully at the light in the crystal, expecting it to blink out and leave them all in the gathering, chilling darkness.

But the light did not waver. Caramon's hand closed around the staff, above his brother's hand. The light gleamed brightly, shedding its radiance upon the torn and bloody black robes, the dull and mud-covered armor.

Raistlin let go of the staff. Slowly, almost falling, he staggered to his feet and drew himself up, standing

without aid, standing alone. The staff, in Caramon's hand, continued to glow.

"Hurry," Raistlin said coldly, "I will keep the Queen from following you. But my strength will not last long."

Caramon stared at him a moment, then at the staff, its light still burning brightly. Finally, drawing a ragged breath, he sheathed his sword.

"What will happen . . . to you?" he asked harshly, kneeling down to lift up Crysania in his arms.

You will be tortured† in mind and in body. At the end of each day, you will die from the pain. At the beginning of each night, I will bring you back to life. You will not be able to sleep, but will lie awake in shivering anticipation of the day to come. In the morning, my face will the first sight you see.

The words curled about Raistlin's brain like a snake. Behind him, he could hear sultry, mocking laughter.

"Be gone, Caramon," he said. "She comes."

Crysania's head rested against Caramon's broad chest. The dark hair fell across her pale face, her hand still clasped the medallion of Paladine. As Raistlin looked at her, he saw the ravages of the fire fade, leaving her face unscarred, softened by a look of sweet, peaceful rest. Raistlin's gaze lifted to his brother's face, and he saw that same stupid expression Caramon always wore—that look of puzzlement, of baffled hurt.

"You blubbering fool! What do you care what becomes of me?" Raistlin snarled. "Get out!"

Caramon's expression changed, or maybe it didn't change. Maybe it had been this way all the time. Raistlin's strength was dwindling very fast, his vision dimmed. But, in Caramon's eyes, he thought he saw understanding. . . .

"Good-bye . . . my brother," Caramon said.

Holding Crysania in his arms, the Staff of Magius in one hand, Caramon turned and walked away. The light of the staff formed a circle around him, a circle of silver that shone in the darkness like the moonbeams of Solinari glistening upon the calm waters of Crystalmir Lake. The silver beams struck the dragon's heads, freezing them, changing them to silver, silencing their screams.

Caramon stepped through the Portal. Raistlin, watching him with his soul, caught a blurred glimpse

Raistlin's imminent punishment here reflects the torture inflicted on Prometheus in Greek myth. Prometheus was chained to a rock, and every day Zeus's eagle would rip him open, but the wounds would heal by the next morning so he could be tortured again.

of colors and life and felt a brief whisper of warmth touch his sunken cheek.

Behind him, he could hear the mocking laughter gurgle into harsh, hissing breath. He could hear the slithering sounds of a gigantic scaled tail, the creaking of wing tendons. Behind him, five heads whispered words of torment and terror.

Steadfastly, Raistlin stood, staring into the Portal. He saw Tanis run to help Caramon, he saw him take Crysania in his arms. Tears blurred Raistlin's vision. He wanted to follow! He wanted Tanis to touch his hand! He wanted to hold Crysania in his arms . . . He took a step forward.

He saw Caramon turn to face him, the staff in his hand.

Caramon stared into the Portal, stared at his twin, stared beyond his twin. Raistlin saw his brother's eyes grow wide with fright.

Raistlin did not have to turn to know what his brother saw. Takhisis crouched behind him. He could feel the chill of the loathsome reptile body flow about him, fluttering his robes. He sensed her behind him, yet her thoughts were not on him. She saw her way to the world, standing open. . . .

"Shut it!" Raistlin screamed.

A blast of flame seared Raistlin's flesh. A taloned claw stabbed him in the back. He stumbled, falling to his knees. But he never took his eyes from the Portal, and he saw Caramon, his twin's face anguished, take a step forward, toward him!

"Shut it, you fool!" Raistlin shrieked, clenching his fists. "Leave me alone! I don't need you any more! I don't need you!"

And then the light was gone. The Portal slammed shut, and blackness pounced upon him with raging, slathering fury. Talons ripped his flesh, teeth tore through muscle, and crunched bone. Blood flowed from his breast, but it would not take with it his life.

He screamed, and he would scream, and he would keep on screaming, unendingly. . . .

Something touched him . . . a hand. . . . He clutched at it as it shook him, gently. A voice called, "Raist! Wake up! It was only a dream. Don't be afraid. I won't let them hurt you! Here, watch . . . I'll make you laugh."

The dragon's coils tightened, crushing out his breath. Glistening black fangs ate his living organs,

This is the most touching scene I think we ever wrote. Having said that, and at the great risk of spoiling this poignant scene, I admit that its origins were not as pure.

Michael Williams worked closely with us in crafting the DRAGONLANCE story. At one point, we thought that Dragons of Autumn Twilight *would end with the heroes leading the refugees through the dwarf kingdom and that the final confrontation would be there rather than at Pax Tharkas. The three of us were sitting around a table bantering ideas for that final climactic scene.*

Flames were shooting up out of a great pit. The heroes were almost certainly doomed as they confronted the terrible, flaming horror approaching them. The flames cast enormous shadows of our heroes up the vast dwarven wall behind them.

So, someone asked what Caramon was doing in this tense moment. Michael, who did not have a high opinion of Caramon's intellect, turned and held his hands up in a silhouette pose and said, "Look, Raist! Bunnies!"

We laughed so hard that we didn't get any more work done that day. Over a year later, we still remembered that scene and got our revenge of sorts on Michael by turning it into the most heartfelt and emotionally powerful moment in the book.

It just goes to show that a writer never can tell from where inspiration will come. —TRH

devoured his heart. Tearing into his body, they sought his soul.

A strong arm encircled him, holding him close. A hand raised, gleaming with silver light, forming childish pictures in the night, and the voice, dimly heard, whispered, "Look, Raist, bunnies. . . ."†

He smiled, no longer afraid.† Caramon was here.

The pain eased. The dream was driven back. From far away, he heard a wail of bitter disappointment and anger. It didn't matter. Nothing mattered anymore. Now he just felt tired, so very, very tired. . . .

Leaning his head upon his brother's arm, Raistlin closed his eyes and drifted into a dark, dreamless, endless sleep.†

Raistlin's sacrifice redeems him, as does Caramon's love. So many people misread this and thought that Raistlin is left to be tormented in the Abyss. Read the last lines closely and you will see that Raistlin is granted peace in sleep. —MW

Raistlin has come to a realization of his own mistake, and it is a mistake for which he will pay with his life and soul. He does not sacrifice himself for some noble cause or selflessly for the world—or even necessarily for Caramon and Crysania. He does so because he has realized that he was wrong and that this is the only way he can make it right. It is enough, however, to win his soul peace. —TRH

CHAPTER II

The drops of water in the water clock dripped steadily, relentlessly, echoing in the silent laboratory. Staring into the Portal with eyes that burned from the strain, Tanis believed the drops must be falling, one by one, upon his taut, stretched nerves.

Rubbing his eyes, he turned from the Portal with a bitter snarl and walked over to look out the window. He was astonished to see that it was only late afternoon. After what he had been through, he would not have been much surprised to find that spring had come and gone, summer had bloomed and died, and autumn† was setting in.

The thick smoke no longer swirled past the window. The fires, having eaten what they fed upon, were dying. He glanced up into the sky. The dragons had vanished from sight, both good and evil. He listened. No sound came from the city beneath him. A haze of

Besides being a literal description of the setting, this paragraph also alludes to the structure of the first DRAGONLANCE trilogy— spring turning to summer, summer turning to autumn, and it was in autumn that Tanis's first great adventure began back in Dragons of Autumn Twilight.

fog and storm and smoke still hung over it, further shadowed by the darkness of the Shoikan Grove.

The battle is over, he realized numbly. It has ended. And we have won. Victory. Hollow, wretched victory.

And then, a flutter of bright blue caught his eye. Looking out over the city, Tanis gasped.

The flying citadel had suddenly drifted into view. Dropping down from the storm clouds, it was careening along merrily, having somewhere acquired a brilliant blue banner that streamed out in the wind. Tanis looked closer, thinking he recognized not only the banner but the graceful minaret from which it flew and which was now perched drunkenly on a tower of the citadel.

Shaking his head, the half-elf could not help smiling. The banner—and the minaret—had once both been part of the palace of Lord Amothus.

Leaning against the window, Tanis continued watching the citadel, which had acquired a bronze dragon as honor guard. He felt his bleakness and grief and fear ease and the tension in his body relax. No matter what happened in the world or on the planes beyond, some things—kender among them—never changed.

Tanis watched as the flying castle wobbled out over the bay, then he was, however, considerably startled to see the citadel suddenly flip over and hang in the air, upside down.

"What is Tas doing?" he muttered.

And then he knew. The citadel began to bob up and down rapidly, like a salt shaker. Black shapes with leathery wings tumbled out of the windows and from doorways. Up and down, up and down bobbed the citadel, more and more black shapes dropping out. Tanis grinned. Tas was clearing out the guards! Then, when no more draconians could be seen spilling out into the water, the citadel righted itself again and continued on its way . . . then, as it skipped merrily along, its blue flag fluttering in the wind, it dove in a wild, unfortunate plunge, right into the ocean!

Tanis caught his breath, but almost immediately the citadel appeared again, leaping out of the water like a blue-bannered dolphin to soar up into the sky once more—water now streaming out of every conceivable opening—and vanish amidst the storm clouds.

Shaking his head, smiling, Tanis turned to see Dalamar gesture toward the Portal. "There he is. Caramon has returned to his position."

Swiftly, the half-elf crossed the room and stood before the Portal once again.

He could see Caramon, still a tiny figure in gleaming armor. This time, he carried someone in his arms.

"Raistlin?" Tanis asked, puzzled.

"Lady Crysania," Dalamar replied.

"Maybe she's still alive!"

"It would be better for her were she not," Dalamar said coldly. Bitterness further hardened his voice and his expression. "Better for all of us! Now Caramon must make a difficult choice."

"What do you mean?"

"It will inevitably occur to him that he could save her by bringing her back through the Portal himself. Which would leave us all at the mercy of either his brother or the Queen or both."

Tanis was silent, watching. Caramon was drawing closer and closer to the Portal, the white-robed figure of the woman in his arms.

"What do you know of him?" Dalamar asked abruptly. "What decision will he make? The last I saw of him he was a drunken buffoon, but his experiences appear to have changed him."

"I don't know," Tanis said, troubled, talking more to himself than to Dalamar. "The Caramon I once knew was only half a person, the other half belonged to his brother. He is different now. He has changed." Tanis scratched his beard, frowning. "Poor man. I don't know . . ."

"Ah, it seems his choice has been made for him," Dalamar said, relief mixed with fear in his voice.

Looking into the Portal, Tanis saw Raistlin. He saw the final meeting between the twins.

Tanis never spoke to anyone of that meeting. Though the visions seen and words heard were indelibly etched upon his memory, he found he could not talk about them. To give them voice seemed to demean them, to take away their terrible horror, their terrible beauty. But often, if he was depressed or unhappy, he would remember the last gift of a benighted soul, and he would close his eyes and thank the gods for his blessings.

Caramon brought Lady Crysania through the Portal. Running forward to help him, Tanis took Crysania in his arms, staring in wonder at the sight of the big man carrying the magical staff, its light still glowing brightly.

"Stay with her, Tanis," Caramon said, "I must close the Portal."

"Do it quickly!" Tanis heard Dalamar's sharp intake of breath. He saw the dark elf staring into the Portal in horror. "Close it!" he cried.

Holding Crysania in his arms, Tanis looked down at her and realized she was dying. Her breath faltered, her skin was ashen, her lips were blue. But he could do nothing for her, except take her to a place of safety.

Safety! He glanced about, his gaze going to the shadowed corner where another dying woman had lain. It was farthest from the Portal. She would be safe there—as safe as anywhere, he supposed sorrowfully. Laying her down, making her as comfortable as possible, he hastily returned to the opening in the void.

Tanis halted, mesmerized by the sight before his eyes.

A shadow of evil filled the Portal, the metallic dragon's heads that formed the gate howled in triumph. The living dragon's heads beyond the Portal writhed above the body of their victim as the archmage fell to their claws.

"No! Raistlin!" Caramon's face twisted in anguish. He took a step toward the Portal.

"Stop!" Dalamar screamed in fury. "Stop him, Half-Elven! Kill him if you must! Close the Portal!"

A woman's hand lunged for the opening and, as they watched in stunned terror, the hand became a dragon's claw, the nails tipped with red, the talons stained with blood. Nearer and nearer the Portal the hand of the Queen came, intent upon keeping this door to the world open so that, once more, she could gain entry.

"Caramon!" Tanis cried, springing forward. But, what could he do? He was not strong enough to physically overpower the big man. He'll go to him, Tanis thought in agony. He will not let his brother die. . . .

No, spoke a voice inside the half-elf. He will not . . . and therein lies the salvation of the world.

Caramon stopped, held fast by the power of that bloodstained hand. The grasping dragon's claw was close, and behind it gleamed laughing, triumphant, malevolent eyes. Slowly, struggling against the evil force, Caramon raised the Staff of Magius.

Nothing happened!

The dragon's heads of the oval doorway split the air with their trumpeting, hailing the entry of their Queen into the world.

Then, a shadowy form appeared, standing beside Caramon. Dressed in black robes, white hair flowing down upon his shoulders, Raistlin raised a golden-skinned hand and, reaching out, gripped the Staff of Magius, his hand resting near his twin's.

The staff flared with a pure, silver light.

The multicolored light within the Portal whirled and spun and fought to survive, but the silver light shone with the steadfast brilliance of the evening star, glittering in a twilight sky.

The Portal closed.

The metallic dragon's heads ceased their screaming so suddenly that the new silence rang in their ears. Within the Portal, there was nothing, neither movement nor stillness, neither darkness nor light. There was simply nothing.

Caramon stood before the Portal alone, the Staff of Magius in his hand. The light of the crystal continued to burn brightly for a moment.

Then glimmered.

Then died.

The room was filled with darkness, a sweet darkness, a darkness restful to the eyes after the blinding light.

And there came through the darkness a whispering voice.

"Farewell, my brother."

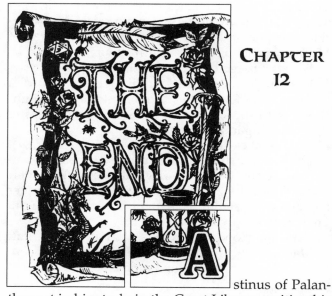

stinus of Palan-
thas sat in his study in the Great Library, writing his
history in the clear, sharp black strokes that had
recorded all the history of Krynn from the first day
the gods had looked upon the world until the last,
when the great book would forever close. Astinus
wrote, oblivious to the chaos around him, or rather—
such was the man's presence—that it seemed as if he
forced the chaos to be oblivious of him.

It was only two days after the end of what Astinus
referred to in the *Chronicles* as the "Test of the Twins"†
(but which everyone else was calling the "Battle of
Palanthas"). The city was in ruins. The only two
buildings left standing were the Tower of High Sorcery and the Great Library, and the Library had not
escaped unscathed.

The fact that it stood at all was due, in large part,
to the heroics of the Aesthetics. Led by the rotund

*One of the fun things
about Tolkien's* Lord of
the Rings *is that he
suggests that the book you
are holding in your hand
is, in fact, descended from
the hobbits'* Red Book of
Westmarch. *It lends a
certain imagined reality to
the reading experience.
Here, we see very much the
same thing going on.*

Bertrem, whose courage was kindled, so it was said, by the sight of a draconian daring to lay a clawed hand upon one of the sacred books, the Aesthetics attacked the enemy with such zeal and such a wild, reckless disregard for their own lives that few of the reptilian creatures escaped.

But, like the rest of Palanthas, the Aesthetics paid a grievous price for victory. Many of their order perished in the battle. These were mourned by their brethren, their ashes given honored rest among the books that they had sacrificed their lives to protect. The gallant Bertrem did *not* die. Only slightly wounded, he saw his name go down in one of the great books itself beside the names of the other Heroes of Palanthas. Life could offer nothing further in the way of reward to Bertrem. He never passed that one particular book upon the shelf but that he didn't surreptitiously pull it down, open it to The Page, and bask in the light of his glory.

The beautiful city of Palanthas was now nothing more than memory and a few words of description in Astinus's books. Heaps of charred and blackened stone marked the graves of palatial estates. The rich warehouses with their casks of fine wines and ales, their stores of cotton and of wheat, their boxes of wonders from all parts of Krynn, lay in a pile of cinder. Burned-out hulks of ships floated in the ash-choked harbors. Merchants picked through the rubble of their shops, salvaging what they could. Families stared at their ruined houses, holding on to each other, and thanking the gods that they had, at least, survived with their lives.

For there were many who had not. Of the Knights of Solamnia within the city, they had perished almost to a man, fighting the hopeless battle against Lord Soth and his deadly legions. One of the first to fall was the dashing Sir Markham. True to his oath to Tanis, the knight had not fought Lord Soth, but had, instead, rallied the knights and led them in a charge against Soth's skeletal warriors. Though pierced with many wounds, he fought valiantly still, leading his bloody, exhausted men time and again in charges against the foe until finally he fell from his horse, dead.

Because of the knights' courage, many lived in Palanthas who otherwise would have perished upon the ice-cold blades of the undead, who vanished

mysteriously—so it was told—when their leader appeared among them, bearing a shrouded corpse in his arms.

Mourned as heroes, the bodies of the Knights of Solamnia were taken by their fellows to the High Clerist's Tower. Here they were entombed in a sepulcher where lay the body of Sturm Brightblade, Hero of the Lance.

Upon opening the sepulcher, which had not been disturbed since the Battle of the High Clerist's Tower, the knights were awed to find Sturm's body whole, unravaged by time. An elven jewel of some type, gleaming upon his breast, was believed accountable for this miracle. All those who entered the sepulcher that day in mourning for their fallen loved ones looked upon that steadily beaming jewel and felt peace ease the bitter sting of their grief.

The knights were not the only ones who were mourned. Many ordinary citizens had died in Palanthas as well. Men defending city and family, women defending home and children. The citizens of Palanthas burned their dead in accordance with ages-old custom, scattering the ashes of their loved ones in the sea, where they mingled with the ashes of their beloved city.

Astinus recorded it all as it was occurring. He had continued to write—so the Aesthetics reported with awe—even as Bertrem single-handedly bludgeoned to death a draconian who had dared invade the master's study. He was writing still when he gradually became aware—above the sounds of hammering and sweeping and pounding and shuffling—that Bertrem was blocking his light.

Lifting up his head, he frowned.

Bertrem, who had not blenched once in the face of the enemy, turned deathly pale, and backed up instantly, letting the sunlight fall once more upon the page.

Astinus resumed his writing. "Well?" he said.

"Caramon Majere and a—a kender are here to see you, Master." If Bertrem had said a demon from the Abyss was here to see Astinus, he could hardly have infused more horror into his voice than when he spoke the word "kender."

"Send them in," replied Astinus.

"*Them*, Master?" Bertrem could not help but repeat in shock.

Astinus looked up, his brow creased. "The draconian did not damage your hearing, did it, Bertrem? You did not receive, for example, a blow to the head?"

"N-no, Master." Bertrem flushed and backed hurriedly out of the room, tripping over his robes as he did so.

"Caramon Majere and . . . and Tassle-f-foot B-burr-hoof," announced the flustered Bertrem, moments later.

"Tasslehoff Burrfoot," said the kender, presenting a small hand to Astinus, who shook it gravely. "And you're Astinus of Palanthas," Tas continued, his topknot bouncing with excitement. "I've met you before, but you don't remember because it hasn't happened yet. Or, rather, come to think of it, it never will happen, will it, Caramon?"

"No," the big man replied. Astinus turned his gaze to Caramon, regarding him intently.

"You do not resemble your twin," Astinus said coolly, "but then Raistlin had undergone many trials that marked him both physically and mentally. Still, there is something of him in your eyes. . . ."

The historian frowned, puzzled. He did not understand, and there was nothing on the face of Krynn that he did not understand. Consequently, he grew angry.

Astinus rarely grew angry. His irritation alone sent a wave of terror through the Aesthetics. But he was angry now. His graying brows bristled, his lips tightened, and there was a look in his eyes that made the kender glance about nervously, wondering if he hadn't left something outside in the hall that he needed—now!

"What is it?" The historian demanded finally, slamming his hand down upon his book, causing his pen to jump, the ink to spill, and Bertrem—waiting in the corridor—to run away as fast as his flapping sandals could take him.

"There is a mystery about you, Caramon Majere, and there are no mysteries for me! I know everything that transpires upon the face of Krynn. I know the thoughts of every living being! I see their actions! I read the wishes of their hearts! Yet I cannot read your eyes!"

The book that Caramon and Tas got from the future is presented back to Astinus. As he points out, it is a book that "he will never write." This book is from an alternate future probability—a future that will not now take place. This structure of time travel resonates very closely with the foundations of the War of Souls, which finds its roots in this trilogy. See Appendix B. —TRH

"Tas told you," Caramon said imperturbably. Reaching into a knapsack he wore, the big man produced a huge, leather-bound volume† which he set carefully down upon the desk in front of the historian.

"That's one of mine!" Astinus said, glancing at it, his scowl deepening. His voice rose until he actually shouted. "Where did it come from? None of my books leave without my knowledge! Bertrem—"

"Look at the date."

Astinus glared furiously at Caramon for a second, then shifted his angry gaze to the book. He looked at the date upon the volume, prepared to shout for Bertrem again. But the shout rattled in his throat and died. He stared at the date, his eyes widening. Sinking down into his chair, he looked from the volume to Caramon, then back to the volume again.

"It is the future I see in your eyes!"

"The future that is this book," Caramon said, regarding it with grave solemnity.

"We were there!" said Tas, bouncing up eagerly. "Would you like to hear about it? It's the most wonderful story. You see, we came back to Solace, only it didn't look like Solace. I thought it was a moon, in fact, because I'd been thinking about a moon when we used the magical device and—"

"Hush, Tas," Caramon said gently. Standing up, he put his hand on the kender's shoulder and quietly left the room. Tas—being steered firmly out the door—glanced backward. "Goodbye!" he called, waving his hand. "Nice seeing you again, er, before, uh, after, well, whatever."

But Astinus neither heard nor noticed. The day he received the book from Caramon Majere was the only day that passed in the entire history of Palanthas that had nothing recorded for it but one entry:

This day, as above Afterwatch rising 14, Caramon Majere brought me the Chronicles of Krynn, Volume *2000. A volume written by me that I will never write.*†

As has been pointed out before, the gods that are known in Krynn at this time are highly fallible, which explains Astinus's surprise at the book from the alternate future. The gods of Krynn are obviously not omniscient or omnipotent. Again, this is a foundation for the War of Souls, which reveals an underlying relationship between the gods of Krynn in the High God. —TRH

The funeral of Elistan represented, to the people of Palanthas, the funeral of their beloved city as well. The ceremony was held at daybreak as Elistan had requested, and everyone in Palanthas attended—old, young, rich, poor. The injured who were able to be moved were carried from their homes, their pallets laid upon the scorched and blackened grass of the once-beautiful lawns of the Temple.

Among these was Dalamar. No one murmured as the dark elf was helped across the lawn by Tanis and Caramon to take his place beneath a grove of charred, burned aspens. For rumor had it that the young apprentice magic-user had fought the Dark Lady—as Kitiara was known—and defeated her, thereby bringing about the destruction of her forces.

Elistan† had wanted to be buried in his Temple, but that was impossible now—the Temple being nothing but a gutted shell of marble. Lord Amothus had offered his family's tomb, but Crysania had declined. Remembering that Elistan had found his faith in the slave mines of Pax Tharkas, the Revered Daughter—now head of the church—decreed that he be laid to rest beneath the Temple in one of the underground caverns that had formerly been used for storage.

Though some were shocked, no one questioned Crysania's commands. The caverns were cleaned and sanctified, a marble bier was built from the remains of the Temple. And hereafter, even in the grand days of the church that were to come, all of the priests were laid to rest in this humble place that became known as one of the most holy places on Krynn.

The people settled down on the lawn in silence. The birds, knowing nothing of death or war or grief, but knowing only that the sun was rising and that they were alive in the bright morning, filled the air with song. The sun's rays tipped the mountains with gold, driving away the darkness of the night, bringing light to hearts heavy with sorrow.

One person only rose to speak Elistan's eulogy, and it was deemed fitting by everyone that she do so. Not only because she was now taking his place—as he had requested—as head of the church, but because she seemed to the people of Palanthas to epitomize their loss and their pain.

That morning, they said, was the first time she had risen from her bed since Tanis Half-Elven brought her down from the Temple of High Sorcery to the steps of the Great Library, where the clerics worked among the injured and the dying. She had been near death herself. But her faith and the prayers of the clerics restored her to life. They could not, however, restore her sight.

Margaret never liked Elistan. She thought he was a boring character after Dragons of Autumn Twilight. *While I was reading the first draft chapters of the second book,* Dragons of Winter Night, *I discovered that Elistan was not anywhere to be found. I went to Margaret and asked, "Where is Elistan?"*

"Oh, we left him behind."

"We can't leave him behind," I said. "He has to be on the boat on the way up toward Ergoth."

"But he's so boring," she replied. "Can't we just kill him?"

"No," I said. "He's the only living cleric in the world, and we need him up in Palanthas to start the religion!"

Well, Margaret finally agreed and went back to those chapters on the ship. She used a crowbar and reinserted Elistan into a cabin on the boat. This is why, if you read that book again, you will see Elistan poke his head out now and again. —TRH

Crysania stood before them that morning, her eyes looking straight into the sun she would never see again. Its rays glistened in her black hair that framed a face made beautiful by a look of deep, abiding compassion and faith.

"As I stand in darkness," she said, her clear voice rising sweet and pure among the songs of the larks, "I feel the warmth of the light upon my skin and I know my face is turned toward the sun. I can look into the sun, for my eyes are forever shrouded by darkness. But if you who can see look too long in the sun, you will lose your sight, just as those who live too long in the darkness will gradually lose theirs.

"This Elistan taught—that mortals were not meant to live solely in sun or in shadow, but in both. Both have their perils, if misused, both have their rewards. We have come through our trials of blood, of darkness, of fire—" Her voice quavered and broke at this point. Those nearest her saw tears upon her cheeks. But, when she continued, her voice was strong. Her tears glistened in the sunlight. "We have come through these trials as Huma came through his, with great loss, with great sacrifice, but strong in the knowledge that our spirit shines and that we, perhaps, gleam brightest among all the stars of the heavens.

"For though some might choose to walk the paths of night, looking to the black moon to guide them, while others walk the paths of day, the rough and rock-strewn trails of both can be made easier by the touch of a hand, the voice of a friend. The capacity to love, to care, is given to us all—the greatest gift of the gods to all the races.

"Our beautiful city has perished in flame." Her voice softened. "We have lost many whom we loved, and it seems perhaps that life is too difficult a burden for us to bear. But reach out your hand, and it will touch the hand of someone reaching out to you, and—together—you will find the strength and hope you need to go on."

After the ceremonies, when the clerics had borne the body of Elistan to its final resting place, Caramon and Tas sought out Lady Crysania. They found her among the clerics, her arm resting upon the arm of the young woman who was her guide.

"Here are two who would speak with you, Revered Daughter," said the young cleric.

Lady Crysania turned, holding out her hand. "Let me touch you," she said.

"It's Caramon," the big man began awkwardly, "and—"

"Me," said Tas in a meek, subdued voice.

"You have come to say good-bye." Lady Crysania smiled.

"Yes. We're leaving today," Caramon said, holding her hand in his.

"Do you go straight home to Solace?"

"No, not—not quite yet," Caramon said, his voice low. "We're going back to Solanthas with Tanis. Then, when—when I feel a little more myself, I'll use the magical device to get back to Solace."

Crysania gripped his hand tightly, drawing him near to her.

"Raistlin is at peace, Caramon," she said softly. "Are you?"

"Yes, my lady," Caramon said, his voice firm and resolute. "I am at peace. At last." He sighed. "I just need to talk to Tanis and get things sorted out in my life, put back in order. For one thing," he added with a blush and a shame-faced grin, "I need to know how to build a house! I was dead drunk most of the time I worked on ours, and I haven't the faintest notion what I was doing."

He looked at her, and she—aware of his scrutiny though she could not see it—smiled, her pale skin tinged with the faintest rose. Seeing that smile, and seeing the tears that fell around it, Caramon drew her close, in turn. "I'm sorry. I wish I could have spared you this—"

"No, Caramon," she said softly. "For now I see. I see clearly, as Loralon promised." She kissed his hand, pressing it to her cheek. "Farewell, Caramon. May Paladine go with you."

Tasslehoff snuffled.

"Good-bye, Crysani—I mean, Rev-revered Daughter," said Tas in a small voice, feeling suddenly lonely and short. "I—I'm sorry about the mess I made of things—"

But Lady Crysania interrupted him. Turning from Caramon, she reached out her hand and smoothed back his topknot of hair. "Most of us walk in the light

and the shadow, Tasslehoff," she said, "but there are the chosen few who walk this world, carrying their own light to brighten both day and night."

"Really? They must get awfully tired, hauling around a light like that? Is it a torch? It can't be a candle. The wax would melt all over and drip down into their shoes and—say—do you suppose I could meet someone like that?" Tas asked with interest.

The secret to Tasslehoff's greatness is that he never tries to be great. He is the example of the greatness of humility and servitude.

"You *are* someone like that,"† Lady Crysania replied. "And I do not think you ever need worry about your wax dripping into your shoes. Farewell, Tasslehoff Burrfoot. I need not ask Paladine's blessing on you, for I know you are one of his close, personal friends. . . ."

"Well," asked Caramon abruptly as he and Tas made their way through the crowd. "Have you decided what you're going to do yet? You've got the flying citadel. Lord Amothus gave it to you.† You can go anywhere on Krynn. Maybe even a moon, if you want."

Lord Amothus gave a flying citadel to a kender? Was he insane? —TRH

"Oh, that." Tas, looking a little awestruck after his talk with Lady Crysania, seemed to have trouble remembering what Caramon was referring to. "I don't have the citadel anymore. It was awfully big and boring once I got around to exploring it. And it wouldn't go to the moon. I tried. Do you know," he said, looking at Caramon with wide eyes, "that if you go up high enough, your nose starts to bleed? Plus it's extremely cold and uncomfortable. Besides, the moons seem to be a lot farther away than I'd imagined. Now, if I had the magical device—" He glanced at Caramon out of the corner of his eye.

"No," said Caramon sternly. "Absolutely not. That's going back to Par-Salian."

"I could take it to him," Tas offered helpfully. "That would give me a chance to explain about Gnimsh fixing it and my disrupting the spell and—No?" He heaved a sigh. "I guess not. Well, anyway, I've decided to stick with you and Tanis, if you want me, that is?" He looked at Caramon a bit wistfully.

Caramon replied by reaching out and giving the kender a hug that crushed several objects of interest and uncertain value in his pouches.

"By the way," Caramon added as an afterthought, "what *did* you do with the flying citadel?"

"Oh"—Tas waved his hand nonchalantly—"I gave it to Rounce."

"The gully dwarf!" Caramon stopped, appalled.

"He can't fly it, not by himself!" Tas assured him. "Although," he added after a moment's profound thought, "I suppose he could if he got a few more gully dwarves to help. I never thought of that—"

Caramon groaned. "Where is it?"

"I set it down for him in a nice place. A very nice place. It was a really wealthy part of some city we flew over. Rounce took a liking to it—the citadel, not the city. Well, I guess he took a liking to the city, too, come to think of it. Anyway, he was a big help and all, so I asked him if he wanted the citadel and he said he did so I just plunked the thing down in this vacant lot.

"It caused quite a sensation," Tas added happily. "A man came running out of this really big castle that sat on a hill right next to where I dropped the citadel, and he started yelling about that being his property and what right did we have to drop a castle on it, and creating a wonderful row. I pointed out that his castle certainly didn't cover the entire property and I mentioned a few things about sharing that would have helped him quite a bit, I'm certain, if he'd only listened. Then Rounce starting saying how he was going to bring all the Burp clan or something like that and they were going to come live in the citadel and the man had a fit of some sort and they carried him away and pretty soon the whole town was there. It was real exciting for a while, but it finally got boring. I was glad Fireflash had decided to come along. He brought me back."

"You didn't tell me any of this!" Caramon said, glaring at the kender and trying hard to look grim.

"I—I guess it just slipped my mind," Tas mumbled. "I've had an awful lot to think about these days, you know."

"I know you have, Tas," Caramon said. "I've been worried about you. I saw you talking to some other kender yesterday. You could go home, you know. You told me once how you've thought about it, about going back to Kendermore."

Tas's face took on an unusually serious expression. Slipping his hand into Caramon's, he drew nearer, looking up at him earnestly. "No, Caramon,"

Campbell points out in his texts on the Hero's Journey that it is the end of the adventure—the coming home—that is often the most difficult part. Odysseus returns only to find his house full of suitors for his wife, but it is more than that. The journey changes the hero so that home no longer is the same to him. This is part of what Tas is expressing here, that his adventures have changed him to the point where it is hard for him to relate to his brothers any longer.
—TRH

he said softly. "It isn't the same.† I—I can't seem to talk to other kender anymore." He shook his head, his topknot swishing back and forth. "I tried to tell them about Fizban and his hat, and Flint and his tree and . . . and Raistlin and poor Gnimsh." Tas swallowed and, fishing out a handkerchief, wiped his eyes. "They don't seem to understand. They just don't . . . well . . . care. It's hard—caring—isn't it, Caramon? It hurts sometimes."

"Yes, Tas," Caramon said quietly. They had entered a shady grove of trees. Tanis was waiting for them, standing beneath a tall, graceful aspen whose new spring leaves glittered golden in the morning sun. "It hurts a lot of the time. But the hurt is better than being empty inside."

Walking over to them, Tanis put one arm around Caramon's broad shoulders, the other arm around Tas. "Ready?" he asked.

"Ready," Caramon replied.

"Good. The horses are over here. I thought we'd ride. We could have taken the carriage, but—to be perfectly honest—I hate being cooped up in the blasted thing. So does Laurana, though she'll never admit it. The countryside's beautiful this time of year. We'll take our time, and enjoy it."

"You live in Solanthas, don't you, Tanis?" Tas said as they mounted their horses and rode down the blackened, ruined street. Those people leaving the funeral, returning to pick up the pieces of their lives, heard the kender's cheerful voice echo through the streets long after he had gone.

"I was in Solanthas once. They have an awfully fine prison there. One of the nicest I was ever in. I was sent there by mistake, of course. A misunderstanding over a silver teapot that had tumbled, quite by accident, into one my pouches. . . ."

Dalamar climbed the steep, winding stairs leading up to the laboratory at the top of the Tower of High Sorcery. He climbed the stairs, instead of magically transporting himself, because he had a long journey ahead of him that night. Though the clerics of Elistan had healed his wounds, he was still weak and he did not want to tax his strength.

Later, when the black moon was in the sky, he would travel through the ethers to the Tower of

High Sorcery at Wayreth, there to attend a Wizard's Conclave—one of the most important to be held in this era. Par-Salian was stepping down as Head of the Conclave. His successor must be chosen. It would probably be the Red Robe, Justarius. Dalamar didn't mind that. He knew he was not yet powerful enough to become the new archmage. Not yet, at any rate. But there was some feeling that a new Head of the Order of the Black Robes should be chosen, too. Dalamar smiled. He had no doubt who that would be.

He had made all his preparations for leaving. The guardians had their instructions: no one—living or dead—was to be admitted to the Tower in his absence. Not that this was likely. The Shoikan Grove maintained its own grim vigil, unharmed by the flames that had swept through the rest of Palanthas. But the dark loneliness that the Tower had known for so long would soon be coming to an end.

On Dalamar's order, several rooms in the Tower had been cleaned out and refurbished. He planned to bring back with him several apprentices of his own—Black Robes, certainly, but maybe a Red Robe or two if he found any who might be suitable. He looked forward to passing on the skills he had acquired, the knowledge he had learned. And—he admitted to himself—he looked forward to the companionship.

But, first, there was something he must do.

Entering the laboratory, he paused on the doorstep. He had not been back to this room since Caramon had carried him from it that last, fateful day. Now, it was nighttime. The room was dark. At a word, candles flickered into flame, warming the room with a soft light. But the shadows remained, hovering in the corners like living things.

Lifting the candlestand in his hand, Dalamar made a slow circuit of the room, selecting various items—scrolls, a magic wand, several rings—and sending them below to his own study with a word of command.

He passed the dark corner where Kitiara had died. Her blood stained the floor still. That spot in the room was cold, chill, and Dalamar did not linger. He passed the stone table with its beakers and bottles, the eyes still staring out at him pleadingly. With a word, he caused them to close—forever.

Finally, he came to the Portal. The five heads of the dragon, facing eternally into the void, still shouted their silent, frozen paen to the Dark Queen. The only light that gleamed from the dark, lifeless metallic heads was the reflected light of Dalamar's candles. He looked within the Portal. There was nothing. For long moments, Dalamar stared into it. Then, reaching out his hand, he pulled on a golden, silken cord that hung from the ceiling. A thick curtain dropped down, shrouding the Portal in heavy, purple velvet.

Turning away, Dalamar found himself facing the bookshelves that stood in the very back of the laboratory. The candlelight shone on rows of nightblue-bound volumes decorated with silver runes. A cold chill flowed from them.

The spellbooks of Fistandantilus—now his.

And where these rows of books ended, a new row of books began—volumes bound in black decorated with silver runes. Each of these volumes, Dalamar noticed, his hand going to touch one, burned with an inner heat that made the books seem strangely alive to the touch.

The spellbooks of Raistlin—now his.

Dalamar looked intently at each book. Each held its own wonders, its own mysteries, each held power. The dark elf walked the length of the bookshelves. When he reached the end—near the door—he sent the candlestand back to rest upon the great stone table. His hand upon the door handle, his gaze went to one, last object.

In a dark corner stood the Staff of Magius, leaning up against the wall. For a moment, Dalamar caught his breath, thinking perhaps he saw light gleaming from the crystal on top of the staff—the crystal that had remained cold and dark since that day. But then he realized, with a sense of relief, that it was only reflected candlelight. With a word, he extinguished the flame, plunging the room into darkness.

He looked closely at the corner where the staff stood. It was lost in the night, no sign of light glimmered.

Drawing a deep breath, then letting it out with a sigh, Dalamar walked from the laboratory. Firmly, he shut the door behind him. Reaching into a wooden box set with powerful runes, he withdrew a silver key and inserted it into an ornate silver doorlock—a

doorlock that was new, a doorlock that had not been made by any locksmith on Krynn. Whispering words of magic, Dalamar turned the key in the lock. It clicked. Another click echoed it. The deadly trap was set.

Turning, Dalamar summoned one of the guardians. The disembodied eyes floated over at his command.

"Take this key," Dalamar said, "and keep it with you for all eternity. Give it up to no one—not even myself. And, from this moment on, your place is to guard this door. No one is to enter. Let death be swift for those who try."

The guardian's eyes closed in acquiescence. As Dalamar walked back down the stairs, he saw the eyes—open again—framed by the doorway, their cold glow staring out into the night.

The dark elf nodded to himself, satisfied, and went upon his way.

The Homecoming

Thud, thud, thud.

Tika Waylan Majere sat straight up in bed.

Trying to hear above the pounding of her heart, she listened, waiting to identify the sound that had awakened her from deep sleep.

Nothing.

Had she dreamed it? Shoving back the mass of red curls falling over her face, Tika glanced sleepily out the window. It was early morning. The sun had not yet risen, but night's deep shadows were stealing away, leaving the sky clear and blue in the half-light of predawn. Birds were up, beginning their household chores, whistling and bickering cheerfully among themselves. But no one in Solace would be stirring yet. Even the night watchman usually succumbed to the warm, gentle influence of the spring night and slept at this hour, his head slumped on his chest, snoring blissfully.

I must have been dreaming, thought Tika drearily. I wonder if I'll ever get used to sleeping alone? Every little sound has me wide awake. Burrowing back down in the bed, she drew up the sheet and tried to go back to sleep. Squinching her eyes tightly shut, Tika pretended Caramon was there. She was lying beside him, pressed up against his broad chest, hearing him breathe, hearing his heart beat, warm, secure. . . . His hand patted her on the shoulder as he murmured sleepily, "It's just a bad dream, Tika . . . be all gone by morning. . . ."

Thud, thud, thudthudthud.

Tika's eyes opened wide. She *hadn't* been dreaming! The sound—whatever it was—was coming from up above! Someone or something was up there—up in the vallenwood!

Throwing aside the bedclothes and moving with the stealth and quiet she had learned during her war adventures, Tika grabbed a nightrobe from the foot of her bed, struggled into it (mixing up the sleeves in her nervousness), and crept out of the bedroom.

Thud, thud, thud.

Her lips tightened in firm resolve. Someone was up there, up in her new house. The house Caramon was building for her up in the vallenwood. What were they doing? Stealing? There were Caramon's tools—

Tika almost laughed, but it came out a sob instead. Caramon's tools—the hammer with the wiggly head that flew off every time it hit a nail, the saw with so many teeth missing it looked like a grinning gully dwarf, the plane that wouldn't smooth butter. But they were precious to Tika. She'd left them right where *he'd* left them.

Thud, thud, thud.

Creeping out into the living area of her small house, Tika's hand was on the door handle when she stopped.

"Weapon," she muttered. Looking around hastily, she grabbed the first thing she saw—her heavy iron skillet.† Holding it firmly by the handle, Tika opened the front door slowly and quietly and sneaked outside.

Tika's skillet is her weapon of choice—and one any foe should flee. —TRH

The sun's rays were just lighting the tops of the mountains, outlining their snow-capped peaks in gold against the clear, cloudless blue sky. The grass sparked with dew like tiny jewels, the morning air was sweet and crisp and pure. The new bright green leaves of the vallenwoods rustled and laughed as the sun touched them, waking them. So fresh and clear and glittering was this morning that it might well have been the very first morning of the very first day, with the gods looking down upon their work and smiling.

But Tika was not thinking about gods or mornings or the dew that was cold upon her bare feet. Clutching the skillet in one hand, keeping it hidden behind her back, she stealthily climbed the rungs of the ladder leading up into the unfinished house perched among the strong branches of the vallenwood. Near the top she stopped, peeping over the edge.

Ah, ha! There *was* someone up here! She could just barely make out a figure crouched in a shadowy corner. Hauling herself up over the edge, still making no sound, Tika padded softly across the wooden floor, her fingers getting a firm grip on the skillet.

But as she crossed the floor, creeping up on the intruder, she thought she heard a muffled giggle.

She hesitated, then continued on resolutely. Just my imagination, she told herself, moving closer to the cloaked figure. She could see him clearly now. It was a man, a human, and by the looks of the brawny arms and the muscular shoulders, it was one of the biggest men Tika had ever seen! He was down on his hands and knees, his broad back was turned toward her, she saw him raise his hand.

He was holding Caramon's hammer!

How dare he touch Caramon's things! Well, big man or no—they're all the same size once they're laid out on the floor.

Tika raised the skillet—

"Caramon! Look out!" cried a shrill voice.

The big man rose to his feet and turned around.

The skillet fell to the floor with a ringing clatter. So did a hammer and a handful of nails.

With a thankful sob, Tika clasped her husband in her arms.

"Isn't this wonderful, Tika? I bet you were surprised, weren't you! Were you surprised, Tika? And say—would you really have wanged Caramon over the head if I hadn't stopped you? That might have been kind of interesting to watch, though I don't think it would have done Caramon much good. Hey, do you remember when you hit that draconian over the head with the skillet—the one that was getting ready to rough up Gilthanas? Tika? . . . Caramon?"

Tas looked at his two friends. They weren't saying a word. They weren't *hearing* a word. They just stood there, holding each other. The kender felt a suspicious moisture creep into his eyes.

"Well," he said with a gulp and a smile, "I'll just go down and wait for you in the living room."

Slithering down the ladder, Tas entered the small, neat house that stood below the sheltering vallenwood. Once inside, he took out a handkerchief, blew his nose, then began to cheerfully investigate the furnishings.

"From the looks of things," he said to himself, admiring a brand-new cookie jar so much that he absent-mindedly stuffed it into a pouch (cookies

included), all the while being firmly convinced that he'd set it back on the shelf, "Tika and Caramon are going to be up there quite a while, maybe even the rest of the morning. Perhaps this would be a good time to sort all my stuff."

Sitting down cross-legged on the floor, the kender blissfully upended his pouches, spilling their contents out onto the rug. As he absent-mindedly munched on a few cookies, Tas's proud gaze went first to a whole sheaf of new maps† Tanis had given him. Unrolling them, one after another, his small finger traced a route to all the wonderful places he'd visited in his many adventures.

I absolutely love maps! Perhaps that part of me found its way into kender, too. —TRH

"It was nice traveling," he said after a while, "but it's certainly nicer coming home. I'll just stay here with Tika and Caramon.† We'll be a family. Caramon said I could have a room in the new house and—Why, what's that?" He looked closely at the map. "Merilon?† I never heard of a city named Merilon. I wonder what it's like. . . .

Of course, we know that Tasslehoff will never settle down, which is what makes his commentary on homecoming so entertaining. —MW

"No!" Tas retorted. "You are through adventuring, Burrfoot. You've got quite enough stories to tell Flint as it is. You're going to settle down and become a respectable member of society. Maybe even become High Sheriff."

The allusion to Merilon is an in-joke. Merilon is a city in the Darksword trilogy that Tracy and I were working on the time. —MW

Rolling up the map (fond dreams in his head of running for High Sheriff), he placed it back in its case (not without a wistful glance). Then, turning his back upon it, he began to look through his treasures.

"A white chicken feather, an emerald, a dead rat—yick, where did I get that? A ring carved to look like ivy leaves, a tiny golden dragon—that's funny, I certainly don't remember putting that in my pouch. A piece of broken blue crystal, a dragon's tooth, white rose petals, some kid's old worn-out, plush rabbit, and—oh, look. Here's Gnimsh's plans for the mechanical lift and—what's this? A book! *Sleight-of-Hand Techniques to Amaze and Delight!* Now isn't that interesting? I'm sure this will really come in handy and, oh, no"—Tas frowned irritably—"there's that silver bracelet of Tanis's again. I wonder how he manages to hang onto anything without me around, constantly picking up after him? He's extremely careless. I'm surprised Laurana puts up with it."

He peered into the pouch. "That's all, I guess." He sighed. "Well, it certainly has been interesting.

Mostly—it was truly wonderful. I met several dragons. I flew in a citadel. I turned myself into a mouse. I broke a dragon orb. Paladine and I became close, personal friends.

"There were some sad times," he said to himself softly. "But they aren't even sad to me now. They just give me a little funny ache, right here." He pressed his hand on his heart. "I'm going to miss adventuring very much. But there's no one to adventure with anymore. They've all settled down, their lives are bright and pleasant." His small hand explored the smooth bottom of one final pouch. "It's time for me to settle down, too, like I said, and I think High Sheriff would be a most fascinating job and—

"Wait. . . . what's that? In the very bottom. . . ." He pulled out a small object, almost lost, tucked into a corner of the pouch. Holding it in his hand, staring at it in wonder, Tas drew in a deep, quivering breath.

"How did Caramon lose this? He was so *very* careful of it. But then, he's had a lot on his mind lately. I'll just go give it back to him. He's probably fearfully worried over misplacing it. After all, what *would* Par-Salian say. . . ."

Studying the plain, nondescript pendant in his palm, Tas never noticed that his other hand— apparently acting of its own accord since *he* had quit adventuring—skittered around behind him and closed over the map case.

"What was the name of that place? Merilon?"

It must have been the hand that spoke. Certainly not Tas, who had given up adventuring.

The map case went into a pouch, along with all of Tas's other treasures; the hand scooping them up hastily and stowing them away.

The hand also gathered up all of Tas's pouches, slinging them over his shoulders, hanging them from his belt, stuffing one into the pocket of his brand-new bright red leggings.

The hand busily began to change the plain, nondescript pendant into a sceptre that was really quite beautiful—all covered with jewels—and looked very magical.

"Once you're finished," Tas told his hand severely, "we'll take it right upstairs and give it to Caramon—"

"Where's Tas?" Tika murmured from the warmth and comfort of Caramon's strong arms.

Caramon, resting his cheek against her head, kissed her red curls and held her tighter. "I don't know. Went down to the house, I think."

"You realize," said Tika, snuggling closer, "that we won't have a spoon left."

Caramon smiled. Putting his hand on her chin, he raised her head and kissed her lips. . . .

An hour later, the two were walking around the floor of the unfinished house, Caramon pointing out the improvements and changes he planned to make. "The baby's room will go here," he said, "next to our bedroom, and this will be the room for the older kids. No, I guess two rooms, one for the boys and one for the girls." He pretended to ignore Tika's blush. "And the kitchen and Tas's room and the guest room—Tanis and Laurana are coming to visit—and. . . ." Caramon's voice died.

He had come to the one room in the house he had actually finished—the room with the wizard's mark carved on a plaque which hung above the door.

Tika looked at him, her laughing face suddenly grown pale and serious.

Reaching up, Caramon slowly took down the plaque. He looked at it silently for long moments, then, with a smile, he handed it to Tika.

"Keep this for me, will you, my dear?" he asked softly and gently.

She looked up at him in wonder, her trembling fingers going over the smooth edges of the plaque, tracing out the arcane symbol inscribed upon it.

"Will you tell me what happened, Caramon?" she asked.

"Someday," he said, gathering her into his arms, holding her close. "Someday," he repeated. Then, kissing the red curls, he stood, looking out over the town, watching it waken and come to life.

Through the sheltering leaves of the vallenwood, he could see the gabled roof of the Inn. He could hear voices now, sleepy voices, laughing, scolding. He could smell the smoke of cooking fires as it rose into the air, filling the green valley with a soft haze.

He held his wife in his arms, feeling her love surround him, seeing his love for her shining before

him always, shining pure and white like the light from Solinari . . . or the light shining from the crystal atop a magical staff. . . .

Caramon sighed, deeply, contentedly. "It doesn't matter anyway," he murmured.

"I'm home."

WEDDING SONG
(A REPRISE)†

But you and I, through burning plains,
   through darkness of the earth,
   affirm the world, its people,
  the heavens that gave them birth,
  the breath that passes between us,
   this new home where we stand,
and all those things made larger by
  the vows between woman and man.

This, of course, was originally in Dragons of Autumn Twilight, *sung at the wedding of Riverwind and Goldmoon. The most fun I ever had with this poem was at a reading I gave for Gen Con in 1994. My friend (and a long-time co-worker) Steve Sullivan had been recently married, and I dedicated the reading of the poem to him and his new wife.*

Such opportunities—to make a gift of imagination and words to people you care about—are the real rewards of doing these kinds of things. As a brief aside, I'd like to say that Margaret and Tracy are among the most generous people I have know, precisely in this way. They were always willing to let others enter the world their imaginations had created; they also made it a practice to sustain and nurture those same people in the daily world in which we all have to live.

It was great going back over these poems. It helped me recall the delight and challenge of the whole project and the friendships I made in the process.
—Michael Williams

ACKNOWLEDGMENTS

We would like to acknowledge the original members of the DRAGONLANCE story design team: Tracy Hickman, Harold Johnson, Jeff Grubb, Michael Williams, Gali Sanchez, Gary Spiegle, and Carl Smith.

We want to thank those who came to join us in Krynn: Doug Niles, Laura Hickman, Michael Dobson, Bruce Nesmith, Bruce Heard, Michael Breault, and Roger E. Moore.

We would like to thank our editor, Jean Blashfield Black, who has been with us through all our trials and triumphs.

And, finally, we want to express our deep thanks to all of those who have offered encouragement and support: David "Zeb" Cook, Larry Elmore, Keith Parkinson, Clyde Caldwell, Jeff Easley, Ruth Hoyer, Carolyn Vanderbilt, Patrick L. Price, Bill Larson, Steve Sullivan, Denis Beauvais, Valerie Valusek, Dezra and Terry Phillips, Janet and Gary Pack, our families, and, last but not least—all of you who have written to us.

AFTERWORD

And so, our travels in Krynn have come to an end.†

We know that this will disappoint many of you, who have been hoping that our adventures in this wonderful land would last forever. But, as Tasslehoff's mother might say, "There comes a time when you have to toss out the cat, lock up the door, put the key under the mat, and start off down the road."

Of course, the key will always remain under the doormat (provided no other kender move into town), and we are not discounting the possibility that someday we might journey down this road in search of that key. But we have Tas's magical time-traveling device in *our* pouches now (fortunately for Krynn!), and there are more worlds we are eager to explore before we return to this one.

We had no idea, when the DRAGONLANCE® project was started, that it would be as successful as it has been. There are many reasons for this, but the main one, I think, is that we had a truly great team working on the project. From the writers to the artists to the game designers to the editors—everyone on the DRAGONLANCE team cared about their work and went above and beyond the call of duty to make certain it succeeded. Tracy says that—somewhere—Krynn really exists and that all of us have been there. We know this is true,† because it is so hard saying good-bye.

Speaking of saying good-bye, we first realized the depth of feeling readers had for our characters and our world we had created when we received the outpouring of letters regarding the death of Sturm.

"I know Sturm doesn't mean anything to you!" one distraught reader wrote. "After all, he's just a figment of your imagination."

Of course, he was much more than that to us. Spending so much time with our characters, they become very real to us, too. We triumph with them, grieve with them, and mourn them. We did not "kill" Sturm arbitrarily. The noble Knight of Solamnia was intended to be a tragic hero from the first inception of the project. Death is a part of life, it is a part we all face and must learn to deal with—even our happy-go-lucky kender.

At the time we wrote this, we did believe that this would be our last DRAGONLANCE book. I cannot remember the circumstances at the time, but it would not be long before Margaret and I would leave our cubicles at TSR and strike out— rather kenderlike—on our own into other books about other lands. This was a heartfelt goodbye and thanks to our readers and is just as warmly felt today.

People have also asked us if War of Souls is our last DRAGONLANCE book. We tell them yes, but that it is probably the fourth *time we have written our last DRAGONLANCE book!*
—TRH

We always felt that this was true. We feel more like we are reporting events that happened elsewhere.
—TRH

Sturm's death is foreshadowed in the first book by the Forestmaster, who looks directly at the knight when she says, "We do not mourn the loss of those who die fulfilling their destinies."

Sturm's brave sacrifice forces the knights to reexamine their values and eventually provides the means to unite them. Sturm died as he lived—courageously, with honor, serving others. His memory lives for those who loved him, just as the light of the Starjewel beams in the darkness. Many times, when his friends are troubled or facing a dangerous situation, the memory of the knight returns to them, giving them strength and courage.

We knew that Flint's death would have a sad impact on Tasslehoff and, indeed, we wept more for Tas when Flint died than we did for the old dwarf, who had led a rich, full life. But something in Tas changed forever (and for the better) when he lost his gruff but tender-hearted friend. This, too, was a necessary change (though Tanis would add here that some things never change—kender among them!). But we knew that Tas would have to face a rough road in the second trilogy. We knew he would need strength and, most of all, compassion to come through it.

We always hoped we would have a chance to tell Caramon's and Raistlin's story, even when we were still working on the first trilogy. When writing the short story, "Test of the Twins," we had the vague outlines in mind of what would eventually become the second trilogy. LEGENDS grew in scope and depth even as we worked on CHRONICLES, and therefore it was quite simple to just keep traveling down the road with those of our characters who still needed us.

It was important to us to show in LEGENDS a quest that was not so much involved with saving a world as it was (as Par-Salian says) with saving a soul. Everyone believed that it was Raistlin's soul we referred to, but, of course, it was his twin's. The archmage had already doomed himself. The only thing that saves him at the end is his brother's love and that small spark of caring in his own heart that even the darkness within him cannot completely extinguish.

But now this road has brought us, as all roads must eventually, to a parting. We authors are traveling down one path, our characters another. We feel confident we can leave them now. They don't need us anymore. Caramon has found the inner resources he needs to cope with life. He and Tika will have many sons and daughters, and we would be surprised if at least one doesn't become a mage.

Undoubtedly Caramon's children will join with Tanis's one son (a quiet, introspective youth) and with Riverwind's and Goldmoon's golden-haired twins in some adventure or other. They might possibly try to discover whatever became of Gilthanas and Silvara. They might journey to the united elven kingdom, brought together at last by Alhana and Porthios, who do—after all—come to develop a deep and enduring love for each other. They may meet up with Bupu's children (she married the Highbulp when he wasn't looking) or they might even travel for a while with "Grandpa" Tasslehoff.

Astinus will chronicle these adventures, of course, even if we do not. And you who are role-playing the DRAGONLANCE games will undoubtedly come to know more about the further adventures than we will. At any rate, you will continue, we hope, to have a marvelous time in that fabled land. But we must be on our way.

We shake hands with Tas (who is snuffling again) and bid him goodbye (checking our pouches first, of course, and relieving Tas of the many personal possessions we have unaccountably "dropped"). Then we watch as the kender goes skipping down the road, his topknot bobbing, and we imagine that we can see him—in the distance—meet up with an old, befuddled wizard, who is wandering about looking for his lost hat—which is on his head.

And then they vanish from our sight. With a sigh, we turn and walk down the new road that beckons us onward.†

At the time Tracy and I were working on this book, we did think it was going to be the last book we would write in the DRAGONLANCE *series. Other authors were taking up the task and adding their visions to our world, and we were involved in writing another fantasy series (The Darksword trilogy).*

How wrong we were!

As Tas says, after adventuring in other places, coming home is the best part of the journey!
—MW

AFTERWORD TO THE ANNOTATED LEGENDS
By Margaret Weis, April 2003

Working with Tracy has always been immense amounts of fun for me. We have a great time when we work on projects. One of my favorite stories about our partnership involves the end of Legends. We were working on an extremely tight deadline with Test of the Twins. We actually wrote the book in a month's time, which is something I'll never do again! Writing away, I was coming to the end of the story when I realized I had a made a dreadful mistake. Caramon had to enter the Portal, and I'd made no provision for him to do this. Raistlin has to go through all this machinations in order to get into the Abyss, and here's Caramon, who is just going to walk in!

I called Tracy in a panic and explained the problem. I was practically in tears.

He calmed me down and said he knew how Caramon entered the Abyss.

"How does he?" I cried, frantic.

"There's something about Caramon that very few people know," Tracy said solemnly.

"Yes, yes, what is it?" I was feverishly taking notes.

"Caramon always carried American Express," said Tracy.

Well, as you know, Caramon does not use American Express to enter the Abyss! Tracy came up with a brilliant solution to my problem. And he made me laugh.

Laughter and tears. To my mind, that's what makes the DRAGONLACE setting a wonderful, living world.

Appendix A:
The Mythic Journey

By Tracy Hickman

Legends, much more so than Chronicles, is a mythic journey. This is, perhaps, why Legends is a far more personal book for many readers: it is a book about their own life journey. It is one reason that I so like to write in this medium. Fantasy is writing Modern Mythology.

The Mythic Story form is as old as mankind. Joseph Campbell in his excellent writings talks about the universality of the Mythic Story as a literary form. All cultures utilize this form of story. It is, in a very real sense, a large part of how we communicate between cultures despite our vast differences. The names of the characters, their circumstances, settings, and even the ethics and morals extolled by the stories are vastly different, yet the foundations of those stories—what Campbell calls the monomyth—remain essentially the same.

Mythos of story is how we make sense of the world. It is the glass through which we view the world around us and the means by which we place ourselves in that world. The Dramatica Theory of Story postulates that such epic tales in their complete form represent the human mind working through a problem from all aspects.[1] If this is true—and I believe it is—then stories teach us about our problems, possible solutions, and their desirable or undesirable outcomes. Can there then be any doubt as to how truly powerful story is in shaping our thoughts, not only of the world without but our place within? This story form has a very real purpose. "It is the business of mythology proper, and of the fairy tale, to reveal the specific dangers and techniques of the dark interior way from tragedy to comedy." Story—epic, mythic story in particular—is ethically based. It teaches us something about ourselves and who we should be.

While this "story within" helps us to come to grips with the complexities of the world around us, it is not necessarily an accurate picture once all the dots have been connected. Reporters are not told to go out and "get the facts," but to "get the story."

1 — Dramatica: A New Theory of Story; (Fourth Edition), Melanie Anne Phillips & Chris Huntley, pg. 15

Facts, raw data, and figures are boring and often confusing. Story makes sense. This is why there are legions of commentators on television news programs who are there to "help us make sense of what is happening." They put everything "in context" (i.e. the story form or the monomyth) so that we can understand its relevance to us. As a result, we have come to believe, at least in western societies, that every complex issue has only two sides. In addition, even though both of those sides should be addressed, one side or the other should have more weight or "rightness"—the so-called "slant of the story." Above all, no matter how complex the issue, it can be boiled down to an understandable three to five minutes in length. We can watch continuous mythmaking hour by hour on CNN. It is no coincidence that their own brochure for the CNN tour is titled: "The Story behind the News."

Campbell's approach to the monomyth of story is very much centered in psychology and defines the common experience of mythos in those terms. I, on the other hand, approach the monomyth form from the perspective of faith and God. Campbell looks at the monomyth and sees psychological wiring. I look at the monomyth and see the fingerprints of God. Regardless of which of our approaches is more correct than the other, the monomyth is a common, innate desire coded into us all—a genetic call to become something greater tomorrow than we are today.

Whichever approach you take, the great underlying story structure—the classic monomyth—is common to us all. It is why readers from many nations and cultures identify with Caramon and Raistlin and can share their experiences. Whichever of us—or perhaps both of us—are correct in our perspectives ultimately may not be important; we all share the monomyth as a way of understanding our world.

THE MONOMYTH CYCLE

2 — Campbell, Joseph: The Hero with a Thousand Faces, pg. 30

3 — Ibid, pg. 35

Caramon's path through the Legends story follows the "formula in the rites of passage: separation-initiation-return."[2] This is his nuclear monomyth. It involves "a separation from the world, a penetration to some source of power, and a life-enhancing return."[3] In many ways, we have three heroes in our

story, and each of them walks the mythic path to their own ends.

DEPARTURE

The first stage of the epic myth begins, appropriately enough, at home in the comfortable and familiar surroundings. This, perhaps, is why most adventures in fantasy roleplaying games used to start in an inn or tavern. Caramon begins his epic journey from the confines of his beloved Inn of the Last Home. Crysania has lived most of her life safely within the confines of the Temple of Paladine in Palanthas. At the time of our story's beginning, Raistlin's journey has long since begun for him. It is only as we take up the road of trials with Caramon and Crysania that we discover Raistlin's road as well.

It is interesting to note, however, that Caramon's adventure begins after having *failed* his previous adventure. Caramon was a Hero of the Lance, a revered and much-honored warrior. In his previous adventure, he, too, left this same home (the separation or departure) and went to unknown lands of power (trials and victories of initiation), only to return once more to this same inn in Solace (reentry). Campbell says that it is this last stage of returning that "the hero may find the most difficult of all."[4] Hero that he was, when this story opens, Caramon is an abject failure; he has retreated into alcoholism in order to flee from the pain of his failures with his brother and, apparently, as a man. So Legends begins most poignantly with a failed adventurer who was unable to effect a return home. Some part of Caramon remains "out there" where he failed his brother.

He is called to adventure by the most unlikely of heralds: Tasslehoff Burrfoot. Like many heralds throughout history, he is one who is judged as "evil" by the world. This herald is also something of a guide to the hero. Caramon certainly seems to be led about by Tasslehoff's whims to the point of falling into the adventure. It is Tasslehoff who issues the call to adventure that Caramon picks up. Crysania is also issued a call—a call that draws her out of her familiar surroundings to take up the unsure path.

4 — *Ibid, pg 36*

The next step in enabling the adventurer is the endowment of supernatural aid. In most mythological structures, this is provided by some mystical figure, but in our story it is actually a device: the device of Time Traveling. This is the talisman that allows Caramon, Crysania, and Tasslehoff to pass from the familiar realm of their homeland into the powerful and mysterious lands of the past and of the potential future.

All that is left, then, is to cross the threshold that is guarded by a being of power. These guardians are the members of the Conclave. Par-Salian and his fellow wizards stand as guardians of the past and future. It is past them that Caramon, Crysania, and Tasslehoff must move in order to walk the passage into the realm of night. This they do, facilitated by the marvelous device.

ADVENTURE: TRIALS AND VICTORIES

"The passage of the magical threshold is a transit into a sphere of rebirth," says Campbell. This truly can be said of Caramon. He is reborn before our eyes, forged anew in the arenas of Istar at the height of its glory and folly. This is his "road of trials" as he deals with his alcoholism and his poor physical condition. Crysania, too, must relinquish her former existence in order to be reborn and gain enlightenment. Raistlin, too, must die as his old self as he progresses down his path—his encounter with Fistandantilus bringing him a rebirth as something he had not previously supposed.

It is a long path, this "road of trials," that our heroes take. It spans multiple epochs of Krynn's history. It takes them to places that might have been and places that should never be. It takes them beyond the circles of the world. Each of them is in a quest for the "ultimate boon," though what that boon is for each of them is different and, in many ways, in conflict with one another. Caramon comes to an understanding of who he truly is and, like Dorothy of Oz, that in his home he had already attained the ultimate boon, even though he had refused to see it. Crysania sacrifices her eyesight so that she may truly see the compassion and acceptance that is the hallmark of her greater faith. Raistlin gains the boon of knowledge and a

bitter boon at that: he knows that he was fundamentally wrong.

REENTRY

It is this return and reintegration with society that "the hero himself may find the most difficult requirement of all."[5]

There are three dangers in this return for the hero. If the hero has won through, there is the danger that his experience may "annihilate all recollection of, interest in, or hope for, the sorrows of the world."[6] Or, if the hero has plucked the boon too quickly by violence, quick device, or luck, then "the powers that he has unbalanced may react so sharply that he will be blasted from within and without."[7] Or, finally, if the hero makes his safe return to the world of his home, "he may meet with such a blank misunderstanding and disregard from those whom he has come to help that his career will collapse."[8] As mentioned before, this last result seemed to be the fate of Caramon at the beginning of the Legends tale: an adventurer who has failed in his return.

It is the second fate that seems to befall Raistlin, and in a literal sense this may be true. However, Raistlin's refusal to return is not so much one of his destruction as a willing acknowledgement of his error and his willingness to pay for it. It is an act of sacrifice, but less based in nobility than it is in ethics. Nevertheless, it is in this understanding that Raistlin actually attains a level of atonement, for having realized his mistake, he is willing to pay for it. In this he earns his final boon: rest from torment.

Caramon and Crysania, both literally and figuratively, cross the returning threshold as they pass back through the portal from the Abyss. Both of them, in doing so, are freed. They are freed to live. Joseph Campbell puts it perfectly in terms of the message of Legends:

> The battlefield is symbolic of the field of life, where every creature lives on the death of another. A realization of the inevitable *guilt of life may so sicken the heart that, like Hamlet or like Arjuna, one may refuse to go on with it.*

5 — *Ibid, pg 36*

6 — *Ibid.*

7 — *Ibid, pg. 37*

8 — *Ibid.*

On the other hand, like most of the rest of us, one may invent a false, finally unjustified, image of oneself as an exceptional phenomenon in the world, not guilty as others are, *but justified in one's inevitable sinning because one represents the good*. Such self-righteousness leads to a misunderstanding, not only of oneself but of the nature of both man and the cosmos. *The goal of the myth is to dispel the need for such life ignorance by effecting a reconciliation of the individual consciousness with the universal will*. And this is effected through a realization of the true relationship of the passing phenomena of time to the imperishable life that lives and dies in all. [9]

9 — *Ibid, pg. 238. Italics added.*

Crysania begins the book like the Kingpriest of Istar, "justified in one's inevitable sinning because one represents the good." Caramon begins his journey with "guilt of life" and refusing "to go on with it." The battlefield in Legends is a wide-ranging one, through both time and space, internal and external, yet through this crucible is forged in Caramon and Crysania a "reconciliation of the individual consciousness with the universal will."

So it is that Caramon and Crysania return successfully to their homes, freed at last to truly live. So, too, does Raistlin refuse to return home but finds in his refusal a level of grace.

Appendix B:
Temporal Kenders

By Tracy Hickman

Time traveling dragons?

Stories of time travel have always fascinated me. I fell in love with the concept when I was old enough to watch the George Pal version of *The Time Machine*. Ever since that moment, my dreams have been occupied by a variety of temporal transports. Some of them were built of cardboard boxes and crayons in a basement room in my parents' home where I would power them with my imagination and cross the eons into ancient pasts and far-flung futures—always to return in time for warm cookies and milk in the afternoon. I read H. G. Wells's *The Time Machine* as soon as I could get my hands on it. I was inspired and thrilled when my "Boy's Life" magazine started publishing an all-too-short-lived serial story about a young Boy Scout finding a time machine. As I grew up, temporal paradox became as important to me as Wonder Bread.

But the idea of time travel in a *fantasy* setting? It was a unique mix to say the least. Time travel had always been the province of scientists (mad or otherwise) with super technology. Time-traveling wizards was not a common theme.

However, the core of all really good time-travel stories, regardless of their setting, revolves around choice and consequence—how the choices made by the characters in the story affect events in the future or, for that matter, the past. It is a common dream shared by all of mankind. If we feel unhappily trapped in the present, we often either blame our past or wish for a better future. As John Whittier put it, "For of all sad words of tongue or pen, the saddest are these: "It might have been!"[1]

Everyone, it would seem, wants to go back, rewind the clock, and set things right. Raistlin *should* rule the universe—just ask him! All our problems would be solved . . . if only things had been different *back then*.

Ah, if it were only that simple. . . .

1 — *John Greenleaf Whittier (1807-1892) Maud Muller, 1856*

Time as a River

Par-Salian and most of the other learned thinkers of their time liked to think of time as a river flowing

quick from its headwaters to the sea. Everyone was bobbing about in this flowing river and pretty much couldn't do anything about it. The Conclave had this nifty time-travel device that was a tinker gnome's joy and a wizard's nightmare, but everyone calmed down once they realized that humans could travel backward in time and it wouldn't really change anything. It was, from their perspective, pretty much like taking a spoonfull of water out of the river, walking it upstream a ways and dropping it back in. The sum volume of the river remained the same, the river's course did not change a bit, and history remained pretty much intact.

Well, all of that is a fine and dandy perspective if you happen to be the one in the river, but for those of us sitting here on the bank it looks a little more complicated than that. The reason that humans cannot change the course of this river of time is that any effect they may have had on the river upstream has *already* affected where they got out of the river downstream.

Let's walk away from the river for a moment, sit under this oak tree, and get hit on the head with an acorn. Ouch! That hurt! Bad oak tree! I would be inclined to think that if I could just go back into the past, chop down that offending oak yesterday, then I would not have been hit on the head with that acorn.

However, on reflection, if I *had* chopped down that oak tree yesterday, then I would not have been hit in the head and would have had no motivation for going back to chop down the oak tree.

If all this makes your head hurt, then it is more than that acorn that just hit us on the head. You are beginning to understand why I find time travel so interesting.

Put in terms of the Legends story: Picture Raistlin sitting near the fireplace in the Inn of the Last Home. He is pondering going back in time to gain the power he needs to challenge the Queen of Darkness. Raistlin's desire and motivation for going back in time and challenging Fistandantilus for his power and knowledge was a result, in part, of his circumstances. The Cataclysm, the secretiveness of the Towers of High Sorcery, the dangerous state of the world in general, the missing true gods . . . all of

these things factored into his decision to go back in time. All of these factors existed and were, in part, *caused* by Raistlin *being* back in time in the first place! His actions while in Istar may have actually contributed to the Cataclysm. In other words, Raistlin's trip back in time has *already* taken place, even though, from his perspective sitting in the Inn of the Last Home, he has not yet left.

The most recent film production of H. G. Wells's *The Time Machine* gives us perhaps the clearest picture of how time travel actually works in Krynn. The time traveler realizes at last that he *cannot* go back in time and save his fiancé because both he and his time machine are the products of that woman's death.

PARALLEL HISTORIES

If your head is still smarting over the acorn incident, come back to the river with me for a few moments. There is something else we need to consider. We walk downstream a little way and find that the river diverges into two branches, left and right, which then run parallel next to each other down the hill. A short way down the hill we see that both of these rivers branch again, making four rivers running in parallel down the hill.

Think of each of these branching points in the river as a moment of decision. Each decision results in one of two possibilities: the water goes to the left or the water goes to the right. The resulting twin rivers represent two separate courses, two separate histories based entirely on the fate of a single decision. Now picture these rivers branching on and on with every decision that not only you make but that each other person in the stream makes—each river a different, yet parallel, River of Time.

That's a *lot* of histories!

Concurrent with the River of Time theory is a second theory of parallel universes running through time. It still works with the river analogy as we now understand it. If Raistlin goes back in time from a specific river branch into the past—remember, he is going into *his own* past—then everything will lead him right back to that *same* branch of the river downstream.

With so many parallel histories—all apparently equally viable—one might ask what the High God thinks of all this? Is there one particular history that is better than another? Is there an optimum branch of the river that yields a better result than the others? I believe that there *is* such an optimum time-line, which is being chronicled by Astinus. If that is the case, then what about all those other histories? What about the conservation of mass and energy in the universe? If Raistlin goes back in time and his atoms go with him, doesn't that mean that there are now *two* of the same atoms in the universe? Would it not be less painful for us just to go back and sit under that oak tree and be pelted by acorns until we pass out?

I honestly don't know the answer to these questions. All I know is that within the context of the story there are parallel histories determined by our choices and that going back in time normally doesn't change anything.

All of this would be quite comforting to Par-Salian—if it weren't for kender.

KENDER DIVERGENCE

What is it about kender? They seem to hold a unique position in the universe. They apparently are not welcomed in the Abyss any more than most major cities. They are as perennial as weeds. Most importantly for our purposes, they have the ability to affect the course of the River of Time.

Maybe it is because of their great innocence. Perhaps it is a gift given to them from the gods for the protection of the world. Or it could be just something they eat. Whatever it is, the effect appears to leave them unaffected by previous historical events. As a result, any kender traveling back in time can radically changed the course of downstream histories and, more importantly, which of the shadowy probability histories becomes the optimum reality.

ONE KENDER'S JOURNEY THROUGH TIME

Perhaps these strange events are best understood through this graphic illustration. The original was created by Tasslehoff on the back of a piece of bark—apparently the only writing surface available

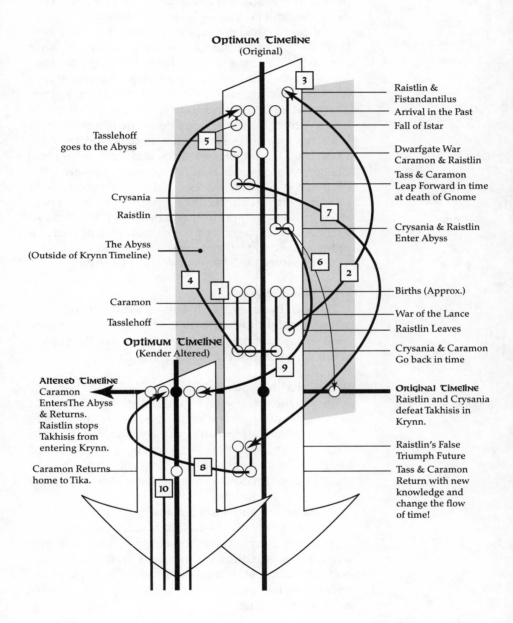

Optimum Timeline
(Original)

Tasslehoff
goes to the Abyss

Crysania

Raistlin

The Abyss
(Outside of Krynn Timeline)

Caramon

Tasslehoff

Optimum Timeline
(Kender Altered)

Altered Timeline
Caramon
EntersThe Abyss
& Returns.
Raistlin stops
Takhisis from
entering Krynn.

Caramon Returns
home to Tika.

Raistlin &
Fistandantilus
Arrival in the Past
Fall of Istar

Dwarfgate War
Caramon & Raistlin

Tass & Caramon
Leap Forward in time
at death of Gnome

Crysania & Raistlin
Enter Abyss

Births (Approx.)

War of the Lance

Raistlin Leaves

Crysania & Caramon
Go back in time

Original Timeline
Raistlin and Crysania
defeat Takhisis in
Krynn.

Raistlin's False
Triumph Future

Tass & Caramon
Return with new
knowledge and
change the flow
of time!

at the time. While we have taken the liberty to clean up the presentation graphically, the convolutions of time travel and the effects of kender on such journeys may still be a little difficult to follow.

The large background arrows with the thick central line represent the flow of time on Krynn, with the past at the top and the future toward the bottom. There are two of these large arrows. The tallest represents the original Optimum Timeline of Krynn. The smaller one to the left represents an alternate history timeline. On either side of the arrow's center lines are four lines representing, from left to right, Tasslehoff, Caramon, Crysania, and Raistlin in time. The gray area in the background represents the Abyss, a place that exists outside the time-flow of Krynn. Natural time flows from top to bottom in straight lines. Temporal travel occurs either forward in time (top to bottom) or back through time (bottom to top) along the curved lines.

Our journey begins, as it were, in the middle. . . .

1. The Births
All of the players in this drama are born in approximately the same era. The War of the Lance runs its course, making heroes of many of them. This is the beginning of the kender's journey.

2. Raistlin's Journey Back in Time
Raistlin determines to challenge the Queen of Darkness—and the rest of the gods—for supremacy in the universe. He journeys back through time to confront and challenge a notorious wizard of unspeakable power. Only in this way can he learn what he needs to know in order to complete his plan.

3. Raistlin Confronts Fistandantilus
Raistlin confronts Fistandantilus at last. The two engage in a terrible wizard combat. The outcome remains a speculation for debate. I prefer to say that both of them lost. What was Raistlin and what was Fistandantilus merge into a single, supremely powerful wizard being.

4. Caramon, Crysania, and Tasslehoff Journey Back
In a monumental mistake—or monumental stroke of fortune—Tasslehoff journeys back in time with

Caramon in an attempt to save Raistlin from Fistandantilus. Crysania, of course, journeys back in order
to save the world without fully understanding
what that entails. They all arrive back in the past
and discover that Raistlin and Fistandantilus are
the same person.

It is interesting to note, for those of us stuck in
linear temporal thought, that the "historical" Fistandantilus known to both Raistlin and Caramon
while they were growing up is, in fact, the mature
Raistlin who has merged with Fistandantilus in the
past. Raistlin was, in effect, urged into the past by
tales of himself.

5. Istar Falls / A Kender in the Abyss
Crysania is unable to stop the Cataclysm. She is
sheltered from its effects by the Tower of High Sorcery, saved with Caramon by Raistlin. The kender,
however, does not fair as well. He is plunged by
the Cataclysm into the Abyss. Being innocent, the
Kender is not allowed to stay, however, and is
returned to the circles of the world of Krynn to join
Caramon and Crysania in confronting Raistlin in
the Dwarfgate Wars.

6. The Cost of Triumph
At the end of the Dwarfgate Wars, Raistlin having
found the Portal, passes with Crysania into the
Abyss in order to confront Takhisis. Had the kender
not interfered, Raistlin and Crysania would have
engaged the Queen of Darkness and Raistlin would
have conquered the world—but at a terrible price.

7. A Kender View of the Future
The price of Raistlin's triumph, however, was to
be his undoing. Tasslehoff, incensed at the death of
his gnomish friend and attempting to get Caramon
home, used the time travel device to transport both
Caramon and himself into the future. This leap into
the future allowed them to view the results of
Raistlin's "victory"—the death of the world.

8. Return of the Kender / Altering Time
Seeing the results of Raistlin's triumph, Tasslehoff
and Caramon returned in time to the one place they
could find a portal and hope to stop Raistlin. Unbe-

knownst to either of them, it was this knowledge of the future that enabled the kinder—consciously, subconsciously, or unconsciously—to empower Caramon and shift the Optimum Timeline. The future history had been changed.

9. Raistlin's Choice

In changing future history, Raistlin and Crysania, too, were shifted into a new optimum timeline. This time, the result would be far different. Raistlin was now aware of his terrible destiny and chose a different future for Krynn at the cost of his own.

10. The New Future

It was Raistlin's choice then, enabled by the presence of a little kender, that saved the future of the world.

CONCLUSION

Interestingly enough, even if we *could* get to the past, it would still be the *present* for those of us who were there. All our actions, everything we think, and the exercise of our free will, takes place only in *this moment*.

2 — Paul H. Dunn, "I Challenge You, I Promise You," 1973

> "Yesterday is but a dream,
> Tomorrow a vision
> But today, well lived
> Makes every yesterday
> A dream of joy
> And every Tomorrow
> A vision of hope."[2]

So it is with each of us. All our will and ability to change rests in this moment, right now. We can change our destiny and repair our past—if we will only decide to change our course—right now.

APPENDIX C:
FAITH AND FANTASY

By Tracy Hickman

Readers—and for that matter, writers—of the DRAGONLANCE Saga all come from a wonderful diverse spectrum of beliefs. Many of you are Christians of one denomination or another. Many of you are of entirely different creeds altogether. Christian, Jewish, Islamic, Taoist, Buddhist, Hindu, and even those of you who profess no religion all deal (and occasionally wrestle with) the question of faith.

People who know that I am a devoted and avowed Christian have occasionally asked me how I can justify my writing fantasy novels with my faith. I have always given them the same answer: there is no difference between my faith and my work. I write what I believe. My faith is in my work. When I say this, I mean that the DRAGONLANCE Saga, for me—and Legends more than any other work—is an allegory of many aspects of my own faith.

My religion is an active, proselytizing faith. I believe that the truths found in its teachings change lives for the better. I would be happy to talk to you about my faith and hope you ask,[1] but that is not the purpose of this appendix. The point here is to give you some insight into where the underlying foundations of the "twins trilogy" came from and how they affected the telling of this tale.

1 — You can contact me through my website at http://www.trhickman.com.

I believe in and accept Christ as my Savior and Redeemer. I also, by the way, have no problem in believing that Mohammed was a prophet, that the Jewish people were chosen of God, and that Buddha was enlightened, as were many spiritual leaders down through mankind's long history. I am a devoted member of the Church of Jesus Christ of Latter Day Saints. As part of my faith, I believe that God loves all His children around the world and wants to help them in whatever ways He can.

Does God limit His great love to any single denomination of worshippers to the exclusion of the rest of His children? No. I believe that there are many faiths around the world that seek and serve God as they understand Him. Where there seems to

be so much trouble in the world is when men get involved in trying to narrowly limit God's grace and love to a select few at the expense of others who do not share their singular viewpoint.

I can certainly recognize the beautiful truths in the following idea from Abd al-Kader:

> "Each time that something comes to your mind regarding Allah—know that He is different from that!" Commentary: If you think and believe that He is what all the schools of Islam profess and believe—He is that, and He is other than that! If you think that He is what diverse communities believe—Muslims, Christians, Jews, Mazdeans, polytheists and others—He is that and He is other than that! And if you think and believe what is professed by the Knowers par excellence—prophets, saints, and angels—He is that! He is other than that! None of His creatures worship Him in all His aspects; none is unfaithful to Him in all His aspects. No one knows Him in all His aspects; no one is ignorant of Him in all His aspects. Those who are among the most knowing regarding Him have said: "Glory to Thee. We have no knowledge except what You have taught us." (Koran 2:32)[2]

2 — "The Spiritual Writings of Abd al-Kader", 1995, Kitab al-Mawaqif, 254, pp. 127-128

From my own faith comes the following similar concept: "We believe all that God has revealed, all that He does now reveal, and we believe that He will yet reveal many great and important things pertaining to the Kingdom of God."[3] We all still have much to learn of the incomprehensible, eternal truth of God and the relationship of our faith to Him.

3 — "The Pearl of Great Price", Articles of Faith 9

The question of faith—or more precisely *true* faith as opposed to false or misdirected faith—seems on the surface to be very much a central theme in Legends. On reflection, however, the question is actually centered on the difference between *persuasion*

and *coercion* in regard to faith. Crysania's journey through the story is defined by this central question, although all the other characters—especially Caramon and Raistlin—are also affected strongly by this central theme.

The nature and depth of Crysania's faith is at the heart of her character, both as a strength and as a flaw. In the beginning of Legends, we see Crysania as being very much taken up in the forms of the temple of Paladine, central to its worldly bureaucracy and dogmatically myopic. What she perceives as the strength of her faith is shown in the course of the story to be her greatest weakness. Her narrow vision of truth and her brittle, unbending view of her own rightness shatter against Raistlin's wider and darker vision. Yet in breaking, she faces at last the higher, deeper, grander, blacker, and more sublime truths outside the narrow vision of her original dogma. It is no accident that in going blind, Crysania at last can truly see.

This lesson is taught first by the Kingpriest of Istar, the archetype for coercion of faith. The Kingpriest, so completely convinced of the rightness of his own cause, asserts with the authority of his power and office at once the *wrongness* of every other point of view. Perhaps, for me, this is the most important point of Legends. It is not the Kingpriest's *faith* that causes the downfall of both himself and his nation. It is his inability to allow for any other faith except his rigidly and narrowly defined faith.

The results of this failing are interesting. Having called down the wrath of the gods, which results in the destruction of Istar, the general reaction of the populace seems to be to blame the gods for what happened. It is not unlike the infant who, lacking sufficient motor control, slams his own fist into his nose and then glares at his mother for hitting him. The people of Krynn seem no more comprehending than this child. It is a natural tendency we all share. It is far easier to lay blame at every other person's feet but never our own. The gods never left Krynn so much as Krynn left the gods. This same theme is very much at the center of the War of Souls trilogy, although the causes were much different in that tale.

So, as Pilate asked Jesus, "What is truth?"[4] It was

4 — *The Bible, John 18:38*

the question, too, that troubled both Crysania and Raistlin through their journeys of light and dark. Crysania finds herself constantly at odds between the rigid dictates of her faith and the reality that she encounters through her experience. Raistlin wants to define truth in his own terms, to rewrite truth if necessary through the enforcement of his magic. Yet ultimately Raistlin's own failing is that he, too, does not fully comprehend the truth and, once realized, nearly pays for it at the cost of his own soul. It is that realization—not of any sense of guilt for what he had done, but that he had an obligation to pay for his debts—that earned him some modicum of redemption from the tortures of the Queen of Darkness.

Each of them reflects their right of choice, their agency given of the gods to choose for themselves the course before them. In the foundation structures of the DRAGONLANCE saga, it is this very agency that gives motion to the world, as the mortals constantly shift the balance through their choices of good, evil, and chaos.

In the theology of my faith, Satan's idea before the beginning of the world was the suppression of agency. In this passage, the Lord God tells Moses about a council in heaven before the earth was formed:

> 1 And I, the Lord God, spake unto Moses, saying: That Satan, whom thou hast commanded in the name of mine Only Begotten, is the same which was from the beginning, and he came before me, saying—Behold, here am I, send me, I will be thy son, and I will redeem all mankind, that one soul shall not be lost, and surely I will do it; wherefore give me thine honor.
>
> 2 But, behold, my Beloved Son, which was my Beloved and Chosen from the beginning, said unto me—Father, thy will be done, and the glory be thine forever.
>
> 3 Wherefore, because that Satan rebelled against me, and sought to

destroy the agency of man, which I,
the Lord God, had given him, and
also, that I should give unto him
mine own power; by the power of
mine Only Begotten, I caused that he
should be cast down;

4 And he became Satan, yea, even the
devil, the father of all lies, to deceive
and to blind men, and to lead them
captive at his will, even as many as
would not hearken unto my voice.[5]

5 — "The Pearl of Great Price", Moses 4:1-4

Satan's plan described here is to "destroy the agency of man," to take away humanity's free will and thereby to *enforce* salvation. This, too, is the plan of both Takhisis and Raistlin, but as evil feeds upon itself they obviously differ strenuously on just what brand of salvation will be forced on the world. It is then ultimately the forcing of faith at the expense of agency that is wrong.

I believe that all truth is of God, that it is our limited understanding that we struggle against. It is our quest for greater understanding and enlightenment that is the true struggle for each of us, not a struggle against one another. It is a difficult path, but as Crysania points out at last ". . . the rough and rock-strewn trails of both can be made easier by the touch of a a hand, the voice of a friend. The capacity to love, to care, is given to us all—the greatest gift of the gods to all the races."

Appendix D:
The Gods of Krynn

by Jeff Grubb

Editor's Note: This article was originally posted to the Dragonlance-L mailing list and is reprinted here with the author's permission. Special thanks to Michael Falconer for sharing Mr. Grubb's response to his e-mail with the Dragonlance-L mailing list.

The big thing to keep in mind about the original Toril gods (yeah, we took the name of the campaign and glued it onto the FORGOTTEN REALMS planet) is that they were only a base from which the gods of the DRAGONLANCE saga evolved. To give an idea of the time frame, these gods showed up in my campaign when I was using the original "little pamphlets" of DUNGEONS & DRAGONS (the wood-grained box, Greyhawk, Blackmoor, and Eldritch Wizardry), combined with some of the early DRAGON magazines.

Now, the original notes are packed away in my archives (read: storage in the basement). The following is what I've gleaned from memory, so it comes with this caveat: I reserve the right to double back on myself when and if I get my original notes out. Several of the names are Biblical in origin, and taken from a book *Everyone in the Bible* by the Reverend William P. Barker, who was also the minister of my church when I was growing up—and who thanks Fred Rogers of "Mr. Roger's Neighborhood" in the introduction. All references are for the original Toril campaign. Later development comes from a number of other talented, creative hands.

In my original campaign, I pulled them together in three groups of seven (Good, Neutral, Evil—this was just before Law and Chaos appeared in the alignment system), because seven was a mystic number. In addition to the gods, there were two "über-gods" who represented the ultimate values of good and evil on Toril. The original creator god was Torallah Eruidan. Paladins in my world flexed their class name into Palidan and the native language of good (remember alignment languages?) was Edantal. The ultimate evil god was Desmos Ben-Shatain. The original conflict between the forces of Good and Evil was the All Saints

War. The name of the All Saints War made it into the DRAGONLANCE universe, but neither Edan nor Desmos made the crossover (which is good because it made the DRAGONLANCE gods the supreme beings of their universe). The symbol of the ultimate good was a seven-candled menorah, while the symbol of ultimate evil was the septagram or seven-pointed star.

Most of the gods' names have a rhythm to them, either a two-beat (Reorx, Chislev, Kiri-Jolith) or a three-beat (Mishakal, Habbakuk, Majere, Gilead). Most have an attribute or descriptor as well (Mantis of the Rose, the Red Condor, The Bison-Headed Minotaur). Since most of these were presented verbally in play to my dungeon group, the rhythm makes them easy to remember. Also, I often pronounced "ch" as a hard "k," so Chislev and Chemosh would be pronounced KIZ-lev and KAY-mosh (though Babylonians don't come after me for slamming Sargon).

Almost all my players were good or neutral, so their gods tended to be tailored to their roles, while the evil gods sort of just existed as opposition. There were no halfling gods, since the halfling of the time were worshipping the same gods as men. There were no gnome gods, because there were no gnome players at the time, and definitely no drow gods, since the drow were just starting to show up in the G- and D-series of AD&D Adventure Modules.

Paladine — Draco Paladin in my campaign. He was the platinum dragon described in the GREYHAWK supplement. I think he gained the Bahamut name when he showed up in the first AD&D *Monster Manual*. When Tracy was doing the original forging of Krynn, I tossed him my campaign's pantheon, and he easily folded it into his mix. Draco Paladin became Paladine. He was the paladin's god in my campaign, venerated by Fenetar the Paladin, run by Frank Dickos, the player who was the one who convinced me to set down my pantheon in the first place.

Takhisis — Draco Cerebus in my campaign, the chromatic dragon Tiamat. Draco Cerebus also went by the name Draco Cerebrint in my campaign. I think the name change came about because of the sudden appearance of a short, gray aardvark in the comics. I don't know where Tracy got the name

Takhisis, though it may be Indonesian. Part of his decision to rename the gods was to separate the cosmology of the DRAGONLANCE setting from the GREYHAWK setting. When I built my mythology (a time when Tracy was first playing as well) neither Bahamut nor Tiamat were so named in the game books, so the idea of creating new versions of them unique to the DRAGONLANCE saga would not be too far a reach. Draco Cerebus may have had the anti-paladin as followers, but that class came and left my campaign several times.

Gilean — Originally called Gilead the Book, as in "Is there no balm in Gilead?" (Jeremiah 8:22). He was the god of sages and most often personified as a lean hooded guy with a big book, sort of like the third spirit from "A Christmas Carol" or Destiny of the Endless. Although the Sandman comic was years later, we were probably pulling from the same sources (and actually, Destiny himself was pulled from a horror collection comic that DC did when I was a kid, so it may well be the same source).

Majere — The Mantis of the Rose was the good monk's god. Parallel development made it also the family name of Caramon and Raistlin. There was an accent on the last e (mah-JAIR-ee). This was a completely invented name, likely playing off "majestic."

Kiri-Jolith — The Bison-Headed Minotaur, god of good fighters and eventually fighters in general. The name was partially manufactured (Kiri) and partially inspired by Joelah, a son of Jeroham from 1st Chronicles.

Mishakal — Mishakal, the good cleric's god and the Healer, was originally male. The pantheon was pretty much an all-boy's club in its original form. Genders and relationships of who was whose child or spouse came with the DRAGONLANCE setting. The name comes from the story of the fiery furnace from the Book of Daniel—Meshach, Shadrach, and Abednego.

Habbakuk — The Fisher King, the good nature god. Christian and Arthurian allegory aside, he was a Kingfisher, because I liked the bird. He was a counter-

balance to the aquatic Zeboim, the only god who my players ever saw in the flesh, as it made its lair in a great glacier to the north. Habbakuk was also the god of rangers (who first appeared in an issue of *The Strategic Review*, DRAGON's predecessor). In the real world, Habakkuk (note the single "b" and the double "k" in the middle) was a prophet in the Bible, one of the "eight minor prophets." His book is a collection of oracles delivered against the backdrop of the Babylonian threat to Judah in 600 B.C. The original Habakkuk was a bard, a temple singer. His book was on the subject of why a good god would allow the evil Babylonians to exist and thrive.

Branchala — The Bard King. He was god of the elves in my campaign and later of bards. The name was purely invented.

Sirrion — Sirrion the Flowing Flame, god of Alchemists. Personified as animated fire in serpentine form or a salamander. The name started with a wizard character in my early campaign named Simon, which morphed into Simeon, who was one of the leaders of the twelve tribes of Israel. The name jumped the track entirely when the "m" turned into a double "r" (and occasionally a single "r" as well).

Reorx the Forge — Dwarf god, who created many of the artifacts used by other gods. He also fit in with the various weaponsmith and armorer classes floating around at the time. I have no idea where the original came from.

Chislev — Known as the Feathered Cleric, a mostly forgotten god. He was never really given much form. I think he was always shown as the same species as his worshippers. His servants were based on the Hopi Kachina spirits, but that's not something that translated into the DRAGONLANCE setting. He was created as a nature god (Chislev was my original druid god), but was eventually worshipped by neutral clerics who were not druids, as Zivilyn took over the druidic role. The name Chislev evolved out of Kislev, the name for the ninth month of the Jewish year. The was also originally male in my campaign.

Zivilyn — The Tree of Life, which grew in the largest forest in my campaign, was a plant god who started as a god of forest creatures (centaurs, pixies, and satyrs), but later became the druid deity. Zivilyn and Chislev seemed to go back and forth, depending on the nature of the "all-neutral-clerics-are-druids" discussion of the day. This may have been inspired by a Biblical name, but I could not tell you at this stage.

Shinare — The Griffon God, also male in his original incarnation. With Branchala, he was one of the younger gods in my pantheon and was worshipped by Merchants. He was sort of Branchala's sidekick (like Donkey was to Shrek). The accent is on the final "e" so that the name rhymes with Majere. Again, this may have been inspired by Biblical names, but it was likely pure invention.

Sargonnas — The Red Condor, god of evil monks, who was set up as opposition to the Mantis of the Rose. He ended up including evil fighters as well. The name was taken from Sargon, King of Babylon in the Book of Isaiah.

Morgion — Though now portrayed as a hooded figure with red eyes, in his early incarnation he was a floating red skull, which in turn was inspired by an old campfire ghost story told at Boy Scout Camp in Arizona, up on the Mogion Rim, which was the origin of the name. Morgion is known in my notes as Morgion of the Dark Brotherhood. What the Dark Brotherhood? Beats the heck outta me. He had the cowl with glowing eyes before he went to the DRAGONLANCE setting, and the Red Skull image became a servant demon. Morgion was a general good choice in my campaign for cultists.

Chemosh — Ram-headed Lord of the Undead, Orcus by any other name, though I don't think that was ever picked up in the DRAGONLANCE setting. In the real world, Chemosh was the supposed god of the Ammonites in the Bible. In 1st and 2nd Kings, Solomon erected an altar to him at Jerusalem, and Josiah destroyed it.

Zeboim — The Dragon Turtle, god of evil and destructive nature. This predates my knowledge of Dave "Zeb" Cook by many years. Zeboim was the progenitor of all dragon turtles, which were the nastiest sea beasts in the game at the time. He was originally a sahuagin god. Sahuagin were hot because they were a major creature rolled out with the Blackmoor supplement. The name was influenced by Biblical names such as Zebidiah and Zebulon.

Hiddukel — The Demon Merchant. He looked like a merchant (in my world merchants wore fur tophats and looked like the Mad Hatter) with the keys to Hell hanging off his belt. All the demons (all six types; there were no devils when he first appeared) worked for him. It is a cool name, because it has the same sounds and rhythm as "Duke of Hell," but the dukes came later to the AD&D party. The servants of Hiddukel could be evil merchants, but they were more likely demons, demonologists, and those who make deals with the devil. It's all very Faustian.

Solinari — Created by Reorx the Forge and worshipped by good wizards. One of the three spheres of magic ("Sol" for sun, "Lune" for moon, and "Nuit" for night), who were thought of more as power sources then as animated gods, which worked for the whole "where-does-magic-come-from" idea. The gods of magic were made into moons when they arrived in Krynn. Solinari ruled over the sphere of white magic. I also called him Solintari in my notes.

Lunitari — God of the neutral sphere of neutral magic and illusionists. His color was originally gray, though it later became red in the DRAGONLANCE saga.

Nuitari — God of the sphere of black magic, worshipped by evil mages. The name is from the French word *nuit*, meaning "night."

Annotated Legends Works Cited

Anthony, Mark, and Ellen Porath, *Kindred Spirits*, Wizards of the Coast, Inc., 1991.

Barker, Rev. William Pierson, *Everyone in the Bible*, Oliphants.

Berberick, Nancy Varian, *Dalamar the Dark*, Wizards of the Coast, Inc., 2000.

Brown, Lesley (ed.), *The New Shorter Oxford English Dictionary*, Oxford University Press, 1993.

Brown, Steven "Stan!", *The Bestiary*, a Dramatic Supplement for the DRAGONLANCE SAGA Game Rules, Wizards of the Coast, Inc., 1998.

Campbell, Joseph, *The Hero with a Thousand Faces*, Princeton University Press, 1972.

Chesterton, Gilbert Keith, *Appreciations and Criticisms of the Works of Charles Dickens*, London, J. M. Dent & sons, ltd, 1911.

Chesterton, Gilbert Keith, "The Glass Walking-stick," and other essays, from the *Illustrated London News*, 1905-1936. London, Methuen, 1955.

Chesterton, Gilbert Keith, *Orthodoxy: The Romance of Faith*, Image Books/Doubleday, 1990.

Chodkiewicz, Michel and Amir Abd Al-Kader, *The Spiritual Writings of Amir Adb Al-Kader: Suny Series in Western Esoteric Traditions*, State University of New York Press, 1995.

Connors, William W., and Sue Weinlein Cook, THE FIFTH AGE Dramatic Adventure Game, TSR, Inc., 1996.

Cook, David "Zeb," Steve Winter, and John Pickens, 2nd Edition ADVANCED DUNGEONS & DRAGONS *Player's Handbook*, TSR, Inc., 1997.

Cook, David "Zeb," *Time of the Dragon* Boxed Set, TSR, Inc., 1989.

Daniell, Tina, *The Companions*, Wizards of the Coast, Inc., 1993.

Dickens, Charles, *A Christmas Carol*, Dover, 1993.

Dunn, Paul H., *I Challenge You . . . I Promise You*, Bookcraft, Inc., 1973.

Eliot, T.S., *The Cocktail Party*, Harvest Books 1964.

Fonstad, Karen Wynn, *The Atlas of the DRAGONLANCE World*, TSR, Inc., 1987.

Goldman, William, *The Princess Bride*, Ballantine Books, 1990.

Haring, Bennie, and Terra, *Otherlands*, an Official DRAGONLANCE game accessory for 2nd Edition *ADVANCED DUNGEONS & DRAGONS*, TSR, Inc., 1990.

Herbert, Mary, *The Clandestine Circle*, Wizards of the Coast, Inc., 2000.

Hickman, Tracy and Margaret Weis, *DRAGONLANCE Adventures*, TSR, Inc., 1987.

James, Peter and Nick Thorpe, *Ancient Inventions*, Ballantine Books, 1995.

Johnson, Harold, and John Terra, J. Robert King, Wolfgang Baur, Colin McComb, Jean Rabe, Norm Ritchie, TALES OF THE LANCE Boxed Set, TSR, Inc., 1992.

King, Stephen, *'Salem's Lot*, Pocket Books, 1999.

King, Stephen, *The Shining*, Pocket Books, 2001.

Knaak, Richard A., *The Citadel*, Wizards of the Coast, Inc., 2000.

Knaak, Richard A., *The Legend of Huma*, Wizards of the Coast, Inc., 2003.

Kirchoff, Mary and Steve Winter, *Wanderlust*, TSR, Inc., 1991.

McKeone, Dixie Lee, *Tales of Uncle Trapspringer*, Wizards of the Coast, Inc., 1998.

McLaren (née Williams), Teri, "The Vallenwoods," *The History of Dragonlance*, edited by Margaret Weis and Tracy Hickman, TSR, Inc., 1995.

Miller, Steve, "Istar: Land of the Kingpriests," Wizards of the Coast, Inc., 2003, published on www.wizards.com.

Miller, Steve and "Stan!", *DRAGONLANCE Classics 15th Anniversary Edition*, TSR, Inc., 1999.

Niles, Douglas, DWARVEN KINGDOMS OF KRYNN Boxed Set, TSR, Inc., 1993.

Phillips, Melanie Anne & Chris Huntley, *Dramatica: A New Theory of Story*; (Fourth Edition), Screenplay Systems Inc., 1993.

Perrin, Don, *Theros Ironfeld*, Wizards of the Coast, Inc.

Pierson, Chris, *Chosen of the Gods*, Wizards of the Coast, Inc. 2001.

Pierson, Chris, *Divine Hammer,* Wizards of the Coast, Inc., 2002.

Pierson, Chris, *Sacred Fire,* Wizards of the Coast, Inc., 2003.

Pierson, Chris, *Spirit of the Wind,* Wizards of the Coast, Inc., 1998.

Siegel, Scott and Barbara, *Tanis: The Shadow Years*, TSR, Inc., 1990.

Simpson, J.A., and Edmund S. Wiener (ed.), *The Oxford English Dictionary, Second Edition,* Oxford University Press., 1989.

Stein, Kevin, *The Brothers Majere*, Wizards of the Coast, Inc., 2003.

Stewart, Doug (ed.) et al, 2nd Edition ADVANCED DUNGEONS & DRAGONS *Monstrous Manual,* TSR, Inc., 1997.

Stewart, Mary, *The Crystal Cave,* Fawcett Crest Edition, 1989.

Tolkien, J.R.R., *The Hobbit*, HarperCollins Publishers, 1995.

Tolkien, J.R.R., *The Lord of the Rings*, Houghton Mifflin Co., 2003.

Twain, Mark, "Fenimore Cooper's Literary Offenses," in *The Unabridged Mark Twain*, Lawrence Teacher (ed.), Running Press, 1976.

Van Belkom, Edo, *Lord Soth*, Wizards of the Coast, Inc., 1998.

Weis, Margaret, *The Soulforge,* Wizards of the Coast, Inc., 1998.

Weis, Margaret and Don Perrin, *Brothers in Arms*, Wizards of the Coast, Inc., 1999.

Weis, Margaret and Don Perrin, Jamie Chambers, and Christopher Coyle, DRAGONLANCE *Campaign Setting*, Wizards of the Coast, Inc., 2003.

Weis, Margaret and Tracy Hickman, *Dragons of Autumn Twilight,* Wizards of the Coast, Inc., 1984.

Weis, Margaret and Tracy Hickman, *Dragons of Spring Dawning,* Wizards of the Coast, Inc., 1985.

Weis, Margaret and Tracy Hickman, *Dragons of Winter Night,* Wizards of the Coast, Inc., 1985.

Weis, Margaret and Tracy Hickman, *The History of* DRAGONLANCE, TSR, Inc., 1995.

Weis, Margaret and Tracy Hickman, *Leaves from the Inn of the Last Home*, TSR, Inc., 1987.

Weis, Margaret and Tracy Hickman, *More Leaves from the Inn of the Last Home*, Wizards of the Coast, Inc., 2000.

Weis, Margaret and Tracy Hickman, Jean Blashfield Black (ed.), *The Annotated Chronicles*, Wizards of the Coast, Inc., 2002

Weis, Margaret et al, *The Cataclysm*, DRAGONLANCE Tales II, Volume 2, TSR, Inc., 1992.

Weis, Margaret et al, *The Reign of Istar*, DRAGONLANCE Tales II, Volume 1, TSR, Inc., 1992.